英國文學名篇選注

An Anthology of
English Literature
Annotated in Chinese

王佐良 李赋宁 周珏良 刘承沛　主编

创于1897 商務印書館 The Commercial Press

图书在版编目(CIP)数据

英国文学名篇选注/王佐良等著. —北京:商务印书馆,1983.7(2023.8重印)
ISBN 978-7-100-00746-7

Ⅰ.①英… Ⅱ.①王… Ⅲ.①英国文学—文学欣赏 Ⅳ.①I561.06

中国版本图书馆CIP数据核字(2014)第255449号

英国文学名篇选注

王佐良 李赋宁
周珏良 刘承沛 主编

商 务 印 书 馆 出 版
(北京王府井大街36号 邮政编码100710)
商 务 印 书 馆 发 行
北 京 通 州 皇 家 印 刷 厂 印 刷
ISBN 978-7-100-00746-7

1983年7月第1版　开本850×1168 1/32
2023年8月北京第14次印刷　印张39½

定价：126.00元

序

这个选本是在商务印书馆1962—65年出版的《英美文学活叶文选》的基础上，加以扩充而成。它以中古以后的英国文学为范围，从十六世纪英国文艺复兴时期起至二十世纪二十年代的现代派文学止，共收名作家五十二人，作品种类包括民谣、诗、诗剧、英文《圣经》、随笔小品、文论、游记、传记、历史、小说、剧本等。

这个选本的目的是向大学英语专业三、四年级学生和懂英语的文学爱好者提供英国文学中最有名的一些篇章，并通过“题解与注释”帮助他们解决一些阅读和欣赏上的困难。

需要说明的是：

一、英国文学的名篇远不止这一些，就是入选的作家也未必都以其最重要的作品在此出现，我们只是根据我们所了解的中国学生的情况，选了一些我们认为对他们比较有用的篇章。当然，这些篇章的绝大多数确是有定评的名文。

二、我们不薄古人，但在选文比例上对较近的时期略有侧重。这也是针对中国学生的需要来安排的。

三、“题解与注释”也是面向中国学生，因此除了一般外国同类选本必注之点外，我们还努力对中国学生有特别困难的地方多加注释。

四、我们力图提供每篇的全文，但做来往往不易。对于有些类别，如长诗、小说、剧本，只能节选。凡节选者在目录上都打有*号。

五、虽然各篇章的注释体例大致相同，但是选注者各有写法，主编者也不强求一律。不同性质的文章需要不同的处理，各有个性的写法也可能使这选本的解说部分有更多可读之处。

最后，有一点个人感想。这个选本的准备过程，如从《英美文学活叶文选》算起，前后约为二十年，参加选注的同志二十多人，都是工作很忙的，有的同志年老体弱，平时轻易不愿担任“外活”，但对这项工作却都乐于支援，没有一个是轻视注释工作的。注释工作是语言、文学研究中的基本功之一，也是硬功夫，从选择版本到解释语句，无不需要扎扎实实的学问和巨大、认真、细致的劳动。他们之所以乐此不疲，我想是因为他们希望我国喜爱和研究英国文学的青年同志能够有一本比较符合中国读者需要的原文选本，这样读者就能从认真阅读原著做起。作为主编人之一，在工作过程中，我是时时受到这些同志的精神的鼓舞的。

这个选本的形成，还有商务印书馆编辑部同志们的心血在内。特别是陈羽纶同志，从《英美文学活叶文选》初创时起，一直到这个选本的最后定稿和出版，都给予了大量的具体的帮助。可以说，整个过程是主编者、选注者和出版者通力合作的过程。我谨在此向所有参与这个选本的工作的同志表示衷心的感谢。

王佐良

1982 年 4 月

目　录

* 选目上打有 * 号者非全文而系选段。

1 ENGLISH AND SCOTTISH POPULAR BALLADS

1. Lord Randal
2. The Wife of Usher's Well
3. The Three Ravens
4. Sir Patrick Spens
5. Robin Hood and the Widow's Three Sons

刘世沐　选注

1. LORD RANDAL

I

'O where hae ye been[1], Lord Randal, my son?
O where hae ye been, my handsome young man?' —
'I hae been to the wild wood; mother, make my bed soon,
For I'm weary wi' hunting, and fain wald[2] lie down.'

II

'Where gat ye[3] your dinner, Lord Randal, my son?
Where gat ye your dinner, my handsome young man?' —
'I dined wi' my true-love; mother, make my bed soon,
For I'm weary wi' hunting, and fain wald lie down.'

III

'What gat ye to your dinner, Lord Randal, my son?
What gat ye to your dinner, my handsome young man?' —
'I gat eels[4] boil'd in broo'[5]; mother, make my bed soon,

For I'm weary wi' hunting, and fain wald lie down.[6]

IV

'What became of your bloodhounds, Lord Randal, my son?
What became of your bloodhounds, my handsome young man?' —
'O they swell'd and they died; mother, make my bed soon,
For I'm weary wi' hunting, and fain wald lie down.'

V

'O I fear ye are poison'd, Lord Randal, my son!
O I fear ye are poison'd, my handsome young man!' —
'O yes! I am poison'd; mother, make my bed soon,
For I'm sick at the heart, and I fain wald lie down.'

2. THE WIFE OF USHER'S WELL

I

There lived a wife[1] at Usher's well,
And a wealthy wife was she;
She had three stout and stalwart sons,
And sent them o'er the sea.

II

They hadna[2] been a week from her,
A week but barely ane[3],
When word came to the carline wife[4]
That her three sons were gane[5].

III

They hadna been a week from her,
A week but barely three,
When word came to the carline wife

That her sons she'd never see.

IV

'I wish the wind may never cease,
Nor fashes[6] in the flood,
Till my three sons come hame[7] to me
In earthly flesh and blood!'

V

It fell[8] about the Martinmas,
When nights are lang and mirk[9]
The carline wife's three sons came hame,
And their hats were o' the birk[10].

VI

It neither grew in syke[11] nor ditch,
Nor yet in ony sheugh[12];
But at the gates o' Paradise
That birk grew fair eneugh[13].

VII

'Blow up the fire, my maidens!
Bring water from the well!
For a' my house[14] shall feast this night,
Since my three sons are well.'

VIII

And she has made to them a bed,
She's made it large and wide;
And she's ta'en her mantle her about[15],
Sat down at the bedside.

IX

Up then crew the red, red cock,
　　And up and crew the gray;
The eldest to the youngest said,
　　' 'Tis time we were away.'

X

The cock he hadna craw'd[16] but once,
　　And clapp'd his wings at a',
When the youngest to the eldest said,
　　'Brother, we must awa[17]'.

XI

'The cock doth craw[18], the day doth daw[19],
　　The channerin' worm[20] doth chide[21];
Gin we be miss'd out o' our place[22],
　　A sair pain we maun bide.[23]' —

XII

'Lie still, lie still but a little wee while[24],
　　Lie still but if we may;
Gin my mother should miss us when she wakes,
　　She'll go mad ere it be day[25].' —

XIII

'Fare ye weel[26], my mother dear!
　　Fareweel to barn and byre[27]!
And fare ye weel, the bonny lass[28]
　　That kindles my mother's fire!'

3. THE THREE RAVENS

I

There were three ravens sat on a tree,
They were as black as they might be.

II

The one of them said to his make[1],
'Where shall we our breakfast take?'

III

'Down in yonder greene field
There lies a knight slain under his shield;

IV

'His hounds they lie down at his feet,
So well do they their master keep[2];

V

'His hawks they flie so eagerly,
There's no fowl[3] dare come him nigh.

VI

'Down there comes a fallow[4] doe
As great with young as she might goe.

VII

'She lift[5] up his bloudy[6] head
And kist[7] his wounds that were so red.

VIII

'She gat him up upon her back

And carried him to earthen lake[8].

IX

'She buried him before the prime[9],
She was dead herself ere evensong time[10].

X

'God send[11] every gentleman
Such hounds, such hawks, and such a leman[12]!'

4. SIR PATRICK SPENS

The Sailing.

I

The king sits in Dunfermline town
    Drinking the blude-red[1] wine;
'O whare[2] will I get a skeely skipper[3]
    To sail this new ship o' mine?'

II

O up and spak[4] an eldern knight[5],
    Sat at the king's right knee[6]:
'Sir Patrick Spens is the best sailor
    That ever sail'd the sea.'

III

Our king has written a braid letter[7],
    And seal'd it with his hand,
And sent it to Sir Patrick Spens,
    Was walking on the strand[8].

IV

‘To Noroway[9], to Noroway,
To Noroway o’er the faem[10];
The king’s daughter o’ Noroway,
’Tis thou must bring her hame[11].’

V

The first word that Sir Patrick read
So loud, loud laugh’d he;
The neist[12] word that Sir Patrick read
The tear blinded his e’e.

VI

‘O wha is this has done[13] this deed
And tauld the king o’ me[14],
To send us out, at this time o’ year,
To sail upon the sea?

VII

‘Be it wind, be it weet, be it hail, be it sleet[15],
Our ship must sail the faem;
The king’s daughter o’ Noroway,
’Tis we must fetch her hame.’

VIII

They hoysed[16] their sails on Monenday[17] morn
Wi’ a’ the speed they may[18];
They hae landed in Noroway
Upon a Wodensday[19].

The Return.

IX

'Mak ready[20] mak ready, my merry men a'!
Our gude ship sails the morn.[21]' —
'Now ever alack, my master dear,
I fear a deadly storm.

X

'I saw the new moon late yestreen[22]
Wi' the auld moon in her arm;
And if we gang[23] to sea, master,
I fear we'll come to harm.'

XI

They hadna sail'd a league, a league,
A league but barely three,
When the lift[24] grew dark, and the wind blew loud,
And gurly[25] grew the sea.

XII

The ankers brak, and the topmast lap[26],
It was sic[27] a deadly storm:
And the waves cam owre[28] the broken ship
Till a' her sides were torn.

XIII

'O where will I get a gude sailor
To tak' my helm in hand,
Till I get up to the tall topmast
To see if I can spy land?' —

XIV

'O here am I, a sailor gude,
To tak' the helm in hand,
Till you go up to the tall topmast,
But I fear you'll ne'er[29] spy land.'

XV

He hadna gone a step, a step,
A step but barely ane,
When a bolt flew out of our goodly ship,
And the saut sea[30] it came in.

XVI

'Go fetch a web o' the silken claith[31],
Another o' the twine,
And wap[32] them into our ship's side,
And let nae[33] the sea come in.'

XVII

They fetch'd a web o' the silken claith,
Another o' the twine,
And they wapp'd them round that gude ship's side,
But still the sea came in.

XVIII

O laith, laith[34] were our gude Scots lords
To wet their cork-heel'd shoon[35];
But lang or[36] a' the play was play'd
They wat[37] their hats aboon[38].

XIX

And mony[39] was the feather bed

That flatter'd on the faem[40];
And mony was the gude lord's son
That never mair[41] cam hame.

XX

O lang, lang may the ladies sit,
Wi' their fans into their hand,
Before they see Sir Patrick Spens
Come sailing to the strand!

XXI

And lang, lang may the maidens sit
Wi' their gowd kames[42] in their hair,
A-waiting for their ain[43] dear loves!
For them they'll see nae mair[44].

XXII

Half-owre, half-owre to Aberdour[45],
'Tis fifty fathoms deep;
And there lies gude Sir Patrick Spens,
Wi' the Scots lords at his feet!

5. ROBIN HOOD AND THE WIDOW'S THREE SONS

I

There are twelve months in all the year,
As I hear many men say,
But the merriest month in all the year
Is the merry month of May.

II

Now Robin Hood is to Nottingham gone,

With a link a down and a day[1],
And there he met a silly old woman[2],
Was weeping on the way.

III

'What news? what news, thou silly old woman?
What news hast thou for me?'
Said she, 'There's three squires in Nottingham town
To-day is condemn'd to die.'

IV

'O have they parishes burnt?' he said,
'Or have they ministers[3] slain?
Or have they robb'd any virgin,
Or other men's wives have ta'en[4]?' —

V

'They have no parishes burnt, good sir,
Nor yet have ministers slain,
Nor have they robbed any virgin,
Nor other men's wives have ta'en.'

VI

'O what have they done?' said bold Robin Hood,
'I pray thee tell to me.' —
'It's for slaying of the King's fallow deer,
Bearing their long bows with thee.[5]' —

VII

'Dost thou not mind[6], old woman,' he said,
'Since thou made me sup and dine?
By the truth of my body,' quoth[7] bold Robin Hood,
'You could tell it in no better time.'

VIII

Now Robin Hood is to Nottingham gone,
With a link a down and a day,
And there he met with a silly old palmer[8],
Was walking along the highway.

IX

'What news? what news, thou silly old man?
What news, I do thee pray?' —
Said he, 'Three squires in Nottingham town
Are condemned to die this day.' —

X

'Come change thy apparel with me, old man,
Come change thy apparel for mine;
Here is forty shillings in good silver,
Go drink it in beer or wine.' —

XI

'O thine apparel is good,' he said,
'And mine is ragged and torn;
Wherever you go, wherever you ride,
Laugh ne'er an old man to scorn.' —

XII

'Come change thy apparel with me, old churl,
Come change thy apparel with mine;
Here are twenty pieces of good broad gold,
Go feast thy brethren with wine.'

XIII

Then he put on the old man's hat,

It stood full high on the crown[9]:
'The first bold bargain that I come at,
It shall make thee[10] come down.'

XIV

Then he put on the old man's cloak,
Was patch'd black, blue, and red;
He thought no shame, all the day long,
To wear the bags of bread[11].

XV

Then he put on the old man's breeks[12],
Was patch'd from ballup to side[13];
'By the truth of my body,' bold Robin can say[14],
'This man lov'd little pride!'

XVI

Then he put on the old man's hose[15],
Were patch'd from knee to wrist[16];
'By the truth of my body,' said bold Robin Hood,
'I'd laugh if I had any list[17].'

XVII

Then he put on the old man's shoes,
Were patch'd both beneath and aboon[18];
Then Robin Hood swore a solemn oath,
'It's good habit[19] that makes a man!'

XVIII

Now Robin Hood is to Nottingham gone,
With a link a down and a down,
And there he met with the proud Sheriff,
Was walking along the town.

XIX

'O save[20], O save, O Sheriff,' he said,
'O save, and you may see!
And what will you give to a silly old man
To-day will your hangman be?'

XX

'Some suits[21], some suits,' the Sheriff he said,
'Some suits I'll give to thee;
Some suits, some suits, and pence thirteen
To-day's a hangman's fee.'

XXI

Then Robin he turns him round about,
And jumps from stock to stone[22];
'By the truth of my body,' the Sheriff he said,
'That's well jumpt, thou nimble old man.'—

XXII

'I was ne'er a hangman in all my life,
Nor yet intends to trade[23];
But curst be he,' said bold Robin,
'That first a hangman was made!

XXIII

'I've a bag for meal, and a bag for malt,
And a bag for barley and corn;
A bag for bread, and a bag for beef,
And a bag for my little small horn.

XXIV

'I have a horn in my pocket,

I got it from Robin Hood,
And still when I set it to my mouth,
For thee it blows little good.'—

XXV

'O wind thy horn[24], thou proud fellow,
Of thee I have no doubt[25];
I wish that thou give such a blast
Till both thy eyes fall out.'

XXVI

The first loud blast that he did blow,
He blew both loud and shrill;
A hundred and fifty of Robin Hood's men
Came riding over the hill.

XXVII

The next loud blast that he did give,
He blew both loud and amain[26];
And quickly sixty of Robin Hood's men
Came shining over the plain.

XXVIII

'O who are yon,' the Sheriff he said,
'Come tripping over the lee[27]?'
'They're my attendants,' brave Robin did say,
'They'll pay a visit to thee.'

XXIX

They took the gallows from the slack[28],
They set it in the glen,
They hang'd the proud Sheriff on that,
And releas'd their own three men.

【简介】 英格兰和苏格兰民谣（English and Scottish Popular Ballads）作为一种诗歌形式是中世纪的产物，始于十二、三世纪，盛于十四、五世纪。当时，就在苏格兰南部，即所谓的“低地”（Lowlands）以及英格兰北部和苏格兰接壤的地区，即所谓的“边区”（Border）流行着无数民谣。这些民谣很多已经失传，保存下来的三百〇五首都是后人搜集所得，构成英国文学中一份极其宝贵的遗产。

这三百多首民谣都是叙事诗，用诗歌的形式来讲述各式各样的故事，内容极为丰富，反映早期英格兰和苏格兰人民生活的各方面，其中不无糟粕，但总的说来是健康的。有的民谣象有名的 *Chevy Chase*（《彻维山的追猎》）或 *Battle of Otterburn*（《奥特本之战》），讲到苏格兰人和英格兰人在边境上的战斗。有些民谣是关于海上生活的，说明苏格兰和英格兰的人民有悠久的航海历史，象 *Sir Patrick Spens*（《帕特里克·斯本士爵士》）即属这一类。很多民谣讲述罗宾汉（Robin Hood）故事。关于这位绿林豪杰我们今天所知道的故事都来自民谣。此外，民谣中有神怪和迷信，有家庭悲剧，有爱情，有仇杀，也有滑稽幽默，等等。

这些民谣是民间文学，并无作者。当时苏格兰南部以及英格兰的北部，和英格兰南部正是不同。这里没有新兴的城市和城市阶层，社会情况比较单纯，比较原始，文艺创作基本上还是人民群众之事，在集体基础上进行，没有宫廷和专业诗人的影响。在这样特殊的社会条件下，民谣就有了一个全盛时代，得到空前的繁荣和发展。

我们不难想象一首民谣产生的经过。民谣的题材十分广泛，史实、传闻以及街头巷尾发生的事件，都可以入民谣。人们在节日或其他集体活动的场合就会运用他们所熟习的方式如问答、唱和等来演唱故事情节，起初可能简单粗糙，后来在传播的过程中得到改进，最后达到比较完善的内容和形式。当然，在传播的过程中也一定有许多民谣因质量不高或其他原故而失传。

这样，民谣从头就是人民群众的集体创作，而且是在口头上进行的。这就使民谣在很多方面不同于专业诗人的作品。首先，民谣自始与书面文字无关，并没有什么固定的底稿。其次，人民群众在集体创作的过程中不会象一个专业诗人那样推敲词句或追求形式上的完美。因此，一首民谣不能拿书面文字的标准去衡量，许多地方可能是粗糙的，例如句子结构，动词时态不规则，诗行、韵脚有缺陷，等等。有时一些词和句是简单的重复，或者是毫无意义的垫词、垫句。但是我们如果记住民谣的口头性质以及民谣是有音乐的、可歌唱的，这些问题就不足为怪，相反地应看作民谣应有的特色，没有这些就不成其为民谣了。

当然，民谣中有一些词的形式是古老的，如 eldern (elder)，shoon (shoes)，gang (go)，Wodensday (Wednesday) 等。也有一些词在读音、拼写或用法上是北方方言，如 blude (blood)，claith (cloth)，lift 用作 sky 的意义等。也还有些词如 fashes (troubles)，carline (old)，在今天的英语里已不存在。象 silly 作 poor，innocent 解或 wife 作 woman 解也不是今天的英语所允许的。这些中世纪英语或北方方言可能给我们造成一些困难，但是这些困难是表面的，通过注释或多读几首民谣也就可以解决。而且由于民谣的写定往往是几百年以后的事情，文字也并不如想象的那么古老。

民谣的语言总是很生动的，但是民谣的艺术还不在于它的生动语言。所有的民谣都善于讲述故事。人们凭记忆来传播民谣，因此故事不能复杂，一般都是环绕一二个中心情节。象《帕特里克·斯本士爵士》的中心情节就是故事中的主人翁奉了国王的使命去挪威求亲，在归途遇风暴而淹没，如此而已，附带的情节极少，又没有人物刻划或心理描写。要想把这样一个故事讲得生动而不平板就十分不容易，但是我们读起这首民谣来觉得故事内容虽不多，故事性却相当强。这是因为民谣的故事有一种戏剧性，有一种结构上的紧凑。首先是动作多，通过动作或具体发生的事来发展故事，一件接一件，始终没有“冷场”的情况。非常有趣的是帕特里克·斯本士爵士接到国王书信后的反应：

The first word that Sir Patrick read
So loud, loud laugh'd he;
The neist word that Sir Patrick read
The tear blinded his e'e.

他心中的矛盾通过一笑一哭的动作来表达，非常形象化。此外，广泛运用对话来讲述故事，也是民谣的特点，通过一问一答来发展故事而又不失之冗长拖沓，也会使简单的情节带有高度戏剧性。

虽然说来民谣是以叙事为主，但它也有不可少的抒情成分。每一首民谣都有它的气氛或调子，是欢乐还是悲伤，是沉重还是轻快，等等，使故事具有一种感染力。象《帕特里克·斯本士爵士》的调子就比较低沉，自始就有一种气氛，预示不幸的结局，最后反复咏叹，更具有抒情性质。

作为诗歌，民谣的重要还在于它的形式。总的说来，民谣的形式是多样的、灵活的，而且与题材密切结合的。但最常见的最有影响的形式就是一节四行，第一二行和第三四行各成一组，韵脚落在第二和第四行的末尾，第一行和第三行稍长，各有四个重音；第二行第四行稍短，各有三个重音。我们可举《厄舍尔井的妇人》的第一节为例：

There lívéd a wífe at Úsher's wéll,
　　And a wéalthy wífe was shé;
She hád three stóut and stálwart sóns
　　And sént them o'ér the séa.

这种形式在民谣里应用很广，我们这里选的五篇民谣中有三篇是应用这种形式的。当然，这种形式并不死板，还可以有些变化。也还有些形式与此截然不同。我们不妨统称之为民谣体。民谣体的重要可以从下列一点看出，即从十八世纪末一直到现代的许多著名诗人，尤其是浪漫主义的诗人，采用民谣的形式和题材写出了精美的诗篇。事实上，在英美诗坛上民谣的传统始终不坠。这也说明十四五世纪的英格兰和苏格兰民谣在英国文学史上占一重要地位，长期以来影响着英美诗歌的发展。

【题解与注释】

1. LORD RANDAL《伦得尔勋爵》

伦得尔显然是一个年轻的贵族。他刚从打猎归来，觉得身体困顿，急于要躺下休息。他的母亲觉得他有点异样，问了他几个问题，伦得尔一一答复，但总是喊累，要求躺下。母亲的结论是儿子已经中了毒，儿子自己也说中了毒，但怎样中毒的，以及是否有救，没有说明。值得注意的是第二节母亲问：Where gat ye your dinner? 伦得尔的答复是 I dined with my true-love. 如果是这样中毒的，便意味着可能的情杀。这一类的事在那种比较原始的社会里是很寻常的。

全篇一共五节，内容与结构都很简单，母亲一问，儿子一答，就构成一节。每节四行，每行看上去很长，但实际上很短，因为每行的后半是固定的重复部分。通过问答和反复来解开情节取得艺术的效果，这正是民谣的特点。

1. hae ye been: = have you been.

2. fain wald: = gladly would.

3. gat ye: = did you get.

4. eels: = snakes.

5. in broo': = in broth.

2. THE WIFE OF USHER'S WELL
《厄舍尔井的妇人》

故事讲到一个母亲思念海上的三个儿子。在一个漫长的冬夜里母亲见到儿子们的鬼魂回来，她忙着张罗接待，但到了天明鸡叫时这些鬼魂就得离去。三个儿子临行时依依不舍，向母亲告别，向粮仓牛舍告别，向照顾母亲的女孩告别。

这里显然是利用了迷信，如鬼魂入梦之类，来描写一个母亲失去三个儿子的悲痛。全篇并无任何悲痛字样，有的倒是儿子们归来的欢乐，形成一种戏剧性的反衬(irony)。故事的细节不多，但所有的细节，如母亲吩咐家人生火，汲水、备餐，铺床，都提高了这一效果。

这首民谣的形式是最常见的一种形式，在《简介》中已有所说明。这里要指出的是一些词句的类似或重复，象第二节和第三节讲到三个儿子死在海上，或第九、第十、第十一节讲到鸡鸣时他们匆匆离去，都是民谣常利用的艺术手段。

1. **wife:** = woman.

2. **hadna:** = had not.

3. **barely ane:** = barely one.

4. **carline wife:** old woman.

5. **gane:** = gone.

6. **fashes:** troubles.

7. **come hame:** = come home.

8. **it fell:** it happened.

9. **lang and mirk:** long and gloomy.

10. **o' the birk:** of the birch.

11. **syke:** marsh

12. **ony shengh:** = any trench.

13. **fair eneugh:** = fair enough.

14. **a' my house:** = all my house.

15. **she's ta'en her mantle her about:** = she has taken her mantle about her.

16. **craw'd:** = crowed.

17. **we must awa':** = we must away, we must go away.

18. **doth craw:** = does crow.

19. **doth daw:** = does dawn, does break.

20. **channerin' worm:** fretting worm.

21. **chide:** make noise, stir.

22. **Gin we be miss'd out o' our place:** If we are not found in our place.

23. **A sair pain we maun bide:** = A sore pain we must endure.

24. **a little wee while:** = a little while.

25. **ere it be day:** = before it is day.

26. **fare ye weel:** = fare you well, farewell to you.

27. **byre:** cowhouse, cowshed.

28. **bonny lass:** handsome girl.

3. THE THREE RAVENS

《三只乌鸦》

这首民谣并不长。它通过三只乌鸦所见，描绘一幅图画：一个战死的骑士，躺在地里，旁边有他的狗在看守，上面有他的鹰在飞翔，最后一个母鹿（喻他的情人）以沉重迂缓的步子走来：

As great with young as she might goe

来到他的身旁，抬起他的头，吻了他的伤口，把他驮在背上，运到一个坑里把他葬了。全篇以一个祝愿收尾："愿上帝赐予每一个骑士这样的狗，这样的鹰，这样的情人。"

这首民谣一共十节，每节只有两行，但这两行只是有意义的文字部分。如果我们参看别的本子便会发现：

There were three ravens sat on a tree,
  Down a down, hay down, hay down,
There were three ravens sat on a tree,
  With a down,
There were three ravens sat on a tree,
They were as black as they might be,
  With a down, derry, derry, derry, down, down.

这里原来的两行变成了七行，原来的第一行重复了三次，中间夹了只有音节没有意义的三行。这可能是原来歌唱时的情况，这也是民谣的特点。而我们现在看到的两行不过是从文字的意义考虑加以整理的结果。

1. to his make: = to his mate.

2. So well do they their master keep: = so well do they watch their master.

3. no fowl: no bird.

4. fallow: brownish-red.

5. lift: = lifted.

6. bloudy: = bloody.

7. kist: = kissed.

8. earthen lake: pit, hole in the ground.

9. prime: early morning, sunrise.

10. evensong time: time for evening prayer (with song).

11. God send: = may God send.

12. leman: = lover, sweetheart.

4. SIR PATRICK SPENS

《帕特里克·斯本士爵士》

这首民谣看来较为古老。Dunfermline 作为苏格兰的首府是十三世纪或更早的事情。故事的情节很简单：帕特里克 · 斯本士爵士是个航海家，国王命他冬季出航挪威为国王求亲。在归航的路上，在苏格兰海岸不远处，遇到风暴，全船沉没，船上所有的人无一生还。历史上有无这么一个人和这么一件事无法考证。

这首民谣传播较广，有许多不同的本子。这里的一个本子较为详细，有二十二节。简单的本子只有十一、二节，所不同的就是在简单的本子里没有提到去挪威求亲（III，IV）这个任务，没有提到启航（VII，VIII），没有与风暴作斗争的描写（XI—XVII），但是重要的细节，如帕特里克爵士接到国王的来信一笑一哭，或者在回程启航时水手们见到风暴预兆：

'I saw the new moon late yestreen
　　Wi' the auld moon in her arm;
And if we gang to sea, master,
　　I fear we'll come to harm.'

以及最后三节（XX，XXI，XXII）描绘妇女们等待他们归来，反复咏叹他们的不幸遭遇，在所有的本子里都是一样的。这些不同本子中的同与不同也说明民谣的艺术和特点。

1. **blude-red:** = blood-red.
2. **whare:** = where.
3. **skeely skipper:** skilful captain.
4. **spak:** = spoke.
5. **eldern knight:** = elder knight.
6. **at the king's right knee:** on the king's right hand.
7. **a braid letter:** a broad letter, a large letter.
8. **was walking on the strand:** = who was walking on the shore.
9. **Noroway:** = Norway.
10. **o'er the faem:** = over the foam, over the sea.
11. **bring her hame:** = bring her home.
12. **neist:** = next.
13. **wha is this has done:** = who is this that has done.
14. **tauld the king o' me:** = told the king about me.
15. **be it wind, be it weet ...:** = whether it be wind, whether it be rain ....
16. **hoysed:** = hoised.
17. **Monenday:** = Monday.
18. **wi' a' the speed they may:** with all the speed they were capable of.
19. **Wodensday:** = Wednesday.
20. **Mak ready:** = make ready, get ready.
21. **Our gude ship sails the morn:** = Our good ship sails in the morning.
22. **late yestreen:** = late yesterday evening.
23. **gang:** = go.
24. **lift:** sky.
25. **gurly:** = growling, surly.

26. The ankers brak, and the topmast lap: = The anchors broke and the top-mast leapt.

27. sic: = such.

28. cam owre: = came over.

29. ne'er: = never.

30. the saut sea: = the salt sea.

31. claith: = cloth; **a web of the silken claith:** = a length of silk.

32. wap: = wrap.

33. let nae: = let not.

34. laith: = loath.

35. cork-heel'd shoon: = cork-heeled shoes.

36. or: = ere, before.

37. wat: = wetted.

38. aboon: = above.

39. mony: = many.

40. flatter'd on the faem: tossed afloat on the sea.

41. never mair: = never more.

42. gowd kames: = gold combs.

43. ain: = own.

44. nae mair: = no more.

45. Half-owre, half-owre to Aberdour: = Half-over, half-over to Aberdeen.

5. ROBIN HOOD AND THE WIDOW'S THREE SONS
《罗宾汉和寡妇的三个儿子》

中世纪末期，即十五世纪，也可能更后一些，繁衍出以罗宾汉为主要人物的一系列民谣。罗宾汉是一个传说中的人物，也可以说是民谣中的人物，纯系人民群众的创造，历史上并无其人。他的英雄业绩，劫富济贫，扶弱抑强，反映人民群众反封建主义，反豪暴势力的思想。有关罗宾汉及其伙伴们的故事流传之广，已家喻户晓，但很少人知道这些故事来自民谣。

有关罗宾汉的民谣不仅是多而成套，而且每一首都有一定长度，情节也比较复杂，故事性比较强。但是和所有的民谣一样，每一首都有其主要情节，并且和其他各首民谣是相互独立的。更重要的是，在形式和技巧上都具有民谣的特点，例如词句的反复，气氛的统一，情节或人物的戏剧性，等等。

在《罗宾汉和寡妇的三个儿子》里，一上来第一段就点出"欢乐的五月"(the merry month of May)，也就是阳光明媚的英格兰，气氛是轻松愉快的。自第二节起到最后第二十九节，分为三大段，每一段都以

Now Robin Hood is to Nottingham gone
With a link a down and a day

开始。不用说这里的第二行是无意义的，但是提示出轻快的节奏或步伐。第一大段讲述罗宾汉了解到寡妇的三个儿子因杀死国王的鹿而将被处死；第二大段讲述罗宾汉说服一个年老的行脚僧（palmer）和他换衣服，化装去救三个年轻人；第三段讲述罗宾汉救了三个年轻人，处死了执法的州官（Sheriff）。

这一类民谣形成较迟，而且以英格兰为背景，文字上没有北方方言的特点，加上情节引人入胜，读起来比较顺利，虽然篇幅长一些并不觉其长。

1. With a link a down and a day: 此行是一种叠唱，并无意义，只是用声韵表示轻快的步法。

2. a silly old woman: = a poor old woman.

3. ministers: clergymen.

4. ta'en: = taken.

5. Bearing their long bows with thee: = Being your men with long bows.

6. Dost thou not mind: = Don't you remember.

7. quoth: said.

8. a silly old palmer: a poor old palmer.

9. crown: top of the head.

10. thee: *i. e.* the hat.

11. bags of bread: *i. e.* the black, blue and red patches sewed to the cloak for keeping bread.

12. breeks: breeches, underbreeches.

13. from ballup to side: = from center or front to side.

14. can say: = did say.

15. hose: = covering for legs or feet, stockings.

16. from knee to wrist: from knee to ankle.

17. if I had any list: if I had any desire.

18. aboon: = above.

19. good habit: good clothing.

20. O save: = O Christ save you.

21. some suits: *i. e.* suits from the condemned.

22. from stock to stone: from stump to stone, that is, nimbly.

23. to trade: to be the hangman and earn the fee.

24. wind thy horn: blow your horn.

25. I have no doubt: I have no fear.

26. amain: with main force, violently.

27. over the lee: over the meadow.

28. slack: hollow, dell.

2 EDMUND SPENSER
1552–1599

1. Amoretti
Sonnets 15, 54, 70 and 75
2. Prothalamium

王佐良　选注

1. AMORETTI

Sonnet 15

Ye tradefull merchants, that with weary toyle[1]
Do seeke most pretious[2] things to make your gain,
And both the Indias[3] of their treasures spoile,
What needeth you to seeke so farre in vaine?
For loe[4] my love[5] doth in her selfe containe
All this world's riches that may farre be found[6].
If saphyres[7], loe her eyes be saphyres plaine;
If rubies, loe her lips be rubies sound;
If pearls, her teeth be pearls both pure and round;
If yvorie, her forhead yvory weene[8];
If gold, her locks are finest gold on ground[9];
If silver, her fair hands are silver sheene[10].
But that which fairest is[11], but few behold:
Her mind, adornd with vertues manifold[12].

Sonnet 54

Of this worlds theatre[1] in which we stay,

My love like the spectator ydly sits[2]
Beholding me that all the pageants play[3],
Disguysing diversly my troubled wits[4].
Sometimes I joy when glad occasion fits,
And mask in myrth lyke to a comedy[5]:
Soone after when my joy to sorrow flits,
I waile and make my woes a tragedy.
Yet she, beholding me with constant eye,
Delights not in my merth nor rues my smart[6]:
But when I laugh she mocks, and when I cry
She laughs and hardens evermore her heart.
What then can move her? if nor merth nor mone[7],
She is no woman, but a sencelesse[8] stone.

Sonnet 70

Fresh spring the herald of loves[1] mighty king,
In whose cote armour[2] richly are displayd
All sorts of flowers the which on earth do spring
In goodly colours[3] gloriously arrayd[4].
Goe to my love, where she is carelesse layd[5],
Yet in her winters bowre[6] not well awake:
Tell her the joyous time wil not be staid[7]
Unlesse she doe him by the forelock take[8].
Bid her therefore her selfe soone ready make,
To wayt on love amongst his lovely crew[9]:
Where every one that misseth then her make[10],
Shall be by him amearest with penance dew[11].
Make hast[12] therefore sweet love, whilest it is prime,
For none can call againe the passéd time.

Sonnet 75

One day I wrote her name upon the strand[1],
But came the waves and washéd it away:

Agayne I wrote it with a second hand,
But came the tyde, and made my paynes his pray[2].
"Vayne man[3]," sayd she, "that doest in vaine assay[4],
A mortall thing so to immortalize[5],
For I my selve shall lyke to this decay[6],
And eek my name bee wypéd out lykewize[7]."
"Not so," quod I[8], "let baser things devize[9],
To dy in dust, but you shall live by fame:
My verse your vertues rare[10] shall eternize,
And in the heavens wryte[11] your glorious name,
Where whenas death shall all the world subdew[12],
Our love shall live, and later life renew[13]."

2. PROTHALAMIUM

Calm was the day, and through the trembling air
Sweet breathing Zephyrus[1] did softly play,
A gentle spirit, that lightly did delay
Hot Titan's beams[2], which then did glister fair;
When I (whom sullen care,
Through discontent of my long fruitless stay
In princes' court, and expectation vain
Of idle hopes, which still do fly away,
Like empty shadows, did afflict my brain)
Walked forth, to ease my pain.
Along the shore of silver streaming Thames;
Whose rutty bank[3], the which his river hems,
Was painted all with variable flowers,
And all the meads[4] adorned with dainty gems,
Fit to deck maidens' bowers,
And crown their paramours[5],
Against the bridal day[6], which is not long:
    Sweet Thames! run softly, till I end my song[7].

There, in a meadow, by the river's side,
A flock of nymphs[8] I chancèd to espy,[9]
All lovely daughters of the flood thereby[10],
With goodly greenish locks, all loose untied,
As each had been a bride:
And each one had a little wicker basket,
Made of fine twigs, entrailèd curiously[11].
In which they gathered flowers to fill their flasket[12],
And with fine fingers cropt full feateously[13]
The tender stalks on high.
Of every sort which in that meadow grew
They gathered some; the violet, pallid blue,
The little daisy, that at evening closes,
The virgin lily, and the primrose true,
With store of vermeil roses[14],
To deck their bridegroom's posies[15],
Against the bridal day, which was not long:
Sweet Thames! run softly, till I end my song.

With that, I saw two swans[16] of goodly hue
Come softly swimming down along the Lee[17];
Two fairer birds I yet did never see;
The snow which doth the top of Pindus[18] strew
Did never whiter shew,
Nor Jove himself, when he a swan would be
For love of Leda[19], whiter did appear;
Yet Leda was, they say, as white as he,
Yet not so white as these, nor nothing near;
So purely white they were,
That even the gentle stream, the which them bare,
Seemed foul to them, and bade his billows spare
To wet their silken feathers[20], lest they might

Soil their fair plumes with water not so fair,
And mar their beauties bright,
That shone as heaven's light,
Against their bridal day, which was not long:
Sweet Thames! run softly, till I end my song.

Eftsoons[21] the nymphs, which now had flowers their fill, [22]
Ran all in haste to see that silver brood[23],
As they came floating on the crystal flood;
Whom when they saw, they stood amazèd still,
Their wondering eyes to fill;
Them seemed they never saw a sight so fair[24]
Of fowls so lovely, that they sure did deem
Them heavenly born, or to be that same pair
Which through the sky draw Venus' silver team[25];
For sure they did not seem
To be begot of any earthly seed[26],
But rather angels, or of angels' breed;
Yet were they bred of summer's heat[27], they say,
In sweetest season, when each flower and weed
The earth did fresh array;
So fresh they seemed as day,
Even as their bridal day, which was not long:
Sweet Thames! run softly, till I end my song.

Then forth they all out of their baskets drew
Great store of flowers, the honour of the field,
That to the sense did fragrant odours yield,
All which upon those goodly birds they threw,
And all the waves did strew,
That like old Peneus' waters[28] they did seem,
When down along by pleasant Tempe's shore[29],
Scattered with flowers, through Thessaly[30] they stream,

That they appear, through lilies' plenteous store,
Like a bride's chamber floor[31].
Two of those nymphs, meanwhile, two garlands bound
Of freshest flowers which in that mead they found,
The which presenting all in trim array,
Their snowy foreheads therewithal they crowned,
Whilst one did sing this lay[32],
Prepared against that day,
Against their bridal day, which was not long:
    Sweet Thames! run softly, till I end my song.

"Ye gentle birds! the world's fair ornament,
And heaven's glory, whom this happy hour
Doth lead unto your lover's blissful bower,
Joy may you have, and gentle hearts' content
Of your love's couplement[33];
And let fair Venus, that is queen of love,
With her heart-quelling son[34] upon you smile,
Whose smile, they say, hath virtue to remove
All love's dislike[35], and friendship's faulty guile
For ever to assoil; [36]
Let endless peace your steadfast hearts accord,
And blessed plenty wait upon your board; [37]
And let your bed with pleasures chaste abound,
That fruitful issue may to you afford[38],
Which may your foes confound,
And make your joys redound
Upon your bridal day, which is not long:
    Sweet Thames! run softly till I end my song."

So ended she; and all the rest around
To her redoubled that her undersong[39],
Which said their bridal day should not be long:

And gentle Echo from the neighbour ground
Their accents did resound.
So forth those joyous birds did pass along,
Adown the Lee, that to them murmured low,
As he would speak[40], but that he lacked a tongue,
Yet did by signs his glad affection show,
Making his stream run slow.
And all the fowl which in his flood did dwell
'Gan[41] flock about these twain, that did excel
The rest, so far as Cynthia doth shend
The lesser stars.[42] So they, enrangèd well, [43]
Did on those two attend,
And their best service lend,
Against their wedding day, which was not long:
Sweet Thames! run softly, till I end my song.

At length they all to merry London came, [44]
To merry London, my most kindly nurse,
That to me gave this life's first native source;
Though from another place I take my name[45],
An house of ancient fame:
There when they came, whereas[46] those bricky towers
The which on Thames' broad, agèd back do ride,
Where now the studious lawyers have their bowers, [47]
There whilom wont the Templar Knights to bide, [48]
Till they decayed through pride:
Next whereunto there stands a stately place,
Where oft I gainèd gifts and goodly grace[49]
Of that great lord[50] which therein wont to dwell,
Whose want too well now feels my friendless case; [51]
But ah! here fits not well
Old woes, but joys, to tell,
Against the bridal day, which is not long:

Sweet Thames! run softly, till I end my song.

Yet therein now doth lodge a noble peer[52],
Great England's glory, and the world's wide wonder,
Whose dreadful name late through all Spain did thunder[53],
And Hercules' two pillars[54] standing near
Did make to quake and fear:
Fair branch of honour, flower of chivalry!
That fillest England with thy triumph's fame,
Joy have thou of thy noble victory,
And endless happiness of thine own name[55],
That promiseth the same;
That through thy prowess and victorious arms[56]
Thy country may be freed from foreign harms;
And great Elisa's[57] glorious name may ring
Through all the world, filled with thy wide alarms,
Which some brave muse may sing
To ages following,
Upon the bridal day, which is not long:
Sweet Thames! run softly, till I end my song.

From those high towers this noble lord issuing,
Like radiant Hesper[58] when his golden hair
In th' ocean billows he hath bathèd fair,
Descended to the river's open viewing,
With a great train ensuing[59].
Above the rest were goodly to be seen[60]
Two gentle knights of lovely face and feature
Beseeming well the bower of any queen[61],
With gifts of wit, and ornaments of nature, [62]
Fit for so goodly stature,
That like the twins of Jove they seemed in sight, [63]
Which deck the baldrick of the heavens bright[64];

They two, forth pacing to the river's side,
Received those two fair brides, their love's delight;
Which, at th' appointed tide[65],
Each one did make his bride,
Against their bridal day, which is not long:
　　Sweet Thames! run softly, till I end my song.

【作者简介】 Edmund Spenser（艾德蒙特·斯宾塞，1552—1599），十六世纪英国重要诗人，求学于剑桥大学，毕业后变成贵族家的门客，结识了名人菲力浦·雪尼爵士，1580年成为英国驻爱尔兰总督的秘书，从此长期居住任地，直到1598年由于爱尔兰人民举行反英起义，他的庄宅被烧，才仓皇奔回英国，不久即病死于伦敦。

他的主要诗作有牧歌体的 *Shepheardes Calender*（《牧童的月历》，1579）和熔传说、寓言和对伊丽莎白女王的颂歌于一炉的 *The Faerie Queene*（《仙后》，1596），两者都是卷帙丰富的长诗，后者尤为其毕生精力所注，但仅完成计划中十二卷的前六卷。此外著名的作品还有长诗 *Colin Clouts Come Home Againe*（《克劳茨回家记》，1595），两首对婚姻的颂歌 *Epithalamium* (1595) 和 *Prothalamium* (1596)，一本以 *Amoretti*（《爱情小唱》，1595）为题的十四行诗集。

他在写诗时，立志重振 Chaucer 所创立的英国诗传统，因此用字古奥，为其友菲力浦·雪尼所病，然而内容丰富，形式完整，音乐性强，在诗律上富于创造性，特别是建立了优美流畅的"斯宾塞体"（即五音步一行的八行加上六音步的一行而成的九行体），影响深远，后世的 Thomson，Byron，Shelley，Keats，Tennyson 等人都曾用它写出佳作，因此人们称斯宾塞为"诗人的诗人"。

十六世纪英国诗剧崛起，许多有诗才的人被吸引到这个新品种之中，但在非戏剧性诗歌的领域中，也是呈现一片英国文艺复兴的蓬勃气象，这当中最有成就的诗人公认为斯宾塞。

【题解与注释】

为了适合我国学生的需要，我们在这里选了篇幅较短而又比较易懂的 *Prothalamium* 一诗和十四行诗四首。

1. AMORETTI

十六世纪九十年代起，十四行诗在英国风行一时，但大多是意大利和法国的十四行诗的仿作，真正写得出色的不过 Sidney，Spenser，Shakespeare 三人，此外 Michael Drayton，Samuel Daniel，Fulke Greville 等人亦间有佳作。这些人所写的十四行诗，大多用来歌颂爱情，往往一整个集子都是献给一个所爱的姑娘的。

斯宾塞的 *Amoretti* 一集共有十四行诗 89 首，出版于 1595 年，也是用来歌颂一个姑娘的，据说就是后来成为他的第二个妻子的 Elizabeth Boyle。他所表达的内容除了描写姑娘的美丽之外，还有心灵更美于外貌的柏拉图思想，文学能使人不朽的文艺复兴时期的信念（见下面所选的第 75 首），等等，其特点在于音乐性强，首首可诵，写法则于优美中见变化；十四行体本来就结构谨严，在斯宾塞笔下更见整体形式之美。

斯宾塞在十四行诗中的脚韵安排是 abab bcbc cdcd ee，这是所谓英国式，与意大利原型不同。这也是一个比较难于处理的形式，斯宾塞则运用自如，足见其诗艺的高超。

这几首诗的本文我们保留了斯宾塞原来的拼法。有些与今不同的形式实是伊丽莎白朝英文的共同形式，如：y = i（toyle / toil, saphyres / saphires, yvory / ivory）；er = ir（vertue / virtue, merth / mirth）；词尾多余的 e（seeke / seek, vaine / vain, containe / contain）；过去分词词尾中用 d 而不用 ed（adornd / adorned, displayd / displayed）；词尾的 -ful 常作 -full（tradefull / tradeful, mortall / mortal）；若干异体词（pray/prey, subdew/ subdue），等等。但作者本人并不一致，如第 15 首第 10 行中就见到 yvorie 与 yvory 两个形式。斯宾塞也曾为了力求古朴而独创或复活某些词，但在这里所选四首诗中少见。在句法方面，几乎完全是十六世纪时书面体英语的通常用法。总之，能读莎士比亚剧本的人读斯宾塞的诗是不会有多少困难的。

标题 Amoretti，意大利语，意为 little loves，或 little love poems，即“爱情小唱”。

Sonnet 15

1. Ye tradefull merchants: 起句即言商人，具见当时英国的海外贸易之兴盛。**weary toyle,** = weary toil.

2. pretious: precious.

3. both the Indias: 指 India 和 the West Indies。这行的正常结构应是 spoil both the Indias of their treasures，即掠取印度和西印度群岛的财宝。

4. loe: = lo，感叹词。

5. my love: 我的所爱的人。

6. that may farre be found: farre = anywhere.

7. If saphyres ...: 以下一连串的比喻，总意是各种珍宝集她一身。

8. weene: 古字，意为假设为，可以看作，即她的额可视为象牙。

9. on ground: = on earth，在人世上。

10. silver sheene: = silver sheen，银的光泽。

11. But that which fairest is …: 最后两行起了变化，从身体外表转到内心之美。

12. adornd with vertues manifold: adorned with manifold virtues，（她的心）有多种美德。

Sonnet 54

1. this worlds theatre: = this world's theatre，当时许多作家将人世看成舞台。斯宾塞之外，莎士比亚也曾写过：

All the world's a stage,
And all the men and women merely players;

—*As You Like It,* II, vii, 139–140

Life's but a walking shadow, a poor player
That struts and frets his hour on the stage,
And then is heard no more.

—*Macbeth,* V, v, 24–26

2. My love like the spectator ydly sits: 我的爱人象一个坐着看戏的旁观者；ydly, = idly.

3. Beholding me that all the pageants play: 看着我扮演各种角色；pageants = roles.

4. Disguysing diversly my troubled wits: disguysing 即 disguising，此行意为用不同方法掩盖我内心的不安。

5. mask in myrth lyke to a comedy: = mask in mirth like to a comedy，戴着欢乐的面具，如演喜剧；lyke to = like.

6. Delights not in my merth nor rues my smart: 既不因我乐而喜，也不因我痛而悲。

7. if nor merth nor mone: 如果欢乐和啼哭都不能打动她；mone= moan.

8. sencelesse: = senseless，无感觉的，冥顽不灵的。

Sonnet 70

1. loves: = love's.

2. cote armour: = coat of arms，（贵族家的）纹章。

3. goodly colours: = splendid colours.

4. arrayd: = arrayed，穿着，装饰着。

5. layd: = laid.

6. winters bowre: = winter's bower，冬天的闺房。

7. wil not be staid: = will not be stayed；stayed，被挡住，停住；整行意为：告

诉她吧，欢乐的时间不会停留。

8. Unlesse she doe him by the forelock take: 除非是她赶紧抓住时机；him 指上文所说的 time；take time by the forelock 现已是成语，意为抓住时机。

9. To wayt on love amongst his lovely crew: 在丽人群中迎候爱神。

10. her make: = her mate, her lover.

11. Shall be by him amearest with penance dew: 将会受到他的惩罚；amearest 受到；penance dew = penance due，应有的惩罚。

12. hast: = haste; **prime** = early morning. 这首诗的主要意思是劝所爱的姑娘要及时接受爱情，否则机缘一纵即逝。

Sonnet 75

此诗写法略有不同，一上来就是叙述体，下面还有一问一答的对话。

1. upon the strand: 在沙滩上。

2. But came the tyde, and made my paynes his pray: 潮水来了，使我的辛苦变为徒劳；**tyde** = tide；**pray** = prey，为（潮水）吞食的牺牲品。

3. Vayne man: 妄想的人。

4. vaine assay: = try in vain，徒然尝试。

5. A mortall thing so to immortalize:（企图）使一个必死的东西变成不朽。

6. shall lyke to this decay: = shall decay like this；将会象这个一样地腐朽；decay 是动词。

7. eek my name bee wypéd out lykewize: 我的名字也会很快被抹掉；eek, eke: = also; wypéd out: = wiped out; lykewise: = likewise.

8. quod I: = quoth I，我回答说。

9. devize: = contrive，费尽心机。

10. your vertues rare: 你的难得的德行，你的不寻常的优点。

11. wryte: = write.

12. whenas death shall all the world subdew: 虽然死亡将征服全世界；**whenas** = whereas; **subdew** = subdue.

13. later life renew: 以后生命将延续下去。

这首诗的主要意思是：依仗我的诗句，我们的爱情可以不朽，你的声名也就永存。这一种文学可以使人不朽的信念体现了文艺复兴时期人文主义的特色，当时用十四行诗表达此意者颇有其人，莎士比亚的 Sonnet 55（“Not marble, nor the guilded monument, / Of Princes shall outlive this powerfull rime”）就是一例。

2. PROTHALAMIUM

此诗出版于 1596 年，原有一个副标题，说是为庆祝贵族 Lord Worcester 的两个女儿的正式订婚（spousall）而作。（现版已将拼法现代化了。）

前一年，斯宾塞曾作另一婚礼颂歌，名 *Epithalamium*，一般认为写得更好。然而 *Prothalamium* 也自有其优点，即以较短的篇幅描写了一个泰晤士河上的盛典，颇富英国的水乡风光，在读者面前展现了伦敦近郊草地和花木的秀丽，而音调优美，特别是一再重复的迭唱：

Sweet Thames! run softly, till I end my song.

成为传诵至今的名句，使人感染到英国文艺复兴初期的新鲜气息。

诗中穿插有几处作者对自己求取功名利禄而不得的感慨，略见当时文人寄居王公大人门下的辛酸，然而着墨无多，还不显得不协调，倒是稍有阴影，使得诗篇不至过分甜美。

此诗结构如下：1—18 行，写当日气候，诗人在河岸上徘徊；19—36 行，写一群仙女准备迎亲；37—72 行，写两位新娘来临；73—126 行，写仙女们接待新娘；127—144 行，写仙女卫护新娘来到伦敦；145—162 行，歌颂女王的宠臣 Lord Essex 与女王本人；163—180 行，写 Essex 及众人出迎，两位新郎迎接了新娘。

1. Zephyrus: 即 Zephyr，和风。

2. Hot Titan's beams: 太阳光；Titans 本是希腊神话里的巨人，但从古罗马诗人 Virgil 与 Ovid 起，作家有用 Titan 作为太阳的名字的，与斯宾塞同时的莎士比亚也这样用过：

And flecked Darkness like a drunkard reels
From forth Day's path and Titan's fiery wheels.

—*Romeo and Juliet*, II, iii

3. rutty bank: = rooty bank; rooty，多根的，即长满了树木花草的（河岸）。**the which his river hems** = which hems the water，它们给河水镶了边；the which = which.

4. meads: = meadows，草地。

5. paramours: 爱人；（非今日‘情夫、情妇’之意）。

6. Against the bridal day: 为了准备婚日的来临；against 在此意为 prepared against.

7. Sweet Thames! run softy, till I end my song: 传诵的名句，词简，意境美，声韵动人。它传达了当时泰晤士河的优美情调。二十世纪的现代派诗人 T. S. Eliot 在其名作 *The Waste Land*（《荒原》，1922）第三章 The Fire Sermon（《火诫》）中就引用此行，以与后来污秽的泰晤士河及其所象征的现代生活相对照。

8. nymphs: 原意是神话中居于山林水泽的仙女，此处借指来迎接新娘的美人们。

9. espy: 窥见。

10. daughters of the flood thereby: 那里的泰晤士河的女儿们，即上述来迎亲的仙女们。

11. entrailèd curiously: 编得很精细的；curiously 在此是古意，仔细地，精心地。

12. flasket: 长形浅篮。

13. cropt full feateously: 摘得十分整齐；feateously，古字，= neatly。

14. the violet … daisy … lily … primrose … roses: 这几行里出现了一连串花名，表现了泰晤士河岸之美，也传达了诗人对于春天来临的喜悦。二百多年以后，年轻的浪漫诗人济慈（Keats）也在一节诗里写下一连串的花：

guess each sweet
Wherewith the seasonable month endows
The grass, the thicket, and the fruit-tree wild:
White hawthorn, and the pastoral eglantine;
Fast fading violets cover'd up in leaves;
And mid-May's eldest child,
The coming musk-rose, full of dewy wine,
The murmurous haunt of flies on summer eves.

—*Ode to a Nightingale*

只是情调有所不同，季节也从春天转入初夏。这样集中、热烈地歌颂各类的花，在英国诗里成为传统，为其特色之一。

15. bridegroom's posies: 新郎的花束，准备送给新娘的。

16. two swans: 指两位新娘。

17. the Lee: 即 the Lea，是流入泰晤士河的一条河。

18. the top of Pindus: Pindus 是希腊 Thessaly 地区的山名。

19. Jove himself, when he a swan would be / For love of Leda: 希腊神话故事，天神 Jupiter（即 Jove）看见 Leda 在洗澡，变作白天鹅接近了她，使她生了孩子，其中一个就是希腊美人 Helen。

20. Seemed foul to them, and bade his billows spare / To wet their silken feathers: 连河水都自惭形秽，嘱咐波浪不要去打湿天鹅的洁白如丝的羽毛。

21. Eftsoons: 古字，= soon afterwards.

22. had flowers their fill: had their fill of flowers，摘够了她们所要的花。

23. that silver brood: 指两位新娘。

24. Them seemed they never saw a sight so fair: = it seemed to them that they had never seen a sight so fair，她们感到似乎从来没有得到过这样美丽的一瞥。

25. draw Venus' silver team: 拉着爱神的车子；silver team 指 chariot。

26. they did not seem / To be begot of any earthly seed: 她们不象是世上凡人所生的；seed，精液。

27. bred of summer's heat: 在夏天的炎热中成孕的；另外，这里还有双关语，隐射新娘之一的 Lady Katherine Somerset 名字中的 Somerset 一字。

28. old Peneus' waters: Peneus 是希腊一条河流名。

29. Tempe's shore: 希腊 Thessaly 地区东北部一狭长山谷的出海处，富林木之胜，风景甚美。

30. Thessaly: 希腊北部一区，中为平原，四围是大山，以多古迹和出勇士著称。

以上用希腊地名，表示一个最美的处所。当时因为正值重新出现了崇拜古希腊文化的热潮，文人言必称希腊，以示典雅。

31. Like a bride's chamber floor:（花投得那样多，布满了河面，看起来几乎）象新房的地板。

32. lay: 歌曲。

33. your love's couplement: 你们爱情的结合；couplement, union of pairs.

34. her heart-quelling son: 指 Venus 之子 Cupid，他也是爱神，凡是被他的箭射中的都必然坠入情网，故云 heart-quelling（刺心）。

35. hath virtue to remove / All love's dislike: 有能力使所爱的人不再厌恶自己；virtue，效力，功效。

36. For ever to assoil: 永远宽恕（机诈的朋友）。

37. And blessed plenty wait upon your board: 上天祝福的丰足食物将在餐桌上侍候你们，即：你们将不缺食。

38. let your bed with pleasures chaste abound, / That fruitful issue may to you afford: 这两行是说祝愿你们早生贵子，但将它写得典雅；pleasures 本是指床上之乐，但诗人又加上似乎矛盾的 chaste，表示这是一种正当而不是淫荡的行为。

39. all the rest around / To her redoubled that her undersong: 她身边的其余仙女唱着她歌里的迭句，即 Sweet Thames 那一行。

40. As he would speak: 此处 he 指河流，即 the Lee。

41. 'Gan: = Began，开始。

42. so far as Cynthia doth shend / The lesser stars: 就象月神使得众星失色那样；Cynthia，月神，女王伊丽莎白也常被称为 Cynthia，因此这里还有对女王的赞颂；shend, put to shame，使之感羞，即使之自惭不如。

43. enrangèd well: 整齐地排列成行。

44. At length they all to merry London came: 此节叙新娘和众仙女来到伦敦情况，同时插入诗人个人对伦敦的观感。

请注意他称伦敦为 merry London，'愉快的伦敦'。

45. from another place I take my name: 诗人生在伦敦，但其家族世居 Althorp 地方。

46. whereas: = where.

47. Where now the studious lawyers have their bowers: 那一带有四个有名的律师组织，它们是 Lincoln's Inn，Gray's Inn，the Inner Temple，和 the Middle Temple，统称 Inns of Court.

48. There whilom wont the Templar Knights to bide: 过去十字军救护团骑士常住之所；Templar Knights 通称 Knights Templar，是保护去耶路撒冷朝圣的基督徒的军事组织，创立于 1118 年，后来形成欧洲各国政治中的重要力量，1312 年为教皇下令解散；whilom，古字，formerly，过去；wont，古字，be accustomed to; used to.

49. a stately place, / Where oft I gainèd gifts and goodly grace: 指 Essex House，诗人曾在那里受到 Lord Leicester 的赏赐与称赞。

50. that great lord: 指 Lord Leicester（c.1532–88），伊丽莎白女王的宠臣。

51. Whose want too well now feels my friendless case: 我现在缺乏朋友援引，更感失去了他之苦恼；按斯宾塞写此诗时，Leicester 已死去七八年。句子倒装，主语应是 my friendless case。

52. a noble peer: 指 Lord Essex (1566–1601)，女王的另一宠臣，曾经显赫一时，但最后由于图叛被斩首。斯宾塞写此诗时，Essex 正得意，所以诗人在下面几行对他大加歌颂，希望能通过他的关系接近女王。

53. Whose dreadful name late through all Spain did thunder: 他的威名不久前震动整个西班牙，指 Lord Essex 曾率海军去占领西班牙的 Cadiz 港。

54. Hercules' two pillars: 指直布罗陀海峡，海峡甚狭，两岸的高岬，被称为大力神的两柱。此行与下行仍是赞 Essex 的军功。

55. endless happiness of thine own name: 隐射 Lord Essex，因他的名字是 Robert Devereux，而后一字与法语 heureux（快乐）相近，故说 happiness 云云。

56. victorious arms: 取得胜利的武器；仍指 Essex 的军功。

57. great Elisa: 指伊丽莎白女王。

58. radiant Hesper: 明亮的晚星；Hesper 即 Hesperns，the evening star。这里诗人在描述 Essex 的英俊。

59. with a great train ensuing: 有一大群人跟随在后，train，一长列的人。

60. goodly to be seen: = gracefully to be seen.

61. Beseeming well the bower of any queen: 适合于住在任何王后的内室；配得上任何高贵的姑娘。

62. gifts of wit, and ornaments of nature: 天生聪敏，又加文采风流。

63. like the twins of Jove they seemed in sight: 看起来象是朱庇特神的双生子。

64. deck the baldrick of the heavens bright: 装饰着明亮的天空所形成的肩带。

65. at th' appointed tide: 在预定的时刻；tide，古用法，时刻。

3 CHRISTOPHER MARLOWE 1569–93

THE TRAGICAL HISTORY OF DR. FAUSTUS

(selections)

杨周翰　选注

Enter Chorus

Not marching in the fields of *Thrasimen*[1],
Where *Mars*[2] old mate the warlike *Carthagens*[3],
Nor sporting in the dalliance of love
In Courts of Kings, where state is overturn'd, [4]
Nor in the pomp of proud audacious deeds[5],
Intends our Muse[6] to vaunt[7] his heavenly verse;
Only this, Gentles: we must now perform
The form[8] of *Faustus's* fortunes, good or bad,
And now to patient judgements we appeal,
And speak for *Faustus* in his infancy.
Now is he born, of parents base of stock,
In *Germany*, within a Town call'd *Rhode*[9]:
At riper years to *Wittenberg*[10] he went,
Whereas[11] his kinsmen[12] chiefly brought him up;
So much he profits in Divinity[13],
The fruitful plot[14] of Scholarism[15] grac'd[16],
That shortly he was grac'd with Doctor's name[17],
Excelling all, whose sweet delight's[18] dispute[19]

In th' heavenly matters of Theology,
Till swoll'n with cunning[20] of a self conceit[21],
His waxen wings[22] did mount above his reach [23],
And melting, [24] heavens[25] conspir'd[26] his over-throw:
For falling to a devilish exercise,
And glutted[27] now with learning's golden gifts,
He surfeits[28] upon cursed Necromancy: [29]
Nothing so sweet as Magic is to him,
Which he prefers before his chiefest bliss[30];
And this the man[31] that in his study sits.

Exit[32].

Scene i

Enter[1] Faustus *in his study.*

Faustus. Settle thy studies[2] *Faustus*, and begin
To sound[3] the depth of that[4] thou wilt profess[5].
Having commenc'd[6], be a Divine in shew[7],
Yet level at the end[8] of every Art,
And live and die in *Aristotle's* works[9].
Sweet *Analitics*[10], 'tis thou hast[11] ravish[12] me,
Bene disserere est finis logicis[13].
Is to dispute well Logic's chiefest end?
Affords this Art[14] no greater miracle?
Then read no more, thou hast attain'd that end;
A greater subject fitteth *Faustus's* wit:
Bid *on kai me on*[15] farewell, *Galen*[16] come:
Seeing[17] *ubi desinit philosophus, ibi incipit medicus.*[18]
Be a Physician, *Faustus*, heap up gold[19],
And be eterniz'd[20] for some wondrous cure:
Summum bonum medicinae sanitas, [21]
The end of Physic is our bodies' health:
Why *Faustus*, hast thou not attain'd that end?
Is not thy common talk sound Aphorisms[22]?

Are not thy bills[23] hung up as monuments,
Whereby whole Cities have escap't the plague,
And thousand desperate maladies been cur'd?
Yet art thou still but *Faustus*, and a man.[24]
Couldst thou make men to live eternally,
Or being dead, raise them to life again,
Then this profession were to be esteem'd.
Physic, farewell: where is *Justinian*[25]?
Si una eademque res legatur duobus, alter rem, alter valorem rei, etc.[26]
A petty case of paltry[27] Legacies:
Exhaereditare filium non potest pater, nisi—[28]
Such is the subject of the *Institute,* [29]
And universal body[30] of the law.
This study fits a Mercenary drudge[31],
Who aims at nothing but external trash, [32]
Too servile and illiberal[33] for me.
When all is done, *Divinity* is best:
Jerome's Bible[34], *Faustus*, view it well:
Stipendium peccati mors est: ha, *Stipendium, etc.*[35]
The reward of sin is death? that's hard:
Si peccasse negamus, fallimur, et nulla est in nobis veritas:[36]
If we say that we have no sin we deceive our selves, and there is no truth in us.
Why then belike[37]
We must sin, and so consequently die,
Ay, [38] we must die, an everlasting death.
What doctrine call you this? *Che sera, sera*:[39]
What will be, shall be; *Divinity* adieu.
These Metaphysics[40] of Magicians,
And Necromantic books are heavenly.
Lines, Circles, Signs, Letters, and Characters, [41]
Ay these are those that *Faustus* most desires.

O what a world of profit and delight,
Of power, of honour, and omnipotence,
Is promised to the Studious Artisan?[42]
All things that move between the quiet Poles[43]
Shall be at my command: Emperors and Kings,
Are but[44] obey'd in their several[45] Provinces[46]:
Nor can they raise the wind, or rend the clouds:
But his[47] dominion that exceeds in this,[48]
Stretcheth as far as doth the mind of man:
A sound Magician is a Demi-god,
Here tire my brains to get a Deity.[49]

Enter Wagner.[50]

Wagner, commend me to[51] my dearest friends,
The German *Valdes* and *Cornelius*,[52]
Request them earnestly to visit me.
Wagner. I will sir.
Faustus. Their conference[53] will be a greater help to me,
Than all my labours, plod[54] I ne'er so fast.

Enter Good Angel *and* Bad Angel.[55]

Good Angel. O *Faustus*, lay that damned[56] book aside,
And gaze not on it lest it tempt thy soul,
And heap God's heavy wrath upon thy head.
Read, read the Scriptures[57]: that[58] is blasphemy.
Bad Angel. Go forward *Faustus* in that famous Art
Wherein all nature's treasury is contain'd:
Be thou on earth as *Jove*[59] is in the sky,
Lord and Commander of these elements.[60]

Exeunt[61] Angels.

Faustus. How am I glutted with conceit[62] of this?
Shall I make spirits fetch me what I please?
Resolve me of all ambiguities?

Perform what desperate enterprise I will?
I'll have them fly to *India*[63] for gold;
Ransack[64] the Ocean for Orient[65] Pearl,
And search all corners of the new-found-world[66]
For pleasant fruits, and princely delicates.[67]
I'll have them read me strange Philosophy,
And tell the secrets of all foreign Kings[68]:
I'll have them wall all *Germany* with Brass,[69]
And make swift *Rhine*[70], circle fair *Wittenberg*:
I'll have them fill the public Schools[71] with silk[72],
Wherewith the Students shall be bravely[73] clad.
I'll levy soldiers with the coin they[74] bring,
And chase the Prince of *Parma*[75] from our Land,[76]
And reign sole King of all our Provinces.[77]
Yea[78] stranger engines[79] for the brunt of war[80],
Than was the fiery keel[81] at *Antwerp* bridge,
I'll make my servile spirits to invent.
Come *German Valdes* and *Cornelius*,
And make me blest with your sage[82] conference.

Enter Valdes *and* Cornelius.

Valdes, sweet *Valdes* and *Cornelius*,
Know that your words have won me at the last,
To practise Magic and concealed Arts.[83]
Yet not your words only, but my own fantasy,[84]
That will receive no object,[85] for my head
But ruminates on Necromantic skill.
Philosophy is odious and obscure,
Both Law and Physic are for petty wits:
Divinity is basest of the three[86],
Unpleasant, harsh, contemptible and vilde[87]:
'Tis magic, magic, that hath ravisht me.
Then gentle friends aid me in this attempt,

And I, that have with concise Syllogisms
Gravel'd[88] the Pastors[89] of the German Church,
And made the flowering pride[90] of *Wittenberg*
Swarm[91] to my Problems[92], as th' infernal spirits[93]
On[94] sweet *Musaeus*[95] when he came to hell,
Will be[96] as cunning as *Agrippa*[97] was,
Whose shadows made all *Europe* honour him.
    Valdes. *Faustus*, these books, thy wit, and our experience,
Shall make all Nations to canonize[98] us:
As Indian *Moors*[99] obey their Spanish Lords,
So shall the spirits of every element,
Be always serviceable to us three:
Like Lions shall they guard us when we please,
Like *Almain* Rutters[100] with their horsemen's staves,[101]
Or Lapland[102] Giants trotting by our sides:
Sometimes like women or unwedded Maids,
Shadowing[103] more beauty in their airy brows,[104]
Than has[105] the white breasts of the Queen of love.[106]
From *Venice* shall they drag huge *Argosies*,[107]
And from *America* the Golden Fleece,[108]
That yearly stuffs old *Phillip's*[109] treasury,
If learned *Faustus* will be resolute.[110]
    Faustus. *Valdes*, as resolute am I in this,
As thou to live, therefore object[111] it not.
    Cornelius. The miracle that magic will perform,
Will make thee vow[112] to study nothing else.
He that is grounded[113] in Astrology,
Inricht[114] with tongues, well seen[115] in Minerals,[116]
Hath all the Principles Magic doth[117] require:
Then doubt not *Faustus* but to be renown'd,
And more frequented[118] for this mystery,[119]
Than heretofore the *Delphian* Oracle.[120]
The spirits tell me they can dry the sea,

And fetch the treasure of all foreign wracks:[121]
Yea all the wealth that our fore-fathers hid,
Within the massy[122] entrails[123] of the earth:
Then tell me, *Faustus*, what shall we three want?
Faustus. Nothing, *Cornelius*; O this cheers my soul:
Come, show me some demonstrations magical,[124]
That I may conjure in some bushy Grove,
And have these joys in full possession.
Valdes. Then haste thee to some solitary Grove,
And bear wise *Bacon's*,[125] and *Albanus's* works,
The *Hebrew* Psalter[126], and new Testament;
And whatsoever else is requisite,
We will inform thee ere[127] our conference cease.
Cornelius. *Valdes*, first let him know the words of Art,
And then all other ceremonies learn'd,[128]
Faustus may try his cunning by himself.
Valdes. First I'll instruct thee in the rudiments,
And then wilt thou be perfecter than I.
Faustus. Then come and dine with me, and after meat[129]
We'll canvass[130] every quiddity[131] thereof:
For ere I sleep, I'll try what I can do:
This night I'll conjure tho[132] I die therefore.

Scene xvii

Thunder and lightning: Enter devils with cover'd dishes[1]*;*
Mephostophilis *leads them into* Faustus *Study:*
Then enter Wagner.

Wagner. I think my Master means to die shortly, he has made his will, and given me his wealth, his house, his goods, and store of golden plate; besides two thousand ducats[2] ready coin'd[3]: I wonder what he means, if death were nigh,[4] he would not frolic[5] thus: he's now at supper with the scholars, where there's such belly-cheer[6], as *Wagner* in his life ne'er saw the like: and see where they come, belike the feast is done.

Exit.

Enter Faustus, Mephostophilis[7], *and two or three Scholars.*

1 Scholar. Master Doctor *Faustus*, since our conference about fair Ladies, which was[8] the beautifullest in all the world, we have determin'd[9] with our selves, that *Helen*[10] of *Greece* was the admirablest Lady that ever liv'd: therefore Master Doctor, if you will do us so much favour, as to let us see that peerless[11] dame of *Greece,* whom all the world admires for Majesty[12], we should think out selves much beholding[13] unto you.

Faustus. Gentlemen,
For that[14] I know your friendship is unfeign'd,[15]
And *Faustus's* custom is not to deny
The just requests of those that wish him well,
You shall behold that peerless dame of *Greece,*
No otherways[16] for pomp[17] and Majesty,
Than when[16] sir *Paris*[18] cross'd the seas with her,
And brought the spoils[19] to rich *Dardania*:[20]
Be silent[21] then, for danger is in words.

Music sound, Mephostophilis *brings in* Helen, *she passeth over the stage.*

2 Scholar. Too simple is my wit[22] to tell her worth,
Whom all the world admires for majesty.

3 Scholar. No marvel tho[23] the angry Greeks pursu'd
With ten years' war the rape[24] of such a queen,
Whose heavenly beauty passeth all compare.[25]

1 Scholar. Now we have seen the pride of Nature's work,
And only[26] Paragon[27] of excellence,

Let us depart, and for this blessed sight[28]
Happy and blest be *Faustus* evermore.

Exeunt Scholars.

Enter an Old Man.

Old Man. O gentle *Faustus* leave this damned Art,
This Magic, that will charm thy soul to hell,
And quite bereave[29] thee of salvation.
Though thou hast now offended like a man,
Do not persever[30] in it like a Devil;
Yet, yet, thou hast an amiable[31] soul,
If sin by custom grow not into nature[32]:
Then[33] *Faustus*, will repentance come too late,
Then thou art banisht from the sight of heaven;
No mortal[34] can express the pain of hell.
It may be this my exhortation[35]
Seems harsh, and all unpleasant; let it not, [36]
For gentle son, I speak it not in wrath,
Or envy of thee[37], but in tender love,
And pity of thy future misery.
And so have hope, that this my kind rebuke,[38]
Checking[39] thy body, may amend[40] thy soul.

Faustus. Where art thou, *Faustus*? wretch, what hast thou done?
Damned art thou *Faustus*, damned, despair and die.

Mephostophilis *gives him a dagger.*[41]

Hell claims his right, and with a roaring voice,
Says, "*Faustus* come, thine hour is almost come,"
And *Faustus* now will come to do thee right.[42]

(Offers to stab htmself.)

Old Man. Ah stay good *Faustus*, stay thy desperate steps.
I see an Angel hover o'er thy head,
And with a vial[43] full of precious grace,

Offers[44] to pour the sane[45] into thy soul,
Then call[46] for mercy, and avoid[46] despair.[47]

Faustus. Ah my sweet friend,
I feel thy words to comfort my distressed soul,
Leave me a while, to ponder on my sins.

Old Man. *Faustus* I leave thee, but with grief of heart,
Fearing the enemy[48] of thy hapless[49] soul.

Exit.

Faustus. Accursed *Faustus*, where is mercy now?
I do repent, and yet I do despair,
Hell strives with grace[50] for conquest in my breast:
What shall I do to shun the snares of death[51]?

Mephostophilis. Thou traitor *Faustus*, I arrest thy soul,
For disobedience to my sovereign Lord,
Revolt[52], or I'll in piece-meal tear thy flesh.

Faustus. I do repent I e'er offended him,
Sweet *Mephostophilis*, intreat thy Lord
To pardon my unjust presumption[53],
And with my blood again I will confirm
The former vow I made to *Lucifer*.

Mephostophilis. Do it then *Faustus*, with unfeigned heart,
Lest greater dangers do attend thy drift[56].

Faustus. Torment[57] sweet friend, that base and crooked age,
That durst dissuade me from thy *Lucifer*,
With greatest torments that our hell affords.

Mephostophilis. His faith[58] is great, I cannot touch his soul;
But what I may afflict his body with,
I will attempt, which is but little worth[59].

Faustus. One thing, good servant, let me crave of[60] thee,
To glut the longing of my heart's desire,
That I may have unto my paramour[61],
That heavenly *Helen*, which I saw of late,
Whose sweet embraces may extinguish clear[62],

Those thoughts that do dissuade me from my vow,
And keep mine oath[63] I made to *Lucifer*[64].

Mephostophilis. This, or what else my *Faustus* shall desire,
Shall be perform'd in twinkling of an eye.

Enter Helen *again, passing over between two Cupids.*

Faustus. Was this the face that launcht[65] a thousand ships,
And burnt the topless[66] Towers of *Ilium*?[67]
Sweet *Helen*, make me immortal with a kiss:[68]
Her lips suck forth my soul, see where it flies.
Come *Helen*, come, give me my soul again,[69]
Here will I dwell, for heaven is in these lips,
And all is dross[70] that is not *Helena*.

Enter Old Man *(aloof)*.

I will be *Paris*, and for love of thee,
In stead of *Troy* shall *Wittenberg* be sack't[71],
And I will combat with weak *Menelaus*[72],
And wear thy colours[73] on my plumed crest.
Yea, I will wound *Achilles*[74] in the heel,
And then return to *Helen* for a kiss.
O thou art fairer than the evening's air,
Clad[75] in the beauty of a thousand stars:
Brighter are thou than flaming *Jupiter*[76],
When he appear'd to hapless *Semele*[77]:
More lovely than the Monarch of the sky[78],
In wanton Arethusa's[79] azur'd[80] arms,
And none but thou shalt be my Paramour.

Exeunt.

Old Man. Accursed *Faustus*, miserable man,
That from thy soul exclud'st the grace of heaven,
And fliest the throne of his tribunal seat[81].

Enter the Devils.

Satan[82] begins to sift[83] me with his pride[84]:

As in his furnace God shall try my faith,
My faith, vile hell, shall triumph over thee,
Ambitious fiends, see how the heavens[85] smiles
At your repulse[86], and laughs[87] your state[88] to scorn,
Hence[89] hell, for hence I fly unto my God.

Exeunt.

Scene xviii

Thunder. Enter (above) Lucifer[1], Belzebub[2], *and* Mephostophilis.

Lucifer. Thus from infernal *Dis*[3] do we ascend
To view the subjects of our Monarchy,
Those souls which sin[4], seals[5] the black sons of hell,
'Mong[6] which as chief, *Faustus*, we come to thee,
Bringing with us lasting damnation,
To wait upon thy soul; the time is come
Which makes it forfeit[7].

Mephostophilis. And this gloomy night,
Here in this room will wretched *Faustus* be.

Belzebub. And here we'll stay,
To mark[8] him how he doth demean[9] himself.

Mephostophilis. How should he, but in desperate lunacy.
Fond[10] worldling, now his heart-blood dries with grief;
His conscience kills it, and his labouring brain,
Begets a world of idle fantasies[11],
To over-reach[12] the Devil, but all in vain;
His store of pleasures must be sauc'd[13] with pain.
He and his servant *Wagner* are at hand,
Both come[14] from drawing *Faustus's* latest will.
See where they come.

Enter Faustus *and* Wagner.

Faustus. Say *Wagner*, thou hast perus'd my will,

How dost thou like it?

Wagner. Sir, so wondrous well,
As in all humble duty, I do yield
My life and lasting service for your love.

Enter the Scholars.

Faustus. Gramercies[15] *Wagner*. Welcome gentlemen.

(*Exit* Wagner.)

1 Scholar. Now worthy *Faustus*: methinks[16] your looks are chang'd.

Faustus. Ah gentlemen.

2 Scholar. What ails *Faustus*?

Faustus. Ah my sweet chamber-fellow, had I[17] liv'd with thee, then had I lived still, but now must die eternally.
Look sirs, comes he not[18]? comes he not?

1 Scholar. O my dear *Faustus* what imports this fear?

2 Scholar. Is all our pleasure turn'd to melancholy?

3 Scholar. He is not well with being over solitary.

2 Scholar. If it be so, we'll have Physicians,
And *Faustus* shall be cur'd.

3 Scholar. 'Tis[19] but a surfeit[20] sir, fear nothing.

Faustus. A surfeit of deadly sin, that hath damn'd both body and soul.

2 Scholar. Yet, *Faustus*, look up to heaven, and remember God's mercy is infinite.

Faustus. But *Faustus's* offence can ne'er be pardonned, the serpent that tempted *Eve*[21] may be saved, but not *Faustus*. Ah gentlemen, hear me with patience, and tremble not at my speeches. Though my heart pant and quiver[22] to remember that I have been a student here these thirty years, O would[23] I had never seen *Wittenberg*, never read book: and what wonders I have done, all *Germany* can witness, yea, all the world: for which *Faustus* hath lost both *Germany* and the world, yea heaven itself: heaven the seat of God, the Throne of the Blessed, the Kingdom of Joy, and must remain in hell for ever. Hell, ah hell for ever. Sweet friends, what shall become of *Faustus* being in hell for ever?

2 Scholar. Yet, *Faustus*, call on God.

Faustus. On God, whom *Faustus* hath abjur'd[24]? on God, whom *Faustus* hath blasphem'd?[25] Ah my God, I would weep, but the Devil draws in my tears. Gush forth blood in stead of tears, yea life and soul: oh he stays my tongue[26]: I would life up my hands, but see they hold 'em, they hold 'em.

All. Who, *Faustus*?

Faustus. Why, *Lucifer* and *Mephostophilis*:
Ah gentlemen, I gave them my soul for my cunning.

All. O God forbid.

Faustus. God forbade it indeed, but *Faustus* hath done it: for the vain pleasure of four and twenty years hath *Faustus* lost eternal joy and felicity. I writ[27] them a bill[28] with mine own blood, the date is expired: this is the time, and he will fetch me.

1 Scholar. Why did not *Faustus* tell us of this before, that Divines[29] might have prayed for thee?

Faustus. Oft have I thought to have done so: but the Devil threatened to tear me in pieces if I nam'd God: to fetch me body and soul[30], if I once gave ear to Divinity: and now 'tis too late. Gentlemen away, lest you perish with me.

2 Scholar. O what may we do to save *Faustus*?

Faustus. Talk not of me, but save your selves and depart.

3 Scholar. God will strengthen me, I will stay with *Faustus*.

1 Scholar. Tempt not God, sweet friend, but let us into[31] the next room, and there pray for him.

Faustus. Ay, pray for me, pray for me: and what noise soever you hear, come not unto me, for nothing can rescue me.

2 Scholar. Pray thou, and we will pray, that God may have mercy upon thee.

Faustus. Gentlemen farewell: if I live till morning, I'll visit you: if not, *Faustus* is gone to hell.

All. Faustus, farewell.

Exeunt Scholars.

(Enter Mephostophilis *below.)*

Mephostophilis. Ay, *Faustus,* now thou hast no hope of heaven,
Therefore despair, think only upon hell;
For that must be thy mansion, there to dwell.

Faustus. O thou bewitching fiend, 'twas thy temptation,
Hath rob'd[32] me of eternal happiness.

Mephostophilis. I do confess it, *Faustus*, and rejoyce;
'Twas I, that when thou wert i' the way to heaven,
Dam'd up[33] thy passage; when thou took'st the book,
To view the Scriptures, then I turn'd the leaves[34]
And led thine eye.[35]
What, weep'st thou? 'tis too late, despair, farewell,
Fools that will laugh on earth, must weep in hell.

Exit.

Enter the Good Angel *and the* Bad
Angel *at several doors.*[36]

Good Angel. Oh *Faustus*, if thou hadst given ear to me,
Innumerable joys had followed[37] thee.
But thou didst love the world.

Bad Angel. Gave ear to me,
And now must taste hell's pains perpetually.

Good Angel. O what will all thy riches, pleasures, pomps,
Avail thee now?

Bad Angel. Nothing but vex[38] thee more,
To want[39] in hell, that had on earth such store.

Music while the Throne[40] *descends.*

Good Angel. O thou hast lost celestial happiness,
Pleasures unspeakable, bliss without end.
Hadst thou affected[41] sweet divinity,
Hell, or the Devil, had had no power on thee.
Hadst thou kept on that way, *Faustus*, behold,
In what resplendant glory thou hadst set[42]
In yonder throne, like those bright shining Saints,
And triumpht over hell: that hast thou lost,
And now poor soul must thy good Angel leave thee,

Exit. (Throne ascends.)

Hell is discovered.[43]

Bad Angel. Now *Faustus*, let thine eyes with horror stare
Into that vast perpetual torture-house,
There are the furies[44] tossing damned souls,
On burning forks: their bodies boil in lead.[45]
There are live quarters[46] broiling[47] on the coals,
That ne'er can die: this ever-burning chair,
Is for the o'er-tortur'd[48] souls to rest them in.
These, that are fed with sops[49] of flaming fire,
Were gluttons, and lov'd only delicates,
And laught to see the poor starve at their gates: [50]
But yet all these are nothing, thou shalt see
Ten thousand tortures that more horrid be.[51]

Faustus. O, I have seen enough to torture me.

Bad Angel. Nay, thou must feel them, taste the smart[52] of all.
He that loves pleasure, must for pleasure fall:
And so I leave thee *Faustus* till anon[53],
Then wilt thou tumble in confusion.[54]

Exit. (Hell closes.)

The Clock strikes eleven.

Faustus. Ah *Faustus*,

Now hast thou but one bare hour to live,
And then thou must be damn'd perpetually.
Stand still, you ever moving Spheres of heaven,
That time may cease, and midnight never come.
Fair nature's eye[55], rise, rise again and make
Perpetual day: or let this hour be but
A year, a month, a week, a natural day[56],
That *Faustus* may repent, and save his soul.
O lente lente currite noctis equi[57]:
The Stars move still[58], Time runs, the Clock will strike,
The devil will come, and *Faustus* must be damn'd.
O I'll leap up to my God: who pulls me down?
See see[59] where Christ's blood streams in the firmament,
One drop would save my soul, half a drop, ah my Christ.
Rend not my heart[60], for naming of my Christ,
Yet will I call on him: O spare me, *Lucifer*.[61]
Where is it now?[62] 'tis gone. And see where God
Stretcheth out his Arm, and bends his ireful[63] Brows:
Mountains and Hills[64], come, come, and fall on me,
And hide me from the heavy wrath of God.
No, no?
Then will I headlong run into the earth:
Gape earth; O no, it will not harbour me.
You Stars[65] that reign'd at my nativity,
Whose influence[66] hath allotted[67] death and hell;
Now draw up[68] *Faustus* like a foggy mist,
Into the entrails of yon labouring cloud,
That when you[69] vomit forth into the air,
My limbs may issue from your smoky mouths,
So that[70] my soul may but ascend to heaven.

The Watch strikes.

Ah half the hour is past: 'twill all be past anon[71]:
O God, if thou wilt not have mercy on my soul,

Yet for Christ's sake, whose blood hath ransom'd me, [72]
Impose some end[73] to my incessant pain:
Let *Faustus* live in hell a thousand years,
A hundred thousand, and at last be sav'd.
No end is limited to damned souls.
Why wert thou not a creature wanting soul?
Or why is this[74] immortal that thou hast?
Ah *Pythagoras's*[75] *Metempsychosis*[76]; were that true,
This soul should fly from me, and I be chang'd
Unto some brutish beast.
All beasts are happy, for when they die,
Their souls are soon dissolv'd in elements,
But mine must live still[77] to be plagu'd in hell.
Curst[78] be the parents that ingendred me;
No *Faustus*, curse thy self, curse *Lucifer*,
That hath depriv'd thee of the joys of heaven.

The clock striketh twelve.

It strikes, it strikes; now body turn to air,
Or *Lucifer* will bear thee quick[79] to hell.
O soul be chang'd into little water drops,
And fall into the Ocean, ne'er be found.

Thunder, and enter the devils.

My God, my God, look not so fierce on me;
Adders[80] and serpents, let me breathe a while:
Ugly hell, gape not[81]; come not *Lucifer*,
I'll burn my books[82]; ah *Mephostophilis*.

Exeunt with him.

(Exeunt Lucifer and devils above.)

Scene xix

Enter the Scholars.

1 Scholar. Come Gentlemen, let us go visit *Faustus*,
For such a dreadful night, was never seen,

Since first the world's creation did begin.
Such fearful shrieks, and cries, were never heard,
Pray heaven the Doctor have escapt the danger.

2 Scholar. O help us heaven, see, here are *Faustus's* limbs[1],
All torn asunder by the hand of death.

3 Scholar. The devils whom *Faustus* serv'd have torn him thus:
For twixt the hours of twelve and one, me thought
I heard[2] him shriek and call aloud for help:
At which self time[3] the house seem'd all on fire,
With dreadful horror of these damned fiends.

2 Scholar. Well Gentlemen, tho *Faustus's* end be such
As every Christian heart[4] laments to think on:
Yet for he was a Scholar, once admired
For wondrous knowledge in our German schools,
We'll give his mangled[5] limbs due burial:
And all the Students clothed in mourning black,
Shall wait upon his heavy[6] funeral.

Exeunt.

Enter Chorus.

Cut is the branch that might have grown full straight,[7]
And burned is *Apollo's*[8] laurel bough,[9]
That sometime grew within this learned man:
Faustus is gone, regard[10] his hellish fall,
Whose fiendful[11] fortune[12] may exhort[13] the wise
Only to wonder at[14] unlawful[15] things,
Whose deepness[16] doth entice[17] such forward wits,[18]
To practise more than heavenly power permits.

(Exit.)

Terminat hora diem, Terminat Author opus.[19]

F I N I S.[20]

【作者简介】 Christopher Marlowe（克里斯托弗·马娄 1564—1593）文艺复兴时期英国剧作家和诗人。他是坎特伯雷城一个鞋商的儿子，曾入剑桥大学读书。他上了六年大学，在这期间他受政府之雇完成过某种政治使命（反对外国天主教势力企图推翻伊丽莎白女王的阴谋），并开始创作。

在他的朋友中，有剧作家 Chapman，Kyd 和政治活动家、探险家、诗人 Walter Raleigh 和数学家 Roydon，Hariot 等，他们都有些无神论的言论。1591 年他同 Kyd 住在一起，1593 年 Kyd 以有无神论言论被捕，供称马娄也有同样言论。1593 年 5 月，马娄在伦敦近郊酒店，由于口角，被人刺死。

马娄从离开大学到死，不过短短六年时间，但他的生活经历正好反映了时代的动荡；他的活动正好说明代表新兴资产阶级的“巨人”性格，他们有思维能力，有热情，多才多艺，学识渊博，既用舌、笔，也用刀剑。

马娄一共留下六部剧作，翻译过罗马诗人 Ovid 的爱情诗和罗马诗人 Lucan 的史诗的第一章，他的长诗 *Hero and Leander* 未完成，他就去世了。在他的戏剧中比较重要的有 *Tamburlaine*（《帖木儿》）上下篇（1587，1588），写蒙古可汗帖木儿征服亚欧许多国家的故事，赢得“上帝之鞭”（the Scourge of God）的称号；*The Jew of Malta*（《马耳他的犹太人》1590）为了财富，不惜毒死自己的女儿和她的爱人，最后自己也落进为谋害土耳其人而设的沸镬而丧命。这两部戏剧写的是对权力和财富的追求，而《浮士德》则是写对知识的追求。这些主题在莎士比亚等的剧作中都有所继承发展。

马娄的戏严格说来只是在舞台上演出一个故事，结构松散，是从中古戏剧向文艺复兴成熟期的过渡。

【题解与注释】

The Tragical History of Doctor Faustus（《浮士德博士的悲剧》，1592—1593）是马娄最受人重视的一部作品，在他死后出版，有两类版本，分别出版于 1604（A–text）和 1616（B–text），互有出入。现在通行本都是根据 W. W. Greg 1950 年 A–text 和 B–text 并列本。

浮士德实有其人，生活在 1488—1541 年间的德国，据传是个魔术师或巫师，慢慢成了一个半神话式的人物。1587 年在法兰克福出版了一部关于他的故事书——Volksbuch，很快（1592）就译成了英文，名为 *The History of the Damnable Life and Deserved Death of Dr. John Faustus*。这部德国作品具有路德派反对天主教的性质。马娄同（至少）另一剧作家把它编成剧本。一般公认至少首尾两部分出自马娄手笔。

这出戏大致可以分成三段。第一段写浮士德对中世纪经院所传授的知识感到不满，向往“魔术”，同魔鬼歃血为约，为了获得知识，他可以驱使魔鬼二十四年，到期魔鬼就把他的灵魂劫往地狱。第二段写二十四年的经历，由若干互不相联的插曲组成：浮士德和魔鬼站在德国皇帝一边，捉弄罗马教皇；在德国皇帝宫中召来马其顿王亚历山大，并和宫廷大臣恶作剧；为 Vanholt 公爵夫人在冬天摄来南方的葡萄等，大都取材于原来的德国故事书。第三段是宏伟的终场。这里选了首尾两部分。

有的评论家认为马娄的英雄都是野心勃勃，追求他们力不胜任的东西，结果失败，咎由自取，所谓 over-reachers。有的人认为对文艺复兴时期的人来说，金钱、权力有很大的诱惑力，但知识的诱惑力最大。这类意见并不全错，也并不全对。我们觉得马娄的浮士德所反映的是，在中世纪的蒙昧之中要获得科学知识，就象婴儿难产一样，是一个痛苦挣扎的过程。浮士德对中世纪的一切“学问”都感到强烈的不满，要追求新知识，有了新知识就有了力量，就可以实现自己的政治抱负，但他又深受中世纪神学的束缚，挣脱不掉这沉重的枷索，这就是他的内心矛盾、痛苦和悲剧。凡是教会反对的——爱情、金钱、权力、知识他都要，而教会除了神学以外，反对一切 curiositas——追求知识的欲望。这出悲剧之所以深刻就在它揭示了蒙昧主义对人们心灵的毒害，以及新生事物——真正的知识——诞生的艰难。

本·琼生（Ben Jonson）称赞马娄的诗，有一句有名的话：Marlowe's mighty line。一语中的，已成定论。马娄的浪漫主义的高昂、奔放、激越而充沛的感情，顿挫跌宕的诗句，变化虽不及莎士比亚（《哈姆雷特》里曾模仿嘲弄过马娄），但开启一代诗剧，岿然独步。他用的无韵诗体，从希腊、罗马脱胎而来，到他手里成为一个铿锵有力的工具。他的诗象他笔下反抗黑暗的人物一样，一往直前，富于朝气，充满能量。

选文出自 *The Complete Works of Christopher Marlowe*, ed. Fredson Bowers, Cambridge University Press, 1973。标点不全是为了指示语法结构，而往往是为了念白停顿，都保留不改；属格标点一律改成现在标法。名词一般大写，不动。拼法一律改成现在拼法。

读法：先通读一遍，参看每段段首的注释，掌握大意，再细读。

无韵体（blank verse）不叶韵，每行十个音节，安排成抑扬（轻重）五步格 iambic pentameter，如第一行

Not márching ín the fiéld of Thrásimén。

每行第一音节常常是重音，如第五行

Nót in the pómp of próud audácious déeds。

马娄这种早期的无韵体，每行往往构成一个意义单位，但偶尔也不然，如十八—十九行：… dispute / In th' heavenly matters，这种写法称为 enjambement 或 run-on line。有时一行诗最后多出一个音节来，称为 feminine ending，但这种诗行在马娄诗中极罕见。

Faustus [ˈfɔːstʌs]（但 Faust [faust]）

Chorus 合唱队，文艺复兴时期英国舞台由一个演员扮演，介绍全剧或一幕的剧情，或发表意见。

1. Thrasimen: 即 Thrasimene 湖，在意大利，迦太基的汉尼拔（Hannibal）大败罗马军队于此（217 B. C.）。

2. Mars: 罗马神话中的战神。文艺复兴时期古希腊、罗马文化广为传播，成为知识界的共同财富，剧中引用随处可见。

mate 一解 join with；一解（O. E. D.）checkmate，defeat；一解 espouse（the cause of）支持；一解 rival or cope with。如按历史事实，应解作 join with，espouse；如把 Mars 理解为罗马军队，则可解作 rival。翻译时须参照各家意见决定取舍。

3. Carthagens: 即 Carthaginians 迦太基（北非帝国）人。

4. Nor sporting ... where state is overturn'd: 可能指马娄前此所写的剧本 Edward II 或 Dido 的剧情。state，political power；overturn'd，'d 即 ed 的缩写（elision），表明不算一个音节，而 25 行 cursed，-ed 作一音节，读为 ['kə:sid]。其他如 19 行 th' heavenly，20 行 swoll'n 等都是 elision。

5. Nor in the pomp of proud audacious deeds: 可能指 Tamburlaine。但开始第 1、2 行不知何所指。注意此行 p、d 音，第 4 行 k 音，第 6 行 v 音，第 8 行 f 音的重复（alliteration），读来铿锵有力。加以每行断句、停顿，这些都是构成 mighty line 的因素。

6. our Muse: 诗神，此处指作者或两位合作者，是全句（1—5 行）的主语。

7. vaunt: display proudly，炫耀。

8. form: course of action，所作所为。

9. Rhode: 即 Roda，属 Saxe-Altenburg，今 Stadtroda，德国城市。

10. Wittenberg: 威登堡，德国城市，马丁·路德在此间大学学习，进行宗教改革活动。莎士比亚剧中的哈姆雷特也在此学习。新教策源地。

11. whereas: = where.

12. his kinsmen: 按英译浮士德故事，浮士德有一个 uncle，富有，无嗣。

13. Divinity: 神学，按上书，威登堡大学的诸校长和十六名硕士口试浮士德，无人能问倒他，一致同意授予神学博士学位。

14. plot: 园地。

15. Scholarism: 即 scholasticism 经院哲学。

16. grac'd: = adorned，这一行可以视为独立片语，The fruitful plot ... being adorned by him，他给经院哲学增添了光采。Grac'd 也有人解作 graz'd 吃草，比喻说法，意为吸取营养，当主要动词，也通。

17. grac'd with Doctor's name: 剑桥大学术语，指获得学位。

18. delight's = delight is.

19. dispute: = disputation，中古大学术语，辩论、答辩，中世纪经院中一种教学形式，训练逻辑思考。

20. cunning: 学问，略有贬意。

21. self conceit: 自满，高傲自大。“满招损”。

22. waxen wings: 用蜡粘连在背上的翅膀，指希腊神话中青年 Icarus 和他的父亲巧匠 Daedalus 被困在迷宫，他父亲制了两付羽翼，粘在各自背上，飞了出去，但 Icarus 不听父亲警告，飞得离太阳太近，蜡熔化了，他坠入爱琴海中，至今称为 Icarian Sea。

23. above his reach: 超过他的能力。

24. melting: 指翅膀。

25. heavens: = the heavens = heaven，上苍。

26. conspir'd: devised，plotted，促成。

27. glutted: 填饱。

28. surfeits: 沉湎于。

29. Necromancy ['nekroumænsi]**:** 魔法，由“死尸”和“占卜”两词构成，即勾来死者的魂魄，向其询问未来。其后人们混淆了希腊文 nekros 死人和拉丁文的 niger 黑，把它叫做 Black magic. 指浮士德所追求的、为教会所禁止的新知识。

30. chiefest bliss: 最高幸福，指灵魂的得救。

31. this the man: = this is the man，指后台帷幕拉开之后而显露的浮士德。

32. Exit: 拉丁文，he (she, it) goes out.

Scene i　这一场写浮士德对经院学问的不满，追求新知识，但内心充满了矛盾。

1. Enter: 祈使语，= let enter.

2. Settle thy studies: 解决你思想上的困惑（study—a state of mental perplexity or anxious thought, O. E. D.），或停止学习吧。

3. sound: 探索，考虑。

4. that: = that which.

5. profess: 将要从事的工作。

6. commenc'd: 术语，晋升（博士）。

7. in shew: being a doctor of divinity, look one，外表得象个神学博士。

8. level at the end: level, aim，瞄准；end，最终目的。探求各种学术的终极目的。

9. Aristotle's work: 希腊哲学家亚里士多德的著作是神学教育中的必修课目。这一句的意思应紧接第 3 行。

10. Analitics: 即 Analytics 逻辑分析，是亚里士多德逻辑学著作中的一种。

11. 'tis thou hast: it is you who have.

12. ravish: 使我神魂颠倒。

13. Bene ...: 拉丁文，意思见下一行。这是浮士德从手持的书里念的一句引语。浮士德对此表示怀疑，所以用疑问句。这段台词拉丁文引语很多，说明作者在中古和近代交替时期所受大学教育中浓厚的中古影响。

14. this Art: 指逻辑学。

15. on kai me on: 希腊文，存在与不存在，生与死，泛指哲学。

16. Galen: 公元二世纪希腊医学家。医学也是中世纪大学一门课目。医学也不能使浮士德满足。

17. seeing: = since.

18. ubi ...: 拉丁文 where the philosopher leaves off, the doctor begins. 语出亚里士多德。

19. heap up gold: 发财致富。又，金子可入药。

20. be eterniz'd: be made immortal，名垂不朽。

21. Summum ...: 拉丁文，义见下行。

22. Aphorisms: 格言录，传说是公元前五世纪希腊名医 Hippocrates 的著作。此处指浮士德精通医道，他的片言只语就能医好疾病。

23. bills: 处方。

24. and a man: 还不是神。

25. Justinian: 查士丁尼，六世纪罗马皇帝，他所颁布的法典为后世所遵从。

26. Si una ...: 拉丁文 If one and the same thing is bequeathed to two persons, one shall have the thing and the other the value of the thing，如果一件遗产分给两个人，一个人得到这件东西，另一个得到东西的代价，或价值相同的东西。

27. paltry: 琐屑可鄙的。

28. Exhereditare ...: 拉丁文 A father cannot disinherit his son unless，父亲不得剥夺儿子的继承权除非…

29. Institute: 查士丁尼法典。上面一句即摘引此法典中一条的大意。这部法典是中世纪大学法科学生必修课本。

30. body: 译自拉丁文 corpus，律法大全。学习法律也不能使浮士德满足。

31. Mercenary drudge: 追逐小利的贩夫走卒。

32. trash: 钱。

33. illiberal: 卑贱；liberal，适合自由人身份的，不同于奴隶的。

34. Jerome's Bible: 圣徒杰罗姆（约 340—420）把《圣经》译成拉丁文。

35. Stipendium ...: 义见下行，引自《新约》《罗马人书》。

36. Si peccasse ...: 义见下行，引自《新约》《约翰一书》。

37. belike: *adv.* perhaps, it is likely that.

38. Ay: yes.

39. Che sera, sera: 意大利文，义见下行。

40. Metaphysics: 超自然的、形而上的学问，魔术。

41. Characters: 符号。这一行都是魔术中使用的符、记。

42. Artisan: 魔法师。

43. quiet Poles: 地球两极固定不动，故称 quiet.

44. but: = only.

45. several: respective，各自的。

46. Provinces: 领域。

47. his: 指魔法师。

48. exceeds in this: 他所能驾驭的还远远不只风和云，凡是人能想到的，他都能做到。

49. Here tire my brains to get a Deity: 这句诗由于版本的差异，引起不同的解释，一般以 my brains 为呼格，即 In this endeavour, exhaust yourselves, my brains, by making me a great magician, to create a new divinity. 让我绞尽脑汁，全力以赴地变成一

个魔法师，以便创造出一个新神。可以看出马娄有否认基督教上帝的思想，用人来代替神，他笔下的英雄人物都是半人半神。

50. Wagner: 浮士德的仆人。

51. commend me to: 代我向…致意。

52. Valdes 和 Cornelius: 浮士德的朋友，魔法师。德文故事书中没有这两个人物，为什么特别点出 German，历来无解。

53. conference: = conversation.

54. plod: study or work on laboriously，用功。让步从句：即使我再努力用功，也不如同他们二人谈一次话更有益。

55. Good Angel, Bad Angel: 善恶两天使。当时人们相信人的灵魂受他们控制，可以理解为浮士德内心矛盾着的两个方面。这种抽象人物是从中世纪戏剧沿袭而来的。

56. damned [-id] **book:** 魔法书。

57. the Scriptures:《圣经》。

58. that: 指 damned book.

59. Jove: 即 Jupiter，罗马神话中的主神，此处指上帝。

60. these elements: = the elements，指水、火、风、土等元素。

61. Exeunt: 拉丁文，they go out.

62. conceit: = the idea (of attaining such skill)，妙想、奇想。

63. India: 此处指"西印度"即美洲。

64. Ransack: 搜刮。

65. Orient: 原意是太阳升起的地方，此处意为光辉夺目的、珍贵的。

66. new-found-world: 西半球。地理发现使欧洲人扩大了视野。

67. delicates: = delicacies，山珍海错。

68. foreign Kings: 马娄本人曾当过政府谍探。

69. I'll have ... with Brass: 这种保卫国土，抵御天主教西班牙入侵英国的情绪在当时很普遍。剧作家格林（Robert Greene）的剧本 *Friar Bacon and Friar Bungay* 中，Bacon 也有要在英国周围树立一道铜墙铁壁的意图。

70. Rhine: 莱因河。按，威登堡在易北河（Elbe）上。

71. public Schools: 指大学课堂。

72. silk: 贵重的丝绸衣服。这是违反中古大学禁欲教规的。杜甫：安得广厦千万间，大庇天下寒士俱欢颜。

73. bravely: 华丽、漂亮。

74. they: 指精灵们。

75. Prince of Parma: 帕尔玛公爵是西班牙派往它的领地尼德兰（荷兰）的总督（1579—1592），对英国是极大威胁。

76. our Land: 从德国人角度说，尼德兰同德国休戚与共。

77. Provinces: 尼德兰分为若干省。

78 yea [jei]: yes, furthermore.

79. stranger engines: invent 的宾语，更新奇的武器。

80. brunt of war: 战争的袭击。

81. fiery keel: 火船，指 1585 年尼德兰人攻打帕尔玛公爵在安特卫普城（Antwerp）的工事时用焚烧着的船只攻破封锁。

82. sage: = wise. 从以上一段台词可以看出浮士德追求魔法的意图是有爱国、反天主教的政治内容的。

83. concealed [-id] **Arts:** 玄妙奥秘的法术。

84. fantasy: 遐想、思考，应是 101 行 won 的主语，but my own fantasy has won me。

85. object: 一般解释为“物质的实体”、“现实”，意思是我的遐想是空灵的。但 object 据 O. E. D. 也有 obstacle 的意思，指自由翱翔的遐想。

86. basest of the three: = baser than the other three.

87. vilde: = vile，可鄙，可耻。

88. gravel'd: = confounded, perplexed，用严格的三段法 syllogism 使他们瞠目结舌。

89. Pastors: 下级教士，当指宗教改革前德国天主教教士。

90. flowering pride: 有才华的俊杰。

91. swarm: 蜂拥而来听我的…。

92. Problems: 逻辑和数学的演讲；或作经院中辩论时提出的问题。

93. infernal spirits: 冥界的幽灵。

94. on: = swarm on.

95. Musaeus: 希腊神话中的歌手、诗人。此处同 Orpheus 混淆了，后者也是希腊神话中的歌手、音乐家，因寻找去世的妻子，来到冥界，他的音乐感动了冥王，把他妻子赦回人间。

96. will be: 主语为 112 行的 I。

97. Agrippa: Cornelius (1485 – 1535) 德国学者，著有《论奥秘哲学》，因而人们盛传他能使死人还魂，下一行 shadows 即指亡魂。

98. canonize: 重音在第二音节，封为圣徒。

99. Moors: 原是北非人，当时常用于一切有色人种，此处当指当时受西班牙统治的美洲土著。

100. Almain Rutters: 德国骑兵。法语称德国为 Allemagne，德国人为 alle mand。Rutter 荷兰语。

101. staves: = staffs，长矛。

102. Lapland: 北欧的极北部分；相传为巨人、魔巫所居。

103. shadowing: = sheltering，蕴藏着。

104. airy brows: 非人间的、天仙般的容貌。

105. has: 原文疑误，应作 have。

106. Queen of love: 指 Venus 爱神。

107. Argosies: 复数。Argosy，大商船，尤其指威尼斯商船。参看莎士比亚《威尼斯商人》。

108. Golden Fleece: 金羊毛，原指希腊神话中 Jason 盗取金羊毛故事，此处意为黄金。

109. Phillip: 即 Philip，指西班牙王菲力普二世 Philip II (1572–1598)。

110. resolute: 有决心。此字数见，说明浮士德内心的矛盾，须要别人随时提醒他下决心。

111. object: = object to，不必提出我必须下决心这样的条件。

112. vow: 立誓。

113. grounded: = versed，精通。

114. Inricht (enriched) **with tongues:** 增添语言才能，尤指拉丁语，作法时要用拉丁语。

115. well seen: = well-versed，精通。

116. Minerals: 例如炼金术和医学中使用的矿物。

117. doth: = does，此处并非加重语气，是由于音节需要的垫字（expletive）。

118. frequented: = resorted to，人们来向我求教。

119. mystery: 秘术。

120. Delphian Oracle: 古希腊人到 Delphi 地方的 Apollo 庙祈求神谕，解答疑难。

121. wracks: 失事的船只。

122. massy: = massive，巨大的。

123. entrails: 内脏，肚皮。

124. magical: = of magic.

125. Bacon: Roger Bacon，十三世纪英国僧侣，传说他用铜造了一个人头，能说话，道出宇宙的秘密。Albanus 也是十三世纪僧侣、魔法师，传说他同 Bacon 共制铜头。works 指他们的著作。

126. Hebrew Psalter [ˈsɔːltə]：希伯来文的《诗篇》，指《旧约》中的《诗篇》（Psalms）[sɑːmz]。**New Testament**：《新约》。人们用《诗篇》第 22、51 篇，《新约》《约翰福音》开始几句话召唤鬼神。

127. ere: = before.

128. learn'd: = learned，修饰 ceremonies，深奥的仪式。

129. meat: = dinner.

130. canvass: 考察，讨论。

131. quiddity: 事物的本质（经院哲学中逻辑学术语），此处指细节。

132. tho: = though.

Scene xvii　全剧接近尾声，浮士德已近老年。这一场写他最后一次施展魔术，召来希腊美人海伦的幽灵，这是他覆灭前最后一次“犯罪”或向诱惑的屈服。老人，据故事书，是浮士德的邻居，一个虔诚的教徒，规劝过浮士德。他在这里代表“信仰”，有中古剧人物“善”的抽象的象征意义。

1. cover'd dishes: 盖着盖子的菜肴。

2. ducats: 钱币名。

3. ready coin'd: 浮士德用魔术铸造的。

4. nigh: = near.

5. frolic: 作乐，指摆酒筵。

6. belly-cheer: 大吃大喝。

7. Mephostophilis: 重音在 -sto-，可能由三个希腊词组成 not loving the light，亦作 Mephistophilis 或 Mephistopheles。在故事书中，他是 Lucifer 派来引诱浮士德的魔鬼。

8. which was: = which one was 或 who was.

9. determin'd: = decided.

10. Helen: 海伦，希腊斯巴达（Sparta）王墨涅劳斯（Menelaus [ˌmeniˈleiəs]）的王后，传说是古代最美的女子，被特洛亚（Troy）王子帕里斯（Paris）诱拐，引起特洛亚战争。海伦象征人间的美、美感、诗意，浮士德和她的拥抱象征对上帝、对宗教信仰的最后挑战。从基督教观点看，海伦是魔鬼的化身，浮士德既与魔鬼拥抱，就万劫不复了。

11. peerless: 无与伦比的。

12. Majesty: 有庄严美妙的涵义。

13. beholding: = beholden，感激。

14. for that: = since，既然，因为。

15. unfeign'd: = true.

16. no otherway than when: = just as when.

17. for pomp: = respecting pomp，就威仪、仪态而论，修饰 peerless。

18. sir Paris: 把帕里斯称为骑士，是因袭中古传奇文学而来。

19. spoils: 掳获物。

20. Dardania: 特洛亚的别名。

21. Be silent: 据故事书，当幽灵出现时，浮士德禁止观者向幽灵发问或说话，否则就会发生危险。

22. wit: 此处指头脑。

23. tho: = then.

24. pursu'd the rape: = took vengeance for the rape. rape：奸污。

25. compare: = comparison.

26. only: 独一无二的。

27. Paragon: 最完美的事物，尤物。

28. for this blessed sight: = on account of this.

29. bereave: 剥夺。

30. persever: 重音在第二音节，即 persevere 坚持。作为一个人，允许你犯错误，若坚持错误，那你就是魔鬼了。

31. amiable: 此处指值得人爱的。

32. custom ... nature: 勿使习惯成为天性。老人劝他不要再搞罪恶的魔法了。grow 假设句，所以不用 grows。

33. Then: 如果你不听劝告，继续迷恋魔法。

34. No mortal: = no man, no one.

35. this my exhortation: = this exhortation of mine，我的这番劝告。

36. let it not: = let it not seem so.

37. envy of thee: = with any ill-will toward you，与 wrath 平行，不是出于对你的恶意。

38. rebuke: 责备。

39. checking: 抑制。

40. amend: 对…有利。

41. dagger: 魔鬼给他匕首，因为自杀是背叛上帝的行为。

42. to do thee right: 向你还债（是对在场的魔鬼说的）。

43. vial: 小瓶，小药瓶，里面装的不是治病的油膏而是上帝的恩惠，可以拯救灵魂。

44. offers: 应作不定式 offer，与 58 行 hover 平行。

45. the same: 指 grace.

46. call, avoid: 祈使句。

47. despair: 绝望也是背叛上帝的一种表现，表示对上帝的仁慈失去信心。参看 68 行。

48. enemy: 指魔鬼。

49. hapless: = unhappy 不幸的。

50. Hell strives with grace: 浮士德内心的斗争文字化。Hell 是魔鬼、无神论、科学知识，Grace 是上帝、宗教，二者在争夺浮士德。

51. to shun the snares of death: 避开死亡的罗网，皈依上帝。

52. Revolt: = turn back，回来，倒向魔鬼吧。

53. presumption: 僭越、非分，指想要背叛魔鬼的念头。

56. drift: 叛离魔鬼的行为，或解作“意图”drive at, aim at。

57. Torment: 动词，祈使句。crooked age 一作 aged man 指方才那老人。折磨那老人去吧，是他怂恿我叛离魔鬼的。

58. His faith: 指老人的信仰。

59. but little worth: 我去折磨老人的肉体，没有什么意义。

60. crave of: = beg of，请求你。

61. unto my paramour: = as my paramour（情人）。

62. clear: = entirely, thoroughly，彻底地。

63. keep mine oath: 与 91 行 extinguish those thoughts 平行。

64. 第 91 行—93 行： 据故事书，浮士德爱上海伦，和她结婚生子。歌德用这个情节，产生出欧福良（Euphorion），象征自由向上的精神。马娄则把这一情节解释为同魔鬼的结合，向魔鬼投降，因为海伦是个幽灵。所以下面有“信守对魔王的誓言”的话头。

65. launcht: = launched，发动。据传说，希腊人聚集了 1200 条船。

66. topless: 高不见顶的。

67. Ilium: 特洛亚的别名。马娄用简单而又宏伟的形象（a thousand ships, topless towers），用两句诗概括了一场十年战争。

68. 第 96 行—98 行：这是马娄最有名的几句诗，不仅表达了惊奇和结合的兴奋，更是对宗教叛逆的赞歌。在《帖木儿》下篇中，马娄也歌颂过海伦之美，在 Dido 剧中他歌颂了爱的不朽（Dido: "And he'll make me immortal with a kiss"），在这二十句诗里，他更是高声歌唱美和爱的赞歌。美和爱——人文主义者的理想，在他看来是不朽的，虽然对它们的追求和对知识的追求一样是违反宗教的禁欲主义和蒙昧主义（suck my soul forth）的，但对理想的追求远远胜过了（在这一霎那）宗教禁条（all is dross that is not Helena）。

69. again: = back，还给我。

70. dross: 渣滓。

71. sack: 洗劫。

72. Menelaus: 海伦的丈夫，见前，他没有什么本领，故称 weak。

73. thy colours: 缎带、徽章之类的标志；plumed crest，顶上插着羽毛的头盔。中古骑士为了赢得意中人垂青，带着她的标志出征。

74. Achilles [əˈkiliːs]：特洛亚战争中希腊阵营的大将，刀枪不入，只有脚跟可以受伤致死。

75. clad: = clothed，穿着。

76. Jupiter: 尤比特，罗马神话中的主神，也是雷电之神、光明之神，故称 flaming。

77. Semele [ˈsemili]：希腊 Thrace 地方的姑娘，尤比特爱上了她。她要求尤比特再来时不要变成凡人，而要显露神的光辉的真身，结果被尤比特的雷电焚殛。hapless = unhappy，见前。

78. Monarch of the sky: 指尤比特。

79. Arethusa [ˌæriˈθjuːzə]：泉水女仙，此处说她拥抱尤比特，古代神话中没有这段恋爱故事。

80. azur'd: 淡蓝色，泉水的颜色，一说指臂上的静脉。这一行用了三个 a 音的头韵（alliteration）。

81. fliest ...: 逃离上帝的审判宝座，逃避上帝的审判。

82. Satan: 撒旦，魔鬼之王。

83. sift: 筛选，此处意为考验，语出《路加福音》22 章 31 节，耶稣警告门徒说撒旦要得到他们，象筛麦子一样，但要求门徒不要丧失信心。

84. pride: 力量。老人见群鬼上场，所以说魔鬼在考验他，在同他较量，上帝也在考验他的信心，但他相信将战胜魔鬼。按故事书，浮士德与魔鬼订约决不听从任何人的劝说而皈依上帝，老人劝他，因此他痛恨老人，要害死老人。老人起着浮士德对立面的作用。

85. the heavens: 作单数，参看序曲 25 注。

86. repulse: 即 being repulsed，指魔鬼之被击退。

87. laugh to scorn: 嘲弄。

88. state: 地位，尊严。

89. Hence: 第一个 hence 相当于动词 go away；第二个 hence 表示地点，从这里。

Scene xviii　这一场分为四段：1. 魔王们的会议；2. 浮士德与学者告别，写浮士德的悔恨；3. 对浮士德的裁决；4. 他的痛苦以及最终的毁灭。

1. Lucifer: 拉丁文“带来光明的人”，启明星；在基督教《圣经》中用以称呼巴比伦王，他要同上帝较量，被打入地狱，变成了魔王、撒旦。

2. Belzebub: 一般作 Beelzebub [biˈelzibʌb]。希伯来文，苍蝇之王，仅次于撒旦的魔鬼。

3. Dis: 罗马神话中冥府之神，此处指地狱。

4. sin: 子句中的主语。后面的逗号完全是为朗读停顿。注意此行 s 头韵。

5. seals: 有两个宾语 which (souls) 和 sons of hell，打上印记把他标为…。

6. ’Mong: = Among，省去一个音节。

7. make it forfeit: it 指浮士德灵魂；forfeit，抵偿、没收。时间到了，要夺去你的灵魂了。

8. mark: 观察，him 和 how … himself 都是宾语。

9. demean: = conduct，看他怎样行动。

10. fond: (= foolish) worldling，愚蠢的凡人。

11. Begets … fantasies: 他的脑子胡思乱想。

12. over-reach: 自作聪明想胜过魔鬼。

13. sauc’d: = paid for dearly，付出极其痛苦的代价。

14. come: 过去分词，与动词 to be 连用。

15. Gramercies: 单数 gramercy，古法语 grant merci，十分感谢。

16. methinks: = it seems to me.

17. chamber-fellow: 大学同屋住的同学。**had I … had I …:** 古语法，= if I had … I should have …

18 comes he not?: 指魔鬼。

19. ’Tis: = it is.

20. surfeit: 饮食过度。下一行 surfeit，过量、过多。

21. Eve: 夏娃，指《圣经》中魔鬼变蛇引诱夏娃的故事。

22. pant and quiver: 跳动，心悸。让步从句。

23. would: = I would, I wish.

24. abjur’d: 发誓放弃。

25. blasphem’d: 亵渎、咒骂。

26. stays my tongue: 让我说不出话来。

27. writ: = wrote，订立。

28. bill: 契约。

29. Divines: 神父。

30. body and soul: 副词。

31. into: 起动词的作用，go into.

32. hath rob’d: = that has robbed.

33. Dam'd up: = dammed up，堵塞住。

34. turn'd the leaves: 浮士德想读《圣经》，魔鬼替他翻篇。

35. 第 98 行： 这行诗的后半多半被编辑者删去。

36. several doors: 两个不同的门。

37. had followed: = would have followed. 第 112—115 行，结构相同。

38. vex: 折磨。

39. To want: 匮乏、缺乏；store，富足。

40. Throne: 从舞台上方缒下一张宝座，其用意见 Good Angel 台词。

41. affected: = devoted yourself to，致力于。

42. set: = sat.

43. Hell is discovered: 指拉开后台帷幕，露出一张黑色的幕代表地狱，或一张绘有地狱图形的幕。

44. furies: 希腊、罗马神话中的三个复仇女神，此处泛指鬼。

45. lead: 熔化了的铅，铅水。

46. live quarters: 肢解了的但仍活着的肢体。

47. broil: 烤、焙。

48. over-tortur'd: 再受到酷刑的。

49. sops: 蘸汁的面包片，此处 = flaming fire。

50. 第 128 行： 指生前眼望着乞丐在门前饿死而自己则狼吞虎咽的人到地狱里被罚吃火。

51. that more horrid be: that are more horrid.

52. smart: 痛苦、苦楚。

53. till anon: = for a short while.

54. confusion 四个音节 [kən'fjuːʒən]：灾难、毁灭。

第 127 行—135 行： 每两行或三行叶韵，可能不是出自马娄手笔。

55. Fair nature's eye: 太阳。

56. a natural day: 普通长度的白天。

57. O lente …: 拉丁文 O slowly, slowly run, horses of the night，语出罗马诗人奥维德（Ovid）情诗（Amores）。马娄把一行情人恨夜短的诗化为浮士德的内心痛苦，暗示他对人生、知识和感官享受的热爱，对神学教条的反叛，历来评家都认为是神来之笔。我们也可以看出古代文学怎样在文艺复兴时期起作用。

58. still: = continually，不停顿地。

59. See see: 基督的血在太空中流动。这一行意象突兀、宏伟、可怖。它同第五场浮士德与魔鬼歃血订约相呼应。它充满了对宗教的强烈批判：号称无边仁慈的基督竟舍不得半滴血来拯救浮士德的灵魂。结合据传马娄说过的话"Christ was a bastard and his mother dishonest"，"the first beginning of religion was only to keep men in awe"，更可以理解这句诗的无比愤懑的含意了。

60. rend not my heart: 不要撕碎我的心。

61. 第 152 行： 浮士德只得向魔王求救，但他一旦向魔王求救，就再也得不到上帝的仁慈了。

62. Where is it now: 指满天的血河。

63. ireful: = angry.

64. Mountains and Hills: 出自《旧约》《何西阿书》，用逃避来抵制神的残暴。

65. Stars: 浮士德出生时当令的星宿。

66. influence: 指对新生儿的性格和命运所产生的影响。

67. allotted: 派定。

68. draw up: 人们相信星宿有此威力。

69. you: 指 stars.

70. so that: = if only.

71. anon: = soon, presently.

72. 第 169 行： 指基督用死来为人类赎罪。

73. impose some end: = put an end to.

74. this: 指人的灵魂。

75. Pythagoras [paiˈθægəræs]**:** 毕达哥拉，公元前六世纪希腊哲学家。

76. Metempsychosis [ˌmetempsiˈkousis]**:** 灵魂转移说，人死后，灵魂转入其他生物躯体。

77. still: = always.

78. Curst: = cursed，受诅咒。

79. quick: = alive，活活地。

80. Adders: 蛇，指魔鬼。

81. gape not: 不要张嘴。

82. books: 魔术书。

Scene xix　学者对浮士德表示同情。尾声。

1. Faustus's limbs: 按故事书，午夜狂风大作，浮士德的房门被刮开，听到他微弱的呼救声，随即寂静。天明，学者们发现室内满地是血和脑浆，尸体抛在院内马粪堆上，四肢撕裂。

2. me thought I heard: = I seem to have heard.

3. At which self time: = at that very moment, at the same time.

4. every Christian heart: 反映作者对浮士德的同情。

5. mangled: 血肉模糊的。

6. heavy: = sorrowful.

7. 第 20 行—27 行： 尾声。有人认为前三句和后五句不同，前三句表示同情惋惜，后五句表示责备，要人引以为戒，因而认为前三句是马娄本意，后五句的意思是故事书所规定的。但也有人指出故事书所警戒的是 the stiff-necked and high-minded，倔强而高傲的人们，马娄则代之以 the wise，墙头草随风倒之辈，说明马娄还是赞赏浮士德这种倔强的人物，因而前后并不矛盾。

8. Apollo: 阿波罗，希腊神话中的日神、诗歌学术之神。

9. laurel bough: 桂枝，月桂树是阿波罗的树，象征学问、诗歌、光明。

10. regard: = pay heed to, take warning by，引以为戒。hellish fall，堕入地狱。

11. fiendful: 受魔鬼影响的。

12. fortune: 遭遇。

13. exhort: 警戒。

14. only to wonder at: 只羡慕。

15. unlawful: 为宗教所禁止的。

16. deepness: 深奥（贬义）。

17. entice: 引诱。

18. forward wits: 有才华而唐突不自量力的人。

19. Terminat ...: 拉丁文，The hour ends the day, the author ends his work。印书商人从早期一部手抄本戏剧末尾引来，其中 Author 用的是英文，照搬未改。

20. Finis: 拉丁文，The End。

4 WILLIAM SHAKESPEARE
1564–1616

I. SONGS FROM THE PLAYS

李赋宁 选注

(1) When Daisies Pied
SPRING

When daisies pied[1] and violets blue
    And ladysmocks all silver-white
And cuckoobuds[2] of yellow hue
    Do paint the meadows with delight,
The cuckoo then, on every tree,
Mocks married men[3]: for thus sings he,
                'Cuckoo;
Cuckoo, cuckoo.' Oh word of fear,
Unpleasing to a married ear!

When shepherds pipe on oaten straws,[4]
    And merry larks are ploughmen's clocks[5];
When turtles tread[6], and rooks, and daws,
    And maidens bleach their summer smocks,

The cuckoo then, on every tree,
Mocks married men; for thus sings he,
'Cuckoo;
Cuckoo, cuckoo': Oh word of fear,
Unpleasing to a married ear!

WINTER

When icicles hang by the wall
And Dick the shepherd blows his nail,[7]
And Tom bears logs into the hall,
And milk comes frozen home in pail,
When blood is nipped, and ways be foul,
Then nightly sings the staring owl,
'Tu-who;
Tu-whit, tu-who'[8]: a merry note,
While greasy Joan doth keel the pot.[9]

When all aloud the wind doth blow,
And coughing drowns the parson's saw[10],
And birds sit brooding in the snow,
And Marian's nose looks red and raw;
When roasted crabs[11] hiss in the bowl,
Then nightly sings the staring owl,
'Tu-who;
Tu-whit, tu-who': a merry note,
While greasy Joan doth keel the pot.

(2) Tell Me Where Is Fancy Bred

Tell me, where is fancy[1] bred,
Or in the heart, or in the head?
How begot, how nourishéd?
Reply, reply.
It is engendered in the eyes,

With gazing fed; and fancy dies
In the cradle where it lies.
Let us all ring fancy's knell:
I'll begin it — Ding, dong, bell.
Ding, dong, bell.

(3) Sigh No More, Ladies

Sigh no more, ladies, sigh no more,
Men were deceivers ever;
One foot in sea, and one on shore,
To one thing constant never.
Then sigh not so,
But let them go,
And be you blithe and bonny[1],
Converting all your sounds of woe
Into Hey nonny, nonny[2].

Sing no more ditties[3], sing no mo[4]
Of dumps[5] so dull and heavy;
The fraud of men was ever so,
Since summer first was leavy[6].
Then sigh not so,
But let them go,
And be you blithe and bonny,
Converting all your sounds of woe
Into Hey nonny, nonny.

(4) Under the Greenwood Tree

Under the greenwood tree
Who loves[1] to lie[2] with me,
And turn his merry note
Unto the sweet bird's throat[3],
Come hither, come hither, come hither:

Here shall he see
No enemy
But winter and rough weather.
Who doth ambition shun
And loves to live i' the sun,
Seeking the food he eats,
And pleased with what he gets,
Come hither, come hither, come hither:
Here shall he see
No enemy
But winter and rough weather.

(5) Blow, Blow, Thou Winter Wind

Blow, blow, thou winter wind,
Thou art not so unkind
As man's ingratitude;
Thy tooth is not so keen,
Because thou art not seen,
Although thy breath be rude[1].
Heigh-ho[2]! sing, heigh-ho! unto the green holly:
Most friendship is feigning, most loving mere folly:
Then, heigh-ho, the holly!
This life is most jolly.

Freeze, freeze, thou bitter sky,
That dost not bite so nigh
As benefits[3] forgot:
Though thou the waters warp[4],
Thy sting is not so sharp
As friend remembered not.
Heigh-ho! sing, etc.

(6) Oh Mistress Mine

Oh mistress mine! where are you roaming?
Oh! stay and hear; your true love's coming,
    That can sing both high and low[1].
Trip no further, pretty sweeting[2];
Journeys end in lovers' meeting,
    Every wise man's son doth know.

What is love? 'tis not hereafter[3];
Present mirth hath present laughter;
    What's to come is still[4] unsure:
In delay there lies no plenty;
Then come kiss me[5], sweet and twenty[6],
    Youth's a stuff will not endure[7].

(7) Take, Oh, Take Those Lips Away

Take, Oh, take those lips away,
    That so sweetly were forsworn[1];
And those eyes, the break of day[2],
    Lights that do mislead the morn[3]:
But my kisses bring again[4], bring again;
Seals of love[5], but sealed in vain, sealed in vain.

(8) Fear No More the Heat o' the Sun

Fear no more the heat o' the sun,
    Nor the furious winter's rages;
Thou thy worldly task hast done,
    Home art gone, and ta'en thy wages:
Golden lads and girls[1] all must,
As chimney-sweepers, come to dust.

Fear no more the frown o' the great;

Thou art past the tyrant's stroke;
Care no more to clothe and eat[2];
To thee the reed is as the oak[3]:
The scepter, learning, physic[4], must
All follow this[5], and come to dust.

Fear no more the lightning flash,
Nor the all-dreaded thunder stone[6];
Fear not slander, censure rash;
Thou hast finished joy and moan:
All lovers young, all lovers must
Consign to thee[7], and come to dust.

No exorciser harm thee!
Nor no witchcraft charm thee!
Ghost unlaid[8] forbear thee[9]!
Nothing ill come near thee!
Quiet consummation have;[10]
And renowned be thy grave!

(9) Full Fathom Five[1]

Full fathom five thy father lies;
Of his bones are coral made[2];
Those are pearls that were his eyes:
Nothing of him that doth fade,
But doth suffer a sea change[3]
Into something rich and strange.
Sea nymphs hourly ring his knell:
Ding-dong.
Hark! now I hear them — Ding-dong, bell.

(10) Where the Bee Sucks, There Suck I

Where the bee sucks, there suck I:

In a cowslip's bell I lie;
There I couch when owls do cry.
On the bat's back I do fly
After summer merrily[1].
Merrily, merrily shall I live now
Under the blossom that hangs on the bough.

(11) Who Is Silvia?

Who is Silvia? What is she,
That all our swains[1] commend her?
Holy, fair, and wise is she;
The heaven such grace did lend her,
That she might admired be.

Is she kind as she is fair?
For beauty lives with kindness.
Love doth to her eyes repair[2],
To help him of his blindness[3],
And, being helped, inhabits there[4].

Then to Silvia let us sing,
That Silvia is excelling;
She excels each mortal thing
Upon the dull earth dwelling.
To her let us garlands bring.

(12) When Daffodils Begin to Peer

When daffodils begin to peer,
With heigh! the doxy[1] over the dale,
Why, then comes in the sweet o' the year;
For the red blood reigns in the winter's pale[2].

The white sheet bleaching on the hedge[3],

With heigh! the sweet birds, oh, how they sing!
Doth set my pugging tooth on edge[4];
For a quart of ale is a dish for a king.

The lark, that tirra-lirra[5] chants,
With heigh! with heigh! the thrush and the jay,
Are summer songs for me and my aunts[6],
While we lie tumbling in the hay.

【作者简介】 William Shakespeare（威廉·莎士比亚，1564—1616），文艺复兴时期英国剧作家和诗人。马克思把莎士比亚和艾斯契拉斯（Aeschylus，古希腊悲剧诗人）看作是"世界上曾经有过的两个最伟大的天才戏剧家"（刘慧义译P. 拉法格，《马克思与文学》）。莎士比亚的戏剧代表作有：*Romeo and Juliet*（《罗密欧与朱丽叶》，1595），*The Merchant of Venice*（《威尼斯商人》，1596），*Julius Cæsar*（《儒略·凯撒》，1599），*As You Like It*（《皆大欢喜》，1600），*Hamlet*（《汉姆雷特》，1601），*King Lear*（《李尔王》，1605），*Macbeth*（《麦克佩斯》，1605），*The Tempest*（《暴风雨》，1611），等。莎士比亚的诗歌作品最有名的是他的Sonnets（十四行诗），共154首，1609年出版。

【题解与注释】

莎士比亚所写的剧本里穿插着一些歌曲（songs）和民歌（lyrics），这些歌谣十分清新、优美，充分显示出莎士比亚作为抒情诗人的才华。即便在一些非常曲折、复杂的剧本里，读者仍会遇到明晰、透亮的歌曲，随着音乐的伴奏，给人以极大的美感享受。莎士比亚剧中的歌曲富于诗意，具有英国乡间泥土的清香，歌颂大自然的美丽和民间的淳朴生活，充满了英国人民的梦幻和向往。它们具有各种类型：黎明曲（aubade），牧歌（pastoral），情歌（love song），民谣（ballad），葬歌（dirge），等。它们反映了莎士比亚的多方面的天才——抒情的本领、幽默和对大自然的图画和音乐的高度敏感。它们音乐性很强，反映了伊丽莎白时代（the Elizabethan age）的音乐发展。有些歌曲表现了当时芭蕾舞曲（ballet）的欢乐，有些表现了赞歌（motet）的严肃，有些还表现了小曲（madrigal）的简练风格。还有一点值得注意的是莎士比亚剧中的歌曲都有它的戏剧目的和作用，并不是可有可无的。莎士比亚的抒情本领是为他的戏剧才能服务的。

我们一共选了十二首歌曲，现说明并注释如下：

(1) When Daisies Pied (Spring & Winter) "当杂色的雏菊"（春和冬）

这首歌曲选自莎士比亚的早期喜剧 *Love's Labour's Lost*（《爱的徒劳》，1594）的结尾，包括两支歌:《春之歌》(Spring)和《冬之歌》(Winter)。英国桂冠诗人John Masefield (1878–1967) 认为这两支歌给英国描绘了一幅最美丽的图画。这两支歌的形式可以看成是一场对话(dialogue)，内容是对话的一方对布谷鸟(the cuckoo)的赞扬，另一方对猫头鹰(the owl)的推崇。布谷鸟代表春天，猫头鹰代表冬天，它们象征着《爱的徒劳》喜剧的又甜又苦的结尾。

1. pied: variegated(杂色的)。雏菊(daisy)一般呈黄心、白色或粉红色花瓣。

2. cuckoobud: "Shakespeare has been variously supposed to refer to the buttercup(金凤花)，marsh-marigold(立金花)，and cowslip(黄花九轮草)."(OED)

3. Mocks married men: The cuckoo's song—"Cuckoo!"—is taken to mean "Cuckold!" (a man whose wife has proved *unfaithful*). 布谷鸟的咕咕歌声好像在嘲笑戴绿头巾的丈夫。

4. oaten straws: the reed pipes(牧笛、簧管)played by shepherds. 牧羊人吹奏的牧笛。

5. larks are ploughmen's clocks: because they sing at sunrise. 云雀在日出时唱歌，因此云雀是庄稼汉的钟表。

6. turtles tread: turtledoves(斑鸠)mate(配偶)。

7. blows his nail: warms his fingers by blowing on them. 向手指头呵热气取暖。

8. Tu-whit, tu-who: cry of owl. 猫头鹰的叫声。

9. keel the pot: stir, to prevent boiling over. 搅动汤锅，防止汤水沸腾溢出。

10. the parson's saw: wise saying. 牧师的格言。

11. roasted crabs: crabapples(野生的酸苹果)。烤熟了的野生酸苹果。

请参看郭沫若先生对《冬之歌》的译文：

"冰柱条条悬挂在岩梢，
牧羊人老李吹他的手爪，
老唐把木柴抱进了厅堂，
送来的牛奶冻在路上；
手足有冻疮，路又不象样，
枭鸟鼓着眼睛，夜：在唱
　　荒唐！
荒唐，荒唐，调子倒满响亮！
正在搅拌砂锅，那油垢的蒋。

寒风四处总吹个不停，
喀嗽声淹没了牧师的讲经，
众鸟栖息在雪里的巢，
玛良的鼻子冻成朵红海椒；
酸林檎在钵子里啾啾地响，
枭鸟鼓着眼睛，夜：在唱
　　荒唐！

荒唐，荒唐，调子倒满响亮！
正在搅拌砂锅，那油垢的蒋。”

(2) Tell Me Where Is Fancy Bred（**“告诉我爱情生长在何方”**）

这首歌曲选自莎士比亚的喜剧《威尼斯商人》(1596—97)，III. ii. 63 ff. 当巴萨尼奥（Bassanio）选择金盒、银盒和铅盒时，他一面独白，乐队一面奏乐唱歌。唱这首歌曲的目的可能是为了帮助巴萨尼奥做出决定。请注意在这首歌里，有不少词和lead‘铅’押韵：bred, head, nourishéd, fed，因此有可能向巴萨尼奥提示，叫他选择铅盒。

1. fancy: love. It is a superficial love or liking for something attractive.（这是一种被美丽的人或物所吸引而发生的肤浅的爱情。）

请参看朱生豪先生对此首歌曲的译文：

“告诉我爱情生长在何方？
还是在脑海？还是在心房？
它怎样发生？它怎样成长？
　　回答我，回答我。
爱情的火在眼睛里点亮，
凝视是爱情生活的滋养，
它的摇篮便是它的坟堂。
让我们把爱的丧钟鸣响，
　　玎珰！玎珰！
　　玎珰！玎珰！”

(3) Sigh No More, Ladies（**“莫再叹息，女士们”**）

这首歌曲选自莎士比亚的喜剧《无事生非》(*Much Ado About Nothing*, 1598–99)，II. iii. 64 ff. 阿拉贡亲王唐·彼德罗命令他的仆人鲍尔萨泽唱这首歌。

1. bonny: smiling, gay（嬉笑的，欢乐的）。

2. nonny: a meaningless word in old ballad refrain, usually “hey, nonny”, “hey nonny nonny”, or “hey nonny no”（古民谣每节收尾的重叠句常出现 hey nonny nonny 这些字眼。它们本身没有意义。这里 hey nonny nonny 指欢乐的歌声）。

3. ditty: a short, simple song（短歌、小曲）。

4. no mo: no more（不再）。古体 *mo* 来自古英语 mā。

5. dumps: sad songs（悲哀的歌曲）。

6. leavy: (archaic form of *leafy*) covered with leaves, having many leaves（*leafy* 的古体。被树叶覆盖着，多树叶的）。

请参看朱生豪先生对这首歌曲的译文：

“不要叹气，姑娘，不要叹气，
　男人们都是些骗子，

一脚在岸上，一脚在海里，
他天性里朝三暮四。
不要叹息，让他们去，
你何必愁眉不展？
收起你的哀丝怨绪，
唱一曲清歌婉转。
莫再悲吟，姑娘，莫再悲吟，
停住你沉重的哀音；
哪一个夏天不绿叶成荫？
哪一个男子不负心？
不要叹息，让他们去，
你何必愁眉不展？
收起你的哀丝怨绪，
唱一曲清歌婉转。”

(4) Under the Greenwood Tree（**“在绿林树下”**）

这首歌曲选自莎士比亚喜剧《皆大欢喜》（*As You Like It*, 1599–1600）II. v. 1 ff. 它生动地说明了被流放的公爵和他的随从们在亚登森林里过着快活的、无忧无虑的生活。

1. Who loves: 等于 he who 或 anyone who.

2. lie: 等于 stay（停留）。

3. And turn his merry note / Unto the sweet bird's throat: improvise his song in harmony with the bird's（与鸟儿的歌声相和谐，即席放声歌唱）。

请参看朱生豪先生对这首歌曲的译文：

“绿树高张翠幕，
谁来偕我偃卧，
翻将欢乐心声，
学唱枝头鸟鸣：
盍来此？盍来此？盍来此？
目之所接，
精神契一，
唯忧雨雪之将至。

孰能敝屣尊荣，
来沐丽日光风，
觅食自求果腹，
一饱欣然意足：
盍来此？盍来此？盍来此？
目之所接，
精神契一，
唯忧雨雪之将至。”

(5) *Blow, Blow, Thou Winter Wind*（**“吹吧，吹吧，你那冬天的风”**）

这首歌曲也选自《皆大欢喜》II. vii. 174 ff. 它的主题是大自然的善与人类的恶之间的对照。这个主题也贯穿在整部《皆大欢喜》剧本之中。

1. Although thy breath be rude: 等于 although your breath (i. e., wind) is violent（尽管你的呼吸是狂暴的）。早期英语在连词 although 引起的转折从句里，动词用虚拟语气，因此用 *be* 代替 *is*。

2. Heigh-ho!: an exclamation of greeting; an exclamation used to give encouragement（招呼别人或鼓励别人时的用语）。

3. benefits: acts of kindness, favours（恩惠）。

4. warp: i. e. roughen by freezing（通过结冰使水面变得不平）。

请参看朱生豪先生对这首歌曲的译文：

“不惧冬风凛冽，
风威远难逮及
人世之寡情；
其为气也虽厉，
其牙尚非甚锐，
风体本无形。
噫嘻乎！且向冬青歌一曲：
友交皆虚妄，恩爱痴人逐。
噫嘻乎冬青！
可乐唯此生。

不愁冱天冰雪，
其寒尚难逮及
受施而忘恩；
风皱满池碧水，
利刺尚难逮比
捐旧之友人。
噫嘻乎！且向冬青歌一曲：
友交皆虚妄，恩爱痴人逐。
噫嘻乎冬青！
可乐唯此生。”

(6) *Oh Mistress Mine*（**“啊我的姑娘”**）

这首歌曲选自莎士比亚的喜剧《第十二夜》（*Twelfth Night*, 1601–2）II. iii. 40 ff. 这是小丑费斯特唱的一首情歌。它的主题是世界文学当中最有普遍性的主题之一：Cape diem（Seize the day，及时行乐）。莎士比亚对这个主题的处理十分清新可爱。

1. high and low: adverb, ‘everywhere’（地点状语，‘到处’）。

2. sweeting: archaic variant of sweetheart（sweetheart‘情人’的古体）。

3. hereafter: adverb, 'in the future', 'in the life after death'（在未来，在来生）。

4. still: 等于 always（永远，总是）。

5. Then come kiss me: 等于 Then come and kiss me.

6. sweet and twenty: 有两种解释：（1）sweet = fair（美丽），twenty = young（年轻）；sweet and twenty = at once fair and young（既美丽又年轻）；（2）and twenty = indeed（的确）；sweet and twenty = sweet indeed. 试比较 Good even and twenty = Good evening! 的强调语气。

7. Youth's a stuff will not endure: stuff 后面是一个定语从句，关系代词 *that* 被省略：Youth is a stuff that will not endure.

请参看朱生豪先生对这首歌曲的译文：

"你到哪儿去，啊我的姑娘？
听呀，那边来了你的情郎，
　嘴里吟着抑扬的曲调。
不要再走了，美貌的亲亲；
恋人的相遇终结了行程，
　每个聪明人全都知晓。

什么是爱情？它不在明天；
欢笑嬉游莫放过了眼前，
　将来的事有谁能猜料？
不要蹉跎了大好的年华；
来吻着我吧，你双十娇娃，
　转眼青春早化成衰老。"

(7) Take, Oh, Take Those Lips Away（**"啊，拿开这张嘴吧"**）

这首歌曲选自莎士比亚的悲喜剧《一报还一报》（*Measure for Measure*, 1604）IV. i. 1 ff. 它感人地表达了玛利安娜被她的未婚夫安哲鲁遗弃后的凄凉心情。在她第一次出场时，童儿唱的就是这首歌。

1. were forsworn: had sworn falsely（发伪誓）。

2. the break of day: the dawn（黎明）。在这行诗里，the break of day 是同一行诗里 those eyes 的同位语。

3. lights that do mislead the morn: lights that attract the morning（吸引清晨的光线）。在这里 lights 和第 3 行的 those eyes 以及 the break of day 都是同位语。情人的目光就象黎明的光线那样，吸引着清晨（指少女自己）。mislead 除有'吸引'的含义外，还当'引入歧途'，'欺骗'解。

4. But my kisses bring again: But give back my kisses（但是把吻还给我）。在这里 kisses 是 bring 的宾语。again = back.

5. Seals of love: confirming tokens of love（证实爱情的标志）。seals of love 是上一行（第 5 行）的 my kisses 的同位语。

请参看朱生豪先生对这首歌曲的译文：

“莫以负心唇，
　婉转弄辞巧；
莫以薄幸眼，
　颠倒迷昏晓；
定情密吻乞君还，
当日深盟今已寒！”

(8) Fear No More the Heat o'the Sun（“不用再怕骄阳晒蒸”）

这首歌曲选自莎士比亚的悲喜剧《辛白林》（*Cymbeline*, c. 1610）IV. ii. 258 ff. 这是一首挽歌，哀悼假死的伊摩琴。

1. Golden lads and girls: golden = gifted in a way that promises future success（有才能的，有出息的）。

2. Care no more to clothe and eat: care = worry, be anxious（再不用为穿衣、吃饭发愁）。

3. To thee the reed is as the oak: To you the inferior thing (the reed) is just as good as the superior thing (the oak). 对于死者来说，芦苇和橡树没有什么区别。意思是说：人死了，好东西和坏东西对他来说都是一样的，都是无所谓的。

4. The scepter, learning, physic: the scepter 指国王，learning 指学者，physic 指医生，意思是‘各行各业’。

5. All follow this: this= this law of nature（所有的人都必须服从这一自然规律）。

6. the all-dreaded thunder stone: all dreaded = dreaded by all（为大家所害怕的）；thunder stone: The sound of thunder was commonly thought to be caused by the falling of stones or meteorites（通常人们认为雷声来自陨石的坠落）。

7. consign to thee: put themselves in your care（把他们自己委托给你照料，意思是说使他们自己和死去的伊摩琴在一起）。

8. Ghost unlaid: unlaid = not appeased（怒气或怨气未消的鬼魂）。

9. forbear thee: spare you（饶恕你，不伤害你）。

10. Quiet consummation have: May you have a quiet conclusion of life（愿你平静地结束生命）。

请参阅朱生豪先生对这首歌曲的译文：

“不用再怕骄阳晒蒸，
　不用再怕寒风凛冽；
世界工作你已完成，
　领了工资回家安息。
才子娇娃同归泉壤，
正象扫烟囱人一样。

不用再怕贵人嗔怒，

　你已超脱暴君威力；
无须再为衣食忧虑，
　芦苇橡树了无区别。
健儿身手，学士心灵，
帝王蝼蚁同化埃尘。

不用再怕闪电光亮，
　不用再怕雷霆暴作；
何须畏惧谗人诽谤，
　你已阅尽世间忧乐。
无限尘寰痴男怨女，
人天一别，埋愁黄土。

没有巫师把你惊动！
　没有符咒扰你魂魄！
野鬼游魂远离坟冢！
　狐兔不来侵你骸骨！
瞑目安眠，归于寂灭；
墓草长新，永留追忆！”

(9) Full Fathom Five（**“五呣的水深处”**）

这首歌曲选自莎士比亚的悲喜剧《暴风雨》(*The Tempest*, 1611–12) I. ii. 396 ff. 魔岛上的小精灵爱丽儿向那不勒斯王子腓迪南唱这首歌。腓迪南听了这首歌后说道："这支歌在纪念我的溺毙的父亲。这一定不是凡间的音乐，也不是地上来的声音。"

1. Full fathom five: a fathom = 6 feet (a nautical measure for the depth of water，航海用的测水深的度量衡，等于六英尺。fathom five= 30 feet). full= '完全的'、'十足的'。

2. Of his bones are coral made: Pieces of red coral are made of his bones (一块块的红珊瑚是他的骨头形成的)。在这里 *coral* 是个集体名词 (collective noun)，因此动词用复数 *are* made。

3. Nothing of him that doth fade, / But doth suffer a sea change: Whatever in him is subject to change undergoes a sea change (他身上没有一个可变化的部分不经历了一场海洋的变化)。nothing but 是双否定结构 (double negative)，其效果等于一个强调的肯定结构 (strong affirmative)。第 4 行的 fade = change gradually. 第 5 行的 suffer = undergo, experience.

请参看朱生豪先生对这首歌曲的译文：

“五呣的水深处躺着你的父亲，
　他的骨骼已化成珊瑚；
　他眼睛是耀眼的明珠；
他消失的全身没有一处不曾

受到海水神奇的变幻，
化成瑰宝，富丽而珍怪。
海的女神时时摇起他的丧钟，（和声）
叮！咚！
听！我现在听到了叮咚的丧钟。”

(10) Where the Bee Sucks, There Suck I
（“蜂儿吮啜的地方，我也在那儿吮啜”）

这首歌曲也选自莎士比亚的《暴风雨》V. i. 88 ff. 小精灵爱丽儿快乐地歌唱着他将要过的自由、幸福的生活。在这里莎士比亚创造了细美、轻盈的芭蕾舞音乐世界和天真、欢乐的童话世界。

1. After summer merrily: after = in pursuit of, in search of（追逐，寻求）。

请参看朱生豪先生对这首歌的译文：

“蜂儿吮啜的地方，我也在那儿吮啜；
在一朵莲香花的冠中我躺着休息；
我安然睡去，当夜枭开始它的呜咽。
骑在蝙蝠背上我快活地飞舞翩翩，
快活地快活地追随着逝去的夏天；
快活地快活地我要如今
向垂在枝头的花底安身。”

(11) Who Is Silvia?（“西尔维娅伊何人”）

这首歌曲选自《维洛那二绅士》（*The Two Gentlemen of Verona*, 1594）IV. ii. 39 ff.

1. swains: young men, lovers（小伙子，情人）。

2. Love doth to her eyes repair: Love (= Cupid) resorts to her eyes（爱神乞援于她的眼睛）。爱神是盲目的。

3. To help him of his blindness: to cure him of his blindness（为了医治好他的盲症）。

4. inhabits there: lives in her eyes（住在她的眼睛里）。

请参看朱生豪先生对这首歌曲的译文：

“西尔维娅伊何人，
乃能颠倒众生心？
神圣娇丽且聪明，
天赋诸美萃一身，
俾令举世诵其名。

伊人颜色如花浓，
伊人宅心如春柔；
盈盈妙目启瞽矇，

创平痍复相思瘳，
寸心永驻眼梢头。

弹琴为伊歌一曲，
伊人美好世无伦；
尘世萧条苦寂寞，
唯伊灿耀如星辰；
穿花为束献佳人。”

(12) When Daffodils Begin to Peer（“当水仙花初放它的娇黄”）

这首歌曲选自《冬天的故事》（*The Winter's Tale*, 1610–11）IV. iii. 1 ff. 卖唱人、小贩、流浪汉奥托里古斯上场时唱着这首歌。这首歌不仅生动地说明了歌唱者的性格，而且使这个剧本从前几场的冬天情调转向后几场的春天气氛。

1. the doxy: (thieves' slang) girl or mistress（小偷的行话：姑娘或情妇）。

2. in the winter's pale: *pale* is a pun on（1）a territory over which one has jurisdiction;（2）lacking in colour（pale 是个双关语:（1）（某一范围内或管辖权下的）地区；（2）苍白的，暗淡、失色的）。

3. The white sheet bleaching on the hedge: Laundry, dried or bleached on hedges, was sometimes stolen by passing vagabonds like Autolycus（晒晾在篱笆上的漂白的布单有时被象奥托里古斯那样的过路的流浪汉所偷窃）。

4. Doth set my pugging tooth on edge: stimulates my desire to steal（激起我偷窃的欲望）。pugging = thieving（偷窃）。

5. tirra-lirra: 云雀的叫声，表示喜悦、愉快。

6. aunts: girls or mistresses（姑娘或情妇）。

请参看朱生豪先生对这首歌曲的译文：

“当水仙花初放它的娇黄，
嗨！山谷那面有一位多娇；
那是一年里最好的时光，
严冬的热血在涨着狂潮。

漂白的布单在墙头晒晾，
嗨！鸟儿们唱得多么动听！
引起我难熬的贼心痒痒，
有了一壶酒喝胜坐龙廷。

听那百灵鸟的清歌婉丽，
嗨！还有画眉喜鹊的叫噪，
一齐唱出了夏天的欢喜，
当我在稻草上左搂右抱。”

II. SONNETS (XVIII, XXIX, XXX, LXV)

王佐良　选注

XVIII

Shall I compare thee[1] to a summer's day?
Thou art more lovely and more temperate.
Rough winds do shake the darling buds of May,
And summer's lease[2] hath all too short a date[3].
Sometime too hot the eye of heaven[4] shines,
And often is his gold complexion dimm'd;
And every fair from fair sometime declines[5],
By chance, or nature's changing course, untrimm'd[6];
But thy eternal summer shall not fade,
Nor lose possession of that fair thou ow'st[7],
Nor shall Death brag thou wander'st in his shade,
When in eternal lines to time thou grow'st[8];
　So long as men can breathe or eyes can see,
　So long lives this, and this gives life to thee.

XXIX

When, in disgrace with Fortune and men's eyes[1],
I all alone beweep[2] my outcast state[3],
And trouble deaf heaven with my bootless[4] cries,
And look upon myself and curse my fate,
Wishing me like to[5] one more rich in hope,
Featur'd[6] like him, like him[7] with friends possess'd[8],
Desiring this man's art[9] and that man's scope[10],
With what I most enjoy contented least[11];
Yet[12] in these thoughts myself almost despising,
Haply[13] I think on thee, and then my state,
Like to the lark at break of day arising
From sullen[14] earth, sings hymns at heaven's gate;

For thy sweet love remember'd such wealth brings
That then I scorn to change my state with kings.

XXX[1]

When to the sessions[2] of sweet silent thought
I summon up[3] remembrance of things past,
I sigh the lack of many a thing I sought,
And with old woes new wail[4] my dear time's waste[5].
Then can I drown an eye[6], unus'd to flow[7],
For precious friends hid in death's dateless night[8],
And weep afresh love's long since[9] cancell'd woe,
And moan th' expense[10] of many a vanish'd sight:
Then can I grieve at grievances foregone[11],
And heavily from woe to woe tell o'er[12]
The sad account of fore-bemoaned[13] moan,
Which I new pay as if not paid before.
　But if the while[14] I think on thee, dear friend,
　All losses are restor'd and sorrows end.

LXV

Since brass[1], nor stone, nor earth, nor boundless sea,
But sad mortality[2] o'ersways their power,
How with this rage[3] shall beauty hold a plea[3],
Whose action[4] is no stronger than a flower?
O, how shall summer's honey breath[5] hold out
Against the wreckful siege of battering days[6],
When rocks impregnable are not so stout[7],
Nor gates of steel so strong, but Time decays[8]?
O fearful meditation! Where, alack,
Shall Time's best jewel[9] from Time's chest[10] lie hid?
Or what strong hand can hold his swift foot[11] back?
Or who his spoil[12] of beauty can forbid?
　O, none, unless this miracle have might,

That in black ink my love may still[13] shine bright.

—*Sonnets*, 1609

【题解与注释】

十四行诗（the sonnet）是一种形式完整、格律严谨、以歌咏爱情为主的小诗，十三、四世纪盛行于意大利，其最主要的代表者为 Petrarch (1304–1374)，十六世纪中叶由 Thomas Wyatt 传入英国，至莎士比亚一代而臻完美。

莎士比亚的十四行诗每行通常有五个“音步”（foot），每个音步一般有一轻一重两个音节。全诗韵脚的安排是 abab，cdcd，efef，gg，亦即这十四行可分四组，即前四行，中四行，后四行和最后两行。每首诗一般只有一个比较简单的主题，但这种分组情况也允许它有一些曲折变化。以上面所选的第十八号而论，前四行算是“起”，中四行是“承”，都是讲岁月无常，青春难再；后四行可以说是“转”，因为全诗到此忽然一变，作者宣告虽然别人美貌难存，他所爱的朋友则将靠他的诗笔而永保朱颜；最后两行是音韵铿锵（互相押韵）的小结，亦即是“合”。当然，不是每首莎士比亚的十四行诗都有这样清楚的起承转合，但是这种小范围内的曲折变化确是它的特点之一。

意大利原型的十四行诗与此不同，它每行十一个音节，韵脚的安排是 abba，abba，cdcdcd，亦即从结构上说，主要是一个八行组加上一个六行组。后来英国写十四行诗的人，虽然在每行五个音步这一点上与莎士比亚一致，在韵脚安排上则颇有不取莎士比亚型而回到意大利型的，如 Milton，Wordsworth，Keats 等都是。

十四行诗在十六世纪的英国曾盛极一时，名家辈出，上述 Wyatt 之外，还有 Sidney，Spenser，Samuel Daniel 等人。但是这种诗体由于范围小而限制大，题材上歌咏爱情又有一套传统，不易写得有新鲜意境，在一班附庸风雅的人手里更是只成为一种时髦的写作练习。

莎士比亚的长处在于他能利用这一束缚重重的诗体而动人地写出了真实感情。这里所选的四首之中，第十八号与第六十五号两首主题相似，即同是表达“唯有文学可以同时间抗衡”的思想；文学既是人所创造的业绩，因此这又是宣告人的伟大与不朽。原来在中古教会的眼里，人不但不是伟大的，而且是生来有罪的；现在诗人却将他从孽种升到几乎与天使相等的地位，大胆地表达了英国文艺复兴时期的人文主义新思想。当时表达这种新思想的不止莎士比亚一人，例如另一诗人 Michael Drayton（1563—1631）就曾在也是一首十四行诗里用这样的两行来结束他对爱人的歌颂：

So shalt thou fly above the vulgar throng,
Still to survive in my immortal song.*

但是比较起来，还是莎士比亚表达得更加生动。第十八号有一种朝露似的新鲜，情调优美而又有足够的思想深度；第六十五号则更进一步，深度增加了，对照十分强烈：

---

* 此诗首行是“How many paltry, foolish, painted things”，是以“Idea”为总题的一束十四行诗中的一首。第二行的 still 当时作“永远”解。

一边是金属、岩石、大地、海洋等自然界坚固事物被时间摧毁，一边则是一朵脆弱的小花承受了时间的一切凶猛袭击而依然美丽如故！

第二十九号与第三十号的主题又大体相似，同是歌颂爱情的伟大力量。一想到爱情，诗人的愤懑不平和怀旧的哀思都消失了。这一点在第二十九号里尤其写得深刻。本来，诗人陷于自怨自艾，羡慕这个人的本领，妒忌那个人的广博，几乎无以自拔，但是一旦在心里看见爱者的形象，他就立刻脱出污泥，自由飞翔天空，不但再无怨尤，而且连国王的宝座也视若粪土了。这是何等的自信！这自信又导致了何等戏剧性的变化！

然而莎士比亚在这四首诗里歌颂的爱人不是女人，而是一个年轻的男子。他的154首十四行诗多数是写给这位男子的，只有少数写给一个黑皮肤的女人。至于这两人是谁，莎士比亚为什么要写这些十四行诗，以及这些诗究竟写于何时，历来学者虽有各种说法，却无定论；可以肯定的事实只是：这些十四行诗在1609年合成一集出版于伦敦，其中多数是超越当时一般十四行体水平的生动、优美、深刻的好诗。

这些诗声韵优美，宜于朗诵，能背更好。文字方面，有一些困难只属于表面形式，如表示亲热的 thou，thee，thy 等（相当于现代的 you，you，your）第二人称单数各格形式，以及与 thou 相当的动词形式，如 art = are，grow'st = growest = grow（用 -'st 形式而不用 -est 只是为了省去一个音节）等等。真正的困难可能有下列两类：1. 词义的变化，still（LXY）作"长远"解，而不似今日之指"仍旧"；fair（XVIII）作"美人"或"美貌"解，不是形容词而是名词；又如 ow'st（owest, XVIII）十七世纪时实即是 own（意为"享有"），而在现代英语中两词意义完全相反；2. 倒装句法，如 By chance, or nature's changing course, untrimm'd (XVIII) 实为 untrimmed by chance …；With what I most enjoy contented least (XXIX) 实为 least contented with what I most enjoy. 这类倒装句法在中外诗里都有，不独莎士比亚一人为然。

SONNET XVIII

1. thee: 十七世纪时，代名词 thou（见第2行）及其变格形式（thee, thine, thy）用于第二人称单数，爱人或谂友相见，一般以此相呼；you（或 ye）及其变格形式（you, yours, your）则专用于第二人称复数，但同时又为第二人称单数的尊称形式。与 thou 相应的第二人称单数动词形式为 -est -st -t，例如第2行 art = are，第10行 ow'st = owe，11行 wander'st = wander，第12行 grow'st = grow.

2. lease:（租用房、地）期限；租借权，使用权。

3. date: 时间长度（现作具体的年、月、日即日期解）。

4. the eye of heaven: 指太阳。

5. every fair from fair sometime declines: 此处两个 fair（名词，非形容词）意义不同，前者指具体的美人，后者指美貌（第10行同）；sometime = sometimes.

6. untrimm'd: 即 untrimmed，为省一音节，故以"'"代 e；意为夺走了美貌；trim 愿意为 dress，因此 untrimmed 作"夺走了华美的外衣"解。此行系倒装句，应解为 untrimmed by chance or nature's changing course.

7. that fair thou ow'st: fair 为美貌之意，参阅注 5；ow'st = owest，当时与 own

实是一字，意为“享有”。（现义为“欠债”，大为不同。）

8. to time thou grow'st: grow'st = growest，与时间合一，与时间同寿，亦即不朽。

SONNET XXIX

1. in disgrace with Fortune and men's eyes: 穷愁潦倒，受人白眼。

2. beweep: = weep over；有些不及物动词在加上前缀 be- 之后，获得及物动词的作用，不需前置词即可直接跟宾语。

3. my outcast state: 我之见弃于人；state 情况，处境。

4. bootless: 无效的。

5. like to: = like，第 11 行同。

6. Featur'd: 容貌（长得象某人），亦有解作处境（如某人）者。

7. like him, like him: 非指同一人，意为“某乙”与“某丙”。（上行的 one 指“某甲”。）

8. with friends possess'd: = possessing friends.

9. art: 此处指本领，技巧。

10. scope: 有两解：广博的才学，或充分的机会。

11. With what I most enjoy contented least: 倒装结构，即 least contented with what I most enjoy，意为本身最为擅长之事，恰是自己最不希罕之处。

12. Yet: 强调词，意为 moreover, even.

13. Haply: = by chance.

14. sullen: 阴沉的。

SONNET XXX

1. 第 1 行至第 4 行之中有十几个 [s] 和 [z] 音，再加上 [ʃ] 和 [θ] 音，造成特殊的音韵效果，使诗行更加优美。

2. sessions: 法律用语；意为“审案”。

3. summon up: 亦是法律用语，意为“传到”。

4. new wail: 即 newly wail，用新泪浇旧愁，哭时间之消逝。

5. waste: 与 past 押韵，因为 16、17 世纪 past 读音为 [pæ:st]，waste 为 [wæ:st].

6. drown an eye: 眼睛里泪水横流。

7. unus'd to flow: 不习惯于流泪，不轻易流泪；unus'd= unused.

8. death's dateless night: 死亡的长夜；dateless，无尽期。

9. long since: = long ago.

10. expense: = loss. 此行费解。过去学者曾作如下注释：“the loss of many an object which being gone hence is no more seen”（Steevens）；“Does not ‘moan the expense’ mean ‘pay my account of moans for’?”（Dowden）；另有人（Malone）甚至以为 sight 是 sigh（叹息）之意。虽然如此，大意仍为：我痛哭已难再见的故人旧物。

11. grieve at grievances foregone: 为过去的伤心事再度伤心；foregone = past.

12. tell o'er: 一一点数，清算；第 8 行的 expense，第 11 行的 account（帐务），

第 12 行的 pay（偿付）以及末行的 losses（亏损），均与此连贯。

13. fore-bemoaned: 过去已经悲叹过的。

14. the while: = meanwhile.

SONNET LXV

1. Since brass: 应解作 since neither brass，与下面一连串的 nor … nor … nor … 相接。整行系省略结构；如不省略，全句应作 Since there is neither brass, nor stone … but that sad mortality oversways. 金属，岩石，大地，海洋，无不为时间战胜。

2. mortality: 死亡。

3. rage: 淫威；**plea**：求情，申辩，与下行 action 贯通。

4. action: 法律用语，意为 case，即申辩的理由；亦有作"力量"解者。

5. honey breath: honey = honeyed，形容词。

第 5，6 两行中，声韵也象内容一样，造成对照。第 5 行中 [s]，[ʃ] 诸音轻柔，表示花朵的嫩弱；到第 6 行则 wreckful 与 battering 两词带来破坏和冲撞的声音，加强了时间无所不摧的威力。

6. the wreckful siege of battering days: days 指时间；时间的猛烈冲击，犹如重兵攻打城池。

7. stout: 坚固。

8. decays: causes to decay.

9. Time's best jewel: 指 beauty.

10. Time's chest: 时间的箱子，或棺木（chest = coffin），莎士比亚时，有一种传说：凡时间之神不拟保存之物，悉投箱中消灭；此行意为：美丽的事物怎样才能避免被遗忘的命运？

11. his swift foot: 时间的飞快的脚步，下行 his spoil of beauty 中的 his 亦指时间。

12. spoil: act of spoiling，劫夺，破坏。

13. still: = always（古义）。

III. THE MERCHANT OF VENICE

张振先　选注

IV, i, 1–400

SCENE I. *Venice. A court of justice.*

Enter the DUKE, *the* Magnificoes, ANTONIO, BASSANIO, GRATIANO, SALERIO, *and* Others.

Duke. What, is Antonio here?

Ant. Ready[1], so please your Grace[2].
Duke. I am sorry for thee; thou art come to answer
A stony adversary[3], an inhuman wretch,
Uncapable of pity, void and empty
From any dram of mercy[4].
Ant. I have heard
Your Grace hath ta'en great pains[5] to qualify[6]
His rigorous course[7]; but since he stands obdurate[8],
And that no lawful means can carry me
Out of his envy's reach[9], I do oppose
My patience to his fury, and am arm'd
To suffer with a quietness of spirit
The very tyranny[10] and rage of his.
Duke. Go one, and call the Jew into the court.
Saler. He is ready at the door; he comes, my lord.

Enter SHYLOCK.

Duke. Make room, and let him stand before our[11] face.
Shylock, the world thinks, and I think so too,
That thou but leadest this fashion of thy malice[12]
To the last hour of act; and then, 'tis thought
Thou'lt show thy mercy and remorse[13] more strange
Than is thy strange apparent[14] cruelty;
And where[15] thou now exacts[16] the penalty,
Which is a pound of this poor merchant's flesh,
Thou wilt not only loose the forfeiture[17],
But, touch'd with human gentleness and love,
Forgive[18] a moiety[19] of the principal,
Glancing an eye of pity on his losses,
That have of late so huddled on his back—
Enow[20] to press a royal merchant[21] down
And pluck commiseration[22] of his state
From brassy bosoms and rough hearts of flint,[23]

From stubborn Turks and Tartars[24], never train'd
To offices of tender courtesy[25].
We all expect a gentle answer, Jew.
Shy. I have possess'd[26] your Grace of what I purpose,
And by our holy Sabbath[27] have I sworn
To have the due and forfeit of my bond.
If you deny it, let the danger[28] light
Upon[29] your charter and your city's freedom[30].
You'll ask me why I rather choose to have
A weight of carrion flesh[31] than to receive
Three thousand ducats. I'll not answer that,
But say it is my humour[32]—is it answer'd?
What if my house be troubled with a rat,[33]
And I be pleas'd to give ten thousand ducats
To have it ban'd?[34] What, are you answer'd yet?
Some men there are love not a gaping pig[35];
Some that are mad if they behold a cat;
And others, when the bagpipe sings i' th' nose[36],
Cannot contain their urine; for affection[37],
Mistress of passion, sways it to the mood
Of what it likes or loathes. Now for your answer:
As there is no firm reason to be rend'red
Why he cannot abide a gaping pig;
Why he, a harmless necessary cat;
Why he, a woollen bagpipe, but of force
Must yield to such inevitable shame
As to offend, himself being offended;
So can I give no reason, nor I will not,
More than a lodg'd hate[38] and a certain[39] loathing
I bear Antonio, that I follow thus
A losing suit[40] against him. Are you answered?
Bass. This is no answer, thou unfeeling man,
To excuse the current[41] of thy cruelty.

Shy. I am not bound to please thee with my answers.
Bass. Do all men kill the things they do not love?
Shy. Hates any man the thing he would not kill?
Bass. Every offence is not a hate at first.
Shy. What, wouldst thou have a serpent sting thee twice?
Ant. I pray you, think you question with[42] the Jew.
You may as well go stand upon the beach
And bid the main flood[43] bate his usual height;
You may as well use question with the wolf,
Why he hath made the ewe bleat for the lamb;
You may as well forbid the mountain pines
To wag their high tops and to make no noise
When they are fretten[44] with the gusts of heaven[45];
You may as well do anything most hard
As seek to soften that—than which what's harder?—
His Jewish heart. Therefore, I do beseech you[46]
Make no moe[47] offers, use no farther means,
But with all brief and plain conveniency[48]
Let me have judgment, and the Jew his will.
Bass. For thy three thousand ducats here is six.
Shy. If every ducat in six thousand ducats
Were in six parts, and every part a ducat,
I would not draw[49] them; I would have my bond.
Duke. How shalt thou hope for mercy, rend'ring none?
Shy. What judgment shall I dread, doing no wrong[50]?
You have among you many a purchas'd slave,[51]
Which, like your asses and your dogs and mules,
You use in abject and in slavish parts[52],
Because you bought them; shall I say to you,
Let them be free, marry them to your heirs—
Why sweat they under burdens?—let their beds
Be made as soft as yours, and let their palates
Be season'd[53] with such viands[54]? You will answer,

'The slaves are ours.' So do I answer you:
The pound of flesh which I demand of him
Is dearly bought, 'tis mine, and I will have it.
If you deny me, fie upon your law!
There is no force in the decrees of Venice.
I stand for judgment; answer; shall I have it?
Duke. Upon[55] my power I may dismiss this court
Unless Bellario, a learned doctor,[56]
Whom I have sent for to determine this,
Come here to-day.
Saler. My lord, here stays without
A messenger with letters from the doctor,
New come from Padua.
Duke. Bring us the letters; call the messenger.
Bass. Good cheer, Antonio! What, man, courage yet!
The Jew shall have my flesh, blood, bones, and all,
Ere thou shalt lose for me one drop of blood.
Ant. I am a tainted wether[57] of the flock,
Meetest[58] for death; the weakest kind of fruit
Drops earliest to the ground, and so let me.
You cannot better be employ'd, Bassanio,
Than to live still, and write mine epitaph.
Enter NERISSA, *dressed like a lawyer's clerk.*
Duke. Came you from Padua, from Bellario?
Ner. From both, my lord. Bellario greets your Grace.
[*Presents a letter.*
Bass. Why dost thou whet thy knife[59] so earnestly?
Shy. To cut the forfeiture from that bankrupt there.
Gra. Not on thy sole[60], but on thy soul[60], harsh Jew,
Thou mak'st thy knife keen; but no metal can,
No, not the hangman's axe, bear half the keenness
Of thy sharp envy. Can no prayers pierce thee?
Shy. No, none that thou hast wit enough to make.

Gra. O, be thou damn'd, inexecrable[61] dog!
And for thy life let justice be accus'd.[62]
Thou almost mak'st me waver in my faith,[63]
To hold opinion with Pythagoras[64]
That souls of animals infuse[65] themselves
Into the trunks of men. Thy currish spirit
Govern'd a wolf who, hang'd for human slaughter,
Even from the gallows did his fell[66] soul fleet[67],
And, whilst thou layest in thy unhallowed dam,[68]
Infus'd itself in thee; for thy desires
Are wolfish, bloody, starv'd, and ravenous.

Shy. Till thou canst rail[69] the seal from off my bond,
Thou but offend'st[70] thy lungs to speak so loud;
Repair thy wit[71], good youth, or it will fall
To cureless[72] ruin. I stand here for law.

Duke. This letter from Bellario doth commend[73]
A young and learned doctor to our court.
Where is he?

Ner. He attendeth here hard by
To know your answer, whether you'll admit him.

Duke. With all my heart. Some three or four of you
Go give him courteous conduct to this place.
Meantime the court shall hear Bellario's letter.

Clerk. [*Reads*] 'Your Grace shall understand that at the receipt of your letter I am very sick; but in the instant that your messenger came, in loving visitation was with me a young doctor of Rome—his name is Balthasar. I acquainted him with the cause in controversy between the Jew and Antonio the merchant; we turn'd o'er many books together; he is furnished with my opinion which, bettered with his own learning—the greatness whereof I cannot enough commend—comes with him at my importunity to fill up your Grace's request in my stead. I beseech you let his lack of years be no impediment to let him lack a reverend estimation[74], for I never knew so young a body with so old a head. I leave him to your gracious acceptance, whose trial shall better publish his commendation.'

Duke. You hear the learn'd Bellario, what he writes;
And here, I take it, is the doctor come.

Enter PORTIA, *dressed like a doctor of laws*.

Give me your hand; come you from old Bellario?

Por. I did, my lord.

Duke. You are welcome; take your place.
Are you acquainted with the difference[75]
That holds this present question in the court?

Por. I am informed throughly[76] of the cause.
Which is the merchant here, and which the Jew?

Duke. Antonio and old Shylock, both stand forth.

Por. Is your name Shylock?

Shy. Shylock is my name.

Por. Of a strange nature is the suit you follow;
Yet in such rule[77] that the Venetian law
Cannot impugn[78] you as you do proceed.
You stand within his danger,[79] do you not?

Ant. Ay, so he says.

Por. Do you confess the bond?

Ant. I do.

Por. Then must the Jew be[80] merciful.

Shy. On what compulsion must I? Tell me that.

Por. The quality of mercy is not strain'd;[81]
It droppeth as the gentle rain from heaven
Upon the place beneath. It is twice blest[82]:
It blesseth him that gives, and him that takes.
'Tis mightiest in the mightiest; it becomes[83]
The throned monarch better than his crown;
His sceptre[84] shows the force of temporal power,[85]
The attribute to awe and majesty,[86]

Wherein doth sit the dread and fear of kings;[87]
But mercy is above this sceptred sway[88],
It is enthroned in the hearts of kings,
It is an attribute to God himself;
And earthly power doth then show likest God's
When mercy seasons[89] justice. Therefore, Jew,
Though justice be thy plea, consider this —
That in the course of justice none[90] of us
Should see salvation; we do pray for mercy,
And that same prayer doth teach us all to render
The deeds of mercy. I have spoke thus much
To mitigate the justice of thy plea,
Which if thou follow,[91] this strict court of Venice
Must needs give sentence 'gainst the merchant there.

Shy. My deeds upon my head![92] I crave the law,
The penalty and forfeit of my bond.

Por. Is he not able to discharge the money?

Bass. Yes; here I tender it for him in the court;
Yea, twice the sum; if that will not suffice.
I will be bound to pay it ten times o'er
On forfeit of my hands, my head, my heart;
If this will not suffice, it must appear
That malice bears down truth[93]. And I beseech you,
Wrest[94] once the law to your authority;
To do a great right, do a little wrong,
And curb this cruel devil of his will.

Por. It must not be; there is no power in Venice
Can alter a decree established;
'Twill be recorded for a precedent,
And many an error[95], by the same example,
Will rush into the state; it cannot be.

Shy. A Daniel[96] come to judgment! Yea, a Daniel!
O wise young judge, how I do honour thee!

Por. I pray you, let me look upon the bond.
Shy. Here 'tis, most reverend Doctor; here it is.
Por. Shylock, there's thrice thy money offer'd thee.
Shy. An oath, an oath! I have an oath in heaven.
Shall I lay perjury upon my soul?
No, not for Venice.
Por. Why, this bond is forfeit;
And lawfully by this the Jew may claim
A pound of flesh, to be by him cut off
Nearest the merchant's heart. Be merciful.
Take thrice thy money; bid me tear the bond.
Shy. When it is paid according to the tenour[97].
It doth appear you are a worthy judge;
You know the law; your exposition
Hath been most sound; I charge you by the law,
Whereof you are a well-deserving pillar,
Proceed to judgment. By my soul I swear
There is no power in the tongue of man
To alter me. I stay here on my bond.[98]
Ant. Most heartily I do beseech the court
To give the judgement.
Por. Why then, thus it is:
You must prepare your bosom for his knife.[99]
Shy. O noble judge! O excellent young man!
Por. For the intent and purpose of the law
Hath full relation to the penalty,
Which here appeareth due upon the bond.
Shy. 'Tis very true. O wise and upright judge,
How much more elder[100] art thou than thy looks!
Por. Therefore, lay bare your bosom.
Shy. Ay, his breast—
So says the bond; doth it not, noble judge?
'Nearest his heart', those are the very words.

Por. It is so. Are there balance here to weigh
The flesh?
Shy. I have them ready.
Por. Have by some surgeon, Shylock, on your charge,
To stop his wounds, lest he do bleed to death.
Shy. Is it so nominated in the bond?
Por. It is not so express'd, but what of that?
'Twere good you do so much for charity[101].
Shy. I cannot find it; 'tis not in the bond.
Por. You, merchant, have you anything to say?
Ant. But little: I am arm'd and well prepar'd.
Give me your hand, Bassanio; fare you well.
Grieve not that I am fall'n to this for you,
For herein Fortune[102] shows herself more kind
Than is her custom. It is still her use[103]
To let the wretched man outlive his wealth,
To view with hollow eye and wrinkled brow
An age of poverty;[104] from which ling'ring penance
Of such misery doth she cut me off.
Commend me to your honourable wife;
Tell her the process[105] of Antonio's end;
Say how I lov'd you; speak me fair in death;
And, when the tale is told, bid her be judge
Whether Bassanio had not once a love.[106]
Repent but you that you shall lose your friend,
And he repents not that he pays your debt;[107]
For if the Jew do cut but deep enough,
I'll pay it instantly with all my heart.[108]
Bass. Antonio, I am married to a wife
Which[109] is as dear to me as life itself;
But life itself, my wife, and all the world,
Are not with me esteem'd above thy life;
I would lose all, ay, sacrifice them all

Here to this devil, to deliver you.
Por. Your wife would give you little thanks for that,
If she were by to hear you make the offer.
Gra. I have a wife who I protest I love;
I would she were in heaven, so she could
Entreat some power to change this currish Jew.
Ner. 'Tis well you offer it behind her back;
The wish would make else an unquiet house.
Shy. [*Aside*] These be the Christian husbands!
I have a daughter —
Would any of the stock of Barrabas[110]
Had been her husband rather than a Christian! —
We trifle time; I pray thee pursue sentence.
Por. A pound of that same merchant's flesh is thine.
The court awards it, and the law doth give it.
Shy. Most rightful judge!
Por. And you must cut this flesh from off his breast.
The law allows it, and the court awards it.
Shy. Most learned judge! A sentence! Come, prepare.
Por. Tarry a little; there is something else.[111,112]
This bond doth give thee here no jot of blood:
The words expressly are 'a pound of flesh'.
Take then thy bond, take thou thy pound of flesh;
But, in the cutting it, if thou dost shed
One drop of Christian blood, thy lands and goods
Are, by the laws of Venice, confiscate[113]
Unto the state of Venice.
Gra. O upright judge! Mark, Jew. O learned judge!
Shy. Is that the law?
Por. Thyself shalt see the act[114];
For, as thou urgest justice, be assur'd
Thou shalt have justice more than thou desir'st.
Gra. O learned judge! Mark, Jew. A learned judge!

Shy. I take this offer then: pay the bond thrice,
And let the Christian go.
Bass. Here is the money.
Por. Soft!
The Jew shall have all justice. Soft! No haste.
He shall have nothing but the penalty.
Gra. O Jew! an upright judge, a learned judge!
Por. Therefore, prepare thee to cut off the flesh.
Shed thou no blood, nor cut thou less nor more
But just a pound of flesh; if thou tak'st more
Or less than a just[115] pound—be it but so much
As makes it light or heavy in the substance,[116]
Or the division of the twentieth part
Of one poor scruple;[117] nay, if the scale do turn
But in the estimation of a hair[118]—
Thou diest, and all thy goods are confiscate.
Gra. A second Daniel, a Daniel, Jew!
Now, infidel, I have you on the hip.[119]
Por. Why doth the Jew pause? Take thy forfeiture.
Shy. Give me my principal, and let me go.
Bass. I have it ready for thee; here it is.
Por. He hath refus'd it in the open court;
He shall have merely justice and his bond.
Gra. A Daniel, still say I, a second Daniel!
I thank thee, Jew, for teaching me that word.
Shy. Shall I not have barely my principal?[120]
Por. Thou shalt have nothing but the forfeiture
To be so taken at thy peril, Jew.
Shy. Why, then the devil give him good of it!
I'll stay no longer question.[121]
Por. Tarry, Jew.
The law hath yet another hold on you.
It is enacted in the laws of Venice,

If it be prov'd against an alien[122]
That by direct or indirect attempts
He seek the life of any citizen,
The party 'gainst the which he doth contrive[123]
Shall seize one half his goods; the other half
Comes to the privy coffer[124] of the state;
And the offender's life lies in the mercy[125]
Of the Duke only, 'gainst all other voice.[126]
In which predicament, I say, thou stand'st;
For it appears by manifest proceeding
That indirectly, and directly too,
Thou hast contrived against the very life
Of the defendant; and thou hast incurr'd
The danger formerly by me rehears'd.[127]
Down, therefore, and beg mercy of the Duke.
Gra. Beg that thou mayst have leave to hang thyself;
And yet, thy wealth being forfeit to the state,
Thou hast not left the value of a cord;
Therefore thou must be hang'd at the state's charge.
Duke. That thou shalt see the difference of our spirit,
I pardon thee thy life before thou ask it.
For half thy wealth, it is Antonio's;
The other half comes to the general state,
Which humbleness[128] may drive unto a fine.[129]
Por. Ay, for the state; not for Antonio.
Shy. Nay, take my life and all, pardon not that.
You take my house when you do take the prop
That doth sustain my house; you take my life
When you do take the means whereby I live.
Por. What mercy can you render him, Antonio?
Gra. A halter gratis[130]; nothing else, for God's sake!
Ant. So please my lord the Duke and all the court
To quit[131] the fine for one half of his goods;

I am content, so he will let me have
The other half in use,[132] to render it
Upon his death unto the gentleman
That lately stole his daughter—
Two things provided more: that, for this favour,
He presently[133] become a Christian;[134]
The other, that he do record a gift,
Here in the court, of all he dies possess'd[135]
Unto his son Lorenzo and his daughter.
Duke. He shall do this, or else I do recant[136]
The pardon that I late pronounced here.
Por. Art thou contented, Jew? What dost thou say?
Shy. I am content.
Por. Clerk, draw a deed of gift.
Shy. I pray you, give me leave to go from hence; I am not
well; send the deed after me,
And I will sign it.
Duke. Get thee gone, but do it.
Gra. In christ'ning[137] shalt thou have two godfathers;
Had I been judge, thou shouldst have had ten more[138],
To bring thee to the gallows, not to the font.[139]
[*Exit Shylock*

【题解与注释】

The Merchant of Venice（1597年写成）是莎士比亚青年时期比较成熟的作品。

威尼斯人Bassanio想去向富家女Portia求婚，找商人Antonio去借钱。商人虽富，但一时手头紧，就去找高利贷者犹太人Shylock去转借。犹太人因在商业竞争上和种族歧视上都和Antonio有矛盾，恨之入骨，想乘机报仇，假意开玩笑似地劝他签订一个契约，约定到时还不上钱，就还身上的一磅肉。

Bassanio借到了钱，求婚成功，但是Antonio的货船途中受阻，因此到期还不上债。Shylock坚决要按契约所订从Antonio胸部割下一磅肉。我们此处所选就是法庭审问的一场。Shylock坚决要报仇，大家限于契约，一筹莫展，眼看着他磨刀就要下手了。这时候Portia女扮男装，以律师的身份首先肯定契约有效，取得了Shylock的信任，然后，以彼之矛攻彼之盾，声明契约只言明一磅肉，但并未言及一滴血，如Shylock割肉时使Antonio流一滴血或与一磅肉的分量有丝毫差异，就必然受到威尼斯法律的严厉惩罚。Shylock的图谋终于失败。

在这剧中，Shylock 一方面是封建式的高利贷者，以金钱为罪恶活动的工具；另一方面他代表被歧视的犹太人，充满了反抗情绪。

舞台说明 **Magnificoes**，古威尼斯共和国的权贵。

Gratiano 和 **Salerio**，是 Bassanio 和 Antonio 的伴从。

1. ready: = here! 有！到！

2. your Grace: 对公爵的尊称，只适用于英国；此处的公爵实即威尼斯城邦之主，因此可作“殿下”解。

3. A stony adversary: 铁石心肠的仇敌。

4. dram of mercy: 一点一滴的怜悯。

5. pains: = trouble.

6. qualify: 减弱。

7. rigorous course: 严峻的行动（指 Shylock 坚决要割一磅肉的事）。

8. obdurate: 硬了心的。在 Shakespeare 戏剧里这个词总是把重音打在第二个音节上。

9. envy's reach: 仇恨所能达到的地方。envy = ill-will, hatred, malice.

10. tyranny: 残暴。

11. our: 公爵为威尼斯之主，所以莎士比亚照英国君主说话习惯，用 we 及 our 自指。

12. thou but leadest this fashion of thy malice: 你不过装作凶恶罢了；malice 与第 10 行的 envy's reach 里的 envy 相对照。

13. remorse: 怜悯心。

14. apparent: 外表看起来好象是显而易见的。

15. where: = whereas.

16. exacts: 当原动词最后一个字母是“t”时，它的第二人称单数常加“s”于“t”之后；因此 exacts = exactest, ‘demandest’.

17. loose the forfeiture: 由于不遵守合同所处的罚款等。loose：解除（= let go）.

18. Forgive: 免掉。

19. moiety: 一部分。

20. Enow: enough.

21. a royal merchant: 皇商。royal = in the service of the King. 这里可见 Duke 的同情是在 Antonio 一方面。

22. commiseration: 怜悯心的表示。

23. brassy bosoms and rough hearts of flint: 铁石心肠。

24. Turks 和 **Tartars:** 常常用来代表最残暴最野蛮的人，这是当时西欧人的错误看法。

25. offices of tender courtesy: 和善、体贴的行为（= acts of kindness and attention）.

26. possess'd: 通知了（= informed）.

27. Sabbath: 犹太教的主日。

28. danger: = harm, damage.

29. light upon: 落在…上面。

30. If you ... freedom: Shylock 这句话很重要。他认为只要按契约办事就有把握为所欲为。他看清 Duke 是为新兴的资产阶级服务的，后者不敢，也不能改动保护私有财产的契约和法律。在这点上也可看出莎士比亚把古威尼斯也加以英国化了，因为这更符合当时英国的情况。

31. carrion flesh: 臭肉。

32. humour: 一时的高兴（就要这么干），个人的脾性。Shylock 所以敢于如此是因为他认为刀把子在他手里，他完全有把握按照契约高兴怎么干就怎么干。因为按照 Shylock 的看法，Antonio 胸部的一磅肉是 3,000 ducats 的代价买来的，因此也是 Shylock 的私产。既是私产，业主当然有权随意处理。Shylock 的这种把债务者的肉看成是债权人货币的转化，在人剥削人的社会里是有长久的传统的。马克思著的《资本论》（人民出版社，1956 年北京版）卷一，第 336 页脚注是这样说的："南北美战争爆发以前不久，奴隶所有者曾在新墨西哥领土内定下如下的法典，规定劳动者只要他的劳动力为资本家所购买，就是'资本家的货币'。在罗马贵族间，这种意见也很流行。他们所垫支于负债平民的货币，已经由生活资料转化为债务者的血和肉了。所以，这种'血和肉'，就是'他们所有的货币'。薛洛克式的十铜表（the Shylock-Law of the Ten Tables），就是这样出来的。"因此这个割肉还债的戏剧就成了金钱就是一切的资本主义制度的典型的讽刺。

33. 第 44—58 行： 大意是说各人有各人的脾气，各人有各人的特殊反应。Shylock 也是如此。

34. ban'd: = baned, poisoned.

35. Some men there are love not a gaping pig: = there are some men *who* do not love a gaping pig.

36. 第 49—50 行： 大意是说有人一听到风笛声就受刺激，以至在人前尿裤子。

37. affection: 心情，好恶。

38. lodg'd hate: 入骨的仇恨。

39. certain: definite，肯定无疑的，强烈的。

40. losing suit: 赔钱的官司，因为 Shylock 即使是打赢了这场官司，他所得的将是一磅"carrion flesh"，所失的却是"three thousand ducats".

41. current: = course. 参看第 8 行的"rigorous course"。

42. question with: 与之争辩。

43. main flood: 海潮的最高潮。

44. fretten: = fretted，为…所激动。

45. the gusts of heaven: 烈风。

46. 第 70—80 行： 大意是说即使做"挟泰山以超北海"那种事也不比软化犹太人 Shylock 的铁石心肠更难。

47. moe: = more.

48. conveniency: = convenience.

49. draw: 提取（款项）。

50. doing no wrong: Shylock 所以能公开理直气壮地这样讲是有根据的。参看第 38—39 行注和第 43 行注。资本主义制度下的法律和其他一切都表示“金钱万能”，钱能买到的，即使是人肉或人命，都是“合法”的。

51. 第 90—103 行： 大意是说既然按当时的法律规定奴隶是奴隶主的私产，那么 Shylock 用高价买到的人肉也应理所当然被视为他的私产。

52. abject ... parts: 低贱的职责。

53. season'd: 调味。

54. viands: 食品。

55. Upon: = in accordance with. Duke 虽同情 Antonio，但因法律所限也无能为力。这点也就更鲜明地反衬出人吃人的法律在资本主义制度下是“合法”的。

56. 第 105—120 行： 这里是个戏剧性的低潮和转折点。Shylock 由于种族歧视所受的污辱，交易场上的损失，女儿的私奔，这一切的刻骨深仇，势在必报。正在这时候忽然有了一线的希望。这个气氛就为 Portia 的出场做好了准备。

57. tainted: 生了传染病的。

wether: 阉羊。

58. meetest: 最适于。

59. whet thy knife: 通常的演法是 Shylock 在台口上不动声色地抬起脚来认真地在他的鞋底子上磨刀。

60. sole 和 soul: 是同音异义词。莎士比亚戏剧里这类的双关语很多。Sole，鞋底子；soul，灵魂。意思是：你不是在你的鞋底上，而是在你的灵魂上磨刀。你的灵魂比铁石还硬，因此磨起刀来会更快。

61. inexecrable: 怎么骂都骂不够的 = execrable，“可诅咒的”，但更强调。

62. And for thy life let justice be accus'd: 让你活在世上，连法庭本身都是有罪的。

63. in my faith: 此处 faith 指基督教。

64. Pythagoras: 古希腊哲学家和数学家，他相信轮回转世之说，如人兽互转等。

65. infuse: 注入。

66. fell: 残酷的。

67. fleet: flit，逃走。

68. And, whilst ... dam: 你还在你的臭娘胎里卧着的时候。unhallowed = 罪恶的，下贱的。

69. rail: 骂。

70. offend'st: 损伤。

71. Repair thy wft: 修补修补你的才智吧。换句话说，等于说：“你不要太伤脑力，想坏字眼来骂我”。

72. cureless: incurable，无法补偿的。

73. commend: 推荐，赞扬。

74. let his lack of years be no impediment to let him lack a reverend esti-

mation: 不要因他年轻就对他不够尊敬；impediment，阻碍；to let him lack，使他得不到。这封信是律师写的，因此措词周到而欠典雅。

75. difference: 争论之点。

76. throughly: = thoroughly，完全的，彻底的。

77. in … rule: 合乎法律上的规定。

78. impugn: 争辩和疑问。

79. danger: = power.

80. must … be: Portia 的意思是说"那可得"，Shylock 听了认为是"那必得"，因此下一行才有"On … must I?"的一问。

81. 第 184—202 行： 这段台词是这一幕里最出名的一段，人们常常背诵的，Portia 在此大谈仁慈之可贵，实际上充满伪善，因为资产阶级最为残酷，上文 Shylock 已指出他们将奴隶当作牛马驱使，下文 Antonio 硬要 Shylock 改信基督教，都是证明。

strain'd: forced，带点勉强的。针对第 183 行 Shylock 所说 On what compulsion must I——"凭什么硬要我这样？"——而言。

82. blest: 被祝福。

83. becomes: 适合（身份）。

84. sceptre: 帝王手中所持之杖，表示威权。

85. temporal power: 世间的权力（以别于上天的权力——divine power）。

86. the attribute to awe and majesty:（帝王的）威严与尊贵的特征。

87. Wherein doth sit the dread and fear of kings: 在这个 sceptre 里有着天下王者使人望而生畏的权威。

88. above this sceptred sway: 超乎帝王的权力之上。

89. seasons: 调剂。

90. none: 按圣经上说所有的人都是有罪的，因此如果不是上帝的慈悲，任何人也不能得救。

91. if thou follow: 如果你一定要按法律把这场官司打下去的话。

92. My deeds upon my head!: 意思是说："我不管什么慈悲不慈悲。我做的事我自己担当"。

93. malice bears down truth: 恶毒硬要压倒真诚。

94. wrest: 扭转一下，灵活地变动一下。

95. error: 不公平的事，非法的事。

96. Daniel: 但以里，古以色列时代年轻的审判官，以能替人伸冤著称。请参看基督教《圣经外传》"The Apocrypha"中的"The History of Susanna".

97. tenour: 契约上所载明的办法。

98. I stay here on my bond: = I take my stand on my bond，我完全凭契约行事。

99. 第 245—304 行： 这段是全幕的最低潮，比第 105—120 行更低，那里出现的一线希望似乎也落了空。Shylock 一手拿着磨得雪亮的尖刀，一手拿着秤肉的天平，马上就要行动了。

100. much more elder: 可与第 163 行的"So young a body with so old a head"对比。莎士比亚经常为了强调而用 more elder 之类不合文法的说法。

101. charity: 对人的慈爱心。

102. Fortune: 命运之神，常常被“人格化”。

103. use: 习惯。

104. An age of poverty: 此处 age 指 old age，穷困的老年。

105. process: 经过。

106. love: 好友。

107. Repent … debt: repent 在此作 grieve 讲。二行意为：只要你对于失去我这样一个朋友感到悲伤，那么我就决不因替你还此恶债而有任何悔恨。

108. heart: 全心全意，整个的人心。这个双关语用在这里更增加了悲惨的气氛。

109. which: = who.

110. Barrabas:（Barabbas）古犹太著名的强盗。参看基督教《新约圣经》马太福音第 27 章第 16 节。

111. 第 305 行： 这个最紧张的时刻，通常演出时是 Shylock 持刀奔向 Antonio，全场惊骇，Portia 一手举着契约，一手止住 Shylock，不动声色地、一个音步一板地说出这段关键性的台词。

112. 第 305—363 行： 这段是全幕最大的转折点和高潮。Shylock 根据一般的人吃人的法律要求割肉还债，Portia 根据法律条文的词句，和保护本教和本邦、歧视异教和异邦的特殊法律，给 Shylock 以决定性的反击。

113. confiscate: = confiscated，被没收。

114. act: 法律的条文。

115. just: 不多不少，整整的。

116. substance: 重量。

117. division of the twentieth part of one poor scruple: 一个 scruple 的二十分之一的一部分；scruple，药剂衡量名，极微之量。

118. But in the estimation of a hair: 纵使（天平上）只有一发之差。

119. on the hip: 抓住了（摔跤用语，抓住之后就要把对方摔倒了）。

120. principal: 本金（即不要利息了）。

121. I'll stay no longer question: 我不准备继续谈了。

122. alien: 异邦人。由于 Shylock 是犹太人，不能当作公民，只算异邦人。

123. contrive: 设计谋害。

124. privy coffer: 王室私用财库。

125. in the mercy: = in the power.

126. voice: 意见。

127. formerly by me rehears'd: 我在前面已经提到过；rehears'd，此处意为叙述过。

128. humbleness: 指低头认罪，改过自新。

129. may drive unto a fine: 就可以减轻到交一些罚款就算了。

130. a halter gratis: 一条免费的绞索。

131. quit: 豁免。

132. in use: 托管。

133. presently: 立刻。

134. Christian: 强迫一个犹太人作基督徒正是宗教歧视的一种表现。

135. all he dies possess'd: 他的全部遗产（在他死时所有的全部财产）。

136. recant: 撤回。

137. christ'ning: 入基督教时的洗礼；洗礼时的监证人称为 godfather（教父）。

138. ten more: 加上前一行的 two 一共有 12 个。这是开玩笑骂人的话，指判刑时的 12 个陪审员。意为：如由我决定，则不让你去受洗变成基督徒，而是把你判处死刑。

139. font: 放圣水的洗礼盘。

IV. JULIUS CÆSAR

张振先　选注

III, ii, 1–273

Scene II. *Rome. The Forum.*

Enter BRUTUS *and* CASSIUS, *with the* Plebeians.[1]

Plebeians. We will be satisfied![2] Let us be satisfied!

Bru. Then follow me, and give me audience[3], friends.
Cassius, go you into the other street,
And part the numbers.[4]
Those that will hear me speak, let 'em stay here;
Those that will follow Cassius, go with him;
And public reasons shall be rendered[5]
Of Cæsar's death.

1 Pleb. I will hear Brutus speak.

2 Pleb. I will hear Cassius, and compare their reasons,
When severally[6] we hear them rendered.

[*Exit* CASSIUS, *with some of the* Plebeians.

BRUTUS *goes into the pulpit.*

3 Pleb. The noble Brutus is ascended. Silence!

Bru. Be patient till the last.[7]
Romans, countrymen, and lovers![8] hear me for my cause,[9] and be silent, that you may hear[10]. Believe me for mine honour, and have respect to[11] mine honour, that you may believe.

Censure[12] me in your wisdom, and awake your senses[13], that you may the better judge. If there be any in this assembly, any dear friend of Cæsar's, to him I say that Brutus' love to Cæsar was no less than his. If then that friend demand[14] why Brutus rose against Cæsar, this is my answer: Not that I lov'd Cæsar less, but that I lov'd Rome more. Had you rather Cæsar were living, and die all slaves, than that Cæsar were dead, to live all free men? As Cæsar lov'd me, I weep for him; as he was fortunate, I rejoice at it; as he was valiant, I honour him; but—as he was ambitious, I slew him. There is tears for his love; joy for his fortune; honour for his valour; and death for his ambition. Who is here so base that would be a bondman[15]? If any, speak; for him have I offended. Who is here so rude[16] that would not be a Roman? If any, speak; for him have I offended. Who is here so vile[17] that will not love his country? If any, speak; for him have I offended. I pause for a reply.

All. None, Brutus, none.

Bru. Then none have I offended. I have done no more to Cæsar than you shall do to Brutus.[18] The question[19] of his death is enroll'd[20] in the Capitol[21]; his glory not extenuated,[22] wherein he was worthy; nor his offences enforc'd[23], for which he suffered death.

Enter MARK ANTONY *and Others with* CÆSAR'S *body.*

Here comes his body, mourn'd by Mark Antony, who, though he had no hand in his death, shall receive the benefit of his dying, a place in the commonwealth[24], as which of you shall not? With this[25] I depart, that, as I slew my best lover for the good of Rome, I have the same dagger for myself, when it shall please my country to need my death.

All. Live, Brutus! live! live!

1 Pleb. Bring him[26] with triumph home unto his house.

2 Pleb. Give him a statue with his ancestors.[27]

3 Pleb. Let him be Cæsar.[28]

4 Pleb. Cæsar's better parts
Shall be crown'd in Brutus.

1 Pleb. We'll bring him to his house with shouts and clamours.

Bru. My countrymen—

2 Pleb. Peace, silence! Brutus speaks.

1 Pleb. Peace, ho!

Bru. Good countrymen, let me depart alone,
And for my sake, stay here with Antony.
Do grace to Cæsar's corpse, and grace his speech
Tending to Cæsar's glories,[29] which Mark Antony,
By our permission, is allow'd to make.
I do entreat you, not a man depart
Save I alone,[30] till Antony have spoke. [*Exit*.

1 Pleb. Stay, ho! and let us hear Mark Antony.

3 Pleb. Let him go up into the public chair[31].
We'll hear him. Noble Antony, go up.

Ant. For Brutus' sake, I am beholding[32] to you.
[*Goes up*.

4 Pleb. What does he say of Brutus?

3 Pleb. He says, for Brutus' sake[33]
He finds himself beholding to us all.

4 Pleb. 'Twere best he speak no harm of Brutus here.

1 Pleb. This Cæsar was a tyrant.[34]

3 Pleb. Nay, that's certain.
We are blest that Rome is rid of him.

2 Pleb. Peace! let us hear what Antony can say.

Ant. You gentle Romans—

All. Peace, ho! let us hear him.

Ant. Friends, Romans, countrymen, lend me your ears;
I come to bury Cæsar, not to praise him.

The evil that men do lives after them;
The good is oft interred with their bones;[35]
So let it be with Cæsar. The noble Brutus
Hath told you Cæsar was ambitious.
If it were so,[36] it was a grievous fault;
And grievously hath Cæsar answer'd it.[37]
Here, under leave of Brutus and the rest—
For Brutus is an honourable man;
So are they all, all honourable men—
Come I to speak in Cæsar's funeral.
He was my friend, faithful and just to me;
But Brutus says he was ambitious,
And Brutus is an honourable man.
He hath brought many captives home to Rome,
Whose ransoms did the general coffers[38] fill;
Did this in Cæsar seem ambitious?
When that the poor have cried, Cæsar hath wept;
Ambition should be made of sterner stuff.[39]
Yet Brutus says he was ambitious;
And Brutus is an honourable man.
You all did see that on the Lupercal[40]
I thrice presented him a kingly crown,[41]
Which he did thrice refuse. Was this ambition?
Yet Brutus says he was ambitious;
And sure he is an honourable man.
I speak not to disprove what Brutus spoke,
But here I am to speak what I do know.
You all did love him once, not without cause;
What cause withholds you, then, to mourn for him?[42]
O judgment, thou art fled to brutish beasts,
And men have lost their reason! Bear with me;[43]
My heart is in the coffin there with Cæsar,
And I must pause till it come back to me.

1 Pleb. Methinks there is much reason in his sayings.

2 Pleb. If thou consider rightly of the matter,
Cæsar has had great wrong.[44]

3 Pleb. Has he, masters!
I fear there will a worse come in his place.

4 Pleb. Mark'd ye his words?[45] He would not take the crown;
Therefore 'tis certain he was not ambitious.

1 Pleb. If it be found so, some will dear abide it.[46]

2 Pleb. Poor soul! his eyes are red as fire with weeping.

3 Pleb. There's not a nobler man in Rome than Antony.

4 Pleb. Now mark him, he begins again to speak.

Ant. But yesterday the word[47] of Cæsar might
Have stood against the world: now lies he there,
And none so poor to do him reverence.[48]
O masters, if I were dispos'd to stir
Your hearts and minds to mutiny[49] and rage,
I should do Brutus wrong, and Cassius wrong,
Who, you all know, are honourable men.
I will not do them wrong; I rather choose
To wrong the dead, to wrong myself and you,
Than I will wrong such honourable men.
But here's a parchment with the seal of Cæsar;
I found it in his closet[50]—'tis his will.
Let but the commons[51] hear this testament,
Which, pardon me, I do not mean to read,
And they would go and kiss dead Cæsar's wounds,
And dip their napkins[52] in his sacred blood;
Yea, beg a hair of him for memory
And, dying, mention it within their wills,
Bequeathing it as a rich legacy
Unto their issue.[53]

4 Pleb. We'll hear the will. Read it, Mark Antony.
All. The will, the will! We will hear Cæsar's will.
Ant. Have patience, gentle friends, I must not read it;
It is not meet[54] you know how Cæsar lov'd you.
You are not wood, you are not stones, but men;
And being men, hearing the will of Cæsar,
It will inflame you, it will make you mad.
'Tis good you know not that you are his heirs;
For if you should, O, what would come of it?
4 Pleb. Read the will; we'll hear it, Antony!
You shall read us the will—Cæsar's will.
Ant. Will you be patient? Will you stay awhile?
I have o'ershot myself[55] to tell you of it.
I fear I wrong the honourable men
Whose daggers have stabb'd Cæsar; I do fear it.
4 Pleb. They were traitors. Honourable men!
All. The will! the testament!
2 Pleb. They were villains, murderers.
The will! Read the will.
Ant. You will compel me, then, to read the will?
Then make a ring about the corpse of Cæsar,
And let me show you him that made the will.
Shall I descend? and will you give me leave?
All. Come down.
2 Pleb. Descend. [ANTONY *comes down.*
3 Pleb. You shall have leave.
4 Pleb. A ring! Stand round.
1 Pleb. Stand from the hearse,[56] stand from the body.
2 Pleb. Room for Antony, most noble Antony!
Ant. Nay, press not so upon me; stand far off.[57]
All. Stand back. Room! Bear back.[58]
Ant. If you have tears, prepare to shed them now.[59]
You all do know this mantle. I remember

The first time ever Cæsar put it on;
'Twas on a summer's evening, in his tent,
That day he overcame the Nervii.[60]
Look! in this place ran Cassius' dagger through;
See what a rent the envious[61] Casca made;
Through this the well-beloved Brutus stabb'd,
And as he pluck'd his cursed steel away,
Mark how the blood of Cæsar follow'd it,
As[62] rushing out of doors, to be resolv'd[63]
If[64] Brutus so unkindly[65] knock'd or no;
For Brutus, as you know, was Cæsar's angel.[66]
Judge, O you gods, how dearly Cæsar lov'd him!
This was the most unkindest[67] cut of all;
For when the noble Cæsar saw him stab,
Ingratitude, more strong than traitors' arms,
Quite vanquish'd him. Then burst his mighty heart;
And in his mantle muffling up his face,[68]
Even[69] at the base[70] of Pompey's[71] statua,[72]
Which[73] all the while ran blood, great Cæsar fell.
O, what a fall was there, my countrymen!
Then I, and you, and all of us fell down,
Whilst bloody treason flourish'd[74] over us.
O, now you weep, and I perceive you feel
The dint[75] of pity. These are gracious drops.[76]
Kind souls, what[77] weep you when you but behold
Our Cæsar's vesture wounded? Look you here,
Here is himself,[78] marr'd as you see with traitors.[79]

1 Pleb. O piteous spectacle!

2 Pleb. O noble Cæsar!

3 Pleb. O woeful day!

4 Pleb. O traitors, villains!

1 Pleb. O most bloody sight!

2 Pleb. We will be reveng'd.

All. Revenge! About![80] Seek! Burn! Fire! Kill!
Slay! Let not a traitor live!

Ant. Stay, countrymen.

1 Pleb. Peace there! Hear the noble Antony.

2 Pleb. We'll hear him, we'll follow him, we'll die withhim.

Ant. Good friends, sweet friends, let me not stir you up
To such a sudden flood of mutiny.
They that have done this deed are honourable.
What private griefs[81] they have, alas, I know not,
That made them do it; they are wise and honourable,
And will, no doubt, with reasons answer you.
I come not, friends, to steal away your hearts;
I am no orator, as Brutus is,
But, as you know me all, a plain blunt[82] man,
That love my friend; and that they know full well
That gave me public leave to speak[83] of him.
For I have neither wit, nor words, nor worth,[84]
Action, nor utterance, nor the power of speech,
To stir men's blood; I only speak right on.[85]
I tell you that which you yourselves do know;
Show you sweet Cæsar's wounds, poor poor dumb mouths,
And bid them speak for me. But were I Brutus,
And Brutus Antony, there were an Antony
Would[86] ruffle up[87] your spirits, and put a tongue
In every wound of Cæsar, that should move
The stones of Rome to rise and mutiny.

All. We'll mutiny.

1 Pleb. We'll burn the house of Brutus.

3 Pleb. Away, then! Come seek the conspirators.

Ant. Yet hear me, countrymen; yet hear me speak.

All. Peace, ho! Hear Antony, most noble Antony.

Ant. Why, friends, you go to do you know not what.

Wherein hath Cæsar thus deserv'd your loves?
Alas, you know not! I must tell you, then:
You have forgot the will I told you of.

All. Most true. The will! Let's stay and hear the will.

Ant. Here is the will, and under Cæsar's seal:
To every Roman citizen he gives,
To every several[88] man, seventy-five drachmas[89].

2 Pleb. Most noble Cæsar! We'll revenge his death.

3 Pleb. O royal[90] Cæsar!

Ant. Hear me with patience.

All. Peace, ho!

Ant. Moreover, he hath left you all his walks,
His private arbours, and new-planted orchards,[91]
On this side[92] Tiber;[93] he hath left them you,
And to your heirs for ever — common pleasures,[94]
To walk abroad and recreate yourselves.
Here was a Cæsar! When comes such another?

1 Pleb. Never, never! Come away, away!
We'll burn his body in the holy place,[95]
And with the brands fire the traitors' houses.
Take up the body.

2 Pleb. Go, fetch fire.

3 Pleb. Pluck down benches.

4 Pleb. Pluck down forms[96], windows, any thing.

[*Exeunt* Plebeians *with the body*

Ant. Now let it work. Mischief, thou art afoot,
Take thou what course thou wilt.

Enter a Servant.

How now, fellow!

Serv. Sir, Octavius[97] is already come to Rome.

Ant. Where is he?

Serv. He and Lepidus[98] are at Cæsar's house.

Ant. And thither will I straight to visit him.

He comes upon a wish.[99] Fortune[100] is merry,
And in this mood will give us any thing.
Serv. I heard him say Brutus and Cassius
Are rid[101] like madmen through the gates of Rome.
Ant. Belike[102] they had some notice of the people,
How I had mov'd them.[103] Bring me to Octavius.
[*Exeunt*.

【题解与注释】

Julius Cæsar 是莎士比亚中年时期的作品之一，一般认为写在 1599 年左右，最早的印本出现在 1623 年的莎士比亚全集（第一对开本），内容主要是写古罗马"前三雄"之一的 Gaius Julius Cæsar（公元前 100—44）战胜政敌 Pompey 之后有独自称王的野心。Brutus 与 Cassius 等恐其称王后实行独裁，破坏古罗马的共和体制，因而合谋刺杀之。Cæsar 的追随者 Antony 挑起群众暴动，联合 Cæsar 的外侄孙 Octavius 和 Lepidus 在内战中击败 Brutus 等，而后古罗马的"后三雄"兴起。

所选的第 3 幕第 2 景是全剧最精彩的一段。主要内容是 Brutus 在刺死 Julius Cæsar 之后，不但未杀 Antony，反而允许后者按古罗马的习俗在名人死后做"祭文"式的演讲，以致授人以机。Antony 乘机挑拨本来拥护 Brutus 的群众起而暴动。

Brutus 的演讲是纯说理式的，而 Antony 的演讲步步深入，挑起群众的感情而达到他自己的政治目的。

这一景里出场的主要人物有：

Marcus Brutus，谋刺 Cæsar 者的领袖之一。在人民群众中声望很高。心地坦率，但理想多于实际。死后他的敌人都说："This was the noblest Roman of them all ..."

Marcus Antonius (Mark Antony)，Cæsar 的追随者。一个口若悬河的演讲家和勇敢的军人。在反对 Brutus 等人的政争中，他是领袖。后来与 Octavius Cæsar 及 Lepidus 联合统治罗马的天下，成为"后三雄"之一。

此处所选，版本主要根据 Peter Alexander 所编的 William Shakespeare: *The Complete Works* (the Tudor edition) London: Collins, 1951.

1. Plebeians: 公民。

2. We will be satisfied: 我们要彻底了解（为什么要刺杀 Cæsar 的）全部情况；satisfied，彻底了解全部情况。

3. give me audience: 请听我讲。

4. part the numbers: 将听众分开。

5. public reasons shall be rendered: 应当公开说明理由；rendered: given.

6. severally: 分头地。

7. till the last: till I finish，等我讲完。

8. lovers: 亲爱的朋友们。

9. 第 13 行：注意对比 Brutus 干巴巴说理式的演讲和 Antony 口若悬河，步步深入，动人情感的演讲。莎士比亚有意造成二者的鲜明对比。Brutus 的演讲用散文，Antony 的演讲用五步无韵诗，也增加了这个对比的气氛。

10. that you may hear: = so that you may hear.

11. have respect to: 请记着，请勿忘。

12. censure: 判断。

13. senses: 理智（Brutus 的演讲重理智）。

14. demand: 要求答复。

15. bondman: 奴隶。

16. rude: 愚昧，不明是非。

17. vile: 卑鄙。

18. I have done no more to Cæsar than you shall do to Brutus:（如果我也有象 Cæsar 那样的野心）你们也可以象我对待 Cæsar 一样来对待 Brutus.

19. question: 判决 Cæsar 当死的案情。

20. enroll'd: 存档。

21. Capitol: 古罗马上议院开会处。

22. extenuated: 缩小。

23. enforc'd: 强调。

24. a place in the commonwealth: 在古罗马共和体中一个自由公民的地位。

25. With this: = with this statement.

26. Bring him: escort him，陪伴他。

27. ancestors: 祖先，指 Lucius Junius Brutus. 人们称 Brutus 的这位祖先为“解放者”，因为他曾为古罗马的人民逐走一个残暴的统治者。

28. Let him be Cæsar: 这是戏剧性的讽刺。Cæsar 的词意是独裁的君主。Brutus 所以要刺杀 Cæsar 正是怕他称王而破坏古罗马共和政体的自由，而现在群众要他象 Cæsar 那样掌政。

29. Do grace to Cæsar's corpse, and grace his speech / Tending to Cæsar's glories: do grace to，尊敬（死者）；grace his speech，请听他说话；这里指古罗马的习俗，名人死后要有人作“祭文”式的演讲，歌颂死者生前的德政。

30. Save I alone: 除我一人之外。

31. public chair: 讲坛。

32. beholding: 感谢。

33. for Brutus' sake: = in the name of Brutus for whom I am acting.

34. tyrant: 暴君。

35. The evll ... their bones: 古谚语，意思是说死者生前所做的恶事会被人们记在心里，但是他生前所做的善事却常会被人忘掉而随死者葬入地下。这里是个伏笔。

36. If it were so: 从这句假设语气开始，Antony 一步一步挑起群众对 Brutus 的怀疑和反感。

37. answer'd it:（用 Cæsar 的生命）还了这笔债。

38. general coffers: 国库。

39. sterner stuff: 意指铁石心肠。

40. Lupercal: 指 the Lupercalia，古罗马敬牧神的赎罪净心节。

41. 第 97 行： 指 Cæsar 在罗马公民庆祝他战胜政敌的节日故意使他的助手 Antony 向他三次献上王冠以试民意，他故意三次拒绝之。

42. to mourn for him: = from mourning for him.

43. Bear with me: 请耐心地体谅我。

44. has had great wrong: = has had great wrong done to him.

45. Mark'd ye his words? 你注意听到他说的话了么？

46. dear abide it: 重重地偿还这笔血债。

47. the word: 指令。

48. And none so poor to do him reverence: 最卑微的人也不屑向死者致敬了。

49. mutiny: 暴动。从这里开始 Antony 就进入主题，挑动群众的情感，使他们起而暴动，反对 Brutus.

50. closet: 私室。

51. the commons: = the common people.

52. napkins: 手帕。

53. issue: 后代子孙。

54. meet: 妥当。

55. o'ershot myself: 扯得太远了。

56. hearse: 担尸架。

57. stand far off: 往后点站。

58. Bear back: 往后站。

59. 第 170 至 198 行： Antony 看到他已经把群众的情感挑起来，他就进一步指着 Cæsar 尸首上的血肉模糊的伤口给群众看，借以煽起他们复仇的怒火。这段演讲词是全景的高潮。

60. the Nervii: 当时欧洲西北部最强的部落。Cæsar 在公元前 57 年大破之，罗马举行了空前盛大的庆祝会。Antony 提起此事，用意在使人们怀念死者的功勋。

61. envious: 恶毒的。

62. as: = as if.

63. to be resolv'd: 为了要断定。

64. If: 是否。

65. unkindly: 残酷无情地。

66. angel: 最亲密的朋友。

67. most unkindest: = unkindest，莎士比亚常用双重的比较级（例如 more better）和双重的最高级形容词，作为一种强调手段。

68. in his mantle muffling up his face: 用衣服盖上自己的脸。

69. even: = exactly.

70. the base: 雕像下的石基。

71. Pompey: 古罗马“前三雄”之一，Cæsar 的政敌，被 Cæsar 战败而死。

72. statua: 雕像。此词在此读成三音节。

73. Which: 先行词是 base 不是 statua. 意思是说石基溅满了往下直淌的鲜血，不是说仇家 Pompey 的雕像也感动得流出血来了。

74. flourish'd: 摇头晃脑，耀武扬威。

75. dint: = dent，印记，此处作力量解。

76. gracious drops: 沉痛的热泪。

77. what: = what for, for what reason.

78. Here is himself: 说到这里，Antony 刷地一下把死者的衣裳掀起来给群众们亲眼看看尸体上的伤口。

79. marr'd ... traitors: 被叛徒们…刺死了。

80. About!: 转身行动！

81. private griefs: 私仇。Antony 在这里故意说刺杀 Cæsar 是为了报私仇，而不是为公。

82. blunt: 笨拙，尤指嘴笨。

83. public leave to speak: = permission to speak in public.

84. 第 222 至 224 行：For I have ... men's blood：这里 Antony 道出了他心目中认为一个演讲家应有的优点：wit 心智灵巧，words 口齿伶俐，worth 说话有分量（亦有作 reputation for excellence 解者），action 姿势合度，utterance 演讲术精湛，the power of speech, To stir men's blood 言词有力，使听众热血沸腾。G. L. Kittredge 不但把以上六点注明，并认为 speech 与 to stir 之间不应有“,”。Arden 版也没有“,”。

85. right on: = straight on.

86. would: who would.

87. ruffle up: 挑起狂怒。

88. several: 一个一个的。

89. drachmas: 古希腊币制单位。

90. royal: 高贵的，慷慨的。

91. orchards: = gardens.

92. On this side: = on this side of.

93. Tiber: 罗马河名。

94. pleasures: 娱乐场所。

95. burn his body in the holy place: 指极其隆重的火葬式。

96. forms: 长凳子。

97. Octavius: 古罗马“后三雄”之一。Julius Cæsar 的外侄孙。

98. Lepidus: 古罗马“后三雄”之一。

99. upon a wish: 正合我意。

100. Fortune: 幸运之神。

101. rid: 奔逃。

102. Belike: 也许。

103. Belike ... mov'd them: = Probably they had some notice of how I had moved the people.

V. HAMLET

李赋宁　选注

II, ii, 307–321

HAMLET. I have of late—but wherefore I know not—lost all my mirth[1], forgone all custom of exercises[2]; and indeed, it goes so heavily with my disposition that this goodly frame[3], the earth, seems to me a sterile promontory[4]; this most excellent canopy,[5] the air[6], look you, this brave[7] o'erhanging firmament, this majestical roof fretted with[8] golden fire—why, it appeareth[9] no other thing to me than a foul and pestilent congregation of vapours. What a piece of work is a man![10] how noble in reason! how infinite in faculties![11] in form and moving[12] how express[13] and admirable! in action how like an angel! in apprehension[14] how like a god! the beauty of the world, the paragon[15] of animals! And yet to me what is this quintessence of dust?[16]

III, i, 56–88

HAMLET. To be, or not to be[17]—that is the question:
Whether 'tis nobler in the mind to suffer[18]
The slings[19] and arrows of outrageous fortune[20]
Or to take arms against a sea of troubles,[21]
And by opposing end them.[22] To die—to sleep—
No more;[23] and by a sleep to say we end[24]
The heartache, and the thousand natural shocks[25]
That flesh is heir to.[26] 'Tis a consummation[27]
Devoutly to be wish'd.[28] To die—to sleep.
To sleep—perchance to dream:[29] ay[30], there's the rub![31]

For in that sleep of death what dreams may come[32]
When we have shuffled off[33] this mortal coil,[34]
Must give us pause. There's the respect[35]
That makes calamity[36] of so long life.[37]
For who would bear[38] the whips and scorns of time,[39]
Th' oppressor's wrong,[40] the proud man's contumely,[41]
The pangs of despis'd love,[42] the law's delay,
The insolence of office,[43] and the spurns[44]
That patient merit of th' unworthy takes,[45]
When he himself might his quietus[46] make
With a bare bodkin?[47] Who would these fardels bear,[48]
To grunt[49] and sweat under a weary life,
But that[50] the dread of something after death[51]—
The undiscover'd country,[52] from whose bourn[53]
No traveller returns[54]—puzzles the will,[55]
And makes us rather bear[56] those ills we have
Than fly to[57] others[58] that we know not of?
Thus conscience[59] does make cowards of us all,
And thus the native hue of resolution[60]
Is sicklied o'er with[61] the pale cast[62] of thought,[63]
And enterprises of great pith[64] and moment[65]
With this regard[66] their currents turn awry[67]
And lose the name of action.[68]

III, ii, 1–46

HAMLET. Speak the speech,[69] I pray you, as I pronounc'd it to you, trippingly[70] on the tongue. But if you mouth it,[71] as many of our players do, I had as live[72] the town crier[73] spoke[74] my lines. Nor do not[75] saw the air too much with your hand,[76] thus,[77] but use all gently[78]; for in the very torrent, tempest, and (as I may say) whirlwind of your passion, you must acquire and beget[79] a temperance[80] that may give it smoothness[81].

O, it offends me to the soul[82] to hear a robustious[83] periwig-pated[84] fellow tear a passion to tatters, to very rags, to split the ears[85] of the groundlings,[86] who (for the most part) are capable of[87] nothing but inexplicable dumb shows[88] and noise. I would have such a fellow whipp'd for o'erdoing[89] Termagant[90]. It out-herods Herod.[91] Pray you avoid it.[92]

PLAYER. I warrant your honour.[93]

HAMLET. Be not too tame neither; but let your own discretion[94] be your tutor[95]. Suit the action to the word, the word to the action; with this special observance,[96] that you o'erstep not[97] the modesty[98] of nature: for anything so overdone is from[99] the purpose of playing, whose end, both at the first[100] and now, was and is, to hold, as 'twere, the mirror up to nature; to show virtue her own feature, scorn[101] her own image, and the very age and body of the time[102] his[103] form and pressure.[104] Now this overdone,[105] or come tardy off,[106] though it make[107] the unskilful[108] laugh, cannot but make the judicious[109] grieve; the censure of the which one[110] must in your allowance[111] o'erweigh a whole theatre of others.[112] O, there be players that[113] I have seen play, and heard others praise, and that highly[114] (not to speak it profanely[115]), that,[116] neither having the accent of Christians, nor the gait of Christian, pagan, nor man, have so strutted and bellowed that[117] I have thought some of Nature's journeymen[118] had made men, and not made them well,[119] they imitated humanity[120] so abominably.[121]

PLAYER. I hope we have reform'd that indifferently[122] with us,[123] sir.

HAMLET. O, reform it altogether! And let those that play your clowns[124] speak no more than is set down for them. For there be of them[125] that will themselves laugh, to set on[126] some quantity[127] of barren[128] spectators to laugh too, though in the mean time[129] some necessary question[130] of the play be then to be considered.[131] That's villanous[132] and shows a most pitiful ambition[133] in the fool[134] that uses it.[135]

【题解与注释】

The Tragical History of Hamlet, Prince of Denmark, 1601（《丹麦王子汉姆雷特的悲剧故事》）根据13世纪初丹麦历史家Saxo Grammaticus的记载，叙述丹麦王子汉姆雷特替父亲报仇，杀死他的篡夺王位的叔父的故事。在莎士比亚创作《汉姆雷特》悲剧以前，伦敦舞台上曾经上演过一个《汉姆雷特》剧本，可惜这个剧本没有留传下来。这个老本子《汉姆雷特》可能和Thomas Kyd的*The Spanish Tragedy*（《西班牙悲剧》，1585年左右所作）有相似之处：替亲人报仇的主题；被谋杀者鬼魂的出现；主人公的装疯；剧中剧的穿插；等等。莎士比亚沿用了这些陈套，把这个古老的丹麦故事又一次搬上了伦敦舞台。但是莎士比亚的伟大贡献，更重要的是在于他的革新，在于他的独创。莎士比亚改造了丹麦的历史故事，改造了故事中主人公的性格，创造了汉姆雷特这个复杂深刻的人物。通过这个人物和他周围环境之间的冲突，莎士比亚反映了文艺复兴时期人文主义思想家的理想和资本主义原始积累时期社会现实之间的无法调和的矛盾。中世纪的丹麦实际上就是指的16、17世纪的英国，丹麦王子汉姆雷特实际上就是文艺复兴时期英国社会上进步青年（具有先进的人文主义思想的青年）的代表。对于这些青年来说，当时英国的政治，英国的社会真是太黑暗了。难怪汉姆雷特说："丹麦是一所监狱"（II，ii，249），"丹麦是一间最坏的囚室"（II，ii，252）。

这里所选莎士比亚悲剧《汉姆雷特》三段都能够说明文艺复兴时期先进的人文主义思想。第一段（II，ii，307—321）歌颂自然界的壮丽，歌颂人的聪明才智，歌颂人的力量。第二段（III，i，56—88）探索生和死的问题，指出思想和行动之间的矛盾。第三段（III，ii，1—46）提出先进的文艺理论：戏剧的目的是反映人生。下面就对这三段文章作进一步的分析。

第一段：汉姆雷特已和他父亲的鬼魂见了面，鬼魂已把他被谋杀的经过告诉给汉姆雷特，并且命他替父报仇（I，v）。汉姆雷特听到这些骇人听闻的罪恶行为，受到极大的震动。他进一步认识到社会的黑暗，人的自私自利，奸诈虚伪的盛行，诚实正直的被损害。他意识到他不仅有责任替父报仇，而且有责任改造这样黑暗罪恶的社会。他的苦闷，他的忧郁加深了。这时他的叔父派了汉姆雷特以前的两个好朋友，Rosencrantz和Guildenstern，来刺探汉姆雷特苦闷的原因。汉姆雷特很快就识破这两个卖友求荣的奸细的可耻行为。他戳穿了他们的面具，迫使他们不得不承认是国王派他们来的。我们选的这段文章是汉姆雷特向他们客观地描述自己心情的转变和行为的反常。他只说了他的苦闷所表现出来的一些现象，他决不会把他苦闷的真正原因告诉给他们。但是在描述这些现象时，汉姆雷特情不自禁地歌颂了宇宙的壮丽，人的才华和力量，同时也发出了理想幻灭的痛苦声音：“大地是伸到茫茫大海里的一座荒凉的山岬，天空也无非是一大堆结聚在一起的乌烟瘴气。”（卞之琳译文）

第二段：这是汉姆雷特最有名的一段独白。这段独白并不说明汉姆雷特想借自杀来逃避替父报仇的责任，而是表达了人文主义思想家对生死问题的思考。汉姆雷特已和演员们约好当天夜间在宫中上演一出小戏，特请国王和王后观赏。他叫演员们演的戏很象他叔父谋害他父亲，娶他母亲的内容，目的在于观察他叔父对这出戏的反应，用以证实鬼魂所说关于谋杀的罪行。若经证明他叔父果然是凶手，那么他就要立刻采取行动替父报仇。他焦急地等待着夜晚的来临，以便进行这个关键性的试验。在这段无事可做的等待期间，他心情更加沉重了。他想到死是一条出路，但是他并未下决心自杀。他权衡着生和死的得失；他想到每个人都掌握着自己的生死命运。拼一死去和罪恶社会作战呢？还是消极地忍受世间的不平和痛苦？“默然忍受命运的暴虐的毒箭，或是挺身反抗人世的无涯的苦难，在奋斗中结束了一切，这两种行为，哪一种是更勇敢的？”（朱生豪译文）。在这里汉姆雷特历数英国资产阶级社会上不平等，非正义的现象：“谁愿意忍受人世的鞭挞和讥嘲，压迫者的凌辱，傲慢者的冷眼，被轻蔑的爱情的惨痛，法律的迁延，官吏的横暴，和微贱者费尽辛勤所换来的鄙视”（朱生豪译文）。汉姆雷特考虑到拿起武器和罪恶社会作斗争，采取行动替父亲报仇，都可能要付出生命作代价，因此他想到生存和死亡的问题。死亡可以结束一切尘世间的痛苦，何乐而不为？但是死亡究竟是个谜，死后可能还有来生，来生可能有更多、更可怕的痛苦在等待着我们，如同睡眠中有噩梦一般。由于这个顾虑，人们宁愿忍受漫长的、痛苦的一生，而不肯轻易用一柄小小的刀子来结束自己的生命。因此，顾虑使我们成为懦夫。汉姆雷特从生死问题转而思索思想和行动之间的关系。思想是指导行动的，但是想得太多却令人踌躇不前，误了大事。这是汉姆雷特对自己的警告。文艺复兴时期的人文主义者，既是思想家，又是行动家。在这段独白里，汉姆雷特决不是在宣传自杀。相反的，他所主张的是拿起武器和罪恶社会战斗，是思想必须付诸行动。这正是文艺复兴时期人文主义思想家所极力主张的。

第三段：这是汉姆雷特向三个演员谈论表演艺术的一段谈话。谈话的时间是当天傍晚，在那三个演员将要演出汉姆雷特准备好用来侦探国王是否凶手的那出戏以前。为了把这出戏演好，真能感动听众，汉姆雷特特别关照参加演出的那三个演员，叫他们要注意表演艺术。汉姆雷特所发表的关于戏剧艺术的意见是先进的文艺复兴时期的文艺观点，和中世纪封建的文艺观点和表演艺术恰成对照。汉姆雷特强调表演不要过火，要有节制，要合乎自然，因为戏剧的目的在于反映人生，在于“给自然照一面镜子”（hold the mirror up to nature）。可见汉姆雷特重视现实主义艺术，强调文艺反映时代精神和社会面貌的作用。在第二幕第二场里，汉姆雷特把演员称为“时代的缩影和简史”（the abstracts and brief chronicles of the time, II, ii, 557–8）。中世纪的教会戏剧通过神怪来宣传宗教，因此和人生及社会现实距离较远。文艺复兴戏剧宣传人文主义思想，戏剧成为反映社会，批判社会，改造社会的有力武器。汉姆雷特的戏剧理论是合乎新时代的要求的。此外，在表演艺术方面，汉姆雷特所提出的一些原则，今天说来，仍有借鉴价值。例如，不要演得太过火，也不要演得太平淡或太懈怠。又如，凭着常识的指导，用动作配合台词，用台词配合动作（Suit the action to the word, the word to the action）等。这些原则是针对英国舞台上中世纪的残余，夸张过火的表演技巧而发的。新时代的戏剧要求彻底改革表演的技术。

版本根据 G. L. Kittredge 所编（Boston，1939），注中参考了 Edward Dowden 和 John Dover Wilson 的解释，并引用了朱生豪和卞之琳的译文。

HAMLET, II, ii, 307–321

1. **mirth:** cheerfulness（愉快的心情）。

2. **custom of exercises:** 游戏作乐的习惯。

3. **this goodly frame:** "这一座美好的框架"（朱生豪译文）——指地球。

4. **a sterile promontory:** "一座荒凉的山岬"（卞之琳译文）——伸入宇宙的大海里。

5. **canopy:** 帐幕——指天空。

6. **the air:** the sky.

7. **brave:** splendid（华丽的）。

8. **fretted with:** embossed with, adorned with（镶嵌着，点缀着）。

9. **appeareth:** 古体 appears.

10. **What a piece of work is a man:** 'Look at a *man*, and see what a masterpiece（杰作）he is!' (Kittredge). *a piece of work*，一件杰作，一件艺术品。

11. **infinite in faculties:** 感官功能（视力、听力等），力量无穷。

12. **form and moving:** "仪表和举止"（卞之琳译文）。

13. **express:** 形容词，"准确的"，"恰好合乎要求的"。

14. **apprehension:** 理解力，洞察力。

15. **paragon:** 最完美的代表。

16. **this quintessence of dust:** 这个从泥土里提炼出来的精华——指人，因为基督教认为人是上帝用泥土塑成的。汉姆雷特对于人的高贵性的信念受到黑暗社会的震撼，他不禁发出痛苦的喊声："可是，照我看来，这个从泥土里提炼出来的精华又算得了什么呢？"

HAMLET, III, i, 56–88

17. **To be, or not to be:** to live, or to die（to be = to exist "生存"）。

18. **In the mind to suffer:** passively to suffer（"默然忍受"——朱生豪译文），与 59 行 to take arms against（拿起武器来反抗）恰成对照。

19. **slings:** 一种投石的武器。

20. **outrageous fortune:** "狂暴的命运"（卞之琳译文）。

21. **a sea of troubles:** 象海洋一样多的苦恼。

22. **by opposing end them:** 通过反抗来结束这些苦恼。

23. **To die—to sleep—no more:** To die is to sleep; to die is to be (exist) no more.

24. and by a sleep to say we end: and by a sleep it is to say that we end.

25. natural shocks: attacks made by nature（自然的打击）。

26. That flesh is heir to: to which (the thousand natural shocks) the human body is an heir（继承人）。意为：肉体所不得不承担的（那些成千的自然的打击）。

27. a consummation: a final settlement of everything（最终的结算）。

28. Devoutly to be wish'd: to be passionately wished for（所热烈期望的）。

29. To sleep—perchance to dream: To sleep is perhaps to dream.

30. ay: yes.

31. the rub: the impediment（阻碍），the difficulty. 原为十柱滚球游戏（bowling）之术语。

32. what dreams may come: 这个名词子句是 68 行动词 must give 的主语。

33. shuffled off: 摆脱掉。

34. this mortal coil: trouble or turmoil of mortal life（尘世间的苦恼和纷扰）。*coil* 也有"绳索"，"羁绊"之意，因此 *mortal coil* 也可能指"肉体"，因为宗教上认为肉体是灵魂的羁绊。

35. respect: consideration（考虑）。

36. calamity: 灾难。

37. of so long life: so long-lived, so lasting（如此长期、持久）。

38. bear: endure（忍受）。

39. the whips and scorns of time: "人世的鞭挞和嘲弄"（卞之琳译文）。*time,* the times, the world we live in.

40. wrong: 名词，"对别人合法权利的侵犯"，"不公正的待遇"。

41. contumely: 轻蔑、骄傲的语言或行为。

42. The pangs of despis'd love: "被轻蔑的爱情的惨痛"（朱），"失恋的痛苦"（卞）。

43. The insolence of office: "官吏的横暴"（朱），"衙门的横暴"（卞）。

44. spurns: kicks（踢开）。

45. That patient merit of th' unworthy takes: (the kicks) that a person of merit patiently receives from the unworthy（一个有真才实学的人忍耐地接受了不学无术之徒对他所施的蛮横无理的待遇）。*of* = from.

46. quietus: make his quietus 意为 settle his own account（清帐），就是说，"脱离人世"。试比较古老的谚语："He that dies pays all debts."

47. a bare bodkin: a mere poniard（只消一把尖刀）。

48. these fardels bear: bear these burdens（担负这些重担）。

49. grunt: groan（呻吟）。

50. But that: unless（除非）。

51. the dread of something after death: dread 是 80 行动词 puzzles 和 81 行动词 makes 的主语。

52. The undiscover'd country: 尚未发现的国土，不可知的地方——指死后的世界。

53. bourn: boundary（疆界）。

54. No traveller returns: "不曾有一个旅人回来过"（朱），活人去了是回不来的。

55. puzzles the will: "迷惑了我们的意志"（朱），使我们不能采取行动。

56. rather bear: 宁愿忍受。

57. fly to: 跑向，投奔。

58. others: 指 other ills（另一些苦难）。

59. conscience: reflection, consciousness（思考，顾虑）。

60. the native hue of resolution: 决心的本来颜色（按，决心的本来颜色为血红色）。

61. Is sicklied o'er with: is covered with a sickly colour（"蒙上了一层病容"——卞）。

62. cast: shade of colour（颜色的深浅、浓淡）。

63. thought: anxious or melancholy thought（焦虑，忧思）。

64. pith: importance. 另一版本作 *pitch*，意为"height"，"elevation"（高度——指苍鹰飞翔的高度）。

65. moment: 亦作 importance 解。

66. With this regard: on this account（由于这个缘故）。

67. their currents turn awry: turn awry their currents 意为 turn their course to one side, deviate from their purpose（改换方向，转移目标）。

68. And lose the name of action: 伟大的事业改变了方向，达不到原来的目的，结果就流产了。流产了的事业当然算不上行动。

HAMLET, III, ii, 1–46

69. the speech: 指汉姆雷特亲自写的那段十五、六行的台词，用来测验他叔父的心理反应。

70. trippingly: easily, naturally（轻快地，自然地）。

71. mouth it: *mouth* 在这里是动词，意为"响亮、夸张地念出来"；*it* 指上面的 *speech*。

72. live: lief. I had as lief 我宁愿。

73. the town crier: "宣布告示的公差"（朱、卞）。

74. spoke: 虚拟式，等于 should speak. I prefer that the town crier should speak my lines.

75. Nor do not: nor. 莎士比亚时代的英语中双重否定常表示强调的否定，并不等于肯定。

76. saw the air too much with your hand: 用过多的手势（过多地"用手把空气劈来劈去"——卞。*saw*，动词，意为"用锯来锯"）。

77. thus: 象这样。

78. use all gently: 用一切（手势、动作等）都要"文静"（卞），"温文"（朱）。

79. acquire and beget: "acquire, through training and practice（通过训练和练习来获得）; beget, through a native artistic impulse（通过天赋的美感来制造）" —Dowden.

80. temperance: 节制。

81. give it smoothness: give gentleness to your passion（使你的热情变得柔和

一些）。

82. it offends me to the soul: 我顶不喜欢，我最讨厌。

83. robustious: noisy（大声喧哗的）。

84. periwig-pated: 头戴假发的（演员在台上表演时要戴假发）。*pate* 意为“头顶”。

85. split the ears: “震裂耳鼓”（卞）。

86. the groundlings: “spectators who sat or stood in the pit (called ‘the yard’), which was the cheapest place in the theatre”（Kittredge）——在池座（the pit）里坐着或站着听戏的观众，他们只花一分钱（a penny）就可以进到戏园里来听戏。Hamlet 认为这些观众的趣味不是很高雅的。

87. capable of: 能够欣赏。

88. inexplicable dumb shows: 不可理解的哑剧（只有手势和动作，没有台词的戏剧表演）。早期英国戏剧中常穿插着哑剧场面（或为闹剧，或为寓言剧），这也是中世纪戏剧的残余。莎士比亚并不反对一切哑剧，他只反对莫名其妙、无法理解的哑剧。

89. o’erdoing: overdoing，演（某角色）演得过火。

90. Termagant: 中世纪基督徒认为伊斯兰教徒所崇拜的偶象之一，在中世纪宗教剧中是一个狂暴的、好说大话的、盛气凌人的角色。

91. It out-herods Herod: *it* 指 *o’erdoing Termagant*（这种过火的表演）。*Herod*（希律）是耶稣诞生时的犹太暴君，在中世纪的奇迹剧里是一个气势汹汹、盛怒咆哮的角色。*out-herods* 是个动词，意为 outdoes Herod in violence（比希律还要凶，还要狂暴）。

92. Pray you avoid it: I beg you to avoid it（我请求你们要避免这种过火的表演）。

93. I warrant your honour: 我向殿下保证。

94. discretion: judgment（判断力）。

95. tutor: 导师，指导。

96. observance: rule（戒规）。

97. o’erstep not: 不可越过。动词 *o’erstep* 在子句里是虚拟式，与 *not* 连用，表示戒规。

98. modesty: moderation（分寸，适度）。

99. from: 要读强音 [frɔm]，意为 away from（脱离），contrary to（违背）。

100. at the first: at first（最初），“when the art of acting was first invented”（Kittredge）.

101. scorn: 应该嘲笑的事物或行为，意同 folly（“荒唐”——卞）。

102. the very age and body of the time: “the times exactly as they are”（Kittredge）——时代和社会的本来面目。一个人的相貌主要由他的年龄（age）和体格（body）来决定。

103. his: 莎士比亚时代的英语常用 *his* 代替 *its*. *his* 在这里指 *the time.*

104. pressure: “impression, as in wax”（Kittredge）——（蜡上的）印记。这句话连贯起来是说“让时代和社会的本相看一看它自己的样子和印记”。

105. Now this overdone: *this* 是 24 行动词 *cannot…make* 的主语。*overdone* 是过去分词，修饰 *this*，意为 if it is overdone.

106. come tardy off: come off tardy, produce an effect slowly（拖沓）。在这里，*come* 也是过去分词，修饰 *this*，等于 having come，意为 if it has come off tardy.

107. though it make: 早期英语，在用 *though, if* 等连词引起的子句中，动词用虚拟式。*make* 在这里是虚拟式。

108. the unskilful: 指观众中缺乏判断力的人。*skill* 古义为 judgment（判断），reason（理智）。

109. the judicious: 有见识的人。

110. the censure of the which one: "the opinion of a single one of whom"（Kittredge）——他们（the judicious）当中的一个人的意见。

111. in your allowance: in approbation of you, in order to win approval of your acting（为了博得观众对你们表演的赞赏）。*allow* 意为 approve（赞赏）。

112. must ... o'erweigh a whole theatre of others: 必然比满园子其他观众的意见更有分量。

113. there be players that: 古体，等于 there are players whom.

114. and that highly: *that* 是个代词，代替 *heard others praise.*

115. not to speak it profanely: *speak profanely,* 说话对上帝不敬。汉姆雷特指的是下面他将要说的话。他说不是上帝造人，而是"大自然临时雇来的笨工匠造出了人"（卞）。这样的说法是违背基督教的教义的，因此是对上帝不敬的。汉姆雷特说这句话的意思是为了避免误会，怕人家说他不敬上帝。

116. that: 等于 who，指 26 行的 *players. that* 是 30 行动词 *have strutted and bellowed* 的主语。

117. have so strutted and bellowed that ...: "那样的大摇大摆，吼啊叫啊"（卞）以至于…

118. some of Nature's journeymen: "大自然临时雇来的（某一个）笨工匠"（卞）。*journeyman* is "an artisan who is not a master of his trade but works for another, (hence) indifferent workman" (Dover Wilson)——不熟练的工匠，雇佣于别人，因此是一个拙劣的手艺人。

119. and not made them well: *they* ...，*them* 和 *they* 都指 31 行 *men.*

120. humanity: 人类，人性。

121. abominably: unnaturally（违背人性地，不自然地）。

122. indifferently: pretty well（相当地）。

123. with us: 在我们戏班里。

124. clowns: 丑角。

125. there be of them: 等于 there are some of them（这些丑角当中有某些人）。

126. set on: "逗引"（卞）。

127. quantity: "small quantity"（Kittredge）——少数。

128. barren: dull，stupid（"没有头脑的"——卞）。

129. in the mean time: 在当时，在那个时刻。

130. necessary question: "紧要问题"（卞）。

131. be then to be considered: 等于 is then to be considered, must then be considered.

132. villanous: ‘vulgar’（Kittredge）——庸俗的，低级趣味的。
133. a most pitiful ambition: “最可鄙的野心”（卞）。
134. fool: 双关语，“丑角”，“傻瓜”。
135. that uses it: 等于 who practises this（这样做的那个丑角或傻瓜）。

VI. THE TRAGEDY OF MACBETH

李赋宁　选注

I, vi, 1–10

After sunset of the same day. Before Macbeth’s castle.
Enter KING DUNCAN, MALCOLM, DONALBAIN, BANQUO,
LENNOX, MACDUFF, ROSS, ANGUS, *and* Attendants.
Duncan. This castle hath a pleasant seat[1]; the air
Nimbly[2] and sweetly recommends itself[3]
Unto our gentle senses.
Banquo. This guest of summer,[4]
The temple-haunting[5] martlet, does approve[6]
By his lov’d mansionry[7] that the heaven’s breath
Smells wooingly[8] here: no jutty[9], frieze,[10]
Buttress,[11] nor coign of vantage,[12] but this bird
Hath made his pendent bed[13] and procreant cradle.[14]
Where they most breed and haunt, I have observed
The air is delicate.[15]

II, ii, 1–74

Later the same night. The court of Macbeth’s castle, with a stairway leading up to the quarters occupied by King Duncan and his sons.
Enter LADY MACBETH.
Lady Macbeth. That which hath made them drunk hath made me

bold,[16]
What hath quench'd[17] them hath given me fire.[18]
—Hark![19]—
Peace![20]—
It was the owl that shriek'd, the fatal bellman,[21]
Which gives the stern'st good-night.[22]—He is about it;[23]
The doors are open, and the surfeited[24] grooms[25]
Do mock their charge with snores.[26] I have drugg'd[27] their possets,[28]
That[29] death and nature[30] do contend about them
Whether they live or die.

Macbeth. [*Within.*] Who's there?[31] what, ho![32]

Lady Macbeth. Alack![33] I am afraid they have awak'd,
And 'tis not done! The attempt,[34] and not the deed,
Confounds[35] us. —Hark!—I laid their[36] daggers ready;
He could not miss them.[37]—Had he not resembled[38]
My father as he slept, I had done't. —My husband!

Enter MACBETH *with a dripping dagger in each hand.*

Macbeth. I have done the deed! —Didst thou not hear a noise?

Lady Macbeth. I heard the owl scream, and the crickets cry. —Did not you speak?

Macbeth. When?

Lady Macbeth. Now.

Macbeth. As I descended?[39]

Lady Macbeth. Ay.[40]

Macbeth. [*Starting.*] Hark!
Who lies i' the second chamber?[41]

Lady Macbeth. Donalbain.[42]

Macbeth. [*Looking on his hands.*] This is a sorry[43] sight.

Lady Macbeth. A foolish thought to say a sorry sight![44]

Macbeth. There's one did laugh in's sleep,[45] and one cried "Murder!"

That[46] they did wake each other. I stood and heard them.[47]
But they did say their prayers, and address'd them[48]
Again to sleep.

Lady Macbeth. There are two lodg'd together.[49]

Macbeth. One cried "God bless us!"[50] and "Amen"[51] the other,
As[52] they had seen me with these hangman's hands.
Listening[53] their fear, I could not say "Amen"
When they did say "God bless us!"

Lady Macbeth. Consider it not so deeply.

Macbeth. But wherefore[54] could not I pronounce "Amen"?
I had most need of blessing;[55] and "Amen"
Stuck[56] in my throat.

Lady Macbeth. These deeds must not be thought
After these ways;[57] so,[58] it will make us mad!

Macbeth. Methought[59] I heard a voice cry "Sleep no more!—
Macbeth does murder sleep—the innocent sleep[60]—
Sleep that knits up[61] the ravell'd[62] sleave[63] of care—
The death of each day's life[64]—sore[65] labour's bath—
Balm of hurt minds—great nature's second course[66]—
Chief nourisher in life's feast"—

Lady Macbeth. What do you mean?

Macbeth. Still[67] it cried "Sleep no more!" to all the house:
"Glamis[68] hath murder'd sleep!—and therefore Cawdor[69]
Shall sleep no more!—Macbeth shall sleep no more!"—

Lady Macbeth. Who was it that thus cried?—Why, worthy thane,
You do unbend[70] your noble strength to think
So brainsickly[71] of things.—Go get some water,
And wash this filthy witness[72] from your hand.—
Why did you bring these daggers from the place?
They must lie there. Go, carry them; and smear
The sleepy grooms with blood.

Macbeth. I'll go no more!

I am afraid to think what I have done:
Look on't again, I dare not.
Lady Macbeth. Infirm of purpose![73]
Give me the daggers. The sleeping and the dead
Are but as[74] pictures.[75] 'Tis the eye of childhood
That fears a painted devil. —If he[76] do bleed,
I'll gild[77] the faces of the grooms withal;[78]
For it must seem their guilt.
[*Exit. Knocking within.*
Macbeth. [*Starting.*] Whence is that knocking? —
How is't with me, when every noise appals[79] me? —
What hands are here![80] Ha![81] they pluck out[82] mine eyes! —
Will all great Neptune's[83] ocean wash this blood
Clean[84] from my hand? No: this my hand will rather[85]
The multitudinous[86] seas incarnadine,[87]
Making the green[88] one red.[89]
Re-enter Lady Macbeth with her hands bloody.
Lady Macbeth. My hands are of your colour, but I shame[90]
To wear a heart so white.[91] —[*Knocking within.*]
I hear a knocking
At the south entry[92]. Retire we[93] to our chamber.
A little water clears us of this deed;
How easy is it, then! Your constancy
Hath left you unattended.[94]—[*Knocking within.*]
Hark! more knocking.
Get on[95] your nightgown,[96] lest occasion[97] call us
And show us to be watchers.[98] Be not lost[99]
So poorly[100] in your thoughts.
Macbeth. To know my deed, 'twere best not know myself.[101]
[*Knocking within.*
Wake Duncan with thy knocking![102] I would thou couldst![103]
[*Exeunt.*

III, ii, 1–56

Later the same afternoon. Lady Macbeth's room in the Royal Palace.

Enter LADY MACBETH *and a* Servant.

Lady Macbeth. Is Banquo gone from court?

Servant. Ay, madam; but returns again[104] to-night.

Lady Macbeth. Say to the king, I would attend his leisure
For a few words.

Servant. Madam, I will. [*Exit.*

Lady Macbeth. Nought's had, all's spent,[105]
Where our desire is got without content.[106]
'Tis safer to be that which we destroy[107]
Than by destruction dwell in doubtful[108] joy.

Enter MACBETH.

How now, my lord! why do you keep alone,
Of sorriest[109] fancies your companions making,
Using[110] those thoughts which should indeed have died
With them they think on?[111] Things without all remedy
Should be without regard.[112] What's done is done.

Macbeth. We have scotch'd[113] the snake, not killed it!
She'll[114] close[115] and be herself,[116] whilst our poor[117] malice[118]
Remains in danger of her former tooth.[119]
But, let the frame of things disjoint![120] both the worlds suffer![121]
Ere[122] we will eat our meal in fear, and sleep
In the affliction of these terrible dreams
That shake us nightly.[123] Better be with the dead,
Whom we, to gain our peace, have sent to peace,
Than on the torture of the mind[124] to lie
In restless ecstasy.[125]—Duncan is in his grave;
After life's fitful fever[126] he sleeps well!

Treason has done his[127] worst; nor steel,[128] nor poison,
Malice domestic,[129] foreign levy,[130] nothing
Can touch him further. —

Lady Macbeth. Come on! —
Gentle my lord, sleek o'er your rugged looks;[131]
Be bright and jovial among your guests to-night.

Macbeth. So shall I, love. And so, I pray, be you. —
Let your remembrance[132] apply to[133] Banquo.
Present him eminence,[134] both with eye and tongue.
Unsafe[135] the while,[136] that[137] we
Must lave our honours in these flattering streams,[138]
And make our faces vizards to[139] our hearts,
Disguising what they[140] are.

Lady Macbeth. You must leave this.

Macbeth. O! full of scorpions is my mind, dear wife! —
Thou know'st that Banquo, and his Fleance,[141] lives.

Lady Macbeth. But in them nature's copy's not eterne.[142]

Macbeth. There's comfort yet; they are assailable.[143]
Then be thou jocund. Ere[144] the bat hath flown
His cloister'd[145] flight, ere to black Hecate's[146] summons[147]
The shard-borne[148] beetle with his drowsy hums
Hath rung night's yawning peal,[149] there shall be done
A deed of dreadful note.[150]

Lady Macbeth. What's to be done?

Macbeth. Be innocent of the knowledge, dearest chuck,[151]
Till thou applaud the deed. — Come, seeling[152] night,
Scarf up[153] the tender eye of pitiful day,
And with thy bloody and invisible hand[154]
Cancel[155] and tear to pieces[156] that great bond[157]
Which keeps me pale! Light thickens,[158] and the crow
Makes wing[159] to the rooky wood;[160]
Good things of day[161] begin to droop[162] and drowse,[163]
Whiles night's black agents[164] to their preys[165] do rouse.[166] —

Thou marvell'st[167] at my words: but hold thee still;[168]
Things bad begun make strong themselves by ill.
So, prithee,[169] go with me. [*Exeunt.*

V, v, 16–28

Later the same day. Within the Castle of Dunsinane. Enter MACBETH, SEYTON, *and* Soldiers, *with drum and colours.*

*   *   *

Seyton. The queen, my lord, is dead.
Macbeth. She should have died hereafter;[170]
There would have been a time for such a word.[171]—
To-morrow, and to-morrow, and to-morrow,
Creeps[172] in this petty pace[173] from day to day,
To the last syllable of recorded time;[174]
And all our yesterdays have lighted[175] fools
The way to[176] dusty death.[177] Out,[178] out, brief candle![179]
Life's but[180] a walking shadow, a poor player
That[181] struts and frets his hour upon the stage,[182]
And then is heard no more: it is a tale
Told by an idiot,[183] full of sound and fury,
Signifying nothing —

【题解与注释】

《麦克佩斯》是莎士比亚的四大悲剧之一。这里选的几段系根据 Joseph Quincy Adams 编辑的 *The Tragedy of Macbeth* (Boston, 1931) 版本，同时也参考了 Adams 的注释。此外，还参考了 Alexander Schmidt 所编的 *Shakespeare-Lexicon* (Berlin & Leipzig, 1923)。

剧本讲的是苏格兰的历史故事。莎士比亚有关英国和苏格兰的历史知识主要来自 Holinshed, *Chronicles of England, Scotland, and Ireland* (1577)。英国女王伊丽莎白逝世（1603）后，苏格兰国王 James 继承了英国王位，称为 James I（詹姆斯一世，1603—1625）。莎士比亚的剧团受到新国王 James I 的保护，成为 the King's Men（国王的仆人）。1606 年夏季，丹麦国王 Christian IV 访问英国，James I 予以隆重的招待。James 命令莎士比亚剧团准备演出新的剧目。很有可能，*The Tragedy of Macbeth* 就是莎士比亚奉 James 命在短期内仓促写成，为了在宫中演出，娱乐贵宾的一出戏。在这个剧本里，莎士比亚明显地向James致敬，取悦于英国的新国王，因为James是*Macbeth*剧中历史人物Banquo的第八代子孙，Banquo是苏格兰历史上有名的英勇、正直的武士，James是Banquo的后裔，当然感到光荣。在*Macbeth*剧中，莎士比亚又预言到James的后代将继承王位，延绵不绝。此外，莎士比亚又在剧中引入女巫作法的场面，以取悦于James。原来James为人十分迷信，他曾写过一本书，名叫*Dæmonologie*（《魔鬼论》，1599），专门论证魔鬼的存在和女巫们的法力。由上列事实推论，*The Tragedy of Macbeth*的写作和上演的年代是1606年夏季。

*The Tragedy of Macbeth*的情节：苏格兰国王Duncan年老、无能，他的臣子Macdonwald叛变，发兵向他进攻，图谋夺取王位。他的两个儿子Malcolm和Donalbain年幼力弱，不能替父出征。幸亏Duncan的堂弟Macbeth英勇善战，他替Duncan平息了Macdonwald的叛乱，又胜利地抵御了挪威国王Sweno的侵略。这样Macbeth解救了苏格兰民族的危难，为国家立下了大功。在凯旋回朝的途中，Macbeth和他的战友Banquo在暴风雨的原野上遇见了三个女巫（weird sisters）。女巫们向Macbeth预言：Macbeth将来要做国王；又向Banquo预言：Banquo的子孙要做国王。Banquo对女巫的话一笑置之，但Macbeth听了女巫的预言，不禁大吃一惊（Macbeth starts violently），原来Macbeth心里早有当国王的念头，被女巫们一语道破，焉得不惊？不过，虽然Macbeth野心勃勃，但他对利用犯罪手段达到做国王的目的却抱着很大的顾虑。Duncan热情洋溢地欢迎了Macbeth的胜利归来。他衷心地向Macbeth表示感谢，以至于下泪。为了向Macbeth致敬，他决定访问Macbeth的府第，打算在那里住宿一宵。Duncan向大家宣布，立他的长子Malcolm为皇储，将来要继承他的王位。根据苏格兰古老的习惯，王位继承一般不是世袭，而是通过选举来决定的。Duncan一旦去世，Macbeth作为民族英雄很可能被选为国王。但是Duncan却不顾古老的习惯，竟然以王位传子，这对Macbeth的野心是一个打击。因此Macbeth起了谋杀Duncan的念头。现在Duncan居然打算到他的府第来过夜，送上门来，这是千载难逢的良机，岂能轻易放过？Macbeth和他的妻子定计谋杀Duncan，并且嫁罪于侍候Duncan睡觉的两名侍卫。Macbeth杀死Duncan后，立即受到良心的谴责。他好象听见空中有声音在喊："Macbeth在谋杀睡眠，Macbeth再也休想睡觉！"（"Macbeth does murder sleep ... Macbeth shall sleep no more!"）的确，从此以后Macbeth丧失了内心的安宁，再也睡不着觉了。Duncan的忠实臣子Macduff和Lennox在黎明前来敲Macbeth府第的门，催Duncan早起上路。他们和Macbeth一起发现Duncan被杀死在床上。Macbeth一怒之下杀死了那两名侍候Duncan睡觉的仆人，企图灭口。Malcolm和Donalbain为了替父报仇，连夜分头逃往英国和爱尔兰，乞求援军。由于他们不辞而别，大家都疑心是他们害死了自己的父亲。于是Macbeth被大家拥戴为苏格兰国王，继承了Duncan的王位。Macbeth虽然如愿以偿，但他心里仍担忧女巫关于Banquo子孙将继承王位那个预言的实现，因此他怂恿几个不满现状的军人，趁Banquo和他的儿子Fleance夜晚从郊外归来，在半途中杀死了Banquo。Fleance逃脱，得以幸免。当晚，Macbeth在宫中大宴群臣，虚席以待Banquo，凶手回报Banquo头上刀伤二十余处，死于沟壑之中。由于Fleance逃脱，Macbeth心中不安，竟然忘记招待宾客。幸亏他的妻子提醒了他，方重新振作精神，打算和他的臣子们开怀畅饮。但忽然间

Macbeth 看见 Banquo 的鬼魂坐在他自己打算坐的座位上，而在座其他宾客却都看不见这个鬼魂。Macbeth 向 Banquo 的鬼魂说："你不能说这事是我干的！不要对着我摇摆你那凝结了血块的头发！"（"Thou canst not say I did it! Never shake Thy gory locks at me!"）虽然有 Macbeth 夫人来解围，使 Macbeth 没有当场泄漏他害死 Banquo 和 Duncan 的秘密，但 Macbeth 在宴会上的奇异行为引起了他的臣子们对他的猜疑。逐渐 Macbeth 发现自己处在众叛亲离之中。为了要知道自己未来的命运，Macbeth 主动地去寻找那三个女巫。这一次他所得到的预言是:（1）要提防 Macduff!（2）要残忍、勇敢、果断，凡是女人生的人都没有力量伤害你。（3）除非是 Birnam 森林移到 Dunsinane 山面前，Macbeth 永远也不会被人征服。听了女巫们的预言后，Macbeth 立即采取行动对付 Macduff。由于 Macduff 已逃亡国外，Macbeth 就凶残地把 Macduff 的妻子和幼儿一同杀死。Macduff 逃往英国，找到了 Duncan 的长子 Malcolm。他们争取到英国国王的援助，发兵讨伐 Macbeth，为民除害，因为 Macbeth 已经堕落成杀人不眨眼的暴君。与此同时，Macbeth 夫人的病日益加深，她患的是夜行病。她在睡眠中走来走去，作着用水洗手的姿势，每次要洗上一刻钟。她叹息地说："这儿还有那血腥味！阿拉伯所出产的一切香料都不能使这小小的一只手变香。"（"Here's the smell of the blood still! All the perfumes of Arabia will not sweeten this little hand."）她在睡梦夜行中独自和她丈夫对话，她重演谋杀 Duncan 那晚她所做的每一个重要动作。她数钟响两下，说：是该行动的时候了（她和丈夫约好在晚上两点钟动手杀害 Duncan）。她永远也忘不了 Duncan 卧在血泊里那个场面。她自言自语地说："可是谁又会料到那个老头子竟流出这么多的血？"（"Yet who would have thought the old man to have had so much blood in him?"）医生叫 Macbeth 夫人的护士提防病人自杀。终于 Macbeth 夫人忍受不了内心的痛苦，趁人不备，结束了自己的生命。这时 Malcolm 和 Macduff 已引来英国军队和苏格兰起义军队会合，把 Macbeth 围困在 Dunsinane 城堡中。Malcolm 命兵士每人折一树枝，拿在手中作为掩护物，浩浩荡荡向 Dunsinane 城堡前进。Macbeth 部下向 Macbeth 报告 Birnam 森林已经移到 Dunsinane 山面前。Macbeth 痛恨女巫们欺骗了自己，决心与敌人拚个你死我活，于是打开了城堡，出城迎战。Macbeth 终于和 Macduff 交锋。Macbeth 认为没有人能够战胜他，除非那人不是女人生的。Macduff 向他说：Macduff 不是女人生的，他未足月就从母亲子宫里取了出来。Macbeth 认识到他又受了女巫们的欺骗。最后 Macduff 杀死了暴君 Macbeth, Malcolm 继任为苏格兰国王。

在 *Macbeth* 悲剧里，莎士比亚塑造了 Macbeth 和 Macbeth 夫人这两个令人难忘的形象。Macbeth 夫人注重实际，意志刚强，一心要想帮助丈夫把苏格兰的王位弄到手。她没有什么道德观念，对谋杀 Duncan 毫无顾虑，以为用一点水就可以洗干净杀人的罪恶。她对丈夫说："A little water clears us of this deed; How easy is it, then!" 可是逐渐她认识到她和她丈夫所犯的罪恶的严重性。她老在那里洗手，因为她意识到她的罪恶是永远也洗不干净的。她绝望地说："唉！这两只手将永远也干净不了吗？"（"What! will these hands ne'er be clean?"）是的，Macbeth 夫人的罪恶是洗不干净的。莎士比亚创造了这样一个妇女形象，来说明野心和犯罪行为给人所带来的内心痛苦和肉体上的折磨。最后，Macbeth 夫人只有自杀一条路好走。和他的妻子相比较，Macbeth 的悲剧更令人惊心动魄。Macbeth 原是一个正直勇敢的军人，他受到大家的爱戴和器重。他对妻子说：“我赢得各阶层的人们对我的好评。”（“I have bought Golden opinions from all sorts of people.”）由于他替苏格兰国家和人民立了功，成为苏格兰的民族英雄，于是就动了做国王的念头。很可能原先他在政治上有他自己的抱负和理想，由于 Duncan 软弱无能，他便有心取而代之。但是他心里所抱的远大志向，按照他的性格，必须用纯洁高尚的手段来实现。（Macbeth 夫人说她丈夫：“你想要追求的高贵东西，你愿意用圣洁的方式去获得。”[“What thou wouldst highly, That thou wouldst holily.”]）他的性格里又“充满了人类仁慈的乳汁，使他不肯抄近路”。（“It is too full o' the milk of human kindness To catch the nearest way.”）他的道德观念很强，心里顾虑重重，又加上他非常富于幻想，因此他经常象一位诗人或哲学家那样来形容、描绘他自己的思想和感情，来分析、评论他自己的动机和行为。在一段类似 Hamlet 考虑生死问题的独自里，Macbeth 幻想一旦 Duncan 被杀害，“怜悯将象一个一丝不挂的新生的婴孩骑在狂风背上，把这桩可怖的谋杀事件随风吹入每个人的眼中，使泪水把大风淹灭”。（“And pity, like a naked new-born babe Striding the blast, ... Shall blow the horrid deed in every eye, That tears shall drown the wind.”）但是他经不起妻子的怂恿和嘲讽，还是犯了那可怕的杀人罪。他选择了一条罪恶、残暴的途径来达到做国王的目的。这是 Macbeth 生平第一次犯罪。一旦走上了犯罪的道路，Macbeth 就和他的正直、诚实永别了。但是他的想像力变得更加敏捷。例如，当他妻子听见猫头鹰叫和蟋蟀悲啼，他却听见空中有声音在喊：“Sleep no more! —Macbeth does murder sleep— ... Macbeth shall sleep no more!”这是他灵魂深处的喊声。此后 Macbeth 在罪恶的泥坑里愈陷愈深，他向他的妻子发出极端痛苦的喊声：“噢，亲爱的妻子，我心里有蠍子在螫！”（“O! full of scorpions is my mind, dear wife!”）尤其是，他对生命感到厌倦，表露出羡慕死人在坟墓里安眠的消极、绝望的心情：“Duncan 躺在他的坟墓里；经过了人生热病的发作以后，他现在睡得很安稳！”（“Duncan is in his grave; After life's fitful fever he sleeps well!”）Macbeth 对生命表示厌倦的感情在他生命的末日达到了顶峰。当他听到他的侍从向他报告 Macbeth 夫人逝世消息时，他对人生作了总结：“熄灭吧，短短的蜡烛！人生不过是个会行走的影子，不过是个技术恶劣的演员，在舞台上趾高气扬地迈着步子，咆哮着度过在台上规定的时间，以后再也不出场了：人生不过是痴人说梦，听起来声色俱厉，其实毫无意义。”（“Out, out, brief candle! Life's but a walking shadow, a poor player That struts and frets his hour upon the stage, And then is heard no more: it is a tale Told by an idiot, full of sound and fury, Signifying nothing.”）这是 Macbeth 对他自己的罪恶、痛苦的一生所作的结论，同时也是莎士比亚对它作的结论。

在 *Macbeth* 悲剧里，莎士比亚企图说明社会罪恶和马基亚维里式的（Machiavellian）利己主义道德标准给善良正直的人所带来的危害和痛苦。资产阶级利己主义的道德标准和不择手段来达到目的的哲学对莎士比亚来说是万恶之源，是一切痛苦和灾难的祸根。Macbeth 也受到这种思想的影响（女巫和 Macbeth 夫人都对他施加影响），他的性格受到腐蚀，日趋堕落。他也学会了伪装、诽谤、欺骗、恐吓、报复这些资产阶级利己主义者所惯用的罪恶伎俩。Macbeth 夫人向 Macbeth 说：“装出一副象无害的鲜花的模样，但是干的是花底下躲藏着的毒蛇所干的事情！”（“look like the innocent flower, But—be the serpent under't!"）Macbeth 夫人所灌输给 Macbeth 的思想是所谓的超道德的思想。她代表的是资产阶级冒险家为了追求利润所表现的"坚强的意志和毅力"。她用轻蔑嘲笑作为手段，把她丈夫逼上了犯罪之路。Macbeth 夫人代表的是家庭对 Macbeth 的影响；那三个女巫可以说是代表社会对 Macbeth 的影响。莎士比亚利用大家都认为是有很大的危害力量的女巫来象征资产阶级利己主义对 Macbeth 的腐蚀作用和败坏影响。Banquo 也看到了女巫，听到了女巫们的预言，但是 Banquo 并没有受女巫们的影响，始终保持他的正直、善良、忠诚、老实的本来面目。Macbeth 经不起女巫的诱惑，受了他们的影响，结果走上了犯罪的道路，丧失了他的正直善良，遭受到最严厉的内心惩罚和最残酷的精神痛苦，到头来众叛亲离，成为人民公敌，落得个悲惨可耻的下场。莎士比亚的作品对今天的读者仍有教育意义。我们要时刻警惕资产阶级思想对我们的侵害和腐蚀。

现将所选的几段 *Macbeth* 选文的具体内容说明如下：

（1）Act I, Scene VI：Duncan 在傍晚时分来到了 Macbeth 的府第前，他和 Banquo 有一段动人的对话，描写 Macbeth 府第环境的优美、清幽、愉快、健康。这段文字一方面表现 Banquo 和 Duncan 心地的纯洁、平静，另一方面又与下面行将发生的谋杀和恐怖场面成为鲜明的对照。

（2）Act II, Scene II：这是 Macbeth 和 Macbeth 夫人谋杀 Duncan 的一场，是整个悲剧中最可怖的一场。当然杀害 Duncan 的实际行动是在幕后进行的，但是全场充满了紧张、恐怖的气氛，使观众屏止了呼吸看下去。同时，莎士比亚把这一对犯罪夫妇的心理刻划得十分深刻。二人的性格呈现出鲜明强烈的对照：Macbeth 夫人着重实际效果，行动果断、迅速；Macbeth 着重考虑行为的意义和犯罪的后果，犯罪后立刻坠入幻想世界，迟迟不能采取有效措施来掩盖自己的犯罪痕迹。请读者注意 Macbeth 的自我分析的特点。例如，他看着自己染上了 Duncan 的鲜血的双手，向他的妻子说："真可怕！真难看！"（"This is a sorry sight."）又如，他说他听见有个声音在喊："不要睡觉了！——Macbeth 在谋杀睡眠——无辜的睡眠——"（"Sleep no more! —Macbeth does murder sleep—the innocent sleep—"）

（3）Act III, Scene II：这一场的内容是 Macbeth 杀死了 Duncan 以后，如愿以偿地做了苏格兰国王，但是他并不感到心满意足。相反地，他忧虑、憔悴，晚上睡不着觉，白天不愿见人，独自个想心思。他羡慕死去的 Duncan 在坟墓里睡得安稳。他痛苦地向他的妻子求援，说他自己心里钻满了蝎子，不断地在螫他的心。这是良心对他的处罚，他不了解，反而以为是由于 Banquo 和 Banquo 的儿子 Fleance 仍旧活着，他自己的王位坐不安稳，因此他决心要把 Banquo 和 Fleance 害死，以除后患，以为这样做就可以拔掉自己心中的肉刺。在 Macbeth 和 Macbeth 夫人的对话里，Macbeth 运用了一系列描写黑夜的极为生动的形象来象征他自己内心世界的黑暗和他的可怕的犯罪心理。

（4）Act V, Scene V：这一段文字表现了 Macbeth 对生命的厌倦，同时也可以看作是莎士比亚对悲剧主人公虚度了的一生所作的结论。一个有理想、有抱负、正直、勇敢的人，由于在罪恶的社会影响面前解除了武装，成为它的俘虏，结果在犯罪的泥坑里愈陷愈深。这样一个人的一生岂不是虚度了吗？请读者注意：莎士比亚并不是在这里宣传悲观厌世的哲学，提倡“人生空虚论”。相反地，他在这里表现了正面积极的思想：人应该充分发挥自己的聪明才智，过一个有意义、有价值的一生。

(1) MACBETH, I, vi, 1–10

1. seat: situation（地位，地势）。

2. Nimbly: in a manner enlivening the spirits（令人精神振奋地）。

3. recommends itself: is agreeable（赏心悦目）。

4. This guest of summer: 指下一行 martlet = a kind of swallow（一种燕子），候鸟，随夏季而来。

5. temple-haunting: resorting to, and dwelling about, temples（盘桓、筑巢于教堂建筑物的周围）。

6. approve: prove, testify（证明）。

7. mansionry: abode（住所）。**By his lov'd mansionry,** by making this a favourite place of abode（以此处为其心爱之住所）。

8. wooingly: invitingly（引人入胜地）。

9. jutty: ledge, or shelf-like projection on the wall of a building（建筑物墙上的突出部分）。

10. frieze:〈建筑〉中楣（圆柱上面墙顶的一部分）。

11. Buttress: wall standing out and built to support another wall（突出的护墙）。

12. coign of vantage: suitable corner（合适的角落）。

13. pendent bed: hanging nest（悬挂在高处的鸟巢）。

14. procreant cradle: cradle for begetting young（为了生小鸟用的摇篮）。

15. delicate: delightful, pleasant（令人愉快的）。

(2) MACBETH,II, ii, 1–74

16. That which hath made them drunk hath made me bold: Lady Macbeth had taken wine to fire her courage（Macbeth 夫人饮酒以壮胆）。

17. quench'd: stupefied（使昏迷不醒）。

18. fire: courage（勇气）。

19. Hark: listen（听）。

20. Peace: keep silent（别做声）。

21. the fatal bellman: a night watchman sent to condemned persons on the night before execution（在犯人被处死刑的前夕特来探望犯人的守夜的人）。在这里 Duncan 好比被判处死刑的犯人，猫头鹰好比给犯人带来死亡噩耗的守夜人。*fatal,* sent by the Fates and foretelling death（被司命运之神所派遣，前来预言死亡的行将来临）。

22. Which gives the stern'st good-night: who (the fatal bellman) bids the severest good-night (i. e., the last good-night of death)（他——带来死亡消息的守夜人——来说最

严厉的晚安——夜间告别时所说的话——也就是最后一次的晚安）。

23. He is about it: Macbeth is engaged in the business of murdering Duncan（Macbeth 正在进行谋杀 Duncan 那件事）。

24. surfeited: fed to excess（吃得过饱的）。

25. grooms: servants（侍者，仆从）。

26. Do mock their charge with snores: by snoring (i. e., sleeping soundly) make a mockery of their duty (of guarding the King)（以鼾声来嘲笑他们警卫国王的职守）。

27. drugg'd: put narcotic drugs in（下了麻药）。

28. possets: evening drinks, composed of hot milk, curdled by some strong infusion, and used to be taken before going to bed（夜间服用的饮料，其成分为热牛奶加酒，以前人们多在临睡前饮用）。

29. That: so that（以至于）。

30. nature: i. e., their natural vitality, their vital forces（他们——国王的两名侍卫——的生命力）。

31. Who's there: Macbeth hears the sound referred to in lines 2 and 3 (i. e., the scream of the owl), he is alarmed at every noise（Macbeth 听见了猫头鹰的尖叫声，他以为有人来了，所以问 Who's there? 他的神经太紧张了，每一个声音都使他有草木皆兵之感）。

32. ho: 唤起人注意的惊叹词。

33. Alack: 表示失望、埋怨、伤心等感情的惊叹词。

34. attempt: an unsuccessful effort or trial, as opposed to a performed deed（未成功的努力或企图，与完成了的行动恰好相反）。

35. Confounds: destroys, ruins（毁灭）。

36. their: the two grooms'（那两名侍卫的）。

37. He could not miss them: Macbeth could not miss the daggers（Macbeth 不会找不到他们的匕首）。

38. Had he not resembled: if Duncan had not looked like（假若 Duncan 不象）。Macbeth 夫人原来打算亲自杀害 Duncan，但因睡熟了的 Duncan 很象她自己的父亲，所以不忍心下手。

39. As I descended: Duncan 睡觉的卧室在楼上。Macbeth 谋杀 Duncan 后，从楼梯上走下来。

40. Ay: yes.

41. second chamber: 楼上有两间卧室。这是 Duncan 睡觉的那间卧室除外的另一间卧室。

42. Donalbain: 人名，Duncan 的次子。

43. sorry: sorrowful，sad（悲惨的）。

44. A foolish thought to say a sorry sight: You are being foolish if you repent of what you have done（假若你懊悔你自己所做的事，那你未免太傻了）。

45. There's one did laugh in's sleep: There was one who laughed in his sleep（有

一个人在睡梦中笑了起来)。Macbeth 说当他犯了谋杀罪后经过 Donalbain 睡觉的卧室时，听见屋内有一个人在睡梦里笑了起来，另外一个人在梦中喊 "Murder!"("杀人了!")。必须指出这两个人并不是 Duncan 的那两名侍卫。他们睡得象死人一样，丝毫未被惊醒。

46. That: so that(以至于)。

47. I stood and heard them: Macbeth heard two persons speaking, and he had to stand there, waiting outside their door with his bloody hands, until they were quiet again and he could creep by without being heard(Macbeth 听见两个人在屋内说话，他只得静静地站在门外，等他们再睡着了，他好轻轻地走过他们的房门，从楼梯上走了下来)。

48. address'd them: made themselves ready(准备好)。

49. There are two lodg'd together: The two princes are lodged together(两位王子睡在一起), i. e., there is nothing in that; the two princes are sleeping in the same room(那没有什么奇怪；两位王子睡在一间卧室里)。

50. God bless us: 上帝保佑我们。这是一句惊叹的话，表示惊讶或恐惧。

51. Amen: 回答别人祈祷的话，表示赞许、肯定祈祷的内容。

52. As: as if(似乎)。两位王子忽然从梦中惊醒，就好象他们在隔壁房间里已经看见了我的刽子手般的双手。

53. Listening: listening to(注意地听，古用法)。

it: this trivial incident (i. e., his inability to say "Amen")(这一件小事，指 Macbeth 不能说出"阿门"这一件事)。

54. wherefore: for what reason, why(为什么)。

55. I had most need of blessing: I had most need of God's blessing, because I had committed a heinous crime(我最需要上帝的赐福，因为我犯了最严重的罪行)。

56. Stuck: 粘(*stick* 的过去式)。

57. After these ways: in this manner(用这种方式)。

58. so: if we do so(假若我们这样做)。

59. Methought: it seemed to me(我觉得)。

60. the innocent sleep: Sleep is compared to an innocent babe(睡眠被比做天真纯洁的婴儿)。

61. knits up: straightens out(使平整)。The cares of the day disorder and entangle the skein of floss-silk, which under the influence of sleep is gathered together again into an ordered plait(白天的烦恼扰乱人的精神，象一束纠缠、杂乱的绒线。在睡眠的影响之下，这一束乱绒线被理出头绪，编成辫子)。

62. ravell'd: tangled, entangled(纠缠，缠结)。

63. sleave: defined by Florio, *A World of Words* (1598), as "any kind of ravelled stuff"; usually a coarse kind of silk(一种粗糙的丝线)。

64. The death of each day's life: *Death* probably suggests "rest", "repose", "comfort", "ease"(*death* 可能有"休息","解脱[烦恼]"的含义)。

65. sore: painful, heavy(痛苦的，沉重的)。

66. second course: the main part of a banquet（第二道菜是一桌酒席最主要的一道菜）。Sleep is the second course in nature's daily banquet. Life's feast has two courses—food and sleep. Macbeth regards the second as even more sustaining to our nature than the first. Life is a banquet, of which the first course is labour, and the second rest（生活的酒席有两道菜：食物和睡眠。Macbeth 认为第二道菜比第一道菜更富于营养。生命好象一桌酒席，第一道菜是劳动，第二道菜是休息）。

67. Still: continuously, without interruption（继续不断地，不停地）。

68. Glamis: [glɑːmz]，Macbeth 的贵族头衔之一是 Thane of Glamis（*thane*，苏格兰的伯爵）。

69. Cawdor: Macbeth 的另一个贵族封号是 Thane of Cawdor.

70. unbend: relax（使松弛，使变弱，使疲累）。

71. brainsickly: madly（疯疯癫癫地）。

72. this filthy witness: i. e., the stains of blood（血痕，血斑，血印）。

73. Infirm of purpose: weak of will（意志薄弱）。

74. but as: only like（仅仅相象）。

75. pictures: i. e., The sleeping and the dead are only pictures of living men, and pictures cannot hurt you. Only a child is afraid of a devil that is not real, but only painted（睡着了的人和死人只不过是活人的图象罢了，图象并不能伤人。只有小孩子才怕画里的魔鬼）。

76. he: 指 Duncan 的尸体。

77. gild: i. e., smear the faces of the grooms with his (Duncan's) blood. Mark the pun on "gild" and "guilt"（用 Duncan 的血来染红那两名侍卫的脸。请读者注意 gild "染红"和 guilt [第 57 行]"有罪"是双关语）。gild 原义为"cover with a golden colour"（涂上金色），转义为"make ruddy"（染红），或"smear with blood"（抹上血）。

78. withal: *adv.*（副词），with this, by means of this（用这个东西）。在这里指 with Duncan's blood（用 Duncan 的血）。

79. appals: strikes with extreme fear（使非常害怕）。

80. What hands are here: Macbeth 注意到他的涂满鲜血的双手。

81. Ha: 表示惊讶或悲哀的感叹词。

82. pluck out: pull out, tear out（挖出眼珠子）。Macbeth 不忍心看他自己的双手，好象这一双血手要把他的眼珠子挖出来。

83. Neptune's: Neptune, Roman sea-god（古罗马人的海神）。

84. Clean: *adv.*（副词），quite, entirely, completely（完全，干干净净地）。

85. rather: *adv.*（副词），on the contrary（相反地）。

86. multitudinous: innumerable, endless（数不清的，无止境的），said of the ocean or any mass of water with reference to its great bulk or to its innumerable ripples（喻海洋之大，或指海中无数之波纹）。The idea is of tumbling seas, with wave over wave like a swaying crowd（意为波浪滚滚的海洋，一浪接着一浪，犹如人山人海）。请读者注意形容词 *multitudinous* 从名词 multitude（人群）而来。

87. incarnadine: *v. t.*（及物动词），dye red（染红）。

88. the green: i. e., the green colour of the seas（海洋的绿色）。

89. one red: one uniform red colour（一整片红颜色），i. e., turning the green colour of the seas into one universal red（把海洋的绿色变成到处都是一片红色）。*green* 和 *red* 都是名词。The imagination of Macbeth dwells upon the conversion of the universal green into one pervading red（Macbeth 的幻想集中在把一整片绿色变成到处是一片红色的意境上）。Macbeth 好比一个染匠，把一整匹绿布染成了一整匹红布。请读者注意 Macbeth 的诗人般的想象力。

90. shame: *v. i.*（不及物动词），am ashamed（感觉羞愧）——古用法。

91. To wear a heart so white: i. e., to be white-livered or cowardly（胆怯，懦弱）。

92. entry: door, gate（门，大门）。

93. Retire we: let us retire, let us go to bed（让我们回到卧室休息去吧）。

94. Your constancy hath left you unattended: i. e., Your usual courage or firmness has deserted you（你平日的勇气或坚定现在都离你而去，在你身上找不着了）。

95. Get on: put on（穿上）。

96. nightgown: a dressing gown, *robe de chambre*, which Elizabethans hastily threw about them when aroused from bed（梳洗时所着之长衣。伊丽莎白时代的人们夜间从床上惊起后，匆忙地披上早晨梳洗时所着的长衣）。

97. occasion: exigency, pressing necessity（紧急的需要）。

98. watchers: persons who remain awake（尚未睡觉的人们）。

99. Be not lost: i. e., do not lose yourself（不要使你自己坠入）。

100. poorly: piteously, despicably（可怜地，可耻的）；without spirit or courage（不勇敢地，懦弱地）。

101. To know my deed, 'twere best not know myself: In reply to Lady Macbeth's 'Be not lost', etc., Macbeth says, in effect: "I would rather lose myself altogether in my thoughts than be brought back to the consciousness of what I have done"（这是 Macbeth 在回答 Macbeth 夫人给他的劝告 "Be not lost So poorly in your thoughts" 时所说的话。实际上，这句话的意思是："我宁愿完全掉进沉思中，不愿回忆起我所做的事情"）。*To know* = in knowing, i. e., if I must know（假若我必须知道我自己所做的事）。*'twere best not know myself* = it would be best to be lost in my thoughts（我最好还是掉进沉思中去）。全句的意思是：Better be lost in thought than look my deed in the face（与其正视我自己的行为，还不如坠入于沉思中）。

102. Wake Duncan with thy knocking: This is addressed to the invisible knocker at the gate（这是 Macbeth 向那位看不见的敲门者说的话）。

103. I would thou couldst: I wish you could wake Duncan up with your knocking（但愿你能用你敲门的声音把 Duncan 唤醒）。Macbeth 深悔自己杀害了 Duncan.

104. again: back（回来）。

105. Nought's had, all's spent: Nothing is obtained, everything is spent（什么东西都没有得到，所有的东西都用光了）。Macbeth 夫人当了王后，但是她并没有获得幸福，反而失去了往日的宁静心情。和她丈夫一样，她也受到良心的谴责，睡不着觉。Joseph Quincy Adams: '"Nought's had" is pathetic enough, but far more pathetic is Lady Macbeth's added confession, "all's spent"—self-esteem, character, soul-salvation, everything that makes life worth living'（"all's spent" 指自尊心，人格，灵魂的得救，总之，一切使生命值得活下去的东西）。

106. Where our desire is got without content: i. e., in the case in which the object of our desire is obtained without peace of mind（在我们并非心安理得地获得了我们所追求的东西的情况下，我们的感觉是：什么都没有得到，一切都用光了）。

107. 'Tis safer to be that which we destroy: Macbeth 夫人羡慕 Duncan 的安稳处境。*that which we destroy* = he whom we kill（被我们所杀的人——指 Duncan）。

108. doubtful: filled with apprehensions or fears（充满了担心或恐惧，提心吊胆的）。

109. sorriest: saddest（最忧郁的）。

110. Using: i. e., occupying yourself with those thoughts（从事于想这些心事）。

111. them they think on: i. e., those on whom they (those thoughts) think（它们所思念的那些人——Duncan 当然也包括在这些人们当中）。

112. Should be without regard: should not be regarded or thought of（不应该在意，可以不在考虑之列）。

113. scotch'd: slightly wounded（使受轻伤）。

114. She: 代替 the snake.

115. close: heal up（使伤口合拢）。

116. be herself: 复元。

117. poor: feeble, useless（微弱的，无效的）。

118. malice: hate, enmity（仇恨，敌意）。

119. in danger of her former tooth: i. e., in danger of being bitten by her again（有被毒蛇重咬一口的危险）。

120. let the frame of things disjoint: let the fabric of the world fall to pieces（让这个世界的结构分崩离析）；*frame* = structure（结构）；*disjoint, v. i.*, fall out of joint, fall to pieces（脱节，崩碎）。

121. both the worlds suffer: i. e., let both the present life and the future life suffer, let personal safety in this world and soul salvation in the next world suffer（让今生和来生都遭殃，让当前个人的平安和死后灵魂的得救都受到损害）。此行另一解：heaven and earth perish（天地都灭亡）。

122. Ere: before, rather than（强似，胜过）。

123. nightly: every night（每夜）。

124. on the torture of the mind: with our minds upon the rack（把我们自己的心灵放在刑具架上受拷问）。

125. restless ecstasy: unceasing agony（无休止的痛苦）。

126. After life's fitful fever: 请读者注意：此处 *f* 声音的重叠、连续出现生动地表达了人生的烦扰和生活的空虚。*fitful*, full of paroxysms（一阵一阵发作的［疾病］）。

127. his: 等于 its（它的——指 Treason "谋反，叛逆"）。

128. steel: 钢刀，宝剑。

129. Malice domestic: treason at home（国内的叛乱）。

130. levy: forces（军队）。

131. sleek o'er your rugged looks: make smooth your wild looks（使你的不安的面容平静下来）。

132. remembrance: thought, regard, consideration, a state of being mindful（注意力）。

133. apply to: be directed to（被放在…上面）。

134. Present him eminence: pay court to him as a most distinguished guest（把他当做上宾，向他致敬）。

135. Unsafe: we being unsafe（由于我们并不安稳）。

136. the while: in the meantime（同时）。

137. that: so that（因此）。

138. lave our honours in these flattering streams: i. e., keep our dignities clear from suspicion by thus flattering others（用阿谀奉承的手段来使别人不疑心我们的高位是通过不正当的途径获得的）。*lave*, wash, bathe（洗涤，冲洗）；*honours*, high rank, dignity, distinction（高位，威严，荣誉）；在这些阿谀奉承的河流里，来把我们的高位洗刷干净，免得别人猜疑。

139. vizards to: masks to conceal（面具，用来遮掩［我们的真心］）。

140. they: 代替 our hearts.

141. Fleance: 人名，Banquo 的儿子。

142. in them nature's copy's not eterne: i. e., Their tenure of life is not permanent（他们对于生命的享用权并不是永恒的）；*nature's copy* = life's copyhold（生命的享用权）；*eterne* = eternal, everlasting（永恒的，永存的）。这句的含义是：Banquo and Fleance will die（Banquo 和 Fleance 总要死的）。

143. assailable: liable to attack（容易受到袭击的）。

144. Ere: before（在…以前）。

145. cloister'd: confined to the precincts of a cloister（局限于修道院的范围之内）。蝙蝠喜黑暗，怕光明。修道院的建筑，墙高院深，光线阴暗，蝙蝠尤其喜欢在这种建筑物附近飞翔。Macbeth 用极为生动的形象来唤起黑夜的寂静、孤独、阴森、可怕的气氛，为他自己的犯罪心理和犯罪行为提供背景。

146. Hecate's: the moon's（月亮的）。*black Hecate* 在这里是拟人化了的黑夜。

147. summons: call（召唤）。

148. shard-borne: borne in flight by its hard scaly wings（在飞行时由它的坚硬

的、鳞片状的翅鞘所支持的）。

149. peal: a mighty sound（巨大、强烈的声音）。这里 Macbeth 把甲虫的鸣声比做钟声，ring a peal 意为 make a sound like a bell（发出象敲钟或摇铃似的声音）。

150. note: character（性质）。

151. chuck: a term of endearment（亲爱的称呼）= chicken（小鸡）。

152. seeling: i. e., that closes the eye-lids（合上了眼皮的）。

153. Scarf up: blindfold（蒙上眼睛）。

154. thy bloody and invisible hand: Macbeth 请求黑夜做他的帮凶。

155. Cancel: 取消。

156. tear to pieces: 撕毁。

157. bond: 契约，债券。The prophecy of the witches regarding Banquo's issue, viewed as a bond given by Fate（女巫们关于 Banquo 后代的预言被看做是命运之神所持有的债券）。Macbeth 害怕命运之神手里的债券，他请求黑夜撕毁这张债券，免得关于 Banquo 子孙做国王的预言得到实现。

158. thickens: grows dim, becomes dark（变暗，变黑）。

159. wing: flight, the act of flying（飞行）。

160. rooky wood: a wood where rooks abound, especially where they roost at night（多乌鸦的树林，尤其是乌鸦在夜间栖息的树林）。这两行诗：Light thickens, and the crow Makes wing to the rooky wood 语言非常朴素有力（例如，*thickens, makes wing, rooky wood* 这些词），在读者脑中唤起一幅暮鸦归巢的图画，极富于诗意。

161. Good things of day: 白昼的善良的生物；*things* = creatures（有生命的东西）。

162. droop: hang down (their head) in weariness（疲倦地垂下他们的头）。

163. drowse: be heavy with sleepiness（沉沉欲睡）。

164. night's black agents: 夜晚的黑色侦探（例如，蝙蝠、狼、刺客，等）。

165. preys: the act of preying, of catching and devouring other creatures（野兽捕食的动作，捕获、吞食其他动物的动作）。

166. rouse: *v. i.*（不及物动词）rise, get up（睡醒起身，起床）。

167. marvell'st: find（something）strange, wonder at（觉得奇怪，诧异）。

168. hold thee still: keep quiet, be silent（不要说话，别问了）。

169. prithee: *int.*（惊叹词）pray, please（我请求你，请）。

(4) MACBETH, V, v, 16–28

170. She should have died hereafter: i. e., A later time would have been more fitting for her to die（她应该死得更晚一些）。

171. such a word: such a message, such news, i. e., the news of her death（这样一个口信，这样一项消息）。

172. Creeps: 代替 creep（爬行）。

173. in this petty pace: i. e., slowly and unregarded（慢吞吞地，并且是不被人们

注意地）。

174. To the last syllable of recorded time: 时间好象一本书，上面写满了字。我们生命中的明天，慢慢地，一天一天地过去，一直走到时间的记录册上的最末一个字；*syllable* = word（字）；*recorded time*, time of which a record may be kept（有记录的时间）。

175. lighted: guided by light（用光亮引路）。*fools* 是 *lighted* 的直接宾语。

176. The way to: i. e., on the way to（走上了通往…的道路）。

177. dusty death: 人死后化为灰尘；*dusty* = reduced to dust（化为灰尘）。

178. Out: *adv.*（副词），especially of fires and lights extinguished（尤其指火或光被熄灭）。

179. brief candle: *Candle* is used as a symbol of life（蜡烛象征人生），*brief candle* symbolizes the transitoriness of life（短蜡烛象征人生的暂短）。Macbeth 的这一段独白表达了他对人生的空虚之感："To-morrow, and to-morrow, and to-morrow." 他对自己的生活感到厌倦，渴望死去："Out, out, brief candle!"

180. but: *adv.*（副词）= only（仅仅）。

181. That: *rel. pron.*（关系代词）= who（他）。

182. struts and frets his hour upon the stage: spends his time striding theatrically and raging on the stage（在舞台上高视阔步、大嚷大叫来度过时间）。

183. it is a tale told by an idiot: Macbeth 回顾自己的一生，得出这样一个结论："人生不过是痴人说梦"（一个白痴所讲的故事）。他对自己罪恶、失败的一生表示厌恶，但他并没有真正认识自己罪恶的性质，也丝毫没有悔过自新的意思。

5 BEN JONSON
1572?–1637

1. Song to Celia

2. To the memory of … Mr. William Shakespeare …

3. Volpone, or the Fox (selections)

杨周翰　选注

1. SONG TO CELIA[1]

Drink to me only with thine eyes,[2]
　　And I will pledge[3] with mine;
Or leave a kiss but[4] in the cup,
　　And I'll not look for wine.
The thirst that from the soul doth[5] rise,
　　Doth ask a drink divine[6]:
But might I[7] of Jove's Nectar sup[8],
　　I would not change for thine.[9]
I sent thee late[10] a rosy wreath[11],
　　Not so much honoring[12] thee,
As giving it hope, that there
　　It could not wither'd be.[13]
But thou thereon did'st only breathe,[14]
　　And sent'st it back to me:
Since when[15] it grows and smells, I swear,
　　Not of itself, but thee.[16]

(From "The Forest", IX, *Ben Jonson*,
Vol, VIII, ed. C. H. Herford and
Percy and Evelyn Simpson)

2. TO THE MEMORY OF MY BELOVED, THE AUTHOR MR.[1] WILLIAM SHAKESPEARE: AND WHAT HE HATH LEFT US.[2]

To draw no envy[3] (Shakespeare) on thy name,
    Am I thus ample[4] to thy Book and Fame[5]:
While I confess thy writings to be such,
    As neither Man nor Muse[6] can praise too much.
'Tis true, and all men's suffrage[7]. But these ways[8]
    Were not the paths[9] I meant unto thy praise[10]:
For seeliest[11] Ignorance on thee may light[12],
    Which, when it sounds at best,[13] but[14] echo's[15] right;
Or blind Affection, which doth ne'er advance[16]
    The truth, but gropes[17], and urgeth[18] all by chance;
Or crafty Malice[19], might pretend this praise,
    And think[20] to ruin, where it seem'd to raise.
These are, as some infamous Bawd or Whore[21]
    Should praise a Matron[22]. What could hurt her[23] more?
But thou art proof against[24] them[25], and indeed
    Above th'ill fortune of them,[26] or the need.[27]
I therefore will begin. Soul of the Age!
    The applause! delight! the wonder of our Stage!
My Shakespeare, rise[28], I will not lodge thee by[29]
    Chaucer, or Spenser, or bid Beaumont lie
A little further,[30] to make thee a room:
    Thou art a Monument, without[31] a tomb,
And art alive still[32], while thy Book doth live,
    And we have wits to read, and praise to give.
That I not mix thee so, my brain excuses;[33]
    I mean with great but disproportion'd Muses:[34]
For, if I thought my judgement were of years,[35]

I should commit[36] thee surely with thy peers,[37]
And tell, how far thou didst our Lyly[38] outshine,
Or sporting[39] Kyd[40], or Marlowe's[41] mighty line.
And though thou hadst small Latin and less Greek,[42]
From thence[43] to honour thee, I would not seek
For names[44]; but call forth thundering[45] Aeschylus,[46]
Euripides,[47] and Sophocles[48] to us,
Paccuvius, Accius[49], him of Cordova dead,[50]
To life again[51], to hear thy Buskin[52] tread,[53]
And shake a Stage[54]: Or when thy Socks[55] were on,
Leave thee alone, for the comparison
Of all[56] that insolent Greece or haughty Rome[57]
Sent forth, or since[58] did from their ashes[59] come[60].
Triumph, my Britain, thou hast one to show,
To whom all Scenes[61] of Europe homage owe[62].
He was not of an age[63], but for all time![64]
And all the Muses still were in their prime,[65]
When like Apollo[66] he[67] came forth to warm
Our ears,[68] or like a Mercury[69] to charm!
Nature[70] herself was proud of his designs,[71]
And joy'd to wear the dressing of his lines!
Which were so richly spun, and woven so fit,
As, since[72], she will vouchsafe no other wit.[73]
The merry Greek, tart Aristophanes,[74]
Neat[75] Terence,[76] witty Plautus,[77] now not please;
But antiquated, and deserted lie
As they were not of Nature's family.
Yet must I not give Nature all: Thy art,
My gentle[78] Shakespeare, must enjoy a part.
For though the Poet's matter Nature be,
His Art doth give the fashion.[79] And that[80] he,
Who casts[81] to write a living line, must sweat,
(Such as thine[82] are) and strike[83] the second heat[84]

Upon the Muses' anvil[85]: turn[86] the same
(And himself with it) that[87] he thinks to frame;[88]
Or[89] for the laurel, he may gain a scorn,
For a good Poet's made, as weel as born.[90]
And such wert thou. Look how the father's face
Lives in his issue,[91] even so the race[92]
Of Shakespeare's mind and manners[93] brightly shines
In his well turned,[94] and true-filed[95] lines:
In each of which[96] he seems to shake a Lance,[97]
As brandish't[98] at the eyes of Ignorance.[99]
Sweet Swan of Avon![100] what a sight it were[101]
To see thee in our waters yet appear,[102]
And make those flights[103] upon the banks of Thames,[104]
That so did take[105] Eliza,[106] and our James[107]!
But stay, I see thee in the Hemisphere[108]
Advanc'd[109] and made a Constellation[110] there!
Shine forth, thou Star of Poets, and with rage,[111]
Or influence,[112] chide or cheer the drooping Stage;[113]
Which[114], since thy flight[115] from hence, hath mourn'd like night,
And despairs day[116], but for[117] thy Volume's[118] light.

(From "Ungathered Verse", XXVI, *Ben Jonson,* Vol. VIII, ed. Herford and Simpson.)

3. *VOLPONE,*[1] *OR THE FOX*

The Argument[2]

Volpone, childless, rich, feigns[3] sick, despairs,
Offers his state to hopes of several heirs,
Lies languishing; His Parasite[4] receives
Presents of all[5], assures, deludes: Then weaves
Other cross-plots[6], which ope'[7] themselves, are told.[8]
New tricks for safety are sought; they thrive: When bold,
Each tempts th' other[9] again, and all are sold.[10]

Act I. Scene I.

Volpone, Mosca.[11]

Vol. Good morning to the day; and, next, my gold:[12]
Open the shrine,[13] that I may see my saint.
Hail the world's soul, and mine.[14] More glad than is[15]
The teeming earth,[16] to see the long'd-for sun
Peep through the horns of the celestial ram,[17]
Am I, to view thy[18] splendour, darkening his.[19]

....

Act I. Scene IV.

....

Mosca, Corbaccio, Volpone.

(Another knocks)

Vol. Who's that, there, now? a third[20]?
Mos. Close,[21] to your couch again:[22] I hear his voice.
It is Corvino,[23] our spruce[24] Merchant.
Vol. Dead.[25]
Mos. Another bout,[26] sir, with your eyes. Who's there?

....

Act I. Scene V.

Mosca, Corvino, Volpone.

Mos. Signior[27] Corvino! come[28] most wisht for! O,
How happy were you, if you knew it, now!
Corv. Why? what? wherein?
Mos. The tardy hour[29] is come, sir.
Corv. He is not dead?
Mos. Not dead, sir, but as good;
He knows no man.
Corv. How shall I do, then?
Mos. Why, sir?
Corv. I have brought him, here, a pearl.
Mos. Perhaps, he has
So much remembrance left, as to know you, sir;

He still[30] calls on you, nothing but your name
Is in his mouth: Is your pearl orient,[31] sir?
Corv. Venice was never owner of the like.[32]
Volp. Signior Corvino.
Mos. Hark.[33]
Volp. Signior Corvino.
Mos. He calls you, step[34] and give it him. H' is here, sir,
And he has brought you a rich pearl.
Corv. How do you, sir?
Tell him,[35] it doubles the twelfe[36] caract.[37]
Mos. Sir,
He cannot understand, his hearing's gone;
And yet it comforts him, to see you—
Corv. Say,
I have a diamant[38] for him, too.
Mos. Best shew't, sir,
Put it into his hand; 'tis only there
He apprehends: He has his feeling, yet.
See, how he grasps it!
Corv. 'Lass,[39] good gentleman!
How pitiful the sight is!
Mos. Tut[40], forget, sir.
The weeping of an heir should still be laughter,
Under a visor.[41]
Corv. Why? am I his heir?
Mos. Sir, I am sworn, I may not shew the will,[42]
Till he be dead: But, here has been Corbaccio,
Here has been Voltore, here were others too,
I cannot number 'em, they were so many,
All gaping here for legacies[43]; but I,
Taking the vantage[44] of his naming you,
(Signior Corvino, Signior Corvino)[45] took
Paper, and pen, and ink, and there I ask'd him,

Whom he would have his heir? Corvino. Who
Should be executor[46]? Corvino. And,
To any question, he was silent too,
I still interpreted the nods, he made
(Through weakness)[47] for consent: and sent home th' others,
Nothing bequeath'd them,[48] but to cry, and curse.
(They embrace)
Corv. O, my dear Mosca. Do's[49] he not perceive us?
Mos. No more than a blind harper.[50] He knows no man,[51]
No face of friend, nor name of any servant,
Who 't was that fed him last[52], or gave him drink:
Not those,[53] he hath begotten or brought up
Can he remember.
Corv. Has he children?
Mos. Bastards,[54]
Some dozen, or more, that he begot on beggars,
Gipseys,[55] and Jews, and black-moors,[56] when he was drunk.
Knew you not that, sir? 'Tis the common fable,[57]
The Dwarf,[58] the Fool, the Eunuch[59] are all his;
H' is the true father of his family,
In all, save me[60]: but he has giv'n 'hem nothing.
Corv. That's well, that's well. Art[61] sure he does not hear us?
Mos. Sure, sir? why, look you, credit[62] your own sense.[63]
The pox[64] approach, and add to your diseases,
If it would send you hence the sooner, sir.
For, your incontinence, it hath deserv'd it[65]
Throughly[66], and throughiy, and the plague[67] to boot.[68]
(You may come near, sir)[69] would you would[70] once close
Those filthy eyes of yours, that flow with slime,[71]
Like two frog-pits[72]; and those same hanging cheeks,
Cover'd with hide, in stead of skin: (nay, help, sir)[73]
That look like frozen dish-clouts,[74] set on end.[75]

Corv. Or, like an old smok'd wall, on which the rain
Ran down in streaks.[76]
Mos. Excellent, sir, speak out;
You may be louder yet: a culvering,[77]
Discharged in his ear, would hardly bore[78] it.
Corv. His nose is like a common sewer, still running.
Mos. 'Tis good! and what his mouth?
Corv. A very draught.[79]
Mos. O, stop it up —
Corv. By no means.
Mos. Pray you let me.
Faith, I could stifie him, rarely,[80] with a pillow,
As well as any woman, that should keep[81] him.
Corv. Do as you will, but I'll be gone.
Mos. Be so;
It is your presence makes him last so long.[82]
Corv. I pray you, use no violence.
Mos. No, sir? why?
Why should you be thus scrupulous? pray you, sir.
Corv. Nay, at your discretion.
Mos. Well, good sir, be gone.
Corv. I will not trouble him now, to take my pearl?[83]
Mos. Puh, nor your diamant. What a needless care
Is this afflicts[84] you? Is not all, here, yours?
Am not I here whom you have made your creature[85]
That owe my being to you?
Corv. Grateful Mosca!
Thou art my friend, my fellow, my companion,
My partner, and shalt share in all my fortunes.
Mos. Excepting one.
Corv. What's that?
Mos. Your gallant[86] wife, sir.
Now is he gone: we had no other means,

To shoot him hence, but this.[87]

Volp. My divine Mosca!
Thou hast today outgone thyself.

(Another knocks)

Who's there?
I will be troubled with no more. Prepare
Me music, dances, banquets, all delights;
The Turk[88] is not more sensual, in his pleasures,
Than will Volpone.[89] Let me see, a pearl?
A diamant? plate[90]? cecchines[91]? good morning's purchase[92];
Why, this is better than rob churches, yet:
Or fat,[93] by eating (once a month) a man.

....

Act III. Scene VII.

Mosca, Corvino, Celia[94], Bonario[95], Volpone.

Mos. Death on me![96] you are come too soon, what meant
you? Did I not say, I would send?

Corv. Yes, but I fear'd
You might forget it, and then they prevent[97] us.

Mos. Prevent? did e'er man haste so, for his horns[98]?
A courtier would not ply it[99] so, for a place.[100]
Well, now there's no helping it, stay here;
I'll presently[101] return.

Corv. Where are you, Celia?
You know not wherefore[102] I have brought you hither?

Cel. Not well, except[103] you told me.

Corv. Now, I will:
Hark hither ......
Nay, now, there is no starting back; and therefore,
Resolve upon it:[104] I have so decree'd.
It must be done. Nor would I move't[105] afore,
Because I would avoid all shifts[106] and tricks,
That might deny me.[107]

Cel. Sir, let me beseech you,
Affect[108] not these strange trials; if you doubt
My chastity, why lock me up, for ever:
Make me the heir of darkness. Let me live,
Where I may please your fears,[109] if not your trust.
Corv. Believe it, I have no such humor[110], I.
All that I speak, I mean; yet I am not mad:
Not horn-mad,[111] see you? Go to, shew yourself
Obedient, and a wife.[112]
Cel. O heaven!
Corv. I say it,
Do so.
Cel. Was this the train?[113]
Corv. I 'have told you reasons;
What the physicians[114] have set down; how much
It may concern me; what my engagements[115] are;
My means; and the necessity of those means,[116]
For my recovery: wherefore, if you be
Loyal and mine, be won,[117] respect my venture.[118]
Cel. Before[119] your honour?
Corv. Honour? tut, a breath;[120]
There's no such thing, in nature: a mere term
Invented to awe fools. What is my gold
The worse, for touching?[121] clothes, for being look'd on?
Why, this's no more.[122] An old, decrepit wretch,
That has no sense, no sinew;[123] takes his meat
With others' fingers; only knows to gape,
When you do scald[124] his gums; a voice; a shadow;
And, what can this man hurt you?
Cel. Lord! what spirit
Is this hath enter'd him?
Corv. And for your fame,
That's such a jig; [125] as if I would go tell it,

Cry it, on the piazza![126] who shall know it?
But he,[127] that cannot speak it; and this fellow,[128]
Whose lips are i' my pocket:[129] save[130] yourself,
If you'll proclaim't, you may. I know no other
Should come to know it.
Cel. Are heaven, and saints then nothing?
Will they be blind, or stupid?
Corv. How?
Cel. Good Sir,
Be jealous still[131], emulate them;[132] and think
What hate they burn with, toward every sin.
Corv. I grant you: if I thought it were a sin,[133]
I would not urge you. Should I[134] offer this
To some young Frenchman,[135] or hot Tuscan[136] blood,[137]
That had read Aretine,[138] conn'd[139] all his prints,
Knew every quirk[140] within lust's labyrinth,[141]
And were profest[142] critique in lechery[143];
And I would look upon him, and applaud him,
This were a sin: but here, 'tis contrary,
A pious[144] work, mere charity,[145] for physic,[146]
And honest polity,[147] to assure mine own.[148]
Cel. O heaven! canst thou suffer such a change?
Volp. Thou art mine honor, Mosca, and my pride,
My joy, my tickling,[149] my delight! go, bring 'em.
Mos. Please you draw near, sir.
Corv. Come on, what —
You will not be rebellious? by that light[150]—
Mos. Sir, signior Corvino, here, is come to see you.
Volp. Oh.
Mos. And hearing of the consultation[151] had,[152]
So lately, for your health, is come to offer,
Or rather, sir, to prostitute[153]—
Corv. Thanks, sweet Mosca.

Mos. Freely, unask'd, or unintreated[154]—
Corv. Well.
Mos. (As the true, fervent instance[155] of his love)
His own most fair and proper[156] wife; the beauty,
Only of price,[157] in Venice—
Corv. 'Tis well urg'd.
Mos. To be your comfortress, and to preserve[158] you.[159]
Volp. Alas, I'm past[160] already! pray you, thank him,
For his good care and promptness, but for that,[161]
'Tis a vain labour,[162] e'en to fight, 'gainst heaven;
Applying fire to a stone[163]: (uh, uh, uh, uh.)[164]
Making a dead leaf grow again. I take
His wishes gently, though; and, you may tell him,
What 'I[165] have done for him: marry,[166] my state is hopeless!
Will him,[167] to pray for me; and t'use his fortune,[168]
With reverence,[169] when he comes to 't.[170]
Mos. Do you hear, sir?
Go to him, with your wife.
Corv. Heart of my father![171]
Wilt thou[172] persist thus? come, I pray thee, come.
Thou seest 'tis nothing: Celia. By this hand,
I shall grow violent. Come, do't, I say.
Cel. Sir, kill me rather: I will take down poison,
Eat burning coals, do anything—
Corv. Be damn'd.
(Heart) I will drag thee hence,[173] home, by the hair;
Cry thee a strumpet,[174] through the streets; rip up[175]
Thy mouth, unto thine ears; and slit[176] thy nose,
Like a raw rotchet[177]—Do not tempt me,[178] come.
Yield, I am loth[179]—(Death)[180] I will buy some slave,[181]
Whom I will kill, and bind thee to him, alive;
And at my window, hang you forth: devising[182]
Some monstrous crime, which I, in capital letters,

Will eat into your flesh, with aqua fortis,[183]
And burning cor'sives,[184] on this stubborn breast.
Now, by the blood, thou hast incens'd,[185] I'll do't.
Cel. Sir, what you please, you may, I am your martyr.
Corv. Be not thus obstinate, I ha' not deserv'd it:
Think, who it is, intreats[186] you. Pray thee, sweet;
(Good 'faith) thou shalt have jewels, gowns, attires,[187]
What thou wilt think, and ask. Do but[188] go kiss him.
Or touch him, but. For my sake. At my suit.[189]
This once. No? not? I shall remember this.
Will you disgrace me, thus? do'you thirst my 'undoing?[190]
Mos. Nay, gentle lady, be advis'd.[191]
Corv. No, no.
She has watch'd her time.[192] God's precious,[193] this is skirvy;
'Tis very skirvy:[194] and you are—
Mos. Nay, good sir.
Corv. An errant[195] locust,[196] by heaven, a locust. Whore,
Crocodile[197], that hast thy tears prepar'd,
Expecting,[198] how thou'lt bid 'em flow.[199]
Mos. Nay, pray you, sir,
She will consider.
Cel. Would my life would serve[200]
To satisfy.
Corv. (S'death)[201] if she would but speak to him,
And save my reputation,[202] 'twere somewhat;[203]
But, spitefully to affect[204] my utter ruin.
Mos. I,[205] now you 'have put your fortune in her hands.
Why i' faith,[206] it is her modesty, I must quit[207] her;
If you were absent, she would be more coming;[208]
I know it: and dare undertake[209] for her.
What woman can, before her husband? pray you,
Let us depart, and leave her, here.
Corv. Sweet Celia,

Thou mayst redeem all,[210] yet; I'll say no more:
If not, esteem yourself as lost. Nay, stay there.[211]
Cel. O god, and his good angels! whither, whither
Is shame fled[212] human breasts? that[213] with such ease,
Men dare put off your[214] honours, and their own?
Is that, which[215] ever was a cause[216] of life,
Now plac'd beneath the basest circumstance[217]?
And modesty an exile made,[218] for money?
Volp.
(He leaps off from his couch)
I,[219] in Corvino, and such earth-fed minds,
That never tasted the true heav'n of love.
Assure thee, Celia, he that would sell thee,
Only for hope of gain, and that uncertain,[220]
He would have sold his part of paradise
For ready money, had he met a cope-man.[221]
Why art thou maz'd, to see me thus reviv'd?
Rather applaud thy beauty's miracle;
'Tis thy great work: that hath, not now alone,
But sundry times, rais'd me,[222] in several shapes,[223]
And, but[224] this morning, like a mountebank,[225]
To see thee at thy window. I, before[226]
I would have left my practice, for thy love,
In varying figures,[227] I would have contended
With[228] the Blue Proteus,[229] or the horned Flood.[230]
Now, art thou welcome.
Cel. Sir!
Volp. Nay, fly[231] me not.
Nor, let thy false imagination
That I was bedrid,[232] make thee think, I am so:
Thou shalt not find it. I am now as fresh,
As hot, as high,[233] and in as jovial plight,[234]
As when (in that so celebrated scene,

At recitation[235] of our comedy,
For entertainment of the great Valois[236])
I acted young Antinous[237]; and attracted
The eyes, and ears of all the ladies, present,
T' admire each graceful gesture, note,[238] and footing.[239]

Song.[240]

Come, my Celia, let us prove,[241]
While we can, the sports of love;
Time will not be ours, for ever,
He,[242] at length, our good[243] will sever;[244]
Spend not then his[245] gifts, in vain.
Suns, that set, may rise again:
But if, once, we lose this light,[246]
'Tis with us perpetual night.
Why should we defer[247] our joys?
Fame, and rumor are but toys.[248]
Cannot we delude[249] the eyes
Of a few poor household spies?[250]
Or his[251] easier[252] ears beguile,
Thus removed,[253] by our wile?
'Tis no sin, love's fruits to steal;[254]
But the sweet thefts to reveal:[255]
To be taken, to be seen,
These[256] have crimes accounted been.

Cel. Some serene[257] blast[258] me, or dire[259] lightning strike
This my[260] offending[261] face.

.........[262]

Cel. If you have ears that will be pierc'd[263]; or eyes,
That can be open'd; a heart,[264] may be touch'd;
Or any part, that yet sounds man,[265] about you:
If you have touch[266] of holy saints, or heaven,
Do me the grace,[267] to let me escape. If not,
Be bountiful[268], and kill me. You do know,

I am a creature, hither ill betray'd,[269]
By one,[270] whose shame I would forget it were.[271]
If you will deign me[272] neither of these graces,
Yet feed your wrath,[273] sir, rather than your lust;[274]
(It[275] is a vice, comes[276] nearer manliness)[277]
And punish that unhappy crime of nature,[278]
Which you miscall[279] my beauty: flay my face,
Or poison it, with ointments,[280] for seducing[281]
Your blood[282] to this rebellion.[283] Rub these hands,
With what[284] may cause an eating leprosy,[285]
E'en to my bones, and marrow: any thing,[286]
That may disfavour[287] me, save in my honour.[288]
And I will kneel to you, pray for you, pay down
A thousand hourly vows,[289] sir, for your health,
Report[290] and think you virtuous—
Volp. Think me cold,
Frozen, and impotent,[291] and so report me?
That I had Nestor's[292] hernia,[293] thou wouldst think.
I do degenerate,[294] and abuse my nation,[295]
To play with opportunity[296], thus long:
I should have done the act, and then have parley'd.[297]
Yield, or I'll force thee.
Cel. O! just God.
Volp. In vain—
(Bonario leaps out from where Mosca plac'd him)
Bon. Forbear,[298] foul ravisher, libidinous[299] swine,
Free the forc'd lady, or[300] thou diest, impostor.[301]
But that[302] I am loth to snatch thy punishment
Out of the hand of justice, thou shouldst, yet,
Be made the timely sacrifice of vengeance,[303]
Before this altar,[304] and this dross,[305] thy idol.[306]
Lady, let's quit the place, it is the den[307]
Of villainy; fear nought,[308] you have a guard:[309]

And he, ere long, shall meet his just reward.
　　Volp. Fall on me, roof,[310] and bury me in ruin,
Become my grave, that wert my shelter. O!
I am unmask'd, unspirited, undone,
Betray'd to beggary, to infamy—

(From *Ben Jonson*, Vol. V., ed. Herford and Simpson.)

【作者简介】 Ben Jonson（本·琼生 1572？—1637）是英国十六世纪末、十七世纪初的剧作家、诗人、演员、学者、批评家、翻译家、诗派的领袖。他的父亲是伦敦的一个绅士，后来当了牧师。琼生是在他父亲死后出生的，两年后母亲改嫁给一个砌砖建筑师傅（bricklayer）。琼生从小自食其力，入Westminster School，该校的副校长 William Camden 是一位古典文学的饱学之士，教导他并赡养他。中学毕业后，他继父不准他进大学，要他当砌砖的瓦工，他去当了兵，随英国军队到尼德兰（荷兰）参加尼德兰人反抗西班牙的战争，表现十分英勇。回到英国后，不过二十来岁，结了婚。五年后，同莎士比亚一样，他被剧团雇佣当了演员，修改剧本。他曾因决斗杀人被判死刑，但因是牧师之子而被赦免，左手拇指打上了犯罪的烙印。1598 年他的喜剧 *Every Man in his Humour* 上演，据说莎士比亚曾担任其中角色。1601 年 James I 继位，琼生发表侮辱苏格兰民族的言论，被投入监狱。此后他改信天主教，1605 年国会火药爆炸案发生，他受到怀疑。同年，他同 Marlowe, Chapman 合写的剧本 *Eastward Ho* 又有开罪国王的言论，都被投入监狱，他被割去一只耳朵，免于一死。他创作了大量诗歌、戏剧，参加笔战。到了晚年，他依附宫廷，得到了俸金，1616 年封为桂冠诗人。他在当时诗人、剧作家中威望极高，俨然成为文坛盟主。早年，莎士比亚、邓、培根等都是他的朋友，后来又有一批青年诗人奉他为领袖，自称 Sons of Ben 或 The Tribe of Ben。1616 年他出版了诗歌全集（*Works*），这在英国文学史上还是首次，前此没有一个作家在生前敢于如此妄自尊大。1616 年他停止了为公共剧场创作戏剧。1618 年他徒步去苏格兰旅行，会见诗人、历史家 Drummond，后者纪录下不少琼生的生平事迹。1637 年他死于贫困，但被隆重安葬于西敏寺，墓碑上刻着 O rare Ben Jonson 四个字。大体说来，琼生 1616 年以前的作品较有价值，后期作品多迎合宫廷贵族趣味，崇尚华丽。他的评论受古典文学理论影响，但很有见地。

【题解与注释】

作为诗人，琼生写过不少应酬之作，包括宴会场合的应景诗、赠友诗、序诗，此外还有散见于剧本或后期“假面剧”（masque）中的抒情歌曲，以及模仿罗马诗人的警句诗等。他的剧作，除了两部悲剧和后期的假面剧外，最成功的是喜剧，讽刺社会上一些道德风尚和现实界某些丑恶现象，其中以 *Volpone*（《狐狸》1606）为最好，其他还有 *The Alchemist*（《炼金术士》1610），*Epicoene*, or *The Silent Woman*（《沉默的女人》1609）。琼生同以后的巴尔扎克（Balzac）一样，认为人都受某种气质或情欲支配，他称之为 humour，如《沉默的女人》中的主角 Morose 的脾气就是怕声音，《炼金术士》、《狐狸》的主角的主导欲望则是贪婪。莎士比亚的喜剧富于浪漫色彩，琼生的喜剧则是讽刺的、现实主义的。总的说来，琼生的戏剧不及莎士比亚和马娄的那样具有深度。

1. Song to Celia (1616)

这是琼生一首有名的抒情诗，曾谱成音乐，可以歌唱。琼生自知写诗有的地方不如邓（参看关于邓的《简介》），有的地方又不如莎士比亚（参看下面的选诗）。的确他的诗无论从意象或思想看，都不及他们。但他的诗歌的特点在于明快，文字干净，说理确切，已有后来古典主义诗歌的兆头，这无疑是受希腊尤其罗马诗歌的训练所致。但他如果决定写一首时尚的情诗，尽管象“一只笨重的大象”“扭动它那柔软的鼻子”，他仍能写得很出色。

To Celia 赞美的是精神爱（Platonic love）。诗的大意是受公元二、三世纪希腊作家 Philostratus 的书信中某些词句的启发而得来的。此诗可以分为两段，每段八行，第二段重复第一段的乐调。

1. Celia ['siːliə]**:** 女子名。

2.（第 1 行）只须用你的眼睛向我“祝酒”，不必用酒。酒是物质的。祈使句，但也起条件从句作用—if，第 3 行同。

thine eyes, thine = thy 你的，eyes 以元音开始，所以改为 thine，取其辅音结尾。正如 eye 前不用 a 而用 an 一样。

3. pledge: = drink a toast 祝酒。

4. but: = only. 以吻代酒。

5. doth (does): 由于音节须要而用的垫词（expletive）非加重语气，以下 6，13 行同。

6. drink divine: = divine drink. 词序颠倒为了叶韵。

7. might I: = if I might.

8. sup: = sip，饮。

of，部分所有格 partitive genitive, = some of. 或竟把 of 略去，意义不变。

Jove's Nectar—Jove 即 Jupiter，天神的美酒。

9.（第 7—8 行）这两行诗可以解为：除非我能喝到天神的蜜酒，我决不用你的

‘酒’去换取任何其他东西；或，即使我能喝到天神的酒，我也不拿它换你的‘酒’。

10. late: = lately 不久前。

11. rosy wreath: 玫瑰花扎的花环。

12. honouring: = in order to honour.

13. that there … wither'd be: hope 的同位语。

there 指 with you，戴在你头上或颈上。

withered be: = be withered = wither 干萎。

14. But …: but if you merely breathe on it. 语气接第 10 行。

did'st breathe: 现在虚拟式，下行 sent'st 同。

15. since when: = after which time = then，起副词作用。

16. of itself, of thee: of 若与 grows 连用，of itself = by itself 自己生长；of thee = on account of you，由于你而生长。Of 与 smells 连用，of itself = 自身发出芬芳；of thee = 散发出你的芬芳，或由于你嗅了它的原故。

2. To the memory of … Mr. William Shakespeare …

To Shakespeare 这首诗发表在 1623 年（莎士比亚死后七年）出版的莎士比亚戏剧集第一对开本（The First Folio）的卷首（卷首还有琼生《致读者》和别人的题诗等）。这是一首纪念诗，琼生在这首诗里热情赞扬了莎士比亚，在一个作家之间、剧团之间相互竞争很厉害的时代，这样客观慷慨是难能可贵的。这不止是一首纪念或应酬诗，也是一篇文学评论，说理性强；以诗为文，启十七、八世纪古典主义诗歌之端。琼生的评论往往中肯，如 Marlowe's mighty line 的确成了千古定评。琼生评论的标准是“自然”，这也成为后来古典主义评论家所遵奉的圭臬。他称莎士比亚为 Soul of the Age; Not of an age but for all time，也成为名句。当然，他在别处也批评莎士比亚“缺乏艺术”，可能也是从古典主义崇尚琢磨的角度说的。此诗用的格律是 couplet，每行轻重音五步，每两行一叶韵。参看卞之琳译文，见《古典文艺理论译丛》3。此诗可分四段，见下面注释。

1. Mr.: = Master.

2. what he hath left us: 遗著。

1—16 行为第一段，引子，表明诗人反对什么样的“赞扬”。他曾说过，错误的地方被错误的人赞扬是极大的侮辱。

3. envy: 反映当时剧团之间、作家之间的竞争。这句话的意思是：我不是为了要招引别人的忌妒。

4. ample: = liberal 慷慨、大方。

5. Fame: 身后的令名。

6. Muse: 诗神，此处指诗人、作家；man 指一般人。

7. suffrage: = consent，这是人人同意的。

8. these ways: 指下面普通人赞扬莎氏的办法。

9. paths: = ways.

10. unto thy praise: in order to praise you.

7—12 行 对莎氏三种不同的称赞：1 出于无知，2 盲目爱戴，3 出于恶意，明褒暗贬。

11. seeliest: = silliest. 现代英语 silly < ME seely = happy > innocent > simple > poor > pitiful. 下译 "可怜的"。

12. light: = alight 降落到。"可怜的无知可能降落到你头上"，有的人称赞你，其实他们不了解你。

13. when it sounds at best: 即使说得天花乱坠。

14. but: = merely.

15. echo's: = echoes 动词，人云亦云。

16. advance: 推进。

17. gropes: 瞎摸。

18. urgeth [-iθ]**:** 两个音节。这半句下译 "乱捧"。

19. crafty Malice: "奸诈的恶意"。名词大写一般都是拟人化（personification）.

20. think: = intend.

21. Bawd, Whore: 娼妓。

22. Matron: 罗马喜剧、诗歌中常见的人物，正经的大户人家的主妇。

23. her: 指 matron.

24. proof against: 不怕。

25. them: 指上面那几类赞美者。

26. Above ... of them: 不怕他们带给你什么灾难，of= from.

27. or the need: = or above the need of them 也不需要他们的赞扬，of 属格。

17—42 行为第二段，把莎氏同古今诗人作家比较。

28. rise: 升到一个应有的崇高地位。

29. lodge thee by: = put you beside，把你葬在 Chaucer, Spenser 旁边，把你同他们相比。

30. bid ... further: 让 Beaumont 挪过去一点，给你让出一个空当儿。按：以上三个诗人都安葬在西敏寺内，莎氏则葬在自己故乡。当时有人写挽诗纪念莎氏，开头几句就作了上述安排，琼生这几句诗就是对此而发，他以为莎氏超出他们之上，不必同他们葬在一起——他们不能和莎氏同日而语。

31. without: 1. 没有埋葬在墓里，仍然活着（即 23 行的意思）；2. 不需要什么华丽的陵墓、外表的装饰。

32. art alive still: = will always live, will live on, so long as your book lasts. 参看莎氏十四行诗，如第 18 首 So long lives this and this gives life to thee. 艺术使人不朽是当时流行的新思想。

33. That I not mix thee so, my brain excuses: = My brain excuses that I do not mix you so. 我不把你同他们混为一谈是有道理的。这句诗的气势一直要贯注到 42 行，不愧为大家手笔。so 指下一句。

34.（第 26 行）这句诗解释上一句的 so.

great but disproportion'd Muses: 上述和以下那些诗人、作家是伟大的，但“比例不调”，即偏才，惟独莎氏是全才。

35.（第 **27—30** 行）把你和同时代作家相比。

of years: 按年代或时代来判断评比。

36. commit: = put you alongside with 把你和……比一比。

37. peers: 卞译“同辈的伙伴”。

38. Lyly (1554?–1606): 剧作家、传奇作家，以文体华丽著称，莎氏早期喜剧颇受他影响。

39. sporting: 卞译“淘气的”。Kyd 的作品十分肃穆壮烈，称不上淘气，这是用 Kyd 姓氏的含义（kid 羔羊）作文字游戏。这种一语双关的习气（punning 或 paronomasia）当时很流行，好象作家们忽然发现语言的奥妙，最突出的是法国拉伯雷。参看下面。

40. Kyd (1558–1594): 以其复仇剧《西班牙悲剧》著称，对莎氏也有影响。

41. Marlowe (1564–1593): 详见另篇。以上三家都对莎氏创作发展起过影响，在当时颇有声名，说莎氏超过他们是极大的恭维，但也符合实际。

42. small Latin and less Greek: 琼生当时以博学闻名，认为莎氏不大懂拉丁文，更不通希腊文，是个缺点。其实莎氏的拉丁文，据晚近评家的看法，还是很不错的，比现在西方受过教育的人高明得多。

43. from thence: 从这方面，即从古代文学中。

44. names: 指希腊、拉丁作家。我不想把你同大量的希腊、拉丁作家相比，只提几个重要作家吧。

45. thundering: 指他的诗铿锵如雷鸣。

46. Aeschylus ['iːskiləs]**:** 埃斯库罗斯。

47. Euripides [juə'ripidiːz]**:** 欧里庇底斯。

48. Sophocles ['sɔfəkliːz]**:** 索福克里斯。

以上是公元前五世纪希腊三大悲剧家。

49. Paccuvius, Accius: 公元前 2—1 世纪罗马悲剧家。

50. him of Cordova dead: 指公元一世纪罗马悲剧家塞内加（Seneca）。他出生于西班牙的科多瓦城，对英国此时悲剧发展产生很大影响。这是拉丁文短语结构，dead 形容 him “已故的科多瓦的他”。这种结构在密尔顿（Milton）诗中极多。

51. To life again: 接 33 行 call forth，把他们召回人间来听听……

52. Buskin: 古希腊、罗马演员穿的厚底靴。此处代表悲剧。

53. tread: 应是动词，在台上迈步的声音，与 shake 平行。

54. shake a Stage: 卞译“震动剧坛”。用姓氏作双关语又一例。大学才子剧作家格林（Robert Greene）出于嫉妒，临终前（1592）遗书警告同行要警惕那只“暴发的乌鸦”（指莎士比亚），说他自认为是 the only Shake-scene in a country（在国内独步剧坛）也是一例。

55. Socks: 古代喜剧演员穿的“轻履”，指喜剧。你的喜剧也超过古代。

56. Leave thee alone ... Of all: 卞译“就让你独自去和他们全体来比一比”。

for the comparison of all = to compare with all.

57. insolent Greece and haughty Rome: “骄希腊，傲罗马”这个著名的短语初见于塞内加，琼生在论培根时又用过。

58. since: = afterwards, in later time.

59. ashes: 指希腊、罗马已故诗人、作家。

60. come: 主语仍是 all that，指上述诗人的后代、后继者。

61. Scenes: 取拉丁文原意，舞台。

62. homage owe: = owe homage 应向莎氏膜拜。

43—65 行为第三段。莎氏之所以伟大在于他是“大自然”的一面镜子，艺术又高超。

63. not of an age: 意思是 not of one age only.

64.（第 43 行）这句诗也是经常被引用的。说得很对。

65. all the Muses ... in their prime: 诗歌（文艺）还在全盛时期，有两种可能的含意：当莎氏出现之时，就象回到了古代诗歌全盛的岁月；或当英国诗歌正在方兴未艾之时，莎氏出现而轰动一时。后一种解释更为可取。

66. Apollo: 希腊神话中的日神、文艺音乐之神、预言之神。

67. he: 指莎氏。

68. to warm our ears: 使我们听到天上的仙乐而感到温暖。

69. Mercury: 罗马神话中的神使，也是催眠催梦之神，故用 charm，使人入迷。

70. Nature: 自然女神经过他诗句的装扮感到欣悦。莎氏的作品非常真实，使人读了感到高兴愉快。

71. designs: 下译“心裁”。

72. since: = afterwards.

73. vouchsafe no other wit: 不屑于雇用其他有才的人（来为她裁制衣服了）。

74. merry Greek, tart Aristophanes: merry Greek 与 tart Aristophanes 同位。Aristophanes [ˌærisˈtɔfəniːz] 阿利斯托芬，公元前五—四世纪希腊喜剧家。

merry 轻松逗趣的。tart 尖刻的。

75. neat: 干净利落的。

76. Terence [ˈterəns]**:** 泰伦斯，公元前二世纪罗马喜剧家。

77. Plautus [ˈplɔːtəs]**:** 普劳塔斯，公元前三—二世纪罗马喜剧家。

78. gentle: 温和，高贵。

79. fashion: = shape 外形。他的作品的内容是“自然”，但没有艺术技巧，内容也就没有形式。

80. that: 连接词，前面省略了“I must say”之类的主句。

81. casts: = aims.

82. thine: = your lines 象你所写的那样的诗句（作品）。

83. strike: 与前一行 sweat 平行。

84. second heat: 打铁不能只趁一次热，要一而再地打。

85. anvil: 打铁砧。

86. turn: 与 strike 平行，转动那要锤打的铁活。

87. the same ... that: = the thing that，指铁活。

88. frame: 打成某种形状。

himself with it 铁活在你手里转动，你自己身体也随之转动。把创作比作打铁，极言其不易。

89. or: = otherwise，否则。下译"桂冠不上头，笑骂落一身。"

90.（第 64 行）也是名句，颠扑不破。罗马诗人贺拉斯（Horace）在《诗艺》（Ars Poetica）中有类似的意思。不过贺拉斯是天才和训练并重，琼生强调苦功（made）（as well as born 表示次要）。

65—80 行第四段写对莎氏的怀念，并表示相信莎氏身后之名是不朽的。

91. issue: 子孙，此处指这部戏剧集。把莎氏比作父亲，作品比作子嗣。

92. race: 族类、后代。此处指产物。

93. manners: = moral character 品质、品德、人格。

94. well turned [-id]**:** 以镟工为喻，磨得光润的。

95. true-filed [-id]**:** 锉平、锉光了的。语出贺拉斯《诗艺》limae labor et mora "花工夫花劳力去磨"。作品文字要经过琢磨才能发出光辉。以上四句的大意是，儿子似父，莎氏的作品也反映出他的思想和品质，在他的光辉的诗句之中。

96. which: 指 lines.

97. shake a Lance: 又是暗切莎氏的姓氏，手摇长矛。

98. as brandish't: = as if brandished 挥舞，摇动。

99. at ... Ignorance: 直指那些无知之辈。

100. Sweet Swan of Avon [ˈeivən]**:** 常被后人引用作为莎氏的别名。Avon 是莎氏家乡的河名。据希腊传说，音乐之神 Apollo 附在天鹅体内，因而天鹅善歌。另说，天鹅垂死，歌声最动听，指莎之遗作。Sweet，可爱的。

101. it were: = it would be.

102. appear: = to see thee appear 看到你出现在。

103. flights: 飞翔。

104. Thames [temz]**:** 泰晤士河，即前一行 our waters.

105. take: = please, delight.

106. Eliza [iˈlaizə]**:** 女王伊丽莎白一世。

107. James: 詹姆斯一世（1625 去世）。

108. Hemisphere: 半球。天球一半在地平线上，一半在其下，此处指上半，即天宇。

109. Advanc'd: 过去分词，升到。

110. Constellation: 星座，从天鹅联想而来，天上有天鹅星座。

111. rage: 如修饰 chide，为"猛烈"，如修饰 cheer，则为"热烈"。

112. influence: 一切天体、星宿对人都有影响。是 with 的宾语。

113. drooping Stage: 衰落的剧坛。戏剧更多供宫廷娱乐。1642 年清教徒封闭伦敦公共剧场。

114. which: 指 Stage.

115. flight: 指莎氏去世或指莎氏 1612 左右脱离舞台生涯。

116. despairs day: = loses hope of day.

117. but for: = except for 若不是（你的全集散发出光辉）。

118. Volume: 指这部全集。

3. Volpone (1606)

这出喜剧写一个威尼斯富翁 Volpone 贪财无餍，伙同他的仆人 Mosca 骗人财物。他没有子嗣，佯称将死，正在考虑遗产继承人问题，以此来引诱一批贪利之徒来奉承他，送他许多珍贵礼物，希望成为继承人。有的人剥夺了自己儿子的继承权，把 Volpone 选为继承人，以博得他的欢心；有的人把自己妻子献给他。主仆二人又商议散布流言说他已死，并已规定仆人为继承人，使那些送礼之人叫苦不迭。仆人想趁此机会弄假成真，但被人告发，受到法律制裁。

这出戏的骗子们一个比一个高强，写得很成功；作者把人们的贪欲"气质"写得淋漓尽致，结果聪明反被聪明误。他在给牛津和剑桥大学的献辞中说，作家应当洞悉人情世故（a master of manners），应当是个好人，应当是个导师，别人如果骂我尖刻，也在所不惜。

这出戏是严格按照三一律写的。地点是威尼斯一地，时间是一天之内，情节是单一的。这出戏除故事梗概外都用无韵诗写成。

琼生戏剧思想深度和语言的诗意都不及马娄和莎士比亚，但对现实生活的讽刺则首屈一指。

下面选的是一个完整的情节：Corvino 献妻。

1. Volpone [vɔl'pəuni]: 意大利文，大狐狸。琼生的人物的姓名多说明人物的性格（"气质"）。这种命名法从中古一直延续到十八世纪。

2. Argument: 故事梗概。这首诗每行第一个字母拼连起来就是剧名 Volpone，这种文字游戏叫 Acrostics.

3. feigns: 假装。

4. Parasite: 寄生虫，此处指仆人 Mosca。罗马喜剧中不可少的人物，多是食客、奴仆。

5. of all: = from all would-be heirs.

6. cross-plots: = perverse plots 刁钻、恶毒的诡计。

7. ope': = open 算一个音节，展现。

8. are told: 指将在剧中演出。

9. Each ... th' other: 彼此互相勾心斗角。

10. sold: 被出卖、揭穿。

Act I. Scene I. 写 Volpone 对金钱的膜拜。

11. Mosca: 意大利文，苍蝇（法语 mouche，拉丁文 musca），Volpone 的仆人。

12.（第 1 行）先向开始的一天道早安，再向金钱道早安。这种拜金思想的描写也见于马娄的《马耳他的犹太人》，莎士比亚《威尼斯商人》里的夏洛克。

13. shrine: 神龛，指藏金币的箱或匣，或舞台后台帷幕后的内室。

14. mine: = my soul 黄金是世界的灵魂，也是我的灵魂。

15.（第 3—7 行）I am more glad to view thy splendour than the teeming earth is to see etc.

16. teeming earth: 万物滋生的大地。

17. ram: 白羊星座，白羊有角故称 horns。这是太阳升起的方向。

18. thy: 指黄金。

19. his: 指太阳，his splendour 太阳的光辉。

Act I. Scene IV. 古典主义戏剧以在场人物的更动决定场次。

Corbaccio [kɔːˈbɑːʧiəu] 意大利文，大乌鸦，象征贪婪。是一个年老绅士，断绝了他儿子 Bonario 的继承权，立 Volpone 为嗣，希望他快死，就可吞掉他的遗产，又不失掉自己的产业。

20. a third: 指在 Corvino 到来之前已有贪婪的律师 Voltore [vɔlˈtɔːre]（秃鹫）和刚打发走的 Corbaccio 两起访客前来请早安送礼，连同 Corvino，一清早就来了三起客人。

21. close: = be still 安静。

22. again: = back to your bed 回到床上去。

23. Corvino [kɔːrˈviːnəu]**:** 意大利文，形容词，象乌鸦一样乌黑。

24. spruce: 衣冠楚楚。

25. Dead: = Say I am dead.

26. bout [baut]**:** 量词，一回、一次，指人在临死前涂油的宗教仪式。前此他已两次假装垂死，涂过油膏了。此处油涂在眼睛上。

Act I. Scene V.

27. Signior [ˈsiːnjɔːr]**:** 意大利文，先生。

28. come: = you are come.

29. tardy hour: 迟迟不到的时刻，死的时刻。

30. still: = constantly 不断地，下同，如 22 行。

31. orient: 光泽纯净。

32. Venice was never owner of the like: 一种修辞说法：象这样的明珠，威尼斯从未有过。

33. Hark: 听。

34. step: 走上前去。

35. Tell him: 对 Mosca 说的。

36. twelfe: 即 twelfth.

37. caract: 即 carat 克拉，宝石的重量单位。

38. diamant: 即 diamond 钻石。

39. 'Lass: = alas.

40. Tut: 古语，惊叹词，表示不同意，"去、去"。

41. visor: 中古骑士头盔上可以启闭的面罩。这句话的意思是继承人哭丧，明哭暗笑（"躲在面罩后哭"）。出自公元前一世纪罗马格言作家 Publilius Syrus.

42. I am sworn I may not ... the will: 我已起过誓不得把遗嘱拿出来。

43. gaping for legacies: 张着大嘴等待遗产。

44. vantage: = advantage 利用他呼唤你的名字的时候。

45.（第 30 行）括号内的台词是 Mosca 模仿 Volpone 的呼叫。32，33 行同。

46. executor: 遗嘱执行人。

47. Through weakness: Volpone 一个劲儿点头，是因为他体力衰退，我却把它理解为同意的表示。

48. Nothing bequeath'd them: 独立短语，什么也没有遗留给他们。

49. Do's: = does.

50. blind harper: 盲竖琴师，瞎子。

51. 第 39—42 行：据注家指出，出自罗马讽刺诗人朱文纳尔 Juvenal. 琼生熟悉古典文学，常从其中移植一些辞句到自己作品中来。

52. last: 上一次，谁喂他吃饭。

53. those: 他的子孙。他连自己的儿孙都记不得了。

54. Bastards: 私生子，没有继承权，用以安慰 Corvino，参看 49 行。

55. Gipseys: = Gypsies 吉卜赛人。

56. black-moors: 黑人。

57. fable: = subject of common talk 人人都说……

58. Dwarf: 侏儒，宫廷、贵族府邸多豢养侏儒以供取乐。

59. Eunuch ['juːnək]**:** 阉人。引自罗马诗人马希尔 Martial.

60. In all, save me: = all of them, except myself. 'hem= them.

61. Art: = Art thou, are you.

62. credit: = trust，不信你自己看吧。

63. sense: = eyes.

64. The pox: 天花。Mosca 骂 Volpone 给 Corvino 听。祈使句：May the pox approach.

65.（第 54 行）第一个 it 重复 incontinence，行为不检点。后一个 it，指 pox.

66. Throughly: = thoroughly.

67. the plague: deserv'd 的又一宾语。

68. to boot: = in addition, besides.

69.（第 56 行）括号内台词向 Corvino 说的。

70. would you would: = I wish you would. 向 Volpone 说的。

71.（第 57—59 行）引自朱文纳尔。

slime: 粘液。

72. frog-pits: 按朱文纳尔原诗，用蟾蜍内脏（viscus）进行占卜，viscus 又 =

womb.

73. nay, help, sir: nay，语气词，“喂，你不要闲着”。help “帮我骂他呀。”

74. dish-clout: = dish cloth 擦碗布。

75. set on end: 倒立着。

76. streaks: 条斑。

77. culvering: = culverin 大炮。

78. bore: 穿眼，打穿。

79. draught: 茅厕。

80. rarely: = splendidly, finely.

81. keep: 养（汉子）。

82. It is your presence makes him ...: 省略关系代词 that，以下 77 行等处同。

83. to take my pearl: 取回我的珠子。珠子攥在 Volpone 手里。

84. afflicts: 使……痛苦。是不是这不必要的担心使你痛苦？

85. creature: 您一手提拔起来的人。

86. gallant: = excellent.

87. but this: = except this 指除了想要染指其妻子的想法之外。

88. Turk: 土耳其人，在当时人心目中代表喜欢寻欢作乐的人。

89. Than will Volpone: = than Volpone will be (sensual).

90. plate: 银盘，是律师 Voltore 所赠。

91. cecchines: = sequins，古意大利金币。

92. purchase: 买卖、生意。

93. fat: 动词，发胖、长肉。

Act III. Scene VII. 写 Corvino 献妻的丑剧。

94. Celia: Corvino 的妻室。

95. Bonario: Corbaccio 之子。

96. Death on me!: 真要命！

97. prevent: 按此字原意：come before. 我怕他们会先我而来。

98. horns: 角，妻子与人通奸，其夫就被说成头上生角。

99. ply it: 寻求、恳求。

100. place: 官职。

101. presently: 马上、很快。

102. wherefore: 为什么。

103. except: = unless，故用虚拟语气 told.

104. Resolve upon it: 祈使句，下决心，作出决定。

105. move't: move it 提出。

106. shifts:（你的）诡计，花招。

107. deny me: 破坏我的计划。

108. affect: = make a show of 不要假装考验我了。

109. please your fears: 安抚你的疑心。

110. humour: 琼生的“气质”论，此处指疑虑情绪。

111. horn-mad: 原意象有角兽类被激怒那样发狂。此处双关：发狂；因妻子不贞而恼怒。

112. obedient, and a wife: 古代诗歌中一种一分为二的修辞手段（hendiadys），即 an obedient wife.

113. train: 诡计。

114. physicians: 医生。Corvino 要治病，治病要钱，把妻子献给 Volpone 就能得到遗产致富。

115. engagements: = commitments 债务。

116. means: 财产，指手头无钱。

117. be won: 听我的话，照我所说去做。

118. venture: 此处意为 hazard，危险处境，或冒险的计划。

119. Before: = above, in spite of，超出，不顾。

120. a breath: 荣誉不过是空话。莎士比亚《亨利四世》上篇福斯塔夫也有同样言论。

121. worse for touching: 我的金子，别人摸一摸，就不值钱了么？

122. this is no more: this 指下一句。这不过是个糟老头子。

123. sinew: 筋腱，精力。

124. scald: 烫。烫痛了他的牙床，他也只会张大了嘴（不会说话）。很形象。

125. jig: = farce. 不值一笑。

126. piazza: 意大利文，广场。

127. But he: = except him，指 Volpone.

128. this fellow: 指 Mosca.

129. whose lips are in my pocket: 我可以花钱买他的缄默。

130. save: = except.

131. be jealous still: = be always apprehensive, always fear heaven. 你随时都应防备上天的责罚。

132. emulate them: 学习圣徒们的榜样。

133.（第 57—66 行）Corvino 这段歪理、狡辩表现出琼生的戏剧讽刺才能。

134. Should I: = If I should，主句在 64 行：This were (would be) a sin.

135. Frenchman: 登徒子之流。

136. Tuscan: 意大利人，含意同上。

137. blood: 尤其 hot blood 常代表 passion 情欲。

138. Aretine [ˈæritiːn]**:** 即 Pietro Aretino (1492–1556) 意大利喜剧家、讽刺诗人，又以写艳情十四行诗著名。

139. con: 仔细阅读。

140. quirk: = sudden twist 弯、曲；扭动。

141. labyrinth: 迷宫。

142. profest (professed): critique 精通的行家。

143. lechery: 淫秽行为。

144. pious: 虔诚的、敬奉上帝的、合乎本分的。

145. mere charity: 纯纯粹粹的仁慈举动。

146. physic: = health 为了（Volpone 的）健康。

147. polity: = policy 权宜的做法。

148. mine own: = my own health.

149. tickling: 痒，一种快感 = pleasure, delight.

150. by that light: 赌咒语。

151. consultation: 医生的诊断。

152: had: 过去分词，修饰 consultation.

153. prostitute: 出卖……为妓，宾语 wife 在 78 行。

154. unintreated: 出于自愿。

155. instance: = proof.

156. proper: = his very own.

157. only of price: 连前一行 beauty，又是 Hendiadys 一例，= the only beauty of price 独一无二希世美人。

158. preserve: 保全你的性命。

159.（第 72—80 行）从 72 行开始的一句到此结束。

160. past: = beyond（cure），无可救药了。

161. but for that: = if not for that 如果不是他这样照顾我。

162. 'Tis a vain labour: = it would be a vain labour，要同天命斗争，那是白费气力的了。

163. applying fire to stone: 以火攻石，不可能。

164. uh: 咳嗽声。

165. 'I: 一个音节。

166. marry: 惊叹词。

167. will him: 请他。will 及物动词。祈使句。

168. his fortune: 指他将要继承的（我的）财产。

169. reverence: 敬爱的心情。

170. comes to it: 继承了产业。

171. Heart of my father: 向妻子咒骂。第 92 行，By this hand；第 96 行，Heart 等都是咒骂词。

172. Wilt thou: 此处 Corvino 不用 you，改用 thou, thee，口气变得严厉。

173. hence: = from this house.

174. Cry thee a strumpet: 向行人高声喊叫你是个婊子。

175. rip up: 撕破你的嘴，直到耳根。

176. slit: 划开、划破。

177. rotchet: 一种鱼。

178. tempt me: 惹我发火，引诱我犯罪。

179. loth (loath) [ləuθ]**:** 不愿。此句未说完。

180. Death: 也是咒骂。106 By the blood 同。

181.（第 100—105 行）大意是我去买个奴隶，把他杀了，把你活活地同他绑在一起，挂到窗外，在你胸前用镪水烫上大字，说你们想要图谋不轨。莎士比亚长诗《鲁克丽斯受辱记》中恶人塔昆也有类似的话（670—672 行）。

182. devising: 捏造，主语是"我"。

183. aqua fortis: 拉丁文，原意"镪水"，硝酸。

184. cor'sives (corrosives): 腐蚀剂。

185. incens'd: = incensed me 激怒了我，惹我发火。

186. intreats (entreats): 前面省略关系代词 who.

187. attires: 衣服。

188. but: = only.

189. suit: = request 请求。

190. thirst my 'undoing: = thirst after my undoing 渴望我完蛋吗？

191. be advis'd: 听他的话吧，放聪明点吧。

192. watch'd her time:（故意）窥伺时机（要我失败）。

193. God's precious: 赌咒语。

194. skirvy: = scurvy 卑鄙。

195. errant: = arrant 十足的、彻头彻尾的，从 errant（迷途的）变来。

196. locust: 一种瘟疫。"你真是个十足的瘟神。"

197. Crocodile: 鳄鱼，传说鳄鱼杀死人以后，先哭一通，然后吃掉。"你假装正经，其实是要害我。"

198. expecting: 等候时机。

199. how etc.: 修饰前一行 prepar'd，眼泪怎么个流法。

200. Would my life ...: = I wish my life ...

201. S'death: = God's death 咒骂语。

202. reputation: 明明是他要毁妻子的名声，反说她毁了他的名声。琼生善于发掘戏剧讽刺（dramatic irony）.

203. 'twere somewhat: = it would be something，这还象话。

204. affect: = effect, cause. 不定式短语常作为完整句子，省略的后半句无非是"真正岂有此理"之类的话。

205. I: = ay= yes.

206. Why i' faith (in faith): = Why, indeed.

207. quit: 原谅。

208. coming: = ready to meet advances, compliant，随和些。

209. undertake: 担保。

210. redeem all: 补救你的一切过失。

211. Nay stay there: 别动。他与苍蝇退下，Celia 也想一起走，他不准她动。

212. flee: 现在完成时。如 come 等动词，辅助动词用 to be. flee 作及物动词。= Has shame fled from human breasts?

213. that: = so that，如果从句。

214. your: 指上帝和天使。

215. that which: 指 shame，羞耻之心。

216 cause: 理由、目标。人应当有尊严，有荣誉感，这是人文主义者的一个信条。

217. basest circumstance: 暗指不如畜生。

218. modesty an exile made: = modesty is made an exile 被流放了。

219. I: = Ay.

Volpone 同 Corvino 本来是一丘之貉，却把自己放在 Corvino 对立面上，又是戏剧讽刺。earth-fed mind 象蛆虫一样的泥土俗流。

220. and that uncertain: that 指 hope of gain, (is) uncertain.

221. cope-man: = dealer 经纪人，善于做生意的人。

222. rais'd me: 使我起死回生。

223. sundry times ... in several shapes: 这些情节并未在剧中出现，剧本严守三一律，只演了 149 行提到的情节。

224. but: = only.

225. mountebank: 江湖郎中。本剧第二幕，在当天上午 Volpone 假扮江湖医生到广场吸引 Celia 到窗前，张罗卖药给她，被 Corvino 赶跑。

226.（第 150—153 行）大意是在我停止向你卖药（打交道）之前，我本想表演一些故事供你取乐。

227. In varying figures: 扮成各种人物。

228. contend with: 同……比赛变换相貌形状。

229. Blue Proteus: 是史诗《奥德赛》中的海上老人（故呈蓝色），能预卜未来，能变换形状，谁也捉他不住。

230. horned Flood: 希腊神话中的河神 Achelous，河有支流，故称 horned（长角的），他同大力神 Hercules 争夺加里冬王（King of Calydon）的女儿，几次变换形状，还是被打败。

以上两个掌故都是说 Volpone 本想扮不同角色。

231. fly: = fly from.

232. bedrid: = bedridden 因病卧床不起。

233. high: = high-spirited.

234. jovial plight: = joyous state.

235. recitation: 预演、演出。

236. Valois ['vælwɑ:]**:** 华洛瓦，法国王朝，此处指亨利三世（1551—1589）在 1574 年接到其父查理九世去世的消息，从国外回法国途中在威尼斯受到当地行政长官和元老的款待。160 行 our，因为 Volpone 是威尼斯人。

237. Antinous [ænti'nəuəs]**:** 公元二世纪罗马皇帝 Hadrian 的宠幸，年轻俊美。

238. note: 音。

239. footing: 台步、舞步。

240. Song: 这也是琼生一首著名的抒情诗，并谱成乐曲，也常被选进诗选。这首诗大部分内容取自罗马抒情诗人 Catullus.

241. prove: 体验、实践。

242. He: 指时间。

243. our good: 幸福、欢乐。

244. sever: 割断、疏远。

245. his: = love's.

246. this light: = love，把爱情比作太阳的光明。

247. defer: 推迟。

248.（第 175 行）不必考虑名声和流言蜚语。

249. delude: 骗过。

250. spies: 等于现在的私人侦探。罗马贵族、富翁派遣暗中监视女眷行动的耳目。

251. his: 指丈夫。

252. easier: 一种张冠李戴的修辞手法（hypallage），实际是 more easily beguile his ears by our wile 用我们狡猾更轻而易举地骗过他的耳目。

253. Thus removed: 修饰 ears，意为我们躲到一个他听不见的地方。

254. 'Tis etc.: It is no sin to steal love's fruits.

255. But the sweet thefts to reveal: But it is sin to reveal the sweet thefts.

256. These: 重复 to be taken 和 to be seen. 古代斯巴达人认为偷窃不犯罪，被人发现捉住才构成犯罪。这里沿用这个说法。

257. serene: 即法语的 serein，热带日落以后的毛毛雨，古人认为是对人有害的雾气。

258. blast: 动词，祈使句，摧毁。

259. dire: 可怕的。

260. This my: = this ... of mine. 早期英语语法。

261. offending: = harmful，给我带来灾难的。

262.（第 186—239 行）略。Volpone 继续同 Celia 纠缠。

263. be pierced 被打动，听得进（我的哀求）。

264. a heart: 后面略去关系代词 that.

265. that yet sounds man: 听起来还象一个人，还有点人的气息。人文主义者认为人应同禽兽有所区别，因此 Celia 的责骂是很重的。

266. touch: 一丁点儿。人不是兽，应当更接近神。

267. grace: = kindness 请你行行好。

268. bountiful: 请你开恩。

269. hither ill betrayed: 被骗到这儿。

270. one: 指她的丈夫。

271. it were: = it ever existed; it 可以理解为 the fact that I am betrayed.

272. deign me: = condescend to show me. 如果哪种恩典你都不肯赏给我（指放了

我或杀了我）。

273. feed your wrath: "满足你的怒气"，消怒，指 252—253 行所提供的办法。

274. feed your lust: 满足你的情欲。

275. It: 指 feeding your wrath.

276. comes: = that comes.

277. nearer manliness: 更象一点人干的事。强调人应有"人性"。

278. crime of nature: 大自然犯的罪，指下一句 my beauty. 上天赋予我美貌，使我遭到这样的不幸，无异是上天造孽。

279. miscall: 误称为，是一种忿怒讽刺口吻。

flay 剥皮。

280. ointments: 药膏，此处指毒药。

281. seducing: 勾引，引诱。

282. blood: 情欲。

283. rebellion: 违反天良的行为。

284. what: 指某种毒药。

285. eating leprosy: 腐蚀人体的麻疯病。

286. any thing: rub with any thing.

287. disfavour: 破坏相貌。

288. save in my honour: = except (that it is done) in my honour. 不过你破我的相应是为了保全我的荣誉（不是侮辱我）。反映人文主义者对人的尊严的重视。

289. pay down ... vows: 花钱请人每小时为你祈祷。

290. report: 向人们宣称（你道德高尚）。

291. impotent: 精力衰竭。

292. Nestor: 荷马史诗《伊利亚特》中希腊军最年老的统帅。

293. hernia: 疝气。

294. degenerate: 退化。

295. abuse my nation: 对不起我的民族，指威尼斯人。

296. play with opportunity: 拖延，不行动。

297. parley: 谈判。我应当先动手，后动口。

298. Forbear: 住手。

299. libidinous: 淫荡的。

300. or: 否则。

301. impostor: 骗子。

302. But that: = If it is not because 如果不是因为我宁愿让法律来惩罚你。

303. timely sacrifice of vengeance: 立刻把你宰了出出气。

304. altar: 祭坛。

305. dross: 渣滓。

306. idol: 偶像。以上三者统指内室和内室的藏金。

307. den: 狗窝。

308. nought: = nothing.

309. a guard: 指 Bonario 自己。

310. roof: 呼格。

6 THE ENGLISH BIBLE

The Old Testament

1. Genesis, Ch. I

2. The Song of Solomon

The New Testament

3. The Gospel According to St, John, Ch, I

4. 1 Corinthians, Ch. XIII

张谷若 选注

1. GENESIS

CHAPTER 1

In the beginning God created the heaven and the earth.[1]

2 And[2] the earth[3] was without form, and void; and darkness
was upon the face of the deep.[4] And the Spirit of God[5] moved
upon the face of the waters.[6]

3 And God said, Let there be light: and there was light.[7]

4 And God saw the light, that it was good: and God divided
the light from the darkness.

5 And God called the light Day, and the darkness he called
Night. And the evening and the morning were the first day.[8]

6 And God said, Let there be a firmament in the midst of the
waters, and let it divide the waters from the waters.

7 And God made the firmament,[9] and divided the waters
which were under the firmament from the waters which were
above the firmament: and it was so.

8 And God called the firmament Heaven. And the evening
and the morning were the second day.[10]

9 And God said, Let the waters under the heaven be gath-

ered together unto one place, and let the dry land appear: and it
was so.
10 And God called the dry land Earth; and the gathering to-
gether of the waters called he Seas:[11] and God saw that it was good.
11 And God said, Let the earth bring forth grass, the herb
yielding seed, and the fruit tree[12] yielding fruit after his kind,[13]
whose seed is in itself, upon the earth: and it was so.
12 And the earth brought forth grass, and herb yielding
seed after his kind, and the tree yielding fruit, whose seed was in
itself, after his kind: and God saw that it was good.
13 And the evening and the morning were the third day.
14 And God said, Let there be lights[14] in the firmament of
the heaven to divide the day from the night; and let them be for
signs,[15] and for seasons, and for days, and years;
15 And let them be for lights in the firmament of the heaven
to give light upon the earth: and it was so.
16 And God made two great lights; the greater light to rule
the day, and the lesser light to rule the night: he made the stars
also.
17 And God set[16] them in the firmament of the heaven to
give light upon the earth,
18 And to rule over the day and over the night, and to divide
the light from the darkness: and God saw that it was good.
19 And the evening and the morning were the fourth day.
20 And God said, Let the waters bring forth abundantly the
moving creature that hath life, and fowl that may fly above the
earth in the open firmament of heaven.[17]
21 And God created great whales,[18] and every living crea-
ture that moveth, which the waters brought forth abundantly, af-
ter their kind, and every winged fowl after his kind: and God saw
that it was good.
22 And God blessed them, saying, Be fruitful, and multiply,
and fill the waters in the seas, and let fowl multiply in the earth.

23 And the evening and the morning were the fifth day.
24 And God said, Let the earth bring forth the living crea-
ture after his kind, cattle, and creeping thing, and beast of the
earth[19] after his kind: and it was so.
25 And God made the beast of the earth after his kind, and
cattle after their kind, and every thing that creepeth upon the
earth after his kind: and God saw that it was good.
26 And God said, Let us make man[20] in our image, after our
likeness:[21] and let them have dominion over the fish of the sea, and
over the fowl of the air, and over the cattle, and over all the earth,[22]
and over every creeping thing that creepeth upon the earth.
27 So God created man in his own image, in the image of
God created he him; male and female created he them.
28 And God blessed them, and God said unto them, Be fruit-
ful, and multiply, and replenish[23] the earth, and subdue it: and
have dominion over the fish of the sea, and over the fowl of the
air, and over every living thing that moveth upon the earth.
29 And God said, Behold, I have given you every herb bear-
ing seed, which is upon the face of all the earth, and every tree, in
the which is the fruit of a tree yielding seed; to you it shall be for
meat.[24]
30 And to every beast of the earth, and to every fowl of the
air, and to every thing that creepeth upon the earth, wherein there
is life, I have given every green herb for meat: and it was so.
31 And God saw every thing that he had made, and, behold, it
was very good. And the evening and the morning were the sixth day.

2. THE SONG OF SOLOMON

CHAPTER 1

The Song of songs, which is Solomon's.[1]
2 Let him kiss me with the kisses of his mouth:[2] for thy love
is better than wine.[3]

3 Because of the savor of thy good ointments thy name is as ointment poured forth,[4] therefore do the virgins love thee.

4 Draw me,[5] we will run after thee:[6] the King hath brought me into his chambers:[7] we will be glad and rejoice in thee, we will remember thy love more than wine: the upright love thee.

CHAPTER 2

8 The voice of my beloved! behold he cometh leaping upon the mountains, skipping upon the hills.

9 My beloved is like a roe or a young hart: behold, he standeth behind our wall, he looketh forth at the windows, showing himself through the lattice.

10 My beloved spake, and said unto me, Rise up, my love, my fair one, and come away.

11 For, lo, the winter is past, the rain is over and gone;

12 The flowers appear on the earth; the time of the singing of birds is come, and the voice of the turtle[8] is heard in our land;

CHAPTER 8

6 Set me as a seal upon thine heart, as a seal[9] upon thine arm: for love is strong as death; jealousy is cruel as the grave: the coals thereof are coals of fire, which hath a most vehement flame.

7 Many waters cannot quench love, neither can the floods drown it: if a man would give all the substance of his house for love, it would utterly be contemned.[10]

3. ST. JOHN

CHAPTER 1

In the beginning was the Word, and the Word was with God, and the Word was God.[1]

2 The same[2] was in the beginning with God.

3 All things were made by him[3]; and without him was not

any thing[4] made that was made.
4 In him was life;[5] and the life was the light[6] of men.[7]
5 And the light shineth[8] in darkness; and the darkness[9] com-
prehended[10] it not.
6 There was a man[11] sent from God,[12] whose name was John.
7 The same came for a witness[13], to bear witness of the
Light, that all men through him might believe.
8 He was not that Light, but was sent to bear witness of
that Light.
9 That was the true Light, which lighteth every man[14] that
cometh into the world.[15]
10 He was in the world, and the world was made by him,
and the world knew him not.[16]
11 He came unto his own,[17] and his own received him not.
12 But as many as received him, to them gave he power[18]
to become[19] the sons of God,[20] even to them that believe[21] on
his name:[22]
13 Which were born, not of blood,[23] nor of the will of the
flesh,[24] nor of the will of man,[25] but of God.
14 And the Word was made flesh,[26] and dwelt among us, (and
we beheld his glory,[27] the glory as of[28] the only begotten of the Fa-
ther,)[29] full of grace and truth.[30]
15 John bare witness of him, and cried,[31] saying, This was
he of whom I spake,[32] He that cometh after me is preferred before
me[33]; for he was before me.[34]
16 And of his fulness have all we received,[35] and grace for
grace.[36]
17 For the law was given by Moses, but grace[37] and truth
came by Jesus Christ.[38]
18 No man hath seen God at any time;[39] the only begotten
Son, which is in the bosom of the Father, he hath declared[40] him.
19 And this is the record of John,[41] when the Jews sent
priests and Lē´vītes[42] from Jerusalem to ask him, Who art thou?

20 And he confessed, and denied not;[43] but confessed, I am
not the Christ.[44]
21 And they asked him, What then?[45] Art thou Ē-lī´ăs?[46] And
he saith, I am not. Art thou that Prophet?[47] And he answered, No.
22 Then said they unto him, Who art thou? that we may give
an answer to them that sent us. What sayest thou of thyself?
23 He said, I am the voice of one crying in the wilderness,
Make straight the way of the Lord, as said the prophet Ē-ṣā´ịăs.[48]
24 And they which were sent were of the Phăr´Ĭ-sēeṣ.[49]
25 And they asked him, and said unto him, Why baptizest thou
then, if thou be not that Christ, nor Ē-lī´ăs, neither that Prophet?
26 John answered them, saying, I baptize with water: but
there standeth one among you, whom ye know not;
27 He it is, who coming after me is preferred before me,
whose shoe-latchet[50] I am not worthy to unloose.
28 These things were done in Bĕth´-ăb´ȧ-rȧ[51] beyond Jor-
dan,[52] where John was baptizing.
29 The next day John seeth Jesus coming unto him, and
saith, Behold the Lamb of God,[53] which taketh away the sin of
the world![54]
30 This is he of whom I said, After me cometh a man which
is preferred before me; for he was before me.
31 And I knew him not:[55] but that he should be made mani-
fest[56] to Ĭṣ´rā-ĕl, therefore am I come baptizing with water.[57]
32 And John bare record,[58] saying, I saw the Spirit descend-
ing from heaven like a dove,[59] and it abode upon him.
33 And I knew him not:[60] but he that sent me to baptize with
water, the same said unto me, Upon whom thou shalt see the Spir-
it descending, and remaining on him, the same is he which bap-
tizeth with the Holy Ghost.
34 And I saw, and bare record that this is the Son of God.[61]
35 Again the next day after,[62] John stood, and two of his dis-
ciples;

36 And looking upon Jesus as he walked, he saith, Behold
the Lamb of God!
37 And the two disciples heard him speak, and they followed
Jesus.
38 Then Jesus turned, and saw them following, and saith
unto them, What seek ye? They said unto him, Răb´bī,[63] (which is
to say, being interpreted, Master,) where dwellest thou?
39 He saith unto them, Come and see.[64] They came and saw
where he dwelt, and abode with him that day: for it was about the
tenth hour.[65]
40 One of the two which heard John speak, and followed
him, was Andrew, Simon Peter's brother.
41 He first findeth his own brother Simon, and saith unto him,
We have found the Mĕs-sī´ăs,[66] which is, being interpreted, the Christ.
42 And he brought him to Jesus. And when Jesus beheld
him, he said, Thou art Simon the son of Jō´nȧ: thou shalt be called
Çē´phăs, which is by interpretation, A stone.
43 The day following Jesus would go forth into Galilee, and
findeth Philip, and saith unto him, Follow me.[67]
44 Now Philip was of Bĕth´sā´ĭ-dȧ, the city of Andrew and
Peter.
45 Philip findeth Nȧ-thăn´ā-ĕl, and saith unto him, We have
found him, of whom Moses in the law,[68] and the prophets,[69] did
write, Jesus of Nazareth,[70] the son of Joseph.
46 And Nȧ-thăn´ā-ĕl said unto him, Can there any good thing
come out of Nazareth?[71] Philip saith unto him, Come and see.
47 Jesus saw Nȧ-thăn´ā-ĕl coming to him, and saith of him,
Behold an Ĭş´rā-ĕl-īte indeed,[72] in whom is no guile!
48 Nȧ-thăn´ā-ĕl saith unto him, Whence knowest thou me?
Jesus answered and said unto him, Before that Philip called thee,
when thou wast under the fig tree, I saw thee.
49 Nȧ-thăn´ā-ĕl answered and saith unto him, Răb´bī, thou
art the Son of God; thou art the King of Ĭş´rā-ĕl.

50 Jesus answered and said unto him, Because I said unto thee, I saw thee under the fig tree believest thou?[73] thou shalt see greater things than these.

51 And he saith unto him, Verily, verily,[74] I say unto you,[75] Hereafter ye shall see heaven open, and the angels of God ascending and descending upon the Son of man.[76]

4. 1 CORINTHIANS

CHAPTER 13

Though I speak with the tongues of men and of angels,[1] and have not charity,[2] I am become as sounding brass, or a tinkling cymbal.

2 And though I have the gift of prophecy,[3] and understand all mysteries, and all knowledge; and though I have all faith, so that I could remove mountains,[4] and have not charity, I am nothing.

3 And though I bestow all my goods to feed the poor,[5] and though I give my body to be burned, and have not charity, it profiteth me nothing.

4 Charity suffereth long,[6] and is kind;[7] charity envieth not;[8] charity vaunteth not itself, is not puffed up,[9]

5 Doth not behave itself unseemly, seeketh not her own,[10] is not easily provoked,[11] thinketh no evil;

6 Rejoiceth not in iniquity, but rejoiceth in the truth;

7 Beareth all things, believeth all things, hopeth all things, endureth all things.

8 Charity never faileth:[12] but whether there be prophecies,[13] they shall fail; whether there be tongues, they shall cease; whether there be knowledge, it shall vanish away.

9 For we know in part,[14] and we prophesy in part.

10 But when that which is perfect is come, then that which is in part shall be done away.

11 When I was a child, I spake as a child, I understood as a

child, I thought as a child: but when I became a man, I put away
childish things.[15]
12 For now we see through a glass, darkly; but then face to
face: now I know in part; but then shall I know even as also I am
known.[16]
13 And now abideth[17] faith, hope, charity, these three; but
the greatest of these is charity.

【作者简介】《圣经》(*The Bible* 或 *The Holy Scriptures*)由两部分组成:(1)《旧约》(*The Old Testament*);(2)《新约》(*The New Testament*)。《旧约》除极少例外的章节，都是用希伯来文（Hebrew）写的。《新约》则是用希腊文写的；不过这种希腊文，和希腊古典文学中所用的那几种都不同，而是由此发展的一种特别希腊文，叫做犹太希腊文（Judæo-Greek）或亥伦尼斯提克希腊文（Hellenistic Greek）。《旧约》译成别种文字，最古老、最重要的叫做 The Septuagint 的希腊文译本。Septuagint 为希腊文，意为 70，这是因为据传说，其书由 72 名犹太人译成。全部《圣经》译为别种文字之最重要者为拉丁文译本，叫做 *The Vulgate*，即通行本之意。这种译本一直为公教（Catholic Church，通称天主教）所用。

《圣经》译为英文，始自第 8 世纪，但都只是一些片断。1382 年后所译而叫做《维克利夫圣经》(Wyclif's Bible）的译本，虽为全帙，并未通行（直至 1850 年始有印本）。到了宗教改革时期，应时势之要求，英文译本才多起来。到了 1611 年，叫做《钦定圣经》(*Authorized Version*）者出，英文圣经始定于一，至今通行。所以叫它是“钦定”，只因此本曾经英国国王詹姆斯第一（James I）指令，用它代替以前所用之英译本，在教堂作礼拜时作诵读之用。

《钦定圣经》以《廷兑勒氏圣经》(*Tyndale's Bible*，出版于 1525—1534 年）及《克菲兑勒氏圣经》(*Coverdale's Bible*，出版于 1535 年）为主要底本，参考 1611 年以前其它英译本、马丁·路得之德文译本、希腊文、拉丁文译本及希伯来文与犹太希腊文原本，实集以前译本之大成而成书。至 1881 年及 1885 年出版之《修订本英文圣经》(*Revised Version*）影响不大。此外新近尚有译本及个人译本。兹不备述。

16、17 世纪，英文译本圣经问世后，其对英人在社会、政治、道德、思想各方面之影响，读 John Richard Green 之 *A Short History of the English People* 第 8 章，可窥见一二。这里只略谈英文圣经，特别是钦定圣经，对英国文字、文学方面之影响。

英国语言学家 Henry Bradley 在他的 *The Making of English* 一书里说，“对近代英语之形成有贡献之作品中，圣经之翻译，自 16 世纪末期之廷兑勒与克菲兑勒至 1611 年之钦定圣经，占有重要之地位。”他举出 beautiful 一字为例。他说，“象 beautiful 这样一个至为熟悉而决不可缺的字，在廷兑勒以前不知道有任何人用过。这个字决不是廷兑勒所造，但是毫无疑问，却是由于他在圣经里用了这个字，这个字才普遍流行起来。”这一个例子可概括其它的例子，Bradley 这个话可以代表别家英国语言学家或语言史家的意见。英国论文家及历史家 T. B. Macaulay 则说，“假使所有用英文写的东西全都毁灭了，而只剩下《英文圣经》这一部书，那这部书自己就足以把英文里全部的美与力显示出来。”英国文学史家 George Saintsbury，在他的《伊丽莎白时代文学史》(*Elizabethan Literature*) 里对此书有更详细的分析与高度的赞扬(他对《修订本圣经》则极贬抑)。至于只读了一部《圣经》而就成为文学家、能写出《天路历程》(*The Pilgrim's Progress*) 那一类书的班扬 (John Bunyan)，则更是尽人皆知。S. H. Butcher 与 A. Lang 等人译荷马时，采用了 Biblical English。

总之，《英文圣经》对英美人的日常生活，对他们的文学所有的影响，是不可估计的，因此也就是研读英美文学的人所必不可少的参考书。

但是《钦定英文圣经》，究竟是三百多年以前的产物，其中有的语法、词汇现象，现在已不通行。而且它既是由翻译而来，而原希伯来文又太古老，文字讹误在所不免，加以它的内容，既属异族，又属异代，今日读之，困难自必不少，故有注释之必要。但其牵涉方面太广，古文字且不论，而对于近代科学，如天文学、地质学、人类学、生物学，以及宗教史、社会史、犹太史，等等，注者皆门外汉，故谫陋之讥，诚所不敢多让，而剽窃之诮，亦且聊以分谤。

现在选《旧约》第一卷《创世纪》第一章，《雅歌》第一、二、八章各节，《约翰福音》第一章及《哥林多前书》第十三章，只可尝鼎一脔。

【题解与注释】

1. GENESIS.

Genesis 原为希腊文，有“原本”、“开始”、“形成”、“创造”等意。*The Septuagint Version* (简写作 The LXX Version) 用以称《旧约》第一卷，拉丁文译本及英文译本因之，汉译《创世纪》。本卷言天地或宇宙之开辟，人类始祖之创造，希伯来族家长制时期之历史，等等。其全名为 *The First Book of Moses, Called Genesis*，因为据传说，其书为摩西所写。但据后来学者研究结果，其实作者非一人，非一时，非一本，主要编辑工作约始于纪元前第 8 世纪，写定于纪元前第 6 世纪。为世界上记载一民族神治（Theocracy）时期社会最完整之作。大凡每个民族都经过这样一个社会时期，不过其时期有长短，势力有大小，方式有不同。但其记载之完整，则恐无过于《旧约》。古代希伯来族，尤其是记叙这个时期社会史的人，是否真信、尽信所记为事实，非此简介所能明，但后来人对于神之看法，则有 Pantheism, Atheism, Deism，等等。其中最极端者为英国 17 世纪之 Ranters，他们目摩西为骗子。这不过只举一例，说明在近代科学发达以前，就已有人指出“神治”时期，最多也不过是“神道设教”而已。但是“神”的影响，至今并不能说阴魂完全已散。不过稍有科学常识者，决不会相信有神。

现在所选的为《创世纪》第一章，内言上帝于六日内创造天地万物。自从地质学、天文学兴起后，特别是达尔文的《物种原始》问世后，《创世纪》里的说法，已从根本上被推翻，虽当时曾有“卫道之士”，与达尔文学说之拥护者之间，引起了一场剧烈的争辩，但到后来，即使教会中人，也不相信这一套，而只认为这是古代希伯来人对于宇宙和万物之起源的看法而已。

On the Sublime 的作者 Longinus，在他那篇文章的第 9 章第 9 节里，指出《创世纪》的头几节，认为表现神灵的伟大光辉，那就是范例。那里说的当然是希伯来文原本，但也适用于英文译本。

第一章

第 1 节　1. In the beginning God created the heaven and the earth: 这一句是总叙，后面第 2 节到第 10 节才分别细叙 the heaven and the earth 是由什么创造出来的，是怎样创造出来的。这里虽只 heaven 和 earth 二字，实则包括了当时所看到而认识的全部世界，等于英语中的 time and space，相当于汉语中的宇宙（上下四方谓之宇，往古来今谓之宙，见《淮南子》）。古人没有抽象概念，只有具体概念，故以 heaven 与 earth 表示时间与空间。（宇宙之为上下四方，往古来今，亦非本意，而为引申意，可参阅《说文解字》。）

In the beginning:《约翰福音》第一句 In the beginning was the Word 之 in the beginning 据此而来，但意义不同。此处之 in the beginning 只表示宇宙之起点，在此起点之时间内，上帝有所行动。在《约翰福音》中之 in the beginning 则说，起始时 the Word 已存在，是 the Word 之存在先于 the beginning，故彼处之 in the beginning 一般解释为等于 before the world was，含有 eternity 之意，是超时间的。这就表示，同样一个词，因前后文不同而意义即不尽同。

God: 古希伯来人所奉者为一神，此处一开始，径直认定上帝之存在，不作任何臆测与推论，此为希伯来人之宇宙创造说（cosmogony）不同于其他民族之处。其他民族之宇宙创造说，如巴比伦、腓尼基、古埃及等，多先之以神族谱系（Theogony），古希腊诗人 Hesiod 之 Theogony 为其中之最著者。希伯来人对于神的概念为：神具无限之力（omnipotence）与慧（omniscience）等等。英人接受这种概念，故 god 一字在英语中，为 emotive word, significant and pregnant，所以英国现代文学批评家 John Middleton Murry 说，英人一听到 god 一字，心中即起种种感情。至于此字前面一般不用定冠词（definite article），其理由据 Otto Jespersen 说，“［英语中］有些字被看作是专有名词…（他把它归到 quasi-proper names，而 quasi-proper names 又属于 articles 的第三类）。God 既为基督教徒…惟一的 god，则其被视为专有名词固甚自然。”但此字在某种情况下，也用定冠词。正象 heaven 和 earth 二字，与此相反，一般用定冠词，the heaven, the earth，而在某种情况下则又不用（参看 Jespersen 或 Christophersen）。

第 2 节　这一节追叙宇宙创造以前的光景。

2. And: 在这儿是 introductory，用以连结前句或前段，前句可表明，也可省略。甚而在英语中，有时一书或一章一开始即有用 and 者。不过在圣经里，这种 and 用得特多，这是由于保存原文形式之故。

3. earth: 这儿的 earth，按照下文所说，是淹没在 waters 之中的（比较《诗篇》第 104 首 第 6 节，Thou coverest it [the earth] with the deep as with a garment）。既是这样，所以说 without form and void。waters 是从希伯来文直译过来的，用以表示水之广漠浩淼、渺迤漫衍。凡属 Semitic 语系之文字（希伯来文为此系之一支），皆用一字之复数形式，以加强该字单数形式所表之意。在英语中，表示流动不息之河水或后浪逐前浪之海水，亦用 waters（如 see the children sport upon the shore, And hear the mighty waters rolling evermore — Wordsworth; The cataract hurled Its headlong waters from the height — Longfellow），和这儿的 waters 相似。但那种用法既都说的是河、海之类，当然不能和这儿的 waters 混而为一。至于 waters 在 mineral waters, still waters, troubled waters, table waters，以及 cross the waters, drink the waters，则都更应别论。

4. the deep: 这个字在《旧约》里，一般用以表示 the Ocean。按照希伯来人的概念，the Ocean 周环世界，并充满 earth 下面的巨洞。但在此处，则用以表示太古洪荒之时，在黑暗中 waters 渺茫无际、深不可测的混沌景象，而注意点在深，故拉丁文以 abyssi，英文以 the deep 译之。

5. the Spirit of God: Spirit 原文有二意：（1）本意，风、气；（2）比喻意，精神、灵。希伯来人的观念，黑暗之中所以有光、无生之物所以有生，都是上帝之气所赋予的。但是这种气的功能、运用，是无形的，是不可抗拒的，故为精神、为灵。以古代人缺乏抽象观念而论，则以 Spirit 为气、风，更合。但这儿的 Spirit 却决不能与后来三位一体（Trinity）中之圣灵（The Holy Spirit 或 Holy Ghost）混而为一。

6. moved upon the face of the waters: 亦译作 was brooding upon the waters，这给人一种鸟展翼覆于巢上的形象。Milton 就采取了这种解释，所以他在 *Paradise Lost* 第 1 卷第 19—22 行说：

… thou from the first
Wast present, and with mighty wings outspread,
Dove-like sat'st brooding on the vast abyss

And mad'st it pregnant: …

在第7卷第233—237行又说：

Matter unformed and void. Darkness profound
Covered the abyss; but on the watery calm
His brooding wings the Spirit of God outspread,
And vital virtue infused, and vital warmth
Throughout the fluid mass, …

这一句表示，圣经文字就其原希伯来本意而论，可有不同解释，但此与屈从经义于教义而牵强附会以解释经文者绝然不同。必须分别清楚。

这一节虽极简质，却把希伯来人想象中天地尚未开辟之前的景象，极形象化地传达了出来。直至近代，法人讲天文的作者，写到星际，一片黑暗，无边无际，其邈远不可思议，尚能令人起一种 awful 之感，何况古代。希伯来人这种想象，更优于其他民族。例如巴比伦神话，说，大神 Marduk 斩龙（dragon），分其体为二，一部为天，一部为地。中国神话则说，天地混沌如鸡子，盘古生其中，一万八千岁，天日高一丈，地日厚一丈，盘古日长一丈。试把这两种想象和希伯来人的想象相比较，优劣自见。

第3节　7. And God said, Let there be light: and there was light: 这里的第二个 and 是用来 introduce a consequence，和第一个 and 之只为 introductory 者不同。上帝只要一发话，结果天地万物立即出现。《诗篇》第33首第6节和第9节说，"By the word of the Lord were the heavens made … For he spake, and it was done; he commanded, and it stood fast，"正是此处的注脚。

第5节　8. And the evening and the morning were the first day: 我们说，日夜、朝夕，英语也说 day and night, morning and evening，都是先说日、朝，后说夜、夕。此处为什么却说 the evening and the morning？原来希伯来人的一日，从 evening 算起，他们的一日是 6 p. m. 到 6 p. m.

第7节　9. firmament: 普通的意思是 vault of heaven with its clouds and stars，相当于汉语之"穹窿"。但是希伯来人并无"天积气耳"或天是 an infinite ethereal space 的概念。在他们的概念中，穹窿是有实体的拱形结构，覆于地上（地是平的），有柱支撑。《约伯记》第38章第18节说，… the sky which is strong as a molten mirror，就是指着这种 firmament 说的。因为是实体，所以才能把 waters 分开，且在 firmament 上面也有水，这种水是渟滀于天上的蓄水库里的，为雨露等之源，下雨等等即把天上的水门或窗户打开而来。英语 firmament 是由拉丁文 firmamentum 沿袭而来，但这两个字都没能把希伯来文表示这种现象的意思传达出来。这说明译事时有所穷。

第8节　10. 在前面和后面，每创造一样东西，都要跟一句 and God saw that it was good，这里没有这一句，应是原希伯来文本漏掉。

第10节　11. Seas: 希伯来人概念，地周围环海（如中国之瀛海，古希腊之 oceanus），且与地下渟滀之水相通（江河泉水所自出），故用复数，以表示其广大、汪洋，且包括所有不同的部分。这种用法和英诗中此字之复数用法相似，如 the multitudinus seas (Shakespeare)，magic casements，opening on the foam of perious seas (Keats)。

比较 the high seas, the four seas, the seven seas 等及上文之 waters。

第 11 节　12. grass ... herb ... and the fruit tree: 这儿可有两种解释：(1)植物界有三种，the grass, the herb, the tree。(2)grass = vegetation，植物界总称，总称下分两类，the herb 与 the fruit-tree.

13. after his kind: his = 现在的 its, kind 是 collective。这一词组 = according to their various species。修订本圣经把 after his kind 改为 after its kind，把 whose seed is in itself 改为 wherein is the seed thereof。

第 14 节　14. Let there be lights: 这儿的 lights，和前面的 light 不同，light 是光，lights 是发光体，日、月、星等。

天体（日、月、星）之创造，后于植物之创造，这当然很怪。注释家有两种解释。(1)六天创造之中，以每三天为一阶段，而每一阶段都以创造 light 开始，不过 light 为两类，一类属于 elemental，一类属于 sidereal。另一种解释是：所创造之物，以有生命、能运动的程度大小定先后。日月星辰亦按固定秩序活动运行，其活动之程度虽远不及动物，却远胜过植物，故列之于二者之间。古代人认为无生命的东西也有生命，在古希腊神话中表现为山、林、泉、石各自有神，在更原始的民族中，表现为拜物教，在语言中，如拉丁文、希腊文、德、法等文中，表现为无生命之物之名词也都有性别。

15. signs: 可能指星座而言（constellations），特别是 signs of the zodiac（汉语叫黄道带或黄道十二宫）。这是古巴比伦人就已有了的东西，而西洋人后世还用以表岁时，如 Chaucer 在 *Canterbury Tales* 的 General Prologue 里，一开始就说 The yonge sonne Hath in the Ram his halve cours yronne (= The young sun has run its half-course in the Ram)。The Ram（汉语叫白羊宫）即十二宫之第一宫。又此处只说大发光体（the greater light）、小发光体（the lesser light），而不说 the sun, the moon，因 the sun, the moon 为偶像迷信崇拜之对象，故避免之。Lesser 为 double comparative，意思与 less 同，但用法不同，lesser 只能用作定语，也就是说，用作形容词，放在名词前面。同时，less 用于 degree, value，或 amount，与 more 相对。这个字主要用于 collective nouns，或 nouns denoting a mass or abstract whole。如说 less money, less noise, less appeal, the moon yields less light than the sun。Lesser 是说 not as great, as important, or less significant as that with which the thing so qualified is compared。如说 a lesser person, woman is the lesser man (Tennyson)。The lesser light 即属于这一类。可与前 the moon yields less light 作比较。

第 17 节　16. set: = placed。希伯来人的概念是，日月星辰是嵌在实体的穹窿内部凹处，每一个发光体都有它自己的地位，并按一定的径路移动。比较后来 Ptolemy 之 sphere 说。

第 20 节　17. the fowl that may fly above the earth in the open firmament of heaven: Fowl 是 collective，在这儿等于 winged things，除了鸟类，还包括 bats, butterflies, beetles 等。Fowl 这种意思到 17 世纪时已废。连 fowl = bird 也都变为 archaic。现在这个字只用来表示某种家禽，如 barn-door fowl (= domestic cock or hen)，且多与它字连用，如 guinea-fowl, water-fowl 等。In the open firmament of heaven，正确

的译法应为 in front of，就是说，in midair, in front, as it were, of the solid firmament of heaven, which was not remote. The winged creatures would continually be visible against the sky.

第 21 节　18. great whales: 修正本改作 great sea-monsters.

第 24 节　19. living creature ... and creeping thing, and beast of the earth: living creature 是总说，cattle and creeping thing and beast of the earth 是分说。Cattle = all domestic animals, including oxen, cows, sheep, horses, asses, camels。现在 cattle 则只限于 bovine animals（牛属），特别是 ox。Creeping thing 不限于 snakes and lizards，并包括小动物，如昆虫等。The beast of the earth = wild beasts，别于 domestic animals。这一句里的 creature, creeping thing 和 beast，都和 cattle 一样，是 collective。Cattle 直到现在，还是复数。

第 26 节　20. man: 在这儿表示 mankind generally，所以后面跟 them。man 包括男女，所以第 27 章说，male and female created he them。关于 man 用于 generic sense，参看 Otto Jespersen, *A Modern English Grammar,* Vol. II. 5. 411。不过他所举的例句里没有这儿这一句。

Let us make man。这里的 us 是有名费解的"疙瘩"之一。这种用法见于《旧约》者，还有三处。在许多解释之中，我们在这儿只选择其中比较最合理的两种：（1）把这种用法看作是 the plural of Majesty。如国王自称为 we，而不用 I，似汉语之"朕"（据说此制已由现英女王伊丽莎白第二之父乔治第六废止）。（2）把这种用法解作是 the plural of Deliberation，亦即用这种方式表示庄重严肃。如把 Let us make man in our own image，改作 Let me (or I will) make man in my own image，而加以比较，则差别自见。

21. In our image, after our likeness: 在这一句里，第一要注意，在创造别的动物时，只说 after its kind（各自为类），而创造人时，则依上帝之形体。第二，In our image, after our likeness 二词组，意义有无分别？有人说，前者较永久，后者较短暂；又有人说，image 表示形体与本质，形貌与精神，likeness 只是外表相似。我认为不必加以区分；这是希伯来文的一种表达方式，即一事而用两个意义相同的词组或句表示（如汉语之骈偶）。这是希伯来文特点之一，尤其多见于含有诗歌性质的文字里。

22. and over all the earth: 应为 over all the beast of the earth，原希伯来文中 the beast of 漏掉了。

第 28 节　23. replenish: = fill。

第 29 节　24. meat: = food。此意现已变为 archaic。

从这一段里，可以看出，上帝让人吃的只是草长的种子（粮）和树结的果子，这也就是说，要人素食，让动物也只食草和树叶。这是古希伯来人相信，人类有一个时期是天真的，不杀生的，野兽也都没有互相残杀的，象中国人想象中的无怀氏、葛天氏之民，欧美人的 golden age。《以赛亚书》第 65 章第 25 节说，"狼与羔羊要同食，狮子和牛一样，只吃草，"这是想回到或复现这种理想的世界。R. Kipling 在 *The Second Jungle Book* 的故事 How Fear Came，也是根据这种理想世界而写的。

2. THE SONG OF SOLOMON, CHAPTER 1, VERSES 1–4; CHAPTER 2, VERSES 8–12; CHAPTER 8, VERSES 6–7.

《旧约》的一部分为诗歌。这些诗歌有的很短，一首一首，散见于各卷之中。另有的则是以类相从，辑为一卷，《诗篇》(The Book of Psalms) 即属此类。《雅歌》(The Song of Solomon) 亦为诗歌而辑为一卷者，但其性质在《圣经》中，则独树一帜，几与其它所有部分都绝然不同。盖《圣经》各卷，几无一不与宗教有关——亦即与神有关，而《雅歌》则独言人事——男女之爱（此据近代之解释）。

《雅歌》之列入'经'(canon) 中，为时最晚，其所以得列入'经'中，从第一世纪前，犹太法学家以寓言诗解释之，即把其中所歌咏的男女之爱，解释为上帝与其人民之间之爱。初期基督教作家，继此精神，又把歌中之新郎解释为基督，而以新娘为基督教会或教会之灵魂。以寓言方式解释经典或诗歌，为古今中外所通行，但这须看原作者是否采用了寓言式。这是一个很复杂的问题，应分别对待。对《雅歌》作寓言解释，即便在这种解释最盛行之时，都曾有人提出反对意见，这当然是当时所绝不许可的。所以到了宗教改革之后，新教教徒才把《雅歌》从桎梏中解放出来，圣经学者才承认了《雅歌》本来所有的自然性质。

但是这种依《雅歌》本来所有的自然性质解释《雅歌》，意见也并非一致。有人认为，这一卷书只是一些零散的情歌，辑在一起。另一种人则以戏剧解释之，把各节各段分为对话，派给不同的脚色。第三种解释，则以为这些章节，是古犹太人在举行婚礼期间及前后，新娘、新郎及伴娘、伴郎所唱的'催妆诗'。还有其它说法。这些说法，虽各有其道理，但也都有窒碍难通之处，故不能说有最后定论。现在在这三段选注中，头一段用'催妆诗'解释，第二、三段则用自成段落的情歌解释。

《雅歌》既为诗歌，原来当然为有节奏之文字（英语谓之 measured beat and strophic rhythm）。英文用散文译之，但亦保存了一些原文的风格，不过其风格仍属散文，其节奏亦为散文节奏（prose rhythm）。（散文节奏，不同于诗的节奏，在英文散文中如出现诗的节奏或韵文节奏，则为疵瑕。）前所选之《创世纪》，文体风格属于庄严典重一派，此所选《雅歌》，则属于清新妍美一类，内容既绝然不同，文体风格因亦迥异。

第一章

第 1 节　1. The Song of songs, which is Solomon's = the best of songs which is Solomon's，说此歌为 Solomon 所作，当然是后人所加。作者为无名氏。这是原始或古代诗歌之通例，不知作者为谁。这类诗歌多属集体创作。

第 2 节　2. Let him kiss me with the kisses of his mouth: kiss 之意为：以唇紧接某处，所以表示敬、爱，成相逢之喜、相别之凄等等，其所接之处则因性质不同而异。如表尊敬则吻足，表相逢之喜则吻颈等等。此处特表明 kisses of his mouth，当然是表示爱，以别于它处。

第2节前半说 let him，后半又说 for thy (= your) love，似指两人，实则一人。所以用不同代名词，有两种解释：一种是把前半中之 him 改为 you，使全句皆为女直呼男而告之之词。另有人则认为，男并不在面前，只是女心中所想，故前半以 him 呼之。但其心中所想者非常强烈，直觉其人如在面前，故由前面之 him 变而为 thy。

3. for thy love is better than wine: 比较本卷第4章第10节：'How much better is thy love than wine!'

第3节　4. thy name is as ointment poured forth: 比较 Ecclesiastes（《传道书》）第7章第1节，'a good name is better than precious ointment.'

第4节　5. Draw me: 比较 Hosea（《何西亚书》）第11章第4节，'I drew them with cords of a man, with bands of love.' 又 St. John's Gospel（《约翰福音》）第12章第22节，'and I, if I be lifted up from the earth, will draw all men unto [= to] me.'

6. We will run after thee: thee = you. 比较 Psalms（《诗篇》）第119篇第32节，'I will run the way of thy commandments.'

7. the King has brought me into his chambers: 比较 Psalms 第45篇第14—15节，'She (= the king's daughter) shall be brought unto (= to) the king … The virgins her companions that follow her shall be brought unto thee … They shall enter into the king's palace!' 这儿 the king，要是依此诗歌为结婚期间之'催妆诗'的说法，则为新郎。因在此期间，新郎称为 the king，而新娘称为 the queen。

现依'催妆诗'之解释，把这几节安排如下：

新娘对还未来到的新郎倾吐爱情：
Let him kiss me with the kisses of his mouth,
For thy love is better than wine.
Because of the savour of thy good ointments
Thy name is as ointment poured forth,
Therefore do the virgins love thee.

新娘第二次对新郎表示爱情，同时伴娘们与之应答：
新娘：Draw me. 伴娘：We will run after thee.
新娘：The king hath brought me into his chamber.
伴娘：We will be glad and rejoice in thee.
We will remember thy love more than wine.
新娘：The upright love thee.

以下另选两段自成段落的。

第二章

第12节　8. the turtle: = the turtle-dove.

第八章

第 6 节　9. 第二个 seal: = seal-ring，象手钏，戴于腕上。

第 7 节　10. it would utterly be contemned: 等于说 the attempt to buy off the tender passion would prove useless.

3. THE GOSPEL ACCORDING TO ST. JOHN

Chapter I.

《新约》极简括言之，可分为两部分，第一部分，即四福音书，记耶稣基督之生死及教导，第二部分记基督教由耶稣门徒及使徒初期建立及传布之经过。而在四福音书中，《约翰福音》有别于其前之三福音书。前三福音书一般总称之为 Synoptic Gospels，而《约翰福音》则单独称之为 Johannine Gospel。因前三福音书，即《马太福音》(St. Matthew's Gospel)、《马可福音》(St. Mark's Gospel)、及《路加福音》(St. Luke's Gospel)，彼此间虽小有不同，而其皆记载耶稣基督之生死言行，则并无二致，《约翰福音》之别于前三福音者，以其除记载耶稣之言行而外，且含有辩护之性质，故包括神学、哲学之论叙。盖《约翰福音》在四福音书中，问世最晚（约作于纪元后 75 年以后），其时只讲一些耶稣表面上的行动言论，已不足使人信服，必须讲出一番大道理来，才能抓住信徒，驳倒敌人。圣约翰即本此意而写此书。其写此书之目的可用他自己的话来说明：These have been written that ye may believe that Jesus is the Christ, the Son of God, and that believing ye may have life in his name（本书第 20 章第 31 节）. 人称圣约翰是基督教神学之祖，就是因为他在这卷书里阐述了要人相信基督的道理。

神学，简单地说，是论述神之本质与属性及其与人和宇宙之关系的学问。一涉及神，且不管有神无神之辩如何，即主张有神论者，其主张亦各派不同，虽似皆持之有故，但皆不免要含 mysticism 意味，而所谓 mysticism 即 belief in spiritual apprehension of truths beyond the understanding，这也就是说，是一种超理智——非理智可解——的精神作用。而英国宗教著作家圣保罗大教堂堂长 William Ralph Inge 则说 The Gospel of St. John is the charter of Christian Mysticism。这样说，似不应该选《约翰福音》里这一章书了。殊不知现在选这一章，就是因为这一章里具有上面所说的性质。这第一是因为:《圣经》既为宗教经典，当然讲的是神，而最能表示出这种经典的特点来的，《约翰福音》至少得算是其中之一。所以不读《圣经》则已，要读《圣经》，则读了这一章，不失为尝鼎一脔，'可'知其味。第二是因为，学英语和研读英国文学的人，应该知道英国文学中有这样一种文章；而且有由这一种文章演绎出来的另一种文章——讲道文（sermon）；讲道文在英国文学史上是占有一席之地的，而且其中也真有好文章，只举一例，如 17 世纪神学作家 Jeremy Taylor 的 *Holy Living* 与 *Holy Dying* 即是。而现在选这一章，除了前面所举的原因而外，还因为《约翰福音》，特别是其中的第 11 章、第 14 章和 15 章，在英国乡村田舍中更是家传户诵，同时英诗人 William Wordsworth 说过，我对《圣经》，特别是《约翰福音》，作了宗教方面的沉思冥想，于是我的信念，就如烟云之轻渺，同时又象金刚之坚固，自然而然就轩翥高举。更因为这一卷书的文章，刚劲有力，庄严朴质，明白畅达。《英国公祷书》(Book of Common Prayer) 里的‘洗礼文’、‘婚礼文’、‘葬礼文’等，无不从此书而出。尤其是一开始那几节，可与《创世纪》相比，同样表现了阳刚之美。至于信仰问题一开始那几节不是此处所讨论的，更不是此处所能尽的，当然不在话下。

第 1 节——第 18 节为全章之导言。

第 1 节　1. In the beginning was the Word, and the Word was with God, and the Word was God: The Word 原为希腊文 ὁ λόγος（o 为定冠词，o 上之 ʽ 表示 h 音）由 λόγος 译为拉丁 Verbum，又由 Verbum 译为英文 The Word。但不论 Verbum，也不论 The Word，都不能传达原文之 λόγος（此为译事有所穷之另一例）。因希腊文 λόγος 一字，不但有‘话’、‘言’、‘语’等意，还有“用语言所表达之意义及道理”之意。汉语用‘道’译之，也只能说译了这个字的一方面。这个希腊字，本是希腊哲学家用过的。柏拉图用它来表示‘神之智慧之显现’。斯多噶学派用它来表示‘宇宙精神内在之力’。（这当然不会概括确切，不过表示希腊哲学家曾用过此字而已。）而在《创世纪》第 1 章里，言上帝创造天地万物之时，只要上帝一‘说’如何如何，事物便如何如何，是上帝之‘言’已含神之意志和能力的表现。在《诗篇》第 33 篇第 6 节里，说‘By the word of the Lord were the heavens made, and all the host of them by the breath of his mouth’；第 107 篇第 20 节说‘He sent his word and healed them’；别的地方，也有同样的说法。在《箴言》第 8 章和第 9 章，则把 Wisdom 完全拟人化。是以犹太人概念中早已有把 Word 视为上帝代表之概念。同时在耶稣生活、传道时期，犹太人又发展了另一种概念，认为上帝不应和人世直接接触，他与人之间应有一媒介。这样，λόγος 一字，既为人所已熟悉，又含有神之意志、力量与智慧之意，又已成为拟人化，适可作神与人之媒介，故圣约翰采用了这个字，而更使它具体化，使之成为 the Will of God manifested in personal action，把它看作和神是二为一，故与宇宙同其长久，同其广大，又一为二，故为耶稣，为神之子。这样，无限（the infinite）与有限（the finite），亦即神与人，也就成了二而一、一而二了。

这种解释，是把圣约翰用这个字的原因、用意，及其用此字所表示之意义最简括地陈叙出来。我们也可以用另一种方式，即寓言式方式（allegorically）来进行解释。这种方式，本来常为讲圣经的人所采用，但他们用得往往不见得恰当，象《旧约：雅歌》选注里所已经说过的那样。

17 世纪荷兰犹太哲学家斯宾诺莎的《论宗教与政治》(*Tractatus Theologico-Politicus*) 一书，主旨在说明，《圣经》中所用的语言，是有意地使用了寓言式或比喻式的。这种提法，现在虽然变得平淡无奇，但用这种方式——寓言式——来解这里 λόγος 这个字，还是有其作用。古犹太人数经亡国，城毁人散，留在故国者，受到罗马皇帝和犹太总督的双重压迫，犹太人自己的僧侣等上层阶级又愚昧朽腐，起义又失败，受到残酷镇压，人民处于水深火热之中，对此世已绝望，自然希望有一个公正、仁慈、坚强的上帝，来主宰世界，但这好象又难实现，于是有一个人出来，言上帝之言，行上帝之行，教世人以天国之道，那这个人岂非上帝之化身，岂非上帝的儿子？所以所谓 λόγος 者，只是一个人，有上帝之精神能力，象上帝的人而已。但又何必采用 λόγος，说耶稣是神的儿子呢？欲对此作解释，还是引用斯宾诺莎较好。他说，先知及门徒是对全民、全人类传播他们的主义的，故其内容一定得适应普通大众的智力。他们的目的，并非启发人的理解力，使之信服，而是鼓动人的想象力使之信仰。所以我们简单地说，上帝之灵或精神，是空虚飘渺，视而不见的，故使群众信服，必使之具体化，于是具体化到耶稣这个人身上（犹太教和基督教绝对不许有偶像），而人又太平常，不足令人生畏起敬，尊崇供奉，于是又把人——即耶稣——神化。

In the beginning: 解释已见《圣经》选注《创世纪》第 1 章。

was: 这儿的 was，还有下面 was with God 之 was，从语法上讲，都是 substantive be; the Word was God 的 was 是 copulative。从意义上讲，这个 was = was already in existence before the creation of the world。比较《箴言》第 8 章第 22—23 节，The Lord possessed me [= Wisdom] in the beginning of his way, before his works of old. I was set up from everlasting, from the beginning, or ever the world was.

with God: = with the Father.

The Word was God: The Word partook of the Divine *nature*, not was identical with the Divine *Person*. 这一句总起来可解释为，the logos [= the Word] existed from all eternity, distinct from the Father, and equal to the Father.

第 2 节　**2. The same:** = He or This (Word), with emphasis. 这一节是把前一节总括起来重叙一遍。

第 3 节　**3. by him:** = through him. The universe was created by the Father through the agency of the Son.

4. not any thing: = not even one; stronger than 'nothing'. Every single thing, however great, however small, throughout all the realms of space, came into being through Him.

第 4 节　**5. In him was life:** He was the well-spring from which every form of life—physical, intellectual, moral, spiritual, eternal—flows.

6. the light: the one true light; absolute truth both intellectual and moral, free from all ignorance and all stain.

7. the light of men: Man shares life with all organic creatures, light is for him alone. Everything could in its measure reveal God: the inanimate world His power and divinity, all animate beings His indwelling life, and man His light, the power to see and show forth moral goodness and spiritual truth.

第 5 节　**8. shineth:** note the present tense. It brings people down to St. John's own day: now, as of old, the light shines—in reason, in conscience.

9. the darkness: By darkness is meant all that the Divine Light does not reach. 'Darkness' is used here in a metaphorical sense for spiritual and moral darkness.

10. comprehended: The darkness remained apart, unyielding, and unpenetrated. 或 Light shines in Darkness, and Darkness, instead of yielding and dispersing, shuts it out. 比较本书第 3 章第 19 节，And this is the condemnation, that light is come into the world, and men loved darkness rather than light, because their deeds were evil.

第 6 节　**11. There was a man:** There arose a man. He arose, came into existence, in time.

12. sent from God: because he was a prophet. 比较 Malachi，第 4 章第 5 节，'I will send Elijah the prophet.'

第 7 节　**13. for a witness:** to bear witness.

第 9 节　**14. every man:** not 'all men' : the Light illumines each one singly, not all collectively. God deals with men separately as individuals, not in masses.

15. That cometh into the world: a Jewish phrase for being born.

第 10 节　**16. and the world knew him not:** and = and yet. 不过要注意 and 比 and yet 更有力量。比较本章第 5 节 'and the darkness comprehended it not' 和本章第 11 节 'and his own received him not'，那两个 and 与此处之 and 相同。

第 11 节　**17. He came unto his own:** i. e. into his own country. 第二个 his own = his own people ('own' used absolutely = one's own property, kinsfolk, friends, or whatever is implied in the context; somewhat archaic except in some phrases).

第 12 节　**18. power:** right, privilege, liberty, authority. People are born with a *capacity* for becoming sons of God; that they have as men. He gives them a *right* to become such; that they receive as Christians.

19. to become: Christ is from all eternity the Son of God, men are empowered to become sons of God.

20. the sons of God: 现在说 children of God. Both St. John and St. Paul insist on the fundamental fact that the relation of believers to God is a filial one.

21. even to them that believe: Explains who are the sons of God. The test of a child of God is belief in God's Son.

22. on his name: 普通说 to believe in，但在 16 世纪时，to believe in 与 to believe on 一般本无分别，只在《圣经》中，believe on 用得比 believe in 较多，而圣约翰用得更多，二者遂微有别，即 believe on 语气更重。故在此处表示 the strongest belief. 至 to believe God 和 to believe in or on God 之分别则为：to believe God is to believe what God says to be true. To believe in or on God expresses not belief only, but the motion to and repose on God. 至于 name，解者谓 names were so significant that a man's name told not merely who he was, but what he was: it was an index of character. So the 'Name of the Lord' is not a mere periphrasis for 'the Lord'; it suggests His attributes and His relations to us as Lord. 不过这种解释似还不够透彻。原来古代有的民族相信一个人的名字就是那个人的生命、灵魂，故咒骂一个人欲其死，即呼其名而咒之，其人即能死。此中国古代所以有'讳'之一说，就是因为怕人之呼其名而咒之（此说见 Ogdon & Richards 合写之 *Meaning of Meaning*）。

第 13 节　**23. Which were born, not of blood:** which = 现在的 who. not of blood: the blood was regarded as the seat of physical life.

24. nor of the will of the flesh: nor from any fleshly impulse.

25. nor of the will of man: nor from the volition of any earthly father. St. John denies thrice that human generation has anything to do with Divine regeneration. Man cannot become a child of God in right of human parentage. 简单言之，人为父母所生，但只凭这一点，并不能成为上帝之儿女。成为上帝之儿女是精神或灵魂之再生，须信仰耶稣才可做到。

第 14 节　26. And the Word was made flesh: was made = became. The Logos [= the Word], existing from all eternity with Father（第 1 节及第 2 节）, not only manifested His power in creation（第 3 节）and in influence on the mind of men（第 9，12，13 节），but manifested Himself in the form of a man of flesh.《圣经》解释家说，在 'The Word became flesh' 这个简短的句子里一下表示出来 The union of the Infinite and the Finite. 即神与人之结合。这是神学家的解释。换一种说法，也就是 the Incarnation of Christ，即基督本为上帝之化身，现又显而为肉体之人身。

27. his glory: 这儿这个 glory 的意思，和它普通的意思不一样，等于希伯来文的 Shekinah（也作 shechinah），上帝出现之时或所在之处所显现的威仪光辉。

28. as of: = exactly like.

29. the only begotten of the Father: The only son really and truly born of God. This marks off His unique Sonship from that of the 'sons of God.'

30. full of grace and truth: Grace here, in its distinctly theological sense, means the *favour* of God towards sinners. It has for its central point the *freeness* of God's gifts: they are not earned, He gives them *spontaneously* through Christ. 'Truth' means not only truth of teaching about God（比较第 4 章第 23 节，But the hour cometh, when the true worshippers shall worship the Father in spirit and in truth；又第 8 章第 32 节，And ye shall know the truth, and the truth shall make ye free；又第 16 章第 13 节，… when he, the Spirit of truth, is come, he will guide you into all truth），but also *reality* —everything was real about Him, and He made our lives real（比较第 6 章第 32 节，Then Jesus said unto them, Verily, verily, I say unto you, Moses gave you not that bread from heaven; but my Father giveth you the true bread from heaven；又第 15 章第 1 节，I am the true vine, and my Father is the husbandman）.

第 15 节　31. and cried: 'cried' indicates strong emotion, characteristic of a prophet.

32. I spake: spake= spoke (archaic).

33. He that cometh after me is preferred before me: He who is coming after me has become superior to me, for he was in existence from all eternity before me. As soon as He appeared as a teacher, He at once eclipsed His forerunner.

34. He was before me: before me both in time and in dignity.

第 16 节　35. And of his fulness have all we received: fullness 为神学名词。It denotes the totality of the Divine powers and attributes. In 'receive of', the 'of' denotes partitive. Cp. 'partake of ', 'take of'. This fullness of the Divine attributes belonged to Christ, and by Him was imparted to the Church; and through the Church each individual believer in his degree receives a portion of it.

'all we' shows that St. John and not John the Baptist is speaking（本书作者为 St. John，而书中又有个 John the Baptist）.

36. grace for grace: one grace succeeding another.

第 17 节 **37. law ... grace ...:** grace is superior to the Law; for the Law could only condemn sinners, grace forgives them. Moses gave the Law 见 Exodus.

38. Jesus Christ: Jesus 为名字，Christ = the God's anointed = Messiah = the Saviour. St. John no longer speaks of the Logos (The Word); the Logos has become incarnate（第 14 节，and the Word was made flesh）, and is spoken of henceforth by the name, which he has borne in history.

第 18 节 **39. at any time:** Here means 'ever yet'. 'No one hath ever yet seen God,' but some shall see Him hereafter.

40. he hath declared: acted as His interpreter. 'He' here is used for emphasis. 比较本章第 33 节，he that sent me ... the same said unto me.

第 19 节 **41. John:** John the Baptist.

42. Levites: 利未人，助祭司行祭礼者。

第 20 节 **43. confessed, and denied not:** 这是 antithetic parallelism.

44. the Christ: 希腊文原有定冠词，但英译多省去，因 Christ 已成为耶稣的名字之一部分。但此字原为称呼，故用作称呼时仍有冠词，the Christ = the Messiah.

第 21 节 **45. What then?:** = 'What then are we to think?' or 'What then art thou?'

46. Art thou Elias?: Elias = Elijah，犹太先知，早已死去，但犹太的 Scribes（犹太法学家）仍对人们说 Elijah 要在救世主来到以前，先莅人世。

47. that Prophet: 指 Deuteronomy 第 18 章第 15 节及 18 节所说的那个人所熟知的 prophet 而言。

第 23 节 **48. Esaias:** = Isaiah，犹太先知，见《旧约：以赛亚书》。

第 24 节 **49. of the Pharisees:** Some of the Pharisees. Pharisees were an ancient Jewish sect distinguished by strict observance of traditional and written law and pretentious to sanctity. They were most opposed to Christ.

第 27 节 **50. shoe-latchet:** (archaic) thong for fastening shoe.

第 28 节 **51. Bethabara:** 近 Galilee 一小地方。确址无考。

52. Jordan: 约旦河。

第 29 节 **53. the Lamb of God:** John the Baptist 这样叫耶稣，是由于 Isaiah 第 53 章第 7—12 节所说：'he is brought as a lamb to the slaughter.' 又 The Acts，第 8 章第 32 节，'He was led as a sheep to the slaughter; and like a lamb dumb before his shearer...' . So 'the Lamb of God' signifies the Servant to God, led as a lamb to the slaughter, bearing the sins of others, one greater than and different from John the Baptist, patient, and gentle under the Shepherd's guidance.

54. which taketh away the sin of the world: 'taketh away' may mean He removes by His presence all thought of sin or evil, and He takes upon Himself the suffering caused by sin.

第 31 节　**55. And I knew him not:** = I also knew him not.

56. that he should be made manifest: This was John the Baptist's second duty: He had (1) to prepare for the Messiah by preaching repentance; (2) to point out the Messiah.

57. baptizing with water: in humble contrast to Him Who baptizeth with the Holy Ghost.

第 32 节　**58. bare record:** 前面第 7、第 8、第 15 节都说 bare witness，第 19 节用 record，第 34 节用 bare record，都是一样的意思。

59. the Spirit … like a dove: 比较 St. Luke，第 3 章第 21—22 节，'The heaven was opened, and the Holy Ghost descended in a bodily shape like a dove upon him, and a voice came from heaven.' 但是 The Acts 第 2 章第 3—4 节又说，'And there appeared unto them cloven tongues like as of fire, and it sat upon each of them. And they were all filled with the Holy Ghost'. Ghost 古英语 = spirit，现只用于 give up the ghost 及 ghostly father. Holy Ghost = Holy Spirit. 比较本书第 4 章第 24 节，'God is a Spirit: and they that worship him must worship him in spirit…'

第 33 节　**60. And I knew him not:** I *also* knew him not, as before. abiding.

remaining:

第 34 节　**61. the Son of God:** = the Messiah.

第 35 节　**62. the next day after:** = on the morrow.

第 38 节　**63. What seek ye, Rabbi:** Notice that He does not ask 'Whom seek ye?' 'Rabbi' was a comparatively modern word when St. John wrote, and therefore required explanation to Gentile readers. St. John often interprets between Hebrew and Greek.

第 39 节　**64. Come and see:** Come and ye shall see.

65. for it was about the tenth hour: Probably 10 p. m. Whether here St. John reckons the hours of the day according to the Jewish method, from sunset to sunset, or according to the modern method, from midnight to midnight, is a dispute never settled.

第 41 节　**66. the Messias:** = the Messiah，为希伯来文，希腊文译作 Christos（χριδτός），拉丁文为 Christus，英语为 Christ，汉语译'基督'，由希腊文或拉丁文而来。

第 43 节　**67. Follow me:** In the Gospels, the words 'follow me' seem always to be the call to become a disciple.

第 45 节　**68. Moses in the law:** 指 Deuteronomy 第 18 章第 15 节而言，那里说，'The Lord thy God will raise up unto thee a Prophet from the midst of thee, of thy brethren, like unto me; unto him ye shall hearken.'

69. the prophets: 比较 St. Luke 第 24 章第 27 节，'And beginning at Moses and all the prophets, he expounded unto them in all the scriptures the things concerning himself.'

70. Jesus of Nazareth: 指他居住之地而言，不是指他出生之地。他生于 Bethlehem.

第 46 节　**71. Can there any good thing come out of Nazareth?:** All Galileans were despired for their want of culture and contact with Gentiles. Here is a Galilean who reproaches Nazareth in particular. Nazareth was a town in Galilee.

第 47 节　72. an Israelite indeed: an Israelite in character as will as by birth. 见 Genesis 第 27 章第 35 节。

第 50 节　73. Because I said ... believest thou?: Do you base your belief in me simply because ...?

第 51 节　74. Verily, verily: the double 'verily' occurs 25 times in this Gospel. It introduces a truth of special solemnity and importance.

75. unto you: plural; all present are addressed.

76. the Son of man: This phrase in all four Gospels is invariably used by Christ Himself of Himself as the messiah. In the Old Testament, the phrase 'Son of Man' has three distinct uses: (1) in the Psalm, for the ideal man; (2) in Ezekiel, as the name by which the Prophet is addressed by God; (3) in the 'night vision' of Daniel（第 7 章第 13，14 节）where 'One like a son of man came with the clouds of heaven ... was given Him dominion, and glory, and a kingdom, that all people, nations, and languages should serve Him. Jesus takes this phrase and uses it of Himself. As contrasted with the Son of God it emphasizes the reality of His human nature; as with 'a son of man', 'sons of men,' His perfect representation of human nature.

4. 1 CORINTHIANS, CHAPTER 13.

这一卷的全名为 The First Epistle of Paul the Apostle to the Corinthians，汉译《保罗达哥林多人前书》，为《新约》中之一卷。

保罗为建立及初期传布基督教最力之使徒。他在小亚细亚及希腊、罗马各地建教，其地之一为希腊的哥林多。哥林多城当时据罗马通东方之孔道，商业繁盛，人民生活奢侈，其地除希腊人外，又有罗马人、犹太人及其他民族。保罗约于公元 51—52 年在哥林多建教后，又到其它地方。哥林多人既复杂，皈依基督教的信徒亦包括各种人。保罗离开其地之后，教会内部派系纷起，势同水火，其它问题亦因之而生。保罗听到这种情况，除派人到哥林多对会务加以整顿而外，又写了这一封信。信约写于公元 57 年以后，其中除指摘派系分裂之不当，兼及其它问题。现在所选即此信的第 13 章，里面谈 charity，最为有名。其中所讲的道理姑不必论，重在它的文字，生动流利，表现了《圣经》中最有代表性的风格之一。

第 1 节　在前一章里，保罗谈到各种神赋之才德（spiritual gifts）；如有的人多智，另有的人明哲，又有的人善于言语，另有的人擅于作奇迹等等，但所有这些才德都不及 charity，为至高无上之美德。

1. speak with the tongues of men and of angels: tongues = languages, tongues of men 是人间的语言，tongues of angels 是天国的语言，是超人间的，这里面包括 ecstatic speech（魂灵出壳、精与神遇之时所说的话）。Brass = musical instruments of brass; brass 是总说，后面 cymbal 是单说。Sounding，发声，这儿特指高噪之声；tinkling 本为铃、钹（cymbal）等清脆叮当之声，但后来 tinkling cymbal 一语，由于此处

所说，变为‘无意义之语言’之意。但这儿这个‘意义’为精神（spiritual）方面的。

2. charity: 可译作‘仁爱’，但须了解为‘真正基督教徒对同类之仁爱’或‘象耶稣基督所行的那种仁爱’，亦即本章所说的 charity. 修订本圣经改作 love. 但过去的人都用 charity，如林肯在第二次就总统职时演说中所说的‘With malice toward none, with charity for all ...’英诗人 William Cowper 在他的诗‘Charity’里所说的‘true charity, a plant divinely nursed,’都与这儿的 charity 同义。

这一节里的‘Though I speak’之‘though’，如改作‘if’，则更合现代用法，后面各‘though’亦然。‘And have not charity’之‘and’，按现代用法应作‘but’. 不过比较‘This is mine, (and) not yours’及‘This is not mine, but yours.’‘I am come’比较‘Is he gone?’及‘Has he gone?’本章其它与此相同之语法现象，不再重复。

第 2 节　3. prophecy: 在前一章里，prophecy 列为 gifts 之一。第 14 章第 39 节也说 ... brethren, covet to prophecy, and forbid not to speak with tongues，可见保罗是重视 prophecy 的。For‘mysteries’，比较第 2 章第 7 节‘... we speak the wisdom of God in a mystery, even the hidden wisdom’，For‘knowledge’，比较第 2 章第 11—12 节，‘... what man knoweth the things of a man, save the spirit of man which is in him? even so the things of God knoweth no man, but the Spirit of God. Now we have received, not the spirit of the world, but spirit which is of God; that we might know the things that are freely given to us of God.’

4. have all faith, so that I could remove mountains: 比较 St. Matthew 第 17 章第 19—20 节，‘Then came the disciples to Jesus ... and said, Why could not we cast him [the devil] out? And Jesus said unto them, Because of your unbelief: for verily I say unto you, If ye have faith as a grain of mustard seed, ye shall say unto this mountain, Remove hence to yonder place; and it shall remove; and nothing shall be impossible unto you.’

第 3 节　5. I bestow all my goods to feed the poor: 这是慈善事业，在英语里也叫 charity，但与本章所说之 charity 有别。这一节说，倾其所有以济贫民，自焚其身以济世人，但若无 charity，则仍无益。‘自焚其身’可能指如殉教者之被焚死而言。

第 4 节　6. Charity suffereth long: 比较 Proverbs（《箴言》）第 10 章第 12 节，‘Hatred stirreth strifes: but love (= charity) covereth all sins.’又同书第 17 章第 9 节，‘He that covereth a transgression seeketh love’；又 1 Thessalonians（《帖撒罗尼迦前书》）第 5 章第 14 节‘Now we exhort you, brethren, ... comfort the feebleminded, support the weak, be patient toward all men.’这儿的‘suffereth long’就指这类‘隐人之恶、扶助弱者，对所有的人忍耐’的‘隐’、‘忍’而言。

7. and is kind: 比较 2 Corinthians 第 6 章第 4—6 节，‘... in all things approving ourselves as the ministers of God, in much patience, in affliction ... in distresses ... By pureness ... by long suffering, by kindness ...’

8. charity envieth not: it is free from envy.

9. is not puffed up: does not give itself airs.

第 5 节　10. seeketh not her own: does not make its own interest its concern.

11. Is not easily provoked: is not provoked to hostility by the conduct of others.

第 8 节　12. Charity never faileth: Charity is imperishable. Never 不但指今世，且由今世而转入来世。

13. whether there be prophecies: if there be any prophecies. Whether 在这儿 = if any，或 whatever.

第 9 节　14. For we know in part: 比较本书第 8 章第 2 节，And if any man think that he knoweth any thing, he knoweth nothing yet as he ought to know.

第 11 节　15. I put away childish things: because those things which he had as a child no longer answered to his needs when he came to man's estate.

第 12 节　16. For now we … as also I am known: his present knowledge is as though he were seeing things reflected in a mirror with uncertainty as to the significance of what he saw; in the future state there will be direct (= face to face) vision. Darkly = dimly, with uncertainty. 比较（《雅各书》James）第 1 章第 23 节，'he is like unto a man beholding his natural face in a glass.'

第 13 节　17. abideth: = continue, stand firm. —eth 是古英语动词第三人称、单数、现在式、indicative mood 的语尾形式之一。Faith, hope, charity, the three, will continue, stand firm. Faith and hope formed with charity a well-known three, the triad, the 'three Christian graces'. Perhaps that is why they are mentioned together here. They are all abiding, but among them there is a distinction: charity is greatest.

7 FRANCIS BACON
1561–1626
Essays

1. Of Marriage and Single Life
2. Of Great Place
3. Of Wisdom for a Man's Self
4. Of Beauty
5. Of Studies

王佐良　选注

1. OF[1] MARRIAGE AND SINGLE LIFE

He that hath wife and children hath given hostages to fortune[2]; for they are impediments to great enterprises, either of virtue or mischief. Certainly the best works,[3] and of the greatest merit for the public, have proceeded from the unmarried or childless men; which both in affection and means[4] have married and endowed the public. Yet it were great reason[5] that those that have children should have greatest care of future times; unto which they know they must transmit their dearest pledges[6]. Some there are, who though they lead a single life, yet their thoughts do end with themselves, and account future times impertinences[7]. Nay, there are some other that account wife and children but as bills of charges.[8] Nay more, there are some foolish rich covetous men, that take a pride in having no children, because they may be thought so much the richer. For perhaps they have heard some talk, *Such a one is a great rich man*, and another except to it[9], *Yea, but he hath a great charge of children;* as if it were an abatement to his riches. But the most ordinary cause of a single life is liberty, especially in certain self-pleasing and humorous minds,[10] which are so sensible of every restraint,[11] as they will go near to think their girdles and garters to be bonds and shackles. Unmarried men are best friends, best masters, best servants; but not always best subjects; for they are light to run away;[12] and almost all fugitives are of that condition. A single life doth well with churchmen; for charity will hardly water the ground where it must first fill a pool. It is indifferent[13] for judges and magistrates; for if they be facile[14] and corrupt, you shall have a servant five times worse than a wife. For soldiers, I find the generals commonly in their hortatives[15] put men in mind of their wives and children;[16] and I think the despising of marriage amongst the Turks maketh the vulgar soldier[17] more base. Certainly wife and children are a kind of discipline of humanity; and single men, though they may be many times more charitable, because their means are less exhaust, yet, on the other side, they are more cruel and hardhearted (good to make severe inquisitors), because their tenderness is not so oft called upon. Grave natures,[18] led by custom, and therefore constant, are commonly loving husbands; as was said of Ulysses,[19] *vetulam suam prœtulit immortalitati.*[20] Chaste women are often proud and froward,[21] as presuming upon the merit of their chastity. It is one of the best bonds both of chastity and obedience in the wife, if she think her husband wise; which she will never do if she find him jealous. Wives are young men's mistresses; companions for middle age; and old men's nurses. So as a man may have a quarrel to marry when he will.[22] But yet he was reputed one of the wise men,[23] that made answer to the question, when a man should marry? *A young man not yet, an elder man not at all.*[24] It is often seen that bad husbands have very good wives; whether it be that it raiseth the price of their husbands' kindness when it comes;[25] or that the wives take a pride in their patience. But this never fails, if the bad husbands were of their own choosing, against their friends' consent; for then they will be sure to make good their own folly.

2. OF GREAT PLACE[1]

Men in great place are thrice servants: servants of the sovereign or state; servants of fame; and servants of business. So as they have no freedom; neither in their persons nor in their actions, nor in their times. It is a strange desire, to seek power and to lose liberty: or to seek power over others and to lose power over a man's self. The rising unto place is laborious; and by pains men come to greater pains;[2] and it is sometimes base; and by indignities men come to dignities. The standing[3] is slippery, and the regress[4] is either a downfall, or at least an eclipse, which is a melancholy thing. *Cum non sis qui fueris, non esse cur velis vivere.*[5] Nay, retire men cannot when they would,[6] neither will they when it were reason;[7] but are impatient of privateness,[8] even in age and sickness, which require the shadow[9]; like old townsmen,[10] that will be still sitting[11] at their street door, though thereby they offer age to scorn.[12] Certainly great persons had need to borrow other men's opinions, to think themselves happy; for if they judge by their own feeling, they cannot find it: but if they think with themselves what other men think of them and that other men would fain be as they are,[13] then they are happy as it were by report;[14] when perhaps they find the contrary within. For they are the first that find their own griefs, though they be the last that find their own faults. Certainly men in great fortunes are strangers to themselves, and while they are in the puzzle of business[15] they have no time to tend their health either of body or mind. *Illi mors gravis incubat, qui notus nimis omnibus, ignotus moritur sibi.*[16]

In place there is license[17] to do good and evil; whereof the latter is a curse: for in evil the best condition is not to will; the second not to can.[18] But power to do good is the true and lawful end of aspiring. For good thoughts (though God accept them) yet towards men are little better than good dreams, except they be put in act; and that cannot be without power and place, as the vantage and commanding ground.

Merit and good works[19] is the end of man's motion; and conscience[20] of the same is the accomplishment of man's rest. For if a man can be partaker of God's theatre,[21] he shall likewise be partaker of God's rest. *Et conversus Deus, ut aspiceret opera quæ fecerunt manus suæ, vidit quod omnia essent bona nimis;*[22] and then the Sabbath.

In the discharge of thy place[23] set before thee the best examples; for imitation is a globe of precepts.[24] And after a time set before thee thine own example; and examine thyself strictly whether thou didst not best at first. Neglect not also the examples of those that have carried themselves ill in the same place;[25] not to set off thyself by taxing their memory, but to direct thyself what to avoid.[26] Reform therefore, without bravery or scandal of former times and persons;[27] but yet set it down to thyself as well to create good precedents as to follow them. Reduce things to the first institution,[28] and observe wherein and how they have degenerate;[29] but yet ask counsel of both times;[30] of the ancient time, what is best; and of the latter time, what is fittest.

Seek to make thy course regular, that men may know beforehand what they may expect; but be not too positive and peremptory; and express thyself well when thou digressest from thy rule.[31] Preserve the right of thy place; but stir not questions of jurisdiction: and rather assume thy right in silence and *de facto*,[32] than voice it with claims and challenges. Preserve likewise the rights of inferior place;[33] and think it more honour to direct in chief than to be busy in all. Embrace and invite helps and advices touching the execution of thy place; and do not drive away such as bring thee information, as meddlers; but accept of them in good part.[34]

The vices of authority are chiefly four; delays, corruption, roughness, and facility.[35]

For delays; give easy access; keep times appointed; go through with that which is in hand, and interlace not business but of necessity.[36]

For corruption; do not only bind thine own hands or thy servants' hands from taking, but bind the hands of suitors[37] also from offering. For integrity used doth the one; but integrity professed, and with a manifest detestation of bribery, doth the other. And avoid not only the fault, but the suspicion. Whosoever is found variable, and changeth manifestly without manifest cause, giveth suspicion of corruption. Therefore always when thou changest thine opinion or course, profess it plainly, and declare it, together with the reasons that move thee to change; and do not think to steal it.[38] A servant or a favourite, if he be inward, and no other apparent cause of esteem,[39] is commonly thought but a by-way to close corruption.

For roughness; it is a needless cause of discontent: severity breedeth fear, but roughness breedeth hate. Even reproofs from authority ought to be grave, and not taunting.

As for facility; it is worse than bribery. For bribes come but now and then; but if importunity or idle respects lead a man,[40] he shall never be without. As Salomon[41] saith, *To respect persons*[42] *is not good; for such a man will transgress for a piece of bread.*

It is most true that was anciently spoken, *A place showeth the man.*[43] And it showeth some to the better, and some to the worse, *Omnium consensu capax imperii, nisi imperasset,*[44] saith Tacitus[45] of Galba;[46] but of Vespasian[47] he saith, *Solus imperantium, Vespasianus mutatus in melius:*[48] though the one was meant of sufficiency,[49] the other of manners and affection. It is an assured sign of a worthy and generous spirit, whom honour amends.[50] For honour is, or should be, the place of virtue; and as in nature things move violently to their place and calmly in their place, so virtue in ambition is violent, in authority settled and calm.[51] All rising to great place is by a winding stair; and if there be factions, it is good to side a man's self whilst he is in the rising, and to balance himself when he is placed.[52] Use the memory of thy predecessor fairly and tenderly; for if thou dost not, it is a debt will sure be paid when thou art gone. If thou have colleagues, respect them, and rather call them when they look not for it, than exclude them when they have reason to look to be called. Be not too sensible or too remembering of thy place[53] in conversation and private answers to suitors; but let it rather be said, *When he sits in place he is another man.*

3. OF WISDOM FOR A MAN'S SELF

An ant is a wise creature for itself, but it is a shrewd[1] thing in an orchard or garden. And certainly men that are great lovers of themselves waste the public.[2] Divide with reason between self-love and society;[3] and be so true to thyself, as thou be not false to others;[4] specially to thy king and country. It is a poor centre of a man's actions, himself. It is right earth.[5] For that only stands fast upon his own centre;[6] whereas all things that have affinity with the heavens,[7] move upon the centre of another, which they benefit. The referring of all to a man's self[8] is more tolerable in a sovereign prince; because themselves are not only themselves, but their good and evil is at the peril of the public fortune.[9] But it is a desperate evil[10] in a servant to a prince, or a citizen in a republic. For whatsoever affairs pass such a man's hands, he crooketh[11] them to his own ends; which must needs be[12] often eccentric to[13] the ends of his master or state. Therefore let princes, or states, choose such servants as have not this mark; except they mean their service should be made but the accessary.[14] That which maketh the effect more pernicious is that all proportion is lost.[15] It were disproportion enough[16] for the servant's good to be preferred before the master's; but yet it is a greater extreme, when a little good of the servant shall carry things[17] against a great good of the master's. And yet that is the case of bad officers, treasurers, ambassadors, generals, and other false and corrupt servants; which[18] set a bias upon their bowl, of their own petty ends and envies, to the overthrow of their master's great and important affairs.[19] And for the most part, the good such servants receive is after the model[20] of their own fortune; but the hurt they sell for that good is after the model of their master's fortune. And certainly it is the nature of extreme self-lovers, as they will[21] set an house[22] on fire, and it were but to roast[23] their eggs; and yet these men many times hold credit with their masters,[24] because their study[25] is but to please them and profit themselves; and for either respect[26] they will abandon the good of their affairs.

Wisdom for a man's self is, in many branches thereof,[27] a depraved thing. It is the wisdom of rats, that will be sure to leave a house somewhat before it fall. It is the wisdom of the fox, that thrusts out the badger, who digged[28] and made room for him. It is the wisdom of crocodiles, that shed tears when they would devour.[29] But that which is specially to be noted is, that those which[30] (as Cicero[31] says of Pompey[32]) are *sui amantes, sine rivali,*[33] are many times unfortunate. And whereas they have all their time sacrificed to themselves, they become in the end themselves sacrifices to the inconstancy of fortune; whose wings they thought by their self-wisdom[34] to have pinioned.[35]

4. OF BEAUTY

Virtue is like a rich stone, best plain set[1]: and surely virtue is best in a body, that is comely, though not of delicate features: and that hath rather dignity of presence,[2] than *beauty* of aspect. Neither is it almost seen, that very *beautiful persons,* are otherwise of great virtue;[3] as if nature, were rather busy not to err, than in labour, to produce excellency.[4] And therefore, they prove accomplished, but not of great spirit; and study rather behaviour, than virtue;[5] but this holds not always;[6] for *Augustus Caesar,*[7] *Titus Vespasianus,*[8] *Philip le Belle of France,*[9] *Edward the Fourth of England,*[10] *Alcibiades of Athens,*[11] *Ismael the Sophy of Persia,*[12] were all high and great spirits; and yet the most *beautiful men* of their times. In *beauty,* that of favour,[13] is more than that of colour, and that of decent and gracious motion, more than that of favour. That is the best part of *beauty*, which a picture cannot express; no nor the first sight of the life.[14] There is no excellent *beauty,* that hath not some strangeness in the proportion. A man cannot tell, whether *Apelles,*[15] or *Albert Durer,*[16] were the more trifler[17]: whereof the one would make a personage by geometrical proportions: the other, by taking the best parts out of divers faces, to make one excellent. Such personages, I think, would please no body, but the painter, that made them. Not but I think a painter, may make a better face, then ever was; but he must do it, by a kind of felicity,[18] (as a musician that maketh an excellent air in music) and not by rule. A man shall see faces, that if you examine them, part by part, you shall find never a good; and yet all together do well. If it be true, that the principal part of *beauty*, is in decent motion, certainly it is no marvel, though persons in years,[19] seem many times more amiable; *Pulchrorum autumnus pulcher:*[20] for no youth can be comely, but by pardon,[21] and considering the youth, as to make up the comeliness.[22] *Beauty* is as summer-fruits, which are easy to corrupt, and cannot last: and, for the most part, it makes a dissolute youth, and an age a little out of countenance:[23] but yet certainly again, if it light well,[24] it maketh virtues shine, and vices blush.

5. OF STUDIES

Studies serve for delight, for ornament, and for ability. Their chief use for delight, is in privateness[1] and retiring;[2] for ornament, is in discourse[3]; and for ability, is in the judgement and disposition of business. For expert men[4] can execute, and perhaps judge of particulars, one by one; but the general counsels, and the plots[5] and marshalling of affairs[6], come best from those that are learned. To spend too much time in studies is sloth[7]; to use them too much for ornament, is affectation[8]; to make judgement wholly by their rules, is the humour[9] of a scholar. They perfect nature, and are perfected by experience: for natural abilities are like natural plants, that need proyning[10] by study; and studies themselves do give forth directions too much at large,[11] except they be[12] bounded in by experience.[13] Crafty men[14] contemn studies, simple men[15] admire[16] them, and wise men use them; for they teach not their own use; but that is a wisdom without them, and above them,[17] won by observation. Read not to contradict and confute; nor to believe and take for granted;[18] nor to find talk and discourse;[19] but to weigh and consider. Some books are to be tasted, others to be swallowed, and some few to be chewed and digested; that is, some books are to be read only in parts; others to be read, but not curiously;[20] and some few to be read wholly, and with diligence and attention. Some books also may be read by deputy,[21] and extracts made of them by others; but that would be[22] only in the less important arguments,[23] and the meaner sort of books; else distilled books are like common distilled waters, flashy things.[24] Reading maketh[25] a full man: conference[26] a ready man;[27] and writing[28] an exact man. And therefore, if a man write little,[29] he had need have a great memory; if he confer little, he had need have[30] a present wit:[31] and if he read little, he had need have[30] much cunning, to seem to know that[32] he doth rot.[33] Histories make men wise; poets witty[34]; the mathematics subtile;[35] natural philosophy[36] deep; moral[37] grave; logic and rhetoric able to contend.[38] *Abeunt studia in mores*.[39] Nay there is no stond[40] or impediment in the wit,[41] but may be wrought out[42] by fit studies: like as[43] diseases of the body may have appropriate exercises. Bowling is good for the stone and reins;[44] shooting[45] for the lungs and breast; gentle walking for the stomach; riding for the head; and the like. So if a man's wit be wandering,[46] let him study the mathematics; for in demonstrations,[47] if his wit be called away never so little,[48] he must begin again. If his wit be not apt to distinguish or find differences, let him study the schoolmen;[49] for they are *cymini sectores*.[50] If he be not apt to beat over matters,[51] and to call up one thing to prove and illustrate another, let him study the lawyers' cases.[62] So every defect of the mind may have a special receipt.[53]

【作者简介】 Francis Bacon（弗兰西斯·培根，1561—1626），曾任大理院院长，封为勋爵，但因受贿为国会弹劾去职。他是大哲学家，"英国唯物主义的真正始祖"（马克思），著有 *Advancement of Learning*（《学术的进展》，1605），*Novum Organum*（《新工具》，1620），*New Atlantis*（《新大西岛》，1627）等书。他又是一个出色的文章家，所写 *Essays*（《随笔》，1625）是英国文学史上著名的散文作品之一。

【题解与注释】

"随笔"（the essay）作为一种文学形式，始于1580年法人蒙田的两卷《随笔》（Montaigne: *Essais*），书出后在英有译本，有仿作，但至培根始出现第一部重要的英文随笔，因此他被目为这一文学形式在英国的创始者。培根的《随笔》初版于1597年，仅有十篇极短的摘记式的小文，经过1612、1625两次增补，最后共收短文58篇。这些文章以当时统治阶级世家子弟为对象，谈的是处世的道理，成功的秘诀，读书、旅行、娱乐、营造等事的实际经验，但也探讨哲理，议论人生。文字写得十分紧凑简约，有时似乎枯燥，实则充满了独到之见，诛心之论。作者用老吏折狱的笔法剖析了当时统治阶级的图谋和动机，而且时有诗情的一闪。

这里所选几篇各有特色。*Of Marriage and Single Life*（《谈婚嫁与单身》）是一个精明强干的人根据本身的经验和对别人的观察，对于婚姻的得失作了各种论断，中间也反映了上层社会的各种世态。

Of Great Place（《谈高位》）揭露了向上爬的艰苦与辛酸："循小梯盘旋而上"，"须做尽不光荣之事，方能达光荣之位"——蝇营狗苟的痛苦，真是慨乎言之！

Of Wisdom for a Man's Self（《谈自谋》）是一篇读了叫人感到可怕的作品。培根深感于他周围的人的自私，用了一些野兽的形象来写出他们为害之烈，并叫我们看出当时统治阶级内部倾轧和争夺的白热化。但是他对这些人的劝告却只是：不可自谋过甚，而要公私兼爱，而所以必须如此，也不过是为了保全自己。无怪乎后来十八

世纪末的诗人 William Blake 在他所读的培根《随笔》的扉页上，写下了这样的批语："Good Advice for Satan's Kingdom"（"这是向魔鬼的王国献的妙计！"）。

Of Beauty（《谈美》）是培根少有的论艺术之作，主旨在将美与品德结合起来，因此说"朴素最美"，"绝色无大德"。而就美本身说，则"举凡最美之人，其部位比例，必有异于常人之处"，"美之要素在于举止"。文章虽短，卓见甚多。

Of Studies（《谈读书》）谈读书的用处和方法，设想周到，一方面提倡读书，一方面又强调读书要结合经验和对自然的观察，具见这位实验科学先驱者的本色。他说得有条有理，头头是道，什么情况都有应付的办法，其自信反映了初露头角的英国资产阶级在文艺复兴时期的抱负，其武断又表露了初期唯物主义的机械性。

* * *

构成培根《随笔》的风格的基础的，是十分简洁的警句格言。几乎每篇随笔的起句都是一上来就将读者紧紧抓住：

He that hath wife and children hath given hostages to fortune.

We take cunning for a sinister or crooked wisdom.

I cannot call riches better than the baggage of virtue.

Men fear death, as children fear to go in the dark.

文章当中，这种言简意赅的警句，也是俯拾即是。但是更值得注意的，是培根虽能雄辩滔滔，却最恨舞文弄墨，写作以准确达意为第一，决不因词害意，而是意重于词。这种简朴、准确、能说明具体事物的实用文体正是当时正在不断出现的自然科学著作所要求的，也有助于后来报纸杂志的普及和近代小说的兴起。

对于中国学生，培根《随笔》的文字大体上是不难的，不过要注意十七世纪英文与现代英文不同的地方，如拼法的差别（proyning = pruning），语法形式的差别（hath = has, maketh = makes, crooketh = crooks，虚拟式 it were = it would be），特别是词义的变化，如 shrewd 一词今作机灵、世故解，培根当时则指狡猾、阴险，两义相近，但褒贬的分寸不同，不可不辨；至于拉丁引语之类，则有注解可查，倒不必望而却步了。

1. OF MARRIAGE AND SINGLE LIFE

1.（标题中的）**of:** = about, concerning，关于；以后各篇标题中的 of 同此。

2. hath given hostages to fortune: 向命运付出了抵押品，意即变得审慎，不敢自由行事；hostage 原意是人质。

3. works: 事业。

4. means: 资财。

5. it were great reason: = it would be very reasonable.

6. their dearest pledges: 他们最亲的抵押品，指子女。

7. account future times impertinences: 认为将来与他们无关。

8. bills of charges: 帐单，意为负担。

9. another except to it: 另一人提出异议。此处 except 是动词，意为反对，不同

意。现代英语中 to take exception to something 即是表达此意。

10. self-pleasing and humorous minds: 那些自娱、任性的人；humorous = capricious, odd, peevish，任性，怪僻。

11. so sensible of every restraint: 对于任何拘束都极为敏感，即不愿受任何拘束。

12. light to run away: 没有累赘，易于跑走。

13. indifferent: 无关紧要。

14. facile: 柔顺，易于为人左右。

15. hortatives: = exhortations，激励语。

16. put men in mind of their wives and children: 使他们的部下记得他们的家小。

17. the vulgar soldier: 普通士兵。

18. Grave natures: 天性庄重的人。

19. Ulysses: 即 Odysseus，荷马史诗 *Odyssey* 中的英雄。在该书第五部，仙女 Calypso 表示愿给 Ulysses 不朽和永恒的青春，如果他肯与她同居，但是 Ulysses 拒绝了而仍回归其老妻 Penelope。

20. *vetulam suam prætulit immortalitati*: 拉丁引语，英译可作：He preferred his old wife to immortality，他爱老妻胜过不朽。语出西塞罗（Cicero, *De Oratore*, i, 44）。

21. froward: 即 forward，傲慢，放肆。

presuming upon the merit of their chastity: 依仗着她们有贞节这个优点。

22. So as a man may have a quarrel to marry when he will: 这样人就可以有理由在他愿意的任何时间结婚；quarrel，此处意为道理，理由；so as = so that.

23. one of the wise men: 指希腊古哲学家 Thales of Miletus (640–550 B. C.).

24. A young man not yet, an elder man not at all: 意为年轻人不必急于结婚，年老人则根本不该结婚。

25. whether it be that it raiseth the price of their husbands' kindness when it comes: 是否这样在她们的丈夫真对她们和善的时候就更显得可贵了。

2. OF GREAT PLACE

1. place: 官位；great place，高官，高位。

2. by pains men come to greater pains: 此处 pains 意为艰辛，全句意为：含辛茹苦，唯得更大辛苦。

3. standing: 立足之处。

4. regress: 退后一步，退行。

5. *Cum non sis qui fueris, non esse cur velis vivere*: 拉丁引语，英译可作：When you are no longer what you were, there is no reason why you should wish to live. 既已非当年之盛，又何必贪生。语出西塞罗（Cicero, *Epist. ad Fam.* vii, 3）。

6. retire men cannot then they would: 倒装句，即 men cannot retire when they want to，人们想隐退的时候却不能隐退。

7. when it were reason: = when it would be the reasonable thing to do.

8. impatient of privateness: 不愿独处。

9. require the shadow: 需要隐退，shadow 指隐蔽处。

10. townsmen: 市民，商人。

11. that will be still sitting: 此处 still 作 always 解。

12. offer age to scorn: 使高年成为嘲笑的对象。

13. other men would fain be as they are: would fain be = would be glad to be，（想到）别人很愿意变成他们自己那样，即羡慕他们的地位。

14. happy as it were by report: as it were = in a manner of speaking, so to speak，可以说是；by report = by what others say, by common talk；可以说是靠听别人的话才感到自己是快乐的。

15. puzzle of business: 事务的纠缠。

16. *Illi mors gravis incubat, qui notus nimis omnibus, ignotus moritur sibi*: 拉丁引语，英译可作 It is a sad fate for a man to die too well known to everybody else, and still unknown to himself. 悲哉斯人之死也，举世皆知其为人，而独无自知之明！语出塞内加（Seneca, *Thyestes*, ii, 401）。

17. license: 机动之权，（做事的）自由。

18. not to will: 无（此）意愿；**not to can**：无（此）能力。

19. good works: 善行。

20. conscience: 意识，= consciousness; **conscience of the same**，意识到上述这一点。

21. God's theatre: 上帝活动的场所；partaker of God's theatre，分享上帝的行动的人，即象上帝一样做事的人。

22. *Et conversus Deus, ut aspiceret opera quæ fecerunt manus suæ, vidit quod omnia essent bona nimis*: 拉丁引语，英译可作：And God turned to look upon the works which his hands had made, and saw that all were very good，上帝回顾他手做的东西，发现一切都很好。（因此在第七天就休息了，这就是安息日（Sabbath）的由来。）基督教《圣经》《创世纪》第二章即作如是语。

23. the discharge of thy place: 在执行你的职务时。

24. imitation is a globe of precepts: 模仿集箴言之大成，意为模仿前任的善举就等于实行了最好的箴言。globe = a complete or perfect body, a good combination.

25. those that have carried themselves ill in the same place: 那些在这同一职位上搞得不好的人。

26. not to set off thyself by taxing their memory, but to direct thyself what to avoid: 不是为了反衬你自己如何好而去重提他们的旧事，而是为了提醒你自己该避免什么。

27. without bravery or scandal of former times and persons: 不夸耀也不诽谤旧时或古人。bravery = show, display.

28. the first institution: 最初的制度。

29. how they have degenerate: 它们是如何变坏了的；degenerate = degenerated.

30. ask counsel of both times: 向古今都请教。

31. express thyself well when thou digressest from thy rule: 在你偏离你自己的规则时，应当清楚说明（理由）。

32. assume thy right in silence and *de facto*: 不事声张地在实际上行使你的职权；de facto，拉丁文，= in actual fact.

33. inferior place: 下级。

34. accept of them in good part: 乐意地接受他们所提供的情况。

35. facility: 柔顺，易信人言。

36. interlace not business but of necessity: 除非必要，不使事务混杂。

37. suitors: 求情的人。

38. do not think to steal it: 不要企图偷偷摸摸地进行。

39. inward, and no other apparent cause of esteem: 只是亲信而另无其他优点。

40. if importunity or idle respects lead a man: 如果一个人易为求情和虚幻的崇拜所左右。

41. Salomon: 即 Solomon，公元前十世纪的以色列王，以智慧著。

42. To respect persons: 崇拜权贵。英语中常说 he is no respecter of persons，意为此人有骨气，不崇拜权贵。

参阅基督教《圣经》《旧约》《箴言》第 28 章第 21 节："看人的情面，乃为不好。人因一块饼枉法，也为不好。"

43. A place showeth the man: 一旦做官就露出其人本相。语出亚理斯多德（Aristotle, *Eth.* N. v. 1.16）。

44. *Omnium consensu capax imperii, nisi imperasset*: 拉丁引语，英译可作：A man whom everybody would have thought fit for empire if he had not been emperor，如他不是皇帝，那末人人都会说他是适于治理帝国的人。语出塔西陀（Tacitus）的《历史》，i，49。

45. Tacitus: 塔西陀，古罗马历史家，公元一世纪时在世。

46. Galba: 生于公元前 3 年，卒于公元 69 年，罗马皇帝（在位仅一年，68—69）。

47. Vespasian: 罗马皇帝（在位 69—79）。

48. *Solus imperantium, Vespasianus mutatus in melius*: 拉丁引语，英译可作：Vespasian was the only emperor who changed for the better，他是唯一的一个登大位而变得更好的皇帝。语出塔西陀的《历史》，i，50。

49. sufficiency: 能力。

50. honour amends: 尊荣使（他）变得更好。

51. virtue in ambition is violent, in authority settled and calm: 有德而大志未酬，德行必狂；居高位而有德，德行和缓。

52. when he is placed: 在他已有了高位之后。

53. Be not too sensible or too remembering of thy place: 不要处处感到并时时不忘你的地位。

3. OF WISDOM FOR A MAN'S SELF

1. shrewd: 阴险，有害的。

2. waste the public: 为害于众。

3. Divide with reason between self-love and society: 合理地兼顾自我与别人。society 在此指与人来往或来往的人，而不是近代意义的"社会"。

4. as thou be not false to others: 此处 as 作 that 用，与前文之 so 相接，意为既忠实于己，又忠实于别人。thou be = thou shalt be.

5. It is right earth: 意为 it is exactly like the earth. 就象地球一样。

6. only stands fast upon his own centre:（而地球）只是呆立在一点上；fast，牢固地，紧紧地；his = its，指地球。按培根不信地动说，所以说地球站住不动。

7. have affinity with the heavens: 与天体相似；heavens = heavenly bodies，天上的星辰日月。

8. a man's self: = oneself.

9. their good and evil is at the peril of the public fortune: 他们行善或作恶，是公众安危祸福之所系。

10. a desperate evil: 大恶行，此处 desperate 作 extremely bad 解。

11. crooketh: = crooks，扭曲。

12. must needs be: needs 在此是副词，意为 necessarily.

13. eccentric to: 背道而驰（古义）。

14. except they mean their service should be made but the accessary: 除非主人们决心只将他们作为驯顺的工具来使用，不让他们擅作主张；but，意为 only; accessary，助手。

15. all proportion is lost: 失去了一切分寸。

16. it were disproportion enough: = it would be disproportion enough（虚拟式），已经够是本末倒置的了。

17. carry things: 胜过，压倒。

18. which: 此处作 who 用。

19. set a bias upon their bowl, of their own petty ends and envies, to the overthrow of their master's great and important affairs: 从他们的卑琐的图谋和私人的恩怨出发，故意将事办坏，犹如作滚球戏时，竭力使球斜行，造成他们主人伟大事业的失败。envies，恶意。

20. after the model: proportionate to，大小如之。

21. as they will: as 此处作 that 用。

22. an house: h 往往被认为是哑辅音（mute consonant），故前用 an；但培根并不一致，以下 23 行出现 *a* house.

23. and it were but to roast: = if it were only to roast.

24. hold credit with their masters: 获得他们主人的信任。

25. study: 努力（古义）。

26. for either respect: 为了这两个目的中的任何一个。

27. in many branches thereof: 就其许多方面来说。

28. digged: = dug.

29. crocodiles, that shed tears when they would devour: 鳄鱼在吞食别的动物时先流眼泪。当时的游记有这样的记载。故"鳄鱼之泪"代表了"假慈悲"。

30. those which: = those who.

31. Cicero: Marcus Tullius（公元前 106—43），古罗马政治家，演说家。

32. Pompey:（公元前 106—48）古罗马大将。

33. *sui amantes, sine rivali*: 拉丁引语，出处在西塞罗的《书信集》(Cicero, *Letters*, III, 8)，意为 lovers of themselves, without a rival，无人匹敌的自爱者（自私者）。

34. self-wisdom: 替自己打算的聪明。

35. pinioned: 割断。

4. OF BEAUTY

1. best plain set: at its best when it is set plainly; set，镶，嵌；plain，朴素的。

2. dignity of presence: 举止大方。

3. are otherwise of great virtue: 而无大德；otherwise = different, not so.

4. rather busy not to err, than in labour, to produce excellency: 务求不出错误，而不是尽力造成优美。

5. study rather behaviour, than virtue: 注意仪表态度，而不是德行。

6. this holds not always: this does not always hold true，并不总是这样。

7. Augustus Caesar: 纪元前 63—纪元后 14，第一个罗马皇帝。

8. Titus Vespasianus: 罗马皇帝（在位 79—81）。

9. Philip le Belle of France: 法王菲力浦四世，1268—1314，在位 1285—1314。

10. Edward the Fourth of England: 英王爱德华四世，1442—83，在位 1461—70；1471—83。

11. Alcibiades of Athens: 公元前五世纪雅典政治家和将领。

12. Ismael the Sophy of Persia: 1499—1524，波斯国王（在位 1502—24），萨瓦维特王朝的创建者。

13. favour: 外貌。

14. no nor the first sight of the life: 也不是第一次见到真人时。the life 指所画的真人。

15. Apelles: 公元前四世纪希腊画家。（可能培根指的是比此人早六十年的希腊画家 Zeuxis，古罗马的西塞罗说他为了画 Helen，集中了五位美女的优点。）

16. Albert Durer: 即 Albrecht Dürer，1471—1528，德国画家。

17. the more trifler: 更为可笑的人。

18. by a kind of felicity: 依靠神来之笔。

19. persons in years: 年事已长的人。

20. ***Pulchrorum autumnus pulcher*:** 拉丁引语，英译可作：The autumn of the beautiful is beautiful，意为美者虽到中年仍是美的。

21. **but by pardon:** 意为 except by making allowance for defect，除非是降低要求。

22. **to make up the comeliness:** 补足其美。

23. **it makes a dissolute youth, and an age a little out of countenance:** 使青年放荡，使老年失态。

24. **if it light well:** 如果光照宜人。

5. OF STUDIES

1. **privateness:** 独处。
2. **retiring:** = retirement，隐居。
3. **discourse:** 议论。
4. **expert men:** 有经验的人。
5. **plots:** = plans，计划，非今日“阴谋”之意。
6. **marshalling of affairs:** 安排事务。
7. **sloth:** 懒惰。
8. **affectation:** 装腔作势。
9. **humour:** 脾气（古义），此处指怪僻。
10. **proyning:** = pruning，修剪枝叶。
11. **too much at large:** 不着边际。
12. **except they be:** = except they should be.
13. **bounded in by experience:** 受经验的限制。
14. **Crafty men:** = men of craft；有一技之长的人，非今日“狡黠者流”之意。
15. **simple men:** 头脑简单、易于受欺的人；simple 在此不作单纯解。
16. **admire:** 古义为“惊奇不已”，强调远过于今之“赞美”。
17. **without them, and above them:** 在书本之外，在书本之上；without = outside.
18. **to take for granted:** 不加疑问地接受，认为当然。
19. **nor to find talk and discourse:** 也不是寻找谈话的材料。
20. **curiously:** with care，仔细地（古义）。
21. **by deputy:** 请人代理。
22. **that would be:** 意为 that ought to be。
23. **arguments:** 书的内容，题材。
24. **flashy things:** 淡而无味的东西。
25. **maketh:** = makes.
26. **conference:** 讨论，谈话。
27. **a ready man:** 敏于应对的人。
28. **writing:** 写笔记，作劄记。

29. if a man write little: 此处 write 是虚拟式。早期英语中，在以 if, though 等连词起引的子句中，动词用虚拟式。下文 confer, read，以及 if a man's wit *be* wandering, if his wit *be* called away, if his wit *be* not apt，与 if he *be* not able 等句中的 be，都属此类。

30. had need have: = would require to have; ought to have.

31. a present wit: 即 ready wit，有急智。

32. that: 此处用法如 what.

33. doth not: = does not.

34. witty: 机灵（古义）。

35. subtile: subtle 的古拼法，此处作深入细致解。

36. natural philosophy: 科学。

37. moral: 指 moral philosophy，伦理学。

38. contend: 辩论。

39. *Abeunt studia in mores*: 拉丁引语，出处在古罗马诗人奥维德（公元前 43—公元 18）的《女英雄书信集》(Ovid, *Heroides*, XV, 83)，意为 Studies pass into the character，凡有所学，皆成性格。

40. stond: 即 stand，名词，阻碍（古义）。

41. in the wit: = in the mind. 下文 wit 一词都指 mind，心智。

42. wrought out: 除去。

43. like as: = as.

44. the stone and reins: 睾丸与肾脏；通常 stones（复数）始作睾丸解，故亦有将 the stone 作膀胱结石解者。

45. shooting: 射箭。

46. if a man's wit be wandering: 如有人不能专心。

47. demonstrations: 推演数学题。

48. never so little: = ever so little, no matter how little.

49. the schoolmen: 欧洲中古经院哲学家。

50. *cymini sectores*: 拉丁引语，意为 dividers of cumin seeds，即 hairsplitters，过分讲究细节的人。

51. to beat over matters: 详细审察事物。

52. the lawyers' cases: 律师经办的案件，特指法律上的先例。

53. receipt: = recipe，药方。

8 JOHN DONNE
1572–1631

1. Song (Go and catch a falling star)

2. The Canonization

3. A Valediction: Of Weeping

4. A Valediction: Forbidding Mourning

5. Holy Sonnet VII (At the round earth's imagin'd corners, blow)

杨周翰　选注

1. SONG

Go[1], and catch a falling star[2],
　　Get with child a mandrake root[3],
Tell me, where all past years are,[4]
　　Or who cleft[5] the Devil's foot,
Teach me to hear Mermaids[6] singing,
　　Or to keep off envy's[7] stinging,[8]
　　　　And find
　　　　What wind[9]
Serves to advance an honest mind.

If thou beest borne to strange sights,[10]
　　Things invisible to see,[11]
Ride[12] ten thousand days and nights,
　　Till age snow[13] white hairs on thee,
Thou, when thou return'st, wilt[14] tell me
　　All strange wonders that befell[15] thee,
　　　　And swear[16]

No where
Lives a woman true,[17] and fair.

If thou findst one, let me know,[18]
Such a Pilgrimage[19] were[20] sweet;
Yet do not, I would not go,
Though at next door we[21] might meet,
Though she were true,[22] when you met her,
And last,[23] till you write your letter,[24]
Yet she
Will be
False, ere I come,[25] to two, or three.[26]

2. THE CANONIZATION[1]

For God's sake hold your tongue, and let me love,[2]
Or chide my palsy,[3] or[4] my gout[5],
My five gray hairs,[6] or ruin'd fortune flout,[7]
With wealth your state, your mind with Arts improve,[8]
Take you a course,[9] get you a place,[10]
Observe[11] his honour,[12] or his grace,[13]
Or the King's real, or his stamped face[14]
Contemplate, what you will, approve,[15]
So[16] you will let me love.

Alas, alas, who's injur'd by my love?[17]
What merchant's ships have my sighs[18] drown'd?
Who says my tears[18] have overflow'd his ground?[19]
When did my colds[20] a forward spring remove?
When did the heats[21] which my veins fill
Add one more[22] to the plaguy Bill[23]?
Soldiers find wars,[24] and Lawyers find out still
Litigious[25] men, which[26] quarrels move,[27]

Though she and I do love.

Call us what you will, we are made such[28] by love;[29]
Call her one, me another fly,[30]
We'are[31] Tapers[32] too, and at our own cost die,
And we in us find the'Eagle and the Dove.[33]
The Phoenix[34] riddle hath more wit[35]
By us,[36] we two being one, are it.
So[37] to[38] one neutral thing[39] both sexes fit,
We die and rise the same, and prove
Mysterious[40] by this love.

We can die by it,[41] if not live by love,
And if unfit for tombs and hearse[42]
Our legend be,[43] it will be fit for verse;
And if no piece of Chronicle[44] we prove,
We'll build in sonnets[45] pretty rooms;[46]
As well a well-wrought urn[47] becomes[48]
The greatest ashes,[49] as half-acre tombs,[50]
And by these hymns,[51] all[52] shall approve[53]
Us *Canoniz'd* for Love:

And thus invoke us;[54] "You whom reverend love
Made one another's hermitage;[55]
You, to whom love was peace,[56] that now is rage;[57]
Who did the whole world's soul contract,[58] and drove[59]
Into the glasses[60] of your eyes
(So made such mirrors,[61] and such spies,
That they did all to you epitomize,)
Countries, Towns, Courts: Beg[62] from above[63]
A pattern[64] of your love!"

3. *A VALEDICTION*[1]*: OF*[2] *WEEPING*

Let me pour forth[3]
My tears before thy face, whilst I stay here,[4]
For thy face coins them,[5] and thy stamp they bear,[6]
And by this Mintage[7] they are something worth,
For thus they be[8]
Pregnant[9] of thee;
Fruits of much grief they are, emblems[10] of more,[11]
When a tear falls, that thou[12] fallst which it bore,
So thou and I are nothing then, when on a divers shore.[13]

On a round ball[14]
A workman that hath copies[15] by, can lay
An Europe, Afrique, and an Asia,[16]
And quickly make that, which was nothing,[17] *All,*[18]
So[19] doth each tear,[20]
Which thee doth wear,
A globe, yea[21] world by that impression[22] grow,
Till thy tears mixt with mine do overflow[23]
This world, by waters sent from thee, my heaven dissolved so.[24]

O more than Moon,[25]
Draw not up seas to drown me in thy sphere,[26]
Weep not me dead,[27] in thine arms, but forbear[28]
To teach the sea, what it may do too soon;[29]
Let not the wind[30]
Example find,
To do me more harm, than it purposeth;[31]
Since thou and I sigh one another's breath,[32]
Who e'er sighs most, is cruellest, and hastes the other's death.

4. A VALEDICTION: FORBIDDING MOURNING

As virtuous men pass mildly away,[1]
And whisper to their souls, to go,
Whilst some of their sad friends do say,
The breath goes now, and some say, no:

So let us melt, and make no noise,
No tear-floods, nor sigh-tempests[2] move,[3]
T'were profanation[4] of our joys
To tell the laiety[5] our love.

Moving of th'earth[6] brings harms and fears,
Men reckon[7] what it did and meant,
But trepidation of the spheres,[8]
Though greater[9] far, is innocent.[10]

Dull sublunary[11] lovers' love
(Whose soul[12] is sense[13]) cannot admit
Absence, because it[14] doth remove
Those things[15] which elemented[16] it.[17]

But we by a love, so much refin'd,[18]
That our selves know not what it is,[19]
Inter-assured[20] of the mind,
Care less,[21] eyes, lips, and hands[22] to miss.

Our two souls therefore, which are one,[23]
Though I must go, endure not yet[24]
A breach,[25] but an expansion,[26]
Like gold to airy thinness[27] beat.[28]

If they be two, they are two so[29]
As stiff twin compasses are two,
Thy soul the fixt foot,[30] makes no show
To move, but doth,[31] if th'other[32] do.[33]

And though it in the centre sit,[34]
Yet when the other far doth roam,
It[35] leans, and hearkens[36] after it,
And grows erect, as that[37] comes home.

Such wilt thou be to me, who must
Like th'other foot,[38] obliquely[39] run;
Thy firmness makes my circle just,
And makes me end, where I begun.[40]

5. HOLY SONNET VII

At the round earth's imagin'd corners, blow[1]
Your trumpets, Angels,[2] and arise, arise
From death, you numberless[3] infinities
Of souls, and to your scatter'd bodies[4] go[5],
All[6] whom the flood[7] did, and fire[8] shall o'erthrow,
All[6] whom war, dearth, age, agues,[9] tyrannies,[10, 11]
Despair, law, chance, hath slain,[12] and you[13] whose eyes,[14]
Shall behold God, and never taste death's woe.
But let them[15] sleep, Lord, and me mourn[16] a space,[17, 18]
For, if above all these[19], my sins abound,[20]
'Tis late[21] to ask abundance of thy grace,[22]
When we are there; here on this lowly ground,[23]
Teach me how to repent; for that's as good
As[24] if thou'hadst seal'd my pardon, with thy blood.[25]

【作者简介】John Donne（约翰·邓，或译邓恩，1571—1631）出生在伦敦的一个富有的商人家庭。四岁丧父，他的母系是天主教徒，同《乌托邦》的作者、天主教的殉教者 Thomas More 有姻亲关系。他的舅父和哥哥都与天主教有牵连而被捕入狱，哥哥死在狱中。邓早年完全是受的天主教教育。他在牛津大学和剑桥大学先后读了六年书，由于他是天主教徒，不能获得学位。90 年代初，他在伦敦学法律，生活放荡。90 年代中，他去意大利、西班牙游历。1596 年随 Essex 伯爵的舰队去西班牙作战，次年又去阿速尔群岛（Azores）作战。1598 年任掌玺大臣 Egerton 的秘书。1601 年他同 Egerton 夫人的侄女 Anne More 秘密结婚，因而失宠入狱。出狱后生活潦倒，大半在这时候他改信了国教并参加反天主教的笔战。1612 年左右被引见国王 James I，国王颇赏识他的才学，希望他能出任教职，但他一直拖延到 1615 年才正式成为国教牧师，任王室牧师，1612 年成为伦敦圣保罗大教堂的教长。他的宣讲极负盛名。他的妻子 1617 年去世，他自己死于 1631 年。

邓的一生反映了他那时代一个侧面。他经历了三个朝代。他出身富裕家庭，早年受文艺复兴时期世俗文化的影响，纵情声色，但也颇有抱负。不过当时有才华的青年多无出路（试看 Marlowe, Greene, Kyd 这批大学才子莫不穷愁潦倒）。在国教确立的英国，他一个天主教徒要在社会上取得地位，不得不依附国教权贵，这使他内心极度困惑。加以 James I 和 Charles I 两朝政治腐败，社会上弥漫着一种怀疑、幻灭的感觉。邓的诗歌（抒情诗、讽刺诗、诗简、宗教诗），散文，布道文，都反映了他内心的挣扎。他诗歌标奇立异，也是一种反抗的表现。

【题解与注释】

下面选了四首爱情诗，一首宗教诗。邓这派诗歌被称为“玄学派”The Metaphysical School，邓是始作俑者。这个名称来源于十七世纪诗人评论家 Dryden，他评论邓说：“他喜弄玄学，不仅在他的讽刺诗中如此，在爱情诗中也如此。爱情诗本应言情，他却用哲学的微妙的思辨，把女性们的头脑弄胡涂了。”十八世纪的 Johnson 进一步阐发了对玄学的见解，他也认为邓这一派的爱情诗不是抒写自然之情，只是炫耀学问，所以他们写的不是诗，只是韵文。Johnson 说他们有聪敏机智（wit），但不是 Pope 所说的机智（把人们常想到的，用巧妙的方式表达出来），而是 discordia concors，即把不和谐的东西聚在一起；The most heterogeneous ideas are yoked by violence together，把杂七杂八的思想生拉硬套，扭在一起，只是为了语不惊人死不休，是雕虫小技。不过，Johnson 说，话又说回，他的奇思妙想（conceits），不多读书，不多思考，也是写不出来的。这派诗歌在十八、十九世纪默默无闻。到了二十世纪，人们对十九世纪英国诗歌那种甜蜜腻人软绵绵的风格感到腻烦，玄学派又被人注意。Grierson 1912 年出版邓的诗集，经过 Eliot 等人的鼓吹，不仅邓的地位又确立了，而且对英国现代诗歌产生了很大影响。Eliot 认为英国诗歌从邓以后日趋衰落，他称之为 dissociation of sensibility，即思想与感情分家，而邓和文艺复兴时代的诗歌既有思想又有感情，溶成一体——unified sensibility.

归纳各家评论，邓这派诗歌的特点大要如下：

所谓 wit 或 conceit，指的是说理辩论多于抒情，把不同的思想、意象、典故交揉在一起，意象则涉及各种知识领域，类比奇特。这种敏捷活泼的思维活动又与强烈的激情——爱的激情、宗教的激情，溶为一体。他的爱情诗不写花容月貌，婉转柔情，也不尚词藻的修饰，而是刚健有力，所谓 strong line，口语化，戏剧化。格律则在繁复的变化之中有不变。但这派诗歌常流于晦涩。本·琼生说邓作为诗人在某些方面是天下第一，但又说由于人们读不懂，难以流传。总之，这一派在英诗中是一支突起的异军，可以说前无古人，而模仿者也必然只能画虎不成。

1. SONG

邓的爱情诗大致可以分为两类，一类是否定的，一类是肯定的。Song 这首诗是前一类，但家喻户晓，并谱了曲，是选家必选的一首。中心思想是世界上没有专一的爱情，诗人所持是怀疑玩世的态度。同邓其他抒情诗一样，中心思想单纯，只有一个，而布局常按辩论程序分成若干段。这里共三段。第一段大意是：这里所举的一切都是不可能办到的。第二段说走遍天涯海角，历尽千年万载，也找不到忠贞不渝的爱。第三段是戏剧性的转折和结束：即使不可能存在的事被人发现了，诗人也不相信。

1. Go: 起句突兀。是祈使句，对话式，口语，富于戏剧性。

2. catch a falling star: 陨星是捉不住的。

3. mandrake root: 蔓德拉草的根象人参一样长成人形，据《圣经》传说，女子服用可以成孕，所以此处联想到 get with child = beget a child on a mandrake root。

4.（第 3 行）: 参看中古法国诗人 Villon 的名句：Mais où sont les neiges d'antan，“去年的雪到哪里去了？”也是无答案的问题。这种提问法和提这类的问题，都是经院辩论的遗风。

5. cleft: 即 clove, cleave 的过去式。劈开。据传魔鬼的脚象牛羊蹄。

6. Mermaid: 美人鱼。此处指古代希腊神话中的海妖（siren），海妖用歌声迷住奥德修斯 Odysseus 的水手们。

7. envy: 嫉妒，此处半拟人化（personification），爱嫉妒的人。

8. stinging: 螫刺，指诽谤。抵御诽谤是不可能的。

9. wind [waind]: 风。什么风能帮助一个老实人提高地位呢？连上句，诗人突然夹进两句对社会风尚的批判。

10.（第 10—11 行） 有人这样解释：If you are strongly drawn to see strange things，如果你极想看些珍奇的事物。也可以解作：如果你出门在外看到些奇景。

11. Things invisible to see: 可以是倒装句，即 to see invisible things，也可以是

sights 的同位语。这一段反映了地理发现后，人们的知识领域扩大了。

12. Ride: 可以是祈使句，也可以理解为 If you ride。

13. snow: 动词，till 后面用虚拟语气。

14. wilt: 第二人称单数，= will. 这是这一段的主句。

15. befell: = happened to.

16. And swear: = And wilt swear.

17. true: 后面的逗号表示读时要停顿，以突出 fair。

18. let me know: 完全是现代口语。

19. Pilgrimage: 中古朝圣旅行，暗示虔诚，但联系下面，则反衬出讽刺的涵义。

20. were: = would be.

21. we: 指我和这样一个女子。

22. Though she were true: = Suppose she were true.

23. last: = will last 她的忠实能够延续到…。

24. you write your letter: 指分别后的通信。意思是她的忠实最多保持到你离开后给她写第一封信的时候。

25. ere I come: = before I come，我作为新情人去同她交往。

26. False to two or three: 又已经对两三个情人不忠了。

2. THE CANONIZATTON

1. Canonization: 天主教把有功于教会的人（如殉教者）封为圣者之谓。诗人把准备殉情的情侣比作殉教的圣徒。这是一首正面的爱情诗。第一段大意是不管人们做什么，不要妨碍我追求爱。第二段提出反问，我和她的爱情损害了什么人呢？第三段，爱把我们结合为一体，我们的爱是神秘的。第四段，准备殉爱，成为爱的圣徒。第五段结束：人们将把我们的爱视为一切爱的范本。此诗的韵脚安排，第一段为：abbacccaa，其他各段都保持 a 韵脚。

2. for God's sake etc.: 这是邓的一句脍炙人口的诗，收入《牛津引语词典》，语气急切，甚至粗鲁。这种语气，贯串全段。对话者 you 不是女方，而是一般世人。暗示人们早在议论纷纷。

3. palsy: 痉挛病。

4. or ... or: = either ... or.

5. gout: 风湿病。

6. five gray hairs: 少量灰白头发。妙在具体五根头发，和“白发三千丈”异曲同工。

7. flout: 动词，蔑视、嘲笑，以 hair, fortune 为宾语。

8.（第 4 行）= Improve your state with wealth and your mind with arts. 富贵、学问是别人的事，我只要爱情。

9. Take you a course: 从事一桩固定的职业。

10. place: 职务、官职。

11. observe: be attentive to，小心伺候，察言观色。

12. his honour: 某位贵族、权贵。

13. his grace: 某位主教。

14. real face, stamped face: 前者指国王本人，后者指铸有国王头像的钱币。两词都是 contemplate（谛视）的宾语。

15. what you will, approve: = approve what you will, approve 验证。

16. So: = so long as 只要。

17.（第 10—15 行）语气一变，用温和委婉的反问。但同前一段一样，也有现实社会的反映。

18. sighs, tears, colds, heats: 这类名词以及夸大的写法都是沿袭意大利 Petrarch (1304–1374) 抒情诗传统，称为 conceit.

19. ground: 土地、地产。难道我的眼泪把谁的土地淹没了，毁坏了？

20. colds: 感冒；爱情的冷却、失意。这会使春天迟迟不来，种田人遭受损失吗？（cold 借用为"寒冷的气候"。）

21. heats: 热病；爱情的炽热。

22. one more: one more person.

23. plaguy Bill: = plague Bill，天气炎热引起瘟疫；Bill 指每个教区每周公布的因瘟疫而死亡者的名单。

24. Soldiers etc.: = Soldiers will find wars 当兵的想打仗，还是有仗可打的。下面接 Though she and I do love.

25. Litigious: 好打官司的。

26. which: = who (men).

27. quarrels move: = move quarrels 挑起争端。

28. such: 指下面的比喻。

29.（从 19 行起）从此以下，口气平和。

30. fly: 灯蛾。

31. We'are: 一个音节。下一行 The'Eagle 也是一个音节。

32. Tapers: 蜡烛。

33. Eagle and Dove: 凶猛和温和的象征。

34. Phoenix: 据传说，凤凰只有一个，寿千年，到期自焚身死，然后从灰烬中再生，成为新凤凰。Riddle 指凤凰再生的传说不可理解。

35. more wit: more meaning，更有意义，更易理解。

36. By us: = by our example. 把爱的极度兴奋比作死亡，从兴奋中恢复过来，比作再生。

37. So: = in such measure，指下一行 We die and rise the same.

38. to = into.

39. one neutral thing: 凤凰是中性的，不分雌雄。

40. Mysterious: 象宗教一样神秘、不可思议、值得崇敬。在西方诗歌里，爱情常和宗教密不可分。

41. it: anticipatory pronoun 先行代词，指句末的 love。

42. hearse: 灵柩。

43. If unfit ... our legend be: legend 指我们这种传奇式的爱情。这句诗的意思是：如果我们的爱不值得铭刻在墓碑上。

44. Chronicle: 编年史。不值得载入史册。

45. sonnet: 十四行诗，此处泛指情诗。

46. pretty rooms: 借用意大利文 stanza 一词的原义（"房间"），实指 stanza，诗段。"在情诗里建造美好的厅堂"，用诗歌来咏唱爱情。

47. urn: 骨灰瓶，此处指爱情小诗。

48. becomes: = suits, befits 适合于。

49. The greatest ashes: 伟大的殉爱者的骨灰。

50. half-acre tomb: 占地很大的陵墓。骨灰瓶、陵墓，都指伟大功勋的见证。

51. hymns: 宗教赞美诗，此处指赞颂爱情的诗。

52. all: 一切人，后代。

53. approve: 承认、确认。

54. invoke us: 接上面 shall，一定会向我们两个圣徒祈祷、祈求。

55. hermitage: 孤独的修道者，此处指虔诚的爱情信奉者。

56. peace: 对你们已死去的人来说，狂热已成过去。

57. that now is rage: that 指 love，指我们这些现在狂热恋爱的人们。

58. contract: 收拢，意思是你们曾是人类灵魂的缩影（即 43 行 epitomize）。

59. drove: = crammed 压挤进去。宾语是 44 行 countries 等。把国家、都市、朝廷，都收入你们眼底，意思是饱览人间一切。

60. glasses: 镜子。

61. So made such mirrors: = your eyes were made in such a way that they were such mirrors and spies that they epitomized all to you. 这两句完全是修饰 41 行 eyes，你们的眼睛就象镜子和侦探，把世间一切都收拢到你们的眼里。

62. Beg: 为我们乞求。

63. above: 上天、上苍。

64. pattern: 模范，使世人都能仿效你们。

3. A VALEDICTION: OF WEEPING

此诗有人以为是作者同他爱妻分别时所写。这首诗的情绪是激昂的，但又有很强的说理。英国当代批评家 Empson 以为此诗充满疑虑，怕对方不忠贞，又自作多情。又，此诗所用的意象全是圆形（钱币、地球、月球）圆形既象征完整，又象征零。

1. Valediction: = farewell 珍重告别。

2. of: = on 说明诗人要发表议论。

3.（第 1 句）祈使句起句。

4. whilst I stay here: = while I am still with you.

5. coins them: 把我的眼泪铸成钱币（我的眼泪里映着你的头像），钱币暗示我的眼泪有了价值。一说 coins = 勾引出，可参考。

6. thy stamp they bear: = they bear thy stamp 我的泪珠刻印着你的肖像。

7. Mintage: 铸造。

8. they be: = they would be; thus 代表条件从句。

9. pregnant: 我的眼泪里孕育着你，被你所充满。

10. emblems: 象征、符号，多用于宗教图画或器物，如等边三角形与圆重叠是一个 emblem，象征三位一体，一只手从一朵云里伸出，象征上帝等。此处含有朕兆之意，预示一滴痛苦之泪会勾起更多的痛苦之泪。

11. of more: = of more grief.

12. that thou: thou 作名词用，= that image of you，你的那个映像。所谓“更多的痛苦”，因为不仅一滴泪滴落了，而且泪上面你的肖像也随之滴落，多了一层痛苦。

13.（第 9 行）此句难解。接上文的意思，可以解作：既然我的眼泪和你的映像都同归于尽（nothing），这就预示（emblem）我们分别之后（when on a divers shore）的命运了：分别无异于死亡。本·琼生（Ben Jonson）说过，邓的诗必因无人能懂（for not being understood）而不传，此为难懂的一例。

on a divers shore：一般解为 diverse shore，即 in different countries.

14.（第 10 行）用制地球仪的比喻说理。地球仪的制作是随地理发现而新兴的一门学问和行业。其法是把绘制好的地图剪贴在空白球体上。邓看来也熟悉这个行当，他在书信中曾谈到过。

15. copies: 一张张绘好的地图。

16. Asia: 亚洲。显然是三个音节，最后音节是长音，与前一行叶韵。

17. nothing: 空白球体。

18. all: 包罗万物的地球。由零变为一切。

19. So: 象工匠制地球仪一样。

20.（第 14—16 行）each tear 主语，指诗人的泪；grow 动词，= make or become; globe 和 world 都是宾语。我的每滴眼泪（上面有你的肖像）同样也变成了地球、世界。

21. yea: 不仅如此；不仅仅是个地球，还是个大千世界。

22. by that impression: 由于有了你的肖像在上边。

23.（第 17—18 行）也是两句难解的诗。This world 根据上文是诗人的泪珠。从 14 行开始，大意应是：“我的每一滴泪都变成了一个世界（这种情况一直持续到）你的眼泪掺和着我的眼泪，把这个世界（诗人的泪）淹没了。” By waters 实际是重复前面的意思，即你的眼泪。

24. my heaven dissolved so: 说明 waters 的来源。My heaven 就是女方，与 thee 同位。据中世纪天文学，第九重天全是水（参看下一首诗 8 注），天溶解了（dissolved），水就倾注下来了。So，语气词，表示极大程度。

25.（第 19 行）接前一段的思路。月亮有吸引潮水的力量，但对方比月亮更强有力。

26. sphere: 天体运行的圆形轨道，引伸为影响范围。

27. dead: 在当时的含义是极度兴奋。

28. forbear: 不要，切勿。

29. what it may do too soon: 诗人要出海远行，对女方说：勿使大海学你的榜样，兴风作浪，把我淹死。

30. wind: 读 [waind].

31. than it purposeth: 比风暴想要给我带来的灾害还多。诗人把叹息比作风暴。
32. sigh one another's breath: 二人同呼吸，一人叹一口气就等于使对方少一口气。

4. A VALEDICTION: FORBIDDING MOURNING

此诗情调比较克制、平和、超脱，但想象仍极突兀，意象仍极奇特。据 Izaak Walton 写的传记，邓于 1611 年随 Robert Drury 出使法国，作此以赠妻子。诗里也流露出忧虑情绪，他妻子果然在他在国外时产一死胎。

1. pass away: 死去。语气平和缓慢，但仍有戏剧性。第一段的场面完全是为了烘托第五行 melt，溶化、溶为一体。

2. tear-floods, sigh-tempests: 参看前诗，此处也把眼泪比作洪水，叹息比作风暴，这种构思（conceit）来源于意大利诗人 Petrarch. 邓极擅长把简单的词拼在一起，使文字简炼，内容浓缩，其他例子如 that thou, an everywhere, a she-sigh, vice-nature. 莎士比亚和文艺复兴时期诗人以至散文家都善于创造性地运用语言。

3. move: = stir up，搅起。

4. profanation: 亵渎、不敬。

5. laiety: = laity ['leiəti] 教会圣职人员以外的普通人。以上两词都把爱情暗比为神圣的宗教。

6. moving of th'earth: 地震。当时人相信地震是由于上帝震怒而引起的，必然带来灾难。

7. reckon: 估计着。

8. trepidaton of the spheres: 据托勒密（Ptolemy）天文学（地球中心说）天体运行的轨道有九圈，最近地球一圈为月球轨道，第八层为众恒星的轨道，第九层为水晶圈，全是水。Trepidation 抖动，摇晃，指第九重天或第八重天的运行发生变化，影响里面几重天，以至春分秋分发生差错。这四句诗的意思是：小小地球的震动引起人们的惊慌，而庞大天体和宇宙的偏移，人们却认为无害。诗人把离别比作庞大天体的偏移，是神秘的、重大的，不足为凡人道的。

9. greater: 指 trepidation 与 moving of the earth 相比。

10. innocent: 按字面原意：无害。

11. sublunary: "月下"，地球上的、凡俗的、可变的、可朽的。

12. soul: = essence 本质。

13. sense: 感官，与精神相对而言。邓歌颂精神的爱（Platonic love，柏拉图式的爱），这是凡夫俗子所不能理解的。

admit: = suffer, stand 忍受。

14. it: 指 absence，离别。

15. those things: 指感官。

16. elemented: = composed 构成。

17. it: 指 13 行人间的爱，凡俗的爱。

18. refined: 精炼，象经过炼金术提炼的一样。

19.（第 18 行）有些"不可言传"的意思。

20. Inter-assured [-id]: 修饰 we. 我们心心相印，互相盟誓（有法律的庄严保证的涵义）。

21. Careless: = careless 修饰 we。不以为意，紧接 to miss+ 宾语 eyes, etc.

22. eye, etc.: 各种感官。

23.（第 21 行）论点一转：我们固然不象凡夫俗子那样分手不得，但却也忍受不了分别，我们不要把它看作分别吧，把它看作扩展吧。

24. endure not yet: 读作 yet endure not.

endure = suffer 忍受。

25. breach: 分裂，分别。

26. expansion: 延展，endure 的宾语，引入另一比喻：把一块黄金打成一片金页（据说一两黄金可打成一片 250 平方英尺的页片）；把他们之间的爱比作黄金。

27. airy thinness: 同凡俗的、沉浊的（sublunary）爱暗比。

28. beat: 过去分词。

29.（第 25 行）以下又引入一个新比喻。按：圆规历来是坚贞（firmitas）的象征（emblem），圆又是完美的象征。据注家考证十一世纪末波斯诗人 Omar Khayyam 的 *Rubaiyat*（《鲁拜集》）中已出现过，其后传入欧洲。以下三段是三个意思：25—28 圆规的两脚是互相牵动的，29—32 分后必合，33—36 由于一只脚坚定不移，另一只才能画一个完美的圆。

they: 指二人的灵魂。

so: = in such a way.

30. fixt (fixed) foot: 圆心脚，定在圆心上不动。

31. doth (does): 代替 moves.

32. th'other: 指圆周脚。圆周脚动，圆心脚也动。

33. do: 条件句，故不用 doth (does).

34. sit: 让步句，故不用 sits.

35. It: 第一个 it 指圆心脚，第二个 it 指圆周脚。

36. hearken: 倾听，倾斜。

37. that: 指圆周脚。

38. th'other foot: 圆周脚。

39. obliquely: 倾斜。

40. ... end, where I begun (began): 画一个整圆，或解作回到圆心脚旁边。

5. HOLY SONNET VII

有人把邓比作圣·奥古斯丁（St. Augustine 354-430），早年放荡不羁，追逐声色名位，晚年皈依宗教，大事忏悔。邓写过两组十四行圣诗，中心主题两个：一、在上帝面前自惭形秽，二、最后审判之可怕。十四行诗本来是由意大利发端的情诗体裁，邓却用它来写宗教题材。他不是直接抒写内心活动，而是通过天主教耶稣会士常用的默祷方式，向上帝和天使致辞来表达悔罪情绪。下面是第二组（共十九首）中的第七首。

1.（第 1 行）这也是一句名诗。据《圣经》《启示录》七章一节："我看见四位天使站在地的四角"，邓套用这句话，却又加上 round 和 imagined（想象中的），多少带有点离经叛道的味道，隐约显出新与旧、科学与宗教的矛盾。评论家多认为邓的宗教诗并没有多少笃信者的虔诚，而多自我戏剧化，并极力争取声音和形象的效果。

2. Angels: 呼格。世界末日，天使们吹响号角，召唤亡魂们听候上帝的最后审判。Blow，祈使句，向天使们所发。

3. you numberless ...: 呼格。你们数不清的、无限多的亡魂。Arise，祈使句，向亡魂们所发。

From death: 基督教认为人死后灵魂分别入地狱、炼狱、天堂，等候世界末日来到，听取上帝的最后审判。

4. scatter'd bodies: 分散在各地的尸体。

5. go: 祈使句，向下两句中的 All 所发，向你们分散各地的尸体走去，死者还魂，听候审判。

6.（第 5—6 行）All: 呼格。一切人们。

7. flood: 指《圣经》中所记载的洪水。上帝因人类犯罪，降洪水把人类淹死，只留下诺亚一家。

8. fire: 指世界末日，上帝要降大火，烧毁大地。洪水指过去，大火指未来。

9. agues [ˈeigjuːz]**:** 疟疾。

10.（第 6—7 行） 这是一系列的人间灾难，莎士比亚十四行诗第 66 首也有类似的罗列。

11. tyrannies: 具体的暴虐行为。

12. hath slain: has killed，受最后一词影响，用单数动词。

13. you: 呼格。

14. whose eyes: 逗号表明读时略作停顿。这些人是信基督的人，他们死后都能复活，见到上帝。语出《新约》保罗致哥林多人的信《哥林多前书》十五章。

15. them: 指以上众人。

16. me mourn: = let me mourn 让我表示哀痛吧。

17.（第 9—14 行）十四行诗前八行（octet）是一个段落，一个意思，后六行（sestet）成一个段落，转入另一个意思。此诗前八行大张旗鼓兴师动众要古往今来已死的、将死的亿兆亡魂都起来听候最后审判，到此突然戏剧性地刹住，一个 180 度急转变，一切声音骚动骤然寂静无声，形成鲜明对比。前面是千军万马，后面是他一人面对上帝。评论家说他自我中心，而这种追求戏剧效果也引起人们对他的虔诚有了怀疑。不过邓仍不失为奇才、怪才。

18. a space: = a while 片刻。

19. above all these: = more than all these 超出这些人之上。

20. if my sins abound: 如果我的罪很多。

21. 'Tis late: 指 12 行 when we are there，当我们来到最后审判席的时候。

22. abundance of thy grace: 你的宽厚的恩泽。

23. lowly ground: 指人世。

24. as good as: 等于⋯了。

25. seal my pardon with thy blood: 用你的血签署了我的赦罪书，指基督用自己的生命为人类赎罪。上帝，请你教导我怎样悔罪吧，这就等于你赦免我的罪了，我获得宽恕了。

9 ANDREW MARVELL
1621–1678

1. To His Coy Mistress
2. The Garden

周珏良　选注

1. TO HIS COY[1] MISTRESS

Had we but world[2] enough, and time,
This coyness, Lady, were no crime.
We would sit down, and think which way
To walk, and pass our long love's Day.
Thou by the Indian Ganges'[3] side
Should'st[4] rubies[5] find; I by the tide
Of Humber[6] would complain. I would
Love you ten years before the Flood[7],
And you should, if you please, refuse
Till the Conversion of the Jews.[8]
My vegetable[9] love should grow
Vaster then empires, and more slow.
An hundred years should go to praise
Thine eyes, and on thy forehead gaze;[10]
Two hundred to adore each breast,
But thirty thousand to the rest;
An age[11] at least to every part,
And the last age should show your heart.
For, Lady, you deserve this state[12],

Nor would I love at lower rate.[13]
But at my back I always hear
Time's wingèd chariot[14] hurrying near;
And yonder all before us lie
Deserts of vast eternity.
Thy beauty shall no more be found,
Nor, in thy marble vault,[15] shall sound
My echoing song; then worms shall try
That long-preserv'd virginity,
And your quaint[16] honour[17] turn to dust,
And into ashes all my lust.[18]
The grave's a fine and private place,
But none I think do there embrace.
Now therefore, while the youthful hue
Sits on thy skin like morning dew,
And while thy willing soul transpires
At every pore with instant fires,[19]
Now let us sport us[20] while we may;
And now, like am'rous birds of prey,
Rather at once our time devour,[21]
Than languish in his slow-chapt pow'r.[22]
Let us roll all our strength, and all
Our sweetness, up into one ball,
And tear our pleasures with rough strife,
Thorough[23] the iron gates of life.
Thus, though we cannot make our sun
Stand still, yet we will make him run.

2. THE GARDEN

I

How vainly men themselves amaze[1]
To win the palm,[2] the oak, or bays;

And their uncessant[3] labours see
Crowned from some single herb or tree[4]:
Whose short and narrow-vergèd shade
Does prudently their toils upbraid;[5]
While all flowers and all trees do close
To weave the garlands of repose.[6]

II

Fair Quiet, have I found thee here,
And Innocence, thy sister dear!
Mistaken long, I sought you then
In busy companies of men.
Your sacred plants,[7] if here below,
Only among the plants will grow.
Society is all but[8] rude,
To this delicious[9] solitude.

III

No white nor red was ever seen
So am'rous[10] as this lovely green.
Fond[11] lovers, cruel as their flame,
Cut in these trees their mistress' name:
Little, alas, they know or heed
How far these beauties hers[12] exceed!
Fair trees, wheresoe'er your barks I wound,
No name shall but your own be found.

IV

When we have run our passion's heat,[13]
Love hither makes his best retreat.[14]
The gods, that mortal beauty[15] chase,
Still[16] in a tree did end their race:
Apollo hunted Daphne so,

Only that she might laurel grow;
And Pan did after Syrinx speed,
Not as a nymph, but for a reed.

V

What wondrous life in this I lead!
Ripe apples drop about my head;
The luscious clusters of the vine
Upon my mouth do crush their wine;
The nectarine,[17] and curious[18] peach
Into my hands themselves do reach;
Stumbling on melons, as I pass,
Ensnared with flowers, I fall on grass.

VI

Meanwhile the mind from pleasure less[19]
Withdraws into its happiness;
The mind, that ocean where each kind
Does straight its own resemblance find;[20]
Yet it creates, transcending these,
Far other worlds and other seas,
Annihilating[21] all that's made
To[22] a green thought in a green shade.

VII

Here at the fountain's sliding foot,
Or at some fruit-tree's mossy root,
Casting the body's vest[23] aside,
My soul into the boughs does glide:
There, like a bird, it sits and sings,
Then whets[24] and combs its silver wings,
And, till prepared for longer flights,
Waves in its plumes the various light.[25]

VIII

Such was that happy garden-state,[26]
While man there walked without a mate:
After a place so pure and sweet,
What other help could yet be meet[27]!
But 'twas[28] beyond a mortal's share
To wander solitary there:
Two paradises 'twere[29] in one
To live in paradise alone.

IX

How well the skillful gardener drew,[30]
Of flowers and herbs, this dial new;
Where, from above, the milder sun
Does through a fragrant zodiac run;[31]
And, as it works, the industrious bee
Computes its time as well as we!
How could such sweet and wholesome hours
Be reckoned but[32] with herbs and flowers!

【作者简介】 Andrew Marvell（安德鲁·马维尔，1621—1678）是英格兰北部约克郡一位加尔文派（Calvinist）教士的儿子，曾在剑桥大学“三一学院”（Trinity College）读书。1642 年英国资产阶级革命开始时他正在欧洲旅行。政治上他站在国会军一边。他是密尔顿的同僚，1657 年被任命做当时政府的拉丁文秘书，是密尔顿的助手，1659 年当选家乡 Hull 地方的国会议员。查理二世复辟后他继续当选，一直到去世。他也曾在英国驻俄国、丹麦、瑞典等国使馆任职。

他生前只以讽刺诗和散文知名。1681 年，他死后四年，他的《各体诗集》（*Miscellaneous Poems*）出版时也没有引起多大注意。直到本世纪二十年代初期，英国十七世纪以 John Donne 为首的“玄理诗人”，因为学者 Herbert J. C. Grierson 选印之于先，诗人兼批评家 T. S. Eliot 评论之于后，因而风行的时候，他作为这派的一员才以抒情诗知名。然而他自有自己的特殊风格，诗里有玄理派诗的形象，如下面选的《致羞涩的姑娘》（*To His Coy Mistress*）中所用的；但也继承了伊丽莎白时代诗人，如斯宾塞（Edmund Spenser），西德尼（Sir Philip Sidney）田园诗的风格，（见下面选的 *The Garden* 一首），而把这个和玄理诗的特点结合起来就酿成了 Marvell 的特殊风格。他写诗多用双行偶句（Couplet）又下启了德莱顿（John Dryden）和蒲伯（Alexander Pope）的诗风。所以他虽非象邓恩、密尔顿那样的大诗人（他传世的诗一共不到一百首），但在文学史上自有不可磨灭的地位，而他的作品至少有好几首是英国文学中的不朽之作，这里选的二首就在其中。

【题解与注译】

1. TO HIS COY MISTRESS

这首诗的主题是极为常见的。我国唐人绝句：“劝君莫惜金缕衣，劝君惜取少年时。花开堪折只须折，莫待无花空折枝。”比 Marvell 略早的英国诗人 Robert Herrick（1591—1674）的脍炙人口的小诗：

Gather ye rosebuds while ye may,
  Old time is still a-flying;
And this same flower that smiles today,
  Tomorrow will be dying.
………
That age is best which is the first,
  When youth and blood are warmer,
But being spent, the worse, and worst
  Time still succeed the former.

Then be not coy, but use your time,
  And while ye may, go marry:
For having lost but once your prime,
  You may forever tarry.

都用的这个主题，还有其他的英国诗，乃至希腊、拉丁文诗也有用这个主题的，可谓熟之又熟，但 Marvell 这首诗又却是一首极清新之作，这是为什么？简单的说是因为 Marvell 对熟题目使用了新作法，在意象（images）的选择和展开上，在对衬迥然不同的意象的奇想上，在全诗的结构上（他使用了类似逻辑中的三段论法），都颇见巧思。但是又不止此，更重要的是诗人能把炽热的激情运用刚强的理智在轻快隽雅的抒情格调下表现出来（a tough reasonableness beneath the slight lyric grace，现代诗人 T. S. Eliot 评 Marvell 的话），这样就以故为新，夺胎换骨，创造出象本诗这样崭新的动人作品来了。

在这首诗里，一位青年劝说他所恋的羞涩姑娘不要迟延，快接受他的爱情，以免枉度了青春。诗以三大段组成，第一段说，如果我们两个人在时间空间上是不受限制的（Had we but world enough, and time,）那么你这么忸怩下去确也不算罪过（This coyness, Lady, were no crime.）我们可以尽量等待下去。第二段说，但是时光是不饶人的（But at my back I always hear / Time's wingèd chariot hurrying near）；不久你的美貌，我的歌声都将不再存在，死亡将使爱情成为不可能了。第三段说，因而乘我们都在青春之际，让我们和时光竞赛，及时地最大限度地夺取生命的乐趣。这说理过程很清楚，但如果只有这一段说道理，却也不成其为诗。那么这首诗的"诗意"到底从何而生？

诗是诉诸感情的东西，要能使读者的感情受到影响，得到美感而且越强烈越好，我们才说它是好诗，否则我们说它没有味道，或者简直不是诗。我们现在看看面前的这一首到底如何？

从第一行到20行为一段。第一、二行如前面所指出的，说明了这一段的主题，提出了空间时间这一对意象。从第三行起就加以发挥。青年人说，既然这么说，好吧，让我们坐下来想想往什么方向走，花费长时间来决定何时相爱，时空两个意象都照顾到。下面的六行运用了新奇的展开意象的手法：既然空间阔大，时间不忙，那就一个到东方印度的恒河（Ganges）之畔去找红宝石，一个就在西欧英国北部的亨伯河（Humber，这河在Marvell的家乡Hull）边去独自埋怨，彼此离得远远的。从时间上说，也可拉得长长的，我要从上古洪水之前十年爱起，而你如果愿意，也可以一直不理睬到世界的结束。下面两行（11—12行）结合时间空间来写，因为时间之长，所以我的爱情，固然和植物（vegetable love）那样缓缓地长，可也会长到疆土辽阔的帝国那样了。下面的六行又集中在时间上，要赞赏、爱慕你这位姑娘要用上好几千年，你的身体每一部分顶少都值得花上一个历史时期（age）去爱慕，最后才能看到你的真心。作这样纵横数万里，上下几千年无尽无休的努力，这青年毫无怨言，因为本段最后两行中说，他的恋人很值得这种礼遇（state）而他自己也不肯以少于这种程度的感情来爱她（at lower state）。这一整段给我们的感觉是这青年正在热恋，苦恋，但是他使用的不寻常的，时常是夸张的意象和似乎轻松的口气又使我们顶少有一半拿不准他是否是严肃的，这就埋下了有戏剧作用的伏笔。

第二段开始引入了时光不饶人的这一主题，口气突变，给读者以出乎意外的感觉。意象的展开速度增快更增加了紧迫感，时光的生翼的车轮紧跟在后面（Time's wingèd chariot hurrying near.），而展开在这一对恋人前面的是时间的无尽和空间的无边。这一意境是用四个字的短诗行"Deserts of vast eternity"（这里deserts指的是荒凉无人的原野，不是沙漠）有力地表现出来的。然而天地悠悠，人却不能永生。姑娘的花容月貌将有一天无可寻觅（Thy beauty shall no more be found），而青年的歌声也不可能在她的墓穴（marble vault）中回响。引入了这个死亡的主题，再加所使用的类乎邓恩诗中的玄理诗派意象使全诗气氛为之一变，带上了严肃强烈的感情。而第一段中的夸张的意象和轻松的口气曾经使我们怀疑这青年是否严肃的，这时起了反衬作用，使读者受到更强烈的严肃感情的感染。而下面六行（26—32行）中死亡意象的发展一步紧似一步，而且紧密结合了时间和空间的两个意象，加强了诗的效果。对人来讲，死亡是时间的终结，而当骸骨化了灰之后，也就是空间的终结，所以说大理石墓穴中将听不见我歌声的回响（Nor, in thy marble vault, shall sound / my echoing song）；而你长保的童贞也将由尸虫来初尝（then worms shall try / That long-preserv'd virginity）；你的矜持将为尘土（And your quaint honour turn to dust）；而我的恋情也将化灰而去（And into ashes all my lust）。31，32 两行把全诗中的四个中心意象：时间、空间、死亡、爱情以诗人的杰出想象力点化出这样的警句：

The grave's a fine and private place,
But none I think do there embrace.

墓穴不错而又很幽静，但谁又能在那里说爱谈情。这是全诗的高潮，就如戏剧中那样，是矛盾发展的顶点，下面就要为矛盾提出个解决的办法了。

第三段青年开始正面祈告姑娘在她青春的容光（youthful hue）犹如清晨的鲜露（morning dew），而她有情的内心（willing soul）中的激情又随时可以迸发为满面羞红（transpires / At every pore with instant fires,）时，应当及时行乐（sport us while we may）。下面的几行中又把时间和空间用典型的玄理诗派的意象（metaphysical images）来表现，38 行中说让我们象相爱着的捕捉小鸟的猛禽（am'rous birds of prey）来“吞食”（devour）时间，即尽量利用时间而不要被时间所慢慢吞吃掉，虚度了青春而无可奈何（Than languish in his slow-chapt pow'r）。下面一个意象更是出奇，上面已把吞噬人的时间形象化为张开的巨颚（slow-chapt），这里又把人世对恋人所横加的限制化为铁铸的囚门（iron gates），冲出了这囚门就在空间上摆脱了枷锁，就可夺得欢乐（tear our pleasures with rough strife），而时间也就无奈我何，因为虽然不能使时光不逝（cannot make our sun stand still），但可以使它快跑，这样就可以使欢乐的时间早日到来。而为了夺门而出，就最好把两人的力量（strength）集中起来，把双方的恋情（sweetness）集中起来成一球体（ball），因为同样体积的东西以球形占面积为最少，这就可以转得快，冲得方便，冲出来后，就可以脱出空间的限制而在时间中自由遨翔了。这样爱情就战胜了时空，战胜了死亡。诗人使用了这些意象，加以发展，表现出强烈的激情，足以感动读者，而意象的瑰丽又给读者以格外的美的享受，这就是一首好诗的效果。

这首诗用的是四轻重诗步的双行偶句（iambic tetrameter couplet），即每行四个轻重音步（iamb），每两行换韵，一般每一行之末都停顿。有的诗行连到下一行意义才完整，读时在行末就不能停顿而要连读下去，这就给人以流动的感觉，并使速度加快，本诗 5—10 行间，26—28 行间，33—34 行间，41—42 行间都是如此。

1. coy: 这个字在英国十六、十七世纪的诗里常带有难为人的意思，而不止于是安静、羞涩。

2. world: 大地或其一部分，泛指空间。

3. Indian Ganges: 印度的恒河。

4. should'st: = shouldest. should 的第二人称单数的古用法。

5. ruby: 红宝石。古代西方人认为红宝石可以使人忘忧和绝去邪念。

6. Humber [ˈhʌmbə]**:** Marvell 家乡 Hull 地方的一条河，在英格兰北部。

7. the Flood: 指《圣经》“创世纪”上记载的上古的洪水。

8. the Conversion of the Jews: 依据基督教的信仰，到了历史某阶段，犹太人也会改信基督教。一般是指事实上不可能的事。

9. vegetable: 如植物般生长得很慢。

10. and on thy forehead gaze: = and to gaze on thy forehead. 因为格律的关系改动句子中的词序，这是诗中常有的事。

11. age: 指一个长时期。

12. state: 适合身分的礼遇。

13. at lower rate: 以不足的感情。

14. Time's wingèd chariot: 在西方的神话里时间常常是被形容成坐在战车里（因为太阳神 Apollo 是乘金色战车的）或生着翅膀的，Marvell 这里是两者并用。wingèd 的 e 注了要发音，是格律的需要。

15. marble vault: 指大理石墓穴。

16. quaint: = fastidious 矜持。

17. honour: = purity, chastity.

18. lust: 情欲。

19. thy willing soul transpires / At every pore with instant fires: 这里是说姑娘的羞涩遮盖不住她的情思（willing soul）使她面泛红色（instant fires）。

20. sport us: = divert ourselves，以此欢娱自己。

21. devour: 原意是吞噬，这里和时光（time）连用，意指要快快利用时光。

22. slow-chapt pow'r: chap 是动物的颚颊，chapt 是把这个字作动词使用。这里已把时间拟物化，整个这个词指的是时光慢慢吞吃人的生命的力量。

23. thorough: = through.

2. THE GARDEN

在这首诗里一个人，也许是诗人自己，在一座有花木林泉之胜的园林里沉思着人生与自然的问题。他的思潮的起伏，常常是对拟人化了的自然的感受和冥想中向自己提出的问题，解决了的或者没有解决的，形成了这首诗的流动的，发展的，而非静止的本体，读来给人以恬适的乐趣。

I

在诗的开始，诗中人就批评了人们无端（vainly）为功利名誉而烦恼，而且偏偏要以自然界的草木如棕榈（palm）、橡叶（oak）和月桂（bays）来作为象征而去争夺（1—4 行）；但这些草木却很可以责人（upbraid）（5—6 行）；况且整个园林的葳蕤花木岂不更使人安适（repose），为什么要去争那些橡冕、桂冠等等呢？（7—8 行）

1. amaze: = perplex 或 craze.

2. the palm: 棕榈枝是古代给予胜利者和优异成就的奖赏。the oak 指 civic crown，是古代奖给在战争中救了同伴性命的战士的橡叶制的冠。bays 是月桂冠，古代奖给诗人和竞技的胜利者的。

3. uncessant: = incessant.

4. crowned: 奖赏。**some single herb or tree**：指上面说的棕榈等。

5. Whose short and narrow-vergèd shade…upbraid: 这里的 whose 指上面月桂冠等。用这些树叶制成的冠冕不过是窄窄的一环，所以叫它做 narrow-verged shade. Verge 一字在十七世纪有伸展的意思。prudently upbraid 意为很有理由责备他们这么干（their toils）。

6.（第 7—8 行）这两行明确地把整个园林里植物（all flowers and all trees）交织成的花木葳蕤（close to weave the garlands of repose；此处 close = unite）的环境也叫做花环（garlands），同以棕榈、橡叶、月桂等个别草木织成的冠冕对比，暗中则是对比世上的功名利禄和园林里的恬静安适。这里用 vainly 和 upbraid 等字明显表出是后者可取而前者不足道。

II

在这一段里，诗中人正面向拟人化了的恬静（Quiet）和无邪（Innocence）申诉情怀，说我在这里才找到了你们，而长期却错误地（mistaken long）在人间的熙熙攘攘中（busy companies of men）去找寻，哪能找到（9—12 行）！代表你们的花木，如在人间（if here below）能生长，那只能在大自然中（the plants）(14 行）。同这意味无穷的静寂之境（delicious solitude）比较起来，世俗的社会只是野蛮而不开化的（rude）（13—16 行）。

7. Your sacred plants: 说 plants sacred to 某人或某神，是指这种花木因而得名，或因而成为神圣的。这里是指代表恬静和无邪的花木。

8. but: = only. rude = unrefined, barbarous.

9. delicious: 这里既指精神上的意味，也指感官上的味道。参看第五段。

III

本段的开始说粉白脂红从来也不如这园林里的翠绿惹人爱（am'rous），这是用象征的说法说男女性爱不如对大自然之爱（17—18 行）。热恋中的恋人，以火热的恋情（cruel as their flame）常常把所爱的人的名字刻在树上（19—20 行）(如莎士比亚 *As You Like It* 一剧中就有这样的情节)，可叹，他们那知道，又那里理会（heed）花木的美好（these beauties）远比她们为甚啊！（21—22 行），美丽的树木，我如在你们的树皮上刻恋人的名字，那只能刻你们的名字了（23—24 行）。

10. am'rous: = amorous 因为这一行的音律是◡/◡/◡/◡/，所以在 amorous 中省去一个音节，使这一行读成：

◡ / ◡ / ◡ / ◡ /
So am'rous as this lovely green

以合乎音律。

11. fond: = infatuated.

12. hers: 指 20 行的 mistress.

IV

这一段紧接上段，说在经历了火热的恋爱之后，爱情就退到自然中来找安宁恬静（25—26 行）。天上的神仙追逐世上的美女，最后追到手的也总就是一棵树木，还不是以情欲始以自然终（27—28 行）。这里用了西方古典神话里的两个典故，Apollo 是太阳神，追求仙女 Daphne，追得她无奈何，只得变成一棵月桂树。Pan 是牧羊人和猎手的保护神，追求女神 Syrinx，把她也逼得变成了芦苇（29—32 行）。这里面有嘲讽的意味在内，因为两个神想得到的是女神，并非月桂芦苇，但结果却如此。对比人生也是如此，爱情尝够了，到底还是大自然中无邪、恬静，这种艺术手法在玄理派诗中是常有的。

13. run our passion's heat: heat 这里是双关语，作“情焰”解，也作“赛跑”（追逐）解。

14. retreat: 也是双关语，作“退隐”解，也作“撤退”（对追逐而言）解。

15. mortal beauty: 因为 Apollo 和 Pan 追求的女神都是 nymph，即一种寄居在海、河、山、林里的二等神仙，比起 Apollo 等大神来还是没有能完全脱去生死的“半仙”之体，所以说 mortal.

16. still: = always.

V

这一段写诗中人在大自然里享受的生活。拟人化了的自然对他好似对待恋人。这一诗节中有浓郁的感官美。成熟的苹果悬在他头上。一串一串又甜又香（luscious）的葡萄自动把类乎醇酒的汁水挤出，送上嘴来（upon my mouth crush their wine）（34—36 行）。而含有仙液般汁水的（nectarine）桃子更是体贴入微（curious），竟自己送到人手中来了（37—38 行）。在这一个花木扶疏，瓜果茂盛的乐境中活动，偶然失步，也就是让瓜绊了一下，或者被花藤缠住，失足摔在草地上是不会摔重的（39—40 行）。在本诗下面第八段里提到《圣经》中的伊甸园，在那里面亚当一失足（英文也是 fall），就被赶出园子，贬到了人间，而在这个园子里失足（I fall on grass）也不过摔在软软的草皮上。此园岂非比伊甸园更乐了？

17. nectarine: 是一种桃子的名字，同时也使人联想起 nectar 一字，那是希腊神话中的神仙的饮料。

18. curious: 这里有稀有的意思，也有充满关心或体贴人的意思。

VI

园中之乐如此，那么是否到此就是止境了呢？大是不然，还有更高的境界。因为身体感官所达到的境界是不能满足心灵的要求的，因而本段一开始就说如上一段所描述的感官享受乐趣之际，心灵却从这些比较起来不足道的快感（pleasure less）转而内向，以获得它独有的快乐（withdraws into its happiness）(41—42 行)，心灵犹如大海，能预先就认识世上一切事物（见下注），但不止如此，它还能超出这些（transcending these）而创造现实中所未有的“陆地和海洋”，意为其他更高的境界（43—46 行）。底下 47—48 两行是脍炙人口的名句：

Annihilating all that's made
To a green thought in a green shade.

这里的关键问题是 green thought 到底是什么意思。green 应理解为新鲜的，引伸为无邪的，没有受到尘俗沾染的。green shade 指的是诗中人处在其中的林园，也就是大自然的象征。所以这两行可以解释为“和处在这样翠绿的大自然环境中的不受尘俗沾染的无邪思想比起来，物质世界就可认为是没有什么价值的了。”但是这两行诗之所以感人，更重要的是 green thought 和 green shade 所显示的意象，代表大自然的一片绿荫，同时又象征无邪的思想，这新鲜无尘的新绿给人以美感，乐趣。

19. less: = lesser.

20. that ocean where each kind / Does straight its own resemblance find: 当时有一种通行而非科学的看法，认为凡陆地上有的，海洋里也有相当的东西，这里是用这个思想，而把心灵同海洋类同起来，把世界同陆地等同起来，认为心灵可以预知世上的一切事物。straight = without delay.

21. amnihilating: = treating as of no value，也可释为 reducing.

22. to: = compared to，与…相比较。

VII

这一段写的是在这翠绿的自然环境中沉思着的灵魂，也就是上段所讲的心灵，在这园林的泉边树下摆脱了肉体的外壳（casting the body's vest aside），他象一只鸟儿一样飞上了树枝，一边歌唱，一边用喙啄着（whets）梳着银色的羽毛；在准备好更长途的飞翔之前（till prepared for longer flight），这银色的羽毛上如水波似地荡漾着各色光采（Waves in its plumes the various light）。这一段形象很美，而且还有一层更深的哲理。依新柏拉图主义（Neo-Platonism）的说法，认为人的魂灵只有通过暂时摆脱肉体的束缚，进入出神状态，才能达到与神相交的境界，从而窥见真理。这一段用意象表达的正是这个思想，所谓更长途的飞翔就是达到与神相交的更高的境界，而第 56 行里讲的一片银白色羽毛实际上是新柏拉图主义哲学里永恒的光芒的象征，而荡漾在上面的光采也就是反映出的大千世界了。意象和哲理这样结合起来就使诗行获得了深一层的内容。

23. vest: 原义是外衣，引申作外壳。

24. whet: = preen，（鸟）用嘴整理（羽毛）。

25. 第 56 行： 这一行是倒装的，正常的词序应为 the various light waves in its plumes. various = varied in colour, waves 是动词，表示光作波状跃动。

VIII

在这绿色的园林里饱尝了感官上的享乐（见 V），又经历了精神上的遨翔，在这一段里诗中人从当前的园林推想到了最古的园林，也就是人类始祖亚当和夏娃所居住的伊甸园（Garden of Eden）。这节一开始就说在这里真好似当年亚当一个人在伊甸园独来独往那样快乐（57—58 行），而在这一个超出尘外（pure）的乐乡里还要什么伴侣呢（59—60 行）？但是一个凡人（mortal）那有偌大福分（share）能独自一人永远在这乐园里遨游呢（61—62 行）？在乐园里一个人独居，那就是双料的乐园，凡人是不能享受到的。于是远古的亚当因为有了个夏娃为伴而吃了智慧之果就同夏娃一起被逐出伊甸园，贬落人间，而诗中人也不能永远处在出神的境界，还是要回到现实中间。

26. garden-state: 这里 garden 指伊甸园。

27. meet: = suitable. 在《圣经》《旧约》《创世纪》里说："And the Lord God said, It is not good that the man should be alone; I will make him a help meet for him"（II 18）. 这里用的就是这个典故。

28. 'twas: = it was，因前述格律关系，把两个字拼在一起，省去一个音节。

29. 'twere: = it were. 这是虚拟语气。

IX

但是诗人回到的现实却也还不是熙熙攘攘的争名夺利之地而是个美好的园林，在这里高手的花匠用各种花草设计了一个日晷（65—66 行），而透过树木浓荫照下来的柔软的阳光（milder sun），移动着照在组成日晷的芬芳花草上（through a fragrant zodiac run），标记出时间（67—68 行）。而辛勤的蜜蜂在它工作时飞在不同的花上采蜜也象阳光和人那样地记录了时间（69—70 行）。最后两行说这快乐而宜人（wholesome）的时光不用花草焉能计算（reckoned）得出来（71—72 行）。这里的含意是，在这里没有花草蜜蜂这些自然界的东西，就计算不出时间，时间也就可算不存在，于是大自然战胜了时间，因之可以说是永存的，和伊甸园也不就是差不了多少了吗？这一段里用的这种说理的方法，是玄理诗意象的特征之一。

30. drew: = designed，设计。

31. the milder sun / Does through a fragrant zodiac run: Zodiac 是黄道带，是古代依日照计时的方法，分十二宫（signs），日照每一个月移动一宫，这里是把日影在园中花木上的移动比作太阳一年在十二宫上的移动。

32. but: = except.

10 JOHN MILTON
1608–1674

1. To Mr. Cyriack Skinner upon His Blindness
2. Paradise Lost, Book I, Lines 105–191

杜秉洲　选注

3. Areopagitica

许国璋　选注

1. TO MR. CYRIACK SKINNER UPON HIS BLINDNESS

杜秉洲　选注

Cyriack, this three years' day[1] these eyes, though clear
　　To outward view[2] of blemish or of spot,[3]
　　Bereft of light,[4] their seeing have forgot,[5, 6]
　　Nor to their idle orbs[7] doth sight appear.
Of sun or moon or star,[8] throughout the year,
　　Or man or woman. Yet I argue not
　　Against Heaven's hand or will,[9] nor bate a jot[10]
　　Of heart or hope, but still bear up[11] and steer
Right onward. What supports me, dost thou ask?
　　The conscience,[12] friend, to have lost them overplied
　　In liberty's defence,[13] my noble task,
Of which all Europe talks[14] from side to side.
　　This thougnt might lead me through the world's vain mask[15]
　　Content, though blind, had I no better guide.[16]

2. PARADISE LOST

Book I, lines 105–191

杜秉洲 选注

[Satan's Speech]

"...What though the field[1] be lost?
All is not lost:[2] the unconquerable will,
And study of revenge, immortal hate,
And courage never to submit or yield,
And what is else not to be overcome?[3]
That glory[4] never shall his wrath or might
Extort from me. To bow and sue for grace
With suppliant knee, and deify his power
Who, from the terror of this arm so late
Doubted his empire[5, 6]—that were low indeed;
That were an ignominy and shame beneath
This downfall;[7] since by fate[8] the strength of gods[9]
And this empyreal substance[10] cannot fail,[11]
Since through experience of this great event,[12]
In arms not worse, in foresight much advanced,
We may with more successful hope[13] resolve
To wage by force or guile[14] eternal war,
Irreconcilable to our grand Foe,
Who now triumphs, and in the excess of joy
Sole reigning holds the tyranny of Heaven."
So spake the apostate Angel,[15] though in pain,
Vaunting aloud, but racked with deep despair;
And him thus answered soon his bold compeer:[16]—
"O Prince! O Chief of many thronèd powers,[17]
That led the embattled[18] Seraphim[19] to war
Under thy conduct,[20] and, in dreadful deeds
Fearless, endangered Heaven's perpetual[21] King,

And put to proof[22] his high supremacy,
Whether upheld by strength, or chance, or fate!
Too well I see and rue the dire event
That with sad overthrow and foul defeat
Hath lost us[23] Heaven, and all this mighty host[24]
In horrible destruction laid thus low,
As far as gods and Heavenly essences[25]
Can perish: for the mind and spirit remains
Invincible, and vigour soon returns,[26]
Though all our glory[27] extinct,[28, 29] and happy state
Here swallowed up in endless misery.
But what if he our Conqueror (whom I now
Of force,[30] believe almighty, since no less
Than such[31] could have o'erpowered such force as ours)
Have left us this our spirit and strength entire,
Strongly to suffer and support[32] our pains,
That we may so suffice[33] his vengeful ire;[34]
Or do him mightier service,[35] as his thralls
By right of war,[36] whate'er his business[37] be,
Here in the heart of Hell to work in fire,
Or do his errands in the gloomy Deep?[38]
What can it then avail, though yet we feel
Strength undiminished, or eternal being
To undergo eternal punishment?"[39]
Whereto with speedy words the Arch-Fiend[40] replied: [41]—
"Fallen Cherub, to be weak is miserable,
Doing or suffering:[42] but of this be sure—
To do aught[43] good never will be our task,
But ever to do ill our sole delight,
As being the contrary to his high will
Whom we resist. If then his Providence[44]
Out of our evil seek to bring forth good,
Our labour must be to pervert that end,

And out of good still[45] to find means of evil;
Which ofttimes may succeed, so as perhaps
Shall grieve him, if I fail not,[46] and disturb
His inmost counsels[47] from their destined aim.
But see! the angry Victor hath recalled
His ministers[48] of vengeance and pursuit
Back to the gates of Heaven; the sulphurous hail,
Shot after us in storm, o'erblown[49] hath laid[50]
The fiery surge that from the precipice[51]
Of Heaven received us falling; and the thunder,
Winged with red lightning and impetuous rage,
Perhaps hath spent his[52] shafts, and ceases now
To bellow through the vast and boundless Deep.
Let us not slip[53] the occasion, whether scorn
Or satiate fury[54] yield it from our Foe.[55]
Seest thou yon dreary plain, forlorn[56] and wild,
The seat of desolation, void of light,
Save what the glimmering of these livid flames
Casts pale and dreadful? Thither let us tend[57]
From off the tossing of these fiery waves;
There rest, if any rest can harbour[58] there;
And, reassembling our afflicted[59] powers,[60]
Consult how we may henceforth most offend[61]
Our Enemy, our own loss how repair,[62]
How overcome this dire calamity,
What reinforcement we may gain from hope,
If not,[63] what resolution from despair."[64]

【作者简介】 John Milton（约翰·密尔顿，1608—1674）十七世纪英国伟大诗人，著名史诗《失乐园》的作者。1632 年毕业于剑桥大学后，拒绝供职于为专制帝王所控制的英国国教会，在家潜心读书，博览希伯来文、希腊文、拉丁文、意大利文典籍，兼攻基督教神学，文学史家誉为英国诗人中学问最渊博者。1641 年起参加英国资产阶级反对教会及王权的活动；1649

年任国务会议拉丁文秘书。在这一时期诗人写了不少拥护革命、保卫自由的文章。其时英王室流亡欧洲，图谋复辟，阴使当时名学者 Salmasius 撰文，斥英国革命政府杀查理一世为非法，文曰《为君主申辩》。传至英国，密尔顿奉命著文反驳，于 1651 年写成《为英国人民申辩》；其后 Salmasius 又作答辩，诗人遂于 1654 年写《再为英国人民申辩》。诗人目力素弱，为了对保皇势力进行严正的笔伐，经常读书写文至深夜，医生屡劝休息，仍坚持不辍，卒至失明。1660 年斯图亚特王朝复辟，诗人一度曾受迫害，经友人援助得释。其后在家专心创作，完成三本宏伟的诗篇：*Paradise Lost*（《失乐园》，1667），*Paradise Regained*（《复乐园》，1671），*Samson Agonistes*（《力士参孙》，1671）。

密尔顿的英文是比较难懂的，就此处选诗而言，有下列特点：

1. 源出拉丁文的单词，多袭用原义：如 empire 在诗里作“权威”解，此乃其词源拉丁文 imperium 的原义，其他很多袭用拉丁文原义的词，已在注中标明。

2. 模仿拉丁文的句法：如第 141 行 Though all our glory extinct，以及第 167 行 if I fail not（假如我没有错的话）。这两句在注里已有解释。

3. 有些单词是古体：如第 179 行的 satiate，现代英文应作 satiated. 在十七世纪以前的作品中有不少 -ate 结尾的词，原系拉丁文过去分词，在英文中也用作过去分词与形容词。

4. 倒装句法：如第 127 行 And hím | thus áns | wered sóon | his bóld | compéer. 这是五音步抑扬格无韵诗行；诗人为了配合音律并加重 him 一词的语势，乃用了这倒装诗句（等于 And thus his bold compeer soon answered him）。

5. 现代英文里不再应用的词语：如所选十四行诗第 1 行内 this three years' day 在十七世纪以前的英文里作 for three years 解。Shakespeare 也用过类似的词，如 I saw not better sport these seven years' day（2 *Henry VI* II, i，2）。

【题解与注释】

1. TO MR. CYRIACK SKINNER UPON HIS BLINDNESS

此诗是十四行诗。密尔顿的十四行诗是按照意大利体的格式写出，与伊丽莎白时代的诗人如 Sidney，Spenser，Shakespeare 等所写的十四行诗在风格，韵律与题材方面均有不同。密尔顿所涉及的题材较广：有抒情，朋友赠答，歌颂妇女以及关于政治方面的诗篇。结构亦较谨严，语多朴素而气势雄壮。就韵律言，本诗分为两部分：一为八行，称为 octave，韵的排列为 abba abba；一为六行，称为 sestet，韵的排列则为 cdc dcd（这六行韵的排列在密尔顿其他十四行诗里有变化）。全诗共有十四行，每行基本上为五音步抑扬格，称为 iambic pentametre.

在这首诗的前八行里，诗人对他的朋友说，他完全失去视觉已经三年了；他的双眼，虽然看起来莹澈无瑕，却已一年四季看不见日月星辰与山川人物；但他并不怨天，也不气馁，仍勇往直前地生活。到了后六行意思一转，诗人设问说："你会问我，是什么支持着我在生活呢？"诗人自解地回答："在我苦恼时，我想着我失去了视觉，是由于我过度疲劳地去完成全欧称赞的，我们捍卫自由的崇高任务。在我没有更好的指导时，就是这种思想可能在这舞台似的人世里引导我这双目失明的人过着知足不辱的生活。"

大约在写这诗的同年里（1655 年）诗人写了另一首关于他失明的十四行诗。在那首诗里诗人完全暴露了他悲观绝望的心情，因为他认为他的诗才不能发展了。无可奈何，诗人只得凭借宗教迷信来安慰自己说，残废了而不能有所作为的人，只要能听从上帝的安排，也是可以真实地服侍天主的（They also serve who only stand and wait）。在 1671 年出版的 *Samson Agonistes* 里诗人可能下意识地借参孙的感叹而发泄了自己深心郁结着的哀怨。诗句说：

O dark, dark, dark, amid the blaze of noon,
Irrecoverably dark ...
As in the land of darkness, yet in light,
To live a life half dead, a living death,
And buried; ...
（啊，黑暗呀，黑暗呀，黑暗呀，在正午烈日的强光里，
不可补救的黑暗呀…
虽在光天化日之下，如同在阴森森的境地，
半生半死，
而被埋在坟墓里；…）

如把上面所引两段迸发出悲愤与绝望心情的诗句与这首十四行诗作一比较，可以看出后者表现了诗人达到的雨过天晴的境界。诗人自知他为了维护自由而牺牲了双目，已尽了人生最崇高的责任；所以不怨天不尤人而能心定神全，乐观地生活下去。

再者，这首诗有些诗行在末尾处没有意义或语法上的停顿，而是有如行云流水，毫无窒碍。这样便使得诗势一气呵成，显得庄严稳重与诗意完全相称。同时诗的层次分明，结构紧密，且语多白描，无藻饰铺张，故能"以质胜文"而又音调清越，真不愧为华兹华斯（Wordsworth）所赞颂的"鼓舞灵魂的诗篇"（soul-animating strain）了。

1. this three years' day: 三年以来。诗人于 1652 年失明，因此可以推断此诗作于 1655 年。

2. To outward view: 在外表上。

3. clear ... of blemish or of spot: 没有损伤或斑点（诗人虽已失明，但双眼外表上仍莹澈无瑕与常人无异）。

4. Bereft of light: 被夺去了光明。

5. their seeing have forgot: 此句主语是 these eyes.

6. forgot: = lost.

7. idle orbs: 不起作用的眼球。

8. Nor … doth sight appear / Of sun, etc.: = Nor doth sight of sun, etc. appear …

9. Heaven's hand or will: 上天的主宰或意志。

10. nor bate a jot: bate 是 abate 一词的简体，意为"减少"。此句意为，并不减少一点。

11. bear up: 此语不单作"忍受"解；它与下文 steer 同是航海用语，意为，朝着一定方向航行。

12. conscience: = consciousness，认识到（某一事实）。

13. overplied / In liberty's defence: 这一短语在此处用作状语，说明失明的经过。overplied，用力过度，指诗人写《为英国人民申辩》正篇（1651 年），耗损目力，卒至失明。

14. talks: 1694 年密尔顿诗集的编者 Edward Phillips 大概鉴于诗人曾在另一首十四行诗内用过 rings（Fairfax, whose name in arms through Europe rings），把原稿的 talks 换为 rings（响彻全欧）。此词的确反映了当时情况，不为过誉，至今多数版本便沿用了此词。其实，诗人所用的 talks（议论纷纷），很朴实，也很生动。

15. world's vain mask: mask 原意是假面具；world's vain mask 即人世间虚幻的假面具戏。在莎士比亚的《皆大欢喜》（*As You Like It*）一剧里也有类似的话，"举世攘攘，不过一舞台而已"（All the world's a stage）。

16. had I no better guide: = if I had no better guide. 这句说：即使我没有更好的引路人在前带路，我只要想到我为了保卫自由而献出了双目这事，也就心安理得，知道如何在这变幻莫测的人间戏剧里处世行事；我虽已失去视觉，而仍有勇气生活下去，理由即在于此。这里引路人（guide）只可能指上帝，仿佛说如无上帝引路，也可凭自己的良知处世，这出于笃信宗教者如密尔顿之口，更足以表示他对当时争取自由的斗争是如何忠诚和勇敢。在 1673 年印行的版本里，没有此诗；因此句在当时被认为不太虔诚，所以诗人只得将全诗割爱了。

2. PARADISE LOST, BOOK I, LINES 105–191

本段选自《失乐园》第一部，第 105—191 行。《失乐园》分十二部，内容如下：Satan 率领一些天使反抗上帝，失败后被打入地狱，在烈火中受罪。这时上帝已创造了大地山河，Adam 与其妻 Eve 在 Eden 乐园里安居。Satan 为了泄恨，潜入 Eden 劝诱 Eve 违反上帝命令，偷食禁果，破坏乐园的法度。其后，Adam 情不自禁，也尝了禁果。因此二人被上帝逐出乐园，谪往世间，胼手胝足，自谋衣食，所谓"失去了乐园"，意即指此。

所选诗行开始时，Satan 在地狱里刚从昏迷中醒来，看见他的亲信 Beëlzebub，说了一段激昂慷慨的话。语句之间表示出不屈不挠一心对抗上帝的决心。他还说，天使本非上帝所造，岂能慑服于暴君威力之下。又说胜利是可期待的，只要大家能同心协力，公开或秘密地与上帝的专制挑战，直到永远！接着 Beëlzebub 答话，他对前途颇为悲观，并以绝望的心情结束他的答话说，象这样永无休止地遭受天罚，活下去有什么好处呢？ Satan 迫不及待地向他说，不要悲观示弱，这样就会永远痛苦。我们只要一息尚存，便能设法扰乱仇敌。现在我们先聚集起来，商议报仇雪耻的办法吧。

Satan 这段话充分流露了一个受迫害的革命者的豪迈气概。这里密尔顿以雄健之笔勾划出 Satan 的英勇挺拔的形象。Satan 原为天宫中天使之长，他敢于率领天使，与上帝作殊死的斗争，正显出他气势磅礴，万古凛烈；斗争失败，毫不气馁，仍神采奕奕，辉同日月；而又复仇心切，有如火山爆发，熔岩奔腾。密尔顿是革命诗人，他创造出 Satan 这样卓越的形象，可说是他热爱自由，痛恨专制的革命性格的升华，真可共天地而不朽了。但是我们必须知道这里对 Satan 的刻划，还不是完整的；在史诗的后几部密尔顿还要叙述 Satan 的堕落。只是在这史诗的头一、二部里 Satan 的革命者的形象光耀夺目，真够使读者惊心动魄的了。

1. field: 战场，在此处作“战役”解。

2. All is not lost: = not all is lost，不是一切都失败了。

3. And what is else not to be overcome?: 此句各家解释不一，大意是，（除了我们的不可驯服的意志，报仇的壮举等等之外）还有其他什么构成我们的不可屈服的精神呢？从第 106 到第 109 行的整句意思是：不是一切都失败了——（还有）不可驯服的意志，报仇的壮举，万古不泯的仇恨，不屈不挠的胆量；除了这些，还有其他什么构成我们的不可屈服的精神呢？

4. That glory: 指上帝战胜撒旦（并使撒旦俯首认罪，不思报仇）获得彻底胜利的光荣。整句意为：上帝永远不可能从我这里取得这种彻底胜利的光荣（因为我还要报仇）。

5. Who … so late / Doubted his empire: 这里 who 指上帝，因为不久前撒旦率天使与上帝战，震撼了上帝的宝座，迫使上帝对他的统治不能不有所疑虑。

6. empire: 在此从拉丁文 imperium 原义，指“权威”，“统治”。

7. an ignominy and shame beneath / This downfall: downfall 指撒旦反抗上帝，失败后被迫堕入地狱；ignominy，为了符合五音步抑扬格，此词末尾元音 y 省去，读 ['ignəmin]；beneath = worse than.

8. by fate: 撒旦认为“命运”的主宰，超过上帝的权威；天使非上帝所造，乃在“命运”注定之日，自然生成。

9. gods: 神灵。

10. empyreal [em'piriəl] **substance:** 指天使，因他们的个体为九霄中物质之精——纯火——所形成，不能毁灭；**empyreal:** fiery, composed of pure fire.

11. fail: = perish，消灭。

12. event: 结局，第 134 行同。

13. successful hope: = hope of success，对胜利的希望。

14. by force or guile: 力胜或智取。

15. the apostate Angel: 叛逆的天使，即撒旦。

16. compeer: 伙伴，即 Beëlzebub [bi(:)'elzibʌb]. 此行为倒装句法，已在前面说明。

17. thronèd powers: 拥护撒旦的天使们。thronèd 指他们有尊贵的地位。

18, embattled: 排列成战阵的。

19. Seraphim: 天使，seraph 的复数。

20. conduct: = command，领导。

21. perpetual: 长久的。虔诚的教徒在祷告上帝时，用 eternal（永恒的）一词。但 Beëlzebub 因附和 Satan 反抗上帝，故不愿尊称上帝为“永恒”而只说“长久”。

22. put to proof: 考验。

23. Hath lost us: 使我们失去了。

24. mighty host: 强大的队伍（指撒旦所统率的天使们）。

25. Heavenly essences: 指天使。**essences**：源出拉丁文 esse，作 being 解。

26. and vigour soon returns: 应解释为 and therefore vigour will soon return to us.

27. glory: 光辉。

28. Though all our glory extinct: 这是一种拉丁文结构；但也可解释为省略了系词“be”。

29. extinct:（象火焰一样）被扑灭了。

30. Of force: 必然地。

31. such: 指 Almighty.

32. support: endure, undergo，忍受。

33. suffice: = satisfy（从拉丁文 sufficere 原义）。

34 ire: 忿怒。

35. mightier service: 指从事指派的工作，而不是仅仅忍辱负重。

36. Or do him mightier service, as his thralls / By right of war ...: 上帝既将反叛的天使战败，根据战胜者的权利，可以将他们俘虏为奴（thralls），并使他们从事劳役。

37. his business: 上帝指派的工作。

38. the gloomy Deep: 浑沌的深渊（Chaos）.

39. or eternal being / To undergo eternal punishment?: = or being eternal, so as to undergo eternal punishment? 此句大意说：即使长生不死，但永受折磨，又有什么好处呢？

40. Fiend: = one who hates，心怀仇恨者（古英文原义）。**Arch-Fiend**：指 Satan.

41. 第 156 行： Beëlzebub 言语之间表示了悲观与绝望，Satan 立即发言（with speedy words）以期改变他的这种情绪。

42. Doing or suffering: 无论是有所作为或任人摆布（主动或被动的境地）。

43. aught: = anything.

44. his Providence: 指上帝。

45. still: = always.

46. if I fail not: 假如我没有错的话。此句系模仿拉丁文句 ni fallor.

47. inmost counsels: 最秘密的计划。

48. His ministers: 指听从上帝吩咐的天使们。

49. o'erblown: = blown over，象暴风雨般已过去了。

50. laid: = put to rest，已使平静下来。

51. precipice: = a headlong fall，头朝下掉将下来（古义）。

52. his: = its；亦可认为是 thunder 拟人化后的人称代词。

53. slip: = let slip，放过。

54. satiate: = satiated，饱和了的。**satiate fury**：盛怒。

55. whether scorn / Or satiate fury yield it from our Foe: = whether it should yield scorn or satiate fury from our Foe. **Foe**：指上帝。

56. forlorn: 空虚的。

57. tend: = make one's way towards，向…行进。

58. harbour: = dwell，栖息于。

59. afflicted: 战败了的（拉丁文原义）。

60. powers: 队伍。

61. offend: = hurt，伤害（拉丁文原义）。

62. our own loss how repair: 倒装结构，即 how we may repair our loss.

63. If not: 假如我们不能从希望中得着任何后援的话。

64. what resolution from despair: 这是省略句。完全的句子，依照上句的结构，是 what resolution we may gain from despair，绝望之余我们也可立下决心干下去，即"知其不可为而为之"之意。

3. *AREOPAGITICA*

许国璋　选注

(1) To the pure all things are pure.

To the pure all things are pure[1]; not only meats and drinks,[2] but all kind of knowledge[3] whether of good or evil; the knowledge cannot defile,[4] nor consequently the books, if the will and conscience be not defiled. For books are as meats and viands[5] are; some of good, some of evil substance; and yet God in that unapocryphal vision said without exception,[6] Rise Peter, kill and eat, leaving the choice to each man's discretion. Wholesome meats to a vitiated stomach differ little or nothing from unwholesome; and best books to a naughty mind are not unappliable to occasions of evil. Bad meats will scarce breed good nourishment in the healthiest concoction[7]; but herein the difference is of bad books,[8] that they to a discreet and judicious reader serve in many respects to discover, to confute, to forewarn, and to illustrate.[9] Whereof what better witness can ye expect[10] I should produce than one of your own now sitting in Parliament, the chief of learned men reputed in this land, Mr. Selden,[11] whose volume of natural and national laws proves, not only by great authorities brought together, but by exquisite reasons and theorems almost mathematically demonstrative, that all opinions, yea, errors,[12] known, read, and collated, are of main service and assistance toward the speedy attainment of what is truest. I conceive, therefore, that when God did enlarge the universal diet of man's body,[13] saving ever the rules of temperance,[14] He then also, as before, left arbitrary the dieting and repasting of our minds;[15] as wherein every mature man might have to exercise his own leading capacity.[16] How great a virtue is temperance, how much of moment through the whole life of man! Yet God commits the managing so great a trust,[17] without particular law or prescription, wholly to the demeanour of every grown man.[18]

(2) Good and evil grow up together.

Good and evil we know in the field of this world grow up together almost inseparably[1]; and the knowledge of good is so involved and interwoven with the knowledge of evil and in so many cunning resemblances hardly to be discerned, that those confused seeds, which were imposed on Psyche as an incessant labour to cull out and sort asunder, [2] were not more intermixed. It was from out the rind of one apple tasted that the knowledge of good and evil as two twins cleaving together leaped forth into the world. And perhaps this is that doom which Adam fell into of knowing good and evil, that is to say of knowing good by evil.[3] As therefore the state of man now is, what wisdom can there be to choose, what continence to forbear, without the knowledge of evil? He that can apprehend and consider vice with all her baits and seeming pleasures,[4] and yet abstain, and yet distinguish, and yet prefer that which is truly better, he is the true warfaring Christian.[5] I cannot praise a fugitive and cloistered virtue, unexercised and unbreathed, that never sallies out and sees her adversary, but slinks out of the race, where that immortal garland is to be run for not without dust and heat. Assuredly we bring not innocence into the world; we bring impurity much rather: that which purifies us is trial, and trial is by what is contrary. That virtue therefore which is but a youngling in the contemplation of evil, and knows not the utmost that vice promises to her followers, and rejects it, is but a blank virtue, not a pure;[6] her whiteness is but an excremental whiteness;[7] which was the reason why our sage and serious poet Spenser, whom I dare be known to think a better teacher than Scotus or Aquinas,[8] describing true temperance under the person of Guion,[9] brings him in with his palmer[10] through the cave of Mammon and the Bower of Earthly Bliss, that he might see and know, and yet abstain. Since therefore the knowledge and survey of vice is in this world so necessary to the constituting of human virtue, and the scanning of error to the confirmation of truth, how can we more safely and with less danger scout into the regions of sin and falsity than by reading all manner of tractates,[11] and hearing all manner of reason? And this is the benefit which may be had of books promiscuously read.[12]

(3) If we think to regulate printing, thereby to rectify manners, we must regulate our recreations and pastimes, all that is delightful to man. No music must be heard, no song be set or sung, but what is grave and Doric.

If we think to regulate printing,[1] thereby to rectify manners, we must regulate our recreations and pastimes, all that is delightful to man. No music must be heard, no song be set or sung, but what is grave and Doric.[2] There must be licensing dancers,[3] that no gesture, motion, or deportment be taught our youth but what by their allowance shall be thought honest;[4] for such Plato was provided of.[5] It will ask more than the work of twenty licensers to examine all the lutes, and violins, and the guitars in every house; they must not be suffered to prattle as they do, but must be licensed what they may say. And who shall silence all the airs[6] and madrigals, that whisper softness in chambers? The windows also, and the balconies must be thought on;[7] there are shrewd books, with dangerous frontispieces, set to sale; who shall prohibit them? shall twenty licensers? The villages also must have their visitors to inquire what lectures the bagpipe and the rebeck reads,[8] even to the ballatry, and the gamut of every municipal fiddler, for these are the countryman's Arcadias and his Monte Mayors.[9] Next, what more national corruption, for which England hears ill abroad, than household gluttony?[10] Who shall be the rectors of our daily rioting[11] and what shall be done to inhibit the multitudes that frequent those houses where drunkenness is sold and harboured?[12] Our garments also should be referred to the licensing of some more sober workmasters to see them cut into a less wanton garb. Who shall regulate all the mixed conversation of our youth, male and female together, as is the fashion of this country? Who shall still appoint[13] what shall be discoursed, what presumed, and no further? Lastly, who shall forbid and separate all idle resort,[14] all evil company? These things will be, and must be;[15] but how they shall be least hurtful, how least enticing, herein consists the grave and governing wisdom of a State. To sequester out of the world into Atlantic and Utopian polities,[16] which never can be drawn into use, will not mend our condition; but to ordain wisely as in this world of evil,[17] in the midst whereof God hath placed us unavoidably. Nor is it Plato's licensing of books will do this,[18] which necessarily pulls along with it so many other kinds of licensing, as will make us all both ridiculous and weary, and yet frustrate[19];

but those unwritten, or at least unconstraining, laws of virtuous education, religious and civil nurture, which Plato there mentions as the bonds and ligaments of the Commonwealth, the pillars and the sustainers of every written statute;[20] these they be which will bear chief sway[21] in such matters as these, when all licensing will be easily eluded. Impunity and remissness,[22] for certain, are the bane of a Commonwealth; but here the great art lies to discern in what the law is to bid restraint and punishment, and in what things persuasion only is to work. If every action which is good or evil in man at ripe years were to be under pittance and prescription and compulsion, what were virtue but a name, what praise could be then due to welldoing, what grammercy to be sober, just, or continent?[23] Many there be that complain of Divine Providence for suffering Adam to transgress.[24] Foolish tongues![25] When God gave him reason, he gave him freedom to choose, for reason is but choosing; he had been else a mere artificial Adam, such an Adam as he is in the motions.[26]

【题解与注释】

在英国诗人中，密尔顿真正是一个不凡的人物。他受过欧洲文艺复兴时期渊博的教育；他从事反对英国君主专制的革命活动整整二十年，这二十年也是为革命奋笔著作的二十年；1660年君主复辟以后，他身处逆境，双目失明，仍然矢志不移，学问不厌，写了两部史诗和一部诗的悲剧（*Paradise Lost*, 1667; *Paradise Regained*, 1671; *Samson Agonistes*, 1671）。这三部名作都是用当时的英语写的，也借用大量欧洲古典语言的语汇和句法，有不少语词是密尔顿自己创造的。题材（《失乐园》与《力士参孙》取自《旧约》,《复乐园》取自《新约》）是古典的，体裁（希腊的史诗和悲剧）也是古典的，却又充满了弱者敢于向权势斗争的精神，充满了用理性去解释神和人之间的冲突的哲学勇敢。密尔顿十二岁从学于博览群史的业师，十七岁入剑桥大学，二十一岁得学士位，二十四岁得硕士位；嗣后，又在乡间家宅（Horton）潜心文学历史六年，古今语言、文学、音乐无不通达。1638年春，游学意大利，访伽利略于佛罗伦萨。十八年的勤学和抒情创作，二十年的革命和革命创作，最后是宁静的史诗创作的十年。学问——革命——创作，组成这个欧洲（说他是英国不能完全体现他的气势）十七世纪中不凡人物的一生的绚丽。

我们大多数人读过密尔顿的诗，他的散文在一般的选本里不常见。这里选的却是密尔顿一篇名文中的几段。名文的题材是“反对书报检查，争取出版自由”，这个题材很有意思，密尔顿又把意思发挥得很透彻，透彻到有时叫人拍案叫绝，请读一读这篇名文的为首两段吧：

They who to states and governors of the Commonwealth direct their speech, High Court of Parliament, or, wanting such access in a private condition, write that which they foresee may advance the public good, I suppose them, as at the beginning of no mean endeavour, not a little altered and moved inwardly in their minds: some with doubt of what will be the success, others with fear of what will be the censure; some with hope, others with confidence of what they have to speak. And me perhaps each of these dispositions, as the subject was whereon I entered, may have at other times variously affected; and likely might in these foremost expressions now also disclose which of them swayed most, but that the very attempt of this address thus made, and the thought of whom it hath recourse to, hath got the power within me to a passion far more welcome than incidental to a preface. Which though I stay not to confess ere any ask I shall be blameless, if it be no other than the joy and gratulation which it brings to all who wish and promote their country's liberty; whereof this whole discourse proposed will be a certain testimony, if not a trophy.

（夫为国献言，大夫条陈于明堂，议政于国会，一介之士则撰文章。文章，大业也。执笔之际，情为之移，神为之奋，或忧其败，或虑其祸，或切盼成功，或信其说必行。余作此文，各种心情悉有之，于此卷首，宜以主要动机，为读者述之。然今既脱稿，不日将见于公众，激越澎湃，不能自已，殊非卷首数语可毕其辞。虽然，余纵不作序，谅世人亦不以余责。此文之作无他，为国之爱慕自由之人，为国之提倡自由之人，为与彼等共雀跃同欢庆耳。全篇文字，可作争取自由之实证，甚或可作赢得自由之丰碑。）

在以雄壮的语言开始了他的出版自由的宣言书之后，密尔顿热情讴歌了著作的神圣不可侵犯。他写道：

I deny not, but that it is of greatest concernment in the Church and Commonwealth, to have a vigilant eye how books demean themselves as well as men; and thereafter to confine, imprison, and do sharpest justice on them as malefactors. For books are not absolutely dead things, but do contain a potency of life in them to be as active as that soul was whose progeny they are; nay, they do preserve as in a vial the purest efficacy and extraction of that living intellect that bred them. I know they are as lively, and as vigorously productive, as those fabulous dragon's teeth, and being sown up and down, may chance to spring up armed men. And yet, on the other hand, unless wariness be used, as good almost kill a man as kill a good book: who kills a man kills a reasonable creature, God's image; but he who destroys a good book, kills reason itself, kills the image of God, as it were, in the eye.

（教会与国家，于书之为好书坏书，公民之为好人坏人，不能不表极大关注，此点余亦承认。治坏人，或予禁闭，或投牢中，或处以极刑。然则书非可以致死者也。书之生命力，乃作者灵魂所赋予。书，作家智慧之精华，如炼金丹，升华净化，臻于至纯，乃纳玉壶，以为珍藏。谚言，龙之齿，植地生幼龙。书之孳衍，与龙似。植书于野，异日或生持矛武士。人可以错杀，好书亦可以错毁。是不可不慎也。杀一人，杀一有理性之生命，杀一上帝之子孙耳。若毁一好书，实毁理性本身，无异毁上帝之目。）

这篇宣言书充满着古典文学的故事和拉丁文法特有的句子结构，确是不易读懂。下面的一些注释，希望能有助于读者了解其哲理之美和文章的气势。

篇名 Areopagitica 是密尔顿创造的一个词。此词原出希腊文，拉丁拼法为 Areopagiticus. Areopagitica 是它的派生形容词，属阴性，在这个阴性形容词前面，省略了它所从属的名词 Oratio，全名应该是 Oratio Areopagitica，意即 Areopagus 的讲演辞。

Areopagus 的原义是古希腊议会里的最高评议会，具有最高法院的职权，对宗教与国家行政进行仲裁。Areopagus 是以雅典郊外的 Ares 的一座山而得名的，原义 Hill of Ares. 古雅典哲人（Isocrates, 436 B. C. 生）曾以此为讲坛，唤醒雅典人革新政制，防御马其顿人的入侵。

密尔顿为什么借用这个希腊体制来作为这篇出版自由宣言书的题目呢？因为希腊文学是这位文艺复兴时期学者和作家旦夕揣摩的文学，这一文学中包含的争取自由反抗专横的精神是他精神生活的一部分，这一文学的语汇几乎是他母语语汇的一部分。

事情的起因是这样的：1643 年六月十四日，成立不到三年的英国革命新政府颁布了出版审查法，而这个审查法仅仅是在两年以前（1641）作为已被推翻的君主政府的可咒诅的敕令被废止过的。现在，出版审查法再度颁发，明令今后一切书刊的出版和重印，必须得到官方的许可，同时对一切未经许可的出版商进行搜查。这是恢复旧制，践踏自由的反动，对于已经写过几本不经审查的小册子的密尔顿，是断难容忍的。密尔顿是革命政府积极的辩护者，但是对于这一反动措施他提出了强烈的抗诉。1644 年九月，密尔顿有三个月的时间公务较轻（他那时任革命政府拉丁文秘书，即外交秘书官），他利用这段时间写了 Areopagitica。那是一本四十页的小四开本。不用说，他没有向官方登记，没有申请许可。一篇痛斥书刊审查法的宣言书，无视一切审查手续公然问世，密尔顿的愤激是可以想象的。上文所引‘激越澎湃，不能自已，殊非卷首数语可毕其辞’，即是说的这种心情。

对于今天的读者，一个有兴趣的问题是：密尔顿当年大声反对的书刊审查，取得了什么效果没有？回答是，审查制不仅没有取消，反而变本加厉。1662 年，君主复辟以后，政府正式任命了审查官。1667 年，密尔顿的《失乐园》由书商送审，第一章 594 行以下数行就险遭扼杀。但是，这些审书吏有谁能看懂这首满是古典景物的长诗，又谁有这个素养把它读完呢？三百多年前的“知制诰”，有谁能看出就在他们的案头，放着不朽的文章，不假良史，不托飞驰，不以隐约而弗务，而自传于后世呢？

(1) TO THE PURE ALL THINGS ARE PURE

1. To the pure all things are pure: 至纯之人，诸物皆纯，邪恶不能移其心。

2. meats and drinks: meats = food.

3. all kind of knowledge: present-day English: all kinds of；但也说 these *kind* of men annoy me = men of this kind annoy me。

4. defile: make foul.

5. viands: meats.

6. yet God in that unapocryphal vision said etc.: 见 *New Testament,* The Acts, 10, 10–12.

And he (Peter) became very hungry, and would have eaten; but while they made ready, he fell into a trance.

And saw heaven opened, and a certain vessel descending unto him, as it had been a great sheet knit at the four corners, and let down to the earth; (as it had been = as if it had been)

Wherein were all manner of four-footed beasts of the earth, and wild beasts, and creeping things, and fowls of the air.

And there came a voice to him, Rise, Peter, kill, and eat.

上述故事出在《新约》，如上面引文。Peter 是耶稣弟子，时耶稣已死。Peter 梦见上帝，赐野兽、爬虫、飞禽作为食物。Peter 不敢吃，因怕其不洁，跪地祈祷不起。上帝说："彼得，起来，宰了吃。"意思是说，洁与不洁，应该人类自己作出选择。密尔顿以此比喻人世之事，事之为善为恶，应由人作出自己的选择。

7. concoction: digestion.

8. but herein the difference is of bad books: = but here is (*or* herein lies) the difference of bad books.

9. they to a discreet and judicious reader serve in many respects to discover, to confute, to forewarn, and to illustrate: 善读书者，即坏书也有各种作用：发隐，明辩，预为警告，以此例彼。

10. Whereof what better witness can ye expect: = of that, what better witness can you expect I should produce. **Witness** 指可以为密尔顿的理论提供证明之人。即下句的 Selden，时为议员。

11. Mr. Selden: John Selden (1584–1654) who like Milton was a writer of political tracts, and a champion of liberty against the Stuarts.

12. that all opinions, yea, errors: *yea* = yes, indeed.

13. when God did enlarge the universal diet of man's body: 即指上文 Peter 梦见上帝时，上帝赐各色食物，由他自己挑。

14. saving ever the rules of temperance: saving = except.

15. He (God) then also, as before, left arbitrary the dieting and repasting of our minds: 物质的食粮既然由人类自己鉴别选择，精神食粮亦同。

16. as wherein every mature man might etc.: = as in this matter every mature man might etc.

17. Yet God commits *the managing so great a trust*: present-day English: the managing *of* so great a trust.

18. commit ... to the demeanour of every grown man: 把这一重大的责任付托给一切成年人自己去处理。

(2) GOOD AND EVIL GROW UP TOGETHER

1. Good and evil we know in the field of this world grow up together almost inseparably: 在此 we know = that we know，或 as we know：就我们所认识的世界而言，善生恶亦生，难于分隔。参看下文 It was from out the rind of one apple tasted that the knowledge of good and evil ... leaped forth into the world. 此句发挥了上文的意思。《旧约》创世纪述 Eve 与 Adam 分食一个苹果，在同一个苹果里蕴藏着善与恶的观念。

2. those confused seeds, which were imposed on Psyche ... to cull out and sort asunder: Psyche，出自公元二世纪 Apuleius 所作传奇 Asino Aureo (Golden Ass) 中 Cupid and Psyche 一章。Psyche 与 Cupid 恋，后被迫分离，Psyche 为了找 Cupid，历尽苦难，其中一难即是要她从一大堆杂粮中把小麦，大麦，小米，罂粟子，豌豆，扁豆，黄豆等一一分离。见 Robert Graves 译本，Penguin, 1950, p.125.

3. this is that doom which Adam fell into of knowing good and evil etc.: = this is that doom of knowing good and evil, that is to say of knowing good by evil. 亚当自天上的乐园堕入（doom）凡人世界，乃识善恶，识善恶者，识恶乃能识善之意。又上文 cleaving together = sticking together.

4. vice with her baits and seeming pleasures: 参看上文 "good is so involved and interwoven with the knowledge of evil and in so many cunning resemblances hardly to be discerned." "邪恶者，诱人以饵，迷人以声色。" "善之与恶，杂厕其间，何处无有，人莫能辨。"

5. warfaring Christian: 战斗的，敢与邪恶交战的耶教信徒，与下文"临阵怯懦，落荒而走"相对（never sallies out and sees her adversary, but slinks out of the race）。

6. a blank virtue, not a pure (virtue): 虚德而非纯德。

7. excremental whiteness: 表相的无疵。

8. Spenser, *whom I dare be known to think* a better teacher than Scotus or Aquinas: = whom I am not afraid to think (that he is). Spenser: Edmund Spenser (1552?–1599) 英国文艺复兴时期在 Chaucer 之后，Shakespeare 之前的大诗人，长诗 *Faërie Queene* 是他的名作。Guion 的故事出此诗第二卷，第七章与第十二章。Duns Scotus, Thomas Aquinas 均系中古世纪经院哲学家。

9. true temperance under the person of Guion etc.: Guion 在 Spenser 原作中拼为 Guyon，是长诗中诸游侠武士之一；Sir Guion 节操自持，不为富贵所淫。至 Cave of Mammon，金玉珠宝，无所不具，Guion 拒之。又至 Bower of Earthly Paradise，芳草奇卉，直是天上，有美女，倩笑薄衣，以金樽敬美酒，Guion 掷之地上，不为美色所动。

10. Palmer: 到耶教圣地耶路撒冷朝过圣，手持棕榈枝，苦修的行脚僧。与 Sir

Guion 同游四方，对他起规劝的作用。

11. tractate, all manner of tractates: 密尔顿所生的时代，是君权与民权，专制与自由，政府与教会，教育是否应由教会控制，离婚是否应予准许等社会问题进行热烈讨论的时代。讨论的文章极多，长的专论称 tractate，短的称 tract.

12. This is the benefit ... of books promiscuously read: 这是好书要读，坏书也要读的好处。

(3) IF WE THINK TO REGULATE PRINTING

1. regulate printing: 管制书刊出版。thereby to rectify manners：以此来整肃人的行为。all that is delightful to man：这是 our recreations and pastimes 的同位语，使一个专指的叙述变成泛指的叙述。

2. No music must be heard ... but what is grave and Doric: but = except; Doric: martial 尚武的，提倡军国教育的音乐。只有这类音乐让听。

3. There must be licensing dancers: = there must be the licensing of dancers；参看上文 the managing so great a task.

4. no gesture ... be taught our youth but what by their allowance shall be thought honest: = no gesture should be taught to our youth except what would be regarded as honest by their consent. 青年的一举一动，都得有他们（按照出版审查法设置的道德风俗审查官）的认可，不经认可，不得传给青年。

5. for such Plato was provided of: = by such consent as was given by Plato (of = by). Plato (427–348 B. C.)，希腊哲学家，他的名著之一是 *The Republic*（《理想国》）。这一著作中有下列对话，论青年教育，主张严格管制，并不准读古人的诗篇：

—Shall we therefore allow our children to listen to any stories written by anyone, and to form opinions the opposite of those we think they should have when they grow up?

—We certainly shall not.

—Then it seems that our first business is to supervise the production of stories, and choose only those we think suitable, and reject the rest. We shall persuade mothers and nurses to tell our chosen stories to their children and so mould their minds and characters rather than their bodies. The greater part of the stories current today we shall have to reject.

—What are you thinking of?

…

—The stories in Homer and Hesiod and the poets. For it is the poets who have always made up stories to tell to men. (*The Republic,* trans. H. D. P. Lee, Penguin, 1953, pp. 114–115.)

柏拉图在这一著名的论断里，反对读诗人的创作，因为这些创作都是虚构的，因而是谎言。密尔顿是反对这种管制的，他认为这是愚蠢的，也是不可行的。

6. And who shall silence all the airs: 在此 shall = is to，谁去抑制这一切歌唱呢？这里，在密尔顿时代的英语，是不能用 will 的，如用 will，那就是说谁又愿意这样做呢？参看下文：

Who shall prohibit them? Shall twenty licensers? 谁去禁止这一切？（纵有）二十个审查官，禁止得了吗？

7. The windows also, and the balconies must be thought on: 窗户也得当心，阳台也得注意。（因为谁知道从窗户里从阳台上会传出什么未经许可的歌声呢？）

8. The villages also must have their visitors to inquire what lectures the bagpipe and the rebeck reads etc.: = the villages too need to have their licensers who will visit them from time to time (visitors) asking (to inquire) what moral lesson (lecture) has been taught by the tunes played by the bagpipe（风笛）and the rebeck（一种提琴）。（不仅如此），每个乡村也得去审查官呀！看看人们吹的拉的是不是富有教育意义呀！

ballatry = balladry.

the gamut of every municipal fiddler = every note played by the municipal fiddler. 从市区来的提琴师拉的高的低的音符（都得问一下有没有教育意义呀！）

9. the countryman's Arcadias and his Monte Mayors: = pastoral songs loved by the countryman（= 农民）.

Arcadia—a pastoral poem originated by the Italian poet Sanazzaro (16th cent.)

Monte Mayor—a Portuguese poet who wrote in imitation of Sanazzaro, also of the 16th century.

10. What more national corruption, for which England hears ill abroad, than household gluttony?: national corruption 指 household gluttony；英国人在当时的欧洲以贪吃著称，密尔顿把它看作有损民族荣誉。

corruption = moral corruption.

for which England hears ill abroad= for which England is heard ill of in foreign countries = the English as a nation have a bad name abroad for being over-fond of eating.

11. rectors of our daily rioting: rector= controller, ruler. 每天发生的狂饮狂闹，前去制止的执法人。

12. houses where drunkenness is sold and harboured: = taverns, alehouses where people can get drunk and protected from law.

13. who shall appoint etc.: who shall decide the rules of, fix the limits of etc.（still = yet）

14. idle resort: getting together for nothing but fun.

15. These things will be, and must be etc.: these things (drinking etc.) will always exist, and there is no way to do away with these things. 这些事情是永远会有的，不可避免的。

but how they shall be etc. …how they might be made least harmful, leading fewer people to evil, in this matter lies (herein consists) the … wisdom of a State. 治国之道，在于使此等事引起的危险减至最小。

1.—15. 从本节首句 If we think to regulate printing, thereby to rectify manners, we must regulate our recreations and pastimes, all that is delightful to man 起，到 These things will be, and must be; but how they shall be least hurtful, how least enticing, herein consists the grave and governing wisdom of a State. 这一大段（密尔顿的散文是很少分段的，有的几乎全篇不分段，这点与中国古文相似），密尔顿用嘲讽的笔调，指出书刊审查的愚蠢，因为书刊审查的目的，无非要整顿社会的风尚（manners）。既如此，音乐与歌唱也得审查，舞蹈的姿态，各人家里的乐器，牧童短曲，甚至在室内哼哼的小调也得审查，窗户里传出什么歌声乐声也得注意；有着诱人的封面的书籍得审查，每个乡村都得有人去检查，看农民们吹的拉的是否具有教育意义？英国人的饕餮，狂闹，到酒铺饮酒，服饰，都得审查。青年谈话，男女杂处，又怎样检查？谁来决定什么可以谈，什么不可？酒食游戏，龙蛇俱集，怎样禁止，怎样区分？这一切是永远会有的。国家只能引导，减少危害，这才是治政之道。

密尔顿当时所讽刺的，还不过是一种设想。但是在密尔顿死后的三个世纪中，这一切又都发生，而且一再发生，这也许是读这篇三百年前的名文的乐趣之一。

16. To sequester out of the world into Atlantic and Utopian polities etc.: to withdraw from this world and build an ideal State in some imaginary land … will not mend our condition.

Atlantic polity —a fabulous island in the Atlantic Ocean, a beautiful and prosperous country. Polity = political organization. Francis Bacon describes that imaginary island in *New Atlantis*（1626）.

Utopian polity—the political organization in Thomas More's *Utopia* (Latin = nowhere) where a kind of communism is practised (1516). 脱离现实世界，寄希望于理想国，于事无补（will not mend our condition）.

17. but to ordain wisely as in this world of evil: = but to arrange things wisely in this world of evil will mend our condition. 承上文，will mend our condition 在此省略。

18. Nor is it Plato's licensing of books will do this: present-day English: Nor is it that etc. Plato's licensing of books etc.; see note 5 above.

19. and yet frustrate: = and yet frustrated (by a sense of being utterly powerless in face of immense difficulties).

20. those unwritten, … laws of virtuous education … which Plato there mentions as … the pillars and the sustainers of every written statute: 此句未完，下句 these they be which will bear chief sway 中的 they 是 unwritten laws 这一主语的重复。

Plato there mentions—See *The Republic*, Book IV: "Above all they must maintain the educational system unchanged; for on education everything else depends, and it is an illusion to imagine that mere legislation without it can effect anything of consequence." (Penguin, 1953, p. 166) 柏拉图的主要意思是：光靠立法来治理国家是不可靠的，成文的法律必须靠有教育的人民加以支持，而人民的教育则是一种道德教养，是一种不成文的法律。

21. these they be which will bear chief sway etc.: 出版管制法总是容易逃过去的。只有不成文的、不具强制性的道德教育中所培育的守法精神，才能在这类事情中起首要作用。注：这里 these = laws of virtuous education; such matters as these（这

类事情）= to ordain wisely as in this world of evil etc.（看到世界上有罪恶，但能治之以方，等等。）

22. impunity and remissness: 犯法者不受制裁，执政者又坐令法纪废弛。

the bane of a Commonwealth: the cause of death to a people's State.

23. If every action which is good or evil in man at ripe years were to be under pittance and prescription and compulsion, what were virtue but a name, what praise could be then due to well-doing, what grammercy to be sober, just, or continent?: 人已成年，而为善为恶悉唯国家法律之严或宽，禁止或许可，有压力或无压力而定，则道德岂非虚名，德行何足赞美，节操自持之品德安得受社会之敬重？

pittance—a small share or allotment，小量的配给，意为由法律来定罪名的大小。

grammercy = great thanks（Old French: grant merci）

continent—abstaining from the indulgence of pleasure. 自持严，不纵情声色。

24. Many there be that complain of Divine Providence for suffering Adam to transgress: = There are many people, however, who will complain that God should have allowed Adam to do wrong (transgress = to overstep the limits of doing right). 指没有听从上帝，偷吃了禁果。

25. Foolish tongues!: They are fools who complain that way.

26. When God gave him reason, he gave him freedom to choose, for reason is but choosing; he had been else (= or else he would have been) **a mere artificial Adam, such an Adam as he is in the motions** (motions= puppet shows)**:** 亚当有罪于天堂。或有怨上帝曰，勿宜听之任之。此等人众，然愚人耳。上帝给亚当以理性，同时给予选择之自由，盖理性者，选择之理性也。亚当如无理性，此亚当不过木偶戏中木人亚当耳。

* * *

密尔顿原文约三万字，这里所选三段包括的哲学含义是：善恶相伴而生，人有理性，乃知选择，否则木偶耳。还有一点值得注意。密尔顿在这一文中反复用了《旧约》偷食禁果，乃知善恶这一主题，这一主题又正是《失乐园》的主题，可见诗人密尔顿和文章家密尔顿是一致的。以古典喻今事，并作了新的阐发，这正是文艺复兴的精神。

11 JOHN BUNYAN 1628–1688

THE PILGRIM'S PROGRESS

Vanity Fair

杨周翰 注释

Then[1] I[2] saw in my dream, that[3] when they[4] were got[5] out of the wilderness,[6] they presently[7] saw a town before them, and the name of that town is Vanity; and at the town there is a fair kept[8] called Vanity Fair:[9] it is kept all the year long[10], it beareth[11] the name of Vanity Fair, because the town where tis[12] kept is lighter than vanity; and also,[13] because all that is there sold, or that cometh thither, is vanity. As is the saying of the wise, *All that cometh is vanity.*[14]

This fair is no new-erected business, but a thing of ancient standing; I will show you the original of it.[15]

Almost five thousand years agone,[16] there were pilgrims walking to the Celestial City, as these two honest persons are; and Beelzebub,[17] Apollyon, and Legion, with their companions, perceiving by the path that the pilgrims made, that their way to the city lay through this town of Vanity, they[18] contrived here to set up a fair; a fair wherein should be sold all sorts of vanity, and that[19] it should last all the year long. Therefore at this fair are all such merchandise[20] sold, as houses, lands, trades, places, honours, preferments,[21] titles, countries, kingdoms, lusts, pleasures, and delights of all sorts, as whores, bawds,[22] wives, husbands, children, masters, servants, lives, blood, bodies, souls, silver, gold, pearls, precious stones, and what not.[23]

And, moreover, at this fair there is at all times to be seen juggling, cheats, games, plays, fools, apes,[24] knaves, and rogues, and that of all sorts.

Here are to be seen too, and that for nothing,[25] thefts, murders, adulteries, false-swearers, and that of a bloodred colour.

And as in other fairs of less moment,[26] there are the several[27] rows[28] and streets under their proper[29] names, where such and such wares are vended:[30] so here likewise, you have the proper places, rows, streets, (*viz.*[31] countries, and kingdoms) where the wares of this fair are soonest[32] to be found: Here is the Britain Row, the French Row, the Italian Row, the Spanish Row, the German Row, where several sorts of vanities are to be sold. But as in other fairs, some one commodity is as the chief of all the fair, so the ware of Rome[33] and her merchandise is greatly promoted[34] in this fair: only our English nation, with some others, have taken a dislike[35] thereat.[36]

Now, as I said, the way to the Celestial City lies just through this town, where this lusty[37] fair is kept; and he that will go to the City, and yet not go through this town, must needs[38] *go out of the World.*[39] The Prince of princes[40] himself, when here,[41] went through this town to his own country, and that upon a fair-day too: yea,[42] and as I think it was Beelzebub, the chief lord[43] of this fair, that invited him to buy of his vanities;[44] yea, would have made[45] him lord of the fair, would he but[46] have done him reverence[47] as he went through the town. Yea, because he was such a person of honour, Beelzebub had him from street to street, and showed him all the kingdoms of the world in a little time, that he might, if possible, allure that Blessed One,[48] to cheapen[49] and buy some of his vanities. But he had no mind to[50] the merchandise, and therefore left the town; without laying out[51] so much as one farthing[52] upon these vanities. This fair therefore is an ancient thing, of long standing, and a very great fair.

Now these Pilgrims, as I said, must needs go through this fair: Well, so they did; but behold, even as they entered into the fair, all the people in the fair were moved,[53] and the town itself as it were in a hubbub about them;[54] and that for several reasons: for,

First, The pilgrims were clothed with such kind of raiment,[55] as was diverse[56] from the raiment of any that traded in that fair. The people, therefore, of the fair, made a great gazing[57] upon them: some said they were fools, some they were Bedlams,[58] and some they are outlandish men.[59]

Secondly, And as they wondered at their apparel, so they did likewise at their speech; for few could understand what they[60] said; they naturally spoke the language of Canaan[61]; but they that kept the fair, were the men of this world: so that from one end of the fair to the other, they seemed barbarians[62] each to the other.[63]

Thirdly, But that which did not a little amuse[65] the merchandisers, was, that these pilgrims set very light by[66] all their wares, they cared not so much as to look upon them: and if they called[67] upon them to buy, they would[68] put their fingers in their ears, and cry, *Turn away mine*[69] *eyes from beholding vanity;* and look upwards, signifying that their trade and traffic[70] was in heaven.

One chanced mockingly, beholding the carriage[71] of the men, to say unto them, *What will ye buy?*[72] But they, looking gravely upon him, said, *We buy the Truth.* At that, there was an occasion[73] taken to despise the men[74] the more; some mocking, some taunting,[75] some speaking reproachfully, and some calling upon others to smite them. At last things came to a hubbub, and great stir in the fair, insomuch that all order was confounded. Now was word presently brought to the great one[76] of the fair, who quickly came down, and deputed some of his most trusty friends to take these men into examination,[77] about whom the fair was almost overturned. So the men were brought to examination; and they that sat upon[78] them, asked them whence they came, whither they went, and what they did there in such an unusual garb?[79] The men told them, that they were pilgrims and strangers in the world, and that they were going to their own country, which was the heavenly Jerusalem;[80] and that they had given none occasion to the men of the town, nor yet to the merchandisers, thus to abuse them, and to let[81] them in their journey. Except it was,[82] for that, when one asked them what they would buy, they said, they would buy the Truth. But they that were appointed to examine them, did not believe them to be any other than Bedlams and mad, or else such as came to put all things into a confusion in the fair. Therefore they took them, and beat them, and besmeared[83] them with dirt, and then put them into the cage,[84] that they might be made a spectacle to all the men of the fair. There therefore they lay[85] for some time, and were made the objects of any man's sport,[86] or malice, or revenge, the great ones of the fair laughing still[87] at all that befell them! But the men[88] being patient, and not rendering railing for railing,[89] but contrariwise, blessing, and giving good words for bad, and kindness for injuries done: some men in the fair that were more observing,[90] and less prejudiced than the rest, began to check and blame the baser sort for their continual abuses done by them to the men; they[91], therefore, in angry manner,[92] let fly[93] at them[94] again,[95] counting them as bad as the men in the cage, and telling them that they seemed confederates,[96] and should be made partakers of their misfortunes. The other[97] replied, that for aught they could see,[98] the men were quiet, and sober, and intended nobody any harm; and that there were many that traded in their fair, that were more worthy to be put into the cage, yea, and pillory[99] too, than were the men that they had abused. Thus, after divers[100] words had passed on both sides, (the men[101] behaving themselves all the while very wisely, and soberly before them) they[102] fell to some blows,[103] among themselves, and did harm one to another. Then were these two poor men brought before their examiners again, and there charged[104] as being guilty of the late hubbub that had been in the fair. So they beat them pitifully,[105] and hanged irons upon them, and led them in chains up and down the fair, for an example and a terror[106] to others, lest any should further speak in their behalf, or join themselves unto them. But Christian and Faithful behaved themselves yet more wisely, and received the ignominy[107] and shame that was cast upon them, with so much meekness and patience, that it won to their side (though but few in comparison of the rest) several of the men in the fair. This put the other party yet into[108] greater rage, insomuch that they concluded[109] the death of these two men. Wherefore they threatened that the cage nor irons[110] should serve their turn,[111] but that they should die, for the abuse they had done, and for deluding[112] the men of the fair.

【作者简介】 John Bunyan（约翰·班扬，1628—1688）是英国文学史上著名的散文家、小说家。他的职业是小炉匠。他青年时期正值英国资产阶级革命，被征入革命的议会军，离开军队后，在故乡（伦敦北百余里的Bedford城）从事传教活动。1660年斯图亚特王朝复辟，当局借口未经许可而传教，把他逮捕入狱，监禁了十二年（1660—1672年）。出狱后，他又一度被捕，拘禁了半年，此后终其生在故乡和伦敦进行传教活动。

他的著作很多，主要有四部。《上帝赐予最大罪人的无限恩惠》（*Grace Abounding to the Chief of Sinners*, 1666年）系作者早期生活的自传；《天路历程》（*The Pilgrim's Progress*, Part I, 1678年；Part II, 1684年）写基督徒及其妻子先后寻找天国的经历；《坏人先生传》（*The Life and Death of Mr. Badman*, 1680年）假托坏人先生以讽刺大资产阶级的行径；《圣战》（*The Holy War*, 1682年）假托上帝与魔鬼争夺人类灵魂的故事揭发当时政治、社会的黑暗，为受迫害的小人物鸣不平。

班扬一生的宗教活动和著作反映了英国资产阶级革命后一部分小资产阶级、农民、手工艺人对大资产阶级和复辟贵族的妥协局面的不满和反抗，资产阶级革命胜利并未给他们带来任何好处。他们斗争的主要形式是“不从国教”（dissent或nonconformity），而当权者由于害怕他们反抗，进行疯狂迫害，象Bedford这样一个小城，一间小小监房在班扬囚禁时最多曾关过六十名“不从国教者”。

由于历史原因，资产阶级革命一上来就是披着宗教外衣进行的。人们的精神、思想、感情无不是在宗教气氛中培养起来的。班扬受的教育不多，他读得最熟的书就是《圣经》和少数宗教、修身的书籍。他的作品因此也必然染上浓厚的宗教色彩，但是透过这层迷雾，我们看到的却是一个充满信心、决不妥协、勇往直前的灵魂。我们在他身上看不出任何没落颓废情绪；反之，他对待生活是严肃的、积极的、乐观的。他在狱中毫不沮丧，学习制鞋带赡养家属，向其他监犯传道，据信，至少《天路历程》中一部分也是在狱中写的。

他的作品在英国散文和小说史上占很重要的地位。文艺复兴时期诗歌已经开花结果，但散文作为表达工具则尚在摸索阶段，有的人仿效法国的绮丽体，有的人仿效拉丁散文的冗长或警炼，有的人则毫无批判地滥用口语，有的人则混杂以上各体，总之当时散文尚未成熟。英国散文成熟是十七世纪后期的事，以两个政治立场截然不同的作家功劳最大，其一是写论说批评文的德莱顿（Dryden），其一是写叙事文的班扬。班扬不仅在语言上，而且在小说技巧上，为十八世纪斯威夫特（Swift）和笛福（Defoe）的小说、散文，铺平了道路。

班扬的语言工夫主要得力于民间口语和《圣经》，特点是简单、明晰、生动、有力。尽管他距离文艺复兴不过一百年，距离今天将近三百年，但在风格上更接近现代散文。他传教、写书，目的是要使最广大的群众听懂、看懂，这就是他的风格特点的由来。本篇选文很能说明这些特点。

【题解与注释】

The Pilgrim's Progress，旧译《天路历程》，以第一部分最为通行。全书开始时写作者梦见主人公基督徒（Christian）背着包袱，背朝家门，手捧一书，正在阅读，忽然大呼一声说：“我怎么办呢？”作者接着写他梦见主人公如何历尽千辛万苦，克服种种魔障，终于到达天国。全书主旨不外是想借此指出一个人如要想到达天国，亦即实现革命理想，必须下定决心，抛弃家室，丢掉包袱，遵循《圣经》的指示，经受各种考验，道德上要坚定才行，并想以此思想来影响当时广大读者。

本节是书中比较精彩的一段，从中可以窥见作者思想和艺术的一斑。本节写主人公经历的许多考验中的一次考验。所谓虚荣市正是复辟时期英国社会的缩影，在这里一切关系都可以归结为买卖关系；有人想要把革命向前推进一步，就被认为是咄咄怪事，这种人必然受到迫害。文中的概括与虚构的形象无不以作者对当时现实的观察为依据，只是他的表现方式是梦幻和寓言（allegory）。把追求革命比作中世纪信徒的朝圣，这是通篇的大寓言；把英国社会比作市集，这是本节的寓言；把这社会的统治者比作魔鬼（Beelzebub, Apollyon, Legion）等《圣经》上的形象，这又是个别形象、更小规模的寓言。但是总而言之，这些寓言后面都有现实根据。这种形式是中世纪以来广泛流传的一种现成形式，作者对他这方法本来不是没有顾虑的，并还引用《圣经》的比喻（parable）为自己辩护，但出书以后，很受欢迎（仅作者生前即印了十一版，其中两版，各印刷两次，总数达十万册以上），并有人模仿（因而他写了第二部分），证明这种形式是当时广大读者所喜爱的。

班扬的词汇、句法有时显得古老，但如前所述，把他和文艺复兴时期散文家，甚至十七世纪一些文人作家比一比，他就显得十分现代化。如果说班扬选用了一定数量在当时也是较古老的词汇，这是文章性质所决定的，大凡传道说教者流都有这种习惯，班扬深受《圣经》影响，要求语言庄严、严肃，在这方面他可以说是很成功的，特别在叙事部分，例如 so they did; but behold, even as they entered into the fair, all the people in the fair were moved，这里不仅选词，而且在字句安排（包括重复）、停顿和韵律方面，都有强烈的英译《圣经》文体的味道。

但是总的说来，班扬的风格更多体现了口语的特点，十分平易近人，条理清晰，但也不妨碍他偶尔插入一段题外话，例如他先把市集来历交代了，接着描写市集情况，人物出现引起骚动，他又分析原因一、二、三，条理十分清楚，但在中间插入一段耶稣故事，使人读来不觉是节外生枝，反如面其人、闻其声。他善于用比，以熟悉的比陌生的，以现实的比想象的，从近比远（如 as ... so ...），使读者一目了然。他的文章有力量、有节奏，这种特点表现在层层积累（如虚荣市上的商品、娱乐、犯罪行为），层层推进（如几个 yea ... yea ... yea ...），最便于朗读。他的文章富于戏剧性，读来极为生动，例如市集中人对来客的反应（all the people in the fair were moved ... were in a hubbub about them ... made a great gazing upon them ... some said ... some (said) ... some (said)），寥寥几笔，他们的惊讶、议论纷纷的情况就跃然纸上。此外，还有许多很亲切的口语特点，如 I will show you, as I said, now, well 等，凡此种种都表明他的写作目的是要真正能够打动人，好象自己在读者、听众群中。

班扬总提醒自己说，必须和穷人在一起，不能离开穷人（"I should often make it my business to be going again and again into the company of these poor people, for I could not stay away."）；他必须战斗，剑不离手，剑在手中，混身是胆（"I fought till my sword did cleave to my hand; and when they were joined together as if the sword grew out of my arm; and when the blood ran through my fingers, then I fought with most courage."）。他的斗争武器之一就是他的作品，这一武器的威力，不论是他的敌或友，都是一致承认的：当时王朝出版检查官（L'Estrange）就说班扬这类作家都是通俗文体的大师（"great masters of the Popular Style"），这种文章最能打动"群氓"的心（"strike home to the capacity and humour of the multitude"）。一百年后约翰逊（Samuel Johnson）对他的传记作者鲍斯威尔（Boswell）说："《天路历程》无论就创造性、想象力、故事的安排来说，都有很大优点，最好的证明就是它受到人们普遍的、不断的欣赏。"（"His *Pilgrim's Progress* has great merit, both for invention, imagination, and the conduct of the story; and it has the best evidence of its merit, the general and continued approbation of mankind.”）

1. Then: 全书共写十几场梦，作者 Bunyan [ˈbʌnjən] 前此已在梦中见到主人公基督徒（Christian）离家后在寻找天国（the Celestial City）途中一些遭遇。虚荣市在全书前半。

2. I: 指作者自己。

3. that: 此处为联接词，接宾语。书中 that 尚有其它用法，如联系代词，可以代替一从句或名词（如第 1 段第 6 行、第 5 段第 1 行）；如代词（如第 4 段第 3 行）；或作 so that 用（如第 7 段第 11 行）等，不一一列举。读者应加区别，以免混淆。

4. they: 指主人公及其旅伴 Faithful. 主人公在全书中共有三个旅伴，1. Pliable，老早放弃此行；2. Faithful，到此被杀害，3. Hopeful，继 Faithful 之后陪伴主人公共入天国。

5. were got: 古代语法，某些动词，如 come，go，become，arrive 等，用助动词 to be 表示过去完成时态。又，读者可注意本文动词均极简单，广用名词，形容词极少，反映了民间口语和英译《圣经》的特色。

6. wilderness: 指前此二人在途中遇见 Talkative 进行一场辩论后，在原野上行走一节故事。

7. presently: 不久。

8. there is a fair kept: 古代语法常有 there+be+n. +participle 的结构。

9. fair: 集市。Vanity Fair 是作者在本书中创造的许多形象中最著名的一个，十九世纪小说家 Thackeray 以此作为他一部小说的书名。

10. all the year long: 以表示与定期的、季节性的集市有别。

11. beareth [ˈbɛəriθ]: 动词现在时第三人称单数 th(eth) 即现代的 s. s 在十七世纪口语中已通行，但英译《圣经》以及教堂宣教时仍保留 th.

12. tis: = ’tis = it is. 较 it is 更口语化。

13. also: 后面的逗点（,）并非语法所需要，而是适应诵读时停顿的需要的，早期文章标点常如此。本文中有些逗点均如此，不列举。

14. *all ... is vanity*: 语出《圣经》。书中援引《圣经》辞句极多，不一一注出。斜体字表示直接引语。

15. original: origin.

of it: its 在十七世纪口语中已常用，但《圣经》中避免之，用 there of, of it. Bunyan 此处受《圣经》风格影响。

16. five thousand years agone: agone，古语，即 ago. 按《圣经》计算，人类在这时被创造。

17. Beelzebub [biˈelzibʌb]: 希伯来语，“苍蝇的主宰”，堕落天使的领袖之一；Apollyon [əˈpɔljən] 希腊语“毁灭者”，Legion 罗马军团，转义为“众”、“群”，此处按《圣经》义作“污鬼”解。三语均出《圣经》，都是魔鬼的化身。

18. they: 主语是 Beelzebub 等，此处 they 乃重复，语法上不需要，系口语特点。

19. and that: 语法上很难交代，可以勉强与前一行 contrived 联系。口语，尤其长句，不能按语法家条例要求。

20. merchandise: 复数。

21. preferments: 升官。

22. bawds: 老鸨。

23. and what not: 等等。

24. apes: = mimics，作模仿性动作的艺人。

25. for nothing: 不必花钱。

26. moment: = importance. Of less moment 较小的，小型的。指真正的市集。

27. several: 古语，= different.

28. rows: 巷。一般注释家认为作者此处蓝本系剑桥市(Cambridge)附近 Stourbridge 市集，此集规模宏大，店铺按类列成巷道，如蒜巷、书商巷、饭铺巷等。

29. proper: 按法语原意解作 own.

30. vended: sold.

31. *viz.*: [viˈdi:liset, ˈneimli]，拉丁语 videlicet，意为 namely，即。作者此处把自己的比喻明确点出，市集中不同的街道比作宗教信仰不同的欧洲各国。

32. soonest: 最容易。

33. Rome: 天主教的象征。

34. promoted: 地位高。

35. dislike: 不赞成，disapproval. 意为不赞成天主教。

36. thereat: at it, at Rome.《圣经》语法，参前。

37. lusty: = merry, cheerful，贬辞；也有人欲横流之意。

38. needs: 副词，加强 must 语气。

39. go out of the World: 人要到天堂而不经过此城，那就只有离开人世，意即不可能不经过此城。

40. The Prince of princes: 万王之王，指耶稣。希伯来语表达"最高级"(the superlative)的方式，其后在英语中扎了根，如'in my heart of hearts'(*Hamlet*).

41. when here: 当他在人世时。

42. yea: 古语，= yes，不仅如此，而且…，与 nay 正相反。

43. the chief lord: 当时英国市集一般由当地市长或由市长委派副手主管，执行法律，判断纠纷。

44. of his vanities: of，在语法中称为 partitive genitive，意为 some of. 参看第 7 段第 11 行。

45. would have made: 以 that 为主语。

46. would he but: = if only he would.

47. done him reverence: to do (pay, make) reverence to someone，表示尊敬，如跪拜。

48. that Blessed [ˈblesid] **One:** 指耶稣。

49. cheapen: 古语，买。指魔鬼引诱耶稣，见《马太福音》第四章。

50. had no mind to: 不想、不愿（买）。

51. laying out: 花钱、投资。

52. farthing: 四分之一便士，一个小钱。

53. moved: 骚动。

54. the town ... about them: 此句省去 was.

in a hubbub: 吵嚷、议论。

55. raiment: 衣服。

56. diverse: = different.

57. made a great gazing: 作者喜用动名词，形成特殊的古朴有力的风格，参看第 1 段第 7 行，第 2 段第 1 行，第 7 段第 14 行，第末段倒数第 2 行等，亦可比较第 6 段最后一行 take a dislike，第 7 段第 13 行 have no mind to. 此处烘托出情节的戏剧性。

58. Bedlams: 疯人。

59. they are outlandish men: 用现在式，可以视为直接引语。见《以赛亚书》第十九章。外国人。

60. they: 指 Christian 与 Faithful.

61. the language of Canaan [ˈkeinən]**:** 迦南即巴勒斯坦，圣地。迦南语言意为真正信徒的语言。

62. barbarians: 外国人。

63. each to the other: 两位旅客与市集中人。

64. Thirdly, But: 按现代句法，应作 But thirdly.

65. amuse: = bewilder，使…惊讶。

66. set very light by: 轻视。

67. they called: 指商人。

68. they would: 指两位旅客。

69. mine: = my，后一词以元音开始时，古代用 mine.

70. trade and traffic: 双声骈比词，即现代英语 business.

71. carriage: 举止、行为。

72. What will ye buy?: 直接引语。下一行 *We buy the Truth* 同。

73. occasion: 尤其指攻击的机会。第 12 段第 16 行，occasion 接近 offence 意。

74. the men: 指二旅客。

75. taunting: 傲慢地谩骂。

76. the great one: 指市集主管，参看第 43 注。

77. examination: 审讯。

78. sat upon: 审问。

79. garb: 衣服，装束。

80. Jerusalem [dʒəˈruːsələm]**:** 耶路撒冷，此处指天国。

81. to let: 古义阻止。

82. Except it was: except (conj.) +it was (it be, it were) + prep. phrase（或 because, for that 从句）是古代语法常有的公式；用 it was，以免重复前述事由。此处附属从句独立成句，目的在使之突出。意思是：除非是因为…

83. besmeared: 抹、涂。

84. cage: 囚笼。

85. lay: = stayed, remained.
86. sport: 戏弄。
87. still: 古语，= always, constantly.
88. the men: 指二旅客。
89. rendering railing for railing: 以骂还骂。
90. observing: = compliant，随和。
91. they: 指 the baser sort.
92. in angry manner: 古语，in an angry manner.
93. let fly: 以恶毒言语比作射箭。比喻出自《旧约》《诗篇》第 64 篇。
94. them: 指市集中较善良的人—the more observing sort.
95. again: 古义 back (adv.)，与最后一段倒数第 14 行义异。
96. confederates: 同盟，同谋。
97. The other: 即 the others, the other party.
98. for aught ... see: = as far as they could see，据他们看。
99. pillory: 立枷。
100. divers: = various, many. 与第 9 段第 2 行义异。
101. the men: 仍指二旅客。
102. they: 指市集上的两派人。
103. fell to some blows: 打起来，动起武来。
104. charged: were charged 被控犯…罪。
105. pitifully: 实际上等于 pitilessly.
106. example and a terror: 以警效尤。
107. ignominy: 耻辱。
108. yet into: into yet.
109. concluded: 决定。
110. the cage nor irons: = neither the cage nor the irons.
111. serve their turn: 适用于他们。
112. deluding: 蒙骗。

12 JOHN DRYDEN
1631–1700

I. *An Essay of Dramatic Poesy*
〔*Shakespeare*〕
〔*Ben Jonson*〕
II. *Preface to Fables*
〔*Chaucer*〕

杜秉洲　选注

III. *Alexander's Feast*
IV. *Absalom and Achitophel*
〔*Achitophel*〕

戴镏龄　选注

I. *AN ESSAY OF DRAMATIC POESY*

杜秉洲　选注

I. PROSE PASSAGES

[SHAKESPEARE]

'To begin, then, with Shakespeare. He was the man who of all modern, and perhaps ancient poets, had the largest and most comprehensive soul.[1] All the images of Nature were still present to him,[2] and he drew them, not laboriously, but luckily;[3] when he describes anything, you more than see it, you feel it too. Those who accuse him to have wanted[4] learning, give him the greater commendation: he was naturally learned;[5] he needed not the spectacles of books to read Nature;[6] he looked inwards, and found her there.[7] I cannot say he is everywhere alike[8]; were he so, I should do him injury to compare him with the greatest of mankind.[9] He is many times flat, insipid;[10] his comic wit degenerating into clenches,[11] his serious swelling into bombast.[12] But he is always great, when some great occasion is presented to him; no man can say he ever had a fit subject for his wit, and did not then raise himself as high above the rest of poets.[13]

Quantum lenta solent inter viburna cupressi.[14]

The consideration of this made Mr. Hales of Eaton[15] say, that there was no subject of which any poet ever writ, but he would produce it much better done in Shakespeare;[16] and however others are now generally preferred before him,[17] yet the age wherein he lived, which had contemporaries with him Fletcher[18] and Jonson, never equalled them to him in their esteem:[19] and in the last King's court,[20] when Ben's[21] reputation was at highest, Sir John Suckling,[22] and with him the greater part of the courtiers,[23] set our Shakespeare far above him.

[BEN JONSON]

'As for Jonson, to whose character I am now arrived, if we look upon him while he was himself (for his last plays were but his dotages[1]), I think him the most learned and judicious writer which any theatre[2] ever had. He was a most severe judge of himself, as well as others. One cannot say he wanted[3] wit, but rather that he was frugal of it.[4] In his works you find little to retrench or alter. Wit, and language, and humour[5] also in some measure,[6] we had before him; but something of art was wanting to the Drama, till he came.[7] He managed his strength to more advantage than any who preceded him. You seldom find him making love in any of his scenes,[8] or endeavouring to move the passions;[9] his genius was too sullen and saturnine[10] to do it gracefully, especially when he knew he came after those[11] who had performed both to such an height. Humour was his proper sphere; and in that he delighted most to represent mechanic people.[12] He was deeply conversant[13] in the Ancients,[14] both Greek and Latin, and he borrowed boldly from them: there is scarce a poet or historian among the Roman authors of those times whom he has not translated in *Sejanus* and *Catiline*.[15] But he has done his robberies so openly, that one may see he fears not to be taxed[16] by any law. He invades authors like a monarch; and what would be theft in other poets, is only victory in him.[17] With the spoils of these writers he so represents old Rome to us, in its rites, ceremonies, and customs, that if one of their poets had written either of his tragedies, we had seen less of it[18] than in him. If there was any fault in his language,[19] 'twas that he weaved it too closely and laboriously, in his comedies especially: perhaps too, he did a little too much Romanize our tongue,[20] leaving the words which he translated almost as much Latin as he found them: wherein,[21] though he learnedly followed their language, he did not enough comply with the idiom of ours.[22] If I would compare him with Shakespeare, I must acknowledge him the more correct poet, but Shakespeare the greater wit. Shakespeare was the Homer, or father of our dramatic poets; Jonson was the Virgil,[23] the pattern[24] of elaborate writing; I admire him, but I love Shakespeare.'[25]

II. PREFACE TO FABLES

[CHAUCER]

In the first place, as he is the father of English poetry, so I hold him in the same degree of veneration as the Grecians held Homer, or the Romans Virgil. He is a perpetual fountain of good sense;[1] learn'd in all sciences;[2] and, therefore, speaks properly[3] on all subjects. As he knew what to say, so he knows also when to leave off;[4] a continence which is practised by few writers, and scarcely by any of the ancients, excepting Virgil and Horace[5]. ...

He must have been a man of a most wonderful comprehensive nature, because, as it has been truly observed of him, he has taken into the compass[6] of his *Canterbury Tales*[7] the various manners and humours[8] (as we now call them) of the whole English nation, in his age. Not a single character has escaped him. All his pilgrims are severally[9] distinguished from each other; and not only in their inclinations, but in their very physiognomies and persons.[10] Baptista Porta[11] could not have described their natures better, than by the marks[12] which the poet gives them. The matter and manner[13] of their tales, and of their telling, are so suited to their different educations, humours, and callings,[14] that each of them would be improper in any other mouth. Even the grave and serious characters are distinguished by their several sorts of gravity: their discourses[15] are such as belong to their age, their calling, and their breeding;[16] such as are becoming of them,[17] and of them only. Some of his persons are vicious,[18] and some virtuous; some are unlearn'd, or (as Chaucer calls them) lewd, and some are learn'd. Even the ribaldry of the low characters is different: the Reeve, the Miller, and the Cook,[19] are several men,[20] and distinguished from each other as much as the mincing Lady-Prioress and the broad-speaking, gap-toothed Wife of Bath.[21] But enough of this;[22] there is such a variety of game[23] springing up before me, that I am distracted in my choice,[24] and know not which to follow. 'Tis sufficient to say according to the proverb, that here is God's plenty.

【作者简介】 John Dryden（约翰·德莱顿，1631—1700），英国十七世纪末期著名的古典主义作家，其作品包括文学评论，政治讽刺诗，讴颂诗，英雄诗剧，喜剧与悲剧等。他在剑桥大学受了古典文学教育，1654 年毕业。1668 年封为皇室的桂冠诗人。他在政治上无骨气，竭力适应于皇室贵族所控制的政治与宗教环境。

德莱顿写过《英雄诗章》（*Heroic Stanza*, 1658）歌颂清教徒领袖克伦威尔，但又写过《正义恢复了》（*Astraea Redux*, 1660）一诗欢迎查理二世即位，斯图亚特王朝复辟。他写过《世俗人的宗教观》（*Religlo Laici*, 1683）以维护英国国教会，后来天主教徒詹姆士二世于 1685 年即位，德莱顿改信天主教，不久便写了《牡鹿与豹》（*The Hind and the Panther*, 1687），贬斥英国国教会而竭力赞扬罗马天主教。德莱顿曾为当时贵族阶级写了一些喜剧反映了宫廷淫佚放荡的生活方式。他写的一些英雄诗剧描写英雄、美人与爱情，剧情光怪陆离，对话荒诞不经，充满了宫廷的感情与意识。

德莱顿文学上的成就在于他的文学评论，政治讽刺诗和讴颂诗。著名的攻击当时辉格党人的讽刺诗如《亚布萨伦与阿琦图菲尔》(*Absalom and Achitophel*, 1681),《奖章》(*The Medal*, 1682)，以及《马克·傅莱克诺》(*MacFlecknoe*, 1682)等笔锋犀利；诗中英雄偶句(heroic couplet)技巧精练有阳刚的气势，十八世纪前期以蒲伯(Alexander Pope, 1688–1744)为首的诗坛曾奉之为诗律的楷模。

德莱顿的文学评论，如《论戏剧诗》(*An Essay of Dramatic Poesy*, 1668)以及其他与批评有关的诗与剧的序言，风格清新，笔锋遒劲，分析能鞭辟入里。德莱顿成功地革新了伊丽莎白王朝遗留下来的绮丽艰深的文体，而为十八世纪以艾狄生(Joseph Addison, 1672–1719)作品为代表的明白晓畅的散文奠定了坚实的基础。

我们在此所选的几小段散文作品，属于德莱顿最有名的文论，读者可以从中看出英国过去文学批评的某些特点，例如不重理论而重具体作品的分析，而分析时又不求全面而只指点几处，个人印象多于系统阐释，文章则用小品笔法，常有警句。德莱顿虽然活动在十七世纪后半，但语言平易处与口语色彩的浓厚都接近现代英语，写得纵横自如，值得学习英文散文的人研究。

【题解与注释】

1. [SHAKESPEARE]

评论莎士比亚与本·琼生的两篇文章选自德莱顿的《论戏剧诗》(*An Essay of Dramatic Poesy*, 1668). 这篇著名的文章以对话的形式写四位朋友，各抒己见，分别比较古希腊与十七世纪戏剧，以及十七世纪法国戏剧与英国伊丽莎白与詹姆士朝代的戏剧，论列其优劣及技巧特点。这四人中，Neander 是作者本人的代言人。他强调薄古厚今，持论要全面。我们所选的评论莎士比亚与本·琼生的两段文章是 Neander 发表的意见的一小部分。Neander 认为莎士比亚以来英国剧作种类多样化而又蓬勃有生气，人物典型多式多样，刻划逼真传神，语言生动有力，能创造性地摹仿人生与自然。谈到莎士比亚时他说：

> "莎士比亚在现代或者古代的诗人中具有最博大而又悟力最强的才智。他的心灵随时洞悉宇宙万象。他能轻巧地刻划出它们而不露斧凿痕迹。他描写人物栩栩如生，象有实体可触一样。有人疵其学识贫乏，实赐予更佳的称誉。他天才卓越，能直观宇宙万物，无需博览群书以知自然。他只须内窥其心，即可发现宇宙真理。"

但 Neander 不是莎士比亚盲目的崇拜者，他很清醒地指出：

“我不能说莎士比亚的剧作篇篇同样精美。假如这样，则世间最伟大的作家较之亦远为逊色了。”

王政复辟时期御用作家对文学语言要求极严格的工整与贵族化的雅致，因之Neander对莎士比亚不免有白璧微瑕之感。他认为莎士比亚行文有时不精心修饰，间或用语俚俗以迎合小市民观众，因之

“他剧作中常有平凡乏味之处；他的喜剧的隽语有时退化为对谑打诨，而严肃的隽语又常臃结为荒诞浮夸。”

但有时Neander能超出当时新古典主义的范畴，发现在莎士比亚不合古典戏剧规则的剧作中实涵蕴着无比的天才。他说：

“每有伟大论题，莎士比亚常作雄文以施其艺。这样便无人敢说莎士比亚在处理与其天才相称的题材而不能超过其他诗人，‘有如翠柏（高耸）于篱边匐生着的枝条之间’一样。因之他的声名无匹于当时。在查理一世当本·琼生文名鼎盛时，莎士比亚亦为朝中多数文士所崇敬而被远列于本·琼生之上。”

以上德莱顿借Neander之口对莎士比亚所发表的评论，曾左右着整个英国十七世纪对莎士比亚的评价。甚至到十八世纪末期新古典主义的著名殿军约翰逊（Samuel Johnson，1709—84）仍把德莱顿这篇评论莎士比亚的短文，奉为颂词的圭臬（model of encomiastic criticism）。约翰逊在他的《莎士比亚戏剧集序言》（1765）中说：

“莎士比亚的这些优点是值得赞扬的：他的戏剧是人生的写照；凡是在追寻其他诗人所唤出的幽灵而致想象迷惑的人，可以领会一下莎士比亚剧里用活人语言所描写出的人的情感。这样便可医好他们精神的癫狂了。”

约翰逊的这段批评大体上仍反映了德莱顿颂词的主要内容。由此可见德莱顿在英国文学批评史上影响的深远了。

1. the largest and most comprehensive soul: 最博大和最能领悟一切的智力。

2. All the images of Nature were still present to him: “still” 在此句为古义，意为：经常地。全句说：宇宙里所有的形象经常呈现在他（的心里）。

Nature: 井然有序的宇宙，这个中世纪遗留下来的观念，在莎士比亚生活的时代仍很流行。

3. drew ... luckily: 巧妙地，不着痕迹地…描写出。

4. to have wanted: 缺少了。

5. was naturally learned: 直观宇宙的万事万物。

6. he needed not the spectacles of books to read Nature: 他不需把书籍作为视镜去研究宇宙；把书本知识作为研究宇宙的张本。

7. he looked inwards, and found her there: 伊丽莎白王朝时代仍流传着人本身（Microcosm 小宇宙）为大自然（Macrocosm 大宇宙）的缩影。此句意为：莎士比亚只要向内心观察，即可发现宇宙的缩影；这是中世纪传下来的唯心看法。

8. everywhere alike: 全都一样，意为处处都好。

were he so: if he were so 的另一种表现法；意即，假如他（的著作）是处处都好的话。

9. I should do him injury to compare him with the greatest of mankind: injury 在此句中的古义为，有意的侮辱。全句说：我即使把他与人类中最伟大的人相比，也将对他是一种侮辱；即如他处处都好，则即与最伟大的作家相比，也是委曲了他。

10. He is many times flat, insipid: 意即，他（的著作里）常有平淡、枯燥之处。

11. his comic wit degenerating into clenches: 这短语属于独立主格（Nominative absolute）的结构。他的喜剧的隽语退化为戏谑打诨。

12. his serious (wit) swelling into bombast: 他的严肃的隽语臃结为荒诞浮夸。

13. no man can say he ever had a fit subject for his wit, and did not then raise himself as high above the rest of poets: wit 在这句里的意义与前句中的 wit（隽语）不同，此处为才智或天才。这句话说："没有人可以说，他（莎士比亚）写作与他天才相称的题目时，而不能大大超过其余的诗人。"

14. *Quantum lenta solent inter viburna cupressi*: 此语德莱顿引自罗马诗人 Virgil (70–19 B. C.) 的《牧歌》（Eclogues）第一章二十五行。英译为：As cypresses do among trailing hedgerow shoots 有如翠柏（高耸）于篱边匐生着的枝条之间。

15. Mr. Hales of Eaton: Eaton 现写为 Eton，即 Eton 学院，为英国有名贵族化中学；Mr. John Hales (1584–1656) 当时为该校的教师（fellow）。

16. there was no subject of which any poet ever writ, but he would produce it much better done in Shakespeare: writ 为 wrote 的古体。produce，提示。but 在现代英文里为 but that，有否定之意，即 if ... not. 此句可译为：不论任何诗人写任何题目，他（Mr. Hales）都可在莎士比亚著作中找出同样的题目写得更为完美；意即莎士比亚写过的任何题目都远比其他诗人写得更好。

17. others are now generally preferred before him: 莎士比亚的诗名在英国十七世纪六十年代处于低潮。

18. Fletcher: John Fletcher (1579–1625) 与莎士比亚同时的剧作家。

19. never equalled them to him in their esteem: equalled 在此句的古义为，认…与…相匹敌。此句可直译为：绝对没有把他们（指 Fletcher 和 Jonson）与他（指莎士比亚）在他们（指与莎士比亚同时的人）崇敬的心情里对等起来；意即，他们更崇拜莎士比亚。

20. in the last King's court: 指查理一世的宫延里。

21. Ben's: Ben Jonson's，详选文第二篇注释。

22. Sir John Suckling: (1609–42)，查理一世王朝的贵族抒情诗人与剧作家。

23. courtiers: 朝臣们。

2. *[BEN JONSON]*

在评论本 · 琼生（1572—1637）这段文章里德莱顿分析了这位比莎士比亚晚生八年的写实主义剧作家的特点，认为在剧作家中本 · 琼生最为博学明辨，在写作方面对己对人批判最严。德莱顿以为琼生并不缺乏想象力，他不过是用之则俭而已。其作品中几无可省改之处。才华，词藻，怪僻个性的描写，前已大约有之，但本 · 琼生善用其才，笃守艺术规律（如戏剧的三一律）为前人所不及。

德莱顿又指出琼生的剧中甚少求爱或热情奔放的场面。他深知前人已在此登峰造极而己则才质沉郁不能优异为之。本·琼生擅描写人物怪僻的个性，最喜塑造工匠平民的形象。他精通古代希腊、罗马文学，在他的 *Sejanus* 与 *Catiline* 二悲剧中大胆翻译、引用所有罗马诗人与史家的著作；公开剽窃，无所顾忌。“他象帝王一样去侵略作家；其他诗人的剽窃，在他作品中便成了战利品”。因之在此二剧中他所描写的古罗马的礼节，典章与风俗，丰富多采，虽当时罗马诗人执笔，亦不能逮。

但德莱顿认为琼生行文过于谨严，有造作的痕迹，其喜剧尤甚。这大概由于他模仿拉丁文有些过分了，致使英文太罗马化；他翻译时常抄用原文；因博学好古，以致忽略尽可能地遵循英文的习惯了。

在此文末尾德莱顿用了比较批评法。他把本·琼生与莎士比亚相对比，因之便突出各自的特点。他认为本·琼生的作品较规范，而莎士比亚的想象则较丰富。莎士比亚如荷马，是英国戏剧诗人的始祖；本·琼生如弗吉尔（Virgil），是精细写作的模范。因之德莱顿很深刻地提出他的感想：他对本·琼生只是肃然起敬，但对莎士比亚则感到他蔼然可亲。

同时德莱顿常用简洁有力的文笔，在分析他们作品时，能单刀直入，一语破的。在论述古代作品对本·琼生的影响时，他说：

“He invades authors like a monarch; and what would be theft in other poets, is only victory in him.”（“他象帝王一样去侵略作家；其他诗人的剽窃，在他作品中便成了战利品。”）这几句话说得机智，清楚地勾画出本·琼生的为人、治学的特点。

1. dotages: 年老糊涂，此处意为琼生最后的一些剧本为其败笔，露出其龙钟老态。

2. any theatre: 任何国家的戏剧界，此处不作具体的某一戏院解。

3. wanted: 缺乏。

4. frugal of it: 用得俭省，即不浪费（自己的才华）。

5. humour: 此处为古义，指人的特别的气质。当时许多英国学者以为人有四种气质，即忧郁，轻佻，迟钝，暴躁；决定于人身上四种流液孰多孰少，而四种流液又相当于宇宙中四大元素，即土，气，水，火。琼生曾写剧本《人人合于气质》及《人人不合气质》，借“气质”来突出人物性格上的某一主要特点。

6. in some measure: = to some extent，在某种程度上。

7. something of art was wanting to the Drama, till he came: 到琼生手上，戏剧才算有了完美的艺术；在他之前，戏剧总象缺少一点艺术。

8. seldom find him making love in any of his scenes: 很少见他在剧本中写爱情，亦即琼生不长于写男女爱情。

9. to move the passions: 深刻地震撼灵魂。

10. saturnine: 沉重的，忧郁的。

11. those: 指莎士比亚等人。

12. mechanic people: 工匠之类。

13. deeply conversant: 精通。

14. the Ancients: 希腊罗马的古典作家。

15. *Sejanus, Catiline*: 皆琼生所作剧本名，以古罗马历史为题材。

16.taxed: 受到惩罚。

17. He invades authors like a monarch; and what would be theft in other poets, is only victory in him: 名句，与上文 borrowed boldly 及 done his robberies so openly 呼应，下文 spoils（战利品）又与此呼应，道出琼生公然利用前人材料，毫无愧色，结果表面上看来是抄袭，实际则是他本人胜利的改作。琼生深通古学，然又不为古学所蔽。参阅本文题解。

18. we had seen less of it: 虚拟式，现代英语应作 we would have seen less of it.

19. fault in his language: 上面谈琼生写得真实，从此起谈琼生的语言。作者的意见是否正确，请看下面第 22 注。

20. Romanize our tongue: 使我们的语言接受过多的拉丁影响，即将英语当作拉丁文来写，所以紧接有 leaving the words ... almost as much Latin as he found them（原来是拉丁文，经他之手后几乎仍是同样的拉丁文）。

21. wherein: = in which, in this matter.

22. the idiom of ours: 英语的特性。此处 idiom（单数）不指个别的成语，而指英语整个的特性。

以上是德莱顿对于琼生语言的意见，有一定道理，但不够全面。事实上，琼生的语言虽有其拉丁影响较重的一面，主要却还是道地的民间英语，这在他的喜剧里尤为明显。德莱顿称赞琼生的古罗马史剧，而特别不喜欢琼生的喜剧，这是因为在英国大资产阶级与大地主阶级达成妥协、斯图亚特王朝复辟之后，伦敦盛行迎合贵族趣味的浮华、淫秽的"风尚喜剧"（the comedy of manners），因此琼生所写的以讽刺世态为题材的现实主义的喜剧也就不合当时上层人士的胃口了。琼生的最大贡献正在这些写实喜剧，而德莱顿之不喜欢它们，不仅说明了他本人的偏见，也代表了当时文学趣味的堕落。

23. Shakespeare was the Homer ... Jonson was the Virgil: 以莎士比亚比荷马，而以琼生比弗吉尔；在当时及以前西欧文人的心目中，古希腊史诗作家荷马比古罗马史诗作家弗吉尔更高一筹，原因是荷马是西方文学的创始者，其"神才"不可企及，而弗吉尔虽是古罗马第一大家，但更多地以功力见长。

24. the pattern: the model，榜样，模范。

25. I admire him, but I leve Shakespeare: 结语有力；admire 强调理性上的佩服，love 则表达感情上的倾倒。这也是常见于英国式文论的典型笔法：从个人观感立论，用词平易；此处则寓批评于称赞之中，也值得读者注意。

3. [CHAUCER]

这两段评论乔叟（Geoffrey Chaucer, 1340?–1400）的文章，选自德莱顿的《古今故事诗集的前言》（Preface to *The Fables, Ancient and Modern*）。这部诗集是他最后的译作，1700 年三月出版，五月德莱顿即逝世。这个集子里面有 Homer，Virgil，Ovid，Boccaccio 的英译，及 Chaucer 的一些故事诗的今译。在此序言里德莱顿对 Homer 与 Virgil，Ovid 与 Chaucer 分别作了精湛的比较，但著名的是他在序言的下半部对乔叟较长的论述。

德莱顿用夹叙夹议的方法把乔叟的时代与生平和他本人对这位诗人的批评融合成娓娓动听的散文，表达其对乔叟热情的欣赏，同时也对乔叟作了一番分析。

德莱顿说：乔叟为英国诗歌之父，流不尽的理性的泉源；而且乔叟博学慎思，论事得体而又能适可而止，实古今之罕有。希腊、罗马文苑中仅 Virgil 与 Horace 能有其才。同时德莱顿认为乔叟的《坎特伯雷故事集》(*Canterbury Tales*) 内的各色人物，无论智贤愚与不肖，都是刻划入微，各如其分，为当时英国社会各阶层人物最典型的艺术形象；因之乔叟这部现实主义的巨著，真不愧为"文学的天府了"(Here's God's plenty)。

德莱顿在这几段评论文章里，没有用骈对的结构和修饰的赘语。字字随意写出，各适其分；因之风格便显得平易自然。此外，这段文章还具有德莱顿所重视的"散文所特有的和谐"(the other harmony of prose)。

1. perpetual fountain of good sense: 理性的不断的源泉。理性二字标出德莱顿的新古典主义立场。

2. all sciences: 一切知识。

3. properly: 恰如其分地。这也是新古典主义者重视的品质。

4. when to leave off: 什么时候该住口，适可而止。自我节制也是新古典主义者提倡的。下文 continence 即指节制。

5. Horace: (公元前 65—8)，古罗马讽刺诗人及文学批评家。

6. compass: 范围。

7. *Canterbury Tales*: 乔叟的名作，《坎特伯雷故事集》，是用"同韵对句"写成的叙事诗集（包括一篇开场白，及二十四首带有引言的叙事诗）。作者于 1387 年开始诗集的规划，写作继续到 1393 或 1394 年。

8. humours: 各种人的特性，气质。参阅上文 Ben Jonson 段注解。

9. severally: separately，个别地。

10. physiognomies and persons: 面貌与身体。

11. Baptista Porta: (1538—1615)，意大利著名相面家。

12. the marks: (相貌上的)特征。

13. matter and manner: 内容与形式。

14. callings: 职业。

15. discourses: 谈吐。

16. breeding: 教养。

17. are becoming of them: 适合他们；现代英语不用此形式，而说 become them; become of 在现代英语中另有意义，如 What's become of him? = What's happened to him?

18. vicious: wicked，坏（人），与 virtuous 相对。

19. the Reeve, the Miller, and the Cook: 管事，磨坊主，厨子，都是《坎特伯雷故事集》中的人物，三人都是所谓"下流人物"(low characters)，每人都讲了一个粗俗、淫秽的故事。

20. several men: 各有分明个性的人；several = separate.

21. the mincing Lady-Prioress and the broad-speaklng, gap-toothed Wife

of Bath: 细声细气的做作的尼庵主和说话粗俗，牙缝奇宽的 Bath 女人；这两人也是《坎特伯雷故事集》中的人物；Bath 是地名，在英格兰西南部，以温泉胜。德莱顿在此只用了几个形容词，就把乔叟诗中的人物的特点点明，颇能传神：mincing 表示故作文雅、高尚、忸忸怩怩；broad-speaking，喜说粗话；gap-toothed，现代版本作 gat-toothed，意为牙与牙间有很大的空缝（teeth set wide apart）.

22. But enough of this: 好了，不必多说了。口语化的省略句。

23. such a variety of game: 这么多的野兽；game 为作为打猎对象的野兽，这里指乔叟诗中众多的人物。

24. distracted in my choice: 不知选择哪个才好；有学者以为 choice 系 chace（即 chase，追捕）之误植，如此则与上文 game 一致，意为可猎之兽甚多，不知追赶哪个才好。

III. ALEXANDER'S FEAST; OR, THE POWER OF MUSIC

戴镏龄　选注

'Twas at the royal feast for Persia won
        By Philip's warlike son:[1]
    Aloft in awful state
    The godlike hero sate[2]
        On his imperial throne;
    His valiant peers[3] were placed around;
Their brows with roses and with myrtles bound:[4]
    (So should desert in arms be crowned.[5])
The lovely Thais,[6] by his side,
Sate like a blooming Eastern bride,
In flower of youth and beauty's pride.
    Happy, happy, happy pair!
        None but the brave,
        None but the brave,
None but the brave deserves the fair.[7]

Chorus.

Happy, happy, happy pair!
None but the brave,
None but the brave,
None but the brave deserves the fair.

Timotheus,[8] placed on high
Amid the tuneful quire,[9]
With flying fingers touched the lyre:
The trembling notes ascend the sky,
And heavenly joys inspire.
The song began from Jove,[10]
Who left his blissful seats above,
(Such is the power of mighty love.)
A dragon's fiery form belied[11] the god:
Sublime on radiant spires he rode,[12]
When he to fair Olympia[13] pressed;
And while he sought her snowy breast,
Then round her slender waist he curled,
And stamped an image of himself,[14] a sovereign of the world.
The listening crowd admire the lofty sound,
A present deity,[15] they shout around;
A present deity, the vaulted roofs rebound:[16]
With ravished ears
The monarch hears,
Assumes the god,
Affects to nod,
And seems to shake the spheres.[17]

Chorus.

With ravished ears
The monarch hears,
Assumes the god,
Affects to nod,

And seems to shake the spheres.
The praise of Bacchus[18] then the sweet musician sung,[19]
Of Bacchus ever fair, and ever young.
The jolly god[20] in triumph comes;
Sound the trumpets, beat the drums;
Flushed with a purple grace
He shows his honest face:[21]
Now give the hautboys[22] breath; he comes, he comes.
Bacchus, ever fair and young,
Drinking joys did first ordain;[23]
Bacchus' blessings are a treasure,
Drinking is the soldier's pleasure;
Rich the treasure,
Sweet the pleasure,
Sweet is pleasure after pain.

Chorus.

Bacchus' blessings are a treasure,
Drinking is the soldier's pleasure;
Rich the treasure,
Sweet the pleasure,
Sweet is pleasure after pain.

Soothed with the sound the king grew vain;[24]
Fought all his battles o'er again;
And thrice he routed all his foes, and thrice he slew the slain.
The master[25] saw the madness rise,
His[26] glowing cheeks, his[26] ardent eyes;[27]
And while he heaven and earth defied,
Changed his hand,[28] and checked his pride.[29]
He chose a mournful Muse,[30]
Soft pity to infuse;
He sung Darius[31] great and good,

By too severe a fate,
Fallen, fallen, fallen, fallen,
Fallen from his high estate,
And weltering in his blood;[32]
Deserted at his utmost need
By those his former bounty fed;[33]
On the bare earth exposed he lies,[34]
With not a friend to close his eyes.
With downcast looks the joyless victor[35] sate,
Revolving in his altered soul[36]
The various turns of chance below:
And, now and then, a sigh he stole,[37]
And tears began to flow.

Chorus.

Revolving in his altered soul
The various turns of chance below;[38]
And, now and then, a sigh he stole,
And tears began to flow.

The mighty master[39] smile to see
That love was in the next degree;[40]
'Twas but a kindred-sound to move,[41]
For pity melts the mind to love.[42]
Softly sweet, in Lydian measures,[43]
Soon he soothed his soul to pleasures.
War, he sung,[44] is toil and trouble;
Honour but an empty bubble;
Never ending, still[45] beginning,
Fighting still, and still destroying;
If the world be worth thy winning,[46]
Think, O think it worth enjoying:
Lovely Thais sits beside thee,

Take the good[47] the gods provide thee.
The many[48] rend the skies with loud applause;
So Love was crowned, but Music won the cause.
The prince, unable to conceal his pain,
Gazed on the fair[49]
Who caused his care,
And sighed and looked, sighed and looked,
Sighed and looked, and sighed again;
At length, with love and wine at once oppressed,[50]
The vanquished victor[51] sunk upon her breast.

Chorus.

The prince, unable to conceal his pain,
Gazed on the fair
Who caused his care,
And sighed and looked, sighed and looked,
Sighed and looked, and sighed again;
At length, with love and wine at once oppressed,
The vanquished victor sunk upon her breast.

Now strike the golden lyre again;[52]
A louder yet, and yet a louder strain.[53]
Break his bands of sleep[54] asunder,
And rouse him, like a rattling peal of thunder
Hark, hark, the horrid[55] sound
Has raised up his head;
As[56] awaked from the dead,
And, amazed,[57] he stares around.
'Revenge, revenge!' Timotheus cries;
'See the Furies[58] arise;
See the snakes that they rear,[59]
How they hiss in their hair,[60]
And the sparkles that flash from their eyes!
Behold a ghastly band,

Each a torch[61] in his hand!
Those are Grecian ghosts, that in battle were slain,
And unburied remain
Inglorious on the plain:[62]
Give the vengeance due
To the valiant crew.
Behold how they toss their torches on high,
How they point to the Persian abodes,
And glittering temples of their hostile gods,'[63]
The princes applaud with a furious joy;
And the king seized a flambeau[64] with zeal to destroy;
Thais led the way,
To light him to his prey,
And, like another Helen,[65] fired another Troy.

Chorus.

And the king seized a flambeau with zeal to destroy;
Thais led the way,
To light him to his prey,
And, like another Helen, fired another Troy.

Thus long ago,
Ere heaving bellows learned to blow,[66]
While organs yet were mute,[67]
Timotheus, to[68] his breathing flute
And sounding lyre,
Could swell the soul to rage, or kindle soft desire.
At last divine Cecilia[69] came,
Inventress of the vocal frame;[70]
The sweet enthusiast,[71] from her sacred store,
Enlarged the former narrow bounds,[72]
And added length to solemn sounds,
With Nature's mother-wit, and arts unknown before.
Let old Timotheus yield the prize,

Or both[73] divide the crown:
He raised a mortal to the skies;[74]
She drew an angel down.[75]

Grand Chorus.

At last divine Cecilia came,
Inventress of the vocal frame;
The sweet enthusiast, from her sacred store,
Enlarged the former narrow bounds,
And added length to solemn sounds,
With Nature's mother-wit, and arts unknown before.
Let old Timotheus yield the prize,
Or both divide the crown:
He raised a mortal to the skies;
She drew an angel down.

IV. ABSALOM AND ACHITOPHEL

[ACHITOPHEL]

Of these the false Achitophel was first,[1]
A name to all succeeding ages curst:[2]
For close[3] designs and crooked counsels fit,[4]
Sagacious, bold, and turbulent of wit,[5]
Restless, unfixed in principles and place,
In power unpleased, impatient of disgrace;
A fiery soul which, working out its way,
Fretted the pigmy body to decay
And o'er-informed the tenement of clay.[6]
A daring pilot[7] in extremity,
Pleased with the danger, when the waves went high,
He sought the storms; but, for a calm unfit,
Would steer too nigh the sands to boast his wit.
Great wits are sure to madness near allied,
And thin partitions do their bounds divide[8];

Else, why should he, with wealth and honour blest,
Refuse his age the needful hours of rest?
Punish a body which he could not please,
Bankrupt of life, yet prodigal of ease[9]?
And all to leave what with his toil he won
To[10] that unfeathered two-legged thing,[11] a son.

—from *Absalom and Achitophel,* 1681

【题解与注释】

III. ALEXANDER'S FEAST; OR, THE POWER OF MUSIC

《亚历山大的宴会》;或,《音乐的力量》。原诗尚有一副题,《一六九七年庆祝圣塞西利阿节日的歌》(*A song in honour of St. Cecilia's Day,* 1697)。

塞西利阿是公元二三〇年殉道的罗马女基督徒,被教会追封为圣徒,故通称圣塞西利阿(St. Cecilia)。英国十七世纪盛行纪念她的节日,十年前即一六八七年德莱顿已为此写过一首歌。圣塞西利阿相传为管风琴的发明者,故在西欧又被奉为音乐赞护神。上述德莱顿的两首歌都是以音乐为主题,本首的副题即是《音乐的力量》,描绘在亚历山大的宴会上一个杰出乐师演奏所产生的奇异的效果。

亚历山大(Alexander the Great,前356—323),马其顿(Macedon 古代希腊东北部国家)国王,后统治全希腊,率兵征服邻近的亚非各个国家。亚历山大具有雄才大略,为著名的君主,然而如这首诗所说,在宴会上不断为一个乐师的演奏所迷惑住了,作者通过这样的描绘的手法,烘托出音乐的感染力,杂以奇闻轶事,绘声绘色,颇为成功。亚历山大尽管了不起,现在却逃不了音乐力量的支配,音乐力量感人之深,可想而知,这正是作者所要说明的。

作者在本诗中用的是歌颂(Ode)这类的体裁,但行句的长短,韵律的格式,较为自由,不受定型限制,这样,可以更好地写情抒怀。至于诗中每节后的合唱迭句(chorus)以及末节的大合唱(grand chorus),则是为了增加作品的音乐性,要知道原诗是在纪念场合供歌唱用,还有乐器伴奏,不是供阅读的。

德莱顿是英国古典主义传统的杰出的代表,他的诗歌除其本身的价值外,还开了一代的风气,所以从历史观点看,也是值得研究者重视的。

1. 'Twas at the royal feast for Persia won By Philip's warlike son: 大意:在亚历山大庆祝波斯被击败的王家宴会上。Philip's warlike son,腓力普的尚武的储君,即亚历山大(腓力普是亚历山大的父亲)。'Twas = It was. 从此处起第一节为全诗的序幕。

2. sate: sit 过去式 sat 的旧体,此处用以与第三行的 state 协韵。

3. peers: 贵族们(= nobles)。

4. Their brows with roses and myrtles bound: 正常结构可作 Their brows being bound with roses and myrtles，他们前额扎有玫瑰花和桃金娘枝。（古代希腊人在宴会上头部作这样的打扮，玫瑰花和桃金娘枝是爱情的象征。）

5. So should desert in arm be crowned: 给战功应该赏以这样的花冠。这是承上行说，用玫瑰花和桃金娘枝扎在额上。desert in arms，作战有功。

6. Thais [ˈθeiis]**:** 古代雅典名伎，得到亚历山大的宠幸，曾随他出征亚洲有关国家。

7. None but the brave deserves the fair: 唯勇士应得美人。在现代英语中，none 接动词复数，即 deserve。这是流传下来的作者的名句之一，本句中仍沿用 deserves.

8. Timotheus: 从此处起第二节引出一个乐师用演奏歌颂亚历山大的半天神化身，听众高呼，国王心领神会，诗人于此介绍音乐魅力的第一步。这个乐师 Timotheus [tiˈmouθjəs/-θĭəs] 是亚历山大同时代的有名演奏者，另有一个同名的诗人及乐器改良家，其时代更早，为公元前 446—357，不可与此相混，见 Smith 的《古典词典》。

9. quire: = choir. tuneful quire，乐队，用 tuneful 有音调优美的联想，不是泛指乐队。

10. began from Jove: 把佐父作为着手演奏的主题。佐父（Jove），古代罗马人用以称天廷的主神，即管理众神的神，相传为亚历山大的父亲，与腓力普私通而生亚历山大。关于帝王出身不凡，历来有许多迷信传说，此处诗人巧妙地用它来敷演成文，联系到音乐上，说佐父在天廷闻乐声而大动情思，化成一条龙，离开自己的宝座下临凡界，使亚历山大的母亲怀了孕。把佐父作为入手的主题，其实是歌颂亚历山大的天神家世：他出自龙种。

11. belied: 乔装，伪装，指天神的真面目隐蔽起来了。A dragon's fiery form belied the god，一条龙闪耀似火的身子把这位天神乔装起来了，即这位天神乔装成一条闪闪的龙。

12. sublime on radiant spires he rode: 指龙在空中游行，头部高耸，身体旋绕发光，好象佐父骑龙降临，其实龙和佐父是一体。sublime 高高在空中（指龙头）；radiant spires 发光的旋绕体（指龙身）；he，指佐父。

13. Olympia: 亚历山大的生母，这是德莱顿此处的拼法，应为 Olympias.

14. stamped an image of himself:（在她身上）打印下自己的形象，即使她怀孕。

15. A present deity: 当今的神呀！（在场臣众受到乐声的鼓舞，就高呼面前的国王是神。）

16. rebound: 把回声传回，把发出的共鸣声传回。

17. shake the spheres: 摇动天空。亚历山大点头（上文 Affects to nod）而天为之动摇，俨然如古代传说中的主神了。

18. The praise of Bacchus: 对酒神（Bacchus）的歌颂。此节借歌颂酒神以描绘宴席上的纵饮狂欢。

19. sung: sing 的过去式，今通作 sang，同 44。

20. The jolly god: 宴乐的神，即酒神。jolly = festive，宴乐的。

21. honest face: 漂亮的面孔。

22. hautboys: = oboes，（复数）一种双簧管，欧巴。give the hautboys breath 吹起双簧管。

23. Drinking joys did first ordain: 最初规定下饮酒的欢乐，对饮酒作乐是首先发出命令的。

24. Soothed with the sound, the King grew vain: 国王（亚历山大）从乐声感到快慰后，自己觉得了不起。此节下面叙述亚历山大因此又燃起战争的热狂，不可一世，乐师于是转入悲调，描述大流士这个巍巍的人物怎样一败不振，众叛亲离，捐命沙场，使亚历山大听了为之叹气流泪。

25. The master: 乐师（Timotheus）.

26. His ... his: 此处两 his 均指 Alexander's.

27. ardent eyes: 燃烧着（战火）的目光。

28. changed his hand:（Timotheus）变动他的手法（即弹起另一个调子）。

29. checked his pride: 抑制他的（=国王的）自豪感。

30. He chose a mournful Muse: 他选用了一段悲哀的乐曲（承上文 changed his hand 说）。Muse，掌管音乐的女神，此处借用为音乐。

31. Darius: 波斯国王大流士第三，是亚历山大的对手并被他击败。

32. weltering in his blood: 在自己血潭中打滚（指大流士为其部下暗杀）。

33. Deserted at his utmost need/ By those his former bounty fed: 在他束手待毙的时刻，被他曾给以恩赐的人所遗弃。at his utmost need，直译是，当他最危急的时刻。

34. On the bare earth exposed he lies: 大流士曝尸原野上。

35. the joyless victor: 丧失了欢乐的胜利者（亚历山大听到大流士的下场后，感到沮丧了）。

36. Revolving in his altered soul: 在他的起了变化的灵魂深处考虑着。

37. a sigh he stole: 他私下里叹气；他低声叹了一口气。

38. The various turns of chances below: 人世上种种运数的转变无常。below= on earth，地上，人世。这一行是上行 revolving 的宾语。

39. The mighty master: 这位大师（指 Timotheus）。

40. love was in the next degree: 接着就是爱情了（转下去就是以爱情为主题的调子）。

41. 'Twas but a kindred-sound to move: 那只是奏一个相似的调子。'Twas，见注一。move，挥弦，弹弦。

42. pity melts the mind to love: 悲悯使心情化为怜爱。但这儿亚历山大从悲生哀，不是施于同一个对象，他因敌人的凄惨失败而发出对人世无常的一般的悲叹，后来却醉倒在和 Thais 的爱情中。

43. Lydian measures: 柔情绵绵的调子。

44. sung: 见注 19。

45. still: 不断地。

46. worth thy winning: 值得你去赢得或获取。

47. good: 利益，好处。

48. many: 随从，扈从。（殆即 meiny 的变体，见 Chambers 世纪英语词典 meinie 条。）

49. The fair: 美人（指 Thais）.

50. with love and wine at once oppressed: 既沉溺于爱，又沉溺于酒。at once，同时。全语修饰下行的 victor.

51. The vanquished victor: 被征服了的胜利者。（指亚历山大，他战胜波斯，却成了 Thais 的俘虏）。

52. again: 指换一个调子，另弹一个调子。此节引出希腊神话中的复仇女神，燃起为死于战事而陈尸原野的希腊士兵复仇的情绪。这儿诗人的说法是：亚历山大在 Thais 的怂恿下，纵火焚烧了波斯人的都城。

53. strain: 乐曲，曲调。

54. bands of sleep: 睡箍。（睡魔象箍一样将人缠住。）

55. horrid: 粗糙刺耳的。

56. as: = as if，仿佛。

57. amazed: 迷惑住。

58. Furies: 希腊神话中司复仇的三个女神，头上的头是缠绕着的蛇，两眼滴血，十分可怖。

59. the snakes that they rear: 复仇女神使之立起的蛇。they = the Furies.

60. How they hiss in their hair: 这些蛇（they）怎样地在她们的（女神们的，their）头发里发出嘶嘶声。

61. Each a torch ... = each with a torch。

62. unburied remain / Inglorious on the plain: 未被埋葬，在原野上蒙受耻辱。古代人认为死尸应该入土，露尸郊原被看成是对死者极不光彩的。参考注 52.

63. their hostile gods: 波斯人的（their）对希腊人怀有敌意的神。

64. flambeau: 火炬。

65. Helen（Troy）: 海伦，古希腊美人，由于被拐诱而引起特洛依城受希腊军队围攻，最后被毁。此处作者认为 Thais 在焚毁波斯都城上所起的作用简直是另一个海伦（another Helen）.

66. Ere heaving be blows learned to blow: 在鼓气风箱试吹奏出乐声之前。（鼓风器古代长期以来只用以吹旺炉火，至于用来振动簧片发音，制造风琴，乃是后来的事。）

67. While organs yet were mute: 风琴还不曾响起来。（即风琴还未作成，承上一行说。）

68. to: 按照，随着，与……相一致。

69. Cecilia: 见注文前绪言。

70. vocal frame: 歌唱的框架，即风琴，相传 Cecilia 发明。Inventress，（女）发明家。

71. The sweet enthusiast: 温柔的热心信徒（指 Cecilia）。

72. Enlarged the former narrow bounds,/And added length to solemn sounds: 此两行指：Cecilia 借助了发明的风琴，使器乐的乐音得到扩大并增加了延续性。

73. both: 指 Timotheus 及 Cecilia 二人。

74. raised a mortal to the skies: 把一个凡人捧抬到天上。Timotheus 曾演奏 Jove，描绘亚历山大的天神家世，使臣民高呼他是当今的神（见注 16）。

75. She drew an angel down: 指根据传说 Cecilia 曾对人说，天使（angel）每夜降临来看她。

【题解与注释】

IV. [ACHITOPHEL]

这一段选自德莱顿的讽刺长诗 *Absalom and Achitophel*，今译作《亚布萨伦与阿琦图菲尔》。中文本《圣经》把 Absalom 译作“押沙龙”，Achitophel 则据另一拼法 Ahitophel 译作“亚希多弗”。据《圣经》、《旧约》、《撒母耳记下》(*2 Samuel*)，亚布萨伦对以色列国王，即他的父亲大卫，实行叛变。阿琦图菲尔本是大卫的谋臣，却倒向亚布萨伦，合谋进攻大卫。

这儿选的是作者讽刺阿琦图菲尔的片段。

德莱顿用亚布萨伦影射英国国王查理二世的私生子蒙茂斯公爵（Duke of Monmouth），用阿琦图菲尔影射沙夫兹勃里伯爵（Earl of Shaftsbury）. 沙夫兹勃里所代表的政治集团要拥立蒙茂斯以继承查理二世。这一切和上述的《圣经》故事很相象，查理二世就是大卫。在这场王位继承之争中，作者处于和沙夫兹勃里敌对阵营中，因而丑化他为阿琦图菲尔。

德莱顿在诗中使用的是同韵对句，得心应手，平易自如，充分挖掘了这种诗体作为讽刺手段的妙用。他的措词雄浑有力，泼辣生动，很能说明他是一个语言的巧匠和讽刺的大师，开通了以后几十年中英国文坛的新风气，并且在这个领域中始终保持了他的卓越地位。

1. Of these the false Achitophel was first: 其中无信义的阿琦图菲尔居首。此承上文有若干煽动反对英国政府的集团说。

2. A name to all succeeding ages curst: 受到千代万世咒骂的名字。《圣经》中记载的 Achitophel 臭名昭著。

3. close: 秘密的，隐蔽的。参下条注。

4. fit: 下接本行的第一个词 for，即 fit for，宜于，长于。For close designs and crooked counsels fit，长于搞阴谋诡计。

5. turbulent of wit: 头脑狂妄。

6. A fiery ... clay: 全诗用同韵对句，偶尔变格，如此处三行一韵。大意：这副浮躁的灵魂，多方为自己经营，使这矮个受尽烦恼的磨折，并拼命地向泥躯壳打气。《圣经》、《创世纪》第二章，“神用地上的尘土造人”故作者用 tenement of clay（泥房子）指人的躯壳。这个政客矮小身体支持不住富于心计的灵魂的驱使；over-informed，过分地激励或打气。（给以过多的生气，过多地激励）。o'er-informed = over-informed.

7. A daring pilot: 指这个政客肆无忌惮，总想冒惊涛骇浪的险，以求一逞。

8. Great ... divide: 天才确是接近疯狂，两者分界只隔一张薄墙。这儿天才用于贬义，因为丧失了理性，德莱顿时代是理性地位逐渐上升的时代。

9. Bankrupt of life, yet prodigal of ease: 生命衰竭，却丝毫不顾安息。

10. leave what with his toil he won to ...: 把他自己辛辛苦苦后捞到的东西留给……

11. unfeathered two-legged thing: 把人看成无翼的两足物，古希腊时代已有这样的说法。

13 DANIEL DEFOE
1659 – 1731

THE LIFE AND STRANGE ADVENTURES OF ROBINSON CRUSOE

selections

夏祖煃　选注

When I waked it was broad day, the weather clear, and the storm abated,[1] so that the sea did not rage and swell as before. But that which surprised me most was, that the ship was lifted off in the night from the sand where she lay,[2] by the swelling of the tide, and was driven up almost as far as the rock which I first mentioned, where I had been so bruised by the dashing me against it[3]. This being within about a mile from the shore where I was, and the ship seeming to stand upright still,[4] I wished myself on board, that, at least, I might have some necessary things for my use.

When I came down from my apartment in the tree[5] I looked about me again, and the first thing I found was the boat,[6] which lay as the wind and the sea had tossed her upon the land, about two miles on my right hand. I walked as far as I could upon the shore to have got to her, but found a neck or inlet of water between me and the boat, which was about half a mile broad; so I came back for the present, being more intent upon getting at the ship, where I hoped to find something for my present subsistence.

A little after noon I found the sea very calm, and the tide ebbed so far out, that I could come within a quarter of a mile of the ship; and here I found a fresh renewing of my grief, for I saw evidently, that if we had kept on board we had been all safe,[7] that is to say, we had all got safe on shore, and I had not been so miserable as to be left entirely destitute of all comfort and company, as I now was. This forced tears from my eyes again; but as there was little relief in that, I resolved, if possible, to get to the ship; so I pulled off my clothes, for the weather was hot to extremity, and took the water.[8] But when I came to the ship, my difficulty was still greater to know how to get on board; for as she lay aground, and high out of the water, there was nothing within my reach to lay hold of. I swam round her twice, and the second time I spied a small piece of a rope, which I wondered I did not see at first, hang down by the fore-chains[9] so low, as that with great difficulty I got hold of it, and by the help of that rope got up into the forecastle of the ship. Here I found that the ship was bulged,[10] and had a great deal of water in her hold, but that she lay so on the side of a bank of hard sand, or rather earth, that her stern lay lifted up upon the bank, and her head low almost to the water. By this means all her quarter was free,[11] and all that was in that part was dry; for you may be sure my first work was to search and to see what was spoiled and what was free.[12] And first I found that all the ship's provisions were dry and untouched by the water; and being very well disposed to eat, I went to the bread-room and filled my pockets with biscuit, and eat it as I went about other things,[13] for I had no time to lose. I also found some rum in the great cabin, of which I took a large dram, and which I had indeed need enough of to spirit me for what was before me.[14] Now I wanted nothing but a boat, to furnish myself with many things which I foresaw would be very necessary to me.

It was in vain to sit still and wish for what was not to be had, and this extremity roused my application.[15] We had several spare yards, and two or three large spars of wood, and a spare top-mast or two[16] in the ship. I resolved to fall to work with these, and flung as many of them overboard as I could manage for their weight, tying every one with a rope, that they might not drive away.[17] When this was done I went down the ship's side, and, pulling them to me, I tied four of them fast together at both ends as well as I could, in the form of a raft; and laying two or three short pieces of plank upon them crossways,[18] I found I could walk upon it very well, but that it was not able to bear any great weight, the pieces being too light. So I went to work, and with the carpenter's saw I cut a spare topmast into three lengths, and added them to my raft, with a great deal of labour and pains; but hope of furnishing myself with necessaries encouraged me to go beyond what I should have been able to have done upon another occasion.[19]

My raft was now strong enough to bear any reasonable weight. My next care was what to load it with, and how to preserve what I laid upon it from the surf of the sea; but I was not long considering this.[20] I first laid all the planks or boards upon it that I could get, and having considered well what I most wanted, I first got three of the seamen's chests, which I had broken open and emptied, and lowered them down upon my raft. The first of these I filled with provisions, viz., bread, rice, three Dutch cheeses, five pieces of dried goat's flesh, which we lived much upon,[21] and a little remainder of European corn, which had been laid by for some fowls which we brought to sea with us, but the fowls were killed. There had been some barley and wheat together, but, to my great disappointment, I found afterwards that the rats had eaten or spoiled it all. As for liquors, I found several cases of bottles belonging to our skipper, in which were some cordial waters,[22] and, in all, about five or six gallons of rack[23]. These I stowed by themselves, there being no need to put them into the chest, nor no room for them.[24] While I was doing this, I found the tide began to flow,[25] though very calm, and I had the mortification to see my coat, shirt, and waistcoat, which I had left on shore upon the sand, swim away; as for my breeches, which were only linen, and open-kneed,[26] I swam on board in them, and my stockings. However, this put me upon rummaging for clothes, of which I found enough,[27] but took no more than I wanted for present use; for I had other things which my eye was more upon, as first tools to work with on shore; and it was after long searching that I found out the carpenter's chest, which was indeed a very useful prize to me, and much more valuable than a ship-loading of gold would have been at that time. I got it down to my raft, even whole as it was, without losing time to look into it, for I knew in general what it contained.

My next care was for some ammunition and arms; there were two very good fowling-pieces in the great cabin, and two pistols; these I secured first, with some powder-horns,[28] and a small bag of shot, and two old rusty swords. I knew there were three barrels of powder in the ship, but knew not where our gunner had stowed them; but with much search I found them, two of them dry and good, the third had taken water; those two I got to my raft with the arms. And now I thought myself pretty well freighted,[29] and began to think how I should get to shore with them, having neither sail, oar, or rudder;[30] and the least capful of wind would have overset all my navigation.[31]

I had three encouragements. 1. A smooth, calm sea. 2. The tide rising and setting in to the shore. 3. What little wind there was blew me towards the land.[32] And thus, having found two or three broken oars belonging to the boat,[33] and besides the tools which were in the chest, I found two saws, an axe, and a hammer, and with this cargo I put to sea. For a mile or thereabouts my raft went very well, only that I found it drive a little distant from the place where I had landed before,[34] by which I perceived that there was some indraft[35] of the water, and consequently I hoped to find some creek or river there, which I might make use of as a port to get to land with my cargo.

As I imagined, so it was; there appeared before me a little opening of the land, and I found a strong current of the tide set into it,[36] so I guided my raft as well as I could to keep in the middle of the stream. But here I had like to have suffered a second shipwreck,[37] which, if I had, I think verily would have broke my heart;[38] for knowing nothing of the coast, my raft ran aground at one end of it upon a shoal, and not being aground at the other end, it wanted but a little that all my cargo had slipped off[39] towards that end that was afloat, and so fallen into the water. I did my utmost by setting my back against the chests to keep them in their places, but could not thrust off the raft with all my strength, neither durst I stir from the posture I was in, but holding up the chests with all my might, stood in that manner near half-an-hour, in which time the rising of the water brought me a little more upon a level;[40] and a little after, the water still rising, my raft floated again, and I thrust her off with the oar I had into the channel, and then driving up higher, I at length found myself in the mouth of a little river, with land on both sides, and a strong current or tide running up. I looked on both sides for a proper place to get to shore, for I was not willing to be driven too high up the river, hoping in time to see some ship at sea, and therefore resolved to place myself as near the coast as I could.

At length I spied a little cove on the right shore of the creek, to which, with great pain and difficulty, I guided my raft, and at last got so near, as that, reaching ground with my oar, I could thrust her directly in; but here I had like to have dipped all my cargo in the sea again; for that shore lying pretty steep, that is to say, sloping, there was no place to land but where one end of my float, if it run on shore, would lie so high and the other sink lower, as before, that it would endanger my cargo again.[41] All that I could do was to wait till the tide was at the highest, keeping the raft with my oar like an anchor to hold the side of it fast to the shore, near a flat piece of ground, which I expected the water would flow over; and so it did. As soon as I found water enough, for my raft drew about a foot of water, I thrust her on upon that flat piece of ground, and there fastened or moored her by sticking my two broken oars into the ground; one on one side near one end, and one on the other side near the other end; and thus I lay till the water ebbed away, and left my raft and all my cargo safe on shore.

My next work was to view the country and seek a proper place for my habitation, and where to stow my goods to secure them from whatever might happen. Where I was, I yet knew not[42]; whether on the continent, or on an island; whether inhabited, or not inhabited; whether in danger of wild beasts, or not.[43] There was a hill, not above a mile from me, which rose up very steep and high, and which seemed to overtop some other hills, which lay as in a ridge from it, northward. I took out one of the fowling-pieces and one of the pistols, and a horn of powder; and thus armed, I travelled for discovery up to the top of that hill, where, after I had with great labour and difficulty got to the top, I saw my fate to my great affliction,[44] viz., that I was in an island environed every way with the sea, no land to be seen, except some rocks which lay a great way off, and two small islands less than this, which lay about three leagues to the west.

I found also that the island I was in was barren, and, as I saw good reason to believe, uninhabited, except by wild beasts, of whom, however, I saw none; yet I saw abundance of fowls,[45] but knew not their kinds; neither, when I killed them, could I tell what was fit for food, and what not. At my coming back, I shot at a great bird which I saw sitting upon a tree on the side of a great wood. I believe it was the first gun that had been fired there since the creation of the world. I had no sooner fired, but from all the parts of the wood there arose an innumerable number of fowls of many sorts, making a confused screaming, and crying every one according to his usual note; but not one of them of any kind that I knew. As for the creature I killed, I took it to be a kind of a hawk, its colour and beak resembling it, but had no talons or claws more than common;[46] its flesh was carrion,[47] and fit for nothing.

Contented with this discovery, I came back to my raft, and

fell to work to bring my cargo on shore, which took me up the rest of that day; and what to do with myself at night, I knew not, nor indeed where to rest; for I was afraid to lie down on the ground, not knowing but some wild beast might devour me, though, as I afterwards found, there was really no need for those fears. However, as well as I could, I barricaded myself round with the chests and boards that I had brought on shore, and made a kind of a hut for that night's lodging; as for food, I yet saw not which way to supply myself, except that I had seen two or three creatures like hares run out of the wood where I shot the fowl.

I now began to consider, that I might yet get a great many things out of the ship, which would be useful to me, and particularly some of the rigging and sails, and such other things as might come to land;[48] and I resolved to make another voyage on board the vessel, if possible. And as I knew that the first storm that blew must necessarily break her all in pieces, I resolved to set all other things apart[49] till I got everything out of the ship that I could get. Then I called a council, that is to say, in my thoughts,[50] whether I should take back the raft, but this appeared impracticable; so I resolved to go as before, when the tide was down; and I did so, only that I stripped before I went from my hut, having nothing on but a chequered shirt and a pair of linen drawers, and a pair of pumps on my feet.

I got on board the ship as before, and prepared a second raft, and having had experience of the first, I neither made this so unwieldy, nor loaded it so hard; but yet I brought away several things very useful to me; as, first, in the carpenter's stores I found two or three bags full of nails and spikes, a great screw-jack, a dozen or two of hatchets, and above all, that most useful thing called a grindstone. All these I secured, together with several things belonging to the gunner, particularly two or three iron crows,[51] and two barrels of musket bullets, seven muskets, and another fowling-piece, with some small quantity of powder more; a large bag full of small-shot, and a great roll of sheet lead;[52] but this last was so heavy, I could not hoist it up to get it over the ship's side. Besides these things, I took all the men's clothes that I could find, and a spare fore-top sail,[53] a hammock, and some bedding; and with this I loaded my second raft, and brought them all safe on shore, to my very great comfort.

I was under some apprehensions during my absence from the land, that at least my provisions might be devoured on shore; but when I came back, I found no sign of any visitor, only there sat a creature like a wildcat upon one of the chests, which, when I came towards it, ran away a little distance, and then stood still. She sat very composed and unconcerned, and looked full in my face, as if she had a mind to be acquainted with me. I presented my gun at her;[54] but as she did not understand it, she was perfectly unconcerned at it, nor did she offer to stir away; upon which I tossed her a bit of biscuit, though, by the way, I was not very free of it, for my store was not great.[55] However, I spared her a bit, I say, and she went to it, smelled of it,[56] and ate it, and looked (as pleased)[57] for more; but I thanked her, and could spare no more, so she marched off.

Having got my second cargo on shore, though I was fain to open the barrels of powder and bring them by parcels, for they were too heavy, being large casks, I went to work to make me a little tent with the sail and some poles which I cut for that purpose; and into this tent I brought everything that I knew would spoil either with rain or sun; and I piled all the empty chests and casks up in a circle round the tent, to fortify it from any sudden attempt,[58] either from man or beast.

When I had done this I blocked up the door of the tent with some boards within, and an empty chest set up on end without; and spreading one of the beds upon the ground,[59] laying my two pistols just at my head, and my gun at length by me, I went to bed for the first time, and slept very quietly all night, for I was very weary and heavy; for the night before I bad slept little, and had laboured very hard all day, as well to fetch all those things from the ship, as to get them on shore.[60]

I had the biggest magazine[61] of all kinds now that ever was laid up, I believe, for one man; but I was not satisfied still, for while the ship sat upright in that posture, I thought I ought to get everything out of her that I could. So every day at low water I went on board, and brought away something or other; but, particularly, the third time I went I brought away as much of the rigging as I could, as also all the small ropes and rope-twine I could get, with a piece of spare canvas, which was to mend the sails upon occasion, the barrel of wet gunpowder; in a word, I brought away all the sails first and last, only that I was fain to cut them in pieces, and bring as much at a time as I could; for they were no more useful to be sails, but as mere canvas only.

But that which comforted me more still was, that at last of all, after I had made five or six such voyages as these, and thought I had nothing more to expect from the ship that was worth my meddling with; I say, after all this, I found a great hogshead of bread, and three large runlets of rum or spirits, and a box of sugar, and a barrel of fine flour; this was surprising to me, because I had given over expecting any more provisions, except what was spoilt by the water. I soon emptied the hogshead of that bread, and wrapped it up parcel by parcel in pieces of the sails, which I cut out; and, in a word, I got all this safe on shore also.

The next day I made another voyage. And now, having plundered the ship of what was portable and fit to hand out,[62] I began with the cables; and cutting the great cable into pieces, such as I could move, I got two cables and a hawser on shore, with all the ironwork I could get; and having cut down the sprit-sailyard, and the mizzen-yard, and everything I could to make a large raft, I loaded it with all those heavy goods, and came away. But my good luck began now to leave me; for this raft was so unwieldy, and so overladen, that after I was entered the little cove[63] where I had landed the rest of my goods, not being able to guide it so handily as I did the other, it overset, and threw me and all my cargo into the water. As for myself, it was no great harm, for I was near the shore; but as to my cargo, it was great part of it lost, especially the iron, which I expected would have been of great use to me. However, when the tide was out I got most of the pieces of cable ashore, and some of the iron, though with infinite labour; for I was fain to dip for it[64] into the water, a work which fatigued me very much. After this I went every day on board, and brought away what I could get.

I had been now thirteen days on shore, and had been eleven times on board the ship; in which time I had brought away all that one pair of hands could well be supposed capable to bring,[65] though I believe verily, had the calm weather held,[66] I should have brought away the whole ship piece by piece. But preparing the twelfth time to go on board, I found the wind begin to rise. However, at low water I went on board, and though I thought I had rummaged the cabin so effectually as that nothing more could be found, yet I discovered a locker with drawers in it, in one of which I found two or three razors, and one pair of large scissors, with some ten or a dozen of good knives and forks;[67] in another, I found about thirty-six pounds value in money,[68] some European coin,[69] some Brazil,[70] some pieces of eight,[71] some gold, some silver.

I smiled to myself at the sight of this money. "O drug![72]" said I aloud, "what art thou good for?[73] Thou art not worth to me, no, not the taking off of the ground;[74] one of those knives is worth all this heap. I have no manner of use for thee; even remain where thou art, and go to the bottom as a creature whose life is not worth saving." However, upon second thoughts,[75] I took it away; and wrapping all this in a piece of canvas, I began to think of making another raft; but while I was preparing this, I found the sky overcast, and the wind began to rise, and in a quarter of an hour it blew a fresh gale from the shore.[76] It presently occurred to me that it was in vain to pretend to make a raft with the wind off shore, and that it was my business to be gone before the tide of flood began, otherwise I might not be able to reach the shore at all. Accordingly I let myself down into the water, and swam across the channel, which lay between the ship and the sands, and even that with difficulty enough, partly with the weight of the things I had about me, and partly the roughness of the water; for the wind rose very hastily, and before it was quite high water it blew a storm.

But I was gotten home to my little tent, where I lay with all my wealth about me very secure. It blew very hard all that night, and in the morning, when I looked out, behold,[77] no more ship was to be seen. I was a little surprised, but recovered myself with this satisfactory reflection, viz., that I had lost no time, nor abated no diligence,[78] to get everything out of her that could be useful to me, and that indeed there was little left in her that I was able to bring away if I had had more time.

I now gave over any more thoughts of the ship, or of anything out of her,[79] except what might drive on shore from her wreck, as indeed divers pieces of her afterwards did; but those things were of small use to me.

* * *

I have already described my habitation, which was a tent under the side of a rock, surrounded with a strong pale of posts and cables; but I might now rather call it a wall, for I raised a kind of wall up against it of turfs,[80] about two feet thick on the outside, and after some time—I think it was a year and a half—I raised rafters from it leaning to the rock, and thatched or covered it with boughs of trees and such things as I could get to keep out the rain, which I found at some times of the year very violent.

I have already observed how I brought all my goods into this pale, and into the cave which I had made behind me. But I must observe, too, that at first this was a confused heap of goods, which as they lay in no order, so they took up all my place;[81] I had no room to turn myself. So I set myself to enlarge my cave and works farther into the earth; for it was a loose sandy rock, which yielded easily to the labour I bestowed on it. And so, when I found I was pretty safe as to beasts of prey, I worked sideways to the right hand into the rock; and then, turning to the right again, worked quite out, and made me a door to come out on the outside of my pale or fortification. This gave me not only egress and regress,[82] as it were a backway to my tent and to my storehouse, but gave me room to stow my goods.

And now I began to apply myself to make such necessary things as I found I most wanted, as particularly a chair and a table; for without these I was not able to enjoy the few comforts I had in the world. I could not write or eat, or do several things with so much pleasure without a table.

So I went to work; and here I must needs observe,[83] that as reason is the substance and original of the mathematics, so by stating and squaring everything by reason, and by making the most rational judgment of things, every man may be in time master of every mechanic art.[84] I had never handled a tool in my life; and yet in time, by labour, application, and contrivance, I found at last that I wanted nothing but I could have made it, especially if I had had tools. However, I made abundance of things even without tools, and some with no more tools than an adze and a hatchet, which, perhaps, were never made that way before,[85] and that with infinite labour. For example, if I wanted a board, I had no other way but to cut down a tree, set it on an edge before me, and hew it flat on either side with my axe, till I had brought it to be thin as a plank, and then dub it smooth with my adze. It is true, by this method I could make but one board out of a whole tree; but this I had no remedy for but patience,[86] any more than I had for the prodigious deal of time and labour which it took me up to make a plank or board.[87] But my time or labour was little worth, and so it was as well employed one way as another.

However, I made me a table and a chair, as I observed above, in the first place, and this I did out of the short pieces of boards that I brought on my raft from the ship. But when I had wrought out some boards, as above, I made large shelves of the breadth of a foot and a half one over another, all along one side of my cave, to lay all my tools, nails, and iron-work; and, in a word, to separate everything at large in their places,[88] that I might come easily at them.[89] I knocked pieces into the wall of the rock[90] to hang my guns and all things that would hang up;[91] so that had my cave been to be seen,[92] it looked like[92] a general magazine of all necessary things; and I had everything so ready at my hand, that it was a great pleasure to me to see all my goods in such order, and especially to find my stock of all necessaries so great.

* * *

This at length put me upon thinking[93] whether it was not possible to make myself a canoe, or *periagua*,[94] such as the natives of those climates make, even without tools, or, as I might say, without hands,[95] viz., of the trunk of a great tree.[96] This I not only thought possible, but easy, and pleased myself extremely with the thoughts of making it, and with my having much more convenience for it than any of the negroes or Indians; but not at all considering the particular inconveniences which I lay under more than the Indians did, viz., want of hands to move it, when it was made, into the water, a difficulty much harder for me to surmount than all the consequences of want of tools could be to them. For what was it to me, that when I had chosen a vast tree in the woods, I might with much trouble cut it down, if, after I might be able with my tools to hew and dub the outside into the proper shape of a boat, and burn or cut out the inside to make it hollow, so to make a boat of it; if,[98] after all this, I must leave it just there where I found it, and was not able to launch it into the water?

One would have thought I could not have had the least reflection upon my mind of my circumstance while I was making this boat, but I should have immediately thought how I should get it into the sea;[99] but my thoughts were so intent upon my voyage over the sea in it, that I never once considered how I should get it off of the land; and it was really, in its own nature, more easy for me to guide it over forty-five miles of sea, than about forty-five fathoms of land, where it lay,[100] to set it afloat in the water.

I went to work upon this boat the most like a fool that ever man did who had any of his senses awake.[101] I pleased myself with the design, without determining whether I was ever able to undertake it. Not but that the difficulty of launching my boat came often into my head,[102] but I put a stop to my own inquiries into it, by this foolish answer which I gave myself, "Let's first make it; I'll warrant I'll find some way or other to get it along when it is done."

This was a most preposterous method; but the eagerness of my fancy prevailed, and to work I went. I felled a cedar tree: I question much whether Solomon[103] ever had such a one for the building of the Temple at Jerusalem.[104] It was five feet ten inches diameter at the lower part next the stump,[105] and four feet eleven inches diameter at the end of twenty-two feet,[106] after which it lessened for awhile, and then panted into branches. It was not without infinite labour that I felled this tree. I was twenty days hacking and hewing at it at the bottom; I was fourteen more getting the branches and limbs, and the vast spreading head of it cut off, which I hacked and hewed through with axe and hatchet, and inexpressible labour.[107] After this, it cost me a month to shape it and dub it to a proportion,[108] and to something like the bottom of a boat, that it might swim upright as it ought to do. It cost me near three months more to clear the inside, and work it so as to make an exact boat of it.[109] This I did, indeed, without fire, by mere mallet and chisel, and by the dint of[110] hard labour, till I had brought it to be a very handsome *periagua*, and big enough to have carried six and twenty men, and consequently big enough to have carried me and all my cargo.

When I had gone through this work, I was extremely delighted with it. The boat was really much bigger than I ever saw a canoe or *periagua*, that was made of one tree, in my life. Many a weary stroke it had cost, you may be sure; and there remained nothing but to get it into the water; and had I gotten it into the water, I make no question but I should have begun the maddest voyage, and the most unlikely to be performed, that ever was undertaken.

But all my devices to get it into the water failed me, though they cost me infinite labour too. It lay about one hundred yards from the water, and not more; but the first inconvenience was, it was uphill towards the creek. Well, to take away this discouragement, I resolved to dig into the surface of the earth, and so make a declivity. This I began, and it cost me a prodigious deal of pains;[111] but who grudges pains, that have their deliverance in view?[112] But when this was worked through, and this difficulty managed, it was still much at one,[113] for I could no more stir the canoe than I could the other boat.

Then I measured the distance of ground, and resolved to cut a dock or canal, to bring the water up to the canoe, seeing I could not bring the canoe down to the water.[114] Well, I began this work; and when I began to enter into it, and calculate how deep it was to be dug, how broad, how the stuff to be thrown out, I found that by the number of hands I had, being none but my own, it must have been ten or twelve years before I should have gone through with it; for the shore lay high, so that at the upper end it must have been at least twenty feet deep; so at length, though with great reluctancy, I gave this attempt over also.

This grieved me heartily; and now I saw, though too late, the folly of beginning a work before we count the cost, and before we judge rightly of our own strength to go through with it.

* * *

My clothes began to decay, too, mightily. As to linen,[115] I had none a good while, except some chequered shirts[116] which I found in the chests of the other seamen, and which I carefully preserved, because many times I could bear no other clothes on but a shirt; and it was a very great help to me that I had, among all the men's clothes of the ship, almost three dozen of shirts. There were also several thick watch-coats[117] of the seamen's which were left indeed, but they were too hot to wear; and though it is true that the weather was so violent hot[118] that there was no need of clothes, yet I could not go quite naked, no, though I had been inclined to it, which I was not,[119] nor could abide the thoughts of it, though I was all alone.

The reason why I could not go quite naked was, I could not bear the heat of the sun so well when quite naked as with some clothes on; nay, the very heat frequently blistered my skin; whereas, with a shirt on, the air itself made some motion, and whistling under that shirt, was twofold cooler than without it. No more could I ever bring myself to go out in the heat of the sun without a cap or a hat. The heat of the sun beating with such violence, as it does in that place, would give me the headache presently, by darting so directly on my head, without a cap or hat on, so that I could not bear it; whereas, if I put on my hat, it would presently go away.[120]

Upon those views, I began to consider about putting the few rags I had, which I called clothes, into some order. I had worn out all the waistcoats I had, and my business was now to try if I could not make jackets out of the great watch-coats which I had by me, and with such other materials as I had; so I set to work a-tailoring, or rather, indeed, a-botching,[121] for I made most piteous work of it.[122] However, I made shift to make two or three new waistcoats, which I hoped would serve me a great while. As for breeches or drawers, I made but a very sorry shift indeed till afterward.[123]

I have mentioned that I saved the skins of all the creatures that I killed, I mean four-footed ones, and I had hung them up stretched out with sticks in the sun, by which means some of them were so dry and hard that they were fit for little, but others it seems were very useful. The first thing I made of these was a great cap for my head, with the hair on the outside, to shoot off the rain;[124] and this I performed so well, that after this I made me a suit of clothes wholly of these skins, that is to say, a waistcoat, and breeches open at knees, and both loose, for they were rather wanting to keep me cool than to keep me warm.[125] I must not omit to acknowledge that they were wretchedly made: for if I was a bad carpenter, I was a worse tailor. However, they were such as I made very good shift with;[126] and when I was abroad, if it happened to rain, the hair of my waistcoat and cap being outermost, I was kept very dry.

After this I spent a great deal of time and pains to make me an umbrella. I was indeed in great want of one, and had a great mind to make one. I had seen them made in the Brazils,[127] where they are very useful in the great heats which are there; and I felt the heats every jot as great here,[128] and greater too, being nearer the equinox.[129] Besides, as I was obliged to be much abroad, it was a most useful thing to me, as well for the rains as the heats. I took a world of pains at it, and was a great while before I could make anything likely to hold; nay, after I thought I had hit the way, I spoiled two or three before I made one to my mind; but at last I made one that answered indifferently well.[130] The main difficulty I found was to make it to let down.[131] I could make it to spread; but if it did not let down too, and draw in, it was not portable for me any way but just over my head,[132] which would not do. However, at last, as I said, I made one to answer, and covered it with skins, the hair upwards, so that it cast off the rains like a pent-house, and kept off the sun so effectually, that I could walk out in the hottest of the weather with greater advantage than I could before in the coolest; and when I had no need of it, could close it, and carry it under my arm.

【作者简介】 Daniel Defoe（笛福，1660？—1731）英国政论家、政治活动家、小说家，出生于伦敦的小屠户—蜡烛商家庭，二十多岁时经营内衣业及其它商业，曾到西班牙、意大利、德国及法国等地旅行。一说他曾参加以新教教徒为主体的蒙莫斯公爵的叛乱。他从事的商业都不成功，1692 年宣告破产，1703 年又第二次破产。由于家庭出身和宗教信仰的影响，他趋向于反对斯图亚特王朝和英国国教教会以及罗马教皇的封建统治。镇压蒙莫斯叛乱的英王詹姆士二世被威廉三世所替代之时，他成为威廉的热烈支持者，加入了威廉的军队，并受到威廉的恩赐，于1695年担任政府中的小税官，并开办了一个砖瓦厂。与此同时，他开始进行政治活动，写了大量的小册子，议论时事朝政。在出身荷兰王族的威廉受到某些狭隘的英国人的攻击时，他写了讽刺打油诗《地道的英国人》(*The True-Born Englishman*)，予以反击。他接受了洛克的政治思想，主张民权和宗教自由。1702年他的小册子《对待非国教徒的最简便的办法》，用说反话的笔法，抨击政府对非国教徒的迫害与限制，因而被捕入狱，并枷号示众。他利用这个机会，发表了《枷颂》(*Hymn to the Pillory*)，受到了民众的欢呼，成为他们心目中的英雄。他因入狱而破产，性格也有所改变。此后他一面办《评论报》(*The Review*)等报纸和写政治小册子，一面受雇于历届政府，充当秘密情报员到苏格兰活动，促进英格兰与苏格兰的联合。1713—1714年先后三次因讥刺政府而被捕。1715年又为辉格党的大臣当密探。但他的公开政治生命在1714年乔治一世登基后就结束了。

1719年，在笛福年近六旬时，他的头一本小说《鲁滨逊飘流记》问世，风行一时。他马上出版了它的续集，一年以后又出版了《鲁滨逊·克鲁梭的严肃的思考》一书。其后数年间他又写了许多小说，比较好的有《辛格顿船长》(*Captain Singleton*),《摩尔·弗兰德斯传》(*Moll Flanders*),《洛珊娜传》(*Roxana*)，和《疫年纪日》(*A Journal of the Plague Year*)等，余外的作品中不少是糟粕。后来他为了躲债(一说亦为了精神失常)而逃匿他乡，于1731年死去。

【题解与注释】

笛福虽曾结识在荒岛孤身独居五年之久的有名的水手亚历山大·塞尔刻克(Alexander Selkirk)，并取得了他的文件资料，但他的《鲁滨逊飘流记》远远超出塞尔刻克在荒岛五年生活的范围。在这本小说的三个主要部分中，叙述了一个水手的大半生。第一部分说鲁滨逊从小逃离家庭去航海，历尽艰险，在巴西开办了种植园；第二部分叙述在一次航行中遇险，流落荒岛多年；第三部分谈到他从荒岛遇救回到英国，在从葡萄牙到法国的途中遇到狼群追袭。其中唯有在荒岛赤手空拳建立家园的叙述最能引人入胜。这里节选了鲁滨逊初到荒岛的较长一段，和一些其它有趣的描绘岛上生活的章节。

笛福创造了鲁滨逊这样一个英雄，歌颂了一个平民百姓的子弟，在孤身一人落难于荒岛的情况下，勇敢机智，百折不挠，以自己勤快的双手创建了象样的生活，开辟了他一个人的王国，在受尽千辛万苦之后，又能回到英国，并成为富豪。笛福在栩栩如生地讲一个“海外奇谈”式的故事时，歌颂了水手鲁滨逊坚毅不拔，战天斗地的丈夫气概，这正与英国资产阶级的时代精神相契合。他们作为在上升中的新兴阶级，冲破封建主义的羁绊，以“勤俭生财”为人生要义，向广大富饶的海外异域开拓殖民王国，索取自然宝藏。

笛福被称为英国现实主义小说的重要创始人，从他刻划鲁滨逊在荒岛落难的遭遇的笔法，可以看出他的享有盛誉是由来有自的。鲁滨逊一到岛上，就设法从大船上取来一切能搬动的生活资料和工具。他利用自然条件为自己修了个家屋，不仅遮风避雨，而且能抗御人兽侵犯。他努力从失败中学习，学会了种粮驯兽，采制食物，制造器皿，缝制衣服；不仅如此，他还着眼于最终回归敌国，想利用从大船上漂来的小艇不成，就自制独木舟，又不成，就另外做一艘小船。如此等等，每一件事、每一个应付困难与危险的方法，都是反复剖析事，娓娓道之，使读者感到很真实，好象自己如果是鲁滨逊的话，也应是这样干的。

笛福用了极大篇幅对想象的鲁滨逊建立家业的活动进行描写，事极怪诞，却都合情合理，这首先是因为他有丰富的生活知识与经验，但也由于他对事物的敏锐观察力和求实精神。他所述的一些可能是为贵族和文人所不屑顾的琐事，却无疑地是工场主、商人和农民及工匠艺徒们所喜闻乐见，耳熟能详的。这也说明了《鲁滨逊》一书为什么能走出书斋、客厅和闺房，深入到作坊店铺中去。

在短短的数段选文中，很难体现《鲁滨逊》一书的全貌。我们尽量不选过去已有选本的段子，又争取体现原书的主要情节和优点。选段的注释，也许能解决一些语言上的疑难。

* * *

1. the weather clear, and the storm abated: = the weather *was* clear, and the storm *was* (or: *had*) abated。

2. that the ship was lifted off in the night from the sand where she lay: 那艘帆船在夜间已经被（海潮）托起，离开了搁浅的沙滩（上文说到大帆船遇到风暴，搁浅在海中沙滩上，水手们一起弃船乘小艇逃命，而小艇又被大浪打翻，鲁滨逊一个人被大浪打到荒岛上，逃得性命，别人都丧身波涛之中了。他栖身于大树上过了一夜）。

3. where I had been so bruised by the dashing me against it: 就在我先前被浪头冲荡到礁石上而受伤累累的地方（the dashing me against it 是较古旧的说法，相当于 by being dashed against it 或 by the waves' dashing me against it.）。

4. This being within about a mile ..., and the ship seeming to stand upright still: = As this was within about a mile ..., and as the ship seemed to stand upright still（原句系带主语的独立结构，即 Nominative Absolute）.

5. When I came down from my apartment in the tree ...: 当我从大树上的寓所走下来后…（称自己栖身一夜的树枝为 apartment，说明鲁滨逊虽身处急难之地，却仍能调侃自己，显示他临危不乱，冷静自持。)

6. the boat: 上文书中叙述鲁滨逊与其他水手们藉小艇逃离大船，而小艇终于被大浪打翻，别人丧生，只有他没有淹死。

7. that if we had kept on board we had been all safe, ...: = that if we had kept on board we would have been all safe 这是较古的虚拟语态形式，下文的 we had all got safe on shore 和 I had not been so miserable ... 均同此 .

8. took the water: 跳到了水里（现作 took *to* the water）。

9. fore-chains: 船首锚链。

10. bulged: 胀破；船板漏水（同 bilged）was bulged = had bulged.

11. all her quarter was free: 船的后部都没有浸水。

12. what was spoiled and what was free:（食品和某些用品被海水浸泡后即不能食用，这是航海者遇难后最关心的事。)

13. and eat it as I went about other things: 当时 eat 的过去时仍可用 eat 的形式，*ate* 尚未成为唯一的正确形式。后文亦有此例。

14. and which I had indeed need enough of to spirit me for what was before me: 我真的很需要喝点酒，好振奋起精神去做当前该做的事情。

15. and this extremity roused my application: 这种极端困厄的处境促使我苦思苦想。

16. a spare top-mast or two: 一两根备用的中桅。

17. drive away: 随波逐流地漂走。

18. crossways: *adv.* 横着。

19. but hope of furnishing myself with necessaries encouraged me to go beyond what I should have been able to have done upon another occasion: 但是我切望获得生活所必需的物品，这就鼓舞我去做平常所做不到的事。

20. but I was not long considering this: 但我没有花多少时间，就想出了办法。以人为主语 + be 动词 + 时间，意思是“花了多少时间”。

21. which we lived much upon: 我们当初在船上时这东西吃得很多。

22. cordial waters:（加香料的）甜酒（*waters* 当作“酒类”或“矿泉水”讲时，习惯用复数形式，如 strong waters 烈性酒；take the waters 服用矿泉水治病）。

23. rack: = arrack [ˈærək]（从椰汁或米酒提炼的）烧酒。

24. nor no room for them: = nor was there any room for them（这种重复否定词的做法，在近代已被认为是属于 sub-standard 的语体，被排除于 educated speech 之外了）。

25. I found the tide began to flow: 在近代英语中应作 I found the tide *beginning*（或 *begin*）to flow，或 I found (that) the tide *had begun* to flow. 而同句中又有 ... to see my coat ... *swim* away ... 并行不悖，可见当时语言尚未充分定型，用法还不十分一致。

26. open-kneed: 没有扎裤腿的（当时水手的一般装束是短裤长略过膝，在膝下扎紧，下面穿中等长度的袜子。）

27. this put me upon rummaging for clothes, of which I found enough: = I found enough of them，这促使我到处搜寻衣服，也找到了不少。

28. powder-horns: 放火药的牛角（尖端开口塞住，利用尖端向枪膛里灌火药）。

29. I thought myself pretty well freighted: 我认为我的木排装载得够满了（myself = my raft，后文亦有以 I 或 me 代表自己的船或木筏的）。

30. having neither sail, oar, or rudder: = having neither sail, oar, *nor* rudder。

31. and the least capful of wind would have overset all my navigation: 只要有一小口风，就会打乱我的航海术。

32. What little wind there was blew me towards the land: 虽然没有多大的风，但这点风却是把我朝岸边送去的。

33. two or three broken oars belonging to the boat: 鲁滨逊在大船上搜寻物品，本已大致就绪，看水观风，准备起行，但忽又找到些木桨，斧锯之类带上。

34. I found it drive a little distant from the place where I had landed before: 我发现木排漂向的地方，离开我以前登陆的地点有一些距离。

35. indraft: 向海岸河口内流去的水流。

36. I found a strong current of the tide set into it: 我发现有一股强劲的潮水向这河口里涌去。

37. I had like to have suffered a second shipwreck: 我差一点又遭到一次毁船事故（had like to 是 like 的古用法）。

38. which··· would have broke my heart: = would have *broken* my heart。

39. ... all my cargo had slipped off ...: = all my cargo *would have slipped off* ...

40. the rising of the tide brought me a little more upon a level: 潮水上涨，使我的排子略为平了一些（me = my raft）。

41. there was no place to land but where ... my cargo again: 没有地方可以登岸，除非是在这样的地方，如果筏子的一头搁上了岸，那么它就会翘得很高，而另一头就会沉得很低，和原先那次一样，···

42. Where I was, I yet knew not: 我到现在还不知道自己是在什么地方。（这是倒装句 where I was 是动词 knew 的宾语从句。I knew not 这种不使用助动词 do 的否定式谓语是较古式的）。

43. whether on the continent, or on an island ... or not: 这里一连三个 whether ... or ...，都是省略句，但句式各不相同，省略句的意思上的主语由第一句的 I 变为第二句的 the place，又变回到第三句的 I。

44. I saw my fate to my great affliction: 我明白了我的命运，这使我极为悲痛。

45. fowls: 现代英语此字的复数形式须作 fowl。

46. but had no talons or claws more than common: 可是这鸟的爪子不象鹰爪，却和普通鸟的爪子一样。

47. carrion ['kæriən]**:** 动物尸体的腐肉，此处意称这鸟的肉味道恶劣，不能供食用。

48. come to land: 弄上岸来。

49. set all other things apart: = set all other things aside 把其它的事都先搁下。

50. I called a council, that is to say, in my thoughts: 我自己在脑子里开了个会。

51. crows: = crowbars 撬棒。

52. sheet lead [led]**:** 铅皮，可熔化制枪弹。

53. a spare fore-top sail: 备用的前樯中桅帆。

54. I presented my gun at her: 我举枪向它瞄准。

55. though, by the way, I was not very free of it, for my store was not great: 然而我没有太大方，因为我自己的存粮也不多。

56. smelled of it: 嗅了嗅它（现代英语中 to smell of something 是"有…的味道"的意思）。

57. as pleased: = as if it were pleased。

58. any sudden attempt: = any sudden attempt on my life。

59. spreading one of the beds upon the ground: 把一床被褥铺在地上…。

60. as well to fetch ... as to get them on shore: 我由大船上弄回那些东西费了很大的力气，而把这些东西（从筏子上）弄到岸上费的劲儿也并不小。

61. magazine: 货仓，仓库（全句的意思是，现在我有了一大批各式各样的货物了，敢说从来没有为单独一个人存储过比这更多的东西）。

62. having plundered the ship of what was portable and fit to hand out ...: 我已经把船上能移动和好搬走的东西全都搬空了。

63. after I was entered the little cove: was entered = had entered。

64. I was fain to dip for it: 我不得不潜水去取锚缆…（be fain to do 有两种意思，一是"愿意、欣然去做"，如上文 I was fain to open the barrels of powder .... 而另一个意思是"不得不做，没有别的法子只好做"，如这里。后一个用法现在较少见。）

65. I had brought away all that one pair of hands could well be supposed capable to bring: 我已经把能指望我单人匹马搬来的东西都搬来了（capable to bring 在现代英语应作 capable of bringing）。

66. had the calm weather held: = if the calm weather had held（hold 这里指好天气维持不变）。

67. a dozen of good knives and forks: 现代英语 of 已略去。

68. I found about thirty-six pounds value in money: 我找到了约值三十六英镑的硬币（thirty-six pounds value = thirty-six pounds' value）。

69. some European coin: 这里 coin 是不可数名词的用法，这种用法仍保留在某些特殊场合（如金融界）和一些习语中，如 false coin（伪造的钱币），pay a man back in his own coin（以其人之道还治其人之身）。

70. some Brazil [brə'zil]**:** = some Brazilian [brə'ziljən] coins 一些巴西钱币。

71. pieces of eight: 一种西班牙古银币，又称 real(e)s（[riəlz] 或 [reiˈɑːlz]）里亚尔，曾通用于西班牙及某些拉丁美洲国家，其形状和重量略同于后来的“墨西哥鹰洋”。

72. drug: 在这里的意思是卖不出手，没有人要的货色，这意思保留在短语 drug on the market 中。

73. O drug! What art thou good for?: 鲁滨逊使用了 apostrophe（呼语）的修辞手段，并从而使用了较古的代词与动词形式 thou (= you) 和 art (= are)，故作古雅，极不自然，不符合鲁滨逊的身份，鲁滨逊在荒岛上亟需取得生活所必需的衣食、工具、武器等物，而视金银如粪土，这本是简单的真理，但迪福不以此为满足，遂不免画蛇添足。

74. Thou art not worth to me, no, not the taking off of the ground: = You are not worth to me the trouble of taking you off (from) the ground. 对于我来说，都不值得费劲把你从地上拾起来。现代英语中这里使用 off 或 off from, off of 常见于方言。此外现代英语中在这样的地方，动名词短语前面一般不用定冠词 the。

75. upon second thoughts: 再一想（笛福是不能听任鲁滨逊把金钱弃之不顾的，既然已经说教了一番，钱还是拿着的好。在这些地方迪福非常识时务）。

76. it blew a fresh-gale from the shore: 从岸的方向刮起了一阵大风。gale 相当于现代风力的八级，fresh 用于风，是“强劲的”的意思。现在刮风已不用 it blew a wind (a storm) 这种说法。

77. behold: 瞧呀！（这个词的命令式用法是《圣经》中常见的，在普通场合使用，是一种拟古的修辞手段。）

78. nor abated no diligence: 也没有偷懒松劲（这里又是 double negative 的一例）。

79. I now gave over any more thoughts of the ship, or of anything out of her: = or any more thoughts of getting anything out of her。

80. for I raised a kind of wall up against it of turfs: = for I raised a kind of wall of turfs up against it, turfs 草皮。

81. which as they lay in no order, so they took up all my place: 这个定语从句中，只有以 as 与 so 开始的两个从句，致使关系代词 which 落空。这是不够严谨的，但在当时很常见。如果把 so, they 两字去掉，语法就正确了。

82. egress and regress [ˈiːgres][ˈriːgres]**:** 出去和回来（这两个字不是常用词，比较书卷气，和句子其它部分的寻常词语并不相称）。

83. I must needs observe: 我必须说明。needs 在这里是副词，现只用于 must needs do something 句型中，意思是“偏要”，“必须”或“不得不”。

84. by stating and squaring everything by reason ... mechanic art: 通过理性对一切事物进行排式子和乘方…（stating 又是“阐明”或“陈述”，squaring 又是“调正”或“摆平”。在这里，笛福使用了一些数学术语，语义双关，似是而非，把活生生的“熟能生巧”的例子，说成了“万用存于一心”。

85. which, perhaps, were never made that way before: 那些器物可能从来没有人用（我）这种方法去做成过。which 在这里指前面相隔很远的 abundance of things 和 some.

86. but my patience: = except my patience。

87. any more than I had for ... or board: = I had no more remedy for it than I had for it ...（全句的意思是，用一整棵树只能修出一块板材，但对这种浪费、正如同对气力和时间的巨大浪费一样，只有以忍耐处之。）

88. to separate everything at large in their places: 把东西大致地分门别类放好。at large 在这里是“笼统地，大致地”。

89. that I might come easily at them: = so that (in order that) I might get hold of them easily; come at 是“取到，拿到”的意思。

90. I knocked pieces into the wall of the rock: 我在石壁上楔了木橛子。

91. and all things that would hang up: 一切能挂的东西（这里动词 hang 意思上应是被动的，但用主动语态，是习惯用法）。

92. had my cave been to be seen, it looked like ...: = if my cave had been seen, it would have looked like ... 此句中除条件从句省去了 if 而使用了倒装句外，had been to be seen 这种动词形式也是很不常见的，后面的 it looked like 也不同于现代用法。

93. This at length put me upon thinking ...: 这件事终于使我开始考虑…（原书上文谈到鲁滨逊企图修理那艘被风浪抛到海滩上的小艇，但是他无法使小艇翻过来正面向上，只得作罢。This 就是指这件事而言。）

94. periagua:（西班牙语）现通作 piragua [piˈrægwə] 南美印第安人的独木舟。

95. or, as I might say, without hands: 或者，也可以说，没有手也能做出来（因为没有工具，就等于没有了手一样）。

96. ...of the trunk of a great tree: 句子的基本结构是 a canoe ... such as the natives ... make ... of the trunk of a great tree。

97. the particular inconveniences which I lay under more than the Indians did: 那些使我比印第安人更受限制的特殊不利条件。

98. what was it to me ... if ... if ...: 要是…，要是…那对我又有什么用呢？

99. but I should have immediately thought how ... sea: 这里 but 的意思是“而不…”。全句的大意是：人们会认为，我在做独木舟时，只要稍稍考虑到具体情况，就不会不马上想到船做好以后怎样把它弄到海里去的问题。

100. where it lay: = from where it lay。

101. I went to work upon this boat the most like a fool that ever man did who had any of his senses awake: 我就象傻到不能再傻的傻瓜一样开始造这条船了（直译为：比任何一个脑子还有一点儿清醒的人都要傻）。

**102. Not but that the difficulty of launching my boat came often into my

head: 使船下水的困难，我并不是没有经常想到。

103. Solomon [ˈsɔləmən]**:** 所罗门，《圣经 · 旧约》中的公元前十世纪的以色列王，大卫之子，以智慧，豪侈著称。

104. the Temple of Jerusalem [dʒəˈruːsələm]：耶路撒冷圣殿，为传说中所罗门王在都城耶路撒冷所兴建，体制极为雄伟。

105. It was five feet ten inches diameter next the stump: = It was five feet ten inches *in* diameter next *to* the stump。

106. and four feet eleven inches diameter at the end of twenty-two feet: 在从根量起长二十二英尺的地方直径四英尺十一英寸。

107. And inexpressible labour: = and *with* inexpressible labour 付出了无可计量的劳动。

108. to a proportion: 使比例大小合适；使粗具规模。

109. to work it so as to make an exact boat of it: 对它进行加工，把它做成一条尺寸精确的船。

110. by the dint of: 现通用 by dint of，通过、依靠。

111. it cost me a prodigious deal of pains: 我为它费尽了力气。

112. but who grudges pains, that have their deliverance in view? 可是巴望从灾难中得到解救的人，怎会吝惜气力呢？

113. it was still much at one: 还跟原来一样。at one 一模一样，相同。

114. to bring the water up to the canoe, seeing I could not bring the canoe down to the water: 既然我不能把独木船弄到水那边去，就想把水引到船这边来。（传说中穆哈默德命令一座山到他面前来，山没有动。他就说："既然山不肯到穆哈默德这里来，穆哈默德就到山那儿去"，然后走了过去。这句话显然套了这个故事。）

115. As to linen: = As for linen（linen [ˈlinin] 本义为亚麻布，后泛指状似亚麻布的细白布衣物，如衬衫、内裤、桌布、床单，等）。

116. chequered ([ˈtʃekəd]) **shirts:** 花格布衬衫（现更常用 checked）。

117. watch-coats: 水手值班时穿的外衣。

118. so violent hot: 这么热，热得这么厉害（按照语法应说 so violently hot，但实际上非正式语言中常这样把一个表示强调的形容词与另一个形容词连在一起使用，如 dreadful sorry, damned embarassing 等）。

119. yet I could not go quite naked, no, though I had been inclined to it, which I was not: = yet, even if I had been inclined to going quite naked, which I was not, I could not have done it.（这种地方描述了鲁滨逊虽孤处荒岛，还是尽可能地保持了文明人的体统。）

120. it would presently go away: 头痛很快就会好了。

121. so I set to work a-tailoring, or rather, indeed, a-botching: 我从而开始

干起裁缝的活儿来，或者不如说是瞎鼓捣一气。

122. I made most piteous work of it: 我干的活儿实在太糟了（这里 piteous 亦是较古的用法）。

123. made but a sorry shift indeed till afterwards: 起先勉强凑合，实在极不象话，到后来才有所改善。

124. to shoot off the rain: 使雨水能顺着毛流掉。

125. for they were rather wanting to keep me cool than to keep me warm: 因为之所以需要它们，是为了防暑，而不是御寒。

126. they were such as I made very good shift with: 这些衣服帽子的缝制，凑合着还很顶用。

127. the Brazils: 巴西当时习惯用复数形式，并在前面用定冠词 the，现已不用。

128. I felt the great heats every jot as great here: 我感觉到这里的炎热季节一点也不亚于巴西。

129. the equinox [ˈiːkwinɔks]**:** 原义为昼夜平分点，即春分或秋分。这里用来指赤道或天球赤道。

130. but at last I made one that answered indifferently well: 可是，终于我做成了一把勉强能过得去的伞。answer 在这里是"符合（我的心意）"的意思。

131. to make it *to* let down: make it *to* spread 现代英语中这里的 to 省略。

132. it was not portable for me any way but just over my head: 除了撑在头顶上以外，没有别的方法携带。

14 JONATHAN SWIFT 1667–1745

1. Gulliver's Travels
Book II, Chapter VI

梅仁毅　选注

2. A Modest Proposal

王佐良　选注

1. GULLIVER'S TRAVELS

梅仁毅　选注

Book II Chapter VI

Several contrivances of the Author to please the King and Queen. He shows his skill in music. The King enquires into the state of Europe, which the Author relates to him. The King's observations thereon.[1]

I USED to attend the King's levee[2] once or twice a week, and had often seen him under the barber's hand, which indeed was at first very terrible to behold; for the razor was almost twice as long as an ordinary scythe. His Majesty, according to the custom of the country, was only shaved twice a week. I once prevailed on[3] the barber to give me some of the suds or lather, out of which I picked forty or fifty of the strongest stumps of hair.[4] I then took a piece of fine wood, and cut it like the back of a comb, making several holes in it at equal distance with as small a needle as I could get from

Glumdalclitch.[5] I fixed in the stumps so artificially[6], scraping and sloping them with my knife towards the points, that I made a very tolerable comb; which was a seasonable supply,[7] my own being so much broken in the teeth, that it was almost useless: neither did I know any artist[8] in that country so nice[9] and exact, as would undertake to make me another.

And this puts me in mind of[10] an amusement wherein I spent many of my leisure hours. I desired the Queen's woman to save for me the combings[11] of her Majesty's hair, whereof in time I got a good quantity, and consulting with my friend the cabinet-maker,[12] who had received general orders to do little jobs for me, I directed him to make two chair-frames, no larger than those I had in my box; and then to bore little holes with a fine awl[13] round those parts where I designed the backs and seats; through these holes I wove the strongest hairs I could pick out, just after the manner of cane chairs in England.[14] When they were finished, I made a present of them to her Majesty, who kept them in her cabinet, and used to show them for curiosities, as indeed they were the wonder[15] of every one who beheld them. The Queen would have had me sit upon one of these chairs, but I absolutely refused to obey her; protesting[16] I would rather die a thousand deaths, than place a dishonourable part of my body on those precious hairs that once adorned her Majesty's head. Of these hairs (as I had always a mechanical genius[17]) I likewise made a neat little purse about five foot[18] long, with her Majesty's name deciphered[19] in gold letters, which I gave to Glumdalclitch, by the Queen's consent. To say the truth, it was more for show than use,[20] being not of strength to bear the weight of the larger coins, and therefore she kept nothing in it but some little toys that girls are fond of.

The King, who delighted in music, had frequent concerts at court, to which I was sometimes carried, and set in my box[21] on a table to hear them; but the noise was so great, that I could hardly distinguish the tunes. I am confident that all the drums and trumpets of a royal army, beating and sounding together just at your ears, could not equal it. My practice was to have my box removed from the places where the performers sat, as far as I could, then to shut the doors and windows of it, and draw the window-curtains; after which I found their music not disagreeable.

I had learned in my youth to play a little upon the spinet.[22] Glumdalclitch kept one in her chamber, and a master attended twice a week to teach her: I call it a spinet, because it somewhat resembled that instrument, and was played upon in the same manner. A fancy came into my head that I would entertain the King and Queen with an English tune upon this instrument. But this appeared extremely difficult; for the spinet was near sixty foot long, each key being almost a foot wide, so that, with my arms extended, I could not reach to above five keys,[23] and to press them down required a good smart stroke with my fist, which would be too great a labour, and to no purpose.[24] The method I contrived was this. I prepard two round sticks about the bigness of common cudgels; they were thicker at one end than the other, and I covered the thicker ends with a piece of a mouse's skin, that by rapping on them[25] I might neither damage the tops of the keys,[26] nor interrupt the sound. Before the spinet a bench was placed, about four foot below the keys, and I was put upon the bench. I ran sideling upon it that way and this,[27] as fast as I could, banging the proper keys with my two sticks, and made a shift to play a jig, to the great satisfaction of both their Majesties: but it was the most violent exercise I ever underwent, and yet I could not strike above sixteen keys, nor, consequently, play the bass[28] and treble together, as other artists do; which was a great disadvantage to my performance.

The King, who, as I before observed, was a prince of excellent understanding, would frequently order that I should be brought in my box, and set upon the table in his closet. He would then command me to bring one of my chairs out of the box, and sit down within three yards distance upon the top of the cabinet, which brought me almost to a level with his face. In this manner I had several conversations with him. I one day took the freedom to tell his Majesty,[29] that the contempt he discovered[30] towards Europe, and the rest of the world, did not seem answerable to those excellent qualities of the mind he was master of.[31] That reason did not extend itself with the bulk of the body:[32] on the contrary, we observed in our country that the tallest persons were usually least provided with it. That among other animals, bees and ants had the reputation of more industry, art and sagacity,[33] than many of the larger kinds. And that, as inconsiderable as he took me to be, I hoped I might live to do his Majesty some signal[34] service. The king heard me with attention, and began to conceive a much better opinion of me[35] than he had ever before. He desired I would give him as exact an account of the government of England as I possibly could; because, as fond as princes commonly are of their own customs[36] (for so he conjectured of other monarchs by my former discourses), he should be glad to hear of any thing that might deserve imitation.

Imagine with thyself, courteous reader, how often I then wished for the tongue of Demosthenes[37] or Cicero,[38, 39] that might have enabled me to celebrate[40] the praise of my own dear native country in a style equal to its merits and felicity.[41]

I began my discourse by informing his Majesty that our dominions[42] consisted of two islands, which composed three mighty kingdoms[43] under one sovereign, besides our plantations[44] in America. I dwelt long upon[45] the fertility of our soil, and the temperature[46] of our climate. I then spoke at large upon the constitution of an English Parliament, partly made up of an illustrious body called the House of Peers, persons of the noblest blood, and of the most ancient and ample patrimonies.[47] I described that extraordinary care always taken of their education in arts and arms, to qualify them for being counsellors born to the king and kingdom, to have a share in the legislature, to be members of the highest court of judicature, from whence[48] there could be no appeal,[49] and to be champions[50] always ready for the defence of their prince[51] and country, by their valour, conduct, and fidelity. That these were the ornament and bulwark of the kingdom,[52] worthy followers[53] of their most renowned ancestors, whose honour had been the reward of their virtue,[54] from which their posterity were never once known to degenerate. To these were joined several holy persons, as part of that assembly, under the title of Bishops, whose peculiar business it is to take care of religion, and of those who instruct the people therein.[55] These were searched and sought out through the whole nation, by the prince and his wisest counsellors, among such of the priesthood as were most deservedly distinguished by the sanctity of their lives,[56] and the depth of their erudition; who were indeed the spiritual fathers of the clergy and the people.

That the other part of the Parliament consisted of an assembly[57] called the House of Commons, who were all principal[58] gentlemen, freely picked and culled out[59] by the people themselves, for their great abilities, and love of their country, to represent the wisdom of the whole nation. And these two bodies make up the most august[60] assembly in Europe, to whom, in conjunction with the prince, the whole legislature is committed.[61]

I then descended to the Courts of Justice, over which the Judges, those venerable sages and interpreters of the law,[62] presided, for determining the disputed rights and properties of men, as well as for the punishment of vice, and protection of innocence. I mentioned the prudent management of our Treasury; the valour and achievements of our forces by sea and land. I computed the number of our people, by reckoning how many millions there might be of each religious sect, or political party among us. I did not omit even our sports and pastimes, or any other particular which I thought might redound[63] to the honour of my country. And, I finished all with a brief historical account of affairs and events in England for about an hundred years past.

This conversation was not ended under five audiences,[64] each of several hours, and the King heard the whole with great attention, frequently taking notes of what I spoke, as well as memorandums of what questions he intended to ask me.

When I had put an end to these long discourses, his Majesty in a sixth audience consulting his notes, proposed many doubts, queries, and objections upon every article.[65] He asked what methods were used to cultivate the minds and bodies of our young nobility, and in what kind of business they commonly spent the first and teachable part of their lives.[66] What course was taken to supply that assembly when any noble family became extinct.[67] What qualifications were necessary in those who are to be created new lords: whether the humour of the prince,[68] a sum of money to a courtlady, or a prime minister, or a design of strengthening a party opposite to the public interest, ever happened to be motives in those advancements.[69] What share of knowledge these lords had in the laws of their country, and how they came by[70] it, so as to enable them to decide the properties of their fellow-subjects in the last resort.[71] Whether they were always so free from avarice, partialities, or want,[72] that a bribe, or some other sinister view, could have no place among them. Whether those holy lords I spoke of were constantly promoted to that rank upon account of their knowledge in religious matters, and the sanctity of their lives, had never been compliers with the times[73] while they were common priests, or slavish prostitute chaplains[74] to some nobleman, whose opinions they continued servilely to follow after they were admitted into that assembly.

He then desired to know what arts[75] were practised in electing those whom I called Commoners.[76] Whether a stranger with a strong purse might not influence the vulgar voters[77] to choose him before their own landlords, or the most considerable gentleman in the neighbourhood. How it came to pass,[78] that people were so violently bent upon getting into this assembly, which I allowed to be[79] a great trouble and expence, often to the ruin of their families, without any salary or pension: because this appeared such an exalted strain of virtue and public spirit,[80] that his Majesty seemed to doubt it might possibly not be always sincere: and he desired to know whether such zealous gentlemen could have any views of refunding themselves for the charges and trouble they were at, by sacrificing the public good to the designs of a weak and vicious prince in conjunction with a corrupted ministry. He multiplied his questions, and sifted[81] me thoroughly upon every part of this head,[82] proposing numberless enquiries and objections, which I think it not prudent or convenient to repeat.

Upon what I said in relation to our Courts of Justice, his Majesty desired to be satisfied in several points: and this I was the better able to do, having been formerly almost ruined by a long suit in Chancery,[83] which was decreed for me with costs.[84] He asked, what time was usually spent in determining between right and wrong, and what degree of expence. Whether advocates[85] and orators had liberty to plead in causes manifestly known to be unjust, vexatious,[86] or oppressive. Whether party in religion or politics[87] were observed to be of any weight in the scale of justice.[88] Whether those pleading orators were persons educated in the general knowledge of equity;[89] or only in provincial, national, and other local customs. Whether they or their judges had any part in penning[90] those laws which they assumed the liberty of interpreting and glossing upon[91] at their pleasure.[92] Whether they had ever at different times pleaded for and against the same cause, and cited precedents to prove contrary opinions. Whether they were a rich or a poor corporation. Whether they received any pecuniary reward for pleading or delivering their opinions. And particularly whether they were ever admitted as members in the lower senate.[93]

He fell next upon[94] the management of our Treasury; and said he thought my memory had failed me,[95] because I computed our taxes as about five or six millions a year, and when I came to mention the issues,[96] he found they sometimes amounted to more than double; for the notes he had taken were very particular in this point, because he hoped, as he told me, that the knowledge of our conduct might be useful to him, and he could not be deceived in his calculations. But, if what I told him were true, he was still at a loss how a kingdom could run out of its estate[97] like a private person. He asked me, who were our creditors; and where we found money to pay them. He wondered[98] to hear me talk of such chargeable[99] and extensive wars; that certainly we must be a quarrelsome people, or live among very bad neighbours, and that our generals must needs be[100] richer than our kings. He asked what business[101] we had out of our own islands, unless upon the score of trade or treaty, or to defend the coasts with our fleet. Above all, he was amazed to hear me talk of a mercenary standing army in the midst of peace, and among a free people. He said, if we were governed by our own consent in the persons of our representatives, he could not imagine of whom we were afraid, or against whom we were to fight; and would hear my opinion, whether a private man's house might not better be defended by himself, his children, and family, than by half a dozen rascals picked up at a venture[102] in the streets, for small wages, who might get an hundred times more by cutting their throats.

He laughed at my odd kind of arithmetic[103] (as he was pleased to call it) in reckoning the numbers of our people by a computation drawn from the several sects among us in religion and politics. He said, he knew no reason, why those who entertain opinions prejudicial to the public,[104] should be obliged to change, or should not be obliged to conceal them. And as it was tyranny in any government to require the first, so it was weakness not to enforce the second: for a man may be allowed to keep poisons in his closet, but not to vend them about as cordials.[105]

He observed that among the diversions[106] of our nobility and gentry I had mentioned gaming.[107] He desired to know at what age this entertainment was usually taken up, and when it was laid down; how much of their time it employed; whether it ever went so high as to affect their fortunes; whether mean vicious people, by their dexterity in that art,[108] might not arrive at great riches, and sometimes keep our very nobles in dependence,[109] as well as habituate them to vile companions,[110] wholly take them from the improvement of their minds, and force them by the losses they received, to learn and practise that infamous dexterity upon others.[111]

He was perfectly astonished with the historical account I gave him of our affairs during the last century, protesting it was only a heap of conspiracies, rebellions, murders, massacres, revolutions, banishments, the very worst effects that avarice, faction,[112] hypocrisy, perfidiousness,[113] cruelty, rage, madness, hatred, envy, lust, malice, and ambition could produce.

His Majesty in another audience was at the pains to recapitulate[114] the sum of all I had spoken, compared the questions he made with the answers I had given, then taking me into his hands, and stroking me gently, delivered himself in these words,[115] which I shall never forget nor the manner he spoke them in:[116] My little friend Grildrig,[117] you have made a most admirable panegyric upon your country; you have clearly proved that ignorance, idleness, and vice, are the proper ingredients for qualifying a legislator; that laws are best explained, interpreted, and applied by those whose interest and abilities lie in perverting,[118] confounding,[119] and eluding[120] them. I observe among you some lines of an institution,[121] which in its original might have been tolerable,[122] but these half erased, and the rest wholly blurred and blotted[123] by corruptions. It doth not appear from all you have said, how any one perfection is required towards the procurement of any one station[124] among you; much less that men are ennobled on account of their virtue, that priests are advanced for their piety or learning, soldiers for their conduct or valour, judges for their integrity, senators for the love of their country, or counsellors for their wisdom. As for yourself (continued the King) who have spent the greatest part of your life in travelling; I am well disposed to hope you may hitherto have escaped many vices of your country. But by what I have gathered from your own relation, and the answers I have with much pains wringed and extorted from you, I cannot but conclude the bulk of your natives to be the most pernicious race of little odious vermin that nature ever suffered to crawl upon the surface of the earth.[125]

【作者简介】 Jonathan Swift（江纳生·斯威夫特，1667—1745），英国十八世纪伟大讽刺作家，出生于爱尔兰首府都柏林的贫苦家庭，在都柏林三一学院（Trinity College, Dublin）毕业后，到其远房亲戚邓波尔爵士（Sir William Temple）家中任私人秘书。因感地位不稳，为前途计，于1694年加入英国国教会为教士。此后他以文人身份参与政治，先为当时执政的辉格党写文章，后投托雷党，担任《审察者报》（*The Examiner*）主编。1712年发表了《盟国的行为》（*The Conduct of the Allies*），强烈反对英国为了西班牙皇位继承权而继续与法国作战。此文对1713年Utrecht和约的缔结起了制造舆论的作用。

1713年斯威夫特失意于政界，回到都柏林，担任圣·帕特里克大教堂教长（Dean of St. Patrick's）。当时的爱尔兰在英国的暴虐统治下，饥民浮于道，乞丐充斥于市，盗匪横行，民不聊生。斯威夫特目睹这种情况，便以他辛辣的文笔写各种小册子，为这个受压迫的民族鸣不平。在十八世纪二十年代他发表了一系列激动整个爱尔兰的文章，最著名的有《布商的信》（*The Drapier's Letters* 1724）和《一个小小的建议》（*A Modest Proposal* 1729）。斯威夫特在爱尔兰问题上的立场和他所进行的斗争，赢得了爱尔兰人民的尊敬。《布商的信》发表后，统治当局曾悬赏三百镑，缉拿作者，但整个都柏林，没有一个人去告密。

1726年出版了斯威夫特有名的寓言小说《格列佛游记》（*Gulliver's Travels*）。

斯威夫特的散文平易有力，然又饶有韵味，其典雅促进了十八世纪英语的规范化，其质朴发展了英国散文中的平易传统，历来公认为英国散文中最重要的大家之一。他对于语言文字的作用，一向重视，曾经主张设立科学院来审定词汇，纠正文风。他反对华而不实，曾说能将"恰当的词放在恰当的位置，就是能称为好的风格"（"Proper words in proper places, makes the true definition of a style."—*Letter to a Young Gentleman, Lately Entered into Holy Orders*）。这一论点对后来英国散文的发展也起了良好影响，而其本人所作，正是这种风格的范例。凡此种种，都说明斯威夫特在英国散文发展史上，占有十分重要的地位。

《格列佛游记》分四卷：第一卷《小人国游记》；第二卷《大人国游记》；第三卷《飞岛国游记》；第四卷《慧马国游记》。全书是以里梅尔·格列佛船长用第一人称进行叙述的。格列佛到达的第一个国家是小人国，那儿的居民身高仅六英寸。格列佛在小人国住了一段时间，通过他的亲身经历和观察，描述了那儿君主和大臣们的贪婪、残忍，党派间的互相倾轧，争权夺利，以至国家间的连绵战祸。所有这些，斯威夫特都是针对时政而发的。格列佛到的第二个国家是大人国，那儿的居民个个象巨塔。离开大人国后，格列佛来到了飞岛国。飞岛国有一块属地，如果居民稍有不顺，飞岛就飞临其上空，或断其阳光，或降落在属地上，将属地居民压成齑粉。这是对英国剥削、统治爱尔兰的殖民主义政策的公开抨击。最后格列佛来到了慧马国。在那儿，居统治地位的是一些具有高度理性的慧马，而另一部分居民则是一些具有人的外形的动物（Yahoos）。这些动物贪婪、忌妒、凶残、心毒，从外表到内心，极为丑恶。在这儿斯威夫特展示给人们，如果人类让贪欲战胜理智，人类就可能堕落成 Yahoo 一样的卑劣的动物。斯威夫特并不是反对整个人类社会，而是猛烈抨击当时社会的种种罪恶，希望有朝一日"理性"（Reason）能占上峰，那时一切邪恶均将消失，人类将永享幸福、和平。这当然只能是一种幻想。

【题解与注释】

《格列佛游记》是一本游记体的讽刺文学作品。在这本书里，作者对十八世纪英国上层社会层出不穷的阴谋倾轧、谄媚贿赂、争权夺利、勾心斗角等作了淋漓尽致的描绘。他的主要抨击目标是当时的资产阶级，笔锋所指，遍及行政、司法、立法制度、侵略战争和殖民主义等方面的罪恶，但作品也透露了他本人的一些保守思想。

这里所选的是小说第二卷《大人国游记》中的一章。大人国国王数度召见格列佛，讯问了英国社会政治制度种种。格列佛是一个"真诚的爱国者"，因此竭力颂扬英国政治制度的优越：议会的尊严，法官的廉直，财政的严明和军队的英勇善战。但国王并没有被这夸耀的言辞所迷惑。他以一连串的反问彻底剥掉英国统治者的外衣，而将其奸诈与腐败揭露出来。

作者首先歌颂自己的王国及其习俗法令，明褒实贬，含义甚深。接着笔锋一转，由含蓄的讽刺转为锐利的剖解，大人国国王一连串的反诘，以一种排山倒海之势，逼得格列佛无言以答。

但是《格列佛游记》又是一本故事书，出版以来，一直吸引着儿童，其原因之一是书中有奇幻的想象与写实的细节的动人的结合。本章的前半便是一个例证。这里既有有趣的奇怪的故事，又有人人可以了解的具体描绘。作者写大人之大，写自己之小，写躯体、用具、居室，尺寸比例，都有法度，很难找出破绽。事虽荒诞，却当作最家常的事情来写，一点不带夸张。这些都显现了斯威夫特深刻的笔力。

1. thereon: on that or it.

2. the King's levee: 君王（起床后）的接见群臣，早朝。

3. prevailed on: 说服。

4. stumps of hair: 头发根。

5. Glumdalclitch: 大人国照顾格列佛的女佣，九岁，身高四十英尺。

6. artificially: 精巧地（= with art，古义）。

7. a seasonable supply: 这（一木梳的）供应非常及时。

8. artist: 艺匠。

9. nice: 精细（古义）。

10. this puts me in mind of: 这使我想起了。

11. combings: 梳下来的头发。

12. cabinet-maker: 专制家具、木柜的匠人。

13. awl: 锥子。

14. after the manner of cane-chairs in England: 仿照英国藤椅的样子。

15. the wonder: 引起赞叹之物。

16. protesting: saying.

17. a mechanical genius: 具有制造器物的才能。

18. five foot: 现代英文作 feet, 当时在数目字之后可用 foot；第 348 页 11 行 sixty foot，和同页 20 行 four foot 同此。

19. deciphered: 刻上文字，图案（古义）。

20. more for show than use: 与其说是为了实用，还不如说是为了陈设。

21. my box: 大人国国王为格列佛做一木盒，上有门窗，内置桌椅，作为他的住处。

22. spinet: 一种长琴，其键与钢琴相似。

23. with my arms extended, I could not reach to above five keys: 我伸直了手臂也最多碰到五个键。

24. to no purpose: 徒劳的。

25. that by rapping on them: that = so that; rapping on them (= the keys) 用较粗一头敲击琴键。

26. the tops of the keys: 琴键的表面。

27. I ran sideling upon it that way and this: 我在乐器上左右敲打；sideling = sidelong（副词）。

28. the bass [beis] **and treble:** 最低音部和最高音部。

29. took the freedom to tell his Majesty: 坦率地对国王陛下讲。

30. discovered: exhibited, showed（古义）。

31. did not seem answerable to those excellent qualities of the mind he was master of:（他对欧洲以及其他地区所表示的轻蔑态度）似乎和他高明的思想不相称（即不应该这样想）。

32. that reason did not extend itself with the bulk of the body: 这个 *that*-clause 是 tell 的宾语，下面第 6，9 两行的 *that*-clause 同此。一个人的躯体可以长的很大，但智力不一定随之增高。

33. industry, art and sagacity: 勤劳，灵巧和聪明。

34. signal: remarkable, striking.

35. to conceive a much better opinion of me: to think more highly of me.

36. as fond as princes commonly are of their own customs: though princes are commonly fond of their customs.

37. Demosthenes [Di'mɔsθəniːz]（公元前 384—322）：古希腊政治家，演说家。

38. how often I then wished for the tongue of Demosthenes or Cicero: 我多么希望能有 Demosthenes 或 Cicero 那样的口才。

39. Cicero ['sisərəu]，**Marcus Tullius**（公元前 106—43）：古罗马政治家，演说家。

40. celebrate: 公开宣扬（古义）。

41. in a style equal to its merits and felicity:（赞扬的）语气与措词要能充分表示我国体制完美，民生康乐。

42. dominions: 领土，版图（现代英语用 territory）.

43. three mighty kingdoms: 即英格兰、苏格兰和爱尔兰。苏格兰于 1707 年与英格兰联合组成大不列颠王国，那时格列佛已从大人国回到了英国；爱尔兰到 1801 年才被英格兰、苏格兰合并。

44. plantations: 殖民地（古义）。

45. dwelt long upon: 详细地叙述了。

46. temperature: temperate state, mildness；温和。

47. of the most ancient and ample patrimonies: 有一份很大的世袭家产。

48. from whence: 现代英语用 from which.

49. from whence there could be no appeal: 一经判决，不得上诉。

50. champions: 战士（古义）。

51. prince:（在此处）= king.

52. That these were the ornament and bulwark of the kingdom: 这些人是王国的光荣，王国的干城；这个 *that*-clause 是正文 described 的宾语。

53. worthy followers: 有出息的后代。

54. whose honour had been the reward of their virtue: 他们的高尚品质使他们得到了贵族的称号。

55. therein: 在那点上，指在宗教方面。

56. sanctity of their lives: 他们洁白无瑕、庄严神圣的生活。

57. That the other part of the Parliament consisted of an assembly: 这个 *that*-clause 仍是前面 described 的宾语。

58. principal: 著名的（现代英语用 prominent, leading）.

59. culled out: 挑选。

60. august [ɔːˈgʌst]: 庄严的。

61. to whom, ... the whole legislature is committed: 上下两院被授权为制订法律的机关；to whom 现代英语用 to which.

62. interpreters of the law: 法律的解释者。

63. redound: 有助于，增加。

64. audience: 一次觐见。

65. every article:（格列佛所谈的）每一点。

66. the first and teachable part of their lives: 他们应该接受教育的少年时代。

67. when any noble family became extinct: 当一个贵族爵位没有后裔继承时。

68. the humour of the prince: 君王的一时兴致（指缺乏考虑的决定）。

69. advancements: 提升，晋爵。

70. came by: 获得。

71. to decide ... in the last resort: 最后决定。

72. free from avarice, partialities, or want: 不贪财，不徇私，又不缺钱用。

73. compliers with the times: 趋时媚世之人。

74. chaplains:（王公贵人府中的）礼拜堂的牧师。

75. arts: 方法（古义）。

76. Commoners: 下议院议员（上议院议员 peers 之对称）。

77. the vulgar voters: 此处 vulgar 作 common 解，与今日用法不同。

78. came to pass: happened.

79. allowed to be: admitted to be.

80. such an exalted strain of virtue and public spirit: 如此高尚的道德品质和为公众服务的精神。

81. sifted: 细细地查问。

82. head: a chief point of discussion；这一点。

83. chancery [ˈtʃɑːnsəri]: 大法官厅（从前英国的最高法院，今属高等法院的一部分）。

84. decreed for me with costs:（这场官司）我打赢了，但诉讼费由我负担；decreed 判决（法律用语）。

85. advocates: 律师（古义）。

86. vexatious: 诬告的（法律用语）。

87. party in religion or politics: 宗教或政治问题中的派别之争；party= party spirit（古义）。

88. to be of any weight in the scale of justice: 在审理案件中是否影响法治精神。

89. **equity:** principles of justice.

90. **penning:** 起草。

91. **glossing upon:** 阐明。

92. **at their pleasure:** 随意的。

93. **the lower senate:** 即 House of Commons，下议院。

94. **fell upon:** = came to，谈到。

95. **my memory had failed me:** 我把事情记错了。

96. **issues:** 支出。

97. **run out of its estate:** 入不敷出。

98. **wondered:** was surprised.

99. **chargeable:** 昂贵（古义）。

100. **must needs be:** 一定是；needs 在此用作副词。

101. **what business:** 指下文所说的 standing army；意即常备军有何用处。

102. **picked up at a venture:** 随便挑来的。

103. **my odd kind of arithmetic:** 我那奇怪的算法。

104. **opinions prejudicial to the public:** 对社会有害的观点，见解。

105. **not to vend them about as cordials:** 而不到处当作补药兜售。

106. **diversions:** 娱乐。

107. **gaming:** 赌博。

108. **their dexterity in that art:** 精通赌术。

109. **sometimes keep our very nobles in dependence:** 有时甚至使我们的贵族负债累累。

110. **habituate them to vile companions:** 使他们惯于与恶棍歹徒为伍。

111. **practise that infamous dexterity upon others:** 用赌术诈骗他人。

112. **faction:** 党派之争。

113. **perfidiousness** [pəːˈfidiəsnis]: 背信弃义。

114. **at the pains to recapitulate:** 煞费苦心地扼要重述一遍。

115. **delivered himself in these words:** 说了下面一段话。

116. **nor the manner he spoke them in:** = nor (shall I ever forget) the manner in which he spoke them.

117. **Grildrig:** 格列佛在大人国的名字。

118. **perverting:** 曲解。

119. **confounding:** 混淆。

120. **eluding:** 逃避（法网）。

121. **some lines of an institution:** 一种制度的某些方面。

122. **tolerable:** 差强人意的。

123. **blurred and blotted:** 制度已被弄得面目全非了。

124. **station:** 职位，身份。

125. **I cannot but conclude the bulk of your natives to be the most pernicious race of little odious vermin that nature ever suffered to crawl upon the surface of the earth:** 这是常被引用的斯威夫特的名言之一，由于放在全章之末，成为特别有力的结论，而且由于这个结论是从格列佛原来对英国的颂扬引出，更是

意味深长；vermin，蚤虱之类（英文中极严重的骂人字眼）；suffered, allowed；容许。

2. A MODEST PROPOSAL

For Preventing the Children of poor People in Ireland from being a Burden to their Parents or Country; and for making them beneficial to the Public.

王佐良　选注

IT IS a melancholy object[1] to those who walk through this great town[2], or travel in the country, when they see the streets, the roads, and cabin doors, crowded with beggars of the female sex, followed by three, four, or six children,[3] all in rags, and importuning every passenger[4] for an alms.[5] These mothers, instead of being able to work for their honest livelihood, are forced to employ all their time in strolling, to beg sustenance[6] for their helpless infants, who, as they grow up, either turn thieves for want[7] of work, or leave their dear native country to fight for the Pretender in Spain,[8] or sell themselves to the Barbadoes.[9]

I think it is agreed by all parties,[10] that this prodigious[11] number of children in the arms, or on the backs, or at the heels of their mothers, and frequently of their fathers, is in the present deplorable state of the Kingdom,[12] a very great additional grievance;[13] and therefore, whoever could find out a fair, cheap, and easy method of making these children sound and useful members of the commonwealth,[14] would deserve so well of the public,[15] as to have his statue set up for a preserver of the nation.[16]

But my intention is very far from being confined to provide only for[17] the children of professed beggars:[18] it is of a much greater extent, and shall take in the whole number of infants at a certain age, who are born of parents in effect[19] as little able to support them, as those who demand our charity in the streets.

As to my own part,[20] having turned my thoughts for many

years upon this important subject, and maturely weighed[21] the several[22] schemes of other *projectors*,[23] I have always found them grossly[24] mistaken in their computation. It is true a child, just dropped from its dam,[25] may be supported by her milk for a solar year[26] with little other nourishment, at most not above[27] the value of two shillings, which the mother may certainly get, or the value in scraps,[28] by her lawful occupation of begging, and it is exactly at one year old that I propose to provide for them, in such a manner, as, instead of being a charge[29] upon their parents, or the parish,[30] or wanting food and raiment for the rest of their lives, they shall, on the contrary, contribute to the feeding, and partly to the clothing, of many thousands.

There is likewise another great advantage in my scheme, that it will prevent those voluntary abortions,[31] and that horrid practice of women murdering[32] their bastard children,[33] alas! too frequent among us, sacrificing the poor innocent babes,[34] I doubt,[35] more to avoid the expense, than the shame, which would move tears and pity in the most savage and inhuman breast.

The number of souls[36] in Ireland being usually reckoned one million and a half, of these I calculate there may be about two hundred thousand couple[37] whose wives are breeders;[38] from which number I subtract thirty thousand couples, who are able to maintain their own children, although I apprehend[39] there cannot be so many under the present distresses of the Kingdom; but this being granted,[40] there will remain an hundred and seventy thousand breeders. I again subtract fifty thousand for those women who miscarry,[41] or whose children die by accident or disease within the year. There only remain an hundred and twenty thousand children of poor parents annually born; the question therefore is, how this number shall be reared and provided for, which, as I have already said, under the present situation of affairs, is utterly impossible by all the methods hitherto *proposed*; for we can neither employ them in handicraft or agriculture:[42] we neither build houses (I mean in the country) nor cultivate land;[43] they can very seldom pick up a livelihood by stealing till they arrive at six years old, except where they are of towardly parts;[44] although I confess they learn the rudiments much earlier,[45] during which time they can however be properly looked upon only as probationers,[46] as I have been informed by a principal gentleman in the county of Cavan,[47] who protested[48] to me, that he never knew above one or two instances under the age of six, even in a part of the Kingdom so renowned for the quickest proficiency in that art.[49]

I am assured by our merchants that a boy or a girl, before twelve years old, is no saleable commodity,[50] and even when they come to this age, they will not yield[51] above three pounds, or three pounds and half a crown at most, on the Exchange,[52] which cannot turn to account either to the parents or the Kingdom,[53] the charge of nutriment and rags having been at least four times that value.

I shall now therefore humbly *propose* my own thoughts, which I hope will not be liable to the least objection.

I have been assured by a very knowing American[54] of my acquaintance in London, that a young healthy child well nursed is at a year old a most delicious, nourishing, and wholesome food, whether stewed, roasted, baked, or boiled; and I make no doubt[55] that it will equally serve[56] in a fricassee or a ragout.

I do therefore humbly offer it to public consideration, that, of the hundred and twenty thousand children already computed, twenty thousand may be reserved for breed, whereof only one fourth part to be males, which is more than we allow to sheep, black cattle, or swine; and my reason is that these children are seldom the fruits of marriage,[57] a circumstance not much regarded[58] by our savages; therefore one male will be sufficient to serve four females. That the remaining hundred thousand may[59] at a year old be offered in sale to the persons of quality and fortune[60] through the Kingdom, always advising the mother to let them suck plentifully in the last month, so as to render them plump and fat for a good table.[61]

A child will make two dishes at an entertainment for friends,[62] and when the family dines alone, the fore or hind quarter[63] will make a reasonable dish, and seasoned[64] with a little pepper or salt will be very good boiled on the fourth day, especially in winter.

I have reckoned, upon a medium,[65] that a child just born will weigh twelve pounds, and in a solar year if tolerably[66] nursed increaseth to twenty-eight pounds.

I grant this food will be somewhat dear,[67] and therefore very proper for landlords, who, as they have already devoured most of the parents, seem to have the best title[68] to the children.

Infants' flesh will be in season[69] throughout the year, but more plentiful in March, and a little before and after; for we are told by a grave author,[70] an eminent French physician, that, fish being a prolific diet,[71] there are more children born in Roman Catholic countries about nine months after Lent,[72] than at any other season; therefore reckoning a year after Lent, the markets will be more glutted than usual, because the number of Popish[73] infants is at least three to one[74] in this Kingdom, and therefore it will have one other collateral[75] advantage by lessening the number of Papists[76] among us.

I have already computed the charge of nursing a beggar's child (in which list I reckon all cottagers,[77] labourers, and four-fifths of the farmers) to be about two shillings per annum,[78] rags included; and I believe no gentleman would repine to give ten shillings for the carcass[79] of a good fat child, which, as I have said, will make four dishes of excellent nutritive meat, when he hath only some particular friend, or his own family to dine with him. Thus the squire will learn to be a good landlord, and grow popular among his tenants,[80] the mother will have eight shillings net profit, and be fit for work till she produces another child.

Those who are more thrifty (as I must confess the times require) may flay[81] the carcass; the skin of which, artificially dressed,[82] will make admirable gloves for ladies, and summer boots for fine gentlemen.

As to our city of Dublin, shambles[83] may be appointed for this purpose, in the most convenient parts of it, and butchers we may be assured will not be wanting, although I rather recommend buying the children alive, and dressing them hot from the knife,[84] as we do roasting pigs.

A very worthy person, a true lover of his country, and whose virtues I highly esteem, was lately pleased in discoursing on this matter to offer a refinement upon my scheme.[85] He said that many gentlemen of this Kingdom having of late destroyed their deer, he conceived that the want of venison might be well supplied by the bodies of young lads and maidens, not exceeding fourteen years of age, nor under twelve, so great a number of both sexes in every county being now ready to starve for want of work and service; and these to be disposed of by their parents if alive, or otherwise by their nearest relations. But with due deference[86] to so excellent a friend, and so deserving a patriot,[87] I cannot be altogether in his sentiments;[88] for as to the males, my American acquaintance assured me from frequent experience, that their flesh was generally tough and lean, like that of our schoolboys, by continual exercise, and their taste disagreeable, and to fatten them would not answer the charge.[89] Then as to the females, it would, I think with humble submission[90], be a loss to the public, because they soon would become breeders themselves. And besides, it is not improbable that some scrupulous people might be apt to censure such a practice (although indeed very unjustly) as a little bordering upon cruelty,[91] which, I confess, hath always been with me the strongest objection against any project, however so well intended.

But in order to justify my friend, he confessed that this expedient was put into his head by the famous Psalmanazar,[92] a native of the island Formosa, who came from thence to London, above twenty years ago, and in conversation told my friend that in his country, when any young person happened to be put to death, the executioner sold the carcass to persons of quality, as a prime dainty, and that, in his time, the body of a plump girl of fifteen, who was crucified for an attempt to poison the emperor, was sold to his Imperial Majesty's prime minister of state, and other great mandarins[93] of the court, in joints from the gibbet,[94] at four hundred crowns.[95] Neither indeed can I deny, that if the same use were made of several plump young girls in this town, who, without one single groat to their fortunes,[96] cannot stir abroad[97] without a chair,[98] and appear at the play-house and assemblies[99] in foreign fineries,[100] which they never will pay for, the Kingdom would not be the worse.

Some persons of a desponding spirit are in great concern about that vast number of poor people, who are aged, diseased, or maimed; and I have been desired to employ my thoughts what course may be taken, to ease the nation of so grievous an encumbrance.[101] But I am not in the least pain upon that matter,[102] because it is very well known that they are every day dying, and rotting, by cold, and famine, and filth, and vermin, as fast as can be reasonably expected. And as to the younger labourers, they are now in almost as hopeful a condition.[103] They cannot get work, and consequently pine away[104] for want of nourishment, to a degree that, if at any time they are accidentally hired to common labour, they have not strength to perform it; and thus the country and themselves are happily delivered from the evils to come.[105]

I have too long digressed,[106] and therefore shall return to my subject. I think the advantages by the proposal which I have made are obvious and many, as well as of the highest importance.

For first, as I have already observed, it would greatly lessen the number of Papists, with whom we are yearly overrun,[107] being the principal breeders of the nation, as well as our most dangerous enemies, and who stay at home on purpose with a design to deliver the Kingdom to the Pretender,[108] hoping to take their advantage by the absence of so many good Protestants,[109] who have chosen rather to leave their country, than stay at home and pay tithes[110] against their conscience to an episcopal curate.[111]

Secondly, the poorer tenants will have something valuable of their own, which by law may be made liable to distress,[112] and help to pay their landlord's rent, their corn and cattle being already seized, and money a thing unknown.

Thirdly, whereas the maintenance of an hundred thousand children, from two years old, and upwards, cannot be computed at less than ten shillings apiece[113] per annum, the nation's stock[114] will be thereby increased fifty thousand pounds per annum, besides the profit of a new dish, introduced to the tables of all gentlemen of fortune in the Kingdom, who have any refinement in taste; and the money will circulate among ourselves, the goods being entirely of our own growth and manufacture.

Fourthly, the constant breeders, besides the gain of eight shillings sterling per annum, by the sale of their children, will be rid of the charge[115] of maintaining them after the first year.

Fifthly, this food would likewise bring great custom[116] to taverns, where the vintners[117] will certainly be so prudent as to procure the best receipts[118] for dressing it to perfection, and consequently have their houses frequented by all the fine gentlemen, who justly value themselves upon their knowledge in good eating; and a skillful cook, who understands how to oblige his guests, will contrive to make it as expensive as they please.

Sixthly, this would be a great inducement to marriage,[119] which all wise nations have either encouraged by rewards, or enforced by laws and penalties. It would increase the care and tenderness of mothers toward their children, when they were sure of a settlement for life[120] to the poor babes, provided in some sort by the public to their annual profit instead of expense. We should soon see an honest emulation[121] among the married women, which of them could bring the fattest child to the market. Men would become as fond of their wives, during the time of their pregnancy, as they are now of their mares in foal, their cows in calf, or sows when they are ready to farrow,[122] nor offer to beat or kick them (as it is too frequent a practice) for fear of a miscarriage.

Many other advantages might be enumerated: for instance, the addition of some thousand carcasses in our exportation of barrelled beef;[123] the propagation of swine's flesh,[124] and improvement in the art of making good bacon, so much wanted among us[125] by the great destruction of pigs, too frequent at our tables,[126] which are no way comparable in taste or magnificence[127] to a well-grown, fat yearling child, which roasted whole will make a considerable figure[128] at a lord mayor's feast or any other public entertainment. But this and many others I omit, being studious of brevity.[129]

Supposing that one thousand families[130] in this city would be constant customers for infants' flesh, besides others who might have it at merry meetings, particularly weddings and christenings, I compute that Dublin would take off annually about twenty thousand carcasses, and the rest of the Kingdom (where probably they will be sold somewhat cheaper) the remaining eighty thousand.

I can think of no one objection, that will possibly be raised against this proposal, unless it should be urged that the number of people will be thereby much lessened in the Kingdom. This I freely own,[131] and it was indeed one principal design[132] in offering it to the world. I desire the reader will observe, that I calculate my remedy for[133] this one individual Kingdom of Ireland, and for no other that ever was, is, or, I think, ever can be upon earth.[134] Therefore let no man talk to me of other expedients: of taxing our absentees at five shillings a pound;[135] of using neither clothes, nor household furniture, except what is of our own growth and manufacture; of utterly rejecting the materials and instruments that promote foreign luxury;[136] of curing the expensiveness of pride, vanity, idleness, and gaming[137] in our women; of introducing a vein of parsimony, prudence, and temperance;[138] of learning to love our country, wherein we differ even from Laplanders,[139] and the inhabitants of Topinamboo;[140] of quitting our animosities and factions,[141] nor act any longer like the Jews, who were murdering one another at the very moment their city was taken;[142] of being a little cautious not to sell our country and consciences for nothing;[143] of teaching landlords to have at least one degree of mercy toward their tenants. Lastly, of putting a spirit of honesty, industry, and skill into our shopkeepers, who, if a resolution could now be taken[144] to buy only our native goods, would immediately unite to cheat and exact upon us in the price, the measure, and the goodness,[145] nor could ever yet be brought to make one fair proposal of just dealing, though often and earnestly invited to it.

Therefore, I repeat, let no man talk to me of these and the like expedients, till he hath at least some glimpse of hope that there will ever be some hearty[146] and sincere attempt to put them in practice.

But as to myself, having been wearied out for many years with offering vain, idle, visionary thoughts,[147] and at length utterly despairing of success, I fortunately fell upon this proposal; which, as it is wholly new, so it hath something solid and real, of no expense and little trouble, full in our own power,[148] and whereby we can incur no danger in disobliging England.[149] For this kind of commodity will not bear exportation, the flesh being of too tender a consistence to admit a long continuance in salt,[150] although perhaps I could name a country which would be glad to eat up our whole nation without it.[151]

After all, I am not so violently bent upon my own opinion, as to reject any offer proposed by wise men, which shall be found equally innocent,[152] cheap, easy, and effectual. But before something of that kind shall be advanced in contradiction to my scheme, and offering a better, I desire the author or authors will be pleased maturely to consider two points. First, as things now stand, how they will be able to find food and raiment for an hundred thousand useless mouths and backs. And secondly, there being a round million[153] of creatures in human figure,[154] throughout this Kingdom, whose whole subsistence put into a common stock,[155] would leave them in debt two millions of pounds sterling, adding those, who are beggars by profession, to the bulk of farmers, cottagers, and labourers, with their wives and children, who are beggars in effect; I desire those politicians, who dislike my overture,[156] and may perhaps be so bold to attempt an answer, that they will first ask the parents of these mortals,[157] whether they would not at this day think it a great happiness to have been sold for food at a year old, in the manner I prescribe, and thereby have avoided such a perpetual scene of misfortunes, as they have since gone through by the oppression of landlords,[158] the impossibility of paying rent without money or trade, the want of common sustenance,[159] with neither house nor clothes to cover them from the inclemencies of weather,[160] and the most inevitable prospect of entailing the like or greater miseries upon their breed for ever.[161]

I profess[162] in the sincerity of my heart that I have not the least personal interest in endeavoring to promote this necessary work, having no other motive than the public good of my country, by advancing our trade, providing for infants, relieving the poor, and *giving some pleasure to the rich.* I have no children by which I can propose[163] to get a single penny; the youngest being nine years old, and my wife past childbearing.[164]

【题解与注释】

《一个小小的建议》是斯威夫特最有名的政论文章，作于 1729 年，先在都柏林出版，接着在伦敦重版，到 1732 年共计印了七次，仅 1730 年一年就达五次之多，可见其流行之广。它是一般英文散文选集必备之作，不过多有删节，我们这里印行的则是全文。

爱尔兰在十六世纪以后沦为英国的属国，十八世纪虽仍保有单独的国会，但完全受伦敦政府的严密控制，人民在经济上受着英国商人和爱尔兰地主的双重剥削。在斯威夫特写此文之际，情形更加恶化。他在 1729 年 8 月 11 日从爱尔兰乡下写信给在伦敦的著名诗人蒲伯（Alexander Pope），这样描述当地的情况：

> 至于这个国家，它经历了三个可怕的歉收年头，现在到处充满了乞丐。但是即使在气候更好的地方，歉收也是常见的事情，可见我们这里的苦难还有更深的原因。试想一个国家将全部收入的三分之二花在国外，而剩下的三分之一又不许用来进行贸易；此外这个国家的女人由于虚荣不肯穿本国出产的衣料，即使国产

品比进口货好得多也是这样。简括言之，这就是爱尔兰的现状。

然而在这大灾三年、饥民遍野的时候，统治阶级的谋臣策士却还在穷苦人民的身上打主意，提出了各种旨在加深他们灾难的建议。这些人就是斯威夫特文章中所着重讽刺的“献策者”（projectors）。当时谈论爱尔兰人口问题的人很多，一些受英国资产阶级经济学中重商学派影响的“政治算学家”（political arithmeticians）扬言人民是“国家的财富”。实际上，他们的意思不过是：每人都象商品一样各有身价。例如有一个叫做 Samuel Madden 的人曾公开对爱尔兰贫民的身价作了估计，说是“每人可值三十镑，价与奴隶及黑人相等”。斯威夫特在此文里就是仿效了这些献策者的口吻，也象他们那样口口声声救国救民，也将人当作“财富”，也为了显示精确而用了各种数字，表面上也相信他们所提的种种主张，只不过将他们的主张略加引伸，推到其逻辑的极端，得出了这样的结论：既然乞丐太多，救济无方，那么为了使贫民由“公众的负担”转变为“国家的财富”，首先应该将他们的婴孩当作食物卖给有钱人吃掉，这样不仅可以解决许多献策者所焦虑的贫民人口过多的问题，而且还可以“给有钱人一点儿乐趣”（giving some pleasure to the rich）。他不止主张吃食一、二婴孩，而是建议将全体贫民所生的婴孩（除了少数留为传种者以外）一律杀掉——设想周到地、步骤分明地、最大规模地杀掉，而且成为今后的常规，贫民的婴孩就象鸡鸭一样，养了只是准备吃掉。这才是解决爱尔兰人口问题的唯一办法！这才是“人民乃国家财富”说在爱尔兰的具体实现！如果说这是极端残酷的建议，那么残酷的其实不是斯威夫特，他只是用献策者们的全部理论和逻辑，揭出了他们和他们的主子全是道地的吃人生番而已！

斯威夫特是一个“处心积虑，必获全胜”的作家。试看这篇文章所暴露情况的广度：乞丐遍地，大批壮丁流亡国外，一切修建和耕作都已停止，六岁的孩子就已精于偷窃之道，地主们普遍“不得人心”（Thus the squire will… *grow popular* among his tenants），有的地主根本住在外国逍遥，住在本国的就在连续大灾之年也仍是穷奢极欲——因此斯威夫特大谈人肉的各种烹调法，并建议他们用人皮作精致的手套和漂亮的凉靴。但是他并未忘记站在他们后面的英国官吏。他深知爱尔兰的地主对他们奉承逢迎，唯恐不力，因此特别意味深长地说：我这个建议毫无得罪英国的危险（…incur no danger in disobliging England）. 斯威夫特写此文时，象是只着眼爱尔兰地主，实际上他同时注视着英国政府。为了怕人还不清楚这一点，他接着写道：有一个国家恨不得能够将我们整个民族一口吞下；如果有需要的话，我完全可以说出这个国家的名字。

这种写法上的扬抑变化是本文的特色之一。总的说来，作者一本正经地以“献策者”自居，采取了用他们的议论暴露他们的用心的嘲讽（irony）方式；论到嘲讽运用之妙，本文是英国文学史上的顶峰之一。提出一个如此残忍的建议，而说得如此“合情合理”，最后又将责任如此不容逃避地牢牢钉在爱尔兰地主与英国政府身上，这不能不说是斯威夫特论辩艺术的一大成就。但是与侧面的嘲讽相辅相成的，还有正面的谴责。在紧要关头，他总要出来指点一下。上面提到的对英国的谴责便是一例。在文章结尾处提到“别的办法大不如我”（let no man talk to me of other expedients）时，一长串的项目当中，也是嘲讽与谴责交错，即使我们原先不甚注意，一读到“不要毫无代价地出卖我们的国家与良心”（not to sell our country and consciences for nothing）就必然会感到他那当面痛斥的力量。这痛斥力量之大，正在于它来得突然，出乎意外。下面的一例更可说明：

> I grant this food will be somewhat dear, and therefore very proper for landlords, who, as they have already devoured most of the parents, seem to have the best title to the children.

作者先是抱歉似地说：这种食物价钱可能昂贵一些，但是我想地主们不会介意；正因昂贵，地主们倒将认为适合他们的身份。我们读到这里，感到作者的辛辣，但以为文章到此而止，不料他却来了一个回马枪，用一个平行结构造成了戏剧性的对照，清楚地指出了：地主们已经吞食了穷孩子的父母，也就最有资格来享用穷孩子本身。这当中“吞食”（devoured）一词象是猛击一掌，令人愕然。然而接着却又是含有嘲讽的文雅字样：the best title to the children（享用这些儿童，最有权利）。一扬一抑，一野一文，因 title 之文而更增 devoured 之野，因 seem to have 之商榷口气而益显 have already devoured 之坚决肯定。这证明了斯威夫特所说“将恰当的词放在恰当的位置”的重要性。同时，我们也看到作者利用句子结构上的特点来造成令人吃惊的突然效果：一般人以为附属子句多半包含次要的意思，而斯威夫特在这里却用它点明了地主们的最大罪行。

但是 devoured 一词之所以用得好，还因为它唤起了野兽吞食的形象。人吃（eat）而兽吞（devour），这分别是明显的。这文章里充满了使人想起野兽的其他用语：devour 表其凶恶，用来形容地主；breed，breeder，dam，carcass，produce (another child)，creatures (in human figure) 等词则一再表明献策者是一个有身份的“上等人”，在他的眼里贫民只是野兽和家畜。更值得注意的，却是整篇文章所采用的冷静、文雅的文字与所建议的可怕罪行之间的明显矛盾。不仅冷静，文雅，不仅头头是道，而且彻底，彻底到要一劳永逸地解决爱尔兰全部贫穷人民的生活问题——既安排了儿童的命运，也安排了儿童的父母的生活。这矛盾，这彻底，都使我们看清了当时英国统治阶级所鼓吹、所推崇的理性的真相。不错，英国资产阶级曾经拿了理性做鞭子去打封建地主和教会，但是现在他们却拿理性做屠刀来杀害一个国家里的几乎全部的穷人了。从头起，他们的“理性王国”就是一个极为残酷的地方；殖民地种植园里的奴隶，遥远的亚非美各洲的受宰割的和平居民，十五世纪以来被不断的圈地运动弄得流离失所、家破人亡的广大英国农民，正在伦敦及英国北部城镇陆续出现的工厂工人，都是身受严重戕害的血淋淋的见证人；现在斯威夫特又提出了爱尔兰的全部贫民的命运，用了英国资产阶级的政治经济学的分析证明只有将穷苦儿童当作好菜吃掉才能解决这个严重的社会问题。骇人听闻的建议！然而斯威夫特使读者看出这又是完全合资产阶级之情，合资产阶级之理的。处在英国资产阶级正占优势的“盛世”，当斯威夫特的朋友大都满足于社会现状，连诗人蒲伯也歌唱“凡是存在的，都是合理的”的时候，斯威夫特能如此深切地关心爱尔兰贫民的命运，用精确、老练的文字写下了如此惊心动魄的控诉，在当时和后世的读者之间造成了十分深刻的印象，这说明了斯威夫特的眼光，这也突出了斯威夫特的成就。

标题　英国十八世纪的政论小册往往有很长的标题。斯威夫特也照通例用了长题。后世读者则为了方便，以简题 *A Modest Proposal* 称之。原题交代了文章的表面用意，象是作者要献出一条妙计，使爱尔兰的贫苦儿童不但不至成为他们父母及国家的负担，反而能有益于社会。然而他又故示谦逊，自称所献之策微不足道，因此用了 modest 一词，它的词义不是“温和”，而是“小小的，没有什么野心的”。又：此小册于 1729 年在都柏林出版时，未署作者姓名，同年在伦敦再版时，始有 By Dr. Swift 字样。

1. a melancholy object: 一种悲惨的景象。

2. this great town: 指爱尔兰首都都柏林（Dublin）.

3. three, four, or six children: 作者列举这些数字，表示贫苦儿童之多，也表示自己严肃从事，十分精确。

4. importuning every passenger: asking every passer-by，央求每个过路行人；passenger 现在一般只作“旅客”讲，与此处用法不同。

5. alms: 施舍（注意此词复数形式，但作单数用）。

6. sustenance: 意同 livelihood，即生活所需。

7. want: 缺乏。下文 wanting food and raiment, butchers will not be wanting 中的 wanting 也都是“缺乏”之意。

8. the Pretender in Spain: 指 James Stuart (1688–1766)，英王 James II 之子，父子都信天主教。James II 于 1688 年为英国资产阶级逐出英国，王位改由其女 Mary 与其婿荷兰国王 William 承继。但 James Stuart 虽随父在外国流亡，仍不放弃承继王位的企图，自称 James III，人称 The Pretender（自称有承继王位权者）。他曾随法军入侵荷兰一带，并组织军队于 1708 及 1715 年在苏格兰登陆，准备夺取英国王位，但都遭失败。爱尔兰人反英情绪强烈，因此贫民在本国无以为生时，有往投 James Stuart 作雇佣军者，但另外也有人卖身去西印度群岛为英国殖民者作仆役、工头等等。

9. the Barbadoes [bɑːˈbeidəuz]: 西印度群岛中一个岛，当时英国殖民地之一。

10. all parties: all people concerned; parties 在此不指政党。

11. prodigious: great；十八世纪作家喜用此词，现代文章中则少见。

12. the Kingdom: 指爱尔兰。

13. grievance: 民怨，造成人民不满的原因。

14. commonwealth: 国家，亦指爱尔兰。

15. deserve so well of the public: 对公众有功，值得大家感谢。

16. preserver of the nation: 保全民族的功臣。

17. to provide ... for: 安排…的生活。

18. professed beggars: professional beggars，以讨饭为职业的人们。

19. in effect: 实际上。

20. As to my own part: as for me，至于我。

21. maturely weighed: 仔细考虑过。

22. several: 各个。

23. projectors: 献策者，提出各种建议的人。当时由于爱尔兰经济情况恶劣，不少人提出各种筹款的建议，其中有设想荒诞者，有事类骗局者，而用心所在，无不以使贫民陷入更大的苦难为终极目的。斯威夫特为了揭露他们，故意模仿他们的口气写了此文。

24. grossly: greatly.

25. dam: 母（一般用来指野兽，斯威夫特用它，是为了表示他同别的献策者一样，是一个把劳动人民看作兽类的"上等人"；同句动词用 dropped from 而不说 born of，也表示不是谈人，而是谈兽）。

26. a solar year: 一整年，作者用 solar（阳历）字样，也是故意为了表示精确：a solar year = 365 天又 5 小时 48 分 46 秒。

27. above: over，超过。

28. value in scraps:（乞讨来的）残羹冷炙的价值。

29. charge: 经济上的负担。

30. the parish:（贫民所属的）教区。

31. abortions: 人工流产，堕胎。

32. horrid practice of ... murdering: 作者在此大叫"可怕"、"谋杀"，但是他所要提出的建议却是还要可怕千百倍的大规模屠杀婴儿。这是一个伏笔。

33. bastard children: 私生子。

34. babes: = babies.（按 babe 是原来拼法，后来才为 baby 所代。）

35. I doubt: I fear，我以为。

36. souls: 人。

37. couple: 单数此处作复数用，一般用于兽类（见牛津大字典 couple 条）。但下文作 couples，一般指人类夫妻。

38. breeders: 有生育能力的女性。（这也是一个一般用于兽类的轻蔑字。）

39. apprehend: understand.

40. this being granted: 承认了这点之后（即接受了有三万对夫妇能够供养自己子女的估计之后）。

41. miscarry: 流产。

42. neither employ them in handicraft or agriculture: 全句应作 employ them neither in handicraft nor in agriculture.

43. we neither build houses ... nor cultivate land: 注意此处所透露的爱尔兰人民生活的惨状。

44. towardly parts: 天生早熟，指年纪很小就有偷窃的能力。

45. learn the rudiments much earlier: 远在（六岁）以前，就已学到（偷窃的）基本知识。

46. probationers: 试用者，实习生。

47. county of Cavan ['kævən]**:** 爱尔兰北部之一郡。

48. protested: 郑重地说。

49. quickest proficiency in that art: 特别擅长那项本领。

50. no saleable commodity: 不是可出售的商品（不能作为商品出售；当时贫民常将子女当作奴婢卖给富人，但十二岁以下的儿童无人愿买）。

51. yield: 赚取（利润）。

52. the Exchange: 交易所，此处似泛指市场。

53. cannot turn to account either to the parents or the Kingdom: cannot be useful or profitable to their parents or Ireland，对于儿童的父母和国家都没有好处。

54. a very knowing American: 一个深知内情的美国人。

55. I make no doubt: I have no doubt.

56. serve: satisfy, do what is required，令人满意。

fricassee [frikə'si:]，燉肉片或炒肉丝（原系法语）。

ragout ['rægu:]，一种肉丁与蔬菜同煮的菜（原系法语）。

57. seldom the fruits of marriage: 很少是正式结婚的产物。

58. not much regarded: 不被重视。（意为野人杂交，无婚姻礼法。）

59. That the remaining hundred thousand may: 此句为一从句，that 接第 21 行的 I do humbly offer it，与第 22 行的 that 一样；此处标点与大写都是十八世纪用法。

60. persons of quality and fortune: 有地位和有钱的人。

61. for a good table: for a good dinner.

62. entertainment for friends: 请朋友吃饭。

63. the fore or hind [haind] **quarter:** 兽类的前腿或后腿，此处指婴儿的一臂或一腿。

64. seasoned: 调味。

65. upon a medium: on the average，平均而论，一般说来。

66. tolerably: 相当好地。

67. I grant this food will be somewhat dear: 这是本文中最常为人引用的一段。图穷匕现，斯威夫特反对当地地主的锋芒毕露了。（请参阅题解）

68. the best title: 最大的权利（即最有资格）。

69. in season: fit for eating，指副食品生产的旺季。

70. a grave author: 指法国文艺复兴时期著名作家拉伯雷（François Rabelais 1494？—1553），他曾行医。称滑稽大师拉伯雷为“严肃的作家”显系嘲讽（irony）.

71. prolific diet: 有助生育的食物。

72. Lent: 四旬斋，约自一月底到三月二十一日左右。天主教徒在斋戒期间只吃鱼，不吃肉。

73. Popish: 天主教的，按此词含有敌视之意。

74. three to one: 三与一之比，按爱尔兰居民多数信天主教，天主教家庭所生的孩子为新教家庭所生孩子数目的三倍。

75. collateral: 附带的。

76. Papists: 罗马教皇的信徒们（此词带有轻视之意，按斯威夫特是装作一个英国人后代的爱尔兰新教徒来写此文的，因此主张减少爱尔兰的天主教徒的人数）。

77. cottagers: 爱尔兰的贫农，他们向地主租一小屋（cottage）居住，同时租一小块土地耕种，故名。

78. per annum: each year，每年（拉丁文）。

79. carcass: dead body（常指兽类，只在要表达鄙视时才用来指人）。

80. Thus the squire will learn to be a good landlord, and grow popular among his tenants: 这样，乡绅老爷会学会如何做一个好东家，从而受到他的佃户们的爱戴。（按：此语透露当时地主与贫农之间的矛盾之大。）

81. flay: 剥皮。

82. artificially dressed: 经过人工处理。

83. shambles: 屠宰场（复数作单数用）。

84. dressing them hot from the knife: 刚一杀完，立即准备上灶（dressing 指洗、切、放作料等烹饪前的准备工作）。

85. refinement upon my scheme: improvement upon my plan，比我的计策更妙的一着。

86. with due deference to: 对…怀着应有的敬意。

87. so deserving a patriot: 一个这样值得人们感谢的爱国志士（用 patriot 一词，意为献此策者有功于国家）。

88. I cannot be altogether in his sentiments: 未敢苟同；窃以为未必尽然。

89. would not answer the charge: 抵不上所花的费用。

90. with humble submission: humbly asking for correction if wrong，如有错误，愿意虚心改正（一种客气话，早已不用）。

91. a little bordering upon cruelty: 有点近乎残忍。

92. Psalmanazar, George (1679?–1763): 当时一个大骗子的假名，此人冒充是台湾人，曾写一本记述台湾的书（*A Historical and Geographical Description of Formosa*，1704），捏造了许多事情。斯威夫特在此段中所谈台湾种种，受此人影响，纯系虚构。

93. mandarins: 官僚们。

94. in joints from the gibbet: 从钉在绞刑架上的尸体上割下来的大块人肉。

95. at four hundred crowns: 价值四百克朗（一克朗值五先令）。

96. without one single groat to their fortunes: 一文不名，一点财产也没有；groat，英国古银币，值四便士（很小的数目）。

97. stir abroad: 出门；abroad 此处意为 out of doors.

98. chair: 轿子。

99. assemblies: 社交场所。

100. foreign fineries: 进口的华丽衣料。当时爱尔兰统治阶级妇女“由于虚荣，不愿穿本国出产的衣料，即使质地超过外国产品也不愿穿”（斯威夫特 1729 年 8 月 11 日致蒲伯函）。

101. to ease the nation of so grievous an encumbrance: 使国家解脱这样难堪的负担。

102. not in the least pain upon that matter: 对于那事一点儿也不着急。按 pain 一词现已不作此用。

103. as hopeful a condition: 同样有希望的情况。（作者继续仿照统治阶级的口气说话，指出这等人会自行灭亡，不用“上等人”发愁，因此事情对统治者有利）。

104. pine away: 消瘦，衰弱下去。

105. thus the country and themselves are happily delivered from the evils to come: 这样国家和他们自己都可以幸运地免受未来灾祸之苦。（亦即他们会很快死去，不至成为国家之祸。）

106. digressed: 谈到题外去了。

107. overrun: 泛滥（指天主教徒人多）。

108. with a design to deliver the Kingdom to the Pretender: 阴谋将国家交给自称有权承继王位的 James Stuart（参阅第 373 页注 8）。

109. to take their advantage by the absence of so many good Protestants: 利用许多善良的新教徒的出走，乘机占得优势。

110. tithes: 十一税，即田租的十分之一归教会，用以供养教士。当时不少祖籍英国（因而是新教徒的）的地主不愿交纳十一税，为此长期居住国外。斯威夫特站在教会立场，不满地主们这种行为。1729 年 12 月 11 日曾写信给蒲伯说："十一税虽是上帝所创立，却是魔鬼所执行。（Although tithes be of divine institution, they are of diabolical execution. ）"

111. episcopal curate: 主教委派的教士。

112. by law may be made liable to distress: 按照法律可以没收偿债（distress 在此是法律用语，意为"扣留财物拍卖，以所得偿付欠债，尤其欠租"）。

113. apiece: each，每人（指每个儿童）。

114. stock: 储备金。

115. rid of the charge: 免去…的费用。

116. custom: 生意、买卖（= 许多顾客）。

117. vintners: wine merchants，此处指酒店老板。

118. receipts [ri'si:ts]**:** 此处 = recipes，食谱。

119. a great inducement to marriage: 对于婚姻的一大激励。（即足以促进婚姻。这一段的讽刺在于表明妇女的作用只在生产一种商品——可以用作食物的婴孩。）

120. settlement for life: 一生的费用。

121. emulation: 竞赛。

122. mares in foal, ... cows in calf, ... sows when they are ready to farrow: 马将产驹，牛将产犊，猪将产豚的时候。（此处将穷人妻子比作家畜。）

123. barrelled beef: 桶装的牛肉。

124. the propagation of swine's flesh：繁殖生猪。

125. so much wanted among us:（是）我们所十分缺乏的。

126. too frequent at our tables: 指爱尔兰有钱人经常吃食猪肉。

127. magnificence: 丰盛。

128. make a considerable figure: 受人注意，颇出风头。

129. being studious of brevity: 由于我讲究扼要，不喜冗长。

130. one thousand families: 由此可见都柏林城内只有一千富户。

131. This I freely own: 这一点我完全承认；freely，无条件地，无保留地。

132. design: 用意。（我提出吃食婴孩，正是为了减少人口。）

133. calculate my remedy for: adapt my remedy to，我所提出的救国之道只适合于。

134. for no other that ever was, is, or ... ever can be upon earth: 不是为过去、现在或将来的任何其他国家。

135. taxing our absentees at five shillings a pound: 对于住在外国的爱尔兰地主按照其收入课以每镑五先令的税金。此处 absentees 主要指 landlords，即在爱尔兰有田租收入而住在国外的地主，当时爱尔兰舆论指摘这等人。认为他们在外国逍遥，使本国资金外流，对本国的经济有害，因此主张按照其收入课以重税。但此词也指身居外国而在爱尔兰领干薪的人，1729 年 11 月（即此文写成的同时）爱尔兰国会通过法律，规定对这些人的薪给（salaries）课以每镑四先令的税金，即是证明。

136. promote foreign luxury: 提倡外国的奢侈品。

137. gaming: 赌博。

138. a vein of parsimony, prudence, and temperance: 一种省俭、审慎和节制（temperance 特指戒酒）的精神。

139. Laplanders: Lapland 的居民，地在北欧斯堪的内维亚半岛的北端。曾分属俄、瑞、挪等国，居民以狩猎为生，分散居住，各自为政。斯威夫特用他们来讽刺爱尔兰人之无爱国心。

140. Topinamboo: 巴西之一区，当时人以为特别野蛮，斯威夫特也是用他们来讽刺爱尔兰人野蛮到无爱国观念。

141. quitting our animosities and factions: 戒除内部的仇视与党争。

142. the Jews, who were murdering one another at the very moment their city was taken: 指公元 70 年罗马帝国大军在大将 Vespasian 与 Titus 率领下进攻耶路撒冷（Jerusalem）城时，城内犹太人还在内哄。

143. not to sell our country and consciences for nothing: 不再毫无代价地出卖我们的祖国和良心。

144. if a resolution could now be taken: 如果通过决议。

145. to cheat and exact upon us in the price, the measure, and the goodness: 在价目、分量和质地方面欺骗我们，使我们吃亏；exact upon us，硬要我们出钱。

146. hearty: 全心全意的。

147. having been wearied out for many years with offering vain, idle, visionary thoughts: 多年来提出了许多无用的、迂阔的、空想的看法，使我已经疲惫不堪。（斯威夫特在此慨乎言之。但他并未绝望，紧接此文之后，他又写《建议女士们经常穿着本国衣料书》—*Proposal that All Ladies Should Appear Constantly in Irish Manufactures*，1729—等文，不断提出为爱尔兰人民利益设想的新建议）。

148. full in our power: 完全在我们能力之内。

149. incur no danger in disobliging England: 不至有得罪英国的危险；disobliging 是 obliging 的反面，obliging 意为有求必应，使客人感到满意；disobliging 表示不

能做到这点。斯威夫特用此词是有深意的，他暗示爱尔兰的统治阶级向来逢迎英国官吏，在他们面前总是小心翼翼，生怕有任何一点不周到的地方。

150. too tender a consistence to admit a long continuance in salt: 肉质太嫩，不能长期放在盐内。

151. I could name a country which would be glad to eat up our whole nation without it: 这里又透露斯威夫特的真意所在，a country 指英国；it 指 salt, without it 意为不用调味，活活吞下。

152. innocent: 无害的，无恶意的。

153. a round million: 一百万整数；round figures，整数。

154. creatures in human figure: 人形的动物，指贫民。斯威夫特一直仿照统治阶级口气，将贫民看作兽类。

155. put into a common stock: 加成一笔总数。

156. overture: 此处特指 proposal（古时用法），即建议。

157. these mortals: 这些人。

158. the oppression of landlords: 这一句所揭出的一连串的贫民苦难，无论在用词与节奏上都表明了作者行文至此，抑制不住自己的心头怒火，因此采取了直接的谴责方式。

159. the want of common sustenance: 缺乏共同的谋生途径（意为没有一笔公共救济金）。

160. the inclemencies of weather: 天气的严酷（指酷寒暴暑之类）。

161. the most inevitable prospect of entailing the like or greater miseries upon their breed for ever: 展望前途，只有一个必然的归宿（entail，带来必然的后果），即后代子孙必将遭受同样的或更大的苦难。此处 breed（后代）与上文 breeder 一样，指兽类。

162. profess: 郑重申明。

163. propose: 计划、打算。

164. my wife past childbearing: 我的妻子已过了生育儿女的年龄。（这最后的一句话也是饱含讽刺。作者竭力表明作此建议非从私利出发，言下之意是别的献策者都有个人目的。同时，他又暗示这种血淋淋的事情不会落到他自己头上，只有别家的婴孩才会给人吃掉，从另一角度证明献策者的极端自私。）

15 WILLIAM CONGREVE 1670 – 1729

The Way of the World
Act IV, Scene 5
Act IV, Scene 12

李赋宁　选注

THE WAY OF THE WORLD

Act IV, Scene 5

Millamant, Mirabell.

Milla. Like Phœbus sung[1] the no less am'rous boy.

Mira. Like Daphne she,[2] as lovely and as coy.

Do you lock yourself up from me, to make my search more curious[3]? Or is this pretty artifice[4] contrived to signify that here the chase must end, and my pursuit be crowned,[5] for you can fly no further?

Milla. Vanity[6]! No — I'll fly and be followed to the last moment. Though I am upon the very verge of matrimony,[7] I expect you should solicit me as much as if I were wavering at the grate of a monastery,[8] with one foot over the threshold. I'll be solicited to the very last, nay,[9] and afterwards.

Mira. What, after the last?

Milla. O, I should think I was poor and had nothing to bestow, if I were reduced to an inglorious ease and freed from the agreeable fatigues of solicitation.

Mira. But do not you know, that when favours are conferred upon instant and tedious solicitation,[10] that they diminish in their value, and that both the giver loses the grace[11] and the receiver lessens his pleasure?

Milla. It may be in things of common application[12], but never sure[13] in love. O, I hate a lover that can dare[14] to think he draws a moment's air independent on[15] the bounty of his mistress. There is not so impudent a thing in nature as the saucy look of an assured man, confident of success. The pedantic arrogance[16] of a very husband[17] has not so pragmatical[18] an air. Ah! I'll never marry, unless I am first made sure of my will[19] and pleasure.

Mira. Would you have 'em[20] both before marriage? Or will you be contented with the first[21] now and stay for[22] the other[23] till after grace[24]?

Milla. Ah, don't be impertinent.[25]—My dear liberty, shall I leave thee? My faithful solitude, my darling contemplation, must I bid you then adieu? Ay-h, adieu—My morning thoughts, agreeable wakings, indolent slumbers, all ye *douceurs,* ye *sommeils du matin,*[26] adieu?—I can't do't,[27] 'tis more than impossible. Positively, Mirabell, I'll lie abed in a morning as long as I please.

Mira. Then I'll get up in a morning as early as I please.

Milla. Ah, idle creature, get up when you will. —And d'ye hear? I won't be called names after I'm married; positively I won't be called names.

Mira. Names?

Milla. Aye, as wife, spouse, my dear, joy, jewel, love, sweetheart, and the rest of that nauseous cant[28] in which men and their wives are so fulsomely familiar—I shall never bear that. —Good Mirabell, don't let us be familiar[29] or fond,[30] nor kiss before folks, like my Lady Fadler[31] and Sir Francis; nor go to Hyde Park[32] together the first Sunday in a new chariot to provoke eyes and whispers,[33] and then never to be seen together again, as if we were proud of one another the first week and ashamed of one another for ever after. Let us never visit together nor go to a play together, but let us be very strange[34] and well bred.[35] Let us be as strange as if we had been married a great while, and as well bred as if we were not married at all.

Mira. Have you any more conditions to offer? Hitherto your demands are pretty reasonable.

Milla. Trifles, —as[36] liberty to pay and receive visits to and from whom I please; to write and receive letters, without interrogatories[37] or wry faces[38] on your part. To wear what I please, and choose conversation with regard only to my own taste; to have no obligation upon me to converse with wits[39] that I don't like, because they are your acquaintance; or to be intimate with fools because they may be your relations. Come to dinner when I please, dine in my dressing-room when I'm out of humour,[40] without giving a reason. To have my closet[41] inviolate;[42] to be sole empress of my teatable, which you must never presume[43] to approach without first asking leave.[44] And lastly, wherever I am, you shall always knock at the door before you come in. These articles subscribed,[45] if I continue to endure you a little longer, I may by degrees[46] dwindle into a wife.[47]

Mira. Your bill of fare[48] is something advanced[49] in this latter account.[50] Well, have I liberty to offer conditions—that when you are dwindled into a wife, I may not[51] be beyond measure enlarged into a husband?[52]

Milla. You have free leave. Propose your utmost; speak and spare not.

Mira. I thank you. *Imprimis*[53] then,[54] I covenant[55] that your acquaintance be general; that you admit no sworn[56] confidante[57] or intimate[58] of your own sex, no she-friend[59] to screen her affairs[60] under your countenance[61] and tempt you to make trial of a mutual secrecy.[62] No decoy-duck[63] to wheedle you a-fop-scrambling[64] to the play in a mask[65]—then bring you home in a pretended fright, when you think you shall be found out—and rail at me for missing the play[66] and disappointing the frolic which you had,[67] to pick me up and prove my constancy.[68]

Milla. Detestable *imprimis*! I go to the play in a mask!

Mira. *Item*,[69] I article,[70] that you continue to like your own face as long as I shall; and while it passes current[71] with me, that you endearour not to new-coin it.[72] To which end,[73] together with all vizards[74] for the day, I prohibit all masks for the night, made of oiled-skins[75] and I know not what—hog's bones,[76] hare's gall, pig-water, and the marrow of a roasted cat. In short, I forbid all commerce[77] with the gentlewoman[78] in What-d'ye-call-it-Court.[79] *Item,* I shut my doors against all bawds with baskets,[80] and pennyworths of muslin, china,[81] fans, atlases,[82] etc. —*Item*, when you shall be breeding[83]—

Milla. Ah! Name it not.

Mira. Which may be presumed, with a blessing on our endeavours[84]—

Milla. Odious endeavours!

Mira. I denounce against all strait lacing,[85] squeezing for a shape,[86] till you mold my boy's head like a sugar-loaf;[87] and instead of a man-child,[88] make me the father to a crooked billet.[89] Lastly, to the dominion of the tea-table I submit, —but with proviso:[90] that you exceed not in your province;[91] but restrain yourself to native and simple tea-table drinks, as tea, chocolate, and coffee, as likewise to genuine and authorized[92] tea-table talk—such as mending of fashions,[93] spoiling reputations,[94] railing at absent friends,[95] and so forth—but that on no account you encroach upon the men's prerogative and presume to drink healths or toast fellows; for prevention of which I banish[96] all foreign forces, all auxiliaries[97] to the tea-table, as orange-brandy, all aniseed, cinnamon citron, and Barbados waters,[98] together with ratafia and the most noble spirit of clary.[99]—But for cowslip-wine, poppy water, and all dormitives,[100] those I allow. These provisos admitted,[101] in other things I may prove[102] a tractable and complying husband.[103]

Milla. O, horrid provisos! filthy strong waters! I toast fellows, odious men! I hate your odious provisos.

Mira. Then we're agreed. Shall I kiss your hand upon the contract?[104] And here comes one[105] to be a witness to the sealing of the deed.

[*Enter* Mrs. Fainall]

Milla. Fainall. what shall I do? Shall I have him? I think I must have him.

Mrs. Fainall. Aye, aye, take him, take him, what should you do?

Milla. Well then—I'll take my death, I'm in a horrid fright—Fainall, I shall never say it—well—I think—I'll endure you.

Mrs. Fainall. Fie, fie! have him, have him, and tell him so in plain terms; for I am sure you have a mind to[106] him.

Milla. Are you? I think I have—and the horrid man looks as if he thought so too.—Well, you ridiculous thing you, I'll have you—I won't be kissed, nor I won't be thanked—here, kiss my hand though.—So, hold your tongue now, and don't say a word.

Mrs. Fainall. Mirabell, there's a necessity for your obedience; —you have neither time to talk nor stay. My mother is coming;[107] and in my conscience, if she should see you, would fall into fits,[108] and maybe not recover time enough[109] to return to Sir Rowland,[110] who as Foible[111] tells me, is in a fair way to succeed.[112] Therefore spare your ecstasies for another occasion, and slip down the back stairs, where Foible waits to consult you.

Milla. Aye, go, go. In the meantime I suppose you have said something to please me.

Mira. I am all obedience.

[*Exit* Mirabell]

Act IV, Scene 12

Lady Wishfort, Waitwell disguised as for Sir Rowland.

Lady. Dear Sir Rowland, I am confounded with confusion[113] at the retrospection of[114] my own rudeness—I have more pardons to ask than the Pope distributes in the Year of Jubilee.[115] But I hope where there is likely to be so near an alliance—we may unbend the severity of decorum—and dispense with a little ceremony.

Wait. My impatience, madam, is the effect of my transport[116]—and till I have the possession of your adorable person,[117] I am tantalized on the rack;[118] and do but hang, madam, on the tenter of expectation.[119]

Lady. You have excess of gallantry, Sir Rowland; and press things to a conclusion, with a most prevailing vehemence. —But a day or two for decency of marriage. —

Wait. For decency of funeral, madam. The delay will break my heart—or if that should fail, I shall be poisoned. My nephew[120] will get an inkling of my designs, and poison me—and I would willingly starve him before I die—I would gladly go out of the world with that satisfaction. —That would be some comfort to me, if I could but live so long as to be revenged on that unnatural[121] viper.[122]

Lady. Is he so unnatural, say you? Truly I would contribute much both to the saving of your life, and the accomplishment of your revenge—Not that I respect myself;[123] though he has been a perfidious wretch to me.

Wait. Perfidious to you!

Lady. O Sir Rowland, the hours that he has died away at my feet, the tears that he has shed, the oaths that he has sworn, the palpitations that he has felt, the trances and the tremblings, the ardours and the ecstasies, the kneelings and the risings, the heart-heavings and the hand-gripings, the pangs and the pathetic regards of his protesting eyes[124]! Oh, no memory can register.

Wait. What, my rival! Is the rebel my rival?[125] a dies.[126]

Lady. No, don't kill him at once, Sir Rowland, starve him gradually inch by inch.

Wait. I'll do't. In three weeks he shall be barefoot;[127] in a month out at knees[128] with begging an alms[129]—he shall starve upward and upward, till he has nothing living but his head, and then go out in a stink like a candle's end upon a saveall.[130]

Lady. Well, Sir Rowland, you have the way. —You are no novice in the labyrinth of love—you have the clue—but as I am a person, Sir Rowland, you must not attribute my yielding to any sinister appetite,[131] or indigestion of widowhood;[132] nor impute my complacency[133] to any lethargy of continence.[134]—I hope you do not think me prone to any iteration of nuptials.[135]—

Wait. Far be it from me[136]—

Lady. If you do, I protest[137] I must recede[138]—or think that[139] I have made a prostitution of decorums,[140] but in the vehemence of passion, and to save the life of a person of so much importance—

Wait. I esteem it so—

Lady. Or else you wrong my condescension[141]—

Wait. I do not, I do not—

Lady. Indeed you do.

Wait. I do not, fair shrine of virtue.[142]

Lady. If you think the least scruple[143] of carnality[144] was an ingredient—

Wait. Dear madam, no. You are all camphire and frankincense,[145] all chastity and odour.

Lady. Or that[146]—

【作者简介】 威廉·康格里夫(William Congreve, 1670–1728)是十七世纪英国剧作家，被公认为复辟时期风尚喜剧(the Restoration comedy of manners）最优秀的代表。他父亲是驻扎在爱尔兰的英国军官，因此威廉早年就在爱尔兰求学，与斯威夫特（Swift）有同窗之谊。康格里夫写的第一个剧本是《老光棍》（*The Old Bachelor*, 1693），是在德莱顿（Dryden）赞助下演出的，受到观众的欢迎。接着康格里夫又写了三个喜剧：《两面派》（*The Double Dealer*, 1693），《以爱还爱》（*Love for Love*, 1695），和他的杰作《如此世道》（*The Way of the World*, 1700）。在这些喜剧里，康格里夫显示出足以和莫里哀（Molière）相媲美的喜剧才能和典雅、机智的舞台对话。他还写了一部悲剧《新婚悼亡》（*The Mourning Bride*, 1697）。当时英国有一位传教士名叫杰里米·考里尔（Jeremy Collier, 1650–1726），写了一篇文章《关于英国舞台道德沦丧和渎亵神灵之管见》（*A Short View of the Immorality and Profaneness of the English Stage*, 1698），猛烈攻击复辟时期英国戏剧之不道德。康格里夫愤怒地答复了这个攻击。1700 年以后，康格里夫结束了他的戏剧创作生涯，但却经常和其他作家来往，包括斯威夫特，斯迪尔（Steele），蒲伯（Pope），以及访英的法国作家伏尔泰（Voltaire）等知名之士。

【题解与注释】

《如此世道》是一部典型的复辟时期风尚喜剧。所谓风尚喜剧，指的是反映上层阶级社会风尚的喜剧。这些上层阶级包括国王查理二世（Charles II）和他手下的朝臣和其他宫廷人物。他们反对清教徒严峻的道德准则，走向男女关系杂乱和性生活绝对自由的另一极端。实际上，复辟时期风尚喜剧对这种上层社会道德败坏的风尚是抱着揭露、谴责、讽刺的态度的。这是一种批判的喜剧，其目的在于革除陋习，用“常识的利剑”（the sword of common sense）来割掉社会的恶疮。尤其是康格里夫的风尚喜剧，具有严肃的道德目的。《如此世道》就是这样一部喜剧。它的主题是两性之间关系的道德问题。康格里夫赞美的是夫妻之间忠诚、真挚的爱情，谴责的是两性之间的不合法的、不道德的、和不负责任的自私的男女关系。《如此世道》歌颂的是正面人物男主角 Mirabell 和女主角 Millamant 之间的纯洁的爱情和婚姻关系。与此相反，它无情地揭露和讽刺了有钱的老寡妇 Lady Wishfort 的荒淫无耻和玩弄女性的花花公子 Fainall 的虚伪、贪婪和不择手段。我们从《如此世道》里选注了两场：第四幕第五场和第四幕第十二场。前一场是有名的“谈判场”（the bargaining scene），即包括 Mirabell 和 Millamant 为婚后共同生活而相互提出一系列有趣条件的精彩对话的一场。后一场写的是 Mirabell 的仆人 Waitwell 化装、冒充贵族 Sir Rowland，并且假装向有钱的老寡妇 Lady Wishfort 求婚，以便充分暴露老寡妇的丑恶嘴脸。在这场戏里，康格里夫有意识地运用了上层社会矫揉造作、虚伪、夸张的求爱语言，来揭露老妇的无耻和假正经，以及仆人的假斯文和愚昧无知。

1. Like Phœbus sung ...: 引自 Edmund Waller (1606–87) 的诗 *The Story of Phœ-*

bus and Daphne Applied。根据希腊神话，Phœbus（即日神 Apollo）追求仙女 Daphne. 为了逃避 Phœbus 的追逐，Daphne 化作月桂树（a laurel tree）.

2. Like Daphne she ...: Mirabell 接着 Millamant 所引的 Waller 的诗行，继续引了下去。Mirabell 自比 Phoebus，而把逃避他的求爱的 Millamant 比作 Daphne. 因此他接着问 Millamant: "Do you lock yourself up from me …?"

3. curious: difficult, intricate, laborious（困难，复杂，费力）。

4. pretty artifice: clever trick（聪明的伎俩）。

5. be crowned: i. e., must be crowned with victory or successfully concluded（必然以胜利结束）。

6. vanity: being excessively proud of oneself, exaggerated self-importance（过度骄傲，过份地自以为了不起）。

7. upon the verge of matrimony: i. e., on the point of being married（即将结婚）。

8. the grate of a monastery: i. e., the grated door of a convent（女修道院的安装着铁条栏杆的大门）。进了修道院就意味着终生不结婚。

9. nay: not only that, but also（不仅如此，而且）。

10. instant and tedious solicitation: i. e., urgent (or pressing) and tiresome (or wearying) begging（迫不及待的、令人厌倦的、苦苦的哀求）。

11. grace: good will, kindness（好心肠、善意）。

12. application: use（用途）。

13. sure: undoubtedly true（毫无疑问地是这样）。

14. can dare: 在这里 *dare* 不是辅助动词（auxiliary verb），而是主要动词（main verb），义为 'have enough courage or audacity'（敢于，胆敢）。

15. independent on: not depending on, independent of（不依赖）。

16. pedantic arrogance: school-masterly arrogance（象男老师那样专横）。

17. a very husband: a husband in the full sense of the word（十足的丈夫，地地道道的丈夫）。

18. pragmatical: conceited, self-important（自高自大，骄傲自满）。

19. will: inclination（爱好，倾心）。

20. 'em: them，指 will and pleasure（爱好和乐趣，倾心和享受）。

21. the first: 指 my will（我的爱好，我所倾心的人）。

22. stay for: wait for（等待）。

23. the other: 指 my pleasure（我的乐趣，我的享受）。

24. after grace: grace = a short prayer in which blessing is asked, or thanks are given, for a meal（饭前或饭后的感恩祷告）。在这里，*after grace* 有 after the marriage ceremony 的含义（试比较成语 dinner without grace 义为"未举行婚礼而同房"）。

25. don't be impertinent: 休得无礼。这是 Millamant 针对 Mirabell 所说的话的含义（即'婚后同房'）而说的。

26. douceurs, sommeils du matin: comforts and morning sleep（ 安 逸 和 睡懒觉）。

27. I can't do't: i. e., I can't get married（我不能结婚）。

28. cant: insincere or almost meaningless talk used merely from convention or habit（仅根据习俗或习惯而说的不诚恳的话或几乎是毫无意义的话）。

29. familiar: intimate（亲热）。

30. fond: very affectionate（多情）。

31. Fadler: 康格里夫剧中人物的姓名大多数都有寓义。这里 Lady Fadler 这个姓的寓义显然是 Fondler（= caresser 抚爱者，来自动词 fondle = caress 抚爱，抚摸）。

32. Hyde Park: a public park in London where fashionable people used to appear, riding in their carriages（伦敦海德公园。过去时髦人物经常乘坐马车在这个公园里抛头露面）。

33. to provoke eyes and whispers: to arouse attention and comments（惹人注目和议论）。

34. strange: distant or reserved（疏远或冷淡）。

35. well bred: courteous（彬彬有礼）。

36. Trifles, —as: small matters, such as（琐碎小事，例如）。

37. interrogatories: questions or inquiries（讯问或调查）。

38. wry faces: twisted faces expressing displeasure（表示不满的脸色）。

39. wits: persons endowed with wit（富于机智的人，才子）。

40. out of humour: out of temper, displeased（情绪不佳）。

41. closet: a small private room（私室，小房间）。

42. inviolate: kept sacred（保持神圣不可侵犯）。

43. presume: take upon oneself to do with overboldness（擅自，胆敢）。

44. leave: permission（许可，同意）。

45. These articles subscribed: these conditions having been agreed to（这些条件被同意后）。

46. by degrees: little by little, gradually（一点一点地，逐渐地）。

47. dwindle into a wife: grow smaller into a wife（缩小成为一个妻子）。照 Millamant 看来，她结婚后将受到许多限制，权利缩小了，自由行动的范围也缩小了，因此她说 dwindle into a wife.

48. bill of fare: a list of the foods served, menu（菜单）。

49. something advanced: somewhat extended（相当长）。

50. in this latter account: in this last statement（在后面这段话里——指后面所提的许多条件）。

51. that when you are dwindled into a wife, I may not ...: in order that when you have dwindled into a wife, I may not ...（为了当你缩小成为妻子时，我不至于…）。

52. be beyond measure enlarged into a hushand: be expanded to an exceedingly great degree into a husband（被过度膨胀成为一个丈夫）。Mirabell 所说的这句话在句子结构上和语义上都和 Millamant 说的那句调皮话成为对偶（antithesis）：I may by degrees dwindle into a wife.

I may not beyond measure be enlarged into a husband.

53. Imprimis: [im'praimis] first of all (in the language of a legal contract). 这是拉丁语，用于法律条文或合同中，义为‘第一，首先’。

54. then: in that case, therefore（那么，因此）。

55. covenant: ['kʌvinənt] make a specific demand as a condition in an agreement（提出具体的要求作为合同的一条）。

56. sworn: devoted, pledged as by an oath（忠诚的，盟誓的）。

57. confidante: female bosom friend entrusted with secrets, especially in love affairs（知己的女友）。

58. intimate: a familiar friend（亲密的朋友）。

59. she-friend: female friend（女友）。试比较 she-ass, she-bear, she-wolf, she-devil 等类似的复合名词，就可以体会到 she-friend 的贬义。

60. screen her affairs: conceal her love affairs（掩盖她的风流韵事）。

61. under your countenance: under your support and approbation（在你的赞助之下）。

62. mutual secrecy: keeping each other's secrets（相互为之保密）。

63. decoy-duck: one employed to allure others into a snare（诱人入圈套的人）。

64. wheedle you a-fop-scrambling: entice you into hoping to attract fops（诱使你抱着吸引花花公子的目的）。这里 a-fop-scrambling 的结构和 a-hunting, a-fishing，等相同。**a** 是一个弱化了的介词（= into）.

65. to the play in a mask: 戴上假面具去看戏。

66. rail at me for missing the play: 责备我没有去看戏。

67. disappointing the frolic which you had: (for) spoiling the fun which you had (in watching the play):（责备我）破坏了你的看戏的乐趣。

68. to pick me up and prove my constancy: in order to take me into your company and test my faithfulness（为了使我陪伴你，并且考验我对你的忠诚）。

69. Item: used to introduce each item in a list（用来引起合同的每一条款）。

70. article: stipulate（规定）。

71. passes current: is received as genuine（作为有流通价值的货币而被接受）。

72. new-coin it: coin it anew or again（重新铸造货币）。

73. To which end: for that purpose, i. e., for the purpose of pleasing me with your pretty face（为了那个目的，即为了用你的美貌讨我的欢心）。

74. vizards: masks for dress, as opposed to cosmetic masks "for the night"（作为服装的一部分的面具，区别于用于夜晚的用化装品制成的面具）。**vizard** 是 **visor** 的变体。

75. oiled-skins: skins smeared with oil（涂抹上油脂的兽皮）。

76. hog's bones, etc.: Cosmetics were made of materials as repulsive as those that Mirabell names（当时化装品就是用象 Mirabell 所说的这些令人作呕的原料制成的）。**pig-water** = pig's urine（猪尿）。

77. commerce: social intercourse, personal dealings（社交，个人的交往）。

78. gentlewoman: formerly, a woman in attendance on a lady of rank（以往指侍候贵妇人的女仆）。

79. in What-d'ye-call-it-Court: 在被你称之为宫廷里的。

80. bawds with baskets: procuresses or female panders carrying baskets（携着提篮的媒婆或拉皮条的女人）。

81. china: any earthenware dishes or crockery（任何用瓷器或陶器制成的碟、盘或其它器皿）。

82. atlases: oriental satins（东方绸缎）。

83. when you shall be breeding: when you are going to bring forth offspring（当你快要生孩子的时候）。

84. with a blessing on our endeavours: thanks to our efforts（由于我们的努力）。

85. strait lacing: wearing tightly laced garments（穿紧身衣）。

86. shape: good figure（好身材）。

87. sugar-loaf: hard lump of sugar in the form of a cone（塔糖，圆锥形的糖块）。

88. man-child: male child, boy, son（男孩，儿子）。

89. crooked billet: a crooked piece of firewood（一根弯曲的柴火）。

90. proviso: [prəˈvaizəu] a condition or stipulation（条件或规定）。

91. province: territory, sphere of influence（领域，势力范围）。

92. authorized: approved（公认的，许可的）。

93. mending of fashions: improving or finding fault with prevailing customs（纠正或指责流行的风尚）。

94. spoiling reputations: backbiting, speaking ill of others behind their backs（诽谤，说别人坏话）。

95. railing at absent friends: 试比较法语成语：Les absents ont toujours tort（人们总是把过错推卸给不在场的人）。

96. banish: send away, prohibit（排斥，禁止）。

97. auxiliaries: foreign or allied armed forces（外国或盟国的援军）。

98. aniseed, cinnamon, ... waters: All of these "waters" are alcoholic drinks（"strong waters"，强性烈酒）。

99. clary: a sweet liqueur made of wine, honey, and spices（混有蜂蜜和香料的烈性甜酒）。

100. dormitives: drinks that help one sleep（催眠的饮料）。

101. These provisos admitted: These conditions having been accepted（如果这些条件被接受了）。

102. I may prove: I may be found to be.

103. a tractable and complying husband: an easily manageable and obedient husband（一个容易控制的、驯服的丈夫）。

104. upon the contract: to show agreement on the contract（为了表示双方在合同上达成了协议）。

105. And here comes one: 指 Mrs. Fainall. 她是剧中正面人物之一，站在 Millamant 和 Mirabell 一边。

106. have a mind to: be strongly inclined to（倾心于）。

107. My mother is coming: i. e., Lady Wishfort is coming.

108. fits: i. e., fainting fits（昏死过去）。

109. time enough: soon enough, in time（及时）。

110. Sir Rowland: Mirabell 的仆人 Waitwell 假装是 Mirabell 的有钱的地主伯父 Sir Rowland，并且假装向 Lady Wishfort 求婚。

111. Foible: 她是 Lady Wishfort 的女仆，嫁给了 Mirabell 的仆人 Waitwell.

112. in a fair way to succeed: likely to succeed（大有成功的希望）。

113. confounded with confusion: overwhel med with shame（羞愧难当）。

114. at the retrospection of: at the remembrance of, when I recall（当我回忆起）。请注意 Lady Wishfort 假斯文的咬文嚼字的习惯。

115. Year of Jubilee: In the Roman Catholic Church, a year (every twenty-fifth year) of indulgence or pardon（罗马天主教的大赦年，免罪年或赦罪年，每隔二十五年轮到一次，或不定期）。

116. the effect of my transport: the result of my strong emotion of love（我的强烈爱情的结果）。

117. the possession of your adorable person: the enjoyment of your most lovely body（享受你极可爱的身体）。

118. I am tantalized on the rack: Waitwell mixes his metaphors. Tantalus, from whose name we derive the word **tantalize** was not tortured on the rack. In Hades he was placed in a pool of water that receded from his lips.（Waitwell 对希腊神话的典故不很熟悉，因此他把 Tantalus 在阴间所受的惩罚和 rack（拷问犯人时拉其四肢使关节脱离的一种刑具）联系起来。实际上，Tantalus 因泄露天机被罚永世站在上有果树的水中，水深及下巴，口渴想喝水时水即减退，腹饥想吃果子时树枝即升高）。

119. on the tenter of expectation: in a state of suspense because of expectation（由于期望而感到心神不安）。

120. My nephew: 指 Mirabell. Waitwell 冒充 Mirabell 的伯父 Sir Rowland.

121. unnatural: lacking in human nature（缺少人性的）。

122. viper: a malignant or treacherous person（阴险毒辣的人）。

123. respect myself: consider myself（考虑我个人）。

124. protesting eyes: declaring eyes, eyes that solemnly affirm his love for me（公开表明态度的眼神）。

125. rival: 情敌。

126. a dies: He dies（他非死不可）。这里 **a** 是英语方言人称代词 **he** 的读音。Waitwell 尽管假装斯文，仍不免露出他的乡下佬的土音。

127. barefoot: wearing nothing on the feet（穷得没有鞋穿）。

128. out at knees: threadbare at knees（裤子膝部磨损到褴褛的程度）。

129. an alms: money or goods given to the poor in charity（救济金，施舍物）。alms（<OE ælmesse）是单数名词。

130. a saveall: a small pan inserted into a candlestick to catch the drippings of the candle（有插烛钉的烛碟）。

131. sinister appetite: evil desire（罪恶的欲望）。

132. indigestion of widowhood: 寡妇的消化不良。

133. complacency: complaisance, compliance, a yielding to a wish or demand（顺从）。

134. lethargy of continence: slowness in controlling one's sexual desire（懒于节欲）。

135. prone to any iteration of nuptials: tending or inclined to any repetition of the wedding ceremony（倾向于重复结婚仪式，即倾向于再结婚）。

136. Far be it from me: I don't think so at all（我一点也不这样想）。

137. protest: affirm solemnly（郑重声明）。

138. recede: i. e., recede or withdraw from my promise（收回我的诺言）。

139. or think that: nor must you think that（你也不要这样想）。

140. make a prostitution of decorums: put etiquette to an infamous use（践踏了礼仪）。

141. wrong my condescension: fail to do justice to my kindness（辜负了我的恩惠）。

142. fair shrine of virtue: beautiful sacred embodiment of chastity（贞节的美丽、神圣的化身）。Waitwell 对 Lady Wisbfort 恭维达到了偶象崇拜的程度。

143. scruple: very small quantity（微量）。

144. carnality: sexual desire（性欲，肉欲）。

145. camphire and frankincense: Camphor was considered an effective antidote to sexual desire（过去人们认为樟脑是消除性欲的有效药物）。**frankincense**（乳香）和下面的 **odour**（香味）都指天主教教堂里为圣母玛丽亚烧的香。这里 Waitwell 把 Lady Wishfort 进一步偶象化，把她比作圣洁的玛丽亚。

146. or that: nor must you think that（你也不要这样想）。Lady Wishfort 还想说下去。实际上，欲盖弥彰，颇有“此地无银三百两”的味道。康格里夫成功地刻画了一个假装正经的老寡妇。

16 JOSEPH ADDISON
1672-1719

SUNDAY IN THE COUNTRY

许国璋　选注

I AM always very well pleased with a country Sunday, and think, if keeping holy the seventh day were only a human institution[1], it would be the best method that could have been thought of for the polishing and civilizing of mankind. It is certain the country people would soon degenerate into a kind of savages and barbarians, were there not such frequent returns of a stated time,[2] in which the whole village meet together with their best faces, and in their cleanliest habits,[3] to converse with one another upon indifferent subjects,[4] hear their duties explained to them, and join together in adoration of the Supreme Being.[5] Sunday clears away the rust of the whole week, not only as it refreshes in their minds the notions of religion, but as it puts both the sexes upon appearing[6] in their most agreeable forms,[7] and exerting all such qualities as are apt to give them a figure[8] in the eye of the village. A country fellow distinguishes himself as much in the churchyard, as a citizen does upon the Change,[9] the whole parish-politics[10] being generally discussed in that place either after sermon or before the bell rings.

My friend Sir Roger, being a good churchman,[11] has beautified the inside of his church with several texts of his own choosing.[12] He has likewise given a handsome pulpit-cloth, and railed in[13] the communiontable at his own expense. He has often told me, that at his coming to his estate[14] he found his parishioners very irregular;[15] and that in order to make them kneel and join in the responses, he gave every one of them a hassock and a common-prayer book: and at the same time employed an itinerant singingmaster, who goes about the country for that purpose, to instruct them rightly in the tunes of the Psalms; upon which they now very much value themselves, and indeed outdo most of the country churches that I have ever heard.

As Sir Roger is landlord to the whole congregation,[16] he keeps them in very good order, and will suffer[17] nobody to sleep in it besides himself; for if by chance he has been surprised into a short nap[18] at sermon,[19] upon recovering out of it he stands up and looks about him, and if he sees anybody else nodding, either wakes them himself or sends his servants to them. Several other of the old knight's[20] particularities[21] break out upon these occasions. Sometimes he will be lengthening out a verse in the singing Psalms half a minute after the rest of the congregation have done with it;[22] sometimes, when he is pleased with the matter of his devotion, he pronounces 'Amen'[23] three or four times to the same prayer; and sometimes stands up when everybody else is upon their knees, to count the congregation, or see if any of his tenants are missing.

I was yesterday very much surprised to hear my old friend, in the midst of the service, calling out to one John Matthews to mind what he was about and not disturb the congregation. This John Matthews it seems is remarkable for being an idle fellow, and at that time was kicking his heels for his diversion. This authority of the knight, though exerted in that odd manner which accompanies him in all the circumstances of life, has a very good effect upon the parish, who are not polite enough[24] to see any thing ridiculous in his behaviour; besides that the general good sense and worthiness of his character make his friends observe these little singularities as foils that rather set off than blemish his good qualities.[25]

As soon as the sermon is finished, nobody presumes to stir till

Sir Roger is gone out of the church. The knight walks down from his seat in the chancel[26] between a double row of his tenants, that stand bowing to him on each side; and every now and then inquires how such a one's wife, or mother, or son, or father do, whom he does not see at church; which is understood as a secret reprimand[27] to the person that is absent.

The chaplain has often told me that, upon a catechizing day,[28] when Sir Roger has been pleased with a boy that answers well, he has ordered a Bible to be given to him next day for his encouragement; and sometimes accompanies it with a flitch of bacon to his mother. Sir Roger has likewise added five pounds a year to[28] the clerk's place;[29] and that he may[30] encourage the young fellows to make themselves perfect in the church service, has promised upon the death of the present incumbent,[31] who is very old, to bestow it according to merit.[32]

The fair understanding between Sir Roger and his chaplain, and their mutual concurrence in doing good, is the more remarkable because the very next village is famous for the differences and contentions that arise between the parson and the squire, who live in a perpetual state of war. The parson is always preaching at the squire; and the squire, to be revenged on the parson, never comes to church. The squire has made all his tenants atheists and tithe-stealers;[33] while the parson instructs them every Sunday in the dignity of his order,[34] and insinuates to them, in almost every sermon, that he is a better man than his patron.[35] In short, matters are come[36] to such an extremity, that the squire has not said his prayers either in public or private this half year; and the parson threatens him, if he does not mend his manners, to pray for him[37] in the face of the whole congregation.

Feuds of this nature, though too frequent in the country, are very fatal to the ordinary people, who are so used to be dazzled with riches, that they pay as much deference to the understanding of a man of an estate,[38] as of a man of learning; and are very hardly brought to regard[39] any truth, how important soever it may be, that is preached to them, when they know there are several men of five hundred[40] a year who do not believe it.

The Spectator, No. 112
July 9, 1711

【作者简介】 Joseph Addison (1672–1710)，十八世纪初英国小品文家。早年以诗名见重于执政的辉格党，曾任国务秘书。1711年辉格党下野，罢官，与友人 Richard Steele 合办一小型文艺刊物，名曰 *The Spectator*（《旁观者》），日出一张，每期一文，表明不谈政治，只从旁观者的角度，取城乡琐闻，官场趣事，历史掌故，诗家名篇，写成清丽可诵的短文，作为茶余酒后的谈资，也作为一种人人可得的通俗读物。其对象主要是当时新兴的资产阶级。这一刊物前后办了两年时间（1711年三月至1712年十二月，1714年又曾短期复刊），出了六百三十多期，开了当时期刊文学的风气。

期刊文学是英国十八世纪一种新兴的文学，而小品随笔则是期刊中最流行的文体。它不是文学的主流，但它却富于各阶层、各种人物的写照；我们可以从中约略看出昨天的英国社会如何构成，进而更好地了解今天英国社会的形形色色。

英国散文，十六、七世纪多以华丽为尚，十七世纪末渐趋平易，到了十八世纪初期，期刊文学大兴，一种简约朴素的文体成为一时风尚。Addison 的小品在当时可算是一种平易畅达的白话，即在今天读来，也还不觉得古奥。这固然应归功于他个人的文学素养，但决定因素还是他的读者：新发迹的商人家庭，购置了家宅和马车以后，颇想增添一点文化教养，但毕竟还没有读过多少书，文章写深了，典故用多了，很可能读不懂，写得太洒脱放浪，又会看不惯，于是象 Addison 所写的一种文体——亲切通俗，但屏除鄙俚之词；典雅优美，但绝不炫耀文采*——就应运而生了。

【题解与注释】

《旁观者》前后共有几十篇随笔写 Sir Roger de Coverley，这是较早的一篇。Sir

---

* "familiar but not coarse, and elegant but not ostentatious"——十八世纪后叶文学批评家 Samuel Johnson 评 Addison 语。

Roger 是虚构的乡间士绅，拥有很多的田产，俨然一乡之主。这篇写他在教堂做礼拜的情形，威势也是不小。你看他在礼拜进行的时候，谁要是打盹，他管得着，谁要是坐的不安稳，他就当场申斥，谁要是缺席，他就要问明原因；等到礼拜结束，人们得让他先走；教堂里某个司仪人死了，后任人要由他决定。这是英国地主阶级在乡村中统治权的一个侧面；这种统治在十八世纪还很牢固——许多小说里都有这类人物的描写——直到工业革命以后，才被资产阶级的政治机器所代替。

Addison 写的是一个比较开明的地主，但是他并不一味为他捧场。作者写他不许别人做礼拜的时候睡觉，自己却不免打盹；要别人赞美诗唱得和谐，自己却把一句诗拖长了半分钟还不觉得难为情；要别人庄严肃静，立跪如仪，自己却不顾礼节，大声呼喝。这又是在威势之外，写他的庸俗、粗鲁、缺乏教养。

文末提到的乡绅与牧师之争，也是英国小说中常可碰到的。在一般情形下，“绅权”与“神权”是互为利用的。乡绅即是一乡中最大的地主，拥有田产（estate），租给佃户（tenants）；这样的田产，通常构成一个教区（parish），教区居民谓之教民（parishioners），教民也即佃户。教区由牧师（parson）管，田产由乡绅（squire）管，但如遇牧师出缺，后任还得由乡绅推荐，教堂的给养维修，也得靠后者支持。因此，牧师与乡绅的关系，还是一种前者依附后者的宾主关系。文中有一句话：“Sir Roger is landlord to the whole congregation”（对整个教众是地主）。这句话说出了乡绅与教堂的关系，也肯定了前者的地位。

1. human institution: 人类创造的制度，即“上帝规定的制度”（divine institution）之反。《旧约》：上帝创造世界，工作六天，第七天休息，因此也规定人类在第七天休息。（参看《旧约》《创世纪》第二章第三节，《出埃及记》第二十章第八至十二节。）

2. frequent returns of a stated time: 指星期日：七日一来复。

3. cleanliest habits: habits 在此是古义 = clothes; cleanly 读作 ['klenli].

4. indifferent subjects: 并无特别选择的题目，即无所不谈。（indifferent 在此是古义。）

5. The Supreme Being: God.

6. puts both the sexes upon appearing: requires both men and women to appear.

7. in their most agreeable forms: in their best clothes and gentlest manners.

8. to give them a figure: to make them appear to the best advantage. 使他们能显得出色。

9. Change: Exchange.（交易所）。

10. parish-politics: 教区里的各种事务和纠纷。

11. being a good churchman: 是一个好的教友（做礼拜逢期必到，乐于捐款，听从牧师的话等）。

12. texts of his own choosing: 从圣经中选择一定段落，刻在教堂墙上，作为格言，也作为装饰。此事由 Sir Roger 出钱捐助，经文也由他选定。

13. railed in: 周围建起栏杆，把祭坛上圣桌（communion-table）围起来。

14. at his coming to his estate: 当他初次接管他这份产业的时候。

15. found his parishioners very irregular: 发现他的教区内的教民不合做礼拜的礼节（该下跪时不下跪，该说“阿门”时不说，赞美诗（Psalms [sɑːmz]）的调子唱得不齐等等）。

16. congregation: 做礼拜的教徒（集体）。

17. suffer: allow.（古用。）

18. surprised into a short nap: 一时昏倦，抵挡不住，就瞌睡一会儿。to be surprised 在此是古义 = to be overcome (by sleep).

19. sermon:（教士）讲道。

20. the old knight: 指 Sir Roger；封为爵士（knight）的人才能称为 Sir 某某。

21. particularities: = peculiarities，怪僻的脾气。与下文 singularities 意义相同。

22. have done with it: have finished it.

23. Amen ['eimen]**:** 祷告结束时一种习惯用语，源出希伯来文，意即“心愿如此！”汉译：“阿门”。

24. who are not polite enough: 态度还不够文雅，即是说还不象城里人那样有教养，因此对 Sir Roger 那种颟顸和粗率的举止不以为意。

25. rather set off than blemish his good qualities: 不仅无损，抑且更明显地衬托出他的优点。

26. chancel: 设在教堂东端的席位，四周围有栏杆，专为有钱势的人做礼拜时坐用。

27. a secret reprimand ['reprimɑːnd]**:** 暗地里的责备。

28. catechizing ['kætikaiziŋ] **day:** 教理问答日。

29. clerk's place: 教堂中做礼拜时的领首人的职位。

30. that he may ...: = in order that he may…

31. present incumbent: 目前在职人。

32. to bestow it according to merit: 将这一职位给予德才兼备的人。

33. The squire has made all his tenants atheists ['eiθiːists] **and tithe-steal ers** ['taið-'stiːləz]**:** 乡绅与牧师不和，叫佃户不要去做礼拜，于是佃户就变为无神论者（atheists）；又叫他们不要把原规定的“什一之赋”（即以田地收入的十分之一作为赋税）交给教会，于是他们又变成这种赋税的盗窃者。

34. instructs them every Sunday in the dignity of his order: 教规庄严，不得触犯，每星期日，谆谆为教民告。

35. patron: 教士与地主有宾主关系，此处 patron 即是“主”的意思。

36. are come: 现代英语用 have come.

37. pray for him: 乡绅半年不做礼拜而不忏悔，牧师声言将为他祷告，求上帝去感化他，借此可把他的恶行公开宣布。

38. a man of an estate: 现代英语作 a man of property，有产者。

39. are very hardly brought to regard ...: 不易使他们尊重…

40. five hundred: five hundred pounds 每年收入五百镑，在当时是一笔大数目。

17 JOHN GAY
1685 – 1732

THE BEGGAR'S OPERA
(selections)

梅仁毅　选注

Act 1. Scene I.
SCENE PEACHUM'S HOUSE.

Peachum[1] sitting at a Table with a large Book of Accounts[2] before him.

AIR I. An old woman cloathed[3] in gray.
THROUGH all the employments[4] of life
　　Each neighbour[5] abuses his brother;
Whore and Rogue they call Husband and Wife:
　　All professions be-rogue[6] one another.
The Priest calls the Lawyer a cheat,
　　The Lawyer be-knaves[7] the Divine[8];
And the Statesman, because he's so great,
　　Thinks his trade as honest as mine.

A Lawyer is an honest employment, so is mine. Like me too he acts in a double capacity,[9] both against Rogues and for 'em[10]; for 'tis but fitting[11] that we should protect and encourage Cheats, since we live by 'em.

SCENE II.

PEACHUM, FILCH.

Filch. Sir, black Moll hath[12] sent word her tryal[13] comes on in the afternoon, and she hopes you will order matters[14] so as to bring her off.[15]

Peach. Why, she may plead her belly[16] at worst; to my knowledge she hath taken care of that security.[17] But as the wench is very active and industrious, you may satisfy her that I'll soften the evidence.

Filch. Tom Gagg, Sir, is found guilty.

Peach. A lazy dog! When I took him the time before, I told him what he would come to[18] if he did not mend his hand.[19] This is death without reprieve. I may venture to book him.[20] (Writes.) For Tom Gagg, forty pounds. Let Betty Sly know that I'll save her from Transportation, for I can get more by her staying in England.

Filch. Betty hath brought more goods into our Lock[21] to-year[22] than any five of the gang; and in truth, 'tis pity to lose so good a customer.

Peach. If none of the gang take her off, she may, in the common course of business,[23] live a twelve-month longer. I love to let women scape. A good sportsman always lets the Hen-Partridges fly, because the breed of the game depends upon them.[24] Besides, here the Law allows us no reward; there is nothing to be got by the death of women—except our wives.[25]

Filch. Without dispute, she is a fine woman! 'Twas to her I was oblig'd for my education,[26] and (to say a bold word) she hath train'd up more young fellows to the business[27] than the Gamingtable.

Peach. Truly, Filch, thy[28] observation is right. We and the Surgeons are more beholden to women[29] than all the professions besides.[30]

AIR II. The bonny gray-ey'd morn, & c.

Filch. 'Tis woman that seduces all mankind.
By her we first were taught the wheedling arts:[31]
Her very eyes can cheat; when most she's kind,
She tricks us of our money with our hearts.
For her, like Wolves by night we roam for prey,[32]
And practise ev'ry fraud to bribe her charms;
For suits of love, like law, are won by pay,
And Beauty must be fee'd into our arms.[33]

Peach. But make haste to Newgate, boy, and let my friends know what I intend; for I love to make them easy one way or other.

Filch. When a gentleman is long kept in suspence, penitence may break his spirit ever after.[34] Besides, certainty gives a man a good air[35] upon his tryal, and makes him risque another without fear or scruple.[36] But I'll away, for 'tis a pleasure to be the messenger of comfort to friends in affliction.

SCENE III.

PEACHUM.

But 'tis now high time to look about me for a decent Execution[37] against next Sessions.[38] I hate a lazy rogue, by whom one can get nothing 'till he is hang'd. A Register of the Gang. (Reading.) Crookfinger'd Jack. A year and a half in the service: Let me see how much the stock owes to his industry;[39] one, two, three, four, five gold Watches, and seven silver ones. A mighty clean-handed fellow! sixteen Snuff-boxes, five of them of true gold. Six dozen of Handkerchiefs, four silver-hilted Swords, half a dozen of Shirts, three Tyeperiwigs, and a piece of Broad Cloth. Considering these are only the fruits of his leisure hours,[40] I don't know a prettier fellow, for no man alive hath a more engaging presence of mind[41] upon the road. Wat Dreary, alias[42] Brown Will, an irregular dog,[43] who hath an underhand way of disposing his goods. I'll try him only for a Sessions or two longer upon his good behaviour.[44] Harry Paddingdon, a poor petty-larceny[45] rascal, without the least genius; that fellow, though he were to live these six months, will never come to the gallows with any credit. Slippery Sam; he goes off the next Sessions, for the villain hath the impudence to have views of following his trade as a Taylor, which he calls an honest employment. Mat of the Mint; listed not above a month ago, a promising sturdy fellow, and diligent in his way; somewhat too bold and hasty, and may raise good contributions on the publick, if he does not cut himself short by murder. Tom Tipple, a guzzling soaking sot,[46] Who is always too drunk to stand himself, or to make others stand. A cart is absolutely necessary for him. Robin of Bagshot, alias Gorgon, alias Bluff Bob, alias Carbuncle, alias Bob Booty.

SCENE IV.

PEACHUM. MRS. PEACHUM.

Mrs. Peach. What of Bob Booty, husband? I hope nothing bad hath betided him.[47] You know, my dear, he's a favourite customer of mine. 'Twas he made me a present of this ring.[48]

Peach. I have set his name down in the black-list, that's all my dear; he spends his life among women, and as soon as his money is gone, one or other of the ladies will hang him for the reward, and there's forty pound lost to us for-ever.[49]

Mrs. Peach. You know, my dear, I never meddle in matters of Death; I always leave those affairs to you. Women indeed are bitter[50] bad judges in these cases, for they are so partial to the brave that they think every man handsome who is going to the Camp[51] or the Gallows.

AIR III. Cold and raw, etc.

If any wench Venus's[52] girdle wear,
　　Though she be never so ugly,[53]
Lillies and roses will quickly appear,
　　And her face look wond'rous smuggly.
Beneath the left ear, so fit but a cord,[54]

(A rope so charming a Zone[55] is!)
The youth in his cart hath the air of a lord,
And we cry, There dies an Adonis![56]

But really, husband, you should not be too hard-hearted, for you never had a finer, braver set of men than at present. We have not had a murder among them all, these seven months. And truly, my dear, that is a great blessing.

Peach. What a dickens is the woman always a whimpring about murder for?[57] No gentleman is ever look'd upon the worse for killing a man in his own defence; and if business cannot be carried on without it, what would you have a gentleman do?

Mrs. Peach. If I am in the wrong, my dear, you must excuse me, for no-body can help the frailty of an over-scrupulous Conscience.

Peach. Murder is as fashionable a crime as a man can be guilty of. How many fine gentlemen have we in Newgate every year, purely upon that article?[58] If they have wherewithal[59] to perswade[60] the jury to bring it in manslaughter, what are they the worse for it?[61] So, my dear, have done upon this subject.[62] Was captain Macheath here this morning, for the bank-notes he left with you last week?

Mrs. Peach. Yes, my dear; and though the Bank hath stopt payment, he was so cheerful and so agreeable! Sure there is not a finer gentleman upon the road than the Captain! If he comes from Bagshot at any reasonable hour he hath promis'd to make one this evening with Polly, and me, and Bob Booty, at a party of Quadrille.[63] Pray, my dear, is the Captain rich?

Peach. The Captain keeps too good company ever to grow rich.[64] Marybone and the Chocolate-houses[65] are his undoing. The man that proposes to get money by play[66] should have the education of a fine gentleman, and be train'd up to it from his youth.

Mrs. Peach. Really, I am sorry upon Polly's account the Captain hath not more discretion. What business hath he to keep company with lords and gentlemen? he should leave them to prey upon one another.

Peach. Upon Polly's account! What, a plague,[67] does the woman mean?—Upon Polly's account!

Mrs. Peach. Captain Macheath is very fond of the girl.

Peach. And what then?

Mrs. Peach. If I have any skill in the ways of women, I am sure Polly thinks him a very pretty man.

Peach. And what then? you would not be so mad to have the wench marry him? Gamesters and highwaymen are generally very good to their whores, but they are very devils[68] to their wives.

Mrs. Peach. But if Polly should be in love, how should we help her, or how can she help herself? Poor girl, I am in the utmost concern about her.

AIR IV. Why is your faithful slave disdain'd?
If love the virgin's heart invade,
How, like a Moth, the simple maid
    Still plays about the flame!
If soon she be not made a wife,
Her honour's sing'd, and then for life,
    She's—what I dare not name.

Peach. Look ye, wife. A handsome wench in our way of business, is as profitable as at the bar of a Temple coffe-house, who looks upon it as her livelihood to grant every liberty but one.[69] You see I would indulge the girl as far as prudently we can. In any thing, but marriage! after that, my dear, how shall we be safe? are we not then in her husband's power? for a husband hath the absolute power over all a wife's secrets but her own. If the girl had the discretion of a court lady, who can have a dozen young fellows at her ear without complying with one, I should not matter it; but Polly is tinder, and a spark will at once set her on a flame. Married! If the wench does not know her own profit, sure she knows her own pleasure better than to make herself a property! My daughter to me should be, like a court lady to a minister of state, a key to the whole gang. Married! If the affair is not already done, I'll terrify her from it, by the example of our neighbours.

Mrs. Peach. May-hap,[70] my dear, you may injure the girl. She loves to imitate the fine ladies, and she may only allow the Captain liberties in the view of interest.

Peach. But 'tis your duty, my dear, to warn the girl against her ruin, and to instruct her how to make the most of her beauty. I'll go to her this moment, and sift[71] her. In the mean time, wife, rip out the coronets and marks of these dozen of cambric handkerchiefs, for I can dispose of them this afternoon to a chap in the city.

SCENE V.

MRS. PEACHUM.

Never was a man more out of the way in an argument, than my husband! Why must our Polly, forsooth, differ from her sex, and love only her husband? And why must our Polly's marriage, contrary to all observation, make her the less followed by other men? All men are thieves in love, and like a woman the better for being another's property.

AIR V. Of all the simple things we do, & c.

A Maid is like the golden oar,
Which hath guineas intrinsical in't
Whose worth is never known, before
It is try'd and imprest in the mint.
A Wife's like a guinea in gold,
Stampt with the name of her spouse;
Now here, now there; is bought, or is sold;
And is current in every house.[72]

SCENE VI.

MRS. PEACHUM, FILCH.

Mrs. Peach. Come hither, Filch. I am as fond of this child, as though my mind misgave me he were my own.[73] He hath as fine a hand at picking a pocket as a woman, and is as nimble-finger'd as a juggler. If an unlucky session does not cut the rope of thy life, I pronounce, boy, thou wilt be a great man in history. Where was your post last night, my boy?

Filch. I ply'd at the Opera, madam; and considering 'twas neither dark nor rainy, so that there was no great hurry in getting chairs and coaches, made a tolerable hand on't.[74] These seven handkerchiefs, madam.

Mrs. Peach. Colour'd ones, I see. They are of sure sale from our ware-house at Redriff among the sea-men.

Filch. And this snuff-box.

Mrs. Peach. Set in gold! A pretty encouragement this to a young beginner.

Filch. I had a fair tug at a charming gold watch. Pox take the Taylors[75] for making the fobs so deep and narrow! It stuck by the way, and I was forc'd to make my escape under a coach. Really, madam, I fear I shall be cut off in the flower of my youth, so that every now and then (since I was pumpt[76]) I have thoughts of taking up[77] and going to sea.

Mrs. Peach. You should go to Hockley in the hole, and to Marybone, child, to learn valour. These are the schools that have bred so many brave men.[78] I thought, boy, by this time, thou hadst lost fear as well as shame.[79] Poor lad! how little does he know yet of the Old-Bailey![80] For the first fact I'll ensure thee from being hang'd; and going to Sea, Filch, will come time enough[81] upon a sentence of transportation. But now, since you have nothing better to do, ev'n go to your book, and learn your catechism;[82] for really a man makes but an ill figure[83] in the Ordinary's[84] paper, who cannot give a satisfactory answer to his questions. But, hark you,[85] my lad, Don't tell me a lye; for you know I hate a lyar. Do you know of any thing that hath past between captain Macheath and our Polly?

Filch. I beg you, Madam, don't ask me: for I must either tell a lye to you or to Miss Polly; for I promis'd her I would not tell.

Mrs. Peach. But when the honour of our family is concern'd—

Filch. I shall lead a sad life with Miss Polly, if ever she come to know that I told you. Besides, I would not willingly forfeit my own honour by betraying any body.[86]

Mrs. Peach. Yonder comes my husband and Polly. Come Filch, you shall go with me into my own room, and tell me the whole story. I'll give thee a glass of a most delicious cordial[87] that I keep for my own drinking.

SCENE VII.

PEACHUM, POLLY.

Polly. I know as well as any of the fine ladies how to make the most of my self and of my man too. A woman knows how to be mercenary,[88] though she hath never been in a court or at an assembly.[89] We have it in our natures, papa. If I allow captain Macheath some trifling liberties, I have this watch and other visible marks of his favour[90] to show for it. A girl who cannot grant some things, and refuse what is most material,[91] will make a poor hand of her beauty,[92] and soon be thrown upon the common.

AIR VI. What shall I do to show how much I love her?
Virgins are like the fair flower in its lustre,
    Which in the garden enamels the ground;
Near it the Bees in play flutter and cluster,
    And gaudy Butterflies frolick around.
But, when once pluck'd, 'tis no longer alluring,
    To Covent-garden[93] 'tis sent, (as yet sweet,)

There fades, and shrinks, and grows past all enduring,
Rots, stinks, and dies, and is trod under feet.

Peach. You know, Polly, I am not against your toying and trifling with a customer in the way of business, or to get out a secret, or so. But if I find out that you have play'd the fool and are married, you jade you, I'll cut your throat, hussy. Now you know my mind.[94]

SCENE VIII.

PEACHUM, POLLY, MRS. PEACHUM.

AIR VII. Oh London is a fine Town.

Mrs. Peachum, (in a very great passion.)

Our Polly is a sad slut! nor heeds what we have taught her.
I wonder any man alive will ever rear a daughter!
For she must have both hoods and gowns, and hoops to swell her pride,
With scarfs and stays, and gloves and lace; and she will have men beside;
And when she's drest with care and cost, all-tempting, fine and gay,
As men should serve a Cowcumber,[95] she flings herself away.

You baggage! you hussy! you inconsiderate jade! had you been hang'd, it would not have vex'd me, for that might have been your misfortune; but to do such a mad thing by choice! The wench is married, husband.

Peach. Married? the Captain is a bold man, and will risque any thing for money; to be sure he believes her a fortune. Do you think your mother and I should have liv'd comfortably so long together, if ever we had been married? Baggage!

Mrs. Peach. I knew she was always a proud slut; and now the wench hath play'd the fool[96] and married, because forsooth she would do like the Gentry. Can you support the expence of a husband, hussy, in gaming, drinking and whoring? have you money enough to carry on the daily quarrels of man and wife about who shall squander most? There are not many husbands and wives, who can bear the charges of plaguing one another in a handsome way.[97] If you must be married, could you introduce no-body into our family, but a highwayman! Why, thou foolish jade, thou wilt be as ill us'd, and as much neglected, as if thou hadst married a Lord![98]

Peach. Let not your anger, my dear, break through the rules of decency, for the Captain looks upon himself in the military capacity,[99] as a gentleman by his profession. Besides what he hath already,[100] I know he is in a fair way[101] of getting, or of dying; and both these ways, let me tell you, are most excellent chances for a wife. Tell me hussy, are you ruin'd, or no?[102]

Mrs. Peach. With Polly's fortune, she might very well have gone off to a person of distinction. Yes, that you might, you pouting slut!

Peach. What, is the wench dumb! Speak, or I'll make you plead by squeezing out an answer from you. Are you really bound wife to him, or are you only upon liking?[103] (Pinches her.)

Polly. Oh! (Screaming.)

Mrs. Peach. How the mother is to be pitied who hath handsome daughters! Locks, bolts, bars, and lectures of morality are nothing to them:[104] they break through them all. They have as much pleasure in cheating a father and mother, as in cheating at cards.

Peach. Why, Polly, I shall soon know if you are married, by Macheath's keeping from our house.[105]

AIR VIII. Grim King of the Ghosts, & c.

Polly. Can Love be controul'd by advice?
Will Cupid[106] our mothers obey?
Though my heart were as frozen as Ice,
At his flame 'twould have melted away.
When he kist me so closely he prest,
'Twas so sweet, that I must have comply'd:

So I thought it both safest and best
To marry, for fear you should chide.

Mrs. Peach. Then all the hopes of our family are gone for ever and ever!

Peach. And Macheath may hang his father and mother-in-law, in hope to get into their daughter's fortune.

Polly. I did not marry him (as 'tis the fashion) cooly and deliberately for honour or money.[107] But, I love him.

Mrs. Peach. Love him! worse and worse! I thought the girl had been better bred. Oh husband, husband! her folly makes me mad! my head swims! I'm distracted! I can't support myself —Oh!

(Faints.)

Peach. See, wench, to what a condition you have reduced your poor mother![108] a glass of cordial, this instant. How the poor woman takes it to heart! Ah, hussy,now this is the only comfort[109] your mother has left!

Polly goes out, and returns with it.

Polly. Give her another glass, Sir; my Mamma drinks double the quantity whenever she is out of order. This, you see, fetches her.[110]

Mrs. Peach. The girl shows such a readiness, and so much concern, that I could almost find in my heart to forgive her.

AIR IX. O Jenny, O Jenny, where hast thou been.
O Polly, you might have toy'd and kist.
By keeping men off, you keep them on.[111]

Polly. But he so teaz'd me,
And he so pleas'd me,
What I did, you must have done.

Mrs. Peach. Not with a highwayman. —You sorry slut!

Peach. A word with you, wife. 'Tis no new thing for a wench to take man without consent of Parents. You know 'tis the frailty of woman, my dear.

Mrs. Peach. Yes, indeed, the sex is frail. But the first time a woman is frail, she should be somewhat nice methinks, for then or never is the time to make her fortune. After that, she hath nothing to do but to guard herself from being found out, and she may do what she pleases.

Peach. Take your self a little easy;[112] I have a thought shall soon set all matters again to rights.[113] Why so melancholy, Polly? since what is done cannot be undone, we must all endeavour to make the best of it.

Mrs. Peach. Well, Polly; as far as one woman can forgive another, I forgive thee. —Your father is too fond of you, hussy.

Polly. Then all my sorrows are at an end.[114]

Mrs. Peach. A mighty likely speech, in troth, for a wench who is just married![115]

AIR X. Thomas, I cannot, & c.

Polly. I, like a ship in storms, was tost;
Yet afraid to put into Land;
For seiz'd in the port the vessel's lost,
Whose treasure is contreband.
The waves are laid,[116]
My duty's paid.
O joy beyond expression!
Thus, safe a-shore,
I ask no more,
My all is in my possession.[117]

Peach. I hear customers in t'other room; go, talk with 'em, Polly; but come to us again, as soon as they are gone. —But, hark ye, child, if 'tis the gentleman who was here yesterday about the repeating watch,[118] say, you believe we can't get intelligence of it,[119] till to-mororw. For I lent it to Suky Straddle, to make a figure with[120] to-night at a tavern[121] in Drury-Lane.[122] If t'other gentleman calls for the silver-hilted sword; you know beetle-brow'd Jemmy hath it on, and he doth not come from Tunbridge till Tuesday night; so that it cannot be had till then.

SCENE IX.

PEACHUM, MRS. PEACHUM.

Peach. Dear wife, be a little pacified.[123] Don't let your passion run away with your senses.[124] Polly, I grant you,[125] hath done a rash thing.

Mrs. Peach. If she had had only an intrigue[126] with the fellow, why the very best families have excus'd and huddled up[127] a frailty of that sort.[128] 'Tis marriage, husband, that makes it a blemish.[129]

Peach. But money, wife, is the true fuller's earth[130] for reputations,[131] there is not a spot or a stain but what it can take out.[132] A rich rogue now-a-days is fit company for any gentleman;[133] and the world, my dear, hath not such a contempt for roguery as you imagine. I tell you, wife, I can make this match turn to our advantage.[134]

Mrs. Peach. I am very sensible husband, that captain Macheath is worth money, but I am in doubt whether he hath not two or three wives already, and then if he should die in a Session or two, Polly's dower[135] would come into dispute.[136]

Peach. That, indeed, is a point which ought to be consider'd.

AIR XI. A Soldier and a Sailor.
A Fox may steal your hens, sir,
A whore your health and pence, sir,
Your daughter rob your chest,[137] sir,
Your wife may steal your rest, sir,
A thief your goods and plate.[138]
But this is all but picking,
With rest, pence, chest and chicken;
It ever was decreed, sir,
If Lawyer's hand is fee'd,[139] sir,

He steals your whole estate.

The Lawyers are bitter enemies to those in our way. They don't care that any body should get a clandestine livelihood but themselves.

SCENE X.

MRS. PEACHUM, PEACHUM, POLLY.

Polly. 'Twas only Nimming Ned. He brought in a damask[140] window-curtain, a hoop-petticoat, a pair of silver candlesticks, a perriwig, and one silk stocking, from the fire that happen'd last night.

Peach. There is not a fellow that is cleverer in his way, and saves more goods out of the fire than Ned.[141] But now, Polly, to your affair; for matters must not be left as they are.[142] You are married then, it seems?

Polly. Yes, Sir.

Peach. And how do you propose to live, child?

Polly. Like other women, Sir, upon the industry of my husband.

Mrs. Peach. What, is the wench turn'd fool? A highway-man's wife, like a soldier's, hath as little of his pay, as of his company.[143]

Peach. And had not you the common views of a gentlewoman in your marriage, Polly?

Polly. I don't know what you mean, Sir.

Peach. Of a jointure,[144] and of being a widow.

Polly. But I love him, Sir: how then could I have thoughts of parting with him?

Peach. Parting with him! Why, that is the whole scheme and intention of all Marriage-articles.[145] The comfortable estate of widow hood,[146] is the only hope that keeps up a wife's spirits. Where is the woman who would scruple to be a wife, if she had it in her power to be a widow whenever she pleas'd?[147] If you have any views of this sort, Polly, I shall think the match not so very unreasonable.

Polly. How I dread to hear your advice! Yet I must beg you to explain yourself.

Peach. Secure what he hath got,[148] have him peach'd the next Sessions, and then at once you are made a rich widow.

Polly. What, murder the man I love! The blood runs cold at my heart[149] with the very thought of it.

Peach. Fye,[150] Polly! what hath murder to do in the affair? Since the thing sooner or later must happen, I dare say,[151] the Captain himself would like that we should get the reward for his death sooner than a stranger. Why, Polly, the Captain knows, that as 'tis his employment to rob, so 'tis ours to take Robbers; every man in his business. So that there is no malice in the case.

Mrs. Peach. Ay, husband, now you have nick'd the matter.[152] To have him peach'd is the only thing could ever make me forgive her.

AIR XII. Now ponder well, ye parents dear.

Polly. Oh, ponder well! be not severe;
So save a wretched wife!
For on the rope that hangs my dear
Depends poor Polly's life.

Mrs. Peach. But your duty to your parents, hussy, obliges you[153] to hang him. What would many a wife give for such an opportunity![154]

Polly. What is a jointure, what is widow-hood to me? I know my heart. I cannot survive him.[155]

AIR XIII. Le printemps rappelle aux armes.[156]

The Turtle thus with plaintive crying,[157]
Her lover dying,
The turtle thus with plaintive crying
Laments her Dove.
Down she drops quite spent[158] with sighing,
Pair'd in death, as pair'd in love.[159]

Thus, Sir, it will happen to your poor Polly.

Mrs. Peach. What, is the fool in love in earnest then? I hate thee for being particular:[160] Why, wench, thou art a shame to thy very Sex.[161]

Polly. But hear me, mother. —If you ever lov'd—

Mrs. Peach. Those cursed Play-books she reads have been her ruin. One word more, hussy, and I shall knock your brains out, if you have any.[162]

Peach. Keep out of the way, Polly, for fear of mischief,[163] and consider of what is propos'd to you.

Mrs. Peach. Away, hussy. Hang your husband, and be dutiful.[164]

SCENE XI.

MRS. PEACHUM, PEACHUM.

(Polly listening.)

Mrs. Peach. The thing, husband, must and shall be done. For the sake of intelligence[165] we must take other measures, and have him peach'd the next Session without her consent. If she will not know her duty, we know ours.

Peach. But really, my dear, it grieves one's heart to take off a great man.[166] When I consider his personal bravery, his fine stratagem, how much we have already got by him, and how much more we may get, methinks I can't find in my heart to have a hand in his death.[167] I wish you could have made Polly undertake it.

Mrs. Peach. But in a case of necessity—our own lives are in danger.

Peach. Then, indeed, we must comply with the customs of the world,[168] and make gratitude give way to interest.[169]—He shall be taken off.

Mrs. Peach. I'll undertake to manage Polly.[170]

Peach. And I'll prepare matters[171] for the Old-Baily.

SCENE XII.

PEACHUM. LOCKIT WITH AN ACCOUNT-BOOK

Lock. In this last affair,[172] brother Peachum, we are agreed. You have consented to go halves in Macheath.[173]

Peach. We shall never fall out[174] about an execution. —But as to that article,[175] pray how stands our last year's account?[176]

Lock. If you will run your eye over it,[177] you'll find 'tis fair and clearly stated.

Peach. This long arrear of the government[178] is very hard upon us![179] Can it be expected that we should hang our acquaintance for nothing, when our betters will hardly save theirs without being paid for it.[180] Unless the people in employment[181] pay better, I promise them for the future, I shall let other rogues live besides their own.

Lock. Perhaps, brother, they are afraid these matters may be carried too far.[182] We are treated too by them with contempt, as if our profession were not reputable.

Peach. In one respect indeed, our employment may be reckoned dishonest, because, like great Statesmen, we encourage those who betray their friends.

Lock. Such language,[183] brother, any where else, might turn to your prejudice.[184] Learn to be more guarded,[185] I beg you.

AIR XXX. How happy are we, & c.

When you censure the age,[186]
Be cautious and sage,
Lest the Courtiers offended should be:
If you mention vice or bribe,
'Tis so pat[187] to all the tribe;
Each cries—That was levell'd at me.[188]

Peach. Here's poor Ned Clincher's name, I see. Sure, brother Lockit, there was a little unfair proceeding in Ned's case:[189] for he told me in the condemn'd hold,[190] that for value receiv'd,[191] you had promis'd him a Session or two longer without molestation.[192]

Lock. Mr. Peachum, —this is the first time my honour was ever call'd in question.[193]

Peach. Business is at an end[194]—if once we act dishonourable.

Lock. Who accuses me?

Peach. You are warm,[195] brother.

Lock. He that attacks my honour, attacks my livelyhood.[196]—And this usage[197]—Sir—is not to be born.[198]

Peach. Since you provoke me to speak—I must tell you too, that Mrs. Coaxer charges you with defrauding[199] her of her information-money, for the apprehending[200] of curl-pated Hugh. Indeed, indeed, brother, we must punctually pay our Spies, or we shall have no Information.

Lock. Is this language to me, Sirrah[201]—who have sav'd you from the gallows, Sirrah! (Collaring each other.)[202]

Peach. If I am hang'd, it shall be for ridding the world of an arrant rascal.[203]

Lock. This hand shall do the office of the halter[204] you deserve, and throttle you—you dog!—

Peach. Brother, brother, —we are both in the wrong—we shall be both losers in the dispute[205]—for you know we have it in our power to hang each other.[206] You should not be so passionate.

Lock. Nor you so provoking.

Peach. 'Tis our mutual interest; 'tis for the interest of the world we should agree.[207] If I said any thing, brother, to the prejudice of your character,[208] I ask pardon.[209]

Lock. Brother Peachum—I can forgive as well as resent.[210]—Give me your hand. Suspicion does not become a friend.[211]

Peach. I only meant to give you occasion to justifie yourself:[212] But I must now step home, for I expect the gentleman about this Snuff-box, that Filch nimm'd[213] two nights ago in the Park. I appointed him at this hour.[214]

【作者简介】 John Gay（约翰·盖伊，1685—1732），英国十八世纪剧作家，生于英格兰西南部得文郡（Devonshire）一个有点地位的家庭。十岁失去双亲，由叔父照顾。中学时，盖伊就酷爱文学，这对他的一生都有影响。后来经叔父介绍，盖伊到伦敦给一个绸布商当学徒。在当学徒期间，他结识了一些作家，并练习写作。一七〇八年他匿名发表了第一首无韵诗《酒》，从此开始了作家的生涯。一七一二年他当上了蒙默思（Monmouth）公爵夫人的秘书。一七一四年经斯威夫特介绍，他到克拉伦顿（Clarendon）勋爵家中任职。同年，发表了《牧羊人的一周》（*The Shepherd's Week*）。这首诗嘲笑陈旧的田园体诗，反映了他对乡村情况颇为熟悉。一七一七年他在漫游欧洲之后，回到英国，在政府中任职，担任管理彩票的官员。

盖伊比较成功的长诗为《琐事》（Trivial，1716年，副题是《逛伦敦大街的艺术》）和《寓言》（Fables，1727年）。《琐事》以一种带有韵律的随笔体，叙述了乔治一世早期统治时伦敦的风俗、景色和蕴藏的危险。《寓言》共有六十六首，五十首发表于一七二七年，还有十六首是在他死后，于一七三八年发表。大部分写得轻松有趣，不少寓意明显。《驮马和运货人》就是其中的一首。这首是献给一个年轻的贵族的，劝他不要依赖祖先的美德。诗中有这么几句，寓意十分明显：

你的地位要求你品质优秀，
人们为此尊崇你的祖先：
如果你由此堕落下来，
他们的美德使你耻辱倍增。

但盖伊最著名的作品是喜歌剧《乞丐的歌剧》。此剧于一七二八年在 Lincoln's Inn Fields 一上演，就轰动全城，头一轮连演六十场。经过约两个世纪，此剧又于一九二〇年六月在伦敦上演，一共演了一千五百场。当年由于《乞丐的歌剧》的成功，盖伊又写了《波莉》（*Polly*，1729年），作为前剧的续编。但由于前剧讽刺了当时执政的英国首相沃波尔，因此宫廷大臣对剧本《波莉》进行审查，下令禁止上演。

盖伊一生写了不少剧本，不过都没有《乞丐的歌剧》有名。他的第一个剧本叫《莫霍克人》（*The Mohocks*，1712年）。这是一部讽刺城镇无赖所作所为的悲喜滑稽剧（Tragi-Comical Farce）。一七一五年二月在 Drury Lane 剧院上演了他的另一个剧《你叫它什么》，这是一个戏中有戏的田园笑剧。一七二四年盖伊写了一个名叫《俘虏》的悲剧，剧中的主角是被米提亚人俘虏的波斯王子索芬尼斯，他几次面临杀身之祸，最后杀死了图谋杀害米提亚国王的叛逆者，夫妻得以团圆。

在盖伊之前，英国舞台为意大利歌剧所垄断。尽管一些剧作家写了不少剧本，企图夺回舞台，但均成效甚微。只有在《乞丐的歌剧》上演后，英国的舞台才出现了深受观众欢迎的、具有英国风味的喜歌剧，因此人称盖伊为喜歌剧的鼻祖。

盖伊死后葬于威斯敏斯特教堂。墓碑上有他自己写的对句：

人生是一玩笑；一切均可证明。
我曾这么想过；现在确知如此。
（Life is a jest; and all things show it.
I thought so once; but now I know it.）

【题解与注释】

《乞丐的歌剧》是盖伊最有名的作品。这是一部有六十九段歌词的喜歌剧，完成于一七二七年十月。剧本完成后盖伊先送给 Drury Lane 剧院，但被拒绝。后来他又送给 Lincoln's Inn Fields 剧院的约翰·里奇。里奇虽然对此剧能否成功没有把握，但还是于一七二八年一月二十九日予以上演。

此剧的创作得助于斯威夫特的启示。斯威夫特曾向蒲伯和盖伊建议，写一个关于'伦敦西门监狱'（Newgate）的田园剧。尽管盖伊最后的成品没有一点田园剧的味道，但全剧却充满了监狱气氛。

全剧以一个乞丐，亦即此剧作者的独白开场。他创作了此剧，并由其乞丐同伴们在圣·乔尔斯教堂（St. Giles）的大屋中多次上演。此时他正向演员表示感谢，感谢他们允许此剧在专业舞台上演出。

紧接着，第一幕头几场介绍了剧中的两个主人公：窝主和告密者皮琼（Peachum）和他的老婆。皮琼是 peach them 两字的谐音，意思是告发他们。尽管皮琼夫妇整天与盗贼为伍，却希望他们漂亮的女儿波莉（Polly）找个有地位的丈夫。可是波莉却背着父母，与拦路大盗麦克希思结婚。当皮琼夫妇发现后，就逼着女儿告发麦克希思，以便把他的财产据为己有。波莉不干，悄悄通知麦克希思逃走。麦克希思逃走前跟同伙见了面，并准备与几个妓女寻欢作乐一番。不幸其中两个出卖了他，他被捕入狱，关在伦敦西门监狱。监狱看守洛克伊特（此名是 lock it 两字的谐音，意思是关起来）的女儿露西恰好是麦克希思的情妇。于是波莉和露西为了争夺麦克希思而互相对骂撕打。与此同时，皮琼和洛克伊特也因分赃不均而发生口角。在露西的帮助下，麦克希思逃出监狱，但很快又为一个女人所出卖而重新入狱。这次他被判死刑，立即执行。就在他被押出处死时，演员突然出来干预，说这是悲剧结局，而歌剧的结局应该是高高兴兴的。于是麦克希思被宣布缓刑。为了表示庆贺，跳起了舞，麦克希思宣布他与波莉已经结婚，全剧到此告终。

此剧情节并不复杂，但饶有兴趣，语言风趣，歌词优美，政治讽刺，大胆辛辣，却又寓于笑语唱词之中，不显过分刺激。作者对伦敦了解颇深，所写情景，真实贴切。所用曲调，大部分是英国乐曲，为人们所喜闻乐见，故此剧深受欢迎。

全剧开始时皮琼的一段独唱，就定下了政治讽刺的基调。他在歌中唱道：

在生活的一切行业之中
　　这个行业指责那个；
妓女和无赖他们叫做夫妻：
　　每个行业都指责别人为无赖。
神父称律师为骗子，
　　律师叫神父是流氓。
而政治家呢，因为他如此伟大，
　　认为他的职业和我的一样光明正大。

这里盖伊强调了当时颇为流行的这样一种观点：卑劣的动机，罪恶的行径，到处可见，并非下层社会所独有。只是地位不同，表现各异。这种观点在第三幕十六场乞丐的一段道白中表达更为清楚。乞丐说道："纵观全剧，你可以看到上层社会和下层社会的行为极为相似，很难说（在时兴的恶习方面）是文质彬彬的绅士模仿拦路抢劫的大盗，还是大盗模仿绅士。"这样，盖伊就把上层的士绅和底层的盗贼看成一丘之貉，彼此彼此。这种对比、抨击，全剧多处出现。如第四场中，皮琼夫人说道："说真的，我替波莉感到遗憾，上尉（注：指麦克希思）应该更为审慎。与勋爵、绅士作伴，跟他有何相干？应该让他们去互相撕打。"又如同一场中皮琼的一席话，"我的女儿对我来说，就象宫中贵妇对于朝中大臣那样，是掌握这一帮人的关键。"而第二幕第十场皮琼和洛克依特为分赃不均而翻脸更是直接影射当政首相沃波尔（Walpole）和他的内弟汤斯黑德大臣（Townshead）之间的明争暗斗。洛克依特唱道：

　　当你抨击这个世道，
　　你要小心、审慎，
否则廷臣你要得罪：
　　谈起恶习或受贿，
　　他们一伙都对得上号；
个个都要嚷起来——这是冲我来的。

歌词点明了廷臣的通病，而且盖伊用了'tribe'，一词，表示这是一伙人，而不是个别人。皮琼把他们的卑鄙说得更清楚。他说，"确实如此，在一种意义上可以说我们的职业并不光明磊落，因为，与伟大的政治家一样，我们也赞成出卖朋友。"短短数语，把政治家之间的勾心斗角、尔虞我诈，揭露得相当深刻。

对于当时上流社会的婚姻、恋爱，金钱关系，盖伊也有不少指责和讥讽。在得知波莉已嫁给麦克希思以后，皮琼以一种关心女儿前途、幸福的口吻，提出一个令人毛骨悚然的建议：攫取丈夫的钱财，尔后告发他，进而可得四十镑赏银，并指出这是很普通的事情。皮琼进一步训斥其女儿道：做妻子的所以精神不垮，是因为寄希望于当寡妇，可以得一份舒适的家产。没有一个女人不愿当个夫人，只要她有把握随时想当寡妇就能当上。一席教导，把婚姻的金钱关系刻划得入木三分。难怪当皮琼太太发现女儿真的爱上了麦克希思以后，怒斥其女道："你是女人的耻辱。"

盖伊所作六十九段歌词，不少行文优美，富有诗意。第一幕第七场波莉表露对麦克希思爱情的独唱，表达了一个少女初恋的痴情。她把初恋比作盛开的花朵，一旦把它掐了，就会枯萎、腐烂、发臭。第十三场麦克希思和波莉分离时的男女声对唱，充分运用了比喻的力量，表达了依依惜别之情。

对话部分，幽默、生动，处处有引人发笑的警句，笑完之后，很有回味之处。在第一幕第二场，皮琼答应救一女贼，这时他说："死个女人，一无所得——除非死的是自己的老婆。"用这种反高潮（anti-climax）的手法，使观众先为之一惊，继而报以一笑，然后回味一下，感到言简意深。在第八场中，皮琼太太得知波莉已经结婚，气得晕死过去。皮琼叫女儿拿来一杯酒，给夫人灌了下去。这时女儿又说："再给她一杯吧。我妈不舒服时，得喝双倍才行。"一句笑话，把皮琼太太性格的一个侧面展现在观众面前。这类妙语，比比皆是，使全剧生动、有力。这也是此剧能在文学史上占有一定地位的一个重要原因。

1. Peachum: 此名是 peach them 两字的谐音，意思是告发他们，这种用有意思的字的谐音取名，本身就表示了人物的特点。

2. book of accounts: 帐簿。

3. cloathed:（旧）clothed.

4. employments: 职业，工作。

5. neighbour: 在这儿不作邻居解，应视作职业或工作，而 brother 应视作相近似的职业。

6. be-rogue: be 作前缀，加在名词前面，表示叫做……，在这儿，意思是叫做无赖。

7. be-knaves: 叫做流氓或无赖。

8. Divine: 牧师。

9. in a double capacity: 以一种双重身分。

10. 'em: 即 them.

11. 'tis but fitting: it is only fitting，完全合情合理。

12. hath: 即 has，古用法。

13. tryal: 即 trial，古拼法。

14. order matters: 作好安排。

15. bring her off: 把她救出来。

16. plead her belly: 以怀孕为理由。

17. hath taken care of that security: 已经怀孕，security 在这儿指怀孕。因为怀孕以后，就不能处死，必须等孩子生了以后才能执行。

18. what he would come to: 他的下场会是怎样。

19. mend his hand: 改进（偷窃）手段。

20. to book him:（到警察局）告发他。

21. lock: 保险籍。

22. to-year: this year.

23. in the common course of business: 按照事情的正常发展。

24. because the breed of the game depends upon them: 因为这种野禽的繁

殖要靠她们。

25. there is nothing to be got by the death of women—except our wives: 注意此处所使用的“反高潮”的修辞手段。作者先用一个破折号表示停顿，好象后面的话是临时想起，加以补充的，然后来了个完全不同的含义，这样就取得很强的效果。此句意思是处死女贼，我们一无所得，除非死的是自己的老婆，才会对我们有些好处。

26. education: 此处作培养、训练解，指把他训练成一个熟练的小偷。

27. to the business: for this profession，指偷窃这一行业。注意作者把偷窃行为称作一种职业，表示这类人之多，而且有一定的组织。

28. thy: 即 your，古用法。

29. we and the Surgeons are more beholden to women: 我们和外科医生对妇女更为感激。这话的含义是由于女贼多，怀孕的多，这两种行业生意兴隆，因此要感激她们。

30. than all the professions besides: than all other professions.

31. wheedling arts: 骗术

32. like Wolves by night we roam for prey: 就如夜间狼群出来到处寻找食物。这是一个生动的比喻，把人们找女人与饿狼找食物相比，带出了贪婪的特征。

33. Beauty must be fee'd into our arms: you have to pay in order to get hold of a woman, beauty 在这儿代表女人，这是一种修辞手段，用事物的一种特征，代表一种事物。

34. penitence may break his spirit ever after: 面临死刑，他可能后悔他干过的坏事，这样即使把他放了出来，他也不敢象过去那样干。

35. a good air: 一付好气派。

36. makes him risque another without fear or scruple: 出来以后会毫无顾忌地再干，不怕再次受审。

37. to look about me for a decent Execution: 看看我周围这批人的情况，决定告发什么人。

38. next Sessions: 下一个开庭期。

39. industry: 勤奋，在这儿是一种讽刺的意思，表示偷得很勤。

40. the fruits of his leisure hours: 不是他的正业，而是他闲余时间偷来的东西。

41. engaging presence of mind: 令人喜欢的镇定、沉着。

42. alias: 化名

43. an irregular dog: 跟别人不太一样的家伙，用‘dog’这个字，皮琼在模仿上流社会的口吻，表示瞧不起这种人。

44. upon his good behaviour: 行为检点。

45. petty-larceny: 轻盗窃罪。

46. a guzzling soaking sot: 大吃狂饮的家伙。

47. nothing bad hath betided him: 他没有发生什么大祸吧，他没有大祸临头吧。

48. 'Twas he made me a present of this ring: it was he who gave me this ring as a present.

49. there's forty pound lost to us for-ever: 我们就要少拿四十镑（这是因为我们没有去告发，因而没拿到这四十镑赏银）。

50. bitter: = bitterly

51. Camp: 意思是 military service。

52. Venus: 维纳斯（罗马神话中爱和美的神）。

53. though she be never so ugly: 虽然没有人比她更丑。

54. so fit but a cord: 一条绞刑用的绳索正合适。

55. Zone: 即 girdle（古时用法）。

56. Adonis: 阿多尼斯（希腊神话中爱神阿芙罗狄蒂所恋的美少年）。

57. What a dickens is the woman always a whimpring about murder for?: 女人到底为什么老要抱怨谋杀呢？ what a dickens 的意思是 what the devil a whimpring, a 在这儿作加重语气用，whimpring 即 whimpering.

58. purely upon that article: simply because of that crime.

59. wherewithal: (Colloq.) money etc. needed for a purpose.

60. perswade: = persuade.

61. what are they the worse for it: 他们并不会怎么样。

62. So…have done upon this subject: 这件事就这么样。

63. to make one ... at a party of Quadrille: 我们的牌局中，他算一个。Quadrille 是十八世纪流行的一种牌戏（四人用四十张牌）。

64. keeps too good company ever to grow rich: 交往的都是些有钱人，钱都花了，存不了什么钱。

65. chocolate-houses: 类似咖啡馆的铺子。

66. to get money by play: 靠赌钱来挣钱。

67. a plague: 咒骂的话，加重语气用（古用法）。

68. devils: 在这儿是 severe 的意思。

69. to grant every liberty but one: 别人要怎么样都行，就是不结婚。

70. may-hap: = perhaps.

71. sift: 细细查问。

72. current in every house: 家家户户都有。

73. my mind misgave me he were my own: 我为他担心，就好象是我自己的孩子似的。

74. made a tolerable hand on't: 小小地偷了点东西。

75. pox take the taylors: taylors 即 tailors，古拼法；这些该死的裁缝。

76. since I was pumpt: pumpt 即 pumped，自从受到盘问以后。

77. taking up: 作为一种职业。

78. these are the schools that have bred so many brave men: 把 Hockley in the hole 和 Marybone 这样一些赌场称作是学校，而且是培养了一大批勇敢的人的学校，作者这儿用的是讽刺的口吻。

79. thou hadst lost fear as well as shame: hadst 是 have 第二人称的古用法，作者把无畏和无耻两种截然相反的品质放在一起，取得较好的效果，这在修辞中叫作对偶。

80. Old-Bailey: 伦敦中央刑事法庭。

81. time enough: 有充分时间，来得及。

82. learn your catechism: 学习（在审讯时）如何对答如流。catechism 原指基督教的基本教义问答。

83. makes ... an ill figure: 出丑。

84. ordinary:（法律）推事。

85. hark you: 你听着。

86. I would not willingly forfeit my own honour by betraying any body: 我不会轻易地出卖别人，使自己名声扫地。Filch 是在暗示，要他讲出来的话，得有代价。

87. cordial: 加香料的甜酒。

88. a woman knows how to be mercenary: 女人知道如何弄钱。

89. at an assembly: 到过社交场合。though she hath never been in a court or at an assembly，这句话把女贼、妓女一类人物和宫廷贵妇、上流淑女等同起来，而且指出前者是向后者学的，但是话又没有明说，而是用了一个"虽然"和"宫廷"、"社交场合"两个地点，含蓄但又达到抨击的效果。

90. other visible marks of his favour: 他送给我的其他东西。

91. a girl who cannot grant some things, and refuse what is most materia!: 一个既不能给人点什么，又不收礼的女孩子…

92. make a poor hand of her beauty: 不会利用她的美貌得利。

93. Covent-garden: 伦敦大菜市。

94. you know my mind: you know what my position is.

95. as men should serve a Cowcumber: 就象人们烧黄瓜一样。作者在这儿用了一个比喻，前面用"drest"（with care and cost），因 drest 也可表示"做菜"，后面用一个"serve"相对称，前面讲女儿打扮完后，跟了别人，后面讲黄瓜做好后，就吃掉，结果也是一样。

96. play'd the fool: 干蠢事。

97. who can bear the charges of plaguing one another in a handsome way: 谁受得了在花钱上相互折磨。in a handsome way 也是一种"反高潮"，因为人们不会预料在这方面相互折磨的。

98. thou wilt be as ill us'd, and as much neglected, as if thou hadst married a Lord: 嫁给一个拦路大盗和嫁给一个勋爵一样，都要受到虐待和打入冷宫，作者又一次把上层和下层等同起来。

99. the Captain looks upon himself in the military capacity: 在军事方面上尉认为他自己…

100. besides what he hath already: 除了他现有的钱财。

101. in a fair way: 有…希望。

102. are you ruin'd or no: are you married or not. 把结婚称作毁灭，这是对当时婚姻制度的尖锐攻击。

103. are you only upon liking: 仅仅是有好感。

104. locks, bolts, bars, and lectures of morality are nothing to them: locks, bolts, bars 指把她们关起来，是有形的；lectures of morality 指精神上的束缚，是无形的。

105. by Macheath's keeping from our house: by not allowing Macheath to come to our house.

106. Cupid: 罗马神话中的爱神。

107. I did not marry him (as 'tis the fashion) cooly and deliberately for honour or money: 这话是对当时的婚姻制度的批评，指出这是一种金钱关系。

108. to what a condition you have reduced your poor mother: 你把你可怜的母亲弄成什么样。

109. this is the only comfort: 指的是甜酒。

110. this ... fetches her: 酒使她苏醒过来。

111. by keeping men off, you keep them on: 这是一个对句，意思是只有跟男的若即若离，才能让他们追求你。

112. take yourself a little easy: 这句是从 take it easy 中变化出来的，意思是别太着急。

113. I have a thought shall soon set all matters again to rights: 现代英语中，此句结构应为 I have a thought which shall soon set all matters right again.

114. all my sorrows are at an end: 我的一切痛苦都成为过去。

115. a mighty likely speech, in troth, for a wench who is just married: 这倒很象一个刚结婚的女孩子的话。

116. the waves are laid: 风浪平息。

117. my all is in my possession: 我的一切均在我掌握之中。

118. repeating watch:（= repeater）打簧表。

119. get intelligence of it: 有消息。

120. to make a figure with: 带着这表出出风头。

121. tavern: 小酒店

122. Drury-Lane: 伦敦一剧院。

123. be a little pacified: 镇静点。

124. Don't let your passion run away with your senses: 不要让感情过分冲动，失去理智。

125. I grant you: 不错；诚然。

126. intrigue: 私通。

127. huddled up: 掩盖。

128. a frailty of that sort: 那样的弱点。把私通称作弱点，也是一种修辞手段，称作委婉法。

129. 'Tis marriage that makes it a blemish: 而结婚倒是一个污点。把私通仅

仅看作弱点，而结婚则是污点，这种对比把当时的男女关系，双方各有打算，作了揭露。

130. fuller's earth: 漂（白）土。

131. money ... is the true fuller's earth for reputations: 金钱是声誉真正的漂白土。这句话的含义是，不管你行为如何，只要有钱，名声就好。

132. there is not a spot or a stain but what it can take out: there is not a spot or a stain which money cannot take out.

133. fit company for any gentleman: 完全配和任何绅士交往。

134. I can make this match turn to our advantage: 我有办法使婚事对我们有利。

135. dower: 嫁妆。

136. come into dispute: 产生争议。

137. chest: 钱柜。

138. plate: 金银餐具。

139. if Lawyer's hand is fee'd: 如果要满足律师的要价。

140. damask: 缎子。

141. saves more goods out of the fire than Ned: Ned 从火灾中弄到的财物比谁都多。这话的意思是 Ned 经常趁火打劫。

142. for matters must not be left as they are: 因为不能让事情就这样算了。

143. hath as little of his pay, as of his company: 拿不到他的钱，也见不到人。

144. jointure: 寡妇所得遗产。

145. marriage-articles:（婚前预定财产权、继承权等的）婚姻契约。

146. the comfortable estate of widowhood: 寡妇那份舒适的家产。

147. where is the woman who would scruple to be a wife, if she had it in her power to be a widow whenever she pleas'd: 没有一个女人不愿当个夫人，只要她有把握随时想当寡妇，就能当上。

148. secure what he hath got: 把他所有的钱财弄到手。

149. the blood runs cold at my heart: 我毛骨悚然。

150. fye: = fie [fai]〔表示嫌恶、震惊等〕呸！咄！

151. I dare say: 我想，大概。

152. you have nick'd the matter: 你算说中了。

153. obliges you: 要求你。

154. what would many a wife give for such an opportunity: 不少妻子为了有这么一个机会，出多少钱都行。

155. I cannot survive him: 他死了，我也活不长。

156. Le printemps rappelle aux armes:（法语）意思是 spring calls to arms.

157. with plaintive crying: 在哀鸣。

158. quite spent: 精疲力竭。

159. pair'd in death, as pair'd in love: 相亲相爱，双双死去。

160. being particular: 特别，与众不同。

161. thou art a shame to thy very sex: 皮琼夫人认为真正的爱情是女性的耻辱，这是对当时那种出于利害关系、金钱目的的婚姻的讽刺，请注意皮琼夫人在这儿用了“thy very sex”，好象她不是一个女的，这样就带出了评论的口气。

162. if you have any: if you have any brain at all. 意思是她干的事表明她毫无头脑。

163. for fear of mischief: 以免伤了你。

164. be dutiful: 做个顺从的孩子。

165. for the sake of intelligence: 为了得到情报。

166. to take off a great man: 杀掉一个出众的人。

167. to have a hand in his death: 参与杀害他。

168. comply with the customs of the world: 遵循这个社会通常的做法。

169. make gratitude give way to interest: 感激让位于私利。皮琼装得道貌岸然，实际上这个主意是他出的，这也是对当时那种唯利是图，不讲信义的风气的抨击。

170. I'll undertake to manage Polly: 我来对付波莉。

171. prepare matters: 准备证据。

172. in this last affair: 这最后一件事，指的是处死麦克希思。

173. to go halves in Macheath: 告发麦克希思所得赏银对半分。

174. fall out: 争吵。

175. as to that article: 至于钱嘛。

176. pray how stands our last year's account: 请问我们去年的帐目如何。

177. run your eye over it: 浏览一下，“it”指的是帐目。

178. this long arrear of the government: 一连串政府欠下来付的尾数。指一次次该给的赏银没有付清。

179. hard upon us: 对我们太苛刻了。

180. when our betters will hardly save theirs without being paid for it: 而社会地位比我们高的人，如果不给他们钱，他们是不会救他们的朋友的。皮琼又一次把他们与上层人物等同起来，揭露上层人物间的关系也是尔虞我诈的关系。

181. in employment: 雇告密者的（人）。

182. these matters may be carried too far: 这种事（指告密）搞得太过份了。

183. such language: 这种话。

184. turn to your prejudice: 对你不利。

185. be more guarded:（说话）更谨慎些。

186. censure the age: 抨击这个世道。

187. pat: 恰当，合适。

188 levell'd at me: 对准我的。

189. a little unfair proceeding in Ned's case: 内德一案，做法有些欠公平。

190. condemn'd hold: 死刑囚犯的牢房。

191. for value receiv'd: 给了你钱。

192. without molestation: 不会抓他。

193. call'd in question: 受到怀疑。

194. business is at an end: 买卖以后就做不成了。

195. warm: 激动。

196. he that attacks my honour, attacks my livelyhood: 谁要指责我的信誉，就是断我的活路。把"honour"和"livelyhood"联系起来，是很少见。但这儿有其用意，意思是一旦没人信得过我，我就没有生财之道了。

197. usage: 指说他不守信誉。

198. to be born: 容忍。

199. defrauding: 骗取。

200. apprehending: 逮捕。

201. sirrah: 古用法，小子（表示轻蔑，生气的称呼）。

202. collaring each other: 互相揪住对方衣领。

203. if I am hang'd, it shall be for ridding the world of an arrant rascal: 我要给绞死的话，那是因为我替世上除掉一个臭名昭著的恶棍。

204. do the office of the halter: 起绞索的作用。

205. we shall be both losers in the dispute: 这样吵下去，我们谁也不会有好结果。

206. we have it in our power to hang each other: 我们都能置对方于死地。一句话点明了政治家们互相勾结的基础。

207. 'Tis our mutual interest ... we should agree: 我们间的利害关系决定我们要一致。这是前面一句话"we have it in our power to hang each other"的必然结论。

208. to the prejudice of your character: 有损于你的声望。

209. I ask pardon: 请你原谅。

210. I can forgive as well as resent: 我可以十分气愤，也能宽大为怀。

211. suspicion does not become a friend: 朋友之间不应怀疑。become 的意思是同…相称。

212. I only meant to give you occasion to justifie yourself: 我原意是给你机会证明你是公正无私的。

213. nimm'd: 应为 nipped，意思是偷。

214. I appointed him at this hour: I asked him to come at this hour.

18 ALEXANDER POPE
1688–1744

1. An Essay on Criticism 〔Conceit; Language; Numbers〕
2. Epistle to Dr. Arbuthnot 〔Atticus〕

王佐良　选注

1. 〔*CONCEIT; LANGUAGE; NUMBERS*〕

Some to *Conceit*[1] alone their taste confine,
And glitt'ring thoughts[2] struck out at every line;
Pleased with a work where nothing's just or fit;[3]
One glaring Chaos[4] and wild heap of wit.[5]
Poets like painters, thus, unskill'd to trace[6]
The naked Nature and the living grace,[7]
With gold and jewels cover every part,
And hide with ornaments their want of art.
True Wit is Nature to advantage dress'd,
What oft was thought, but ne'er so well express'd;[8]
Something, whose truth convinced at sight we find,[9]
That gives us back the image of our mind.
As shades more sweetly recommend[10] the light,
So modest plainness sets off[11] sprightly wit.
For works may have more wit than does 'em good,
As bodies perish through excess of blood.
Others for *Language* all their care express,
And value books, as women men, for Dress:
Their praise is still,[12] — The Style is excellent:
The Sense, they humbly take upon content.[13]

Words are like leaves; and where they most abound,
Much fruit of sense beneath is rarely found:
False Eloquence, like the prismatic glass,
Its gaudy colours spreads on every place;
The face of Nature we no more survey,
All glares alike, without distinction gay:
But true expression, like th' unchanging Sun,
Clears and improves whate'er it shines upon,
It gilds all objects, but it alters none.
Expression is the dress of thought, and still
Appears more decent,[14] as more suitable;
A vile conceit[15] in pompous words express'd
Is like a clown in regal purple[16] dress'd:
For diff'rent styles with diff'rent subjects sort,[17]
As several garbs with country, town, and court.[18]
Some by old words to fame have made pretence,[19]
Ancients in phrase,[20] mere moderns in their sense;
Such labour'd nothings, in so strange a style,
Amaze[21] th' unlearn'd, and make the learned smile.
Unlucky, as Fungoso[22] in the play,
These sparks[23] with awkward vanity display
What the fine gentleman wore yesterday;
And but so mimic ancient wits at best,
As apes our grandsires, in their doublets drest.[24]
In words, as fashions, the same rule will hold;
Alike fantastic, if too new, or old:
Be not the first by whom the new are tried,
Nor yet the last to lay the old aside.[25]

But most by *Numbers*[26] judge a Poet's song;
And smooth or rough, with them is right or wrong:
In the bright Muse though thousand charms conspire,[27]
Her voice is all these tuneful fools[28] admire;
Who haunt Parnassus[29] but to please their ear,

Not mend their minds; as some to Church repair.
Not for the doctrine, but the music there.
These equal syllables alone require,[30]
Though oft the ear the open vowels[31] tire;
While expletives[32] their feeble aid do join;[33]
And ten low words oft creep in one dull line:[34]
While they ring round the same unvaried chimes,
With sure returns of still expected rhymes;[35]
Where'er you find "the cooling western breeze",[36]
In the next line, it "whispers through the trees":
If crystal streams "with pleasing murmurs creep",
The reader's threatened (not in vain) with "sleep":[37]
Then, at the last and only couplet fraught
With some unmeaning thing they call a thought,
A needless Alexandrine[38] ends the song
That, like a wounded snake, drags its slow length along.[39]
Leave such to tune their own dull rhymes, and know
What's roundly smooth or languishingly slow;
And praise the easy vigour of a line,
Where Denham's strength, and Waller's sweetness[40] join.
True ease in writing comes from art, not chance,
As those move easiest who have learned to dance.
'Tis not enough no harshness gives offence,
The sound must seem an Echo to the sense:[41]
Soft is the strain when Zephyr[42] gently blows,
And the smooth stream in smoother numbers flows;
But when loud surges lash the sounding shore,
The hoarse, rough verse should like the torrent roar:
When Ajax[43] strives some rock's vast weight to throw,
The line too labours, and the words move slow;
Not so, when swift Camilla[44] scours the plain,
Flies o'er th' unbending corn, and skims along the main.
Hear how Timotheus'[45] varied lays surprise,

And bid alternate passions fall and rise!
While, at each change, the son of Libyan Jove[46]
Now burns with glory, and then melts with love,
Now his fierce eyes with sparkling fury glow,
Now sighs steal out, and tears begin to flow:
Persians and Greeks like turns of nature found,[47]
And the world's victor[48] stood subdued by Sound!
The power of Music all our hearts allow,[49]
And what Timotheus was, is DRYDEN now.[50]

—from *An Essay on Criticism*, 1711

2. 〔*ATTICUS*[1]〕

Peace to all such![2] but were there[3] One[4] whose fires[5]
True Genius[6] kindles, and fair Fame inspires,
Blest with each Talent, and each Art to please,[7]
And born to write, converse, and live with ease:
Shou'd such a man, too fond to rule alone,
Bear, like the *Turk,*[8] no brother near the throne,
View him with scornful,[9] yet with jealous eyes,
And hate for Arts[10] that caus'd himself to rise;
Damn with faint praise, assent with civil leer,[11]
And without sneering, teach the rest to sneer;
Willing to wound, and yet afraid to strike,
Just hint a fault, and hesitate dislike;[12]
Alike reserv'd to blame, or to commend,[13]
A tim'rous foe, and a suspicious friend;
Dreading ev'n[14] fools, by Flatterers besieg'd,[15]
And so obliging that he ne'er oblig'd;[16]
Like *Cato,*[17] give his little Senate[18] laws,
And sit attentive to his own applause;[19]
While Wits and Templars[20] ev'ry sentence raise,[21]
And wonder with a foolish face of praise.[22]

Who but must laugh, if such a man there be?
Who would not weep, if *Atticus* were he?[23]

—from *An Epistle to Dr. Arbuthnot,* 1735

【作者简介】 Alexander Pope（亚历山大·蒲伯，1688—1744），十八世纪英国重要诗人，善写"英雄双韵体"诗（the heroic couplet），在这一体裁内达到空前的完美，曾用它翻译荷马史诗，并写了《论批评》(*An Essay on Criticism,* 1711)，《夺发记》(*The Rape of the Lock,* 1712-1714)，《人论》(*An Essay on Man,* 1733-1734)，《致阿勃斯诺特医生书》(*An Epistle to Dr. Arbuthnot,* 1735)，《群愚史诗》(*The Dunciad,* 1743）等优秀作品。

蒲伯一生多病，由于生在天主教家庭而绝望仕途，又因才华太露而遭受各方面的长期攻击，以至他本人曾经感慨系之地称自己一生为"长期的病症"：

The Muse but served to ease some friend, not Wife,
To help me through this long disease, my Life.

—*An Epistle to Dr. Arbuthnot*

他对社会上的某些人物多所讥刺，然而不及社会本身。对于当时由资产阶级所控制的社会秩序，他毋宁是赞成的，曾有诗云：

One truth is clear, WHATEVER IS, IS RIGHT.

凡是现存的，都是正确的；资产阶级既然打了天下，他们的天下也就是合理的；一句话清楚地道出了蒲伯的思想立场。

在文学上，他崇奉新古典主义，重节制，讲法则，唯鄙陋之务去，文雅之是尚，这也是与当时提倡理性的社会合拍的。他本人所作无不精心雕琢，意境虽不高远，气魄亦无雄奇，但文字与音韵都达到技巧上的高度圆熟。他在《论批评》中提出一个关于好诗的定义，认为卓越的诗句须是：

What oft was thought, but ne'er so well express'd;

亦即内容虽是人们熟悉的，文字却是空前出色的。蒲伯本人的诗完全实现了他自己的主张。

蒲伯的名声，曾经有过起伏。十八世纪他在世时，虽然有人攻击他的学识与人品，他的诗才则是大家折服的。十九世纪，浪漫派兴起，他所代表的新古典主义诗歌成了攻击目标，唯有拜伦一人力排众议，肯定他的优点。到了十九世纪中叶，名诗人兼批评家安诺德（Matthew Arnold）竟说蒲伯的诗根本不算诗，只能当作散文来看。二十世纪二十年代，浪漫派的诗风衰竭，蒲伯又受到重视，人们重新发现了他的许多优点，认识了他在英国诗歌史上的重要地位——在“英雄双韵体”的运用上，他的艺术成就至今无人超越。

【题解与注释】

1. CONCEIT; LANGUAGE; NUMBERS

选自 *An Essay on Criticism*，它是蒲伯早年所写，也是他的成名之作，发表于1711年，那时他还只二十三岁。

写诗来论文学在欧洲有许多先例，著名的如古罗马贺拉斯的《诗艺》(Horace: *Ars Poetica*)，欧洲文艺复兴时期意大利维达的《诗学》(Vida: *Poetica*)，十七世纪法国布瓦洛的《诗艺》(Boileau: *L'Art poétique*) . 蒲伯在本诗里的许多意见是从这三本书里取来的。他的主旨在论述文学批评之道，认为一个批评家必须有高尚的趣味 (taste)，而这趣味是可以培养的，但是趣味必须不违背自然 (Nature)，只有这样才有真正的机智 (wit) 可言。话虽如此，他却将重点放在趣味与机智上面，而这正是英国十八世纪新古典主义者的共同趋势，因此此诗可以看作新古典主义对于文学——特别是对于文学批评——的意见的全面阐明。

诗的内容虽然主要是掇拾人言，新意不多，诗的写法却显示了蒲伯的非凡才能，有无数特别机智、俏皮、精辟的诗句，后来为人经常引用。但它又毕竟是蒲伯的早年作品，还留下不少僵硬及不合语法之处，音韵亦不尽协调。

历来批评家对于此诗大都是推崇的。可以举 Dr. Johnson 在 *Lives of the Poets* 中的话为例：

> One of his greatest though of his earliest works is the *Essay on Criticism*, which, if he had written nothing else, would have placed him among the first critics and the first poets, as it exhibits every mode of excellence that can embellish or dignify didactic composition, selection of matter, novelty of arrangement, justness of precept, splendour of illustration, and propriety of digression.

而作为英国文论的代表作，则一直到二十世纪它还出现在几本重要的文学批评选集里。

原诗分为三个部分：一，第1—200行，论述文学批评的重要与一个良好的批评家如何养成；二，第201—559行，论述评论之所以不当的十大原因 (骄傲，浅学，枝节，挑剔或奉承，崇古或厚今，偏颇，怪僻，易变，党见，妒忌)；三，第560—744行，论述文学批评的准则并简要回顾欧洲文学批评的历史。

我们所选的片断 (第289—383行) 取自原诗第二部分有关“枝节”一段，诗人在其中论述批评家只注意局部而不顾全体之害，并举三例说明所谓枝节何指。这三例就是：过分着重奇思怪喻 (conceit)，孤立注意文字 (language)，一味考究音韵 (numbers)。这些都是当时批评的流弊，蒲伯除了指出必须从全局立论之外，又对每例本身所涉及的问题作了分析和论断，主张恰当，得体，文字服从思想，声调追随意义。这些含有不少至今有益的意见。

此外，还可以注意蒲伯诗作的声韵之美。尤其在本诗论到音韵的时候，他本人的诗行产生了特殊的拟声效果，例如：

And ten low words oft creep in one dull line,

一行十个单音的普通字构成了特别慢的行进速度，又如在提到别的拙劣的诗人喜用 Alexandrine 体诗（每行 6 个音步，即 12 或 13 个音节）之后，他紧接写了一行

That, like a wounded snake, drags its slow length along,

正是 Alexandrine 体的示范，而且音形义结合，不仅诗行的长度似蛇，声调之缓慢亦如受伤的蛇在爬行，更增加了讽刺效果。

（标题） 非原有，是我们根据内容所加；三字解释见下。

1. Conceit: 此处是十八世纪用法，指文学作品中的奇思怪喻，十七世纪玄学派诗人（the Metaphysical Poets）所追求的一类便是，例如堂恩（John Donne）曾以圆规的两脚来比喻离别中的夫妻，便是有名的 conceit:

If they be two, they are two: so
  As stiff twin compasses are two,
Thy soul the fixed foot, makes no show:
  To move, but doth, if th' other do.

—*A Valediction: Forbidding Mourning*

十八世纪此风已不盛，但尚有残余，因此重规矩、讲文雅的蒲伯要竭力纠正之。

2. glitt'ring thoughts: 即指 conceits; **struck out** 突出。

3. just or fit: 这正是蒲伯等新古典主义者所着重的品质。

4. Chaos: confusion and disorder.

5. wit: 此字在本诗出现多次，意义不一，在此意同 imagination 或 fancy，即在不同事物之间发现相似处的能力，因此实指 conceit.

6. to trace: to draw.

7. The naked Nature and the living grace: 真面目的大自然和天生的优雅。

8. True Wit is Nature to advantage dress'd, What oft was thought, but ne'er so well express'd: 蒲伯的名句。此处 Wit 意义不同于第 292 行，指文雅的机智；由于新古典主义者特别推重机智，故在此行中又泛指一切好诗。诗之好者，不在有多少新意，而在写法特妙。蒲伯此意为当时许多新古典主义者所共有，早见于布瓦洛（Boileau）与屈莱顿（Dryden），同时代人中艾狄生（Addison）也说："Wit and fine writing do not consist so much in advancing things that are new as in giving things known an agreeable turn."（*Spectator*, No 253）

9. Something, whose truth convinced at sight we find: 句子结构不甚清楚，可以解为 Something, of whose truth we find (ourselves) convinced at first sight，即初一读到就完全相信了它的真实。

10. recommend: 使之更显出色。

11. sets off: 衬托出。

注意蒲伯以此行末字 wit 与上行 light 押韵，音律不调，为其青年时败笔之一。

12. still: always（古义）；第 318，349 行同。

13. take upon content: 不加细察就接受下来。

14. decent: becoming，恰当，合式。

15. conceit: 此处可解为"意思"，但亦可释作"奇思怪喻"如前。

16. in regal purple: 穿着国王的袍服（**purple** = crimson，欧洲古时国王穿深红色）。

17. sort: be of the same class with，配合。

18. As several garbs with country, town, and court: 就象是在乡，进城，入朝都要有不同服装（反映蒲伯写的是统治阶级人士）。

19. Some by old words to fame have made pretence: 有人想靠用古字出名；**made pretence to,** laid claim to.

20. phrase: 泛指文字，而非指语法上的所谓"短语"。

21. amaze: 使无知者惊为天人；此字当时意为 to overwhelm one with wonder，意思比今天强烈。

22. Fungoso: 系十七世纪剧作家 Ben Jonson (1572–1637) 在所作 *Every Man Out of his Humour* (1601) 一剧中的人物，剧作者"人物介绍"中说他是"a student, one that has revelled in his time, and follows the fashion afar off, like a spy."

23. sparks: 浮华人物的鄙称。

24. in their doublets drest: dressed in our grandfathers' clothes; doublets 是古时男人穿的外衣。

25. 第 335—336 两行：反映蒲伯的写作态度：不可太新，也不可过旧。

26. Numbers: 原指诗中的音节（metrical periods or feet），此处泛指诗的音韵；蒲伯曾另有名句说明其从小就会做诗云：

> I lisped in numbers, for the numbers came.
>
> —*An Epistle to Dr. Arbuthnot*

27. conspire: combine（此处特义）。

28. tuneful fools: 这些只讲音韵的笨虫们。

29. Parnassus: 缪斯（the Muses）所聚居的山，相传在希腊 Phocis 地方。这里意为"诗歌的圣地"。

30. These equal syllables alone require: 这些人只要求音节均匀。注意从此起蒲伯故意利用声音模拟他所讽刺的种种毛病。

31. open vowels: 开豁的元音，即要张大口才能发出的元音，如 [ɑː]，[ou]，[ɔː]，[au] 等；tire 的宾语是 ear；意为听了过久的开豁元音，使耳朵感到单调，因而疲倦。

32. expletives: 为了强调或为了韵律而加上的赘词；德莱顿（Dryden）曾批评人说："He creeps along with ten little words in every line, and helps out his numbers with *For to* and *Unto*, and all the pretty expletives he can find, till he drags them to the end of another line …".

33. 第 346，347 行 **join** 与 **line** 押韵，因当时 join 读如 [dʒʌin]，line 读如 [lʌin].

34. And ten low words oft creep in one dull line: 措词如上行注引 Dryden 之

言；关于其拟声特点，参阅本诗题解。

35. With sure returns of still expected rhymes: 总是那样机械地押韵，毫无变化；**still,** always，如上。

36. 第 350—353 四行：俏皮地用模仿的手法挖苦了那些拙劣的诗人不仅押韵呆板，用词也陈腐俗套；其实这正是新古典主义者的末流所为。蒲伯成名之后，有模仿他而未得其妙者，也往往落入这等所谓十八世纪的"诗语"（poetic diction）的俗套。

37. The reader's threatened (not in vain) with "sleep", 此行意义双关，一方面说那些拙劣诗人用 sleep 去同 creep 押韵；另一方面，又指他们的诗是那样沉闷，真的会使读者昏昏欲眠。**The reader's** = The reader is.

38. Alexandrine，诗体名，每行六个音步，十二或十三个音节；十二世纪时，法国诗人 Alexandre de Bernay 完成前人 Lambert le Court 未竟之功，用这个诗体写成歌颂古希腊亚历山大的武功的长诗 *Alexandriade, ou Chanson de Geste D'Alexandre le grand*，从此人们称此诗体为 Alexandrine.

39. That, like a wounded snake, drags its slow length along, 此行就是用的 Alexandrine 体，共有 12 音节。参阅本诗题解。

40. Denham's strength, and Waller's sweetness, 从此起蒲伯提出他认为好诗的正面例子。在这方面他继承了特莱顿的看法，后者曾在 *Essay of Dramatic Poesy* 中说："[The Greek and Roman poets] can produce … nothing so even, sweet, and flowing, as Mr. Waller; nothing so majestic, so correct, as Sir John Denham …"

Sir John Denham (1615–1668)，曾作 *Cooper's Hill* 等诗，格调不甚高，唯有四行咏 Thames 河的诗至今有名：

O could I flow like thee, and make thy stream
My great example, as it is my theme;
Tho' deep yet clear, tho' gentle, yet not dull,
Strong without rage, without o'erflowing full.

Edmund Waller (1605–1687)，在英国诗歌史上有重要地位，由于他重兴"英雄双韵体"，使诗风复归工整。本人所作有抒情诗"Go, lovely rose"及咏老年的诗至今传诵。

蒲伯在这里提倡一种既刚且柔的诗风，要将有力与优美结合起来，故在第 360 行特别标出 the easy vigour of a line，作为他的主张。

41. The sound must seem an Echo to the sense: 音韵须作意义的回声。下面他举例说明，仍用拟声手法。

42. Zephyr: ['zefə] 微风，一般指西风。

43. Ajax ['eidʒæks]：荷马史诗中所写的希腊英雄，力大，善掷巨石（见 Homer, *Iliad*, VII, 268–271; XII, 380–385）。

44. Camilla [kə'milə]：维琪尔史诗中所写的女英雄，行动敏捷如飞，所过处田野则麦穗不倒，海水则波不沾履（见 Virgil: *Aeneid*, VII, 808–811）。

45. Timotheus [ti'məuθjəs]：特莱顿所作名诗《亚历山大的盛宴》（Dryden: *Alexander's Feast*）中的乐师，他用不同的音乐（varied lays）唤起听众不同的感情（bid alternate passions fall and rise). 亚历山大虽能征惯战，听了也深受感动。德莱顿此诗写得十分出色，韵律能传达各种乐声与情绪。下文都指此诗中的情景。

46. the son of Libyan Jove: 即指亚历山大，古时传说他是利比亚一神（Zeus Ammon of Libya）所生；Jove 即 Jupiter, king of gods，此处借用来指利比亚的主要神祇。

47. Persians and Greeks like turns of nature found: 波斯人与希腊人发现他们虽对战多年，但是天性相同，同样受音乐感动；**like,** similar; **turns of nature,** natural inclination; **found** 是本句动词。

48. the world's victor: 也指亚历山大；Sound，指音乐。

49. allow: 承认。

50. And what Timotheus was, is Dryden now: 过去 Timotheus 所奏音乐的力量，现在可在德莱顿的诗里寻到。蒲伯对于德莱顿一直钦佩，曾说："I learned versification wholly from Dryden's works, who had improved it much beyond any of our former poets."（Spence, *Anecdotes*）. 所以在这专论音韵的一段，他以歌颂德莱顿的诗才作结。

2. ATTICUS

选自 *An Epistle to Dr. Arbuthnot* (1735). John Arbuthnot (1667–1735) 为当时女王 Queen Anne 的御医，与蒲伯、斯威夫特等友善，有文才，也是当时闻人之一。他曾在 1734 年重病时函劝蒲伯在写讽刺诗时要与人为善，蒲伯乃写此诗答之，表白其与人争皆出自卫，而素无损人之意。此诗通篇出色，为蒲伯最好作品之一。

原诗虽在 1735 年才出版，其中有若干片断则早已写好，此处所选一段（第 193—214 行）早在 1722 年 12 月已在杂志 *St. James's Journal* 发表，后来也不断单独成篇印行，成为英国文学中最有名的讽刺片断之一。

讽刺的对象是当时有名的文人政客艾狄生（Joseph Addison, 1672–1719），他不仅会写小品文，有诗才，在政治上也有势力，曾任辉格党组成的内阁次官。他原来同蒲伯友好，但后来逐渐疏远，原因之一是蒲伯不是辉格党人，艾狄生不以亲信视之；1715 年后两人关系更坏，那时蒲伯正译荷马史诗，而艾狄生以其权势地位帮助别人出版另一译本，后来蒲伯又听说艾狄生雇人写文攻击他，更加气愤，于是写了这一部分的初稿，并将它寄给艾狄生本人。

因为艾狄生是非同小可的对手，蒲伯十分讲究战术。一上来他称赞艾狄生，然而着重其得天之厚；接着转入攻击，主要指出他忌才；然而艾狄生又不敢明忌，只是阴损，诗人乃以一连串的对仗句法揭穿他的伪善；再就谈到他身边的党羽（his little Senate），指出他有一个小集团，然后在这大段揭露之后用了既平行又对照的两行作了有力的一结，然又隐含器重之意（Who would not weep, if Atticus were he! 意思是艾狄生原是大家佩服的，现在则叫人失望了），为以后的交情留下余地。

蒲伯运用"英雄双韵体"之妙，到此几已登峰造极。英雄双韵体诗并非新创，早经十四世纪的乔叟（Chaucer）、十六七世纪的斯宾塞（Spenser）与马娄（Marlowe）等大诗人用过，但后来"素体无韵诗"（blank verse）盛行，到十七世纪 Edmund Waller (1606–1687) 起来纠正当时粗犷不协律的诗风，才重振了英雄双韵体，又经过德莱顿（Dryden）的改进，它终于成为十八世纪英国的主要诗体，到了蒲伯手里达到最高的完美。这一诗体每行五个音步，每步两个音节，一轻一重；两行成一组，互相押韵。其好处是整齐优美，但易陷于单调呆板。蒲伯的贡献在于：一方面他使它更工整，例如他的句子一般是一行一句，很少跨越；另一方面他又使它更多变化，特别是利用了行中的停顿（caesura），不仅每行之中常有一顿，往往每半行之中也有一顿，顿的位置不一，这样不仅增加了各种音节配合的机会，而且还使他能将重要的词紧放在顿之前后，获得特别的强调效果，例如：

Damn with faint praise, assent with civil leer,

这里对仗整齐，一行中两个部分相矛盾，而每个部分之内又有矛盾，写出艾狄生阴阳两面，欲大骂先小捧，明里点头，暗里横眼，然又一切正确，叫人抓不住错处。蒲伯的讽刺确实尖锐，艺术确实高超，只不过都用来发泄个人私怨，而不及社会的大不义，人群的大悲愤，因此其诗虽工，其格还不够高。

（标题） 非原有，系后人抽出此段时根据内容所加。

1. Atticus: 原是古罗马政论家 Cicero 之友 Titus Pomponius Atticus（公元前 109—132 年），蒲伯借用来指艾狄生。

2. Peace to all such!: 让这些人安息吧；针对上文所谈诸人说的，这些人都曾攻击蒲伯，蒲伯在此表示不与他们争。

3. were there: 整段都用虚拟式，以 were there 开始，以 there be 与 were he 结束，故弄玄虚，表示这是假想人物，才会这样之坏，但读者一看，知道实有其人，更增讽刺的效果。

4. one: a person，一个人；十八世纪通例，重要名词大写。

5. fires: 灵感。

6. Genius: kindles 的宾语；Fame, inspires 的宾语。

7. each Art to please: 有各种悦世之才。

8. like the *Turk*: 当时英国人对土耳其人有许多传说，其一就是土耳其苏丹惧怕兄弟争夺皇位，将他们一律处死或放逐。此处指艾狄生怕别人与他竞争。

9. scornful: 也形容 eyes；既看不起，又妒忌人。

10. Arts: 伎俩；自己靠某些伎俩飞黄腾达，可是看见别人也用它们，就表示非常厌恶。

11. Damn with faint praise, assent with civil leer: 蒲伯最常为人引用的名句：civil，客气。参阅本诗题解最后部分。

12. hesitate dislike: 明明不喜欢，却要吞吞吐吐半天才说出。

13. Alike reserv'd to blame, or to commend: 既不愿骂人，又不肯赞人。

14. ev'n: even.

15. 第 207，208 行：两行中 besieg'd 与 oblig'd 押韵，oblige 读如 [əbˈliːdʒ] 是当时英国上流社会模仿法语发音的结果。

16. And so obliging that he ne'er oblig'd: 也是蒲伯名句之一，意为似乎有求必应，实则口惠而实不至；**ne'er** = never.

17. *Cato*: 艾狄生曾写一有关古罗马元老 Cato（公元前 95—46 年）的悲剧，即以主角名为题，在1713年上演，获得巨大成功。

18. his little Senate: 指艾狄生左右的一群党羽，用Senate一字是继续上文Cato的故事，古罗马有上议院，但Cato自己又有一批追随者，帮他决策，俨然另一上议院，故云。

19. And sit attentive to his own applause: 坐着仔细听别人对自己的歌颂；attentive一字传神。

20. Templars: 学习法律的人，多系富家子弟，往往也喜文艺。艾狄生身边，有不少这样的人。

21. ev'ry sentence raise: 将艾狄生的每句话都大捧一气。

22. And wonder with a foolish face of praise: 带着赞美的蠢相称羡不已；wonder, marvel.

23. 第213—214两行：总结全段，既整齐，又有对照：上行laugh，下行weep，是对照；上行such a man，下行Atticus，是一致；既下判断，又留余地。蒲伯从1715年左右起意写此，到1735年最后修改，二十年中精心琢磨，五易其稿，才达到现在这样的完美。

19 SAMUEL JOHNSON
1709–1784

1. LETTER TO LORD CHESTERFIELD

2. THE PREFACE TO THE DICTIONARY OF THE ENGLISH LANGUAGE (concluding part)

3. THE LIVES OF THE ENGLISH POETS (selections)

李赋宁　选注

1. LETTER TO LORD CHESTERFIELD

February 7, 1755.

My Lord

I have been lately informed, by the proprietor of *The World*,[1] that two papers, in which my Dictionary is recommended to the public, were written by your Lordship. To be so distinguished,[2] is an honour, which, being very little accustomed to favours from the great,[3] I know not well how to receive, or in what terms to acknowledge.[4]

When, upon some slight encouragement,[5] I first visited your Lordship, I was overpowered, like the rest of mankind, by[6] the enchantment of your address;[7] and could not forbear to wish[8] that I might boast myself *Le vainqueur du vainqueur de la terre;*[9] — that I might obtain that regard for which I saw the world contending; but I found my attendance[10] so little encouraged, that neither pride[11] nor modesty[12] would suffer[13] me to continue it. When I had once addressed your Lordship in public,[14] I had exhausted all the art of pleasing which a retired and uncourtly scholar[15] can possess. I had done all that I could; and no man is well pleased to have his all[16] neglected, be it ever so little.[17]

Seven years, my Lord, have now past,[18] since I waited in your outward rooms, or was repulsed from your door;[19] during which time I have been pushing on my work through difficulties, of which it is useless to complain, and have brought it, at last, to the verge of publication, without one act of assistance, one word of encouragement, or one smile of favour.[20] Such treatment I did not expect, for I never had a Patron[21] before.

The shepherd in Virgil grew at last acquainted with Love, and found him a native of the rocks.[22]

Is not a Patron,[23] my Lord, one who looks with unconcern on a man struggling for life in the water, and, when he has reached ground, encumbers him with help? The notice which you have been pleased to take of my labours,[24] had it been early, had been kind;[25] but it has been delayed till I am indifferent, and cannot enjoy it; till I am solitary,[26] and cannot impart it; till I am known, and do not want it.[27] I hope it is no very cynical asperity[28] not to confess obligations where no benefit has been received, or to be unwilling that the Public should consider me as owing that to a Patron, which Providence has enabled me to do for myself.

Having carried on my work thus far with so little obligation to any favourer of learning,[29] I shall not be disappointed though I should conclude it, if less be possible, with less;[30] for I have been long wakened from that dream of hope, in which I once boasted myself with so much exultation, my Lord,

your Lordship's most humble,

most obedient servant,

Sam: Johnson[31]

2. *THE PREFACE TO THE DICTIONARY OF THE ENGLISH LANGUAGE*

In hope of giving longevity to that which its own nature forbids to be immortal,[1] I have devoted this book,[2] the labour of years, to the honour of my country, that we may no longer yield the palm of philology, without a contest, to the nations of the continent.[3] The chief glory of every people arises from its authors:[4] whether I shall add anything by my own writings to the reputation of English literature, must be left to time:[5] much of my life has been lost under the pressures of disease; much has been trifled away; and much has always been spent in provision for the day that was passing over me;[6] but I shall not think my employment useless or ignoble, if, by my assistance, foreign nations, and distant ages, gain access to the propagators of knowledge, and understand the teachers of truth;[7] if my labours afford light to the repositories of science,[8] and add celebrity to Bacon, to Hooker, to Milton, and to Boyle.[9]

When I am animated by this wish, I look with pleasure on my book, however defective, and deliver it to the world with the spirit of a man that has endeavoured well. That it will immediately become popular I have not promised to myself: a few wild blunders, and risible absurdities, from which no work of such multiplicity was ever free, may, for a time, furnish folly with laughter, and harden ignorance into contempt;[10] but useful diligence will at last prevail,[11] and there never can be wanting some who distinguish desert;[12] who will consider that no dictionary of a living tongue ever can be perfect, since, while it is hastening to publication, some words are budding, and some falling away;[13] that a whole life cannot be spent upon syntax and etymology, and that even a whole life would not be sufficient;[14] that he, whose design includes whatever language can express,[15] must often speak of what he does not understand; that a writer will sometimes be hurried by eagerness to the end, and sometimes faint with weariness under a task, which Scaliger compares to the labours of the anvil and the mine;[16] that what is obvious is not always known, and what is known is not always present;[17] that sudden fits of inadvertency will surprise vigilance, slight avocations will seduce attention, and casual eclipses of the mind will darken learning;[18] and that the writer shall often in vain[19] trace his memory, at the moment of need, for that which yesterday he knew with intuitive readiness, and which will come uncalled into his thoughts tomorrow.[20]

In this work, when it shall be found[21] that much is omitted, let it not be forgotten that much likewise is performed; and though no book was ever spared out of tenderness to the author,[22] and the world is little solicitous to know whence proceeded the faults of that which it condemns;[23] yet it may gratify curiosity[24] to inform it, that the English Dictionary was written with little assistance of the learned, and without any patronage of the great; not in the soft obscurities of retirement, or under the shelter of academic bowers, but amidst inconvenience and distraction, in sickness and in sorrow.[25] It may repress the triumph of malignant criticism[26] to observe,[27] that if our language is not here fully displayed, I have only failed in an attempt, which no human powers have hitherto completed.[28] If the lexicons of ancient tongues,[29] now immutably fixed, and comprised in a few volumes, be yet, after the toil of successive ages, inadequate and delusive;[30] if the aggregated knowledge, and co-operating diligence of the Italian academicians,[31] did not secure them from the censure of Beni;[32] if the embodied critics of France,[33] when fifty years had been spent upon their work,[34] were obliged to change its economy,[35] and give their second edition another form, I may surely be contented without the praise of perfection, which, if I could obtain, in this gloom of solitude, what would it avail me?[36] I have protracted my work till most of those, whom I wished to please, have sunk into the grave, and success and miscarriage are empty sounds:[37] I, therefore, dismiss it with frigid tranquillity, having little to fear or hope from censure or from praise.[38]

【作者简介】 Samuel Johnson（塞缪尔·约翰逊，1709—1784），英国古典主义重要作家之一。他思想保守，但在散文写作和文学批评方面有不小的贡献，同时又是优秀的学者和语言学家。他的散文风格独树一帜，既具有拉丁文散文的典雅、气势和音调的铿锵，又兼备英文散文的雄健、朴素和简练等特点。他的文章，结构整齐匀称如精心营造的建筑物，风貌庄严高昂，但却又亲切动人。他的文学批评从常识判断出发，在某些方面突破了古典主义文艺理论的藩篱。例如在他著名的论文 *The Preface to Shakespeare*（《莎士比亚戏剧集》序言，1765）里，他认为古典主义戏剧所奉为天经地义的"三一律"戒规，不足为训。莎士比亚违反了"三一律"仍不失为伟大的剧作家。在评价文学作品时，法则和条规固然有些帮助，但观察体会尤其重要，不能为法则条规所代替。在文艺领域内，理性必须辅以幻想，方能认识真理，全面正确地反映人生。此外，约翰逊又把文学批评和传记文学结合起来，为文学创作开扩了新的领域，写了一部卓越的 *The Lives of the English Poets*（《英国诗人传》，1779—1781）。在语言学方面，约翰逊独力编纂了 *The Dictionary of the English Language*（《英语词典》，1755）。这部词典，虽然其中某些词的词源不甚可靠，但对词义所下的定义比较准确（某些反映约翰逊个人爱憎和偏见或故意诙谐的词除外），为了解释词义所引用的例句比较丰富（这在约翰逊以前人们所编词典中少见），出版后，被人们奉为权威性的著作。从那时起，英语词汇的词义和拼法才固定下来，逐渐趋于统一。因此，这部词典在使英语规范化方面，起了重要的作用。约翰逊编辑的莎士比亚戏剧集，不以版本见胜，但他对这些剧本，在有关历史背景、情节和人物性格等方面所加的注释却脍炙人口。这一著作刺激、促进了英国学者对于莎士比亚的研究。约翰逊的谈话非常机智、锋利、精辟、发人深省，他的忠实朋友 James Boswell（詹姆斯·鲍斯威耳，1740—1795）所作著名传记 *The*

Life of Samuel Johnson（《塞缪尔·约翰逊传》，1791）翔实生动地记载了他的谈话，使他跃然纸上，活在读者心里。

【题解与注释】

1. Letter to Lord Chesterfield

约翰逊的散文著作和作品，除上述的 *The Preface to Shakespeare* 和 *The Lives of the English Poets* 外，最优秀的还有他的信札 *Letter to Lord Chesterfield*（《致吉斯特非尔德爵爷书》，1755）和 *The Preface to the Dictionary of the English Language*（《英语词典》序言，1755）等。*Letter to Lord Chesterfield* 是英国历代散文中最有名的范文中的一篇。它表现了新兴资产阶级的作家向封建贵族宣布独立自主的反抗精神，因此可以看作欧洲文学史中作家的"独立宣言"。这篇文章写得既锋利又含蓄，不亢不卑，但却充分发泄了作者愤慨的感情，表现了作者不向权贵低头的骨气和克服困难的毅力和信心。这篇文章雄健有力，亲切动人，语言精练，对仗工整，由此可以窥见约翰逊散文风格之一斑。*The Preface to the Dictionary of the English Language* 是学术著作，发表了约翰逊对语言学和词典学的一些见解。我们所选的是这篇文章的结尾数段。在这几段文字里，既有议论，又有叙事，更有抒情。约翰逊谈到他编词典的甘苦，在多么艰难的条件下他独立进行工作，终于完成了这部词典。他对他自己的工作感到自豪，同时他也感到这部词典仍有不少缺点，因此他有些担心，怕读者会对他的词典否定过多。这几段文字也很能说明约翰逊散文风格的特点：句子结构匀称整齐，用词精练、典雅，口气庄重、诚恳，感情深沉、含蓄。总的印象是雄健、朴实，但又典雅、精美。约翰逊的散文的确兼有拉丁文散文和英文散文的优点，把二者圆满地结合起来。

Letter to Lord Chesterfield 是约翰逊写给 Lord Chesterfield 的一封信。Chesterfield 伯爵（1694—1773）是当时英国一个显赫人物。他是贵族、政客，又是作家。当时文人想要出名，在文坛上露头角，必须有达官贵人提携、援引。约翰逊对于伦敦穷困文人的生活是很熟悉的，因为他自己一直在与贫穷和饥饿相挣扎。1747 年约翰逊拟就了一个编纂英语词典的计划，把这个计划送呈 Chesterfield 伯爵，希望得到他的赞许和资助。谁料 Chesterfield 对此计划并不真感兴趣，也未答复约翰逊的请求。约翰逊无可奈何，只得自力更生。他单枪匹马，独立作战达七年之久，词典终于编成。而当词典出版前夕，Chesterfield 忽然在当时销路很广的一家报纸 *The World*（《世界》，1753—1756 年发行）上发表了两篇文章，把约翰逊的词典捧上了天，并说今后英国语言学界必须奉约翰逊为独裁者，为最高的权威。Chesterfield 可能是衷心赞服约翰逊的成就，但他也可能是盼望约翰逊把他新编成的词典献给自己，这样他就可以装成约翰逊的援引人、提携人（patron），就可以把约翰逊的声誉，分一半到自己身上。约翰逊毫不客气地否认了 Chesterfield 或任何别人是他的提携人。他说："I never had a Patron before"（第 443 页，第 9 行）。约翰逊用反语口气问 Chesterfield，一位提携人岂能坐视行将溺水者在水中挣扎而无动于衷，反而当此人已达到岸边，却多余地伸出援助之手？我

们这里所选注的 *Letter to Lord Chesterfield* 的本文系根据 The Oxford World's Classics（牛津大学世界名著丛书）第 282 号，R. W. Chapman 编选的 *Selected Letters of Samuel Johnson*（1925 年出版）。

1. The World: 当时销路很广的一家报纸（2,500 份），1753—1756 年在伦敦发行。

2. distinguished: 受到推崇。

3. being very little accustomed to favours from the great: 由于对大人物的垂青很不习惯。（此处分词片语表示原因。）

4. or in what terms to acknowledge: 或如何措辞来表示感激。

5. When, upon some slight encouragement: 这句话的词序表示 *upon some slight encouragement*（受到了些许鼓励）只是附带说明、轻轻带过的插入语。若把这个片语放在句首，就会产生不适当的强调效果。用表示时间的副词 when 开始一句话或一段话，是非常自然的方式，因为这个时间副词也同时具有连词的作用。放在句首，可使文气运行流畅，接合自如。

6. overpowered ... by: overwhelmed by，倾倒于。

7. the enchantment of your address: 你的应接谈吐（*address*，名词），引人入胜（*enchantment*，魔力，讨人喜欢的本领）。

8. and could not forbear to wish: and I could not help wishing，我不禁发愿（*forbear*，退避）。其它版本在 *and* 后，*could* 前，加一 I 字。

9. Le vainqueur du vainqueur de la terre:（法语）conqueror of the conqueror of the earth（征服世界的人的征服者）。这句话来自十七世纪法国古典主义文学批评家 Boileau（布瓦洛，1636—1711）的 *L'Art poétique*（《诗歌的艺术》，1674），第 3 章，第 272 行："Je chante le vainqueur des vainqueurs de la terre"（I sing the praise of the conqueror of the conquerors of the earth）. Boileau 这句话又引自十七世纪法国作家 Georges de Scudéry (1601–1668) 的史诗 *Alaric*，第 1 章。Boileau 引这句诗，目的在于嘲笑 Scudéry 浮夸的文风。约翰逊在转引时稍加变动，把 des vainqueurs 改为 *du vainqueur*. 帝王将相为征服世界的人，而诗人文学家却能感动帝王将相，说服他们，打动他们的心，因此诗人文学家就变成征服世界的人的征服者。在这里，约翰逊把 Chesterfield 比做世界征服者，把他自己比做世界征服者的征服者，用意是说他不禁发愿，想要赢得 Chesterfield 对他的赏识，受到 Chesterfield 的资助和提携。

10. attendance: act of waiting upon（another）（侍候），company（陪伴），visit（拜访）。

11. pride: self-respect（自尊心）。

12. modesty: bashfulness, shyness（怕羞，不好意思的心理）。

13. suffer: allow（允许）。

14. addressed your Lordship in public: 当着众人向你致意。

15. a retired and uncourtly scholar: 一个与世无争、不善逢迎的读书人。

16. his all: all that he can do.

17. be it ever so little: however little his all (all that he can do) may be（无论他所能做的如何微不足道）。

18. have now past: 其它版本作 passed（度过）。

19. was repulsed from your door: 吃了你的闭门羹，被拒于你的门外。

20. without one act of assistance, one word of encouragement, or one smile of favour: 在这封信里，约翰逊惯用的排偶结构有时发展为三组对偶。例如，此处三个抽象名词 *assistance, encouragement* 和 *favour* 相互对应，另外三个比较具体的名词 *act, word* 和 *smile* 也排列得很匀称。为了收到累进强调的效果，约翰逊一连用了三个词 *assistance*（资助）*encouragement*（鼓励），*favour*（赞赏——approval）。他又连用了 *one act of*（一桩行动），*one word of*（一句话）和 *one smile of*（一副微笑）。这样一来，抽象的、空泛的词就变得具体生动了。这个修辞手法颇值得学习。

21. Patron: 赏识者，恩人；特别指帮助提携文人等的王公贵人。

22. The shepherd in Virgil grew at last acquainted with Love, and found him a native of the rocks: 这个典故出自古罗马诗人 Virgil（维吉尔，公元前 70—19）的 *Eclogue*（《牧歌》），VIII，第 43 行。James Rhoades 的英文译文写道："Now know I what Love is: 'mid savage rocks / Tmaros or Rhodope brought forth the boy, / Or Garamantes in earth's utmost bounds — / No kin of ours, nor of our blood begot"（我现在认识爱神了：这个男孩——指爱神 Cupid——出生在 Tmaros 或 Rhodope 的荒山岩石堆里，或者出生在远达地球边界的 Garamantes 地方。他不是我们的亲戚，也不和我们同血统）。在 Virgil 的《牧歌》里，牧童因失恋而抱怨爱神为蛮荒野人，和文明的罗马人不同种族，也不同血统，因此没有共同的思想感情。爱神既生长在荒山岩石间，他的心肠也变得象岩石一样硬。无怪乎牧童无法打动牧女的心，无从享受到爱情的幸福。约翰逊巧妙地引用了这个典故。他把自己比做牧童（*shepherd*），把 Chesterfield 比作爱神（*Love*）. 标榜为文人的提携者、赏识者（*Patron*）的人，原来是个蛮荒野人，心肠象岩石一样硬。还有一个含义：既然爱神生长在蛮荒之地，那么在文明世界里（罗马），爱神是绝迹的。同样，既然文人的赏识者生长在遥远的蛮邦，那么在文明的英国就找不到真正的赏识者。这个含义，从上下文里是可以看出的。上文："for I never had a Patron before"（第 2 页，第 13 行），下文 "Is not a Patron ..."（第 2 页，第 16 行）。

23. Is not a Patron ...: 这句是反语问话，无情地揭露了所谓的"恩人"或"赏识者"的真面目：见人在水中为生命挣扎，而漠不关心；俟其平安抵岸，重以援助相累（不及时、不需要的帮助反而成了负担）。这正是 Chesterfield 的行为，也是一般自命为文人们的赏识者的写照。无怪乎约翰逊要感慨在文明国度里竟然找不到一个真正的赏识者。

24 The notice which you have been pleased to take of my labours: 这句话也是讽刺口吻：you have been pleased to take notice of my work（你居然高兴，注意起我的作品来了）。"be pleased to do" 这个词组通常用来表示说话人对当事人的恭敬态度。例如，COD（《简明牛津词典》）的例句：Your lordship was pleased to doubt my veracity（蒙大人不见弃，居然怀疑我说的不是实话）。说话人的恭敬态度，显然是一种讽刺。

25. had it been early, had been kind: 在这句话里 *it* 指 *notice*（你对我的作品

所给予的注意）。全句是条件句：If it had been（或 had come）early, it would have been kind（假若你给予我作品的注意来得早些，这种注意就会是善意的）。*had been*（代替 would have been）是早期现代英语中的虚拟式。

26. till I am solitary: 约翰逊的妻子在三年前（1752）就已去世。

27. till I am indifferent, and cannot enjoy it; till I am solitary, and cannot impart it; till I am known, and do not want it: 这是全篇文章的顶峰。约翰逊坚决拒绝了 Chestefield 伯爵所给予他的词典的注意。在这里约翰逊又使用了三个词组相互对偶的修辞手法，收到了最能感动读者的效果。同时也最充分地表现了约翰逊倔强、孤傲的个性。Chesterfield 对约翰逊词典的注意，等于雨后送伞，其实是多余的。约翰逊说："我已无动于衷（*indifferent*），对此关心无法消受（*cannot enjoy it*）；我已孑然一身（*solitary*），无法与人共享（*cannot impart it*）；我已成名（*known*），对此并不需要（*do not want it*）.". 这句话的确是全篇文章最精彩之笔。首先，它的结构非常整齐匀称。其次，选词非常恰当（*indifferent, solitary, known*），情感和口气层层加深、加强（*cannot enjoy it, cannot impart it, do not want it*）。最后一句 *do not want it*，声如霹雳，发泄了多年来积累在心里的愤慨和怨气。同时这句话也说得最为响亮，充满了信心和自豪感，的确是作家独立宣言的号角。我们想要学会用最简单的词汇表达最丰富、最强烈的感情，这句 *do not want it* 是我们学习的好范例。

28. cynical asperity: *cynical*，不相信人性是善的；*asperity*，严厉的、苛求于人的性格。约翰逊说他并不是不相信 Chesterfield 对他是一番好意，或苛求于 Chesterfield. 但是他既然并没有从 Chesterfield 那里受到任何恩惠（*no benefit has been received*），当然就没有必要来承他的情（*confess obligations*）. 既然上帝（*Providence*）使约翰逊自己完成了工作，并没有凭借任何赏识者的援助，那么他当然不肯让读者设想此事应归功于任何"恩人"（*unwilling that the Public should consider me as owing that to a Patron, which Providence has enabled me to do for myself*）. 在这句话里，约翰逊有意识地用了两个难词（*cynical asperity*）和比较复杂曲折的句型（*not to confess obligations where no benefit has been received / consider me as owing that to a Patron, which Providence has enabled me to do for myself*），目的在于加强理直气壮的严肃口吻。

29. favourer of learning: 提倡、奖励学术的人。*favourer of learning* 可以看作是 *Patron* 一字的同义词。

30. though I should conclude it, if less be possible, with less: even if I should end my work with less obligation to a patron, if less obligation is possible（纵然在我结束我的工作期间，从赏识者那里我将得到比以前更少的资助，假若更少的资助是可能的话）。

31. in which I once boasted myself with so much exultation, my Lord, your Lordship's most humble, most obedient servant, Sam: Johnson：在那种梦想之下我曾经一度得意地夸耀自己是爵爷您最卑顺的门下士约翰逊。在这封信的结尾，约翰逊巧妙地利用了书信的收尾套语 *your Lordship's most humble, most obedient servant* 和他自己的签名 *Sam: Johnson*，并将它们同书信本文最后一句连结起来，似卑实亢，再一次向"赏识者"宣告独立。

2. THE PREFACE TO THE DICTIONARY OF THE ENGLISH LANGUAGE

1. that which its own nature forbids to be immortal: 指 language，因为语言随时都在变迁，新旧不断交替，因此它的本性（*its own nature*）就使它不得永恒（*immortal*）.

2. I have devoted this book: 我把这部书（指约翰逊用了七年时间所编成的英语词典）献给。

3. that we may no longer yield the palm of philology, without a contest, to the nations of the continent: 为了使我国人不再把语言科学方面的冠军地位，不加竞赛就让给大陆上的国家。"大陆上的国家"特别指法国和意大利。这两个国家都成立了国家学院，从事词典和语法编纂工作。英国当时没有类似的机构，但约翰逊不甘示弱，单枪匹马编成一部词典，来和大陆上的国家在语言学方面较量一下。

4. The chief glory of every people arises from its authors: 大意是：作家是每个民族最大的骄傲（每个民族的主要荣誉来自他们的作家）。

5. must be left to time: 必须由时间来决定，必须经过时间的考验。

6. much of my life has been lost under the pressures of disease; much has been trifled away; and much has always been spent in provision for the day that was passing over me: 我的生命有一大部分是在疾病的压迫下丧失掉了；有一大部分被荒嬉掉了；还有一大部分总是为了筹谋当天的衣食而消耗掉了。这三句话包含了多少辛酸痛苦。约翰逊的大半生都在疾病（瘰疬）和穷困中挣扎度过。在这里，约翰逊又用了三句排偶的修辞手法，来抒发他的强烈感情。这三句可以和"Letter to Lord Chesterfield"中的 *till I am indifferent*…那三句媲美。

7. the propagators of knowledge / the teachers of truth: 知识的传播者 / 真理的教导者。这些人也就是上文所说的给每个民族增加光荣的作家们（*authors*）。约翰逊的志向就是通过他编的词典，使外国人（*foreign nations*）和遥远的后代读者（*distant ages*）将有可能接近知识的传播者，领会真理的教导者。这些当然都指的是英国作家们。

8. afford light to the repositories of science: 照亮知识（*science*）的宝库（*repositories*）. *Science*，古义为"知识"。

9. add celebrity to Bacon, to Hooker, to Milton, and to Boyle: 增加 *Bacon, Hooker, Milton, Boyle* 等人的声誉（由于约翰逊词典的帮助，有更多的读者将能读懂上列这些英国作家）。Francis Bacon（弗兰西斯·培根，1561—1626），英国科学家兼散文家。Richard Hooker（理查·胡克，1554？—1600），英国宗教家。John Milton（约翰·弥尔顿，1608—1674），英国诗人。Robert Boyle（罗伯特·波义耳，1627—1691），英国科学家，伦敦皇家学会创始人之一。

10. a few wild blunders, and risible absurdities, from which no work of such multiplicity was ever free, may, for a time, furnish folly with laughter,

and harden ignorance into contempt: 一些荒唐的错误和可笑的谬论（这是一部如此复杂的著作所难免的），诚然会暂时给愚人提供谈笑的资料，无知之徒也要横加轻蔑。这句话对仗工稳：*wild blunders* 对 *risible absurdities; furnish folly with laughter* 对 *harden ignorance into contempt.* 约翰逊很喜欢用抽象名词来指人。例如，*folly* 指 foolish people, *ignorance* 指 ignorant people，等。

11. useful diligence will at last prevail: 有益的勤奋（指约翰逊自己编词典的劳动）终于取得胜利。

12. distinguish desert: 分辨得出真才实学。

13. falling away: 消失。

14. that a whole life cannot be spent upon syntax and etymology, and that even a whole life would not be sufficient:（他们将会认为）一个人不可能把毕生的时光都用在句法和词源学上面，即使毕生以赴，也仍会感到时间不足。

15. that he, whose design includes whatever language can express: 一个人，他的计划包括语言所能表达的一切事物。

16. that a writer will sometimes be hurried by eagerness to the end, and sometimes faint with weariness under a task, which Scaliger compares to the labours of the anvil and the mine: 有时作者过于心急，仓促结束工作，有时在艰巨的工作下由于疲惫而昏晕（这项工作 Scaliger 比作铁砧上和矿坑里的劳动）。Julius-Cæsar Scaliger（尤利·凯撒·斯卡理吉，1484—1558）是文艺复兴时期意大利著名的学者和文学批评家，有《诗论》等著作。Scaliger 把作家的劳动比作铁匠和矿工的劳动，喻其艰难辛苦也。

17. that what is obvious is not always known, and what is known is not always present:（对于作家来说）一目了然的事物并不就一定知道，知道了的事物并不就一定记得起来。——这恐怕是比较普遍的现象。

18. that sudden fits of inadvertency will surprise vigilance, slight avocations will seduce attention, and casual eclipses of the mind will darken learning: 忽然一阵疏忽会使警惕性措手不及，而被俘虏，些许消遣会使注意力分散，头脑一时的蒙蔽会使学问暗淡失色。约翰逊在此又运用了他所惯用的三句话相互对仗的修辞手法，以达到列举的目的。

19. shall often in vain: *shall* 在较古老的文体里，有时用来表示可能发生的事情，相当于当代英语中的 may 或 will 的含义。

20. and that the writer shall often in vain trace his memory, at the moment of need, for that which yesterday he knew with intuitive readiness, and which will come uncalled into his thoughts tomorrow: 作家需要回忆某一事物之时，往往苦思而不得，而昨日则信手拈来，毫不费力（*knew with intuitive readiness*，一下子凭直觉就能领会），明天又不需召唤径现脑中。这句话发挥了上面（第 21—22 行）*what is known is not always present* 的意思。

21. when it shall be found: *shall* 在此处也表示可能发生的事情。

22. no book was ever spared out of tenderness to the author: 从来没有读者

因爱惜作者而原谅过他的书。

23. the world is little solicitous to know whence proceeded the faults of that which it condemns: 世人不愿过问他们所否定的作品中的过错从何而来。

24. curiosity: 约翰逊在此又用抽象名词代替人物。*curiosity* 指“具有好奇心的人们”。

25. that the English Dictionary was written with little assistance of the learned, and without any patronage of the great; not in the soft obscurities of retirement, or under the shelter of academic bowers, but amidst inconvenience and distraction, in sickness and in sorrow: 在这里约翰逊又提到在多么艰苦的条件下他独立进行编纂词典的工作：“没有学者的帮助”，“没有大人物的奖励”。这工作“不是在安适的、恬静的隐居生活中”（*not in the soft obscurities of retirement*），“或是在学府的荫庇下”（*under the shelter of academic bowers*），“而是在艰苦和烦扰当中，在疾病和悲伤当中”（*but amidst inconvenience and distraction, in sickness and in sorrow*）进行的。

26. repress the triumph of malignant criticism: 抑制恶毒的批评者的得意忘形。此处抽象名词 *criticism* 指 critics（批评者）。

27. observe: say, especially by way of comment（述说，论述）。

28. if our language is not here fully displayed, I have only failed in an attempt, which no human powers have hitherto completed: 如果说我的书没有展示出我们的民族语言的全貌，那么我所没有做到的，也只不过是以前从来没有人能够做到的。

29. the lexicons of ancient tongues: 古代语言（指希腊语和拉丁语）的词典。

30. delusive: 不可靠。

31. the aggregated knowledge, and co-operating diligence of the Italian academicians: 意大利学院的院士们的集体智慧和协作的努力。指意大利的 Accademia della Crusca（克鲁斯加学院，成立于 1582 年）集体所编的词典 *Vocabolario degli Accademici della Crusca*（1612 年出版）。

32. Beni: Paolo Beni (1552–1625)，是意大利的文学批评家，他和克鲁斯加学院的院士们有过一场热烈的争论。他认为今人胜过古人，文艺复兴时期意大利诗人 Tasso 胜过古代希腊罗马的诗人。他并曾攻击过克鲁斯加学院所编的词典。

33. the embodied critics of France: 组成一个团体的（*embodied*）法国批评家们（指法兰西学会会员们而言）。

34. when fifty years had been spent upon their work: 指法兰西学会会员们集体所编法语词典而言。法兰西学会成立于 1635 年，法兰西学会法语词典出版于 1694 年，其间相隔 59 年。

35. change its economy: 改变他们的著作（指他们所编的词典）的原则或计划。

36. which, if I could obtain, in this gloom of solitude, what would it avail me: *which* 指前面 *the praise of perfection.* 即使我能得到别人的称赞，说我的词典编得尽善尽美，在我孤独凄凉的生活当中，这种称赞对我会有什么好处呢？——约翰逊的妻子已于三年前（1752）去世。

37. success and miscarriage are empty sounds: 成功和失败（对我来说）都毫无意义。

38. I, therefore, dismiss it with frigid tranquillity, having little to fear or hope from censure or from praise: 由于我既不害怕批评，又不盼望称赞，因此我冷淡地、安闲地打发掉我的作品。——虽然约翰逊说他不介意读者的批评，我们读了他的文章仍能体会到他的既自信而又感信心不足的矛盾心理。注意最后这句话的结构非常简练，若要说全了，就是：having little to fear from censure or little to hope from praise.

3. THE LIVES OF THE ENGLISH POETS

I. [The Father of English Criticism]
(from *Life of Dryden*)

1 DRYDEN may be properly considered as the father of English criticism, as the writer who first taught us to determine upon principles the merit of composition. Of our former poets the greatest dramatist[1] wrote without rules, conducted[2] through life and nature by a genius that rarely misled, and rarely deserted him. Of the rest, those who knew the laws of propriety had neglected to teach them.

2 Two *Arts of English Poetry*[3] were written in the days of Elizabeth[4] by Webb and Puttenham,[5] from which something might be learned, and a few hints had been given by Jonson[6] and Cowley;[7] but Dryden's *Essay on Dramatic Poetry*[8] was the first regular and valuable treatise on the art of writing.

3 He who,[9] having formed his opinions in the present age of English literature, turns back to peruse this dialogue,[10] will not perhaps find much increase of knowledge or much novelty of instruction; but he is to remember[11] that critical principles were then in the hands of a few, who had gathered them partly from the Ancients,[12] and partly from the Italians and French. The structure of dramatic poems was not then generally understood. Audiences applauded by instinct, and poets perhaps often pleased by chance.

4 A writer who obtains his full purpose loses himself in his own lustre.[13] Of an opinion which is no longer doubted, the evi-

dence ceases to be examined.[14] Of an art[15] universally practised, the first teacher is forgotten. Learning once made popular is no longer learning: it has the appearance of something which we have bestowed upon ourselves, as the dew appears to rise from the field which it refreshes.[16]

5 To judge rightly of an author we must transport ourselves to his time, and examine what were the wants of his contemporaries, and what were his means of supplying them.[17] That which is easy at one time was difficult at another.[18] Dryden at least imported his science,[19] and gave his country what it wanted[20] before; or rather, he imported only the materials, and manufactured them[21] by his own skill.

6 The dialogue on the Drama[22] was one of his first essays of criticism, written when he was yet a timorous candidate for reputation,[23] and therefore laboured with that diligence which he might allow himself somewhat to remit[24] when his name gave sanction to his positions,[25] and his awe of the public[26] was abated,[27] partly by custom,[28] and partly by success. It will not be easy[29] to find in all the opulence[30] of our language a treatise so artfully[31] variegated[32] with successive representations of opposite probabilities,[33] so enlivened with imagery,[34] so brightened with illustrations.[35] His portraits of the English dramatists are wrought[36] with great spirit[37] and diligence.[38] The account of Shakespeare may stand as a perpetual model of encomiastic[39] criticism; exact without minuteness,[40] and lofty without exaggeration.[41] The praise lavished by Longinus,[42] on the attestation of the heroes of Marathon[43] by Demosthenes,[44] fades away before it.[45] In a few lines is exhibited a character, so extensive in its comprehension[46] and so curious in its limitations,[47] that nothing can be added, diminished, or reformed;[48] nor can the editors and admirers of Shakespeare, in all their emulation of reverence,[49] boast of much more than of having diffused and paraphrased this epitome of excellence,[50] of having changed Dryden's gold for baser metal,[51] of lower value

though of greater bulk.[52]

7 In this, and in all his other essays on the same subject, the criticism of Dryden is the criticism of a poet; not a dull collection of theorems,[53] nor a rude detection of faults,[54] which perhaps the censor was not able to have committed;[55] but a gay and vigorous dissertation,[56] where delight is mingled with instruction, and where the author proves his right of judgement by his power of performance.[57]

8 The different manner and effect with which critical knowledge may be conveyed was perhaps never more clearly exemplified than in the performances of Rymer and Dryden. It was said of a dispute between two mathematicians, 'malim cum Scaligero errare, quam cum Clavio recte sapere';[58] that 'it was more eligible to go wrong with one than right with the other.'[59] A tendency of the same kind every mind must feel at the perusal of Dryden's prefaces[60] and Rymer's discourses. With Dryden we are wandering in quest of Truth, whom we find, if we find her at all, drest in the graces of elegance; and if we miss her, the labour of the pursuit rewards itself: we are led only through fragrance and flowers. Rymer, without taking a nearer, takes a rougher way; every step is to be made through thorns and brambles, and Truth, if we meet her, appears repulsive by her mien and ungraceful by her habit.[61] Dryden's criticism has the majesty of a queen; Rymer's has the ferocity of a tyrant.

II. [The Metaphysical Poets]
(from *Life of Cowley*)

1 The metaphysical poets were men of learning, and to show their learning was their whole endeavour; but, unluckily resolving to show it in rhyme, instead of writing poetry they only wrote verses,[62] and very often such verses as stood the trial of the finger better than of the ear;[63] for the modulation[64] was so imperfect that they were only found to be verses by counting the syllables.

2 If the father of criticism[65] has rightly denominated poetry τέχνη μιμητική, *an imitative art*,[66] these writers[67] will without great wrong[68] lose their right to the name of poets, for they cannot be said to have imitated anything: they neither copied nature nor life; neither painted the forms of matter[69] nor represented the operations of intellect.[70]

3 Those however who deny them to be poets allow[71] them to be wits.[72] Dryden confesses of himself and his contemporaries that they fall below Donne in wit,[73] but maintains that they surpass him in poetry.

4 If Wit[74] be well described by Pope as being 'that which has been often thought, but was never before so well expressed',[75] they certainly never attained nor ever sought it, for they endeavoured to be singular[76] in their thoughts, and were careless of their diction. But Pope's account of wit is undoubtedly erroneous; he depresses[77] it below its natural dignity, and reduces it from strength of thought to happiness of language.[78]

5 If by a more noble and more adequate conception that be considered as Wit which is at once natural and new,[79] that which though not obvious is, upon its first production, acknowledged to be just;[80] if it be that, which he that never found it, wonders how he missed;[81] to wit of this kind the metaphysical poets have seldom risen. Their thoughts are often new, but seldom natural; they[82] are not obvious, but neither are they just; and the reader, far from wondering that he missed them,[83] wonders more frequently by what perverseness of industry[84] they were ever found.[85]

6 But Wit, abstracted from[86] its effects upon the hearer, may be more rigorously and philosophically[87] considered as a kind of *discordia concors;*[88] a combination of dissimilar images, or discovery of occult resemblances[89] in things apparently unlike.[90] Of wit, thus defined, they have more than enough.[91] The most heterogeneous ideas are yoked by violence together;[92] nature and art are ransacked for illustrations, comparisons, and allusions;[93] their

learning instructs, and their subtilty[94] surprises; but the reader commonly thinks his improvement dearly bought, and, though he sometimes admires, is seldom pleased.

7 From this account of their compositions it will be readily inferred that they were not successful in representing or moving the affections.[95] As they were wholly employed on something unexpected and surprising they had no regard to that uniformity of sentiment, which enables us to conceive and to excite the pains and the pleasure of other minds:[96] they never enquired what on any occasion they should have said or done, but wrote rather as beholders than partakers of human nature;[97] as beings[98] looking upon good and evil, impassive and at leisure;[99] as Epicurean deities[100] making remarks on the actions of men and the vicissitudes of life,[101] without interest and without emotion. Their courtship was void of fondness and their lamentation of sorrow.[102] Their wish was only to say what they hoped had been never said before.

8 Nor was the sublime more within their reach than the pathetic;[103] for they never attempted that comprehension and expanse of thought[104] which at once fills the whole mind, and of which the first effect is sudden astonishment, and the second rational admiration. Sublimity is produced by aggregation, and littleness by dispersion.[105] Great thoughts are always general, and consist in positions not limited by exceptions,[106] and in descriptions not descending to minuteness. It is with great propriety that subtlety, which in its original import[107] means exility of particles,[108] is taken in its metaphorical meaning for nicety of distinction.[109] Those writers who lay on the watch for novelty[110] could have little hope of greatness; for great things cannot have escaped former observation.[111] Their attempts[112] were always analytic: they broke every image into fragments,[113] and could no more represent by their slender conceits and laboured particularities[114] the prospects of nature[115] or the scenes of life, than he who dissects[116] a sun-beam with a prism[117] can exhibit the wide efful-

gence[118] of a summer noon.[119]

9 What they wanted however of[120] the sublime they endeavoured to supply by hyperbole;[121] their amplification[122] had no limits: they left not only reason but fancy behind them,[123] and produced combinations of confused magnificence[124] that not only could not be credited, but could not be imagined.[125]

10 Yet great labour directed by great abilities is never wholly lost: if they frequently threw away their wit upon false conceits,[126] they likewise[127] sometimes struck out[128] unexpected truth:[129] if their conceits were far-fetched,[130] they were often worth the carriage.[131] To write on their plan[132] it was at least necessary to read and think. No man could be born a metaphysical poet, nor assume the dignity of a writer[133] by descriptions copied from descriptions, by imitations borrowed from imitations, by traditional imagery and hereditary similes,[134] by readiness of rhyme[135] and volubility of syllables.[136]

11 In perusing the works of this race of authors[137] the mind is exercised either by recollection or inquiry;[138] either something already learned is to be retrieved,[139] or something new is to be examined. If their greatness seldom elevates[140] their acuteness often surprises;[141] if the imagination is not always gratified, at least the powers of reflection and comparison are employed; and in the mass of materials, which ingenious absurdity[142] has thrown together, genuine wit and useful knowledge may be sometimes found, buried perhaps in grossness of expression,[143] but useful to those who know their value,[144] and such as, when they are expanded to perspicuity[145] and polished to elegance,[146] may give lustre to works[147] which have more propriety though less copiousness of sentiment.[148]

12 This kind of writing,[149] which was, I believe, borrowed from Marino[150] and his followers, had been recommended[151] by the example of Donne,[152] a man of very extensive and various knowledge, and by Jonson,[153] whose manner resembled that of Donne

more in the ruggedness of his lines[154] than in the cast of his sentiments.[155]

13 When their reputation was high they[156] had undoubtedly more imitators than time has left behind.[157] Their immediate successors, of whom any remembrance can be said to remain, were Suckling,[158] Waller,[159] Denham,[160] Cowley,[161] Cleveland,[162] and Milton.[163] Denham and Waller sought another way to fame, by improving the harmony of our numbers.[164] Milton tried the metaphysic style only in his lines upon Hobson the Carrier.[165] Cowley adopted it, and excelled his predecessors; having as much sentiment and more music. Suckling neither improved versification nor abounded in conceits.[166] The fashionable style[167] remained chiefly with Cowley: Suckling could not reach it, and Milton disdained it.[168]

* * *

【题解与注释】

The Lives of the English Poets（共52篇）当中有不少篇好文章，以“Life of Savage”（《沙维支传》），“Life of Milton”（《密尔顿传》），“Life of Dryden”（《德莱顿传》），“Life of Pope”（《蒲伯传》），“Life of Swift”（《斯威夫特传》）最为重要。现选注两篇：一篇为［The Father of English Criticism，英国文学批评之父］，选自“Life of Dryden”；另一篇为［The Metaphysical Poets，玄学诗人］，选自“Life of Cowley”（《考黎传》）。John Dryden（约翰·德莱顿，1631—1700）是英国古典主义文学最重要的作家之一。他是诗人、剧作家，又是杰出的散文家和文学批评家。德莱顿曾被誉为“英国文学批评之父”。第一篇选文［The Father of English Criticism］的内容就是论德莱顿对于英国文学批评的贡献，以及他的文学批评的特点。现就此内容作如下的说明：

第一段说德莱顿是第一个教导我们如何按照文学批评的原则来判断作品的价值的人，因此我们有理由把他看作英国文学批评的创始者。在以前的英国诗人当中，莎士比亚只凭他的天才来创作，并不按照规则（rules）来办事。其他的诗人，即使知道什么是正确典雅的法则（laws of propriety），也并没有把这些法则教导给别人。第二段说德莱顿的*Essay on Dramatic Poetry*（《论诗剧》）是英国文学批评史中第一部正式的、有价值的关于创作艺术的论文。第三段说在德莱顿的时代，文学批评的原则只是掌握在少数人的手里，还没有传播和普及。少数人从古代希腊罗马作家和当代意大利和法兰西作家那里采集了一些文学批评的原则，但是诗剧的结构（structure）并不为大众所理解。听众的赞赏和诗人的受欢迎都有一定程度的盲目性和偶然性。第四段说学问一旦为群众所掌握就变成群众自己的东西，人们不再记得谁是这门学问的创始者。约翰逊在这里表现出他是一个轻视群众的资产阶级知识分子。他说普及了的学问就不再是学问，这学问就好象是我们自己固有的东西，犹如滋润田野的露水就好象来自田野，而非上天所赐。约翰逊轻视群众的观点是错误的，因为一切学问（知识、理论）都来自群众的实践。他的比喻也不科学，因为露水当然是从田野里蒸发出的水汽上升，经冷却凝固而复降落田野之上而来。事实上，学问（露水）来自群众（田野），经过有学问的人加以归纳总结（犹如水汽冷却凝固的过程），然后还给群众，变成群众自己的东西，犹如露水变成田野自己的东西一般。这个道理很明显，只是约翰逊对这种社会现象和自然现象的解释反映了他的资产阶级唯心主义的观点。第五段很有道理。约翰逊说评价一个作家必须回到那个作家所生活的时代，必须研究当时人们的要求，看出该作家通过何种方式来满足这些要求。同一件工作在乙时期做来是容易的，但在甲时期做来却困难重重。现在要写一部诗剧论不能算是一件难事，但在德莱顿的时代却是一桩极不简单的工作。假若说德莱顿并没有许多创造和发明，但他至少是把这门学问（science，指诗剧的理论），从法国和意大利输送到了英国，从而填补起他本国学科的空白点。但更确切地来说，德莱顿仅从国外输入文学批评的原料，更重要的是，他用他自己的本领制造出一套适合于本国需要的戏剧理论。第六段说德莱顿这篇论戏剧的对话（指他的 *Essay on Dramatic Poetry*）是他早年的著作，可以看出他的勤奋好学。他这篇论文交错地提出了对立的论点，用了大量的比喻和实例使文章写得十分生动。他对于英国剧作家各人特点的描述写得既细心又大胆，翔实而又有独到见解。尤其值得称赞的是他对于莎士比亚的评论。这个评论可以算作赞颂批评永恒的典范，准确而不琐碎，热情而无浮夸。德莱顿只写了几句话就把莎士比亚最本质的特点完全刻画了出来：莎士比亚对于社会和人生的理解是极其广阔的，但是他却具有一些奇特的局限性。德莱顿的原话是："He (Shakespeare) was the man who of all modern, and perhaps ancient poets, had the largest and most comprehensive soul … when he describes any thing, you more than see it, you feel it too … he was naturally learned; he needed not the spectacles of books to read nature; … I cannot say he is every where alike; … He is many times flat, insipid; his comic wit degenerating into clenches, his serious swelling into bombast. But he is always great, when some great occasion is presented to him; no man can say he ever had a fit subject for his wit, and did not then raise himself as high above the rest of poets."（"在所有的现代诗人当中，或许在所有的古代诗人们的行列里，没有一个人象他［莎士比亚］那样具有最大的和最广阔的心灵…当他描写一件事情，你不仅看见这件事情，而且也在心里感觉到这件事情…他的知识是自然而然获得的；他不需要戴上书本的眼镜来观察自然；…我不敢说他的作品处处皆是天衣无缝；…他在许多地方显得平淡、乏味；他的喜剧幽默变成无聊的文字游戏，他庄严的豪语变成浮夸之辞。但是当他面对着伟大事件时，他总是伟大的、崇高的；凡人都会承认当他［莎士比亚］的创作才能遇到了合适的题材时，他总是高出于其他诗人之上，使他们望尘莫及。"）约翰逊认为：德莱顿对于莎士比亚所作的这段评语真是增一分则太长，减一分则太短，可谓千古定论。后来的人赞扬莎士比亚也不过用更多的字眼重复了德莱顿的话，也不过用更多的铜铁代替了德莱顿的纯金而已。第七段强调德莱顿的文学批评是诗人所写的文学批评（the criticism of Dryden is the criticism of a poet），既不是一束枯燥的定理，也不是一片无礼貌的指责，而是愉快生动的说理。写这种批评文章的人用自己的诗才证明自己绝对有发言的权利。最后一段进一步说明德莱顿的文学批评文章写得真实、愉快、生动。读者读他的批评文章能够得到很大的美感享受，就好象读优美的诗歌一样。在这里约翰逊也展示了他自己的诗才，用非常生动、鲜明的形象语言把德莱顿的文学批评文章拿来和莱莫（Thomas Rymer, 1641–1713）的相对照。我们读德莱顿的文章犹如在花园里漫步，处处是芬芳的花香；读莱莫的文章犹如在荆棘丛里前进，寸步维艰。我们跟随德莱顿追求真理，所找到的真理美丽、娴雅；即使未能找到真理，寻找的过程也是一种很大的乐趣。我们若随莱莫去找寻真理，所找到的真理丑恶粗俗，拒人于千里之外。最后约翰逊总结德莱顿和莱莫的区别，说道："德莱顿的文学批评具有皇后般的庄严华贵；而莱莫的批评却具有暴君般的凶恶与残虐。"约翰逊对于德莱顿的文学批评才能显然评价过高。德莱顿对于莎士比亚的评语固然中肯，但若认为它是千古定论或赞颂批评永恒的典范，后人无法超越，则未免誉之过甚，不合乎人类文化发展之规律。此外，约翰逊为了要说明德莱顿的优点，却夸大了莱莫的缺点，因此对此二人皆未能作到公允，也就难令读者信服。事实上，莱莫是一位很有学问的历史家兼文学批评家。他是亚里斯多德的忠实信徒，推崇理性和规律，是英国古典主义文艺理论早期重要代表人之一。莱莫的文学批评方法着重分析作品（史诗、悲剧等）的情节、结构和语言。这是值得肯定的。但是他的分析有时未免太细、太琐碎。更严重的是他把作品支解成许多片段，忽视作品的整体和全貌。由此可见分析必须和综合相结合才能对作品作出既精确又全面的评价。归根结蒂，莱莫和德莱顿的区别就在于莱莫的文学批评只有分析，没有综合；德莱顿的文学批评却是综合多于分析。莱莫过分重视条规，德莱顿更看重天才和想象力。在认识了莱莫和德莱顿两人的批评方法的根本区别以后，我们最后仍同意约翰逊的话："the criticism of Dryden is the criticism of a poet." 至于约翰逊骂莱莫凶恶残虐犹如暴君，我们却不能完全同意。诚然莱莫曾经指摘和攻击过莎士比亚的戏剧作品，而且说了比较重的话，但是他仍是凭理性和条规作出判断（尽管他的判断并不完全正确），约翰逊没有权利给他加上暴君的罪名。

第二篇选文［The Metaphysical Poets］论述了英国文学史上一个重要的诗歌流派（玄学诗人）的特点和创作方法。第一段说玄学诗人博学，他们喜欢卖弄他们的学问。他们所写的诗固然合乎诗的格律，但节奏并不悦耳，很难称得上是诗。第二段说：亚里斯多德给诗歌所下的定义是：诗歌是一种模仿的艺术，玄学诗人既不模仿自然，也不模仿生活，既不描绘物质的形态，也不表现心灵的活动，因此玄学诗人很难称得上是诗人。第三段说玄学诗人虽然不能称为诗人，但他们却都是才子（wits）. 第四段说玄学诗人的才气并不表现在他们的语言上面，而是表现在他们构思的新奇。在这里约翰逊引了蒲伯（Pope）对于才气（wit）所下的定义，并对蒲伯的定义加以批评，这很能说明约翰逊具有高超的见解。约翰逊说蒲伯把才气不解释为"思想的力量"（strength of language），而说成是"语言的巧妙"（happiness of language），这无疑是错误的，因为如此势必贬低才气的价值。可见约翰逊看重诗歌的思想内容，胜过它的艺术形式。第五段很重要，因为约翰逊在这里给才气下了一个正确、全面的定义：才气必须是既新颖又自然的思想。用这个标准来衡量，玄学诗人也难算做才子，因为他们的思想固然新颖，但却并不自然。他们所说的道理并不明显，也就难以说服读者，难以感动别人。第六段说：假若不考虑对读者或听众所起的效果，就才气本身来说，我们可以给它下一个更加严格、更加抽象的定义：才气是在不和谐的事物之间看出隐蔽的和谐关系的本领，是把不协调的形象结合起来、串连起来的本领。按照这个标准，玄学诗人的才气就显得是很高的了。他们把极为庞杂的思想勉强地套在一根缰绳上；他们旁征博引，从自然界和古人的作品里列举许多事例来说明他们新颖、离奇的构思。他们的博学可以给读者提供知识，他们的妙想往往使读者拍案叫绝，但读者常会感到付出代价过大，得不偿失。第七段说玄学诗人一心追求新奇的思想，势必忽视通常的思想感情，结果是他们对生活采取旁观态度，对善恶不置可否。他们无动于衷地看着人们的行动和生活当中的变化，他们的作品也就是冷冰冰的，毫无生活气息。这不能不说是严重的缺点。约翰逊又用他所惯用的对仗句型指出了这个缺点"他们的求婚缺乏爱情，他们的悼亡缺少悲伤"（"Their courtship was void of fondness and their lamentation of sorrow"），因为他们一心只想道前人之所未道（"Their wish was only to say what they hoped had been never said before"）. 第八段说玄学诗人既不善于写悲惨的故事，也不善于写崇高的事件。约翰逊对崇高的美（the sublime）作出这样的说明：崇高美来自具有概括性和普遍性的思想，这种思想一下子就占据了读者整个的心灵，其效果开始时是突然的惊怖，随后变为理性上的心悦诚服（"that comprehension and expanse of thought which at once fills the whole mind, and of which the first effect is sudden astonishment, and the second rational admiration"）. 接着，约翰逊说崇高美有赖于聚集（aggregation）、综合；细巧美依靠分散（dispersion）、分析。崇高伟大的思想总是概括的道理或普遍的真理。玄学诗人一意追求新奇的思想，欲云前人之所未云。他们立意如此创作，很难收到崇高伟大的效果，因为伟大的思想（概括的道理或普遍的真理）势必为前人所已见或所已云（"for great things cannot have escaped former observation"）. 玄学诗人所用的创作方法总是通过分析，而无综合。他们把每一个形象分裂成许多碎块。通过他们纤细的想象（slender conceits）和雕琢的细节（laboured particularities），自然界的面貌和生活的景象很难表现出来，正象通过三棱镜把日光剖析（dissect）成为七色，很难显示出夏日中午时日光的灿烂夺目，广阔壮丽（the wide effulgence of a summer noon）. 第九段说玄学诗人为了弥补崇高伟大之不足，于是借助于夸张的修辞（hyperbole），结果使他们的作品不但令人无法相信，甚至令人无从想象。第十段谈论玄学诗人的优点和价值。约翰逊特别称赞他们的创造性和对英国诗歌艺术的革新。此外，玄学诗人肯读书，肯思索，这也是他们的长处。约翰逊说：要想成为一个玄学诗人，甚至于要想成为任何一个名实相符的作家，抄袭别人的描写，模仿别人的创作，依靠传统的形象和世代相传的比喻，但凭作诗押韵本领的熟练，那是绝对办不到的。约翰逊这番话说得极是。第十一段继续谈论玄学诗人的优点。在这里约翰逊对玄学诗人的确抱着批评继承的态度。约翰逊时代的英国古典主义诗歌缺少的是创造性的思想和革新的艺术形式。不过约翰逊对于玄学诗人们的诗歌形式并不欣赏，认为他们的语言粗俗（grossness of expression），必须使它成为明澈通畅（perspicuity）、典雅秀丽的（elegance）语言。但约翰逊认为可以继承玄学诗人们对事物的洞察力（acuteness），继承他们有用的知识（useful knowledge）和真正的才气（genuine wit）. 玄学诗人使读者思考、探究问题，通过回忆和对比（recollection and comparison），使读者研究新的问题，认识新的道理，这是约翰逊特别希望他同时代的英国诗人努力向十七世纪的英国玄学诗人们学习的。第十二段说玄学诗派的源流可能来自十六世纪意大利作家 Marino. 在英国玄学诗人的代表是十七世纪英国诗人 Donne 和 Jonson. 第十三段论述那些属于玄学诗派的英国诗人。约翰逊提到这些英国诗人：Suckling, Waller, Denham, Cowley, Cleveland 和 Milton. 但是 Denham 和 Waller 着重韵律的和谐，为英诗另辟途径，开十八世纪英国新古典主义诗歌（及蒲伯为代表）之先河。密尔顿写玄学诗仅偶一为之，不屑多作尝试。Suckling 学玄学诗，但并未学到家。唯独 Cowley 学玄学诗而青出于蓝。Cowley 的诗既有玄学诗人们那么新颖、丰富的思想，又有象 Denham 和 Waller 那样和谐的音乐，因此 Cowley 受到约翰逊的特别赞赏。

以上两篇选文的本文都是根据 Samuel Johnson, *Lives of the English Poets*, ed. George Birkbeck Hill, in three vols., vol. I, pp. 410–413 (Dryden); pp.19–22 (Cowley), Oxford Clarendon Press, 1905.

I. [THE FATHER OF ENGLISH CRITICISM]

1. the greatest dramatist: 指威廉·莎士比亚（William Shakespeare, 1564–1616）而言。

2. conducted: 过去分词，修饰 dramatist。

3. *Arts of English Poetry*:《英国诗论》。

4. Elizabeth: 英国女王伊丽莎白（1558—1603 年在位）。

5. Webb and Puttenham: William Webbe, *A Discourse of English Poetrie*（《论英国诗》，1586 年出版）；George Puttenham, *The Arte of English Poesie*（《英国诗论》，1589 年出版）。

6. Jonson: Ben Jonson (1572–1637), *Timber; or Discoveries Made upon Men and Matter, as They Have Flowed out of His Daily Reading*（《木材：日常读书中有关人物和事件的新发现》，1641 年出版）。

7. Cowley: 指 Abraham Cowley (1618–1667) 所写的若干篇序言（Prefaces）而言。

8. Dryden's *Essay on Dramatic Poetry*: John Dryden (1631–1700), *Essay on Dramatic Poetry*（《论诗剧》，1668 年出版）。

9. He who: 等于 anyone who。

10. this dialogue: Dryden 的 *Essay on Dramatic Poetry* 这篇论文是用对话体写的。

11. he is to remember: 等于 he must remember.

12. the Ancients: 古人，特指古代希腊罗马的作家。

13. A writer who obtains his full purpose loses himself in his own lustre: 一个圆满地完成了他的任务的作家（意为他的作品受到群众的热爱和欢迎），会淹没在他自己的荣誉中（意为群众只记得他的作品中的人物和事件，而忘却了作者本人）。

约翰逊这句格言式的议论有一定的道理。例如我们读了荷马的史诗，我们心中永远忘记不了的是 Achilles 和 Hector 的比武，是 Odysseus 的海上奇遇，我们根本忘了作者荷马的存在。

14. Of an opinion ...: 这句的结构是：The evidence of an opinion which is no longer doubted ceases to be examined（一种已为众人所接受，再也无人怀疑的意见，不会再有人去查对这种意见的根据是什么）。

15. Of an art ...: 这句的结构是：The first teacher of an art universally practised is forgotten（一种普遍地为人们实践的技艺，再也不会有人去追问谁最初把这种技艺教给人们）。

16. which it refreshes: it 代替 the dew（为露水所滋润的田野）。

17. supplying them: them 代替 wants（满足作家同时代人们的需要）。

18. at another: 等于 at another time。

19. his science: 他的这门科学（指关于诗剧的理论和创作方法）。

20. wanted: 缺少。

21. manufactured them: them 代替 materials（把原料制成成品）。

22. The dialogue on the Drama: 指 Dryden 的 *Essay on Dramatic Poetry* 这篇用对话体写的论文。

23. a timorous candidate for reputation: 兢兢业业的声誉候选人（意为勤奋努力的尚未成名的作家）。

24. remit: 放松。

25. when his name gave sanction to his positions: sanction 等于 authority（权威性）；positions 等于 statements, assertions（论断）。

26. his awe of the public: the public 指 the reading public（他对于读者们的畏惧）。

27. abated: 减弱。

28. partly by custom: 部分由于习以为常。

29. It will not be easy: 等于 it is perhaps not easy.

30. opulence: 等于 rich store（丰富的宝藏）。

31. artfully: 等于 skilfully（巧妙地）。

32. variegated: 使之丰富多彩。

33. successive representations of opposite probabilities: 把一切对立的可能性（可能提出的相对立的论点）都一个接着一个地发表了出来。

34. enlivened with imagery: 用形象化的比喻使之生动。

35. brightened with illustrations: 用事例增加光彩。

36. wrought:（古体）等于 worked（made, done，制做出来）。

37. spirit: 冲劲，精力充沛，生动活泼。

38. diligence: 勤奋好学。

39. encomiastic: 赞美的，颂扬的。

40. exact without minuteness: 准确而不琐碎。

41. lofty without exaggeration: 崇高而不夸张。

42. The praise lavished by Longinus: Longinus（Dionysius Cassius Longinus，约公元后 210—273，希腊修辞学家，世传著有《论崇高美》一文，为欧洲文学批评史上一部重要著作）所给予的大量称赞（*De Sublimi*, xvi）.

43. on the attestation of the heroes of Marathon: 对马拉松战役英雄们的宣誓（所给予的大量称赞）。前置词 on 和过去分词 lavished 发生关系；the heroes of Marathon 指抵抗波斯帝国侵略的希腊卫国战士们而言。Marathon（平原名）位于雅典城外东北方 24 英里；马拉松战役发生在公元前 490 年；结果希腊人击溃强大的波斯军队（希腊方面死伤 192 人，波斯方面伤亡 6, 403 人）。马拉松战役粉碎了波斯帝国侵略欧洲的计划，巩固了希腊的国防，为雅典的繁荣富强奠定了基础，因此是世界史上有名的决定性战役之一。

44. by Demosthenes: 为 Demosthenes（公元前 384 或 383—322 古希腊最优秀的演说家。他鼓舞、激发雅典人民的爱国思想，号召他们抵抗马其顿对希腊的侵略）所写的（*De Corona*, 263. II.）。

45. fades away before it: it 代替 the account of Shakespeare (by Dryden). 在 Dryden 所写关于莎士比亚的评述面前，Longinus 对 Demosthenes 所写有关马拉松战役英雄们宣誓所作的赞扬变得暗淡失色。

46. so extensive in its comprehension: 他的理解力是如此的广阔。

47. so curious in its limitations: 他的局限性是如此的奇特。

48. reformed: 被改变，被改进。

49. emulation of reverence: 对莎士比亚致敬的竞赛（莎士比亚作品的编辑者和莎士比亚的崇拜者竞相对莎士比亚致以崇敬的颂赞）。

50. having diffused and paraphrased this epitome of excellence: 传播了和解释、发挥了这个优点的总结；this epitome of excellence 指 Dryden 对于莎士比亚的优点的总结。

51. having changed Dryden's gold for baser metal: 用更平凡的金属代替了 Dryden 的纯金。Dryden's gold 指 this epitome of excellence; baser metal 指 the editors and admirers of Shakespeare 对于 this epitome of excellence 的传播、解释和发挥（diffusion and paraphrase）。

52. of lower value though of greater bulk: 尽管体积更大，但价值却更为低下。这个成分修饰 baser metal，意为别人对于莎士比亚优点的解释和发挥虽然字数更多（though of greater bulk），但其价值远不及 Dryden 对莎士比亚优点的总结。

53. not a dull collection of theorems: 不是一套枯燥乏味的条规或公式。

54. nor a rude detection of faults: 也不是对于缺点或错误的无礼貌的揭发。影射 Thomas Rymer 在 *A Short View of Tragedy*（《浅论悲剧》，1693 年出版）论文中对莎士比亚的悲剧《奥赛罗》（*Othello*）的无情的攻击。

55. which perhaps the censor was not able to have committed: which 代替 faults. 意为这些缺点或错误只是有才能的作家才能犯的；指责这些缺点、错误的人（censor，可能影射 Thomas Rymer），他自己也许就不具备犯这些缺点、错误的才能。

56. a gay and vigorous dissertation: 一篇活泼、有力的论文。

57. the author proves his right of judgement by his power of performance: 作者以他自己的实践能力证明他自己有作出判断的资格。意为 Dryden 的文学批评论文本身就是优美的文学作品。他的高超的实践（写作）才能证明了他有资格判断别人作品的优劣。

58. 'malim cum Scaligero errare, quam cum Clavio recte sapere':（拉丁文）"我宁愿和 Scaliger 一起犯错误，不愿和 Clavius 在一起作出正确的判断" Clavius（十六世纪意大利天文学家）奉 Gregory XIII（罗马教皇，1572—1585 在位）之命修改历法，著有论历法的专著，长达 800 页，其中包括极为详尽的推算和查对公式。Joseph Justus Scaliger（法国历史学家，1540—1609）根据哥白尼的新天文学知识，彻底纠正了世界古代史中计算年代的错误，使历史这门学科变得更为精确，更加科学。Scaliger 的科学方法具有普遍的指导意义，而 Clavius 不过是个见树不见林的计算匠而已。

59. 'it was more eligible to go wrong with one than right with the other': "与某甲同错较与某乙同对更为恰当"。*eligible* 等于 desirable, suitable（令人满意，合适，恰当）。

60. Dryden's prefaces: Dryden 的批评论文大多数是他写在他的创作和译作前面的序言（prefaces）.

Rymer's discourses, Rymer 的批评论文主要有：*The Tragedies of the Last Age Considered*（《论前一时代的悲剧作品》，1678 年出版）；*A Short View of Tragedy*（《浅论悲剧》，1693 年出版），等。

61. habit:（古义）等于 dress（衣裳）。

II. [THE METAPHYSICAL POETS]

62. instead of writing poetry they only wrote verses: 他们没有写出真正的诗（*poetry*），却只写下了一些诗行（*verses*）；poetry 着重指诗歌的内容，verse 指诗歌的外表或形式，因此 verse, versifier 等词通常含有贬意。

63. such verses as stood the trial of the finger better than of the ear: 这样一些诗行，它们通过了手指头的考验（意为用手指头数每一行诗中所规定的音节数目，合乎规定就算通过了这个考验），而没有通过耳朵的考验（意为用耳朵听起来，这些诗行没有诗歌应有的节奏与和谐，所以说不能通过耳朵的考验）。

64. modulation: 等于 rhythmical movement（节奏）。

65. the father of criticism: 指亚里斯多德（Aristotle，公元前 384—322，古希腊最伟大的哲学家之一）而言。亚里斯多德著有《修辞学》和《诗论》。

66. denominated poetry … an imitative art: 把诗歌命名为一种模仿的艺术。此句中两个希腊字即是 an imitative art 之意，语出亚里斯多德《诗论》，第 1 章，第 2 节："史诗和悲剧，喜剧和迪色拉姆抒情诗（赞美酒神的抒情诗），以及横笛和竖琴所发出的各种形式的音乐，概括起来说都是不同方式的模仿。"

67. these writers: 指 the metaphysical poets 而言。

68. without great wrong: 等于 *with reason, justifiably*（有理由，合理地）。

69. the forms of matter: 物质的形态。指自然界的景物而言。

70. the operations of intellect: 心灵的活动，指思想感情而言。

71. allow: 承认。

72. wits: 才子。

73. fall below Donne in wit: 在才气方面不及 John Donne（1572—1631，十七世纪英国玄学诗人最重要的代表）。

74. Wit: 这个词是十七、十八世纪英国文学批评的流行术语。它强调文学作品中思想和语言（内容和形式）的恰当、妥善、机智、娴雅，因此是古典主义文艺创作的重要标准之一。现举十七、十八世纪英国批评家对 Wit 所下定义数条：Davenant（1651 年）："Wit is the laborious, and the lucky resultances of thought having towards its excellence ... as well a happiness, as care"（意为 Wit 是用心构思，勤奋写作的结果，但它的表现却很自然，仿佛毫不经心，类乎天籁）。Dryden（1677 年）："The definition of Wit ... is only this: That it is a propriety of Thoughts and Words; or in other terms, Thought and Words, elegantly adapted to the Subject"（Dryden 强调思想和语言的合适、恰当、娴雅、切题）。Dryden（1697 年）又曾给 Wit 下过这样的定义："solid Sense and Elegant Expression"（"坚实的思想和娴雅的表达"）。Pope（1704 年）："True Wit, I believe, may be defined a justness of thought, and a facility of expression"（蒲伯强调思想的正确和表达的熟练）。

75. 'that which has been often thought, but was never before so well expressed': Pope, *Essay on Criticism*（1709 年）："True Wit is Nature to advantage dress'd, What oft was thought, but ne'er so well express'd"（蒲伯在这里特别强调 Wit 的表达方面，对于思想方面，他只要求通常性和普遍性，并不要求独创性）。

76. singular: 独特的。

77. depresses: 贬低。

78. reduces it from strength of thought to happiness of language: 把 Wit 的含义从有力的思想降低到巧妙的语言。

79. that be considered as Wit which is at once natural and new: that（代词）为 which 从句所修饰；be considered 是虚拟式，用在 *if*（条件）从句中；at once 等于 at the same time（同时既…，又…）。

80. that which though not obvious is, upon its first production, acknowledged to be just: 乍一创作出来，虽不明显，但即被认为是正确的。

81. if it be that, which he that never found it, wonders how he missed: it 代替 Wit; he 指任何人（= anyone）；which 代替 that，同时又是 missed 的直接宾语。这句整个的意思是：任何人自己虽未想到，但经诗人一语道破，不禁有深得我心之感，不禁要问为什么自己没有想到此层。

82. they: 代替 their thoughts（他们的思想）。

83. he missed them: he 代替 the reader（读者）；them 代替 their thoughts.

84. perverseness of industry: 等于 misapplication of diligence（勤奋努力的误用，用得不正当）。

85. they were ever found: they 代替 their thoughts; found 等于 invented（发明，发现）。

86. abstracted from: 从…脱离开来。

87. rigorously and philosophically: 严格地，而且科学地（philosophically）。

88. *discordia concors:*（拉丁文）和谐的不和谐（harmonious discord）。

89. occult resemblances: 等于 hidden similarities（隐藏的类似之点）。

90. apparently unlike: 表面上看来不相同。

91. Of wit, thus defined, they have more than enough: 如此界说的 Wit，他们（they 代替 the metaphysical poets）则用之不尽，取之不竭。

92. The most heterogeneous ideas are yoked by violence together: 极不相同的概念勉强地（by violence）被套在一起（are yoked together）。

93. nature and art are ransacked for illustrations, comparisons, and allusions: 为了寻求例证（illustrations），比拟（comparisons）和隐喻（allusions），自然界（nature）和各种技艺（art）被（他们）搜索遍了（are ransacked）。

94. subtilty: 系 subtlety 的古拼法，意为钻牛角尖（hair-splitting）的本领。

95. not successful in representing or moving the affections: 不善于表现感情或打动（读者的）感情。

96. that uniformity of sentiment, which enables us to conceive and to excite the pains and the pleasure of other minds: 思想感情（sentiment）的共同性（uniformity = sameness），这种共同性使我们能够体会（conceive），并且激发（excite）别人心中的痛苦和快乐。

97. beholders ... partakers of human nature: 人性的旁观者（beholders），人性的参预者（partakers）。

98. as beings: 与本行 *as beholders* 平行；beings 意为人们（people）。

99. looking upon good and evil, impassive and at leisure: 无动于衷地（impassive），悠闲地（at leisure）看待善恶。

100. as Epicurean deities: 与第 16 行 as beholders 平行。Epicurean deities 意为象神（deities = gods）一样高高在上的伊庇鸠鲁派哲学家。伊庇鸠鲁派哲学与斯多噶派哲学（Stoicism）有相似之点，即主张对快乐与痛苦无动于衷（ataraxia）. 伊庇鸠鲁派哲学家 Diogenes of Oenoanda 有四句铭言："上帝没有什么可怕。死了就没有感觉了。善是可以达到的。恶是可以忍受的。"这四句话可以说明伊庇鸠鲁派哲学所主张的无动于衷的人生态度。

101. the vicissitudes of life: 人生境遇的转变（指顺逆，苦乐，成功失败，富贵贫贱等方面而言）。

102. Their courtship was void of fondness and their lamentation of sorrow: 他们诗歌中的求婚（courtship）缺乏（void of）爱情（fondness），他们诗歌中的悼亡（lamentation）缺少悲哀（sorrow）。

103. Nor was the sublime more within their reach than the pathetic: 写悲惨事件（the pathetic）不在他们能力范围之内（not ... within their reach），写崇高伟

大的事件（the sublime）也并不更属于他们能力范围内的事（nor … more within their reach）。

104. comprehension and expanse of thought: 思想的概括性（comprehension）和普遍性（expanse）。具有概括性和普遍性的思想立即占据读者的整个心灵（which at once fills the whole mind），其效果最初为骤然的惊怖（of which the first effect is sudden astonishment），随后为理性上的心悦诚服（the second [effect is] rational admiration）。

105. Sublimity is produced by aggregation, and littleness by dispersion: 崇高美（sublimity）来自聚集（aggregation），细巧美（littleness）来自分散（dispersion）.

106. consist in positions not limited by exceptions:（伟大的思想）在于不受例外限制的命题（positions = propositions）.

and in descriptions not descending to minuteness:（伟大的思想）也在于不下降到细文末节（minuteness）的描写。

107. original import: 原来的含义。

108. exility of particles: 分子（particles）的细小（exility = thinness）。

109. nicety of distinction: 辨异（distinction）的精细（nicety）。

110. lay on the watch for novelty: 守候着新奇事物。

111. great things cannot have escaped former observation: 伟大的事件不可能逃过前人的观察（意为势必为前人所曾观察到）。

112. Their attempts: their 指 the metaphysical poets 而言。

113. they broke every image into fragments: 他们把每一个形象分裂成为碎块（fragments）。

114. by their slender conceits and laboured particularities: 用他们纤细的想象（slender conceits）和雕琢的细节（laboured particularities）.

115. the prospects of nature: 自然界的面貌。

116. dissects: 剖析。

117. prism: 三棱镜。

118. wide effulgence: 广阔的光辉。

119. a summer noon: 等于 the summer sun at noon（夏日中午的太阳光）。

120. wanted … of: 等于 lacked in（在…方面缺少）。

121. hyperbole: [haiˈpəːbəli]:（修辞学用语）夸张。

122. amplificaton: 发挥。

123. they left not only reason but fancy behind them: 他们不仅脱离理性，而且也超出幻想之外。

124. combinations of confused magnificence: 乱七八糟的（confused）华丽词句（magnificence）的组合（combinations）。

125. not only could not be credited, but could not be imagined: 不但令人无法相信（credited），甚至令人无从想象（imagined）。

126. threw away their wit upon false conceits: 把他们的聪明才智（wit）浪费（threw away）在不自然的想象上面（upon false conceits）。

127. likewise: 等于 also。

128. struck out: 产生出来，创造出来。

129. unexpected truth:（人们所）料想不到的真理。

130. if their conceits were far-fetched: 即使（if = even though）他们的想象（conceits）是勉强的，牵强的（far-fetched 原意为从远处取来的）。

131. worth the carriage: 值得运送（值得传达给读者）。

132. on their plan: 等于 according to their plan。

133. assume the dignity of a writer: 具有（assume）作家的资格（dignity = worth）。

134. traditional imagery and hereditary similes: 世代相传的形象和承袭的比喻。

135. readiness of rhyme: 押韵的敏捷。

136. volubility of syllables: 音节（syllables，此处指 rhythm 节奏）的流利圆滑（volubility）。

137. this race of authors: 这类具有某种共同性的作家们（指 the metaphysical poets 而言）。

138. recollection or inquiry: 回忆（recollection）或发现（inquiry，意为通过探索、调查、研究而发现）。

139. retrieved: 通过记忆重新获得或被召唤回来。

140. If their greatness seldom elevates: 即使他们所写的伟大事件或壮烈事迹（greatness，此处指伟大的题材和伟大的效果而言）很少有激发起读者崇高感情的时候（seldom elevates）。

141. their acuteness often surprises: 他们的洞察力（acuteness）往往令读者拍案称奇（surprises）。

142. ingenious absurdity: 聪明的（ingenious = clever）滑稽（absurdity 意为不伦不类的滑稽效果），此处指产生这种滑稽效果的本领。

143. buried ... in grossness of expression: 被粗俗的语言所掩盖。

144. their value: their 指 genuine wit 和 useful knowledge 而言。同样，第 13 行 they 指（those sentences which contain）genuine wit and useful knowledge（这些包含真正才气和有用知识的句子）。

145. expanded to perspicuity:（当这些句子）被扩充（expanded），达到明澈通畅（perspicuity）的程度。

146. polished to elegance:（当这些句子）被雕琢（polished）到典雅（elegance）的程度。

147. such as ... may give lustre to works: 等于 such genuine wit and useful knowledge as may give brightness to works（这样的真正才气和有用知识，它们可以增加作品的光辉）。

148. works which have more propriety though less copiousness of senti-

ment: 那些（较玄学诗人们的作品）更为妥善（have more propriety），但在思想感情方面（sentiment）没有（玄学诗人们的作品）那么丰富（less copiousness）的作品（这些作品当然指的是蒲伯时代和约翰逊时代的英国古典主义诗歌）。

149. This kind of writing: 指 the metaphysical school of poetry（玄学派诗）而言。

150. Marino: Giovanni Battista Marino (1569–1625)，意大利诗人，他的文章风格矫揉造作，华而不实，与欧洲古典主义文学所推崇的典雅朴素的风格恰成对照。

151. recommended: 等于 made acceptable（推荐使其被接受），或 made popular（推广使其被爱好）。

152. Donne: 见第 468 页第 73 注。

153. Jonson: Ben Jonson (1572–1637)，十七世纪英国剧作家，抒情诗人，兼文学批评家，在当时曾与莎士比亚齐名。

154. ruggedness of his lines: 他的诗行（lines）音节的不和谐（ruggedness）.

155. cast of his sentiments: 他的思想感情（sentiments）的类型或性质（cast = type, quality）.

156. their ... they: 指 the metaphysical poets 而言。

157. more imitators than time has left behind:（他们的）模仿者多于经过时间的淘汰而流传下来的作家们。

158. Suckling: Sir John Suckling (1609 –1642)，十七世纪英国骑士派诗人（Cavalier poet）。

159. Waller: Edmund Waller (1606–1687)，十七世纪英国诗人，通常与 Denham 并提，他们的贡献在于使英雄排偶诗体（the heroic couplet）趋向完美境地。

160. Denham: Sir John Denham (1615–1669)，参阅上条注。

161. Cowley: Abraham Cowley (1618–1667)，十七世纪英国骑士派诗人，散文作家，同时也是英国皇家学会最早成员之一，擅长医学和植物学。

162. Cleveland: John Cleveland (1613–1658)，十七世纪英国诗人。

163. Milton: John Milton（约翰 · 密尔顿 1608—1674），十七世纪英国最伟大的诗人兼政论家。他的最重要的作品是长诗《失乐园》(*Paradise Lost*，1667 年出版）。

164. by improving the harmony of our numbers: 通过提高（improving）我国（英国）诗行（numbers = verses）的音乐性（harmony）。

165. lines upon Hobson the Carrier: 密尔顿在 1631 年写了两首打油诗："On the University Carrier"，"Another on the Same". 这两首诗写的是剑桥大学赶大车送信的年老的车夫 Hobson 因伦敦发生鼠疫，交通断绝，被迫休假。这位常年劳动的老人实在闲不住，密尔顿说他："Ease was his chief disease, and to judge right, He died for heaviness that his cart went light"（安逸是他的主要疾病，说实话，他因自己赶的大车变轻了心情变重了而逝世）。

166. neither improved versification nor abounded in conceits: 既未改进韵律，又未多用譬喻或典故。

167. The fashionable style: 指玄学派诗体而言。

168. Milton disdained it: 密尔顿不屑于模仿玄学派诗体。

20 SAMUEL RICHARDSON
1689–1761

THE HISTORY OF CLARISSA HARLOWE

1. Letter XXVIII
2. Letter LXXXVI

吴景荣 选注

Letter XXVIII — Mr. Lovelace to John Belford, Esq.

At Mrs. Sinclair's, Monday Afternoon.

ALL's right, as heart can wish! In spite of all objection — in spite of a reluctance next to fainting — in spite of all foresight, vigilance, suspicion — once more is the charmer of my soul[1] in her old lodgings!

Now throbs away every pulse! Now thump, thump, thumps my bounding heart for something![2]

But I have not time for the particulars of our management.[3]

My beloved is now directing some of her clothes to be packed up — never more to enter this house! Nor ever more will she, I dare say, when once again out of it!

Yet not so much as a condition of forgiveness![4] The Harlowe-spirited fair one[5] will not *deserve* my mercy! She will wait for Miss Howe's[6] next letter; and then, if she find a *difficulty in her new schemes*[7] [thank her for nothing], will — will what?[8] Why even *then* will take time to consider whether I am to be forgiven, or for ever rejected. An indifference[9] that revives in my heart the remembrance of a thousand of the like nature. And yet Lady Betty[10] and Miss Montague[11] [*a man would be tempted to think, Jack, that they wish her to provoke my vengeance*] declare that I ought to be satisfied with such a proud suspension![12]

They are entirely attached to her. Whatever she says, *is*, *must be*, Gospel! They are guarantees for her return to Hampstead[13] this night. They are to go back with her. A supper bespoken[14] by Lady Betty at Mrs. Moore's.[15] All the vacant apartments there, by my permission (for I had engaged them for a month certain), to be filled with them and their attendants, for a week at least, or till they can prevail upon the dear perverse, as they hope they shall, to restore me to her favour, and to accompany Lady Betty to Oxfordshire.

The dear creature has thus far condescended that she will write to Miss Howe and acquaint her with the present situation of things.

If she write, I shall see what she writes. But I believe she will have other employment soon.[16]

Lady Betty is sure, she tells her, that she shall prevail upon her to forgive me; though she dares say that I deserve not forgiveness. Lady Betty is too delicate to inquire strictly into the nature of my offence. But it must be an offence against *herself,* against *Miss Montague,* against the *virtuous of the whole sex,* or it could not be so highly resented.[17] Yet she will not leave her till she forgive me, and till she see our nuptials privately celebrated.[18] Meantime, as she approves of her *uncle's expedient,* she will address her as *already my wife before strangers*.[19]

Stedman, her solicitor, may attend her for orders, in relation to her Chancery affair,[20] at Hampstead. Not one hour they *can* be favoured with, will they lose from the company and conversation of so dear, so charming a new relation.[21]

Hard then if she had not obliged them with her company,[22] in their coach and four,[23] to and from their Cousin Leeson's, who longed (as they themselves had done) to see a lady so justly celebrated.

"How will Lord M.[24] be raptured when he sees her, and can salute her as his niece!

"How will Lady Sarah bless herself! She will now think her loss of the dear daughter she mourns for happily supplied!"[25]

Miss Montague dwells upon every word that falls from her lips. She perfectly adores her new cousin: "For her cousin she *must* be. And her cousin will she call her! She answers for equal admiration in her sister Patty.[26]

"Ay, cry I (whispering loud enough for her to hear), how will my cousin Patty's dove's eyes[27] glisten and run over, on the very first interview! So gracious, so noble, so unaffected a dear creature!"

"What a happy family," chorus we all, "will ours be!"

These and such-like congratulatory admirations every hour repeated: her modesty hurt by the ecstatic praises: — "Her graces are too natural to herself for her to be proud of them: but she must be content to be punished for excellences that cast a shade upon the *most* excellent!"[28]

In short, we are here, as at Hampstead, all joy and rapture: all of us, except my beloved; in whose sweet face [her almost fainting reluctance to re-enter these doors not overcome] reigns a kind of anxious serenity! But how will even that be changed in a few hours![29]

Methinks I begin to pity the half-apprehensive beauty! But avaunt, thou unseasonably-intruding pity![30] Thou hast more than once already well-nigh undone me! And, adieu, reflection! Begone, consideration! and commiseration! I dismiss ye all, for at least a week to come! Be remembered her broken word![31] Her flight, when my fond soul was meditating mercy to her! Be remembered her treatment of me in her letter on her escape to Hampstead! Her Hampstead virulence![32] What is it she ought not to expect from an unchained Beelzebub, and a plotting villain?[33]

Be her preference of the single life to *me* also remembered! That she despises me! That she even refuses to be my WIFE! A proud Lovelace to be denied a *wife!* To be more proudly rejected by a daughter of the *Harlowes!*[34] The ladies of my own family [she thinks them the ladies of my family] supplicating in vain for her returning favour to their despised kinsman, and taking laws from her still prouder punctilio.[35]

Be the execrations of her vixen friend[36] likewise remembered, poured out upon me from *her* representations, and thereby made her *own* execrations!

Be remembered still more particularly the Townsend plot,[37] set on foot between them, and now, in a day or two, ready to break out; and the *sordid threatenings* thrown out against me by that little fury.[38]

Is not *this* the crisis for which I have been long waiting? Shall Tomlinson,[39] shall these women, be engaged; shall so many engines be set at work, at an immense expense, with infinite contrivance; and all to no purpose?

Is not *this* the hour of her trial—and in *her*, of the trial of the virtue of her whole sex, so long premeditated, so long threatened? Whether her frost be frost indeed?[40] Whether her virtue be principle?[41] Whether, if *once subdued, she will not be always subdued?* And will she not want the very crown of her glory, the proof of her till now allsurpassing excellence, if I stopped short of the ultimate trial?[42]

Now is the end of purposes long overawed, often suspended, at hand. And need I to throw the sins of her cursed family into the too weighty scale?[43]

Abhorred be force![44]*—be the thoughts of force! There's no triumph over the will in force!* This I know I have said.[1] But would I not have avoided it, if I could? Have I not tried every other method? And have I any other recourse left me? Can she resent the *last outrage* more than she has resented a *fainter effort?* And if her resentments run ever so high, cannot I repair by matrimony? She will not refuse me, I know, Jack; the haughty beauty will not refuse me, when her pride of being corporally inviolate is brought down; when she can tell no tales,[45] but when (be her resistance what it will) even her own sex will suspect a yielding in resistance;[46] and when that modesty, which may fill her bosom with resentment, will lock up her speech.[47]

But how know I, that I have not made my own difficulties?[48]

Is she not a woman? What redress lies for a perpetrated evil? Must she not *live?* Her piety will secure her life.[49] And will not *time* be my friend? What, in a word, will be her behaviour afterwards? She cannot fly me! She must forgive me—and as I have often said, *once forgiven, will be for ever forgiven.*

Why then should this enervating pity unsteel my foolish heart?

It shall not. All these things will I remember; and think of nothing else, in order to keep up a resolution, which the women about me will have it I shall be still unable to hold.[50]

I'll teach the dear charming creature to emulate me in contrivance! I'll teach her to weave webs and plots against her conqueror! I'll show her, that in her smuggling schemes she is but a spider compared to me, and that she has all this time been spinning only a cobweb!

What shall we do now! We are immersed in the depth of grief and apprehension! How ill do women bear disappointment![51] Set upon going to Hampstead, and upon quitting for ever a house she re-entered with infinite reluctance; what things she intended to take with her ready packed up; herself on tiptoe to be gone; and I prepared to attend her thither; she begins to be afraid that she shall not go this night; and in grief and despair has flung herself into her old apartment; locked herself in; and through the keyhole Dorcas[52] sees her on her knees—praying, I suppose, for a safe deliverance.

And from what? And wherefore these agonizing apprehensions?

Why, here, this unkind Lady Betty, *with* the dear creature's knowledge, though to her concern, and this mad-headed Cousin Montague *without* it, while she was employed in directing her package, have hurried away[53] in the coach to their own lodgings [only, indeed, to put up some night-clothes, and so forth, in order to attend their sweet cousin to Hampstead]; and, no less to my surprise than hers, are not yet returned.

I have sent to know the meaning of it.

In a great hurry of spirits, she would have had me to go myself.

Hardly any pacifying her! The girl, God bless her! is wild with her own idle apprehensions! What is she afraid of?

I curse them both for their delay. My tardy villain, how he stays![54] Devil fetch them! Let them send their coach, and we'll go without them. In her hearing I bid the fellow tell them so. Perhaps he stays to bring the coach, if anything happens to hinder the ladies from attending my beloved this night.

Devil take them, again say I! They *promised* too they would not stay, because it was but two nights ago that a chariot was robbed at the foot of Hampstead Hill; which alarmed my fair one when told of it!

Oh! here's Lady Betty's servant with a billet.

To Robert Lovelace, Esq. *Monday Night.*

EXCUSE us, dear nephew, I beseech you, to my dearest kinswoman. One night cannot break squares.[55] For here Miss Montague has been taken violently ill with three fainting fits, one after another. The hurry of her joy, I believe, to find your dear lady so much surpass all expectation [never did family-love, you know, reign so strong as among us], and the too eager desire she had to attend her, have occasioned it: for she has but weak spirits, poor girl! well as she looks.

If she be better, we will certainly go with you to-morrow morning, after we have breakfasted with *her*, at your lodgings. But, whether she be, or not, I will do myself the pleasure to attend your lady to Hampstead: and will be with you for that purpose about nine in the morning. With due compliments to your most worthily beloved, I am

Yours affectionately,

ELIZAB. LAWRANCE.[56]

Faith and troth, Jack, I know not what to do with myself: for here, just now having sent in the above note by Dorcas, out came my beloved with it in her hand: in a fit of frenzy! True, by my soul!

She had indeed complained of *her head* all the evening.

Dorcas ran to me, out of breath, to tell me that her lady was coming in some strange way: but she followed her so quick, that the frighted wench had not time to say in what way.

It seems, when she read the billet—Now indeed, said she, am I a lost creature! O the poor Clarissa Harlowe!

She tore off her head-clothes; inquired where I was: and in she came, her shining tresses flowing about her neck; her ruffles[57] torn, and hanging in tatters about her snowy hands; with her arms spread out; her eyes wildly turned, as if starting from their orbits. Down sunk she at my feet, as soon as she approached me; her charming bosom heaving to her uplifted face; and clasping her arms about my knees, Dear Lovelace, said she, if ever—if ever—if ever—and, unable to speak another word, quitting her clasping hold, down prostrate on the floor sunk she, neither in a fit nor out of one.

I was quite astonished. All my purposes suspended for a few moments, I knew neither what to say, nor what to do. But, recollecting myself, Am I *again,* thought I, in a way to be overcome, and made a fool of! If I now recede, I am gone for ever.

I raised her: but down she sunk, as if quite disjointed; her limbs failing her—yet not in a fit neither. I never heard of or saw such a dear unaccountable: almost lifeless, and speechless too for a few moments. What must her apprehensions be at that moment! And for what? A high-notioned dear soul![58] Pretty ignorance! thought I.

Never having met with so sincere, so unquestionable a repugnance. I was staggered—I was confounded. Yet how should I know that it would be so till I tried! And how, having proceeded thus far, could I stop, were I *not* to have had the women to goad me on,[59] and to make light of circumstances, which they pretended to be better judges of than I?

I lifted her, however, into a chair; and in words of disordered passion, told her, all her fears were needless: wondered at them: begged of her to be pacified: besought her reliance on my faith and honour: and revowed all my old vows, and poured forth new ones.

At last, with a heart-breaking sob, I see, I see, Mr. Lovelace, in broken sentences she spoke, I see, I see—that at last—at last—I am ruined! Ruined, if *your* pity—let me implore your pity! And down on her bosom, like a half-broken-stalked lily, top-heavy with the overcharging dews of the morning, sunk her head, with a sigh that went my heart.

All I could think of to reassure her, when a little recovered, I said.

Why did I not send for their coach, as I had intimated? It might return in the morning for the ladies.

I had actually done so, I told her, on seeing her strange uneasiness. But it was then gone to fetch a doctor for Miss Montague, lest his chariot should not be so ready.

Ah! Lovelace! said she, with a doubting face; anguish in her imploring eye.

Lady Betty would think it very strange, I told her, if she were to know it was so disagreeable to her to stay one night for *her* company in a house where she had passed *so many*!

She called me names upon this. She had called me names before. I was patient.

Let her go to Lady Betty's lodgings, then; *directly* go; if the person I called Lady Betty was really Lady Betty.[60]

IF, my dear! Good Heaven! What a villain does that IF show you believe me to be![61]

I cannot help it. I beseech you once more, let me go to Mrs. Leeson's, if *that* IF ought not to be said.[62]

Then assuming a more resolute spirit—I will go! I will inquire my way! I will go by myself! And would have rushed by me.[63]

I folded my arms about her to detain her; pleading the bad way I heard poor Charlotte[64] was in; and what a farther concern her impatience, if she went, would give to poor Charlotte.

She would believe nothing I said, unless I would instantly order a coach (since she was not to have Lady Betty's, nor was permitted to go to Mrs. Leeson's), and let her go in it to Hampstead, late as it was;

and all alone; so much the better: for in the house of *people* of whom Lady Betty, upon inquiry, had heard a bad character [*dropped foolishly this, by my prating new relation, in order to do credit to herself, by depreciating others*];[65] everything, and every face, looking with so much meaning vileness, as well as *my own* [*thou art still too sensible, thought I, my charmer!*], she was resolved not to stay another night.

Dreading what might happen as to her intellects, and being very apprehensive that she might possibly go through a great deal before morning (though more violent she could not well be with the worst she dreaded), I humoured her, and ordered Will to endeavour to get a coach directly, to carry us to Hampstead; I cared not at what price.

Robbers, with whom I would have terrified her, she feared not—*I* was all her fear, I found; and this house her terror: for I saw plainly that she now believed that Lady Betty and Miss Montague were both impostors.

But her mistrust is a little of the latest to do her service![66]

And, O Jack, the rage of love, the rage of revenge, is upon me! By turns they tear me! The progress already made—the women's instigations—the power I shall have to try her to the utmost, and still to marry her, if she be not to be brought to cohabitation—let me perish, Belford, if she escape me now!

Will is not yet come back. Near eleven.

Will is this moment returned. No coach to be got, either *for love or money*.[67]

Once more she urges—To Mrs. Leeson's let me go, Lovelace! Good Lovelace, let me go to Mrs. Leeson's! What is Miss Montague's illness to my terror?[68]—For the Almighty's sake, Mr. Lovelace!—her hands clasped.

O my angel! What a wildness is this! Do you know, do you see, my dearest life, what appearances your causeless apprehensions have given you? Do you know it is past eleven o'clock?

Twelve, one, two, three, four—any hour—I care not. If you

mean me honourably, let me go out of this hated house!

Thou'lt observe, Belford, that though this was written afterwards, yet (as in other places) I write it as it was spoken and happened, as if I had retired to put down every sentence as spoken. I know thou likest this lively *present-tense* manner, as it is one of my peculiars.

Just as she had repeated the last words, *If you mean me honourably, let me go out of this hated house,* in came Mrs. Sinclair, in a great ferment. And what, pray, madam, has *this house* done to you? Mr. Lovelace, you have known me some time; and, if I have not the niceness of this lady, I hope I do not deserve to be treated thus!

She set her huge arms akembo: *Hoh!* madam,[69] let me tell you, I am amazed at your freedoms with my character! And, Mr. Lovelace [holding up, and violently shaking, her head], if you are a gentleman, and a man of honour—

Having never before seen anything but obsequiousness in this woman, little as she liked her, she was frighted at her masculine air, and fierce look—God help me! cried she—what will become of me now! Then, turning her head hither and thither, in a wild kind of amaze, Whom have I for a protector! What will become of me now!

I will be your protector, my dearest love! But indeed you are uncharitably severe upon poor Mrs. Sinclair! Indeed you are! She is a gentlewoman born, and the relict of a man of honour; and though left in such circumstances as oblige her to let lodgings, yet would she scorn to be guilty of a wilful baseness.

I hope so—it may be so—I may be mistaken—but—but there is no crime, I presume, no treason, to say I don't like her house.

The old dragon[70] straddled up to her, with her arms kemboed[71] again, her eyebrows erect, like the bristles upon a hog's back, and, scowling over her shortened nose, more than half hid her ferret eyes.[72] Her mouth was distorted. She pouted out her blubber-lips, as if to bellow up wind and sputter into her horse-nostrils: and her chin was curdled, and more than usually prominent with passion.

With two *hoh-madams* she accosted the frighted fair one; who, terrified, caught hold of my sleeve.

I feared she would fall into fits; and, with a look of indignation, told Mrs. Sinclair that these apartments were mine; and I could not imagine what she meant, either by listening to what passed between me and my spouse, or to come in uninvited; and still more I wondered at her giving herself these strange liberties.

I may be to blame, Jack, for suffering this wretch to give herself these airs; but her coming in was without my orders.

The old beldam, throwing herself into a chair, fell a blubbering and exclaiming. And the pacifying of her, and endeavouring to reconcile the lady to her, took up till near one o'clock.

And thus, between terror, and the late hour, and what followed, she was diverted from the thoughts of getting out of the house to Mrs. Leeson's, or anywhere else.

Letter LXXXVI—Miss Clarissa Harlowe to Miss Howe

In the midst of these agreeablenesses, the coach came to the door. The pretended Lady Betty besought me to give them my company to their Cousin Leeson's. I desired to be excused: yet suspected nothing. She would not be denied.[1] How happy would a visit so condescending make her Cousin Leeson! Her Cousin Leeson was not unworthy of my acquaintance: and would take it for the greatest favour in the world.

I objected my dress.[2] But the objection was not admitted. She bespoke[3] a supper of Mrs. Moore to be ready at nine.

Mr. Lovelace, vile hypocrite, and wicked deceiver! seeing, as he said, my dislike to go, desired her ladyship not to insist upon it.

Fondness for my company was pleaded. She begged me to oblige her: made a motion to help me to my fan herself: and, in short, was so very urgent,[4] that my feet complied against my speech and my mind: and being, in a manner, led to the coach by her, and made to step in first, she followed me; and her pretended niece, and the wretch, followed her: and away it drove.

Nothing but the height of affectionate complaisance passed all the way: over and over, what a joy would this unexpected visit give her Cousin Leeson! What a pleasure must it be to such a mind as mine to be able to give so much joy to everybody I came near!

The cruel, the savage seducer (as I have since recollected) was in rapture all the way; but yet such a sort of rapture as he took visible pains to check.

Hateful villain! How I abhor him! What mischief must be then in his plotting heart! What a devoted victim[5] must I be in all their eyes!

Though not pleased, I was nevertheless just then thoughtless of danger; they endeavouring thus to lift me up above all apprehension of that, and above myself too.

But think, my dear, what a dreadful turn all had upon me, when, through several streets and ways I knew nothing of, the coach slackening its pace, came within sight of the dreadful house of the dreadfullest woman in the world,[6] as she proved to me.

Lord be good unto me! cried the poor fool, looking out of the coach. Mr. Lovelace!—Madam! turning to the pretended Lady Betty—Madam! turning to the niece, my hands and eyes lifted up—Lord be good unto me!

What! What! What, my dear!

He pulled the string. What need to have come this way? said he. But since we are,[7] I will but ask a question. My dearest life, *why* this apprehension?

The coachman stopped: *his* servant, who, with one of hers, was behind, alighted. Ask, said he, if I have any letters? Who knows, my dearest creature, turning to me, but we may already have one from the captain? We will not go out of the coach! Fear nothing—why so apprehensive? Oh! these fine spirits! cried the execrable insulter.

Dreadfully did my heart then misgive me: I was ready to faint. Why this terror, my life? You shall not stir out of the coach—but one question, now the fellow has drove[8] us this way.

Your lady will faint, cried the execrable Lady Betty, turning to him. My dearest niece! (niece I *will* call you, taking my hand) we must alight, if you are so ill. Let us alight—only for a glass of water and hartshorn[9]—indeed we must alight.

No, no, no—I am well—quite well. Won't the man drive on? I am well—quite well—indeed I am. *Man,* drive on, putting my head out of the coach. *Man,* drive on! though my voice was too low to be heard.

The coach stopped at the door. How I trembled!

Dorcas came to the door, on its stopping.

My dearest creature, said the vile man, gasping, as it were for breath, you shall *not* alight. Any letters for me, Dorcas?

There are two, sir. And here is a gentleman, Mr. Belton, sir, waits for your honour; and has done so above an hour.

I'll just speak to him. Open the door. You shan't step out, my dear. A letter perhaps from the captain already! You shan't step out, my dear.

I sighed as if my heart would burst.

But we *must* step out, nephew: your lady will faint. Maid, a glass of hartshorn and water! My dear, you *must* step out. You will faint, child—we must cut your laces.[10] [I believe my complexion was all manner of colours by turns]. Indeed, you must step out, my dear.

He knew, he said, I should be well, the moment the coach drove from the door. I should *not* alight. By his soul, I should not.

Lord, Lord, nephew, Lord, Lord, cousin, both women in a breath, what ado you make about nothing! You *persuade* your lady to be afraid of alighting! See you not that she is just fainting?

Indeed, madam, said the vile seducer, my dearest love must not be moved in this point against her will. I beg it may not be insisted upon.

Fiddle-faddle,[11] foolish man! What a pother[12] is here! I guess how it is: you are ashamed to let us see, what sort of people you carried your lady among — but do you go out, and speak to your friend, and take your letters.

He stepped out; but shut the coach door after him, to oblige me.

The coach may go on, madam, said I.

The coach *shall* go on, my dear life, said he — but he gave not, nor intended to give, orders that it should.

Let the coach go on! said I. Mr. Lovelace may come after us.

Indeed, my dear, you are ill! Indeed you must alight — alight but for one quarter of an hour — alight but to give orders yourself about your things. Whom can you be afraid of, in my company and my niece's? These people must have behaved shockingly to you! Please the Lord, I'll inquire into it! I'll see what sort of people they are!

Immediately came the old creature to the door. A thousand pardons, dear madam, stepping to the coach-side, if we have any way offended you. Be pleased, ladies [to the other two], to alight.

Well, my dear, whispered *the* Lady Betty, I now find that a hideous description of a person we never saw,[13] is an advantage to them. I thought the woman was a monster — but, really, she seems tolerable.

I was afraid I should have fallen into fits: but still refused to go out. Man! — Man! — Man! cried I, gaspingly, my head out of the coach and in, by turns, half a dozen times running, drive on! — Let us go!

My heart misgave me beyond the power of my own accounting for it; for still I did not suspect these women. But the antipathy I had taken to the vile house, and to find myself so near it, when I expected no such matter, with the sight of the old creature, made me behave like a distracted person.

The hartshorn and water was brought. The pretended Lady Betty made me drink it. Heaven knows if there were anything else in it!

Besides, said she, whisperingly, I must see what sort of creatures the *nieces*[14] are. Want of delicacy cannot be hid from me. You could not surely, my dear, have this aversion to reenter a house, for a few minutes, in our company, in which you lodged and boarded several weeks, unless these women could be so presumptuously vile, as my nephew ought not to know.

Out stepped the pretended lady; the servant, at her command, having opened the door.

Dearest madam, said the other to me, let me follow you (for I was next the door). Fear nothing: I will not stir from your presence.

Come, my dear, said the pretended lady: give me your hand; holding out hers. Oblige me this once.

I will bless your footsteps, said the old creature, if once more you honour my house with your presence.

A crowd by this time was gathered about us; but I was too much affected to mind that.

Again the pretended Miss Montague urged me; standing up as ready to go out if I would give her room. Lord, my dear, said she, who can bear this crowd? What will people think?

The pretended lady again pressed me, with both her hands held out—Only, my dear, to give orders about your things.

And thus pressed, and gazed at (for then I looked about me), the women so richly dressed, people whispering; in an evil moment, out stepped I, trembling, forced to lean with both my hands (frightened too much for ceremony) on the pretended Lady Betty's arm—O that I had dropped down dead upon the guilty threshold![15]

We shall stay but a few minutes, my dear!—but a few minutes! said the same specious jilt—out of breath with her joy, as I have since thought, that they had thus triumphed over the unhappy victim!

Come, Mrs. Sinclair, I think your name is, show us the way—following her, and leading me. I am very thirsty. You have frighted me, my dear, with your strange fears. I must have tea made, if it can be done in a moment. We have further to go, Mrs. Sinclair, and must return to Hampstead this night.

It shall be ready in a moment, cried the wretch. We have water boiling.

Hasten, then. Come, my dear, to me, as they led me through the passage to the fatal inner house. Lean upon me—how you tremble! how you falter in your steps! Dearest Niece Lovelace (the old wretch being in hearing), why these hurries upon your spirits? We'll be gone in a minute.

And thus she led the poor sacrifice into the old wretch's too well-known parlour.

Never was anybody so gentle, so meek, so low-voiced, as the odious woman; drawling out, in a puling accent,[16] all the obliging things she could say: awed, I then thought, by the conscious dignity of a woman of quality; glittering with jewels.

The called-for tea was ready presently.

There was no Mr. Belton, I believe: for the wretch went not to anybody, unless it were while we were parleying in the coach. No such person, however, appeared at the tea-table.

I was made to drink two dishes, with milk, complaisantly urged by the pretended ladies helping me each to one. I was stupid to their hands;[17] and, when I took the tea, almost choked with vapours; and could hardly swallow.

I thought, *transiently* thought, that the tea, the last dish particularly, had an odd taste. They, on my palating it, observed that the milk was *London milk;* far short in goodness of what they were accustomed to from their own dairies.

I have no doubt that my two dishes, and perhaps my hartshorn, were prepared for me; in which case it was more proper for their purpose, that *they* should help me, than that I should help *myself.* Ill before, I found myself still more and more disordered in my head; a heavy torpid pain increasing fast upon me. But I imputed it to my terror.

Nevertheless, at the pretended lady's motion, I went upstairs, attended by Dorcas; who affected to weep for joy that once more she saw my *blessed* face, that was the vile creature's word; and immediately I set about taking out some of my clothes, ordering what should be put up, and what sent after me.

While I was thus employed, up came the pretended Lady Betty, in a hurrying way. My dear, you won't be long before you are ready. My nephew is very busy in writing answers to his letters: so, I'll just whip away, and change my dress, and call upon you in an instant.

O madam! I *am* ready! I am *now* ready! You must not leave me here: and down I sunk, affrighted, into a chair.

This instant, this instant, I will return — before you can be ready — before you can have packed up your things — we would not be late — the robbers we have heard of may be out — don't let us be late.

And away she hurried before I could say another word. Her pretended niece went with her, without taking notice to me of her going.[18]

I had no suspicion yet that these women were not indeed the ladies they personated; and I blamed myself for my weak fears. It cannot *be*, thought I, that *such* ladies will abet treachery against a poor creature they are so fond of. They must undoubtedly *be* the persons they *appear* to be — what folly to doubt it! The air, the dress, the dignity of women of quality. How unworthy of them, and of my charity, concluded I, is this ungenerous shadow of suspicion!

So, recovering my stupefied spirits, as well as they could be recovered (for I was heavier and heavier;[19] and wondered to Dorcas what ailed me; rubbing my eyes, and taking some of her snuff, pinch after pinch, to very little purpose), I pursued my employment: but when that was over, all packed up that I designed to be packed up; and I had nothing to do but to *think;* and found them tarry so long; I thought I should have gone distracted. I shut myself into the chamber that had been mine; I kneeled, I prayed; yet knew not what I prayed for: then ran out again: It was almost dark night, I said: where, where was Mr. Lovelace?

He came to me, taking no notice at first of my consternation and wildness [what they had given me made me incoherent and wild]: All goes well, said he, my dear! A line from Captain Tomlinson!

All indeed did go well for the villainous project of the most cruel and most villainous of men!

I *demanded* his aunt! I *demanded* his cousin! The evening, I said, was closing! My head was very, *very* bad, I remember I said—and it grew worse and worse.

Terror, however, as yet kept up my spirits; and I insisted upon his going himself to hasten them.

He called his servant. He raved at the *sex* for *their* delay:[20] 'twas well that business of consequence seldom depended upon such parading, unpunctual triflers!

His servant came.

He ordered him to fly to his Cousin Leeson's, and to let Lady Betty and his cousin know how uneasy we both were at their delay: adding, of his own accord, Desire them, if they don't come instantly, to send their coach, and we will go without them. Tell them I wonder they'll serve me so!

I thought this was considerately and fairly put. But now, indifferent as my head was,[21] I had a little time to consider the man and his behaviour. He terrified me with his looks, and with his violent emotions, as he gazed upon me. Evident *joy-suppressed* emotions, as I have since recollected. His sentences short, and pronounced as if his breath were touched. Never saw I his abominable eyes look as then they looked—triumph in them!—fierce and wild; and more disagreeable than the women's at the vile house appeared to me when I first saw them: and at times, such a leering, mischief-boding cast![22] I would have given the world to have been a hundred miles from him.[23] Yet his behaviour was decent—a decency, however, that I might have seen to be struggled for[24]—for he snatched my hand two or three times, with a vehemence in his grasp that hurt me; speaking words of tenderness through his shut teeth, as it seemed; and let it go with a beggar-voiced humble accent, like the vile woman's just before; half-inward; yet his words and manner carrying the appearance of strong and almost convulsed passion! O my dear! What mischiefs was he not then meditating!

I complained once or twice of thirst. My mouth seemed parched.

At the time, I supposed that it was my terror (gasping often as I did for breath) that parched up the roof of my mouth. I called for water: some table-beer was brought me: beer, I suppose, was a better vehicle (if I were not dosed enough before) for their potions. I told the maid that she knew I seldom tasted malt-liquor: yet, suspecting nothing of this nature, being extremely thirsty, I drank it, as what came next: and instantly, as it were, found myself much worse than before; as if inebriated, I should fancy: I know not how.

His servant was gone twice as long as he needed: and just before his return, came one of the pretended Lady Betty's with a letter for Mr. Lovelace.

He sent it up to me. I read it: and then it was that I thought myself a lost creature; it being to put off her going to Hampstead that night, on account of violent fits which Miss Montague was pretended to be seized with; for then immediately came into my head his vile attempt upon me in this house; the revenge that my flight might too probably inspire him with on that occasion, and because of the difficulty I made to forgive him,[25] and to be reconciled to him; his very looks wild and dreadful to me; and the women of the house such as I had more reason than ever, even from the pretended Lady Betty's hint, to be afraid of: all these crowding together in my apprehensive mind, I fell into a kind of frenzy.

I have not remembrance how I was for the time it lasted: but I know that, in my first agitations, I pulled off my head-dress, and tore my ruffles in twenty tatters, and ran to find him out.

When a little recovered, I insisted upon the hint he had given of their coach. But the messenger, he said, had told him that it was sent to fetch a physician, lest his chariot should be put up, or not ready.

I then insisted upon going directly to Lady Betty's lodgings.

Mrs. Leeson's was now a crowded house, he said: and as my earnestness could be owing to nothing but groundless apprehension [and O what vows, what protestations of his honour did he then make!], he hoped I would not add to their present concern. Charlotte, indeed, was used to fits, he said, upon any great surprises, whether of joy or grief; and they would hold her for a week together, if not got off in a few hours.

You are an observer *of eyes,* my dear, said the villain; perhaps in secret insult: saw you not in Miss Montague's now and then, at Hampstead, something wildish?[26] I was afraid for her then. Silence and quiet only do her good: your concern for *her*, and her love for *you*, will but augment the poor girl's disorder, if you should go.

All impatient with grief and apprehension, I still declared myself resolved not to stay in that house till morning. All I had in the world, my rings, my watch, my little money, for a coach; or, if one were not to be got, I would go on foot to Hampstead that night, though I walked it by myself.

A coach was hereupon sent for, or pretended to be sent for. Any price, he said, he would give to oblige me, late as it was; and he would attend me with all his soul. But no coach was to be got.

Let me cut short the rest. I grew worse and worse in my head; now stupid, now raving, now senseless. The vilest of vile women was brought to frighten me. Never was there so horrible a creature as she appeared to me at the time.

I remember I pleaded for mercy. I remember that I said *I would be his — indeed I would be his* — to obtain his mercy. But no mercy found I! My strength, my intellects, failed me — and then such scenes followed — O my dear, such dreadful scenes! — fits upon fits (faintly indeed and imperfectly remembered) procuring me no compassion — but death was withheld from me. That would have been too great a mercy!

Thus was I tricked and deluded back by blacker hearts of my own sex than I thought there were in the world; who appeared to me to be persons of honour: and, when in his power, thus barbarously was I treated by this villainous man!

I was so senseless, that I dare not aver that the horrid creatures of the house were personally aiding and abetting: but some visionary remembrances I have of female figures, flitting, as I may say, before my sight; the wretched woman's particularly. But as these confused ideas might be owing to the terror I had conceived of the worse than masculine violence she had been permitted to assume to me, for expressing my abhorrence of her house; and as what I suffered from his barbarity wants not that aggravation;[27] I will say no more on a subject so shocking as this must ever be to my remembrance.

I never saw the personating wretches afterwards. He persisted to the last (dreadfully invoking Heaven as a witness to the truth of his assertion) that they were really and truly the ladies they pretended to be; declaring that they could not take leave of me when they left town, because of the state of senselessness and frenzy I was in. For their intoxicating, or rather stupefying potions, had almost deleterious effects upon my intellects, as I have hinted; insomuch that, for several days together, I was under a strange delirium; now moping, now dozing, now weeping, now raving, now scribbling, tearing what I scribbled as fast as I wrote it: *most* miserable when now and then a ray of reason brought confusedly to my remembrance what I had suffered.

【作者简介】 塞缪尔·理查逊（Samuel Richardson, 1689–1761）是英国印刷铺当学徒出身，以后当上了老板；由于偶然的机缘，才在五十多岁时走上写作的道路。他一生用书信体体裁写了三部小说：*Pamela* (1740)，*Clarissa* (1748)，和 *Sir Charles Grandison* (1754)。这三部小说中，不管从艺术角度，还是从整个欧洲影响来说，*Clarissa* 应推第一。这是两百多年来西方文坛的定论。

【题解与注释】

Clarissa Harlowe 的遭遇，使西欧千千万万人为之哭泣，点燃了伤感主义（sentimentalism）的火焰。亨利·菲尔丁（Henry Fielding）向来是瞧不起理查逊的，但是对 *Clarissa* 这部著作，也不得不表示钦佩。狄德罗（Diderot）竟把理查逊比作荷马（Homer）. 甚至十九世纪法国名作家巴尔扎克（Balzac）和乔治·桑（George Sand）也赞扬他。

Clarissa 之所以受到如此重视，主要因为当时整个西欧对唯理主义已经厌倦，打开了通向伤感主义的闸门；更重要的是：*Clarissa* 的主题思想是激动人心的。爱情和残酷现实的矛盾，妇女的人格经历了严峻的考验。Clarissa 是那么一个温顺的少女，在封建式家庭压力下，在阶级社会中种种邪恶势力的包围和迫害下，为了自身的尊严，也是为了女性的尊严，不屈服，不动摇，抵制了强暴和诱惑，甚至在遭到人身凌辱之后仍然是严不可犯。这就是理查逊作为伟大艺术家为妇女塑造的形象，为人们带来的崇高信息。

Clarissa 出版于 1748 年，全书共分四卷。女主人翁出身于英国中产阶级家庭。她的父亲强迫她同一个丑陋鄙俗的有钱人结婚。因此她逃离家庭，与 Lovelace 同来伦敦。Lovelace 把她骗到一个名叫 Mrs. Sinclair 的家里去住。这家实际上是个妓院。Clarissa 曾设法逃出火坑，但 Lovelace 耳目众多，手段卑鄙，最后又把她弄回来了，并设下骗局，暗下麻药，致 Clarissa 神志昏迷，遂遭污辱。Clarissa 的亲友中也有人认为木已成舟，劝她妥协的，但她对 Lovelace 已深恶痛绝，誓死不从。

理查逊写的是“书信体小说”（the epistolary novel），即小说由若干封信组成，一切情节、人物的性格和内心活动，都通过书信来表达。这里我们选了两封信，内容互相呼应。一封是 Lovelace 对 Clarissa 下毒手之前写的。这封信描绘了 Lovelace 的复杂心理。另一封是 Clarissa 给她的密友 Miss Howe 写的，叙述她的最后一段遭遇。

理查逊生在两百多年前。英语在语法、结构、词义上都已经起了相当大的变化。那时还用 thou，thy，ye，thine 等，现在不用了；还有些词语及习语也已经不用了，例如 avaunt，troth，dove's eye，break squares 等等；有些词现在虽然还用，但词义已发生变化。对此，我们作了一些注释。

1. LETTER XXVIII　LOVELACE TO BELFORD

（from *Clarissa Harlowe*, Vol 3）

1. the charmer of my soul: 指 Clarissa.

2. Now thump, thump, thumps my bounding heart for something: 前两个 thump 是副词，thumps 才是动词。意思是：“现在砰、砰地响，我狂跳着的心为某一桩事砰砰地响。”这表示他进行罪恶勾当以前的心理状态。

3. But I have not time for the particulars of our management: 但是我现在没有时间去谈我们处理的细节。（指 Lovelace 与 Mrs. Sinclair 定计诱骗 Clarissa 的具体办法。）

4. Yet not so much as a condition for forgiveness: 现在连一个宽恕的条件都谈不到。（指 Clarissa 根本鄙视 Lovelace，决不宽恕他以往的行为，更谈不到提什么条件了。）

5. The Harlowe-spirited fair one: 指 Clarissa，说她具有 Harlowe 家族那种高傲的性格以及缺乏克制的特点。

6. Miss Howe: 与 Clarissa 经常通讯的密友。

7. if she find a difficulty in her new schemes: Clarissa 一直想摆脱 Lovelace 的

控制，到伦敦躲避。这里指她打算逃去 Mrs. Sinclair 这个罪恶地方的方法。Lovelace 通过偷拆信件等恶劣办法已事先知道。

8. will—will what?: What will she do then? Will she marry me?

9. indifference: 指 Clarissa 在是否可以宽恕 Lovelace 过去的行为这个问题还未表态。（实际上她已下决心了）

10. Lady Betty: 即 Lady Elizabeth Lawrance.

11. Miss Montague: Lady Betty's niece.

12. proud suspension: 指 Clarissa 不肯表态。Lovelace 认为她这种态度使他的心定不下来，实在太傲慢了。

13. Hampstead: Mrs. Moore 和 Lady Betty, Miss Montague 都住在那一带。

14. bespoken: 安排（旧义）。

15. Mrs Moore: Clarissa 的姨妈。

16. But I believe she will have other employment soon: 但是我相信她不久会有（除了写信之外）其它要做的事。这里，Lovelace 暗示她会在被辱后同意跟他结婚。

17. or it could not be so highly resented: it 指 offence，大意是：不然的话 Clarissa 也不会这样生气。

18. Yet she will not leave her till she forgive me, and till she see our nuptials privately celebrated: Yet Lady Betty will not leave Clarissa until she (Clarissa) forgives me (Lovelace) and until she sees our wedding privately celebrated.

19. as she approves of her uncles's expedient etc.: as Lady Betty approves of Clarissa's uncle's expedient（指取得结婚特殊许可证，私下举行仪式）she, (Lady Betty) will address her (Clarissa) as already my wife before strangers.

20. her Chancery affair: 指 Lady Betty 通过她的律师要处理的法律事务。

21. Not one hour they can be favoured with, etc.: 这是倒装句。Not one hour which they be favoured with, will they lose from the company etc. 如不用倒装句，应为 they will not lose even one hour (which they can favour with) from the company etc. 这里 they 指 Lady Betty 和 Miss Montague（实际上是冒充的）；their new relation 指 Clarissa. 她们故意把 Clarissa 看作新的亲戚，以便进一步进行欺骗。

22. Hard then if she … etc.: It would have been hard for them then if she had not obliged them with her company.

23. coach and four: 四轮马车（由四匹或四匹以上的马驾着）。

24. Lord M.: Lord Montague.

25. She will now think her loss of the dear daughter she mourns for happily supplied: 她现在会认为她所哀悼的爱女的亡故已经幸福地得到补救了。（在 Clarissa 身上可以看到她亡女的形象。）

26. She answers for equal admiration in her sister Patty: 她（Miss Montague）保证她妹妹 Patty 对 Clarissa 也会有同样的敬慕。

27. dove's eyes: 温柔的眼睛（旧用法）。

28. but she must be content to be punished for excellences that cast a

shade upon the most excellent: 但是由于她的优秀品质，连最优秀的人都觉得有些逊色，这就应该使她受到惩罚而无怨。（Lovelace 暗示要对她下手了。）

29. But how will even that be changed in a few hours: 但在几小时之内，连这一点（指 Clarissa 貌似安详，心实焦虑）也会怎样地起变化啊！（Lovelace 指他对 Clarissa 施兽行后引起的变化。）

30. But avaunt, thou unseasonably-intruding pity: avaunt 意即‘滚开’，为古老用法。Lovelace 以为自己开始对 Clarissa 怀着怜悯之情，这样就会使他下不了毒手。

31. Be remembered her broken word: 等于 Let her broken word be remembered. 她的失信要牢记在心。（指 Clarissa 曾逃离过这个罪恶地方。）

32. Hampstead virulence: Clarissa 曾逃出火坑，住 Hampstead，后又被 Lovelace 骗回。在 Hampstead 时，Clarissa 曾在给 Miss Howe 信内痛骂 Lovelace，所以 Lovelace 认为很恶毒。

33. What is it she ought not to expect from an unchained Beelzebub and a plotting villain?: Beelzebub 是《圣经》内提到的魔王。弥尔顿（Milton）在他的 *Paradise Lost* 里提到 Beelzebub，说他在恶魔里的地位仅次于 Satan. “unchained Beelzebub” 和 “a plotting villain” 都是 Clarissa 给 Miss Howe 信内写 Lovelace 的话。

34. A proud Lovelace to be denied a wife! To be more proudly rejected by a daughter of the Harlowes!: Lovelace 出身贵族家庭，骄傲不可一世，现被中产阶级家庭出身的 Clarissa 严词拒绝，因此怀恨在心。

35. taking laws from her still prouder punctilio: 把她那些更为傲世凌人的拘泥小节行为看作金科玉律。

36. her vixen friend: 指 Miss Howe。

37. Townsend plot: Miss Howe 曾建议由 Mrs. Townsend 和她两个儿子（还包括她儿子所在轮船的水手）将 Lovelace 狠揍一顿。原话如此：“and the horrid villain shall be repaid broken bones, at least, for all his vileness”. 这封信落入 Lovelace 之手。

38. and the sordid threatenings thrown out against me by that little fury: “that little fury” 指 Miss Howe, fury 是 “ferociously angry woman”（旧用法），她在给 Clarissa 信内说过要把 Lovelace 揍一顿。

39. Tomlinson: Captain Tomlinson，是 Lovelace 的同伙。

40. whether her frost be frost indeed?: 是否她真是那么冷若冰霜？

41. whether her virtue be principle?: 她的道德是否就是那么一成不变的原则？

42. the ultimate trial: 指 rape.

43. And need I to throw the sins of her cursed family into the too weighty scale: 我还需要把她可诅咒的家庭的种种罪过（指 Clarissa 父亲的专横，哥哥的粗暴等等）都放在已过重的天平上去称吗？（意即就 Clarissa 本人对 Lovelace 的鄙视和辱骂已够使他采取这一步骤了！）

44. abhorred be force! etc.: 指用暴力征服女人并不是意志上取得胜利。这种想法，在 Lovelace 心中时隐时现。

45. when she can tell no tales: 当她不能说别人闲话的时候（指 rape 以后 Clarissa 再也无颜说什么了。）

46. even her own sex will suspect a yielding in resistance: 即使妇女们自己也不免会疑心她没有抗拒到底。

47. and when that modesty, which may fill her bosom with resentment, will lock up her speech: 那种羞惭之情虽然会使她愤恨不已，却会把她的口堵住了。

48. But how know I, that I have not made my own difficulties?: 但是也许我自己的困难就是我自己制造出来的？（Lovelace 认为他一直没有使 Clarissa 屈服，可能是由于他自己优柔寡断。）

49. Her piety will secure her life: 意即 Clarissa 是一个虔诚的基督徒，不会自杀。

50. and think of nothing else, in order to keep up a resolution, which the women about me will have it I shall be still unable to hold: 为人使自己决心不动摇，再不想其它别的了，我身边那些女人（指妓院的女人）都认为我仍然不会干到底。

51. How ill do women bear disappointment!: 妇女们多么经不起失望啊！

52. Dorcas: 妓院女仆。

53. this unkind Lady Betty, with the dear creature's knowledge, though to her concern, and this mad-headed Cousin Montague without it, ... have hurried away etc.: 这位无情的 Lady Betty 和神经病的 Montague 表妹已经匆匆走了，前者是让我那可爱的人儿（Clarissa）知道的，虽然引起她的恐惧，后者则是不告而别。

54. My tardy villain, how he stays: 我那慢吞吞的坏蛋（指他的车夫），他怎样呆那么久？

55. one night cannot break squares: 过一夜不能算出乎常规之外。（break squares 意即‘出乎常规’，旧用法）。

56. Elizabeth Lawrence: 即 Lady Betty。

57. ruffles: 衣服绉边（特别指手腕处）。

58. A high-notioned dear soul: 一个有崇高道德观念的可爱的人儿。

59. Were I not to have had the women to goad me on: 如果没有这班女人一直逼着我干。

60. Let her go to Lady Betty's lodgings, then; directly go; if the person I called Lady Betty was really Lady Betty.: 让她到 Lady Betty 的寓所，马上去；如果我（Lovelace）称呼为 Lady Betty 的真是 Lady Betty.

61. What a villain does that IF show you believe me to be!: 那‘如果’两个字多么说明你认为我是个怎样的坏蛋啊！

62. if that IF ought not to be said: 假如那‘如果’两个字是不应该说的话。

63. I will go by myself! And would have rushed by me: 我（Clarissa）自己一个人走。（她）真的可能冲过我走出去了。（如果我不去阻拦她。）

64. Charlotte: 指 Miss Montague.

65. dropped foolishly this, by my prating new relation, in order to do credit to herself, by depreciating others.: 这句话是由一个多话的亲戚为了贬低别人从而抬高自己偶然地、愚蠢地说出来的。

66. But her mistrust is a little of the latest to do her service: 但是现在这种怀疑已经太晚，无济于事了。

67. for love or money: 等于 for love or for money = by any means.

68. What is Miss Montague's illness to my terror?: Miss Montague 的病跟我的恐惧来比算得了什么呢？（Clarissa 需要马车，但马车没有来，因为 Miss Montague 有病要请医生。）

69. Hoh! madam!: 嗬！太太！（Hoh！表示惊讶和愤怒，现不用）

70. old dragon: 指 Mrs Sinclair.

71. Kemboed: 现用 akimbo

72. ferret eyes: 审问的目光。

2. LETTER LXXXVI CLARISSA TO MISS HOWE

1. She would not be denied: 假 Lady Betty 坚持要 Clarissa 到 Mrs. Leeson 那儿去。

2. I objected my dress: 我以服装不整为理由提出反对。近代英语应该说："I objected on grounds of my dress."

3. bespoke: arranged for.（旧用法）

4. urgent: 作殷勤解，表示热切希望进行某项活动。（旧用法）

5. a devoted victim: 心甘情愿的牺牲品。

6. dreadful house of the dreadfullest woman in the world: 指 Mrs. Sinclair 的妓院；dreadfullest 现应为 most dreadful。

7. since we are: since we are here.

8. has drove: has driven.

9. hartshorn: 鹿茸。

10. we must cut your laces: 我们必须把你的紧身带剪开。（叫你透口气）

11. fiddle-faddle: fuss, mess

12. pother: fuss, mess

13. I now find that a hideous description of a person we never saw, is an advantage to them: 我现在发现一个从没有见过面的人被描写得非常可怕，是对他们有利的。（指 Mrs. Sinclair 不如想象的丑恶。）

14. nieces: 指妓院里那些女人。

15. O that I had dropped down dead upon the guilty threshold: 我真愿意当时在邪恶的门限上倒地死去。

16. in a puling accent: 以一种哀求的语调。（puling 为旧用法）

17. I was stupid to their hands: "stupid" 是毫无知觉之意（古用法）。

18. without taking notice to me of her going: 没有向我告辞就走了。

19. for I was heavier and heavier: 因为我觉得头脑越来越昏。

20. He raved at the sex for their delay: 他由于她们（指假 Lady Betty 和 Miss Montague）拖延不来，（假装）骂起女人来。

21. indifferent as my head was: 虽然我的头脑有点飘飘然。

22. mischief-boding cast: 预示要为非作歹的一班人。

23. I would have given the world to have been a hundred miles from him: 只要他能远离十万八千里，我当时什么代价都愿意付。

24. a decency, however, that I might have seen to be struggled for: 然而我当时也许可以看得出来他这种规规矩矩的行为是经过思想斗争才表现出来的。

25. because of the difficulty I made to forgive him: 由于我不肯轻易宽恕他。

26. saw you not in Miss Montague's now and then at Hampstead, something wildish?: 在 Hampstead 你难道没有时常看见 Miss Montague 的眼睛多少有些怪吗？（现代英语应为 Did you not see ...?）

27. what I suffered from his barbarity wants not that aggravation: 他野蛮行为给我造成的痛苦不需要细说了。

21 HENRY FIELDING
1707 – 1754

JOSEPH ANDREWS

刘承沛　选注

1. from *Book I, Chapter XII*

[*The rescue of Joseph by the stage-coach occupants*]

The poor wretch,[1] who lay motionless a long time, just began to recover his senses as a stage-coach[2] came by. The postilion[3] hearing a man's groans, stopped his horses, and told the coachman, he was certain there was a *dead* man lying in the ditch; for he heard him groan. "Go on, sirrah,[4]" says the coachman, "we are confounded[5] late, and have no time to look after dead men." A lady, who heard what the postilion said, and likewise heard the groan, called eagerly to the coachman, to stop and see what was the matter. Upon which he bid the postilion alight, and look into the ditch. He did so, and returned, "That there was a man sitting upright as naked as ever he was born."[6] — "O J — sus,[7]" cry'd the lady, "a naked man! dear coachman, drive on and leave him." Upon this the gentlemen got out of the coach; and Joseph begged them to have mercy upon him:[8] for that he had been robbed,[9] and almost beaten to death. "Robbed," cries[10] an old gentleman; "let us make all the haste imaginable, or we shall be robbed too." A young man, who belonged to the law[11] answered, "He wished they had passed by[12] without taking any notice: but that now they might be proved to have been last in his company,[13] if he should die, they might be called to some account for his murder.[14] He therefore thought it advisable to save the poor creature's life, for their own sakes, if possible; at least, if he died, to prevent the jury's finding that they fled for it.[15] He was therefore of opinion[16], to take the man into the coach, and carry him to the next inn.[17]" The lady insisted, "That he should not come into the coach. That if they lifted him in, she would herself alight: for she had rather stay in that place to all eternity, than ride with a naked man." The coachman objected, "That he could not suffer[18] him to be taken in, unless somebody would pay a shilling for his carriage[19] the four miles." Which the two gentlemen refused to do. But the lawyer, who was afraid of some mischief happening to himself if the wretch was left behind in that condition, saying, no man could be too cautious in these matters,[20] and that he remembered very extraordinary cases[21] in the books,[22] threatened the coachman, and bid him deny taking him up at his peril;[23] for that if he died, he should be indicted[24] for his murder; and if he lived, and brought an action against him,[25] he would willingly take a brief in it.[26] These words had a sensible[27] effect on the coachman, who was well acquainted with the person who spoke them;[28] and the old gentleman above mentioned, thinking the naked man would afford him frequent opportunities of showing his wit[29] to the lady, offered to join with the company in giving a mug of beer for his fare; till partly alarmed by the threats of the one, and partly by the promises of the other, and being perhaps a little moved with compassion at the poor creature's condition, who stood bleeding and shivering with the cold, he at length[30] agreed; and Joseph was now advancing to the coach, where seeing the lady, who held the sticks of her fan[31] before her eyes, he absolutely refused, miserable as he was,[32] to enter, unless he was furnished with sufficient covering,[33] to prevent giving the least offence to decency.[34] So perfectly modest[35] was this young man; such mighty effects had the spotless example of the amiable Pamela,[36] and the excellent sermons of Mr. Adams[37] wrought upon him.

Though there were several great coats about the coach, it was not easy to get over this difficulty which Joseph had started. The two gentlemen complained they were cold, and could not spare a rag; the man of wit saying, with a laugh, that charity began at home;[38] and the coachman, who had two great coats spread under him, refused to lend either, lest they should be made bloody; the lady's footman desired to be excused for the same reason, which the lady herself, notwithstanding her abhorrence of a naked man,[39] approved: and it is more than probable, poor Joseph, who obstinately adhered to his modest resolution, must have perished, unless[40] the postilion, (a lad who hath been since transported[41] for robbing a hen-roost)[42] had voluntarily stripped off a great coat,[43] his only garment, at the same time swearing a great oath, (for which he was rebuked by the passengers) "That he would rather ride in his shirt all his life, than suffer a fellow-creature to lie in so miserable a condition."

Joseph, having put on the great coat, was lifted into the coach, which now proceeded on its journey. He declared himself almost dead with the cold, which gave the man of wit an occasion to ask the lady, if she could not accommodate him with a dram.[44] She answered with some resentment, "She wondered at his asking her such a question; but assured him she never tasted any such thing."

The lawyer was enquiring into the circumstances of the robbery, when the coach stopped,[45] and one of the ruffians putting a pistol in, demanded their money of the passengers; who readily gave it them; and the lady, in her fright, delivered up a little silver bottle, of about a half-pint size, which the rogue, clapping it to his mouth, and drinking her health, declared held some of the best Nantes[46] he had ever tasted: this the lady afterwards assured the company was the mistake of her maid; for that she had ordered her to fill the bottle with Hungary water.[47]

As soon as the fellows were departed, the lawyer, who had, it seems, a case of pistols in the seat of the coach, informed the company, that if it had been day-light, and he could have come at his pistols, he would not have submitted to the robbery; he likewise set forth, that he had often met highwaymen when he travelled on horse-back, but none ever durst[48] attack him; concluding, that if he had not been more afraid for the lady than for himself,[49] he should not have now parted with his money so easily.

As wit is generally observed to love to reside in empty pockets;[50] so the gentleman, whose ingenuity we have above remark'd, as soon as he had parted with his money, began to grow wonderfully facetious.[51] He made frequent allusions to Adam and Eve,[52] and said many excellent things on figs and fig-leaves;[53] which perhaps gave more offence to Joseph than to any other in the company.

The lawyer likewise made several very pretty jests, without departing from his profession.[54] He said, "If Joseph and the lady were alone, he would be more capable of making a *conveyance*[55] to her, as his *affairs* were not *fettered* with any *incumbrance;*[56] he'd warrant, he soon suffered[57] a *recovery*[58] by a writ of *entry,*[59] which was the proper way to create *heirs in tail;*[60, 61] that for his own part, he would engage to make so *firm a settlement* in a coach, that there should be no danger of an *ejectment;*"[62] with an inundation of the like gibberish,[63] which he continued to vent till the coach arrived at an inn, where one servant-maid only was up in readiness to attend the coachman, and furnish him with cold meat and a dram. Joseph desired to alight, and that he might have a bed prepared for him, which the maid readily promised to perform; and being a good-natur'd wench, and not so squeamish[64] as the lady had been, she clapt a large faggot[65] on the fire, and furnishing Joseph with a great coat belonging to one of the hostlers,[66] desired him to sit down and warm himself, whilst she made his bed. The coachman, in the meantime, took an opportunity to call up a surgeon, who lived within a few doors: after which, he reminded his passengers how late they were, and after they had taken leave of Joseph, hurried them off as fast as he could.

2. *Book II, Chapter XVI*

A very curious adventure, in which Mr. Adams gave a much greater instance of the honest simplicity of his heart than of his experience in the ways of this world.

Our travellers had walked about two miles from that inn,[67] which they had more reason to have mistaken for a castle, than Don Quixote[68] ever had any of those in which he sojourned;[69] seeing they had met with such difficulty in escaping out of its walls; when they came to a parish,[70] and beheld a sign of invitation[71] hanging out. A gentleman sat smoking a pipe at the door; of whom Adams enquired the road, and received so courteous and obliging an answer, accompanied with so smiling a countenance,[72] that the good parson, whose heart was naturally disposed to love and affection,[73] began to ask several other questions; particularly the name of the parish, and who was the owner of a large house whose front they then had in prospect.[74] The gentleman answered as obligingly as before; and as to the house, acquainted[75] him it was his own. He then proceeded in the following manner: "Sir, I presume by your habit[76] you are a clergyman: and as you are travelling on foot, I suppose a glass of good beer will not be disagreeable to you; and I can recommend my landlord's within,[77] as some of the best in all this county.[78] What say you,[79] will you halt a little and let us take a pipe together? there is no better tobacco in the kingdom." This proposal was not displeasing to Adams, who had allayed[80] his thirst that day, with no better liquor than what Mrs. Trulliber's[81] cellar had produced; and which was indeed little superior either in richness or flavour to that which distilled from those grains her generous[82] husband bestowed[83] on his hogs. Having therefore abundantly thanked the gentleman for his kind invitation, and bid Joseph and Fanny follow him, he entered the alehouse, where a large loaf and cheese, and a pitcher of beer, which truly answered the character given of it,[84] being set before them, the three travellers fell to eating[85] with appetites infinitely more voracious[86] than are to be found at the most exquisite eating-houses in the parish of St. James's.[87]

The gentleman expressed great delight in the hearty and cheerful behaviour of Adams; and particularly in the familiarity with which he conversed[88] with Joseph and Fanny, whom he often called his children, a term he explained to mean no more than his parishioners;[89] saying, he looked on all those whom God had entrusted to his cure,[90] to stand to him in that relation. The gentleman, shaking him by the hand, highly applauded[91] those sentiments. "They are indeed," says he, "the true principles of a Christian divine;[92] and I heartily wish they were universal:[93] but on the contrary, I am sorry to say the parson of our parish, instead of esteeming his poor parishioners as a part of his family, seems rather to consider them as not of the same species with himself.[94] He seldom speaks to any, unless[95] some few of the richest of us; nay, indeed he will not move his hat to the others. I often laugh, when I behold him on Sundays, strutting[96] along the churchyard like a turkey-cock,[97] through rows of his parishioners; who bow to him with as much submission, and are as unregarded as a set of servile courtiers[98] by the proudest prince in Christendom.[99] But if such temporal[100] pride is ridiculous, surely the spiritual is odious[101] and detestable: if such a puffed-up empty human bladder,[102] strutting in princely robes, justly moves one's derision:[103] surely in the habit of a priest it must raise our scorn."

"Doubtless," answer'd Adams, "your opinion is right; but I hope such examples are rare. The clergy[104] whom I have the honour to know, maintain a different behaviour; and you will allow me, sir, that the readiness which too many of the laity[105] show to contemn[106] the order,[107] may be one reason of their avoiding too much humility."[108] "Very true, indeed," says the gentleman; "I find, sir, you are a man of excellent sense, and am happy in this opportunity of knowing you: perhaps our accidental meeting may not be disadvantageous to you neither. At present, I shall only say to you, that the incumbent of this living[109] is old and infirm;[110] and that it is in my gift.[111] Doctor, give me your hand; and assure yourself of it at his decease."[112] Adams told him, "he[113] was never more confounded[114] in his life, than at his utter incapacity[115] to make any return to such noble and unmerited generosity."[116] "A mere trifle, sir," cries the gentleman, "scarce[117] worth your acceptance; a little more than three hundred a year. I wish it was double the value for your sake." Adams bowed, and cried from the emotions of his gratitude; when the other asked him, "if he was married, or had any children, besides those in the spiritual sense he had mentioned." "Sir," replied the parson, "I have a wife and six[118] at your service."[119] "That is unlucky," says the gentleman; "for I would otherwise have taken you into my own house as my chaplain;[120] however, I have another in the parish, (for the parsonage-house is not good enough) which I will furnish for you. Pray[121] does your wife understand a dairy[122]?" "I can't profess she does,"[123] says Adams. "I am sorry for it," quoth[124] the gentleman; "I would have given you half a dozen cows, and very good grounds to have maintained them." "Sir," said Adams, in an ecstacy, "you are too liberal;[125] indeed you are." "Not at all," cries the gentleman, "I esteem riches[126] only as they give me an opportunity of doing good; and I never saw one whom I had a greater inclination to serve."[127] At which words he shook him heartily by the hand, and told him he had sufficient room[128] in his house to entertain him and his friends. Adams begged he might give him no such trouble; that they could be very well accommodated in the house where they were; forgetting they had not a sixpenny piece among them.[129] The gentleman would not be denied; and informing himself how far they were travelling, he said it was too long a journey to take on foot, and begged that they would favour him, by suffering[130] him to lend them a servant and horses; adding withal, that if they would do him the pleasure of their company only two days,[131] he would furnish them with his coach and six.[132] Adams turning to Joseph, said, "How lucky is this gentleman's goodness to you, who I am afraid would be scarce able to hold out on your lame leg;"[133] and then addressing the person who made him these liberal promises, after much bowing, he cried out, "Blessed be the hour which first introduced me to a man of your charity; you are indeed a Christian of the true primitive kind,[134] and an honour to the country wherein you live. I would willingly have taken a pilgrimage[135] to the Holy Land[136] to have beheld you: for the advantages which we draw from your goodness, give me little pleasure, in comparison of what I enjoy for your own sake; when I consider the treasures you are by these means laying up[137] for yourself in a country that passeth not away.[138] We will therefore, most generous sir, accept your goodness, as well the entertainment you have so kindly offered us at your house this evening, as the accommodation[139] of your horses tomorrow morning." He then began to search for his hat, as did Joseph for his; and both they and Fanny were in order of departure,[140] when the gentleman stopping short, and seeming to meditate by himself for the space of about a minute, exclaimed thus: "Sure never any thing was so unlucky;[141] I had forgot that my house-keeper was gone abroad,[142] and hath locked up all my rooms; indeed I would break them open for you, but shall not be able to furnish you with a bed; for she has likewise put away all my linen.[143] I am glad it entered into my head,[144] before I had given you the trouble of walking there; besides, I believe you will find better accommodations here than you expect. Landlord, you can provide good beds for these people, can't you?" "Yes and please your worship,"[145] cries the host, "and such as no lord or justice of the peace[146] in the kingdom need be ashamed to lie in." "I am heartily sorry," says the gentleman, "for this disappointment. I am resolved[147] I will never suffer[148] her to carry away the keys again." "Pray, sir, let it not make you uneasy," cries Adams, "we shall do very well here; and the loan[149] of your horses is a favour we shall be incapable of making any return to." "Ay!" said the squire, "the horses shall attend you here, at what hour in the morning you please." And now after many civilities[150] too tedious to enumerate,[151] many squeezes by the hand, with most affectionate looks and smiles at each other, and after appointing the horses at seven the next morning, the gentleman took his leave of them,[152] and departed to his own house. Adams and his companions returned to the table, where the parson smoked another pipe, and then they all retired to rest.

Mr. Adams rose very early, and called Joseph out of his bed, between whom a very fierce dispute ensued,[153] whether Fanny should ride behind Joseph, or behind the gentleman's servant; Joseph insisting on it, that he was perfectly recovered, and was as capable of taking care of Fanny as any other person could be. But Adams would not agree to it, and declared he would not trust her behind him;[154] for that he was weaker than he imagined himself to be.

This dispute continued a long time, and had begun to be very hot, when a servant arrived from their good friend to acquaint them, that he was unfortunately prevented from lending them any horses; for that his groom[155] had, unknown to him, put his whole stable under a course of physick.[156]

This advice[157] presently[158] struck the two disputants dumb;[159] Adams cried out, "Was ever any thing so unlucky as this poor gentleman? I protest[160] I am more sorry on his account than my own. You see, Joseph, how this good-natur'd[161] man is treated by his servants; one locks up his linen, another physicks his horses; and I suppose by his being at this house last night, the butler had locked up his cellar. Bless us! how good nature is used[162] in this world! I protest I am more concerned[163] on his account than my own." "So am not I,"[164] cries Joseph; "not that I am much troubled about walking on foot; all my concern is, how we shall get out of the house; unless God sends another pedlar to redeem us.[165] But certainly, this gentleman has such an affection for you, that he would lend you a larger sum than we owe here; which is not above four or five shillings." "Very true, child," answered Adams; "I will write a letter to him, and will even venture to solicit[166] him for three half-crowns;[167] there will be no harm in having two or three shillings in our pockets; as we have full forty miles to travel, we may possibly have occasion for them."[168]

Fanny being now risen, Joseph paid her a visit, and left Adams to write his letter, which having finished, he dispatched a boy with it to the gentleman, and then seated himself by the door, lighted his pipe, and betook himself to meditation.[169]

The boy staying longer than seemed to be necessary, Joseph, who with Fanny was now returned to the parson, expressed some apprehensions,[170] that the gentleman's steward had locked up his purse too. To which Adams answered, "It might very possibly be; and he should wonder at no liberties, which the devil might put into the head of a wicked servant to take with so worthy a master:"[171] but added, "that as the sum was so small, so noble a gentleman would be easily able to procure it in the parish; tho'[172] he had it not in his own pocket. Indeed," says he, "if it was four or five guineas,[173] or any such large quantity of money, it might be a different matter."

They were now sat down to breakfast over some toast and ale, when the boy returned, and informed them, that the gentleman was not at home. "Very well!" cries Adams; "but why, child, did you not stay till his return? Go back again, my good boy, and wait for his coming home; he cannot be gone far, as his horses are all sick; and besides he had no intention to go abroad; for he invited us to spend this day and to-morrow at his house. Therefore go back, child, and tarry till his return home." The messenger departed, and was back again with great expedition;[174] bringing an account, that the gentleman was gone a long journey, and would not be at home again this month. At these words, Adams seemed greatly confounded, saying, "This must be a sudden accident, as the sickness or death of a relation, or some such unforeseen misfortune;" and then turning to Joseph, cried, "I wish you had reminded me to have borrowed this money last night." Joseph smiling, answered, "he was very much deceived, if the gentleman would not have found some excuse to avoid lending it.[175] I own,"[176] says he, "I was never much pleased with his professing so much kindness for you at first sight: for I have heard the gentlemen of our cloth[177] in London tell many such stories of their masters. But when the boy brought the message back of his not being at home, I presently[178] knew what would follow; for whenever a man of fashion[179] does not care to fulfil his promises, the custom is, to order his servants that he will never be at home to the person so promised. In London they call it *denying him*. I have myself denied Sir Thomas Booby[180] above a hundred times; and when the man hath danced attendance[181] for about a month, or sometimes longer, he is acquainted in the end, that the gentleman is gone out of town, and could do nothing in the business." "Good Lord!"[182] says Adams, "what wickedness is there in the Christian world? I profess almost equal to[183] what I have read of the heathens.[184] But surely, Joseph, your suspicions of this gentleman must be unjust; for, what a silly fellow must he be, who would do the devil's work for nothing? and canst thou[185] tell me any interest[186] he could possibly propose to himself[187] by deceiving us in his professions?"[188] "It is not for me," answered Joseph, "to give reasons for what men do, to a gentleman of your learning.[189]" "You say right," quoth Adams; "knowledge of men is only to be learnt from books; Plato[190] and Seneca[191] for that; and those are authors, I am afraid, child, you never read." "Not I, sir, truly," answered Joseph; "all I know is, it is a maxim among the gentlemen of our cloth that those masters who promise the most, perform the least;[192] and I have often heard them say, they have found the largest vails[193] in those families where they were not promised any. But, sir, instead of considering any farther these matters, it would be our wisest way to contrive some method[194] of getting out of this house: for the generous gentleman, instead of doing us any service, hath left us the whole reckoning to pay."[195] Adams was going to answer, when their host came in, and, with a kind of jeering smile, said, "Well, masters! the squire hath not sent his horses for you yet. Laud[196] help me! how easily some folks make promises!" "How!" says Adams, "have you ever known him do any thing of this kind before?" "Ay marry have I,"[197] answered the host; "it is no business of mine, you know, sir, to say any thing to a gentleman to his face: but now he is not here, I will assure you, he hath not his fellow within the three next market-towns.[198] I own, I could not help laughing, when I heard him offer you the living; for thereby hangs a good jest.[199] I thought he would have offered you my house next; for one is no more his to dispose of than the other."[200] At these words, Adams blessing himself, declared, "he had never read of such a monster; but what vexes me[201] most," says he, "is that he hath decoyed us into running up a long debt with you,[202] which we are not able to pay; for we have no money about us; and, what is worse, live at such a distance, that if you should trust us, I am afraid you would lose your money, for want of our finding any conveniency of sending it."[203] "Trust you, master!" says the host, "that I will with all my heart; I honour the clergy too much to deny trusting one of them for such a trifle; besides, I like your fear of never paying me. I have lost many a debt in my lifetime; but was promised to be paid them all in a very short time. I will score[204] this reckoning for the novelty of it.[205] It is the first I do assure you of its kind. But what say you, master, shall we have t'other pot[206] before we part? It will waste but a little chalk more;[207] and if you never pay me a shilling, the loss will not ruin me." Adams liked the invitation very well; especially as it was delivered with so hearty an accent.[208]—He shook his host by the hand, and, thanking him, said, "he would tarry another pot,[209] rather for the pleasure of such worthy company than for the liquor;" adding, "he was glad to find some Christians left in the kingdom; for that he almost began to suspect that he was sojourning in a country inhabited only by Jews[210] and Turks."[211]

The kind host produced[212] the liquor, and Joseph with Fanny retired into the garden; where while they solaced themselves with amorous discourse,[213] Adams sat down with his host; and both filling their glasses, and lighting their pipes, they began that dialogue which the reader will find in the next chapter.

【作者简介】 Henry Fielding（亨利·菲尔丁，1707—1754），英国小说家，他写的*Joseph Andrews*（《约瑟夫·安德路斯》，1742），*Jonathan Wild*（《大伟人江奈生·魏尔德》，1743），*Tom Jones*（《汤姆·琼斯》，1749）和

Amelia（《阿米利亚》，1751）等四部小说，确立了日后英国小说的特定形式。在组织结构、事物描绘、人物塑造、情节安排、以及对现实生活的批评等方面，菲尔丁为后来的小说家树立了楷模。十九世纪初叶英国诗人和小说家司各脱（Sir Walter Scott）称菲尔丁为英国小说家之父，是恰如其分的。

菲尔丁从事小说写作之前，写过许多剧本。当时英国戏剧处于低潮，菲尔丁以他锋利的笔法，以反对派的立场，创作了政治讽刺剧，批评当代的社会、政治、以至戏剧界本身。他最后写的 *The Historical Register* (1737) 对英国政府和英国首相本人都作了露骨的攻击，终于遭当局之忌，以致 1737 年 5 月英国议会通过剧本审查法案（the Licensing Act），规定一切剧本上演前必须经过政府审查。至此，英国戏剧受到进一步的窒息。菲尔丁以后改写小说，给英国文学留下了几部不朽的著作。

【题解与注释】

Joseph Andrews 发表于 1742 年。在这以前，菲尔丁的同时代人塞缪尔·理查逊（Samuel Richardson, 1689–1761）于 1740 年发表了小说《潘米拉》（*Pamela, or Virtue Rewarded*）.

《潘米拉》说的是十五岁的女仆潘米拉在女主人去世以后，如何抗拒了少爷的威逼利诱，从而保全了自己的贞操，最后感动了少爷，把她娶作妻子，从此享受荣华富贵。理查逊在这本小说里所宣扬的婚姻道德观念，恰好反映了当时上升着的资产阶级的踌躇满志和市侩气息。因此，此书问世，大受欢迎。

但是，在菲尔丁这样一位充满批判精神的作家看来，理查逊笔下的潘米拉不过是个矫揉造作的势利鬼。她口口声声大谈自己的贞洁，实际上则无时无刻不在盘算着如何勾引住那位少爷，尽量设法把自己的贞节卖得更大的价钱。为了揭露潘米拉的虚伪性，菲尔丁创作了《约瑟夫·安德路斯》，淋漓尽致地嘲弄了潘米拉所代表的道德观念。他把约瑟夫写成是潘米拉的哥哥，而且恰巧是在潘米拉所勾引的那位少爷的婶婶家当男仆。少爷的叔父死后，婶婶对约瑟夫起了欲念，但是约瑟夫断然拒绝了，历尽苦难，回到乡间和心爱的姑娘结了婚。

虽然在小说的开头和结尾，作者都十分明显地讽刺了理查逊的潘米拉，但是《约瑟夫·安德路斯》作为一本好小说，还在于它对当时的社会风尚作了真实的描述和深刻的批判。这里选注的第一卷第十二章中的几段，说的是约瑟夫离开主人回家途中第二天发生的事。在路上他遭到歹徒的拦劫，衣服财物被夺，还挨了一顿毒打，呻吟于道旁沟中。这时来了一辆驿车，其中乘客对约瑟夫的不同态度，反映了各人的思想意识和精神面貌。菲尔丁以其春秋之笔，借各人的对话，三言两语，就把每一个人刻划得惟妙惟肖。作者对资产阶级社会上层人物的鞭挞和对劳苦人民的同情，见之于笔端，是毫不含糊的。

选注第二部分是 *Joseph Andrews* 第二卷第十六章的全文。这一章主要是讲 Parson Adams 为人心地善良淳朴，轻易地相信一位从不相识的乡绅的甜言蜜语。当时 Adams 带着 Joseph 和 Fanny 在赶路，来到一个村庄。这乡绅主动地向 Adams 许诺了好些事情，Adams 信以为真，连声感谢，结果乡绅一走了之，一件事也没有替他们办到。Adams 明明是受了骗，却一直不相信世界上会有那样的坏人。在本书的序言中，菲尔丁特别提到他立意要把 Parson Adams 塑造成为一位完美的单纯的人（a character of perfect simplicity）. 菲尔丁在这个角色上的创造是十分成功的。

FROM BOOK I CHAP. XII

1. The poor wretch: 即 Joseph Andrews，当时已被歹徒打伤，失去知觉。

2. stage-coach: 驿车；这是一种四轮马车，用四至六匹马牵引；车厢内和顶篷上都有座位，是当时重要的长途交通工具。

3. postilion [pəs'tiljən]**:** 马车夫的助手，骑在领头的马背上驾驭驿车，车夫（coachman）本人则坐在车前端的驭者座位上。

4. sirrah ['sirɑː]**:** sir 的鄙薄的称呼，对后辈及仆役用。

5. confounded: 咒骂语，用以强调语气，类似"该死的"、"要命的"等说法。

6. "That there was a man sitting upright ...": 菲尔丁这里所用的虽是直接引语的引号，但是语法上却是间接引语；That 是连接词，时态是用的过去时。现代英语一般的做法，语法上如果是间接引语，则不应有引号。

7. J—sus: 即 Jesus. 用耶稣基督的名字赌咒被认为是亵渎的事。这位太太竟然这样做了，但作者却不愿写出这字的全文。

8. to have mercy upon him: 可怜他。

9. for that he had been robbed: 按现在通行的英语，应是 for he had been robbed.

10. cries: 这里作者用了现在时，语法上称为 historical present，使对话显得更为生动，本书中常有这种用法。

11. A young man, who belonged to the law: 一位当律师的年轻人。

12. "He wished they had passed ...": He 即为律师本人，这种间接引语用引号的做法同第 500 页第 10 行所见，今日英语体例当无引号。

13. be proved to have been last in his company: 被人证明他们在他死前是最后和他在一起的人。

14. be called to some account for his murder: 被要求对于他的被害担负一定的责任。

15. to prevent the jury's finding that they fled for it: 防止陪审团查出他们曾经故意逃跑。

16. He was of opinion: 他认为应该…

17. inn: 客栈，当时驿站上都有客栈，供旅客食宿。

18. suffer: 容忍。

19. carriage: 车费。

20. no man could be too cautious in these matters: 在这些事情上，越小心谨慎越好。

21. cases: 案件。

22. books: 诉讼案件的档案材料。

23. bid him deny taking him up at his peril: 如不让约瑟夫上车，他要承担严重的责任。

24. be indicted [in'daitid]**:** 被控告。

25. brought an action against him: 起诉控告他。

26. take a brief in it: 受理此案。

27. sensible: 明显的。

28. who was well acquainted with the person who spoke them: 他很熟悉说这话的人的脾气。

29. showing his wit: 卖弄他的才智，意为可以乘机戏弄那位太太。

30. at length: 终于。

31. sticks of her fan: 她的折扇的扇骨。作者在这里是说这位太太并没有用扇子遮住眼睛，而是从扇骨缝里向约瑟夫窥视。

32. miserable as he was: 尽管他已困苦不堪。

33. covering: 蔽体之物。

34. to prevent giving the least offence to decency: 免得他有伤风化。

35. modest: 循规蹈矩。

36. Pamela: 即理查逊笔下的贞洁的女仆，书中约瑟夫的妹妹。此处作者是在讲反话。

37. Mr. Adams: 即 Peter Adams，是作者在这本小说里塑造的一位善良纯朴、急公好义的传教士，约瑟夫的好朋友。

38. charity began at home: 讲究仁爱要从家里做起，意思是说，要先己后人；眼前大家都是出门在外，自顾不暇，不能帮别人的忙。

39. notwithstanding her abhorrence of a naked man: 尽管她不能容忍裸体的男人。

40. unless: = if not.

41. transported: 被放逐。

42. hen-roost: 鸡舍。

43. unless the postilion had voluntarily stripped off a great coat: 要不是马车夫的助手自愿地脱下一件大衣的话。

44. to ask the lady, if she could not accommodate him with a dram: 问这位太太是否真的不能够给他一点儿烈酒挡寒。

45. when the coach stopped: 这时驿车停了下来。

46. Nantes: 一种烈酒，以产于法国 Nantes 地方，故名。

47. Hungary water: 一种矿泉水。

48. durst: 即现在通行的 dared。

49. if he had not been more afraid for the lady than for himself: 他自己倒不害怕，所耽心的是这位太太的安全。(否则他是不会这么容易就把钱交出去的)。

50. As wit is generally observed to love to reside in empty pockets: 人们都说，才智喜欢呆在空口袋里；意思指穷急智生；但此处 wit 双关，也指俏皮话。

51. facetious [fəˈsiːʃəs]**:** 诙谐，打趣。

52. made frequent allusions to Adam and Eve: 不断地提到亚当和夏娃的故事。按基督教《圣经·创世纪》第三章第七节说，亚当和夏娃是上帝创造的第一对男女，并叫他们结为夫妻。最初两人赤身露体，等到吃了禁果，才有了视觉，于是采撷无花果树叶，编成围腰以遮羞。

53. figs and fig-leaves: 无花果和无花果树叶。figs 又可解为"无聊的闲谈"，fig-leaves 又可解为"遮羞之物"。

54. without departing from his profession: 不离他的本行，此处律师利用英国财产法的法律术语来打趣，以下几行的斜体字都属于法律术语。

55. conveyance: 产业过户或产业所有权的转移。

56. as his affairs were not fettered with any incumbrance: 因为他的产业未与任何人发生纠葛。此语双关，也可解释为"他赤条条一丝不挂"。

57. suffered: 承受。

58. recovery: 重新获得对自己产业的所有权。

59. a writ of entry: 接管产权的证明书。entry 也是双关语。

60. which was the proper way to create heirs in tail: 而这是构成产业分享人的正确途径。按当时英国法律，产业所有人办理局部的产业过户时，先由所有人立过户证明书，再由接受者填写接管证明书，此后产业即由两人所共有。

61. heirs in tail: 产业共有人，指夫妻、亲子等共同拥有一份产业的人。律师说这番话是在开约瑟夫和那位太太的玩笑，暗示他们可以成为夫妻。

62. he would engage to make so firm a settlement in a coach, that there should be no danger of an ejectment: 此语又是双关。其一是他将在驿车里把过户的事情安排停当，使产业共有人绝无被逐的危险。另一含义则是他将在马车里做好安排，使约瑟夫不可能遭到太太的拒绝。

63. an inundation of the like gibberish: 一派类似这样的胡言乱语。

64. squeamish: 过分拘谨。这是挖苦那位太太的话。

65. faggot: 木柴。

66. hostlers: 客栈里管理来往马匹的人。

BOOK II CHAP. XVI

67. that inn: 前一章中 Adams 等人借宿的客店。因为 Adams 无钱付食宿费，几经周折，最后才从一个小贩那里借到六先令六便士，连同 Adams 自己的六个便士，付了食宿账，才得从客店脱身。

68. Don Quixote: 唐·吉诃德，西班牙小说家塞万提斯创造的有名的浪漫、不切实际的人物。菲尔丁写 *Joseph Andrews* 时，有意按照唐·吉诃德的形象来塑造 Parson Adams.

69. sojourned [ˈsʌdʒənd]**:** 暂住。

70. parish: 乡，小于 county 的行政单位。

71. a sign of invitation: 指酒店的招牌。

72. countenance: 脸上的表情。

73. whose heart was naturally disposed to love and affection: 他的心肠天生慈爱。

74. in prospect: = in view.

75. acquainted: 告诉。

76. habit: 衣着。

77. I can recommend my landlord's within: 我可以向你推荐里面这位店主的酒。

78. county: 县。

79. What say you: = What do you say，你认为怎样。

80. allayed [əˈleid]**:** 压制。

81. Mrs. Trulliber: 小说中另一牧师 Trulliber 的妻子，全心全意地崇拜她那鄙吝的丈夫。

82. generous: 慷慨的。这里是作者故意说反话。

83. bestowed [bisˈtəud]**:** 赐与。

84. truly answered the character given of it:（这啤酒）果然名不虚传。

85. fell to eating: 大嚼起来。

86. voracious [vəuˈreiʃəs]**:** 狼吞虎咽的。

87. the parish of St. James's: 指伦敦繁华的西区。

88. conversed: 谈话。

89. parishioners [pəˈriʃənəz]**:** 一个牧师所管辖的教民。

90. cure: 教牧。

91. applauded: 赞赏。

92. a Christian divine: 基督教的神职人员。

93. universal: 普遍，一律如此。

94. not of the same species with himself: 与己不同的异类。

95. unless: = except.

96. strutting: 昂首阔步。

97. turkey-cock: 公火鸡。

98. servile courtiers: 卑微的廷臣。

99. Christendom [ˈkrisəndəm]**:** 基督教的天下。

100. temporal: 尘俗的，转瞬即逝的。

101. odious: 可恨。

102. puffed-up empty human bladder: 吹涨了的空皮囊，虚张声势的躯壳。

103. moves one's derision: 令人发笑。

104. the clergy: 神职人员，牧师们的总称。

105. the laity ['leiiti]: 俗人，非神职人员。

106. contemn: 蔑视。

107. the order: 神职人员。

108. avoiding too much humility: 避免过分的谦逊。

109. the incumbent of this living: 占着本乡牧师位置（即 living）的人，这个乡里的牧师。

110. old and infirm: 年老体衰。

111. in my gift:（这位置）是由我来给予的。

112. at his decease: 在他去世的时候。

113. he: 指 Adams 本人。

114. confounded: 愧怍，惶恐。

115. utter incapacity: 完全无能为力。

116. noble and unmerited generosity: 崇高而无端的慷慨。

117. scarce: = scarcely.

118. a wife and six: 一个妻子和六个孩子。

119. at your service: 供你差遣。

120. chaplain: 家庭牧师。

121. pray: 请问。

122. dairy: 牛奶房（牛奶加工业务）。

123. I can't profess she does: 我不敢说她懂得。

124. quoth [kwəuθ]: = said.

125. liberal: 慷慨。

126. riches: 财富。

127. I never saw one whom I had a greater inclination to serve: 我从来没有见过象你这样使我乐于为之效劳的人。

128. room: 空间，余地。

129. had not a sixpenny piece among them: 三个人合起来还凑不起六便士的钱。

130. suffering: = permitting.

131. if they would do him the pleasure of their company only two days: 如果他们不嫌弃，到他家住两天。

132. coach and six: 六马牵引的马车。

133. to hold out on your lame leg: Joseph 此时腿部的伤还未痊愈，因此这样说。

134. a Christian of the true primitive kind: 真正淳朴的基督徒。

135. pilgrimage ['pilgrimidʒ]: 朝觐。

136. the Holy Land: 圣地（指耶路撒冷，耶稣诞生之地）。

137. laying up: 储存，积蓄。

138. a country that passeth not away: 永存的国度（基督教的天国，指人死后去处），passeth = passes；此句意思有如汉语“为来世积德”。

139. accommodation: 提供。

140. in order of departure: 准备动身。

141. Sure never any thing was so unlucky: 再没有比这更不巧的事了。

142. was gone abroad: 出门去了。

143. linen: 指床单、桌布等麻织物。

144. it entered into my head: 我忽然想了起来。

145. Yes and please your worship: 一定照办，大人。

146. justice of the peace: 兼管司法的乡绅。

147. resolved: determined.

148. suffer: permit.

149. loan: 借与。

150. civilities: 客气话。

151. enumerate [iˈnjuːməreit]**:** 一一列举。

152. took his leave of them: 向他们告辞。

153. ensued: followed.

154. he would not trust her behind him: 他（Adans）不放心让她骑在 Joseph 身后。

155. groom: 管马人。

156. put his whole stable under a course of physick: 让他所有的马匹都吃了药。physick = physic 药。

157. advice: information.

158. presently: immediately.

159. struck the two disputants dumb: 把这两位进行着争辩的人弄得哑口无言。

160. protest: 严正地声明。

161. good-natur'd: = good-natured.

162. used: 利用，作践。

163. concerned: troubled，着急。

164. So am not I: 我可不是这样。

165. unless God sends another pedlar to redeem us: 除非上帝再差遣一个小贩来搭救我们。Joseph 此处是指前一章所发生的事，当时 Adams 和 Joseph, Fanny 三个人被困在一家客店，没有钱付账，出不了店门。后来有个小贩替他们付了房饭钱。

166. solicit: ask.

167. half-crowns: 英币单位，一个 crown 是五先令，一个 half-crown 是二先令六便士。

168. have occasion for them: 有用得着它们的时候。Adams 认为用借来的钱付了账还可以剩下两三个先令来做四十英里的盘缠，其实这是远远不够的。作者借此说他不懂世情。

169. betook himself to meditation: 开始沉思起来。

170. apprehensions: 挂虑。

171. he should wonder at no liberties, which the devil might put into the head of a wicked servant to take with so worthy a master: 他一点也不奇怪，一个邪恶的仆人听了魔鬼的话，会对一位善良的主人任意胡作妄为，什么事也干得出来。

172. tho': = though.

173. guineas: 英币单位，一个 guinea 合一镑一先令。当时四、五个英镑是一大笔钱。

174. with great expedition: 非常迅速地。

175. he was very much deceived, if the gentleman would not have found some excuse to avoid lending it: 如果那位先生不会找个借口避免把钱借给他们，那他就是大错了。Joseph 的意思是说，那位先生肯定不会借钱给他们。注意此处先用第三人称 he 称 Joseph 本人，但在下句则改了第一人称 I. 这种写法在 Fielding 的时候是常见的。

176. own: 承认，坦白地说。

177. the gentlemen of our cloth: 穿我们这种衣服的人，干我们这一行的人，因 Joseph 是仆人，此处即指仆人。

178. presently: = at once.

179. a man of fashion: 上流社会的人。

180. Sir Thomas Booby: Joseph 的已故主人。

181. hath danced attendance: = has been kept waiting 久候。

182. Lord: 上帝。

183. equal to: 相当于 . 此处是说基督教国家所见到的邪恶，和他所读到的有关野蛮人的情况简直不相上下。

184. heathens: 不信教的野人。

185. canst thou: = can you.

186. interest: 好处。

187. propose to himself: 为自己求谋。

188. professions: 公开的表示，话语。

189. a gentleman of your learning: 象你这样有学问的人。

190. Plato ['pleitəu]**:** 柏拉图（428–348 B. C.），希腊大哲学家。

191. Seneca ['senikə]**:** 塞尼伽（4 B. C. –65 A. D.），罗马哲学家。

192. those masters who promise the most, perform the least: 许愿最多的主人做得最少。

193. vails: 小费，赏赐。

194. contrive some method: 想出个办法，

195. hath left us the whole reckoning to pay: 丢下全部的账款由我们来付。

196. Laud: 即 Lord. 作者采用此一拼法，表明说话的人言谈粗犷。

197. Ay marry have I: = I certainly have，我当然知道（他干过类似这样的事）。marry = (the Virgin) Mary，即以耶稣生母之名发誓，是一种古旧的惊叹词，此处用来表示愤慨或鄙薄。

198. he hath not his fellow within the three next market-towns: 邻近三个市镇里也找不出第二个象他这样的角色。

199. thereby hangs a good jest: 这里头有桩很可笑的事。

200. one is no more his to dispose of than the other: 这两件东西（牧师的职位和店主的房子）他都同样无权处置。

201. he ... me: 都指说话人 Adams.

202. decoyed us into running up a long debt with you: 把我们骗得欠你一大笔债。

203. for want of our finding any conveniency of sending it: 因为我们找不到什么方便的途径把钱给你送来。

204. score:（用粉笔）记下。

205. for the novelty of it: 只是因为它新鲜好玩（才记下这笔账）。

206. t'other pot: = the other pot. 指当时手边的另一盅酒。

207. It will waste but a little chalk more: 这只不过是再浪费一点儿粉笔（指记账时用粉笔写下）。

208. accent: 口吻。

209. tarry another pot: 再耽搁一下把这盅酒喝掉，再耽搁一盅酒的时间。

210. Jews: 犹太人，不信基督教而信犹太教。

211. Turks: 土耳其人，一般信伊斯兰教，Adams 是基督教牧师，认为异教总是邪恶的。

212. produced: 拿出来。

213. amorous discourse: 谈情说爱。

22 LAURENCE STERNE
1713–1768

A SENTIMENTAL[1] *JOURNEY THROUGH FRANCE AND ITALY*[2]
(selections)

杨周翰 选注

MARIA[3]
MOULINES.[4]

I never felt what the distress of plenty[5] was in any one shape till now — to travel it[6] through the Bourbonnois,[7] the sweetest part of France — in the hay-day of the vintage,[8] when Nature is pouring her abundance into every one's lap, and every eye is lifted up — a journey through each step of which music beats time to *Labour,*[9] and all her children are rejoicing as they carry in[10] their clusters[11] — to pass through this with my affections flying out, and kindling at every group before me — and every one of 'em was pregnant with adventures.[12]

Just heaven! — it would fill up twenty volumes — and alas! I have but a few small pages left of this[13] to crowd it into — and half of these must be taken up with the poor Maria my friend, Mr. Shandy,[14] met with near Moulines.

The story he had told of that disorder'd[15] maid affect'd[16] me not a little in the reading[17]; but when I got[18] within the neighbourhood where she lived, it returned so strong into my mind, that

I could not resist an impulse which prompted me to go half a league[19] out of the road to the village where her parents dwelt to enquire after her.

'Tis going, I own,[20] like the Knight of the Woeful Countenance,[21] in quest of melancholy adventures — but I know not how it is, but[22] I am never so perfectly conscious of the existence of a soul within me, as when I am entangled in them.[23]

The old mother came to the door, her looks told me the story before she open'd her mouth — She had lost her husband; he had died, she said, of anguish,[24] for the loss of Maria's sense about a month before. — She had feared at first, she added, that it[25] would have plunder'd her poor girl of what little understanding was left — but, on the contrary, it had brought her more to herself[26] — still she could not rest — her poor daughter, she said, crying,[27] was wandering somewhere about the road —

— Why does my pulse beat languid[28] as I write this? and what made La Fleur,[29] whose heart seem'd only[30] to be tuned to joy, to pass the back of his hand twice across his eyes,[31] as the woman stood and told it? I beckon'd to the postilion[32] to turn back into the road.[33]

When we had got within half a league of Moulines, at a little opening[34] in the road leading to a thicket,[35] I discovered Maria sitting under a poplar[36] — she was sitting with her elbow in her lap, and her head leaning on one side within her hand — a small brook ran at the foot of the tree.

I bid the postilion go on with the chaise[37] to Moulines — and La Fleur to bespeak[38] my supper — and that I would walk after him.

She was dress'd in white, and much as my friend[39] described her, except that her hair hung loose, which before was twisted within a silk net. — She had, superadded likewise to her jacket, a pale green ribband[40] which fell across her shoulder to the waist; at the end of which hung her pipe.[41] — Her goat had been as faithless as her lover; and she had got a little dog in lieu of him, which she had kept tied by a string to her girdle; as I look'd at her dog, she drew him towards her with the string. — "Thou shalt not leave me, Sylvio,[42]" said she. I look'd in Maria's eyes, and saw she was thinking more of her father than of her lover or her little goat; for as she utter'd them[43] the tears trickled down her cheeks.

I sat down close by her; and Maria let me wipe them[44] away as they fell with my handkerchief. — I then steep'd it in my own[45] — and then in hers — and then in mine — and then I wip'd hers again — and as I did it, I felt such undescribable emotions within me, as I am sure could not be accounted for from any combinations of matter and motion.[46]

I am positive[47] I have a soul; nor can all the books with which materialists[48] have pester'd[49] the world ever convince me of the contrary.

MARIA

When Maria had come a little to herself, I ask'd her if she remember'd a pale thin person of a man[50] who had sat down betwixt her and her goat about two years before? She said, she was unsettled[51] much at that time, but remember'd it upon two accounts[52] — that ill as she was she saw the person pitied her; and next, that her goat had stolen his handkerchief, and she had beat him[53] for the theft — she had wash'd it, she said, in the brook, and kept it[54] ever since in her pocket to restore it to him in case she should ever see him again, which, she added, he had half promised her. As she told me this she took the handkerchief out of her pocket to let me see it; she had folded it up neatly in a couple of vine leaves,[55] tied round with a tendril[56] — on opening it, I saw an *S*[57] mark'd in one of the corners.

She had since that, she told me, stray'd as far as Rome, and walk'd round St. Peter's[58] once — and return'd back — that she found her way alone across the Apennines[59] — had travell'd over all Lombardy[60] without money — and through the flinty[61] roads of Savoy[62] without shoes — how she had borne it, and how she had got supported,[63] she could not tell — but *God tempers the wind*, said Maria, to the shorn[64] lamb.

Shorn indeed! and to the quick,[65] said I; and wast thou[66] in my own land, where I have a cottage, I would take thee to it and shelter thee: thou shouldst eat of[67] my own bread, and drink of[68] my own cup — I would be kind to thy Sylvio — in all thy weaknesses[69] and wanderings I would seek after thee and bring thee back — when the sun went down I would say my prayers, and when I had done thou shouldst play thy evening song upon thy pipe, nor would the incense[70] of my sacrifice be worse accepted for entering heaven along with that of a broken heart.

Nature melted[71] within me, as I utter'd this; and Maria observing, as I took out my handkerchief, that it was steep'd too much[72] already to be of use, would needs[73] go wash it in the stream. — And where will you dry it, Maria? said I — I'll dry it in my bosom, said she — 'twill do me good.

And is your heart still so warm, Maria? said I.

I touch'd upon the string on which hung all her sorrows — she look'd with wistful disorder[74] for some time in my face; — and then, without saying any thing, took her pipe, and play'd her service to the Virgin[75] — The string I had touch'd ceased to vibrate[76] — in a moment or two Maria returned to herself — let her pipe fall — and rose up.

And where are you going, Maria? said I. — She said to Moulines. — Let us go, said I, together. — Maria put her arm within mine, and lengthening the string, to let the dog follow, in that order we entered Moulines.

MARIA
MOULINES

Tho' I hate salutations and greetings in the market-place,[77] yet when we got into the middle of this, I stopp'd to take my last look and last farewell of Maria.

Maria, tho' not tall, was nevertheless of the first order of fine forms[78] — affliction had touch'd her looks with something that was scarce earthly[79] — still she was feminine — and so much was there about her of all that the heart wishes, or the eye looks for in woman,[80] that could the traces[81] be ever worn out of her brain, and those of Eliza's[82] out of mine, she should *not only eat of my bread and drink of my cup,* but Maria should lay in my bosom, and be unto me as a daughter.[83]

Adieu, poor luckless maiden! — imbibe the oil and wine[84] which the compassion of a stranger, as he journeyeth on his way, now pours into thy wounds — the being[85] who has twice bruised thee can only[86] bind them up for ever.

THE BOURBONNOIS[87]

There was nothing from which I had painted out for myself so joyous a riot of the affections,[88] as in this journey in the vintage, through this part of France; but pressing through this gate of sorrow[89] to it, my suffering has totally unfitted[90] me: in every scene of festivity I saw Maria in the back-ground of the piece,[91] sitting pensive under her poplar; and I had got almost to Lyons[92] before I was able to cast a shade across her —

— Dear sensibility![93] source inexhausted[94] of all that's precious in our joys, or costly[95] in our sorrows! thou chainest thy martyr down upon his bed of straw[96] — and 'tis thou who lifts him up to HEAVEN[97] — eternal fountain[98] of our feelings! — 'tis here[99] I trace thee — and this is thy divinity[100] which stirs within me — not that,[101] in some sad and sickening moments, "*my soul shrinks back upon herself, and startles at destruction*" — mere pomp of words![102] — but that[103] I feel some generous joys and generous cares beyond myself — All comes from thee, great, great SENSORIUM[104] of the world! which vibrates,[105] if a hair of our heads but falls upon the ground, in the remotest desert of thy creation. — Touch'd with thee, Eugenius[106] draws my curtain when I languish — hears my tale of symptoms,[107] and blames the weather for the disorder of his nerves. Thou giv'st a portion of it[108] sometimes to the roughest peasant who traverses[109] the bleakest mountains — he finds the lacerated lamb of another's flock — This moment I behold him leaning with his head against his crook,[110] with piteous inclination looking down upon it — Oh! had I come one moment sooner![111] — it bleeds to death — his[112] gentle heart bleeds with it —

Peace to thee, generous swain![113] — I see thou walkest off with anguish — but thy joys shall balance[114] it — for happy is thy cottage — and happy is the sharer[115] of it — and happy are the lambs which sport[116] about you.

【作者简介】 Laurence Sterne [stəːn]（劳伦斯·斯泰恩，或译斯特恩，1713—1768）英国小说家。出生在爱尔兰。他父亲是一个下级军官。斯泰恩童年随父母过着军队的生活，居无定所。十一岁那年，由伯父资助在英国北部约克郡的哈利法克斯（Halifax）读了八年书。其间伯父和父亲相继去世，后由堂兄资助进了剑桥大学。斯泰恩家族在约克郡很有地位，作者曾祖父是约克大主教，他一个叔父是约克教区的副主教。作者大学毕业后在 1738 年任本郡塞顿（Sutton in the Forest）的牧师，达 21 年之久。1741 年结婚，生了两个女儿，其一早夭。1760 年他到伦敦，夤缘得到约克郡科克斯瓦德（Coxwold）终身牧师职位。1762—1764 因患肺病与妻女去法国养病，1765 年又去法、意旅行疗养，回到英国后于 1768 年病逝于伦敦。

斯泰恩写过两部“小说”。《商第传》（*Tristram Shandy*）共出了九卷，从 1759 年开始陆续发表，到 1767 年中断，并未完成。它名为《商第的生平和见解》，但主人公到第四卷才出世，到第六卷才到穿裤子的年龄，此后就销声匿迹了。这部书主要写的是商第的父亲 Walter，他的叔父 Toby，他叔父从军时的随从下士 Trim，医生 Slop，主人公的母亲和寡妇 Wadham 等一批颇为怪诞的性格。它打破了当时已趋定型的小说格式，打乱时空秩序，充满长篇插话，写到第三卷的一半，才想起写序言。书里有时插进一张白页、一张黑页、一张虎皮纹书页，有表格、符号、线条、图解，不一而足。作者曾说，人应当“先感受，而后去理解”。这句话反映了当时一种相当普遍存在的情绪，即对“理性王国”的失望，也正是后来浪漫主义的先导。这部小说第一二卷一出版就风靡一时，作者所到之处，不论国内国外，都大受奉承。狄德罗模仿他，歌德赞赏他。后来，马克思也多次提到他。

另一部“小说”《感伤旅行》开始于1767年，原定写四卷，法国和意大利游记各两卷，只完成了一半，作者就去世了。

此外他还发表了布道文四卷和书信集，后者中以《致伊莱莎书信》（Journal to Eliza）最著名。Eliza是英国一个印度殖民官吏Draper的妻子，作者在伦敦与她相识，其时他54岁，Eliza只有22岁，同年她奉丈夫之命回到印度。作者当时病魔缠身，妻女都在法国，他很思念女儿Lydia，他写给Eliza的信一半写他对她的爱慕，一半也是寄托他对女儿的思念。

斯泰恩反对理性，背叛礼教，歌颂感情（这作为历史现象是很好理解的），在艺术手法上大胆突破。历来评家对他毁誉参半，攻击他的说他自作多情，其实是跳梁小丑，最厉害的是萨克雷（Thackeray）。赞扬他的也有，上面已经提到。到了当代，则多是褒奖。伍尔芙夫人（V. Woolf）说，总的说来，斯泰恩为人敏感，富于同情，有人情味，他信奉正直、纯朴，但做得过火一些，因而使人怀疑他是否真诚。这种评价还是公允的。

【题解与注释】

Sentimental Journey 名为游记，其实并没有写多少所见所闻，而是以某些极琐细的事情为引线，抒写自己的情绪。约翰逊（Samual Johnson）说：你读斯泰恩，读的是他的情，故事不过是个引子。所以与其说它是客观世界的纪录，不如说是作者内心世界的描写，更近于诗歌。他反对一般的游记，尤其反对斯末莱特（Smollett）写的法意游记，因为他到处感到不满，对一切批判，缺乏同情。他在《商第传》中还讽刺过他。1767年11月12日他给友人詹姆斯夫人的信关于《感伤旅行》写道：“我写此书的目的是要教导我们比现在更好地去爱这世界，爱我们的同类，因此它涉及的是那些能帮助达到这一目标的温存的情感。”他在本书中也说“这是一次探求自然的、充满爱心的、悄悄的旅行。”他在这本书上花了很大工夫，稿子一改再改。他给友人信中说，这部书耗尽了他的身心，因为一个作家想要感动别人，自己首先要感动。另外，在表现手法上也别具匠心，就拿这部书的开头说吧，它是从一段对话的半路开始的。他知道人们要求他写悲怆、纯朴、可爱的“自然”；他也知道人们对他哪些地方不满意，所以他致友人信中说：“如果有人认为我这书不干净，那么上帝对他们发发慈悲吧，他们的想象力太炽热了。”

作者在两部“小说”里都自称Yorick，这是从莎士比亚《哈姆雷特》剧中掘墓人挖出的一具骷髅得来，他生前是丹麦王的弄臣 Yorick。由此可见作者的态度是要在滑稽幽默嘻笑之中来寄托爱、同情、伤感。

由于作者精心琢磨，文字清澈如水，平易如谈话，使人感到舒服。

下面选的一段，本身比较完整。Maria 这个人物在《商第传》已提到过（9 卷 24 章），在那里她是一个聪明可爱的乡村姑娘，和一个青年相爱。他们订婚之事由牧师公布后，由于牧师捣鬼，未能结婚。她受到打击后，精神不正常，常带着一头山羊，在溪边吹笛唱歌，唱赞美圣母的诗，以自我安慰，四乡的人多次为她祷告祈福，没有效果，父母绝望，作者对她寄予无限同情。

1. Sentimental: 据《牛津大字典》（以下简称 OED）sentiment 第 9 义指高雅、温柔的情感（refined and tender emotion），第一例句就是 1768 *Sentimental Journey*, a people...so renowned for sentiment and fine feelings. Sentimental 据 OED 可以修饰人、人的脾气和行为，表现高雅崇高的感情。最早（1749）是褒义，到十九世纪才逐渐具有贬义。我们一般译为“感伤”，贬义多于褒义，“多情”“善感”可能更切近些。

2. Italy: 这部分游记，没有写。

3. Maria: 见题解。

4. Moulines: 即现在的 Moulins [mulɛ̃]，法国中部 Allier 省的省会，此省旧称 Bourbonnais，见下。

5. distress of plenty: 丰富得使人发愁。这是 Sterne 过火处的一例。

6. travel it: 作“及物动词”用，其实就是旅行。这种用法，OED 就引此句为例句。

7. Bourbonnais [burbɔnɛ]**:** 原属古老的波旁家族，因而得名。

8. vintage: 葡萄收割季节。

9. Labour: 拟人化，故大写，指劳动者。我每走一步就象为他们的劳动打拍子，击节，表示主客观欢乐的协调。

10. in: 副词。从葡萄园里收进来。

11. clusters: 一球球葡萄。对田园风光的美化当时开始盛行，反映对贵族上层社会的不满。也是“'Tis a quiet journey of the heart in pursuit of Nature”的具体表现。

12. pregnant with adventures: 每个劳动者都充满了兴奋。Adventure = exciting experience.

13. this: 本子、簿册。“只剩下几页空白页了。”

14. Shandy: 即《商第传》中的 Uncle Toby（Toby 的名字出自莎士比亚《第十二夜》中一个滑稽人物），他在法国旅行遇到过 Maria。作者称 Shandy 为“我的朋友”，因为作者自己是 Yorick，而 Yorick 是商第家的朋友、座上客。

15. disorder'd: 神经不正常。

16. affected: 受感动。

17. in the reading: 指当我读《商第传》中关于 Maria 的事迹时。

18. got: 当我亲身到了这个地方。

19. league: 约二公里。

20. I own: 我承认。

21. Knight: 指堂吉诃德。按：西班牙的塞万提斯（Cervantes）和法国的拉伯雷

（Rabelais）对作者都有影响。

22. but: = except that.

23. entangled in them: 指 melancholy adventures。吉诃德抱着一副赤诚去济弱锄强，但屡屡失败，故称 melancholy。Entangled 指作者也被纠缠进吉诃德式的行动中去。背后的意思是：有同情心的人才有灵魂。参看 45 注。

24. anguish: 郁闷，痛苦。

25. it: 指 Maria 的父亲之死。

26. brought her more to herself: 反倒使她清醒了些。

27. crying: 指老妇。

28. languid: 微弱无力。作者处处突出个人感受，是故作多情？还是真情实感？

29. La Fleur [la floer]: 意为"花"。在《商第传》中提到过他的身世，在此书中是作者雇用的仆人，一路服侍他。

30. only: 他的心只会弹出欢乐的曲调，指他一向乐观。

31. pass his hand across his eyes: 用手背抹眼泪。

32. postilion [pɔsˈtiliən]: 马车夫。作者在旅途中雇了一辆马车，此指赶车人。

33. Why does ... turn back into the road: 表现作者对 La Fleur 的体贴，不让他过分伤心，也免得老妇人说下去更伤心。这些微妙的笔触是 Sterne 的一个特点。

34. opening: 岔路（引向灌木林）。

35. thicket: 灌木林。

36. poplar: 白杨，象征悲哀、死亡。

37. chaise [ʃeiz]: 马车。

38. bespeak: 预定。

39. my friend: 见 14 注。

40. ribband: = ribbon 宽带。

41. pipe: 笛子，系在宽带一端。

42. Sylvio: 狗名。田园诗歌中常把乡村青年男女取名为 Sylvio, Sylvia.

43. uttered them: 指 the words，对狗说的那句话。她若仅仅对狗说话，不会落泪，证明她是在思念亡父。

44. them: the tears，接 with my handkerchief.

45. in my own: 指 in my own tears。Steep = soak，吸。此处重复动作，确似演戏，追求效果。

46. matter and motion: 指 David Hartley (1705–1757) 一派哲学。Hartley 认为人的头脑是物质，通过震动，使人产生意识，意识通过联想产生好恶等感情。他反对天性、灵魂等说法。Sterne 反对这种物质机械运动的解释，主张人有灵魂。

47. positive: = certain.

48. materialists: 指上述那派用物质运动解释感情的哲学家。

49. pester: = infest，象害虫一样侵扰。

50. a pale thin person of a man: 见注 14。

51. unsettled: 心神不定，精神不正常。

52. upon two accounts: = on account of two things.

53. him: 指山羊。

54. kept it: 作者着意烘托爱的力量。前一节她失去爱，导致精神失常和不幸，此处商第先生对她表示同情，引起她的感激。

55. vine leaves: 葡萄叶。

56. tendril: 葡萄蔓。

57. S: 绣着 Shandy 的第一个字母。

58. St. Peter's: 罗马圣彼得大教堂。Maria 去罗马显然是要在宗教中寻求安慰和爱。在 Sterne 看来，宗教和爱是分不开的。早年他在约克钟情于一个歌女，同她通信，并寄给她一篇布道文，内容是关于《旧约》《列王纪》(上)里以利亚救活一个寡妇的儿子的故事，信里说那歌女温柔仁慈的性格同以利亚一样。

59. the Apennines ['æpinainz]**:** 纵贯意大利的亚平宁山脉。

60. Lombardy ['lɔmbədi]**:** 意大利北部伦巴底地区。

61. flinty: 多燧石的。

62. Savoy [sə'vɔi]**:** 法国东南与意、瑞交界地区。

63. supported: 获得衣食，挣扎着活下来。

64. shorn: shear 过去分词，脱了毛的，剪了毛的。这句话"上帝让风吹得温和些，以免吹坏了脱毛的羔羊"原是法国谚语，经 Sterne 采用已成为英语中的一句谚语。

65. to the quick:(羊毛已剪)到了肉了，已引起痛苦。

66. wast thou: = if you were.

67. of: 部分所有格(partitive genitive), some of.

68. of: = from；也可作为部分所有格，那么 cup = 酒。

69. weaknesses: 发病。

70. incense: 宗教仪式里所焚烧的香。这句话的意思是：我为你作的牺牲象香烟一样升到天上，纵然随伴着一颗破碎的心，上帝也不会不接受的。Sacrifice 指上面所设想的那些细节。A broken heart 意义双关：伤心，同情；破碎的心，不完整的心，既非全心全意，上帝是不会接受的。这一段描绘了一幅茅屋田园、充满着爱的景象，表现一种理想。作者在结婚前向未婚妻求婚时也描绘了这样一幅图画：远离城市；生活在一个浪漫色彩浓厚的金色太阳照耀的茅屋里，充满爱和友情，一个天真无邪的乐园。他说："我们应从大自然学习如何生活"。

71. melted: 作者选词无不着眼于温情。

72. too much: 评论家说 Sterne 感情泛滥，自作多情，自我戏剧化，以至虚伪，多从这类笔调得出结论。

73. needs: 副词 = of necessity 必然。

74. wistful disorder: 勾起心事而不安起来。

75. service to the Virgin: 对圣母玛利亚的礼拜所奏的乐调，暗示对仁爱、贞洁祝祷。

76. vibrate: 颤动。此词当时常用来描写感情。

77. market-place: 引自《新约》《马可福音》12 章 38 节，耶稣警戒人们要防备

"文士"（scribes）和法利赛人（Pharisees 伪善者），这些人专爱在市集上向人问安问好。

78. forms: 仪表、外表。

79. affliction touch'd ... scarce earthly: 痛苦赋予她某种非凡的、天上的美。

80. so much ... for in woman: 指人间的美。

81. traces: 痕迹，不幸的遭遇在她头脑里留下的痕迹。

could the traces: = if the traces could.

82. Eliza [i'laizə]: 即 Mrs. Draper，见作者简介。

83. she should not ... as a daughter: Sterne 同妻子关系不好，时常思念在法国随伴其妻的女儿 Lydia。他对 Eliza 的感情也有父女成分。

84. oil and wine:《新约》《路加福音》10 章 33—34 节，善良的撒玛利亚人看见一个遇盗被劫而受伤的人，就发了慈心，用酒和油倒在他的伤口，为他医治。

85. the being: 指作者自己。"两次给你创伤"指上文勾引起她的悲哀之事。

86. only: 除此之外别无它法。

87. The Bourbonnois: 现代拼法 Bourbonnais。用定冠词是因为有波旁家族领地的意思。取这个地区为本节标题，表示作者旅行到此，但这一节根本没有任何故事，而是一首感情或敏感的赞歌，近于狂诗（rhapsody）。这类情调很受当时人欢迎。

88. riot of the affections: 感情的喧闹，指欢乐感情。

89. gate of sorrow: 指 Maria 引起的悲伤。进入这个充满欢乐景象的地区却是通过一座悲伤之门。

90. unfitted: = unhinged 失常以至不能欣赏欢乐的画面。

91. piece: 一幅画图。

92. Lyons ['laiənz] 或 [ljɔ̃]：里昂，法国南部城市。

93. sensibility: 呼格。据 OED，18 世纪至 19 世纪初，这个词的涵义是 Capacity for refined emotion; readiness to feel compassion for suffering, and to be moved by the pathetic in literature or art. "具有能体验高贵而细致感情的能力；对苦难容易感到同情，容易受悲怆的文学艺术所感动"。有敏感多情的意思。

94. inexhausted: = inexhaustible。Sensibility 是珍贵的欢乐取之不尽的源泉。

95. costly: 代价高昂的。Sensibility 也给我们带来代价高昂的痛苦和悲伤。

96. bed of straw: 监狱中的草荐。Sensibility 把人们象殉教者那样锁在草褥上。

97. Heaven: 上帝。但 Sensibility 也使人们通向上帝。

98. eternal fountain: 指 heaven。

99. here: = in heaven。在天上，在上帝那里，我追溯到了 sensibility。

100. divinity: 神性。Sensibility 既来源于上帝，因而有神性，我内心之所以能激动就是由于这神性的作用。

101. not that: = not in the sense that. 起作用的意思不是说在悲哀的时候"我的灵魂畏缩，害怕毁灭"（引语出自 Addison 悲剧 *Cato*）。Sterne 认为这种个人的内向的恐惧的反应不是真正的 Sensibility。

102. mere pomp of words: 不过是冠冕堂皇的话。

103. but that: 而是说 sensibility 的真正意义指的是超出个人的对别人的忧和乐

都能感受到的能力。

104. Sensorium: 感觉中枢。既指 sensibility，也指上帝。Sterne 仍是反对 Hartley 一派哲学（即人的头脑中的物质颤动引起感觉）而认为上帝是感觉的源泉。

105. vibrates: 颤动。即使我们在最遥远的地方落下一根头发，上帝（感觉中枢）也会颤动（感觉到，息息相通）。《新约》《马太福音》10 章 29—31 节，耶稣对门徒说：不值钱的麻雀，不得上帝的允许，也不会落到地上（死去）。你们头上的头发，上帝也数过，所以不要怕，你们比麻雀贵重得多。Sterne 从这里得到启发。

106. Eugenius [juːˈdʒiːnjəs]: 在《商第传》里，是 Yorick 的朋友。他当我悲伤的时候，出于同情，或不忍见到，把帷幕拉上。

107. symptoms: 症状、症候。他听我谈（tale）我的病痛，引起了他的同情，使他难过（disorder of his nerves），他却假意说天气不好使他感觉不舒服。作者处处歌颂温存、体贴、同情心。

108. it: 指同情心。

109. traverse: = cross, pass 经过、穿越。即使一个普通农夫，Sensorium（上帝）也赋予他同情心。当他发现别人羊群一只羊羔受了伤……

110. crook: 牧羊人用的弯头杖。这一句是作者所想象或见到（behold）的情景：农夫倚着弯头杖，低着头，用怜悯的眼光，谛视着受创伤的羊羔。

111. Oh! etc.: 这是设想农夫说的话。"我早来一会儿就好了，就能救活它了，现在它流血过多，快要死了。" Sterne 大力歌颂无私的同情。

112. his: 指农夫。这是作者的话。

113. swain: 田园诗歌中常用来称谓乡村青年。此处即指上述农夫。

114. balance: 抵偿。你的欢乐将抵得过你的悲伤。

115. sharer: 与你分享茅屋幸福生活的人——妻子、朋友。

116. sport: 动词，嬉戏。

23 THOMAS GRAY
1716–1771

ELEGY[1]

Written in a Country Churchyard

杨周翰　选注

The Curfew[2] tolls the knell of parting day,
The lowing[3] herd[4] wind slowly o'er the lea,[5]
The plowman homeward plods his weary way,
And leaves[6] the world to darkness and to me.

Now fades the glimmering landscape on the sight,[7]
And all the air a solemn stillness holds,[8]
Save[9] where the beetle[10] wheels[11] his droning flight,[12]
And drowsy tinklings[13] lull the distant folds;[14]

Save that from yonder ivy-mantled tow'r[15]
The moping[16] owl does to the moon complain
Of such[17] as, wand'ring near her secret bow'r,[18]
Molest[19] her ancient solitary reign.[20]

Beneath those rugged elms, that yew-tree's shade,
Where heaves the turf[21] in many a mould'ring heap,
Each in his narrow cell[22] for ever laid,[23]
The rude[24] Forefathers of the hamlet[25] sleep.

The breezy call of incense-breathing[26] Morn,

The swallow twitt'ring from the straw-built shed,[27]
The cock's shrill clarion,[28] or the echoing horn,[29]
No more shall rouse them from their lowly bed.[30]

For them[31] no more the blazing hearth shall burn,
Or busy housewife ply her evening care:[32]
No children run to lisp[33] their sire's return,
Or climb his knees the envied[34] kiss to share.

Oft did the harvest to their sickle yield,
Their furrow[35] oft the stubborn glebe[36] has broke;[37]
How jocund did they drive their team[38] afield!
How bow'd the woods beneath their sturdy stroke[39]!

Let not[40] Ambition[41] mock their useful toil,
Their homely joys, and destiny obscure;[42]
Nor Grandeur hear with a disdainful smile,
The short and simple annals[43] of the poor.

The boast of heraldry,[44] the pomp[45] of pow'r,
And all that beauty, all that wealth e'er gave,[46]
Awaits[47] alike th' inevitable hour,
The paths of glory lead but[48] to the grave.

Nor you, ye Proud,[49] impute to These[50] the fault,[51]
If Mem'ry[52] o'er their Tomb no Trophies raise,
Where through the long-drawn aisle[53] and fretted vault[54]
The pealing anthem[55] swells the note of praise.

Can storied urn[56] or animated bust[57]
Back to its mansion[58] call the fleeting breath?[59]
Can Honour's voice provoke[60] the silent dust,[61]
Or Flatt'ry soothe[62] the dull cold ear of Death?

Perhaps[63] in this neglected spot is laid
Some heart once pregnant[64] with celestial fire;[65]
Hands,[66] that the rod of empire[67] might have sway'd,
Or wak'd to ecstasy the living lyre.[68]

But Knowledge to their eyes her[69] ample page[70]
Rich with the spoils of time[71] did ne'er unroll;
Chill Penury[72] repress'd their noble rage,[73]
And froze the genial current[74] of the soul.

Full many a gem[75] of purest ray serene,
The dark unfathom'd caves of ocean bear:
Full[76] many a[77] flower[78] is born to blush unseen,
And waste its sweetness[79] on the desert air.

Some village Hampden,[80] that with dauntless breast
The little Tyrant of his fields withstood;
Some mute inglorious Milton[81] here may rest,
Some Cromwell guiltless[82] of his country's blood.

Th' applause of list'ning senates[83] to command,[84]
The threats of pain and ruin to despise,
To scatter plenty[85] o'er a smiling[86] land,
And read their hist'ry in a nation's eyes,[87]

Their lot forbade: nor circumscrib'd[88] alone
Their growing virtues, but their crimes confin'd;[89]
Forbade[90] to wade through slaughter to a throne,
And shut the gates of mercy on mankind,

The struggling pangs of conscious truth to hide,[91]
To quench the blushes of ingenuous shame,[92]
Or heap the shrine of Luxury and Pride

With incense kindled at the Muse's flame.[93]

Far[94] from the madding crowd's ignoble strife,[95]
Their sober wishes never learn'd to stray;[96]
Along the cool sequester'd[97] vale of life
They kept the noiseless tenor[98] of their way.

Yet ev'n these bones from insult[99] to protect[100]
Some frail memorial[101] still[102] erected nigh,
With[103] uncouth rhymes[104] and shapeless sculpture deck'd,
Implores the passing tribute of a sigh.[105]

Their name, their years, spelt by th' unletter'd muse,[106]
The place of fame and elegy supply:[107]
And many a holy text[108] around she[109] strews,
That[110] teach the rustic moralist[111] to die.[112]

For[113] who to dumb Forgetfulness a prey,
This pleasing anxious being e'er resign'd,[114]
Left[115] the warm precincts of the cheerful day.
Nor cast[116] one longing ling'ring look behind?

On[117] some fond breast[118] the parting soul relies,
Some pious drops[119] the closing eye requires;[120]
Ev'n from the tomb the voice of Nature[121] cries
Ev'n in our Ashes[122] live their[123] wonted Fires.[124]

For[125] thee,[126, 127] who mindful of th' unhonour'd Dead
Dost in these lines their artless[128] tale relate;
If chance,[129] by lonely contemplation led,
Some kindred Spirit[130] shall inquire thy fate,

Haply[131] some hoary-headed[132] Swain[133] may say,

"Oft have we seen him at the peep of dawn
Brushing with hasty steps the dews away
To meet the sun upon the upland lawn.

"There at the foot of yonder nodding beech[134]
That wreathes[135] its old fantastic roots so high,
His listless length[136] at noontide would he stretch,
And pore upon[137] the brook that babbles[138] by.

"Hard by you wood, now[139] smiling as in scorn,
Mutt'ring his wayward fancies[140] he would rove,
Now[139] drooping, woeful wan,[141] like one forlorn
Or craz'd with care,[142] or cross'd[143] in hopeless love.

"One morn I miss'd[144] him on the custom'd[145] hill,
Along the heath and near his fav'rite tree;
Another[146] came; nor[147] yet beside the rill,[148]
Nor up the lawn, nor at the wood was he;[149]

"The next with dirges[150] due in sad array[151]
Slow[150] through the church-way path we saw him borne.[152]
Approach and read (for thou can'st read)[153] the lay,[154]
Grav'd on the stone beneath yon aged[155] thorn.[156]"

THE EPITAPH[157]

Here rests his head upon the lap of Earth
A Youth,[158] to Fortune and to Fame unknown.[159]
Fair Science[160] frown'd not[161] on his humble birth,
And Melancholy mark'd[162] him for her own.

Large was his bounty,[163] and his soul sincere;
Heav'n did a recompense[164] as largely[165] send:

He gave to Mis'ry[166] (all he had) a tear,[167]
He gain'd from Heav'n ('twas all he wish'd) a friend.[168]

No farther seek[169] his merits to disclose,
Or draw his frailties from their[170] dread abode,[171]
(There they[172] alike in trembling hope repose,)
The bosom of his Father and his God.

【作者简介】 Thomas Gray（托玛斯·葛雷，1716—1771）是英国十八世纪后半的一位诗人。他一生只写过十几首诗，他的《墓园挽歌》不仅名噪一时，蔚为风气，而且影响到外国和后世。他性情孤僻，不务声名，一生事迹平淡无奇，绝大部分时间生活在剑桥大学，以教读研究为业，任该校历史和近代语教授，曾谢绝桂冠诗人的封号。他对文学、历史、考古以及当时的科学（如植物学、昆虫学）都感兴趣，晚年在当时风气的影响下，还从事搜集并翻译冰岛、威尔斯古代诗歌的工作，并写了一些以冰岛和威尔斯古代传说为题材的诗歌。他除作诗歌外，还写过游记，又是书信名家。

【题解与注释】

《墓园挽歌》发表于1750年。它常被誉为英国十八世纪、甚至英国历来的诗歌中的一首最好的诗。今天看来，这首诗的突出地位不难理解。第一，它凝聚了一个时期中的某种社会情绪；其次，它用比较完美的形式表达了这种情绪，在一定程度上解决了如何革新旧传统的问题，具有较高的艺术成就。

约翰逊（Samuel Johnson）曾说《墓园挽歌》中的"情绪在每个人的心中都可以找到回声"。可见诗中所表达的情绪是比较普遍的。诗中突出地体现了对农民的同情，这一点是和英国走向产业革命的过程分不开的。同时，诗中也表现出对黑夜、坟墓、死亡的兴趣，尤其是前三节和最后部分。一方面，诗人惋惜农民贫困的遭遇，使他们不能发挥天才，并对权贵表示抗议；但是另一方面诗人勾画了一个理想化了的农民生活景象，歌颂他们的"淳朴"，并退一步设想，认为农民的无权正好使他们免于罪恶，最后拿出了古老的人道主义武器——这一切都赋予全诗以一层消极无奈、甚至不健康的色调，这种情绪在当时十分普遍，竟形成了一个诗歌流派，所谓墓园派诗歌，究其原因，应归于这些文人作家战斗性不强。葛雷在思想上可以说是介乎同情农民的启蒙作家和消极不满的消极浪漫主义作家之间的一个过渡人物。

但是，葛雷又是在古典主义诗歌传统中成长起来的，怎样把古典主义对内容和形式的要求，与新的内容调和起来，就成了他必须解决的问题。他写诗歌颂威尔斯人反对侵略的壮举（*The Bard*），或歌颂他所钦佩的古代和英国的诗人（*The Progress of Poesy*）都用古典的“颂歌体”（the ode），内容和形式没有太大矛盾。但在《伊顿远眺》（*Ode on a Distant Prospect of Eton College*）中就显出一定的不和谐，颂歌体用在回忆童年的快乐还可以，而用以写哀伤就很不舒展。英国古典主义诗人 Dryden 和 Pope 最常用的诗格是五步一行、两行一押韵的 heroic couplet，在他们手中已成为说理讽刺的工具。葛雷一派的诗人 Edward Young 或更早的 James Thomson 则采用了 Milton 的素体诗（blank verse），从古典主义趣味来看，不够整洁；二人的思想感情远不及 Milton 有力，压不住经过 Milton 所锤炼的诗格。在选择这首诗的形式时，放弃了古典形式，而采取了从十六世纪 Wyatt 起即常用的哀挽诗（the elegiac stanza）.

古典主义诗人喜欢援引希腊、罗马神话、历史、文学掌故，从古代文学中找他们的理想，同时这种喜欢用典的风气意在投合贵族嗜好。但在十八世纪后半这种方法已不能满足时代需要，约翰逊评十八世纪早期作家 Gay 的一首咏扇诗就说人们对 Venus, Diana, Minerva 的故事已不感兴趣．葛雷原稿中曾有古罗马历史典故，后来取消，也是一种企图摆脱古典主义的表现。

但是古典主义的崇尚理性的精神为葛雷所保留，表现为一种思想明晰，结构匀称，条理清楚，步伐整齐的特点（参看注解中有关结构部分）。他固然缺乏浪漫主义的奔放热情，但也没有缥缈、暧昧等缺点。诗中也保留了一定的说理特点。

古典主义很强调艺术形式的完美，删除芜杂，不浪费笔墨，要求精益求精。罗马的贺拉斯（Horace）就曾警告诗人不要犯平庸的毛病，建议把诗稿压上九个年头，不要急于发表。本诗写好八年没有发表，不时修改，但是由于不胫而走，葛雷怕流传讹误，才正式发表。举两个例子，可以看出他怎样修改这首诗。例如原稿第 100 行以后有四行诗写农民在傍晚也曾看见他在林边散步，这一内容并不增加读者对人物的性格的认识，被删去了。又如原稿第 116 行以后也曾有四行诗形容墓边花鸟风景，是多余的，破坏了艺术效果，也删去了。此外，删去的诗节还很多，其中有的诗行被保留了，大部分则抛弃了。读者可以从全篇思路的安排，考虑一下全诗的整洁性。在整洁之中又有一定的曲折，例如每段自成一个思想上、句法上的整体，但又有变化（如第 65 行）；每行也是完整的，很少在一行的中途断句（enjambment），但仍有一定的停顿（caesura）.

这种精益求精的精神表现在语言功夫上特别明显。葛雷认为诗歌应有其独特的语言，这种语言的特点表现在这首诗里就是优雅而不堆砌雕琢，流畅而不松散，明晰但有余味，音韵和谐但不单调。因此，诗人虽然下了很大苦功，全诗效果还是比较自然。

语言作为形式，和内容的结合，也达到相当完美的程度。（内容，如前所述，并非全部都是可取的，这一点应加注意。）这种结合特别突出地表现在音和韵两方面。全诗在设韵方面绝大部分都以长音词为韵脚，以烘托出全诗的哀婉情绪，十分相称；但也随内容的变化而变化，有时诗人用短音词为韵脚，如第 20，41—44 等行，似是为了传达一种断然无可挽回的情绪；又如第 57—60 行表现了一定程度的愤慨；或如第 109 行表现了戏剧性等。在词音方面，全诗长音特多，而重音又往往是长音，这也和全诗的基本情调吻合的。但在以长音为重音的总倾向中，也仍然间隔着短音，参差有致。试以第 1 行为例，cur-，to-，par-，day 把回荡的钟声，黄昏时刻缓缓逝去的暮霭，完全烘托出来，而以短音 knell 安置在正中，衬出钟声每一击本身的短暂（虽然它余音如缕），同时使白昼一去断然不返的思想也暗示出来。除元音以外，作者全诗中时时点缀一些双声字，以增强音乐性。此外，如颜色、光暗、动植物、生活图景、其它形象和比喻的选择，也都体现了诗人的匠心。诗人在语言上的这种推敲功夫，结合诗中内容，使这首诗在英国诗歌中占有独特的地位。

葛雷在发挥古典主义对诗歌语言严格要求这一优点的同时，也未能免除古典主义诗歌的抽象性，例如抽象名词、品德的拟人化等在本诗中也到处可见，古代传说中的、已失去生命力的个别形象（如诗神）也不免再现，因此有些部分就不够具体生动。

1. Elegy: 在古希腊，原意是箫歌，内容是尚武的，逐渐也用来纪念战争中的阵亡者，而成为哀歌、挽歌。这种格律在罗马常被诗人采用来写爱情诗。在近代欧洲文学中，elegy 往往只作哀歌解。

全诗用所谓 iambic pentameter 诗行写成，每行五步（foot），每步一轻音、一重音；但有时，尤其在开始，可以一重一轻。四行成一段（stanza），按 a b a b 押韵。

Country Churchyard，指 Buckinghamshire 的 Stoke Pogis 地方的乡村墓地，诗人的母亲住在 Stoke Pogis，诗人常从剑桥大学到此度假。诗人及其母均葬于此地

2. Curfew: 诗中某些重要名词，按十八世纪习惯，都用大写。宵禁钟声，晚八点钟敲，是中世纪遗留下来的风俗。读者可以注意这行诗的五个重音中，有四个是长音；在整首诗里，诗人用长音的时候极频繁；读者也可注意全诗长短重音间隔有致。这首诗是英国文学里最著名的诗歌中的一首，这第一句又是全诗中最著名的佳句，读者还可注意，本诗作者很少在一行的中间断句。（参看题解）

knell，丧钟，指白日已尽，晚钟好象是送别白昼的丧钟。

3. lowing: 牛鸣，不可与第 20 行 lowly 中的 low 相混。注意这一行中的“l”声。音调的考究是此诗一个重要的艺术特点。其它双声例如第 3 行“pl”和“w”，第 10 行“m”，第 14 行“h”等。

4. herd: 牛群。

5. lea: 草地。

6. leaves: 主语为 plowman. 这行诗的内容和意境，并非作者所独创，诗人 William Collins (1721–1759) 1746 年发表 *Ode to Evening*，以及其他诗人，已创造过这样的意境，说明这种孤独情绪已成一种风气。在表达方式方面古典主义诗人遵循罗马贺拉斯的论调，认为内容固然重要，而表达方式即使不更重要，至少也同等重要，对内容往往人同此感，但只有真正诗人才能表达得好，即蒲伯（Pope）所说 What oft was thought, but ne'er so well expressed，因此他们刻意在表达方式上用功，争相竞胜。（参看题解）

7. sight: 眼睛、视线。眼睛已看不清昏暗中的景色了。

8. holds: 统治了。主语为 stillness，宾语为 air. 诗中往往因音节排列的关系，动词放在最后，同时动词前主语、宾语位置往往先后不一致，或主语在先，或宾语在先，读者应能辨别下列各行中的主语和宾语：第 26，34—35，38，47，49—50，53—54，57—58，61—65，81—82，90，93—94，103，122 行。

9. Save: 除了。以下六行写寂静夜晚中，唯一的声响。

10. beetle: 甲虫。Collins 在 *Ode to Evening* 中有句云："Now air is hushed, save where the weak-eyed bat … / Or where the beetle winds / His small but sullen horn." 而 Collins 又脱胎于 Milton, *Lycidas* 28："What time the grey-fly［即 beetle］winds her sultry horn"，Gray 和十八世纪许多英国诗人一样，特别服膺 Milton, Shakespeare 等作家，常套引他们的诗句，所谓"寻章摘句"，本诗中这种例子甚多，其主旨已如前述，以下不一一列举。

11. wheels: 旋转飞翔。

12. droning flight: 飞翔时嗡嗡作响。

13. tinkling: 羊颈上的铃声。

14. folds: 羊圈。

15. ivy-mantled tow'r: 为长青藤所缠绕的教堂塔楼。tow'r = tower，省去 e，表示这个词只作一个音节计算。其他如第 2 行 o're（over），第 11 行 bow'r 第 61 行 Th' applause 等，可以类推。

16. moping: 烦躁不安。

17. such: 可以指人，但更可能指其它动物、飞禽、昆虫之类。

18. bow'r (bower): 闺房、绣房，因此不可随意闯入。

19. Molest: 损害。用词极佳。

20. 以上三段是"开篇"，目的在设景。以下四段点出墓中埋葬的人物，表示惋惜，并追忆其生前生活。

21. turf: 墓园的地上长着一层乱草，这片草地上拱起了（heaves）一堆堆（heap）的坟墓，这些坟墓已坍塌败坏（mouldering）.

22. cell: 指墓穴。

23. Each … laid: 形容下一行 Forefathers.

24. rude: 朴质的、没有文化的。

25. hamlet: 小村落。

26. incense-breathing: 吐出芬芳。incense 不作焚香解。

27. straw-built shed: 茅棚，作储藏农具、饲养牲畜等之用。

28. clarion: 鸡啼在英诗中常比作司晨号角。

29. horn: 清晨打猎人的号角声。

30. lowly bed: 以死亡比睡眠，以坟墓比床榻，以上三句均写清晨的声音，这些声音已不能把死者从长眠中唤醒；lowly 双关语。

31. For them: 可参看诗人 James Thomson (1700–1748)《四季诗》（*The Seasons*）中《冬季》（*Winter*, 1726）一章第 276 行以下，写一走投无路的农民在暴风雪中倒毙，临终时想到妻子为他升火烤衣，孩子们在窗前张望父亲归来的情景，此处与《冬季》中所写极相似。这些都是当时流行的"感伤"情绪的流露。

32. housewife [ˈhʌzif] **ply her evening care:** 忙着晚上的家务事，如把火添旺、烧晚饭等。

33. lisp: 以牙牙学语的口齿喊出父亲回来了。

34. envied: 争着、抢着分享的。

35. furrow: 此处可能作犁解。

36. glebe: 土地、田地。

37. broke: = broken 松（土）。

38. team: 指两三头套在一起的耕畜。写下地耕田。

39. stroke: 指伐木运斧。

40. Let not: 以下四段对“大人物”发出警告，在死亡面前贫富平等。第 29—32 行四行诗曾被 Robert Burns 用作他的 *The Cotter's Saturday Night* 的序诗。

41. Ambition: 包括野心勃勃的和野心已遂的人们。此处是抽象概念的拟人化，故大写，下同。

42. destiny obscure: = obscure destiny 默默无闻的命运或一生。在诗歌中，因押韵、音节或其他艺术效果的关系，常颠倒词序或句法，参看上面第 6，10，14，24，25，26，28 等行。

43. annals: 编年史，此处指一生的历史。

44. heraldry: 指世袭贵族。

45. pomp: 显赫的声势。

46. gave: = yielded，所能获致的。

47. Awaits: 主语为 the inevitable hour（死亡）。初稿作 await，义亦通。修改后，说法与第 36 行相反，而内容相同。

48. but: = only.

49. you, ye Proud: you 用于独立的呼格（vocative）；与名词或形容词合用时，常用 ye 如 Ye blessed creatures (Wordsworth).

50. These: 指埋葬在这里的农民。

51. impute the fault: 把过错归于。所谓过错，指第 38—40 行。

52. Mem'ry: Memory，指人们为了纪念死者，把能代表他生前光荣的物品（Trophies）如军旗、雕象之类，悬挂或安放在教堂内他的墓上。这是英国许多大教堂内常见的景象。

53. aisle: 从教堂大门通向神坛的主要甬路称 nave，其左右两侧平行甬路称 aisles. 此处泛指教堂内的甬路。

54. fretted vault: 教堂内部雕刻缛丽的堂顶。

55. pealing anthem: 大风琴奏出的洪亮的赞美歌。参看 Milton, *Il Penseroso*，161—163 行。

56. storied urn: 指“大人物”墓上的一种装饰——一个石雕或浮雕的瓮，上面刻着他生平某些事迹。

57. animated bust: 指墓上（或其它地方）设置的死者半身石象。Animated 意为栩栩如生。

58. mansion: 宅邸，此处指已死的躯体。Its，指 breath。

59. fleeting breath: 短促的生命。

60. provoke: 召唤，此处指重新赋予生机。

61. dust: 按照基督教《圣经》所说：人是上帝用泥土造成，死后复归泥土。此处指死者。

62. soothe: 以甜言蜜语打动死神，使他闭而不闻的耳朵听从人们请求。

63. 以下七段，诗人惋惜这些淳朴农民的遭遇使他们的潜力与天才未能发挥，但又对他们的地位使他们不致犯大罪这一点表示庆幸。

64. pregnant: filled.

65. celestial fire: 可能指宗教的热诚。农民中可能产生宗教家；也有解作诗才者，则与第48行重复。

66. hands: 虽是复数，但动词仍借用 is laid.

67. rod of empire: 掌握统治大权。从罗马人开始，作为刑具的棒或一束棒（fasces）即成为权力的象征。农民中可能产生治国之材。

68. lyre: 音乐、诗歌的象征。农民中可能产生大诗人、大音乐家。

69. her: 指知识。

70. page: 书本。

71. spoils of time: 人类历来积累下来的经验、智慧。

72. Penury: 贫困。

73. rage: 渴望，理想。

74. genial current: 诗人把农民的创造力比作川流，故用 froze. Genial 原意为"适宜生物滋衍的"，引伸为富于创造力的。贫困使农民不能发挥其创造力。

75. gem: 诗人把农民比作埋藏在海底的明珠。

76. full:〈古〉副词，加重语气。

77. many a: 参看第14行，形式是单数，实际内容是复数。

78. flower: 把农民比作在荒漠中自生自灭、无人赏识的香花，即李贺所谓"无人柳自春"。这一意象十七、八世纪诗人用者极多，如 Waller, Pope, Philips, Young 等。

79. sweetness: 芬芳。

80. Hampden: John Hampden (1594–1643)，Milton, Cromwell 都是十七世纪英国资产阶级革命时期的革命领袖。Hampden 以反对查理一世的横征暴敛受到迫害而著名，故第57—58行说有些农民反抗地主，表现了大无畏的精神，不愧为农民中的 Hampden.

81. mute inglorious Milton: 不谓 Milton 不光荣，而是说农民中可能产生过 Milton 这样的革命诗人，但没有机会发表自己的思想（mute），没有获得象 Milton 那样的光荣。

82. guiltless: 可以有两种相反的解释：（1）农民中可能产生象克伦威尔这样的革命英雄，但手上没有象克伦威尔那样沾着同胞的血；（2）克伦威尔本人就不能算是沾上同胞的血的罪人。二说以前者为是，我们不能希望诗人正确理解十七世纪历史事件的意义。Hampden, Milton, Cromwell 均以 may rest here 为谓语。在初稿中，诗人用三个罗马历史人物 Cato, Tully, Caesar. Gray 的修改说明引用古代神话、历史典故的古典主义方法。已不能适应时代的需要。（参看题解）

83. senates: Senate 罗马元老院（立法机关），此处指议会。

84. to command, to despise, to scatter, (to) read 均为第65行 forbade 的宾语。

to command: 赢得。

85. To scatter plenty: 造福，施舍。

86. smiling: 是造福、施舍的结果；由于得到恩惠，国人（land）笑逐颜开。

87. (to) read their hist'ry ln a nation's eyes: read 意为 declare, relate; history 即 life-history, career. 可以引伸为 great deeds. in a nation's eye，举国上下，有目共睹。

88. nor circumscrib'd: 主语仍是 Their lot. 他们的命运不仅限制了他们的优秀品德的发展。nor … alone，相当于 not … only.

89. confin'd: 主语为 lot，宾语为 crimes.

90. Forbade: 主语仍是 lot，宾语为 to wade，(to) shut, to hide, to quench，(to) heap. 每一宾语代表一种罪恶行为。

91. to hide: 真理挣扎着要出世（pangs），自己也明知其为真理（conscious），但以种种原因不敢吐露真情（hide），极言虚伪、谎言之徒的矛盾痛苦。联系全句主语，意为穷人无须不老实。

92. ingenuous shame: = natural sense of shame，天生的羞耻之心。

93. 第 71—72 行： 二句大意是：以诗歌奉承权贵。诗人以古代祭礼为比喻："把在诗神的火焰上燃着的香（实物，与第 17 行芬芳的气息不同）堆到富贵人的神坛上（奉献给他们）"。

94. 以下五段大意是：虽然他们一生平静无波，死后也不应被人遗忘。

95. Far from the madding crowd' s ignoble strife: 他们的愿望（wishes）不是去（far from）干疯狂的人群所干的不光彩的、你争我夺的勾当。十九、二十世纪小说家哈代（Thomas Hardy）曾以前五个词作为他一部小说的标题。要是把 strife 后的逗号（,）取消，第 73、74 两行将自相矛盾，不合逻辑。又，Far from 固然可以说是形容 wishes，但按意义说，应该说是 They being far …

96. stray: 脱离正道。

97. sequester'd: 与世隔绝，平静。

98. tenor: continuous course，持续的进程。主语为 memorial（第 78 行）；谓语为 implores …（第 80 行）；erected（第 78 行），deck'd（第 79 行），是形容词，形容主语。

99. insult: 指被人铲平或践踏之类。

100. protect: 指 erected 之目的。

101. frail memorial: 例如，一块薄碑，或朴素的墓碑。

102. still: 古义 always.

103. deck'd with: 装饰着。

104. uncouth rhymes: 鄙陋的诗句。

105. Implores … sigh: 恳求过路人馈赠（tribute）一声叹息。

106. unletter'd muse:（乡村的）没有什么学问的诗人。

107. supply the place of: 代替了。

108. holy text:《圣经》上的辞句。

109. she: 指第 81 行的诗神。

110. That: 指 holy texts，用复数动词。

111. rustic moralist: 指读墓铭的乡人。

112. to die: = how to die，以什么态度对待死亡。

113. 以下两段一问一答，皆从 to die 衍绎出来。

114. For who ... resign'd: 有两种解释：（1）who, being a prey to dumb Forgetfulness，任何人死后都要被人遗忘；（2）who ever resigned this pleasing anxious being *so as to become* a prey to dumb Forgetfulness? 有谁愿意舍弃这可爱而又令人不安的生命，被人遗忘，再不被人提起（dumb）呢？以第二种解释为佳。

115. Left: 动词，主语仍是 who.

116. Nor cast: = and did not cast, without casting.

117. on: 接动词 relies.

118. fond breast: fond = affectionate. 具有慈爱心肠的人。

119. pious drops: = dutiful tears.

120. requires: 主语是 eye，宾语是 drops.

121. voice of Nature: 天性的呼声。

122. our Ashes: 在我们死后。

123. their: 指先我们而物故的墓中人。

124. Fires: 精神、"天性"、要求等。

125. 以下至终章均诗人假设自己死后的情景。"墓园派"（Graveyard school）诗歌的特点之一是对贫苦人的同情，具有一定程度的民主性；另一特点是沉浸于对死亡、孤独的玄想之中。这两种特点都统一于他们的软弱性。（参看题解）

126. 第 93—116 行 For thee ... aged thorn（第 116 行）：是完整的一句，其中主语是 Swain（第 97 行）。

127. For thee: = As for thee；"至于你自己"。此处诗人自己对自己说话。

128. artless: 朴素的。

129. chance: = by chance.

130. kindred Spirit: = person like you.

131. Haply:〈古〉即 perhaps.

132. hoary-headed: 白发的。

133. Swain: 乡下人。

134. beech: 一种英国常见的大树。

135. wreathes: 盘成环状。

136. listless length: 百无聊赖的身躯。躺卧。注意双声。

137. pore upon: 专心注视。

138. babbles: 小儿学语貌，此处指流水潺湲呜咽。注意此行 b 音。

139. now ... now: 时而…时而。

140. wayward fancies: 飘忽而不可捉摸的遐想。

141. woeful wan: = sad and pale.

142. craz'd with care: 忧愁得近于疯癫。

143. cross'd: 受挫折。

144. miss'd: 我发现他不见了。

145. custom'd: = accustomed，他常去的。

146. Another: 指另一天到来了。

147. nor: = neither.

148. rill: 小溪。

149. 以上八行，后人刻在诗人墓碑上，作为墓铭。

The next，指第三天。

dirges，葬歌。

due，死者应得的，恰当的。形容 dirges.

150. with dirges, Slow: (= slowly)，均形容 borne（第 114 行）。

151. in sad array: 穿着丧服，或作悲哀的行列。指送殡人，但送殡人一词未在句中出现。

152. borne: i. e. in his coffin.

153. for thou can'st read: 询问者（第 96 行）必然是个读过书的人；当时并非人人识字。

154. lay: 短歌，此处指诗，也就是最后三段的墓铭。

155. aged [ˈeidʒid]**:** 双音节。

156. thorn: = hawthorn tree.

157. The Epitaph: 仍是诗人想象中（参见第 93 行注）乡人指点给访客看的诗人墓铭。

158. A Youth: 全句主语。作者开始写此诗时，年 28 岁。

159. unknown: 形容 a youth.

160. Science: 指一般知识。

161. frown'd not: 不因他出身微贱而歧视他。他有一定的学问。

162. mark'd: 忧郁女神在他（青年）身上打上她的标志以表明他是属于她的。青年天性忧郁。

163. bounty: 恩泽，此处指这青年有博爱的性格。

164. recompense: send 的宾语，指第 124 行的 friend.

165. as largely: = as liberally, as generously，与前一行 large 相呼应。他对人表示（付出）善意，上天也以同样丰厚（as largely）的报酬答谢他。第 121—122 两行又与第 123—124 两行呼应。

166. Mis'ry: misery，受苦难的一切。

167. a tear: 同情心、博爱、人道的象征；不可作"仅仅一滴眼泪"解；同情心是他全部的人格。

168. a friend: 可以指人世间的朋友，或上帝。

169. seek: 命令式。Seek to disclose his merits no farther（no more）.

170. their: 指 frailties. 意谓不要再揭示他的长处和弱点了，上面已经交代清楚。

171. dread abode: 指死后所居之处（即第 128 行 bosom）；dread 是过去分词（dreaded），因为是弱点，所以"怕"上帝惩罚。

172. they: 指 merits 和 frailties. 人死后居留一地，等候上帝的末日审判，行善（merits）的人有希望（hope）上天堂，有罪（frailties）的人唯恐（trembling）下地狱。

24 OLIVER GOLDSMITH
1730-1774

A VISIT TO WESTMINSTER[1] ABBEY

杨周翰　选注

From Lien Chi Altangi[2] to Fum Hoam,[3] First President of the Ceremonial Academy[4] in China

I am just returned from Westminster Abbey, the place of sepulture[5] for the philosophers, heroes, and kings of England. What a gloom do monumental inscriptions,[6] and all the venerable remains[7] of deceased merit[8] inspire! Imagine a temple[9] marked with the hand of antiquity, solemn as religious awe, adorned with all the magnificence of barbarous profusion,[10] dim windows, fretted[11] pillars, long colonnades, and dark ceilings. Think, then, what were my sensations at being introduced to such a scene. I stood in the midst of the temple, and threw my eyes round on the walls, filled with the statues, the inscriptions, and the monuments[12] of the dead.

Alas! I said to myself, how does pride attend the puny[13] child of dust[14] even to the grave! Even humble as I am, I possess more consequence[15] in the present scene than the greatest hero of them all: they have toiled for an hour to gain a transient immortality, and are at length retired to the grave, where they have no attendant but the worm, none to flatter but the epitaph.[16]

As I was indulging such reflections, a gentleman, dressed in black,[17] perceiving me to be a stranger, came up, entered into conversation, and politely offered to be my instructor and guide through the temple. 'If any monument,' said he, 'should particularly excite your curiosity, I shall endeavour to satisfy your demands.' I accepted with thanks the gentleman's offer, adding, that 'I was come[18] to observe the policy, the wisdom,[19] and the justice of the English, in conferring rewards upon deceased merit. If adulation[20] like this,' continued I, 'be properly conducted, as[21] it can no ways injure those who are flattered,[22] so it may be a glorious incentive[23] to those who are now capable of enjoying it. It is the duty of every good government to turn this monumental pride[24] to its own advantage; to become strong in the aggregate[25] from the weakness of the individual.[26] If none but the truly great have a place in this awful repository,[27] a temple like this will give the finest lessons of morality, and be a strong incentive to true ambition. I am told, that none have a place here but characters of the most distinguished merit.' The man in black seemed impatient at my observations; so I discontinued my remarks, and we walked on together to take a view of every particular monument in order as it lay.[28]

As the eye is naturally caught by the finest objects, I could not avoid being particularly curious about one monument, which appeared more beautiful than the rest. 'That,' said I to my guide, 'I take to be the tomb of some very great man. By the peculiar excellence of the workmanship, and the magnificence of the design, this must be a trophy[29] raised to the memory of some king who has saved his country from ruin, or law-giver, who has reduced[30] his fellow-citizens from anarchy[31] into just subjection.[32]' 'It is not requisite.' replied my companion smiling, 'to have such qualifications in order to have a very fine monument here. More humble abilities will suffice.'—'What! I suppose then, the gaining two or three battles,[33] or the taking half a score towns, is thought a sufficient qualification?'—'Gaining battles, or taking towns,' replied the man in black, 'may be of service; but a gentleman may have a very fine monument here without ever seeing a battle[34] or a siege.' 'This, then, is the monument of some poet, I presume, of one whose wit[35] has gained him immortality? '—'No, sir,' replied my guide, 'the gentleman who lies here never made verses; and as for wit, he despised it in others, because he had none himself.' 'Pray tell me then in a word,' said I peevishly, 'what is the great man who lies here particularly remarkable for? '—'Remarkable, sir!' said my companion; 'why, sir, the gentleman that lies here is remarkable, very remarkable[36]—for a tomb in Westminster Abbey.'—'But, head of my ancestors![37] how has he got here? I fancy he could never bribe the guardians of the temple to give him a place. Should he not be ashamed to be seen among company, where even moderate merit[38] would look like infamy[39]?'—'I suppose,' replied the man in black, 'the gentleman was rich, and his friends,[40] as is usual in such a case, told him he was great. He readily believed them; the guardians of the temple, as they got by the self-delusion,[41] were ready to believe him too; so he paid his money for a fine monument; and the workman, as you see, has made him one of the most beautiful. Think not, however, that this gentleman is singular[42] in his desire of being buried among the great; there are several others in the temple, who, hated and shunned by the great while alive, have come here, fully resolved to keep them company now[43] they are dead.'

As we walked along to a particular part of the temple, 'There,' says the gentleman, pointing with his finger, 'that is the Poets' Corner;[44] there you see the monuments of Shakespeare, and Milton, and Prior,[45] and Drayton.'[46] 'Drayton!' I replied, 'I never heard of him before; but I have been told of one Pope;[47] is he there? ' 'It is time enough,' replied my guide, 'these hundred years;[48] he is not long dead; people have not done[49] hating him yet.' 'Strange,' cried I, 'can any be found to hate a man, whose life was wholly spent in entertaining and instructing his fellow-creatures? ' 'Yes,' says my guide, 'they hate him for that very reason. There are a set of men called answerers of books,[50] who take upon them to watch the republic of letters, and distribute reputation by the sheet;[51] they somewhat resemble the eunuchs[52] in a seraglio,[53] who are incapable of giving pleasure themselves, and hinder those that would. These answerers have no other employment but to cry out Dunce,[54] and Scribbler;[55] to praise the dead, and revile the living; to grant a man of confessed abilities some small share of merit; to applaud twenty blockheads, in order to gain the reputation of candour; and to revile the moral character[56] of the man whose writings they cannot injure. Such wretches are kept in pay by some mercenary bookseller, or more frequently the bookseller[57] himself takes this dirty work off their hands, as all that is required is to be very abusive and very dull. Every poet of any genius is sure to find such enemies; he feels, though he seems to despise, their malice; they make him miserable here,[58] and in the pursuit of empty fame, at last he gains solid anxiety.'[59]

'Has this been the case with every poet I see here?' cried I 'Yes, with every mother's son of them,' replied he, 'except[60] he happened to be born a mandarine.[61] If he has much money, he may buy reputation from your book-answerers, as well as a monument from the guardians of the temple.'

'But are there not some men of distinguished taste, as in China, who are willing to patronize[62] men of merit, and soften the rancour of malevolent dulness[63]?' 'I own there are many,' replied the man in black, 'but, alas, Sir, the book-answerers crowd about them, and call themselves the writers of books; and the patron is too indolent to distinguish; thus poets are kept at a distance, while their enemies eat up all their rewards at the mandarine's table.'

Leaving this part of the temple, we made up to[64] an iron gate, through which my companion told me we were to pass, in order to see the monuments of the kings. Accordingly I marched up without further ceremony,[65] and was going to enter, when a person who held the gate in his hand told me I must pay first. I was surprised at such a demand; and asked the man, whether the people of England kept a show? whether the paltry sum he demanded was not a national reproach?[66] whether it was not more to the honour of the country to let their magnificence or their antiquities be openly seen, than thus meanly to tax a curiosity[67] which tended to their own honour?[68] 'As for your questions,' replied the gate-keeper, 'to be sure they may be very right because I don't understand them; but, as for that there[69] threepence, I farm[70] it from one—who rents it from another—who hires it from a third—who leases it from the guardians of the temple, and we all must live.' I expected, upon paying here, to see something extraordinary, since what I had seen for nothing filled me with so much surprise: but in this I was disappointed; there was little more within than black coffins, rusty armour, tattered standards,[71] and some few slovenly figures in wax.[72] I was sorry I had paid, but I comforted myself by considering it would be my last payment. A person attended us, who, without once blushing, told an hundred lies; he talked of a lady[73] who died by pricking her finger; of a king with a golden head,[74] and twenty such pieces of absurdity. 'Look ye there, gentlemen,' says he, pointing to an old oak chair, 'there's a curiosity[75] for ye; in that chair the kings of England were crowned: you see also a stone underneath, and that stone is Jacob's pillow.[76]' I could see no curiosity either in the oak chair, or the stone: could I,[77] indeed, behold one of the old kings of England seated in this, or Jacob's head laid upon the other, there might be something curious in the sight; but in the present case there was no more reason for my surprise than if I should pick a stone from their streets, and call it a curiosity, merely because one of the kings happened to tread upon it as he passed in a procession.[78]

From hence our conductor led us through several dark walks and winding ways, uttering lies, talking to himself, and flourishing a wand which he held in his hand. He reminded me of the black magicians of Kobi.[79] After we had been almost fatigued with a variety of objects, he at last desired me to consider attentively a certain suit of armour, which seemed to show nothing remarkable. 'This armour,' said he, 'belonged to General Monk.'[80] — Very surprising, that a general should wear armour. — 'And pray,' added he, 'observe this cap, this is General Monk's cap.' — 'Very strange indeed, very strange, that a general should have a cap also. Pray, friend, what might this cap have cost originally?' — 'That, sir,' says he, 'I don't know; but this cap is all the wages I have for my trouble.' — 'A very small recompense[81] truly,' said I. 'Not so very small.' replied he, 'for every gentleman puts some money into it, and I spend the money.' — 'What, more money! still more money!'

— 'Every gentleman gives something, Sir.' — 'I'll give thee nothing,' returned I: 'the guardians of the temple should pay you your wages, friend, and not permit you to squeeze thus from every spectator. When we pay our money at the door to see a show, we[82] never give more as we are going out. Sure, the guardians of the temple can never think they get enough. Show me the gate; if I stay longer, I may probably meet with more of those ecclesiastical[83] beggars.'

Thus leaving the temple precipitately,[84] I returned to my lodgings, in order to ruminate[85] over what was great, and to despise what was mean, in the occurrences of the day.[86]

— Letter XIII, *The Citizen of the World,* 1762

【作者简介】 Oliver Goldsmith（奥利佛·哥尔斯密，1730—1774）是英国十八世纪后半一位多才多艺的作家。他写过诗歌（*The Deserted Village,* 1770; *The Traveller,* 1764），小说（*The Vicar of Wakefield,* 1766），戏剧（*The Good Natur'd Man,* 1767; *She Stoops to Conquer,* 1773），散文（*The Citizen of the World,* 1762; *Essays,* 1765），以至历史、传记，还编纂过科学史。

哥尔斯密对十八世纪英国大资产阶级和贵族妥协的局面表示不满，在法国启蒙思想影响下，以理性为武器，对英国现实进行批判，进一步要求民主。特别是在产业革命时期，社会贫富分化更加剧烈，他对社会下层抱有深厚同情。但哥尔斯密也表现了中下层知识分子的软弱性，他的批判往往多从社会风俗道德着眼，幻想通过开明政治崇文黜武，使道德教育复归淳朴来改进社会。有时，他也流于感伤。

【题解与注释】

英国的随笔或小品文（the essay）创始于培根，十八世纪初，在 Addison 和 Steele 手中臻于成熟。十八世纪，统治阶级间的党争激烈，城市中等阶级要求文化，促成了期刊杂志的繁荣。为杂志写文章成了文人谋生手段之一。哥尔斯密适应当时的需要，继承了 *The Spectator*（《旁观者》，Addison 和 Steele 所编）等期刊文学的传统，也写了许多文章，内容从对社会政治、风俗习惯的批评，到人物的素描，以及文学评论、游记、随感之类，无所不包。在风格上，他和前辈以及同辈的主要随笔作家有很大区别。Steele 朝气蓬勃，Addison 工整冷静，二人都喜欢引经据典；Samuel Johnson 选词深奥，讲求对仗，有时显得臃肿；哥尔斯密的特点在于流畅、闲适、生动，稍有讽刺，略带感伤，偶尔也有奇笔（surprise）。这种风格更接近十九世纪散文家 Charles Lamb. 他随笔中的某些人物，如本文中的黑衣人（Man in Black），其它文章中的破落贵族（Beau Tibbs），富裕市侩（The Pawnbroker's Widow）等，可以说是狄更斯（Charles Dickens）小说中某些人物的雏型。

The Citizen of the World 写于 1760—1761 年，在 *The Public Ledger* 杂志中陆续发表，原名 *Chinese Letters*，1762 年收成集子出版，改名 *The Citizen of the World.*

对东方（包括中国）的兴趣是十八世纪欧洲文坛的普遍现象。启蒙作家在寻求一个理想的社会制度的探索中，在当时的欧洲，找不到他们的理想，于是就向古代或遥远的东方以及美洲、非洲瞩望。他们听了传教士、商人、使臣、旅行家带回来的传说，读了他们带回来的文学作品和哲学著作的译本，东方的文明和智慧使他们感到惊讶，东方在他们心目中成了他们梦寐以求的“理性王国”之所在。他们纷纷著书，用这假想的“理性王国”来和欧洲现实比较。他们假托东方异域，有的写小说，有的编剧本，而很多人则用书信体裁来抒发议论。法国这类作品最多，其著名者如孟德斯鸠（Montesquieu）的《波斯人信札》（*Lettres Persanes*）、葛拉菲尼夫人（Mme de Graffigny）的《秘鲁妇人信札》（*Lettres d'une Péruvienne*）、达让侯爵（Marquis d'Argens）的《中国人信札》（*Lettres Chinoises*）。哥尔斯密无疑受到这类作品的启发，但是直接提供人物姓名的则是同时的英国作家 Horace Walpole 的 *A Letter from Xo Ho, a Chinese Philosopher at London, to his friend Lien Chi, at Peking*, 1757。

作者终于改用 *The Citizen of the World* 为书名，反映出他向世界各国吸取有益思想、研究各国社会制度的利弊以截长补短的要求，反映出当时进步思想家视野的广阔。具体说，“世界公民”指的是写信人，即第二信中的 the philosophic wanderer（“云游四方的哲学家”）；他和 *The Traveller* 一诗中的旅行家是一类的人物。

上面选的第十三封信原来没有题目，是全集中写得比较好的一封，它的主旨是在说明只有生前建立过利国利民的功业的人才配垂名后世，嘲笑和否定统治阶级帝王将相的荣誉和特权，戳穿了官方历史的虚伪。这篇文章也反映了当时文人的遭遇和资本主义无孔不入的商业化过程。作者处处强调教育作用，因此他把哲学家、诗人看成是最有用的人，这是当时进步知识分子——启蒙思想家诗同的特征。为了制造中国气氛，作者有意识地选择他所理解的中国人的观点来设问、对比，并选择“中国”词汇来烘托出中国情调。当然作者对中国（乾隆中叶以前的中国）的了解是很肤浅的，仅限于崇拜祖先、孔子、缠足等等，今天看来显得十分可笑。

1. **Westminster Abbey:** 伦敦著名大教堂。某些帝王、贵族、名臣、诗人埋葬于此。

2. **Lien Chi Altangi:** 参看题解。汉字待考。哥尔斯密所增部分显然不是汉字，含义待考。

3. **Fum Hoam:** 名出法文《中国故事集》，1725 年译成英语出版。汉字待考。

4. **Ceremonial Academy:** 似乎是礼部和国子监的混合物。

5. **sepulture:** 墓葬。

6. **monumental inscriptions:** 墓铭。

7. **remains:** 尸体。

8. **deceased merit:** 立过功业的古人。

9. **temple:** 非基督教的庙宇，如古希腊、罗马或中国的庙宇。Lien Chi 的中国词汇中无 church, cathedral, abbey.

10. **barbarous profusion:** 琳瑯满目，但在中国人眼中看来，缺乏文化教养、野蛮。

11. **fretted:** 带有图案雕饰的。

12. **monuments:** 雕像、铭刻、坟墓、碑志等任何纪念死者的标志，不可永远译作“纪念碑”。

13. **puny:** 微弱、渺小。

14. **child of dust:** 按基督教《圣经》，上帝用泥土造人。Child of dust 指人。

15. **possess more consequence:** = am more important. 人死后就没有作为了。

16. **epitaph:** 墓志铭，往往只记死者的优点，故云 flatter.

17. **a gentleman in black:** 是文集中的一个著名人物，据说其形象的根据是作者的父亲和作者自己。他的特点是外严内慈，不肯当牧师，但是总穿黑色衣服。在本文中，他的特点并不突出。

18. **I was come:** = I came, I have come.

19. **policy 与 wisdom:** 义同。

20. **adulation:** 阿谀，指对死者的尊崇。

21. **as ... so ...:** 无因果关系；一方面…一方面…；既…也…

22. **those who are flattered:** 指死者。

23. **incentive:** = stimulus，刺激；可以激发生者去追求荣誉。

24. **monumental pride:** 死后的光荣。

25. **in the aggregate:** 作为一个团体，此处指：使国家民族强大。

26. **from the weakness of the individual:** 以免一个人的力量不足。

27. **awful repository:** 令人肃然起敬的庙堂。repository 贮藏所，指死者尸骨的贮藏所，即教堂。

28. **in order (in the order) as it lay:** = one by one，依次。

29. **trophy:** 此处 = monument.

30. **reduced:** 改变；改变了国内混乱局面，加惠于国民。

31. **anarchy:** 混乱、无政府状态。

32. just subjection: 受到正义的统治。

33. the gaining two or three battles: 打了二、三次胜仗；这种动名词的用法（前面加冠词）在十八世纪很普遍。

34. seeing a battle: 参加战斗。

35. wit: 文学的才华。

36. remarkable, very remarkable: 呼应上文 what is the great man... remarkable for（以何见长），接下文 for a tomb in Westminster Abbey（奇特、难解）。这个人也竟然埋在这里，很难理解。

37. head of my ancestors: 作者所设想的中国人的赌咒话。

38. moderate merit: 没有什么特殊功绩的人。

39. infamy: 相形之下也显得象声名狼藉的人了。

40. his friends: 奉承他的人们。

41. got by the self-delusion: 不介意、无视这种自欺欺人之谈。

42. singular: 唯一的。

43. now: = now that, since.

44. the Poets' Corner: 在教堂东南角，英国许多著名诗人埋葬于此，或设衣冠冢。莎士比亚、弥尔顿在此有衣冠冢。

45. Prior, Matthew (1664–1721)**:** 托利党外交家、古典主义诗人，名噪一时。葬于西敏寺。

46. Drayton Michael (1563–1631)**:** 文艺复兴时期小诗人，有十四行诗、历史叙事诗。也葬于西敏寺。

47. Pope, Alexander (1688–1744)**:** 英国十八世纪主要诗人，属古典派，当时名气很大。

48. It is time enough, these hundred years: 还早，还可等上一百年。

49. done: 结束。

50. answerers of books: 书评家。作者故意铸造此词，怕这位中国哲学家不懂 reviewer 之类的词。

51. by the sheet: 十八世纪期刊不象近代期刊，每期往往只有一个"印张"，几页，故云。

52. eunuchs [ˈjuːnək]**:** 阉奴。孟德斯鸠曾描写过这些被摧残的人。哥尔斯密目的也在加强东方色彩。二者都反映了当时对东方理解有限。

53. seraglio [seˈrɑːliəu]**:** 意大利文，后宫。

54. Dunce: 傻子、蠢才。

55. Scribbler: 劣等作家。

56. revile the moral character: 糟踏人家名誉，骂人家不道德。

57. bookseller: 十八世纪出版商的称谓。mercenary，只图赢利。

58. here: 指在坟墓中。意谓作家已死，评论家还不饶他。

59. empty fame ... solid anxiety: 可怜作家生前追求虚名，不料死后倒扎扎实实地受人折磨。

60. except: = unless.

61. mandarine: 中国（清代）官员，此处指达官贵人。

62. patronize: 鼓励，给以物质资助。

63. malevolent dulness: 恶意而乏味的书评家。

64. made up to: = went up to.

65. without further ceremony: 不再客套。

66. a national reproach: 民族的耻辱。

67. to tax a curiosity: 向参观者索费。

68. which tended to their honour: 参观者看完以后，对传播他们国家的光荣有利。

69. that there: 俗语，= that, the threepence just mentioned.

70. farm: 承包。

71. tattered standards: 破烂的军旗，以纪念武功。

72. figures in wax: 蜡制的人像。

73. a lady: 指 Lady Elizabeth Russell.

74. a king with a golden head: 可能指英王 Henry V，他死后坟头放一木雕像，头部用金属制，但非用金，而是用银。

75. a curiosity: 此处指一件古董。有时则指足以视为珍奇之点。

76. Jacob's pillow: 典出《圣经·旧约》《创世纪》第二十八章，雅各梦见天使沿着梯子从天上下来，又沿着梯子上去，当时他头下枕的是一块石头。寺中之石，附会得名。此石又名 the Stone of Scone（苏格兰城堡），历代苏格兰国王在此石上加冕，十三世纪末搬到英国，英王也在这石上加冕。

77. could I: = if I could.

78. procession: 节日的仪仗行列。

79. Kobi: 即 Gobi，中亚细亚的戈壁大沙漠，马可波罗曾于十三世纪经过，据说曾见鬼魂作怪，大声呼唤人名。black magicians 可能指操纵这些鬼怪的人。

80. General Monk (1608–1670): 英国资产阶级革命时期将领，后又投靠复辟王朝。

81. recompense: 报酬。作者误认为看守人得到一顶破帽子作为工作的报酬。

82. we: 指在中国。

83. ecclesiastical: 教会的。

84. precipitately: 匆忙地。

85. ruminate: 反刍、反复思考。

86. occurrences of the day: 这一天内所遇到的事情。

25 RICHARD BRINSLEY SHERIDAN 1751–1816

THE SCHOOL FOR SCANDAL

杨周翰 选注

ACT I

Scene I.—LADY SNEERWELL'S[1] *House.*
Discovered[2] LADY SNEERWELL *at the dressing-table;*
SNAKE[3] *drinking chocolate.*

Lady Sneer. The paragraphs,[4] you say, Mr. Snake, were all inserted?

Snake. They were, madam; and as I copied them myself in a feigned hand,[5] there can be no suspicion whence they came.

Lady Sneer. Did you circulate the report of Lady Brittle's[6] intrigue[7] with Captain Boastall?[8]

Snake. That's in as fine a train[9] as your ladyship could wish. In the common course of things, I think it must reach Mrs. Clackitt's[10] ears within four and twenty hours; and then, you know, the business is as good as done.[11]

Lady Sneer. Why, truly, Mrs. Clackitt has a very pretty talent, and a great deal of industry.

Snake. True, madam, and has been tolerably successful in her day.[12] To my knowledge she has been the cause of six matches being broken off, and three sons disinherited; of four forced elopements, and as many close confinements;[13] nine separate maintenances,[14] and two divorces. Nay, I have more than once traced[15] her causing a *tête-à-tête*[16] in the *Town and Country Magazine,* when the parties, perhaps, had never seen each other's face before in the course of their lives.

Lady Sneer. She certainly has talents, but her manner is gross.

Snake. 'Tis very true.—She generally designs well, has a free tongue and a bold invention; but her colouring is too dark,[17] and her outlines often extravagant.[18] She wants that delicacy of tint,[19] and mellowness of sneer, which distinguishes your ladyship's scandal.

Lady Sneer. You are partial,[20] Snake.

Snake. Not in the least—everybody allows[21] that Lady Sneerwell can do more with a word or a look than many can with the most laboured detail,[22] even when they happen to have a little truth on their side to support it.

Lady Sneer. Yes, my dear Snake; and I am no hypocrite to deny[23] the satisfaction I reap from the success of my efforts.[24] Wounded myself in the early part of my life by the envenomed tongue[25] of slander,[26] I confess I have since known no pleasure equal to[27] the reducing others[28] to the level of my own injured reputation.

Snake. Nothing can be more natural. But, Lady Sneerwell, there is one affair in which you have lately employed me, wherein, I confess, I am at a loss to guess your motives.

Lady Sneer. I conceive[29] you mean with respect to my neighbour, Sir Peter Teazle,[30] and his family?

Snake. I do. Here are two young men, to whom Sir Peter has acted as a kind of guardian[31] since their father's death; the eldest[32] possessing the most amiable character, and universally well spoken of[33]; the youngest,[34] the most dissipated[35] and extravagant[36] young fellow in the kingdom without friends or character:[37] the former an avowed admirer of your ladyship's,[38] and apparently your favourite; the latter attached to[39] Maria,[40] Sir Peter's ward, and confessedly[41] beloved by her. Now, on the face of these circumstances, it is utterly unaccountable to me why you, the widow of a City knight,[42] with a good jointure,[43] should not close with[44] the passion[45] of a man of such character and expectations[46] as Mr. Surface;[47] and more so why you should be so uncommonly earnest to destroy the mutual attachment subsisting between his brother Charles and Maria.

Lady Sneer. Then at once to unravel this mystery,[48] I must inform you, that love has no share whatever in the intercourse between Mr. Surface and me.

Snake. No!

Lady Sneer. His real attachment is to Maria, or her fortune; but finding in his brother a favoured rival,[49] he has been obliged to mask his pretensions,[50] and profit by my assistance.[51]

Snake. Yet still I am more puzzled why you should interest yourself[52] in his success.

Lady Sneer. How dull you are! Cannot you surmise[53] the weakness[54] which I hitherto, through shame, have concealed even from you? Must I confess, that Charles, that libertine, that extravagant,[55] that bankrupt in fortune and reputation, that he it is for whom I'm thus anxious and malicious,[56] and to gain whom I would sacrifice everything?

Snake. Now, indeed, your conduct appears consistent: but how came you and Mr. Surface so confidential?[57]

Lady Sneer. For our mutual interest. I have found him out[58] a long time since.[59] I know him to be artful, selfish, and malicious — in short, a sentimental knave;[60] while with Sir Peter, and indeed with all his acquaintance, he passes for a youthful miracle of prudence,[61] good sense, and benevolence.

Snake. Yes; yet Sir Peter vows he had not his equal in England — and above all, he praises him as a man of sentiment.[62]

Lady Sneer. True — and with the assistance of his sentiment and hypocrisy,[63] he has brought Sir Peter entirely into his interest[64] with regard to Maria; while poor Charles has no friend in the house, though, I fear, he has a powerful one in Maria's heart, against whom we must direct our schemes.

Enter[65] SERVANT.

Serv. Mr. Surface.

Lady Sneer. Show him up. [*Exit*[66] SERVANT.

Enter JOSEPH SURFACE.

Joseph S. My dear Lady Sneerwell, how do you do to-day? Mr. Snake, your most obedient.[67]

Lady Sneer. Snake has just been rallying[68] me on our mutual attachment; but I have informed him of our real views. You know how useful he has been to us, and, believe me, the confidence[69] is not ill placed.

Joseph S. Madam, it is impossible for me to suspect a man of Mr. Snake's sensibility and discernment.

Lady Sneer. Well, well, no compliments now; but tell me when you saw your mistress, Maria — or, what is more material[70] to me, your brother.

Joseph S. I have not seen either since I left you; but I can inform you that they never meet, Some of your stories have taken a good effect on Maria.

Lady Sneer. Ah! my dear Snake! the merit of this belongs to you: but do your brother's distresses[71] increase?

Joseph S. Every hour. I am told he has had another execution in the house yesterday. In short, his dissipation and extravagance exceed anything I have ever heard of.

Lady Sneer. Poor Charles!

Joseph S. True, madam; notwithstanding his vices one can't help feeling for[72] him. Poor Charles! I'm sure I wish it were in my power to be of any essential service[73] to him; for the man who does not share in the distresses of a brother, even though merited by his own misconduct, deserves —

Lady Sneer. O Lud![74] you are going to be moral, and forget that you are among friends.

Joseph S. Egad,[75] that's true! — I'll keep that sentiment till I see Sir Peter; — however, it certainly is a charity to rescue Maria from such a libertine, who, if he is to be reclaimed,[76] can be so only by a person of your ladyship's superior accomplishments and understanding.

Snake. I believe, Lady Sneerwell, here's company coming: I'll go and copy the letter I mentioned to you.—Mr. Surface, your most obedient. [*Exit* SNAKE.

Joseph S. Sir, your very devoted.[77]—Lady Sneerwell, I am very sorry you have put any farther confidence in that fellow.

Lady Sneer. Why so?

Joseph S. I have lately detected him in frequent conference[78] with old Rowley, who was formerly my father's steward, and has never, you know, been a friend of mine.

Lady Sneer. And do you think he would betray us?

Joseph S. Nothing more likely:—take my word for't,[79] Lady Sneerwell, that fellow hasn't virture enough to be faithful even to his own villany.[80]—Ah! Maria!

Enter MARIA.

Lady Sneer. Maria, my dear, how do you do?—What's the matter?

Maria. Oh! there is that disagreeable lover of mine, Sir Benjamin Backbite,[81] has just called[82] at my guardian's, with his odious uncle, Crabtree;[83] so I slipt out, and ran hither to avoid them.

Lady Sneer. Is that all?

Joseph S. If my brother Charles had been of the party, madam, perhaps you would not have been so much alarmed.

Lady Sneer. Nay, now you are severe;[84] for I dare swear the truth of the matter is, Maria heard *you* were here.—But, my dear, what has Sir Benjamin done, that you would avoid him so?

Maria. Oh, he has done nothing—but 'tis for what he has said: his conversation is a perpetual libel on all his acquaintance.

Joseph S. Aye, and the worst of it is, there is no advantage[85] in not knowing him—for he'll abuse a stranger just as soon as his best friend; and his uncle's as bad.[86]

Lady Sneer. Nay, but we should make allowance[87] — Sir Benjamin is a wit and a poet.

Maria. For my part, I confess, madam, wit loses its respect with me,[88] when I see it in company with malice. — What do you think, Mr. Surface?

Joseph S. Certainly, madam; to smile[89] at the jest[90] which plants a thorn in another's breast is to become a principal[91] in the mischief.

Lady Sneer. Pshaw! — there's no possibility of being witty without a little ill nature; the malice of a good thing[92] is the barb[93] that makes it[94] stick.[95] — What's your opinion, Mr. Surface?

Joseph S. To be sure, madam; that conversation, where the spirit of raillery is suppressed, will ever appear tedious and insipid.

Maria. Well, I'll not debate how far scandal may be allowable; but in a man, I am sure, it is always contemptible. We[96] have pride, envy, rivalship, and a thousand motives to depreciate each other; but the male slanderer must have the cowardice of a woman before he can traduce[97] one.[98]

Enter SERVANT.

Serv. Madam, Mrs. Candour[99] is below,[100] and if your ladyship's at leisure, will leave her carriage.[101]

Lady Sneer. Beg her to walk in. — [*Exit* SERVANT.] — Now, Maria, here is a character to your taste; for though Mrs. Candour is a little talkative, everybody allows her to be the best natured and best sort of woman.

Maria. Yes, — with a very gross affectation[102] of good nature and benevolence, she does more mischief than the direct malice of old Crabtree.

Joseph S. I'faith[103] that's true, Lady Sneerwell: whenever I hear the current running against the characters of my friends,[104] I never think them in such danger as when Candour undertakes their defence.[105]

Lady Sneer. Hush! — here she is!

Enter MRS. CANDOUR.

Mrs. Can. My dear Lady Sneerwell, how have you been this century?[106] — Mr. Surface, what news do you hear? — though indeed it is no matter,[107] for I think one hears nothing else but scandal.

Joseph S. Just so, indeed, ma'am.

Mrs. Can. O Maria! child, — what, is the whole affair off between you and Charles? His extravagance,[108] I presume — the town talks of nothing else.

Maria. Indeed! I am very sorry, ma'am, the town is not better employed.[109]

Mrs. Can. True, true, child: but there's no stopping people's tongues. I own I was hurt to hear it, as I indeed was to learn, from the same quarter,[110] that your guardian, Sir Peter, and Lady Teazle have not agreed lately as well as could be wished.

Maria. 'Tis strangely impertinent[111] for people to busy themselves so.

Mrs. Can. Very true, child: — but what's to be done? People will talk[112] — there's no preventing it. Why, it was but yesterday I was told that Miss Gadabout[113] had eloped with Sir Filigree[114] Flirt.[115] — But, Lord! there's no minding[116] what one hears; though, to be sure, I had this from very good authority.[117]

Maria. Such reports are highly scandalous.

Mrs. Can. So they are, child — shameful, shameful! But the world is so censorious, no character escapes.[118] — Lord, now who would have suspected your friend, Miss Prim,[119] of an indiscretion?[120] Yet such is the ill-nature of people, that they say her uncle stopt her last week, just as she was stepping into the York diligence[121] with her dancing-master.[122]

Maria. I'll answer for't[123] there are no grounds for that report.

Mrs. Can. Ah, no foundation in the world,[124] I dare swear; no more, probably, than for the story circulated last month, of Mrs. Festino's[125] affair[126] with Colonel Cassino;[127] — though, to be sure, that matter was never rightly cleared up.

Joseph S. The licence of invention[128] some people take is monstrous indeed.

Maria. 'Tis so, — but, in my opinion, those who report such things are equally culpable.[129]

Mrs. Can. To be sure they are; tale-bearers are as bad as the tale-makers — 'tis an old observation,[130] and a very true one: but what's to be done, as I said before? how will you prevent people from talking? To-day, Mrs. Clackitt assured me, Mr. and Mrs. Honeymoon were at last become mere man and wife,[131] like the rest of their acquaintance. She likewise hinted that a certain widow, in the next street, had got rid of her dropsy[132] and recovered her shape[133] in a most surprising manner. And at the same time, Miss Tattle,[134] who was by, affirmed, that Lord Buffalo had discovered his lady at a house of no extraordinary fame;[135] and that Sir H. Boquet and Tom Saunter were to measure swords[136] on a similar provocation.[137] — But, Lord, do you think I would report these things? — No, no! tale-bearers, as I said before, are just as bad as the tale-makers.

Joseph S. Ah! Mrs. Candour, if everybody had your forbearance and good-nature!

Mrs. Can. I confess, Mr. Surface, I cannot bear to hear people attacked behind their backs; and when ugly circumstances come out against our acquaintance,[138] I own I always love to think the best.[139] — By-the-by, I hope 'tis not true that your brother is absolutely ruined?[140]

Joseph S. I am afraid his circumstances[141] are very bad indeed, ma'am.

Mrs. Can. Ah! I heard so — but you must tell him to keep up his spirits; everybody almost is in the same way — Lord Spindle,[142] Sir Thomas Splint, Captain Quinze, and Mr. Nickit[143] — all up,[144] I hear, within this week; so if Charles is undone, he'll find half his acquaintance ruined too, and that, you know, is a consolation.

Joseph S. Doubtless, ma'am — a very great one.

Enter SERVANT.

Serv. Mr. Crabtree and Sir Benjamin Backbite.

[*Exit* SERVANT.

Lady Sneer. So, Maria, you see your lover pursues you; positively you shan't escape.

Enter CRABTREE *and* SIR BENJAMIN BACKBITE.

Crabt. Lady Sneerwell, I kiss your hand[145] — Mrs. Candour, I don't believe you are acquainted with my nephew, Sir Benjamin Backbite? Egad! ma'am, he has a pretty wit, and is a pretty poet too; isn't he, Lady Sneerwell?

Sir Benj. B. Oh, fie,[146] uncle!

Crabt. Nay, egad, it's true; I back him[147] at a rebus[148] or a charade[149] against the best rhymer[150] in the kingdom. — Has your ladyship heard the epigram he wrote last week on Lady Frizzle's[151] feather[152] catching fire? — Do, Benjamin, repeat it, or the charade you made last night extempore[153] at Mrs. Drowzie's[154] conversazione.[155] Come now; — your first is the name of a fish, your second a great naval commander, and —

Sir Benj. B. Uncle, now — prythee[156] —

Crabt. I'faith, ma'am, 'twould surprise you to hear how ready he is at all these fine sort of things.[157]

Lady Sneer. I wonder,[158] Sir Benjamin, you never publish anything.

Sir Benj. B. To say truth, ma'am, 'tis very vulgar to print; and as my little productions are mostly satires and lampoons[159] on particular people, I find they circulate more by giving copies in confidence[160] to the friends of the parties.[161] However, I have some love elegies,[162] which, when favoured with this lady's smiles,[163] I mean to give the public.

Crabt. 'Fore Heaven,[164] ma'am, they'll immortalize you! — you will be handed down to posterity, like Petrarch's[165] Laura, or Waller's[166] Sacharissa.

Sir Benj. B. Yes, madam, I think you will like them, when you shall see them on a beautiful quarto page,[167] where a neat rivulet of text[168] shall meander through a meadow of margin.[169] 'Fore Gad,[170] they will be the most elegant things of their kind!

Crabt. But, ladies, that's true—have you heard the news?

Mrs. Can. What, sir, do you mean the report of —

Crabt. No, ma'am, that's not it—Miss Nicely[171] is going to be married to her own footman.[172]

Mrs. Can. Impossible!

Crabt. Ask Sir Benjamin.

Sir Benj. B. 'Tis true very, ma'am; everything is fixed, and the wedding liveries[173] bespoke.[174]

Crabt. Yes—and they do say there were pressing reasons for it.

Lady Sneer. Why, I have heard something of this before.

Mrs. Can. It can't be—and I wonder any one should believe such a story, of so prudent a lady as Miss Nicely.

Sir Benj. B. O Lud! ma'am, that's the very reason 'twas believed at once. She has always been so cautious and so reserved, that everybody was sure there was some reason for it at bottom.

Mrs. Can. Why, to be sure, a tale of scandal is as fatal to the credit[175] of a prudent lady of her stamp,[176] as a fever is generally to those of the strongest constitutions.[177] But there is a sort of puny[178] sickly reputation, that is always ailing,[179] yet will outlive the robuster characters of a hundred prudes.

Sir Benj. B. True, madam,—there are valetudinarians[180] in reputation as well as constitution; who, being conscious of their weak part, avoid the least breath of air,[181] and supply their want[182] of stamina[183] by care and circumspection.

Mrs. Can. Well, but this may be all a mistake. You know, Sir Benjamin, very trifling circumstances often give rise to the most injurious tales.

Crabt. That they do, I'll be sworn,[184] ma'am. Did you ever hear how Miss Piper came to lose her lover and her character last summer at Tunbridge?[185] — Sir Benjamin, you remember it?

Sir Benj. B. Oh, to be sure! — the most whimsical circumstance.

Lady Sneer. How was it, pray?

Crabt. Why, one evening, at Mrs. Ponto's assembly,[186] the conversation happened to turn on the breeding Nova Scotia[187] sheep in this country. Says a young lady in company, I have known instances of it — for Miss Letitia[188] Piper, a first cousin[189] of mine, had a Nova Scotia sheep that produced her twins. — What! cries the Lady Dowager[190] Dundizzy[191] (who you know is as deaf as a post), has Miss Piper had twins? — This mistake, as you may imagine, threw the whole company into a fit of laughter. However, 'twas the next morning everywhere reported, and in a few days believed by the whole town, that Miss Letitia Piper had actually been brought to bed of[192] a fine boy and a girl; and in less than a week there were some people who could name the father, and the farmhouse where the babies were put to nurse.[193]

Lady Sneer. Strange, indeed!

Crabt. Matter of fact,[194] I assure you. — O Lud! Mr. Surface, pray is it true that your uncle, Sir Oliver, is coming home?

Joseph S. Not that I know of,[195] indeed, sir.

Crabt. He has been in the East Indies a long time. You can scarcely remember him, I believe? Sad comfort whenever he returns, to hear how your brother has gone on!

Joseph S. Charles has been imprudent, sir, to be sure; but I hope no busy people[196] have already prejudiced Sir Oliver against him.[197] He may reform.

Sir Benj. B. To be sure he may: for my part, I never believed him to be so utterly void of principle as people say; and though he has lost all his friends, I am told nobody is better spoken of by the Jews.[198]

Crabt. That's true, egad, nephew. If the Old Jewry was a ward,[199] I believe Charles would be an alderman:[200] — no man more popular there, 'fore Gad! I hear he pays as many annuities as the Irish tontine;[201] and that whenever he is sick, they have prayers for the recovery of his health in all the synagogues.[202]

Sir Benj. B. Yet no man lives in greater splendour. They tell me, when he entertains his friends he will sit down to dinner with a dozen of his own securities;[203] have a score of tradesmen[204] waiting in the antechamber, and an officer[205] behind every guest's chair.

Joseph S. This may be entertainment to you, gentlemen, but you pay very little regard to the feelings of a brother.

Maria. Their malice is intolerable. — Lady Sneerwell, I must wish you a good morning: I'm not very well. [*Exit* MARIA.

Mrs. Can. Oh dear! she changes colour very much.

Lady Sneer. Do, Mrs. Candour, follow her: she may want assistance.

Mrs. Can. That I will, with all my soul, ma'am. Poor dear girl, who knows what her situation may be![206]

[*Exit* MRS. CANDOUR.

Lady Sneer. 'Twas nothing but that she could not bear to hear Charles reflected on,[207] notwithstanding their difference.

Sir Benj. B. The young lady's *penchant*[208] is obvious.

Crabt. But, Benjamin, you must not give up the pursuit for that: — follow her, and put her into good humour. Repeat her some of your own verses. Come, I'll assist you.

Sir Benj. B. Mr. Surface, I did not mean to hurt you; but depend on't[209] your brother is utterly undone.

Crabt. O Lud, ay! undone as ever man was. Can't raise[210] a guinea![211]

Sir Benj. B. And everything sold, I'm told, that was movable.

Crabt. I have seen one[212] that was at his house. Not a thing left but some empty bottles that were overlooked, and the family pictures, which I believe are framed in the wainscots[213] —

Sir Benj. B. And I'm very sorry, also, to hear some bad stories against him. [*Going.*

Crabt. Oh! he has done many mean things, that's certain.

Sir Benj. B. But, however, as he's your brother — [*Going*.

Crabt. We'll tell you all another opportunity.[214]

[*Exit* CRABTREE *and* SIR BENJAMIN.

Lady Sneer. Ha! ha! 'tis very hard for them to leave a subject they have not quite run down.[215]

Joseph S. And I believe the abuse was no more acceptable[216] to your ladyship than Maria.

Lady Sneer. I doubt[217] her affections are farther engaged[218] than we imagine. But the family are to be here this evening, so you may as well dine where you are, and we shall have an opportunity of observing farther; in the meantime, I'll go and plot mischief, and you shall study sentiment.[219] [*Exeunt*.

【作者简介】 Richard Brinsley Sheridan（谢立丹，1751—1816）是英国十八世纪后半期杰出的喜剧作家。二十三岁写了第一部喜剧 *The Rivals*（《情敌》，1775），到二十八岁一共写了五、六部喜剧，基本结束了他的创作活动。此后，他一方面从事政治活动，一方面办剧院，曾任议员和政府要职。1794 年发表议会演说，反对英国政府出兵干涉法国革命后的雅各宾专政；1798 年又发表议会演说，要求言论自由。谢立丹的这些政治活动反映了当时英国新兴工业资产阶级的要求。谢立丹的青年朋友，诗人拜伦曾夸张地说："谢立丹所做的和愿意做的一切都是最出色的。他写过最出色的喜剧（《造谣学校》）…发表过人们在英国所能撰拟的、所能听到的最出色的演说（著名的弹劾哈斯丁的演说）。"

【题解与注释】

英国戏剧自莎士比亚以后，经过资产阶级革命时期的消沉，在复辟时期（1660—1688）曾又一度活跃，出现了描写上层社会风尚的喜剧，内容大多猥亵。这种戏剧不久激起反对。十八世纪上半盛行 Steele, Lillo 等人的新戏，宣扬中产阶级道德，带有强烈感伤成分。但是整个说来，十八世纪是英国戏剧贫乏的时期。除了 Fielding（菲尔丁）的政治讽刺剧以外，谢立丹的成就最为突出，他的批判精神接近菲尔丁以及同时代的法国剧作家博马舍（Beaumarchais）.

谢立丹的主要剧本有 *The Rivals*，讽刺当时社会上有产者想在浪漫的幻想之中追求生活意义的风尚；*The Critic*（《批评家》，1779）以戏中戏的形式讽刺当时流行的感伤情调的戏剧和当时文艺批评界的劣迹。

谢立丹的最光辉的成就是五幕喜剧 *The School for Scandal*（《造谣学校》，1777）。它揭露了英国贵族资产阶级社会的种种败德：虚伪、荒淫、以恶意中伤别人的名誉为生活的乐事。剧本写一个年事已长的贵族 Sir Peter Teazle 娶了一个乡间出身的年轻妻子，带到伦敦的上流社会，结果她沾染上挥霍和打情骂俏的恶习，几乎弄到家庭关系破裂。勾引她的是一个表面善良稳重，而实际自私自利的青年 Joseph Surface。他一方面暗中勾引 Lady Teazle，一方面又看中 Sir Peter Teazle 所监护的少女 Maria 的资财，宣称要向她求婚。Joseph 的弟弟 Charles 表面挥霍放荡，但心地善良，和 Maria 相互爱慕，只是 Charles 被"造谣学校"的中心人物 Lady Sneerwell 看中，她和 Joseph 合谋一方面想败坏 Lady Teazle 的名誉，一方面想拆散 Charles 和 Maria 的婚姻。这时，Surface 兄弟的叔父在海外经商致富回国，想考验一下两个侄儿中哪个值得继承他的遗产。他假扮放高利贷的犹太人去收买 Charles 家藏的画像，发现 Charles 毫不惋惜地把历代祖宗肖像都廉价抛售，只留一张叔父的画像，因而很受感动。他又假扮一个穷亲戚去向 Joseph 借钱，Joseph 装穷，并且说他之所以穷，都是因为叔父太吝啬。Joseph 引诱 Lady Teazle 的勾当以及他想要 Maria 的真正意图，最后也被揭穿。

作者在剧中揭露了资产阶级的虚伪自私，强调了伦敦"上流社会"的荒淫无耻对一个天真纯朴的乡村少女的腐蚀作用。作者虽然没有正面提出十八世纪流行的回到淳朴的大自然去的口号，但是在着力描写了大都市"上流社会"的败德时，暗示了城市和乡村的对照。整个伦敦"上流社会"便是一所"造谣学校"，其缩影便是斯尼尔威尔夫人的客厅，其中人物皆饱食终日无所用心，以诽谤别人的名誉为消遣。在作者笔下，他们的面目刻划得很鲜明。他们恶意中伤别人的名誉的一种办法可以称为"联珠法"，从一个对象串联到另一个对象；另一个办法是"滚雪球法"，从一点捕风捉影的谣言开始，愈滚愈大，愈说愈真。谢立丹不仅讽刺了造谣者，而且通过造谣的对象进一步揭穿这个魑魅魍魉的社会的底蕴。这客厅一场也正是这部喜剧取名的来由，是英国戏剧中一个著名的场面。

谢立丹的语言以明快、锋利、俏皮著称，但十八世纪英语和今天比较仍有一定区别。

1. Sneerwell: 含有嘲笑、鄙视之意。作者常通过人名的含意，点出人物性格。

2. Discovered: 幕启时，人物已在台上。

3. Snake: Lady Sneerwell 门下客，剧中次要人物。

4. paragraphs: 送到报馆去刊登的几则新闻。

5. feigned hand: 假冒的，不是他通常的、为人所熟识的笔迹。

6. Brittle: 脆，容易破碎之意。非剧中人物。

7. intrigue: 男女私情。

8. Boastall: 由 boast 和 all 二字组成，非剧中人物。

9. in as fine a train: in as good order or condition，进行得很顺利。

10. Clackitt: 由 Clack 和 it 二字组成，唧唧呱呱乱说之意。非剧中人物。

11. as good as done: = practically done，事情简直就算成了。

12. in her day: 在她的“全盛”时期。

13. close confinements: 严密监禁，例如禁止女儿出门交际。

14. separate maintenance: 夫妻分居，男方提供赡养费。

15. traced: 找线索，此处指侦察出来。

16. causing a tête-à-tête: tête-à-tête [ˈteitɑːˈteit] 法语，“head to head”，private interview. 在刊物上登载捏造的消息，诬指某人与某妇人幽会。

17. colouring is too dark: 渲染得太浓了。

18. outlines often extravagant: 轮廓往往夸张，不适度，不近情理。

19. delicacy of tint: 色彩轻淡。

20. partial: 偏爱，偏心；此处意为“过奖了”。

21. allows: 承认，公认。

22. laboured detail: 费尽力气捏造的细节；与上文 a word, a look 对照。

23. I am no hypocrite to deny: 我是个实心眼的人，我承认。

24. efforts: 此处指破坏别人名誉的行为或努力。

25. envenomed tongue: 毒舌、含毒的话。

26. slander: 诽谤，此处指诽谤者。

27. equal to: as great as.

28. the reducing others ...: 十八世纪用法，= the reducing of others. 把别人降低到和我相同的（即名声败坏的）地位；愿意别人和我一样名声败坏。

29. I conceive: I think.

30. Teazle: <tease，原意为把呢绒上的毛绒梳起来，后来多作戏谑逗惹解。

31. guardian: 监护人，受托管理未成年人的财产、教育等。受监护者称为 ward，见本段。Sir Peter Teazle 监护着三个青年：Joseph 和 Charles Surface 兄弟，和 Maria.

32. the eldest: = the elder.

33. well spoken of: 受人夸奖。

34. the youngest: = the younger.

35. dissipated: 冶游放荡。

36. extravagant: 挥霍，与上文中 extravagant 的意义不同。

37. without ... character: 没有品德，或声名狼藉。

38. of your ladyship's: 尊称，= of yours. 很仰慕夫人。

39. attached to: 爱慕、爱，下文 attachment 意同。

40. Maria: [məˈraiə].

41. confessedly: 据说。

42. City knight: 伦敦城的资本家。City 指伦敦的商业金融区；knight 不指通常的“骑士”，指商人因有钱而受封为“爵士”者。

43. jointure: 男子死后，妻子独自继承的产业。

44. close with: 同意。

45. passion: 爱情。

46. expectations: 继承财产的希望。

47. Mr Surface: 指哥哥 Joseph Surface；弟弟在剧中仅称名（Charles），不称姓。

48. unravel this mystery: 揭开这一秘密，解释这一疑团。

49. finding in his brother a favoured rival: = finding that his brother is a rival and is favoured by Maria.

50. mask his pretensions: 掩盖自己的意图。

51. assistance: 指拆散 Charles 与 Maria.

52. interest yourself: 费力，make efforts towards his success.

53. surmise: 猜到。

54. weakness: 喜爱，指爱上 Charles.

55. extravagant: *n.* 纨袴子弟。

56. malicious: 施毒计。

57. how came you ...?: = how did you and Mr. Surface become so confidential?

58. found him out: 发现他的秘密。

59. since: = ago.

60. a sentimental knave: = a rogue addicted to superficial emotions，表面上装出对道德问题高度敏感的坏人，伪善者。按 sentimental 一词，十八世纪时有情感纯正、高尚，富于同情心之意，与今日之作感情虚浮不真解迥异。

61. he passes for a youthful miracle of prudence: 人皆视之为少年老成，人间奇迹。

62. a man of sentiment: = a tender-hearted man.

63. his sentiment and hypocrisy: 此处，sentiment 已成反语，意为 insincerity.

64. brought ... into his interest: = won ... over.

65. Enter: 上场（剧本说明中常用语）。

66. Exit:（一人）下场（剧本说明中常用语）。exeunt,（多人）下场。

67. your most obedient: = I am your most obedient servant，客套语"您好"。或如下文 Snake 对话中，意为"再见"，"告辞"。

68. rally: 嘲笑、戏弄。

69. confidence: 把秘密告诉 Snake.

70. material: important.

71. distresses: 法律名词，即 distraints，扣押财产，强迫偿债；下文 execution 意同。也可解作普通的不幸，如下文 Joseph 的对话。

72. feel for: 同情、可怜。

73. of any essential service: 对他确实有所帮助；参考 your obedient servant 中 servant 的含义。

74. Lud [ˈlʌd]: 十八、九世纪流行的、造作的惊叹词，即 Lord，"上帝呀！"

75. Egad [iˈgæd]: = By God.

76. reclaimed: 浪子回头，改过自新。

77. your very devoted: 与 your most obedient 结构、意义均同。

78. conference: = conversation.

79. take my word for't: = take my word for it, believe me.

80. (not) faithful even to his own villany: 连干坏事都（不能）始终如一。

81. Backbite: 背后诽谤别人的人；剧中一贵族青年，追求 Maria.

82. has just called: = who has just called.

83. Crabtree: 这种树的果子味酸，喻其性格乖僻，不随和，爱挑剔。

84. severe: 责备过严。

85. there is no advantage ...: 不认识他也无好处，他对素不相识的人照样诽谤。

86. as bad: as bad as he.

87. make allowance: 原谅几分。

88. wit loses its respect with me: = I will not respect wit（才华、才子）。

89. smile: 表示同意，不加批评。

90. jest: 开玩笑，以损害别人。

91. to become a principal ...: 等于作恶的主犯之一。

92. a good thing: 指 wit.

93. barb: 钩、刺。

94. it: 指 good thing.

95. stick: 钩住东西。玩笑必须带刺，才能使人难忘。

96. we: 指女人。

97. traduce: 诽谤。

98. one: 指女人。

99. Candour: 坦率。

100. below: 在楼下，在门外。

101. leave her carriage: 下车进来拜会。

102. gross [grəus] **affectation:** 她故作天性善良，到了过火的程度。

103. I'faith: = In faith, truly, indeed.

104. the current running against the characters of my friends: 许多人说我的朋友们的坏话。

105. when Candour undertakes their defence: Candour 越替他们辩护（越糟）。

106. this century: = this long time.

107. no matter: = of no importance.

108. His extravagance: i. e. is the cause.

109. not better employed: 没有别的事可干了。

110. from the same quarter: from the same source of information. 同一个人告诉我。

111. impertinent: 多管闲事，不礼貌。

112. People will talk: 没法子禁止人们乱说。

113. Gadabout: 游来荡去。非剧中人物。

114. Filigree: 细金属丝制成的装饰，喻其纤巧脆弱。

115. Flirt: 调情。非剧中人物。

116. there's no minding: 不必计较。

117. I had this from very good authority: = I heard this from a very reliable source.

118. censorious ... escapes: 人们太爱挑剔，任何人都难保全名誉。

119. Prim: 正经、刻板，特别指妇女。非剧中人物。

120. indiscretion: 不检点的行为。

121. the York diligence: 开往 York 城的马车。

122. dancing-master: 教舞蹈的教师。

123. answer for't: 我敢担保。

124. in the world: 毫无（根据）。

125. Festino [fesˈtiːnəu]**:** 意大利文，意为节日庆祝娱乐活动。

126. affair: 不正当的男女关系。

127. Cassino [kəˈsiːnəu]**:** 意大利文，意为娱乐室、音乐室、舞厅、或一种纸牌游戏。Cassino 与 Festino 均非剧中人物。

128. licence of invention ... take: 乱造谣言。

129. culpable: 应受处罚。

130. an old observation: 一句老话。

131. mere man and wife: 平平凡凡地做了夫妻。

132. dropsy: 膨胀病，此处指怀孕。

133. shape: 正常的体形。

134. Tattle: 闲扯，乱谈。非剧中人物。

135. a house of no extraordinary fame: 男女幽会场所。

136. measure swords: 决斗。

137. on a similar provocation: 由于类似原因。

138. ugly circumstances come out against ...: 不利于…的丑闻传播开来的时候。

139. think the best: 往好的方面想。

140. ruined: 破产。

141. circumstances: 经济情况。

142. Spindle: 纺线轴；**Splint，**夹板。均有瘦长意。

143. Quinze, Nickit: 前者是一种纸牌游戏，后者（Nick）是掷骰子的术语。以上四人均非剧中人物。

144. all up: 全部破产。

145. I kiss your hand: "上流社会"男子见女子时的一种社交礼节。

146. fie [fai]**:** 早期英语中表示不同意或责备或嫌弃的惊叹词。

147. back him: 押他的注，认为他能操必胜左券。

148. rebus [ˈriːbəs]**:** 一种字谜。

149. charade [ʃəˈrɑːd]**:** 法语，也是一种字谜游戏。

150. rhymer: 只讲押韵的诗人。

151. Frizzle: 鬈毛。非剧中人物。

152. feather: 帽子上的羽毛装饰。

153. extempore [eks'tempəri]**:** 拉丁语，即席，即兴。

154. Drowzie: 沉闷、昏昏欲睡。

155. conversazione ['kɔnvəˌsætsi'əuni]**:** 意大利语，文人、艺术家的晚会。

156. prythee: 或作 prithee ['priði(:)]，古语，由 pray 及 thee（you）二词组成，意为 I pray thee，我请求你。

157. these fine sort of things: 古代语法的复数。

158. I wonder: 我有些纳闷、奇怪、不理解。

159. lampoons: 讽刺作品。

160. in confidence: 私下。

161. parties: 当事人，受到讽刺的对象。

162. elegy: 古希腊、罗马的一种诗体，每行有固定数量的音步，内容不一定哀挽。

163. favoured ... smiles: 得到 Maria 的赞许之后。

164. 'Fore Heaven: = Before Heaven，我敢对天发誓。

165. Petrarch ['pi:trɑ:k]**:** 十四世纪意大利著名诗人，写了许多十四行体抒情诗歌，赞美他的情人 Laura ['lɔ:rə].

166. Waller ['wɔlə]**:** 十七世纪英国诗人，Sacharissa [sækə'risə]（"甜蜜"）是他所歌颂的美人。

167. quarto page: 四开单张。

168. rivulet of text: 诗的本文将象一条小溪流。

169. a meadow of margin: 诗页的四周将印上花饰，如开满繁花的草地。

170. 'Fore Gad: = Before God.

171. Nicely: 口味很高，喜欢挑剔之意，非剧中人物。

172. footman: 仆人。

173. liveries: 仆人穿的制服。

174. bespoke: 定做。

175. credit: 信誉。

176. of her stamp: 象她这种，象她这一类型的。

177. constitution: 体质、健康状况。

178. puny: 发育不完全，孱弱。

179. ailing: 挂着一点病，不好也不死。

180. valetudinarians ['væliˌtju:di'nεəriənz]**:** 身体虚弱的人。

181. breath of air: 风。

182. want: = lack.

183. stamina: 精力。

184. I'll be sworn: 我确信。

185. Tunbridge: Tunbridge Wells 之简称，在伦敦附近，Kent 郡，矿泉疗养、娱乐胜地。当时英国有许多这类地方，如 Bath，供有钱的时髦人之用。

186. Mrs. Ponto's assembly: 在上述地方，往往有人开办一些娱乐场所，assembly（或作 assembly-room）即这种场所，可以举办舞会等。

187. Nova Scotia [ˈnəuvəˈskəuʃə]**:** 拉丁语，意为新苏格兰，加拿大东部滨海省分。

188. Letitia: 读音 [liˈtiʃiə].

189. first cousin: 父、母的兄、弟、姊、妹的子女。

190. Dowager [ˈdauədʒə]**:** 贵族的或有钱的、年龄较大的寡妇。

191. Dundizzy [dʌnˈdizi]**:** 昏瞶之意，非剧中人物。

192. to be brought to bed of: 分娩。

193. to be put to nurse: 送出去喂养。

194. Matter of fact: = It is a fact.

195. Not that I know of: = Not as far as I know.

196. busy people: 多嘴多舌、好管闲事的人。

197. prejudiced ... him: 在…面前说了他的坏话。

198. better spoken of by the Jews: 放高利贷的人都说他的好话。Charles 常向他们借债，照顾他们的营业。

199. ward: 古代伦敦分为若干坊（ward），Old Jewry 即其中之一，政府把犹太人集中此处。

200. alderman: 此处指一坊的行政长官。

201. Irish tontine [tɔnˈtiːn]**:** 为偿付爱尔兰国债而举办的公债，每年偿还本金（annuities）一部分给债券持有者，最后一个未死的债券持有者得到全部剩余本金。

202. synagogues: 犹太人的教堂。

203. securities: 借款的保证人。

204. tradesmen: 来向他讨帐的各种店主。

205. officer: 来逮捕他或保证人（当他还不出债的时候）的警官。极言其满不在乎地挥霍。

206. Who knows what her situation may be!: 谁知道她又处于什么情况！意为她也有难以告人之隐。

207. reflected on: 受人评论。

208. penchant [pɑ̃ːʃɑ̃]**:** = inclination.

209. depend on't: 你可以确信。

210. raise: 举债。

211. guinea [ˈgini]**:** 值一镑一先令的钱数。

212. I have seen one: 我遇到一个到过他家的人，并听此人说。

213. framed in the wainscots [ˈweinskəts]**:** 镶在板墙上，无法取下出卖。

214. another opportunity: = another time.

215. run down: = exhausted，把要说的话全说完。

216. no more acceptable ... than: = as unpleasant… as.

217. I doubt: = I am afraid.

218. farther engaged: 她对 Charles 的爱情比我们想象的要深。

219. study sentiment: 研究高尚的情操，意为“你去钻研怎样装作一个富于同情心的好人吧！”

26 EDWARD GIBBON
1737 – 1794

THE HISTORY OF THE DECLINE AND FALL OF THE ROMAN EMPIRE, CHAPTER I (SELECTIONS)

许国璋　选注

CHAPTER I.

THE EXTENT AND MILITARY FORCE OF THE EMPIRE IN THE AGE OF THE ANTONINES.

IN the second century of the Christian Æra, the empire of Rome comprehended[1] the fairest part of the earth, and the most civilised portion of mankind. The frontiers of that extensive monarchy were guarded by ancient renown and disciplined valour. The gentle, but powerful, influence of laws and manners[2] had gradually cemented the union of the provinces. Their peaceful inhabitants enjoyed and abused the advantages of wealth and luxury. The image of a free constitution[3] was preserved with decent reverence. The Roman senate appeared to possess the sovereign authority, and devolved on the emperors all the executive powers of government. During a happy period of more than fourscore years, the public administration was conducted by the virtue and abilities of Nerva, Trajan, Hadrian, and the two Antonines.[4] It is the design of this and of the two succeeding chapters, to describe the prosperous condition of their empire; and afterwards, from the death of Marcus Antoninus, to deduce the most important circumstances of its decline and fall: a revolution[5] which will ever be remembered, and is still felt by the nations of the earth.

[**Augustus's policy of moderation**]

The principal conquests of the Romans were achieved under the republic;[6] and the emperors, for the most part, were satisfied with preserving those dominions which had been acquired by the policy of the senate, the active emulation of the consuls,[7] and the martial enthusiasm of the people. The seven first centuries[8] were filled with a rapid succession of triumphs; but it was reserved for Augustus to relinquish the ambitious design of subduing the whole earth, and to introduce a spirit of moderation into the public councils. Inclined to peace by his temper and situation, it was easy for him to discover that Rome, in her present exalted situation, had much less to hope than to fear from the chance of arms[9]; and that, in the prosecution of remote wars, the undertaking became every day more difficult, the event more doubtful, and the possession more precarious and less beneficial.[10] The experience of Augustus added weight to these salutary reflections,[11] and effectually convinced him that, by the prudent vigour of his counsels, it would be easy to secure every concession[12] which the safety or the dignity of Rome might require from the most formidable barbarians.[13] Instead of exposing his person and his legions to the arrows of the Parthians, he obtained, by an honourable treaty, the restitution of the standards and prisoners which had been taken in the defeat of Crassus.[14, 15]

[**Further conquests hardly practicable**]

His generals, in the early part of his reign, attempted the reduction of Æthiopia and Arabia Felix.[16] They marched near a thousand miles to the south of the tropic; but the heat of the climate soon repelled the invaders and protected the unwarlike natives of those sequestered regions. The northern countries of Europe scarcely deserved the expense and labour of conquest. The forests and morasses of Germany were filled with a hardy race of barbarians, who despised life when it was separated from freedom[17]; and though, on the first attack, they seemed to yield to the weight of the Roman power, they soon, by a signal act of despair, regained their independence, and reminded Augustus of the vicissitude of fortune. On the death of that emperor his testament[18] was publicly read in the senate. He bequeathed, as a valuable legacy to his successors, the advice of confining the empire within those limits which nature seemed to have placed as its permanent bulwarks and boundaries: on the west the Atlantic Ocean[19]; the Rhine and Danube on the north; the Euphrates on the east; and towards the south the sandy deserts of Arabia and Africa.[20]

Happily for the repose of mankind, the moderate system recommended by the wisdom of Augustus was adopted by the fears and vices of his immediate successors.[21] Engaged in the pursuit of pleasure or in the exercise of tyranny, the first Cæsars seldom showed themselves to the armies, or to the provinces; nor were they disposed to suffer that[22] those triumphs which *their* indolence neglected should be usurped by the conduct and valour of their lieutenants. The military fame of a subject was considered as an insolent invasion of the Imperial prerogative; and it became the duty, as well as interest, of every Roman general, to guard the frontiers entrusted to his care, without aspiring to conquests which might have proved no less fatal to himself[23] than to the vanquished barbarians.

[**The conquest of Britain**]

The only accession[24] which the Roman empire received during the first century of the Christian æra was the province of Britain. In this single instance the successors of Cæsar and Augustus were persuaded to follow the example of the former, rather than the precept of the latter.[25] The proximity of its situation to the coast of Gaul[26] seemed to invite their arms; the pleasing, though doubtful, intelligence[27] of a pearl fishery attracted their avarice; and as Britain was viewed in the light of a distinct and insulated world, the conquest scarcely formed any exception to the general system of continental measures. After a war of about forty years, undertaken by the most stupid, maintained by the most dissolute, and terminated by the most timid of all the emperors,[28] the far greater part of the island submitted to the Roman yoke. The various tribes of Britons possessed valour without conduct, and the love of freedom without the spirit of union. They took up arms with savage fierceness, they laid them down, or turned them against each other with wild inconstancy; and while they fought singly, they were successively subdued. Neither the fortitude of Caractacus,[29] nor the despair of Boadicea,[30] nor the fanaticism of the Druids,[31] could avert the slavery of their country, or resist the steady progress of the Imperial generals, who maintained the national glory, when the throne was disgraced by the weakest or the most vicious of mankind. At the very time when Domitian, confined to his palace, felt the terrors which he inspired, his legions, under the command of the virtuous Agricola,[32] defeated the collected force of the Caledonians[33] at the foot of the Grampian hills; and his fleets, venturing to explore an unknown and dangerous navigation, displayed the Roman arms round every part of the island. The conquest of Britain was considered as already achieved; and it was the design of Agricola to complete and ensure his success by the easy reduction of Ireland, for which, in his opinion, one legion and a few auxiliaries were sufficient. The western isle might be improved into a valuable possession, and the Britons would wear their chains with the less reluctance, if the prospect and example of freedom was on every side removed from before their eyes.

But the superior merit of Agricola soon occasioned his removal from the government of Britain; and for ever disappointed this rational, though extensive, scheme of conquest. Before his departure the prudent general had provided for security as well as for dominion. He had observed that the island is almost divided into two unequal parts by the opposite gulfs or, as they are now called, the Friths of Scotland. Across the narrow interval of about forty miles he had drawn a line of military stations, which was afterwards fortified, in the reign of Antoninus Pius, by a turf rampart,[34] erected on foundations of stone. This wall of Antoninus, at a small distance beyond the modern cities of Edinburgh and Glasgow, was fixed as the limit of the Roman province. The native Caledonians preserved, in the northern extremity of the island, their wild independence, for which they were not less indebted to their poverty than to their valour. Their incursions were frequently repelled and chastised; but their country was never subdued. The masters of the fairest and most wealthy climates of the globe[35] turned with contempt from gloomy hills assailed by the winter tempest, from lakes concealed in a blue mist, and from cold and lonely heaths, over which the deer of the forest were chased by a troop of naked barbarians.

[Trajan's military exploits]

Such was the state of the Roman frontiers, and such the maxims of Imperial policy, from the death of Augustus to the accession of Trajan. That virtuous and active prince had received the education of a soldier, and possessed the talents of a general.[36] The peaceful system of his predecessors was interrupted by scenes of war and conquest; and the legions, after a long interval, beheld a military emperor at their head. The first exploits of Trajan were against the Dacians, the most warlike of men, who dwelt beyond the Danube, and who, during the reign of Domitian, had insulted, with impunity, the majesty of Rome. To the strength and fierceness of barbarians they added a contempt for life, which was derived from a warm persuasion[37] of the immortality and transmigration of the soul. Decebalus, the Dacian king, approved himself[38] a rival not unworthy of Trajan; nor did he despair of his own and the public fortune, till, by the confession of his enemies,[39] he had exhausted every resource both of valour and policy. This memorable war, with a very short suspension of hostilities, lasted five years; and as the emperor could exert, without control, the whole force of the state, it was terminated by the absolute submission of the barbarians. The new province of Dacia, which formed a second exception to the precept of Augustus, was about thirteen hundred miles in circumference. Its natural boundaries were the Dniester, the Theiss, or Tibiscus, the Lower Danube, and the Euxine Sea.[40] The vestiges of a military road may still be traced from the banks of the Danube to the neighbourhood of Bender, a place famous in modern history,[41] and the actual frontier of the Turkish and Russian Empires.

Trajan was ambitious of fame; and as long as mankind shall continue to bestow more liberal applause on their destroyers than on their benefactors, the thirst of military glory will ever be the vice of the most exalted characters. The praises of Alexander,[42] transmitted by a succession of poets and historians, had kindled a dangerous emulation in the mind of Trajan. Like him, the Roman emperor undertook an expedition against the nations of the East, but he lamented with a sigh[43] that his advanced age scarcely left him any hopes of equalling the renown of the son of Philip. Yet the success of Trajan, however transient, was rapid and specious.[44] The degenerate Parthians, broken by intestine discord, fled before his arms. He descended the river Tigris in triumph, from the mountains of Armenia to the Persian Gulf. He enjoyed the honour of being the first, as he was the last, of the Roman generals, who ever navigated that remote sea. His fleets ravaged the coasts of Arabia; and Trajan vainly flattered himself that he was approaching towards the confines of India. Every day the astonished senate received the intelligence of new names[45] and new nations that acknowledged his sway. They were informed that the kings of Bosphorus, Colchos, Iberia, Albania, Osrhoene, and even the Parthian monarch himself, had accepted their diadems from the hands of the emperor; that the independent tribes of the Median and Carduchian hills had implored his protection; and that the rich countries of Armenia, Mesopotamia, and Assyria, were reduced into the state of provinces. But the death of Trajan[46] soon clouded the splendid prospect; and it was justly to be dreaded that so many distant nations would throw off the unaccustomed yoke, when they were no longer restrained by the powerful hand which had imposed it.

[Hadrian, succeeding Trajan, resigns Trajan's conquests]

It was an ancient tradition that, when the Capitol[47] was founded by one of the Roman kings, the god Terminus[48] (who presided over boundaries, and was represented according to the fashion of that age by a large stone) alone, among all the inferior deities, refused to yield his place to Jupiter himself. A favourable inference was drawn from his obstinacy, which was interpreted by the augurs as a sure presage that the boundaries of the Roman power would never recede. During many ages, the prediction, as it is usual, contributed to its own accomplishment.[49] But though Terminus had resisted the majesty of Jupiter, he submitted to the authority of the emperor Hadrian.[50] The resignation of all the eastern conquests of Trajan was the first measure of his reign. He restored to the Parthians the election of an independent sovereign; withdrew the Roman garrisons from the provinces of Armenia, Mesopotamia, and Assyria; and, in compliance with the precepts of Augustus, once more established the Euphrates as the frontier of the empire. Censure,[51] which arraigns[52] the public actions and the private motives of princes, has ascribed to envy a conduct which might be attributed to the prudence and moderation of Hadrian. The various character of that emperor, capable, by turns, of the meanest and the most generous sentiments, may afford some colour to the suspicion. It was, however, scarcely in his power to place the superiority of his predecessor in a more conspicuous light, than by thus confessing himself unequal to the task of defending the conquests of Trajan.[53]

[Hadrian compared with his successor: Antoninus Pius]

The martial and ambitious spirit of Trajan formed a very singular contrast with the moderation of his successor. The restless activity of Hadrian was not less remarkable when compared with the gentle repose of Antoninus Pius. The life of the former was almost a perpetual journey; and as he possessed the various talents of the soldier, the statesman, and the scholar, he gratified his curiosity in the discharge of his duty. Careless of the difference of seasons and of climates, he marched on foot, and bareheaded, over the snows of Caledonia, and the sultry plains of the Upper Egypt; nor was there a province of the empire which, in the course of his reign, was not honoured with the presence of the monarch. But the tranquil life of Antoninus Pius was spent in the bosom of Italy; and, during the twenty-three years that he directed the public administration, the longest journeys of that amiable prince extended no farther than from his palace in Rome to the retirement of his Lanuvian villa.[54]

[Summary of Roman policy of moderation]

Notwithstanding this difference in their personal conduct the general system of Augustus was equally adopted and uniformly pursued by Hadrian and by the two Antonines. They persisted in the design of maintaining the dignity of the empire, without attempting to enlarge its limits. By every honourable expedient they invited the friendship of the barbarians; and endeavoured to convince mankind that the Roman power, raised above the temptation of conquest, was actuated only by the love of order and justice. During a long period of forty-three years their virtuous labours were crowned with success; and, if we except a few slight hostilities that served to exercise the legions of the frontier, the reigns of Hadrian and Antoninus Pius offer the fair prospect of universal peace.[55] The Roman name was revered among the most remote nations of the earth. The fiercest barbarians frequently submitted their differences to the arbitration of the emperor; and we are informed by a contemporary historian that he had seen ambassadors who were refused the honour which they came to solicit, of being admitted into the rank of subjects.

The terror of the Roman arms added weight and dignity to the moderation of the emperors. They preserved peace by a constant preparation for war; and while justice regulated their conduct, they announced to the nations on their confines that they were as little disposed to endure as to offer an injury. The military strength, which it had been sufficient for Hadrian and the elder Antoninus to display, was exerted against the Parthians and the Germans by the emperor Marcus. The hostilities of the barbarians provoked the resentment of that philosophic monarch, and, in the prosecution of a just defence, Marcus and his generals obtained many signal victories, both on the Euphrates and on the Danube. The military establishment of the Roman empire, which thus assured either its tranquillity or success, will now become the proper and important object of our attention.

[**Philosophy of Roman arms**]

In the purer ages of the commonwealth,[56] the use of arms was reserved for those ranks of citizens who had a country to love, a property to defend, and some share in enacting those laws which it was their interest, as well as duty, to maintain. But in proportion as the public freedom was lost in extent of conquest, war was gradually improved into an art, and degraded into a trade. The legions themselves, even at the time when they were recruited in the most distant provinces, were supposed to consist of Roman citizens. That distinction was generally considered either as a legal qualification or as a proper recompense for the soldier;[57] but a more serious regard was paid to the essential merit of age, strength, and military stature. In all levies, a just preference was given to the climates of the north over those of the south; the race of men born to the exercise of arms was sought for in the country rather than in cities, and it was very reasonably presumed that the hardy occupations of smiths, carpenters, and huntsmen would supply more vigour and resolution than the sedentary trades which are employed in the service of luxury After every qualification of property had been laid aside, the armies of the Roman emperors were still commanded, for the most part, by officers of a liberal birth and education;[58] but the common soldiers, like the mercenary troops of modern Europe, were drawn from the meanest, and very frequently from the most profligate, of mankind.

That public virtue, which among the ancients was denominated patriotism, is derived from a strong sense of our own interest in the preservation and prosperity of the free government of which we are members. Such a sentiment, which had rendered the legions of the republic almost invincible, could make but a very feeble impression on the mercenary servants of a despotic prince; and it became necessary to supply that defect by other motives, of a different, but not less forcible nature—honour and religion. The peasant, or mechanic, imbibed the useful prejudice that he was advanced to the more dignified profession of arms, in which his rank and reputation would depend on his own valour; and that, although the prowess of a private soldier must often escape the notice of fame, his own behaviour might sometimes confer glory or disgrace on the company, the legion, or even the army, to whose honours he was associated. On his first entrance into the service, an oath was administered to him with every circumstance of solemnity. He promised never to desert his standard, to submit his own will to the commands of his leaders, and to sacrifice his life for the safety of the emperor and the empire. The attachment of the Roman troops to their standards was inspired by the united influence of religion and of honour. The golden eagle, which glittered in front of the legion,[59] was the object of their fondest devotion; nor was it esteemed less impious than it was ignominious, to abandon that sacred ensign in the hour of danger.[60] These motives, which derived their strength from the imagination, were enforced by fears and hopes of a more substantial kind. Regular pay, occasional donatives,[61] and a stated recompense, after the appointed term of service, alleviated the hardships of the military life, whilst, on the other hand, it was impossible for cowardice or disobedience to escape the severest punishment. The centurions[62] were authorised to chastise with blows, the generals had a right to punish with death, and it was an inflexible maxim of Roman discipline, that a good soldier should dread his officers far more than the enemy. From such laudable arts did the valour of the Imperial troops receive a degree of firmness and docility, unattainable by the impetuous and irregular passions of barbarians.

[Military exercises and discipline]

And yet so sensible were the Romans of the imperfection of valour without skill or practice, that, in their language, the name of an army was borrowed from the word which signified exercise.[63] Military exercises were the important and unremitted object of their discipline. The recruits and young soldiers were constantly trained, both in the morning and in the evening, nor was age or knowledge allowed to excuse the veterans from the daily repetition of what they had completely learnt. Large sheds were erected in the winter quarters of the troops, that their useful labours might not receive any interruption from the most tempestuous weather; and it was carefully observed, that the arms destined to this imitation of war should be of double the weight which was required in real action. It is not the purpose of this work to enter into any minute description of the Roman exercises. We shall only remark that they comprehended whatever could add strength to the body, activity to the limbs, or grace to the motions. The soldiers were diligently instructed to march, to run, to leap, to swim, to carry heavy burdens, to handle every species of arms that was used either for offence or for defence, either in distant engagement or in a closer onset; to form a variety of evolutions; and to move to the sound of flutes in the Pyrrhic or martial dance.[64] In the midst of peace, the Roman troops familiarised themselves with the practice of war; and it is prettily remarked by an ancient historian who had fought against them, that the effusion of blood was the only circumstance which distinguished a field of battle from a field of exercise. It was the policy of the ablest generals, and even of the emperors themselves, to encourage these military studies[65] by their presence and example; and we are informed that Hadrian, as well as Trajan, frequently condescended to instruct the inexperienced soldiers, to reward the diligent, and sometimes to dispute[66] with them the prize of superior strength or dexterity. Under the reigns of those princes, the science of tactics was cultivated with success; and as long as the empire retained any vigour, their military instructions were respected as the most perfect model of Roman discipline.

[Composition of a Roman legion]

Nine centuries of war had gradually introduced into the service many alterations and improvements. The legions, as they are described by Polybius,[67] in the time of the Punic wars, differed very materially from those which achieved the victories of Cæsar, or defended the monarchy of Hadrian and the Antonines. The constitution of the Imperial legion may be described in a few words. The heavy armed infantry, which composed its principal strength, was divided into ten cohorts,[68] and fifty-five companies, under the orders of a correspondent number of tribunes[69] and centurions. The first cohort, which always claimed the post of honour and the custody of the eagle, was formed of eleven hundred and five soldiers, the most approved for valour and fidelity. The remaining nine cohorts consisted each of five hundred and fifty-five; and the whole body of legionary infantry amounted to six thousand one hundred men. Their arms were uniform, and admirably adapted to the nature of their service; an open helmet, with a lofty crest; a breast-plate, or coat of mail; greaves on their legs, and an ample buckler on their left arm. The buckler was of an oblong and concave figure, four feet in length, and two and a half in breadth, framed of a light wood, covered with a bull's hide, and strongly guarded with plates of brass. Besides a lighter spear, the legionary soldier grasped in his right hand the formidable *pilum*, a ponderous javelin, whose utmost length was about six feet, and which was terminated by a massy triangular point of steel of eighteen inches. This instrument was indeed much inferior to our modern fire-arms; since it was exhausted by a single discharge, at the distance of only ten or twelve paces. Yet, when it was launched by a firm and skilful hand, there was not any cavalry that durst[70] venture within its reach, nor any shield or corslet[71] that could sustain the impetuosity of its weight. As soon as the Roman had darted his *pilum*, he drew his sword, and rushed forwards to close with the enemy. It was a short well-tempered Spanish blade, that carried a double edge, and was alike suited to the purpose of striking or of pushing; but the soldier was always instructed to prefer the latter use of his weapon, as his own body remained less exposed, whilst he inflicted a more dangerous wound on his adversary. The legion was usually drawn up eight deep; and the regular distance of three feet was left between the files as well as ranks. A body of troops, habituated to preserve this open order, in a long front and a rapid charge, found themselves prepared to execute every disposition which the circumstances of war, or the skill of their leader, might suggest. The soldier possessed a free space for his arms and motions, and sufficient intervals were allowed, through which seasonable reinforcements might be introduced to the relief of the exhausted combatants. The tactics of the Greeks and Macedonians were formed on very different principles. The strength of the phalanx[72] depended on sixteen ranks of long pikes, wedged together in the closest array. But it was soon discovered, by reflection as well as by the event, that the strength of the phalanx was unable to contend with the activity of the legion.

[The Roman cavalry described]

The cavalry, without which the force of the legion would have remained imperfect, was divided into ten troops or squadrons; the first, as the companion of the first cohort, consisted of an hundred and thirty-two men; whilst each of the other nine amounted only to sixty-six. The entire establishment formed a regiment, if we may use the modern expression, of seven hundred and twenty-six horse,[73] naturally connected with its respective legion, but occasionally separated to act in the line, and to compose a part of the wings of the army. The cavalry of the emperors was no longer composed, like that of the ancient republic, of the noblest youths of Rome and Italy, who, by performing their military service on horseback, prepared themselves for the offices of senator and consul; and solicited, by deeds of valour, the future suffrages of their countrymen. Since the alteration of manners and government, the most wealthy of the equestrian order[74] were engaged in the administration of justice, and of the revenue; and whenever they embraced the profession of arms, they were immediately entrusted with a troop of horse, or a cohort of foot. Trajan and Hadrian formed their cavalry from the same provinces, and the same class of their subjects, which recruited the ranks of the legion. The horses were bred, for the most part, in Spain or Cappadocia. The Roman troopers despised the complete armour with which the cavalry of the East were encumbered. *Their* more useful arms consisted in a helmet, an oblong shield, light boots, and a coat of mail. A javelin, and a long broad sword, were their principal weapons of offence. The use of lances and of iron maces they seemed to have borrowed from the barbarians.

[**Auxiliaries to the legions**]

The safety and honour of the empire was principally entrusted to the legions, but the policy of Rome condescended to adopt every useful instrument of war. Considerable levies[75] were regularly made among the provincials,[76] who had not yet deserved the honourable distinction of Romans. Many dependent princes and communities, dispersed round the frontiers, were permitted, for a while, to hold their freedom and security by the tenure of military service. Even select troops of hostile barbarians were frequently compelled or persuaded to consume their dangerous valour in remote climates, and for the benefit of the state. All these were included under the general name of auxiliaries; and howsoever they might vary according to the difference of times and circumstances, their numbers were seldom much inferior to those of the legions themselves. Among the auxiliaries the bravest and most faithful bands were placed under the command of præfects[77] and centurions, and severely trained in the arts of Roman discipline; but the far greater part retained those arms, to which the nature of their country, or their early habits of life, more peculiarly adapted them.[78] By this institution each legion, to whom a certain proportion of auxiliaries was allotted, contained within itself every species of lighter troops, and of missile weapons; and was capable of encountering every nation with the advantages of its respective arms and discipline. Nor was the legion destitute of what, in modem language, would be styled a train of artillery. It consisted in ten military engines of the largest, and fifty-five of a smaller size; but all of which, either in an oblique or horizontal manner, discharged stones and darts with irresistible violence.

[A Roman camp; a Roman legion on march]

The camp of a Roman legion presented the appearance of a fortified city. As soon as the space was marked out,[79] the pioneers carefully levelled the ground, and removed every impediment that might interrupt its perfect regularity. Its form was an exact quadrangle; and we may calculate that a square of about seven hundred yards was sufficient for the encampment of twenty thousand Romans; though a similar number of our own troops would expose to the enemy a front of more than treble that extent. In the midst of the camp, the prætorium, or general's quarters, rose above the others; the cavalry, the infantry, and the auxiliaries occupied their respective stations; the streets were broad and perfectly straight, and a vacant space of two hundred feet was left on all sides, between the tents and the rampart. The rampart itself was usually twelve feet high, armed with a line of strong and intricate palisades, and defended by a ditch of twelve feet in depth as well as in breadth. This important labour was performed by the hands of the legionaries themselves; to whom the use of the spade and the pick-axe was no less familiar than that of the sword or *pilum*. Active valour may often be the present of nature; but such patient diligence can be the fruit only of habit and discipline.[80]

Whenever the trumpet gave the signal of departure, the camp was almost instantly broken up, and the troops fell into their ranks without delay or confusion.[81] Besides their arms, which the legionaries scarcely considered as an encumbrance, they were laden with their kitchen furniture, the instruments of fortification, and the provision of many days. Under this weight, which would oppress the delicacy of a modern soldier, they were trained by a regular step to advance, in about six hours, near twenty miles. On the appearance of an enemy, they threw aside their baggage,[82] and, by easy and rapid evolutions, converted the column of march into an order of battle. The slingers and archers skirmished in the front; the auxiliaries formed the first line, and were seconded or sustained by the strength of the legions; the cavalry covered the flanks, and the military engines were placed in the rear.

[**Total strength of Roman army: its distribution**]

Such were the arts of war, by which the Roman emperors defended their extensive conquests, and preserved a military spirit, at a time when every other virtue was oppressed by luxury and despotism. If, in the consideration of their armies, we pass from their discipline to their numbers, we shall not find it easy to define them with any tolerable accuracy. We may compute, however, that the legion, which was itself a body of six thousand eight hundred and thirty-one Romans, might, with its attendant auxiliaries, amount to about twelve thousand five hundred men. The peace establishment of Hadrian and his successors was composed of no less than thirty of these formidable brigades; and most probably formed a standing force of three hundred and seventy-five thousand men. Instead of being confined within the walls of fortified cities, which the Romans considered as the refuge of weakness or pusillanimity, the legions were encamped on the banks of the great rivers, and along the frontiers of the barbarians. As their stations, for the most part, remained fixed and permanent, we may venture to describe the distribution of the troops.[83] Three legions were sufficient for Britain. The principal strength lay upon the Rhine and Danube, and consisted of sixteen legions, in the following proportions: two in the Lower, and three in the Upper Germany; one in Rhætia, one in Noricum, four in Pannonia, three in Mæsia, and two in Dacia. The defence of the Euphrates was entrusted to eight legions, six of whom were planted in Syria, and the other two in Cappadocia. With regard to Egypt, Africa, and Spain, as they were far removed from any important scene of war, a single legion maintained the domestic tranquillity of each of those great provinces. Even Italy was not left destitute of a military force. Above twenty thousand chosen soldiers, distinguished by the titles of City Cohorts and Prætorian Guards, watched over the safety of the monarch and the capital. As the authors of almost every revolution that distracted the empire, the Prætorians will very soon and very loudly demand our attention; but, in their arms and institutions, we cannot find any circumstance which discriminated them from the legions, unless it were a more splendid appearance, and a less rigid discipline.

[The Roman navy]

The navy maintained by the emperors might seem inadequate to their greatness; but it was fully sufficient for every useful purpose of government. The ambition of the Romans was confined to the land; nor was that warlike people ever actuated by the enterprising spirit which had prompted the navigators of Tyre,[84] of Carthage, and even of Marseilles, to enlarge the bounds of the world, and to explore the most remote coasts of the ocean. To the Romans the ocean remained an object of terror rather than of curiosity;[85] the whole extent of the Mediterranean, after the destruction of Carthage and the extirpation of the pirates, was included within their provinces. The policy of the emperors was directed only to preserve the peaceful dominion of that sea, and to protect the commerce of their subjects. With these moderate views Augustus stationed two permanent fleets in the most convenient ports of Italy, the one at Ravenna, on the Adriatic, the other at Misenum, in the Bay of Naples. Experience seems at length to have convinced the ancients that, as soon as their galleys exceeded two, or at the most three ranks of oars, they were suited rather for vain pomp than for real service. Augustus himself, in the victory of Actium, had seen the superiority of his own light frigates (they were called Liburnians) over the lofty but unwieldy castles of his rival. Of these Liburnians he composed the two fleets of Ravenna and Misenum, destined to command, the one the eastern, and the other the western division of the Mediterranean; and to each of the squadrons he attached a body of several thousand marines. Besides these two ports, which may be considered as the principal seats of the Roman navy, a very considerable force was stationed at Frejus, on the coast of Provence, and the Euxine was guarded by forty ships, and three thousand soldiers. To all these we add the fleet which preserved the communication between Gaul and Britain, and a great number of vessels constantly maintained on the Rhine and Danube, to harass the country or to intercept the passage of the barbarians. If we review this general state of the Imperial forces, of the cavalry as well as infantry, of the legions, the auxiliaries, the guards, and the navy, the most liberal computation[86] will not allow us to fix the entire establishment by sea and by land at more than four hundred and fifty thousand men; a military power which, however formidable it may seem, was equalled by a monarch of the last century, whose kingdom was confined within a single province of the Roman empire.

We have attempted to explain the spirit which moderated, and the strength which supported, the power of Hadrian and the Antonines. We shall now endeavour, with clearness and precision, to describe the provinces once united under their sway, but, at present, divided into so many independent and hostile states.

[Here Gibbon goes on to describe the various provinces comprising the Roman empire. These are:

Spain, the western extremity of the empire;
Ancient Gaul, which was of greater extent than modern France;
Britain, which comprehended England, Wales, and the Lowlands of Scotland;
Rhætia, Noricum, Pannonia, Dalmatia, Dacia, Mæsia, Thrace, Macedonia, and Greece;
The provinces of Asia, including Syria, Phoenicia, Palestine;
Egypt;
Africa north of the Sahara; and
The islands in the Mediterranean.

Having done this, Gibbon concludes the opening chapter of his *History of the Decline and Fall of the Roman Empire* with a paragraph describing the extent of the empire.]

[The concluding paragraph]

This long enumeration of provinces, whose broken fragments have formed so many powerful kingdoms, might almost induce us to forgive the vanity or ignorance of the ancients.[87] Dazzled with the extensive sway, the irresistible strength, and the real or affected moderation of the emperors, they permitted themselves to despise, and sometimes to forget, the outlying countries which had been left in the enjoyment of a barbarous independence; and they gradually assumed the licence of confounding the Roman monarchy with the globe of the earth. But the temper, as well as knowledge, of a modern historian require a more sober and accurate language. He may impress a juster image of the greatness of Rome by observing that the empire was above two thousand miles in breadth, from the wall of Antoninus and the northern limits of Dacia to Mount Atlas and the tropic of Cancer; that it extended in length more than three thousand miles, from the Western Ocean to the Euphrates; that it was situated in the finest part of the Temperate Zone, between the twenty-fourth and fifty-sixth degrees of northern latitude; and that it was supposed to contain above sixteen hundred thousand square miles, for the most part of fertile and well-cultivated land.

【作者简介】 Edward Gibbon（爱德华·吉朋，1737—1794），幼时多病，不假师训，恣情浏览。十四岁，已读英文欧洲古代史七家，渐及土耳其东方史，十六岁到瑞士洛桑，居四年，读法国史家与希腊拉丁史家。1764 年，吉朋二十七岁，游罗马，登坎毕朵岭，在夕阳中俯视坏垣断壁，感古今盛衰，立志写罗马帝国衰亡史，1787 年全书成，前后二十三年。

【题解与注释】

英国历史家中有吉朋，英国的诗家中有莎士比亚，两者都是峰巅的人物，这个地位是不争的。吉朋的《罗马衰亡史》是一部二百多万字的历史巨著，它写了欧洲历史上一千三百多年（从纪元后二世纪到十五世纪）的沧桑变幻，可以说为这段历史刻石制碑。知道这块碑的人不一定很多，驻足细读的可能更少，但是在这上面储存的信息——疆域，兵制，征战，变乱，治绩，都邑，民族，方物，教制，等等——是十分丰富又是饶有哲理的，稍稍读几段，便觉气势不凡。请看第一章的第一段：

“耶稣降生后第二世纪，罗马帝国拥天下之沃野平川，生民教化，世莫有二。历朝军威，余烈犹存；军纪严明，军士奋勇，故边疆远及八荒，守卫无虞。法制文治，立法宽而执法严，故州郡一心，协洽无懈。庶民安居乐业，生活富足，且及奢侈逸乐矣。古时所订宪法，予民自由，是时仍受尊重，但仅有其表而已。中枢国会，名义上享有最高主权，然政府行政之权，已委诸皇帝。纳尔凡帝，特莱强帝，海德梁帝，又安东尼前后二帝，兹五帝者，德行高而治国有方，凡八十年，是罗马帝国之盛世。本书第一、二、三诸章，述五帝民富国泰之治；第四章起，自安东尼后帝逝世，叙罗马帝国衰落之经过，覆亡之缘由，追溯往史，揭其梗要。盖此乃欧洲史上翻天覆地不可磨灭之变化，其影响所及今日各国犹感觉之。”

吉朋又善于用动态描写。他写罗马兵制，绝无“守则”“操典”一类文字的枯燥，而是写出发军号响了以后的活动（见 593 页第 2 段）：

“出发之军号既响，全营撤帐，军士整队，秩然有序，不稍迟误。重兵在肩，已习以为常，复有锅炊之具，筑垒之具，及备用粮草，均须担负以行。然以训练有素，步伐整齐，虽有辎重之荷，仍能六小时行军二十英里。今世惯养之兵士，恐不能胜此。”

吉朋巨著中可选的本末记事是很多的。有名的是叙基督教兴起，伊斯兰之勃发，君士坦丁城的攻占诸章。但是从章法和详实细密看，从文章的气势看，吉朋自己最珍视的是数易其稿的头上三章。这三章之中，有的选本（例如《牛津英国文学选》）选了第三章，我这里选的是开宗明义的第一章。这一章分三部分：军略、兵制、州郡藩属，其中第三部分删了几页。文章中的小标题是我加的。

吉朋的《衰亡史》的版本是完善的。在吉朋生前，就亲自校阅了第一版和第二版。这部史书所涉及的原始文献，本来是英国大学里历史学科和希腊罗马文献学科的研究对象。在上一个世纪里，各家注释本是不少的。也还有法国历史家和政治家基佐（François Guizot）的法译注释本（1812），考订原始史料甚详。他的注释很多被后来英国注家所吸收，例如 W. Smith 所编的 1854 年牛津本。最权威的英国注释本是 J. B. Bury 的七卷本（1896—1900）。1910 年出版的 Oliphant Smeaton 六卷万人丛书本则吸收了 Guizot 与 Bury 之长。我这次据以排印第一章原文的是 J. H. Fowler 所编的《安东尼前后二帝的时代：吉朋罗马帝国衰亡史第一章至第三章》，1938 年出版。我在注释中采用他的地方约 10 处，均予注明（J. H. F.）。此外，我主要参考《牛津古典文史备要》，1937 年本（*The Oxford Companion to Classical Literature*, ed. Sir Paul Harvey, 1937）。这本《备要》有详细的传记和分目长篇，非常有用。

[*THE EXTENT AND MILITARY FORCE OF THE EMPIRE*]

1. Æra: = era; similarly, Æthiopia = Ethiopia (2.26).
comprehend: = embrace, include.

2. manners: = civil rule, civilization (J. H. F.)

3. image of a free constitution = semblance of a free constitution; that is, the constitution is free in name only, not in reality.

4. Nerva (96–98)**, Trajan** (98–118)**, Hadrian** (117–138)**, Antoninus Pius** (138–161) **and the adopted son of Antoninus, Marcus Aurelius** (161–180)**:** all Roman emperors. The last two named = the two Antonines.

5. revolution: = a great change in human affairs.

[*AUGUSTUS'S POLICY OF MODERATION*]

6. under the republic: = during the days when Rome was still a republic, that is, during the six centuries from the founding of Rome as a republic (510 B. C.) to 27 B. C. when Augustus Octavianus became emperor (27 B. C.–14 A. D.)

7. consuls: = the two highest magistrates of the republic, elected annually.

8. The seven first centuries: Rome was traditionally founded by Romulus in 753 B. C. In the ensuing seven centuries Rome extended its dominion to include the whole of Western Europe and Armenia and Mesopotamia, and also North Africa.

9. had much less to hope than to fear from the chance of arms: wars could be uncertain; Rome, with already a vast empire to govern, had more to lose than to gain from further wars.

10. and the possession more precarious than beneficial: even if Rome were to gain more territories from conquests, it would be uncertain (precarious) if Rome could keep hold of them. (Rome would not be able to station sufficient troops there to maintain its rule.)

11. salutary reflections: wise considerations, ideas that lead to beneficial results.

12. concession: by a barbarian people who agreed to surrender to Rome a piece of land which in Rome's view was necessary for the empire's defence, or to give back war booties taken in war with Rome.

13. barbarians: = any non-Roman or non-Greek people, and also, later, any non-Christian people, not necessarily a wild, uncivilized people.

14. in the defeat of Crassus: the defeat of Marcus Licinius Crassus, Roman consul whose army was completely routed by Parthian archers in 53 B. C. Parthians = soldiers of Parthia (帕提亚，即安息), an Asian empire which at its height (1st century B. C.) extended from the Eurphrates across Afghanistan to the Indus and from the Oxus to the Indian Ocean. (Oxus = today's Amu Darya)

15. Instead of exposing his person and his legions to the arrows of the Parthians, he (Augustus) obtained, by an honourable treaty, the restitution of the standards and prisoners which had been taken in the defeat of Crassus: Augustus saw the wisdom of not going to war with the Parthians, whose archers were deadly. (He chose not to expose his person to their arrows.) By peaceful negotiations he made the Parthians agree to return the Roman flags (standards) and prisoners captured during the war of 53 B. C.

16. Arabia Felix: southeastern Arabia. (J. H. F.)

[*FURTHER CONQUESTS HARDLY PRACTICABLE*]

17. Despised life when it was separated from freedom: would rather die as soon as deprived of freedom.

18. testament: the advice bequeathed by a great statesman to his nation.

19. on the west the Atlantic Ocean: the Rhine and Danube on the north (*not* on the north the Rhine and Danube): to achieve variation of prose rhythm.

20. This paragraph that ends here is a good example of cohesion. The main point is that Augustus's counsel of moderation was also the result of experience, not just philosophical insight. Conquests into the deep south were impossible because of the intense heat; conquests into Germany were equally impossible because the hardy Germans would rather die than live enslaved. On his death Augustus left word that he wanted the nation to be content with the empire as it was. Quite appropriately, the paragragh ends with a description of the empire's boundaries.

21. The moderate system recommended by ... Augustus was adopted by the fears and vices of his immediate successors: Augustus died in A. D. 14; his immediate successors were Tiberius, an able ruler, and the less capable emperors Caligula and Claudius, and the wicked Nero. The less capable rulers refrained from war out of fear; while Nero was simply preoccupied with vice.

22. Nor were they disposed to suffer that: to allow it to happen.

23. Might have proved no less fatal to himself: might have brought death to the general who did aspire to conquest. In fact three generals were checked and recalled in the course of their victories. One was put to death. (J. H. F.)

[*THE CONQUEST OF BRITAIN*]

24. The only accession: = the only territorial acquisition.

25. The successors of Cæsar and Augustus were persuaded to follow the example of the former, rather than the precept of the latter: Julius Cæsar, Roman dictator until his assasination in 44 B. C., landed briefly in Britain in 55 B. C. and returned to conquer it in the following year. However, he left no troops to garrison the conquest. The "accession" Gibbon speaks of apparently refers to the conquest led by Emperor Claudius I, in 43 A. D. Augustus's advice against further imperial expansion has already been noted.

26. Gaul: refers in this case to the Gaul north of the Alps, what is today France, Switzerland, Belgium and the Netherlands, but especially France. Gaul had been a Roman province long before Britain was brought under Roman rule.

27. intelligence: = information.

28. undertaken by the most stupid (Claudius)**, maintained by the most dissolute** (Nero)**, and terminated by the most timid** (Domitian) **of all the emperors:** (J. H. F.)

29. Caractacus: Caractacus(Latin name for Caradoc), king and leader of resistance in the west of Britain, was taken during the reign of Claudius to Rome, where his noble spirit won him a pardon. He figures in a play by Beaumont and Fletcher, *Bonduca*.

30. Boadicea: queen of east Britain who led a revolt against the Romans and took her own life when she was defeated in 61 A. D. She is the subject of a poem by Tennyson.

31. the Druids: priests of the Celts in Britain and Gaul, who formed the core of rebellions against Rome.

32. the virtuous Agricola: Agricola was governor of Britain (78 A. D. – 85 A. D.) and was praised by the Roman historian Tacitus as an enlightened governor who sought to Romanize Britain without harshness or oppression. (Tacitus was Agricola's son-in-law.)

33. Caledonians = Roman name for that part of the island of Great Britain which lies north of the Firths of Clyde and Forth. The Clyde and the Forth are both rivers in Scotland.

the Grampian hills: mountains in Scotland separating the Highlands from the Lowlands.

34. turf rampart: one of the several Roman walls built to keep off invaders from the north.

35. The masters of the fairest and most wealthy climates of the globe: the Romans who inhabit Italy and Gaul. It is not difficult to see where Gibbon's emotional affiliations lie: he identifies himself more as a continental European than as a Briton.

[*TRAJAN'S MILITARY EXPLOITS*]

36. had received the education of a soldier, and possessed the talents of a general: 出身戎伍，而具将才。

37. warm persuasion: passionate belief.

38. approved himself: = demonstrated himself to be.

39. by the confession of his enemies: apparently by the confession of his internal enemies.

40. the Euxine Sea: ancient Greek name of the Black Sea.

41. Bender, a place famous in modern history: a town in Russian Moldavia which the Turks captured in the 16th century. In the 18th century a Swedish king lived near it as the unwelcome guest of the Turkish government.

42. the praises of Alexander: Alexander, son of Philip of Macedon, and the greatest conqueror in ancient times, was the centre of many mediaeval legends.

43. Trajan lamented with a sigh etc.: Gibbon probably had in mind the legend that Alexander lamented with a sigh that the world was too small for him to conquer.

44. specious: making a fair show, presenting a splendid spectacle.

45. the astonished Senate received the intelligence of new names: the government in Rome received with astonishment reports of Trajan's mounting military successes.

46. the death of Trajan: Trajan died on his way home from a campaign against the Parthians.

[*HADRIAN, SUCCEEDING TRAJAN, RESIGNS TRAJAN'S CONQUESTS*]

47. Capitol: (not to be confused with capital, nor with the Congressional Building in

Washington D. C.): English for Latin *Capitolium*, the southwestern summit of the Capitoline Hill in Rome; on this summit was erected the great temple of Jupiter, the special guardian of the city.

48. the god Terminus: a deity inferior in rank to Jupiter, he had the audacity to compete with Jupiter in the order of precedence. A favourable meaning was read into this legend: since Terminus stood for boundary, his refusal to yield was taken to mean that the boundaries of Roman power would never fall back.

49. the prediction, as it is usual, contributed to its own accomplishment: here Gibbon is obviously speaking as a philosopher: man invents an idea and wills himself to act on it.

50. (Terminus) submitted to the authority of the emperor Hadrian: Hadrian resigned the recent conquests made by Trajan and in so doing must have moved back boundary stones of the empire.

51. censure: (here) historical opinion (not necessarily unfavourable).

52. arraign: give a reason to.

53. It was, however, scarcely in his power to place the superiority of his predecessor in a more conspicuous light, than by etc.: Hadrian could not have demonstrated Trajan's superiority more clearly than by admitting his inability to defend the new boundaries.

[*HADRIAN COMPARED WITH HIS SUCCESSOR*] *ANTONINUS PIUS*

54. to the retirement of his Lanuvian villa: to the solitude or privacy of his country-house at Lanuvium. (J. H. F.)

[*SUMMARY OF ROMAN POLICY OF MODERATION*]

55. the fair prospect of universal peace: the Roman-ruled peace during which differences between the smaller nations were submitted to the Roman emperor for arbitration, sometimes called Pax Romana.

[*PHILOSOPHY OF ROMAN ARMS: POLICY OF RECRUITMENT*]

56. In the purer ages of the commonwealth: in the days of the Roman republic, when the political and military machinery was much less sophisticated than it later became.

57. as a proper recompense for the soldier: a recruited soldier would be granted Roman citizenship, a status which brought material advantages.

58. officers of a liberal birth and education: a liberal birth: that of a son of a gentleman's family, not the family of a slave or even of an artisan; liberal education: one directed towards the cultivation of mind and manners, not a technical or professional education.

profligate: abandoned to vice, that is, to drinking and lust

59. The golden eagle, which glittered in front of the legion, etc.: the golden eagle on the legion's standard.

60. Nor was it esteemed less impious than it was ignominious, to abandon that sacred ensign, in the hour of danger: it would be considered as much an act against god as an act against one's code of honour, to yield to the enemy the flag of one's legion during time of war.

61. donatives = gifts.

62. centurion = 百人纵队的队长。

[*MILITARY EXERCISES AND DISCIPLINE*]

63. the name of an army was borrowed from the word which signified exercise: Latin: *exercitus*. (J. H. F.)

64. The soldiers were diligently instructed to etc.: this sentence, with as many as 8 to-phrases, nonetheless achieves a most pleasing rhythm. Note the arrangement:

to march,
to run,
to leap,
to swim,
to carry heavy burdens,
to handle every species of arms that was used
    either for offence or for defence,
    either in distant engagement or in a closer onset;
to form a variety of evolutions; and
to move to the sound of flutes in the Pyrrhic or martial dance.

Note also the punctuation: the six to-phrases before the first semicolon all refer to the performance of the individual soldier; the last two describe group movements.

65. military studies: detailed examination in the art of war.

66. to dispute: to contend.

[*COMPOSITION OF A ROMAN LEGION*]

67. Polybius: historian of the Punic Wars (wars fought between Rome and the African power, Carthage, which lasted off and on from 264–146 B. C.)

68. cohort: division of a Roman army: one tenth of a legion. (J. H. F.)

69. tribunes: the six chief officers of the legion. (J. H. F.)

70. durst: past tense of *dare*, now considered archaic.

71. corslet: = protective body covering of leather or steel.

72. the phalanx: Greek (Macedonian) military formation, consisting of 16 ranks of infantry soldiers, armed with long pikes (spears), 13 to 18 feet in length, so that the formation had the look of an impenetrable thicket of shafts. The Greek phalanx had much less flexibility than the Roman legion.

[*THE ROMAN CAVALRY DESCRIBED*]

73. seven hundred and twenty-six horse: horse = cavalry.

74. equestrian order: Roman 'Knights'. In the early ages of Rome the richest members of the State served in the cavalry; gradually they formed a powerful class of citizens engaged not only in the profession of arms but also in the administration of justice, and also of revenue (that is, as bankers). When in the cavalry, they were invariably given important posts.

[*AUXILIARIES TO THE LEGIONS*]

75. levies: conscription of men for military service.

76. provincials: people in the provinces, non-Roman tribes.

77. præfects: officers in command of the auxiliaries in the Roman army. (J. H. F.)

78. but the far greater part retained those arms to which the nature of their country, or the early habits of life, more peculiarly adapted them: the majority of these barbarian auxiliaries continued to use their own weapons which they had become used to in their home training.

[*A ROMAN CAMP; A ROMAN LEGION ON MARCH*]

79. As soon as the space was marked out, the pioneers carefully levelled the ground, and removed every impediment that might interrupt its perfect regularity: here Gibbon uses what I think might be called *dynamic description*. Instead of describing a camp as it stands, Gibbon presents the reader with one that is being constructed.

80. Active valour may often be the present of nature; but such patient diligence can be the fruit only of habit and discipline: the second observation is Gibbon's own, an experience he probably acquired during the two years he served with the English Militia (1760–1762).

81. Whenever the trumpet gave the signal of departure, the camp was almost instantly broken up, and the troops fell into their ranks without delay or confusion: another example of dynamic description. Here too his Militia experience must have been useful.

82. On the appearance of an enemy, they threw aside their baggage etc.: yet another example of dynamic description. In a modern-day exercise book the description would merely begin with "When in battle, the slingers and archers skirmished in the front etc."

[*TOTAL STRENGTH OF ROMAN ARMY; ITS DISTRIBUTION*]

83. we may venture to describe the distribution of the troops: this is done under five headings, which thanks to the varied sentences still make interesting reading:

Three legions were sufficient for Britain.

The principal strength lay upon the Rhine and the Danube, and consisted of sixteen legions.

The defence of the Euphrates was entrusted to eight legions.

With regard to Egypt, Africa, and Spain, a single legion maintained the tranquility of each.

Even Italy was not left destitute of a military force.

This is what H. W. Fowler would call *elegant variation*; but then the variation in this case seems entirely appropriate for each different region.

84. As the authors of almost every revolution that distracted the empire: many a time in Rome's dismal history a chief conspirator from the Prætorian Guards would murder the reigning emperor and then sell the throne to the highest bidder. Prætorian Guards = 京都警卫军.

[*THE ROMAN NAVY*]

85. Tyre: ancient trading centre of Phoenicia, modern Lebanon.

86. To the Romans the ocean remained an object of terror rather than of curiosity: the Romans believed that the Rock of Gibraltar marked the end of the earth. Roman ambition was always towards the East.

87. the most liberal computation etc.: Gibbon's computation of total strength of Roman infantry, cavalry, the guards and the navy puts it at 450,000 men, a military power which he says "was equalled by a monarch of the last century (i. e. the 17th C.), whose kingdom was confined within a single province of the Roman empire." However, the number of military personnel in most West European nations today is considerably less.

[*THE CONCLUDING PARAGRAPH*]

88. This long enumeration of provinces, whose broken fragments have formed so many powerful kingdoms, might almost induce us to forgive the vanity or the ignorance of the ancients: if the numerous small kingdoms which formed modern Europe had reason to be proud of their wealth and military might, then how much more reason the Romans would have for being vain about their vast empire?

27 WILLIAM BLAKE
1757–1827

王佐良　选注

1. LAUGHING SONG

When the green woods laugh with the voice of joy,
And the dimpling[1] stream runs laughing by;
When the air does laugh with our merry wit,
And the green hill laughs with the noise of it;

When the meadows laugh with lively green,
And the grasshopper laughs in the merry scene,
When Mary and Susan and Emily[2]
With their sweet round mouths sing "Ha, Ha, He!"

When the painted birds[3] laugh in the shade,
Where our table with cherries and nuts is spread,

Come live and be merry, and join with me,
To sing the sweet chorus of "Ha, Ha, He!"

—*Songs of Innocence,* 1789

2. HOLY THURSDAY[1]

Is this a holy thing[2] to see
In a rich and fruitful land,
Babes[3] reduc'd[4] to misery,
Fed with cold and usurous hand?[5]

Is that trembling cry a song?
Can it be a song of joy?
And so many children poor?
It is a land of poverty!

And their sun does never shine,
And their fields are bleak and bare,
And their ways are fill'd with thorns:
It is eternal winter there.

For where-e'er[6] the sun does shine,
And where-e'er the rain does fall,
Babe can never hunger there,
Nor poverty the mind appall.[7]

—*Songs of Experience,* 1794

3. THE CHIMNEY SWEEPER

A little black thing among the snow,
Crying ' 'weep! 'weep! '[1] in notes of woe!
"Where are thy father and mother? say?"
"They are both gone up to the church to pray.

"Because I was happy upon the heath,[2]
"And smil'd[3] among the winter's snow,
"They clothed me in the clothes of death,[4]
"And taught me to sing the notes of woe.[5]

"And because I am happy and dance and sing,[6]
"They think they have done me no injury,
"And are gone to praise God and his Priest and King,
"Who make up a heaven of our misery."[7]

—*ibid.*, 1794

4. THE TIGER

Tiger! Tiger! burning bright
In the forests of the night,[1]
What immortal hand or eye
Could frame thy fearful symmetry?[2]

In what distant deeps or skies
Burnt the fire of thine eyes?
On what wings dare he[3] aspire?[4]
What the hand dare seize the fire?[5]

And what shoulder,[6] and what art,
Could twist the sinews of thy heart?[7]
And when thy heart began to beat,
What dread hand? and what dread feet?[8]

What the hammer?[9] what the chain?
In what furnace was thy brain?[10]
What the anvil? what dread grasp
Dare its deadly terrors clasp?[11]
When the stars threw down their spears,

And water'd heaven with their tears,[12]
Did he smile his work to see?
Did he who made the Lamb[13] make thee?

Tiger! Tiger! burning bright
In the forests of the night,
What immortal hand or eye,
Dare frame thy fearful symmetry?

—*ibid.*, 1794

5. LONDON

I wander thro'[1] each charter'd[2] street,
Near where the charter'd Thames does flow,
And mark[3] in every face I meet
Marks of weakness, marks of woe.[4]

In every[5] cry of every Man,
In every Infant's cry of fear,
In every voice, in every ban,[6]
The mind-forg'd manacles[7] I hear.

How the Chimney-sweeper's cry
Every black'ning[8] Church appalls;[9]
And the hapless Soldier's sigh[10]
Runs in blood down Palace walls.

But most[11] thro' midnight streets I hear
How the youthful Harlot's curse
Blasts[12] the new born Infant's tear,
And blights[13] with plagues the Marriage hearse.[14]

—*ibid.*, 1794

6. AND DID THOSE FEET IN ANCIENT TIME

And did those feet in ancient time
Walk upon England's mountains green?
And was the holy Lamb of God[1]
On England's pleasant pastures seen?

And did the Countenance Divine[2]
Shine forth upon our clouded hills?
And was Jerusalem[3] builded[4] here
Among these dark Satanic Mills?[5]

Bring me my Bow of burning gold:
Bring me my Arrows of desire:[6]
Bring me my Spear: O clouds unfold!
Bring me my Chariot of fire.

I will not cease from Mental Fight,[7]
Nor shall my Sword sleep in my hand
Till we have built Jerusalem
In England's green and pleasant Land.

—Preface to *Milton,* 1808

7. [THE PRICE OF EXPERIENCE]

"What is the price of Experience? do men buy it for a song?[1]
"Or wisdom for a dance in the street[2]? No, it is bought with the price
"Of all that a man hath, his wife, his children.
"Wisdom is sold in the desolate market where none come to buy,
"And in the wither'd field where the farmer plows for bread in vain.

"It is an easy thing to triumph in the summer's sun[3]
"And in the vintage & to sing on the waggon loaded with corn.
"It is an easy thing to talk of patience to the afflicted,[4]
"To speak the laws of prudence to the houseless wanderer,[5]
"To listen to the hungry raven's cry in wintry season[6]
"When the red blood is fill'd with wine & with the marrow of lambs.[7]

"It is an easy thing to laugh at wrathful elements,[8]
"To hear the dog howl at the wintry door, the ox in the slaughter house moan;
"To see a god on every wind & a blessing on every blast;[9]
"To hear sounds of love in the thunder storm that destroys our enemies' house;[10]
"To rejoice in the blight that covers his field, & the sickness that cuts off his children,
"While our olive & vine sing & laugh round our door, & our children bring fruits & flowers.

"Then the groan & the dolor[11] are quite forgotten, & the slave grinding at the mill,[12]
"And the captive in chains, & the poor in the prison, & the soldier in the field
"When the shatter'd bone hath laid him groaning among the happier dead.[13]

"It is an easy thing to rejoice in the tents of prosperity:[14]
"Thus could I sing & thus rejoice: but it is not so with me."[15]

— *Vala*, Night the Second, 1793–1804

【作者简介】 William Blake（威廉·布莱克，1757—1827），英国十八、九世纪之交的重要诗人兼画家，一生清贫，靠刻字雕画为生，深受法国革命所带来的民主思想的影响，对于当时英国社会的罪恶性质有一个手工业者的切身体会，了解甚深，谴责也特别严厉。他热爱儿童，本人所作也表现一片赤子之心。此外，他轻理性，重灵感，有其神秘主义的一面，然又反对官方教会，是非之感强烈，宗教的象征往往结合民主的激情。他在世时并无诗名，所作绝大部分系自刻自印，其中短诗合集 *Songs of Innocence*（《天真之歌》，1789）与 *Songs of Experience*（《经验之歌》，1789—1794）文字素朴，形象鲜明，用意深远，久为后世读者所喜爱；长诗如：*The French Revolution* (1791)，*America* (1793), *Vala, or the Four Zoas* (1793–1804), *Milton* (1804–1808), *Jerusalem* (1804–1820) 等虽然大多难懂，近年来也受到学者们更多的注意。

【题解与注释】

我们在此所选的六首短诗，除第一首 *Laughing Song* 来自 *Songs of Innocence*，第六首 *And Did Those Feet in Ancient Time* 来自长诗 *Milton* 的序言部分外，其余四首都见 *Songs of Experience.*《经验之歌》实是《天真之歌》的续篇，初次印行时是同后者合订在一起问世的，而且作者特别标了这样一个总名：SONGS OF INNOCENCE and OF EXPERIENCE / Shewing the Two Contrary States of the Human Soul. 在内容上，两者合起来也确实表现了"人的灵魂的两种相反的状态"，有不少诗题两集都有，如 *The Chimney Sweeper* 与 *Holy Thursday*，然而情景前乐后苦；前一集有 *Infant Joy*，后一集却换成 *Infant Sorrow*；前一集有 *The Little Boy Lost*，但紧接着有 *The Little Boy Found*，后一集则只有 *A Little Boy Lost*；凡此皆系有意为之，总的情绪是《天真之歌》比较愉快，而《经验之歌》则充满沉痛和激越的调子。值得注意的是：两集写成和刻印之间，爆发了法国革命；布莱克对革命寄予深切的同情，本人的思想也受到很大的冲击，革命之前他主要是用孩子似的"天真"眼光来看世界的，革命之后他更清楚地理解到英国人民的苦难，"经验"深刻了，人生的痛苦也增加了。

布莱克的诗有很高的音乐性，如 *The Tiger* 一诗除内容引人注意外，也以一种"打铁似的乐调"（anvil music）著称。

另选长诗 *Vala* 中的一小段，略窥布莱克中期作品之一斑。

各诗版本据 *The Complete Writings of William Blake* (ed. Geoffrey Keynes, London, 1957). 选注者在注释过程中曾参阅几家解释，主要是 David V. Erdman: *Blake Prophet Against Empire* (Princeton, New Jersey, 1954)。

1. LAUGHING SONG

此诗选自 *Songs of Innocence*，调子愉快，代表布莱克在法国革命爆发以前的心情。诗中表现了英国民间生活的乐趣，情调类似莎士比亚的短歌 "Winter"（*Love's Labour's Lost*, V, ii）.

1. dimpling: 河流也在笑，故有酒窝似的微波。

2. Mary, Susan, Emily: 初稿曾作 Edessa, Lyea, Emilie；这一改动使人名大众化，表示是一群民间的小姑娘。

3. painted birds: 有各色美丽羽毛的鸟。

2. HOLY THURSDAY

此诗是 *Songs of Experience* 之一，文字极为简单容易，而形象鲜明，尤其 Fed with cold and usurous hand 一针见血，直指伪善的慈善家，实际上即是商业资本家，看出诗人了解之深，谴责之严；所写的是儿童，作者不仅为他们发言，而且在最后指出只有在一个充满阳光和雨露的地方，儿童才会幸福。通篇含意深远，形式整齐，是高度的朴素与深厚的感情的动人的结合。

写此诗以前不久，诗人曾在 *Songs of Innocence* 中写过一诗，题名也是 *Holy Thursday*，内容也是有关儿童，叙述他们在节日穿着整齐，同慈善家们（the aged men, wise guardians of the poor）坐在一起，在圣保罗大教堂唱赞美诗，纯洁而快乐，诗人称之为 these flowers of London town。

然而法国革命一爆发，诗人的眼睛给海峡对岸的火光照亮了，回顾伦敦，虽然圣节又到，而儿童几乎都成饿莩了！慈善家们虽然仍旧活动，却都露出高利贷者的冰冷脸色。这一变化表示诗人的思想提高了，诗也更加深刻动人了。

1. Holy Thursday: 庆祝耶稣升天节，即 Ascension Day. 十八世纪时，每逢升天节儿童排队往礼拜堂唱赞美诗，慈善家也对贫苦儿童有所施舍。

2. a holy thing: 一上来就针对 holy 一字发言，直截了当地谴责杀害儿童的罪恶社会，反证其毫无神圣可言。

3. babes: 诗中常用，即 babies.

4. reduc'd: reduced.

5. Fed with cold and usurous hand: fed 表示某些儿童受到一些救济，然而救济者的手是冰冷的，而且是放高利贷者的罪恶黑手！在诗人眼中，慈善家的本质便是这样。这里 usurous 一字用得极好，具体，突出，意味深长。《牛津大字典》（*O. E. D.*）并无此字，只有 usurious, usurous 是布莱克特创的。

6. where-e'er: wherever; **does shine**，强调真有阳光；下行 **does fall**，强调真是雨水充足。

7. appall = terrify，这是一个力量很强的及物动词，其宾语为 the mind.

3. THE CHIMNEY SWEEPER

穷孩子爬进烟囱去扫烟，直到出口，大叫一声 'weep!（"扫烟的！"）才算完事，不但一头一脸尽是煤烟，大有窒息的危险，而且有时烟囱刚刚熄火，更有烫伤皮肤的痛苦。多数烟囱小，身体大了过不去，因此扫烟的孩子须年纪特小，身体特瘦。这种惨不忍睹的情况不仅震撼了诗人，也曾促使一些正直人士指责政府。1788 年国会总算通过一个法案，但也不过规定八岁以下的孩子不得扫烟，扫烟的孩子必须每周沐浴一次，雇主不得逼令他们爬入生火未熄的烟囱等等，未能解除他们的痛苦，而且从反面证实了他们受着非人的折磨。他们所扫烟囱，大部分固系住宅，但也有教堂（布莱克对此特别反感）、官署以及正在逐渐多起来的工厂。

布莱克写过两首以“The Chimney Sweeper”为题的诗，一首见 *Songs of Innocence*，一首见 *Songs of Experience*，后者即是此处所选。两诗相隔不过四、五年，但在内容上形成对照。第一首诗也谈到扫烟囱孩子的痛苦，他们感到象是被关闭在黑色的棺材里，但正在此时，天使出现了：

And by came an Angel who had a bright key,
And he open'd the coffins and set them all free;
Then down a green plain leaping, laughing, they run,
And wash in a river, and shine in the Sun.
Then naked and white, all their bags left behind,
They rise upon clouds and sport in the wind;
And the Angel told Tom, if he'd be a good boy,
He'd have God for his father, and never want joy.

意思是，上帝会搭救他们。但是不过几年之后，当布莱克来写第二首诗的时候，他似乎特别针对这点，做了翻案文章。上帝不仅不能救扫烟囱的孩子，而且同教士和国王合伙，把天堂建筑在他们的痛苦之上。两相对照，看出在法国革命刚刚爆发的动荡岁月里，布莱克对于穷孩子的痛苦，感触更深了，抗议也更强烈了。

诗本身也是从头就充满了对照：当孩子在烟囱里号哭的时候，他的父母倒去教堂感谢上帝；孩子小时在野地玩得快乐，父母却让他穿上黑衣去扫烟囱；因为孩子在每年一定的节日（详下）还会跳舞唱歌，父母以为他没有受到损害；最后一行将宗教和政治的压迫放在一起，并用最简捷的手法指出国王和教士们的天堂是无数扫烟囱孩子（注意诗人用了复数 our）的痛苦所造成的。

诗人用了最简单的语言，平铺直叙，然而口气里充满嘲讽；这嘲讽主要靠形象与情景的对比而得，力量又大过正面的谴责。

1. 'weep!: 乃 Sweep（即 chimney sweep = chimney sweeper）的简体。扫烟囱的孩子在街上要人雇他，高呼此字；扫完烟囱从顶上爬出，报告工作完成，也叫此字。这是一个极惨的声音，在听觉上又与 weep（哭泣）同音。

2. the heath: 野地。童年游玩在自由、快乐的野地上，而现在却钻爬着气闷、黑暗的烟囱，形成两个世界。

3. smil'd: smiled.

4. clothes of death: 指黑色衣服，黑乃死亡之色。

5. to sing the notes of woe: to cry "'weep!"

6. because I am happy and dance and sing: 为什么此处扫烟囱的孩子忽然快乐起来，甚至跳舞唱歌？一个解释是：儿童的快乐天性是怎样也压抑不住的，即在极度苦难之中，也要迸发歌声。但是也另有一解，即布莱克此处指的是五月节的情况，那时扫烟儿同挤奶妇都在街上跳舞，为了得到慈善家的一点施舍。这是当时风俗。布莱克本人曾在 1784 年为 *Wit's Magazine* 刻过一面，就是这个风俗的写照。此面曾经印制，见牛津大学出版的 *Johnson's England* (ed. A. S. Turberville, I, 176). 因此这里他是指一年一度的应景作乐，而且事情本身就又是对扫烟儿的侮辱。

7. Who make up a heaven of our misery: = Who make a heaven out of our misery. 初稿中本行曾作 Who wrap themselves up in our misery，后划去，可以反证此行应作“他们的天堂建筑在我们的苦难上”解。

4. THE TIGER

此诗为 *Songs of Experience* 之一，作于 1793 年以前，在布莱克的笔记本上，曾有两个稿子，连同正式定稿，共有三稿，可见他写得精心。三稿出入不大，有助于阐释的重要差别将在注中说明。

此诗向受读者注意，是布莱克最有名的作品之一，但是对于内容有各种解释，例如“老虎”究竟象征什么，至今尚无定论。

诗中显然有对上帝的歌颂，创造可怕的老虎与和善的小羊的同是上帝，老虎之威势已令人惊怖如此，则其创造者的力量可想而知。但是诗的重点似乎不在崇拜上帝，而且即以上帝而论，布莱克所崇拜的也决非官方教会所标榜的。诗人所深切感到的，倒是老虎所代表的破坏力之巨大，巨大得使得宇宙星座摇坠，天空泪如雨下，因此引起他热烈的赞颂。布莱克对于法国革命的理想心向往之，所作长诗 *The French Revolution* (1791) 鲜明地表明他站在法国人民一边，后来别的文人如 Wordsworth 等骂激进的雅各宾党人，他则始终拥护；他的诗里虽然出现许多神秘的象征，但又总有一种严峻的是非之感。一个对革命同情，对时局敏感的诗人在 1794 年左右赞颂破坏力，这个破坏力可能是指当时法国人民所代表的革命的暴力。

1. burning bright In the forests of the night: 可以照字面解释，即老虎的眼睛在暗中发出特亮的光；但尚有深意。《圣经》《旧约》中有一段话：Deliver him that is spoiled out of the hand of the oppressor, lest my fury go out like fire, and burn that none can quench it, because of the evil of your doings … But I will punish you according to the fruit of your doings, saith the Lord: and I will kindle a fire in the forest thereof, and it shall devour all things round about it. (*Jeremiah*, 21: 12–14) 亦即这老虎所代表的森林里的火焰是指被压迫者反对压迫者的怒火。注意起句突兀，所用各字响亮有力，一开始即显出“打铁似的乐调”。

2. What immortal hand or eye Could frame thy fearful symmetry: 谁的非凡的手能够制出——谁的非凡的眼力又能设想出——你这可怕的形体？ immortal 此处作非凡解；symmetry 一般作“对称”解，此处指老虎身体部位的匀称与机体的健全，总起来即指形体。

3. he: 与第 3 行 What immortal hand or eye 及第 8 行 What the hand 同指老虎的创造者。

4. dare he aspire: 他敢飞得多高？与第 5 行 In what distant deeps or skies 呼应。

5. seize the fire: 谁的手抓得住——创造得出——这样的怒火？

6. what shoulder: 谁有这么大的力气？ **what art,** 谁又有这么高超的技巧？

7. twist the sinews of thy heart: 制造出你的坚强的心脏？ **twist**，扭弯；**sinews**，筋，腱，但此字复数常作“力量”解。

8. What dread hand? and what dread feet?: 未完句，大意可能是：谁的可怕的手和脚能够操纵你，控制你？

dread 在此是形容词，= dreadful, terrible.

一本作 What dread hand Form'd thy dread feet?（谁的可怕的手制出你的可怕的脚？）

9. What the hammer?: 在本节中，诗人用铁匠来比喻老虎的创造者，因此出现本行的 hammer（锤），chain（链），第 14 行的 furnace（打铁炉）及第 15 行的 anvil（砧）等字样。音韵方面，也是突兀、有力，宛似一下一下的铁锤打在砧上，故曰 anvil music.

10. thy brain: 你的脑子是在什么打铁炉里铸炼出来的？

11. what dread grasp Dare its deadly terrors clasp?: 这样使人恐怖的老虎，谁的强有力的大手竟能将它完全控制？ grasp 指“手臂”，初稿曾作 arm，后又划去。

12. When the stars threw down their spears, And water'd heaven with their tears: 两行费解；一个解释是：铁匠抡锤大打，打掉了铁中杂质，一时火花四冒，犹如流星乱坠；当时儿童看见流星，称之为 angels' tears（天使的眼泪）。但这两行还有更深的象征意义，布莱克在长诗 *The French Revolution*（1791）中，称法国封建贵族所组成的反革命武力为国王的 starry hosts（群星），有句云：

Thy Nobles have gather'd thy starry hosts round this rebellious city, (I. 100)
…………………
Can the fires of Nobility ever be quench'd, or the stars by a storming night? (I.181)

这只是贵族们的自夸。当人民的代表发言时，诗人让他这样预言人民的胜利：

Then the valleys of France shall cry to the soldier:
    'Throw down thy sword and musket,
'And run and embrace the meek peasant.' Her Nobles
    shall hear and shall weep, and put off
The red robe of terror, the crown of oppression, the shoes of contempt, and unbuckle
The girdle of war from the desolate earth, … (II. 220–223)

两诗所作时间接近，正是法国革命激烈展开，获得布莱克关注的日子，因此这两行可能是指反革命的贵族们被革命的人民战败之事。

另有一种解释是：老虎眼睛比星光还亮，群星黯淡无光，因此丢掉武器，哭泣不已。

13. Lamb: 在布莱克诗中，Lamb（小羊）代表和平，良善，纯洁。这行的意思是：上帝既制造暴力，又创造和平。在 *Songs of Innocence* 中有 *The Lamb* 一诗，可与本诗参照一读：

Little Lamb, who made thee?
Dost thou know who made thee?

Gave thee life, and bid thee feed
By the stream and o'er the mead;
Gave thee clothing of delight,
Softest clothing, wooly, bright;
Gave thee such a tender voice,
Making all the vales rejoice?
Little Lamb, who made thee?
Dost thou know who made thee?

这里向的同本诗的

What immortal hand or eye
Could frame thy fearful symmetry?

是一类问题，不过一则情景恬静和平，一则森然可怖而已。

5. LONDON

印本初见于 *Songs of Experience*，作于1793年以前，初稿保存在诗人的笔记本上。

这首诗曾被称为 'mightiest brief poem'（Oliver Elton），近年来颇受英美批评家推崇，由于它显示了作者理解伦敦社会的罪恶性质的惊人的洞察力。布莱克本来是热爱伦敦的，曾经称之为 "golden London And her silver Thames, throng'd with shining spires And corded ships"（'King Edward the Third', *Poetical Sketches*, 1769－1778）；但是现在法国革命爆发了，英国政府加紧镇压国内的民主活动，伦敦城显示出一副完全不同的面目：阴暗，恐怖，凄惨，哀号着无数扫烟囱的孩子和受伤的士兵；尤其叫夜行街头的诗人感到触目惊心的是被饥饿逼得在黑暗中出卖肉体的年轻妓女。另一方面，整个伦敦城已经落入商业资本家手中，连过去是十分美丽的泰晤士河现在也被享有专利权的商人所霸占了。布莱克用极其生动的形象，沉痛而又激越的声音，富有感染力地表达了这一切，全诗不过十六行，文字朴素，而内容之丰富与深刻如是！

1. thro': through.

2. charter'd: chartered，意义有多种解释，主要是两种：1. 为大公司所专利的，独占的。2. 有明文规定和保障的，如说 "the chartered liberty of Englishmen". 今从一解。

3. mark: 动词，"注意到"；下行 marks 则为名词，"印记"。

4. marks of woe: 此处布莱克可能是呼应基督教《圣经·旧约》中 Ezekiel 书所载上帝之言："Go through the midst of the city, through the midst of Jerusalem, and set a mark upon the foreheads of the men that sigh and that cry for all the abominations that be done in the midst thereof."（第九章第四节）

5. every: 本节共用五个 every，着重这是穷苦人民无人可免的命运。

6. ban: 有二解：1，禁令（当时伦敦 Pitt 政府所颁发的）；2，结婚公告。

7. mind-forg'd manacles: 心灵所铸成的镣铐；**-forg' d，**-forged. 在初稿上，mind-forg'd manacles 原作 german-forg'd links，后 german 与 links 两字被划去，改如今本；german 指当时英国王室，他们原来是德国境内 Hanover 地方的统治者；兼指当

时为英国政府服务的德国雇佣军，也正是当时英国人民所痛恨的。因此，mind-forg'd manacles 意为伦敦 Pitt 政府费尽心机制造的镣铐，其作用是禁止人民起来反抗。

另有一解，即 mind 指资产阶级的“理性”。布莱克总的态度是反对理性（证据如他在培根《随笔》上的批语：“Rational Truth is not the Truth of Christ, but of Pilate”；另有诗“Mock on, Mock on Voltaire, Rousseau”嘲笑伏尔泰、卢梭等启蒙主义者）。

8. black'ning: blackening.

9. appalls: 及物动词，“使震骇”，其宾语为 Church；此字现在英国拼法作 appals.

10. hapless Soldier's sigh: 不幸士兵的悲鸣。按 sigh 在当时的意义比今天的“叹息”强烈。十八世纪英国在海外扩张，侵略的战争频仍，士兵死伤甚众，伤兵回国后大半沦为乞丐，充塞城乡道路，成为一大社会问题。

11. most: = most of all.

12. Blasts:“使凋缩”；骇得初生儿都不敢哭了。另有一解：象风那样把初生儿的泪水吹散。

13. blights:“残害”，“破坏”。

14. the Marriage hearse: 新婚的柩车。新婚如何与柩车结合在一起？这正是诗人联想敏捷之处。只要受难的少女还在街头卖笑，一切新娘都将无幸福可言，因为爱情已经死去，神圣的结婚受到瘟疫（plagues 中可能包括花柳病）的残害，于是婚车变成了柩车。

6. AND DID THOSE FEET IN ANCIENT TIME

这是长诗 *Milton* 序文部分的一个片断，上下都是散文，只有这几行是诗，向来单独成篇，有的编者还以 Jerusalem 一字标题。

此诗前半追怀未受资本主义工业化摧残的和平美丽的英国，后半表示要同丑恶的现实作殊死的斗争，决心建立一个新的社会。虽然布莱克又照例用了一些基督教中人常用的字眼，这些都有他特加的含义。其中曾在后世批评家中引起争论的 dark Satanic mills 一词是布莱克最有名的诗语之一。

全诗形象鲜明，对照强烈：原来是愉快的绿色大地，现在出现了黑色的魔鬼的工厂；针对着这黑暗势力，诗人要用最明亮的黄金的弓和火焰的飞车去同它作战。这些工厂是冰冷的“理性”的产物，诗人的武器则是热烈的“欲望”。

1. the holy Lamb of God: 小羊代表善良与和平。

2. the Countenance Divine: 指上帝，因此大写。

3. Jerusalem: 基督教的圣城；布莱克经常用此字来指他所憧憬的美好社会；此处特指过去英国，诗人将它理想化了。

4. builded: = built.

5. dark Satanic Mills: 黑暗的、服从魔鬼意旨的磨房（代表工厂）。

6. desire:“欲望”；敌人仗理性来攻（工厂都是培根与牛顿以来的科学产物），因此须用欲望破之，这欲望所代表的实是感情、想象与信仰所组成的精神世界。

7. Mental Fight: 思想战，即争取人心的战争，敌方是培根、牛顿所代表的自然科学和卢梭、伏尔泰、吉朋（Gibbon）所代表的理性主义；布莱克由于极端憎恨十八世纪英国产业革命所带来的社会，因而也就敌视成为那个社会的哲学基础的理性主义。

7. THE PRICE OF EXPERIENCE

此节选自长诗 *Vala, or the Four Zoas*，是诗中人物 Enion 说话的一部分。我们选它，是为了使读者见到布莱克长诗的不同风格：它们的诗行每行都比前面的短诗长，而音节数目又各行不一，没有脚韵，却有一种滔滔向前的气势，是惠特曼式自由体诗的先驱。从内容讲，往往象征与神话色彩浓厚，但近年来经学者研究，已有各种阐释。我们在此选的一段谈的是人为了取得经验所付出的惨重代价，同时有一种正直人的决心，决不随波逐流，幸灾乐祸。这一点，可同前面的《经验之歌》对照来看，两者的用意是一致的。

1. do men buy it for a song?: 人们是否能用一曲歌为代价取得经验？一曲歌代表欢乐、愉快，同时也表示不付任何代价。英文中有 buy（or sell）something for a song 的成语，意为非常廉价地买（或卖）了某物。

2. or wisdom for a dance in the street?: 接上行，主要句子结构是 do men buy wisdom for a dance in the street，意思亦如上行，即人能否不付任何代价而只用欢乐来取得智慧？智慧来自经验，而 dance in the street 则形象地表达了大众欢腾的情景。

3. It is an easy thing to triumph in the summer's sun: 此行与下行都表示人处顺境而兴高采烈是容易的事。

4. to talk of patience to the afflicted: 劝告受难的人要忍受。

5. to speak the laws of prudence to the houseless wanderer: 对无家的流浪者大谈审慎之道。

6. to listen to the hungry raven's cry ... 此处两行表示温饱的人听见饿鸟冻殍的号叫而无动于衷。

7. When the red blood is fill'd with wine & with the marrow of lambs: 当身上灌满了酒和肉的时候，red blood 指人身上的血液，the marrow of lambs 字面意思是羔羊的骨髓，实即好的羊肉；但布莱克经常用 lamb 来指善良的牺牲品，因此可能还隐含着民脂民膏的意思。

8. wrathful elements: 愤怒的自然界力量，指风雨雷电之类。

9. To see a god on every wind & a blessing on every blast:（不但不害怕自然力的袭来，而且）感到大风和雷轰只是带来了神灵的保祐。

10. To hear sounds of love in the thunder storm that destroys our enemies' house: 雷雨毁了自己仇人的屋子，因此听起来只觉得雷声可爱。这行更进一步说明上行的意思，下两行亦同，即对仇人是灾祸的对自己只是快乐。请注意诗人用了农村生活里的具体形象，而不只是泛泛议论。

11. dolor [ˈdəulə]**:** 忧伤，悲哀（文学用语，现代英语中罕见）。

12. the slave grinding at the mill: 在磨房里（艰苦地）推着磨石的奴隶（指磨房工人，但布莱克常用 mill 一词代表各类工厂，上面所选第六首中的 dark Satanic Mills 即是一例，因此又可能泛指一切工人）。

注意 18 行的 are quite forgotten 也是下面 the slave, the captive, the poor, the soldier 等主语的谓语，意为处于顺境的幸福人忘了人世上还有各种苦难和不幸。

13. When the shatter'd bone hath laid him groaning among the happier dead: 士兵在战斗中受伤骨碎，躺在战场上呻吟，感到还不如身旁的死人幸福，所以诗人说 the happier dead.

14. tents of prosperity: 繁荣兴旺的帐篷里，指幸福的环境里。

15. Thus could I sing & thus rejoice: but it is not so with me：我也可以这样唱，这样乐，但我不屑为之。请注意诗人用了虚拟式的 could 一词，表示他也完全可以这样，如果他愿意的话；然而事实却不如此。结语 not so with me 简单明了，斩钉截铁。

总起来说，这一段诗行数不多，然而诗人表达了人世的艰辛，一般人为取得经验和智慧所付出的代价如何惨重，真正善良和正直的人又如何决不以别人的痛苦为自己的快乐，写得酣畅、透彻，得力于那涌流而前的长诗行的节奏，也得力于所用的形象和形象之间的衬托与对照（冬与夏，饥饿的狗与丰足的人家，暴风雨所带来的两种心情，等等，在欢乐的阳光后面总有灾难和死亡的阴影），确是深刻而动人的力作，而且非布莱克莫为。

28 ROBERT BURNS (1759–1796)

1. For A' That An' A' That
2. Scots Wha Hae
3. My Luve Is Like a Red, Red Rose
4. Auld Lang Syne
5. Mary Morison

王佐良　选注

6. Tam o' Shanter

徐　序　选注

1. FOR A' THAT AN' A' THAT[1]

TUNE:[2] For A' That

Is there for honest poverty[3]
　That hings his head,[4] an' a' that?[5]
The coward[6] slave, we pass him by —
　We dare be poor for a' that!
For a' that, an' a' that,
　Our toils obscure,[7] an' a' that,
The rank is but the guinea's stamp,[8]
　The man's the gowd[9] for a' that.

What though on hamely[10] fare we dine,
　Wear hoddin grey,[11] an' a' that?
Gie[12] fools their silks, and knaves their wine —
　A man's a man for a' that.
For a' that, an' a' that,

Their tinsel show,[13] an' a' that,
The honest man, tho' e'er sae poor,[14]
Is king o' men[15] for a' that.

Ye see yon[16] birkie[17] ca'd[18] "a lord,"
Wha[19] struts, an' stares, an' a' that?
Tho' hundreds worship at his word,[20]
He's but a cuif[21] for a' that.
For a' that, an' a' that,
His ribband,[22] star, an' a' that,
The man o' independent mind,
He looks an' laughs at a' that.

A prince can mak a belted knight,[23]
A marquis, duke, an' a' that!
But an honest man's aboon his might[24] —
Guid faith,[25] he mauna fa' that![26]
For a' that, an' a' that,
Their dignities, an' a' that,
The pith o' sense[27] an' pride o' worth,[28]
Are higher rank than a' that.

Then let us pray that come it may
(As come it will for a' that),
That Sense and Worth o'er a' the earth,
Shall bear the gree[29] an' a' that!
For a' that, an' a' that,
It's comin[30] yet for a' that,
That man to man, the world o'er
Shall brithers[31] be for a' that.

2. SCOTS WHA HAE

Scots, wha hae wi' Wallace[1] bled,
Scots, wham[2] Bruce[3] has aften led,
Welcome to your gory bed[4]
Or to victorie![5]

Now's the day, and now's the hour:
See the front o' battle lour,[6]
See approach proud Edward's power[7] —
Chains and slaverie![8]

Wha will be a traitor knave?
Wha can fill a coward's grave?
Wha sae base[9] as be a slave? —
Let him turn, and flee!

Wha for Scotland's King and Law
Freedom's sword will strongly draw,
Freeman stand, or Freeman fa',[10]
Let him follow me!

By Oppression's woes and pains,[11]
By your sons in servile chains,[12]
We will drain our dearest veins,[13]
But they shall be[14] free!

Lay the proud usurpers low!
Tyrants fall in every foe![15]
Liberty's in every blow![16] —
Let us do, or die![17]

3. A RED, RED ROSE

O, my luve is like a red, red rose,
  That's newly sprung in June.
O, my luve is like the melodie,[1]
  That's sweetly play'd in tune.[2]

As fair art[3] thou, my bonie lass,
  So deep in luve am I,
And I will luve thee[4] still, my dear,
  Till a'[5] the seas gang dry.

Till a' the seas gang dry, my dear,
  And the rocks melt wi'[6] the sun!
And I will luve thee still, my dear,
  While the sands o' life shall run.[7]

And fare thee weel,[8] my only luve!
  And fare thee weel, a while[9]!
And I will come again, my luve,
  Tho'[10] it were ten thousand mile!

4. AULD LANG SYNE

Chorus[1]

For auld lang syne, my dear,
  For auld lang syne,
We'll tak a cup o' kindness yet,[2]
  For auld lang syne!

Should auld acquaintance be forgot,
  And never brought to mind?[3]

Should auld acquaintance be forgot,
And auld lang syne?

And surely ye'll be your pint-stowp,[4]
And surely I'll be mine,
And we'll tak a cup o' kindness yet,
For auld lang syne!

We twa hae[5] run about the braes,
And pou'd the gowans[6] fine,
But we've wander'd monie a weary fit,[7]
Sin'[8] auld lang syne.

We twa hae paidl'd in the burn[9]
Frae morning sun till dine,[10]
But seas between us braid[11] hae roar'd
Sin' auld lang syne.

And there's a hand, my trusty fiere,[12]
And gie's a hand o' thine,[13]
And we'll tak a right guid-willie waught,[14]
For auld lang syne.

5. MARY MORISON

O Mary, at thy window be!
It is the wish'd, the trysted hour.[1]
Those smiles and glances let me see,
That make the miser's treasure poor.
How blythely wad I bide the stoure,[2]
A weary slave frae sun to sun.[3]
Could I the rich reward secure —
The lovely Mary Morison!

Yestreen,[4] when to the trembling string
The dance gaed thro' the lighted ha',[5]
To thee my fancy took its wing,
I sat, but neither heard or saw:
Tho' this was fair, and that was braw,[6]
And yon the toast of a' the town,[7]
I sigh'd, and said amang them a':[8] —
"Ye are na[9] Mary Morison!"

O, Mary, canst thou wreck his peace[10]
Wha[11] for thy sake wad gladly die?
Or canst thou break that heart of his
Whase only faut is loving thee?[12]
If love for love thou wilt na gie,[13]
At least be pity to me shown:
A thought ungentle canna[14] be
The thought o' Mary Morison.

6. TAM O' SHANTER

A TALE

Of Brownyis and of Bogillis full is this Buke.

— GAVIN DOUGLAS[1]

When chapman billies[2] leave the street,
And drouthy[3] neebors, neebors meet,
As market-days are wearing late,
An' folk begin to tak the gate;[4]
While we sit bousing at the nappy,[5]
An' getting fou and unco happy,[6]
We think na on the lang Scots miles,[7]
The mosses, waters, slaps, and styles,[8]
That lie between us and our hame,[9]
Whare sits our sulky, sullen dame,[10]

Gathering her brows like gathering[11] storm,
Nursing her wrath[12] to keep it warm.

This truth fand[13] honest TAM O' SHANTER,
As he frae Ayr ae night did canter:[14]
(Auld Ayr, whom ne'er a town surpasses,[15]
For honest men and bonie lasses).[16]

O Tam, had'st thou but been sae[17] wise,
As taen thy ain wife Kate's[18] advice!
She tauld thee weel thou was a skellum,[19]
A blethering, blustering, drunken blellum;[20]
That frae November till October,
Ae market-day thou was nae sober;[21]
That ilka melder wi'[22] the miller,[23]
Thou sat as lang as thou had siller;
That ev'ry naig was ca'd a shoe[24] on
The 'smith and thee gat roarin fou[25] on;
That at the Lord's house, even on Sunday,
Thou drank wi' Kirkton Jean[26] till Monday.
She prophesied[27] that, late or soon,
Thou would be found, deep drown'd in Doon,[28]
Or catch'd wi' warlocks in the mirk,[29]
By Alloway's auld, haunted kirk.[30]

Ah, gentle dames, it gars me greet,[31]
To think how monie counsels[32] sweet,
How monie lengthen'd, sage[33] advices
The husband frae the wife despises[34]!

But to our tale: — Ae market-night,
Tam had got planted[35] unco right,
Fast by an ingle, bleezing[36] finely,

Wi' reaming swats, that drank divinely;[37]
And at his elbow, Souter Johnie,[38]
His ancient, trusty, drouthy cronie:[39]
Tam lo'ed him like a very brither;[40]
They had been fou for weeks thegither.[41]
The night drave on wi' sangs and clatter;[42]
And ay[43] the ale was growing better:
The landlady and Tam grew gracious,[44]
Wi' secret favours, sweet and precious:[45]
The Souter tauld his queerest[46] stories;
The landlord's laugh was ready chorus:[47]
The storm without might rair and rustle,[48]
Tam did na mind the storm a whistle.[49]

Care,[50] mad[51] to see a man sae happy,
E'en drown'd himsel amang the nappy.[52]
As bees fiee hame wi' lades o'[53] treasure,
The minutes wing'd their way[54] wi' pleasure:
Kings may be blest[55] but Tam was glorious,
O'er a' the ills o' life victorious![56]
But pleasures are like poppies[57] spread:
You seize the flow'r, its bloom is shed;[58]
Or like the snow falls in the river,
A moment white — then melts for ever;
Or like the borealis race,[59]
That flit ere[60] you can point their place;
Or like the rainbow's lovely form
Evanishing[61] amid the storm.
Nae man can tether time or tide,[62]
The hour approaches Tam maun ride:[63]
That hour, o' night's black arch the key-stane:[64]
That dreary hour Tam mounts his beast[65] in;
And sic a night he taks the road[66] in,

As ne'er poor sinner was abroad[67] in.

The wind blew as 'twad blawn its last;[68]
The rattling showers rose on the blast;[69]
The speedy gleams the darkness swallow'd;[70]
Loud, deep, and lang the thunder bellow'd;[71]
That night, a child might understarnd,
The Deil[72] had business on his hand.

Weel mounted on his gray mare Meg,[73]
A better never lifted leg,
Tam skelpit on thro' dub and mire,[74]
Despising wind, and rain, and fire;
Whiles holding fast his guid blue bonnet,[75]
Whiles crooning o'er an auld Scots sonnet,[76]
Whiles glow'ring round wi' prudent[77] cares,
Lest bogles catch him unawares:[78]
Kirk-Alloway was drawing nigh,[79]
Whare ghaists and houlets nightly cry.[80]

By this time he was cross the ford,[81]
Whare in the snaw the chapman smoor'd;[82]
And past the birks and meikle stane,[83]
Whare drunken Charlie brak's neck-bane;[84]
And thro' the whins, and by the cairn,[85]
Whare hunters fand the murder'd bairn;[86]
And near the thorn, aboon[87] the well,
Whare Mungo's mither hang'd hersel.[88]
Before him Doon pours all his floods;[89]
The doubling[90] storm roars thro' the woods;
The lightnings flash from pole to pole,[91]
Near and more near the thunders roll;
When, glimmering thro' the groaning[92] trees,

Kirk-Alloway seem'd in a bleeze,[93]
Thro' ilka bore the beams were glancing,[94]
And loud resounded mirth[95] and dancing.

Inspiring bold John Barleycorn,[96]
What dangers thou canst make us scorn![97]
Wi' tippenny,[98] we fear nae evil;
Wi' usquabae,[99] we'll face the Devil!
The swats sae ream'd[100] in Tammie's[101] noddle,
Fair play, he car'd na deils a boddle.[102]
But Maggie stood, right sair astonish'd,[103]
Till, by the heel and hand admonish'd,[104]
She ventur'd[105] forward on the light;
And, vow! Tam saw an unco[106] sight!

Warlocks[107] and witches in a dance:
Nae cotillion, brent new[108] frae France,
But hornpipes, jigs, strathspeys, and reels,[109]
Put life and mettle in their heels.[110]
A winnock-bunker[111] in the east,
There sat Auld Nick, in shape o' beast;[112]
A touzie tyke,[113] black, grim, and large,
To gie them music was his charge:[114]
He screw'd the pipes and gart them skirl,[115]
Till roof and rafters a' did dirl.[116]
Coffins stood round, like open presses,[117]
That shaw'd[118] the dead in their last dresses;
And, by some devilish cantraip sleight,[119]
Each in its cauld hand[120] held a light:
By which heroic Tam was able
To note upon the haly table,[121]
A murderer's banes, in gibbet-airns;[122]
Twa span-lang, wee, unchristen'd bairns;[123]

A thief new-cutted frae a rape[124]—
Wi' his last gasp his gab did gape;[125]
Five tomahawks, wi' bluid red-rusted;[126]
Five scymitars, wi' murder crusted;[127]
A garter which a babe had strangled;[128]
A knife a father's throat had mangled[129]—
Whom his ain son o' life bereft[130]—
The grey-hairs yet stack to the heft;[131]
Wi' mair of horrible and awefu',[132]
Which even to name wad be unlawfu'.[133]

As Tammie glowr'd, amaz'd,[134] and curious,
The mirth and fun grew fast an furious;[135]
The piper loud and louder blew,
The dancers quick and quicker flew,
They reel'd, they set, they cross'd, they cleekit,[136]
Till ilka carlin swat and reekit,[137]
And coost her duddies to the wark,[138]
And linket at it in her sark![139]

Now Tam, O Tam! had thae been queans,[140]
A' plump and strapping in their teens![141]
Their sarks, instead o' creeshie flannen,[142]
Been snaw-white seventeen hunder linen![143]—
Thir breeks o' mine, my only pair,[144]
That ance were plush, o' guid[145] blue hair,
I wad hae gien them off my hurdies,[146]
For ae blink o' the bonie burdies![147]
But wither'd beldams, auld and droll,[148]
Rigwoodie hags wad spean a foal,[149]
Louping and flinging on a crummock,[150]
I wonder did na turn thy stomach![151]

But Tam kend what was what fu' brawlie:[152]
There was ae winsome wench and wawlie,[153]
That night enlisted in the core,[154]
Lang after kend on Carrick shore[155]
(For monie a beast to dead she shot,
An' perish'd monie a bonie boat,[156]
And shook baith meikle corn and bear,[157]
And kept the country-side in fear).

Her cutty sark, o' Paisley harn,[158]
That while a lassie[159] she had worn,
In longtitude tho' sorely scanty,[160]
It was her best, and she was vauntie[161]...
Ah! little kend thy reverend grannie,[162]
That sark she coft for her wee Nannie,[163]
Wi' twa pund Scots ('twas a' her riches),[164]
Wad ever grac'd[165] a dance of witches!

But here my Muse her wing maun cour,[166]
Sic flights are far beyond her power:[167]
To sing how Nannie lap and flang[168]
(A souple jade she was and strang),[169]
And how Tam stood like ane bewitch'd,[170]
And thought his very een enrich'd;[171]
Even Satan glowr'd, and fidg'd fu' fain,[172]
And hotch'd and blew wi' might and main:[173]
Till first ae caper, syne anither,[174]
Tam tint his reason a' thegither,[175]
And roars out, "Weel done, Cutty-sark! "[176]
And in an instant all was dark:
And scarcely had he Maggie rallied,[177]
When out the hellish legion sallied.[178]

As bees bizz out wi' angry fyke,[179]
When plundering herds assail their byke;[180]
As open pussie's mortal foes,[181]
When, pop! she starts before their nose;[182]
As eager runs the market-crowd,[183]
When "Catch the thief!" resounds aloud:
So Maggie runs, the witches[184] follow,
Wi' monie an eldritch skriech and hollow.[185]

Ah, Tam! Ah, Tam! thou'll get thy fairin![186]
In hell they'll roast thee like a herrin![187]
In vain thy Kate awaits thy comin![188]
Kate soon will be a woefu'[189] woman!
Now, do the speedy utmost, Meg,[190]
And win the key-stane of the brig;[191]
There, at them thou thy tail may toss,[192]
A running stream they dare na cross!
But ere the key-stane she could make,
The fient[193] a tail she had to shake;
For Nannie, far before the rest,
Hard upon noble Maggie prest,[194]
And flew at Tam wi' furious ettle;[195]
But little wist she Maggie's mettle![196]
Ae spring brought off her master hale,[197]
But left behind her ain grey tail:
The carlin claught her by the rump,[198]
And left poor Maggie scarce a stump.[199]

Now, wha[200] this tale o' truth shall read,
Ilk man, and mother's son, take heed:[201]
Whene'er to drink you are inclin'd,[202]
Or cutty sarks rin in your mind,[203]
Think! ye may buy the joys o'er dear:[204]

Remember Tam o'Shanter's mare.

【作者简介】Robert Burns（罗伯特·彭斯，1759—1796），苏格兰大诗人，农民出身，在田间劳动了大半生，后为生活所逼做税关职员，曾因同情法国革命受上级传讯。一生经济困难，三十七岁时即于贫病交加中死去。他从小爱好吟哦，稍长用苏格兰方言写诗，1786 年诗集 Poems, Chiefiy in the Scottish Dialect 出版，受到苏格兰文坛的普遍称赏。后又长期在业余从事苏格兰民间歌谣的搜集、整理工作，大量将近失传的民歌靠他的努力得以保存，这是彭斯在文学史上伟大功绩之一。他本人的诗更是开文学史上的新页，最出色的是根据民歌调子写的短诗，例如宣扬法国革命思想的 *For A' That An' A' That*，歌颂苏格兰爱国主义的 *Scots Wha Hae*，以及以 *A Red, Red Rose* 为代表的大量的爱情诗，但还有许多其他优秀作品，如尖锐讽刺教会的 *Holy Willie's Prayer*，关怀老驴的 *The Auld Farmer's New Year Morning Salutation to His Auld Mare Maggie*，诗札如 *Epistle to J. Lapraik*，长篇叙事诗如 *The Twa Dogs, Tam o' Shanter, The Jolly Beggars*，不仅遍涉各类，而且体体皆精，只有少量他为了社交应酬而用英文写的诗比较逊色。

【题解与注释】

这里选的是五首短诗和一首长诗。短诗可分三类。第一、二两首表达彭斯的民主思想，是一类；第四首是怀友之作，自成一类；第三、五两首倾吐爱情，又是一类。长诗则是根据民间传说写成的叙事诗，显示了彭斯诗才的另一面。这些诗都是传诵已久的名作，其共同的特点是：通过劳动人民的眼睛来看世界，情感真挚、热烈，文字朴素、新鲜，音乐性特强。

这些诗都是用苏格兰方言写的，然而方言化的程度不一。苏格兰方言的元音开豁，适宜于歌谣体。

对于一个已知英语的人，苏格兰方言并不难懂，尤其是在朗诵的时候，许多词的发音与英语中相当的词近似，如 aften / often, amang / among, auld / old, brithers / brothers, gie / give, gowd / gold, guid / good, hamely / homely, luve / love, maunav/must not, monie / many, sae / so, twa / two, wad / would, wha / who, wham / whom, weel / well 等等，绝大多数只是在元音上略有差别。但有不少单词（如 birkie, cuif, fiere 等）和某些成语（如 guid-willie waught, mauna fa'that 等）不是通过英语所能猜出意义的，需要查阅注释或工具书。

1. FOR A' THAT AN' A' THAT

此诗写于 1795 年，发表在 1799 年，亦即法国革命爆发不久，英国统治阶级一面组织反法联军，一面加紧镇压国内民主活动的动荡和恐怖的年代。彭斯曾在1792年底因革命官行受税关当局的传讯，1793年英法正式宣战，与他有来往的苏格兰民主人士Muir等被控叛国罪在爱丁堡受审，次年流放海外；另一方面，过去与彭斯交往的上层社会人士因为他有革命思想而与之疏远，贵妇Mrs. Dunlop还同他绝交。在这种政治空气紧张、社会压力沉重的情况下，彭斯却仍然宣扬法国革命的大道理。

此诗所根据的民歌For A' That在彭斯之前曾经多次改编，各有不同内容，其一是对于苏格兰过去，Stuart王朝的怀念。彭斯见过这个本子。但等他自己动手改编的时候，他却完全摈弃这种向封建国王效忠的情绪，而代之以强调自由、平等、博爱的资产阶级革命时期的进步思想。同时，他保存并发挥了原歌的曲调特点，出色地使用for a' that. an' a' that的叠句来嘲笑懦夫，财主，豪绅，爵爷，大臣，直至国王本人，到后来又用它来豪迈地宣告全世界人民成为兄弟的一天必将到来，有一种天不怕地不怕的硬朗、乐观的精神，曾为人称作"人类的马赛曲"。

标题　多数编者用本诗首行作题，即Is There For Honest Poverty.

1. for A' That: 即in spite of all that；本诗中时时出现，成为回旋不已的叠句，带有反抗、嘲笑、不屑等的豪放调子。

2. Tune: 曲调名；彭斯的诗多据民歌改编，能唱，故有曲调名。

3. Is there for honest poverty: 有省略，意为is there any one who ...; **for,** because of; **honest,** honourable，正大光明的。

4. That hings his head: who hangs his head，垂头丧气的人。

5. an' a' that: and all that，意为诸如此类的事；这几字亦是回旋之一，多次出现。

6. coward: 作形容词用，懦弱的；**we pass him by**，我们不齿他。

7. obscure: humble，卑微的。

8. the guinea's stamp: 金币上的花纹，意为权位只是外表；guinea ['gini]，金币，值21先令。

9. gowd: gold.

10. hamely: homely; **hamely fare**，粗茶淡饭。

11. hoddin grey: coarse grey cloth，灰色粗呢衣服（贫苦农民所穿）。

12. Gie: give.

13. tinsel show: 无价值的华美外表。

14. tho' e'er sae poor: though ever so poor，不管多么穷。

15. ling o' men: 有用的人；**o',** of.

16. yon: yonder.

17. birkie: a fellow，带轻蔑意。

18. ca'd: called,

19. Wha: who; **an',** and.

20. Tho' hundreds worship at his word: 虽然他一呼百诺；**tho',** though。

21. He's but a cuif: he's only a fool.

22. ribband: = riband = ribbon，绶带（代表爵位）；**star**，勋章上的星。

23. A prince can mak a belted knight: 国王可以封人为爵士；**mak,** make;

belted，系皮带的（表示有爵位）。

24. aboon his might: above his power，超乎国王权力之上，不受他管。

25. Guid faith: good faith，赌咒语。

26. he mauna fa' that!: he must not claim that；不许他得到那种权力，即国王虽能封官赐爵，但无力左右好人。

27. The pith o' sense: 真知灼见；**pith**，精华；**sense**，见识。

28. pride o' worth: 高尚的人品；**pride**，自豪感；**worth**，有贡献。这几个词连同上文，合指有真才实学、人品高尚的人，与仅有华美外表对比。

29. gree: prize; **bear the gree**，夺得胜利。

30. It's comin: It is coming.

31. brithers: brothers.

2. SCOTS WHA HAE

此诗作于1793年，发表于1794年，与第一首属同一时期。苏格兰原系独立国家，1707年起为英国合并，引起苏格兰人民的激烈反对，到1745年还爆发了最后一次抗英起义。在这首诗里彭斯缅怀英烈，慷慨悲歌，号召为自由而战。它的特点是：每行音节不多（一般七个音节，每三行之后有一行只五个音节，作为有力的一结），用字也少，但平行句成串出现，不断的问句象步步紧逼的挑战，节奏缓而有力，到每小节之末则又突然高昂，到全诗最后一行达到呼喊立即行动的高潮。

但是此诗的重点不在抗英。1793年8月底，彭斯在将此诗寄给 *A Select Collection of Original Scottish Airs* ——一种民歌汇刊——的主编 George Thomson 时，曾经写信说明他原先本不想写此诗，但是后来：

> the accidental recollection of that glorious struggle for Freedom, associated with the glowing ideas of some other struggles of the same nature, *not quite so ancient*, roused my rhyming Mania.
>
> （偶然想起那场争取自由的光荣斗争，又联想到另外一些同样性质的斗争，它们在时间上并不那样遥远，这就挑起了我写诗的狂热。）

这里着重点是彭斯本人特加的；他所指的时间较近、性质相同的斗争毫无疑问是正在使得英国统治阶级谈虎色变的法国革命。诗的重点在于自由，在于抗击一切暴君，外来的以及本国的。彭斯之热烈向往民主革命，在此又得一证明。

标题 **Scots Wha Hae**, Scots who have；此诗彭斯原题为 Robert Bruce's march to Bannockburn，多数编者则取第一行前三字为题；也有不用前三字而另标 Bruce at Bannockburn 者。

1. Wallace: Sir William (1272–1305)，苏格兰民族英雄，曾大败英军，后为奸人出卖，被英军所执处死。

2. wham: whom; **aften,** often.

3. Bruce, Robert (1274–1329): 苏格兰国王，1314年在 Bannockburn 地方大破英军。

4. Welcome to your gory bed: 来吧，准备躺在血泊里吧；**gory,** bloody; **bed**，死亡之床。

5. Victorie: Victory；最后一音节重读，与第 8 行 slaverie，第 12 行 flee，第 16 行 me，第 20 行 free，第 24 行 die（读作 ['di:]）押韵。

6. lour: 即 lower（动词），look dark and angry，此行意为大战就要爆发。

7. proud Edward's power: 骄横的英王的权势；Edward，指英王 Edward II (1284–1327).

8. slaverie: slavery，最后一音节重读。

9. sae: so; **base**，卑鄙。

10. fa': fall；此行意为生作自由人，死作自由魂。

11. By Oppression's woes and pains: 凭被压迫者的苦难来起誓；By, I swear by, "凭…起誓"，下行的 by 同此（英文中此类说法甚多，如 By God，By Jove，By George 等）。

12. servile chains: 奴役的锁链。

13. drain our dearest veins: 流尽我们宝贵的血；**veins**，血管。

14. they shall be: = they must be; shall 重读。

15. Tyrants fall in every foe: 杀一个敌人，少一个暴君。

16. Liberty's in every blow: 每一次打击敌人都争来更多自由。

17. Let us do, or die! 五个单音字，十分坚决有力；do 与 die 是双声；die，与上面 victorie, slaverie, flee, me, free 等字押韵。

3. A RED, RED ROSE

这是彭斯爱情诗里最有名的一首，作于 1794 年，发表于 1796 年。它原来也有几个苏格兰古民歌的本子，经过彭斯加工、改写，才去掉它们的芜杂和庸俗（例如有一个旧本子用类似本诗头上四行的一段来歌颂一个荡妇），集中它们的精华，成为现在这样的抒情绝唱。它清新，咏美人而无一丝脂粉气；它明白如话，但又有足够的分量与深度，经得起不断玩味、思索；它自然，但又有完整的形式：诗中叠字复句的运用更有无限匠心，尤其第八、九两行——Till a' the seas gang dry——的重复实是意味深长的天才之笔，因为这一重复出现在全诗的正中，划分了而又衔接了两个不同的境界：前八行是你我之间的恋爱，只牵涉两人，情调虽热烈而轻快；后八行则将岩石、海洋和太阳都卷了进来，爱情有了一个宇宙背景，不仅空间扩大，时间上也延长了；最后又回到原来的两人，这时爱情深化了，人生经验也丰富了，于是结句——Tho' it were ten thousand mile! ——在我们读者面前展开了一条千里万里的尘土和风雪的旅途，但是行人不论怎样遥远，却一定要回来，会回来，因为经过这样上天入地，爱情是经受得起一切考验了。从一朵红红的玫瑰开始，以通到天涯海角去的大路作结，其间有转折，有深化，显示出对于爱情的高度洞察力，唯有民歌才能供给这样深厚的感情和成熟的智慧作为再创造的基础，唯有天才诗人才能从这基础出发，写出如此新鲜、如此深情的不朽诗篇！

1. **melodie:** melody，曲调。

2. **in tune:** 谐和地。

3. **art:** are; **thou:** you; **bonie:** pretty; **lass:** girl.

4. **thee:** you（作宾语用）。

5. **a':** all; **gang,** go；直到海枯。

6. **wi':** with；直到石烂。

7. **the sands o' life shall run:** 只要我还活着；**sands**，时间（古代用沙漏计时）；**o',** of.

8. **weel:** well; **fare thee weel**，再见吧。

9. **a while:** 暂时。

10. **Tho':** though；纵使路程遥远。

4. AULD LANG SYNE

此诗始作于1788年，改写于1793年，发表于1796年。彭斯自称是听了一位老人唱一支古民歌时当场录下而成，并且加了这样的按语：

> Light be the turf on the breast of the heaven-inspired Poet who composed this glorious Fragment! There is more of the fire of native genius in it, than in half a dozen of modern English Bacchanalians.
>
> （*Letter to Mrs. Dunlop,* 7th December, 1788）

（写这一辉煌的断片的天才诗人应为埋骨的青山增色！这诗燃烧着民间天才之火，纵使拿出六七个近代英国的骚人墨客的大作，也无法同它相比。）

这是不易之论。诗里响彻了 auld lang syne 的回音，这三字无论音义都带给听众一种感喟和怀念。起节突然两问，也是奇笔。第三四节叙儿时嬉乐及后来沧桑，虽用差不多的情景互相呼应，但是第四节的 But seas between us braid hae roar'd（如今大海的怒涛将我们隔开）却又深入一层。也正因有这点人生艰辛的沉重之感，才使这首"劝君更进一杯酒"式的叙旧诗更有感染力。后来此诗经过谱曲，成为世界名歌之一。

标题　**Auld Lang Syne**：许久以前；**auld,** old; **lang syne,** long since, long ago.

1.（重唱部分）**Chorus:** 民歌的重唱部分，此诗每段之后都要唱这四行一遍。

2.（重唱部分）**We'll tak a cup o' kindness yet:** 我们要再干一杯友情的酒；**tak,** take; **o',** of; 彭斯当时，苏格兰民间唱此行时，亦有将 cup 一字改为 kiss 者。

3. **brought to mind:** 回想到。

4. **pint-stowp**，装一品特酒的容器；stowp 一般拼作 stoup；此行意为你一定会畅饮开怀。

5. **twa:** two; **hae:** have; **braes:** a small hill.

6. **pou'd:** pulled; **gowans:** wild daisies，雏菊（一种野花）。

7. **monie:** many; **fit,** foot；流浪得脚疲人倦。

8. **Sin':** since.

9. **paidl'd:** paddled, waded，趟水；**burn**（名词）：a rivulet，小河。

10. Frae: from; **dine:** 吃晚饭的时候。

11. braid: broad.

12. flere: comrade，友伴。

13. gie's: give us; **a hand o' thine:** your hand.

14. guid-willie waught: 意如 a cup of kindness; **guid-willie:** good will，亲善的 **waught:** a deep draught，浮一大白。

5. MARY MORISON

此诗是彭斯少时所作，他自己并不满意，但是自 1800 年发表以来，后世的多数读者却喜爱它。它的感情不及《红红的玫瑰》深挚，音乐性也不如彭斯其他短诗，然而写得文雅，而且形式完整（如每一节都以 Mary Morison 两字结束），不少地方写得新颖巧妙（例如 Or canst thou break that heart of his/Whase only faut is loving thee?）。显示了彭斯轻快、活泼的一面。

Mary Morison，或云即是彭斯青年时的女友 Elison Begbie，但当时彭斯所住的 Mauchline 地方确有一姑娘名 Mary Morison，1791 年 8 月因肺病去世。

1. the trysted hour: 约好的时间。

2. wad I bide the stoure: 甘心忍受一切苦难；**wad,** would; **stoure,** dust.

3. frae: from; **frae sun to sun:** from day to day.

4. Yestreen: last night.

5. gaed: went; **thro':** through; **ha':** hall.

6. Tho': though; **braw:** gaily dressed，装束华丽。

7. yon: yonder; **the toast of a' the town:** 全城举杯相敬的美人。

8. amang: among; **a':** all.

9. na': not.

10. his peace: a man's peace，一个男人心里的宁静。

11. Wha: who.

12. Whase only faut is loving thee: 他如有过错，不过错在敢将你爱；**whase:** whose; **faut:** fault.

13. thou wilt na gie: you will not give.

14. ungentle: unkind; **canna:** cannot,

6. TAM O' SHANTER

这是彭斯根据民间传说写成的叙事诗，它不仅讲了一个有趣的故事，而且用幽默、生动的语调冲淡了原传说中的迷信色彩。它是彭斯最有名的作品之一，其中苏格兰方言的运用达到了戏剧化的新高峰，至今都常有人朗诵。

此诗的情节可以分为六个部分。

第一部分从第 1 行至第 36 行，描写汤姆爱喝酒，尽管他的老婆多次劝他不要贪杯，而且还警告他：

……总有一朝，
你会葬身在杜河的滚滚波涛，
要不就在黑夜给鬼魂抓走，
在阿罗微古老阴森的教堂后头！*

但他还是当作耳边风，见酒就喝。

第二部分从第37行至第58行，描述汤姆趁赶集之机又来到酒店，紧靠着壁炉，一杯又一杯地喝着冒泡的啤酒，还有亲如兄弟的鞋匠约翰来作伴，他和酒店的老板娘也谈得很投机，快乐得连门外刮着大风也不知晓。

第三部分从第59行起止104行，描述了汤姆的这种欢乐犹如昙花一现，好景不长，他又得动身去上路了。这正是黑暗到顶的二更天，加上狂风怒号，大雨倾盆，雷声震得人发颤，有谁敢在这样的黑夜里赶路呀！但汤姆幸喜有匹好马叫梅琪，他坐在马背上小心翼翼细听四周的动静，前面就是阿罗微教堂，那可是个可怕的地方，曾发生过一些惨事。忽然，树林里闪出一片亮光，它照明了整个教堂，呵，还传来了舞会的快乐的笑声！

第四部分从第105行至第142行，作者饶有兴趣地描述汤姆由于喝了酒，壮了胆，敢于偷看前面灯光下一群男女妖怪随着魔鬼尼克的花笛声，在昏天黑地里乱跳乱蹦。他们的四周放着一大排敞着盖的棺材，其中死人高举着烛火；还有圣餐桌上放着死人的骨头、儿童的骷髅等等悲惨可怕的东西，使汤姆看了又惊又怕，但他到底还是看了个究竟。

第五部分从第143行起至第192行，描述魔鬼把花笛越吹越响，群妖的舞步越跳越欢，女妖们一个个直冒热汗，索性把外面的破衣都脱掉，只留下汗衣贴身上。可是她们都是丑恶的老妖婆，只有一个名叫南尼的粗壮的母夜叉，打动了汤姆的心。她身穿一件多年前做闺女时买的粗布短背心，身段灵活，使汤姆瞧得发呆。忽然，魔鬼又把花笛狂吹，群妖跳得如醉如狂，我们的汤姆也如着了迷，他脱口大叫：“好哇！好个半截汗衫！”这一叫非同小可，刷一下灯火全灭，汤姆一看着了慌，赶紧让他的梅琪向前跑，可是妖魔们也已出动了。

第六部分从193行到224行，描写群妖追赶汤姆的情况。他们象一群愤怒的马蜂、眼睛发红的猎犬，嚎叫着直往前扑。汤姆骑马狂奔，急于冲过大石桥，因为他知道妖精们见了流水就不能再进。但是桥头未到，事情已不妙，只见说时迟，那时快，那南尼恶狠狠腾空跃起，想抓住梅琪。梅琪刹一下把主人安全驮上桥，自己却被南尼死命抓住了尾巴，从此她就成了一匹没尾的马。最后诗人劝告众人：

每当好酒叫你实在嘴馋，
每当你胡思女人的短汗衫，
想想这代价！别为了一时的欢娱，
就忘记汤姆·奥桑特的好母驴！

1. 引诗 Of Brownyis and of Bogillis full is this Buke. —GAVIN DOUGLAS: **browny-**

---

* 王佐良译文，下同，皆见《彭斯诗选》，人民文学出版社，1959年

is, brownies，仙童，棕仙；**bogillis,** bogles，妖怪；**buke,** book；全句意为本书充满仙童妖怪之类；句子引自苏格兰十五世纪作家 Gavin Douglas (1475?–1522) 的作品。

2. billies: peddler fellows，小贩。

3. drouthy: thirsty，爱喝酒的；**neebors, neighbours**，邻居；此行照通常词序应作 thirsty neighbours meet neighbours.

4. an': and; **tak the gate:** take the road，上路去。

5. bousing: boozing，痛饮；**nappy:** strong ale，浓烈的啤酒。

6. fou: drunk，醉的；**unco:** very; **unco happy:** 非常快乐。

7. na: not; **lang:** long; **Scots:** 苏格兰的；**Scots miles:** 苏格兰的里程。

8. mosses: 沼泽；**slaps:** gaps (in walls)，围墙断处；**styles:** stiles，篱。

9. hame: home.

10. whare: where; **sulky:** 绷着脸的；**sullen:** 愠怒的；**dame:** 老婆，夫人。

11. gathering her brows: 皱起眉头。

12. wrath: 愤怒，此行原意是：好生保持着她的愤怒，不使它冷下去。

13. fand: found，知道，发现。

14. frae: from; **Ayr:** 地名；**ae:** one; **ae night:** one night; **canter:** 骑马慢跑。

15. auld: old; **ne'er:** never; **surpasses:** 胜过，超越。

16. bonie: bonnie, beautiful; **lasses:** girls.

17. had'st: have 的单数第二人称过去式，与主语 thou 连用；此行作者用的是虚拟式；**sae:** so.

18. taen: taken; **thy:** your, thou 的所有格，你的；**ain:** own; **Kate:** 女人名。

19. tauld: told; **thee:** you,［古］thou 的宾格，你；**weel:** well; **skellum:** good-for-nothing，无用之人，饭桶。

20. blethering: chattering，饶舌；**blustering:** 大吵大嚷；**blellum:** babbler，胡说乱道的人。此行有三个以 bl- 开始的词，形成头韵，增强了滑稽效果。

21. nae: not; **sober:** 未喝醉的，清醒的。

22. ilka: every; **melder:** the amount of corn processed at a single grinding（一次磨面的数量称为 melder）；**wi':** with.

23. siller: silver, money.

24. ev'ry: every; **naig:** nag，小马；**ca'd:** driven，钉进；**shoe:** 蹄铁。

25. 'smith: iron smith，铁匠；**gat:** got; **roarin:** roaring，此处修饰 **fou:**（drunk，喝醉），表示喝得烂醉。

26. Kirkton Jean: 女人名。

27. prophesied: 预告；此行中的 she 系指汤姆的老婆 Kate.

28. drown'd: drowned，淹没；**Doon:** 河流名。

29. catch'd: catched, caught，被抓住；**warlocks:** wizards，男巫；**mirk:** night.

30. Alloway，地名；**haunted:** 闹鬼的；**kirk**：教堂。

31. gars: makes; **greet:** weep，哭泣，流泪。

32. monie: many; **counsels:** 劝告。

33. lengthen'd: lengthened，长的；**sage:** 明智的。

34. despises: 藐视。

35. planted: 安身在。

36. fast: 靠近；**ingle:** fireplace，壁炉；**bleezing:** blazing，烧得旺的。

37. reaming: frothing，发着泡沫的；**swats:** new ale，鲜啤酒；**divinely:** 非凡地，绝好地。

38. at his elbow: 在他手边；**Souter:** Cobbler，皮匠，补鞋匠；**Johnie:** John，人名。

39. ancient: old; **trusty:** 可信赖的；**drouthy:** 渴；**cronie:** crony，亲密的朋友。

40. lo'ed: loved; **brither:** brother.

41. thegither: together.

42. drave: drove，疾驰；**sangs:** songs; **clatter:** 谈笑。

43. ay: always.

44. gracious: 亲热。

45. favours: 恩情；**precious:** 珍贵的。

46. queerest: 最奇怪的。

47. chorus: 齐唱，意为店主人的笑声就象是配合鞋匠所说故事的齐唱。

48. rair: roar，怒号；**rustle:** 发沙沙声。

49. Tam did na mind the storm a whistle: Tam did not mind the storm a bit. 汤姆毫不在乎室外的风暴。

50. Care: 忧虑之神（此处是拟人化的用法）。

51. mad: 生气。

52. e'en: even; **himsel:** himself; **amang the nappy:** among the strong ale，在啤酒之中。

53. flee: 逃；lades：所载物；**o'**：of.

54. wing'd: winged, **winged their way:** 飞走。

55. blest: 有福。

56. o'er: over; **a':** all; **victorious:** 胜利的；此行意为 victorious over all the troubles of life.

57. poppies: 罂粟花。

58. flow'r: flower; **shed:** 脱落。

59. borealis: boreal，北方的；borealis 即 aurora borealis 北极光；**race:** 疾行。

60. flit: 掠过；**ere:** 在…之前。

61. evanishing: 消失。

62. tether: 拴住；**tide:** 潮流。

63. approaches: 接近；**maun:** must; **ride:** 骑，骑马上路。

64. arch: 拱门；**key-stane:** key-stone，拱顶石；此行意为黑夜的顶点。

65. dreary: 阴郁；**mounts:** 登上；**beast:** 牲畜（此处指马）。

66. sic: such; **taks:** takes, **take the road:** 出发，动身。

67. sinner: 罪人；**abroad:** 在外面。

68. 'twad: it would; **blawn:** blown; blawn its last，吹出了最后一口气。

69. **rattling:** 发格格声的；**showers:** 阵雨；**blast:** 一阵（风），一股（气流）。

70. **swallow'd:** swallowed，吞食，吞没。

71. **bellow'd:** bellowed，吼叫，轰鸣。

72. **Deil:** devil，魔鬼。

73. **weel mounted:** well mounted; **mare:** 母马；**Meg:** 马名。

74. **skelpit:** slapped，拍打；thro: through; **dub:** puddle，水坑，泥潭；**mire:** 淤泥。

75. **whiles:** while; **guid:** good; **bonnet:** 帽子。

76. **crooning:** 低声歌唱；**Scots:** 苏格兰方言的；**sonnet:** 十四行诗。

77. **glow'ring:** staring，凝视；**prudent:** 谨慎的。

78. **lest:** 唯恐；**bogles:** hobgoblins，怪物；**unawares:** 没察觉地。

79. **Kirk-Alloway:** Alloway 地方的教堂；**nigh:** near.

80. **ghaists:** ghosts，鬼；**houlets:** owls，枭。

81. **ford:** 可涉水处。

82. **snaw:** snow; **the chapman smoor'd:** the peddler smothered，小贩窒息而死。

83. **birks:** birches，桦；**meikle stane:** big stone.

84. **Charlie:** 人名；**brak's neck-bane:** broke his neck bone，折断他的脖子。

85. **whins:** furze (an evergreen shrub)，荆豆；cairn: stones heaped up as a memorial,（用作纪念或路标等的）圆锥形石堆。

86. **murder'd:** murdered; **bairn:** child.

87. **thorn:** 荆棘；**aboon:** above.

88. **Mungo:** 人名；**mither:** mother; **hang'd:** hanged; **hersel:** herself.

89. **pours:** 灌，注；**floods:** 水；**his** 指 Doon 河的。

90. **doubling:** 加倍（猛烈）的。

91. **lightnings:** 闪电；**flash:** 发出闪光；**from pole to pole:** 从一极到另一极，从一端到另一端。

92. **groaning:** 呻吟着的。

93. **bleeze:** blaze，一阵闪耀。

94. **bore:** hole; **beams:** 束，a beam of light，一束光；**glancing:** 射着光。

95. **resounded:** 鸣响；**mirth:** 欢笑。

96. **bold:** 勇敢的；**John Barleycorn:** 麦酒先生，啤酒先生。

97. **canst:** can（主语为 thou 时用）；**scorn**：藐视。

98. **tippenny:** twopenny (of drink)，两便士（的酒）。

99. **usquabae:** whisky，威士忌酒。

100. **ream'd:** reamed，起泡沫。

101. **Tammie:** Tom 的爱称；**noddle:** 脑袋瓜。

102. **car'd:** cared; **boddle:** a very small copper coin，小铜钱，全句意为：他一点也不怕鬼。

103. **Maggie:** 马名的爱称；**sair:** sore, very; **astonish'd:** astonished.

104. **admonish'd:** admonished，告诫；**by the heel and hand admonish'd:** 受

到汤姆脚踢手打的驱使。

105. ventur'd: ventured，冒险（向前）。

106. vow:（拟声词），叫声，表示惊讶或大喜；**unco:** strange，奇妙的。

107. warlocks: wizards，男巫。

108. cotillion: 交谊舞；**brent:** brand, **brent new:** brand new，崭新的。

109. hornpipes: 号笛；**jigs:** 快步舞；**strathspeys:** slow Highland dance，斯特拉斯贝舞曲（一种苏格兰舞）；**reels:** 旋转。

110. mettle: 精神；**heels:** 脚后跟。

111. winnock-bunker: window seat，窗下座位。

112. Nick: 人名，指魔鬼；**in shape o' beast:** 形状如兽。

113. touzie: 蓬松的（毛发）；**tyke:** shaggy dog，粗毛狗。

114. gie: give; **his charge:** 他的职务。

115. screw'd: screwed，旋转；**gart:** made; **skirl:** screech，尖叫。

116. rafters: 椽；**dirl:** rattle，发出格格声。

117. coffins: 棺材；**presses:** 压榨机。

118. shaw'd: showed.

119. cantraip: cantrip, charm, trick，符咒，魔力；**sleight:** 诡计。

120. cauld: cold; **cold hand:** 冷手（指死人的手）。

121. haly: holy，神圣的；**haly table:** 圣餐桌。

122. banes: bones; **gibbet:** 绞刑架；**airns:** irons，镣铐。

123. twa: two; span-lang: (i. e., the distance from outstretched thumb to little finger)，手掌张开时，大拇指和小指两端的距离，通常为9英寸或23厘米；**wee:** 小小的；**unchristen'd, unchristened:** 尚未命名的。

124. rape: rope.

125. gasp: 喘息；**gab:** mouth; **gape:** 张口。

126. tomahawks: 斧；**bluid:** blood; **redrusted:** 长着红锈。

127. scymitars: 短弯刀；wi' murder crusted: crusted with the blood of people murdered，被谋害的人的血结成了一层硬壳。

128. garter: 吊袜带；**strangled:** 勒死（其宾语为 babe）。

129. throat: 咽喉；**mangled:** 乱砍。

130. bereft: 使丧失；**whom his ain son o' life bereft:** whom his own son bereft of life，他亲生的儿子夺走了他的生命。

131. stack: stuck，沾在；**heft:** haft，刀把。

132. mair: more; **awefu':** awful，可怕的。

133. wad: would; **unlawful:** 犯法的。

134. glowr'd: glowered，凝视；**amaz'd:** amazed，惊奇。

135. mirth: 欢笑；**furious:** 强烈的。

136. reel'd: reeled，旋转；**set:** 相对而舞；**cross'd:** crossed，交叉而过；**cleekit:** joined hands，携手。这几字都是讲舞蹈中的动作。

137. carlin: old woman; **swat:** sweated，流汗；**reekit:** reeked，冒烟，发臭气。

138. coost: cast，扔；**duddies**：破衣服；**wark:** work; 全行意为 cast off her clothes for the work，扔掉她的衣服准备大跳一场。

139. linket: tripped lightly，轻快地跳舞；**sark:** shirt，（只穿衬衫）。

140. thae: those; queans: girls；此行意为：如果这些不是老太婆，而是姑娘们。

141. plump: 丰满；**strapping:** 身体高大而匀称的；**teens:** 十多岁（十三至十九岁）。

142. creeshie flannen: greasy flannel，油污的绒布。

143. snaw-white: snow-white; **seventeen hunder linen:** 细亚麻布，在一架有一千七百（seventeen hunder = seventeen hundred）条线的织机上织的。

144. thir: these; **breeks:** breeches，马裤；**pair:** 一对，一条（指裤子）。

145. ance: once; **plush:** 长毛绒；**guid:** good.

146. gien: given; **hurdies:** buttocks，臀部。

147. blink: 一瞥；**bonie:** bonnie，美丽的；**burdies:** maidens，少女。

148. wither'd: withered，枯萎了的；**beldams:**（貌丑、凶悍的）老太婆；**droll**：古怪离奇的。

149. rigwoodie: bony，瘦的；**hags:** 老丑妇，妖怪；**spean:** wean，断奶，意为她们又丑又干瘪，连小驹也不愿吃她们的奶；**foal:** 驹，（指一岁以下的马、驴、骡）。

150. louping: leaping，跃；**flinging:** 跳来跳去；**crummock:** staff，拐杖；on a crummock，拄着拐杖。

151. turn thy stomach: 使你作呕。

152. kend: 知道，懂得；**what was what**：事情的真相；**fu':** full; **brawlie:** finely；意为他完全了解实况。

153. winsome: 迷人的；**wench:** 少女；**wawlie:** strapping，身体高大而匀称的。

154. enlisted: 加入；**core:** corps，队，舞队。

155. Carrick: 地名；**shore:** 岸。

156. perished monie a bonie boat: 许多好船沉没。

157. baith: both; **meikle:** much; **bear:** barley，大麦。

158. cutty: short; **Paisley:** 带有苏格兰 Paisley 地方特色的花纹的；**harn:** yarn，纱，纱线。

159. lassie: 少女；**while a lassie:** 在她年轻时。

160. longtitude: 长度；**sorely:** 极，非常；**scanty:** 不足的。

161. vauntie: proud.

162. reverend: 可尊敬的；**grannie:** grandmother.

163. coft: bought; **Nannie:** 即这里所谈的舞者年轻时叫的名字。

164. pund Scots: 苏格兰金镑；'twas a' her riches: it was all her riches，这就是她的全部财产。

165. grac'd: graced，增光。

166. Muse: 诗神；**wing:** 翅膀；**maun:** must; **cour:** lower.

167. Sic flights are far beyond her power: 诗人自嘲，说是诗才有限，飞不上高处。

168. **lap:** 拍打；**flang:** flung，（fling 的过去式），跳来跳去。

169. **souple:** supple，灵活；**jade:**（贬）女人；**strang:** strong.

170. **ane:** one; **bewitch'd:** bewitched，着了迷的；**stood like ane bewitch'd:** 站在那里，象是一个着了迷的人。

171. **een:** eyes; **enrich'd:** enriched，大饱眼福。

172. **Satan:** 撒旦；**glowr'd:** glowered，怒视；**fidg'd:** fidget，坐立不安；**fu'fain:** (fidgeted) with pleasure，高兴（得乱动）。

173. **hotch'd:** hotched; **jerked:** 急扭，猛拉；**wi' might and main:** 竭尽全力。

174. **caper:** 跳跃；**syne:** then; **anither:** another.

175. **tint his reason a' thegither:** lost his reason altogether，完全失去了理智。

176. **weel done:** well done，跳得好呵！ **Cutty-sark:** 短汗衫（指女妖南尼）。

177. **scarcely:** 刚刚；**rallied:** 振作。

178. **hellish:** 凶恶的；**legion:** 大批人马；**sallied:** 出发。

179. **bizz out:** buzz out，嗡嗡叫着而飞出；**fyke:** fuss，忙乱。

180. **plundering:** 掠夺的；**herds:** herdsmen，牧人；**assail:** 攻击；**byke:** hive，蜂房。

181. **open:** begin to bark，吠声大作；**pussie:** hare，野兔；**mortal foes:** 不共戴天之敌。

182. **pop:**（拟声词）；she starts before their nose，兔子就在猎犬的面前窜过。

183. **eager:** 渴望的；**the market-crowd:** 市场里的群众。

184. **witches:** 女巫。

185. **eldritch:** unearthly，来自地狱的，可怕的；**skriech:** scream，嘶叫；**hollow:** holler，叫喊。

186. **fairin:** deserts，应得的后果，报应。

187. **roast:** 烤；**herrin:** herring，鲱鱼。

188. **vain:** 徒然的；**comin:** coming.

189. **woefu':** woeful，悲哀的。

190. **speedy:** 迅速的；**utmost:** 极度的行动；**Meg:**（马名）梅琪的爱称。

191. **brig:** bridge.

192. **toss:** 扔；**there, at them thou thy tail may toss:** 到了那里你就可以向那群妖怪翘尾巴了。

193. **fient:** fiend，魔鬼，此行意为：梅琪想用它的尾巴将魔鬼摔掉。

194. **Hard upon noble Maggie prest:** 紧追好马梅琪不放；**prest:** pressed.

195. **furious:** 狂怒的；**ettle:** intent，决心。

196. **wist:** 懂得；**mettle:** 气概。

197. **spring:** 跳（名词）；**hale:** whole，完整无恙。

198. **carlin:** 女巫；**claught:** clutched，抓住；**rump:** 尾部。

199. **scarce a stump:** 连尾巴根也一点不剩。

200. **wha:** who.

201. **heed:** 注意。

202. **whene'er:** whenever; **inclin'd:** inclined，倾向，喜爱。

203. **rin:** run; **rin in your mind:** 在你的心里翻腾。

204. **ye:** you; **o'er:** over; **o'er dear:** 过分昂贵（的代价）。

29 WILLIAM WORDSWORTH
1770–1850

1. *We Are Seven*
2. *The Tables Turned*

吴千之　选注

3. *Lines Composed a Few Miles Above Tintern Abbey*
4. *My Heart Leaps Up*
5. *I Wandered Lonely as a Cloud*
6. *[France](from The Prelude)*
7. *Sonnet: Composed upon Westminster Bridge*
8. *Sonnet: London, 1802*
9. *Sonnet: The World Is Too Much With Us*

张隆溪　选注

1. WE ARE SEVEN

A simple child,[1]
That lightly draws its breath,
And feels its life in every limb,[2]
What should it know of death?

I met a little cottage Girl:
She was eight years old, she said;
Her hair was thick with many a curl
That clustered round her head.

She had a rustic, woodland air,[3]
And she was wildly clad;[4]
Her eyes were fair, and very fair;
Her beauty made me glad.

"Sisters and brothers, little Maid,
How many may you be?"
"How many? Seven in all," she said
And wondering looked at me.

"And where are they? I pray you tell."
She answered, "Seven are we;
And two of us at Conway dwell,
And two are gone to sea.

"Two of us in the church-yard lie,
My sister and my brother;
And, in the church-yard cottage, I
Dwell near them with my mother."

"You say that two at Conway[5] dwell,
And two are gone to sea,
Yet ye are seven! — I pray you tell,
Sweet Maid, How this may be."

Then did the little Maid reply,
"Seven boys and girls are we;
Two of us in the church-yard lie,
Beneath the church-yard tree."

"You run about, my little Maid,
Your limbs they are alive;[6]
If two are in the church-yard laid,

Then ye are only five."

"Their graves are green they may be seen,"
The little Maid replied,
"Twelve steps or more from my mother's door,
And they are side by side.

"My stockings there I often knit,
My kerchief there I hem;
And there upon the ground I sit,
And sing a song to them.

"And often after sunset, Sir,
When it is light and fair,[7]
I take my little porringer,[8]
And eat my supper there.

"The first that died was sister Jane;
In bed she moaning lay,[9]
Till God released her of her pain;
And then she went away.[10]

"So in the church-yard she was laid;
And, when the grass was dry,
Together round her grave we played,
My brother John and I.

"And when the ground was white with snow,
And I could run and slide,
My brother John was forced to go,
And he lies by her side."

"How many are you, then," said I.

"If they two are in heaven?"
Quick was the little Maid's reply,
"O Master! We are seven."

"But they are dead; those two are dead!
Their spirits are in heaven!"
'Twas throwing words away;[11] for still
The little Maid would have her will,
And said, "Nay, we are seven!"

2. THE TABLES TURNED

An Evening Scene on the Same Subject

Up! up! my Friend, and quit your books;
Or surely you'll grow double[1]:
Up! up! my Friend, and clear your looks[2];
Why all this toil and trouble?

The sun, above the mountain's head,
A freshening lustre mellow
Through all the long green fields has spread[3],
His first sweet evening yellow.

Books! 'tis a dull and endless strife:
Come, hear the woodland linnet,[4]
How sweet his music! on my life,[5]
There's more of wisdom in it.

And hark! how blithe the throstle sings![6]
He, too, is no mean preacher:
Come forth into the light of things[7],
Let Nature be your Teacher.[8]

She has a world of[9] ready wealth,
Our minds and hearts[10] to bless —
Spontaneous wisdom breathed by health,
Truth breathed by cheerfulness.[11]

One impulse from a vernal wood[12]
May teach you more of man,
Of moral evil and of good,
Than all the sages can.

Sweet is the lore[13] which Nature brings;
Our meddling intellect
Mis-shapes the beauteous forms of things: —
We murder to dissect.[14]

Enough of Science and of Art;
Close up those barren leaves;[15]
Come forth, and bring with you a heart
That watches and receives.

3. LINES COMPOSED A FEW MILES ABOVE TINTERN ABBEY ON REVISITING THE BANKS OF THE WYE DURING A TOUR. JULY 13, 1798

Five years have passed; five summers, with the length
Of five long winters! and again I hear
These waters, rolling from their mountain-springs
With a soft inland murmur.[1] — Once again
Do I behold these steep and lofty cliffs,
That on a wild secluded scene[2] impress
Thoughts of more deep seclusion; and connect

The landscape with the quiet of the sky.
The day is come when I again repose
Here, under this dark sycamore,[3] and view
These plots of cottage-ground, these orchard-tufts,[4]
Which at this season, with their unripe fruits,
Are clad in one green hue, and lose themselves[5]
'Mid groves and copses. Once again I see
These hedge-rows, hardly hedge-rows, little lines
Of sportive wood run wild:[6] these pastoral farms,
Green to the very door; and wreaths of smoke
Sent up, in silence, from among the trees!
With some uncertain notice,[7] as might seem
Of vagrant dwellers[8] in the houseless woods,
Or of some Hermit's cave, where by his fire
The Hermit[9] sits alone.
These beauteous forms,
Through[10] a long absence, have not been to me
As is a landscape to a blind man's eye:
But oft, in lonely rooms, and 'mid the din
Of towns and cities, I have owed to them
In hours of weariness, sensations sweet,
Felt in the blood, and felt along the heart;
And passing even into my purer mind,
With tranquil restoration:[11] — feelings too
Of unremembered pleasure: such, perhaps,
As have no slight or trivial influence
On that best portion of a good man's life,
His little, nameless, unremembered, acts
Of kindness and of love.[12] Nor less, I trust,
To them I may have owed another gift,
Of aspect more sublime[13]; that blessed mood
In which the burthen of the mystery,
In which the heavy and the weary weight

Of all this unintelligible world,
Is lightened: — that serene and blessed mood,
In which the affections gently lead us on, —
Until, the breath of this corporeal frame[14]
And even the motion of our human blood
Almost suspended, we are laid asleep
In body, and become a living soul:
While with an eye made quiet by the power
Of harmony, and the deep power of joy,
We see into the life of things.[15]
                                        If this
Be but a vain belief, yet, oh! how oft —
In darkness and amid the many shapes[16]
Of joyless daylight; when the fretful stir
Unprofitable, and the fever of the world,[17]
Have hung upon the beatings of my heart —
How oft, in spirit, have I turned to thee,
O sylvan[18] Wye! thou wanderer through the woods,
How often has my spirit turned to thee!

    And now, with gleams of half-extinguished thought,[19]
With many recognitions dim and faint,
And somewhat of a sad perplexity,[20]
The picture of the mind revives again:
While here I stand, not only with the sense
Of present pleasure, but with pleasing thoughts
That in this moment there is life and food
For future years. And so[21] I dare to hope,
Though changed, no doubt, from what I was when first
I came among these hills; when like a roe[22]
I bounded o'er the mountains, by the sides
Of the deep rivers, and the lonely streams,
Wherever nature led: more like a man

Flying from something that he dreads than one
Who sought the thing he loved. For nature then
(The coarser pleasures[23] of my boyish days,[24]
And their glad animal movements all gone by)
To me was all in all.[25]—I cannot paint
What then I was. The sounding cataract
Haunted me like a passion:[26] the tall rock,
The mountain, and the deep and gloomy wood,
Their colours and their forms, were then to me
An appetite;[27] a feeling and a love,
That had no need of a remoter charm,
By thought supplied, nor any interest
Unborrowed from the eye.[28]—That time is past,
And all its aching joys[29] are now no more,[30]
And all its dizzy raptures. Not for this
Faint[31] I, nor mourn nor murmur; other gifts
Have followed; for such loss, I would believe,
Abundant recompense. For I have learned
To look on nature, not as in the hour
Of thoughtless youth; but hearing oftentimes
The still, sad music of humanity,
Nor harsh nor grating, though of ample power
To chasten and subdue.[32] And I have felt
A presence[33] that disturbs me with the joy
Of elevated thoughts; a sense sublime
Of something far more deeply interfused,
Whose dwelling is the light of setting suns,
And the round ocean and the living air,
And the blue sky, and in the mind of man:
A motion and a spirit, that impels
All thinking things, all objects of all thought,
And rolls through all things.[34] Therefore am I still
A lover of the meadows and the woods,

And mountains; and of all that we behold
From this green earth; of all the mighty world
Of eye, and ear,[35]—both what they half create,[36]
And what perceive; well pleased to recognize
In nature and the language of the sense[37]
The anchor[38] of my purest thoughts, the nurse,
The guide, the guardian of my heart, and soul
Of all my moral being.

Nor perchance,
If I were not thus taught, should I the more
Suffer my genial spirits[39] to decay:
For thou[40] art with me here upon the banks
Of this fair river; thou my dearest Friend,
My dear, dear Friend; and in thy voice I catch
The language of my former heart, and read
My former pleasures in the shooting lights
Of thy wild eyes. Oh! yet a little while
May I behold in thee what I was once,
My dear, dear Sister! and this prayer I make,
Knowing that Nature never did betray
The heart that loved her; 'tis her privilege,
Through all the years of this our life, to lead
From joy to joy: for she can so inform[41]
The mind that is within us, so impress[42]
With quietness and beauty, and so feed
With lofty thoughts, that neither evil tongues,
Rash judgments, nor the sneers of selfish men,
Nor greetings where no kindness is, nor all
The dreary intercourse of daily life,
Shall e'er prevail against us, or disturb
Our cheerful faith, that all which we behold
Is full of blessings. Therefore let the moon
Shine on thee in thy solitary walk;

And let the misty mountain-winds be free
To blow against thee: and, in after years,
When these wild ecstasies[43] shall be matured
Into a sober pleasure; when thy mind
Shall be a mansion for all lovely forms,
Thy memory be as a dwelling-place
For all sweet sounds and harmonies; oh! then,
If solitude, or fear, or pain, or grief,
Should be thy portion, with what healing thoughts
Of tender joy wilt thou remember me,
And these my exhortations! Nor, perchance —
If I should be where I no more can hear
Thy voice, nor catch from thy wild eyes these gleams
Of past existence[44] — wilt thou then forget
That on the banks of this delightful stream
We stood together; and that I, so long
A worshipper of Nature, hither came
Unwearied in that service: rather say
With warmer love — oh! with far deeper zeal
Of holier love. Nor wilt thou then forget,
That after many wanderings, many years
Of absence, these steep woods and lofty cliffs,
And this green pastoral landscape, were to me
More dear, both for themselves and for thy sake!

4. MY HEART LEAPS UP

My heart leaps up when I behold
    A rainbow in the sky:
So was it when my life began;
So is it now I am a man;
So be it when I shall grow old,
    Or let me die!

The Child is father of the Man;[1]
And I could wish my days to be
Bound each to each by natural piety.[2]

5. *I WANDERED LONELY AS A CLOUD*

I wandered lonely as a cloud
That floats on high o'er vales and hills,
When all at once I saw a crowd,
A host, of golden daffodils;
Beside the lake, beneath the thess,
Fluttering and dancing in the breeze.

Continuous[1] as the stars that shine
And twinkle on the milky way,
They stretched in never-ending line
Along the margin of a bay:[2]
Ten thousand saw I at a glance,
Tossing their heads in sprightly dance.

The waves beside them danced; but they
Outdid the sparkling waves in glee;
A poet could not but be gay,
In such a jocund company;
I gazed — and gazed — but little thought
What wealth the show to me had brought:

For oft, when on my couch I lie
In vacant[3] or in pensive mood,
They flash upon that inward eye
Which is the bliss of colitude;[4]
And then my heart with pleasure fills,
And dances with the daffodils.

6. *from THE PRELUDE*

[France]

O pleasant exercise[1] of hope and joy!
For mighty were the auxiliars[2] which then stood
Upon our side, us who were strong in love!
Bliss was it in that dawn to be alive,
But to be young was very Heaven! O times,
In which the meagre, stale, forbidding ways
Of custom, law, and statute, took at once
The attraction of a country in romance![3]
When Reason seemed the most to assert her rights[4]
When most intent on making of herself
A prime enchantress[5]— to assist[6] the work,
Which then was going forward in her name!
Not favoured spots alone, but the whole Earth,
The beauty wore of promise[7]— that which sets
(As at some moments might not be unfelt[8]
Among the bowers of Paradise[9] itself)
The budding rose[10] above the rose full blown.
What temper[11] at the prospect did not wake
To happiness unthought of? The inert[12]
Were roused, and lively natures[13] rapt away!
They who had fed[14] their childhood upon dreams,
The play-fellows of fancy, who had made
All powers of swiftness, subtilty, and strength
Their ministers,[15]— who in lordly wise[16] had stirred
Among the grandest objects of the sense,
And dealt with whatsoever they found there
As if they had within some lurking right
To wield it;[17]— they, too, who of gentle mood
Had watched all gentle motions, and to these

Had fitted their own thoughts, schemers more mild,
And in the region of their peaceful selves; —[18]
Now was it that both[19] found, the meek and lofty
Did both find helpers to their hearts' desire,
And stuff at hand, plastic as they could wish, —
Were called upon to exercise their skill,
Not in Utopia[20], — subterranean fields, —
Or some secreted island, Heaven knows where!
But in the very world, which is the world
Of all of us, — the place where, in the end,
We find our happiness, or not at all![21]

——Book Eleventh

7. COMPOSED UPON WESTMINSTER BRIDGE, SEPTEMBER 3, 1802

Earth has not anything to show more fair:
Dull would he be of soul who could pass by
A sight so touching in its majesty:[1]
This City[2] now doth, like a garment, wear
The beauty of the morning: silent, bare,
Ships, towers, domes, theatres, and temples lie
Open unto the fields,[3] and to the sky;
All bright and glittering in the smokeless air.
Never did sun more beautifully steep[4]
In his first splendour, valley, rock, or hill;
Ne'er saw I, never felt, a call so deep!
The river[5] glideth at his own sweet will:
Dear God! the very houses seem asleep;
And all that mighty heart[6] is lying still!

8. LONDON, 1802

Milton[1]! thou shouldst be living at this hour:

England hath need of thee: she is a fen
Of stagnant waters:[2] altar, sword, and pen,[3]
Fireside, the heroic wealth of hall and bower,[4]
Have forfeited[5] their ancient English dower
Of inward happiness. We are selfish men
O! raise us up, return to us again;
And give us manners,[6] virtue, freedom, power.
Thy soul was like a Star, and dwelt apart:[7]
Thou hadst a voice whose sound was like the sea,
Pure as the naked heavens,[8] majestic, free;
So didst thou travel on life's common way
In cheerful godliness; and yet thy heart
The lowliest duties[9] on herself did lay.

9. THE WORLD IS TOO MUCH WITH US

The world[1] is too much with us; late and soon,
Getting and spending, we lay waste our powers;[2]
Little we see in Nature that is ours;[3]
We have given our hearts away, a sordid boon![4]
This Sea that bares her bosom to the moon,
The winds that will be howling[5] at all hours
And are up-gather'd now like sleeping flowers[6],
For this, for everything, we are out of tune;
It moves us not. — Great God! I'd rather be
A pagan suckled in a creed outworn,[7]
So might I,[8] standing on this pleasant lea,[9]
Have glimpses that would make me less forlorn;[10]
Have sight of Proteus[11] rising from the sea;
Or hear old Triton[12] blow his wreathèd horn.

【作者简介】威廉·华兹华斯（William Wordsworth,1770–1850），英国浪漫主义诗人，“湖畔派”（the Lake poets）的魁首，生于英格兰北部肯勃兰的小城考克茅斯

（Cockermouth）一位律师的家庭。幼时丧父母，就学于风景胜地“湖区”的霍克斯海德（Hawkshead），同农家子弟为伍，游憩于湖光山色之间，性情深受大自然陶冶。十七岁入剑桥大学，二十一岁卒业。一七九〇年去法国、瑞士、意大利旅行，饱览阿尔卑斯山景色，并亲身来到法国大革命的风暴中心。他一七九二年重访法国，进一步受到法国革命思想影响，回国后写过一些充满民主思想的好诗。诗人后来回顾这一时期时，曾写下这样壮丽的诗句：

Bliss was it in that dawn to be alive,
But to be young was very heaven!

——*Prelude*, XI, 108–109

（能活在那黎明时光是何等幸福，
但能在那时是个青年更胜似天堂！

——《序曲》，第十一章第108—109行）

由于英国对法国的宣战、雅各宾党的恐怖专政、日益沉重的家庭负担以及友人的馈赠带来的优裕条件等种种原因，诗人在政治上日趋消极，以至保守。十八世纪最后五年，华兹华斯越来越转向自然，在湖区与另一位浪漫主义诗人柯尔律治（Coleridge）结下了莫逆之交，同妹妹多萝西（Dorothy）及柯尔律治一起遍游英格兰北部、苏格兰、威尔士、爱尔兰等地，创作了许多脍炙人口的写景抒情诗。从一七九八年与柯尔律治合作发表《抒情歌谣集》（*Lyrical Ballads*）第一版起至一八〇七年前后，是华兹华斯诗才的全盛时期。一八一三年他接受政府的长期津贴，一八四三年又被封为桂冠诗人，自此诗才江河日下，所作也内容空虚，晦涩难读。

华兹华斯是英国浪漫派诗歌理论的创始人。他的诗论主要见于一八〇〇年第二版《抒情歌谣集》序和一八一五年《诗集》新版序。华兹华斯的名篇甚多，不少是我国读者所熟悉的。这里我们选注了《我们七个》（*We Are Seven*, 1798），《全局改观》（*The Tables Turned*, 1798），《丁登寺旁》（*Lines Composed a Few Miles Above Tintern Abbey*, 1798），《彩虹》（*My Heart Leaps Up*, 1802），《水仙》（*I Wandered Lonely as a Cloud*, 1804），《序曲》（*The Prelude*, 1805）片断以及几首十四行诗（sonnets），从中可以窥见诗人世界观、创作观与艺术风格之一斑。

【题解与注释】

1. WE ARE SEVEN

这首诗写于一七九八年春，女主人公是作者一七九三年游览威尔士时遇见的一个农村小姑娘。小姑娘本来一家七兄妹，死了两个，按成年人的推理，应该算五个，但八岁的小姑娘不是凭数学逻辑，而是凭直觉和感情判断事物。死去的一兄一姐幼时与她一同生活，一同游戏，生时情同手足，死后又躺在离家门仅十数步远的墓地里，仍是天天“相会”的伴侣，自然不该从七兄妹中除名。正是这童心的天真纯洁和这淡淡的忧伤，打动了诗人的心，使他久久不能忘怀，数年之后终成名篇。一八四一年诗人旧地重游，不仅故人已无踪影，当年的古堡建筑也只剩下一片残迹。在重版此诗时，诗人不禁感慨系之，还为此加写过一段序言。

诗人采风，路遇村中儿童，随便问问年龄和家中人口，这本是极平凡的事，诗中的小姑娘也没有作什么语出惊人的回答。在凡夫俗子看来，这里似乎找不到可以入诗的题材，但从平淡无奇的事物中悟出不平凡的哲理，升华为诗，这正是华兹华斯的特色和他诗论中主张的一条重要原理。童心的可爱、可贵，则又是以华兹华斯为代表的浪漫派诗人喜爱的主题，间接地反映了诗人对浑浊的成人世界和冷酷的理性社会的反感。这首诗正可作为代表华兹华斯诗论和浪漫主义思潮的一个范例。

本诗采用的形式是歌谣体（ballad），四行一节，一、三行各四音步，二、四行各三音步，abab 韵，这种形式很适于表现民间叙事的内容。全诗语言浅近，对话部分更近似口语，是华兹华斯优秀诗篇的又一特征。

1. A simple child: 此行音步不完整。当初柯尔律治曾建议以“A little child, dear brother Jem”开头，华兹华斯认为 dear brother Jem 不伦不类，略去未用，最后就成了目前这样的残句。也有的版本将此行改为“A simple child, dear brother Tim”，Tim 与 limb 押韵，显系后人取柯尔律治之意的伪托。

2. 第 2—3 行：意指童年生命力旺盛，呼吸轻快，四肢充满活力。

3. air: 神态，仪表。**rustic, woodland air:** 乡下人和林区人的粗犷气。

4. clad: = clothed; **wildly clad:** 衣着散乱，有一股子野性。

5. Conway: 威尔士西北部港口。

6. Your limbs they are alive: = Your limbs are alive (full of life)，用代词重复名词主语是不规范的口语中常见的形式，在叙事歌谣中也常常出现，修辞学上称为冗言（pleonasm），是一种加强语气的手段。这一节意思是：“小姑娘，你现在活蹦乱跳，四肢灵活，可别忘记你的兄姐已经入土，所以你们兄妹只能算五个了。”

7. light and fair: 指月明天晴。

8. porringer: 儿童喝粥、喝汤用的带把小碗。

9. she moaning lay: = she lay moaning.

10. went away: 指死去。下面第 59 行 *was forced to go* 同。

11. ’Twas (= It was) **throwing words away:** 白废口舌。

2. THE TABLES TURNED

这是感性对理性、自然对书斋的挑战。诗人劝告朋友放下书本，奔向自然，体现了浪漫主义的新思想。自从牛顿对宇宙作出力学的解释以来，整个十七、十八世纪英国思想界都是以崇尚理智与逻辑的经验主义占主导地位，而笛卡尔的唯理主义也有相当影响。十七、十八世纪英国文学中的新古典主义以蒲伯（Alexander Pope）、约翰逊（Samuel Johnson）等为代表，追求形式的完美合理，格律的严谨，文坛上充斥着书卷气，缺乏来自自然和民间的新鲜气息。法国启蒙思想家如卢梭（Rousseau）等的思想和法国大革命的炮声，打破了整个欧洲的沉闷空气，激发了一场思想解放运动。崇拜自然，反对矫饰，提倡个性解放，打破理念的羁绊，成了一代新人的时尚。本诗标题“全局改观”即指当时思想界这种翻天覆地的大变化。本诗表面上以作者友人为对象，实际上是对整个文学界、知识界的号召。诗中多处出现感叹句，体现了诗人顺应时代变迁的紧迫感，口语体的语言则传达了忠告的殷切。诗人成功地运用对比手段，描绘了大自然与感性世界的美妙诱人，讥讽了学究生活与理性世界的无益、无聊。

1. grow double: 指长期伏案会变成佝偻驼背。

2. clear your looks: 换上笑容（舒展你的愁眉，不要愁眉苦脸）。

3. 第 5—7 行： 这三行是倒装结构，宾语 A freshening lustre mellow 提前。意为：西山的夕阳将柔美的晚霞洒满绿色的田野，使人神清目爽。

4. linnet: 红雀。

5. on my life: 口语中表示强调的感叹词，意为“我敢担保”，“说真的”。

6. 第 13 行： 华兹华斯反对用冷僻古奥的诗语（poetic diction），主张诗应以白话为自己的语言，但也适当使用 **hark** (= listen)，**behold** (= look) 这类已十分常见的诗语。

throstle 即 song thrush，画眉。

7. 第 15 行： 作者劝友人走出阴暗的书斋，进入光明的世界。

8. 第 16 行： 这一行可谓全诗主题所在，也是作者自然观的真谛。

9. She: = Nature; **a world of:** 无数的。

10. minds: 指理性所在，**hearts:** 指感性所在。全句大意是：大自然有取之不尽的现成财富来丰富我们的感情和理智。

11. 第 19—20 行： 这两行大意是：健康状态自发产生的智慧，愉悦中获得的真理。字里行间处处埋伏着理性与非理性、书斋与自然的强烈对比。按照传统观念，智慧与真理只能是闭门苦读的结果，而浪漫派诗人则提出全新的见解，主张从自然的领悟中学习；而 breathe 一词则说明大自然赋予的智慧与真理犹如宜人的清风，毫无令人窒息的感觉。

12. impulse from a vernal wood: 春天的树林给人的刺激。

13. lore: 知识，学问。

14. 第 26—28 行：intellect（智力，理智）本应助人更好地认识自然，但在浪漫主义者看来，它只能干扰（meddle with）和歪曲（misshape）自然美。大自然的美只能靠直觉去感受，因此诗人斩钉截铁地断言：剖析等于扼杀。这是对理性主义的大胆宣战。

15. barren leaves: 毫无生机的书页。

3. LINES COMPOSED A FEW MILES ABOVE TINTERN ABBEY, ON REVISITING THE BANKS OF THE WYE DURING A TOUR. JULY 13, 1798

1793 年八月，二十三岁的华兹华斯曾独自徒步旅行，到英格兰西部蒙茅斯郡（Monmouthshire）去游历了风景秀丽的怀河（the Wye）河谷和古老的丁登寺（Tintern Abbey)。五年之后偕其妹 Dorothy 重游故地，风景依旧，而诗人却意识到自己的感受与昔日已有所不同，于是发为深远的幽思。其中既有对少年时代的留恋缅怀，又有对现在的评价和对未来的期待，一种淡淡的优伤和对人生恬然自适的静观态度与诗人对自然的渴求和信念完美地揉合在一起，使这首诗成为代表华兹华斯艺术风格与思想观念最典型的作品之一。

华兹华斯主张诗要写得朴实自然，不要刻意雕琢，他的许多作品也的确做到了这一点。《丁登寺旁》是一首 150 余行的长诗，完全是在风景和诗情的激发下一气呵成，流畅而幽婉，没有一点斧凿痕。诗人自己曾愉快地记叙这首诗的写作过程：

> No poem of mine was composed under circumstances more pleasant for me to remember than this. I began it upon leaving Tintern, after crossing the Wye, and concluded it just as I was entering Bristol in the evening, after a ramble of 4 or 5 days, with my sister. Not a line of it was altered, and not any part of it written down till I reached Bristol.

在形式上，这首诗是无韵体（blank verse），每行十音节，五音步抑扬格（iambic pentameter）。莎士比亚的戏剧和弥尔顿的史诗都是用无韵体写成的，但到了新古典主义时期，英雄双韵体（heroic couplets）成为主要的格律形式，直到浪漫派诗歌兴起之后，无韵体才重新受到重视。华兹华斯和其他一些浪漫派诗人都用无韵体写过不少名篇。

1. 第 1—4 行：诗人起首便用了 **Five years, five summers** 和 **five long winters，**三次重复极言阔别之久，而旧地重游的喜悦也跃然纸上。

soft inland murmur: 内河潺潺的低诉。

2. wild secluded scene: 野外幽静的景色。以下至第 8 行大意为：在一片幽静的野外风景里，河岸两旁的峭壁激起人更为幽远的思绪，并使河谷中的景色与浩浩长空的静穆融为一体。

3. sycamore: 槭树。

4. orchard-tufts: 栽满果树的小山坡。这里的 **tuft** = toft.

5. clad: = clothed; **lose themselves:** 由于果树的果实尚未成熟，都是一片绿色，所以与别的灌木无法分辨开来。

6. sportive wood run wild: 此句描写蔓生的枝条形成天然树篱，极为生动。在华兹华斯笔下，自然界的一草一木似乎都具有灵性。

7. uncertain notice: 袅袅炊烟从树间升起，而四围一片沉寂，使人对那缕缕青烟的来源不敢断然肯定。**notice** 可解为 sign or indication.

8. vagrant dwellers: 浪游者。

9. Hermit: 隐士。林中的烟使人觉得象是丛林中有浪游者或隐士在生火。以上描写是诗人重访旧地所见。

10. Through: throughout, during.

11. 第 25—30 行：自然界中见到的美景（即第 22 行 **These beauteous forms**）在诗人蛰居喧闹的都市，感到孤寂无聊时，可以通过回想带给他慰藉。这是华兹华斯一个重要的思想，可参见下面《水仙》一诗。

purer mind: 这里不是与 **heart** 和 **blood** 相比，而是指 a purer（more serene）state of mind.

tranquil restoration: 恢复恬静的心绪。华兹华斯似乎认为最理想的心理状态应是达到物我交融，与大自然完全和谐一致。在《抒情歌谣集》1800年序中，他指出诗是激情的自然流露，但诗人处于激情中往往不能写作，而要在恬静状态中回想、体会当初的激情，才写得出好诗来："I have said that poetry is the spontaneous overflow of powerful feelings: it takes its origin from emotion recollected in tranquillity."

12. 第30—35行 feelings too ... of love: 自然界中所见的美景还使我在孤寂中重新感到快乐，当初引起快乐的情景虽已淡漠了，但对我们的生命却无形中有不可忽视的影响，使我们做出善意与爱的举动。此数行诗意可与《序曲》中这几行相参照：

The soul
Remembering how she felt, but what she felt
Remembering not, retains an obscure sense
Of possible sublimity.

—*The Prelude*, II. 315–318

13. Of aspect more sublime: of a higher quality.

14. this corporeal frame: the human body，人的肉体。

15. 从第37行 that blessed mood 到第49行 the life of things: 大意是：在这种平静的心绪中，人世上许多阴暗而不可理解的事物在我们心灵上的沉重负担也减轻了；高尚的感情引导着我们，我们几乎暂时忘掉了自己的血液在流动和自己肉体的存在，而变成纯粹的精神；我们坚信万物的和谐而充满了欢乐，于是以平静的眼光观察，可以洞见事物的本质。此数行可以与《序曲》中这几行相参照：

Difference
Perceived in things, where, to the unwatchful eye,
No difference is, and hence, from the same source,
Sublimer joy.

—*The Prelude*, II. 299–302

16. shapes: manifestations, experiences，白日所见的东西或经历的事情。

17. the fretful stir Unprofitable, and the fever of the world: 无益的烦恼和人生的热病。此句似化用莎士比亚悲剧中的两处名句：

How weary, stale, flat and *unprofitable*
Seem to me all the uses of this world!

—*Hamlet*, I. ii. 133–134

After life's fitful *fever* he sleeps well.

—Macbeth, III. ii. 23

18. sylvan: 多树木的，来自拉丁文 *silva*（树林）。

19. with gleams of half-extinguished thought: 诗人旧地重游，又唤起了对过去的回忆，就象已半灭的余烬重又炽燃起来。

20. sad perplexity: 诗人显然意识到眼前所见与记忆中的美景已有所不同，于是产生茫然怅惘的情绪。

21. so: that it will be so.

22. roe: 一种小鹿。

23. coarser pleasures: 指儿时的游戏。

24. my boyish days: 诗人的第一个时期，当时与大自然完全是一体，以至没有意识到自然的存在。

25. To me was all in all: 这是诗人的第二个时期，他意识到了自然的存在，并全心热爱大自然。这就是诗人五年前的情形。

26. a passion: 热烈追求的对象。

27. An appetite: 引起强烈欲望的东西。

28. Unborrowed from the eye: 不靠视觉获得的。诗人用 passion 和 appetite 等字，都强调当时对自然的官能上的感受，而与后来由沉思得来的 remoter charm 相对照。

29. aching joys: joys so intense as to have an aching effect. 把性质相反的两个词放在一起以获得强烈对比的效果，修辞学上称为矛盾修饰法（oxymoron）。下一行 dizzy raptures 同。

30. now no more: 这是诗人的第三个时期，他这时意识到自己与自然和儿时的自我都可能有了一定的距离。

31. Faint: 沮丧。

32. 第 91—93 行 The still, sad music of humanity ... chasten and subdue: 人生的忧伤象低沉的音乐，也是万物和谐中的一部分，所以虽使人变得严肃而节制，却并没有使诗人灰心懊丧。

33. A presence: something present in Nature.

34. 第 95—102 行 a sense ... through all things: 在华兹华斯的自然观中，无论有生命或无生命的事物，无论人或自然，都互相联系在一个和谐的整体中，他似乎感到一种宇宙间的精神（*a spirit*）运行在整个人与自然的王国里。参见《序曲》：

I felt the sentiment of Being, spread
O'er all that moves and all that seemeth still.

—*The Prelude*, II. 401–402

35. the mighty world of eye and ear: 通过眼、耳感觉到的奇妙的世界。**mighty:** wonderful, miraculous.

36. what they half create: 华兹华斯曾说此行是套用扬格（Edward Young）*Night Thoughts* 中的一行诗，扬格说人的感觉"half create the wondrous world they see". 人的感官不是仅仅被动地接受自然景物的刺激，而且也主动地进行选择，因此也是一种创造。

37. the language of the sense: 感官对自然的解释；人对自然界万物的感受。

38. anchor: 支撑。

39. my genial spirits: 我天性中快活的精神。参见 Milton, *Samson Agonistes*, 594:

So much I feel my *genial spirits* droop.

40. thou: 诗人之妹 Dorothy.

41. inform: animate or give life to.

42. impress: affect the mind.

43. wild ecstasies: 即第 84 和 85 行中的 **aching joys** 和 **dizzy raptures.**

44. If I should be ... past existence: 诗人在这里想到死亡，这是构成这首诗基调中的阴影部分。

4. MY HEART LEAPS UP

此诗写于 1802 年，于 1807 年首次发表。在这首短诗里，华兹华斯表现了希望永葆儿童时代的天真纯洁和对自然的热爱的愿望。他的朋友柯尔律治（Coleridge）有一段话可以作为此诗的题解：

> To carry on the feelings of childhood into the powers of manhood; to combine the child's sense of wonder and novelty with the appearances which every day perhaps for forty years have made familiar, — this is the character and privilege of genius.
>
> —*Biographia Literaria*, iv.

1. The Child is father of the Man: 此处的意思不仅是说每个人都先有童年才有成年，而且成年人性情中纯洁美好的部分都是保持了在童年时期形成的东西。参见 Milton, *Paradise Regained*, iv. 220:

> The childhood shews the man,
> As morning shews the day.

2. natural piety: 既然儿童是成人的父亲，每一个今天也是来自昨天，成年人就应当尊敬自己的童年和少年时代，使自己的精神发展连贯一致。

5. I WANDERED LONELY AS A CLOUD

这首诗写于 1804 年，发表于 1807 年。诗人在独自漫游时，忽然发现湖边一大片金黄色的水仙在微风中摇曳起舞，大自然中这奇妙的美景不仅使诗人心旷神怡，而且将成为美好的回忆，在他孤寂无聊的时候给他以安慰和快乐。

在 Dorothy Wordsworth 的日记里，曾记叙了他们兄妹看到一片水仙花的情形（见 1802 年四月十五日的记载）：

> When we were in the woods beyond Gowbarrow Park, we saw a few daffodils close to the water side ... As we went along there were more, and yet more; and, at last, under the boughs of the trees, we saw that there was a long belt of them along the shore, about the breadth of a country turnpike road. I never saw daffodils **so** beautiful. They grew among the mossy stones, about and above them; some rested their heads upon these stones, as on a pillow for weariness; and the rest tossed and reeled and danced, and seemed as if they verily laughed with the wind that blew upon them over the lake. They looked so gay, ever glancing, ever changing.

1. Continuous: 延伸一片。

2. the margin of a bay: 一湾湖水。

3. vacant: 茫然；无聊。

4. that inward eye which is the bliss of solitude: 诗人认为，在孤寂中回想自然中的美景是一种幸福。参见 *Tintern Abbey* 第 25 至 30 行。

6. [France] from *THE PRELUDE* **or Growth of a Poet's Mind**

华兹华斯曾计划写作一部哲理性的长诗，表现自己"关于人、自然和社会"的思想，题名为《隐士》(*Reduse*)，但此计划并未完成。《序曲》的写作开始于 1798 年，于 1805 年夏完成，原是计划中那部长诗的序诗。正象它的副标题表明的那样，这是描述"诗人心灵的成长"的自传性作品，在这方面，法国启蒙思想家卢梭（Rousseau）著名的《忏悔录》(*Confessions*) 在当时已是极有影响的著作。华兹华斯生前一直不时修改这部《序曲》，直到他死后才于 1850 年首次发表，至于 1805 年稿的本来面目，直到 1926 年塞林可特（Ernest de Sélincourt）整理诗人手稿后发表的版本，才第一次为世人所见。

《序曲》共分十四章，记叙了诗人从童年到成熟的内心经历，我们在这里从第十一章"法国"(France) 选取一个片断，由此可以看见青年时代的华兹华斯曾经怎样热情地赞美过法国大革命。

1. exercise: the state or condition of being in active operation. 参见 Keats, *Hyperion*, 107–8:

Godlike exercise
Of influence benign.

2. auxiliars: allies.

3. O times ... in romance: 在革命时代，古老的法国突然焕发了青春，好象具有传奇之国的动人魅力。

meagre: wanting in fullness, harsh. **stale:** worn out.

4. assert her rights: 坚持她（理性）的权利。

5. making of herself A prime enchantress: = making a prime enchantress of herself，使她自己成为一位最有魅力的女神。

6. to assist: = in order to assist.

7. the whole Earth, The beauty wore of promise: 此处采用了倒装句法，等于 the whole Earth wore the beauty of promise，整个大地都充满了美好的希望。

8. might not be unfelt: 用双重否定达到强烈的肯定，比 might be felt 语气更强。这种修辞手段称为间接肯定法（litotes）.

9. Paradise: 即《圣经》中的伊甸乐园（the Garden of Eden），人类的始祖居住的乐土。诗人在此把法国革命带给人类的新的希望与创世之初的极乐世界相比。

10. The budding rose: 含苞欲放的玫瑰，用以比喻未来的希望与前途。

11. temper: temperament, disposition；性情；气质。从此行起，华兹华斯描述了各种性格的人都受到革命的感召和鼓舞。

12. The inert: 生性不活泼的人。

13. lively natures: 性格活跃的人。**rapt away，**欣喜若狂。

14. They who had fed ...: 诗人在这里（第 125 至第 132 行）描写富于热情和幻想的一类人。

15. had made All powers ... Their ministers: 使敏捷的思想和健壮的体格的各种能力都听从他们支配。

subtilty: = subtlety.

ministers: servants（古义）。

16. in lordly wise: 以主人的姿态。

17. And dealt with ... To wield it: 此数行大意是：性格活泼外向的人好象身上（within）潜藏着某种权利（some lurking right），可以自由处置他们在感性世界中发现的一切。

18. 诗人在这几行中描写了性情温和的另一类人。他们注意各种细微的变化（*all gentle motions*），并使自己的思想适应这类变化，他们并不主张激烈的行动（*schemers more mild*），各人安于探索自己能够探索的领域。

19. both: 指上述两类不同性格的人，亦即此行中之 **the meek and lofty.**

20. Utopia: 乌托邦（自希腊文 ου，没有；τορος，地方）。英国人文主义者托马斯 · 莫尔（Sir Thomas More）发表于 1516 年的一部空想社会主义著作中的理想国之名，后来用以指任何不切实际的美好幻想。华兹华斯在此坚信法国革命使人类建立理想王国的愿望就要成为现实，而且就要在这个世界上（**in the very world**）实现。

21. the place where, in the end, We find our happiness, or not at all: 诗人把实现幸福的希望完全寄托在这个现实的世界上，而不是寄希望于上帝或天堂，这表现了华兹华斯青年时代对于法国革命提供的前景抱着坚定信念和乐观态度。

7. COMPOSED UPON WESTMINSTER BRIDGE, SEPTEMBER 3, 1802

据华兹华斯自己说，这首十四行诗是他去法国的途中在马车上写的（Composed on the roof of a coach, on my way to France）. 十四行诗（sonnet）在十六世纪由意大利传入英国，成为伊丽莎白时代和十七世纪英国诗人们喜爱的一种诗体，但在十八世纪古典主义时代，十四行诗不再受到重视，直到浪漫主义诗歌的兴起，才使这种体裁重新成为一种重要的抒情诗形式。华兹华斯和济慈（John Keats）都写过许多优美的十四行诗。在这首诗里，华兹华斯用朴实而充满感情色彩的语言描绘了夏秋之交从泰晤士河（the Thames）上的威斯敏斯特大桥眺望伦敦城清晨的景色。整个伦敦好象还在沉睡，清朗的天空中晨光熹微，泰晤士缓缓流向远方，一切是那么明净、庄重、优美。这首诗写得音韵和谐，徐缓的节奏能很好地传达庄重而恬静的情感内容，因此是十四行诗中最著名的佳品之一。

1. Dull would he be ... in its majesty: 见到如此动人的壮丽美景而无动于衷的人，灵魂可能是呆滞愚钝的。**pass by.** 此处意为漠然地从旁走过。

2. This City: 即 London.

3. Open unto the fields: 由于清晨空气明净，伦敦城的建筑从郊外的远处也可以望得清楚。**fields，**此处指伦敦郊区。

4. steep: bathe.

5. The river: 指 the Thames.

6. that mighty heart: 喧嚷的伦敦城就象一个巨人，它那沸腾的生活就象是一颗巨大心脏在跳动。

8. LONDON, 1802

1802年的英国状况是以经济困难、政治矛盾和与法国战争的失利为特点的，正如一位历史学家所说："It is indeed from these fatal years that we must date that war of classes, that social severance between employers and employed, which still forms the main difficulty of English politics"（Green, *History of the English People*）. 在这首著名的十四行诗里，华兹华斯热烈歌颂英国革命时代的大诗人弥尔顿，希望弥尔顿的自由精神能够冲破沉闷的现实，重新振作起英国人的民族性。在这里，我们看到在行吟湖畔、陶醉于自然风光的华兹华斯之外，还有一个抨击丑恶现实、讴歌自由的华兹华斯。

1. Milton: 弥尔顿（1608—1676），十七世纪英国革命时代的伟大诗人，曾担任共和政府的拉丁文秘书，负责宣传工作，著《为英国人民声辩》等书痛斥王党对英国革命的污蔑。他最著名的作品是长诗《失乐园》、《力士参逊》等。

2. a fen Of stagnant waters: 一潭死水。

3. altar: 指教会；**sword:** 指军队；**pen:** 指文职工作。

4. Fireside: 指家庭。**the heroic wealth of hall and bower:** the wealthy upper classes of noble lineage. hall and bower，分别指贵族和贵妇人。用具体名词来代替一类事物，这是一种常用的修辞手段，称为代称（synecdoche）.

5. Have forfeited: 丧失了。

6. manners: morals. 指导行为的崇高准则。

7. dwelt apart: 在王政复辟之后，弥尔顿仍保持对革命的坚定信念，不愿与王党同流合污，因此象一颗独立的孤星。

8. the naked heavens: the clear unclouded sky. 参见华兹华斯 *Intimations of Immortality*, 13："When the heavens are bare".

9. The lowliest duties: 弥尔顿愿为公众的事业做最平凡的工作，他曾在一首著名的十四行诗（*On His Blindness*）中说：

They also serve who only stand and wait.

9. THE WORLD IS TOO MUCH WITH US

这首诗作于1806年，于1807年发表。在这首诗里华兹华斯清楚地表明，主张走向自然和讴歌自然的浪漫主义具有深刻的社会背景，那就是反对随着商业资本主义的发展必然出现的唯利是图、锱铢必争的市侩气息。这种计较利害得失的庸俗气息破坏了人与自然的和谐，枯竭了人的内心，甚至使宗教也浸透了实利主义，因此诗人宁愿选择一种诗意的泛神论信仰，投入自然的怀抱。

1. The world: 即 worldliness，汲汲于利害得失，一味追求钱财。

2. we lay waste our powers: 耗尽自己的精力。

3. that is ours: that appeals to us.

4. a sordid boon: a mean, mercenary bargain. 诗人相信我们本来都有能理解和热爱自然的心，但陷入利害打算之中就会失去这种美好品性，换来的只是冷冰冰的心肠。

5. will be howling: are eager to howl. 这里的 will 是表意动词（notional verb）.

6. up-gather'd now like sleeping flowers: 诗人认为风也是有灵性的，甚至在没有风的时候，他也设想风儿不过是睡着了，就象花儿在夜里把花瓣收拢起来一样。

up-gather'd: held in restraint; composed to rest.

7. suckled in a creed outworn: 在一种古老的信条中哺育出来的。

8. So might I: if so（即成为一个 Pagan）I might.

9. lea: meadow.

10. forlorn: forsaken, left solitary. 诗人认为未受现代社会腐蚀的古人与自然和谐一致，他们随时可以看见（*glimpses*）自然中的精灵，因此在自然里不会感到孤寂。

11. Proteus: 为海王 Neptune 看管驾车的海豹的一个神话人物，据说他会无穷的变化。参见 Milton, *Paradise Lost*, iii. 603 –604：

call up unbound
In various shapes old Proteus from the sea.

12. Triton: 海王 Neptune 与 Amphitrite 之子，是半人半鱼的神话人物，据说他可以吹一个大海螺做的号角来使海面平静。此行诗句是化用 Spenser, *Colin Clouts Come Home Againe*, 245:

Triton blowing loud his wreathed horn.

30 SAMVUEL TAYLOR COLERIDGE
1772–1834

1. The Rime of the Ancient Mariner
2. Kubla Khan

张隆溪　选注

1. THE RIME OF THE ANCIENT MARINER

In Seven Parts

Argument

How a Ship, having first sailed to the Equator, was driven by storms to the cold Country towards the South Pole; how the Ancient Mariner cruelly and in contempt of the laws of hospitality killed a Seabird and how he was followed by many and strange Judgments: and in what manner he came back to his own Country.

PART I

An ancient Mariner meeteth three Gallants bidden to a wedding-feast, and detaineth one.

It is a ancient Mariner,
And he stoppeth one of three[1].
'By[2] thy long grey beard and glittering eye,
Now whereforea[3] stopp'st thou me?

'The Bridegroom's doors are opened wide,
And I am next of kin;
The guests are met, the feast is set:
May'st[4] hear the merry din.'

He holds him with his skinny hand,

'There was a ship,' quoth[5] he.
'Hold off, unhand me, grey-beard loon! '[6]
Eftsoons[7] bis hand dropped he.

The wedding-Guest is spellbound by the eye of the old seafaring man, and constrained to hear his tale.

He holds him with his glittering eye[8]—
The Wedding-Guest stood still,
And listens like a three years' child:
The Mariner hath his will.

The Wedding-Guest sat on a stone:
He cannot choose but hear;
And thus spake on that ancient man,
The bright-eyed Mariner.[9]

The Mariner tells how the ship sailed southward with a good wind and fair weather, till it reached the Line.

'The ship was cheered, the harbour cleared,[10]
Merrily did we drop[11]
Below the kirk,[12] below the hill,
Below the lighthouse[13] top.

'The Sun came up upon the left,[14]
Out of the sea came he!
And he shone bright, and on the right
Went down into the sea.

'Higher and higher every day,
Till over the mast at noon[15] —'
The Wedding-Guest here beat his breast,
For he heard the loud bassoon.[16]

The Wedding-Guest heareth the bridal music: but the Mariner continueth his tale.

The bride hath paced into the hall,
Red as a rose is she;[17]
Nodding their heads before her goes
The merry minstrelsy.

The Wedding-Guest he beat his breast,[18]
Yet he cannot choose but hear;
And thus spake[19] on that ancient man,
The bright-eyed Mariner.

The ship driven by a storm toward the South Pole.

'And now the STORM-BLAST came, and he[20]
Was tyrannous and strong:
He struck with his o'ertaking wings,
And chased us south along.

'With sloping masts and dipping prow,[21]
As who pursued with yell and blow
Still[22] treads the shadow of his foe,
And forward bends his head,
The ship drove fast, loud roared the blast,
And southward aye[23] we fled.

'And now there came both mist and snow,
And it grew wondrous cold:[24]
And ice, mast-high, came floating by,
As green as emerald.[25]

The land of ice, and of fearful sounds where no living thing was to be seen.

'And through the drifts[26] the snowy clifts[27]
Did send a dismal sheen:[28]
Nor shapes of men nor beasts we ken[29] —
The ice was all between.

'The ice was here, the ice was there,
The ice was all around:
It cracked and growled, and roared and howled,
Like noises in a swound![30]

Till a great seabird,

'At length did cross an Albatross,[31]

called the Albatross, came through the snowfog, and was received with great joy and hospitality.

Thorough[32] the fog it came;
As if it had been a Christian soul,[33]
We hailed it in God's name.

'It ate the food it ne'er had eat,[34]
And round and round it flew.
The ice did split with a thunder-fit;[35]
The helmsman steered us through!

And lo! the Albatross proveth a bird of good omen, and followeth the ship as it returned northward through fog and floating ice.

'And a good south wind sprung[36] up behind;
The Albatross did follow,
And every day, for food or play,
Came to the mariner's hollo!

'In mist or cloud, on mast or shroud,[37]
It perched for vespers nine;[38]
Whiles[39] all the night, through fog-smoke white,
Glimmered the white Moon-shine.'

The ancient Mariner inhospitably killeth the pious bird of good omen.

'God save thee, ancient Marner!
From the fiends, that plague thee thus!—
Why lookest thou so? '—With my cross-bow
I shot the ALBATROSS.[40]

PART II

The Sun now rose upon the right:[41]
Out of the sea came he,
Still hid[42] in mist, and on the left
Went down into the sea.

And the good south wind still blew behind,
But no sweet bird did follow,

Nor any day for food or play
Came to the mariners' hollo!

His shipmates cry out against the ancient Mariner, for killing the bird of good luck.

And I had done a hellish thing,
And it would work 'em[43] woe:
For all averred,[44] I had killed the bird
That made the breeze to blow.[45]
Ah wretch[46]! said they, the bird to slay,
That made the breeze to blow!

But when the fog cleared off. they justify the same, and thus make themselves accomplices in the crime.

Nor dim nor red, like God's own head,[47]
The glorious Sun uprist:[48]
Then all averred, I had killed the bird
That brought the fog and mist.
I was right, said they, such birds to slay,
That bring the fog and mist.[49]

The fair breeze continues; the ship enters the Pacific Ocean. and sails northward, even till it reaches the Line.

The fair breeze blew, the white foam flew,
The furrow followed free;[50]
We were the first that ever burst
Into that silent sea.

The ship hath been suddenly becalmed.

Down dropped the breeze, the sails dropped down,
'Twas[51] sad as sad could be;
And we did speak only to break
The silence of the sea!

All in a hot and copper[52] sky,
The bloody Sun, at noon,
Right up above the mast did stand,
No bigger than the Moon.

Day after day, day after day,
We stuck, nor breath nor motion;
As idle as a painted ship
Upon a painted ocean.[53]

And the Albatross begins to be avenged.

Water, water, every where,
And all the boards did shrink;
Water, water, every where,
Nor any drop to drink.[54]

The very deep[55] did rot: O Christ!
That over this should be!
Yea, slimy things did crawl with legs
Upon the slimy sea.[56]

About, about, in reel and rout[57]
The death-fires[58] danced at night;
The water, like a witch's oils,[59]
Burnt green, and blue and white.

A Spirit had followed them: one of the invisible inhabitants of this planet, neither departed souls nor angels; concerning whom the learned Jew, Josephus, and the Platonic Constantinopolitan, Michael Psellus, may be consulted. They are very numerous, and there is no dimate or element without one or more.

And some in dreams assuréd[60] were
Of the Spirit[61] that plagued us so;
Nine fathom deep[62] he had followed us
From the land of mist and snow.

And every tongue, through utter drought,[63]
Was withered at the root;
We could not speak, no more than if
We had been choked with soot.

The shipmates, in their sore distress, would fain throw the guilt on the ancient Mariner: in sign whereof they hang the dead sea-bird round his neck.

Ah! well a-day![64] what evil looks
Had I from old and young!
Instead of the cross, the Albatross
About my neck was hung.

PART III

"There pass'd a weary time. Each throat[65]
Was parch'd, and glazed each eye,
A weary time! A weary time!
How glazed each weary eye![66]

The andent Mariner beholdeth a sign in the element afar off.

When looking westward I beheld
A something in the sky.

At first it seem'd a little speck,
And then it seem'd a mist:
It moved and moved, and took at last
A certain shape, I wist.[67]

A speck, a mist, a shape, I wist!
And still it near'd and near'd:
As if it dodged a water-sprite,[68]
It plunged and tack'd and veer'd.[69]

At its nearer approach, it seemeth him to be a ship; and at a dear ransom he freeth his speech from the bonds of thirst.

With throats unslaked, with black lips baked,[70]
We could nor laugh nor wail;
Through utter drought all dumb we stood!
I bit my arm, I suck'd the blood,[71]
And cried, A sail! a sail!

With throats unslaked, with black lips baked,
Agape[72] they heard me call:

A flash of joy;

Cramercy[73] they for joy did grin,[74]

And all at once their breath drew in,
As they were drinking all.

And horror follows. For can it be a ship that comes onward without wind or tide?

'See! see! (I cried) she tacks no more!
Hither,[75] to work us weal,
Without a breeze, without a tide,
She steadies with upright keel! '

The western wave was all a-flame;
The day was well nigh done:
Almost upon the western wave
Rested the broad bright sun;
When that strange shape drove suddenly
Betwixt us and the sun.

It seemeth to him but the skeleton of a ship.

And straight the sun was fleck'd with bars,[76]
(Heaven's Mother send us grace!)
As if through a dungeon grate[77] he peer'd,
With broad and burning face.

Alas! (thought I, and my heart beat loud)
How fast she nears and nears!
Are those her sails that glance in the sun,
Like restless gossameres[78]

And its ribs are seen as bars on the face of the setting sun. The spectre woman and her deathmate, and no other on board the skeleton ship.

Are those her ribs through which the sun
Did peer, as[79] through a grate?
And is that Woman all her crew?
Is that a Death? and are there two?
Is Death that woman's mate?

Her lips were red, her looks were free,[80]
Her locks were yellow as gold:

Her skin was as white as leprosy,[81]
The night-mare Life-in-Death[82] was she,
Who thicks[83] man's blood with cold.

Like vessel, like crew!

Death, and Lifein-Death, have diced for the ship's crew, and she (the latter) winneth the ancient Mariner.

The naked hulk[84] alongside came,
And the twain were casting dice;
'The game is done! I've, I've won! '
Quoth she, and whistles thrice.

No twilight within the courts of the sun.

The sun's rim dips; the stars rush out:
At one stride comes the dark;
With far-heard whisper, o'er the sea,
Off shot the spectre-bark.

At the rising of the moon,

We listen'd and look'd sideways up![85]
Fear at my heart, as at a cup,
My life-blood seem'd to sip![86]
The stars were dim, and thick the night,
The steersman's face by his lamp gleam'd white;
From the sails the dew did drip —
Till clomb above the eastern bar[87]
The hornéd[88] moon, with one bright star
Within the nether tip.[89]

One after another,

One after one, by the star-dogg'd moon,[90]
Too quick for groan or sigh,
Each turn'd his face with a ghastly pang,
And cursed me with his eye.

His shipmates drop down dead.

Four times fiffy living men,
(And I heard nor sigh nor groan)
With heavy thump, a lifeless lump,
They dropp'd down one by one.

But Life-in-Death begins her work on the ancient Mariner.

The souls did from their bodies fly,—
They fled to bliss or woe!
And every soul, it pass'd me by,
Like the whizz of my cross-bow!"

PART IV

The wedding-guest feareth that a spirit is talking to him.

"I fear thee, ancient Mariner!
I fear thy skinny hand!
And thou art long, and lank, and brown,
As is the ribb'd[91] sea-sand.

'I fear thee and thy glittering eye,
And thy skinny hand, so brown,'—

But the ancient Mariner assureth him of his bodily life, and proceedeth to relate his horrible penance.

Fear not, fear not, thou Wedding-Guest!
This body dropped not down.

Alone, alone, all, all alone,
Alone on a wide wide sea![92]
And never a saint took pity on
My soul in agony.

He despiseth the creatures of the calm,

The many men, so beautiful!
And they all dead did lie:
And a thousand thousand slimy things
Lived on; and so did I.

And envieth that they should live, and so many lie dead.

I looked upon the rotting sea,
And drew my eyes away;
I looked upon the rotting deck,
And there the dead men lay.

I looked to heaven, and tried to pray;
But or ever a prayer had gushed,[93]
A wicked whisper came, and made

My heart as dry as dust.

I closed my lids, and kept them close,
And the balls[94] like pulses beat;
For the sky and the sea, and the sea and the sky
Lay like a load on my weary eye,
And the dead were at my feet.

But the curse liveth for him in the eye of the dead men.

The cold sweat melted from their limbs,
Nor rot nor reek[95] did they:
The look with which they looked on me
Had never passed away.

An orphan's curse would drag to hell
A spirit from on high;
But oh! more horrible than that
Is the curse in a dead man's eye!
Seven days, seven nights,[96] I saw that curse,
And yet I could not die.

The moving Moon went up the sky,
And nowhere did abide[97]:
Softly she was going up,
And a star or two beside[98]—

In his loneliness and fixedness he yearneth towards the journeying Moon, and the stars that still sojourn, yet still move onward; and everywhere the blue sky belongs to them, and is their appointed rest, and their native country and their own natural homes, which they enter unannounced, as lords that are certainly expected and yet there is a silent joy at their arrival.

Her beams bemocked the sultry main,[99]
dike April hoar-frost spread;
But[100] where the ship's huge shadow lay,
The charméd[101] water burnt alway[102]
A still[103] and awful red.

By the light of the moon he beholdeth God's creatures of the great calm.

Beyond the shadow of the ship,
I watch'd the water-snakes:
They moved in tracks of shining white,
And when they rear'd[104] the elfish light
Fell off in hoary flakes.[105]

Within the shadow of the ship
I watch'd their rich attire:[106]
Blue, glossy green, and velvet black,
They coil'd and swam; and every track
Was a flash of golden fire.

Their beauty and their happiness.

He blesseth them in his heart.

O happy living things! no tongue
Their beauty might[107] declare:
A spring of love gush'd from my heart,[108]
And I bless'd them unaware![109]
Sure my kind saint[110] took pity on me,
And I bless'd them unaware.

The spell begins to break.

The selfsame[111] moment I could pray;
And from my neck so free[112]
The Albatross fell off, and sank
Like lead into the sea.

PART V

"Oh sleep! it is a gentle thing,
Belov'd from pole to pole!
To Mary Queen[113] the praise be given!
She sent the gentle sleep from Heaven,
That slid into my soul.

By grace of the holy Mother, the ancient

The silly[114] buckets on the deck,
That had so long remain'd,

Mariner is refreshed with rain.

I dreamt that they were fill'd with dew;
And when I awoke, it rain'd.

My lips were wet, my throat was cold,
My garments all were dank;[115]
Sure I had drunken[116] in my dreams,
And still my body drank.

I moved, and could not feel my limbs:
I was so light — almost
I thought that I had died in sleep,
And was a blessed[117] ghost.

He heareth sounds and seeth strange sights and commotions in the sky and the element.

And soon I heard a roaring wind:
It did not come anear;[118]
But with its sound it shook the sails,
That were so thin and sere.

The upper air burst into life!
And a hundred fire-flags sheen,[119]
To and fro they were hurried about;
And to and fro, and in and out,
The wan stars danced between.

And the coming wind did roar more loud,
And the sails did sigh like sedge;[120]
And the rain pour'd down from one black cloud;
The moon was at its edge.[121]

The thick black cloud was cleft, and still
The moon was at its side:
Like waters[122] shot from some high crag,
The lightning fell with never a jag,[123]

A river steep and wide.

The bodies of the ships crew are inspirited, and the ship moves on;

The loud wind never reach'd the ship,
Yet now the ship moved on!
Beneath the lightning and the moon
The dead men gave a groan.

They groan'd, they stirr'd, they all uprose,
Nor spake, nor moved their eyes;
It had been strange,[124] even in a dream,
To have seen those dead men rise.

The helnmsman steer'd, the ship moved on;
Yet never a breeze up-blew;[125]
The mariners all 'gan[126] work the ropes,
Where they were wont to do:
They raised their limbs like lifeless tools —
We were a ghastly crew.

The body of my brother's son
Stood by me, knee to knee:[127]
The body and I pull'd at one rope,
But he said nought to me."

But not by the souls of the men, nor by demons of earth or middle air, but by a bless ed troop of antgelic spirits, sent down by the invocation of the guardian saint.

"I fear thee, ancient Mariner!"
"Be calm, thou Wedding-Guest!
'Twas not those souls that fled in pain,
Which to their corses[128] came again,
But a troop of spirits blest:

For when it dawn'd — they dropp'd their arms,
And cluster'd round the mast;
Sweet sounds rose slowly through their mouths,

And from their bodies pass'd.

Around, around, flew each sweet sound,
Then darted to the sun;
Slowly the sounds come back again,
Now mix'd now one by one.[129]

Sometimes a dropping from the sky
I heard the skylark sing;
Sometimes all little birds that are,
How they seem'd to fill the sea and air
With their sweet jargoning![130]

And now 'twas like all instruments,
Now like a lonely flute;
And now it is an angel's song.
That makes the heavens be mute.

It ceased; yet still the sails made on
A pleasant noise till noon,
A noise like of[131] a hidden brook
In the leafy month of June,
That to the sleeping woods all night
Singeth a quiet tune.

Till noon we quietly sail'd on,
Yet never a breeze did breathe:
Slowly and smoothly went the ship,
Moved onward from beneath.

The lonesome spirit from the south-pole carries on the ship as far as the Line, in

Under the keel nine fathom deep,
From the land of mist and snow,
The spirit slid; and it was he

obedience to the angelic troop, but still requireth vengeance.

That made the ship to go,
The sails at noon left off their tune,
And the ship stood still also.[132]

The sun, right up above the mast,
Had fix'd her to the ocean;
But in a minute she 'gan[133] stir,
With a short uneasy motion —
Backwards and forwards half her length,[134]
With a short uneasy motion.

Then like a pawing[135] horse let go,
She made a sudden bound:
It flung the blood into my head,
And I fell down in a swound.

The Polar Spirit's fellow demons, the invisible inhabitants of the element, take part in his wrong; and two of ihem relate, one to the other, that penance long and heavy for the ancient Mariner hath been accorded to the Polar Spirit, who returneth southward.

How long in that same fit[136] I lay,
I have not to declare;
But ere my living life[137] return'd,
heard, and in my soul discern'd
Two voices[188] in the air.

'Is it he? ' quoth one, 'is this the man?
By Him who died on cross,[139]
With his cruel bow he laid full low[140]
The harmless Albatross.

'The spirit who bideth[141] by himself
In the land of mist and snow,
He loved the bird that loved the man
Who shot him[142] with his bow. '

The other was a softer voice,

As soft as honey-dew:[143]
Quoth he, 'The man hath penance done,
And penance more will do.'

PART VI

First Voice

'But tell me, tell me! speak again,
Thy soft response[144] renewing —
What makes that ship drive on so fast?
What is the ocean doing?'

Second Voice

'Still[145] as a slave before his lord,
The ocean hath no blast;
His great bright eye most silently
Up to the moon is cast —

If he may know which way to go;
For she guides him, smooth or grim.[146]
See, brother, see! how graciously
She looketh down on him.'

First Voice

The Mariner hath been cast into a trance; for the angelic power causeth the vessel to drive northward, faster than human life could endure.

'But why drives on that ship so fast,
Without or wave or wind?'[147]

Second Voice

'The air is cut away before,
And closes from behind.
Fly, brother, fly! more high, more high!
Or we shall be belated:[148]
For slow and slow that ship will go,
When the Mariner's trance is abated.'[149]

The supernatural motion is retarded; the Mariner awakes, and his penance begins anew.

I woke, and we were sailing on,
As[150] in a gentle weather:
'Twas night, calm night, the moon was high;
The dead men stood together.

All stood together on the deck,
For a charnel-dungeon[151] fitter:
All fix'd on me their stony eyes,
That in the moon did glitter.

The pang, the curse, with which they died,
Had never pass'd away:
I could not draw my eyes from theirs,
Nor turn them up to pray.

The curse is finally expiated.

And now this spell was snapt:[152] once more
I view'd the ocean green,
And look'd far forth, yet little saw
Of what had else been seen.[153]

Like one that on a lonesome road
Doth walk in fear and dread,
And having once turn'd round, walks on,
And turns no more his head;
Because he knows a frightful fiend
Doth close behind him tread.

But soon there breathed a wind on me,
Nor sound nor motion made:
Its path[154] was not upon the sea,
In ripple or in shade.[155]

It raised my hair, it fann'd my cheek

Like a meadow-gale[156] of spring—
It mingled strangely with my fears,
Yet it felt like a welcoming.

Swiftly, swiftly flew the ship,
Yet she sail'd softly too:
Sweetly, sweetly blew the breeze—
On me alone it blew.

And the ancient Mariner beholdeth his native country.

Oh! dream of joy! is this indeed[157]
The lighthouse top I see?
Is this the hill? is this the kirk?
Is this mine own countree?[158]

We drifted o'er the harbour-bar,[159]
And I with sobs did pray—
'O let me be awake, my God!
Or let me sleep alway.'

The harbour-bay was clear as glass,[160]
So smoothly it was strewn!
And on the bay the moonlight lay,
And the shadow of the moon.

The rock shone bright, the kirk no less,
That stands above the rock:
The moonlight steep'd[161] in silentness
The steady weathercock.

The angelic spirits leave the dead bodies,

And the bay was white with silent light,
Till rising from the same,
Full many shapes, that shadows[162] were,
In crimson colours came.

And appear in their own forms of light.

A little distance from the prow
Those crimson shadows were:
I turn'd my eyes upon the deck —
Oh, Christ! what saw I there!

Each corse lay fiat, lifeless and fiat,
And, by the holy rood![163]
A man all light, a seraph[164]-man,
On every corse there stood.

This seraph-band,[165] each waved his hand:
It was a heavenly sight!
They stood as signals to the land,
Each one a lovely light:

This seraph-band, each waved his hand,
No voice did they impart[166]
No voice; but oh! the silence sank
Like music on my heart.

But soon I heard the dash of oars,
I heard the pilot's cheer;
My head was turn'd perforce[167] away,
And I saw a boat appear.

The pilot, and the pilot's boy,
I heard them coming fast:
Dear Lord in Heaven! it was a joy
The dead men could not blast.[168]

I saw a third — I heard his voice:
It is the Hermit[169] good!
He singeth loud his godly hymns

That he makes in the wood.
He'll shrieve[170] my soul, he'll wash away
The Albatross's blood.

PART VII

The Hermit of the Wood

"This Hermit good lives in that wood
Which slopes down to the sea.
How loudly his sweet voice he rears![171]
He loves to talk with marineres
That come from a far countree.

He kneels[172] at morn, and noon, and eve—
He hath a cushion plump:
It is the moss that wholly hides
The rotted old oak-stump.

The skiff-boat[173] near'd: I heard. them talk,
'Why, this is strange, I trow![174]
Where are those lights so many and fair,
That signal made but I now? '[175]

Approacheth the ship with wonder.

'Strange, by my faith! ' the Hermit said—
'And they answer'd not our cheer!
The planks look warp'd![176] and see those sails,
How thin they are and sere!
I never saw aught like to them,[177]
Unless perchance it were

Brown skeletons of leaves that lag[178]
My forest-brook along:
When the ivy-tod[179] is heavy with snow,
And the owlet whoops to the wolf below
That[180] eats the she-wolf's young.'

'Dear Lord! it hath a fiendish look —
(The pilot made reply)
I am a-fear'd'[181] — 'Push on, push on!'
Said the Hermit cheerily.

The boat came closer to the ship,
But I nor spake nor stirr'd;
The boat came close beneath the ship,
And straight[182] a sound was heard.

The ship suddenly sinketh.

Under the water it rumbled on,
Still louder and more dread:[183]
It reach'd the ship, it split the bay;
The ship went down like lead.

The ancient Marirer is saved in the pilot's boat.

Stunn'd[184] by that loud and dreadful sound,
Which sky and ocean smote,
Like one that hath been seven days drown'd,
My body lay afloat;
But swift as dreams, myself I found
Within the pilot's boat.

Upon the whirl, where sank the ship,
The boat spun round and round;
And all was still, save that the hill
Was telling of the sound.[185]

I moved my lips — the pilot shriek'd,[186]
And fell down in a fit;
The holy Hermit raised his eyes,
And pray'd where he did sit.

I took the oars: the pilot's boy,

Who now doth crazy go,
Laugh'd loud and long, and all the while
His eyes went to and fro.[187]
'Ha! ha!' quoth he, 'full plain I see,
The Devil knows how to row.'

And now, all in my own countree,
I stood on the firm land!
The Hermit stepp'd forth from the boat,
And scarcely he could stand.

The ancient Mariner earnestly entreateth the Hermit to shrieve him; and the penance of life falls on him.

'O shrieve me, shrieve me, holy man!'
The Hermit cross'd his brow.
'Say quick,' quoth he, 'I bid thee say —
What manner of man art thou?'

Forthwith this frame of mine[188] was wrench'd
With a woeful agony,
Which forced me to begin my tale;
And then it left me free.

And ever and anon throughout his future life an agony constraineth him to travel from land to land;

Since then, at an uncertain hour,[189]
That agony returns:
And till my ghastly tale is told,
This heart within me burns.

I pass, like night, from land to land;
I have strange power of speech;
That moment that his face I see,
I know the man that must hear me:
To him my tale I teach.

What loud uproar bursts from that door![190]

The Wedding-Guests are there:
But in the garden-bower the bride
And bride-maids singing are:
And hark the little vesper bell,[191]
Which biddeth me to prayer!

O Wedding-Guest! this soul hath been
Alone on a wide wide sea:
So lonely 'twas, that God himself
Scarce[192] seemed there to be.

O sweeter than the marriage-feast,
'Tis sweeter far to me,
To walk together to the kirk
With a goodly company!—

To walk together to the kirk,
And all together pray,
While each to his great Father bends,
Old men, and babes, and loving friends
And youths and maidens gay!

And to teach, by his own example, love and reverence to all things that God made and loveth.

Farewell, farewell! but this I tell
To thee, thou Wedding-Guest!
He prayeth well, who loveth well[193]
Both man and bird and beast.

He prayeth best, who loveth best
All things both great and small;
For the dear God who loveth us,
He made and loveth all.

The Mariner, whose eye is bright,

Whose beard with age is hoar,[194]
Is gone: and now the Wedding-Guest
Turned from the bridegroom's door.

He went like one that hath been stunned,
And is of sense forlorn:[195]
A sadder[196] and a wiser man,
He rose the morrow morn.[197]

2. *KUBLA KHAN*

In Xanadu[1] did Kubla Khan[2]
A stately pleasure-dome[3] decree:[4]
Where Alph,[5] the sacred river, ran
Through caverns measureless to man[6]
Down to a sunless sea.
So twice five miles[7] of fertile ground
With walls and towers were girdled round:
And here were gardens bright with sinuous rills[8]
Where blossomed many an incense-bearing[9] tree;
And here were forests ancient as the hills,
Enfolding sunny spots of greenery.[10]

But oh! that deep romantic chasm[11] which slanted
Down the green hill athwart[12] a cedarn cover!
A savage place! as holy and enchanted
As e'er[13] beneath a waning moon was haunted
By woman wailing for her demon-lover!
And from this chasm, with ceaseless turmoil seething,[14]
As if this earth in fast thick pants[15] were breathing,
A mighty fountain momently[16] was forced;
Amid whose swift half-intermitted[17] burst
Huge fragments vaulted like rebounding hail,

Or chaffy grain beneath the thresher's flail:[18]
And 'mid[19] these dancing rocks at once and ever
It[20] flung up momently the sacred river.
Five miles meandering with a mazy[21] motion
Through wood and dale the sacred river ran,
Then reached the caverns measureless to man,
And sank in tumult to a lifeless ocean:
And 'mid this tumult Kubla heard from far
Ancestral voices prophesying war!
The shadow[22] of the dome of pleasure
Floated midway on the waves;
Where was heard the mingled measure[23]
From the fountain and the caves.
It was a miracle of rare device,
A sunny pleasure-dome with caves of ice!

A damsel with a dulcimer[24]
In a vision once I saw:
It was an Abyssinian maid,[25]
And on her dulcimer she played,
Singing of Mount Abora.[26]
Could I revive[27] within me
Her symphony and song,
To such a deep delight 'twould win me,[28]
That with music loud and long,
I would build that dome in air,
That sunny dome! those caves of ice!
And all who heard should see them there,
And all should cry, Beware! Beware!
His flashing eyes, his floating hair![29]
Weave a circle round him thrice,
And close your eyes with holy dread,[30]
For he on honey-dew hath fed,

And drunk the milk of Paradise.[31]

【作者简介】 塞缪尔·泰勒·柯尔律治（Samuel Taylor Coleridge，1772—1834），英国浪漫派诗人和批评家，生于德汶郡的 Ottery St. Mary 一个乡村牧师家庭。柯尔律治博闻强记，极富于想象。青年时代曾同情法国革命，并曾于 1794 年与友人计划到美国宾夕法尼亚州去建立一个乌托邦式的大同社会 Pantisocracy，后因经费不足而作罢。他与华兹华斯的友谊以及他们于 1798 年合作发表的《抒情歌谣集》，对于浪漫主义运动在英国的兴起和发展都有重要意义。如果说华兹华斯代表着浪漫主义诗歌中返回自然的主要倾向，那末柯尔律治代表的则是通过瑰丽的想象创造一种神秘气氛或异国情调的倾向，柯尔律治为数极少然而至今传诵的诗篇，都明显地体现了这种倾向。

柯尔律治的个人生活颇为不幸，为镇风湿痛而服鸦片酊（laudanum）又上了瘾，对他产生了极有害的影响，也妨碍了他诗才的发展。他最好的诗几乎都是在 1797 至 1798 的一年多时间里写成的，在那以后，他逐渐丧失了青年时代的激进思想和政治热情，也几乎没有再写出什么好诗来。但是，柯尔律治却是一位颇有思想深度的理论家和文学批评家。他曾到德国去研习语言和文学，深受德国哲学和浪漫主义文学的影响。他的《文学传记》(*Biographia Literaria*）以及他论莎士比亚的批评文字，包含着许多精辟的见解，在文学批评史上很有影响，至今仍是值得一读的重要文献。

【题解与注释】

1. THE RIME OF THE ANCIENT MARINER

《古舟子咏》是柯尔律治最著名的作品，初次发表在 1798 年的《抒情歌谣集》里，1816 年诗人作了一次修订，增加了印在页边的故事梗概（Glosses）。在《文学传记》第十四章里，柯尔律治谈到他与华兹华斯计划写作两类作品，一类是以朴实的语言描绘普通的乡村生活，另一类则是充分运用奇特的想象，描绘超自然的事物，《古舟子咏》就属于后一类作品。就想象的奇特和创造一种戏剧性的紧张情绪和神秘气氛而言，这首诗成功地达到了目的。但诗人并非仅仅是讲了一个离奇古怪的故事。当时曾有一位著名女作家巴波尔德夫人（Mrs. Barbauld）指责这首诗缺乏道德寓意，柯尔律治却回答说此诗的毛病正在于道德的寓意太多。事实上，诗人通过老水手恩将仇报射杀海鸟后遭逢的可怕灾难以及后来的忏悔和得救，探索了罪与罚的伦理问题，突出了爱的力量，确实含有道德的寓意。

在形式上，《古舟子咏》是采用歌谣体写成的，每节四行，一、三行四音步，二、四行三音步并押韵。歌谣体本是起源于民间叙事诗的一种体裁，常常用朴实无华的语言叙述一个具有戏剧性情节的传说或故事，中世纪时的许多民谣就是典型的例子。歌谣体在十八世纪末和十九世纪初的复兴，是浪漫主义文学中一个值得注意的现象，这一方面是对十八世纪新古典主义诗歌规整精巧而充满宫廷气息的英雄双韵体的反动，另一方面也是平民精神觉醒的反映。华兹华斯与柯尔律治合作的诗集题为《抒情歌谣集》，并不是没有道理的。

卷首的 Argument 一词在此意为“概要”。

1. one of the three: 指去参加婚礼的年轻人。在这首诗里多次出现数字，一方面可以把一个虚构的故事讲得绘声绘色，煞有介事，另一方面还因为自古以来三、五、七、九等奇数就被迷信者认为具有神奇的或魔法般的力量。参见下面第 76，133，198，261 等行。

2. By: 凭着。

3. wherefore: why.

4. May'st: you may.

5. quoth: said（古体）。老水手毫不理会年轻人的话而径直开始讲自己的故事，这种简捷的写法是歌谣体的一个特点。

6. Hold off!: 走开！ **unhand:** 放手；**loon:** worthless fellow; rascal（古义）。

7. Eftsoons: immediately; soon afterwards（古体）。

8. He holds him with his glittering eye: 诗中多次描写老水手目光炯炯，似乎有施催眠术的力量，使年轻人不得不停下步来听他讲述自己的故事。

9. Mariner: 在此应读如 marinere，与第 18 行的 **here** 押韵。参见第 517 行。柯尔律治在初稿中都用 marinere 这种古体拼写法。

10. cheered: 指船离港启航时港口上人们欢呼相送；**cleared:**（船）离开码头。

11. drop:【航海术语】趁退潮出海。

12. kirk: church，这是苏格兰和英格兰北部方言中的一个词，那里是产生丰富民谣的地方，诗人用这个词显然是有意增加古歌谣的色彩。教堂位于山脚下，所以首先从水手们的眼里消失。

13. lighthouse: 灯塔位于山巅，所以最后从乘船离去的水手们视野里消失。

14. The Sun came up upon the left: 太阳从左边升起，因为船是向南航行。

15. Till over the mast at noon: 船到赤道时，太阳在正午正位于船的上方。

16. bassoon: 巴松管（一种低音管乐器）。

17. Red as a rose Is she: 这是民歌中常用的句子。参见 Robert Burns 著名的诗句：O my Luve's like a red, red rose. 诗人在这里插入婚礼欢乐场面的一节描写，与老水手讲的充满悲剧性的故事形成互相反衬的对照。

18. The Wedding-Guest he beat his breast: 这里的 he 是重复主语 The Wedding-Guest，修辞学上称为冗言（pleonasm），也是歌谣体的一个特点。

19. spake: spoke（古体）。

20. he: 用 **he** 来指风暴，预示着航船已进入一个神奇世界，那里的一切都具有灵性。

21. With sloping masts and dipping prow: 此节描写狂风驱赶着航船，极为形象生动。

22. Still: always（古义）。

23. aye: always, ever.

24. wondrous cold: extremely cold.

25. As green as emerald: 碧绿有如翡翠。

26. drifts:（雾和雪的）团。

27. clifts: cliffs，指冰山。

28. dismal sheen: 惨淡的光。

29. ken: see, discern（古义）。

30. swound: swoon（古体）。

31. Albatross: 信天翁，一种很大的海鸟。

32. Thorough: through（古义）。

33. soul: human being.

34. ne'er had eat: had never eaten.

35. thunder-fit: 霹雳一声。

36. sprung: sprang.

37. shroud:（船桅的）左右支索。

38. vespers nine: nine evenings；注意奇数 nine 的使用。

39. Whiles: while（古体）。

40. 第 79—82 行： 老水手快讲到自己的犯罪时，精神极为痛苦，这时插入年轻人一句问话，非常简练然而十分有效地描绘了老水手的整个状态。他的回答用最少的字赶快说出了犯罪的事实。第 81 行分为两半，一半问，一半答，节奏迅速，情绪紧张，使读者的注意力全部集中到最后一行：I shot the ALBATROSS.

41. The Sun now rose upon the right: 这时船已绕过南美洲南端的合恩角（Cape Horn）向北行驶，因此太阳从船的右方升起。

42. Still hid: always hidden. **Still:** always（古义），第 87 行同。

43. 'em: = them，指同船的水手们。**work ' em woe，** 给他们带来灾祸。

44. averred: 断言；宣称。

45. made the breeze to blow: 此行中的 to 是民谣中古体的用法，按现代英语用法应略去。

46. wretch: a worthless or vile fellow.

47. like God's own head: 此短语修饰下行之 **Sun.**

48. uprist: uprose（古体）。

49. 第 101—102 行： 众水手并无定见，对于射杀海鸟也并不感到怜惜，因此与老水手成为犯罪的同伙。在这里为他们后来受到的报复埋下了伏笔。

50. The furrow followed free: 注意此行连用三个以 f 音开头的词，取得特殊的音韵效果。这种头韵（alliteration）也是古歌谣体中常常使用的修辞手法。

51. 'Twas: it was.

52. copper: 铜黄色。这个形容词有力地传达出烈日炎炎的天空给人那种灼热难耐的感觉。

53. As idle as a painted ship Upon a painted ocean: 这是柯尔律治的名句，描写无风的海面和静止不动的船，短短两行构成一幅给人深刻印象的画面。

54. Water, water, every where, ... any drop to drink: 注意此节中运用重复强调法（epizeuxis），使人更真切地感觉到处于四面茫茫一片死海中的极端单调、厌倦和焦躁不安。

55. deep: sea.

56. Yea, slimy things ... the slimy sea: 这是诗中描写可怖而且可厌的景象著名的两行。重复 slimy 一词，加上 crawl with legs，几乎使人产生一种生理上的反感。

57. in reel and rout: 飞舞盘旋。

58. The death-fires: 指海面上出现的各种磷光，水手们称之为 St. Elmo's fire，又称"死火"，因为他们迷信这种磷光预兆船员中有人很快会死亡。

59. witch's oils: 旧时的迷信，认为女巫作法时要在一口大锅里煮蛇、蝎、蟾蜍等毒虫，熬出毒油来。参见莎士比亚著名悲剧 *Macbeth*, Ⅳ. ⅰ.

60. assured: 在此应读如三音节词。

61. the Spirit: 为信天翁复仇的精灵。

62. Nine fathom deep: 在水下九㖊深处。注意此处奇数九的使用。fathom 在数词后常可不加 s 用作复数，一个 fathom 相当于 6 英尺或 1.829 米，主要用作测量水深的长度单位。

63. drought: thirst.

64. well a-day: alas（古体）。

65. 第 143—148 行： 在描写水手们即将遭遇的惩罚之前，此节概略重述了他们此刻的处境。词句的重复突出了他们的焦躁、不安和痛苦。

66. glazed each eye: 人人的眼睛都象蒙上了一层釉，变得呆滞模糊。

67. wist: knew.

68. water-sprite: 水中的精灵；水妖。

69. It plunged and tacked and veered: 此行描写无人驾驶的空船在水中左转右旋，渐渐漂近。*tacked*,〔航海术语〕顺风向转舵。

70. unslaked: unmoistened，焦渴的；baked：被烈日晒得坚硬的。

71. I bit my arm, I sucked the blood: 老水手为了润喉，以便能叫出声来而咬破手臂，吮自己的血。

72. Agape: 张大着口。

73. Gramercy!: 谢谢老天爷！〔来自法语 *grandmerci*〕.

74. for joy did grin: 快乐得露出笑脸。嘴唇干裂时不能大笑，只能稍微咧嘴露齿，故用 grin 一词。柯尔律治自己曾有解释：

> I took the thought of 'grinning for joy' from poor Burnett's remark to me, when we had climbed to the top of Plinlimmon, and were nearly dead with thirst. We could not speak from the constriction, till we found a little puddle under a stone. He said to

me, 'You grinned like an idiot.' He had done the same.

75. Hither: 到这里。**weal**，幸运。此节中的 **she** 指从远处驶来的那只奇怪的船。

76. straight: straightway, immediately. **flecked with bars:** 布上斑驳的一条条暗影。

77. dungeon-grate: 地牢的窗格。**he**，指太阳。

78. restless gossameres: 飘摇不定的游丝。

79. as: as if.

80. free: 妖娆的；放荡的。

81. leprosy: 麻风病。**as white as leprosy:** 参见 Exodus, iv. 6: "And he [Moses] put his hand into his bosom; and when he took it out, behold, his hand was **leprous as snow**."

82. Life-in-Death: 这极为可怕的形象象梦魇（*Nightmare*），大概是从柯尔律治服食了鸦片酊后的幻觉之中产生的。诗人的描写也是将生与死揉合在一起，鲜红的嘴唇和金黄的头发似乎代表着生，而患麻风一般病态的白色皮肤又明明是死的痕迹。批评家 Dowden 关于这个形象曾说："She it was who with her numbing spell haunted Coleridge himself in after days." 参见柯尔律治死前不久为自己写的 Epitaph:

Stop, Christian passer-by! …
O, lift one thought on prayer for S. T. C.;
That he who many a year with toil of breath
Found death in life, may here find life in death.

83. thicks: thickens（古体）。

84. hulk: 废船。

85. looked sideways up: 那只怪船忽然远去，水手们心中恐惧，不敢正视，只敢斜着眼偷看。

86. Fear at my heart … seemed to sip: 此处将恐惧拟人化，写成一个吸血的魔鬼。

87. clomb: climbed（古体）。the eastern bar：地平线，此处指海平面。

88. hornéd:（月亮）如钩的。此处读如双音节词。

89. Within the nether tip: 水手们的迷信，认为新月下面出现一颗星是不祥之兆。

90. star-dogged Moon: 诗人自己曾有注："It is a common superstition among sailors that something evil is about to happen whenever a star dogs the Moon."

91. ribbed: 退潮留下浪痕的。

92. Alone, alone, all, all alone, Alone on a wide wide sea: 此两行中单词的多次重复（修辞学上称为 *repetitio crebra*）有力地传达了老水手的极度孤寂之感。

93. or: before; **gusht:** gushed；涌上心头。

94. balls: 眼球。

95. Nor rot nor reek: 既没有腐烂，也没有发臭。

96. Seven days, seven nights: 此处又用了奇数七。《古舟子咏》全诗也是分为七个部分。

97. abide: stay.

98. beside: besides, in addition.

99. bemocked the sultry main: 海面上酷热难耐，月光却象白霜（即下行 hoarfrost）撒在海面，象是嘲弄大海。**main,**【诗】大海。

100. But: except.

101. charméd: 着了魔的（此处读如双音节词）。

102. alway: always.

103. still: 持久的。

104. reared:（海蛇）从水面上竖起身子来。

105. in hoary flakes: 月光之下，水泡从海蛇身上撒落下来时发出闪烁的光芒，象星星点点的霜花。

106. rich attire: 艳丽的服饰，指海蛇的斑纹。

107. might: could.

108. A spring of love gushed from my heart: 老水手心中涌出的爱使他为海中的生物祝福，这在他的遭遇中形成一个新的转折点，使他开始摆脱可怕的诅咒和惩罚。柯尔律治所指的道德寓意，就是爱的力量可以战胜罪恶，净化人的心灵。

109. unaware: unawares.

110. my kind saint: my patron saint.

111. self-same: exactly the same.

112. free: freely.

113. Mary Queen: 指圣母玛利亚。

114. silly: simple, homely; empty.（古义）。

115. dank: 湿漉漉的。

116. drunken: drunk.

117. blessed: 有福的。在此处读如双音节词。

118. anear: near.

119. a hundred fire-flags sheen: 此行描写空中有无数道闪光，象旗帜在飞舞。hundred 言甚多而非实指。

120. sedge: 蓑衣草。这种草在狂风吹动时常常发出尖锐的呼啸声。

121. The Moon was at its edge: 月亮被乌云遮掩，只露出一点边。第 323 行 *at its side* 意义相同。

122. waters: 一股股奔流的瀑布。*shot*，飞湍而下。

123. with never a jag: without a single break.

124. It had been strange: It would have been strange.

125. up-blew: 开始吹起来。

126. 'gan: began.

127. knee to knee: side by side.

128. corses: corpses（古体）。

129. Now mixed, now one by one: 此行描写附在死去的水手们身上的天使唱出的歌声，先上达天庭，然后传下回声，有时形成优美的和声，有时形成单音的旋律。

130. jargoning: twittering, warbling（古义）。

131. like of: as of.

132. 第 377—383 行： 柯尔律治先写船越过赤道向南行驶（见第 30 行），然后绕过南美洲南端向北行驶（见第 83 行），并到达赤道（见第 103—106 行页边的散文概要），但后来的描写似乎船仍在南半球，这里又写船到达赤道，所以前后有些矛盾。不过这并不妨碍诗本身的优美。

133. 'gan: began. 此行的 *she* 指船。

134. half her length: 船前后摆动的幅度达到船身长度的一半。

135. pawing:（马）不耐烦地用蹄刨着地面。

136. fit: 昏迷状态。

137. ere: before. **my living life:** 这里的 living 一词并不是多余的，而是故意强调并与控制着老水手的 Life-in-Death 形成对比。

138. Two voices: 这两个声音显然分别代表着 Justice 和 Mercy.

139. By Him who died on cross: 凭基督的名义（告诉我）*Him* 即 Christ.

140. laid full low: 射杀。

141. bideth: abides, dwells.

142. him: 指 the bird. 此行使老水手射杀信天翁的罪过显得更为残忍。

143. honey-dew: 甘露。

144. response: answer.

145. Still: 安静的，平静的。

146. For she guides him smooth or grim: 因为大海潮水的涨落都是月亮指引的，所以大海象是睁大了眼睛望着月亮，希望月亮指示它应该怎样行动。*she* 指月亮，*him* 指海。

147. Without or wave or wind: 既没有浪涛，也没有风。注意此行的头韵效果。

148. Or we shall be belated: Or else we shall be too long delayed.

149. abated: 减退；消除。

150. As: as if.

151. charnel-dungeon: house or vault where dead bodies are piled.

152. this spell was snapped: 魔法突然解除了。

153. little saw of what had else been seen: saw little of what would have been seen if I was not in fear.

154. Its path: 指风吹水面留下的痕迹。

155. In ripple or in shade: 风吹过时，或刮起一片细浪，或使一片水纹变得颜色更深。

156. meadow-gale: breeze. 这是柯尔律治自己创造的一个词。

157. 第 464—466 行： 注意此处写老水手望见陆地上的目标时，先后顺序十分严谨（参见第 23—24 行）。

158. countree: country.

159. harbour-bar: 港口的浅滩或沙洲。

160. clear as glass: 水平如镜。

161. steeped: bathed. 月光如水，所以用这个动词来写洒在风向标（*weathercock*）上的月光。

162. shadows: reflections. 光辉的天使们在水面上映出的倒影。

163. by the holy rood: 凭圣十字架起誓。*rood*, Christ's cross.

164. seraph: 六翼天使。按希伯莱人的说法，天使分为九个等级，seraph 是最高一级。

165. seraph-band: 一队天使。band，一群；一队。

166. impart: give forth, utter.

167. perforce（副词）**:** 不由自主。

168. blast: blow up; destroy. 老水手心中感到极大的快乐，船上虽然有许多尸体，却不能破坏这种快乐心情。

169. Hermit: 隐士，尤指为宗教原因潜心修行者。

170. shrieve: hear the confession and give absolution for the sins confessed.

171. rears: raises.

172. kneels: 跪下来祈祷。

173. skiff-boat: 领港员驾的小船。

174. I trow:（古）I trust; I believe.

175. but now: 刚才。

176. warped:（因受热曝晒而）翘曲变形。

177. aught like to them: anything like them.

178. lag: 指枯黄的残叶在水上漂浮。

179. ivy-tod: ivy bush.

180. That: 指上行之 **owlet.**

181. a-feared:（古）afraid.

182. straight: straightway, immediately（参见第 177 行）。

183. more dread: more dreadful.

184. Stunned: rendered unconscious.

185. save the hill was telling of the sound: 只有岸边的山上传来回声。**save:** except.

186. 第 560 行： 在以下几小节里，诗人通过 Pilot, Hermit 和 the Pilot's boy 的反应间接写出历尽苦难的老水手样子的可怕。这种写法使读者有充分的余地自己去想象，比直接描述更为有力。

187. His eyes went to and fro: 因为恐惧和惊奇而不断转动眼睛。

188. Forthwith: immediately; **this frame of mine:** my body. 老水手回想自己犯的罪和受的惩罚，痛苦万分，觉得自己的肉体都被撕裂了。

189. at an uncertain hour: at irregular intervals; from time to time.

190. 第 591 行： 婚礼欢乐场面在这里重新出现，似乎使读者由一个神奇的幻想世界又回到现实之中，但从下面的描写看来，这种欢乐场面已失去了它的魅力。长诗结束时不是简单地回到现实，而是通过老水手讲述的故事，对生活有了更深刻的认识，增添了严肃的气氛。

191. vesper bell: 晚祷的钟声。

192. Scarce: scarcely; hardly. *seeméd*，在此读如双音节词。

193. He prayeth well, who loveth well: 老水手给年轻人的临别赠言：只有有爱的行动的人，他的祈祷才不是没有效力的空话。**prayeth:** = prays; *loyeth* = loves；这种古老拼法是模仿《圣经》的文体（the biblical style），使说的话更具庄严和古雅的意味。

194. with age is hoar: 由年老而灰白。

195. of sense forlorn: bereft of feeling.

196. sadder: more serious; of a temperament more grave.

197. morrow morn:〔诗〕next morning. 在听完老水手讲的故事之后，本来要去参加婚礼宴会的年轻客人对寻欢作乐失去了兴趣，变得更为严肃，也更有思想（*A sadder and a wiser man*）。他对于周围世界似乎失去了感觉，而将沉思人生的哲理和永恒的事物。在这里我们可以窥见柯尔律治本人的思想和个性特征，与他的朋友华兹华斯比较起来，他更突出的确实是奇特瑰丽的想象和严肃的哲理的沉思。

2. KUBLA KHAN:
Or a Vision in a Dream. A Fragment

正象诗的副标题所表明的，《忽必烈汗》是梦境的一个片断，然而这却是一场充满奇谲恣肆的幻想和浪漫的异国情调的诗人之梦。柯尔律治曾自述写作此诗的经过，说在1797年某夏日，他因身体不适服用了一点鸦片酊，药性发作后沉沉睡去，睡前正读讲到忽必烈下令建造宫殿和御花园的一篇游记，睡梦中写成二、三百行的一首长诗，醒来时还清楚地记得。于是诗人赶紧追记下来，但不幸因有客来访而中断，所得的终于只有目前这五十四行。柯尔律治这场梦是真是假，这并不要紧，但《忽必烈汗》这首诗写得象梦一样汗漫缥缈，却是确定无疑的。诗人自己称这首诗是“心理描写的奇品”（a psychological curiosity），它的确是浪漫诗的新奇之作，既无叙述故事的情节，也不在于传达某种寓意，它的完整性完全在于诗人心理或情调上的统一。这首诗虽以忽必烈为名，其实却并未描绘这位声名赫赫的蒙古皇帝的霸业，只不过把这位传奇英雄式的人物与瑰丽的花园、深不可测的山洞、操琴的阿比西尼亚姑娘和受到神意鼓舞的诗人等等揉合在一起，创造出一种奇幻的气氛和旋律的美。在这一点上，《忽必烈汗》对于近代诗风的影响是不容忽视的。

1. *Xanadu* ['zænədu]: 关于此地名，现在尚无定说，有人认为指上都，即今内蒙古自治区正蓝旗东约二十公里，元世祖忽必烈即位时称开平府，至元五年改号上都。忽必烈定都北京后，上都仍为行宫所在地。又有人认为指大都，即今北京，为元代首都。

2. Kubla Khan: 忽必烈（1215？—1294），成吉思汗之孙，公元1279年灭宋建元，称世祖。Khan，汗或可汗，蒙古帝王的称号。

3. pleasure-dome: a great palace for entertainment.

4. decree: 下令修建。

5. Alph: 柯尔律治诗中这条圣河并非实有，而是诗人想象力的产物。但有的批评家指出（如 J. L. Lowes, *The Road to Xanadu*, 1927），Alph 与古典作家所提到的河流 Alpheus 和 Nile 有些相似之处，也许无意中受了古希腊、罗马文学的影响。

6. measureless to man: 深不可测的。

7. twice five miles: 方圆五英里。

8. sinuous rills: 蜿蜒曲折的小河。

9. incense-bearing: 开出香花的。

10. greenery: 指葱翠的新绿，与上文苍郁的老林（*forests ancient as the hills*）相对比。

11. chasm [ˈkæzəm]: a deep opening or crack.

12. athwart: across. *cedarn*，雪松的。

13. e'er: ever. 此两行描写在残月下哭着等待阴间的情人（*demon-lover*）而踌躇徘徊的女人，用以烘托这片野景（*savage place*）的浪漫气氛。

14. 第 17—19 行：此三行描写岩间涌出的飞泉，象大地急促地呼吸喷出来似的。

15. thick pants: gasping breaths in quick succession.

16. momently: every moment.

17. half-intermitted: 几乎不间断的。

18. 第 21—22 行：这两行描写形成水帘的瀑布象落地后又飞溅起来的冰雹，或象打谷时连枷下飞扬起来的谷壳。

19. 'mid: = amid. these dancing rocks，在不断涌出的河水冲击之下，岩石好象也在跳荡。

20. It: 此句主语重复，代词 it 即指后面的 river. 在诗中常常出现这种情形。

21. mazy: 迷津般蜿蜒曲折的。

22. shadow: reflection. 水中倒影。

23. mingled measure: 和谐的乐音。参见 William Collins, *The Passions: an Ode for Music*，第 64 行：

Through glades and glooms the mingled measure stole:

24. dulcimer: 类似洋琴的一种古老乐器。由此行起，柯尔律治描写弹琴的阿比西尼亚少女和一位充满灵感的诗人，与忽必烈了无关系，批评家们对这位少女究系何人也众说纷纭；但此诗既为梦境的片断，在浪漫的情调中与前面的描写仍是统一的。

25. Abyssinian maid: 阿比西尼亚少女。Abyssinia 位于非洲东部，东北临红海，现称埃塞俄比亚（Ethiopia）.

26. Mount Abora: 批评家们认为此山即弥尔顿《失乐园》中的 Mount Amara，阿比西尼亚王曾将其儿女置于此山中，使他们免受外界的搅扰。见 Milton, *Paradise Lost*, iv, 280–282：

Nor where Abassin Kings their issue guard,
Mount Amara, though this by some supposed
True Paradise,……

十八世纪约翰逊（Samuel Johnson）的小说 *Rasselas* 也描写了这同一地方，称其名为 Amhara.

27. Could I revive: If I could revive.

28. To such a deep delight 'twould win me: it would bring me such a deep delight. 在以下数行，诗人慨叹说，要是他能够重新唱出那位阿比西尼亚少女所唱的优美动人的歌，他心中的欢乐就能使他有神奇的力量在诗中重现忽必烈豪华的宫殿和花园，人们也会怀着敬畏之情把他看成象古代预言诗人那样受神灵感召的歌手。在这种感慨之中，我们似乎听到柯尔律治在哀叹自己的诗才已渐渐消失，因为他完成了《古舟子咏》、《忽必烈汗》和《克利斯托贝尔》（*Christabel*）第一部分之后，的确再也难写出同样出色的作品了。参见他的《沮丧之歌》（*Dejection: an Ode*）第76—86行：

There was a time when, though my path was rough,
    This joy within me dallied with distress,
And all misfortunes were but as the stuff
    Whence Fancy made me dreams of happiness:
For hope grew round me, like the twining vine,
And fruits, and foliage, not my own, seemed mine.
But now afflictions bow me down to earth:
Nor care I that they rob me of my mirth;
    But oh! each visitation
Suspends what nature gave me at my birth,
    My shaping spirit of Imagination.

29. His flashing eyes, his floating hair: 诗人充满灵感时似有神灵附体，象神话中的狂女一样目光闪耀，长发在风中飘舞。

30. Weave a circle ... with holy dread: 古代迷信，被神灵或妖魔附体的人应当被隔离开来，而闭着眼绕行三圈似乎就是把他与众人隔离开的做法。

31. For he on honey-dew hath fed, And drunk the milk of Paradise: 在柏拉图（Plato）论诗的灵感的《伊安篇》（*Ion*）里，曾把诗人比做酒神的女信徒们，可以从诗神的河水中汲取乳蜜。见 *Ion*, 534 a–b:

For all good poets, epic as well as lyric, compose their beautiful poems not by art, but because they are inspired and possessed. And as the Corybantian revellers when they dance are not in their right mind, so the lyric poets are not in their right mind when they are composing their beautiful strains: but when falling under the power of music and metre they are inspired and possessed; like Bacchic maidens who draw milk and honey from the rivers when they are under the influence of Dionysus but not when they are in their right mind. And the soul of the lyric poet does the same, as they themselves say; for they tell us that they bring songs from honeyed fountains, culling them out of the gardens and dells of the Muses; they, like the bees, winging their way from flower to flower.

31 JANE AUSTEN
1775–1817

PRIDE AND PREJUDICE
(selections)

周珏良　选注

CHAPTER I

It is a truth universally acknowledged,[1] that a single man in possession of a good fortune,[2] must be[3] in want of a wife.

However little known the feelings or views[4] of such a man may be on his first entering a neighbourhood,[5] this truth is so well fixed in the minds of the surrounding families,[6] that he is considered as the rightful property of some one or other of their daughters.[7]

"My dear Mr. Bennet,[8]" said his lady to him one day, "have you heard that Netherfield Park[9] is let[10] at last?"

Mr. Bennet replied that he had not.[11]

"But it is," returned she; "for Mrs. Long[12] has just been here, and she told me all about it."

Mr. Bennet made no answer.

"Do not you want to know who has taken it?" cried his wife impatiently.

"*You* want to tell me,[13] and I have no objection to hearing it."

This was invitation enough.[14]

"Why, my dear, you must know, Mrs. Long says that Netherfield is taken by a young man of large fortune from the north of England;

that he came down on Monday in a chaise and four[15] to see the place, and was so much delighted with it that he agreed with Mr. Morris[16] immediately; that he is to take possession before Michaelmas,[17] and some of his servants are to be in the house[18] by the end of next week."

"What is his name?"

"Bingley."

"Is he married or single?"

"Oh! single, my dear, to be sure! A single man of large fortune; four or five thousand a year.[19] What a fine thing for our girls!"

"How so?[20] how can it affect them?"

"My dear Mr. Bennet," replied his wife, "how can you be so tire-some[21]! You must know that I am thinking of his marrying one of them."

"Is that his design[22] in settling[23] here?"

"Design! nonsense, how can you talk so! But it is very likely that he *may* fall in love with one of them, and therefore you must visit him as soon as he comes."

"I see no occasion for[24] that. You and the girls may go, or you may send them by themselves, which perhaps will be still better, for as you are as handsome[25] as any of them, Mr. Bingley might like you the best of the party.[26]"

"My dear, you flatter me.[27] I certainly have had my share of beauty,[28] but I do not pretend to be any thing extraordinary[29] now. When a woman has five grown up daughters, she ought to give over thinking of her own beauty."[30]

"In such cases,[31] a woman has not often much beauty to think of."

"But, my dear, you must indeed go and see Mr. Bingley when he comes into the neighbourhood.[32]"

"It is more than I engage for, I assure you."[33]

"But consider your daughters. Only think what an establish-ment[34] it would be for one of them. Sir William and Lady Lucas[35] are determined to go, merely on that account,[36] for in general you know they visit no new comers. Indeed you must go, for it will be impossible for *us*[37] to visit him, if you do not."

"You are over scrupulous surely. I dare say Mr. Bingley will be very glad to see you; and I will send a few lines by you[38] to assure him of my hearty consent to his marrying whichever he chooses of the girls; though I must throw in a good word for[39] my little Lizzy.[40]"

"I desire you will do no such thing.[41] Lizzy is not a bit better than the others; and I am sure she is not half so handsome as Jane, nor half so good humoured as Lydia.[42] But you are always giving her the preference."[43]

"They have none of them much to recommend them,"[44] replied he; "they are all silly and ignorant like other girls; but Lizzy has something more of quickness[45] than her sisters."

"Mr. Bennet, how can you abuse your own children in such a way?You take delight in vexing me.[46] You have no compassion on my poor nerves."

"You mistake me, my dear. I have a high respect for your nerves. They are my old friends.[47] I have heard you mention them with consideration[48] these twenty years at least."

"Ah! you do not know what I suffer."

"But I hope you will get over it, and live to see many young men of four thousand a year[49] come into the neighbourhood."

"It will be no use to us, if twenty such[50] should come since you will not visit them."

"Depend upon it,[51] my dear, that when there are twenty, I will visit them all."

Mr. Bennet was so odd a mixture of quick parts,[52] sarcastic humour, reserve, and caprice, that the experience of three and twenty years had been insufficient to make his wife understand his character. *Her* mind was less difficult to develope.[53] She was a woman of mean understanding, little information, and uncertain temper.[64] When she was discontented she fancied herself nervous. The business of her life was to get her daughters married; its solace was visiting and news.[55]

CHAPTER LVI

One morning, about a week after Bingley's engagement with Jane had been formed, as he and the females of the family were sitting together in the dining room, their attention was suddenly drawn to the window,[56] by the sound of a carriage; and they perceived a chaise and four driving up the lawn. It was too early in the morning for visitors,[57] and besides, the equipage did not answer to that of any of their neighbours.[58] The horses were post;[59] and neither the carriage, nor the livery[60] of the servant who preceded it, were familiar to them. As it was certain, however, that somebody was coming, Bingley[61] instantly prevailed on Miss Bennet to avoid the confinement of such an intrusion,[62] and walk away with him into the shrubbery. They both set off, and the conjectures of the remaining three continued,[63] though with little satisfaction,[64] till the door was thrown open,[65] and their visitor entered. It was Lady Catherine de Bourgh.

They were of course all intending to be surprised;[66] but their astonishment was beyond their expectation; and on the part of Mrs. Bennet and Kitty, though she was perfectly unknown to them, even inferior to what Elizabeth felt.[67]

She entered the room with an air more than usually ungracious,[68] made no other reply to Elizabeth's salutation, than a slight inclination of the head, and sat down without saying a word.[69] Elizabeth had mentioned her name to her mother, on her ladyship's[70] entrance, though no request of introduction had been made.[71]

Mrs. Bennet all amazement, though flattered by having a guest of such high importance, received her with the utmost politeness.[72] After sitting for a moment in silence, she said very stiffly[73] to Elizabeth,

"I hope you are well, Miss Bennet. That lady I suppose is your mother.[74]"

Elizabeth replied very concisely[75] that she was.

"And that I suppose is one of your sisters."

"Yes, madam," said Mrs. Bennet, delighted to speak to a Lady Catherine.[76] "She is my youngest girl but one. My youngest of all,[77] is lately married, and my eldest is somewhere about the grounds,[78] walking with a young man, who I believe will soon become a part of the family.[79]"

"You have a very small park here," returned Lady Catherine after a short silence.

"It is nothing in comparison of Rosings,[80] my lady, I dare say; but I assure you it is much larger than Sir William Lucas's."

"This must be a most inconvenient sitting room for the evening, in summer; the windows are full west.[81]"

Mrs. Bennet assured her that they never sat there after dinner; and then added,

"May I take the liberty of asking your ladyship whether you left Mr. and Mrs. Collins well."[82]

"Yes, very well. I saw them the night before last."

Elizabeth now expected that she would produce a letter for her from Charlotte, as it seemed the only probable motive for her calling. But no letter appeared, and she was completely puzzled.

Mrs. Bennet, with great civility, begged her ladyship to take some refreshment; but Lady Catherine very resolutely, and not very politely, declined[83] eating any thing; and then rising up, said to Elizabeth,

"Miss Bennet, there seemed to be a prettyish kind of a little wilderness[84] on one side of your lawn. I should be glad to take a turn in it, if you will favour me with your company.[85]"

"Go, my dear," cried her mother, "and shew her ladyship about the different walks.[86] I think she will be pleased with the hermitage.[87]"

Elizabeth obeyed, and running into her own room for her parasol,[88] attended her noble guest[89] down stairs. As they passed through the hall, Lady Catherine opened the doors into the dining-parlour and drawing-room, and prornouncing them, after a short survey, to be decent looking rooms,[90] walked on.

Her carriage remained at the door, and Elizabeth saw that her waiting-woman was in it. They proceeded in silence along the gravel walk that led to the copse,[91] Elizabeth was determined to make no effort for conversation with a woman, who was now more than usually insolent and disagreeable.[92]

"How could I ever think her like her nephew[93]?" said she, as she looked in her face.

As soon as they entered the copse, Lady Catherine began in the following manner:—

"You can be at no loss, Miss Bennet, to understand the reason of my journey hither.[94] Your own heart, your own conscience, must tell you why I come."

Elizabeth looked with unaffected[95] astonishment.

"Indeed, you are mistaken, Madam. I have not been at all able to account for the honour of seeing you here.[96]"

"Miss Bennet," replied her ladyship, in an angry tone, "you ought to know, that I am not to be trifled with.[97] But however insincere *you* may choose to be, you shall not find me so.[98] My character has ever been celebrated for its sincerity and frankness,[99] and in a cause of such moment[100] as this, I shall certainly not depart from it.[101] A report[102] of a most alarming nature, reached me two days ago. I was told, that not only your sister was on the point of being most advantageously married,[103] but that you, that Miss Elizabeth Bennet, would, in all likelihood,[104] be soon afterwards united to[105] my nephew, my own nephew, Mr. Darcy. Though I *know* it must be a scandalous falsehood;[106] though I would not injure him so much as to suppose the truth of it possible,[107] I instantly resolved on setting off for this place, that I might make my sentiments known to you."

"If you believed it impossible to be true," said Elizabeth, colouring with astonishment and disdain,[108] "I wonder you took the trouble of coming so far.[109] What could your ladyship propose by it?"

"At once to insist upon having such a report universally contra dicted.[110]"

"Your coming to Longbourn,[111] to see me and my family," said Elizabeth, coolly, "will be rather a confirmation[112] of it; if, indeed, such a report is in existence."

"If![113] do you then pretend to be ignorant of it? Has it not been industriously[114] circulated by yourselves?[115] Do you not know that such a report is spread abroad?"

"I never heard that it was."

"And can you likewise declare, that there is no *foundation* for it?"

"I do not pretend to possess equal frankness with your ladyship.[116] *You* may ask questions, which *I*[117] shall not choose to answer."

"This is not to be borne. Miss Bennet, I insist on being satisfied.[118] Has he, has my nephew, made you an offer of marriage?"

"Your ladyship has declared it to be impossible."

"It ought to be so; it must be so, while he retains the use of his reason. But *your* arts and allurements[119] may, in a moment of infatuation,[120] have made him forget what he owes to himself and to all his family.[121] You may have drawn him in."

"If I have, I shall be the last person to confess it."[122]

"Miss Bennet, do you know who I am? I have not been accustomed to such language as this.[123] I am almost the nearest relation[124] he has in the world, and am entitled to know all his dearest concerns.125"

"But you are not entitled to know *mine*;[126] nor will such behaviour as this ever induce me to be explicit."[127]

"Let me be rightly understood.[128] This match, to which you have the presumption to aspire,[129] can never take place. No, never. Mr. Darcy is engaged to *my daughter*. Now what have you to say?"

"Only this;[130] that if he is so, you can have no reason to suppose he will make an offer to me."

Lady Catherine hesitated for a moment, and then replied,

"The engagement between them is of a peculiar kind. From their infancy, they have been intended for each other.[131] It was the favourite wish of *his* mother, as well as of her's.[132] While in their cradles, we plan ned the union: and now, at the moment when the wishes of both sisters would be accomplished, in their marriage, to be prevented by a young woman of inferior birth, of no importance in the world, and wholly unallied to the family![133] Do you pay no regard to the wishes of his friends? To his tacit engagement[134] with Miss De Bourgh?[135] Are you lost to every feeling of propriety and delicacy?[136] Have you not heard me say, that from his earliest hours he was destined for his cousin?[137]"

"Yes, and I had heard it before. But what is that to me? If there is no other objection to my marrying your nephew, I shall certainly not be kept from it, by knowing that his mother and aunt wished him to marry Miss De Bourgh. You both did as much as you could, in planning the marriage. Its completion depended on others. If Mr. Darcy is neither by honour nor inclination[138] confined to his cousin, why is not he to make another choice? And if I am that choice, why may not I accept him?"

"Because honour, decorum,[139] prudence,[140] nay, interest,[141]. forbid it. Yes, Miss Bennet, interest; for do not expect to be noticed by his family or friends, if you wilfully[142] act against the inclinations of all. You will be censured, slighted, and despised, by every one connected with him. Your alliance will be a disgrace[143]; your name will never even be mentioned by any of us."

"These are heavy misfortunes,[144]" replied Elizabeth. "But the wife of Mr. Darcy must have such extraordinary sources of happiness necessarily attached to her situation,[145] that she could, upon the whole, have no cause to repine.[146]"

"Obstinate, headstrong girl! I am ashamed of you! Is this your gratitude for my attentions to you last spring[147]? Is nothing due to me on that score?[148]

"Let us sit down. You are to understand, Miss Bennet, that I came here with the determined resolution of carrying my purpose;[149] nor will I be dissuaded from it. I have not been used to submit to any person's whims. I have not been in the habit of brooking[150] disappointment."

"*That* will make your ladyship's situation at present more pitiable;[151] but it will have no effect on *me*."

"I will not be interrupted.[152] Hear me in silence. My daughter and my nephew are formed for each other. They are descended on the maternal side,[153] from the same noble line;[154] and, on the father's, from respectable, honourable, and ancient, though untitled families.[155] Their fortune[156] on both sides is splendid. They are destined for each other by the voice of every member of their respective houses; and what is to divide them? The upstart pretensions[157] of a young woman without family,[158] connections,[159] or fortune. Is this to be endured! But it must not, shall not be.160 If you were sensible of your own good,[161] you would not wish to quit the sphere, in which you have been brought up."

"In marrying your nephew, I should not consider myself as quitting that sphere. He is a gentleman; I am a gentleman's daughter; so far we are equal."

"True. You *are* a gentleman's daughter. But who was your mother? Who are your uncles and aunts? Do not imagine me ignorant of their condition."

"Whatever my connections may be," said Elizabeth, "if your nephew does not object to them, they can be nothing to *you*.[162]"

"Tell me once for all, are you engaged to him?"

Though Elizabeth would not, for the mere purpose of obliging Lady Catherine, have answered this question; she could not but say, after a moment's deliberation,

"I am not."

Lady Catherine seemed pleased.

"And will you promise me, never to enter into such an engagement?"

"I will make no promise of the kind."

"Miss Bennet, I am shocked and astonished. I expected to find a more reasonable young woman.[163] But do not deceive yourself into a belief that[164] I will ever recede. I shall not go away, till you have given me the assurance I require."

"And I certainly *never* shall give it. I am not to be intimidated into anything so wholly unreasonable. Your ladyship wants Mr. Darcy to marry your daughter; but would my giving you the wished-for promise, make *their* marriage at all more probable? Supposing him to be attached to me,[165] would *my* refusing to accept his hand, make him wish to bestow it on his cousin? Allow me to say, Lady Catherine, that the arguments with which you have supported this extraordinary application[166], have been as frivolous as the application was ill-judged.[167] You have widely[168] mistaken my character, if you think I can be worked on by such persuasions as these. How far your nephew might approve of your interference in *his* affairs, I cannot tell; but you have certainly no right to concern yourself in mine. I must beg, therefore, to be importuned no farther on the subject."

"Not so hasty, if you please. I have by no means done.[169] To all the objections I have already urged, I have still another to add. I am no stranger to the particulars of your youngest sister's infamous elopement. I know it all; that the young man's marrying her, was a patchedup business, at the expence of your father and uncles.[170] And is *such* a girl to be my nephew's sister? Is *her* hushand,[171] is the son of his late father's steward, to be his brother? Heaven and earth!—of what are you thinking? Are the shades of Pemberley[172] to be thus polluted?[173]"

"You can *now* have nothing farther to say," she[174] resentfully answered. "You have insulted me, in every possible method. I must beg to return to the house."

And she rose as she spoke. Lady Catherine rose also, and they turned back. Her ladyship was highly incensed.[175]

"You have no regard, then, for the honour and credit[176] of my nephew! Unfeeling, selfish girl! Do you not consider that a connection with you, must disgrace him in the eyes of everybody?"

"Lady Catherine, I have nothing farther to say. You know my sentiments."

"You are then resolved to have him?"

"I have said no such thing. I am only resolved to act in that manner, which will, in my own opinion, constitute my happiness, without reference to *you,* or to any person so wholly unconnected with me."

"It is well. You refuse, then, to oblige me. You refuse to obey the claims of duty, honour, and gratitude. You are determined to ruin him in the opinion of all his friends, and make him the contempt[177] of the world."

"Neither duty, nor honour, nor gratitude," replied Elizabeth, "have any possible claim on me,[178] in the present instance. No principle of either,[179] would be violated by my marriage with Mr. Darcy. And with regard to the resentment of his family, or the indignation of the world, if the former *were* excited by his marrying me, it would not give me one moment's concern—and the world in general would have too much sense to join in the scorn.[180]"

"And this is your real opinion! This is your final resolve! Very well. I shall now know how to act. Do not imagine, Miss Bennet, that your ambition will ever be gratified. I came to try you. I hoped to find you reasonable; but depend upon it I will carry my point."

In this manner Lady Catherine talked on, till they were at the door of the carriage, when turning hastily round, she added,

"I take no leave of you, Miss Bennet. I send no compliments to your mother. You deserve no such attention. I am most seriously displeased."

Elizabeth made no answer; and without attempting to persuade her ladyship to return into the house, walked quietly into it herself. She heard the carriage drive away as she proceeded up stairs. Her mother impatiently met her at the door of the dressing-room, to ask why Lady Catherine would not come in again and rest herself.

"She did not choose it," said her daughter, "she would go."

"She is a very fine-looking woman! and her calling here was prodigiously[181] civil! for she only came, I suppose, to tell us the Collinses[182] were well. She is on her road somewhere, I dare say, and so passing through. Meryton,[183] thought she might as well call on you. I suppose she had nothing particular to say to you, Lizzy?"

Elizabeth was forced to give into[184] a little falsehood here; for to acknowledge the substance of their conversation was impossible.[185]

【作者简介】 Jane Austen（珍妮·奥斯汀，1775—1817），英国现实主义小说家。她是乡村牧师的女儿，一生住在乡间，对乡村士绅地主的生活了解很深，平生写过六部小说，多以此为背景，而更以婚姻问题为中心题材。但她的作品并不单调乏味，相反地，在她的作品里不仅反映了她所熟悉的那一部分英国社会生活，而且情节结构精密紧凑，人物描写深刻生动，戏剧场面精采，对话巧妙，加上她那略带嘲讽口气的清丽的散文，颇为英国人民所乐读，在我国也颇受欢迎。

【题解与注释】

Pride and Prejudice（《傲慢与偏见》）出版于1813年，是Austen最著名的小说，也是英国文学中的名著。书中主要情节是Bennet太太五个女儿的婚事，而以她第二个女儿Elizabeth和Darcy先生的结合为中心，后者的傲慢曾引起前者的偏见，始而似乎相斥，终而相爱。这里从全书中选了两章，第一段是全书的开场。这里Austen以简练的笔法，点出全书主题：女大当嫁，并以戏剧的场面，巧妙的对话描绘了Bennet先生和太太两个人，一个玩世不恭，一个庸俗愚昧，使读者如闻其声，如见其人，而全章中充斥的温厚的讽刺又是全书的特色。这是英国文学中有名的篇章之一。

这里选的第二段是全书原本第三卷第十四章（版本根据R. W. Chapman编的牛津版），现代版本则是第五十六章。Lady Catherine de Bourgh是Darcy先生的姨母，听到Darcy在追求Elizabeth，勃然大怒（理由在本文中有交代），特地跑来找Elizabeth加以阻拦，孰知后来反倒促成了两人的婚事。这一段也是全书中精采的戏剧性场面之一，其中对Catherine夫人的盛气凌人，骄横无礼，和Elizabeth的从容应对，不屈于威势，以及最后的Elizabeth大获全胜，Catherine夫人铩羽而去的描写，笔酣墨畅，使人读了真堪浮一大白。当然此段之妙也还不止文章。对Catherine夫人这一个贵族阶级代表人物的讽刺，从思想内容上讲，也不无可取的。

CHAPTER I

1. a truth universally acknowledged: 公认的真理。

2. a single man in possession of a good fortune: 拥有丰厚财产的单身汉。

3. must be: 这里意为“定然”。

4. the feelings or views: 思想感情。

5. his first entering a neighbourhood: 他初搬到某地。

6. The surrounding families: 前后左右的邻居人家。

7. is considered as the rightful property of some one or other of their daughters: the rightful property 意为“合法财产”，也就是说被认为要和其中一家的女儿结婚，为她所有。

8. my dear Mr. Bennet: 当时社会上夫妇之间互称 Mr. 某某或 Mrs. 某某是很普通的。

9. Netherfield Park: 这是 Bennet 家附近的一所住宅的名字。英国的许多住宅，往往有自己的名字，就和过去中国地主、官僚和资本家的许多房子叫做某某别墅，某某山庄一样。

10. let: 租出去。

11. he had not: 他没有听到。

12. Mrs. Long: Bennet 家的朋友。

13. You want to tell me: 本段中用斜体印的字都表示语气要加重。所以这里的意思是“是你要告诉我的”。

14. This was invitation enough: 在 Bennet 太太看来，虽然从上面 Bennet 先生的答话里看不出多少热情，但是只要他并不拒绝听她讲，这就足够使她讲下去了，也就是说等于请她（invitation）讲下去了。

15. a chaise and four: 用四匹马拉的车。

16. Mr. Morris: 是 Netherfield Park 的房东。**agreed with Mr. Morris:** 同意了 Morris 先生的（出租）条件。

17. Michaelmas: 9 月 29 日。

18. are to be in the house: 就要派到这所房子里来。

19. four or five thousand a year: 一年有四、五千镑（的收入）。

20. How so?: 怎么会如此呢?

21. tiresome: 惹人着急。

22. design: 目的。

23. settling: 定居。

24. no occasion for: 没有理由去（访问）。

25. handsome: 漂亮。

26. party: 所有的人里。

27. you flatter me: 你是捧我。Bennet 太太完全没有听出她丈夫在讽刺她。

28. I certainly *have* had my share of beauty: 我当然有过漂亮的时候。

29. anything extraordinary: 出色的人。

30. When a woman has five grownup girls … give over thinking of her own beauty: Bennet 太太这里说女儿大了，做妈妈的就不该想自己的美貌了，她暗含的意思是说自己仍然是很漂亮的，所以下面 Bennet 先生才那样讥讽她。

31. In such cases … to think of: Bennet 先生这句话是说等到女儿们都长成人，妈妈往往是老了，也没有什么漂亮不漂亮可说了。

32. when he comes into the neighbourhood: 他搬来之后。

33. It is more than I engage for, I assure you: engage for 意为“保证”；assure 意为“老实说”。全句的意思是“老实向你说，我不能保证做到。”

34. establishment: 这个字在此地的意义是“婚事”，是个较旧的用法。

35. Sir William and Lady Lucas: Bennet 家邻居的一对夫妇。

36. merely on that account: “只是为了这一桩”，意指为了他们女儿的婚事。

37. *us*: 斜体字是加重的意思，这里的“我们”，Bennet 太太指的是她和她的女儿们。

38. will send a few lines by you: 请你带封短信去。

39. throw in a good word for: 替（某人）说句好话。

40. Lizzy: Elizabeth，他们的第二个女儿，小说的女主角。Bennet 先生认为她最有头脑，因之最喜欢她。

41. I desire you will do no such thing: 我希望你别这么干。

42. Jane, Lydia: 他们的第一、第五个女儿。

43. give *her* the preference: 特别喜欢她。

44. They have … to recommend them: recommend = 使别人喜欢。全句意思是说他的几个女儿都没有什么出色的地方，能使别人喜欢她们。

45. has something more of quickness: 比（她的姐妹们）伶俐些。

46. You take delight in vexing me: 你拿气我开心。

47. “You mistake me, … They are my old friends”: mistake me = 你误会了我的意思。your nerves = 你的神经。这三句总的意思是说：你错会了意了。我一向对你的神经十分尊重（因为你总不断提起）。它已经成了我听惯了的事（老朋友）了。

48. with consideration: 关切地。

49. young men of four thousand a year: 一年有四千镑收入的年轻人。

50. twenty such: 二十个这样的人。

51. depend upon it: 放心。

52. quick parts: 敏捷的才能。

53. develope: = discover，此处意为“弄清楚”，是个较旧用法；develope，现代英文拼作 develop.

54. of mean understanding, little information, and uncertain temper: 见识浅，知识少，没有准脾气。

55. its solace was visiting and news: 串门儿和打听消息是她生活中的安慰。

CHAPTER LVI

56. their attention was suddenly drawn to the window: 他们的注意力忽然被吸引到窗户那个方向。

57. too early in the morning for visitors: 当时的习俗认为早晨去拜访人家是不礼貌的。

58. the equipage did not answer to that of any of their neighbours: answer to = 相当。全句意为：这辆车又和哪一家邻近人家的车都不相象。

59. The horses were post: post horses 是旅店所养，租给走远程的客人车上用的。这里用来暗示坐车的人从远处来。

60. livery: 有钱人家给仆人穿的号衣，各家不同。

61. Bingley: 他这时已和 Bennet 家的大女儿 Jane（即 Miss Bennet）订婚。

62. to avoid the confinement of such an intrusion: 以避免有人闯了来（intrusion 是此意）脱不了身（confinement 意为受拘束）。

63. the conjectures of the remaining three continued: 剩下的三个人（即 Bennet 太太，Elizabeth 和她的妹妹 Kitty）仍在那儿猜测（是谁来了）。

64. with little satisfaction: 找不到满意的回答。

65. the door was thrown open: 门被摔开。暗示 Lady Catherine 之无礼。

66. were all intending to be surprised: 都是准备要吃上一惊的。

67. and on the part of Mrs. Bennet and Kitty ... even inferior to what Elizabeth felt: = on the part of Mrs. Bennet and Kitty, though she (*i. e.* Lady Catherine) was perfectly unknown to them, *the astonishment was* not as much as what Elizabeth felt. On the part of = 就…而言。even inferior to = 尚不及。

68. with an air more than usually ungracious: 带上一副比平时更加讨人厌的神气。Lady Catherine 对比她地位低的人一向是颐指气使的，所以这里说比平时更加讨人厌。

69. a slight inclination of the head, and sat down without saying a word: 微微地侧一下头，一句话不说就坐了下来。到人家里不理人，主人不请就自己坐下来。这里极意写她的傲慢无礼。

70. her ladyship: 对贵妇人的尊称。

71. though no request of introduction had been made: 虽然（Lady Catherine）没有要求（Elizabeth）介绍。

72. Mrs. Bennet all amazement ... received her with the utmost politeness: 在一片惶恐之中，Bennet 太太…极端客气地接待她。

73. stiffiy: 僵硬地。

74. That lady I suppose is your mother: 这句话的口气是十分无礼的。下面的 "And *that* I suppose is one of your sisters." 口气也一样。

75. concisely: 简单地，不多费话地。Elizabeth 对 Catherine 夫人的无理态度十分生气，所以也还她个不客气，用一句话回答了她。

76. a Lady Catherine: 一位 Catherine 夫人这样的人。

77. my youngest of all: 我最小的女儿。

78. my eldest is somewhere about the grounds: 我大女儿在园子里。Bennet 太太这里使用的语言是很不得体的，而且不等人问，就大谈自己的女儿们，这也表明 Bennet 太太的没教养。

79. a part of the family:（我们）一家人。

80. Rosings: Catherine 夫人宅邸的名字。

81. the windows are full west: 窗子正朝西。Lady Catherine 来了就先说 Bennet 家花园小，然后又说客厅朝西，夏天晚上一定不舒服，这些笔墨都是用来写她的骄横无礼。

82. May I take the liberty ... Mr. and Mrs. Collins well: 请问夫人临来时，Collins 先生和夫人可好。Collins 先生是 Bennet 家的远亲，Lady Catherine 所在地方的牧师。Collins 太太就是下面将提到的 Charlotte.

83. very resolutely, and not very politely declined: 非常坚决而不很礼貌地拒绝了。

84. a prettyish kind of a little wilderness: 还不错的一片小小野景儿。

85. if you will favour me with your company: 如你愿意陪我一下的话。

86. walks: 散步的小径。

87. hermitage: 园子里幽静处的小屋。

88. parasol: 遮阳伞。

89. her nohle guest: 她的尊贵的客人。这里 noble 一字表示客人有爵位，也带有讽刺意味。

90. decent looking rooms: 看来还不错的几间屋子。

91. copse: 小树林。

92. insolent and disagreeable: 无礼而讨人嫌。

93. her nephew: 指 Darcy 先生。此时 Elizabeth 对 Darcy 先生已有好感。

94. You can be at no loss, ... to understand the reason of my journey hither: 你不会不了解我的来意。

95. unaffected: 不是装出来的。

96. to account for the honour of seeing you here: 解释怎么能在这里有幸见到您。

97. I am not to be trifled with: 不能允许拿我要着玩。

98. you shall not find *me* so: = you shall not find *me* insincere. 这里 shall 有"决不会"的意思。

99. has been celebrated for its sincerity and frankness: 一向以真诚坦率著称。

100. a cause of such moment: 一件如此重要的事。

101. depart from it: = depart from my character.

102. report: 消息。

103. advantageously married: 嫁一个（有钱的）好丈夫。

104. in all likelihood: 十分可能。

105. united to: = married to.

106. scandalous falsehood: 无耻谰言。

107. though I would not injure him so much as to suppose the truth of it possible: 虽然我不认为这种事是真实的，那样想是侮辱我外甥（即 Darcy 先生）。

108. colouring with astonishment and disdain: 因为惊异和厌恶而变了颜色。

109. I wonder you took the trouble of coming so far: 我不了解您为什么要老远地跑到这儿来。

110. having such a report universally contradicted: 向有关的人否认这种消息。

111. Longbourn: Bennet 家的住宅。

112. confirmation: 证实。

113. If!:（你说）假如（有这种消息）。这是接上句"if, indeed, such a report is in existence"来的。

114. industriously: 努力地。

115. yourselves: 指 Bennet 一家人。

116. I do not pretend to possess equal frankness with your ladyship: 我不装成和夫人同样地坦白直爽。这里 Elizabeth 口气里带有讽刺。

117. *you, I*: you 和 I 两字用斜体，读起来加重，造成讽刺口气。

118. I insist on being satisfied: 我坚决要求给我满意的回答。

119. *your* arts and allurements: 你的手段和伎俩。

120. a moment of infatuation: 在被迷住的时刻。

121. what he owes to himself and to all his family: 他对自己和亲朋的责任。

122. If I have, I shall be the last person to confess it: 如果我真那样干了，我是决不会承认的。

123. have not been accustomed to such language as this: 不惯于听这种话。

124. almost the nearest relation: 差不多是最近的亲属。Darcy 先生有个妹妹，Catherine 夫人是他姨母，除他妹妹之外是最亲的人，所以如此说。

125. all his dearest concerns: 他一切最贴身的事情。

126. But you are not entitled to know *mine*: 可是你无权知道我的（一切最贴身的事情）。

127. nor will such behaviour as this ever induce me to be explicit:（你）这种行为更不能使我明言。

128. Let me be rightly understood: 你要清楚地了解我的意思。

129. have the presumption to aspire: 胆敢希冀。

130. only this: 只有这句话要说。

131. From their infancy, they have been intended for each other: 从小就打算他们是一对儿。

132. her's: 现代拼法为 hers.

133. and now, ... and wholly unallied to the family!: both sisters, Catherine 夫人指自己和 Darcy 先生的母亲；她们是姊妹。这句话是惊叹的口气。意思是说：当两个老姊妹为了儿女亲事的一片用心（wishes 应作此解）就将实现的时候，竟然被一个出身低（of inferior birth），没有地位，又毫不沾亲带故的（wholly unallied to the family）女孩子阻挠了，这真是不可想象的。

134. tacit engagement: 对于婚事的默契。

135. Miss De Bourgh: Catherine 夫人的女儿。

136. lost to every feeling of propriety and delicacy: 不顾任何体统和廉耻。

137. he was destined for his cousin: 注定了要娶他表妹的。

138. neither by honour nor inclination: 既无义务又无意愿；confined = bound.

139. decorum: 体面。

140. prudence: 远见。

141. interest: 利益。

142. wilfully: 硬要。

143. your alliance will be a disgrace: 你们的结合将是见不得人的。

144. heavy misfortunes: 严重的不幸，

145. must have such extraordinary sources of happiness necessarily attached to her situation: 必有由于她的处境而特有的欢乐源泉。

146. repine: 不满意。

147. my attentions to you last spring: 指同年春季 Elizabeth 访问 Collins 夫妇（见前注）时，曾受过她的款待。

148. Is nothing due to me on that score?: 我那样款待你，难道不应当报答我吗？

149. carrying my purpose: 达到我的目的。

150. brooking: 忍受。

151. pitiable: 可怜。

152. I will not be interrupted: 不许打断我。

153. on the maternal side: 在母系上。

154. noble line: 贵族世家。

155. untitled families: 没有爵位的人家。

156. fortune: 财产。

157. upstart pretensions: 高攀的妄想。

158. without family: 家世值不得提起的。

159. connections: 社会关系，也就是说有钱有势的亲戚朋友。

160. But it must not, shall not be: 不应当，不允许这样。

161. If you were sensible of your own good: 如果你能为自己着想。

162. they can be nothing to *you*: 在谈话之间，Elizabeth 一直以客气的口气称呼 Catherine 夫人为 your ladyship. 这里改用 you，而且是加重了口气的（从使用斜体字上可见），表示 Elizabeth 十分生气，所以改了称呼。

163. I expected to find a more reasonable young woman: 我原想你是个明白

道理的女孩子。

164. do not deceive yourself into a belief that ...: 不要骗自己以为…。

165. attached to me: 对我有感情。

166. application: 请求。

167. ill-judged: 不恰当的。

168. widely: 大大地。

169. I have by no means done: 我还没有完。

170. I am no stranger to ... at the expence of your father and uncles: Your youngest sister's infamous elopement，指 Elizabeth 的小妹妹 Lydia 与人私奔的事；am no stranger to the particulars，意谓不但知道，而且很详细地知道。a patched-up business, at the expence (= expense) of your father and uncles，意谓这桩丑事（婚事）是你的父亲和舅父花了钱才弥补上的。Catherine 夫人态度无理，但是一直使用的是上层社会的所谓有教养的语言，到了这里用了 patched-up business（遮羞的勾当）这一不含蓄的字眼，也表示她是更为激动了。

171. *her* husband: 指 Lydia 的丈夫 Wickham. 他是 Darcy 的父亲的管家的儿子。

172. shades of Pemberley: Pemberley 是 Darcy 的庄园的名字。shades 指那里的幽雅景色。

173. polluted: 沾污。

174. she: 指 Elizabeth.

175. incensed: 冒火。

176. honour and credit: 荣誉和名声。

177. contempt: 被鄙视的人。

178. have... claim on me: 都对我说（不）着；have 在现代英文中应作 has.

179. either: 指三者（duty, honour, gratitude）中的任何一个；一般 either 只能指二者之一，此处是特殊用法。

180. to join in the scorn: 参加一起来轻蔑。

181. prodigiously: 大大地。

182. The Collinses: Collins 一家人。

183. Meryton: Bennet 家所在的地区名。

184. give into: 等于现代英文的 give in to.

185. for to acknowledge the substance of their conversation was impossible: 说出她们谈话的内容是绝对不成的。意指 Elizabeth 决不能让她母亲知道 Darcy 向她求婚的事和 Lady Catherine 的来意。

32 WALTER SCOTT
1771－1832

IVANHOE
Chapters I & XXIX

丁往道　选注

CHAPTER I

Thus communed these[1]; while to their lowly dome
The full-fed swine return'd with evening home[2];
Compell'd, reluctant, to the several sties,
With din obstreperous[3] and ungrateful cries.
Pope's "Odyssey[4]."

IN that pleasant district of merry England[5] which is watered by the river Don, there extended in ancient times a large forest, covering the greater part of the beautiful hills and valleys which lie between Sheffield and the pleasant town of Doncaster.[6] The remains of this extensive wood are still to be seen at the noble seats of Wentworth, of Wharncliffe Park, and around Rotherham.[7] Here haunted of yore[8] the fabulous Dragon of Wantley[9]; here were fought many of the most desperate battles during the Civil Wars of the Roses;[10] and here also flourished in ancient times those bands of gallant outlaws[11] whose deeds have been rendered so popular in English song.

Such being our chief scene, the date of our story refers to a period towards the end of the reign of Richard I.,[12] when his return from his long captivity[13] had become an event rather wished than hoped for by his despairing subjects, who were in the mean time subjected to every species of subordinate oppression. The nobles, whose power had become exorbitant during the reign of Stephen,[14] and whom the prudence of Henry the Second had scarce reduced into some degree of subjection to the crown, had now resumed their ancient license[15] in its utmost extent; despising the feeble interference of the English Council of State,[16] fortifying their castles, increasing the number of their dependants, reducing all around them to a state of vassalage,[17] and striving by every means in their power to place themselves each at the head of such forces as might enable him to make a figure in the national convulsions[18] which appeared to be impending.

The situation of the inferior gentry, or Franklins,[19] as they were called, who, by the law and spirit of the English constitution, were entitled to hold themselves independent of feudal tyranny, became now unusually precarious. If, as was most generally the case, they placed themselves under the protection of any of the petty kings[20] in their vicinity, accepted of feudal offices in his household, or bound themselves, by mutual treaties of alliance and protection, to support him in his enterprises, they might indeed purchase temporary repose; but it must be with the sacrifice of that independence which was so dear to every English bosom, and at the certain hazard of being involved as a party in whatever rash expedition the ambition of their protector might lead him to undertake. On the other hand, such and so multiplied were the means of vexation and oppression possessed by the great barons,[21] that they never wanted the pretext, and seldom the will,[22] to harass and pursue, even to the very edge of destruction,[23] any of their less powerful neighbours who attempted to separate themselves from their authority, and to trust for their protection, during the dangers of the times, to their own inoffensive conduct[24] and to the laws of the land.

A circumstance which greatly tended to enhance the tyranny of the nobility and the sufferings of the inferior classes arose from the consequences of the Conquest by Duke William of Normandy.[25]

Four generations[26] had not sufficed to blend the hostile blood[27] of the Normans and Anglo-Saxons, or to unite, by common language and mutual interests, two hostile races, one of which still felt the elation of triumph, while the other groaned under all the consequences of defeat. The power had been completely placed in the hands of the Norman nobility by the event of the battle of Hastings,[28] and it had been used, as our histories assure us, with no moderate hand. The whole race of Saxon princes and nobles had been extirpated or disinherited, with few or no exceptions; nor were the numbers great who possessed land in the country of their fathers, even as proprietors of the second or of yet inferior classes.[29] The royal policy had long been to weaken, by every means, legal or illegal, the strength of a part of the population which was justly considered as nourishing the most inveterate antipathy to their victor. All the monarchs of the Norman race had shown the most marked predilection for their Norman subjects; the laws of the chase,[30] and many others equally unknown to the milder and more free spirit of the Saxon constitution,[31] had been fixed upon the necks of the subjugated inhabitants, to add weight, as it were,[32] to the feudal chains with which they were loaded. At court,[33] and in the castles of the great nobles, where the pomp and state of a court was emulated, Norman-French was the only language employed; in courts of law, the pleadings and judgments were delivered in the same tongue. In short, French was the language of honour, of chivalry, and even of justice, while the far more manly and expressive Anglo-Saxon was abandoned to the use of rustics and hinds,[34] who knew no other. Still, however, the necessary intercourse between the lords of the soil, and those oppressed inferior beings by whom that soil was cultivated, occasioned the gradual formation of a dialect, compounded betwixt the French and the Anglo-Saxon, in which they could render themselves mutually intelligible to each other; and from this necessity arose by degrees the structure of our present English language, in which the speech of the victors and the vanquished have been so happily blended together; and which has since been so richly improved by importations from the classical languages,[35] and from those spoken by the southern nations of Europe.

This state of things I have thought it necessary to premise for the information of the general reader, who might be apt to forget that, although no great historical events, such as war or insurrection, mark the existence of the Anglo-Saxons as a separate people subsequent to the reign of William the Second,[36] yet the great national distinctions betwixt them and their conquerors, the recollection of what they had formerly been, and to what they were now reduced, continued, down to the reign of Edward the Third,[37] to keep open the wounds which the Conquest had inflicted, and to maintain a line of separation betwixt the descendants of the victor Normans and the vanquished Saxons.

Now fitted the halter, now traversed the cart,
And often took leave, but seem'd loath to depart.[38]

The sun was setting upon one of the rich grassy glades of that forest which we have mentioned in the beginning of the chapter. Hundreds of broad-headed, short-stemmed, wide-branched oaks, which had witnessed perhaps the stately march of the Roman soldiery,[39] flung their gnarled arms over a thick carpet of the most delicious greensward; in some places they were intermingled with beeches, hollies, and copsewood of various descriptions, so closely as totally to intercept the level beams of the sinking sun; in others they receded from each other, forming those long sweeping vistas in the intricacy of which the eye delights to lose itself,[40] while imagination considers them as the paths to yet wilder scenes of silvan solitude.[41] Here the red rays of the sun shot a broken and discoloured light, that partially hung upon the shattered boughs and mossy trunks of the trees, and there they illuminated in brilliant patches the portions of turf to which they made their way. A considerable open space, in the midst of this glade, seemed formerly to have been dedicated to the rites of Druidical superstition;[42] for, on the summit of a hillock, so regular as to seem artificial, there still remained part of a circle of rough, unhewn stones, of large dimensions. Seven stood upright; the rest had been dislodged from their places, probably by the zeal of some convert to Christianity, and lay, some prostrate near their former site, and others on the side of the hill. One large stone only had found its way to the bottom, and, in stopping the course of a small brook which glided smoothly round the foot of the eminence, gave, by its opposition, a feeble voice of murmur to the placid and elsewhere silent streamlet.

The human figures which completed this landscape were in number two, partaking, in their dress and appearance, of that wild and rustic character which belonged to the woodlands of the West Riding of Yorkshire[43] at that early period. The eldest of these men had a stern, savage, and wild aspect. His garment was of the simplest form imaginable, being a close jacket with sleeves, composed of the tanned skin of some animal, on which the hair had been originally left, but which had been worn off in so many places that it would have been difficult to distinguish, from the patches that remained, to what creature the fur had belonged. This primeval vestment reached from the throat to the knees, and served at once all the usual purposes of body-clothing; there was no wider opening at the collar than was necessary to admit the passage of the head, from which it may be inferred that it was put on by slipping it over the head and shoulders, in the manner of a modern shirt, or ancient hauberk. Sandals, bound with thongs made of boar's hide, protected the feet, and a roll of thin leather was twined artificially round the legs, and, ascending above the calf, left the knees bare, like those of a Scottish Highlander.[44] To make the jacket sit yet more close to the body, it was gathered at the middle by a broad leathern belt, secured by a brass buckle; to one side of which was attached a sort of scrip, and to the other a ram's horn, accoutred with a mouthpiece, for the purpose of blowing. In the same belt was stuck one of those long, broad, sharp-pointed, and two-edged knives, with a buck's-horn handle, which were fabricated in the neighbourhood, and bore even at this early period the name of a Sheffield whittle. The man had no covering upon his head, which was only defended by his own thick hair, matted and twisted together, and scorched by the influence of the sun into a rusty dark-red colour, forming a contrast with the overgrown beard upon his cheeks, which was rather of a yellow or amber hue. One part of his dress only remains, but it is too remarkable to be suppressed; it was a brass ring, resembling a dog's collar, but without any opening, and soldered fast round his neck, so loose as to form no impediment to his breathing, yet so tight as to be incapable of being removed, excepting by the use of the file. On this singular gorget was engraved, in Saxon characters, an inscription of the following purport: "Gurth, the son of Beowulph, is the born thrall[45] of Cedric of Rotherwood."

Beside the swineherd, for such was Gurth's occupation, was seated, upon one of the fallen Druidical monuments, a person about ten years younger in appearance, and whose dress, though resembling his companion's in form, was of better materials, and of a more fantastic description. His jacket had been stained of a bright purple hue, upon which there had been some attempt to paint grotesque ornaments in different colours. To the jacket he added a short cloak, which scarcely reached half-way down his thigh; it was of crimson cloth, though a good deal soiled, lined with bright yellow; and as he could transfer it from one shoulder to the other, or at his pleasure draw it all around him, its width, contrasted with its want of longitude,[46] formed a fantastic piece of drapery. He had thin silver bracelets upon his arms, and on his neck a collar of the same metal, bearing the inscription, "Wamba, the son of Witless, is the thrall of Cedric of Rotherwood." This personage had the same sort of sandals with his companion, but instead of the roll of leather thong, his legs were cased in a sort of gaiters, of which one was red and the other yellow. He was provided also with a cap, having around it more than one bell, about the size of those attached to hawks, which jingled as he turned his head to one side or other; and as he seldom remained a minute in the same posture, the sound might be considered as incessant. Around the edge of this cap was a stiff bandeau of leather, cut at the top into open-work, resembling a coronet, while a prolonged bag arose from within it, and fell down on one shoulder like an old-fashioned nightcap, or a jelly-bag, or the head-gear of a modern hussar. It was to this part of the cap that the bells were attached; which circumstance, as well as the shape of his head-dress, and his own half-crazed, half-cunning expression of countenance, sufficiently pointed him out as belonging to the race of domestic clowns or jesters, maintained in the houses of the wealthy, to help away the tedium of those lingering hours which they were obliged to spend within doors.[47] He bore, like his companion, a scrip attached to his belt, but had neither horn nor knife, being probably considered as belonging to a class whom it is esteemed dangerous to entrust with edge-tools. In place of these, he was equipped with a sword of lath,[48] resembling that with which harlequin operates his wonders upon the modern stage.

The outward appearance of these two men formed scarce a stronger contrast than their look and demeanour.[49] That of the serf, or bondsman, was sad and sullen; his aspect was bent on the ground[50] with an appearance of deep dejection, which might be almost construed into apathy, had not the fire which occasionally sparkled in his red eye manifested that there slumbered, under the appearance of sullen despondency, a sense of oppression, and a disposition to resistance.[51] The looks of Wamba, on the other hand, indicated, as usual with his class, a sort of vacant curiosity, and fidgety impatience of any posture of repose,[52] together with the utmost self-satisfaction respecting his own situation[53] and the appearance which he made. The dialogue which they maintained between them was carried on in Anglo Saxon, which, as we said before, was universally spoken by the inferior classes, excepting the Norman soldiers and the immediate personal dependants of the great feudal nobles. But to give their conversation in the original would convey but little information to the modern reader, for whose benefit we beg to offer the following translation:

"The curse of St. Withold upon these infernal porkers![54]" said the swineherd, after blowing his horn obstreperously, to collect together the scattered herd of swine, which, answering his call with notes equally melodious,[55] made, however, no haste to remove themselves from the luxurious banquet of beech-mast and acorns on which they had fattened, or to forsake the marshy banks of the rivulet, where several of them, half plunged in mud, lay stretched at their ease, altogether regardless of the voice of their keeper. "The curse of St. Withold upon them and upon me!" said Gurth; "if the two-legged wolf[56] snap not up some of them ere nightfall, I am no true man. Here, Fangs! Fangs!" he ejaculated at the top of his voice to a ragged, wolfish-looking dog, a sort of lurcher, half mastiff, half greyhound, which ran limping about as if with the purpose of seconding his master in collecting the refractory grunters; but which, in fact, from misapprehension of the swineherd's signals, ignorance of his own duty, or malice prepense,[57] only drove them hither and thither, and increased the evil which he seemed to design to remedy. "A devil draw the teeth of him,[58]" said Gurth, "and the mother of mischief[59] confound the ranger of the forest,[60] that cuts the fore-claws off our dogs,[61] and makes them unfit for their trade! Wamba, up and help me an thou beest a man[62]; take a turn round the back o' the hill to gain the wind on them[63]; and when thous't got the weather-gage, thou mayst drive them before thee as gently as so many innocent lambs."

"Truly," said Wamba, without stirring from the spot, "I have consulted my legs upon this matter, and they are altogether of opinion that to carry my gay garments through these sloughs[64] would be an act of unfriendship to my sovereign person and royal wardrobe;[65] wherefore, Gurth, I advise thee to call off Fangs, and leave the herd to their destiny, which, whether they meet with bands of travelling soldiers, or of outlaws, or of wandering pilgrims, can be little else than to be converted into Normans before morning,[66] to thy no small ease and comfort.[67]"

"The swine turned Normans to my comfort!" quoth Gurth; "expound that to me, Wamba, for my brain is too dull and my mind too vexed to read riddles."

"Why, how call you those grunting brutes running about on their four legs?" demanded Wamba.

"Swine, fool — swine," said the herd; "every fool knows that."

"And swine is good Saxon,[68]" said the Jester; "but how call you the sow when she is flayed, and drawn, and quartered,[69] and hung up by the heels, like a traitor?"

"Pork," answered the swineherd.

"I am very glad every fool knows that too," said Wamba,"and pork, I think, is good Norman-French[70]; and so when the brute lives, and is in the charge of a Saxon slave, she goes by her Saxon name; but becomes a Norman, and is called pork when she is carried to the castle hall to feast among the nobles. What dost thou think of this, friend Gurth, ha?"

"It is but too true doctrine, friend Wamba, however it got into thy fool's pate.[71]"

"Nay, I can tell you more," said Wamba in the same tone: "there is old Alderman Ox[72] continues to hold his Saxon epithet[73] while he is under the charge of serfs and bondsmen such as thou, but becomes Beef, a fiery French gallant,[74] when he arrives before the worshipful jaws that are destined to consume him. Mynherr Calf, too, becomes Monsieur de Veau[75] in the like manner: he is Saxon when he requires tendance, and takes a Norman name when he becomes matter of enjoyment."

"By St. Dunstan,[76]" answered Gurth, "thou speakest but sad truths; little is left to us but the air we breathe, and that appears to have been reserved with much hesitation, solely for the purpose of enabling us to endure the tasks they lay upon our shoulders. The finest and the fattest is for their board;[77] the loveliest is for their couch[78]; the best and bravest supply their foreign masters with soldiers, and whiten distant lands with their bones,[79] leaving few here who have either will or the power to protect the unfortunate Saxon. God's blessing on our Master Cedric, he hath done the work of a man in standing in the gap[80]; but Reginald Front-de-Bœuf[81] is coming down to this country in person, and we shall soon see how little Cedric's trouble will avail him. Here, here," he exclaimed again, raising his voice, "So ho! so ho! well done, Fangs! thou hast them all before thee now, and bring'st them on bravely, lad."

"Gurth," said the Jester, "I know thou thinkest me a fool, or thou wouldst not be so rash in putting thy head into my mouth.[82] One word to[83] Reginald Front-de-Bœuf or Philip de Malvoisin, that thou hast spoken treason against the Norman—and thou are but a castaway swineherd; thou wouldst waver on one of these trees as a terror to all evil speakers against dignities.[84]"

"Dog, thou wouldst not betray me," said Gurth, "after having led me on to speak so much at disadvantage?"

"Betray thee!" answered the Jester; "no, that were the trick of a wise man; a fool cannot half so well help himself.[85] But soft, whom have we here?" he said, listening to the trampling of several horses which became then audible.

"Never mind whom," answered Gurth, who had now got his herd before him, and, with the aid of Fangs, was driving them down one of the long dim vistas which we have endeavoured to describe.

"Nay, but I must see the riders," answered Wamba; "perhaps they are come from Fairyland with a message from King Oberon.[86]"

"A murrain take thee[87]!" rejoined the swineherd; "wilt thou talk of such things, while a terrible storm of thunder and lightning is raging within a few miles of us? Hark, how the thunder rumbles! and for summer rain, I never saw such broad downright flat drops fall out of the clouds; the oaks, too, notwithstanding the calm weather, sob and creak with their great boughs as if announcing a tempest. Thou canst play the rational[88] if thou wilt; credit me for once, and let us home ere the storm begins to rage, for the night will be fearful."

Wamba seemed to feel the force of this appeal, and accompanied his companion, who began his journey after catching up a long quarter-staff which lay upon the grass beside him. This second Eumæus[89] strode hastily down the forest glade, driving before him, with the assistance of Fangs, the whole herd of this inharmonious charge.

CHAPTER XXIX

Ascend the watch-tower yonder, valiant soldier,
Look on the field, and say how goes the battle.

SCHILLER'S[90] *Maid of Orleans.*

A moment of peril is often a moment of open-hearted kindness and affection. We are thrown off our guard by the general agitation of our feelings, and betray the intensity of those[91] which, at more tranquil periods, our prudence at least conceals, if it cannot altogether suppress them. In finding herself once more by the side of Ivanhoe, Rebecca[92] was astonished at the keen sensation of pleasure which she experienced, even at a time when all around them both was danger, if not despair. As she felt his pulse, and inquired after his health, there was a softness in her touch and in her accents, implying a kinder interest than she would herself have been pleased to have voluntarily expressed.[93] Her voice faltered and her hand trembled, and it was only the cold question of Ivanhoe, "Is it you, gentle maiden?" which recalled her to herself,[94] and reminded her the sensations which she felt were not and could not be mutual.[95] A sigh escaped,[96] but it was scarce audible; and the questions which she asked the knight concerning his state of health were put in the tone of calm friendship. Ivanhoe answered her hastily that he was, in point of health, as well, and better, than he could have expected. "Thanks," he said, "dear Rebecca, to thy helpful skill."

"He calls me *dear* Rebecca," said the maiden to herself, "but it is in the cold and careless tone which ill suits the word.[97] His war-horse, his hunting hound, are dearer to him than the despised Jewess!"

"My mind, gentle maiden," continued Ivanhoe, "is more disturbed by anxiety than my body with pain. From the speeches of these men who were my warders just now, I learn that I am a prisoner, and, if I judge aright of the loud hoarse voice which even now despatched them hence on some military duty, I am in the castle of Front-de-Bœuf. If so, how will this end, or how can I protect Rowena[98] and my father?"

"He names not the Jew or Jewess," said Rebecca, internally; "yet what is our portion in him,[99] and how justly am I punished by Heaven for letting my thoughts dwell upon him!" She hastened after this brief self-accusation to give Ivanhoe what information she could; but it amounted only to this, that the Templar Bois-Guilbert[100] and the Baron Front-de-Bœuf were commanders within the castle; that it was beleaguered from without,[101] but by whom she knew not. She added, that there was a Christian priest within the castle who might be possessed of more information.

"A Christian priest!" said the knight, joyfully; "fetch him hither, Rebecca, if thou canst. Say a sick man desires his ghostly counsel[102]—say what thou wilt, but bring him; something I must do or attempt, but how can I determine until I know how matters stand without?"

Rebecca, in compliance with the wishes of Ivanhoe, made that attempt to bring Cedric into[103] the wounded knight's chamber which was defeated, as we have already seen, by the interference of Urfried,[104] who had been also on the watch to intercept the supposed monk. Rebecca retired to communicate to Ivanhoe the result of her errand.

They had not much leisure to regret the failure of this source of intelligence, or to contrive by what means it might be supplied; for the noise within the castle occasioned by[105] the defensive preparations, which had been considerable for some time, now increased into tenfold bustle and clamour. The heavy yet hasty step of the men-at-arms traversed the battlements, or resounded on the narrow and winding passages and stairs which led to the various bartisans and points of defense. The voices of the knights were heard, animating their followers, or directing means of defense, while their commands were often drowned in the clashing of armour, or the clamorous shouts of those whom they addressed. Tremendous as these sounds were, and yet more terrible from the awful event which they presaged,[106] there was a sublimity[107] mixed with them which Rebecca's high-toned mind[108] could feel even in that moment of terror. Her eye kindled, although the blood fled from her cheeks; and there was a strong mixture of fear, and of a thrilling sense of the sublime, as she repeated, half-whispering to herself, half-speaking to her companion, the sacred text—"The quiver rattleth—the glittering spear and the shield—the noise of the captains and the shouting!"

But Ivanhoe was like the war-horse of that sublime passage, glowing with impatience at his inactivity, and with his ardent desire to mingle in the affray of which these sounds were the introduction. "If I could but drag myself," he said, "to yonder window, that I might see how this brave game is like to go! If I had but bow to shoot a shaft, or battle-axe to strike were it but a single blow for our deliverance[109]! It is in vain—it is in vain—I am alike nerveless and weaponless[110]!"

"Fret not thyself,[111] noble knight," answered Rebecca, "the sounds have ceased of a sudden; it may be they join not battle."

"Thou knowest nought of it," said Wilfred, impatiently; "this dead pause[112] only shows that the men are at their posts on the walls, and expecting an instant attack; what we have heard was but the distant muttering of the storm: it will burst anon in all its fury.[113] Could I but reach yonder window!"

"Thou wilt but injure thyself by the attempt, noble knight," replied his attendant. Observing his extreme solicitude, she firmly added, "I myself will stand at the lattice, and describe to you as I can what passes without."

"You must not—you shall not![114]" exclaimed Ivanhoe. "Each lattice, each aperture, will be soon a mark for the archers; some random shaft..."

"It shall be welcome!" murmured Rebecca, as with firm pace she ascended two or three steps, which led to the window of which they spoke.

"Rebecca, dear Rebecca!" exclaimed Ivanhoe, "this is no maiden's pastime; do not expose thyself to wounds and death, and render me for ever miserable for having given the occasion; at least, cover thyself with yonder ancient buckler, and show as little of your person at the lattice as may be."

Following with wonderful promptitude the directions of Ivanhoe, and availing herself of the protection of the large ancient shield, which she placed against the lower part of the window, Rebecca, with tolerable security to herself, could witness part of what was passing without the castle, and report to Ivanhoe the preparations which the assailants were making for the storm. Indeed, the situation which she thus obtained[115] was peculiarly favourable for this purpose, because, being placed on an angle of the main building, Rebecca could not only see what passed beyond the precincts of the castle, but also commanded a view of the outwork[116] likely to be the first object of the meditated assault. It was an exterior fortification of no great height or strength, intended to protect the posterngate,[117] through which Cedric had been recently dismissed by Frontde-Bœuf. The castle moat divided this species of barbican[118] from the rest of the fortress, so that, in case of its being taken, it was easy to cut off the communication with the main building, by withdrawing the temporary bridge. In the outwork was a sallyport corresponding to the postern of the castle, and the whole was surrounded by a strong palisade. Rebecca could observe from the number of men placed for the defense of this post, that the besieged entertained apprehensions for its safety;[119] and from the mustering of the assailants in a direction nearly opposite to the outwork, it seemed no less plain that it had been selected as a vulnerable point of attack.[120]

These appearances she hastily communicated to Ivanhoe, and

added, "The skirts of the woods seem lined with archers, although only a few are advanced from its dark shadow."

"Under what banner?" asked Ivanhoe.

"Under no ensign of war which I can observe," answered Rebecca.

"A singular novelty,[121]" muttered the knight, "to advance to storm such a castle without pennon or banner displayed! Seest thou who they be that act as leaders?"

"A knight, clad in sable armour, is the most conspicuous," said the Jewess; "he alone is armed from head to heel, and seems to assume the direction of all around him."

"What device does he bear on his shield[122]?" replied Ivanhoe.

"Something resembling a bar of iron, and a padlock painted blue on the black shield."

"A fetterlock and shackle-bolt azure,[123]" said Ivanhoe; "I know not who may bear the device, but well I ween[124] it might now be mine own. Canst thou not see the motto[125]?"

"Scarce the device itself at this distance,"[126] replied Rebecca; "but when the sun glances fair upon his shield it shows as I tell you."

"Seem there no other leaders?" exclaimed the anxious inquirer.

"None of mark and distinction[127] that I can behold from this station," said Rebecca; "but doubtless the other side of the castle is also assailed. They appear even now preparing to advance — God of Zion[128] protect us! What a dreadful sight! Those who advance first bear huge shields and defenses made of plank; the others follow, bending their bows as they come on. They raise their bows! God of Moses, forgive the creatures Thou hast made!"

Her description was here suddenly interrupted by the signal for assault, which was given by the blast of a shrill bugle, and at once answered by a flourish of the Norman trumpets from the battlements, which, mingled with the deep and hollow clang of the nakers (a species of kettle-drum), retorted in notes of defiance the challenge of the enemy. The shouts of both parties augmented the fearful din, the assailants crying, "St. George for merry England![129]" and the Normans answering them with loud cries of *"En avant De Bracy! Beau-seant![130] Beau-seant! Front-de-Bœuf à la rescousse!"* according to the war-cries of their different commanders.

It was not, however, by clamour that the contest was to be decided, and the desperate efforts of the assailants were met by an equally vigorous defense on the part of the besieged. The archers,[131] trained by their woodland pastimes to the most effective use of the long-bow, shot, to use the appropriate phrase of the time, so "wholly together," that no point at which a defender could show the least part of his person escaped their cloth-yard shafts.[132] By this heavy discharge, which continued as thick and sharp as hail, while, notwithstanding, every arrow had its individual aim, and flew by scores together against each embrasure and opening in the parapets, as well as at every window where a defender either occasionally had post, or might be suspected to be stationed—by this sustained discharge, two or three of the garrison were slain and several others wounded. But, confident in their armour of proof,[133] and in the cover which their situation afforded,[134] the followers of Front-de-Bœuf and his allies showed an obstinacy in defense proportioned to the fury of the attack,[135] and replied with the discharge of their large cross-bows, as well as with their long-bows, slings, and other missile weapons,[136] to the close and continued shower of arrows; and, as the assailants were necessarily but indifferently protected, did considerably more damage than they received at their hand. The whizzing of shafts and of missiles on both sides was only interrupted by the shouts which arose when either side inflicted or sustained some notable loss.

"And I must lie here like a bedridden monk," exclaimed Ivanhoe, "while the game that gives me freedom or death is played by the hand of others! Look from the window once again, kind maiden, but beware that you are not marked[137] by the archers beneath. Look out once more, and tell me if they yet advance to the storm.[138]"

With patient courage, strengthened by the interval which she had employed in mental devotion,[139] Rebecca again took post at the lattice, sheltering herself, however, so as not to be visible from beneath.

"What dost thou see, Rebecca?" again demanded the wounded knight.

"Nothing but the cloud of arrows flying so thick as to dazzle mine eyes, and to hide the bowmen who shoot them."

"That cannot endure," said Ivanhoe; "if they press not right on to carry the castle by pure force of arms, the archery may avail but little against stone walls and bulwarks. Look for the Knight of the Fetterlock, fair Rebecca, and see how he bears himself; for as the leader is, so will his followers be.[140]"

"I see him not," said Rebecca.

"Foul craven![141]" exclaimed Ivanhoe; "does he blench from the helm when the wind blows highest?"

"He blenches not!—he blenches not!" said Rebecca, "I see him now; he leads a body of men close under the outer barrier of the barbican. They pull down the piles and palisades;[142] they hew down the barriers with axes. His high black plume floats abroad[143] over the throng, like a raven over the field of the slain. They have made a breach in the barriers—they rush in—they are thrust back! Front-de-Bœuf heads the defenders; I see his gigantic form above the press.[144] They throng again to the breach, and the pass is disputed hand to hand, and man to man.[145] God of Jacob! it is the meeting of two fierce tides—the conflict of two oceans moved by adverse winds!"

She turned her head from the lattice, as if unable longer to endure a sight so terrible.

"Look forth again, Rebecca," said Ivanhoe, mistaking the cause of her retiring; "the archery must in some degree have ceased, since they are now fighting hand to hand. Look again, there is now less danger."

Rebecca again looked forth, and almost immediately exclaimed,"Holy prophets of the law[146]! Front-de-Bœuf and the Black Knight fight hand to hand on the breach, amid the roar of their followers, who watch the progress of the strife. Heaven strike with the cause of[147] the oppressed and of the captive!" She then uttered a loud shriek, and exclaimed, "He is down!—he is down!"

"Who is down?" cried Ivanhoe; "for our dear Lady's sake, tell me which has fallen?"

"The Black Knight," answered Rebecca, faintly; then instantly again shouted with joyful eagerness: "But no—but no! the name of the Lord of Hosts[148] be blessed! he is on foot again, and fights as if there were twenty men's strength in his single arm. His sword is broken—he snatches an axe from a yeoman—he presses Front-de-Bœuf with blow on blow. The giant stoops and totters like an oak under the steel of the woodman[149]—he falls—he falls!"

"Front-de-Bœuf?" exclaimed Ivanhoe.

"Front-de-Bœuf," answered the Jewess. "His men rush to the rescue, headed by the haughty Templar[150]; their united force compels the champion to pause. They drag Front-de-Bœuf within the walls."

"The assailants have won the barriers, have they not?" said Ivanhoe.

"They have—they have!" exclaimed Rebecca; "and they press the besieged hard upon the outer wall; some plant ladders, some swarm like bees, and endeavour to ascend upon the shoulders of each other; down go stones, beams, and trunks of trees upon their heads, and as fast as they bear the wounded to the rear, fresh men supply their places in the assault. Great God! hast Thou given men Thine own image that it should be thus cruelly defaced by the hands of their brethren!"

"Think not of that," said Ivanhoe; "this is no time for such thoughts. Who yield? who push their way?"

"The ladders are thrown down," replied Rebecca, shuddering; "the soldiers lie grovelling under them like crushed reptiles. The besieged have the better."

"St. George strike for us!" exclaimed the knight; "do the false yeomen give way?"

"No!" exclaimed Rebecca, "they bear themselves right yeomanly. The Black Knight approaches the postern with his huge axe; the thundering blows which he deals, you may hear them above all the din and shouts of the battle. Stones and beams are hailed down on the bold champion: he regards them no more than if they were thistle-down or feathers!"

"By St. John of Acre,"[151] said Ivanhoe, raising himself joyfully on his couch, "methought there was but one man in England that might do such a deed!"

"The postern gate shakes," continued Rebecca — "it crashes — it is splintered by his blows — they rush in — the outwork is won. O God! they hurl the defenders from the battlements — they throw them into the moat. O men, if ye be indeed men, spare them that can resist no longer!"

"The bridge — the bridge which communicates with the castle — have they won that pass?" exclaimed Ivanhoe.

"No," replied Rebecca; "the Templar has destroyed the plank on which they crossed; few of the defenders escaped with him into the castle — the shrieks and cries which you hear tell the fate of the others. Alas! I see it is still more difficult to look upon victory than upon battle.[152]"

"What do they now, maiden?" said Ivanhoe; "look forth yet again — this is no time to faint at bloodshed."

"It is over for the time,"[153] answered Rebecca; "our friends strengthen themselves within the outwork which they have mastered, and it affords them so good a shelter from the foemen's shot that the garrison only bestow a few bolts on it from interval to interval, as if rather to disquiet than effectually to injure them."

"Our friends," said Wilfred, "will surely not abandon an enterprise so gloriously begun and so happily attained. Oh, no! I will put my faith in the good knight whose axe hath rent heart-of-oak[154] and bars of iron. Singular," he again muttered to himself, "if there be two who can do a deed of such *derring-do!*[155] A fetterlock, and a shackle-bolt on a field sable — what may that mean? Seest thou nought else,[156] Rebecca, by which the Black Knight may be distinguished?"

"Nothing," said the Jewess; "all about him is black as the wing of the night raven. Nothing can I spy that can mark him further; but having once seen him put forth his strength in battle, methinks I could know him again among a thousand warriors. He rushes to the fray as if he were summoned to a banquet. There is more than mere strength — there seems as if the whole soul and spirit of the champion were given to every blow which he deals upon his enemies. God assoilzie[157] him of the sin of bloodshed! It is fearful, yet magnificent, to behold how the arm and heart of one man can triumph over hundreds."

"Rebecca," said Ivanhoe, "thou hast painted a hero; surely they rest but to refresh their force, or to provide the means of crossing the moat. Under such a leader as thou hast spoken this knight to be, there are no craven fears, no cold-blooded delays,[158] no yielding up a gallant emprize,[159] since the difficulties which render it arduous render it also glorious. I swear by the honour of my house — I vow by the name of my bright lady-love, I would endure ten years' captivity to fight one day by that good knight's side in such a quarrel as this!"

"Alas!" said Rebecca, leaving her station at the window, and approaching the couch of the wounded knight, "this impatient yearning after action — this struggling with and repining at your present weakness, will not fail to injure your returning health. How couldst thou hope to inflict wounds on others, ere that be healed which thou thyself hast received?[160]"

"Rebecca," he replied, "thou knowest not how impossible it is for one trained to actions of chivalry to remain passive as a priest, or a woman, when they are acting deeds of honour around him. The love of battle is the food upon which we live — the dust of the melee is the breath of our nostrils[161]! We live not — we wish not to live-longer than while we are victorious and renowned.[162] Such, maiden, are the laws of chivalry to which we are sworn, and to which we offer all that we hold dear."

"Alas!" said the fair Jewess, "and what is it, valiant knight, save an offering of sacrifice to a demon of vain glory,[163] and a passing through the fire to Moloch?[164] What remains to you as the prize of all the blood you have spilled, of all the travail and pain you have endured, of all the tears which your deeds have caused, when death hath broken the strong man's spear, and overtaken the speed of his war-horse?[165]"

"What remains?" cried Ivanhoe. "Glory, maiden—glory! which gilds our sepulchre and embalms our name."

"Glory!" continued Rebecca; "alas! is the rusted mail[166] which hangs as a hatchment[167] over the champion's dim and mouldering tomb, is the defaced sculpture of the inscription which the ignorant monk can hardly read to the inquiring pilgrim—are these sufficient rewards for the sacrifice of every kindly affection, for a life spent miserably that ye may make others miserable? Or is there such virtue in the rude rhymes of a wandering bard, that domestic love, kindly affection, peace and happiness, are so wildly bartered, to become the hero[168] of those ballads which vagabond minstrels sing to drunken churls over their evening ale?"

"By the soul of Hereward!"[169] replied the knight, impatiently, "thou speakest, maiden, of thou knowest not what. Thou wouldst quench the pure light of chivalry, which alone distinguishes the noble from the base, the gentle knight from the churl and the savage; which rates our life far, far beneath the pitch of our honour,[170] raises us victorious over pain, toil, and suffering, and teaches us to fear no evil but disgrace. Thou art no Christian, Rebecca; and to thee are unknown those high feelings which swell the bosom of a noble maiden when her lover hath done some deed of emprize which sanctions his flame.[171] Chivalry! Why, maiden, she is the nurse of pure and high affection, the stay of the oppressed,[172] the redresser of grievances, the curb of the power of the tyrant. Nobility were but an empty name without her, and liberty finds the best protection in her lance and her sword."

"I am, indeed," said Rebecca, "sprung from a race whose courage was distinguished in the defense of their own land,[173] but who warred not, even while yet a nation, save at the command of the Deity, or in defending their country from oppression. The sound of the trumpet wakes Judah no longer, and her despised children are now but the unresisting victims of hostile and military oppression.[174] Well hast thou spoken, Sir Knight: until the God of Jacob shall raise up for His chosen people[175] a second Gideon, or a new Maccabeus,[176] it ill beseemeth the Jewish damsel to speak of battle or of war."

The high-minded maiden concluded the argument in a tone of sorrow, which deeply expressed her sense of the degradation of her people, imbittered perhaps by the idea that Ivanhoe considered her as one not entitled to interfere in a case of honour, and incapable of entertaining or expressing sentiments of honour and generosity.

"How little he knows this bosom,"[177] she said, "to imagine that cowardice or meanness of soul must needs be its guests,[178] because I have censured the fantastic chivalry of the Nazarenes![179] Would to Heaven[180] that the shedding of mine own blood, drop by drop, could redeem the captivity of Judah! Nay, would to God it could avail to set free my father, and this his benefactor,[181] from the chains of the oppressor! The proud Christian should then see whether the daughter of God's chosen people[182] dared not to die as bravely as the vainest Nazarene maiden, that boasts her descent from some petty chieftain of the rude and frozen north![183]"

She then looked towards the couch of the wounded knight.

"He sleeps," she said; "nature exhausted by[184] sufferance and the waste of spirits, his wearied frame embraces the first moment of temporary relaxation to sink into slumber. Alas! is it a crime that I should look upon him, when it may be for the last time? When yet but a short space,[185] and those fair features will be no longer animated by the bold and buoyant spirit which forsakes them not even in sleep[186]! When the nostril shall be distended, the mouth agape, the eyes fixed and bloodshot; and when the proud and noble knight may be trodden on by the lowest caitiff of this accursed castle, yet stir not when the heel is lifted up against him! And my father!—oh, my father! evil is it with his daughter,[187] when his gray hairs are not remembered because of the golden locks of youth! What know I but[188] that these evils are the messengers of Jehovah's wrath to the unnatural child[189] who thinks of a stranger's captivity before a parent's? who forgets the desolation of Judah,[190] and looks upon the comeliness of a Gentile[191] and a stranger? But I will tear this folly from my heart, though every fibre bleed[192] as I rend it away!"

She wrapped herself closely in her veil, and sat down at a distance from the couch of the wounded knight, with her back turned towards it, fortifying, or endeavouring to fortify, her mind not only against the impending evils from without, but also against those treacherous feelings which assailed her from within.

【作者简介】 Walter Scott（瓦尔特·司各特，1771—1832）是英国十九世纪初浪漫主义时期的著名的诗人、小说家和戏剧家。他生于苏格兰首府爱丁堡的一个律师家里，就读于爱丁堡大学，二十一岁时成为律师。他从小就喜爱诗歌。从1796年起，陆续发表了他所翻译的外国诗和搜集到的苏格兰民歌，接着出版了他自己创作的诗，享有盛名。但他的主要成就在历史小说。第一本Waverley（威佛利）出版于1814年，以后共出版三十种左右。他实际上是苏格兰和英国文学中历史小说的首创者。他的历史小说在当时就取得巨大的成功，以后还影响了所有欧洲国家和美国的文学。此外，他还写了一些剧本，以及关于文学和历史的著作多种。

【题解与注释】

Ivanhoe（现译《艾凡赫》）出版于1819年，被认为是司各特的最有代表性的一部历史小说。它以十二世纪的英国为背景，描写当时的盎格鲁·撒克逊人和在上一世纪征服了英国的诺曼人之间的民族矛盾，以及统治阶层和劳苦农民之间的阶级矛盾。它通过各式各样的人物和错综复杂的情节，展开了一幅描绘中世纪社会生活的广阔画面。

国王理查一世（又名狮心王理查）因参加十字军而离开英国。其弟约翰企图利用这一时机夺取王位。与此同时，盎格鲁·撒克逊贵族塞得利克打算联合本族人恢复撒克逊王朝。理查一世秘密返国。他得到一些诺曼人和塞得利克之子艾凡赫，及绿林豪杰洛克司雷（即罗宾汉）等盎格鲁·撒克逊人的支持，终于战胜了约翰集团，稳住了自己的王位。塞得利克等人也适应形势，决定和诺曼统治者妥协。

本书的一个特色是，除了描写盎格鲁·撒克逊和诺曼贵族之外，还着重地刻画了受歧视、受迫害的普通人物，如农奴葛尔兹，小丑汪巴，绿林英雄洛克司雷、犹太女子蕊贝卡。作者以满腔的同情，把他们塑造成栩栩如生的正面人物。

司各特的创作方法，可以说是现实主义和浪漫主义的结合。他搜集了大量的史料，同时又让自己的丰富的想象力自由驰骋。因而他的作品虽失之于不尽符合历史真实，却得之于离奇曲折，色彩缤纷，对读者有巨大的吸引力。

本书的语言，总的说来，趋于古雅。其中不少词藻和说法，不仅在今天，就是在作者所生活的十九世纪初叶，都显得陈旧。这当然是为了渲染中世纪的气氛而有意使用的。

早在清代末年（1905）本书就由林纾（琴南）介绍到中国，他把书名译为《撒克逊劫后英雄略》。他对这部著作十分推崇，说和友人“谈论英伦文家，则盛推司各特，以为可侪吾国之史迁。顾司氏出语隽妙，凡史莫之或逮矣。”又说“此篇为人不过十五，为日月之，而变幻离合，令读者若历十余稔之久。”近来有新译本，书名译为《艾凡赫》。

这里从原书中选了第一章和第二十九章。前者对时代背景有所说明，后者则为一场战斗的描写。

CHAPTER I

1. Thus communed these: 他们这样地交谈着。

2. with evening home: 夜晚已经来临。

3. With din obstreperous: 吵吵嚷嚷地。

4. Pope's "Odyssey":《奥德赛》原为古代希腊诗人荷马所作的长篇史诗，十八世纪英国诗人 Alexander Pope（蒲伯）将其译为英文，并使之符合英诗的一种格律。（本书每章都以几行古诗开始。）

5. merry England: 令人愉快的英格兰（merry 在此处意为 pleasant）。

6. Sheffield, Doncaster: 英格兰中部的两个城市。

7. seats: 所在地，地址。**Wentworth, Wharncliffe Park** 和 **Rotherham** 皆为市镇名。

8. of yore: 在古时。

9. the Dragon of Wantley: 相传约克郡有一龙，吞食儿童和牲畜，一武士名 More of More Hall 将其杀死。此故事见于十七世纪一讽刺性民谣中。

10. the Civil Wars of the Roses: 玫瑰战争。这是十五世纪英国两个家族之间

争夺王位的战争。双方分别以白玫瑰和红玫瑰为族徽，故有此名。

11. those bands of gallant outlaws: 指 Robin Hood（罗宾汉）一伙劫富济贫的绿林豪侠。传说他们在十二世纪活跃于英格兰中部。

12. Richard I: 理查一世，1189—99 年为英国国王，又名 Richard Coeur de Lion 或 Richard the Lion-Hearted（狮心王理查）。

13. his long captivity: 理查一世参加十字军东侵后，回国途中被奥地利公爵所俘，长期拘留。

14. Stephen: 斯梯芬，征服英国的威廉王之孙，1135—54 年为英国国王。Henry the Second，亨利二世，1154—89 年为英国国王，是理查一世之父。

15. license: 不受任何约束的自由。

16. the English Council of State: 枢密院（国王设立的谘询机构）。

17. vassalage: 附庸或封臣的身份。中世纪的大封建主将土地分给他的臣属，并要求他们承担一定义务。这种臣属叫 vassal。

18. national convulsions: 全国范围的动荡（指由于理查一世不在国内而将发生的对王位的争夺。）

19. Franklins: 自由农民（非贵族出身的土地所有者）。

20. the petty kings: 土皇帝们（即封建领主）。

21. such and so multiplied ... the great barons: 大贵族们所有的令人烦恼和压迫人的手段是这样而又如此之多。这是一个倒装的从句，正常词序是：the means of ... were such and so multiplied。

22. they never wanted the pretext, and seldom the will: 他们从不缺乏借口，也很少缺乏意志。

23. to the very edge of destruction:（把比他们的弱小的邻人迫害）到毁灭的边缘。

24. to trust for their protection ... to their own inoffensive conduct: 靠安分守己来保护他们自己。

25. the Conquest by Duke William of Normandy: 诺曼底（今法国西部）公爵威廉对英国的征服（即发生于 1066 年的诺曼征服，此后诺曼贵族成了英国的统治者）。

26. Four generations: 从诺曼征服到理查一世继承王位有一百二十余年。如以三十年为一代，则已经过四代。

27. the hostile blood: 敌对的血液（即敌对的种族）。

28. the battle of Hastings: 哈斯丁斯战役。威廉率大军渡海在英国登陆，在哈斯丁斯与英军决战，英军败绩，英王哈罗德战死。it had been used ... with no moderate hand，使用权力的手法并不温和（即十分严厉）。

29. of yet inferior classes: 更为低下的阶级（此处 yet 和 still 同义）。

30. the laws of the chase: 狩猎法。诺曼统治者制订严酷的法律，禁止人民进入他们的狩猎场地或伤害其中的动物。

31. the Saxon constitution: 撒克逊人的法律。

32. as it were: 就好象是 = as if it were actually so.

33. At court: 在宫廷里。

34. rustics and hinds: 农民和农村的技工。

35. the classical languages: 指希腊文和拉丁文。

36. William the Second: 威廉二世（征服英国的威廉公爵之子，1087—1100 年为英国国王）。

37. Edward the Third: 爱德华三世（1327—77 年为英国国王）。

38. but seem'd loath to depart: 不愿离开。这两行诗引在此处，暗示作者不断地用自己的口气说话。

39. the stately march of the Roman soldiery: 罗马部队的庄严的行军。一世纪时罗马征服不列颠，至五世纪初撤走。

40. the eye delights to lose itself: 久看不厌。

41. yet wilder scenes of silvan solitude: 寂静的森林中更为荒凉的场所。

42. the rites of Druidical superstition: 古代克尔特（Celts）祭师的迷信仪式。

43. the West Riding of Yorkshire: 约克郡的西区。

44. a Scottish Highlander: 苏格兰（北部）高地人。

45. the born thrall: 生下来就是奴隶。十二世纪时英国仍有奴隶，一般是庄园主的家奴。

46. its want of longitude: 它缺少长度，很短（longitude = length，旧义）。

47. to help away the tedium ... within doors: 帮助他们（富人）消磨掉他们不得不在室内度过的漫长而单调的时间。

48. a sword of lath: 木制的剑。

49. The outward appearance ... than their look and demeanour: 这两个人在外表上的差别并不比他们在神情和举止上的差别大。(**scarce** = scarcely，旧的用法。)

50. his aspect was bent on the ground: 他的眼睛朝地上看。

51. there slumbered ... and a disposition to resistance: 在那儿（眼神里）潜伏着一种被压迫感和反抗的倾向（倒装句，slumbered 的主语为 a sense ... 和 a disposition ...）。

52. fidgety impatience of any posture of repose: 不安于静止休息，老是想动。

53. respecting his own situation: 对于他自己的境况。

54. The curse of St. Withold upon these infernal porkers!: 这些该死的肥猪！

55. with notes equally melodious: 用同样好听的声音（反话，实际上是不好听）。

56. the two-legged wolf: 两脚狼（指贪婪而残忍的人）。

57. from misapprehension ... or malice prepense: 由于它误解了猪倌的信号，不清楚自己的职责，或者是有意害人。

58. A devil draw the teeth of him: 但愿魔鬼来拔掉它的牙！

59. the mother of mischief: 万恶之母，恶魔。

60. the ranger of the forest: 森林守护官。

61. that cuts the fore-claws off our dogs: 他把我们的狗的前爪砍掉。根据当时的诺曼法律，为了保护森林中的动物以便国王打猎，放牧人的狗必须砍掉前爪。

62. an thou beest a man:（= if you be a man）做一个（象样的）人。当时第二人称后的动词常加 -st，

63. to gain the wind on them: 占上风，占有利的地位。下面的 got the weather-gage 同义。

64. through these sloughs: 穿过这些泥沼地。

65. my sovereign person and royal wardrobe: 我的玉体和龙袍（此处 sovereign 和 royal 同义）。

66. can be little else than ... before morning: 只会在明天早晨以前变成诺曼人（被诺曼人吃掉）。

67. to thy no small ease and comfort: 这对你是件很舒服的事。

68. And swine is good Saxon: swine 是个地道的撒克逊词。

69. flayed, and drawn, and quartered: 剥了皮，取出内脏，切成四块。

70. and pork ... is good Norman-French: pork 是个地道的诺曼法语词。在诺曼征服之后，许多法语词进入英语。

71. however it got into thy fool's pate: 不管它（这个道理）怎样进了你这个傻瓜的脑袋。

72. old Alderman Ox: 市参议员牛先生。Wamba 故意用尊称，下面他还说 Mynherr Calf：小牛老爷。

73. to hold his Saxon epithet: 保持他的撒克逊尊号。Ox 是个撒克逊词。

74. a fiery French gallant: 火红的法国君子。*Beef* 一词来自法文。

75. Monsieur de Veau:（法文）小牛肉先生。

76. By St. Dunstan: 对圣·顿士丹发誓。顿士丹为十世纪的英国坎特伯雷主教。

77. The finest and the fattest is for their board: 最好的、最肥的（牲口）给他们（诺曼人）食用。

78. The loveliest is for their couch: 最美的（人）供他们床上用。

79. The best and bravest ... with their bones: 最出色的、最勇敢的人为他们的外国主人当兵，他们的尸骨使遥远的国土变白（葬身异国）。

80. standing in the gap: 挺身而出（以保护撒克逊人）。

81. Reginald Front-de-Bœuf: 约翰亲王派的一个诺曼贵族骑士。

82. putting thy head into my mouth: 冒险把你的头放在我的嘴里，我随时可以咬死你（由 put one's head into the lion's mouth 变来）。

83. One word to ...: 只要我对…说一声。Philip de Malvoisin 是另一个诺曼贵族。

84. thou wouldst waver ... against dignities: 你就会吊死在树上，好使那些说坏话骂贵人的人害怕。

85. a fool cannot half so well help himself: 一个傻子为自己也做不出这种事。

86. King Oberon: 俄勃伦王（传说中仙国的国王）。

87. A murrain take thee!: 你这个该死的！（murrain 原义为瘟疫。）

88. Thou canst play the rational: 你能懂情理。

89. This second Eumæus: 这个尤米阿斯第二。尤米阿斯是希腊传说中的英雄尤利西斯的忠诚的猪倌，此处指 Gurth.

CHAPTER XXIX

90. Schiller: 席勒（1759—1805），德国剧作家和诗人。

91. betray the intensity of those ...: 透露出…感情的强烈程度（those 代表 feelings）。

92. Rebecca: 犹太族商人 Isaac 之女。他们父女出于同情照顾在比武中受伤的 Ivanhoe，在归途中被诺曼贵族 De Bracy 俘虏，带至另一诺曼贵族 Front-de-Bœuf 的古堡中。

93. voluntarily expressed: 有意要表现出的。

94. recalled her to herself: 使她清醒。

95. the sensations ... could not be mutual: 她所有的感情并不是，也不可能是，双方都有的。

96. A sigh escaped: 情不由己地叹息了一声。

97. ill suits the word: 和这个字（dear）不相称。

98. Rowena: 撒克逊王族的后裔。Ivanhoe 之父 Cedric 是她的监护人。他们也是在途中被诺曼贵族 De Bracy 俘虏，带到同一古堡中。

99. what is our portion in him: 我们在他心上占的分量有多少？

100. the Templar Bois-Guilbert: 圣殿骑士 Bois-Guilbert。圣殿骑士团是十二世纪初十字军中的一个宗教军事组织。

101. from without: 从外面。

102. ghostly counsel: 神父的指导（ghostly 指由神父或僧侣进行的，是古义）。

103. made that attempt to bring Cedric into ...: Cedric 化装成一神父，从古堡中逃出。Rebecca 在堡内遇见这个假神父，请他去见受伤的 Ivanhoe，为他所拒绝。

104. Urfried: 一个受迫害的撒克逊妇女，住在该古堡内。

105. occasioned by ...: 由…而造成的。

106. the awful event which they presaged: 那些嘈杂的声音所预兆的可怕的事件（指即将发生的战斗）。

107. a sublimity: 一种崇高庄严的气氛。

108. high-toned mind: 高尚的心。

109. were it but a single blow for our deliverance: 为了挽救我们自己即使是砍一下也好。

110. I am alike nerveless and weaponless: 我既没有精力，又没有武器。

111. Fret not thyself: 不要苦恼。

112. this dead pause: 这个突然的停顿。

113. it will burst anon in all its fury: 它（战斗的风暴）即将猛烈地开始。

114. You must not —you shall not!: 你绝不要去——不许你去！

115. the situation which she thus obtained: 她所在的位置。

116. commanded a view of the outwork: 能看到堡垒外围的一个突出部分。

117. the postern-gate: 后门。

118. this species of barbican: 这种外围的碉楼。

119. the besieged entertained apprehensions for its safety: 被围攻者担心它的安全。

120. a vulnerable point of attack: 易于攻击之点。

121. A singular novelty: 新奇少见的事。

122. What device does he bear on his shield?: 他的盾牌上有什么图案？中古时期的武士在盾牌上绘制各种图案，作为个人、家族或团体的标志。

123. A fetterlock and shackle-bolt azure: 天蓝色的马腿锁和链闩。这是 Ivanhoe 纠正 Rebecca 的话。

124. well I ween: 我真希望。

125. the motto:（盾牌图案上的）箴言。

126. Scarce the device itself at this distance: 离得这么远，我连图案都还看不清呢。

127. None of mark and distinction: 没有一个值得注意和与众不同的人。

128. God of Zion: 和下面的 God of Moses，God of Jacob，都是犹太人对上帝的称呼。Zion 读 [ˈzaiən]。

129. St. George for merry England!: 圣乔治保佑英国！圣乔治被认为是英国的护神。

130. En avant De Bracy! ...:（法语）De Bracy，冲啊！为圣殿骑士团而战！Front-de-Bœuf 又冲上去了！（Beau-seant 是圣殿骑士团的旗帜的名称。）

131. The archers: 弓箭射手。前来进攻这个古堡的射手是 Locksley 手下的绿林好汉们。Locksley 是 Robin Hood（罗宾汉）的化名。

132. cloth-yard shafts: 手拉弓（long-bow）用的长箭。

133. armour of proof: 穿不透的盔甲。

134. in the cover which their situation afforded: 在他们的位置的掩护下。

135. defense proportioned to the fury of the attack: 和进攻的凶猛程度相当的防守。

136. missile weapons: 投掷或发射的武器。

137. beware that you are not marked: 留神不要被看见或注意到。

138. if they yet advance to the storm: 他们是否在前进，准备攻占这个堡垒。

139. mental devotion: 默默的祈祷。

140. as the leader is, so will his followers be: 领袖怎么样，部下也就会怎么样。

141. Foul craven!: 可恶的懦夫！

142. piles and palisades: 尖桩和木栅。
143. His high black plume floats abroad: 他头盔上的高高的黑羽毛在飘动。
144. above the press: 高于（作战的）人群。
145. the pass is disputed hand to hand, and man to man: 进行肉搏战来争夺这个通道。
146. Holy prophets of the law!:（感叹语）神圣的先知们！（此处 law 指戒律。）
147. strike with the cause of ...: 为…一方而战。
148. the Lord of Hosts: 上帝。
149. like an oak under the steel of the woodman: 象栎树被樵夫的刀砍倒一样。
150. the haughty Templar: 那个高傲的圣殿骑士（指 Bois-Guilbert）。
151. By St. John of Acre: 发誓的话。
152. it is still more difficult ... than upon battle: 观看胜利比观看战斗还要困难（因为一方胜利，另一方伤亡就多）。
153. It is over for the time: 这种（看见流血要晕倒的）情绪暂时过去了。
154. hath rent heart-of-oak: 砍倒了勇士。
155. derring-do: 拼死的勇气。
156. Seest thou nought else: 你没看见别的什么吗？
157. assoilzie:（= assoil）宽恕（古词）。
158. no cold-blooded delays: 不会有冷酷的故意的拖延。
159. no yielding up a gallant emprize: 不会放弃一个英勇的业迹。
160. ere that be healed which ... received: 在你自己受的伤愈合之前（此处 which 引起的从句修饰 that）。
161. the dust of the mêlée ... our nostrils!: 鏖战的飞尘就是我们的生命！
162. We live not ... victorious and renowned: 不胜利，不扬名，就不如不活。
163. save an offering ... vain glory: 除了对虚荣这个魔鬼献上祭品之外。
164. a passing through the fire to Moloch: 从火中走向莫洛克神。相传对莫洛克神要用儿童作为祭品，故相当于死神。
165. death hath broken ... his war-horse: 死亡把武士的长矛折断，比他的战马跑得更快（意思是武士逃不脱死亡）。
166. the rusted mail: 生了锈的铠甲。
167. a hatchment: 绘有死者的盾形纹章的菱形板（放在死者的门前）。
168. domestic love ... to become the hero: 把家庭的爱、温情、和平、幸福，统统抛弃，只是为了成为一个英雄。
169. By the soul of Hereward!: 发誓的话。
170. which rates our life ... of our honour: 它（骑士的精神）把生命看得远比荣誉的高度为低（即荣誉重于生命）。
171. sanctions his flame: 使他有权爱她。
172. the stay of the oppressed: 被压迫者的支持者。

173. in the defense of their own land: 保卫他们自己的土地（指犹太人的故乡，即下句提到的 Judah，今巴勒斯坦一带）。

174. victims of hostile and military oppression: 敌对的军事占领的受害者。十一世纪十字军东侵前，犹太人地区早被异族占领。在十字军战争期间，曾建立由十字军控制的耶路撒冷王国。

175. His chosen people: 上帝的特选子民（犹太人）。

176. a second Gideon, or a new Maccabeus: Gideon 和 Maccabeus 都是古代以色列的领袖，曾把以色列从异族压迫下拯救出来。it ill beseemeth… or of war，谈论战斗或战争对犹太姑娘是不适宜的。

177. How little be knows this bosom: 他对（我的）这个胸怀太不了解了。

178. must needs be its guests: 必然是它的客人（必然存在于我的胸怀之中）。

179. the Nazarenes: 基督教徒。

180. Would to Heaven: 但愿上天能使…。

181. and this his benefactor: 这个帮助过他的人。Ivanhoe 曾帮助 Rebecca 的父亲逃脱受诺曼贵族迫害的危险。

182. the daughter of God's chosen people: 指 Rebecca 自己。

183. that boasts her descent ... and frozen north: 她自夸是粗鲁而寒冷的北方的某个小头人的后代（即英国王族的后代，指 Rowena）。

184. nature exhausted by ...,: 精力被…耗尽。

185. yet but a short space: 不久之后。

186. forsakes them not even in sleep: 即使在睡眠中（这种精神）也不离开他的面容。

187. evil is it with his daughter: 他的女儿被邪念缠住了。

188. What know I but: 我知道。are the messengers of Jehovah's wrath，传达了上帝的愤怒。

189. the unnatural child: 没有天性的孩子。

190. Judah:（古代）犹太国。

191. Gentile: 非犹太人。

192. every fibre bleed: 每根纤维都流血（极度痛苦）。

33 CHARLES LAMB
1775–1834

1. A Bachelor's Complaint of the Behayiour of Married People

丁往道　选注

2. Preface to the Last Essays

徐燕谋　选注

1. A BACHELOR'S COMPLAINT OF THE BEHAVIOUR OF MARRIED PEOPLE

As a single man, I have spent a good deal of my time in noting down the infirmities[1] of married people, to console myself for those superior pleasures, which they tell me I have lost by remaining as I am.

I cannot say that the quarrels of men and their wives ever made any great impression upon me, or had much tendency to strengthen me in those anti-social resolutions, which I took up long ago upon more substantial considerations. What oftenest offends me at the houses of married persons where I visit, is an error of quite a different description[2];—it is that they are too loving.

Not too loving neither[3]: that does not explain my meaning. Besides, why should that offend me? The very act of separating themselves from the rest of the world, to have the fuller enjoyment of each other's society,[4] implies that they prefer one another to all the world.

But what I complain of is, that they carry this preference so undisguisedly, they perk it up in the faces of us single people so shamelessly, you cannot be in their company a moment without being made to feel, by some indirect hint or open avowal, that *you* are not the object of this preference. Now there are some things which give no offence, while implied or taken for granted merely; but expressed, there is much offence in them. If a man were to accost the first homely-featured[5] or plain-dressed young woman of his acquaintance, and tell her bluntly, that she was not handsome or rich enough for him, and he could not marry her, he would deserve to be kicked for his ill manners; yet no less is implied in the fact, that having access[6] and opportunity of putting the question to her, he has never yet thought fit to do it. The young woman understands this as clearly as if it were put into words; but no reasonable young woman would think of making this the ground of a quarrel.[7] Just as little right have a married couple to tell me by speeches, and looks[8] that are scarce less plain[9] than speeches, that I am not the happy man, — the lady's choice. It is enough that I know I am not: I do not want this perpetual reminding.

The display of superior knowledge or riches may be made sufficiently mortifying; but these admit of a palliative[10]. The knowledge which is brought out to insult me, may accidentally improve me; and in the rich man's houses and pictures, — his parks and gardens, I have a temporary usufruct[11] at least. But the display of married happiness has none of these palliatives: it is throughout pure, unrecompensed, unqualified[12] insult.

Marriage by its best title is a monopoly[13], and not of the least invidious sort. It is the cunning of most possessors of any exclusive privilege to keep their advantage as much out of sight as possible, that their less favoured neighbours, seeing little of the benefit, may the less be disposed to question the right. But these married monopolists[14] thrust the most obnoxious part of their patent into our faces,[15]

Nothing is to me more distasteful than that entire complacency and satisfaction which beam in the countenances of a new-married couple,—in that of the lady particularly: it tells you, that her lot is disposed of[16] in this world: that you can have no hopes of her. It is true, I have none; nor wishes either, perhaps: but this is one of those truths which ought, as I said before, to be taken for granted, not expressed.

The excessive airs which those people give themselves, founded on the ignorance of us unmarried people, would be more offensive if they were less irrational.[17] We will allow them to understand the mysteries belonging to their own craft[18] better than we who have not had the happiness to be made free of the company:[19] but their arrogance is not content within these limits. If a single person presume to offer his opinion in their presence, though upon the most indifferent subject,[20] he is immediately silenced as an incompetent person. Nay,[21] a young married lady of my acquaintance, who, the best of the jest was, had not changed her condition above a fortnight before[22], in a question on which I had the misfortune to differ from her, respecting the properest mode of breeding oysters for the London market, had the assurance to ask with a sneer, how such an old bachelor as I could pretend to know any thing about such matters.

But what I have spoken of hitherto is nothing to the airs which these creatures give themselves when they come, as they generally do, to have children. When I consider how little of a rarity children are,[23]—that every street and blind alley swarms with them,—that the poorest people commonly have them in most abundance,—that there are few marriages that are not blest with at least one of these bargains,[24]—how often they turn out ill, and defeat the fond hopes of their parents, taking to vicious courses, which end in poverty, disgrace, the gallows,&c.—I cannot for my life tell[25] what cause for pride there can possibly be in having them. If they were young phoenixes,[26] indeed, that were born but one in a year, there might be a pretext. But when they are so common—

I do not advert to the insolent merit which they assume with their husbands on these occasions. Let them look to that. But why *we*, who are not their natural-born subjects,[27] should be expected to bring out spices, myrrh, and incense,[28]—our tribute and homage of admiration,—I do not see.

'Like as the arrows[29] in the hand of the giant, even so are the young children: ' so says the excellent office[30] in our Prayer-book appointed for the churching of women.[31] 'Happy is the man[32] that hath his quiver full of them: ' So say I; but then don't let him discharge his quiver upon us that are weaponless[33];—let them be arrows, but not to gall and stick us. I have generally observed that these arrows are double-headed: they have two forks, to be sure to hit with one or the other. As for instance, when you come into a house which is full of children, if you happen to take no notice of them (you are thinking of something else, perhaps, and turn a deaf ear to their innocent caresses[34]), you are set down as[35] untractable, morose, a hater of children. On the other hand, if you find them more than usually engaging,—if you are taken with their pretty manners, and set about in earnest to romp and play with them, some pretext or other is sure to be found for sending them out of the room: they are too noisy or boisterous, or Mr.—does not like children. With one or other of these forks the arrow is sure to hit you.

I could forgive their jealousy, and dispense with toying with their brats,[36] if it gives them any pain; but I think it unreasonable to be called upon to *love* them, where I see no occasion,[37]—to love a whole family, perhaps, eight, nine, or ten, indiscriminately,—to love all the pretty dears because children are so engaging.

I know there is a proverb, 'Love me, love my dog:[38]' that is not always so very practicable, particularly if the dog be set upon you to tease you or snap at you in sport.[39] But a dog, or a lesser thing,—any inanimate substance, as a keep-sake, a watch or a ring, a tree, or the place where we last parted when my friend went away upon a long absence, I can make shift to[40] love, because I love him, and any thing that reminds me of him; provided it be in its nature indifferent[41], and apt to receive whatever hue fancy can give it.[42] But children have a real character and an essential being of themselves:[43] they are amiable or unamiable *per se;*[44] I must love or hate them as I see cause for either[45] in their qualities. A child's nature is too serious a thing to admit of its being regarded as a mere appendage to another being,[46] and to be loved or hated accordingly: they stand with me upon their own stock,[47] as much as men and women do. O! but you will say, sure it is an attractive age,—there is something in the tender years of infancy that of itself charms us. That is the very reason why I am more nice about them. I know that a sweet child is the sweetest thing in nature, not even excepting the delicate creatures which bear them;[48] but the prettier the kind of a thing is, the more desirable it is that it should be pretty of its kind.[49] One daisy differs not much from another in glory;[50] but a violet should look and smell the daintiest.—I was always rather squeamish in my women and children.[51]

But this is not the worst: one must be admitted into their familiarity at least, before they can complain of inattention. It implies visits, and some kind of intercourse. But if the husband be a man with whom you have lived on a friendly footing before marriage,—if you did not come in on the wife's side,[52]—if you did not sneak into the house in her train,[53] but were an old friend in first habits of intimacy before their courtship was so much as thought on,—look about you—your tenure is precarious[54]—before a twelvemonth shall roll over your head,[55] you shall find your old friend gradually grow cool and altered towards you, and at last seek opportunities of breaking with you. I have scarce a married friend of my acquaintance, upon whose firm faith I can rely, whose friendship did not commence *after the period of his marriage*. With some limitations they can endure that:[56] but that the good man[57] should have dared to enter into a solemn league of friendship in which they were not consulted, though it happened before they knew him,—before they that are now man and wife ever met,—this is intolerable to them. Every long friendship, every old authentic intimacy, must be brought into their office to be new stamped with their currency,[58] as a sovereign Prince calls in the good old money that was coined in some reign before he was born or thought of, to be new marked and minted with the stamp of his authority, before he will let it pass current in the world.[59] You may guess what luck generally befalls such a rusty piece of metal as I am in these *new mintings*.[60]

Innumerable are the ways which they take to insult and worm you out of their husband's confidence. Laughing at all you say with a kind of wonder, as if you were a queer kind of fellow that said good things, *but an oddity*,[61] is one of the ways;—they have a particular kind of stare for the purpose;—till at last the husband, who used to defer to your judgment, and would pass over some excrescences of understanding and manner for the sake of a general vein of observation (not quite vulgar) which he perceived in you,[62] begins to suspect whether you are not altogether a humorist,[63]—a fellow well enough to have consorted with in his bachelor days,[64] but not quite so proper to be introduced to ladies. This may be called the staring way; and is that which has oftenest been put in practice against me.

Then there is the exaggerating way, or the way of irony: that is, where they find you an object of especial regard[65] with their husband, who is not so easily to be shaken from the lasting attachment founded on esteem[86] which he has conceived towards you; by never-qualified exaggeration to cry up all that you say or do,[67] till the good man, who understands well enough that it is all done in compliment to him, grows weary of the debt of gratitude[68] which is due to so much candour, and by relaxing a little on his part, and taking down a peg or two in his enthusiasm,[69] sinks at length to that kindly level of moderate esteem,[70]—that 'decent affection and complacent kindness'[71] towards you; where she herself can join in sympathy with him[72] without much stretch and violence to her sincerity.[73]

Another way (for the ways they have to accomplish so desirable a purpose are infinite) is, with a kind of innocent simplicity, continually to mistake what it was which first made their husband fond of you. If an esteem for something excellent in your moral character was that which riveted the chain which she is to break,[74] upon any imaginary discovery of a want of poignancy[76] in your conversation, she will cry, 'I thought, my dear, you described your friend, Mr. —, as a great wit.' If, on the other hand it was for some supposed charm in your conversation that he first grew to like you, and was content for this to overlook some trifling irregularities in your moral deportment,[76] upon the first notice of any of these she as readily exclaims, 'This, my dear, is your good Mr. —.' One good lady whom I took the liberty of expostulating with for not showing me quite so much respect as I thought due to her husband's old friend, had the candour to confess to me that she had often heard Mr. — speak of me before marriage, and that she had conceived a great desire to be acquainted with me, but that the sight of me had very much disappointed her expectations; for from her husband's representations[77] of me, she had formed a notion that she was to see a fine, tall, officer-like looking man (I use her very words); the very reverse of which proved to be the truth. This was candid; and I had the civility not to ask her in return, how she came to pitch upon[78] a standard of personal accomplishments for her husband's friends which differed so much from his own; for my friend's dimensions[79] as near as possible approximate to mine; he standing five feet five in his shoes, in which I have the advantage of him by about half an inch;[80] and he no more than myself exhibiting any indications of a martial character[81] in his air or countenance.

These are some of the mortifications which I have encountered in the absurd attempt to visit at their houses. To enumerate them all would be a vain endeavour: I shall therefore just glance at the very common impropriety of which married ladies are guilty, — of treating us as if we were their husbands, and *vice versa*.[82] I mean, when they use us with familiarity, and their husbands with ceremony. *Testacea*,[83] for instance, kept me the other night two or three hours beyond my usual time of supping, while she was fretting because

Mr. — did not come home, till the oysters were all spoiled, rather than she would be guilty of the impoliteness of touching one in his absence. This was reversing the point of good manners:[84] for ceremony is an invention to take off the uneasy feeling which we derive from knowing ourselves to be less the object of love and esteem with a fellow-creature than some other person is.[85] It endeavours to make up, by superior attentions in little points, for that invidious preference which it is forced to deny in the greater.[86] Had *Testacea* kept the oysters back for me, and withstood her husband's importunities to go to supper,[87] she would have acted according to the strict rules of propriety. I know no ceremony that ladies are bound to observe to their husbands, beyond the point of[88] a modest behaviour and decorum: therefore I must protest against the vicarious gluttony[89] of *Cerasia,*[90] who at her own table sent away a dish of Morellas,[91] which I was applying to with great good will, to her husband at the other end of the table, and recommended a plate of less extraordinary gooseberries to my unwedded palate[92] in their stead. Neither can I excuse the wanton affront of — .

But I am weary of stringing up all my married acquaintance by Roman denominations.[93] Let them amend and change their manners, or I promise to record the full-length English of their names, to the terror of all such desperate offenders in future.

2. PREFACE TO THE LAST ESSAYS

By a friend of the late Elia

This poor gentleman,[1] who for some months past had been in a declining way,[2] hath at length paid his final tribute to nature.[3]

To say truth, it is time he were gone. The humour of the thing,[4] if ever there was much in it, was pretty well exhausted; and a two years'and a half existence[5] has been a tolerable duration for a phantom.[6]

I am at liberty to confess,[7] that much which I have heard objected to my late friend's writings was well founded.[8] Crude they are, I grant you[9]—a sort of unlicked,[10] incondite[11] things—villainously pranked in an affected array of antique modes and phrases.[12] They had not been *his*, if they had been other than such;[13] and better it is, that a writer should be natural in a self-pleasing quaintness, than to affect a naturalness (so called) that should be strange to him.[14] Egotistical they have been pronounced by some who did not know, that what he tells us, as of himself, was often true only (historically) of another;[15] as in a former Essay[16] (to save many instances)—where under the *first person* (his favourite figure[17]) he shadows forth[18] the forlorn estate[19] of a country-boy placed at a London school, far from his friends and connections—in direct opposition to his own early history. If it be egotism to imply and twine with his own identity the griefs and affections of another[20]—making himself many, or reducing many unto[21] himself—then is the skilful novelist, who all along[22] brings in his hero or heroine, speaking of themselves, the greatest egotist of all; who yet has never, therefore, been accused of that narrowness. And how shall the intenser[23] dramatist escape being faulty, who, doubtless under cover of passion uttered by another, oftentimes gives blameless vent to his most inward feelings,[24] and expresses his own story modestly?

My late friend was in many respects a singular character.[25] Those who did not like him, hated him; and some, who once liked him, afterwards became his bitterest haters. The truth is, he gave himself too little concern what he uttered, and in whose presence.[26] He observed neither time nor place, and would e'en out with[27] what came uppermost. With the severe religionist he would pass for[28] a free-thinker; while the other faction[29] set him down for[30] a bigot, or persuaded themselves that he belied his sentiments.[31] Few understood him; and I am not certain that at all times he quite understood himself. He too much affected that dangerous figure[32]—irony, He sowed doubtful speeches, and reaped plain, unequivocal hatred. He would interrupt the gravest discussion with some light jest; and yet, perhaps, not quite irrelevant in ears that could understand it. Your long and much talkers[33] hated him. The informal habit of his mind, joined to an inveterate impediment of speech,[34] forbade him to be an orator; and he seemed determined that no one else should play that part[35] when he was present. He was *petit*[36] and ordinary in his person and appearance. I have seen him sometimes in what is called good company, but where he has been a stranger, sit silent, and be suspected for an odd fellow; till some unlucky occasion provoking it, he would stutter out some senseless pun (not altogether senseless, perhaps, if rightly taken[37]), which has stamped his character for the evening. It was hit or miss[38] with him; but nine times out often he contrived by this device to send away a whole company his enemies. His conceptions rose kindlier than his utterance, and his happiest *impromptus*[39] had the appearance of effort.[40] He has been accused of trying to be witty, when in truth he was but struggling to give his poor thoughts articulation. He chose his companions for some individuality of character which they manifested. Hence, not many persons of science, and few professed *literati*[41], were of his councils.[42] They were, for the most part, persons of an uncertain fortune;[43] and, as to such people commonly nothing is more obnoxious than a gentleman of settled (though moderate) income, he passed with most of them for a great miser. To my knowledge this was a mistake. His *intimados,*[44] to confess a truth, were in the world's eye[45] a ragged regiment. He found them floating on the surface of society; and the colour, or something else, in the weed[46] pleased him. The burrs[47] stuck to him — but they were good and loving burrs for all that.[48] He never greatly cared for the society of what are called good people. If any of these were scandalised (and offences were sure to arise) he could not help it. When he has been remonstrated with for not making more concessions[49] to the feelings of good people, he would retort by asking, what one point did these good people ever concede to[50] him? He was temperate in his meals and diversions, but always kept a little on this side of abstemiousness.[51] Only in the use of the Indian weed[52] he might be thought a little excessive. He took it, he would say, as a solvent of speech.[53] Marry[54] — as the friendly vapour ascended how his prattle would curl up sometimes with it! the ligaments[55] which tongue-tied him[56] were loosened, and the stammerer proceeded a statist![57]

I do not know whether I ought to bemoan or rejoice that my old friend is departed.[58] His jests were beginning to grow obsolete, and his stories to be found out. He felt the approaches of age; and while he pretended to cling to life, you saw how slender were the ties left to bind him. Discoursing with him latterly[59] on this subject, he expressed himself with a pettishness[60] which I thought unworthy of him. In our walks about his suburban retreat[61] (as he called it) at Shacklewell,[62] some children belonging to a school of industry had met us, and bowed and curtseyed, as he thought, in an especial manner to *him*. 'They took me for a visiting governor,[63] he muttered earnestly. He had a horror, which he carried to a foible,[64] of looking like anything important and parochial.[65] He thought that he approached nearer to that stamp[66] daily. He had a general aversion from being treated like a grave or respectable character, and kept a wary eye upon the advances of age that should so entitle him.[67] He herded always, while it was possible, with[68] people younger than himself. He did not conform to the march of time,[69] but was dragged along in the procession.[70] His manners lagged behind his years.[71] He was too much of the boy-man.[72] The *toga virilis*[73] never sate gracefully on[74] his shoulders. The impressions of infancy had burnt into him, and he resented the impertinence of manhood. These were weaknesses; but such as they were, they are a key to explicate some of his writings.

【作者简介】 Charles Lamb（查理 · 莱姆，1775—1834），英国著名小品文家，出身寒微。父亲为伦敦名律师撒尔特（Samuel Salt）的侍役，外祖母为赫福德郡（Hertfordshire）富绅管家。莱姆幼年在公立基督学校（Christ's Hospital）攻读，和柯勒律治（Coleridge）同学友好。莱姆十七岁入东印度公司当会计，五十岁以老病退休。他的姐姐玛丽有疯病，时时发作，莱姆和她很友爱，共居到老。玛丽也有文才。莱姆和她合作写成了《莎氏乐府本事》(*Tales from Shakespeare*)，出版于1807年。这本书对于莎士比亚的戏剧起了很好的普及作用。自1820年到1823年，莱姆经常以小品文投稿于"伦敦杂志"，(the *London Magazine*).这些文章于1823年编成一集出版，定名为《伊利亚文集》(*The Essays of Elia*).《伊利亚文后集》(*The Last Essays of Elia*)出版于1833年。

莱姆的小品文有独特的风格，源出于法国小品文家蒙田(Montaigne).莱姆长于抒写个人思想感情，追往怀旧的作品，缠绵悱恻，庄谐并陈，很能感动读者。莱姆对于英国17世纪散文作家富勒(Fuller)、勃朗(Browne)、勃登(Burton)有特殊爱好，并且熟习莎士比亚和与莎氏同时代剧作家的作品，行文的时候，古词古语，名言轶闻，不知不觉地奔赴腕底。赫士列特(Hazlitt)论莱姆的"以故为新"的作风，虽似肯定，实际对他的违反时代精神，深表不满。莱姆早年和当时进步人士如高德温(Godwin)、李·恒特(Leigh Hunt)等都有交往，然而他的文章绝少反映政治。

【题解与注释】

这里选了两篇莱姆的散文:《一个单身汉对已婚者的行为的抱怨》和《伊利亚文后集自序》。前者选自《伊利亚文集》，后者选自《伊利亚文后集》。

Elia本来是莱姆早年工作过的"南海公司"的一个意大利籍职员。在莱姆于1820年开始为《伦敦杂志》写稿时，他借用了这个名字。

收集在这两本书中的小品文，大都描写或谈论莱姆所认识的人士，以及他自己的见闻和想法。他的语气亲切委婉，他的文笔淡雅幽默，使得他的文章读起来象是一个朋友在和你谈心，而不是一个陌生人在对你演说。这个特点在第一篇文章中很清楚地反映出来。

莱姆给他的朋友约翰·泰勒(John Taylor)的一封信中曾经说过他的文章"不需要序言；它们可以说都是序言。一篇序言也不过是与读者的谈话而已。"虽然如此，他还是为《伊利亚文后集》写了这篇自序。在自序里他对自己的风格特点作了辩解，也谈到了他为人的大概。正象他自己所说的，这篇自序给读者提供了一把了解他的作品的钥匙。

1. A BACHELOR'S COMPLAINT OF THE BEHAVIOUR OF MARRIED PEOPLE

1. infirmities: 缺点。

anti-social resolutions，指他过独身生活的决心。

2. a different description: 另外一种。

3. Not too loving neither: 此处 neither = either.

4. each other's society: 在一起（society 在此处和 company 同义）。

5. homely-featured: 相貌一般。

6. having access: 有办法。此处 access 和 opportunity 意思相似。

7. the ground of a quarrel: 吵架的借口。

8. looks: 表情。

9. that are scarce less plain: 同样地清楚（**scarce:** = scarcely，旧的用法）。

10. admit of a palliative: 有减轻的可能；有缓和的余地。

11. usufruct:（对别人的财物的）使用权。此处指可以看看别人的花园等。

12. unqualified: 不折不扣的。

13. Marriage by its best title is a monopoly: 婚姻，说得最好听，是一种专利。

14. married monopolists: 享有婚姻这一专利权的人，即结了婚的人。

15. thrust the most ... into our faces: 把他们的专利权的最可恶的部分摆到我们面前。

16. her lot is disposed of: 她的命运已经决定了。

17. would be more offensive ... irrational: 越显得有道理，就越叫人生气。

18. their own craft: 他们自己那一伙。

19. to be made free of the company: 摆脱他们。

20. the most indifferent subject: 一个最不重要的，最不相干的问题。

21. Nay: 相当于 well, why（旧义）。

22. had not changed ... before: 改变她的生活（结婚）还不到半个月。

23. how little of a rarity children are: 小孩子丝毫也不希罕。

24. these bargains: 便宜货（指孩子）。

25. I cannot for my life tell: 我无论如何也说不出。

26. phoenixes: 凤凰。传说在一时期内只可能有一只凤凰，活五百年后自己焚死，从灰烬中另一凤凰诞生。

27. their natural-born subjects: 生下来就是他们的臣民。

28. to bring out spices, myrrh, and incense: 献香祝福，即表示赞美。

29. Like as the arrows ...: 引自《圣经》中《诗篇》第 127 首。全诗大意是：孩子是上帝所赐，有孩子的人是幸福的。

30. the excellent office: 那极好的祷告词。

31. the churching of women: 妇女生孩子后到教堂感谢上帝。

32. Happy is the man...: 引自上述同一首赞美诗。

33. don't let him discharge ... weaponless: 不要让他把箭朝着我们这些毫无武器的人放。意思是有孩子的人不要用孩子来对付没有孩子的人。

34. their innocent caresses: 此处 caresses 指声音、话语。

35. you are set down as: 你就被认为是。

36. dispense with toying with their brats: 不和他们的孩子玩（brat 有贬义）。

37. where I see no occasion: 我没有理由要爱他们。

38. Love me, love my dog: 既然爱我，就该爱我的狗（又译"爱屋及乌"）。意思是只有在尊重我所喜欢的人或物时，才是真正地尊重我。

39. in sport: 闹着玩。

40. make shift to: 相当于 try to.

41. provided it be in its nature indifferent: 假使那东西本身是无所谓的，没有个性的。

42. apt to receive whatever hue fancy can give it: 可以接受想象加给它的任何色彩。意思是你怎样看待它都可以。

43. have a real character ... of themselves: 有他们自己的个性。

44. *per se*: 拉丁文，相当于 in themselves.

45. see cause for either: 有爱或恨的理由。

46. to admit of ... another being:（不）容许把他看作仅仅是另一个人的附属物。

47. they stand with me upon their own stock: 对我来说他们是独立的人。此处 stock 有"基础"的意思。

48. the delicate creatures which bear them: 指他们的母亲。

49. pretty of its kind: 有它独特的美好之处。

50. One daisy differs not much from another in glory: 此语可能是暗引《圣经·哥林多书》中的一句话：There is one glory of the sun, and another glory of the moon, and another glory of the stars: for one star differeth from another star in glory.

51. squeamish in my women and children: 对和我有来往的妇女与儿童有点吹毛求疵。

52. if you did not come in on the wife's side: 如果你不是由于女方的关系而和他们成了朋友。

53. in her train: 跟在她的后面。in first habits of intimacy，极为亲密。

54. your tenure is precarious: 你作为一个朋友的资格随时可被取消。

55. before a twelvemonth shall roll over your head: 在一年之内，一年还没过去。

56. they can endure that: 此处 they 指妻子们。

57. the good man: 指丈夫。

58. to be new stamped with their currency: 和她们的钱币一起重新铸造，指需要得到她们的认可。

59. let it pass current in the world: 在世界上流通。

60. new mintings: 重新铸造，指得到妻子们的认可。

61. an oddity: 一个怪人。

62. would pass over some excrescences ... perceived in you: 不计较你的某些不正常的想法和举止，因为他看到你有一种并不一般的观察力。

63. a humorist: 爱开玩笑，不太严肃的人。

64. well enough to have consorted with ... days: 在做单身汉时很可以交为朋友。

65. an object of especial regard: 特别受到尊重的人。

66. the lasting attachment founded on esteem: 以敬重为基础的持久的友情。

67. to cry up all that you say or do: 对你的一言一行都大加称赞。

68. grows weary of the debt of gratitude: 不想欠更多的感激之债。他感激他的妻子，因为她夸奖他的朋友。

69. taking down a peg or two in his enthusiasm: 降低热情。

70. sinks at length ... moderate esteem: 最后降到只是稍示尊敬的客气的水平。

71. that 'decent affection and complacent kindness': 引自苏格兰作家 John Home (1722–1808) 所著悲剧 *Douglas*，意思是'颇为得体的感情和流露自满的客气'。

72. join in sympathy with him: 和他一致。

73. without much stretch ... sincerity: 对她的诚意来说也并无歪曲或损害。

74. riveted the chain which she is to break: 拴牢她所要打断的链子（指友谊）。

75. a want of poignancy: 不够深刻、尖锐。

76. overlook some trifling irregularities ... deportment: 不计较你品行上某些细小的毛病。

77. representations: 描写。

78. pitch upon: 选择。

79. dimensions: 身材（高矮、胖瘦等）。

80. I have the advantage of him ... inch: 我比他还高半英寸。

81. a martial character: 军人气概。

82. and *vice versa*: 反之亦然，即用对待朋友的办法来对待她们的丈夫。

83. *Testacea*: 即 Mrs. Shell-fish，由拉丁字"贝壳类动物"变来，指她把蠔留给丈夫吃，而不顾客人挨饿。

84. reversing the point of good manners: 颠倒了礼貌的目的。

85. ceremony is an invention ... some other person is: 礼仪是一种创造，用来消除当我们知道我们受某人喜爱和尊敬的程度不如另外一个人时所产生的不安之感。

86. It endeavours to make up ... the greater: 它（礼仪）在小处极为殷勤注意，以弥补在大处它不可能给予的那种令人生气的偏爱。

87. withstood her husband's importunities to go to supper: 顶住她丈夫的要吃晚饭的迫切请求。

88. beyond the point of: 除……之外。

89. the vicarious gluttony: 替别人表现出的贪馋，指她把好吃的黑樱桃送到她丈夫面前。

90. *Cerasia*: 即 Mrs. Cherry，由拉丁字 cerasus（樱桃）变来。

91. Morellas: 黑樱桃。

which I was applying to，我正在那盘菜上下功夫。

92. my unwedded palate: 我这个单身汉的嘴。

93. Roman denominations: 罗马式的名字，指前面用的拉丁名字。

2. PREFACE TO THE LAST ESSAYS

1. this poor gentleman: 指 Elia.

2. in a declining way: 奄奄一息。

3. hath ... paid his final tribute to nature: 已经死去（委婉语）。hath = has（古）。

4. the humour of the thing: 这里“thing”指 the life of the poor gentleman,

5. a two years' and a half existence: 也可以说 a two and a half years' existence.

6. phantom: 指 Elia.

7. at liberty to confess: 可以随便承认。（因为 Elia 已死）。

8. well founded: 有根据的。

9. I grant you: = I admit.

10. unlicked: 不象样的。

11. incondite [inˈkɔndit]**:** 拙劣的。

12. villainously pranked in an affected array of antique modes and phrases: 用矫揉造作的一套古调古语恶俗地装点着的。

13. They had not been *his*, if they had been other than such: 如果不是那样，就不是他的作品了。（照现代语法，主句里的 had not been 应作 would not have been.）

14. better it is, that a writer should be natural ina self-pleasing quaintness, than to affect a naturalness (so called) that should be strange to him: 一位作家如能从容于自适的带有古意的风格比起勉强装出跟他性情不相投的一种所谓自然风格总要好些。

15. what he tells us, as of himself, was often true only (historically) of another: 他告诉我们的关于自己的事实往往（实际上）不是他自己的，而是另一人的。（按莱姆的小品文虽多自传性质的，但事实和虚构往往交织着，读者不能把它们当作自传读。）

16. a former Essay: 指“Christ's Hospital”一文。这篇文章是用第一人称写的。莱姆在这篇文章中说：“I was a poor friendless boy. My parents, and those who should care for me, were far away.”这和他早年的历史完全不符。

17. his favourite figure: 他最喜欢用的写作方法，即用第一人称来写作。（figure 有 person 的意义）。

18. shadows forth: 隐约讲到。

19. estate: = condition（古义）

20. to imply and twine with his own identity the griefs and affections of another: 把另一人的悲欢情绪与他自己纠结在一起作为自己的悲欢情绪。

21. unto: = to（古）。

22. all along: 一贯。

23. intenser: = more emotional (than the novelist).

24. under cover of passion uttered by another oftentimes gives blameless vent to his most inward feelings: 在抒发他人的情感的掩护下往往无可指责地发泄了他自己内心的情感。(借他人的酒杯，浇自己的块垒。)

25. singular character: 怪僻的人物。

26. gave himself too little concern what he uttered, and in whose presence: 太不考虑他讲的是什么，和在什么人面前讲。

27. would e'en out with: = would utter directly.

28. pass for: 充作。

29. the other faction: 其它一派人(指 free-thinkers)。

30. set him down for: 把他认为。

31. belied his sentiments: 不忠实于他的感情。

32. affected that dangerous figure —irony，运用那有危险性的笔法——讽刺。

33. long and much talkers: those who talk long and much 转来的。

34. an inveterate impediment of speech: 口吃的宿疾。

35. play that part: 指 the part of an orator.

36. petit [pə'tiː]: 小(法)。

37. if rightly taken: 是 if the pun is rightly taken 的简略。

38. hit or miss: 随随便便的。

39. *impromptus*: 即席发言(从拉丁 in promptu 来)。

40. had the appearance of effort: 有格格不吐的样子。

41. *literati*: 文人(复)(拉丁)。

42. were of his councils: = were among his friends.

43. persons of an uncertain fortune: 没有固定财产的人。

44. *intimados* [inti'mɑːdəuz]: 知己朋友(西班牙语)。

45. in the world's eye: 在世界上一般人的目光中。

46. weed: 衣服(古)。

47. burrs: = burs，依草附木的人(指 Elia 的朋友们)。

48. for all that: 虽然如此。

49. making ... concessions to: 对…让步。

50. concede to: 对…让步。

51. kept a little on this side of abstemiousness: 不放纵嗜欲，但也不过于啬刻。

52. Indian weed: 烟草。

53. solvent of speech: 谈话的溶媒。

54. Marry: 古惊叹词。

55. ligaments: 韧带。

56. which tongue-tied him: 使他箝口结舌的。

57. statist: 政治家(古)。

58. is departed: 用助动词 be 和内动词的过去分词来表示完成时态是较古的结构，现在只有 go, come, arrive, depart 等内动词还偶尔用这种结构。

59. latterly: 近来。

60. pettishness: 别扭；不快情绪。

61. retreat: 退隐的地方。

62. Shacklewell: 伦敦郊区。

63. visiting governor: 来访问的学校监督。

64. carried to a foible: = carried to a fault，做得过火。

65. had a horror ... of looking like anything important and parochial: 不愿有要人或教区官吏的气息。

66. stamp: 类型。

67. kept a wary eye upon the advances of age that should so entitle him: 刻刻担心着老之将至，惟恐高年会使人们认为他是一位严肃可敬的人物。（这里的 so 是替代词，如果不用 so，就得说 that should entitle him to being treated like a grave or respectable character. 句子要变得很累赘。）

68. herded ... with: 跟…交游。

69. did not conform to the march of time: 不按照时代的步伐前进。

70. dragged along in the procession: 落在行列后面。

71. his years: 他的年龄。

72. boy-man: 不失赤子之心的成人；有稚气的成人。

73. *toga virilis* [ˈtəugə viˈrailis]**:** 成人的外衣。（拉丁）

74. sate: = sat（古）。**sit gracefully on**：有衣服称身的意义。

34 WILLIAM HAZLITT
1778 – 1830

ON THE IGNORANCE OF THE LEARNED

吴千之　选注

"For the more languages a man can speak,
His talent has but sprung the greater leak:[1]
And, for the industry[2] he has spent upon't,[3]
Must full as much some other way discount.
The Hebrew,[4] Chaldee,[5] and the Syriac,[6]
Do, like their letters, set men's reason back,
And turn their wits that strive to understand it
(Like those that write the characters) left-handed.[7]
Yet he that is but able to express
No sense at all in several languages,
Will pass for[8] learneder than he that's known
To speak the strongest reason in his own."

Butler.

The description[9] of persons who have the fewest ideas of all others are mere authors and readers. It is better to be able neither to read nor write than to be able to do nothing else. A lounger[10] who is ordinarily seen with a book in his hand is (we may be almost sure) equally without the power or inclination to attend either to what passes around him or in his own mind. Such a one may be said to carry his understanding about with him in his pocket, or to leave it at home on his library shelves. He is afraid of venturing on any train of reasoning,[11] or of striking out any observation[12] that is not mechanically suggested to him by passing his eyes over certain legible characters;[13] shrinks from the fatigue of thought, which, for want of[14] practice, becomes insupportable to him; and sits down contented with an endless, wearisome succession of words and half-formed images,[15] which fill the void of the mind, and continually efface one another. Learning is, in too many cases, but a foil to common sense;[16] a substitute for true knowledge. Books are less often made use of as "spectacles" to look at nature with,[17] than as blinds to keep out its strong light and shifting scenery from weak eyes and indolent dispositions. The book-worm wraps himself up in his web of verbal generalities,[18] and sees only the glimmering shadows of things reflected from the minds of others. Nature *puts him out*.[19] The impressions of real objects, stripped of disguises of words and voluminous roundabout descriptions, are blows that stagger him; their variety distracts,[20] their rapidity exhausts him; and he turns from the bustle, the noise, and glare, and whirling motion of the world about him (which he has not an eye to follow in its fantastic changes, nor an understanding to reduce to fixed principles),[21] to the quiet monotony of the dead languages, and the less startling and more intelligible combinations of the letters of the alphabet,[22] It is well,[23] it is perfectly well. "Leave me to my repose,"[24] js the motto of the sleeping and the dead. You might as well ask the paralytic to leap from his chair and throw away his crutch, or, without a miracle,[25] to "take up his bed and walk,"[26] as expect the learned reader to throw down his book and think for himself. He clings to it for his intellectual support; and his dread of being left to himself is like the horror of a vacuum.[27] He can only breathe a learned atmosphere, as other men breathe common air. He is a borrower of sense.[28] He has no ideas of his own, and must live on those of other people. The habit of supplying our ideas from foreign sources "enfeebles all internal strength of thought,"[29] as a course of dram-drinking[30] destroys the tone of the stomach.[31] The faculties of the mind,[32] when not exerted, or when cramped by custom and authority,[33] become listless, torpid, and unfit for the purposes of thought or action. Can we wonder at the languor and lassitude which is thus produced by a life of learned sloth[34] and ignorance; by poring over lines and syllables that excite[35] little more idea or interest than if they were the characters of an unknown tongue,[36] till the eye closes on vacancy,[37] and the book drops from the feeble hand! I would rather be a wood-cutter, or the meanest hind,[38] that all day "sweats in the eye of Phoebus, and at night sleeps in Elysium,"[39] than wear out my life so, 'twixt[40] dreaming and awake. The learned author differs from the learned student in this, that the one transcribes what the other reads. The learned are mere literary drudges.[41] If you set them upon original composition, their heads turn, they don't know where they are. The indefatigable readers of books are like the everlasting copiers of pictures, who, when they attempt to do anything of their own, find they want an eye quick enough, a hand steady enough, and colours bright enough, to trace the living forms of nature.

Any one who has passed through the regular gradations of a classical education,[42] and is not made a fool by it, may consider himself as having had a very narrow escape. It is an old remark, that boys who shine at school do not make the greatest figure when they grow up and come out into the world. The things, in fact, which a boy is set to learn at school, and on which his success depends, are things which do not require the exercise either of the highest or the most useful faculties of the mind. Memory (and that of the lowest kind) is the chief faculty called into play in conning over and repeating lessons by rote[43] in grammar, in languages, in geography, arithmetic, etc., so that he who has the most of this technical memory,[44] with the least turn[45] for other things, which have a stronger and more natural claim upon[46] his childish attention, will make the most forward[47] school-boy. The jargon containing the definitions of the parts of speech, the rules for casting up an account,[48] or the inflections[49] of a Greek verb, can have no attraction to the tyro[50] of ten years old, except as[51] they are imposed as a task upon him by others, or from his feeling the want of sufficient relish or amusement in other things. A lad with a sickly constitution and no very active mind, who can just retain[52] what is pointed out to him, and has neither sagacity to distinguish nor spirit to enjoy for himself, will generally be at the head of his form.[53] An idler at school, on the other hand, is one who has high health and spirits, who has the free use of his limbs, with all his wits about him,[54] who feels the circulation of his blood and the motion of his heart, who is ready to laugh and cry in a breath,[55] and who had rather chase a ball or a butterfly, feel the open air in his face, look at the fields or the sky, follow a winding path, or enter with eagerness into all the little conflicts and interests of his acquaintances and friends, than doze over a musty spelling-book, repeat barbarous distichs[56] after his master, sit so many hours pinioned to a writing-desk,[57] and receive his reward for the loss of time and pleasure in paltry prize-medals at Christmas and Midsummer.[58] There is indeed a degree of stupidity which prevents children from learning the usual lessons, or ever arriving at these puny academic honours. But what passes for stupidity is much oftener a want of interest, of a sufficient motive to fix the attention and force a reluctant application to the dry and unmeaning pursuits of school-learning.[59] The best capacities are as much above this drudgery as the dullest[60] are beneath it. Our men of the greatest genius have not been most distinguished[81] for their acquirements at school or at the university.

"Th' enthusiast Fancy was a truant ever."[62]

Gray[63] and Collins[64] were among the instances of this wayward disposition. Such persons do not think so highly of the advantages, nor can they submit their imaginations so servilely to the trammels of strict scholastic discipline. There is a certain kind and degree of intellect[65] in which words take root, but into which things have not power to penetrate. A mediocrity[66] of talent, with a certain slenderness of moral constitution,[67] is the soil that produces the most brilliant specimens of successful prize-essayists[68] and Greek epigrammatists.[69] It should not be forgotten that the least respectable character among modern politicians[70] was the cleverest boy at Eton.[71]

Learning is the knowledge of that which is not generally known to others, and which we can only derive at second-hand from books or other artificial sources. The knowledge of that which is before us, or about us,[72] which appeals to[73] our experience, passions, and pursuits, to the bosoms and businesses of men,[74] is not learning. Learning is the knowledge of that which none but the learned know. He is the most learned man who knows the most of what is farthest removed from common life and actual observation, that is of the least practical utility, and least liable to[75] be brought to the test of experience, and that, having been handed down through the greatest number of intermediate stages, is the most full of uncertainty, difficulties, and contradictions. It is seeing with the eyes of others, hearing with their ears, and pinning our faith on[76] their understandings. The learned man prides himself in the knowledge of names and dates,[77] not of men or things. He thinks and cares nothing about his next-door neighbours, but he is deeply read in[78] the tribes and castes[79] of the Hindoos[80] and Calmuc Tartars.[81] He can hardly find his way into the next street, though he is acquainted with the exact dimensions of Constantinople[82] and Pekin. He does not know whether his oldest acquaintance is a knave or a fool, but he can pronounce a pompous lecture on all the principal characters in history. He cannot tell whether an object is black or white, round or square, and yet he is a professed master[83] of the laws of optics[84] and the rules of perspective.[85] He knows as much of what he talks about as a blind man does of colours. He cannot give a satisfactory answer to the plainest questions, nor is he ever in the right[86] in any one of his opinions upon any one matter of fact that really comes before him, and yet he gives himself out for[87] an infallible judge on all those points, of which it is impossible that he or any other person living should know anything but by conjecture.[86] He is expert in all the dead and in most of the living languages;[89] but he can neither speak his own fluently, nor write it correctly. A person of this class, the second Greek scholar of his day,[90] undertook to point out several solecisms[91] in Milton's Latin style;[92] and in his own performance there is hardly a sentence of common English. Such was Dr.—. Such is Dr.—. Such was not Porson.[93] He was an exception that confirmed the general rule,[94]—a man that, by uniting talents and knowledge with learning, made the distinction between them more striking and palpable.

A mere scholar, who knows nothing but books, must be ignorant even of them. "Books do not teach the use of books."[95] How should he know anything of a work who knows nothing of the subject of it? The learned pedant[96] is conversant with[97] books only as they are made of other books, and those again of others, without end. He parrots those who have parroted others. He can translate the same word into ten different languages, but he knows nothing of the *thing* which it means in any one of them. He stuffs his head with authorities[98] built on authorities, with quotations quoted from quotations, while he locks up his senses, his understanding, and his heart. He is unacquainted with the maxims and manners of the world; he is to seek in[99] the characters of individuals. He sees no beauty in the face of nature or of art. To him "the mighty world of eye and ear"[100] is hid; and "knowledge," except at one entrance,"-quite shut out." His pride takes part with[101] his ignorance; and his self-importance rises with the number of things of which he does not know the value, and which he therefore despises as unworthy of his notice. He knows nothing of pictures,—"of the colouring[102] of Titian,[103] the grace of Raphael,[104] the purity of Domenichino,[105] the *corregiescity*[109] of Correggio,[107] the learning of Poussin,[108] the airs of Guido,[109] the taste of the Caracci,[110] or the grand contour[111] of Michael Angelo,"[112]—of all those glories of the Italian and miracles of the Flemish school,[113] which have filled the eyes of mankind with delight, and to the study and imitation of which thousands have in vain devoted their lives. These are to him as if they had never been, a mere dead letter,[114] a by-word;[115] and no wonder, for he neither sees nor understands their prototypes[116] in nature. A print of Rubens'[117] Watering-place, or Claude's[118] Enchanted Castle, may be hanging on the walls of his room for months without his once perceiving them; and if you point them out to him he will turn away from them. The language of nature, or of art (which is another nature), is one that he does not understand. He repeats indeed the names of Apelles[119] and Phidias,[120] because they are to be found in classic authors, and boasts of their works as prodigies,[121] because they no longer exist; or when he sees the finest remains of Grecian[122] art actually before him in the Elgin Marbles,[123] takes no other interest in them than as they lead to a learned dispute,[124] and (which is the same thing) a quarrel about the meaning of a Greek particle.[125] He is equally ignorant of music; he "knows no touch of it,"[126] from the strains of the all accomplished Mozart[127] to the shepherd's pipe upon the mountain. His ears are nailed to his books; and deadened with the sound of the Greek and Latin tongues, and the din and smithery[128] of school-learning. Does he know anything more of poetry? He knows the number of feet[129] in a verse, and of acts in a play; but of the soul or spirit he knows nothing. He can turn a Greek ode into English, or a Latin epigram into Greek verse; but whether either is worth the trouble he leaves to the critics. Does he understand "the act and practique part of life"[130] better than "the theorique"? No. He knows no liberal or mechanic art,[131] no trade or occupation, no game of skill or chance.[132] Learning "has no skill in surgery,"[133] in agriculture, in building, in working in wood or in iron;[134] it cannot make any instrument of labour, or use it when made; it cannot handle the plough or the spade, or the chisel or the hammer; it knows nothing of hunting or hawking,[135] fishing or shooting, of horses or dogs, of fencing[136] or dancing, or cudgel-playing,[137] or bowls,[138] or cards, or tennis, or anything else. The learned professor of all arts and sciences cannot reduce any one of them to practice, though he may contribute an account of them to an Encyclopedia. He has not the use of his hands or of his feet; he can neither run, nor walk, nor swim; and he considers all those who actually understand and can exercise any of these arts of body or mind as vulgar and mechanical men, — though to know almost any one of them in perfection requires long time and practice, with powers originally fitted,[139] and a turn of mind particularly devoted to them. It does not require more than this to enable the learned candidate[140] to arrive, by painful study, at a doctor's degree and a fellowship,[141] and to eat, drink, and sleep the rest of his life!

The thing is plain. All that men really understand is confined to a very small compass;[142] to their daily affairs and experience; to what they have an opportunity to know, and motives to study or practise. The rest is affectation and imposture. The common people have the use of their limbs; for they live by their labour or skill. They understand their own business and the characters of those they have to deal with; for it is necessary that they should. They have eloquence to express their passions, and wit at will to express their contempt and provoke laughter. Their natural use of speech is not hung up in monumental mockery,[143] in an obsolete language; nor is their sense of what is ludicrous,[144] or readiness at finding out allusions to express it, buried in collections of *Anas*.[145] You will hear more good things on the outside of a stage-coach[146] from London to Oxford than if you were to pass a twelvemonth with the undergraduates, or heads of colleges, of that famous university; and more *home* truths[147] are to be learnt from listening to a noisy debate in an alehouse than from attending to a formal one in the House of Commons.[148] An elderly country gentlewoman will often know more of character, and be able to illustrate it by more amusing anecdotes taken from the history of what has been said, done, and gossiped in a country town for the last fifty years, than the best blue-stocking[149] of the age will be able to glean from that sort of learning which consists in an acquaintance with all the novels and satirical poems published in the same period. People in towns, indeed, are woefully deficient in a knowledge of character, which they see only *in the bust,* not as a whole-length.[150] People in the country not only know all that has happened to a man, but trace his virtues or vices, as they do his features, in their descent through several generations, and solve some contradiction in his behaviour by a cross in the breed[151] half a century ago. The learned know nothing of the matter, either in town or country. Above all, the mass of society have common sense, which the learned in all ages want. The vulgar[152] are in the right when they judge for themselves; they are wrong when they trust to their blind guides. The celebrated nonconformist divine,[153] Baxter,[154] was almost stoned to death by the good women of Kidderminster,[155] for asserting from the pulpit that"hell was paved with infants' skulls"; but, by the force of argument, and of learned quotations from the Fathers,[156] the reverend preacher at length prevailed over the scruples of his congregation,[157] and over reason and humanity.[158]

Such is the use which has been made of human learning. The labourers in this vineyard[159] seem as if it was their object to confound all common sense, and the distinctions of good and evil, by means of traditional maxims and preconceived notions[160] taken upon trust,[161] and increasing in absurdity with increase of age. They pile hypothesis on hypothesis, mountain high, till it is impossible to come at the plain truth on any question. They see things, not as they are,[162] but as they find them in books, and "wink and shut their apprehensions up,"[163] in order that they may discover nothing to interfere with their prejudices or convince them of their absurdity. It might be supposed that the height of human wisdom consisted in[164] maintaining contradictions and rendering nonsense sacred. There is no dogma, however fierce or foolish, to which these persons have not set their seals,[165] and tried to impose on the understandings of their followers, as the will of Heaven, clothed with all the terrors and sanctions[166] of religion. How little has the human understanding been directed to find out the true and useful! How much ingenuity has been thrown away in the defence of creeds and systems! How much time and talents have been wasted in theological controversy, in law, in politics, in verbal criticism,[167] in judicial astrology,[168] and in finding out the art of making gold![169] What actual benefit do we reap from the writings of a Laud[170] or a Whitgift,[171] or of Bishop Bull[172] or Bishop Waterland,[173] or Prideaux'[174] Connections, or Beausobre,[175] or Calmet,[176] or St. Augustine,[177] or Puffendorf,[178] or Vattel,[179] or from the more literal[180] but equally learned and unprofitable labours of Scaliger,[181] Cardan,[182] and Scioppius?[183] How many grains of sense are there in their thousand folio[184] or quarto[185] volumes? What would the world lose if they were committed to the flames tomorrow? Or are they not already "gone to the vault of all the Capulets"?[186] Yet all these were oracles in their time, and would have scoffed at you or me, at common sense and human nature, for differing with them.[187] It is our turn to laugh now.

To conclude this subject. The most sensible people to be met with in society are men of business and of the world,[188] who argue from what they see and know, instead of spinning cobweb distinctions[189] of what things ought to be. Women have often more of what is called *good sense* than men. They have fewer pretensions; are less implicated in theories; and judge of[190] objects more from their immediate and involuntary impression on the mind, and, therefore, more truly and naturally. They cannot reason wrong; for they do not reason at all. They do not think or speak by rule;[191] and they have in general more eloquence and wit, as well as sense, on that account. By their wit, sense, and eloquence together, they generally contrive to govern their husbands. Their style, when they write to their friends (not for the booksellers), is better than that of most authors.—Uneducated people have most exuberance of invention and the greatest freedom from prejudice. Shakespear's was evidently an uneducated mind, both in the freshness of his imagination and in the variety of his views; as Milton's was scholastic, in the texture[192] both of his thoughts and feelings. Shakespear had not been accustomed to write themes at school in favour of virtue or against vice. To this we owe the unaffected but healthy tone of his dramatic morality.[193] If we wish to know the force of human genius we should read Shakespear. If we wish to see the insignificance of human learning we may study his commentators.

—*Edinburgh Magazine,* July, 1818

【作者简介】 William Hazlitt（威廉·赫兹列特，1778—1830），英国散文家、批评家。政治上积极主张民主共和，同情法国大革命，崇拜拿破仑，并著 *Life of Napoleon*（《拿破仑传》，1828）。赫兹列特与其同时代的散文家 Charles Lamb 同为英国的小品文大师，其文体气势磅礴，感情洋溢。一生著作极多，重要的文学批评与小品文集有 *Characters of Shakespeare's Plays*（《莎士比亚戏剧人物论》，1817），*Lectures on English Poets*（《论英国诗人讲演集》，1818—1819），*Table Talk*（《席间杂谈》，1821—1822）*The Plain Speaker*（《直言者》，1826）等；其中名文有"On the Feeling of Immortality in Youth"（"论青春不朽之感"），"On Going a Journey"（"谈旅行"），"On the Ignorance of the Learned"（"论学者之无知"）等篇。

【题解与注释】

"On the Ignorance of the Learned"最初发表在 1818 年 7 月的 *Edinburgh Magazine*《爱丁堡杂志》上，以后又收入小品文集 *Table Talk*。在这篇文章里，赫兹列特揭示了许多学者脱离实际，不晓世事的致命弱点，抒发了他对大自然、对感性世界的憧憬和酷爱。他的思想反映了产业革命时代重实用、轻理论的新思潮，也反映了重情感、轻理性的浪漫主义思想。尽管作者对书本知识的否定和对感性常识的推崇失之过偏，但是他以不可抗拒的说服力量，道出了时代的要求，并且豪迈地宣告了旧思想的失败（"Or are they not already 'gone to the vault of all the Capulets'？"）和新思想的胜利（"It is our turn to laugh now."）。赫兹列特本人善于读书，对大自然和社会生活又有多方面的了解，他既能文、又能画，因此那些不切实际的学者们在他所展现的生活大图面前黯然失色。作者紧紧地抓住博学者无知这个似乎是自相矛盾的主题，成功地运用了似非而是的对比手段（即英文所谓的 paradox）。文章虽因反复阐发主题而略嫌冗长，但作者文思极广，侃侃而谈，毫不使人腻烦。文中机智的警句，通俗的类比，充满生活气息的写实，对文、史、诗、画的引证和议论，汇成滔滔大江，使文章读来有气势，有风趣，有哲理，高精炼于浩瀚之中。

赫兹列特的警句值得我们特别注意，例如：

Such a one may be said to carry his understanding about with him in his pocket, or to leave it at home on his library shelves.

A mere scholar, who knows nothing but books, must be ignorant even of them.

If we wish to know the force of human genius we should read Shakespear.

If we wish to see the insignificance of human learning we may study his commentators.

赫兹列特还喜用引语，有明引也有暗引，用时往往不注出处，甚至也不讲究字句的准确，而是将引语融化于自己的文字中，来增添文章的丰采；这也是赫兹列特小品文的一个特点。

引文　此十二行出自英国诗人 Samuel Butler (1612–1680) 的长诗 *Hudibras*.

1. His talent has but sprung the greater leak: to spring a leak，发现漏洞：全句意为：愈益暴露其才学的疏浅。

2. industry: 工夫。

3. upon't: = upon it.

4. The Hebrew ['hi:bru:]: = the Hebrew language，古希伯来文，在现代英语中只说 Hebrew.

5.(the) Chaldee [kæl'di:]：古加尔底亚文。

6. the Syriac ['siriæk]：古叙利亚文。

7. turn their wits ... left-handed: 使他们的聪明才智变得迟钝起来。这里 left-handed 是双关语，一方面用它的原义（用左手，反手）指那些东方文字自右至左的写法，一方面用它的转义指头脑、才智的迟钝不灵。

8. pass for: 充作，被当作。

9. description: = kind, class，种类。

10. lounger: 游手好闲者。

11. venturing on any train of reasoning: 敢于进行任何（独立的）推理和思考。

12. striking out any observation: 提出任何（独立的）见解。

13. legible characters: 易于辨认的文字；意即：对这些人来说，辨认文字要比思考问题容易。

14. for want of: = for lack of，由于缺乏…下文（第 780 页，第 14 行）动词 want 亦作 lack 解。

15. half-formed images: 模糊不清的形象。

16. a foil to common sense: 常识的衬托，意为恰是常识的反面。

17. "spectacles" to look at nature with: 作者此处实际在引用十七世纪英国文学家 John Dryden 论莎士比亚的名言："He needed not the spectacles of books to read nature”.（*An Essay of Dramatic Poesy*）

18. verbal generalities: 空泛的言词。

19. Nature *puts him out*: 自然界（即指客观世界）使他偏促不安。

20. their variety distracts (him): 它们的千变万化使他无所适从。

21. to reduce (which) to fixed principles: 将其归结为固定的原理。

22. the alphabet: 字母（总称），此处指古代或东方的文字。

23. It is well: 意为：这种情况本来是很自然的，毫不足怪。

24. “Leave me to my repose”: 语出英国诗人 Thomas Gray 的诗作 *Descent of Odin*，71，原文为：

Now my weary lips I close;
Leave me, leave me to repose.

25. without a miracle: 不靠仙术。

26. “take up his bed and walk”: 出自《圣经》“约翰福音”第 4 章，第 8 节，原文为：

Rise, take up thy bed, and walk.

27. the horror of a vacuum: 惧怕真空。

28. sense: 判断力，理智。

29. “enfeebles all internal strength of thought”: “削弱思维的内在力量”；见十八世纪英国文学家 Oliver Goldsmith 的哲学诗 *The Traveller*, 270:

Praise too dearly lov'd, or warmly sought,
Enfeebles all internal strength of thought.

30. a course of dram-drinking: 一大口烈酒。

31. the tone of the stomach: 胃的正常功能。

32. the faculties of the mind: 思维的机能。

33. cramped by custom and authority: 为因循守旧和迷信权威所束缚。

34. learned sloth: 因博学而思想怠惰。

35. excite: 唤起。

36. tongue: = language.

37. the eye closes on vacancy: 两眼对着虚无的空间闭合起来。

38. the meanest hind: 最卑贱的长工；hind 原指英国北部庄园的役丁。

39. “sweats in the eye of Phoebus, and at night sleeps in Elysium”: 语出莎士比亚历史剧《亨利五世》（*Henry V*, IV, i, 269–270）. Phoebus ['fi:bəs] 是希腊的太阳神，Elysium [i'liziəm] 是希腊神话中人死后安息之处。莎士比亚以前者指太阳，以后者比喻夜眠的宁静；“at night” 莎士比亚原文为 “all night”，此处指农民白天劳动，夜间安眠。

40. 'twixt: = between，现已不用。

41. literary drudges: 专作抄录编目等工作的文字匠。

42. a clssical education: 以学习希腊文拉丁文古典著作为主的人文主义教育。

43. conning over and repeating ... by rote: 死记死背。

44. technical memory: = mechanical memory，机械的，不需思考的记忆力。

45. turn: 才能。

46. have a stronger and more natural claim upon: 具有（对儿童的）更强烈也是更自然的吸引力。

47. forward: 优越的，名列前茅的。

48. casting up an account: 作一次计算。

49. inflections: 动词变位的各种词尾。

50. tyro [ˈtaiərou]: 初学者。

51. except as: = unless.

52. retain: 记住。

53. form: 班级。

54. with all his wits about him: 机灵敏锐。

55. in a breath: 同时。

56. barbarous distichs [ˈdistiks]: 用陌生的语言写的诗句。

57. pinioned to a writing-desk: 束缚在书桌旁。

58. Christmas and Midsummer: 圣诞节（十二月二十五日）和仲夏节（六月二十四日）。

59. force a reluctant application to the dry and unmeaning pursuits of school-learning: 勉强用心于枯燥无味的学校科目。

60. dullest: 最笨的。

61. distinguished: 出众。

62. Th' enthusiast Fancy was a truant ever: 意为头脑灵活的人永远不受学校束缚，出处不详。

63. Gray, Thomas (1716–1771): 十八世纪英国诗人，为英国浪漫主义的先驱。

64. Collins, William (1721–1759): 英国诗人。

65. There is a certain kind and degree of intellect ...: 全句意为：有一种（或一定程度的）智力，它善于熟记语汇，却无法把握事物。

66. A mediocrity [ˌmiːdiˈɔkriti] **of talent:** 平庸之才。

67. a certain slenderness of moral constitution: 缺乏德行。

68. prize-essayists: 在学校中得作文奖者。

69. Greek epigrammatists: 仿作希腊格言诗的学生。

70. the least respectable character among modern politicians: 似指 George Canning (1770–1827)，后曾出任英国首相。

71. Eton: 伊登公学，英国贵族子弟的学校。

72. about us: 在我们四周的。

73. appeals to: = is attractive to, is useful to.

74. the bosoms and businesses of men: 人们的情感和事务。这里作者实际是在引用十七世纪英国散文家 Francis Bacon 的话："They [My Essays] come home to men's business and bosoms."（*Essays*, Dedicatory Address）

75. least liable to: 极不可能，最不易于。

76. pinning our faith on: 寄我们的信赖于。

77. dates: 指名人生卒、作品、历史事件等的日期。

78. is deeply read in: 在…方面博览群书。

79. castes: 印度封建社会的种姓阶级。

80. Hindoos [ˈhinduːz]**:** 信奉印度教的印度人。

81. Calmuc Tartars [ˈkɔː lmək ˈtɑːtəz]**:** 中亚细亚一民族，为鞑靼人之一族。

82. Constantinople [ˌkɔnstænti ˈnoupl]**:** 君士坦丁堡，土耳其古城，今名 Istambul（伊斯坦布尔）。

83. a professed master: 自封的专家。

84. optics: 光学。

85. perspective: 透视学。

86. in the right: 正确的。

87. gives himself out for: 宣称自己是。

88. by conjecture: 靠猜测。

89. dead languages: 指现代已不再使用的语言，如梵文、拉丁文等。

90. the second Greek scholar of his day: 当时位居第二的希腊文学者，指 Thomas Bentley (1693?–1742).

91. solecisms [ˈsɔlisizmz]**:** 文字上的谬误。

92. Milton's Latin style: 弥尔顿的拉丁文体；英国大诗人弥尔顿（1608—1674）精通拉丁文，不少诗文均用拉丁文创作。

93. Porson, Richard (1759–1808)**:** 英国研究希腊、拉丁文化的著名学者。

94. an exception that confirmed the general rule: 此语通常为：an exception that proves the rule，意指某一孤立的例外，不仅不能推翻常规，反而使常规更显得颠扑不破。

95. "Books do not teach the use of books": 此处 Hazlitt 实际上又在引用 Bacon 的名言："… for they [studies] teach not their own use"（*Of Studies*）. 意为书本并不以其本身的用处告人。

96. pedant: 书呆子，咬文嚼字的人。

97. conversant with: 通晓。

98. authorities: 权威性的著作或引语。

99. is to seek in: 对…茫然无知。

100. "the mighty world of eye and ear": 耳目所能闻见的实际世界，语出英国诗人 William Wordsworth（华兹华斯，1770—1850）的长诗 *Lines Composed a Few Miles above Tintern Abbey*，原文为：

All the mighty world
Of eye, and ear,—both what they half create,
And perceive.

101. takes part with: 与…成正比。

102. "of the colouring ...": 出处不详。

103. Titian [ˈtiʃiən] (1477–1576)**:** 意大利大画家。

104. Raphael [ˈræfeiəl] (1483–1520)**:** 意大利大画家。

105. Domenichino (1581–1641)**:** 意大利画家。

106. ***corregiescity*:** Correggio 画作所特具的风格。

107. Correggio (1494–1534)**:** 意大利画家。

108. Poussin, Nicolas (1594–1665)**:** 法国画家。

109. Guido (Guido Reni) (1575–1642)**:** 意大利画家。

110. the Caracci: 十六世纪意大利一画派名。

111. contour: 线条。

112. Michael Angelo [ˌmaikəlˈændʒilou] (1475–1564)**:** 意大利大画家。

113. Flemish school: 十五世纪初至十七世纪初 Flanders（法兰德斯，欧洲古国，为现今比利时东、西法兰德斯省与法国北方之一部分）的画派。

114. dead letter: 原意为一纸具文，即已不生效的旧法令，但此处作者用其字面的意义，即一无意义的古老名词。

115. by-word: 人云亦云之语。

116. prototypes: 原型，范本。

117. Rubens: Peter Paul (1577–1640)**:** 法兰德斯画家。

118. Claude, (Claude Lorrain) (1600–1682)**:** 法国风景画家。

119. Apelles: 公元前四世纪希腊画家，为古代艺术大师之一。

120. Phidias（约公元前 500—约 430)**:** 希腊雕刻家。

121. prodigies: 奇迹。

122. Grecian: = Greek，专指古希腊的建筑与浮雕的形容词。

123. the Elgin Marbles: 1801—1803 年间英国爱尔琴伯爵自希腊掠夺来的一套古希腊大理石雕塑品，今存伦敦英国博物馆。

124. a learned dispute: 学术上的争论。

125. a Greek particle: 希腊文中的一个小品词。

126. "knows no touch of it": 意为毫无所感，引语出处不详。

127. Mozart [ˈmoutsɑːt]**, Wolfgang Amadeus** (1756–1791)**:** 莫扎特，奥地利大音乐家。

128. smithery: 原指打铁时发出的响声和强光。

129. feet: 音步，诗行中的韵律单位。

130. "the act and practique part of life": 语出莎士比亚："The art and practique part of life, Must be the mistress to this theorique"（*Henry V*, I. i. 51–52）. Hazlitt 照例有个别字引错，如此处 art 引作 act.

131. liberal or mechanic art: 艺术或技术。

132. game of skill or chance: 凭技术或凭运气的游戏，前者如球类游戏，后者如纸牌游戏。

133. Learning "has no kill in surgery": 见莎剧《亨利四世》上集，"Honour has no skill in surgery, then? No, what is honour?"（*Henry IV*, I, V. i. 135）

134. working in wood or in iron: 木匠活或铁匠活。

135. hawking: 以鹰捕猎。

136. fencing: 剑术。

137. cudgel-playing: 击棍游戏。

138. bowls: 木球游戏。

139. with powers originally fitted: 有适合于这些技艺的天赋。

140. learned candidate: 应考学位或应征教师职位的学者。

141. fellowship: 英牛津、剑桥等大学学院中的高级教师职位，任职者称为 fellow.

142. compass: = sphere，范围。

143. Their natural use of speech is not hung up in monumental mockery: 他们没有处处学舌（指仿古用典之类），而忘了如何自然地说话；hung up 搁置不用。

144. their sense of what is ludicrous: = their sense of humour 他们的幽默感。

145. *Anas*: 名言轶事集。

146. stage-coach: 长途公共马车，因其按站换马，故名。

147. *home* truths: 浅显而真切的道理。

148. the House of Commons: 英国下议院；上议院称 the House of Lords.

149. blue-stocking: 女学者，女文人。

150. only *in the bust*, not as a whole-length:（人像艺术用语）只见半身，不见全身。

151. a cross in the breed: 原意杂交，此处指品德高下不同的人家相互通婚。

152. the vulgar: 平民；vulgar 在此处无今日作"卑俗"解之贬意。

153. nonconformist divine: 英国不从国教派教会的牧师。

154. Baxter, Richard (1615–1691)**:** 英国不从国教派教会牧师。

155. Kidderminster: 英格兰西部市镇名。

156. the Fathers: 头五世纪基督教传道者的尊称。

157. prevailed over the scruples of his congregation: 说服了教民，使他们不再疑虑。

158. reason and humanity: 理智和人性。

159. The labourers in this vineyard: 这处果园里的园丁们，指在学术园地里工作的学者们。

160. preconceived notions: 先入之见。

161. taken upon trust: = taken for granted，被视为天经地义。

162. not as they are: 不是如其原状地。

163. "wink and shut their apprehensions up": 意为：闭上眼睛，不愿正视并认识事物。wink，闭目不视（古义）。语出自英国剧作家 John Marston (1575?–1634) 的 *Antonio's Revenge,* Prologue: "who winks and shuts his apprehension up".

164. consisted in: 主要在于。

165. to set their seals to: 原意盖印认可，此处意为视为定论。

166. sanctions: 奖惩，此处指惩罚。

167. verbal criticism: 对文字细节的评论。

168. judicial astrology: 占星学。

169. the art of making gold: 古代的炼金术。

170. Laud, William (1573–1645): 英国坎特伯雷大主教。

171. Whitgift, John (1530?–1604): 同上。

172. Bishop Bull, George Bull (1634–1710): 英国圣大卫教堂主教。

173. Bishop Waterland, Daniel Waterland (1683–1740): 英国神学家。

174. Prideaux, Humphrey (1648–1724): 英国东方学家，著有 *Connection of the Old and New Testaments in the History of the Jews*,（《新旧约在犹太历史方面的关系》，1716—18），简称 *Connections.*

175. Beausobre, Isaac de (1659–1738): 法国新教神学家。

176. Calmet, Augustin (1672–1757): 法国神学家。

177. St. Augustine (Aurelius Augustinus) (354–430): 基督教初期哲学家和传道者。

178. Puffendorf (Pufendorf), Samuel von (1632–1694): 德国法学家，政论家，历史学家。

179. Vattel, Emerich de (1714–1767): 瑞士政论家。

180. literal: 从具体文字出发，此处意为比较脚踏实地。

181. Scaliger, Joseph Justus (1540–1609): 法国新教神学家。

182. Cardan, Jerome (1501–1576): 意大利医生，数学家，哲学家，星象学家。

183. Scioppius (Schoppe), Kaspar (1576–1649): 德国论辩家。

184. folio: 对开本。

185. quarto: 四开本。

186. "gone to the vault of all the Capulets": 见莎剧《罗密欧与朱丽叶》: Thou shalt be borne to that same ancient vault where all the kindred of the Capulets lie.（*Romeo and Juliet* IV. i. 111–112）意为那些学者所写的无数大书都已尘封土埋，为世遗忘。

187. differing with them: 与他们见解不一。

188. men of the world: 通世故的人。

189. spinning cobweb distinctions: 探求细微末节的差别。

190. judge of: = judge.

191. by rule: 按定规。

192. texture: 原意为细部的构造，此处意为质地。

193. dramatic morality: 戏剧中所表现的道德准则。

35 GEORGE GORDON BYRON
1788–1824

1. [The Isles of Greece]
(from *Don Juan, Canto III)*

王佐良　选注

2. [Haidée's Death]
(from *Don Juan, Canto IV)*

徐　序　选注

1. [THE ISLES OF GREECE]

1

The isles of Greece, the isles of Greece!
Where burning Sappho[1] loved and sung,[2]
Where grew the arts of war and peace,[3]
Where Delos rose, and Phœbus[4] sprung[5]!
Eternal summer gilds them yet,
But all, except their sun, is set.

2

The Scian[6] and the Teian muse,[7]
The hero's harp,[8] the lover's lute,[9]
Have found the fame your shores refuse;[10]
Their place of birth alone is mute
To sounds which echo further west

Than your sires'[11] 'Islands of the Blest.'[12]

3

The mountains look on Marathon[13] —
And Marathon looks on the sea;
And musing there an hour alone,
I dream'd that Greece might still be free;
For standing on the Persians' grave,
I could not deem myself a slave.

4

A king sate on the rocky brow[14]
Which looks o'er sea-born Salamis;[15]
And ships, by thousands, lay below,
And men in nations;[16] — all were his!
He counted them at break of day —
And when the sun set where were they?[17]

5

And where are they? and where art thou,
My country?[18] On thy voiceless shore
The heroic lay[19] is tuneless now —
The heroic bosom beats no more!
And must thy lyre, so long divine,
Degenerate into hands like mine?[20]

6

'Tis something, in the dearth of fame,[21]
Though link'd among a fetter'd race,[22]
To feel at least a patriot's shame,
Even as I sing, suffuse my face;
For what is left the poet here?
For Greeks a blush — for Greece a tear.

7

Must *we* but weep o'er days more blest?
Must *we* but blush?[23] — Our fathers bled.
Earth! render back from out thy breast
A remnant of our Spartan dead![24]
Of the three hundred grant but three,
To make a new Thermopylæ!

8

What, silent still? and silent all?
Ah! no; — the voices of the dead
Sound like a distant torrent's fall,
And answer, 'Let one living head,
But one arise, — we come, we come! '[25]
''Tis but the living who are dumb.

9

In vain — in vain: strike other chords;
Fill high the cup with Samian wine![26, 27]
Leave battles to the Turkish hordes,
And shed the blood of Scio's vine![28]
Hark! rising to the ignoble call[29] —
How answers each bold Bacchanal![30]

10

You have the Pyrrhic[31] dance as yet;
Where is the Pyrrhic phalanx[32] gone?
Of two such lessons, why forget
The nobler and the manlier one?
You have the letters Cadmus[33] gave —
Think ye he meant them for a slave?

11

Fill high the bowl with Samian wine!
    We will not think of themes like these!
It made Anacreon's song divine:[34]
    He served — but served Polycrates[35] —
A tyrant;[36] but our masters then
Were still, at least, our countrymen.

12

The tyrant of the Chersonese[37]
    Was freedom's best and bravest friend;
That tyrant was Miltiades![38]
    Oh! that the present hour would lend
Another despot of the kind!
Such chains as his were sure to bind.[39]

13

Fill high the bowl with Samian wine!
    On Suli's rock, and Parga's shore,[40]
Exists the remnant of a line
    Such as the Doric mothers[41] bore;
And there, perhaps, some seed is sown
The Heracleidan[42] blood might own.

14

Trust not for freedom to the Franks[43] —
    They have a king who buys and sells;
In native swords, and native ranks,[44]
    The only hope of courage dwells;
But Turkish force, and Latin fraud,
Would break your shield, however broad.

15

Fill high the bowl with Samian wine!
Our virgins dance beneath the shade—
I see their glorious black eyes shine;
But gazing on each glowing maid,
My own the burning tear-drop laves,[45]
To think such breasts must suckle slaves.

16

Place me on Sunium's marbled steep.[46]
Where nothing, save[47] the waves and I,
May hear our mutual murmurs[48] sweep;
There, swan-like, let me sing and die:[49]
A land of slaves shall ne'er be mine—
Dash down yon[50] cup of Samian wine![51]

—*Don Juan*, Canto III, 1821

2. [HAIDÉE'S DEATH]

26

Juan[1] and Haidée[2] gazed upon each other
With swimming looks[3] of speechless tenderness,[4]
Which mixed all feelings, friend, child, lover, brother,
All that the best can mingle and express
When two pure hearts are poured in one another,
And love too much, and yet cannot love less;
But almost sanctify the sweet excess[5]
By the immortal wish and power to bless.

27

Mixed in each other's arms, and heart in heart,
Why did they not then die?—they had lived too long

Should an hour come to bid them breathe apart;[6]
Years could but bring them cruel things or wrong;[7]
The world was not for them, not the world's art
For beings passionate as Sappho's[8] song;[9]
Love was born *with* them, *in* them, so intense,
It was their very spirit—not a sense.[10]

28

They should have lived together deep in woods,
Unseen as sings the nightingale; they were
Unfit to mix in these thick solitudes[11]
Called social, haunts of Hate, and Vice, and Care:
How lonely every freedom creature broods!
The sweetest songbirds nestle in a pair;
The eagle soars alone; the gull and crow
Flock o'er their carrion,[12] just like men below.

29

Now pillowed cheek to cheek, in loving sleep,
Haidée and Juan their siesta[13] took,
A gentle slumber,[24] but it was not deep,
Forever and anon[15] a something shook
Juan, and shuddering o'er his frame[16] would creep;
And Haidée's sweet lips murmured like a brook
A wordless music, and her face so fair
Stured with her dream, as rose leaves with the air;

30

Or as the stirring of a deep clear stream
Within an Alpine hollow,[17] when the wind
Walks o'er it, was she shaken by the dream,
The mystical usurper of the mind[18]—
O'erpowering[19] us to be whate'er may seem

Cood to the soul which we no more can bind;
Strange state of being! (for 'tis still to be)[20]
Senseless to feel, and with sealed eyes to see.[21]

31

She dreamed of being alone on the seashore,
Chained to a rock;[22] she knew not how, but stir
She could not from the spot, and the loud roar
Grew, and each wave rose roughly, threatening her;
And o'er her upper lip they seemed to pour,[23]
Until she sobbed for breath,[24] and soon they were
Foaming o'er her lone head,[25] so fierce and high —
Each broke to drown her,[26] yet she could not die.

32

Anon — she was released, and then she strayed
O'er the sharp shingles[27] with her bleeding feet,
And stumbled almost every step she made;
And something rolled before her in a sheet,[28]
Which she must still pursue howe'er afraid;
'Twas white and indistinct, nor stopped to meet
Her glance nor grasp,[29] for still she gazed and grasped,
And ran, but it escaped her as she clasped.[30]

33

The dream changed — in a cave she stood, its walls
Were hung with marble icicles; the work
Of ages[31] on its water-fretted halls,
Where waves might wash, and seals[32] might breed and lurk;
Her hair was dripping, and the very balls
Of her black eyes[33] seemed turned to tears, and murk
The sharp rocks looked[34] below each drop they caught,
Which froze to marble as it fell,[35] she thought.

34

And wet, and cold, and lifeless at her feet,
Pale as the foam that frothed on his dead brow,
Which she essayed in vain[36] to clear (how sweet
Were once her cares, how idle[37] seemed they
Lay Juan, nor could aught[38] renew the beat
Of his quenched heart; and the sea dirges low
Rang in her sad ears like a mermaid's song,[39]
And that brief dream appeared a life too long.[40]

35

And gazing on the dead, she thought his face
Faded, or altered into something new —
Like to her father's features, till each trace
More like and like to Lambro's aspect[41] grew —
With all his keen worn look and Grecian grace;[42]
And starting, she awoke, and what to view?
Oh! Powers of Heaven! what dark eye meets she there?
'Tis — 'tis her father's — fixed upon the pair![43]

36

Then shrieking, she arose, and shrieking fell,
With joy and sorrow, hope and fear, to see
Him whom she deemed a habitant where dwell
The ocean-buried,[44] risen from death,[45] to be
Perchance the death of one she loved too well:[46]
Dear as her father had been to Haidée,
It was a moment of that awful kind —
I have seen such — but must not call to min.

37

Up Juan sprung to Haidée's bitter shriek,

And caught her falling,[47] and from off the wall,
Snatched down his saber,[48] in hot haste to wreak,
Vengeance on him who was the cause of all:[49]
Then Lambro, who till now forebore to speak,
Smiled scornfully, and said, "Within my call,
A thousand scimitars await the word;[50]
Put up, young man, put up your silly sword."

38

And Haidée clung around him; "Juan, 'tis —
'Tis Lambro — 'tis my father! Kneel with me —
He will forgive us — yes — it must be — yes.
Oh! dearest father, in this agony
Of pleasure and of pain — even while I kiss
Thy garment's hem with transport,[51] can it be
That doubt should mingle with my filial joy?
Deal with me as thou wilt,[52] but spare this boy.[53]"

39

High and inscrutable the old man stood,
Calm in his voice, and calm within his eye —
Not always signs with him of calmest mood:[54]
He looked upon her, but gave no reply;
Then turned to Juan, in whose cheek the blood
Oft came and went,[55] as there resolved to die;
In arms, at least, he stood, in act to spring[56]
On the first foe whom Lambro's call might bring.

40

"Young man, your sword"; so Lambro once more said:
Juan replied, "Not while this arm is free."
The old man's cheek grew pale, but not with dread,
And drawing from his belt a pistol, he

Replied, "Your blood be then on your own head."[57]
Then looked close at the flint,[58] as if to see
'Twas fresh — for he had lately used the lock[59] —
And next proceeded quietly to cock.[60]

41

It has a strange quick jar upon the ear,
That cocking of a pistol, when you know
A moment more will bring the sight to bear
Upon your person,[61] twelve yards off, or so;
A gentlemanly distance,[62] not too near,
If you have got a former friend for foe;
But after being fired at once or twice,
The ear becomes more Irish, and less nice.[63]

42

Lambro presented,[64] and one instant more
Had stopped this Canto, and Don Juan's breath,[65]
When Haidée threw herself her boy before;
Stern as her sire:[66] "On me," she cried, "let death
Descend — the fault is mine; this fatal shore
He found[67] — but sought not. I have pledged my faith;
I love him — I will die with him: I knew
Your nature's firmness — know your daughter's too."[68]

43

A minute past, and she had been all tears,
And tenderness, and infancy[69]; but now
She stood as one who championed human fears —
Pale, statue-like, and stern, she wooed the blow;[70]
And tall beyond her sex, and their compeers,[71]
She drew up to her height, as if to show
A fairer mark;[72] and with a fixed eye scanned

Her father's face — but never stopped his hand.[73]

44

He gazed on her, and she on him: 'twas strange
How like they looked! the expression was the same;
Serenely savage, with a little change
In the large dark eye's mutual darted flame;[74]
For she, too, was as one who could avenge,
If cause should be[75] — a lioness, though tame;
Her father's blood before her father's face
Boiled up, and proved her truly of his race.

45

I said they were alike, their features and
Their stature differing but in sex and years;
Even to the delicacy of their hand
There was resemblance, such as true blood wears;[76]
And now to see them, thus divided, stand
In fixed ferocity, when joyous tears,
And sweet sensations, should have welcomed both,[27]
Show what the passions are in their full growth.[78]

46

The father paused a moment, then withdrew
His weapon, and replaced it; but stood still,
And looking on her, as to look her through,
"Not *I*," he said, "have sought this stranger's ill,[79]
Not *I* have made this desolation: few
Would bear such outrage, and forbear to kill;
But I must do my duty — how thou hast
Done thine, the present vouches for the past.[80]

47

"Let him disarm; or, by my father's head,[81]
His own shall roll before you like a ball!"
He raised his whistle as the word he said,
And blew; another answered to the call,
And rushing in disorderly, though led,
And armed from boot to turban,[82] one and all,
Some twenty of his train came, rank on rank;
He gave the word, "Arrest or slay the Frank."[83]

48

Then, with a sudden movement, he withdrew
His daughter; while compressed within his clasp,
'Twixt her and Juan[84] interposed the crew;
In vain she struggled in her father's grasp —
His arms were like a serpent's coil: then flew
Upon their prey, as darts an angry asp,
The file of pirates; save the foremost,[85] who
Had fallen, with his right shoulder half cut through.

49

The second had his cheek laid open; but
The third, a wary, cool old sworder,[86] took
The blows upon his cutlass, and then put
His own well in;[87] so well, ere you could look,[88]
His man[89] was floored, and helpless at his foot,
With the blood running like a little brook
From two smart saber gashes, deep and red —
One on the arm, the other on the head.

50

And then they bound him where he fell, and bore

Juan from the apartment: with a sign
Old Lambro bade them take him to the shore,
Where lay some ships which were to sail at nine.
They laid him in a boat, and plied the oar
Until they reached some galliots,[90] placed in line;
On board of one of these, and under hatches,[91]
They stowed him, with strict orders to the watches.[92]

51[93]

The world is full of strange vicissitudes,
And here was one exceedingly unpleasant:
A gentleman so rich in the world's goods,
Handsome and young, enjoying all the present,
Just at the very time when he least broods
On such a thing is suddenly to sea sent,[94]
Wounded and chained, so that he cannot move,
And all because a lady fell in love.

* * *[95]

56

Afric[96] is all the sun's, and as her earth
Her human clay is kindled;[97] full of power
For good or evil, burning from its birth,
The Moorish blood partakes the planet's hour,[98]
And like the soil beneath it will bring forth:
Beauty and love were Haidée's mother's dower;
But her large dark eye showed deep Passion's force,
Though sleeping like a lion near a source.

57

Her daughter, tempered with a milder ray,[99]
Like summer clouds all silvery, smooth, and fair,
Till slowly charged with thunder they display

Terror to earth, and tempest to the air,
Had held till now her soft and milky way;[100]
But overwrought with passion and despair,
The fire burst forth from her Numidian veins,[101]
Even as the simoom[102] sweeps the blasted plains.

58

The last sight which she saw was Juan's gore,
And he himself o'ermastered[103] and cut down;
His blood was running on the very floor
Where late he trod, her beautiful, her own;
Thus much she viewed an instant and no more[104] —
Her struggles ceased with one convulsive groan;
On her sire's arm, which until now scarce held
Her writhing, fell she like a cedar felled.

59

A vein had burst,[105] and her sweet lips' pure dyes
Were dabbled with the deep blood which ran o'er;
And her head drooped, as when the lily lies
O'ercharged with rain: her summoned handmaids bore
Their lady to her couch with gushing eyes;[106]
Of herbs and cordials they produced their store,[107]
But she defied all means they could employ,
Like one life could not hold, nor death destroy.[108]

60

Days lay she in that state unchanged, though chill —
With nothing livid,[109] still her lips were red;
She had no pulse, but death seemed absent still;
No hideous sign proclaimed her surely dead;
Corruption came not in each mind to kill
All hope; to look upon her sweet face bred

New thoughts of life,[110] for it seemed full of soul—
She had so much, earth could not claim the whole.[111]

61—68[112]

69

Twelve days and nights she withered thus; at last,
Without a groan, or sigh, or glance, to show
A parting pang, the spirit from her passed:
And they who watched her nearest could not know
The very instant,[113] till the change that cast
Her sweet face into shadow, dull and slow,
Glazed o'er her eyes—the beautiful, the black—
Oh! to possess such luster—and then lack![114]

70

She died, but not alone; she held within
A second principle of life,[115] which might
Have dawned a fair and sinless child of sin;[116]
But closed its little being[117] without light,
And went down to the grave unborn, wherein
Blossom and bough lie withered with one blight;
In vain the dews of Heaven descend above
The bleeding flower and blasted fruit of love.[118]

71

Thus lived—thus died she; never more on her
Shall sorrow light, or shame.[119] She was not made
Through years or moons the inner weight to bear,[120]
Which colder hearts endure till they are laid
By age in earth;[121] her days and pleasures were
Brief, but delightful—such as had nor stayed
Long with her destiny; but she sleeps well
By the seashore, whereon she loved to dwell.

72

That isle is now all desolate and bare,
Its dwellings down, its tenants passed away;
None but her own and father's grave is there,
And nothing outward tells of human clay;[122]
Ye could not know where lies a. thing so fair,[123]
No stone is there to show, no tongue to say
What was;[124] no dirge, except the hollow sea's,
Mourns o'er the beauty of the Cyclades.[125]

73

But many a Greek maid in a loving song
Sighs o'er her name; and many an islander
With her sire's story makes the night less long;[126]
Valor was his, and beauty dwelt with her:
If she loved rashly, her life paid for wrong —
A heavy price must all pay who thus err,
In some shape; let none think to fly the danger,[127]
For soon or late Love is his own avenger.

— *Don Juan*, Canto IV, 1821

【作者简介】 George Gordon Byron（拜伦，1788—1824），英国十九世纪大诗人，与雪莱（Shelley）同为浪漫主义诗歌的杰出代表。他虽出身贵族，十岁承继爵位，因此称 Lord Byron（拜伦勋爵），然而反抗暴政，讽刺伪善，初入上议院即为破坏机器的手工业者辩护，后又参加意大利与希腊的民族独立运动，终致在赴希腊参加独立战争的中途，于一小岛上染疾身故。

拜伦诗才广，作品多，除了抒情小诗多首之外，有东方各国纪游长诗 *Childe Harold's Pilgrimage*（《恰尔德·哈罗德游记》，第一、二章，1812；第三章，1816；第四章，1818）；充满异国情调、描绘叛逆性格的故事长诗如 *The Giaour*（《邪教徒》，1813），*The Corsair*（《海盗》，1814），*Lara*（《莱拉》，1814）等；力探人生的苦楚、强调反抗命运的诗剧如 *Manfred*（《曼弗莱德》，1817），*Cain*（《该隐》，1821）等；尖锐的政治讽刺诗如攻击英国王

室及其御用文人的 *The Vision of Judgment*（《审判的幻象》，1822）和讥刺当时欧洲反动君主所组织的“神圣同盟”的 *The Age of Bronze*（《青铜世纪》，1822）。但是拜伦最重要的作品，也是世界文学上公认的杰作，却要数以全欧洲为背景的讽刺史诗 *Don Juan*（《唐璜》，1819—1824）。由于诗人早死，史诗并未完成，然而所完成的十六章、一万六千行已充分显示了作者对于当时欧洲的现实理解之深，揭发之广，而情节动人，言论辛辣，又创造出一种夹叙夹议的新诗体。

拜伦在整个欧洲产生了巨大影响。从意大利到俄罗斯，一时爱好自由、反抗专制的青年诗人无不景仰这位身殉希腊独立事业的义士，但是拜伦在早期作品中渲染 the Byronic hero（“拜伦式的英雄”），也传播了孤傲自高、轻蔑群众等极端个人主义情绪。

【题解与注释】

1. [THE ISLES OF GREECE]

此诗原是 *Don Juan* 第三章（1819 年写成，1821 年出版）中的一支歌曲，但与原诗的情节无关；歌曲本身激昂慷慨，久已单独成篇，为拜伦最著名的作品之一。在我国，它早在清末就有了马君武、苏曼殊、胡适等几个旧体诗译本，以“希腊歌”、“哀希腊”为题，曾经传诵一时。

关于拜伦与希腊的关系，最好借鲁迅先生的话来说明：“裴伦〔按即拜伦〕平时，又至有情愫于希腊，思想所趣，如磁指南。特希腊时自由悉丧，入突厥〔按即土耳其〕版图，受其羁縻，不敢抗拒。诗人惋惜悲愤，往往见于篇章，怀前古之光荣，哀后人之零落，或与斥责，或加激励，思使之攘突厥而复兴，更睹往日耀灿庄严之希腊，如所作《不信者》〔按即《邪教徒》〕暨《堂详》〔按即《堂璜》〕二诗中，其怨愤谯责之切，与希冀之诚，无不历然可征信也。”（《摩罗诗力说》）

对于希腊，西欧的文人学者多有感情，但常从景仰希腊古文明出发；拜伦也爱希腊的古文明，但他始终着眼当代希腊人民在土耳其统治下的苦难，号召他们起来斗争。他在 1809—1811 年间曾亲身到过希腊，停留甚久，当时写 *Childe Harold's Pilgrimage* 就曾这样呼吁：

Greece! change thy lords, thy state is still the same;
Thy glorious day is o'er, but not thy years of shame.

—Canto II, 76

后来，在 1813 年出版的长篇叙事诗 *The Giaour*（即鲁迅提到的《不信者》）里，他又写下这些富于刺激性的诗行：

Say, is not this Thermopylæ?
These waters blue that round you lave,—

Oh servile offspring of the free,
Pronounce what sea, what shore is this?
The gulf, the rock of Salamis!
These scenes, their story not unknown,
Arise, and make again your own;
Snatch from the ashes of your sires
The embers of their former fires;
And he who in the strife expires
Will add to theirs a name of fear
That Tyranny shall quake to hear,
And leave his sons a hope, a fame,
They too will rather die than shame:
For Freedom's battle once begun,
Bequeath'd by bleeding Sire to Son,
Though baffled oft is ever won.
Bear witness, Greece, thy living page!
Attest it many a deathless age!

这里的情绪以及某些细节（例如提到 Thermopylæ, Salamis 的战役）都与《哀希腊》一致，更加证明拜伦对于希腊争自由的斗争关注已久，后来终于离开意大利去参加希腊独立军，不仅出力出钱，而且尽心调停希腊内部派别之争，促成他们一致对外，这些都不是突然的冲动，而是有长远思想基础的革命义举。

《哀希腊》一诗集中地表现了这种思想信念。这里，拜伦以一个希腊诗人的名义发言（因此诗中有 My country, our countrymen 等字样），怀古只是为了讽今，而讽今又只是为了唤起斗争。学生初读本诗时，常苦典故与专用名词过多；其实中外诗人中颇多喜欢用典的人，用得恰当，典故与地名之类能够使诗行更加紧凑，或更加深远，古今并存，也增加历史的魅力，弥尔顿还曾利用地名造成意境与声韵上的特别效果；而拜伦在本诗，所用典故（如荷马，莎弗，古希腊的方阵）都是英国人熟悉的，所用地名（如 Marathon, Thermopylæ, Salamis）也是名垂欧洲史册的，并无生僻之处，他利用它们只是为了用具体的人和事来唤起许多联想，使读者痛感过去如此光华灿烂的希腊现在竟沦为奴隶之邦，来使他们深思，使他们奋起。值得注意的是，他利用过去著名战役的典故，特别强调希腊人民必须进行武装斗争。他所作的对比不仅鲜明、强烈，而且手法敏捷：

For standing on the Persians' grave,
I could not deem myself a slave.

Of the three hundred grant but three,
To make a new Thermopylæ!

以上是两行之间产生对比，还有一行之内，就并陈两种心情，两个世界：

For Greeks a blush — for Greece a tear.

Must *we* but blush? — Our fathers bled.

To think such breasts must suckle slaves

这里对照分明，联结紧密，给人以当头棒喝，写法有如拜伦本人所服膺的蒲伯（Pope），用了这样一些对比，又用了一系列的挑战性的问题——二者结合起来，就是用了“激将法”——他勉励希腊人民团结一致，起来驱逐土耳其的统治者。同时，诗人又在不少地方透露出自己的柔情和忧郁，欲言又止。音韵上也是激越之中含有沉吟，使诗篇有些变化，增加深度。由于这一切，本诗获得了一种情感和意境上的戏剧性。拜伦诗才长处之一就是能将抒情诗写得戏剧化；在《哀希腊》里，他将自己的这一长处表现得特别动人。

标题　非原有，系后人取诗之第一行另加。

1. Sappho [ˈsæfou]:（莎弗，公元前七世纪），古希腊杰出的女抒情诗人，其作品特点之一是感情十分强烈，故拜伦称之为 burning（“燃烧着热情的”）。

2. sung: sang.

3. arts of war and peace: 文治武功；arts 指本领。

4. Delos [ˈdiːlɔs]: 爱琴海中岛名；**Phœbus** [ˈfiːbəs]: 即 Phœbus Apollo，希腊神话中诗歌与音乐之神，相传生在 Delos 岛。

5. sprung: sprang.

6. The Scian [saiən] **muse:** 指史诗《伊利亚特》（*Iliad*）与《奥德赛》（*Odyssey*）的作者荷马（Homer）；形容词 Scian 从名词 Scio 派生，Scio 即古 Chios，相传为荷马出生地；muse，诗神，通译“缪斯”。

7. The Teian [tiːən] **muse:** 指古希腊抒情诗人阿那克里昂（Anacreon [əˈnækrĭən]，公元前六世纪）；Teian 从 Teos 派生，Teos 为 Anacreon 出生地。

8. The hero's harp: 亦指荷马，由于荷马写的是英雄史诗，所以用大型乐器 harp（竖琴）来代表。

9. the lover's lute: 指阿那克里昂，由于他写的是爱情诗，所以用体型较小、声调优美的 lute（琵琶）来代表。

苏曼殊译此行云：“壮士弹坎侯，静女揄鸣筝。”

10. the fame your shores refuse: 意为他们已到处有名，唯独他们的故土希腊忘了他们的荣誉。

11. sires': 祖先的。

12. 'Islands of the Blest': 拜伦自注：古希腊诗人以此名称现在的 Cape de Verd islands or the Canaries；此行意为古希腊诗人现已誉满天下，早已超过他们同时人所知的地区范围；**blest** = blessed.

13. Marathon [ˈmærəθən]: 马拉松，地名，在雅典东北。公元前 490 年波斯大军入侵希腊，但进至 Marathon 时为雅典人击败，故下文（第 17 行）有 the Persians'grave 一语。

14. A king: 指波斯王 Xerxes [ˈzəːksiːz]（公元前 519？—465），他曾在公元前 480 年 9 月 29 日坐在山上俯视 Salamis 岛旁的海战，本以为强大的波斯舰队必胜，不料败于英勇的希腊海军之手，一日之间，灰飞烟灭，受歼殆尽；**sate:** = sat; **rocky brow:** edge of a cliff; 实际上 Xerxes 是坐在 Aegaleos 山上。

15. Salamis ['sæləmis]: 岛名，在雅典以西，上述公元前 480 年著名海战发生的地点。

16. men in nations: 当时 Xerxes 的大军中有被他征服、驱使的亚非各国队伍，故云。

17. And when the sun set where were they?: 从第 19 行到此行，都是关于 Salamis 战役，写得十分戏剧化。

拜伦自注此行时，引了下列诗行：

Deep were the groans of Xerxes, when he saw
This havoc; for his seat, a lofty mound
Commanding the wide sea, o'erlook'd the hosts.
With rueful cries he rent his royal robes,
And through his troops embattled on the shore
Gave signal of retreat; then started wild
And fled disorder'd.

—Aeschylus

按这是古希腊三大悲剧诗人之一的埃斯库罗斯（公元前 525—456）所作剧本《波斯人》中一段的英译，描写波斯王惊惶失措的情形。

埃斯库罗斯曾亲身参加 Salamis 的海战。

18. And where are they? and where are thou, My country?: 与上文接得紧密，而时间忽然由古到今（are 代替了 were），题目亦由古时波斯的败北转到今天希腊的受奴役。

19. lay: poem or song.

20. And must thy lyre, so long divine, Degenerate into hands like mine?: 古希腊出过多少高明的诗人，难道现在竟沦落到要由我这样不成材的人来歌咏她么？"吁嗟乎，欲作神圣希腊歌，才薄其奈希腊何！"（马君武译）lyre，七弦琴，古希腊人用以和诗的乐器，这里代表诗歌。

21. in the dearth of fame: 在这个耻辱的时候；dearth，缺少。

22. link'd among a fetter'd race: 被锁在一个受奴役的民族之内。

23. Must *we* but blush? — Our fathers bled: 此行对照鲜明：今天我们羞辱难堪，昔日祖先则光荣流血；blush 与 bled 两词双声（都以 bl- 起音），增加了这个对照的效果。

24. Spartan dead: 指公元前 480 年由斯巴达王 Leonidas [li(:)'ɔnidæs] 率领在 Thermopylæ [θə:'mɔpili:] 地方力拒波斯入侵大军的斯巴达三百勇士。Thermopylæ 是通往希腊东部的关隘，三百勇士以寡敌众，在该处坚守三日，虽后路断绝，仍血战不屈，终于全体牺牲，但因此为希腊军赢得了时间。

诗人在此缅怀英烈，呼吁希腊人奋起复国，说：那三百壮士只要给我三个，就可以再来一次壮烈的 Thermopylaæ 战役！

25. Let one living head, But one arise,—we come, we come!: 只要有一个活人（one living head）起来，我们（死者）立即行动！

这里诗人紧接上文，以牺牲了的斯巴达勇士的名义发言，表明今天活着的希腊人是如何懦怯，以此刺激他们起来斗争。

26. Samian [ˈseimiən] **wine:** Samos 岛上所产的酒。Samos 是希腊群岛中较大的一个。

27. Fill high the cup with Samian wine! 此行在本诗重复几次，因此对于 Samian wine 的涵义值得研究。Samian 词从 Samos. Samos 为爱琴海上一大岛名，其地盛产酿酒的葡萄，故诗人云 Samian wine. 这是理由之一，但可能尚有深意在焉。希腊人在公元前 494 年曾与波斯人在 Lade 岛旁进行海战，结果大败，原因之一是希腊联军内部不和，Samos 与 Lesbos 两岛派来的水师临阵叛变。拜伦不断重复 Samian 一词，可能是为了刺激当时的希腊人，意为他们如不全力反抗土耳其异族统治，则其可耻就象古时 Samos 岛人的叛变。这样，最后一行 Dash down yon cup of Samian wine 的用意也就更为深刻，即劝告希腊人不仅要摈弃逸乐，而且要断绝叛乱，如此同心协力，才有胜利之可言。

28. Leave battles to the Turkish hordes, And shed the blood of Scio's vine!: 这两行意为：打仗让土耳其人去管吧，我们且饮酒作乐！

诗人意存讽刺，当时希腊正处于土耳其“蛮人”（hordes）的奴役之下，但是希腊人不去战场流血，而只饮希腊葡萄（vine）之血，何等羞耻！

29. the ignoble call: 指请大家饮酒的号召，不是号召去作战，而是号召去作乐，故曰 ignoble.

30. Bacchanal [ˈbækənæl]**:** 酗酒之徒；bold 是讽刺之词。

31. Pyrrhic [ˈpirik] **dance:** 古希腊流传下来的战舞，原来舞者穿盔甲。

32. Pyrrhic phalanx: 步兵的方阵，相传希腊西北部 Epirus 城邦的君主 Pyrrhus 曾在公元前三世纪用这种方阵击败罗马军队。

33. Cadmus [ˈkædməs]**:** 古希腊传说中的人物，大约生在公元前十四世纪，据说他曾从腓尼基人学得字母，传入希腊；**letters，**字母，即文字。

34. It made Anacreon's song divine: it 指 Samian wine；阿那克里昂歌颂醇酒和爱情，其诗清新优美，故曰 divine（“此曲只应天上有”）。

35. He served—but served Polycrates: 阿那克里昂在波斯入侵时，不愿为奴，往依 Samos 岛的统治者 Polycrates [pɔˈlikrətiːz].

36. a tyrant: 霸主，与今日此词之作“暴君”解略有不同；Polycrates 在公元前六世纪之初独霸 Samos 岛，建立强大的海军，远交近攻，与波斯抗衡，又礼贤下士，奖励文艺，有一时盛名，后（公元前 523 年左右）中波斯官吏之计，被执处死。

37. the Chersonese [ˈkəːsəniːs]**:** 地名，即今之 Gallipoli，在 Dardanelles 海峡北边。

38. Miltiades [milˈtaiədiːz]**:** 上文所述马拉松之役中希腊方面的统帅之一，其名与马拉松同垂不朽。

39. Such chains as his were sure to bind: 意为：如果 Miltiades 复生，他那样有为的领袖一定能使希腊人团结起来；此处用 chains 系针对上文 Miltiades. 是一 tyrant 而言，意为他一方面固系独裁者，要压迫我们，另一方面又是将才，会率领我们团结起来对外作战，一如马拉松当年。“束民如连锁，岂串民崩离。”（苏曼殊译）

40. Suli's rock, Parga's shore: 都在西 Epirus，即今日阿尔巴尼亚南部；Suli [ˈsuːli]，区域名；Parga [ˈpɑːgɑː]，其中一城名。早在 *Childe Harold's Pilgrimage* (Canto II, 42)，拜伦就提到过这个地区给他的深刻印象：Morn dawns: and with it stern Albania's hills, Dark Suli's rocks ... 如今他写此诗，这个地区的居民正在英勇袭击土耳其占领军，所以他认为爱好自由的古希腊人的真正的后代（a line）存在那里。

41. Doric mothers: 指斯巴达勇士的母亲们，相传她们教子忠勇卫国：“凯旋执盾而归，或战死卧盾以还！”Dorians 是希腊地区最早的居民的一族，后来进入 Eurotas 河谷，改称 Lacedaemonians，建立了 Sparta 城。

42. The Heracleidan [ˌherəˈklaidən] **blood:** 也指古希腊人的血统；Heracleidan 词从 Heraclidae，即传说中大力神 Hercules 之后；**own，**承认。

43. Franks: 东地中海一带人民对西欧人的统称，下文（第 83 行）Latin fraud 亦泛指西欧人的欺诈，并非只指法国人或拉丁族人。

这一节诗是拜伦对希腊人的劝告，要他们自力斗争，而不可指望西欧的外交援助。拜伦一贯有此思想，早在 1810 年左右写的 *Childe Harold's Pilgrimage* 里，他就指出：

> Hereditary bondsmen! know ye not
> Who would be free themselves must strike the blow?
> By their right arms the conquest must be wrought?
> Will Gaul or Muscovite redress ye? no!
> True, they may lay your proud despoilers low,
> But not for you will Freedom's altars flame.
>
> —Canto II, 76

这里的 Gaul 与 Franks 同指西欧人。

44. native ranks: 当地（希腊）的队伍；“可托唯有希腊军，可托唯有希腊刀。”（马君武译）

45. My own the burning tear-drop laves: 热泪充满（洗涤着）我自己的眼睛；laves. washes.

46. Sunium's marbled steep: 指雅典保护神 Athena 的庙，建在 Sunium [ˈsuːniəm]，即今之 Cape Colonni，在雅典东南、Attica 半岛的最南端。

47. save: except.

48. our mutual murmurs: 指大海的潮声与诗人的歌声，“独有海中潮，伴我声悲嘶。”（苏曼殊译）

49. There, swan-like, let me sing and die: 英国有一种传说，天鹅将死时唱歌；还有人将诗人比作天鹅（例如 the Swan of Avon = Shakespeare, the Mantuan Swan = Virgil）。

拜伦此行，在激越之中，又微露忧郁，这是浪漫诗人常有的情调。

50. yon: yonder.

51. Dash down yon cup of Samian wine!: 掷碎那个装Samos酒的杯子！

2. [HAIDÉE'S DEATH]

《唐璜》在拜伦作品中占有特殊重要的地位，前已言及。这里我们选了第四章的一个比较完整的部分，内容集中于海黛之死。

前三章的故事情节大致如下：一个叫唐璜的西班牙青年贵族，由于被一个名叫朱丽亚的少妇爱上了，惹得她的高龄丈夫大举问罪，为此唐璜离开了家乡去航海远行，不料船只在海上遇险，最后只剩下唐璜一个人，幸亏他会游泳，游到了希腊一个小岛。在那里他被一个少女搭救，这少女是海盗头子兰勃洛的独生女儿海黛。她把唐璜放在洞中，让他好生养息，后来两人发生爱情，在那美丽的小岛上过着幸福生活。欲知下文如何，请看所选段落。

26节　**1. Juan:** Don Juan，人名，唐璜。

2. Haidée: 人名，海黛。

3. swimming looks: 荡漾的目光。

4. speechless tenderness: 无言的温柔。

5. sanctify the sweet excess: 使得过分的甜蜜也变成神圣的了。

27节　**6. they had lived too long Should an hour come to bid them breathe apart:** 意为不如在他们快乐时就死去，如果再活下去，则难保不会有分离之时。

7. Years could but bring them cruel things or wrong: 未来的岁月只可能带来残酷和灾难；but, only。

8. Sappho: 古希腊女诗人，所写抒情诗以热情著。参见第三章 The Isles of Greece 注。

9. beings passionate as Sappho's song: 象莎弗诗中所写的那样热情的人；beings：人。

10. very spirit—not a sense: 不是一种感觉，而是整个的精神。

28节　**11. these thick solitudes:** 这繁华的孤独，指社会。

12. the gull and crow Flock o'er their carrion: 海鸥和乌鸦才喜欢成群结队地围着腐尸而飞。结合前几行，意为高傲的自由人喜欢离群独处，所以唐璜、海黛也应该孤处深林之中。

29节　**13. siesta:** 午睡。

14. gentle slumber: 微睡。

15. Forever and anon: 不时地。

16. his frame: his body。

30节　**17. an Alpine hollow:** 阿尔卑斯山谷。

18. The mystical usurper of the mind: 头脑里的神秘的篡位者，指梦。

19. O'erpowering: overpowering，压制，制服。

20. 'tis still to be: 仍然是一种生存，仍然有生命。

21. Senseless to feel, and with sealed eyes to see: 此处诗人故意用一些互相

矛盾的说法（修辞格称为 oxymoron），意为似乎无知觉，实际仍有感觉；似乎闭了眼，但仍能看得见。

31 节　**22. Chained to a rock:** 被拴在岩石上；**stir she could not,** she could not stir，她动弹不得。

23. o'er her upper lip they seemed to pour: they (waves) seemed to pour over her upper lip：海浪好象直扑她的嘴唇。

24. sobbed for breath: 吸不上气而抽泣。

25. Foaming o'er her lone head:（海浪）朝她孤单单的头上泼来。

26. Each broke to drown her: 每一个浪头打在她身上，都把她淹没了。

32 节　**27. sharp shingles:** 尖的卵石。

28. something rolled before her in a sheet: 有一个披着白床单的东西在她的前面滚动。

29. nor stopped to meet Her glance nor grasp: 一直不停，因此她既看不清楚，也抓不住。

30. it escaped her as she clasped: 刚抓住它，它又滑脱了。

33 节　**31. the work Of ages:** 多年的水滴所形成的。

32. seals: 海豹。

33. the very balls Of her black eyes: 她的黑眼珠。

34. murk The sharp rocks looked: 尖石岩看起来阴沉沉的。

35. froze to marble as it fell: 眼泪一落下就凝成云石。

34 节　**36. essayed in vain:** 想做也徒劳，这儿是指海黛想给唐璜擦干眉头上的海水的泡沫。

37. idle: 无用的，**low idle seemed they now,** they 是指 cares，她过去那样快乐地给予唐璜的照顾现在似乎是多余的了。

38. aught: 任何东西。

39. mermaid's song:（传说中的）美人鱼的歌声。

40. And that brief dream appeared a life too long: 这短短一梦比一生还长。

35 节　**41. Lambro' s aspect:** 兰勃洛的脸，兰勃洛是海盗头子，海黛之父。

42. Grecian grace: 希腊人的优雅。

43. fixed upon the pair: 紧盯着这一对男女，pair 指海黛和唐璜两个人。

36 节　**44. whom she deemed a habitant where dwell The ocean-buried:** 她认为她的父亲已葬身在海底了。

45. risen from death: 回生了。

46. to be Perchance the death of one she loved too well: 也许来杀死她最爱的人；perchance, perhaps。

37 节　**47. caught her falling:** 接住她，使她不致跌倒。

48. saber: sabre，马刀，长剑。in hot haste，火急地。

49. on him who was the cause of all: 对于这个造成这一切的人（进行惩罚）。

50. A thousand scimitars await the word: 千把短刀等待着我一句话，我一叫

就有成千的武士来抓你。

38 节　**51. with transport: with happiness:** 怀着狂喜。

52. Deal with me as thou wilt: deal with me as you will：随便您怎样处置我。

53. spare this boy: 饶了这个青年的命；boy 指唐璜。

39 节　**54. Not always signs with him of calmest mood:** 意为他表面冷静，而内心正是最不冷静。

55. in whose cheek the blood Oft came and went: 唐璜的脸色一时通红，一时苍白；Oft, often。

56. In arms, at least, he stood, in act to spring: 他仗剑站着，准备立即扑向（任何敢于动手的人）。

40 节　**57. Your blood be then on your own head:** 那末你送命就别怪旁人，意为你就要对自己的死亡负责。

58. flint: 打火石（当时手枪要靠打火石发火）。

59. lock: flintlock，旧式手枪上的燧发机。

60. cock: 扳起（枪枝）的击铁，准备击发。

41 节　**61. bring the sight to bear Upon your person:** 向着你瞄准；sight，瞄准器。

62. A gentlemanly distance: i. e. dueling distance，西方绅士们决斗时，双方相距十二码，故云。

63. more Irish, and less nice: 诗人指爱尔兰青年性暴烈，易冲动，经常决斗，因此对于枪声也就不在乎了。

42 节　**64. presented:**（举枪）瞄准。

65. one instant more Had stopped this Canto, and Don Juan's breath: 一瞬间就要结束了这一章和唐璜的生命。

66. Stern as her sire: stern as her father。

67. this fatal shore He found: but sought not，这个要命的海岸他是碰上的，不是有意来找的。

68. know your daughter's too: know your daughter's nature's firmness too，要知道你女儿的性格也象你一样坚韧的。

43 节　**69. infancy:** 幼年期，此处指孩子气。

70. wooed the blow: 自招打击，挺身愿代唐璜死。

71. tall beyond her sex, and their compeers: i. e. she was the match in height of Lambro and Juan，她高过一般女子和男子，即她可以同兰勃洛和唐璜比高。

72. A fairer mark: 一个更加美丽的靶子。

73. never stopped his hand: 不阻拦她父亲的（拿着枪的）手。

44 节　**74. Serenely savage, with a little change In the large dark eye's mutual darted flame:** 暴怒而不形于色，只是大而黑的眼睛里略有变化，从中射出彼此对视的火焰。

75. If cause should be: 只要有理由。

45 节　**76. such as true blood wears:** 就如亲血统所常表现的那样。

77. when joyous tears, And sweet sensations, should have welcomed both: 他们原该流着欢乐的眼泪和怀着甜蜜的感情彼此欢迎。

78. Show what the passions are in their full growth: 表现出他们的情感处于高潮，何等激昂。

46 节 79. Not I, ... have sought this stranger's ill: 我并不故意来找这陌生人的碴。

80. how thou hast Done thine, the present vouches for the past: 至于你是怎样尽了你的本份的，只要看你现在的行为就可以了。

47 节 81. by my father's head: 拿我父亲的头起誓。

82. armed from boot to turban: 全身武装；turban，男用头巾，包头布，当时海盗喜在头上包布。

83. the Frank: 当时西亚、东欧一带人对西欧人的称呼，并非专指法兰西族。

48 节 84. 'Twixt her and Juan: between Haidée and Juan.

85. save the foremost: 除了第一个，即第一个当即被唐璜砍倒。注意此节与下节所写的战斗场面。拜伦的诗笔不仅长于描叙风物和发表议论，而且善于写戏剧性的行动。

49 节 86. a wary, cool old sworder: 一个沉着、冷静的老剑手。

87. put His own well in: thrust his own sword home，即这个老剑手先架住唐璜的来剑，接着顺势狠刺了唐璜几下。

88. ere you could look: 还没等你看清。

89. His man: 指唐璜。

50 节 90. galliots: a small, fast galley, propelled both by oars and sails，旧时地中海的平底小船。

91. under hatches: 被关在船舱内。

92. watches: 值班的看守人。

51 节 93. 这一节是拜伦在发议论，略有一点玩笑口吻。这样，也松弛了刚才描写打斗的紧张空气，使诗篇多点变化。

94. when he least broods On such a thing is suddenly to sea sent: 在他根本没有料到会有这样的事的时候，突然被人送到了海上。

52—55 节 95. 内容涉及旁事，与本处故事无关，故删。

56 节 96. Afric: 非洲

97. Her human clay is kindled:（象非洲的土地一样）非洲的人也是燃烧的，即热血沸腾，易于激动的；human clay，人体，指人。

98. The Moorish blood partakes the planet's hour: 摩尔人的血分享着行星的时辰，意为非洲炽热，因此北非的摩尔人也是性情暴烈。

57 节 99. tempered with a milder ray: 受着比较和煦的阳光的陶冶，意为海黛与她的非洲母亲不同，生长在希腊，所以性情略为平和。

100. Had held till now her soft and milky way: 她一直到现在都是温柔而平和的。

101. her Numidian veins: 她那流着非洲的血的血管；Numidian, North African，北非的。

102. simoom: a violent, hot, dust-laden desert wind，西蒙风（非洲和阿拉伯沙漠地带的干热风）。

58 节　103. o'ermastered: overmastered，被制服了。

104. Thus much she viewed an instant and no more: 她在一瞬间看到了这一切，可是接着什么也看不见了。

59 节　105. A vein had burst: 一条血管破裂了。拜伦对此有注云：

"A vein had burst, and her sweet lips' pure dyes." This is no very uncommon effect of the violence of conflicting and different passions. The Doge Francis Foscari, on his deposition in 1457, hearing the bells of St. Mark announce the election of his successor, "mourut subitement d'une hémorragie causée par une veine qui s'éclata dans sa poitrine," (see Sismondi and Daru, vols. i. and ii.) at the age of eighty years, when *"Who would have thought the old man had so much blood in him?"* Before I was sixteen years of age, I was witness to a melancholy instance of the same effect of mixed passions upon a young person, who, however, did not die in consequence, at that time, but fell a victim some years afterwards to a seizure of the same kind, arising from causes intimately connected with agitation of mind.

（这是各种矛盾感情激烈冲突的常见的后果。窦什·弗兰西斯·弗斯加里在1457年被废黜，他听到圣·马可教堂的钟声宣布继任的人选时，立即由于胸中一条血管的爆裂致死，时年八十岁，"谁会想到这个老头儿有这么多血？"（见莎士比亚所作剧本《麦克白》五幕一场）在我还不到十六岁的时候，我见过一个年轻人由于矛盾感情产生同样后果的惨况，不过他并没有立即死亡，而是在此后一些年里一遇到心情激动，立即引起同样的症状。）——此注译文录自查良铮译《唐璜》，人民文学出版社，1980年版，上卷，第323页。

106. gushing eyes: 不断流泪的眼睛。

107. Of herbs and cordials they produced their store: 她们把所备的草药和补品全都拿了出来。

108. Like one life could not hold, nor death destroy: 象一个既不能活又不会死的人。

60 节　109. With nothing livid: 她脸色并不发青。

110. to look upon her sweet face bred New thoughts of life: 看着她的甜脸，使人重新生起她还会活下去的希望。

111. She had so much, earth could not claim the whole: 她的生命太丰富了，大地都不能要求得到她的全部灵魂。

61—68 节 112. 诗人描写了海黛一度苏醒，后又入睡的状态，与故事无密切联系，故删。

69 节　113. could not know The very instant: 不知道她究竟死在何刻。

114. Oh! to possess such luster —and then lack!: 呵，她的眼睛原来是那样明亮，现在却一点光采也没有了！

70 节　115. she held within A second principle of life: 她身子里还另有一个生命，即她已怀孕。

116. a fair and sinless child of sin: 美丽而无罪的罪孽儿（称为 child of sin，是因为按照世俗的看法，未经正式结婚而生的孩子是罪孽儿，但诗人又点出这个孩子其实是无罪的）。

117. its little being: 这胎儿的小小生命。

118. The bleeding flower and blasted fruit of love: 流血的花和凋残的爱情之果，指海黛与其胎儿。注意诗人在此用了一连串 bl-，fl-，fr-，l- 等音，用头韵增强了诗意。

71 节　119. never more on her Shall sorrow light, or shame: 悲哀与羞辱都不会再降临到她身上。

120. the inner weight to bear: 承受得住内心的负担（指痛苦、忧虑之类）。

121. Which colder hearts endure till they are laid By age in earth: 而较冷的人是能够忍受人生困苦的，直到老年入土。

拜伦在这节和下节诗里总结海黛的一生，写得富于浪漫情思，哀感动人。

72 节　122. nothing outward tells of human clay: 地面上没有东西会告你此地曾有过人。

123. lies a thing so fair: 埋着一个如此美的（少女）。

124. no tongue to say What was: 没有人来说曾经发生的事。

125. the beauty of the Cyclades: 希腊群岛的美人，指海黛。

这一节继续上节的哀思，一样富于感染，结句象是长叹息。我国已故诗人查良铮译了《唐璜》全诗，这两节译文如下：

七一

她如此生——如此死了。从此不再有
　　悲伤或羞辱来烦扰她。她的天性
原不象较冷的人能经年累月地
　　忍辱负重，单等老年来给送终；
她的岁月和欢情虽然够短暂，
　　却竭尽她的命运所容许的一生
愉快地度过，——她终于静静地安眠，
在她常常爱去散步的那个海边。

七二

如今那海岛全然零落而荒凉，
　　房屋坍塌了，居住的人都已亡故：
只有她和她父亲的坟墓还在，
　　但也没有一块碑石把他们记述；
谁知哪儿埋下了如此美的少女，

她的往事再也没有人能够说出；
呵，在那儿听不见挽歌，除了海啸
在为那已死的希腊美人哀悼。

73节　**126. With her sire's story makes the night less long:** 讲她父亲的故事消磨长夜。

127. let none think to fly the danger: 任何人也不要希图逃脱这危险。

选段至此中止。以后的故事是唐璜被海盗刺伤后，被运到土耳其拍卖为奴，在那里他又被苏丹的第四位夫人看中了，硬把他打扮成少女，送进土耳其苏丹后宫去当女奴，后来他摆脱了苏丹夫人的威诱，逃了出来，又卷入伊斯迈战役。他参加了俄军，在这次战役中立了功，同时又从哥萨克骑兵的刀下拯救了一个土耳其幼女。战役结束后，唐璜被派带着捷报去彼得堡，受到女皇叶卡捷琳娜的宠爱，后来她又派他出使英国。诗的最后六章详细叙述了唐璜在英国的见闻，诗人也利用这个机会多方揭露和讽刺了英国上层社会的伪善和冷酷。

36 PERCY BYSSHE SHELLEY
1792–1822

1. Ozymandias
2. Song to the Men of England
3. Sonnet: England in 1819
4. Ode to the West Wind
5. A Lament
6. To —

周珏良　选注

1. OZYMANDIAS

I met a traveller from an antique land[1]
Who said: Two vast and trunkless legs of stone[2]
Stand in the desert ... Near them, on the sand,
Half sunk, a shattered visage[3] lies, whose frown,
And wrinkled lip, and sneer of cold command,[4]
Tell that its sculptor well those passions read[5]
Which yet survive, stamped on these lifeless things,
The hand that mocked them, and the heart that fed:[6]
And on the pedestal[7] these words appear:
'My name is Ozymandias, king of kings:[8]
Look on my works, ye Mighty, and despair!'
Nothing beside remains. Round the decay
Of that colossal wreck,[9] boundless and bare
The lone and level sands stretch far away.

2. SONG TO THE MEN OF ENGLAND

I

Men of England, wherefore plough
For the lords who lay ye low[1]?
Wherefore weave with toil and care
The rich robes your tyrants wear?

II

Wherefore feed, and clothe, and save,
From the cradle to the grave,
Those ungrateful drones[2] who would
Drain your sweat — nay, drink your blood?

III

Wherefore, Bees of England,[3] forge
Many a weapon, chain, and scourge,
That these stingless drones[4] may spoil
The forced produce[5] of your toil?

IV

Have ye leisure, comfort, calm,
Shelter, food, love's gentle balm[6]?
Or what is it ye buy so dear
With your pain and with your fear?

V

The seed ye sow, another reaps;
The wealth ye find, another keeps;
The robes ye weave, another wears;
The arms[7] ye forge, another bears.

VI

Sow seed, — but let no tyrant reap;
Find wealth, — let no impostor heap;[8]
Weave robes, — let not the idle wear;
Forge arms, — in your defence to bear.

VII

Shrink to your cellars, holes, and cells;
In halls ye deck another dwells.[9]
Why shake the chains ye wrought? Ye see
The steel ye tempered glance on ye.[10]

VIII

With plough and spade, and hoe and loom,
Trace your grave, and build your tomb,
And weave your winding-sheet, till fair
England be your sepulchre.[11]

3. SONNET: ENGLAND IN 1819

An old, mad, blind, despised, and dying king,[1] —
Princes, the dregs of their dull race,[2] who flow
Through public scorn, — mud from a muddy spring,[3] —
Rulers who neither see, nor feel, nor know,
But leech-like[4] to their fainting country[5] cling,
Till they drop, blind in blood, without a blow,[6] —
A people starved and stabbed[7] in the untilled[8] field, —
An army, which liberticide and prey[9]
Makes as a two-edged sword to all who wield, —
Golden and sanguine laws which tempt and slay;[10]
Religion Christless, Godless — a book sealed;[11]

A Senate,[12] — Time's worst statute unrepealed, —
Are graves,[13] from which a glorious Phantom may
Burst, to illumine our tempestuous day.[14]

4. ODE TO THE WEST WIND

I

O wild West Wind, thou breath of Autumn's being[1],
Thou, from whose unseen presence[2] the leaves dead
Are driven, like ghosts from an enchanter fleeing,

Yellow, and black, and pale, and hectic red,[3]
Pestilence-stricken multitudes:[4] O thou,
Who chariotest[5] to their dark wintry bed

The wingèd seeds,[6] where they lie cold and low,
Each like a corpse within its grave, until
Thine azure sister of the Spring[7] shall blow

Her clarion[8] o'er the dreaming earth, and fill
(Driving sweet buds like flocks to feed in air)[9]
With living hues and odours plain and hill:

Wild Spirit, which art[10] moving everywhere;
Destroyer and preserver; hear, oh, hear![11]

II

Thou on whose stream, mid the steep sky's commotion,[12]
Loose clouds like earth's decaying leaves are shed,
Shook[13] from the tangled boughs of Heaven and Ocean,

Angels of rain and lightning:[14] there are spread

On the blue surface of thine aëry surge,
Like the bright hair uplifed from the head

Of some fierce Maenad, even from the dim verge
Of the horizon to the zenith's height,
The locks of the approaching storm.[15] Thou dirge

Of the dying year,[16] to which this closing night
Will be the dome of a vast sepulchre,
Vaulted with all thy congregated might

Of vapours, from whose solid atmosphere
Black rain, and fire, and hail will burst: oh, hear![17]

III

Thou who didst waken from his summer dreams
The blue Mediterranean, where he[18] lay,
Lulled by the coil of his crystàlline streams,[19]

Beside a pumice isle[20] in Baiae's bay,
And saw in sleep old palaces and towers
Quivering within the wave's intenser day,

All overgrown with azure moss and flowers
So sweet, the sense faints picturing them![21] Thou
For whose path the Atlantic's level powers

Cleave themselves into chasms,[22] while far below
The sea-blooms and the oozy woods which wear
The sapless foliage of the ocean, know

Thy voice, and suddenly grow gray with fear,
And tremble and despoil themselves: oh, hear![23]

IV

If I were a dead leaf thou mightest bear;
If I were a swift cloud to fly with thee;
A wave to pant beneath thy power, and share

The impulse of thy strength, only less free
Than thou, O uncontrollable![24] If even[25]
I were as in my boyhood, and could be

The comrade of thy wanderings over Heaven,[26]
As then,[27] when to outstrip thy skiey speed
Scarce seemed a vision;[28] I would ne'er have striven

As thus with thee in prayer in my sore need.[29]
Oh, lift me as a wave, a leaf, a cloud!
I fall upon the thorns of life! I bleed![30]

A heavy weight of hours has chained and bowed
One too like thee: tameless, and swift, and proud.[31]

V

Make me thy lyre, even as the forest is:[32]
What if my leaves are falling like its own![33]
The tumult of thy mighty harmonies[34]

Will take from both[35] a deep, autumnal tone,
Sweet though in sadness. Be thou, Spirit fierce,
My spirit! Be thou me, impetuous one![36]

Drive my dead thoughts over the universe
Like withered leaves to quicken a new birth![37]
And, by the incantation of this verse,

Scatter, as from an unextinguished hearth
Ashes and sparks, my words among mankind![38]
Be through my lips to unawakened earth

The trumpet of a prophecy! O, Wind,[39]
If Winter comes, can Spring be far behind?

5. A LAMENT

I

O world! O life! O time[1]!
Oa whose last steps[2] I climb,
    Trembling at that where I has stood before;
When will return the glory of your prime[3]?
    No more — Oh, never more!

II

Out of the day and night
A joy has taken flight;
    Fresh spring, and summer, and winter hoar,[4]
Move my faint heart with grief, but with delight
    No more[5] — Oh, never more!

6. TO —

I

One word[1] is too often profaned
    For me to profane[2] it,
One feeling[3] too falsely disdained[4]
    For thee to disdain it;
One hope is too like despair
    For prudence to smother,[5]

And pity from thee more dear
Than that from another.

II

I can give not what men call love,
But wilt thou[6] accept not
The worship the heart lifts above[7]
And the Heavens reject not, —
The desire of the moth for the star,
Of the night for the morrow,
The devotion to something afar[8]
From the sphere of our sorrow?[9]

【作者简介】 Percy Bysshe Shelley（雪莱，1792—1822），英国的浪漫主义诗人。他生于贵族家庭，早年深受卢梭（Jean Jacques Rousseau），潘恩（Thomas Paine）和葛德文（William Godwin）等人的思想影响。在牛津大学就学时，因发表 *The Nccessity of Atheism*（《无神论的必然性》）一文被开除。不久赴爱尔兰参加民族独立运动，后来住在意大利，一直到乘舟海行，在风暴中遇难。

雪莱的诗才是很壮阔的。他既有富于政治思想性的诗，充满对专制暴政的抗议和对自由和理想社会的追求，也有优美的抒情诗，特别是爱情诗，显示了不羁的想象，瑰丽的色彩和动人的音韵，使他成为英国文学史上最有才华的抒情诗人之一。

根据马克思的女儿爱莲诺的记载，马克思对雪莱的评价很高，称他为彻底的革命者，说他将永远属于社会主义的前锋之列。恩格斯在《英国工人阶级状况》一书中曾记载雪莱和拜伦的诗都是英国工人所喜爱的，并称他为天才和先知。这也是革命者和进步人类对他的基本评价。

雪莱的主要作品有 *Queen Mab*（《麦布女王》，1813），*The Revolt of Islam*（《伊斯兰的叛变》，1818），*Prometheus* [prəˈmiːθjuːs] *Unbound*（《解放了的普罗米修斯》，1819），*The Cenci* [ˈtʃentʃi]（《沉西》，1819），*The Mask of Anarchy*（《暴政的化装游行》，1819）以及许多抒情名作如 *Ode to the West Wind*（《西风颂》，1819），*To a Skylark*（《云雀歌》，1820）和这里所选的一些篇章等等。散文作品 *A Defense of Poetry*（《诗辩》，1821）是他的重要文

学理论著作。

【题解与注释】

1. OZYMANDIAS

Ozymandias 是在埃及尼罗河上古都底比斯（Thebes [θi:bz]）的古埃及王拉默西斯第二（Rameses [ˈræmisi:z] II）的陵墓的名字。拉默西斯第二做了六十七年国王（公元前 1292—1225），和埃及周围的许多国家进行了战争，以“武功”著名，曾被当时的史诗歌颂。他进行了巨大的建筑计划，主要是几座庙宇。他自己的陵墓也是有名的古建筑物之一，后来只剩下一座倾倒了的他本人的黑花岗石坐像，完整时大约有五十几尺高。雪莱这首诗中提到的就是这座石像。

本诗是商籁体（sonnet），或称十四行诗体。

1. antique land: 古国，指埃及。

2. trunkless legs of stone: 失去了躯体的石雕人腿。

3. visage: 人面。此字在现代英文口语中已不常用。

4. sneer of cold command: 带有冷酷权威的嘲笑表情。

5. tell that its sculptor well those passions read: those passions 指上文提到的 sneer of cold command 和使雕像中人双眉紧皱（frown 一字就是此意）、嘴唇紧闭（wrinkled lip）的那些激情；read 此处可了解为“揣摩”。

6. Which yet survive, stamped on these lifeless things, /The hand that mocked them, and the heart that fed: which 指上文的 those passions. stamped on these lifeless things 是说这些激情表现在（stamp 一字的本义是打印，这里可以了解为表现）无生命的东西上（指 shattered visage 等）。Survive 的宾语为 the hand 和 the heart. 前者指雕刻家的手，后者指埃及皇帝的心。这里的 mock 一字应作“模仿”解，是个较古的用法。模仿这些激情的雕刻家和孕育（fed）它们的埃及皇帝拉默西斯第二都不复存在，而这些激情尚留人间，暗指世间仍有暴虐、专制、压迫。雪莱的抗暴思想是很明显的。

7. pedestal: 雕像的基座。

8. 第 10 行： 公元前一世纪希腊史家戴阿多勒（Diodorus Siculus）曾记载拉默西斯第二墓上雕像的铭文，英译如下：I am Ozymandias, king of kings; if any one wishes to know what I am and where I lie, let him surpass me in some of my exploits. 雪莱此地基本上用的是原铭文，而有所更动。本诗第 11 行的意思是：不服气，要和我比一下的人们（ye mighty 原义为刚强的人，所以可了解为刚强不服气的人），你们看看我的功绩（原铭文的 exploits 一字和诗中的 works 一字都是此义），也就只好望洋兴叹了吧（despair 一字原义是沮丧，失望，此地是说无法媲美，因而沮丧，亦即望洋兴叹）。此外，也可以把 ye mighty 解释为 the gods，那么第 11 行的意义就是说拉默西斯自炫功绩，认为自己比天上诸神还高了。

9. colossal wreck: 指这个破碎的巨大雕像。

2. *SONG TO THE MEN OF ENGLAND*

雪莱在1819年写了不少针对当时英国政治局势的、有战斗性的诗。特别是在1819年8月16日在Manchester发生的St. Peter's Field的惨案（这个惨案一般称为"Peterloo"）更激起了雪莱的正义的愤怒。那一天约有六万人举行和平集会，提出要求普选权，要求议会每年开会，反对谷物法案（Corn Law）等改革要求。Manchester当局下令命武装骑警向手无寸铁的人群冲击，结果死了十余人，受伤数百人。当时雪莱在意大利，听到消息之后，气愤之下，在九月底写出长篇名诗*The Mask of Anarchy*，其中有号召英国人民起来推翻暴虐统治的有名的几行：

"Rise like lions after slumber
In unvanquishable number.
Shake your chains to earth, like dew。
Which in sleep have fallen on you:
Ye are many, they are few."

此外他还马上写了这首"Song to the Men of England"，急送伦敦，想印成小册子，在失业工人中散发。但是出版商不敢承印，这首诗一直到雪莱死后多时，1839年才发表。

1. lay ye low: 压迫你们。

2. drones: 雄蜂。蜜蜂中的雄蜂是不管采蜜的，这里用来指坐享其成，寄生的统治阶级。

3. Bees of England: 指英国劳动人民。

4. these stingless drones: 指无能的统治阶级。spoil，掠夺。

5. forced produce: 努力得来的成果。

6. love's gentle balm: 爱情的温柔安慰。

7. arms: 武器。

8. heap: 聚敛。

9.（第25—26行）: 这是个条件句，意思是：如果你们畏缩不前，躲在家里，那么别人就要掠夺你们，你们造的房子就由别人来住了。

10.（第27—28行）: 这两行是一问一答。意思是说你们为什么必须挣脱身上你们自己制的枷锁（shake the chains ye wrought）呢？你们不是看见了你们炼出来的钢铁的寒光正在闪烁地照着你们吗？ glance在这里意为闪烁发光，也有威逼的意思。

11.（第29—32行）: 结尾这一段和上面一段相连，大意是说如果不起而反抗，那么你们就只好在压迫剥削下劳动到死了。犁、铲、锄、织机在这里是劳动的象征。诗人说用它们来为自己选墓，筑坟，织裹尸布（winding-sheet），意为劳动到死。sepulchre，墓穴。

3. SONNET: ENGLAND IN 1819

这首诗也是雪莱在 1819 年秋天写的。在诗中他严厉谴责了压迫、剥削人民的英国统治者，表示了对人民的同情。在诗末他并且预言人民革命风暴的即将到来。

1. 第 1 行： 当时英王 George III 年过八旬，双目失明，已经疯了将近十年，由太子摄政。他是被人民所痛恨的，雪莱这一行写的是实况。

2. dregs of their dull race: 他们的愚蠢的种族的渣滓。

3. flow /Through public scorn, —mud from a muddy spring, —: 意思是说这些王公亲贵在全国人民的痛恶（public scorn）之下，还是依然如故地一代一代混了下去，如泥浆之出于浊流。

4. leech-like: 水蛭能吸人血，这些人也吸人民的血。

5. fainting country: 人民被他们弄得奄奄一息。

6. Till they drop, blind in blood, without a blow, —: 水蛭附在人身上吸血，吸得过多了，就自己掉下来。王公贵人吸人民的血，吸多了，也总有一天要垮台。

7. starved and stabbed: 受饥饿、遭屠杀。

8. untilled: 没有耕种的，荒芜了的。

9. 第 8 行： 灭绝自由（liberticide）和掠夺人民（prey）使得军队在它的控制者的手中（to all who wield）成为一把两刃的刀（two-edged sword）. 所以称之为两刃，是因为军队是用来一方面毁灭自由，一方面掠夺人民，有两方面的恶作用。而这两面又是一体的两用，所以动词 make 用的是单数。

10. 第 10 行： 法律的作用只是收买（tempt 在这里应作此解）和屠杀（slay）所以称之为 golden（金黄的）和 sanguine（血色的）。

11. 第 11 行： 在宗教上既不信耶稣（Christless），也不奉上帝（Godless），于是宗教变成不可理解的东西（a sealed book）。

12. Senate: 指议会。这又是个无能机构，连当代最坏的法律也不能废止（unrepealed）. 这里指的是禁止不信奉英国国教的人和天主教徒任公职的法律。

13. are graves: 它的主语是上面提到的 king, princes, people, army, laws, religion, senate 等等。把他们综合起来，称之为 graves，是因为下面雪莱把自由比之为"光荣的幽灵"（glorious Phantom），而在黑暗的现状下（皇帝遭人痛恨，王公亲贵贪得无餍，军队残暴，法律失效，宗教不存，议会无能和人民遭受痛苦等），预伏着人民将来斗争的希望，他们终将起来，犹如死人的灵魂在"最后审判日"（Judgmentday）都要从坟墓里走出来，得到最后的公平。

14. tempestuous day: 人民斗争的风暴的日子。

4. ODE TO THE WEST WIND

如前面所述，雪莱在 1819 年写了不少战斗性的政治诗，这首《西风颂》也是其中之一。但这首诗不仅是一首政治诗，它也是雪莱最好的抒情诗之一，无论思想内容上还是艺术形式上都是如此。如果有一本英诗选，每个诗人只选一首为代表，雪莱的诗就应选这一首。

雪莱自注说这首诗是1819年秋季一天傍晚在意大利佛罗伦萨（Florence）附近Arno河边的树林中遇上雨雹交加的风暴，有感写成。它从自然界的风暴连系到人世间革命斗争的风暴，在1815年神圣同盟结成后，欧洲复辟潮流猖獗时，预言革命风暴必定到来，写出自己沸腾的感情，和有时不免感伤的浪漫情趣，从思想内容，到意象的运用，诗行的格律，成为一个完整体使读者从各方面得到美感，是一首杰出的诗。

这首诗的格律是但丁《神曲》所用的三行诗节（Terze Rima）和莎士比亚的十四行体的混合。每一大段十四行，分为四个三行的诗节，一个双行偶句（couplet），每行都是五步轻重律的（iambic pentameter），韵脚为（aba bcb cdc ded ee）. 在全诗中雪莱使用跨行（run-on line）乃至跨节的诗行很多，既表达了奔放的感情，又适合于不受羁束的狂烈西风的形象，形成内容和形式的统一。至于细节上的声音之美则可供仔细玩味的地方就更多了。

I

这一段写西风的威力和它的作用，第十四行点出破坏者（destroyer）和护持者（preserver），这是贯串全诗的两个主题，也是诗人认为西风具有的两种特性。这一段写西风吹扫落叶（2—5行）是他作为破坏者行事；也写西风把种子深吹入土，等到春暖发芽开花，尽到它护持者的责任（6—12行）。这一整段只是一个句子，在第十四行谓语里的动词hear才出现。

1. thou breath of Autumn's being: 这里把Autumn大写是人格化了的。being = existence, life. 把西风叫做秋的呼吸，也就是说它代表了秋天的肃杀之气，同时秋季也是种子成熟后埋储起来，等到春天发芽的季节，因而使得西风成为护持者。

2. unseen presence: 风是看不见但感觉得到的，所以说在它看不见的“面前”（presence）. 这里把西风吹落叶比做魔师（enchanter）驱鬼，极写西风的强烈，树叶的迅速飘散。

3. hectic red: 如肺病患者面颊那样火红。

4. pestilence-stricken multitudes: multitudes指大堆的枯叶。枯叶被西风很快地吹跑，好象是害怕瘟疫（pestilence-stricken），所以赶忙躲开。

5. chariotest: 现代英语应作chariot. chariot是古代的战车，做为动词是运载的意思。wintry bed，冬日的眠床，指种子冬天埋在地下。lie cold and low睡在冷处，毫不动弹。

6. winged seeds: 种子被风吹起如同长了翅膀。

7. Thine azure sister of the Spring: 意大利所处的阿尔卑斯山以南全年多西风。雪莱这首诗写的是夏末秋初的西风，而等到冬末刮西风时，又是意大利西海岸春季的开始了，所以这里称呼那时的西风做秋季的西风为“春季的姊妹”（azure sister of the Spring）. Azure是天蓝色，因为春季地中海一带天常是蔚蓝的，所以用来形容春风。

8. clarion: 号角。根据基督教《圣经》的记载，到了最后审判的日子，天使将吹起号角，一切死人都将复苏，听候上帝的裁判。这里暗用这个典故，把发芽的种子比做被唤起的亡人，也和第 8 行的 each like a corpse within its grave 呼应。

9. (Driving sweet buds like flocks to feed in air): 这里把春天的蓓蕾比做羊群，把蓓蕾吸收空气比做羊群吃草，也就是把春风比做牧羊人，所以用“赶去”（driving）一字。

10. art: = are 古用法。

11. hear, oh, hear: 这里诗人向西风呼唤，要它听它歌唱，下面同此。

II

这一段用云、雨、冰雹、闪电来衬托描写西风的威力，这些同雪莱的诗才一样是飘忽不羁的东西，诗人一路写来，用中国古典文学批评习用的话说，就是“纯以神运”，所以读时使人沉浸于一片反映自然之美的意象间，得到极大的艺术享受。可是分析起来，有时却不如本书中其他选入的诗人如 A. Marvell 的作品那样具有严格的理性，乃至逻辑性。近代英美文学批评家，颇有以此诟病雪莱的。问题之发生在对于意象（imagery）运用方法的不同。雪莱的是浪漫主义的，而 Marvell 的，以及 John Donne 的则是玄理诗派的（metaphysical），读者读时知道如何区别，如何不同要求，理解起来也就容易了。具体的问题在下面的注释里将较详细讲到。这一段有两句，第一句到 23 行为止，写西风吹云，酝酿着风暴，第二句到段末，写雨雹，闪电的到来。

12. 第 15—17 行： on whose stream，指乱云被西风的气流（stream）带起。mid the steep sky's commotion，在高空的动荡之中。Loose clouds like earth's decaying leaves are shed, /Shook from the tangled boughs of Heaven and Ocean，乱云象腐朽的叶子从天和海的缠结交错的枝桠上（tangled boughs）飞坠下来（shed）. 这里的问题在 tangled boughs of Heaven and Ocean 如何解释。诗里所讲的自然现象是在高空有一个厚而比较稳定的云层；下面则是较小块，被急风所吹动的乱云，雪莱把上面的稳定的云层叫做交错缠结的海和天的枝桠因为它是太阳把海水热成蒸汽，升到天空所形成，又因为把乱云比做落叶，而叶是从枝桠上落下的，所以反过来把乱云的来源，高空的云层，就比做枝桠，因此就有了这一“海和天的枝桠”的意象了。

13. shook: = shaken.

14. angels of rain and lightning: 指上面的 loose clouds，把它们比做散布雨水和雷电的天使。

15. there are spread .../The locks of the approaching storm: 这里面的一个形象是 Maenad ['mi:nad] 意为“疯狂的女人”。她是希腊酒神 Bacchus 的女祭司，举动疯狂（fierce）. 这几行诗里把乱云比做她的被风吹起的头发（hair uplifted）. even = just. even from the dim verge/Of the horizon to the zenith's height，从看不清的地平线上直到天巅。The locks of the approaching storm. 这里的 locks 还是指乱云，因为上边提到 Maenad 的头发，所用“卷发”一字，但它们又是挟着风雨来的，所以叫它做“面

临的风暴的卷发”。这是雪莱使用意象的很典型方法。

16. Thou dirge/Of the dying year: 这里thou仍是西风；秋风一起，一年将尽，所以称西风为“残年（the dying year）的挽歌（dirge），”当然风不能等同于一首歌，这里当然是说西风吹起了残年的挽歌。

17. to which this closing night ... and hail will burst: oh, hear!: 这里雪莱又使用了一个与死亡有关的形象，把风暴之夕傍晚的天空（this closing night）比做巨大墓穴的圆顶（the dome of a vast sepulchre）笼罩住西风所挟带着的全部〔形成雨雹的〕蒸汽的威力（Vaulted with all thy congregated might/OF vapour）. 从这种浓密的大气（solid atmosphere）将迸裂（burst）出雨、闪电（fire）和冰雹。

III

本诗第一段写西风作用于枯叶，第二段写西风作用于乱云，本段则写西风作用于波浪。先写平静的地中海（29—36行）然后写澎湃的大西洋（36—42行）。

18. he: 指地中海。

19. Lulled by the coil of his crystalline streams: 被自己的晶莹的水流（crystalline streams）的波漩（coil）所催眠而沉睡在夏季的梦中（his summer dreams）. 意思是说地中海夏日是平静的，等到西风一起才被吹动。

20. pumice isle: 白色浮石构成的岛。Baiae's ['beiji:z] bay 在意大利那不勒斯（Naples）附近的一个休假地。古代为罗马皇帝常去的地方。

21. And saw in sleep ... the sense faints picturing them!: 地中海从梦中被西风吹醒，所以在睡眼朦胧中看见（saw in sleep）强烈阳光照耀下（within the wave's intenser day）颤动（quivering）在水波中的古宫殿、城堡的影子。这些古建筑物上长满了美丽的青苔和香花，美到感官都说不出好在那里了（the sense faints picturing them）.

22. Thou/For whose path the Atlanties level powers/Cleave themselves into chasms: 大西洋的波涛经大风一吹翻起巨浪，好象被劈成了巨壑一样（Cleave themselves into chasms）. level powers 指平时是横流的（level）有力的波涛（powers）.

23. 第38—42行： 对这一部分，雪莱自己有一条注：“The phenomenon alluded to at the conclusion of the third stanza is well known to naturalists. The vegetation at the bottom of the sea, of rivers, and of lakes, sympothizes with that of the land in the change of seasons, and is consequently influenced by the winds which announce it.” 这里写的是海底的植物也因西风的威力而战栗变色（grow gray with fear, /And tremble）而落叶（despoil themselves）.

IV

这一段起写诗人因西风而发生的感慨。

24. 第43—47行： 在这里诗人向西风说但愿（If I were ...）自己也象枯叶被风

带走（bear），象飞云那样随风翱翔，象波浪那样在风力下喘息（pant），并且，虽然不象不羁（uncontrollable）的雨风那样自由自在，（only less free/Than thou，）也能分得它的一分猛烈的威力（and share/The impulse of thy strength）.

25. If even/I were as in my boyhood, … in my sore need: 这一句的大意是说，如我还能象童年那样和你西风的奔放相比，那我就不至于象现在这样请求你在痛苦之中加以援手。

26. and could be/The comrade of thy wanderings over Heaven: 能做你遨游天上的伴侣。

27. as then: 如那时（指童年时）

28. when to outstrip thy skiey speed/Scarce seemed a vision: 那时能赶上你在天上的迅速飞翔（thy skiey speed）并不象是梦想（vision）. skiey 也可拼作 skyey，

29. in my sore need: 在需要帮助的痛苦之中。

30. I fall upon the thorns of life! I bleed：在上一行，诗人请求西风把他象波浪、树叶、乱云那样吹到天上。但是现实终是现实，在狂想高潮过后他仍回到现实。落在了生命的痛苦之中（thorns of life），遍体鳞伤（I bleed）.

31. 第 55—56 行： 所以如此，是因为岁月的负担（heavy weight of hours）压垮了（chained and bowed）原来和你西风一样不驯（tameless），高傲（proud）飞逸（swift）的诗人。

V

在这末节里诗人请求西风帮助他扫去暮气，把他的诗句传播到四方，唤醒沉睡的大地。最后以高扬的信心结束全篇，唱出有名的诗句“风啊，寒冬已到，春光还用久等！”

32. Make me thy lyre, even as the forest is: lyre 是七弦的竖琴。西风吹落叶是秋声，是音乐，诗人请求西风给他助力，把诗句传播到四方，就象把他当做一只竖琴来演奏一样。

33. What if my leaves are falling like its own: what if = 就是……也何妨。its own 指树叶。my leaves 指诗人的消极思想，参看 64 行。

34. thy mighty harmonies: 指风声

35. take from both: both 指树和诗人自己。

36. 第 61—62 行： 诗人希望和西风合而为一，意思是要借到西风那样的威力。

37. 第 63—64 行： 西风吹掉落叶，就使春天新叶的生长到来得快些。诗人希望西风扫去自己的消极的思想（dead thoughts），使积极的思想能抬头。

38. 第 65—67 行： 诗人愿借西风之力使自己的诗具有法力（the incantation of this verse）把他的话象未熄灭的炉火中的火花（as from an unextinguished hearth/Ashes and sparks）一样传给人类。

39. 第 68—69 行： 诗人愿通过自己的口向未觉醒的大地（unawakened earth）

吹起预言的号角。他的预言就是最后一行诗里的 If winter comes, can Spring be far behind?

5. *A LAMENT*

这首是雪莱的著名的抒情诗。写作的时期大约在 1821 年。此行词极平易，情感极真，意境极远。

1. time: 时光

2. whose last steps: whose 指上文的 world, life, time 等，last steps 意为最后阶段。

3. the glory of your prime: 指少年时期的光明灿烂。此时雪莱虽只有二十八九岁，但已饱经沧桑，自觉已没有少年心境。

4. hoar: 指苍白色。在英诗中常用来形容冬天。也用来形容老年。

5. No more—Oh, never more! 全诗以呼喊始，以悲叹终，同样是词简情真，而且此行重复两次，也使此诗获得情绪上与形式上的完整。

6. *TO—*

这首诗是雪莱最完美的爱情诗之一。诗中以爱情比做崇拜（worship），比做顶礼（devotion），认为侮辱爱情就等于是亵渎神明（profaned），不落一般情诗蹊径，意境至为阔大。诗的写作时期大约在 1821 年，发表则在雪莱去世之后。

1. one word: 指 love 一字。

2. profaned: 被污渎。

3. one feeling: 指爱慕之情。

4. falsely disdained: 被错误地加以轻侮。

5.（第 5—6 行）: 这两行的意思是说诗人明知自己获得对方爱情的希望极小，几乎接近绝望（despair），因此祈求对方不再考虑世俗的礼法（prudence），而使这一点点希望也受到扼杀（smother）.

6. wilt thou: = will you.

7. lifts above: 献上的。

8.（第 13 —15 行）: "The desire ..."，"The devotion ..." 和上文的 "the worship" 都是同位语。"The desire of the moth for the star" 这一行是雪莱的名句，常被用来代表他独特的浪漫主义风格。

9. the sphere of our sorrow: 我们的痛苦的境地。

37 JOHN KEATS
1795–1821

周珏良　选注

1. Sonnets:

1) On First Looking into Chapman's Homer

2) On the Grasshopper and Cricket

3) When I Have Fears

4) Bright Star

2. Ode to a Nightingale

3. To Autumn

1. SONNETS

1) On First Looking Into Chapman's Homer

Much have I travell'd in the realms of gold,[1]
And many goodly states and kingdoms[2] seen;
Round many western islands have I been
Which bards in fealty to Apollo hold.[3]
Oft of one wide expanse[4] had I been told
That deep-brow'd Homer ruled as his demesne;[5]
Yet did I never breathe its pure serene[6]
Till I heard Chapman speak out loud and bold:
Then felt I like some watcher of the skies[7]
When a new planet swims into his ken;[8]
Or like stout Cortez[9] when with eagle eyes[10]
He star'd at the Pacific — and all his men
Look'd at each other with a wild surmise[11] —
Silent, upon a peak in Darien.[12]

2) On the Grasshopper and Cricket

The poetry of earth is never dead:
When all the birds are faint with the hot sun,[1]
And hide in cooling trees,[2] a voice will run
From hedge to hedge about the new-mown mead;[3]
That is the Grasshopper's — he takes the lead
In summer luxury, — he has never done
With his delights;[4] for when tired out with fun[5]
He rests at ease beneath some pleasant weed.
The poetry of earth is ceasing never:
On a lone winter evening, when the frost
Has wrought a silence,[6] from the stove there shrills
The Cricket's song, in warmth increasing ever,
And seems to one in drowsiness half lost,
The Grasshopper's among some grassy hills.[7]

3) When I Have Fears

WHEN I have fears that I may cease to be[1]
Before my pen has glean'd my teeming brain,[2]
Before high-piled books,[3] in charactery,
Hold like rich garners[4] the full ripen'd grain;
When I behold, upon the night's starr'd face,[5]
Huge cloudy symbols of a high romance,[6]
And think that I may never live to trace
Their shadows, with the magic hand of chance;[7]
And when I feel, fair creature of an hour,[8]
That I shall never look upon thee more,
Never have relish in the faery power
Of unreflecting love;[9] — then on the shore
Of the wide world I stand alone, and think
Till love and fame to nothingness do sink.

4) Bright Star

BRIGHT star, would I were stedfast as thou art—
Not in lone splendour hung aloft the night[1]
And watching, with eternal lids apart,[2]
Like nature's patient, sleepless Eremite,[3]
The moving waters at their priestlike task
Of pure ablution[4] round earth's human shores,
Or gazing on the new soft-fallen mask
Of snow upon the mountains and the moors—
No—yet still stedfast, still unchangeable,
Pillow'd upon my fair love's ripening breast,
To feel for ever its soft fall and swell,
Awake for ever in a sweet unrest,[5]
Still, still to hear her tender-taken breath,
And so live ever—or else swoon to death.

2. ODE TO A NIGHTINGALE

I

My heart aches, and a drowsy numbness[1] pains
My sense, as though of hemlock[2] I had drunk,
Or emptied some dull opiate[3] to the drains[4]
One minute past, and Lethe-wards[5] had sunk:
'Tis not through envy of thy happy lot,
But being too happy in thine happiness,[6]—
That thou, light wingèd Dryad[7] of the trees,
In some melodious plot[8]
Of beechen green,[9] and shadows numberless,
Singest of summer in full-throated ease.[10]

II

O, for[11] a draught of vintage![12] that hath been

Cool'd a long age in the deep-delved earth,[13]
Tasting of Flora[14] and the country green,[15]
Dance, and Provençal song,[16] and sunburnt mirth![17]
O, for a beaker[18] full of the warm South,[19]
Full of the true, the blushful[20] Hippocrene,[21]
With beaded bubbles[22] winking at the brim,
And purple-stainèd mouth;
That I might drink, and leave the world unseen,
And with thee fade away into the forest dim:

III

Fade far away, dissolve, and quite forget
What thou among the leaves hast never known,
The weariness, the fever, and the fret[23]
Here, where men sit and hear each other groan;
Where palsy shakes a few, sad, last grey hairs,
Where youth grows pale, and spectre-thin, and dies;[24]
Where but to think is to be full of sorrow
And leaden-ey'd despairs,[25]
Where Beauty cannot keep her lustrous eyes,
Or new Love pine at them[26] beyond tomorrow.

IV

Away! away! for I will fly to thee,
Not charioted by Bacchus[27] and his pards,
But on the viewless[28] wings of Poesy,
Though the dull brain perplexes and retards:
Already with thee! tender is the night,
And haply the Queen-Moon is on her throne,
Cluster'd around[29] by all her starry Fays;[30]
But here there is no light,
Save what from heaven is with the breezes blown
Through verdurous glooms[31] and winding mossy ways.

V

I cannot see what flowers are at my feet,
Nor what soft incense hangs upon the boughs,
But, in embalmèd darkness,[32] guess each sweet[33]
Wherewith the seasonable month[34] endows
The grass, the thicket, and the fruit-tree wild;
White hawthorn, and the pastoral eglantine;
Fast fading violets cover'd up in leaves;
And mid-May's eldest child,
The coming musk-rose, full of dewy wine,
The murmurous haunt of flies on summer eves.

VI

Darkling[35] I listen; and, for many a time
I have been half in love with easeful Death,
Call'd him soft names in many a musèd rhyme,[36]
To take into the air my quiet breath;[37]
Now more than ever seems it rich to die,
To cease upon the midnight with no pain,
While thou art pouring forth thy soul[38] abroad
In such an ecstasy!
Still[39] wouldst thou sing, and I have ears in vain—
To thy high requiem[40] become a sod.[41]

VII

Thou wast not born for death, immortal Bird!
No hungry generations tread thee down;[42]
The voice I hear this passing night was heard
In ancient days by emperor and clown:[43]
Perhaps the self-same song that found a path
Through the sad heart of Ruth,[44] when, sick for home,
She stood in tears amid the alien corn;

The same that oft-times hath
Charm'd magic casements, opening on the foam
Of perilous seas, in faery lands forlorn.[45]

VIII

Forlorn![46] the very word is like a bell
To toll me back from thee to my sole self![47]
Adieu! the fancy[48] cannot cheot so well
As she is famed to do deceiving elf.[49]
Adieu! adieu! thy plaintive anthem fades
Past the near meadows, over the still stream,
Up the hill-side; and now 'tis buried deep
In the next valley-glades:
Was it a vision, or a waking dream?
Fled is that music: — Do I wake or sleep?

3. TO AUTUMN

I

Season of mists and mellow fruitfulness[1],
Close bosom-friend of the maturing sun;[2]
Conspiring with him how to load and bless
With fruit[3] the vines that round the thatch-eves run;
To bend with apples the moss'd cottage-trees,
And fill all fruit with ripeness to the core;
To swell the gourd, and plump the hazel shells
With a sweet kernel; to set budding more,
And still more, later flowers for the bees,
Until they think warm days will never cease,
For Summer has o'er-brimm'd their clammy cells.[4]

II

Who hath not seen thee oft amid thy store?[5]

Sometimes whoever seeks abroad[6] may find
Thee sitting careless on a granary floor,
Thy hair sort-lifted by the winnowing wind;
Or on a half-reap'd furrow sound asleep,
Drows'd with the fume of poppies[7], while thy hook
Spares the next swath and all its twined flowers[8];
And sometimes like a gleaner thou dost keep
Steady thy laden head across a brook;
Or by a cyder-press, with patient look,
Thou watchest the last oozings[9] hours by hours.

III

Where are the songs of Spring? Ay, where are they?
Think not of them, thou hast thy music too, —
While barred clouds bloom the soft-dying day,[10]
And touch the stubble-plains with rosy hue;[11]
Then in a wailful choir[12] the small gnats mourn
Among the river sallows,[13] borne aloft
Or sinking as the light wind lives or dies;
And full-grown lambs loud bleat from hilly bourn;[14]
Hedge-crickets sing; and now with treble[15] soft
The red-breast[16] whistles from a garden-croft;[17]
And gathering swallows[18] twitter in the skies.

【作者简介】 济慈（John Keats, 1795–1821）是英国浪漫主义诗人，和拜伦、雪莱同时。他出身贫苦，做过医生的学徒，后来才以写诗为业。他向往希腊和英国伊丽莎白时代的文学，爱读荷马史诗和斯宾塞（Edmund Spenser），莎士比亚，密尔顿的作品，自己的创作受益很多。他对当时英国社会的现实不满，希望在一个“永恒的美的世界”中寻找安身立命之处，但他对人生态度是严肃的，不是有人认为的那样的唯美主义者。他和当时的激进文人利·亨特（Leigh Hunt）是朋友，参加他为首的文艺活动，因此受到保守派文人的攻击。他的诗特别以文辞声调之美著称，虽然一生创作的时期不过短短五年，最好的诗差不多都是 1919 一年中写出来的，但留下了许多不朽的篇章，在艺术上对后代的英国诗人影响很大。

【题解与注释】

1. SONNETS

1) On First Looking into Chapman's Homer

在 1816 年夏天的某日，济慈的朋友克拉克（Charles Cowden Clark）借到了一本古本的恰帕曼（George Chapman）的荷马史诗。（他的荷马史诗英译本出版于 1598—1616 间）请济慈来同读，他们两人一同读了一夜。济慈读得极高兴，天亮才离去。到克拉克吃早饭时济慈已写好了这首十四行诗送给他读了。它是济慈早期诗的代表作。

这首诗的主题是发现了新天地的狂喜。济慈是不懂得希腊文的，他第一次接触荷马的著作，其心情之欢畅可想而知。何况荷马又是他向往已久的，一旦实现了宿愿，欣喜之情又非一般可比了（7—8 行）。诗中使用的两个意象具体生动地表现了诗人的感情，一是天文家发现了新星（9—10 行），一是探险家发现了新大洋（11—14 行）。而后者写得更为形象，探险家立在达连湾（Darien）的岩石上俯视着汪洋无际的太平洋，这不是诗人在他接触了荷马这一史诗的高峰后，感到自己的诗境更为无限开阔，犹如发现了一个太平洋一般的形象吗?

1. Much have I travell'd in realms of gold: 在全诗里济慈把自己比作一个探险家，探索者，探索的地域则是伟大的文学作品。realms of gold 指伟大作品价值贵重如黄金，其灿烂也如黄金。

2. goodly states and kingdoms: goodly = beautiful. 这里的 states 和 kingdoms 和上一行的 realms 一样都是指伟大的文学。

3. Round many western islands have I been/Which bards in fealty to Apollo hold: 这里的 I have been round many western islands 指的是诗人自己曾涉猎过许多希腊文学作品，因为古希腊在许多岛上而且这些岛上的诗人（bards）是臣服（in fealty to）于希腊诗神 Apollo 的，到这些岛上去漫游也就是在希腊文学中涉猎。

4. wide expanse: 广大的领域。

5. deep-brow'd Homer ruled as his demesne: 浓眉的荷马作为他的领地而统治着。指荷马的史诗。

6. pure serene: 指荷马的风格既清且纯。

7. watcher of skies: 指观星者，即天文家。

8. swims into his ken: 进入他的视界。

9. Cortez: 指 Hernando Cortez (1485–1547) 西班牙探险家，是发现墨西哥的人。这里济慈的记忆有误，发现太平洋的是 Vasco Nuñez de Balboa (1475–1517)，西班牙人。

10. eagle eyes: 在济慈的第一稿里用的是“wond'ring eyes”. 济慈的朋友 Leigh Hunt 在他的回忆录中说济慈曾见过一幅意大利文艺复兴时名画家 Titian (1477–1576)

画的 Cortez 像，“鹰目”这一形象就是在那幅画里看到的。

11. with a wild surmise: 作出各种奇特的猜想。

12. Darien: 达连湾在加勒比海，巴拿马和哥伦比亚之间。

2) On the Grasshopper and Cricket

在济慈的朋友 Leigh Hunt 家中，常常有出题赛诗的事。他们的朋友克拉克记载说，有一天晚上，话题转到了蟋蟀上，大家说它是“壁炉边的欢乐的小蝈蝈”，Hunt 于是提议以此为题来写一首十四行诗，接着和济慈两人就即席赋起诗来，写好后，Hunt 读济慈诗的头一行就说：“一起便不凡，”读到十行和十一行时说：“妙绝，妙绝！”

本世纪初美国“意象派”（imagist）诗人和批评家 Amy Lowell 在她的《济慈传》里说这首诗清新可喜。“开始就展现了一幅美妙的图画，生动而富于启发！使人觉得看得见，摸得着，闻得到”（“The opening is an excellent picture, vivid and suggestive; one can see it, feel it, and smell it.”），这是对这首诗很好的注脚。

这首诗风格很象我国南宋诗人范成大，杨万里。若对照起来读会很有启发。

1. faint with the hot sun: 因天热而懒洋洋的。

2. cooling trees: 荫凉的树里。

3. new-mown mead: 新修剪的草地，mead = meadow，是诗里用的字。

4. he takes the lead/In summer luxury, —he has never done/With his delights: 他在暑天带头尽情歌唱。他的欢乐永远也唱不尽。天气越热蝈蝈（也叫蝼蝈）就唱得越欢，这里把写实和想象美妙地结合了起来。

5. tired out with fun: 耍够了。

6. when the frost/Has wrought a silence: 冬天的霜冻凝成一片静寂。这又冷又静的境界反衬出下面蟋蟀在炉灶旁尖声的歌唱（shrills the Cricket's song）. 带来了渐浓的暖意（in warmth inereasing ever）也带来了声响，这里的 cricket 也可能指的是我国北方叫做“灶马”的昆虫。

7. And seems to one in drowsiness half lost,/The Grass-hopper's among some grassy hills: seems to one in drowsiness half lost，对一个半睡着了的人。The Grashopper's 指 the grasshopper's song.

3) When I Have Fears

这首诗作于 1818 年，正是济慈诗才成熟的年头，同年他的弟弟汤姆（Tom）因肺病转重卧床，济慈大部时间是看护、陪伴他，直到十二月里汤姆去世。济慈自己也有肺病，这时他又热恋着 Fanny Brawne。这首诗就是在这个背景下写的。这首十四行诗在结构上正好依照诗和爱情两大主题分成前八行，后六行两大段，而贯串全诗的则是诗人面对死亡的威胁而沉思着这两个主题。两大段各自的开头一行，即全诗的第一行和第九行里，作者一方面说担心自己在杰作未完之前就死去（cease to be），另一方面则说担心自己死了，再也看不见 Fanny (I shall never look upon thee more)，享受她的爱情，都是点题的地方。最后二行半说，既然如此，那就独自一个站在苍茫的大地边缘，这样的沉思，直到爱情和荣誉（这里指的也是诗，因为他的诗是他荣誉的来源）都化为无物吧。这首诗十四行一共只有一个句子，以名誉不立、爱情不成的忧虑始，以进入超脱于这些烦恼的境界终，首尾结构完满。我国晋代诗人陶渊明有几句诗：“纵浪大化中，不喜亦不惧，应尽便须尽，无复独多虑。”很可参看。

1. may cease to be: 不复存在；死亡。

2. Before my pen has glean'd my teeming brain: 在我的这枝笔把充满我头脑中的〔诗〕(my teeming brain）收集（glean'd）起来之前。

3. high-piled books: 堆得高高的书本。in charactery = in writing.

4. garners: 谷仓。the full ripened grain 这里济慈把成熟的谷物来比自己成熟的诗作。

5. the night's starr'd face: 满布星斗的天空。

6. Huge cloudy symbols of a high romance: 崇高的浪漫色彩诗篇（a high romance）的巨大而若隐若显的象征（huge cloudy symbols）.

7. I may never live to trace/Their shadows, with the magic hand of chance: 这里诗人以作画来比喻写诗，所以 trace their shadows 的意思就是描述上一行说的 cloudy symbols. 为什么需要用具有魔力的，无意得之的手笔（the magic hand of chance）才能描绘出来呢？因为这是不易捕捉，若隐若显的 symbols，或者说灵感，没有神来之笔怎么能办得到呢。

8. fair creature of an hour: 指 Fanny Brawne. 济慈既感到自己生命不长，因而觉得 Fanny 的美貌也不能长在，所以说 of an hour.

9. Never have relish in the faery power/Of unreflecting love: 并不能纵情领略（have relish in）无忧无虑的爱情（unreflecting love）的魅力（faery power）.

4) Bright Star

这首诗过去常被认为是济慈的绝笔，后来经人考证，写成当在 1819 年，而在 1820 年济慈因发现肺病严重，需要转地疗养，由友人陪同到意大利去时，在途中把它修改抄录在他朋友的一本莎士比亚集的空白页上，因而引起误会。

济慈在 1818 年 6 月给他弟弟汤姆的一封信里说他刚游过的湖泊区（Lake Country）的自然风景“纯洁了一个人的感觉力，使它成为类似北极星那样，永远睁着眼睛，坚定地注视着那至高无上的威力所创造的奇迹。”* 这段话是对这首诗里的意象的来源的说明。这诗前八行是一段，后六行是一段，前一段感叹自己若能象北极星那样永恒不移（stedfast）就好了，但是目的可不是和它那样象一个信奉基督的隐士（eremite）日夜不眠地望着冲涤着人间大地（earth's human shores）的污浊罪恶（at their priest

---

* 这一段的原文是：“refines one's sensual vision into a sort of north star which can never cease to be open lidded and stedfast over the wonders of the great Power.”

like task of pure ablution）的浩瀚的海洋（waters），成者注视着使山川洁白无瑕，银装素裹的新雪（the new soft-fallen mask/Of snow upon the mountains and the moors-）.这里的意境极高、极远、极美，可是诗人却别有希冀，他但愿自己在爱情上能永远坚定，永远不变（still stedfast, still unchangeable），死生以之（And so live ever — or else swoon to death.）。这一主题是在后六行中形象地而不是叙述地表达出来的。这后六行的描写极秾丽，极温柔。诗人但愿自己能永远枕在美丽的恋人的丰满成熟的胸膛（my fair love's ripening breast），永远感到那轻轻的起伏（11 行），永远醒在甜美的不安（sweet unrest）之中，永远，永远听着她那娇弱的呼吸（tender-taken breath），就这样活下去，要不然就沉醉着死去（swoon to death）.

这是一首杰出的情诗。这时济慈热恋着 Fanny Brawne，但是已经证明患了不治之症，活不了多久了。在诗里爱情，死亡，和永恒的主题交织在一起，用了绝妙的意象表达出来，最后一行提出两种愿望，长生不死，或者在甜蜜的热恋中（in a sweet unrest）死去，这听来有些矛盾，但都达到一种永恒的境界。联系到前八行北极星所日夜注视的大洋、白雪也是一种永恒的境界，就促成了这首诗的完整性。

1. in lone splendour hung aloft the night: 夜晚在孤独的光辉中高悬在上，这里指北极星。

2. eternal lids apart: 永不合拢的眼皮。

3. Like nature's patient, sleepless Eremite: eremite = hermit；早期基督教的苦修的隐士。这里把北极星比做苦行夜祷的修士。

4. The moving waters at their priestlike task/Of pure ablution: 这里把海洋的冲洗崖岸比做宗教的沐浴仪式（ablution），引申做荡涤污浊罪恶的意思。

5. a sweet unrest: 热恋因而是甜蜜的，也因而是使人心境不能平静的。

2. ODE TO A NIGHTINGALE

《夜莺颂》是济慈在 1819 年五月里写成的，当时他住在伦敦的一个朋友家里。朋友家附近有个夜莺结了巢，济慈非常喜欢这个鸟的叫声。一天早饭后，他搬了一把椅子，在一棵李树下的草地上坐了两三个钟头，在几张纸上写了一些诗行，经他的朋友帮他整理出来，就成为这首公认的杰作，在这以前几个月，济慈的弟弟汤姆去世。这时，他自己身体也不好，杂志上对他的作品的恶毒的批评和他另一个弟弟乔治一家不久以前离英去美，也增加了他的烦恼。同时，他爱上了 Fanny Brawne，又多了一个不安的根源。这首诗中的感情丰富而多变化，和济慈此时的心境是有关系的。诗中表现了诗人对人生疾苦的体会和同情，但也表现他希望借诗、酒之力逃避现实的消极思想。从艺术性来讲，这首诗在文字和形象以及音律的美妙上，都是佳作。

I

诗的第一段写诗人听到夜莺之歌而发生的夹杂痛苦和快乐的感情。

1. drowsy numbness: 似困倦的麻木。

2. hemlock: 一种毒药，服了先使人全身麻木，然后死亡。古希腊大哲学家苏格拉底（Socrates）就是服此药死去的。

3. opiate: 含鸦片的麻醉剂，饮了能使人麻木，所以叫它做 dull cpiate.

4. to the drains: 饮尽。

5. Lethe-wards: lethe ['li:θi] 是希腊神话中冥间的一道河，死人的鬼魂喝了这条河的水就忘记了过去的事。Lethe-wards 意为向 Lethe 而去，也就是说忘记了人间的一切。Lethe 是济慈喜用的字。

6. 第 5—6 行： 这两行说明上述的 numbness 固然有痛苦的成分，但更有快乐的成分，后者是诗人因夜莺之乐（happy lot）而乐于是产生的。

7. Dryad ['draiəd]**:** 希腊神话中的树木的精灵，此处指夜莺。

8. melodious plot: 夜莺唱出优美歌声的地点。

9. beechen green: 山毛榉树的绿荫。

10. full-throated ease: 高兴时就放开喉咙唱，人物皆然，所以说：full-throated. 又因唱得从容不迫，所以说：in full-throated ease.

II

第二段写诗人想借美酒之力脱离人世烦恼与夜莺共入深林。

11. for: 这里和第 15 行的 for 字都是"但愿能得到"的意思。

12. vintage: 酒。这个意义只有在诗里才用。

13. 第 12 行： 藏酒要在凉爽的地窖里，又要多年才好，所以这里如此说。

14. Flora: 百花的女神，也象征繁殖。

15. country green: 绿色的田野，亦即 Flora 往来之地。

16. Provençal song: Provence 在法国南部沿地中海处，气候温暖，中古时以行吟诗人（troubadours）的爱情诗歌出名。

17. sunburnt mirth: 温暖地带受日晒很多的人们的欢乐气氛。

18. beaker: 大酒杯。

19. the warm South: 温暖的南方美酒。

20. blushful: 人腼腆则面红，这里用来形容酒红如人面。

21. Hippocrene ['hipokri:n]**:** 希腊神话中文艺女神缪斯（the Muses）姊妹所居 Helicon 山上的泉水名，饮了可以给人以诗才。这里拿来比南方的美酒，因为诗人认为酒可以给人以诗的灵感。

22. beaded bubbles: 酒杯边上如珠形的泡沫。

III

第三段写诗人希望借助酒力逃避人世的痛苦。这一段第一行的 fade 一字正和上一段末行（20行）中的同一字相呼应，加强了诗人想解脱人间烦恼的感情。

23. the weariness, the fever, and the fret: 厌倦，焦躁，不安。

24. 第26行： 这一行一般认为是指诗人死去不久的弟弟汤姆和患着肺结核病的诗人自己，但当然它更是广泛地适用于当时社会上所有的贫苦青年。

25. leaden-eyed despairs: 眼光呆滞无神叫 leaden. 所以这里称使人眼里失去光彩的绝望为 leaden-eyed despairs.

26. new Love: 初恋的爱人；**them** 指 eyes.

IV

但是酒也不能使诗人达到夜莺的欢乐境界，于是他转而想借诗的力量，想在诗的幻界中达到所求，最后终于达到目的（35行 Already with thee! 表明了这一点）。

27. Bacchus: 希腊神话中的酒神，他乘坐由豹（pards 是 leopards 的古字）驾驶的车子。这一行的意思是说想借酒之力求得快乐。

28. viewless: 目不能见的。

29. cluster'd around: 被拥戴。

30. starry Fays: 指捧月的星星。Fays = fairies.

31. verdurous glooms: 指月影下的绿荫。

V

在黑夜林中，诗人听着莺歌欣赏着花草的芬芳。

32. embalmed darkness: 芬芳的黑夜。

33. each sweet: 各种香味。

34. seasonable month: 当前的月份。

此行由于 m 音多，表达了夏天晚间醉卧花丛的情调，用声音表达情感是济慈诗的特色之一。

VI

诗人此时欢乐至极，于是想到若此时在夜莺歌声中无痛苦死去（easeful death），避免人生忧患之再来，岂不甚好。

35. darkling: 副词，意为 in the dark.

36. mused rhyme: 着意吟出的诗句。

37. my quiet breath: 我的生命。

38. pouring forth thy soul: 倾吐着心怀。

39. still: = always，是此字的古义。

40. requiem: 安慰亡灵的音乐，此地指夜莺的歌声。

41. sod: 坟上的土和草。

这行诗的大意是说我死之后，夜莺之歌仍将永久不歇，但我则将如埋我骨之黄土（sod），对夜莺的慰灵之曲不听不闻了。

VII

诗人想象到自己之死，相比之下也联想到夜莺之歌则几乎是永生不灭的。

42. 第 62 行： 这一行的意义是说尽管人生痛苦（hungry generations），但夜莺的欢乐歌声则将永生。

43. by emperor and clown: 帝王和小丑，泛指一切人。

44. Ruth:《圣经》《旧约》"路得记"。（The Book of Ruth），路得是大卫王的祖先，丈夫死后，离开自己的家乡，随着婆母过活，曾在波阿斯的田里拾取麦穗，后来嫁给了波阿斯。这里所说的在异乡的麦田里（amid the alien corn）落思乡之泪，则是济慈的想象，原书里没有的。

45. 第 68—70 行： 这三行是脍炙人口的名句，一般被认为典型地代表了浪漫主义诗歌的特色，在欧洲中古的传奇文学里常有孤立在大海中的城堡，受魔法的控制，里面住着被幽囚的公主，如有虔诚勇敢的骑士到来，解除魔法，就能得公主为妻，济慈这里指的就是在这种城堡中被囚的公主为夜莺的歌声吸引，打开窗户来倾听；charmed magic casements 的意思是：使得在受魔法（magic）控制的城堡的窗边（casements）的人被吸引住（charmed）；forlorm 在这里的意思是渺无人迹。

VIII

夜莺的歌声渐远渐歇，诗人从幻想的境界又回到现实中来。

46. forlorn: 这里义为孤单。这个字的声音象钟声，使诗人又回到现实世界中来。

47. my sole self: 自己孤身一人。

48. the fancy: 奇想力。

49. deceiving elf: 惯于弄鬼的家伙，指上面说的 the fancy.

3. TO AUTUMN

这首诗是济慈诗中著名的一首，不少批评家认为是他的"颂"体诗中最完美的。写这首诗后两天，1819 年 9 月 22 日，济慈给他好友 John Hamilton Reynolds 一封信并附上这首诗，信里说："现在这季节真美——空气多好。爽利得适度，真的，不开玩笑，真是宜人天气——暗蓝的天空——我从来也没有这么喜欢过收割过的田野——是啊，比春天的那种冰冷的绿色好多了，不知怎地，收割过的田野看上去很温暖——就象有的图画看上去温暖一样。我在星期天散步时得到很深的印象，就写了这诗。”*

这就是济慈写诗的背景，因之诗的主题也就是秋季的温暖和丰硕。诗一开始就说这是“多雾和成熟丰收的季节，”然后通过一系列的意象，使读者如身历其境，直接感受到声、色、形象各方面的美，获得深刻的美感。诗人没有把他自己的感受用叙述的方法强加给读者，而是通过形象由读者自己去体会，我国古人评诗常说：“景中见情，情中见景。”这首诗可说是“景中见情”的杰作了。

I

诗分三大段，头一段开宗明义就说：“Season of mists and mellow fruitfulness, / Close bosom friend of the maturing sun;”点出诗的主题。秋季是多雾和丰收、成熟的季节，而太阳则既是温暖的来源又是使得世上的生物得以成熟的主宰，所以叫它 maturing sun. 秋季和太阳既然作用是一样的，因之就称它为太阳的“挚友”（Close bosom friend）了。下面接着用一系列使我们几乎能看得见，听得到，摸得着的形象在我们面前展开一幅暖气洋溢的丰硕景象。

首先是秋的季节和太阳一起安排打点（conspiring）给围绕着茅檐（thatch-eaves）的葡萄藤添上果实，然后又给苹果树挂满压弯了树枝的累累果实，并且使得各类的果实都熟得透到了心子里（fill all fruit with ripeness to the core.）；葫芦涨大了肚子（swell the gourd），榛子壳挤满了甜美的榛子仁（plump the hazel shells/With a sweet kernel.）这是何等的滋生丰硕景象。这一段最后三行半又引进了晚放的鲜花（later flowers）使得辛勤采蜜的蜜蜂觉得温暖的日子会永远延长下去（Until they think the warm days will never cease）因为夏季已经使得蜂房里的蜜满得要溢出来了。这里把丰硕和温暖两个意象用蜜蜂连系起来，使得这幅画图更加秾丽。

1. 第 1 行：注意这头一整段只是一句，而且没有谓语的。

2. maturing sun: 使生物成熟起来的太阳。

3. bless with fruit: = make happy with fruit，这里 bless 的用法和说人 be blessed with a child 一样，下面的 ripeness, swell, plump 都和这里的 bless 一字同样暗含着滋生养育的意象。

4. clammy cells: 蜜多了溢出来，所以蜂房是粘粘的。

---

* 这段信的原文如下：

“How beautiful the season is now — How fine the air. A temperate sharpness about it. Really, without joking, chaste weather — *Dian* [= Diana，暗蓝色] skies — I never liked stubble-fields so much as now — Aye better than the chilly green of the Spring. Somehow, a stubble-field looks warm — in the same way that some pictures look warm. This struck me so much in my Sunday's walk that I composed upon it.”

II

这一段换了一个角度，写的是丰收季节里的劳动的人，通过人的形象来描绘收获和温暖。谁出去跑跑（seeks abroad）就会看见劳动者无忧无虑地（careless）坐在谷仓的地上，头发轻轻地被扬谷的微风（winnowing wind）吹起；（13—15 行）或者在尚未收割完的田地里暂时熟睡（16—18 行）；或者是收起了地里剩下的麦穗，顶在头上渡过小溪（19—20 行）；或者在榨机旁耐心地等着苹果汁最后滴干（21—22 行）。这一些形象以人为中心共同构成了一幅温暖的浮雕丰收图。

5. store: 收获的东西。

6. seeks abroad: = goes out of one's house.

7. Drows'd with the fume of poppies: 因嗅到田间杂生的罂粟花香而沉睡。hook 镰刀。

8. spares the next swath and all its twined flowers: 留着（spares）下一把庄稼（swath）和缠结在上面的野花未割下来。这一行很使人想起清朝孔尚任《桃花扇》传奇里的"山荆野草带花桃"的句子。

9. oozings: 榨出的汁水。

III

这一段从秋色写到秋声。一开始就说不要惋惜春天歌声之消失，秋季也自有它的音乐（24 行），然后列举在落日照红了收割完毕的田野时的各种虫鸟声音的交奏，有河边柳间的白翎子（gnats）随轻风抑扬（as the light wind lires or dies）的哀音（mourn），山间绵羊的鸣声，树丛里的蟋蟀叫，园里的知更鸟和天上的麻雀的鸣声，本诗首写秋色，再写"秋人"，最后写秋声，而始终以丰硕温暖为总气氛，首尾完具，效果统一，是首完美的好诗。

10. barred clouds bloom the soft-dying day: 受阳光照耀的带云的傍晚天空光华灿烂。

11. rosy hue: 玫瑰色

12. a wailful choir: 哀鸣

13. sallows: = willows

14. hilly bourn: 山里面

15. treble: 尖音

16. red-breast: 知更鸟。

17. garden-croft 园地。

18. gathering swallows: 归巢的燕子。

38 WILLIAM COBBETT
1762–1835

RURAL RIDES
(selections)

王佐良　选注

MARLBOROUGH

Marlborough,
Tuesday noon, Nov. 6, 1821.

I left Uphusband this morning at 9, and came across to this place (20 miles) in a post-chaise.[1] Came up[2] the valley of Uphusband, which ends at about 6 miles from the village, and puts one out upon the Wiltshire downs,[3] which stretch away towards the West and South-west, towards Devizes[4] and towards Salisbury.[5] After about half a mile of down we came down into a level country; the flints[6] cease, and the chalk[7] comes nearer the top of the ground. The labourers along here seem very poor indeed. Farm houses with twenty ricks[8] round each, besides those standing in the fields; pieces of wheat,[9] 50, 60, or 100 acres in a piece; but, a group of women labourers, who were attending the measurers to measure their reaping work,[10] presented such an assemblage of rags as I never before saw even amongst the hoppers at Farnham,[11] many of whom are common beggars. I never before saw *country* people, and reapers too, observe, so miserable[12] in appearance as these. There were some very pretty girls, but ragged as colts and as pale as ashes. The day was cold too, and frost hardly off the ground;[13] and their blue arms and lips would have made any heart ache but that of a seat-seller or a loan-jobber.[14]

OXFORD

Burghclere (Hants),
Sunday, 18th Nov. 1821.

Upon beholding the masses of buildings, at Oxford, devoted to what they call "*learning*", I could not help reflecting on the drones[1] that they contain and the wasps[2] they send forth! However, malignant as some are, the great and prevalent characteristic is *folly*: emptiness of head; want of talent[3]; and one half of the fellows[4] who are what they call *educated* here, are unfit to be clerks in a grocer's or mercer's shop. — As I looked up at what they call *University Hall*,[5] I could not help reflecting[6] that what I had written, even since I left Kensington[7] on the 29th of October, would produce more effect, and do more good in the world, than all that had, for a hundred years, been written by all the members of this University,[8] who devour, perhaps, not less than *a million pounds a year*, arising from property,[9] completely at the disposal of the"Great Council of the Nation";[10] and I could not help exclaiming to myself: "Stand forth, ye big-wigged, ye gloriously feeding Doctors![11] Stand forth, ye *rich* of that church[12] whose *poor* have had given them *a hundred thousand pounds a year*, not out of your riches, but out of the *taxes*, raised, in part, from the *salt* of the labouring man![13] Stand forth and face me, who have, from the pen of my leisure hours, sent, amongst your flocks,[14] a hundred thousand sermons in ten months![15] More than you have all done for the last half century!" — I exclaimed in vain. I dare say (for it was at peep of day) that not a man of them had yet endeavoured to unclose his eyes.

AN ENGLISH SPRING

Kensington,
Friday, 4 Jan. 1822.

Even in winter the coppices[1] are beautiful to the eye, while they comfort the mind with the idea of shelter and warmth. In spring they change their hue from day to day during two whole months, which is about the time from the first appearance of delicate leaves of the birch[2] to the full expansion of those of the ash[3]; and even before the leaves come at all to intercept the view, what in the vegetable creation[4] is so delightful to behold as the bed of a coppice bespangled with primroses and bluebells[5]? The opening of the birch leaves is the signal for the pheasant[6] to begin to crow, for the blackbird[6] to whistle, and the thrush[6] to sing; and just when the oak-buds[7] begin to look reddish, and not a day before, the whole tribe of finches[8] burst forth in songs from every bough, while the lark,[9] imitating them all, carries the joyous sound to the sky.[10]

A RIDE IN THE RAIN

Fareham (Hants),
Saturday, 2 August, 1823.

Here I am in spite of St. Swithin![1] — The truth is, that the Saint is like most other oppressors: *rough* him! *rough* him! and he relaxes. After drying myself, and[2] sitting the better part of four hours at Singleton, I started in the rain, boldly setting the saint at defiance,[3] and expecting to have not one dry thread[4] by the time I got to Havant, which is nine miles from Fareham, and four from Cosham. To my most agreeable surprise, the rain ceased before I got by Selsey, I suppose it is called, where Lord Selsey's house and beautiful and fine estate is. On I went, turning off to the right to go to Funtington and Westbourne, and getting to Havant to bait[5] my horse, about four o'clock,

CASTLEREAGH[1]

Foot's Cray,
Thursday, 28th July, 1825.

The sight of the house[2] crowded my mind with subjects of recollection: I remembered poor Finnerty;[3] I remembered Reynolds, Oliver, and Edwards:[4] I remembered the shouts, and huzzas,[5] and clapping of hands, with which this fellow[6] had, upon his return from the Continent, been received by a crew,[7] the most corrupt and villainous (with some few honourable exceptions) that ever disgraced the face of this earth: I remembered the "ignorant impatience of taxation,"[8] and the "digging of holes one day and filling them up the next":[9] I remembered the cool statement of the number of "soldiers wanted to collect the taxes in Ireland";[10] I remembered his words when he, with SIDMOUTH,[11] brought in the *Power-of-Imprisonment Bill*,[12] in 1817, of which he was to be one of the executors: I remembered the treatment of KNIGHT[13] and OGDEN[14] under that Bill, and of many other worthy men, not forgetting poor REILEY,[15] who, in a fit of despair, put an end to his life in his dungeon: I remembered the "*basest populace*"[16] applied to the virtuous, just, and generous people of England, who saved from ignominy the hapless and ill-treated Queen:[17] I remembered the 16th of August at Manchester,[18] and the Oldham Inquest:[19] I remembered the two voyages of myself and wife and children across the Atlantic: I remembered that, when the lightning twice struck the ship in which I was, I still thought myself safer than in my native country, which I so truly loved: I remembered how poor little RICHARD[20] (whose hand I held at this moment) had asked his mother (he being then only three years old) why she cried, and how he had asked why his good papa had gone away and left her, and *what it was* that had made his dear papa not to come to kiss him before he went away: I remembered all these things, and others innumerable; and, despising from my soul the hypocritical cant of "*liberality*",[21] I wished to take this very child, and, in triumph, show him *the spot where Castlereagh fell!*

A SHOOTER

Thursley,
Wednesday, 26 Oct. 1825.

I was once acquainted with a *famous shooter* whose name was William Ewing. He was a barrister of Philadelphia,[1] but became far more renowned by his gun than by his law cases. We spent scores of days together a shooting,[2] and were extremely well matched,[3] I having excellent dogs and caring little about my reputation as a shot, his dogs being good for nothing, and he caring more about his reputation as a shot[4] than as a lawyer. The fact which I am going to relate respecting this gentleman, ought to be a warning to young men, how they become enamoured of this species of vanity. We had gone about ten miles from our home, to shoot where partridges were said to be very plentiful. We found them so. In the course of a November day, he had, just before dark, shot, and sent to the farm-house, or kept in his bag, *ninety-nine* partridges. He made some few *double shots,*[5] and he might have a *miss* or two,[6] for he sometimes shot when out of my sight, on account of the woods. However, he said that he killed at every shot; and, as he had counted the birds, when we went to dinner at the farm-house and when he cleaned his gun, he, just before sun-set, knew that he had killed *ninety-nine* partridges, every one upon the wing,[7] and a great part of them in woods very thickly set with largish trees.[8] It was a grand achievement; but, unfortunately, he wanted to make it a *hundred.* The sun *was setting*, and, in that country, darkness comes almost at once; it is more like the going out of a candle than that of a fire; and I wanted to be off, as we had a very bad road to go, and as he, being under strict petticoat government,[9] to which he most loyally and dutifully submitted, was compelled to get home that night, taking me with him, the vehicle (horse and gig[10]) being mine. I, therefore, pressed him to come away, and moved on myself towards the house (that of old John Brown, in Bucks county, grandfather of that General Brown, who gave some of our whiskered heroes such a rough handling last war, which was waged for the purpose of "Deposing James Madison")[11], at which house I would have stayed all night, but from which I was compelled to go by that watchful government,[12] under which he had the good fortune to live. Therefore I was in haste to be off. No: he would kill the *hundredth* bird! In vain did I talk of the bad road and its many dangers for want of moon. The poor partridges, which we had scattered about, were *calling* all around us; and just at this moment, up got one under his feet, in a field in which the wheat was three or four inches high. He shot and *missed*. "That's it," said he, running as if to *pick up* the bird. "What!" said I, "you don't think you *killed*, do you? Why there is the bird now, not only alive, but *calling*, in that wood"; which was at about a hundred yards distance. He, in that *form of words* usually employed in such cases, asserted that he shot the bird and saw it fall; and I, in much about the same form of words, asserted, that he had *missed*, and that I, with my own eyes, saw the bird fly into the wood. This was too much! To *miss* once out of a hundred times! To lose such a chance of immortality! He was a good-humoured man; I liked him very much; and I could not help feeling for him, when he said, "Well, Sir, I killed the bird; and if you choose to go away and take your dog away, so as to prevent me from *finding* it, you must do it; the dog is *yours*, to be sure." "The *dog*,[13]" said I, in a very mild tone, "why, Ewing, there is the spot; and could we not see it, upon this smooth green surface, if it were there?" However, he began to *look about;* and I called the dog, and affected[14] to *join him in the search*. Pity for his weakness got the better of my dread of the bad road.[15] After walking backward and forward many times upon about twenty yards square with our eyes to the ground, looking for what both of us knew was not there, I had *passed* him (he going one way and I the other), and I happened to be turning round just after I had passed him, when I saw him, putting his hand behind him, *take a partridge out of his bag and let it fall upon the ground!* I felt no temptation to detect him,[16] but turned away my head, and kept looking about. Presently he, having returned to the spot where the bird was, called out to me, in a most triumphant tone: "*Here*! *here*! Come here!" I went up to him, and he, pointing with his finger down to the bird, and looking hard in my face at the same time, said, "There, Cobbett; I hope that will be a *warning* to you never to be obstinate again!" "Well," said I, "come along": and away we went as merry as larks.[17] When we got to Brown's, he told them the story, triumphed over me most clamorously; and, though he often repeated the story to my face, I never had the heart to let him know, that I knew of the imposition[18] which puerile vanity[19] had induced so sensible and honourable a man to be mean enough to practise.

THE "EDUCATION" CANTERS

Burghclere,

Monday Morning, 31 October, 1825.

But, the *"education"* canters[1] are the most curious fellows of all.[2] They have seen "education" as they call it, and *crimes,* go on *increasing together,* till the gaols, though of six times their former dimensions, will hardly suffice; and yet, the canting creatures still cry, that crimes arise from want of what they call "*education!*" They see the FELON[3] *better fed and better clad* than the HONEST LABOURER. They see this; and yet they continually cry, that the crimes arise from a want of "*education!*" What can be the cause of this perverseness[4]? It is not perverseness: it is *roguery,*[5] *corruption,* and *tyranny*. The tyrant, the unfeeling tyrant,[6] squeezes the labourers for gain's sake;[7] and the corrupt politician and literary or tub rogue,[8] find an excuse for him[9] by pretending, that it is *not want of food and clothing,* but *want of education,* that makes the poor, starving wretches thieves and robbers.[10] If the press, if only the press, were to do its duty, or but a tenth part of its duty, this hellish system could not go on. But, it favours the system by ascribing the misery to wrong causes. The causes are these: the taxgatherer presses the landlord; the landlord the farmer; and the farmer the labourer. Here it falls at last;[11] and this class[12] is made so miserable, that a *felon's* life is better than that of a *labourer*. Does there want any other cause to produce crimes? But, on these causes, so clear to the eye of reason,[13] so plain from experience, the press scarcely ever says a single word; while it keeps bothering our brains about *education* and *morality;* and about ignorance and immorality leading to *felonies*. To be sure[14] immorality leads to felonies. Who does not know that? But, who is to expect *morality* in a *half-starved man,* who is *whipped if he do not work,*[15] though he has not, for his whole day's food, so much as I and my little boy snapped up in six or seven minutes upon Stoke-Charity down?[16] Aye! but, if the press were to ascribe the increase of crimes to the true causes, it must go *further back*. It must go to the *cause of the taxes*. It must go to the debt,[17] the dead-weight,[18] the thundering standing army,[19] the enormous sinecures,[20] pensions,[21] and grants;[22] and this would suit but a very small part of *a press,*[23] which lives and thrives principally by one or the other of these.

REFLECTIONS IN AN ENGLISH INN

East Everley (Wiltshire)

Sunday, 27th August, 1826. Evening.

Everley is but about three miles from Udgarshall, so that we got here in the afternoon of Friday; and, in the evening a very heavy storm came and drove away all flies, and made the air delightful. This is a real *Down*-country.[1] Here you see miles and miles square without a tree, or hedge, or bush. It is country of *greensward*.[2] This is the most famous place in all England for *coursing*.[3] I was here, at this very inn, with a party *eighteen years ago*; and, the landlord, who is still the same, recognized me as soon as he saw me. There were *forty brace*[4] *of grey-hounds* taken out into the field on one of the days, and every brace had one course, and some of them two. The ground is the finest in the world; from two to three miles for the hare to run to cover,[5] and not a stone nor a bush nor a hillock. It was here proved to me, that the hare is, by far, the swiftest of all English animals; for I saw three hares, in one day *run away*[6] from the dogs. To give dog and hare a fair trial, there should be but *one* dog. Then, if that dog got so close as to compel the hare *to turn,* that would be a proof that the dog ran fastest. When the dog, or dogs, never get near enough to the hare to induce her to *turn*, she is said, and very justly, to"*run away*"from them[7]; and, as I saw three hares do this in one day, I conclude, that the hare is the swiftest animal of the two.

This inn is one of the nicest, and, in summer, one of the pleasantest, *in England;* for, I think, that my *experience* in this way[8] will justify me in speaking thus positively.[9] The house is large, the yard and the stables good, the landlord[10] a *farmer* also, and, therefore, no cribbing your horses in hay or straw and yourself in eggs and cream.[11] The garden, which adjoins the south side of the house, is large, of good shape, has a terrace on one side, lies on the slope, consists of well-disposed[12] clumps of shrubs and flowers, and of *short-grass* very neatly kept. In the lower part of the garden there are high trees, and, amongst these, the *tulip-tree*[13] and the live-oak.[14] Beyond the garden is a large clump of lofty *sycamores,*[15] and, in these a most populous rookery,[16] in which, of all things in the world, I delight. The village, which contains 301 souls,[17] lies to the north of the inn, but adjoining its premises.[18] All the rest, in every direction, is bare *down or open arable.*[19] I am now sitting at one of the southern windows of this inn, looking across the garden towards the rookery. It is nearly sun-setting; the rooks are skimming[20] and curving[21] over the tops of the trees; while, under the branches, I see a flock of several hundred sheep, coming nibbling their way in[22] from the Down, and going to their fold.

Now, what ill-natured devil could bring Old Nic Grimshaw[23] into my head in company with these innocent sheep? Why, the truth is this: nothing is *so swift as thought:* it runs over a life-time in a moment; and, while I was writing the last sentence of the foregoing paragraph, *thought* took me up at the time when[24] I used to wear a smock-frock[25] and to carry a wooden bottle like that shepherd's boy; and, in an instant, it hurried me along through my no very short life of adventure, of toil, of peril, of pleasure, of ardent friendship and not less ardent enmity; and after filling me with wonder, that a heart and mind so wrapped up in every thing belonging to the gardens, the fields and the woods, should have been condemned[26] to waste themselves away amidst the stench, the noise and the strife of cities, it brought me *to the present moment,* and sent my mind back to what I have yet to perform about Nicholas Grimshaw and his *ditches!*[27]

My sons set off about three o'clock to-day, on their way to Herefordshire, where I intend to join them, when I have had a pretty good ride in this country. There is no pleasure in travelling, except on horseback, or on foot. Carriages take your body from place to place; and, if you merely want to be *conveyed*, they are very good; but they enable you to see and to know nothing at all of the country.

INHERITANCE IN THE PUBLIC CARCASS

Heytesbury (Wilts),
Thursday, 31st August 1826.

A little further on, however, I came to a very famous inn, called DEPTFORD INN, which is in the parish of Wyly. I stayed at this inn till about four o'clock in the afternoon. I remembered Wyly very well, and thought it a gay place when I was a boy. I remembered a very beautiful garden belonging to a rich farmer and miller. I went to see it; but, alas! though the *statues* in the water and on the grass-plat[1] were still remaining, every thing seemed to be in a state of perfect carelessness and neglect. The living[2] of this parish of Wyly was lately owned by DAMPIER[3] (a brother of the *Judge*[4]), who lived at, and I believe had the living of, MEON STOKE in Hampshire. This fellow, I believe, never saw the parish of Wyly but once, though it must have yielded him a pretty good fleece.[5] It is a Rectory,[6] and the great tithes[7] must be worth, I should think, six or seven hundred pounds a year, at the least. It is a part of our system to have certain *families,* who have no particular merit; but who are to be maintained, without why or wherefore,[8] at the public expense, in some shape, or under some name, or other, it matters not much what shape or what name. If you look through the old list of pensioners, sinecurists, parsons, and the like, you will find the same names everlastingly recurring. They seem to be a sort of creatures[9] that have an *inheritance in the public carcass,*[10] like the maggots that some people have in their skins. This family of DAMPIER seems to be one of those. What, in God's name, should have made one of these a Bishop and the other a Judge! I never heard of the smallest particle[11] of talent that either of them possessed. This Rector of Wyly was another of them. There was no harm in them that I know of, beyond that of living upon the public; but, where were their merits? They had none, to distinguish them,[12] and to entitle them to[13] the great sums they received; and, under any other system than such a system as this, they would, in all human probability, have been gentlemen's servants or little shopkeepers. I dare say there is some of the *breed*[14] left; and, if there be, I would pledge my existence[15] that they are, in some shape or other, feeding upon the public. However, thus it must be, until that change come which will put an end to men paying *fourpence* in tax upon a pot of beer.[16]

A WATERING PLACE

Hayden,
Saturday Night, 30 Sept. 1826.

The Warwickshire Avon[1] falls into the Severn here, and on the sides of both, for many miles back, there are the finest meadows that ever were seen. In looking over them, and beholding the endless flocks and herds, one wonders *what can become of all the meat!* By riding on about eight or nine miles farther, however, this wonder is a little diminished; for here we come to one of the devouring WENS:[2] namely, CHELTENHAM, which is what they call a "*watering place*"; that is to say, a place to which East India plunderers, West India floggers,[3] English tax-gorgers,[4] together with gluttons, drunkards, and debauchees of all descriptions,[5] *female* as well as male, resort, at the suggestion of silently laughing quacks,[6] in the hope of getting rid of the bodily consequences of their manifold sins and iniquities.[7] When I enter a place like this, I always feel disposed to squeeze up my nose with my fingers. It is nonsense, to be sure; but I conceit[8] that every two-legged creature, that I see coming near me, is about to cover me with the poisonous proceeds of its impurities.[9] To places like this come all that is knavish and all that is foolish and all that is base; gamesters, pick-pockets, and harlots; young wife-hunters in search of rich and ugly and old women, and young husband-hunters in search of rich and wrinkled or half-rotten men, the formerly[10] resolutely bent, be the means what they may, to give the latter heirs to their lands and tenements. These things are notorious; and, Sir William Scott,[11] in his speech of 1802, in *favour of the non-residence of the Clergy,*[12] expressly said, that they and their families ought to appear at *watering places,* and that this was amongst the means of *making them respected by their flocks!*[13] Memorandum:[14] he was a member for Oxford[15] when he said this!

SINGING BIRDS

Horncastle,
April 13, 1830, Morning.

There is one deficiency, and that, with me, a great one, throughout this country of corn and grass and oxen and sheep, that I have come over during the last three weeks; namely, the want[1] of singing-birds. We are now just in that season when they sing most. Here, in all this country, I have seen and heard only about four sky-larks, and not one other singing bird of any description,[2] and of the small birds that do not sing I have seen only one *yellowhammer,*[3] and it was perched on the rail of a pound[4] between Boston and Sibsey. Oh! the thousands of linnets[5] all singing together on one tree in the sand-hills of Surrey! Oh! the carolling[6] in the coppices and the dingles of Hampshire and Sussex and Kent! At this moment (5 o'clock in the morning) the groves at Barn-Elm are echoing with the warblings of thousands upon thousands of birds. The *thrush* begins a little before it is light; next the *blackbird;* next the *larks* begin to rise; all the rest begin the moment the sun gives the signal; and from the hedges, the bushes, from the middle and the topmost twigs of the trees, comes the singing of endless variety; from the long dead grass comes the sound of the sweet and soft voice of the *white-throat* or *nettle-tom,*[7] while the loud and merry song of the *lark* (the songster himself out of sight) seems to descend from the skies. MILTON, in his description of paradise,[8] has not omitted the "song of earliest birds". However, every thing taken together, here, in Lincolnshire, are more good things than man could have had the conscience to *ask* of God.

And now, if I had time and room to describe the state of men's *affairs,* in the country through which I have passed, I should show, that the people at Westminster[9] would have known how to turn paradise itself into hell.

THE CONDITION OF ENGLAND

Spittal, near Lincoln,
19 April 1830.

When I was at St. Ives, in Huntingdonshire, an open country, I sat with the farmers, and smoked a pipe by way of preparation for evening service,[1] which I performed on a carpenter's bench in a wheelwright's shop[2]; my friends, the players,[3] never having gained any regular settlement in that grand mart for four-legged fat meat,[4] coming from the Fens,[5] and bound to the Wen.[6] While we were sitting, a hand-bill was handed round the table, advertising *farming stock* for sale; and amongst the implements of husbandry 'an *excellent fire-engine,*[7] *several steel-traps,*[8] and *spring-guns'*[9]*!* And that is the life, is it, of an *English farmer?* I walked on about six miles ofthe road from Holbeach to Boston. I have before observed upon[10] the inexhaustible riches of this land. At the end of about five miles and three-quarters I came to a public-house,[11] and thought I would get some breakfast; but the poor woman, with a tribe of children about her, had not a morsel of either meat or bread! At a house called an inn, a little further on, the landlord had not meat except a little bit of chine[12] of bacon; and though there were a good many houses near the spot, the landlord told me that the people were become so poor that the butchers had left off killing meat[13] in the neighbourhood. Just the state of things that existed in France on the eve of the Revolution. On that very spot I looked round me and counted more than two thousand fat sheep in the pastures! How long, how long, good God! is this state of things to last? How long will these people starve in the midst of plenty? How long will fire-engines, steel-traps, and spring-guns be, in such a state of things, a protection to property?

THE STATE-DOCTORS

Worcester,
18 May 1830.

Thus have I come through countries of corn and meat and iron and coal; and from the banks of the Humber[1] to those of the Severn[2], I find all the people, who do not share in the taxes,[3] in a state of distress, greater or less, *Mortgagers*[4] all frightened out of their wits; *fathers* trembling for the fate of their children; and *working people* in the most miserable state, and, as they ought to be, in the *worst of temper*. These will, I am afraid, be the *state-doctors*[5] at last!

The farmers are cowed down: the poorer they get, the more cowardly they are. Every one of them sees the cause of his suffering, and sees general ruin at hand; but every one hopes, that by some trick, some act of meanness, some contrivance,[6] *he shall escape*. So that there is no hope of any change for the better but from the *working people*.[7] The farmers will sink to a very low state; and thus the Thing[8] (barring *accidents*[9]) may go on, until neither farmer nor tradesman will see a joint of meat on his table once in a quarter of a year. It appears likely to be precisely as it was in France: it is now just what France was at the close of the reign of Louis XV.[10] It has been the fashion to ascribe the *French Revolution* to the writings of Voltaire, Rousseau, Diderot,[11] and others. These writings had *nothing at all* to do with the matter: no, *nothing at all*. The *Revolution* was produced by *taxes,* which at last became unbearable; by debts of the State; but, in fact, by the despair of the people, produced by the weight of the taxes.

It is curious to observe how ready the supporters of tyranny and taxation are to ascribe rebellions and revolutions to disaffected[12] leaders; and particularly to writers; and, as these supporters of tyranny and taxation have had the press at their command; have had generally the absolute command of it, they have caused this belief to go down from generation to generation. It will not do[13] for them to ascribe revolutions and rebellions to the ture cause; because then the rebellions and revolutions would be justified; and it is their object to cause them to be condemned. Infinite delusion has prevailed in this country, in consequence of the efforts of which I am now speaking. Voltaire was just as much a cause of the French Revolution as I have been the cause of imposing these sixty millions of taxes.[14] The French Revolution was produced by the grindings of taxation; and this I will take an opportunity very soon of proving, to the conviction of every man in the kingdom[15] who chooses to read.

【作者简介】 William Cobbett（威廉·科贝特，1762—1835），十九世纪初年英国最有影响的政论家之一，出身农家，从小在田间劳动，后来当过兵，去过北美洲和法国，回英后主办《政治纪闻》报（*Cobbett's Weekly Political Register*）议论时局。当时法国革命爆发不久，英国庇特（William Pitt）政府在欧洲大陆组织联军进攻法国，在国内则镇压民主活动，推行劫贫济富的纸币政策。科贝特本来思想保守，至此乃觉醒奋起，1805年以后抨击政府更为激烈，所作社论深获贫民之心，《政治纪闻》报销数激增，当局乃课以重税阻其流行，科贝特本人亦受追捕，入狱二年，被迫流亡美国又二年，至1831年还以七十高龄被政府以煽动叛乱罪起诉，然而搏斗如故，对于豪门贵族和靠公债发财的新富口诛笔伐不辍，而且还特别到英格兰北部工业城镇旅行演讲，深入劳动人民之间，受到他们的热烈欢迎。

由于科贝特深爱英国和英国人民，自身又具有英国人民的某些典型特点，因此曾被称为“典型的约翰牛”（“the pattern John Bull of his century”—Thomas Carlyle）。他爱英国的美丽山水和英国人民之间的淳朴风俗，因此同糟蹋英国风物的商业和金融资本家势不两立，但同时他又充满了怀古思想，始终觉得过去的英国事事如意。马克思曾经说他是“大不列颠的最保守又最激进的人；他是古老的英国最纯真的化身，同时又是年轻的英国的最勇敢的预告者”。

科贝特没有进过学校，全靠自学成了一个文章能手，著作极多，最大量的是政论，其次在历史、农业、经济、一般社会问题方面都写了许多书，此外还编过字典和英语与法语的语法，其中《英语语法》一书由于立论浅近，例句新颖，至今都值得学习英语者一读。科贝特凡有著述，文字都十分吸引人，风格质朴有力，词句明白如话，在十九世纪初年浪漫派美文极盛之时，独树一帜，杰出地继承和发扬了以十八世纪笛福与斯威夫特为代表的平易文体。欲知科贝特的散文的特点，首先应读 *Rural Rides*（《骑马乡行记》），它在科贝特的众多作品之中最受文学史家和文章风格研究者的推崇。

【题解与注释】

《骑马乡行记》是科贝特在1821—1830年间出游英格兰、苏格兰各地的零星记载，原来陆续发表在《政治纪闻》报上，到1830年才汇集出版。作者为了深入了解英国农村和城镇的真实情况，曾经不断出行，每次都是骑着马，深入内地，到处注意土壤、庄稼、林木和牛羊牧放的情况，到处交朋友，访古迹，问民生疾苦，一到旅店，喘息未定，即将马背所见，疾书成文，夹叙夹议，充满了一种热腾腾的“此时此地”的实感。但是文中并无多少风景描写，多的是英国人民当时的困苦的纪录：到处是乞丐，农民住处不如猪圈，吃得不如罪犯，却养肥了一群吃公债和拿干薪的新贵！科贝特忧国之心如焚，刚刚神往于春天早晨百鸟齐喧的境界，但是一想到眼前人事，立刻又恨官僚和商人将英国变成了地狱。当时英国正处在历史的一大转折点，法国革命和工业革命的影响激荡不已，反对拿破仑的战争刚打完，工业资本家开始得势，列宁称为“世界上第一次广泛的、真正群众性的、政治性的无产阶级革命运动”（见《列宁全集》中文版第29卷，第276页）的宪章运动就要在英国广大城乡树起斗争的红旗。《骑马乡行记》的难得之处，正在它写下了处在这样一个重要历史时期的英国农村的实况。

然而它却不止是历史记录；除了题材的重要和纪载的真实性之外，这儿还有犀利、明快的文笔。这文笔的第一特点是通俗：科贝特用字简单，句法合于民间口语，从人生最常见的事物采取妇孺皆晓然又新鲜活泼的比喻，尤其会用一二绰号似的名词去画龙点睛似地揭出一个可恨的制度、一类可鄙的人物、一座可憎的城市——伦敦则称为 the Wen（毒瘤），公债客则称为 fundlords，当时英国政府所采取的政治和经济制度则统称为 the THING. 当浪漫派的华丽散文风靡一时之际，科贝特的散文却以平易质朴取胜，它的长处在于既有山水小品文的情致，又有政论文的辛辣和力量。当时另一散文大名家赫兹列特（Hazlitt）曾经盛赞他，说：

> He is not only unquestionably the most powerful political writer of the present day, but one of the best writers in the language. He speaks and thinks plain, broad, downright English. He might be said to have the clearness of Swift, the naturalness of Defoe, and the picturesque satirical description of Mandeville, if all such comparisons were not impertinent. A really great and original writer is like nobody but himself.
>
> （他不仅毫无疑问是当今最坚强有力的政论家，而且是英文中最好的作家之一。他的文章同他的思想一样，是朴素的，开朗的，直截了当的。我们可以说：他有斯威夫特的明白晓畅，笛福的自然流利，曼特维尔的画笔生采而意存讽世——如果这类比拟不是不伦不类的话。一个真正伟大的、有创造力的作家只象他自己，而不象任何别人。）

事实上，在英国散文的演进史上，科贝特不仅上承斯威夫特与笛福，而且下启萧伯纳，在用词与句法上比多数十九世纪英文散文作家都接近二十世纪的风格，值得有志于英语的人学习。

科贝特的散文也有它的缺点：噜嗦，跑野马，有一定程度的单调。有一个英国批评家曾说他的文章中有“绝好英文的巨大浪费”（“a prodigal waste of good English”— Walter Raleigh, *Style*, p.106）. 但毕竟誉之者多，毁之者少。

这里所选的片断按照写作的时间先后排列，每节前后有删节，但本身是完整的，前面的写作时间与地点也照原书，但一律加上了年代，而每节上面的小标题则是选注者加的。文章当中的大写字和斜体字也都出自原书，用尽一切办法（包括印刷形式上的）来强调自己的意思正是科贝特的风格的特点之一，因此一仍其旧。

MARLBOROUGH

这一节叙述当时英国农村的惨状，年轻农妇衣不蔽体，面如死灰。

1. post-chaise: 驿站与驿站间的马车。

2. Came up: 省略了主词 I. 这在日记、书信等随意文体是常见的事。

3. downs: 英国南部常见的无树多草的丘陵地，多用作牛羊牧放之处。

4. Devizesd [diˈvaiziz]**:** 地名。

5. Salisbury [ˈsɔːlzbəri]**:** 地名。

6. flints: 硬石。

7. chalk: 白垩，指地质。

8. ricks: 麦堆。

9. pieces of wheat: 大面积的麦田；piece = enclosed portion of land.

10. attending the measurers to measure their reaping work: 等待验收者来给她们所割的麦子过秤。

11. hoppers at Farnham: Farnham 地方的打草的人；按 Farnham [ˈfɑːnəm] 为科贝特出生地。

12. I never before saw *country* people, and reapers too, observe, so miserable: 作者在这句用的是口语体的句法，observe 是插入语，意为“请注意”。

13. frost hardly off the ground: 地上仍然霜重。

14. but that of a seat-seller or a loan-jobber: 除了那些卖官鬻爵、买空卖空之徒的心以外；seat-seller 指以国会议员席位作交易的人；loan-jobber，借款给政府的银行家或靠公债进行投机的人。

OXFORD

在这一节中，科贝特大骂脱离实际的牛津大学师生之无用、有害。文字泼辣。

1. drones: 雄蜂，亦指懒汉。

2. wasps: 黄蜂，亦指恶毒的人。

3. want of talent: 缺乏才干。

4. fellows: 可能指牛津各学院的教师（每个学院都有若干主要教师，称 fellows）；也可能只是泛指“人们”（那些家伙）。

5. *University Hall*: 指牛津大学的某一校舍，按该校并无一屋以此两词命名。

6. reflecting: 想起。

7. Kensington: 地名，伦敦西郊的一区，科贝特在该区居住。

8. members of this University: 牛津大学的全体师生。

9. arising from property: 从地产而来的（收入）。按牛津许多学院都拥有广大田产。

10. the “Great Council of the Nation”: 照字面似指英国议会，但也可能指牛津大学本身，该校最高评议组织称 Hebdomadal Council.

11. ye gloriously feeding Doctors: 你们这些大鱼大肉吃得过瘾的博士们！ gloriously 此处意为 with intense delight; ye 是 you 的古时形式，作第二人称主格用。

12. that church: 指英国国教会。十九世纪初，牛津各学院的教员多半是牧师担任，由于其待遇优厚，故科贝特称之为 ye rich of that church.

13. the salt of the labouring man: 劳动者的汗水。

14. your flocks: 你们所管的教民们。基督教会自比羊群，而视卫护、指引者耶稣为"好牧童"（the Good Shepherd）. 牧师因亦自视为牧童，而以教民为羊群。

15. a hundred thousand sermons in ten months: 十个月中（发出）布道文十万篇。科贝特 1819 年从美回英时，曾将革命家潘恩（Tom Paine）的骨灰带回，潘恩被当时许多人认为无神论者，科贝特因之亦受到猜疑，为了在贫农间维持他的声誉（他们一般是怕接近无神论者的），同时又为了与官方教会抗衡，科贝特乃写了布道文多篇，除每月印发外，又汇集成书出版，书名 *Twelve Sermons*. 这里的数字十万篇指其布道文印行之大量，而非确实的统计。

AN ENGLISH SPRING

这一节写英国农村的春天，从中可见科贝特对于树木和鸣禽的爱好。文字充满了春天来临的喜悦和新鲜之感。

1. coppices: 低矮的树丛。

2. birch: 桦木。

3. ash: 白杨。

4. the vegetable creation: 指植物世界。

5. bespangled with primroses and bluebells: 缀满了嫩黄的樱草花和蓝色的吊钟花。

6. pheasant: 雉；**blackbird**：画眉；**thrush**：鹞；三者都是会唱歌的鸟，但歌声不同，因此作者用的动词也不同：crow,（象鸡那样）啼；whistle，尖声嘶叫；sing，歌唱。

7. oak-buds: 橡树叶子。

8. finches: 碛鹞。

9. lark: 云雀。

10. carries the joyous sound to the sky: 云雀不仅歌声嘹亮，而且飞得最高，故云。

A RIDE IN THE RAIN

这一小节写科贝特冒雨出游，寥寥数语，豪兴跃然纸上。就在这种场合，他也不忘抵抗压迫者，具见平民政治家的本色。

1. Here I am in spite of St. Swithin!: 尽管雨神肆虐，我毕竟到了此地！St. Swithin，司雨之神。

2. *rough him!*: 顶他！

3. setting the saint at defiance: 违抗雨神。

4. not one dry thread: 衣服上无一处不湿，全身淋透。

5. balt: give food to.

CASTLEREAGH

Castlereagh（见下注）自杀后，科贝特骑马过其旧居，有感书此。他是坚决主张打落水狗的，不因敌人已死就讲宽恕。整段只有一句话（sentence），一气呵成，痛快淋漓。文章也反映了当时英国政府镇压民主运动的残酷与人民斗争的激烈。

1. Castlereagh: Robert Stewart (1769–1822)，反动政客，袭爵而称 Lord Castlereagh ['kɑ:slrei] 及 Marquis of Londonderry，曾主持镇压 1798 年的爱尔兰人民武装起义，后为陆军大臣（1805—1809 年），外交大臣（1812—1821 年）及下院领袖（1812—1821 年），对外主持侵略，对内实行高压，最为人民痛恨。拜伦、雪莱都有诗骂他。1822 年在十目所视、十手所指、举国反对的情况下，神经崩溃，终于自杀。

2. the house: 指 Castlereagh 所住之屋。

3. Finnerty: Peter (1766–1822)，印刷商人，由于参加激进活动曾两次判刑入狱。

4. Reynolds, Oliver, and Edwards: 三人都是当时英国政府派遣打入群众运动的暗探，无不罪行累累。Reynolds, Thomas (1771–1836)，爱尔兰人，1816 年伦敦贫民在 Spa Fields 聚会，事后被捕多人，他出庭为官方作证。Oliver, William (?–1827?)，又名 Richards 及 Jones，曾受 Castlereagh 派遣，挑起 1816 年的"达比夏暴动"（Darbyshire insurrection），结果三人处死。Edwards, George，与 1820 年的伦敦凯图街事件（the Cato Street Conspiracy）有关，当时有一群志士计划袭击内阁，拟一举而扑灭全体大臣，但由于 Edwards 告密，功败垂成，领袖 Arthur Thistlewood 等人英勇就义。

注意　Edwards 后面的标点":"。这个标点有两种用法，一是总起一句，后列细节时用，如本段第一句便是，这是一般比较熟悉并与现代汉语一致的用法；另一种用法则是在有一系列平行或对照事项时点断其中的每项用，如本段多数情形便是，而在每项之中又有并列细节时则用";"点断。

5. huzzas: 欢呼声。

6. this fellow: 指 Castlereagh. 1815 年三月，Castlereagh 参加标志封建势力复辟的维也纳会议后回国，由于他操纵会议获得成功，登陆时曾受到当权派人士的盛大欢迎。

7. a crew: 一帮，指 Castlereagh 的同僚，包括另一民愤极大的反动政客 Sidmouth. 他们都是 Lord Liverpool 所组内阁（1812—1827 年）中的大臣，因此科贝特称之为 the most corrupt and villainous（最腐化、最狠毒的）。

8. "ignorant impatience of taxation": "由于无知而对纳税感到不满"，这是 Castlereagh 在 1816 年在国会辩论时说的话，曾引起强烈的反对。

9. "digging of holes one day and filling them up the next": 这是科贝特仿照 Castlereagh 的口气写的话，讽刺他的所谓失业救济，不过象是驱使贫民今天挖个洞，明天又把它填满罢了，无补生产，也不能解决失业问题。由于 Castlereagh 提倡以这类工作救济贫民，科贝特还送了他一个绰号，叫做“the great hole-digger”.

10. the cool statement of the number of “soldiers wanted to collect the taxes in Ireland”: 也指 Castlereagh 的言论。1815 年反对拿破仑的战争结束之后，大批军队复员，但是政府无法安顿他们，不少人沦为乞丐，Castlereagh 则扬言可以派他们去爱尔兰强迫人民交税。同时，这话也隐射他在爱尔兰镇压 1798 年人民起义的事。这里用 cool 一字也是为了挖苦，表示 Castlereagh 说得悠然自得，冷静非凡。

11. SIDMOUTH: Henry Addington (1757–1844)，内政大臣（1812—1821 年），以反动、残暴著称，1817，1819 年的几项镇压人民的法令都是由他制订的。

12. *the Power-of-Imprisonment Bill*: 即 Sidmouth 制订的镇压法令之一，1817 年由 Castlereagh 在下院提出，原想利用它来逮捕科贝特，但科贝特事先得讯，法令颁布时他已渡洋逃往美国。

13. KNIGHT: John (1763–1838)，曼彻斯特城的老工人，曾因参加民主活动几度入狱，受到拷打，引起各地人民的强烈抗议。Castlereagh 不但授意监禁他，而且诬蔑他为“疯子”。

14. OGDEN: William (1753–1822)，曼彻斯特印刷工人，曾在 1817 年参加当地劳动人民组织的步行赴伦敦向国会请愿的示威性的“毯子进军”（the Blanketeers March），事后被捕入狱，因上重枷而得疝气，不久身死。

15. REILEY: 或作 Riley，名 Thomas, Huddersfield 地方的成衣匠，生年不详，1817 年 7 月被捕，当局始终不予审讯，几度申请被拒，于是在狱中自杀身死。

16. “*basest populace*”: Castlereagh 语，用来咒骂支持 Queen Caroline（见下）的群众。

17. the bapless and ill-treated Queen: 指英王乔治第四之妻，Queen Caroline (1768–1821). 乔治为摄政王时，已不喜 Caroline 而与之分居，及至登极，又诬她不贞，拒给王后名号。乔治本人荒淫残暴，反对他的民主人士遂群起为 Caroline 执言，科贝特尤其全力支持，曾为她写公开信谴责乔治。

18. the 16th of August at Manchester: 1819 年 8 月 16 日，曼彻斯特工人六万人在 St. Peter's Field 集会，要求进行国会改革，忽遭军警袭击，死伤六百人，举国震动，称为 Peterloo 惨案。

19. the Oldham Inquest: 上述惨案中死者之一名 John Lees，系曼彻斯特北边 Oldham 地方人，死后检尸时，群情愤激，当地陪审员宣布其死因为“蓄意谋杀”（wilful murder），公开谴责政府。

20. RICHARD (1804–1875): 科贝特第四子，亦即他钟爱的幼子，曾多次侍父出游。

21.“*liberality*”: “宽宏大量”。Castlereagh 自杀后，不少“绅士”风度的上层人士认为人既死去，也就不必多计较他在世时所作所为，以示“宽宏大量”。科贝特则坚决反对，在此强调宣告：“我从灵魂深处鄙视这种伪善的宽大论！”

A SHOOTER

这节叙述一个有名射手的行径，写他如何因为虚荣而骗人。文章写得通俗、清楚，用的是口语体，读了如闻其声，如见其人；当中还有许多幽默、讽刺的笔触，透露了科贝特对于这类资产阶级人士了解的深刻。

1. a barrister of Philadelphia: 美国费拉德尔非亚城的一个律师。这里所记原是科贝特过去在美国的见闻之一，现在他在英国乡间看见人们因打猎而发生争执，不觉回忆起在美国的往事。

2. a shooting: 即 shooting 之意，a 为前置词，即 on 之变体，现已不常用。用时往往随 go, set 等动词出现，如 he went a begging, they set the bells a ringing.

3. well matched: 搭配得很好。

4. a shot:（好）枪手。

5. double shots: 一枪打下两只。

6. a *miss* or two: 一两次未射中。

7. every one upon the wing: 每一只都打在翅膀上。

8. largish trees: 较大（而不是很大）的树；后缀 -ish 表示“近乎”，“趋向”。

9. petticoat government: 老婆的管束。

10. gig: 由一匹马牵引的两轮马车。

11. that General Brown, who gave some of our whiskered heroes such a rough handling last war, which was waged for the purpose of “Deposing James Madison”: 这里的将军指美国人 Jacob Brown (1775–1828)，战争指 1812 年的美英战争，当时美国总统是詹姆士 · 麦迪孙；our whiskered heroes（我们的胡子兵）指英军；a rough handling，一顿痛打。

12. that watchful government: 仍指律师夫人的严厉的管束，watchful 表示经常警惕地注视着。

13. The *dog*: 科贝特接 Ewing 所说“狗是你的”而言，但下面另谈别事，因此这两字孤立成句。这在口语中是常有的事。

14. affected: 假装。

15. Pity for his weakness got the better of my dread of the bad road: 我已不在乎晚上走坏路的危险，倒是可怜起他的毛病来了；got the better of，胜过，盖倒。

16. I felt no temptation to detect him: 我无意去戳穿他。

17. as merry as larks: 兴高采烈地。

18. imposition: 欺骗，在此为 to practise 的宾语。

19. puerile vanity: 幼稚（可笑）的虚荣心。

THE“EDUCATION”CANTERS

在这一节里，科贝特驳斥“教育救国论”。文字犀利，如长刀一劈到底。

1. the “*education*” canters: 标榜“教育”的论客们；canter 字从 cant（口头

禅，满口仁义道德）。

2. the most curious fellows of all: 最怪的人；curious 此处意为 strange, odd.

3. FELON: 罪犯。

4. perverseness: 一贯邪恶，屡犯不改。

5. *roguery*: 奸诈。

6. the unfeeling tyrant: 全无心肝的暴君；unfeeling 意为麻木不仁。

7. squeezes the labourers for gain's sake: 为贪得而压榨劳动人民。

8. literary or tub rogue: 文氓或教痞。

9. him: 指上文 tyrant.

10. that makes the poor, starving wretches thieves and robbers: 使那些穷苦饥饿的可怜人变成盗贼。

11. Here it falls at last: 最后一切部落在这里（贫农头上）。

12. this class: 指贫农（labourers）阶层。

13. reason: 有理智的人。

14. to be sure: 不错（承认对方论点时说）。

15. *if he do not work*: 假如他敢不作工的话；此处 do 是虚拟式。

16. I and my little boy snapped up in six or seven minutes upon Stoke-Charity down: 指本文另一处所记当天早晨科贝特与其子 Richard 在丘陵地骑在马背上吃早餐的一事。

17. the debt: 指英国政府由于筹措军费所负的国债。对法战争耗费极大，国债在战前仅为二亿四千万镑，而 1815 年停战时增到八亿六千万镑。

18. the dead-weight: 英国政府所发为数惊人的津贴、养老金的总称，有时也用来称呼领受这种金钱的优闲寄生的海陆军退休军官。

19. the thundering standing army: standing army = 常备军，thundering，吼叫如雷（挖苦语）。

20. sinecures: 领干薪的职位。遥领名义，或雇人代理，本人不必工作，坐领高薪的职位，称为 sinecures. 这类“肥缺”向为若干上层家族的囊中物，小儿老妇都可顶名，如 Lord Addington 之子十二岁任 Clerk of the Pell，年薪三千镑，曼彻斯特公爵太夫人任 Collector of Customs，年薪亦三千镑，而 Camden 侯爵任 Teller of the Exchequer，不做一事而年入二万三千镑。科贝特一生就是对这等分赃制度不断加以攻击。

21. pensions: 退休金。

22. grants: 津贴。

23. and this would suit but a very small part of a press: 但是这却是对大多数报纸不相宜的。

REFLECTIONS IN AN ENGLISH INN

这一段兼有写景的真实和抒情的亲切。科贝特坐在一家乡村的小旅店里，面对绿草地和羊群，耳听归鸦的叫声，不禁在那美丽的黄昏时节想起自己的一生。他爱好田野和花草，但是却命定要住在嘈杂、肮脏的城市里！虽然如此，文章却并无感伤情调，因为这一些回忆只使科贝特更加坚决地要同操纵选举的反动政客去进行斗争。

1. *Down-country*: 长满短草的丘陵地，是英格兰南部风景的特色之一。

2. *greensward*: 大片绿草地。

3. *coursing*: 赛狗，狗的赛跑。

4. *forty brace*: 四十对，即八十只（狗）。注意 brace 多数形式如单数，不加 s。

5. cover: 树林等可以躲藏之处。

6. *run away*: 在此有特别涵义，见作者本人在下文（第 22—23 行）的解释。

7. she is said ... to "*run away*" from them: 科贝特在这里解释"run away"在打猎、养狗的人们之间的特别涵义，"跑得（使狗）无法追踪"。

8. my *experience* in this way: 科贝特曾经游历各地，到过许多旅店，因此自觉在这一点上经验丰富。

9. positively: 肯定地。

10. landlord: 此处指旅店主人。

11. no cribbing your horses in hay or straw and yourself in eggs and cream: 你的马只管痛快吃草，你自己也放开吃鸡蛋和奶油好了，不必拘束。

12. well-disposed: well-arranged.

13. *tulip-tree*: 百合树（花似郁金香）。

14. live-oak: 一种原生北美洲的槲树。

15. sycamores: 枫树。

16. rookery: 鸦巢。

17. souls: 人。

18. adjoining its premises: 紧接旅店的园地；premises 指不动产，即房屋园地之类。

19. *open arable*: 开阔的耕地。

20. skimming: 轻掠而过。

21. curving: 从高向低而飞。

22. coming nibbling their way in: 沿途吃着草走回来。

23. Nic Grimshaw: Nicholas Grimshaw，律师，Preston 城的市长，政治上反动，1826 年（即科贝特写作此节的一年）主持该城国会议员选举，科贝特参加竞选，由于 Grimshaw 的操纵而失败，因此十分恨他。

24. thought took me up at the time when ...: 一下子想到了那个…时候。

25. smock-frock: 农民所穿的宽大外衣。

26. should have been condemned: 竟然命定要。

27. what I have yet to perform about Nicholas Grimshaw and his *ditches*: 为了对付 Grimshaw 和他操纵选举的诡计我还有许多事情该做；his ditches, Grimshaw 为了阻止有人接近选民，规定投票时选民须经特别的通道直达投票站，为此特辟了一些沟渠式的通道，时人称为 Grimshaw's ditches.

INHERITANCE IN THE PUBLIC CARCASS

这一节指出英国有某些上层家族，每个成员都是吮吸公众的血的寄生虫，世代如此，早成特权。

1. grass-plat: 草地；plat，一片地。

2. living: 牧师的职位及其收入。

3. DAMPIER: Rev. John (1768–1854)，牧师，共领六个教区（parishes），即一人而兼六职。父为 Durham 教长兼医院院长，二兄一为主教，一为法官。这一家以全体成员皆能拥要职、吃干薪著称。

4. *Judge*: 指 Sir Henry Dampier，上述牧师之兄。

5. fleece: 收入（名词），原意羊毛，教士所管辖的教民称 flocks（羊群），因此科贝特用此词来指他们从教民身上搜括来的收入。按此词一般作名词用时，不指收入，只有作动词用时，始含诈取财物之意。动词转为名词，是近代英文方便处之一，科贝特则是有意为之，表示这种收入是诈取来的不义之财。

6. Rectory: 教区长的职位及其收入，做 rector 的教士享用一个教区（parish）的 tithes（见下）。

7. tithes ['taiðz]**:** 什一税。此字原义为十分之一，当时英国每年从地产收入等项抽取十分之一，作为教会经费及神职人员的生活费。

8. without why or wherefore: 不问理由。

9. creatures: 此处指蛆虫之类。

10. *inheritance in the public carcass*: 承继（吮吸）公众的死尸之权。

11. the smallest particle of talent: 一点点才能。

12. to distinguish them: 使他们显得出色。

13. to entitle them to: 使他们有理由应该享用。

14. *breed*: 名词，种（轻蔑语）。

15. pledge my existence: 以我生命担保。

16. *fourpence* in tax upon a pot of beer: 一大杯啤酒抽税四便士。这个税额极高，超过酒价本身，而且由于啤酒是英国一般人的饮料，这样高的税就剥夺了劳动人民的最后的小小享受。

A WATERING PLACE

英国有不少温泉胜地（watering place），此节所写的 Cheltenham 即为其一。科贝特揭穿真相，使读者看出这等胜地实际只是藏垢纳污之处。

1. Avon. Severn: 都是河名。

2. WENS: 毒疮。科贝特向以 Wen 字称呼城市，尤其是伦敦。

3. floggers: 鞭挞者，指英国殖民地的奴隶主。

4. tax-gorgers: 吞吃税款的人。

5. of all descriptions: of all kinds.

6. quacks: 江湖郎中，骗人的庸医。

7. the bodily consequences of their manifold sins and iniquities: 他们的各

种恶事邪行在他们身上留下的后果（指各种恶疾、传染病）。

8. conceit: 想象（动词）。

9. poisonous proceeds of its impurities: 他的肮脏身体所发出的毒物。此处 its 指上文 creature.

10. the formerly: = the former，前者，指 wife-hunters 与 husband-hunters.

11. Sir William Scott:（1745—1836），历史教授及政客，代表牛津大学任国会议员多年，一贯反动，其女嫁恶行多端的内政大臣 Sidmouth.

12. *the non-residence of the Clergy*: 教士不必居住教区的制度。

13. *flocks*: 教民。

14. Memorandum: 注，按（指出应加注意事项，写在句前）。

15. a member for Oxford: 代表牛津大学的国会议员。

SINGING BIRDS

这是一段有名的文章，作者回忆起春天百鸟争喧的情景，但是一想到眼前人事，他又立刻痛恨伦敦当局将天堂变成地狱了。

1. want: lack，缺乏。

2. of any description: of any kind.

3. *yellow-hammer*: 金翼啄木鸟。

4. pound: 牛栏。

5. linnets: 梅花雀。

6. carolling: singing joyously，快乐地歌唱。

7. *the white-throat or nettle-tom*: 白喉莺。

8. MILTON, in his description of paradise: 见 *Paradise Lost*, Book IV, lines 264–268：

The Birds their quire apply; aires, vernal aires,
Breathing the smell of field and grove, attune
The trembling leaves, while Universal Pan
Knit with *Graces* and *Hours* in dance
Led on th' Eternal Spring.

第一行前五字意为：许多鸟儿唱起歌来（quire = choir，歌队；apply，发挥或添加）。后面几行形容在繁花似锦的春天，天神（Pan）与仙子们（Graces，优雅女神；Hours，季节女神）跳舞的欢乐情景。这一切都发生在天堂。

9. the people at Westminster: 指英国当权派。Westminster 是伦敦的一区，国会所在地。

THE CONDITION OF ENGLAND

英国人民苦难之又一景：丰足中的饥饿。科贝特照例写得具体：满山是肥羊，而酒店之中只见一大群饥饿儿童围着一个毫无办法的母亲打转！看到这种情形，他不禁呼喊起来，短促的句子反映了他心上的焦灼感。

1. evening service: 晚祷。科贝特常在劳动人民中间自动代替教士主持祷告。

2. wheelwright's shop: 制造或修理车轮或轮车的工匠的作场。

3. my friends, the players: 科贝特在该处遇到一个旅行的演戏班子，players 指这个班子中的演员。

4. that grand mart for four-legged fat meat: 那个大规模的羊市；mart = market-place; four-legged fat meat 指羊。

5. the Fens: 剑桥郡一带的低洼地。

6. the Wen: 恶疮，指伦敦。

7. *fire-engine*: 救火器。

8. *steel-traps*: 钢制的陷阱，防盗贼用。

9. *spring-guns*: 暗枪，触动弹簧即发，防盗贼及私人者用。

10. observed upon: remarked on，谈到过。

11. public-house: 酒店。

12. chine: backbone，带肉的后脊骨。

13. left off killing meat: 已经停止屠宰。

THE STATE-DOCTORS

科贝特在此节谴责劳动人民以外的各阶层，指出只有劳动人民才能拯救国家。他对于法国革命原因的分析只从税收一点着眼，反映了他认识的片面。

1. Humber: 河名，在英国北部。

2. Severn: 河名，在英国西南部。

3. share in the taxes: 分享税款，指拿干薪、领政府津贴、吃公债利息等等行为。

4. *Mortgagers*: 抵押了财产的人。

5. *state-doctors*: 诊治国家的医生。

6. contrivance: 计策，办法。

7. but from the *working people*: except from the working people.

8. the Thing: 这是科贝特特别选来指当时英国政府所推行的政治、经济政策与制度的字眼，多年运用，已为他的成语。注意此字极为通俗，人人皆懂，这正是科贝特风格的特色之一。

9. barring *accidents*: 除非有意外事件。

10. Louis XV: 法王路易十五。他死后不久，在路易十六朝内，革命爆发。

11. Voltaire, Rousseau, Diderot: 伏尔泰（1694—1778），卢梭（1712—1778），狄德罗（1713—1784），三人都是有名的法国资产阶级民主思想家。

12. disaffected: 心怀不满的。

13. It will not do:（那样做）是不合适的。

14. Voltaire was just as much a cause of the French Revolution as I have been the cause of imposing these sixty millions of taxes: 伏尔泰之不是法国革命的原因，正犹我之不是硬要人民交出六千万镑税款的原因一样。

15. to the conviction of every man in the kingdom: 使英国每个人都深信不疑。

39 ALFRED TENNYSON
1809–1892

殷宝书　选注

1. BREAK, BREAK, BREAK

Break, break, break,
　　On thy cold grey stones, O Sea!
And I would[1] that my tongue could utter
　　The thoughts that arise in me.

O well for[2] the fisherman's boy,
　　That he shouts with his sister at play!
O well for the sailor lad,
　　That he sings in his boat on the bay!

And the stately ships go on
　　To their haven under the hill;[3]
But O for[4] the touch of a vanished hand,[5]
　　And the sound of a voice that is still!

Break, break, break,
　　At the foot of thy crags, O Sea!
But the tender grace of a day[6] that is dead

Will never come back to me.

2. THE BROOK

An Idyl

'Here, by this brook, we parted; I[1] to the East
And he[2] for Italy — too late[3] — too late:
One whom the strong sons of the world[4] despise;
For lucky rhymes to him were scrip and share,[5,6]
And mellow metres more than cent for cent;[7]
Nor could he understand how money breeds,
Thought[8] it a dead thing; yet himself could make
The thing that is not as the thing that is.[9]
O had he lived! In our schoolbooks we say,
Of those that held their heads above the crowd[10]
They flourish'd then or then;[11] but life in him
Could scarce be said to flourish, only touch'd
On such a time as goes before the leaf,
When all the wood stands in a mist of green,[12]
And nothing perfect: yet the brook he loved,
For which, in branding summers of Bengal,
Or ev'n the sweet half-English Neilgherry air[13]
I panted, seems, as I re-listen to it,
Prattling the primrose fancies of the boy,[14]
To me that loved him; for "O brook," he says,
"O babbling brook," says Edmund in his rhyme,
"Whence come you?" and the brook, why not? replies.

I come from haunts of coot[15] and hern,[16]
    I make a sudden sally
And sparkle out among the fern,
    To bicker down[17] a valley.
By thirty hills I hurry down,

Or slip between the ridges,
By twenty thorps,[18] a little town,
And half a hundred bridges.
Till last by Philip's farm[19] I flow
To join the brimming river,
For men may come and men may go,
But I go on for ever.

'Poor lad, he died at Florence, quite worn out,[20]
Travelling to Naples. There is Darnley bridge,
It has more ivy; there the river; and there
Stands Philip's farm where brook and river meet.

I chatter over stony ways,
In little sharps and trebles,[21]
I bubble into eddying bays,
I babble on the pebbles.

With many a curve my banks I fret
By many a field and fallow,
And many a fairy foreland set
With willow-weed and mallow.[22]

I chatter, chatter, as I flow
To join the brimming river,
For men may come and men may go,
But I go on for ever.

'But Philip chatter'd more than brook or bird;
Old Philip; all about the fields you caught
His weary daylong chirping, like the dry
High-elbow'd grigs[23] that leap in summer grass.

I wind about, and in and out,
With here a blossom sailing,
And here and there a lusty trout,
And here and there a grayling,

And here and there a foamy flake
Upon me, as I travel
With many a silvery waterbreak[24]
Above the golden gravel,

And draw them all along, and flow
To join the brimming river,
For men may come and men may go,
But I go on for ever.

'O darling Katie Willows, his one child!
A maiden of our century,[25] yet most meek;
A daughter of our meadows, yet not coarse;
Straight, but as lissome as a hazel wand;
Her eyes a bashful azure, and her hair
In gloss and hue the chestnut, when the shell
Divides threefold to show the fruit within.[26]

'Sweet Katie, once I did her a good turn,[27]
Her and her far-off cousin and betrothed,
James Willows, of one name and heart with her.
For here I came, twenty years back — the week
Before I parted with poor Edmund; crost[28]
By that old bridge which, half in ruins then,
Still makes a hoary eyebrow for the gleam[29]
Beyond it, where the waters marry — crost,
Whistling a random bar of Bonny Doon,[30]
And push'd at Philip's garden-gate. The gate,

Half-parted from a weak and scolding[31] hinge,
Stuck; and he clamour'd from a casement, "Run"[32]
To Katie somewhere in the walks below,
"Run, Katie!" Katie never ran: she moved
To meet me, winding under woodbine bowers,
A little flutter'd, with her eyelids down,
Fresh apple-blossom,[33] blushing for a boon.[34]

'What was it? less of sentiment than sense
Had Katie; not illiterate; nor of those[35]
Who dabbling in the fount of fictive tears,
And nursed by mealy-mouth'd philanthropies,[36]
Divorce the Feeling from her mate the Deed.

'She told me. She and James had quarrell'd. Why?
What cause of quarrel? None, she said, no cause;
James had no cause: but when I prest the cause,
I learnt that James had flickering jealousies
Which anger'd her. Who anger'd James? I said.
But Katie snatch'd her eyes at once from mine,[37]
And sketching with her slender pointed foot
Some figure like a wizard's pentagram[38]
On garden gravel, let my query pass
Unclaim'd,[39] in flushing silence, till I ask'd
If James were coming. "Coming every day,"
She answer'd, "ever longing to explain,
But evermore her father came across
With some long-winded tale, and broke him short;[40]
And James departed vext with him and her."
How could I help her? "Would I — was it wrong?"
(Claspt hands and that petitionary grace
Of sweet seventeen subdued me ere she spoke)
"O would I take[41] her father for one hour,

For one half-hour, and let him talk to me!"
And even while she spoke, I saw where James
Made towards us, like a wader in the surf,
Beyond the brook, waist-deep in meadow-sweet.

'O Katie, what I suffer'd for your sake!
For in I went, and call'd old Philip out
To show the farm: full willingly he rose:
He led me thro' the short sweet-smelling lanes
Of his wheat-suburb, babbling as he went.
He praised his land, his horses, his machines;
He praised his ploughs, his cows, his hogs, his dogs;
He praised his hens, his geese, his guinea-hens;
His pigeons, who in session[42] on their roofs
Approved him, bowing at their own deserts:[43]
Then from the plaintive mother's teat he took
Her blind and shuddering puppies, naming each,
And naming those, his friends, for whom they were:[44]
Then crost the common into Darnley chase
To show Sir Arthur's deer. In copse and fern
Twinkled the innumerable ear and tail.
Then, seated on a serpent-rooted beech,
He pointed out a pasturing colt, and said:
"That was the four-year-old I sold the Squire."
And there he told a long long-winded tale
Of how the Squire had seen the colt at grass,
And how it was the thing his daughter wish'd,
And how he sent the bailiff[45] to the farm[46]
To learn the price, and what the price he ask'd,
And how the bailiff swore that he was mad,
But he stood firm; and so the matter hung;
He gave them line:[47] and five days after that
He met the bailiff at the Golden Fleece,[48]

Who then and there had offer'd something more,
But he stood firm; and so the matter hung;
He knew the man; the colt would fetch its price;
He gave them line: and how by chance at last
(It may be May or April, he forgot,
The last of April or the first of May)
He found the bailiff riding by the farm,
And, talking from the point,[49] he drew him in,
And there he mellow'd all his heart with ale,
Until they closed a bargain, hand in hand.

'Then, while I breathed in sight of haven,[50] he,
Poor fellow, could he help it? recommenced,
And ran thro' all the coltish chronicle,
Wild Will, Black Bess, Tantivy, Tallyho,
Reform, White Rose, Bellerophon, the Jilt,
Arbaces, and Phenomenon, and the rest,
Till, not to die a listener,[51] I arose,
And with me Philip, talking still; and so
We turn'd our foreheads from the falling sun,
And following our own shadows thrice as long[52]
As when they follow'd us from Philip's door,
Arrived, and found the sun of sweet content[53]
Re-risen in Katie's eyes, and all things well.

I steal by lawns and grassy plots,
I slide by hazel covers;
I move the sweet forget-me-nots
That grow for happy lovers.

I slip, I slide, I gloom, I glance,
Among my skimming swallows;
I make the netted sunbeam dance

Against my sandy shallows.

I murmur under moon and stars
In brambly wildernesses;
I linger by my shingly bars;[54]
I loiter round my cresses;

And out again I curve and flow
To join the brimming river,
For men may come and men may go,
But I go on for ever.

Yes, men may come and go; and these are gone,
All gone. My dearest brother, Edmund, sleeps,
Not by the well-known stream and rustic spire,
But unfamiliar Arno,[55] and the dome
Of Brunelleschi;[56] sleeps in peace: and he,
Poor Philip, of all his lavish waste of words[57]
Remains the lean P. W. on his tomb:
I scraped the lichen from it: Katie walks[58]
By the long wash of Australasian seas
Far off, and holds her head to other stars,
And breathes in converse seasons. All are gone.'

So Lawrence Aylmer,[59] seated on a stile
In the long hedge, and rolling in his mind
Old waifs of rhyme, and bowing o'er the brook
A tonsured head in middle age forlorn,
Mused, and was mute. On a sudden a low breath
Of tender air made tremble in the hedge
The fragile bindweed-bells and briony rings;
And he look'd up. There stood a maiden[60] near,
Waiting to pass. In much amaze he stared

On eyes a bashful azure, and on hair
In gloss and hue the chestnut, when the shell
Divides threefold to show the fruit within:
Then, wondering, ask'd her 'Are you from the farm? '
'Yes,' answer'd she. 'Pray stay a little: pardon me;
What do they call you? ' 'Katie.''That were strange.
What surname? ' 'Willows.' 'No! ' 'That is my name.'
'Indeed! ' and here he look'd so self-perplext,
That Katie laugh'd, and laughing blush'd, till he
Laugh'd also, but as one before he wakes,
Who feels a glimmering strangeness in his dream.
Then looking at her; 'Too happy, fresh and fair,
Too fresh and fair in our sad world's best bloom.
To be the ghost of one who bore your name
About these meadows, twenty years ago.'

'Have you not heard? ' said Katie, 'we came back.
We bought the farm we tenanted before.
Am I so like her? so they said on board.[61]
Sir, if you knew her in her English days,
My mother, as it seems you did, the days
That most she loves to talk of, come with me.
My brother James is in the harvest-field:
But she[62] — you will be welcome — O, come in! '

3. ULYSSES

It[1] little profits that an idle King,
By this still hearth,[2] among these barren crags,
Matched with an agèd wife[3], I mete and dole[4]
Unequal laws[5] unto a savage race[6]
That hoard, and sleep, and feed, and know not me.[7]
I cannot rest from travel; I will drink

Life to the lees.[8] All times I have enjoyed
Greatly, have suffered greatly, both with those
That loved me, and alone; on shore, and when[9]
Through scudding drifts[10] the rainy Hyades[11]
Vexed the dim sea. I am become a name;[12]
For always roaming with a hungry heart
Much have I seen and known — cities of men
And manners, climates, councils, governments,
Myself not least, but honored of them all[13] —
And drunk[14] delight of battle with my peers,[15]
Far on the ringing plains of windy Troy.[16]
I am a part of all[17] that I have met;
Yet all experience is an arch wherethrough
Gleams that untraveled world whose margin fades[18]
Forever and forever when I move.
How dull it is to pause, to make an end,
To rust unburnished, not to shine in use!
As though to breathe were life![19] Life piled on life
Were all too little,[20] and of one to me
Little remains;[21] but every hour is saved
From that eternal silence, something more[22]
A bringer of new things; and vile it were[23]
For some three suns[24] to store and hoard myself,
And this grey spirit yearning[25] in desire
To follow knowledge like a sinking star,
Beyond the utmost bound of human thought.

This is my son, mine own Telemachus,[26]
To whom I leave the scepter and the isle —
Well-loved of me,[27] discerning to fulfill
This labor, by slow prudence to make mild
A rugged people,[28] and through soft degrees
Subdue them to the useful and the good.[29]
Most blameless is he, centered in the sphere

Of common duties, decent not to fail
In offices of tenderness, and pay
Meet adoration to my household gods,[30]
When I am gone. He works his work, I mine.
  There lies the port; the vessel[31] puffs her sail;
There gloom the dark, broad seas. My mariners,
Souls that have toiled, and wrought, and thought with me —
That ever with a frolic welcome took[32]
The thunder and the sunshine, and opposed[33]
Free hearts, free foreheads[34] — you and I are old;
Old age hath yet his honor and his toil.
Death closes all; but something ere the end,
Some work of noble note, may yet be done,
Not unbecoming men that strove with Gods.[35]
The lights begin to twinkle from the rocks;
The long day wanes; the slow moon climbs; the deep.
Moans round with many voices. Come, my friends,
'Tis not too late to seek a newer world.
Push off, and sitting well in order smite
The sounding furrows;[36] for my purpose holds
To sail beyond the sunset, and the baths
Of all the western stars,[37] until I die.
It may be that the gulfs will wash us down;
It may be we shall touch the Happy Isles,[38]
And see the great Achilles, whom we knew.
Though much is taken, much abides; and though
We are not now that strength which in old days
Moved earth and heaven, that which we are, we are[39] —
One equal temper of heroic hearts.[40]
Made weak by time and fate, but strong in will
To strive, to seek, to find, and not to yield.

4. TITHONUS

The woods decay, the woods decay and fall,
The vapours weep their burthen to the ground,[1]
Man comes and tills the field and lies beneath,[2]
And after many a summer dies the swan.
Me only cruel immortality
Consumes[3]: I wither slowly in thine arms,
Here at the quiet limit of the world,[4]
A white-hair'd shadow[5] roaming like a dream
The ever silent spaces[6] of the East,
Far-folded[7] mists, and gleaming halls of morn.

Alas! for this grey shadow, once a man[8] —
So glorious in his beauty and thy choice,
Who[9] madest him thy chosen[10], that[11] he seem'd
To his great heart none other than a God!
I ask'd thee, 'Give me immortality.'
Then didst thou grant mine asking with a smile,
Like wealthy men who care not how they give.[12]
But thy strong Hours[13] indignant[14] work'd their wills,
And beat me down and marr'd and wasted me,
And tho' they could not end me, left me maim'd
To dwell in presence of immortal youth,
Immortal age beside immortal youth,[15]
And all I was, in ashes.[16] Can thy love,
Thy beauty, make amends, tho' even now,
Close over us, the silver star,[17] thy guide,
Shines in those tremulous eyes[18] that fill with tears
To hear me? Let me go: take back thy gift:
Why should a man desire in any way
To vary from the kindly[19] race of men,

Or pass beyond the goal of ordinance[20]
Where all should pause, as is most meet for all?

A soft air fans the cloud apart; there comes
A glimpse of that dark world[21] where I was born.
Once more the old mysterious glimmer[22] steals
From[23] thy pure brows, and from thy shoulders pure,
And bosom beating with a heart renew'd.[24]
Thy cheek begins to redden thro' the gloom,
Thy sweet eyes brighten slowly close to mine,
Ere yet they blind the stars,[25] and the wild team[26]
Which love thee, yearning for thy yoke, arise,
And shake the darkness from their loosen'd manes,
And beat the twilight into flakes of fire.
Lo! ever thus thou growest beautiful
In silence, then before thine answer given
Departest,[27] and thy tears are on my cheek.

Why wilt thou ever scare me with thy tears,
And make me tremble lest a saying learnt,
In days far-off, on that dark earth, be true?[28]
'The Gods[29] themselves cannot recall their gifts,

Ay me! ay me! with what another heart
In days far-off, and with what other eyes
I used to watch — if I be he that watch'd[30] —
The lucid outline forming round thee; saw
The dim curls kindle into sunny rings;
Changed with thy mystic change, and felt my blood
Glow with the glow that slowly crimson'd all
Thy presence and thy portals, while I lay,
Mouth, forehead, eyelids, growing dewy-warm
With kisses balmier than half-opening buds

Of April,[31] and could hear the lips that kiss'd
Whispering[32] I knew not what of wild and sweet,[33]
Like that strange song I heard Apollo sing,[34]
While Ilion like a mist rose into towers.

Yet hold me not for ever in thine East:
How can my nature longer mix with thine?
Coldly thy rosy shadows bathe me, cold
Are all thy lights, and cold my wrinkled feet
Upon thy glimmering thresholds, when the steam
Floats up from those dim fields about the homes
Of happy men that have the power to die,
And grassy barrows[35] of the happier dead.[36]
Release me, and restore me to the ground;
Thou seest all things, thou wilt see my grave:
Thou wilt renew thy beauty morn by morn;
I earth in earth[37] forget these empty courts,[38]
And thee[39] returning on thy silver wheels.

【作者简介】 丁尼生（Alfred Tennyson, 1809–1892）生于英国中东部Lincolnshire州近海的Somersby教区。父亲是牧师，家境小康。1828年入剑桥大学，与海拉姆（A. H. Hallam）结为契友。1830年还在校读书时，开始出诗集。1832年的诗集遭到当时批评家严厉的批评，1833年至友海拉姆又病死；因在精神上诗人连受刺激，以后十年内未发表诗作。在这期间，生活很潦倒，虽然还在写诗。1842年再发表新诗时，引起读者普遍注意，批评家一致赞扬，从此在诗坛上奠定了自己的地位。1850年华兹华斯逝世，丁尼生被任命为后继的英国桂冠诗人。同年发表长诗*In Memoriam*，纪念亡友海拉姆，以后出的重要诗集还有*Maud*（1855年），*Enoch Arden*（1864年），和*Idylls of the King*（1869—1872年）等。

丁尼生诗的体裁大致可分为三类：一是抒情的，如本诗选中的*Break, Break, Break*；一是叙述的，如本诗选中的*The Brook*；一是独白的，如本诗选中的*Ulysses*和*Tithonus*. 诗人对人生颇多伤感，或有美中不足之感，好象中国词中所说的那样，“月有阴晴圆缺，人有悲欢离合，此事古难全”。丁尼生在诗的技巧上，尤其在音律上，才力很高，修养极深，虽有时失诸雕琢，过分注意形式上的和谐。

【题解与注释】

1. BREAK, BREAK, BREAK

这首短诗在 1842 年发表，是悼念亡友海拉姆的。海拉姆是丁尼生在剑桥大学的同学，又是他妹妹的未婚夫，不幸在二十二岁时死于维也纳。丁尼生长时期地思念他，并在 1850 年发表长诗 *In Memoriam* 纪念他。这首短诗，情意凄恻而缠绵，语言精炼而清新。诗中所用格律，每行基本上是三个重音的轻重格。但第三节和第四节的第三行，各有四个重音，诗中有些音步是两个音节的轻重格，第一节和第四节的第一行——Break, break, break——又只有重音并无轻音搭配，所以节奏多变化。一般说，三个音节的音步读起来要快些，但这首诗并不快，因为长音较多。读者应注意元音的配合：诗里有许多诗行前部多圆唇音，如 [ou]，[u:]，[au] 等，行末多近合唇音，如 [i:] 等；这样配合正可以使人联想到如哭如泣。

标题　波浪因拍岸而破碎，象征着诗人的心碎。

1. I would: = I wish；我愿…。

2. O well for ...: = O it would be well for ...，…那倒很好呵！

3. 第 9—10 行：船只的归来和上文提过的渔家兄妹的游戏，少年水手的歌唱。都是欢乐景象，和诗人心中的悲痛，恰成对比。

4. But O for: = But how I wish for，但是我多么希望…。

5. a vanished hand: 人死了，手当然也不在了。

6. the tender grace of a day: 大意是良辰美景。

2. THE BROOK

本诗（1855 年发表）以农村为背景，记述一段失恋故事。故事中有十几节描写溪水的歌谣体小诗穿插于其间，烘托出农村的宁静气氛，但也加强了物是人非的惆怅。

全诗几乎都是叙述人 Lawrence Aylmer 的独白。大致可分五大段：

1.（第 1—73 行）：Aylmer 离开故乡 20 年后，又回到故乡，在散步到一条小溪时，想起当年这小溪附近的农庄上有关的几个人：*a*）Edmund，讲话人的弟弟，是一个年轻诗人；*b*）Philip，这一农庄上的佃户，是一个爱说闲话的老农；*c*）美丽的 Katie，是 Philip 的女儿，已和 James 订了婚。Aylmer 先在这一段介绍这几个人物。

2.（第 74—118 行）：然后故事的情节展开了：Katie 的未婚夫 James 对 Katie 和 Edmund 的关系起了疑心，与 Katie 发生口角，Katie 想丢开 Edmund，却又难于转环，于是求助于 Aylmer.

3.（第 119—156 行）：Aylmer 帮助了 Katie，拉走了碍事的 Philip，给她和

James 找着一个较长的晤面时间，以便解除二人之间的误会。

4.（第 157—196 行）： Katie 和 James 和好了，结婚了，以后便移居到澳大利亚去。Edmund 因失恋而出国，不久在意大利的旅途中抑郁以死。Aylmer 也到印度去了。现在他才回来，旧地重游，抚今追昔，不胜感慨。

5.（第 197—228 行）： Aylmer 正叹息间，忽见篱边有一少女，金发花颜，依稀似当年的 Katie. 问之，才知道是 James 和 Katie 的长女。据云全家已自国外归来，仍住原来老 Philip 的农庄上。于是这新生一代的出现，结束了这一段悲哀的故事。

全诗情节简单，文字朴素，近似浪漫主义时期的华兹华斯。读者可参阅华氏的 *Michael* 等短篇记事诗。

1. I: 指本诗后面提出的 Lawrence Aylmer.

2. he: 指 Edmund Aylmer, Lawrence 的弟弟。

3. too late: 说 Edmund 走得太迟了，早走也许不会爱上了 Katie，也就没有失恋的后果了。

4. strong sons of the world: 指有钱有势的人。

5. 第 4—8 行： Edmund 无钱无势，只会作诗。

6. scrip and share: 证券、股票，害人的财产。

7. cent for cent: 对本对利，相当于本钱那样多的利润，指害人的收入。

8. thought: = having thought (regarded)，认为。

9. could make the thing ... that is: 能使不存在的东西象实际存在的东西一样，能够无中生有，能用想象创造诗中人物和意境。

10. held their heads above the crowd: 高出一般常人。

11. flourish'd then or then: 在这时或另一时发迹了。

12. only touch'd on such a time ... in a mist of green: 将近林木发青但尚未生叶的时候（比喻 Edmund 的命运刚要开始兴旺，可还未兴旺之时）。

13. Neilgherry air: 位于印度南部的 Nilgiri ['nilgiri] Hills，以风景著称。Aylmer 回忆在印度时的生活。

14. 第 19 行： 小溪在背诵 Edmund (the boy) 原先作的诗。下面引的诗，都假定是 Edmund 作的。

15. coot: 一种水鸟。

16. hern: = heron，苍鹭。

17. bicker down: 潺潺流下。

18. thorps: 村。

19. Philip's farm: 位于小溪与大河汇流处。

20. 第 35—36 行： Edmund 想旅居 Naples，却已死在 Florence。

21. sharps and trebles: 作出尖锐的流水声。

22. mallow: 一种野草。

23. grigs: 一种蚱蜢。

24. waterbreak: 微波。

25. a maiden of our century: 本世纪的少女；新女性。

26. and her hair in gloss and hue ... within: 栗果外部有带刺的壳，壳裂开，才见有两三瓣栗果，果呈棕色，有光泽，果内有仁。这里拿光泽的栗果色比 Katie 头发的色泽。

27. did her a good turn: 帮过她一回忙。

28. crost: = crossed.

29. 第 80—81 行： 通过拱桥，人们从远处可望到桥外二水汇合处；那座古桥好象老人的白眉毛，照临着下面（其实是桥外）一片发亮的波澜（犹如发亮的眼睛）。

30. a random bar of Bonny Doon: Bonny Doon（美丽的丘溪，苏格兰语），一只苏格兰歌曲名。a random bar，随便的一节（歌曲）。

31. scolding: = noisy. 指开门时门枢发出的吱吱声。

32. he clamour'd from a casement, "Run": he 指 Edmund. Edmund 在 Philip 家里要求 Katie 和他私奔。

33. fresh apple-blossom: 初开的苹果花，形容主语 she，与 she 同位。

34. blushing for a boon: 因所求难于启齿，Katie 羞得脸绯红。

35. nor of those ...,: 有些人惯于流假眼泪，爱说不坦白的话，使感情脱离了实际行动，Katie 可不是这种人。

36. mealy-mouth'd philanthropies: 搞慈善事业的人，假仁慈，言不由衷。

37. snatch'd eyes ... from mine: 急忙躲开我的眼光。

38. a wizard's pentagram: 据说巫士作法，绘五星符，拘鬼神。这里只指 Katie 用脚尖在地上乱画一阵。

39. unclaim'd: 不睬理。

40. broke him short: 打断他的话。

41. take: 带走。

42. in session: 鸽子叫，仿佛坐在那里，正在开会。

43. Approved him, bowing at their own deserts: 鸽子们同意 Philip 的赞许。在点头表示确有它们自己的优点（长得壮实）。

44. for whom they were: 这些小狗将要被送给的那些朋友。

45. bailiff: 地主的管家。

46. farm: 指 Philip 的田庄。

47. He gave them line: Philip 放长线，给他们从长考虑的时间。

48. the Golden Fleece: 乡村酒店名。

49. talking from the point: 先不谈正题；from = away from; point，正题。

50. in sight of haven: 眼见事情有希望了。

51. to die a listener: 听得太累了。

52. our own shadows thrice as long ...,: 我们的影子已三倍长于…；天晚了，影子比出来时更长了。

53. the sun of sweet content: Katie 眼光露出满意的光辉来。

54. shingly bars: 砂洲。

55. Arno [ˈɑːnəu]：意大利中部一条小河名。

56. Brumelleschi: 意大利一个小地名，Edmund 埋在这里的教堂墓地里。

57. 第 191—192 行： Philip 生前话语是滔滔不绝的，而墓碑上却只剩下 P. W. (Philip Willows) 两个字母了。

58. Katiewalks ...,: Katie 已远在澳大利亚，那里的星辰属于南天，那里的季候正和英国相反。

59. Lawrence Aylmer: 讲故事的人。注意，so 前没有引号。

60. a maiden: Katie 的女儿，也叫 Katie.

61. so they said on board: 在我们乘船回国的途中有人说过这样的话。

62. she: Katie，小 Katie 的母亲。

3. ULYSSES

尤利西斯（Ulysses）是伊撒卡（Ithaca）岛的国王，著名的希腊传统故事中的英雄。在荷马史诗《伊利亚特》里，他是重要角色之一；在《奥德赛》里，他是主角。丁尼生这首诗的情节见但丁神曲（地狱篇第二十六节）。尤利西斯在围攻特洛伊城十年并取得胜利后，扬帆回国。因他得罪了海神，便又经受十年海上风暴冲击，遇到许多惊心动魄的情节，才又回到故国伊撒卡，和他的妻子珀涅罗庇（Penelope）与儿子堤莱莫克斯（Telemachus）欢聚在一起。据但丁《神曲》说，他回家后，并不安于家中的安静生活，还要遨游汪洋大海，探寻亡魂所在的西方乐岛。在本诗中，丁尼生描绘尤利西斯正要扬帆出海，作他的最后一次探险。

本诗第一段讲尤利西斯颇感家中安居的无聊，他应老当益壮，宁知白首之心；第二段讲他想到自己的儿子循规蹈矩，安分守己，满可以管理他这个小小王国了；第三段讲船只水手都已准备停当，日落月出，涛声阵阵，正是尤利西斯扬帆出走的时候了。

诗人丁尼生虽在记述尤利西斯的心情，却突出了一般人的“老骥伏枥，志在千里”之意。

全诗采用无韵体诗段形式。因无韵脚故全诗无阻碍思路的丁东声响；因有节奏回环，故读者很快地被引入诗境；因句法错落，形成诗段，故他们的感情也就跟随诗的内容起伏而共同起伏。

1. It: 是引词，指下面 that ... I mete ...。

2. still hearth: 安静的炉火，指家里。

3. agèd wife: 指 Penelope [pi'nelepi]。

4. mete and dole: 执行；**mete** = measure, **dole** = give.

5. Unequal laws: 不同的，指有赏有罚，是 mete and dole 的宾语。

6. savage race: 指伊撒卡岛国的人民，蔑视语。

7. know not me（诗）**:** = don't know me.

8. drink life to the lees: 把生命之酒喝得一干二净；lees，酒缸下沉的渣滓。

9. and (when ...): 连接两个状语结构；一个是 on shore，一个是 when ... the rainy Hyades Vexed the dim sea。

10. through scudding drifts: 通过急风暴雨。

11. the rainy Hyades [ˈhaiədiːz]**:** 靠近昴宿星团有七颗亮星的毕星团。据说这一星团在日出时出现，预示着天将大雨。

12. I am become a name: 我已是有名无实的人了。am become = have become. name，空有其名。

13. Myself not least, but honored …: 我也不算最无足道的而是其中颇受尊敬的人。Myself 和前面一些名词同位。not least, but honored = who is not least but honored ….

14. And drunk: 和前面的 I have 相接。

15. peers: = companions.

16. Troy: 特洛伊城，希腊人围困十年才攻下的那座城。

17. I ampart of all: 我和大家分享一切苦与乐。

18. 第 19—20 行： 然而经验好象大门，有经验的人便可以从大门向外看，看到那闪烁在远处他未曾到过的世界；wherethrough = through which.

19. As though to breathe were life!: 好象生活的目的就是呼吸！

20. life piled on life were all too little: 充满活力的生命也不算太长。life piled on life，直译为"生活堆积着生活"。

21. and of one to me little remains: = and little of the life of mine remains.

22. something more: 前面应加 if it (every hour) is something more, …

23. vile it were: = it would be vile. it 指下面的 to store …。

24. suns: = days.

25. and this gray spirit yearning: = with this gray head yearning

26. Telemachus [tiˈlemekes]**:** Ulysses 的儿子。

27. well-loved of me: 我所爱的；of me（古），现用 by me.

28. to make mild a rugged people: = to make a rugged people mild.

29. to the useful and the good: 成为有用的好人。

30. my household gods: 古希腊人每家供奉不同的保护神。

31. the vessel: 说明 Ulysses 讲话前已作好航行准备。

32. 第 47—49 行： 他们（我的水手们）欢快地以开朗的情怀，旷达的心胸迎接迅雷烈日，并与之进行斗争。

33. opposed: resisted, competed with；句法上与 took 并列，以 the thunder and the sunshine 为宾语。

34. Free hearts, free foreheads: 尤利西斯以此喻昔日与他共历艰险的水手。free hearts 指勇气，free foreheads 指经得起风霜的皮肤、筋骨。

35. Not unbecoming men strove with Gods: 同那些敢与神争高低的人相称；ot unbecoming men 修饰前面的 something.

36. smite the somding furrows: 在惊涛骇浪中击桨。

37. holds to sail beyond the sunset and the bathsofall the western stars: 坚持驶向落日与西方星宿沐浴的处所之外去。

38. the Happy Isles:（神话）幸福岛远在直布罗陀海峡以西，是死人灵魂的归宿之地。中国神话也说人死归西天。可能古人认为太阳是生命的根源，人死便应反其道而走向西方。

39. that which we are, we are: 我们一向是好汉，今天也还是好汉。

40. One equal temper of heroic hearts: 我们都是同样肝胆所铸造。temper，铸造。

4. TITHONUS

据希腊神话，黎明女神 Eos [ˈiːɔs] 爱一尘世少年 Tithonus [tiˈθəunəs]，并请求天神宙斯赐以长生，但因一时疏忽，未请求不老。于是 Tithonus 是长生了，却日见衰朽，越来越觉得生活乏味，因而请求速死。诗人用 Tithonus 独白口气，叙述这段故事。他不愿为神而永生，只想在老死之前，离开寂寞的天空，回到熙熙攘攘的地面去过真实的生活，这是本诗比较可取的一点。

这首诗结构紧凑，文字典雅，声调悠扬，就艺术性说，成就是很高的；诗人所用的无韵体和密尔顿比，也无逊色。试以第 18—23 行、第 50—63 行为例，听那句子与诗行的穿插，重音与节奏的交错，元音开闭的配合，都已达到美妙境界。

本诗发表在 1860 年，但可能是 1842 年以前在诗人潦倒时期写的。

1. 第 2 行： 水气因化露而消逝。

2. lies beneath: 死后埋在土里。

3. consumes: 消耗，侵蚀。

4. quiet limit of the world: 黎明女神之宫。

5. shadow: Tithonus 衰朽如影子。

6. spaces: 是 roaming 的宾语。

7. far-folded: 隐蔽在远处的。mists, halls 和 spaces 是同位语。

8. Alas! for this grey shadow, once a man: 唉，这个灰色影子过去曾是一个伟男子。

9. who: 先行词是上行领有位 thy，古用法。

10. thy chosen: 你的意中人。

11. that: 与前面的 so 相呼应，是状语从句（表示程度）的连接词。

12. who care not how they give: 指虽赐与长生，却忘掉了不老。仿佛有责难口气：富人施舍时并不考虑受惠者的实际需要与利益。丁尼生把天神宙斯的赐与改为 Eos 的赐与。

13. Hours: 司时间的神，她们是黎明女神的侍者。

14. thy strong Hours indignant: 你的强有力的侍者时间神，一怒之下。indignant = being indignant.

15. immortal age beside immortal youth: 与上文 left me 相连，作 left 的直接宾语。immortal age 指 Tithonus 自己，immortal youth 指 Eos。

16. And all I was, in ashes: 也和上文 left 相连：left all (that I was) in ashes，把

我原来的身体弄得只余下一点灰烬了。

17. the silver star: 黎明星（Lucifer）.

18. those tremulous eyes: 指黎明时闪烁不定的光辉。

19. kindly: 自然的，一般的，不反常的。

20. the goal of ordinance: ordinance 是神的意旨，这里指神给人规定的寿数；goal 是终点，这里指人寿的限度。

21. that dark world: 指地球，尘世。

22. the old mysterious glimmer: 指曙光。

23. steals from ...: 从…流泄出来。

24. with a heart renew'd: 黎明女神每天都有一颗新生的心。

25. they blind the stars: 黎明女神出现后，群星隐蔽潜形。

26. the wild team: 指黎明女神马车上的马匹。

27. before thine answer given Departest ...: 前文 Tithonus 向 Eos 提出请求说，"Let me go, take back thy gift，" Eos 并不回答，便起身走了。

28. be true: 主语是 a saying。

29. the Gods ...: 与 saying 同位。

30. If I be he that watch'd: 如果当时守望…的那个人还是我（但是我已衰朽不堪了，几乎不愿设想那还是我）。

31. mouth,. of April: 是绝对主格，在主句后叙述详细情节的。试在 mouth 前加上 with，结构便更清楚。

32. Whispering: 与 the lips 组成宾语复合结构。

33. I knew not what of wild and sweet: = something wild and sweet which I knew not how to describe，窃窃私语着难以形容的热烈而又甜蜜的情话。

34. Apollo sing: Apollo 神给 Troy (Ilium) 国王筑城垣时，以手挑琴，石块自动筑城。

35. grassy barrows: 坟。

36. the happier dead: 活人能死是幸福，死了的人更幸福。

37. earth in earth: earth 与 I 同位。earth 指人是泥造的（基督教传说）；in earth 指人死了，埋在土里。

38. these empty courts: 指黎明女神之宫。

39. thee: 是 forget 的宾语。forget 前省略去 will，意为：我愿忘掉。从第 72 行起，Tithonus 表示不愿再长此衰老不堪，情愿死去，既然死了，也就忘掉黎明女神的宫殿和她夜夜驾银车归来的情景了。

40 ROBERT BROWNING
1812–1889

王佐良　选注

1. MY LAST DUCHESS

Ferrara

That's my last Duchess painted on the wall,
Looking as if she were alive. I call
That piece a wonder, now: Frà Pandolf's[1] hands
Worked busily a day, and there she stands.[2]
Will't please you sit and look at her?[3] I said
'Frà Pandolf' by design[4] for never read[5]
Strangers like you that pictured countenance,[6]
The depth and passion of its earnest glance,[7]
But to myself they turned[8] (since none puts by
The curtain[9] I have drawn for you, but I)
And seemed as they would ask me, if they durst,[10]
How such a glance came there; so, not the first
Are you to turn and ask thus.[11] Sir, 'twas not
Her husband's presence only, called that spot
Of joy into the Duchess' cheek:[12] perhaps

Frà Pandolf chanced to say, 'Her mantle laps
Over my lady's wrist too much,'[13] or 'Paint
Must never hope to reproduce the faint
Half-flush that dies along her throat: '[14] such stuff
Was courtesy, she thought, and cause enough
For calling up that spot of joy.[15] She had
A heart — how shall I say? — too soon made glad,
Too easily impressed; she liked whate'er
She looked on, and her looks went everywhere.[16]
Sir, 'twas all one![17] My favour at her breast,[18]
The dropping of the daylight in the West,
The bough of cherries some officious fool[19]
Broke in the orchard for her, the white mule
She rode with[20] round the terrace — all and each
Would draw from her alike the approving speech,
Or blush, at least. She thanked men, — good![21] but thanked
Somehow — I know not how — as if she ranked
My gift of a nine-hundred-years-old name
With anybody's gift.[22] Who'd stoop to blame
This sort of trifling?[23] Even had you skill
In speech — (which I have not) — to make your will
Quite clear to such an one,[24] and say, 'Just this
Or that in you disgusts me; here you miss,
Or there exceed the mark'[25] — and if she let
Herself be lessoned so, nor plainly set
Her wits to yours, forsooth, and made excuse,[26]
— E'en then would be some stooping;[27] and I choose
Never to stoop. Oh sir, she smiled, no doubt,
Whene'er I passed her; but who passed without
Much the same smile? This grew;[28] I gave commands;[29]
Then all smiles stopped together.[30] There she stands
As if alive. Will't please you rise? We'll meet
The company below, then. I repeat,

The Count your master's known munificence
Is ample warrant that no just pretence
Of mine for dowry will be disallowed;[31]
Though his fair daughter's self, as I avowed
At starting, is my object.[32] Nay, we'll go
Together down,[33] sir. Notice Neptune, though,
Taming a sea-horse, thought a rarity,[34]
Which Claus of Innsbruck[35] cast in bronze for me!

2. MEETING AT NIGHT

The grey sea and the long black land;
And the yellow half-moon large and low;
And the startled[1] little waves that leap
In fiery ringlets from their sleep,
As I gain the cove with pushing prow,[2]
And quench its speed i' the slushy sand.[3]

Then a mile of warm sea-scented beach;
Three fields to cross till a farm appears;
A tap at the pane, the quick sharp scratch
And blue spurt of a lighted match,[4]
And a voice[5] less loud, thro' its joys and fears,[6]
Than the two hearts beating each to each![7]

3. PARTING AT MORNING

Round the cape of a sudden came the sea,[1]
And the sun look'd over the mountain's rim:
And straight was a path of gold for him,[2]
And the need of a world of men for me.[3]

4. HOME-THOUGHTS, FROM ABROAD

Oh, to be in England
Now that April's there,[1]
And whoever wakes in England
Sees, some morning, unaware,[2]
That the lowest boughs and the brushwood sheaf
Round the elm-tree bole[3] are in tiny leaf,[4]
While the chaffinch sings on the orchard bough
In England—now!

And after April, when May follows,
And the whitethroat builds, and all the swallows!
Hark, where my blossom'd pear-tree in the hedge
Leans to the field and scatters on the clover
Blossoms and dewdrops—at the bent spray's edge[5]—
That's the wise thrush; he sings each song twice over,
Lest you should think he never could recapture
The first fine careless rapture![6]
And though the fields look rough with hoary dew,
All will be gay when noontide wakes anew
The buttercups, the little children's dower[7]
—Far brighter than this gaudy melon-flower![8]

5. THE LOST LEADER

Just for a handful of silver he left us,
Just for a riband to stick in his coat[1]—
Found the one gift[2] of which fortune bereft us,
Lost all the others[3] she lets us devote;
They, with the gold to give, doled him out silver[4]
So much was theirs who so little allowed:[5]

How all our copper had gone for his service![6]
Rags — were they purple, his heart had been proud![7]
We that had loved him so,[8] followed him, honoured him,
Lived in his mild and magnificent eye,[9]
Learned his great language, caught his clear accents,
Made him our pattern to live and to die![10]
Shakespeare was of us, Milton was for us,
Burns, Shelley, were with us,[11] — they watch from their graves!
He alone breaks from the van[12] and the freeman,
— He alone sinks to the rear and the slaves!

We shall march prospering, — not thro' his presence;
Songs may inspirit us, — not from his lyre;
Deeds will be done, — while he boasts his quiescence,[13]
Still bidding crouch whom the rest bade aspire:[14]
Blot out his name, then,[15] — record one lost soul more,
One task more declined, one more footpath untrod,
One more devils'-triumph and sorrow for angels,
One wrong more to man, one more insult to God!
Life's night begins: let him never come back to us!
There would be doubt, hesitation and pain,
Forced praise on our part[16] — the glimmer of twilight,
Never glad confident morning again!
Best fight on well, for we taught him,[17] — strike gallantly,
Aim at our heart ere we pierce through his own[18]
Then let him receive the new knowledge[19] and wait us,
Pardoned in Heaven, the first by the throne![20]

6. THE ITALIAN IN ENGLAND

That second time they hunted me[1]
From hill to plain, from shore to sea,
And Austria, hounding far and wide

Her blood-hounds[2] thro' the country-side,
Breathed hot and instant on my trace,—
I made six days a hiding-place
Of that dry green old aqueduct
Where I and Charles,[3] when boys, have plucked
The fire-flies from the roof above,
Bright creeping thro' the moss they love.
—How long it seems since Charles was lost!
Six days the soldiers crossed and crossed
The country in my very sight;
And when that peril ceased at night,
The sky broke out in red dismay
With signal-fires;[4] well, there I lay
Close covered o'er in my recess,
Up to the neck in ferns and cress,
Thinking on Metternich our friend,[5]
And Charles's miserable end,
And much beside,[6] two days; the third,
Hunger o'vercame me when I heard
The peasants from the village go
To work among the maize; you know,
With us, in Lombardy, they bring
Provisions packed on mules, a string
With little bells that cheer their task,
And casks, and boughs on every cask
To keep the sun's heat from the wine;
These I let pass in jingling line,
And close on them, dear noisy crew,[7]
The peasants from the village, too;
For at the very rear would troop
Their wives and sisters in a group
To help, I knew; when these had passed,
I threw my glove to strike the last,

Taking the chance:[8] she did not start,
Much less cry out, but stooped apart
One instant, rapidly glanced round,
And saw me beckon from the ground:
A wild bush grows and hides my crypt;
She picked my glove up while she stripped
A branch off, then rejoined the rest
With that; my glove lay in her breast:[9]
Then I drew breath: they disappeared:
It was for Italy I feared.[10]

An hour, and she returned alone
Exactly where my glove was thrown.
Meanwhile came many thoughts; on me
Rested the hopes of Italy;
I had devised a certain tale[11]
Which, when 'twas told her, could not fail
Persuade a peasant of its truth;
I meant to call a freak of youth
This hiding, and give hopes of pay,
And no temptation to betray.
But when I saw that woman's face,
Its calm simplicity of grace,
Our Italy's own attitude[12]
In which she walked thus far, and stood,
Planting each naked foot so firm,
To crush the snake and spare the worm[13] —
At first sight of her eyes, I said,
"I am that man upon whose head
They fix the price,[14] because I hate
The Austrians over us: the State[15]
Will give you gold — oh, gold so much,
If you betray me to their clutch!

And be your death,[16] for aught I know,
If once they find you saved their foe.
Now, you must bring me food and drink,
And also paper, pen, and ink,
And carry safe what I shall write
To Padua, which you'll reach at night
Before the Duomo[17] shuts; go in,
And wait till Tenebræ[18] begin;
Walk to the third Confessional,[19]
Between the pillar and the wall,
And kneeling whisper, *Whence comes peace*?[20]
Say it a second time; then cease;
And if the voice inside returns,
From Christ and Freedom; what concerns
The cause of Peace? — for answer, slip
My letter where you placed your lip;[21]
Then come back happy we have done
Our mother[22] service — I, the son,
As you the daughter of our land!"

Three mornings more, she took her stand
In the same place, with the same eyes:
I was no surer of sun-rise
Than of her coming:[23] we conferred
Of her own prospects,[24] and I heard
She had a lover — stout and tall,
She said — then let her eyelids fall,
"He could do much"25 — as if some doubt
Entered her heart, — then, passing out,
"She could not speak for others — who
Had other thoughts; herself she knew:"
And so she brought me drink and food.
After four days, the scouts pursued

Another path: at last arrived
The help my Paduan friends contrived
To furnish me: she brought the news.
For the first time I could not choose
But kiss her hand and lay my own
Upon her head — "This faith was shown
To Italy, our mother; — she
Uses my hand and blesses thee!"[26]
She followed down to the sea-shore;
I left and never saw her more.

How very long since I have thought[27]
Concerning — much less wished for — aught
Beside the good of Italy
For which I live and mean to die!
I never was in love; and since
Charles proved false, what shall now convince
My inmost heart I have a friend?
However, if I pleased to spend
Real wishes on myself — say, Three[28] —
I know at least what one should be;
I would grasp Metternich[29] until
I felt his red wet throat distil
In blood thro' these two hands: and next,
— Nor much for that am I perplexed —
Charles, perjured traitor, for his part,
Should die slow of a broken heart
Under his new employers: last
— Ah, there, what should I wish? For fast
Do I grow old and out of strength. —
If I resolved to seek at length
My father's house again,[30] how scared
They all would look, and unprepared!

My brothers live in Austria's pay
—Disowned me long ago, men say:
And all my early mates who used
To praise me so—perhaps induced
More than one early step of mine—
Are turning wise;[31] while some opine
"Freedom grows License,"[32] some suspect
"Haste breeds Delay,"[33] and recollect
They always said, such premature
Beginnings never could endure!
So, with a sullen "All's for best,"
The land seems settling to its rest.
I think, then, I should wish to stand
This evening in that dear, lost land,
Over the sea the thousand miles,
And know if yet that woman smiles
With the calm smile; some little farm
She lives in there, no doubt; what harm
If I sate on the door-side bench,
And, while her spindle made a trench
Fantastically in the dust,[34]
Inquired of all her fortunes—just
Her children's ages and their names,
And what may be the husband's aims
For each of them—I'd talk this out,
And sit there, for an hour about,
Then kiss her hand once more, and lay
Mine on her head, and go my way.

So much for idle wishing[35]—how
It steals the time! To business now![36]

【作者简介】劳勃特·勃朗宁（Robert Browning, 1812–1889），英国十九世纪中叶诗人，出身富裕家庭，终生不事生产，写诗过日。在英国文学史上，他与丁尼生（Alfred Tennyson）齐名，在政治上倾向于资产阶级自由党中的激进派，在同他妻子伊丽莎白·勃朗宁（也是著名诗人）长期寄居意大利期间，曾同情当地人民反抗奥地利占领者的革命斗争。

勃朗宁写了许多长诗，颇有特色；他尝试过诗剧的创作，则无多建树；他的短诗之中，有两类颇值一读。一类是抒情诗。他的诗笔一般晦涩，但在一些抒情短诗里他却做到以白描见长。另一类是戏剧性的独白诗，用活跃的口语词语和节奏，模拟人物口吻，一时独步诗坛，无人能及。在题材上，诗人所歌咏的，除了爱情之外，多是处在奇幻处境里的人物的心理状态，但也有反对教会与贵族专制的作品。

【题解与注释】

1. MY LAST DUCHESS

勃朗宁的代表作之一，描写文艺复兴时期意大利境内 Ferrara 公国公爵的残忍性格，通过他对来客的一席话，道出他杀死自己年轻妻子的暴行。

来客是一位伯爵的使者。伯爵想将女儿嫁给公爵，派了使者来谈判婚事。公爵接见使者之后，带他看自己收藏的艺术品，两人站在被杀死的公爵夫人的画像之前，公爵作了一番说明。

这番话透露的是这样的一个性格：似乎彬彬有礼，实则野蛮嗜杀；象是爱好艺术，文雅之至，却可以为了妒忌而将自己美丽的妻子处死；作高贵的君主姿态，却同商人一样贪钱。勃朗宁以为十五六世纪意大利的某些领袖人物具有这种所谓“文艺复兴时期的性格”。他的兴趣主要是在他们性格的所谓复杂性，但是通过此诗我们读者也可以看出这些人的残酷。这当中不仅有当时旧的统治势力的残酷，而且有当时新的统治势力的残酷。公爵虽说是贵族，自称有“九百年光荣的家世”（见第 33 行），实则是如当时佛罗伦萨（Florence）的统治者梅狄启（the Medici family）一样的亦王亦商的人物。

全诗用“英雄排偶句”（the heroic couplet）写成，即每两行一韵，每行一般为十个音节。语言全用口语体，插入语甚多，边叙边议，但到紧要关头又故意语焉不详。刚刚说完前妻之死，立即转到眼前婚事，讨价还价之声未息，又夸耀了一件艺术品，说明他将杀妻、娶妻、买画、买雕刻品诸事都同等看待，平白无故地杀害了一个善良纯洁的妇女并不引起他心头任何波动，只不过增加了他向客人夸耀的谈话资料而已。对妻子如此，对人民的残酷也就可想而知。

1. Frà Pandolf: Brother Pandolf，假想的画家的名字。当时画家多为教士，所以名前有 Frà（教兄）称号。

2. there she stands: 指画像，故动词用现在时。

3. Will't please you sit and look at her?: Will it please you to sit and look at her? 请您坐着欣赏她的国像吧。

4. by design: 有意识地；意为我知你必有此一问，所以预先有意识地告诉了你画家的名字。

5. never read: 倒装句，主语为 Strangers like you，宾语为 countenance; read 在此作 looked at 解。

6. that pictured countenance: 那张画上的面容。

7. The depth and passion of its earnest glance: 为上语之同位语，引申“面容”之意：她那顾盼间所流露出来的厚意深情。

8. But to myself they turned:（客人们不理解画像的表情）总要转过身来问我。

9. since none puts by the curtain: 因为只有我才有权利拉开盖住画像的帷幕，意即客人看此像时，总有我本人陪伴在旁。

10. if they durst: 如果他们有勇气的话；durst 为 dare 的过去时的形式之一。

11. not the first Are you to turn and ask thus: = You are not the first to turn and ask as you did.

12. 'twas not Her husband's presence only, called that spot Of joy into the Duchess' cheek: 公爵夫人的脸上露出那片欣喜的红晕，不只是因为丈夫在旁；照通常语法，called 前应有 that.

13. 'Her mantle laps Over my lady's wrist too much': 夫人的外套将她的手盖住太多了，意为她的手应该多露出一些；her 与 my lady 都指公爵夫人。在称呼当中，用第三人称代替第二人称，表示尊敬。

14. dies along her throat:（那片淡淡的红晕）沿着喉部逐渐消失掉。

15. such stuff Was courtesy, she thought, and cause enough For calling up that spot of joy: 她以为那类的话是温文有礼，值得（cause enough = 有足够的理由）为之感到高兴。公爵本人的意思是那类奉承算得什么，何必降低身份去注意，至于因此而脸上泛红，那就更加有失公爵夫人的尊严了。

16. she liked whate'er She looked on, and her looks went everywhere: 她什么都想看，看了什么都喜欢。可见公爵夫人的年轻和真挚，然而公爵却不以为然，嫌她不够高傲，缺乏贵族气派。

17. 'twas all one!: 指下面所列举的东西在公爵夫人的眼里等同看待。

18. My favour at her breast: 我送给她的胸饰（珠宝之类）。

19. some officious fool: 某个多事的蠢才。

20. the white mule She rode with: 自第 25 行至此不过五行，短短几语，公爵无意中说出了公爵夫人在世时如何热爱生活，这就使读者后来听到她的不幸结局时，更感公爵的残酷。

21. She thanked men,—good!: 她向人道谢——那很好！ Good 是插入语，是公爵对她行为的评语。

22. as if she ranked My gift of a nine-hundred-years-old name With anybody's gift: 象是她把我送给她的九百年光荣的家世同任何别人送给她的礼物同等看待。公爵在说 anybody 一字时，表示了特别的轻蔑。

23. Who'd stoop to blame This sort of trifling?: 谁能降低身份去指责这类的

小事呢？ stoop 表明公爵在众人之上。

24. such an one: 指公爵夫人。

25. here you miss, Or there exceed the mark: 这儿你做得不够，那儿你又过了份；mark 是 miss 和 exceed 两个动词的宾语。

26. and if she let Herself be lessoned so, nor plainly set Her wits to yours, forsooth, and made excuse: 即使她听你的教训，不公然同你顶嘴，或提出一个借口；wits = mind; forsooth 是插入语，意为“真是！”

27. E'en then would be some stooping: = Even then there would be some stooping；在公爵的心目中，辱没身份是一个大人物决不干的事。

28. This grew: 这情况越来越严重了。

29. I gave commands: 我下了命令。

30. Then all smiles stopped together: 三个短句紧接，口气坚决，与上文的文雅纡徐完全不同。杀妻的罪行就以这样的三句话带过了。

31. The Count your master's known munificence Is ample warrant that no just pretence Of mine for dowry will be disallowed: 令东伯爵大人素以慷慨闻世，敢信不会拒绝我对于嫁妆的正当要求；pretence = claim. 公爵刚说完如何杀了前妻，就又对后妻的嫁妆提出了要索。凶残可见，贪婪可闻。

32. Though his fair daughter's self, as I avowed At starting, is my object: 虽然我一开始就已申明，我（所追求的）目的只是伯爵的美丽的小姐本人。

33. Nay, we'll go Together down: 请别客气，我们一块儿走下楼去（大概此时使者让公爵先走，公爵表示礼貌，挽他并排同行）。

34. Notice Neptune, though, Taming a sea-horse, thought a rarity: 请看海神驯马的铜像，据说是绝世的杰作。公爵夸耀了杀妻行为，做完了嫁妆交易，现在带客人出门，又来最后自表一番收藏家的眼力。

35. Claus of Innsbruck: Innsbruck 地方的名雕刻匠 Claus（也是一位假想的人物）。Innsbruck 在今奥地利境内，为当时 Tyrol 邦的首都，以雕刻出名。

2. MEETING AT NIGHT

此诗用白描手法写一人乘船渡海，上岸越过田野，在一农舍会见爱人的欣喜心情，着墨无多，一气呵成。景物写得具体，无一语提心到情，但心情自见。

1. startled: 惊醒了的，表示夜间一切沉静，海亦入眠，但由于诗中的“我”即将会见爱人，连醒来的海浪也是欢腾鼓舞的，故下文有 leap In fiery ringlets 的明亮、活跃的形象。

2. As I gain the cove with pushing prow: 当我的疾驶的船头到达海湾的时候。

3. quench its speed i'the slushy sand: 在海岸的泥沙里停住船的行进，亦即停船在沙滩上；此行故意重复了 s 与 sh 的声音，表示船行的速度，最后的 slushy 的声音又传达了小船受阻逐渐停住的情况。

**4. A tap at the pane, the quick sharp scratch And blue spurt of a lighted

match: 窗上轻敲一下,〔窗内〕擦一根火柴，蓝色的火焰忽地一亮；此行中 scratch 与 spurt 都是用声音加强动作效果的“拟声词”。

5. a voice: 指室内人的欣喜叫声。

6. thro' its joys and fears: 由于欣喜和害怕；thro' = through; its 指 voice；一则以喜，一则以忧，可见这会面是秘密的，期待已久的。

7. Than the two hearts beating each to each:（室内人只轻轻叫了一声，话声还不及）两颗心相对而跳（那样响）。诗人只在这最后一行才点明主题，但他仍然只让具体动作来表达人物的心情。

3. PARTING AT MORNING

上诗述夜间见面之欢，此诗为其续文，叙次晨离别之苦，写得含蓄。

1. Round the cape of a sudden came the sea: 转过岬地，忽见大海。第一行写得戏剧化。两人一齐走着，忽然大海在望。正是这大海要将行者带走，隔在两人之间。

2. And straight was a path of gold for him: 读者很容易以为此诗的说话者是在家坐守的女人，以为 him 指远行人，path of gold 指其锦绣前程。这样看，是将此诗看作“闺怨”一类。但是诗人本人却曾在 1889 年 2 月 22 日写信回答一个读者的询问时指出诗中说话者是远行的男人，这个男人原以为两人相见，爱情无尽，现在看来，欢娱一纵即逝，难得永久（Browning: “It is *his* confession of how fleeting is the belief ... that such raptures are self-sufficient and enduring—as for the time they appear.”）因此 him 指太阳，path of gold 指太阳越升越高，到处放出金光，它所走的路象是金子铺的。

3. And the need of a world of men for me: 而我（远行的男人）则需要埋在各种琐事里，到处与别的男人打交道，才能填满空虚的心。

4. HOME-THOUGHTS, FROM ABROAD

勃朗宁最闻名的短诗之一。他写此诗时，身在意大利，意大利的春天虽也风光明媚，但是阳光过于灼热，色彩过于浓艳，诗人不禁怀念起北方故国四五月的光景来了。诗中除了回忆英国的花木之外，更神往于会唱歌的鸟儿。

1. Oh, to be in England Now that April's there: 这两行构成一个惊叹句，= Oh, what a wonderful thing it would be to be in England now that April is there!

2. Sees, some morning, unaware: 不知不觉地在某一个早晨看见（花开了），表示英国经过一个漫长的冬天之后，春天悄悄地来临了。

3. bole: 树干。

4. in tiny leaf: 刚长出嫩叶。

5. at the bent spray's edge: 在弯曲的小枝干的一端。

6. The first fine careless rapture: 第一次唱时所感到的无忧无虑的莫大欢欣。

7. The buttercups, the little children's dower: 金凤花（是）小孩子们的财宝。

8. Far brighter than this gaudy melon-flower: 比这种大红大绿的意大利花要好看得多。

5. THE LOST LEADER

“失去的领袖”指的是英国名诗人华兹华斯（William Wordsworth），即所谓“湖畔诗人”的首领。他在年轻时候曾同情法国资产阶级革命，但后来当雅可宾党人专政的时候，他转而反对，不久完全变成了一个顽固的保守党人。1813 年他接受英国政府给他的一份干薪，1842 年接收政府所颁的养老金每年三百镑，1843 年又继任桂冠诗人。这一系列的行为激怒了勃朗宁。勃朗宁本人在政治上属于自由党，在文学上喜欢雪莱、拜伦、赫兹列特等人，又曾与激进文人利 · 亨特（Leigh Hunt）相过从，这些人都曾指责过华兹华斯的变节（apostasy），勃朗宁在此诗用“失去的领袖”也是此意，对华兹华斯的攻击是有力的，尤其头上几行，十分尖锐。

但是勃朗宁仍然十分佩服华兹华斯的诗才，因此提到 his mild and magnificent eye, his great language, his clear accents 等等，而到诗篇之末，他又说华兹华斯死后将会被上帝第一个宽恕。勃朗宁后来年纪大了，更悔年少孟浪，在回答读者信时曾说此诗虽有意以华兹华斯为模特儿，但许多说法未必完全适合“那个伟大的诗人”，云云（见其 1875 年 2 月 24 日致 Grosart 函）。

1. Just for a riband to stick in his coat: 仅仅为了在衣服上挂一根缎带，意为仅仅为了获得一官半职；riband = ribbon，代表地位（如爵士身份）的缎带。

2. the one gift: 指金钱，这正是命运之神（fortune）不给我们穷小子的东西。

3. all the others: = all the other gifts，我们所有的其他一切（品质）他都失去了；后面的 she 指 fortune，命运之神；devote，供奉。

4. They, with the gold to give, doled him out silver: 那些可以拿出金子的人只拿了一点银子施舍给他；此诗中有明显的 they 与 we 之分，they 指统治者，有钱人；we 指向往于法国资产阶级革命的人；gold 之后用 silver，表示只用一点小钱；doled out,（打发乞丐似地）施舍（几个小钱）。

5. So much was theirs who so little allowed: 他们占有很多东西，然而轻易不肯给人半点。

6. all our copper had gone for his service:（他们把）从我们身上搜刮去的全部铜子儿都用来酬谢他的效劳了。

7. Rags—were they purple, his heart had been proud!: 破衣——只要是贵人穿过的，即使是破衣，他也会穿着感到骄傲！ purple，深红色，古代西欧各国的君主穿深红袍。本行语法有两个特点，一是 rags 为了突出而立在句首，后面用 they 来代它作主词；二是虚拟式动词用了一个十八世纪的旧形式，had been proud 在十九世纪中叶以及现在应作 would have been proud。

8. We that had loved him so: 过去曾经那样爱他的我们这些人；so = so much.

9. Lived in his mild and magnificent eye: 在他的温和、庄严的眼光的照耀下生活；这是勃朗宁对华兹华斯的赞语。

10. Made him our pattern to live and to die: 以他为我们的榜样，象他那样生。象他那样死。

11. Shakespeare was of us, Milton was for us, Burns, Shelley, were with us: 过去许多伟大作家都站在我们这一边；注意这行中用了几个不同的介词：of us，属于我们，即我们的一员；for us，为我们说话、做事；with us，同我们在一起。这两行也代表了勃朗宁对于这几个大作家与人民关系的正确看法。勃朗宁曾在1846年8月22日写信给他爱人Elizabeth Barrett说："I would at any time have gone to Finchley to see a curl of his〔Byron's〕hair or one of his gloves, I am sure—while Heaven knows I could not get up enthusiasm enough to cross the room if at the other end of it all Wordsworth, Coleridge, and Southey were condensed into the little China bottle yonder." 表示他对Wordsworth等人的极端厌恶。

12. the van: 先锋队；= vanguard。

13. quiescence: 清静无为，与前半行的行动（Deeds will be done）相对照。勃朗宁此语说得不错，华兹华斯向来标榜自己的灵感来自在大自然中的沉思。

14. Still bidding crouch whom the rest bade aspire: 他老是叫人们退缩投降，而其余的人则鼓励他们向前；still在此是古义，= always。

15. Blot out his name, then: 抹掉他的名字吧。从此起诗人表示弃绝华兹华斯。下文有一长列的强烈的谴责语：lost soul（迷途的灵魂），devil's triumph（魔鬼的胜利），sorrow for angels（天使的哀愁），one wrong more to man（对于人类的另一罪行），one more insult to God（对于上帝的另一侮辱）。

16. Forced praise on our part:（甚至于）我们还不得不称赞他的诗才。

17. for we taught him: 在过去是我们教会他战斗的。

18. Aim at our heart ere we pierce through his own: 对准我们的胸膛刺来吧，否则我们一定要刺穿他的胸膛；ere = before; his own = his own heart，此行另版作"Menace our heart ere we master his own"，意思一样，而失去了有力的形象。

19. let him receive the new knowledge: 让他知道这新的情况吧（即我们决意同他战斗的决心）。

20. Pardoned in Heaven, the fist by the throne: 得到了上帝的宽恕，成为上帝宝座之旁最亲近的人。这里勃朗宁表示宽大为怀，表示华兹华斯死后仍会得救。

6. THE ITALIAN IN ENGLAND

这是勃朗宁直接写意大利人民抗奥斗争的绝少数作品之一。1815年维也纳会议和巴黎和约签订以后，欧洲反动势力卷土重来，意大利境内朗巴第和威尼西亚地区重新为奥地利帝国统治。意大利爱国志士组织烧炭党（the Carbonari）及其它秘密会社进行斗争，到1830年左右更形活跃；奥地利统治者除了加紧正面镇压之外，还在意大利全境建立了广泛的特务网，收买意奸为其通风报信，诗中提到的Charles即为这种叛卖民族利益的败类之一。然而爱国志士由于有广大人民的支持，不仅制裁了这些意奸，而且给奥国军队以沉重的打击，终于替十九世纪四十年代的民族独立奠定了胜利的基础。

此诗用一个暂时避居英国的意大利革命者的口吻（因此题名“在英国的意大利人”），描写了他在某次遭遇奥军追捕时为一农村少妇搭救脱险的经过。革命者的斗志和少妇的善良、坚定的形象都写得动人。有关意大利民间风俗的背景描绘又增加了诗篇的现实感。文字是口语体，叙述很有戏剧性，在十九世纪英诗中是一篇有一定的积极意义、艺术性也较高的叙事诗。

1. That second time they hunted me: 一上来就是富于戏剧性的一笔，表明这个说话的革命者出生入死，受追捕是家常便饭。

2. Her blood-hounds: 奥地利的猎犬，指军警。

3. Charles: 儿时游伴名，后来变成意奸，因此第 11 行提到 Charles was lost，第 20 行又提到 Charles's miserable end。

4. The sky broke out in red dismay With signal-fires: 天空给报警的烽火照得通红，叫人看着焦急。

5. Metternich our friend: Metternich 是当时奥国首相名，系当时欧洲反动势力的头子之一，为意大利人民所深恶痛绝，此处称之为“我们的朋友”是一种但丁式的挖苦语。

6. And much beside: 以及许多其它事情；beside = besides.

7. dear noisy crew: 可爱的说说笑笑的一群，指下文 the peasants from the village. 这几行写意大利乡村风俗如画。

8. Taking the chance: 碰碰运气一试。

9. my glove lay in her breast: 她将我的手套藏在胸口衣服内。

10. It was for Italy I feared: 我担心的是意大利，意为我不怕自己被人发现，只怕我被捕对于祖国的解放事业不利。

11. I had devised a certain tale: 我本来已经编好了回答她的话，即下文的 a freak of youth（年轻人的一时孟浪），give hopes of pay（愿意出钱酬谢她），等等。但后来一看她的诚恳、坚定的神情，我改变了主意，将真实情况告诉了她。

12. Our Italy's own attitude:（她的态度就是）我们祖国意大利的态度，下文 she 指意大利。

13. To crush the snake and spare the worm: 杀死大敌，赦免小奸。

14. They fix the price: 他们（奥国人）悬赏捉我。

15. the State: 指奥国政府。

16. And be your death: = And it would be the death of you,（如果奥国人发现你救他们的敌人，那么）你就会给杀死。

17. the Duomo:（意大利语），大教堂。

18. Tenebræ（拉丁文）: 黑暗；此处指罗马天主教会在复活节一周中最后三日（即周四至周六）每晚午夜以后的祷告仪式，行礼时烛光逐渐熄灭，教堂归于一片黑暗。

19. Confessional: 天主教堂中神甫听忏悔的神龛。

20. *Whence comes peace?*: 和平来自何处？此语及下文 *From Christ and Freedom* 与 *what concerns the cause of Peace* 都是意大利革命者传递消息时的暗语。

21. where you placed your lip: 在神龛里有一小孔，进去忏悔的人跪下可以凑着小孔说话并吻神甫的手；此行的意思是：通过这个小孔传递密信。

22. Our mother: 我们的祖国，指意大利。

23. I was no surer of sun-rise Than of her coming: 我相信她一定会回来，就象我相信日出一样。

24. we conferred Of her own prospects: 我们谈到了她自己的将来。

25. "He could do much": 注意这里用了虚拟式动词，表示她的爱人现在不愿干革命工作，所以下文又有 She could not speak for others — who had other thoughts; herself she knew（别人怎样她难说，各有各的想法，但她知道自己是坚定的）。

26. she Uses my hand and blesses thee: 祖国通过我来祝福你。

27. How very long since I have thought: 这里另起一节，叙述脱险以后到了英国回想往事时的感喟。

28. Three: 指三个愿望。

29. grasp Metternich: 扼死奥国首相；下文 I felt his red wet throat distil In blood thro' these two hands 写得十分有力。

30. If I resolved to seek at length My father's house again: 意为我如重回祖国的话。

31. turning wise: 挖苦语，指他儿时的伴侣现已大多变节。

32. "Freedom grows License,": 自由会产生放肆（变节者的言论）。

33. "Haste breeds Delay": 匆忙反而迟缓（也是变节者的言论，意为现在还不必立即去争取自由独立）。

34. while her spindle made a trench Fantastically in the dust: 当她的织布机不断转动，轮子在泥地上形成一个奇形的凹道的时候；fantastically 原意是"奇幻地"，此处用来表达热闹、滑稽的家庭情景。

35. So much for idle wishing: 好了，空想到此为止吧！

36. To business now: 现在该做正事了！意为：是行动的时候了！表示意大利爱国者虽然身处异国，仍在积极进行革命工作。这是有力的一结，同时又使读者展望斗争的未来。

41 CHARLES DICKENS
1812-1870

DAVID COPPERFIELD
(selections)

吴千之 选注

Chapter IV I Fall into Disgrace

. . . .

There has been some talk on occasions[1] of my going to boarding-school.[2] Mr. and Miss Murdstone had originated it, and my mother had of course agreed with them.[3] Nothing, however, was concluded on the subject yet. In the meantime I learnt lessons at home.

Shall I ever forget those lessons! They were presided over nominally by my mother, but really by Mr. Murdstone and his sister, who were always present, and found them[4] a favourable occasion for giving my mother lessons in that miscalled firmness,[5] which was the bane of both our lives. I believe I was kept at home for that purpose. I had been apt enough to learn, and willing enough, when my mother and I had lived alone together. I can faintly remember learning the alphabet at her knee. To this day, when I look upon the fat black letters in the primer,[6] the puzzling novelty of their shapes[7] and the easy good-nature of O and Q and S[8], seem to present themselves again before me as they used to do. But they recall[9] no feeling of disgust or reluctance. On the contrary, I seem to have walked along a path of flowers as far as the crocodilebook,[10] and to have been cheered by the gentleness of my mother's voice and manner all the way. But these solemn lessons which succeeded[11] those, I remember as the death-blow at my peace, and a grievous daily drudgery and misery. They were very long, very numerous, very hard—perfectly unintelligible, some of them, to me—and I was generally as much bewildered by them as I believe my poor mother was herself.

Let me remember how it used to be, and bring one morning back again.

I come into the second best parlour after breakfast, with my books, and an exercise-book, and a slate. My mother is ready for me at her writing-desk, but not half so ready as Mr. Murdstone in his easychair by the window (though he pretends to be reading a book), or as Miss Murdstone,[12] sitting near my mother stringing steel beads.[13] The very sight of these two has such an influence over me, that I begin to feel the words I have been at infinite pains to[14] get into my bead, all sliding away, and going I don't know where. I wonder where they *do* go, by the bye?[15]

I hand the first book to my mother. Perhaps it is a grammar, perhaps a history or geography. I take a last drowning look at the page[16] as I give it into her hand, and start off aloud at a racing pace while I have got it fresh. I trip over a word.[17] Mr. Murdstone looks up. I trip over another word. Miss Murdstone looks up. I redden, tumble over half a dozen words, and stop. I think my mother would show me the book if she dared, but she does not dare, and she says softly:

'Oh, Davy, Davy! '

'Now, Clara,' says Mr. Murdstone, 'be firm with the boy. Don't say, "Oh, Davy, Davy!" That's childish. He knows his lesson, or he does not know it.'[18]

'He does *not* know it,' Miss Murdstone interposes awfully.[19]

'I am really afraid he does not,' says my mother.

'Then, you see, Clara,' returns Miss Murdstone, 'you should just give him the book back, and make him know it.'

'Yes, certainly,' says my mother; 'that is what I intend to do, my dear Jane. Now, Davy, try once more, and don't be stupid,'

I obey the first clause of the injunction[20] by trying once more, but am not so successful with the second, for I am very stupid. I tumble down before I get to the old place, at a point where I was all right before, and stop to think. But I can't think about the lesson. I think of the number of yards of net in Miss Murdstone's cap,[21] or of the price of Mr. Murdstone's dressing-gown, or any such ridiculous problem that I have no business with, and don't want to have anything at all to do with. Mr. Murdstone makes a movement of impatience which I have been expecting for a long time. Miss Murdstone does the same. My mother glances submissively at them, shuts the book, and lays it by as an arrear[22] to be worked out when my other tasks are done.

There is a pile of these arrears very soon, and it swells like a rolling snowball. The bigger it gets, the more stupid I *get*. The case is so hopeless, and I feel that I am wallowing in such a bog of nonsense, that I give up all idea of getting out, and abandon myself to my fate.[23] The despairing way in which my mother and I look at each other, as I blunder on[24] is truly melancholy. But the greatest effect in these miserable lessons[25] is when my mother (thinking nobody is observing her) tries to give me the cue[26] by the motion of her lips. At that instant Miss Murdstone, who has been lying in wait[27] for nothing else all along, says in a deep warning voice:

'Clara!'

My mother starts, colours,[28] and smiles faintly. Mr. Murdstone comes out of his chair, takes the book, throws it at me or boxes my ears with it, and turns me out of the room by the shoulders.

Even when the lessons are done, the worst is yet to happen, in the shape of an appalling sum.[29] This is invented for me, and delivered to me orally by Mr. Murdstone, and begins: 'If I go into a cheesemonger's shop,[30] and buy five thousand double-Gloucester cheeses at fourpence-halfpenny each, present payment'—at which I see Miss Murdstone secretly overjoyed. I pore over[31] these cheeses without any result or enlightenment until dinner-time, when, having made a Mulatto of myself[32] by getting the dirt of the slate into the pores of my skin, I have a slice of bread to help me out with the cheeses,[33] and am considered in disgrace for the rest of the evening.[34]

. . . .

Chapter XI I Begin Life on My Own Account, and Don't Like It

. . . .

The counting-house clock[35] was at half-past twelve, and there was general prepacation for going to dinner, when Mr. Quinion[36] tapped at the counting-house window, and beckoned to me to go in. I went in, and found there a stoutish, middle-aged person, in a brown surtout[37] and black tights[38] and shoes, with no more hair upon his head (which was a large one and very shining) than there is upon an egg, and with a very extensive face, which he turned full upon me.[39] His clothes were shabby, but he had an imposing shirt-collar on.[40] He carried a jaunty sort of stick,[41] with a large pair of rusty tassels[42] to it; and a quizzing-glass[43] hung outside his coat — for ornament, I afterwards found, as he very seldom looked through it, and couldn't see anything when he did.

'This,' said Mr. Quinion, in allusion to myself, 'is he.'

'This,' said the stranger, with a certain condescending roll in his voice,[44] and a certain indescribable air of doing something genteel,[45] which impressed me very much, 'is Master Copperfield.[46] I hope I see you well, sir? '

I said I was very well, and hoped he was. I was sufficiently ill at ease, Heaven knows; but it was not in my nature to complain much at that time of my life, so I said I was very well, and hoped he was.

'I am,' said the stranger,'thank Heaven, quite well. I have received a letter from Mr. Murdstone, in which he mentions that he would desire me to receive into an apartment in the rear of my house, which is at present unoccupied — and is, in short, to be let as a — in short,[47]' said the stranger, with a smile, and in a burst of confidence,[48] 'as a bedroom — the young beginner whom I have now the pleasure to—'And the stranger waved his hand, and settled his chin in his shirt-collar.

'This is Mr. Micawber,' said Mr. Quinion to me.

'Ahem!' said the stranger, 'that is my name.'

'Mr. Micawber,' said Mr. Quinion, 'is known to Mr. Murdstone. He takes orders for us on commission,[49] when he can get any. He has been written to by Mr. Murdstone, on the subject of your lodgings, and he will receive you as a lodger.'

'My address,' said Mr. Micawber, 'is Windsor Terrace,[50] City Road. I—in short,' said Mr. Micawber, with the same genteel air, and in another burst of confidence—'I live there.'

I made him a bow.

'Under the impression,' said Mr. Micawber,'that your peregrinations in this metropolis[51] have not as yet been extensive, and that you might have some difficulty in penetrating the arcana of the Modern Babylon[52] in the direction of the City Road—in short,' said Mr. Micawber, in another burst of confidence, 'that you might lose yourself—I shall be happy to call this evening, and install you in the knowledge of the nearest way.'[53]

I thanked him with all my heart, for it was friendly in him to offer to take that trouble.

'At what hour,' said Mr. Micawber, 'shall I—'

'At about eight,' said Mr. Quinion.

'At about eight,' said Mr. Micawber. 'I beg to wish you good day,[54] Mr. Quinion. I will intrude no longer.'

So he put on his hat, and went out with his cane under his arm: very upright, and humming a tune when he was clear of[55] the counting-house.

Mr. Quinion then formally engaged me to be as useful as I could[56] in the warehouse of Murdstone and Grinby, at a salary, I think, of six shillings a week. I am not clear whether it was six or seven. I am inclined to believe, from my uncertainty on this head,[57] that it was six at first and seven afterwards. He paid me a week down[58] (from his own pocket, I believe), and I gave Mealy[59] sixpence out of it to get my trunk carried to Windsor Terrace that night: it being too heavy for my strength, small as it was. I paid sixpence more for my dinner, which was a meat pie and a turn at a neighbouring pump[60]; and passed the hour which was allowed for that meal, in walking about the streets.

At the appointed time in the evening, Mr. Micawber reappeared. I washed my hands and face, to do the greater honour to his gentility,[61] and we walked to our house, as I suppose I must now call it, together; Mr. Micawber impressing the names of streets, and the shapes of corner houses[62] upon me, as we went along, that[63] I might find my way back, easily, in the morning.

Arrived at his house in Windsor Terrace (which I noticed was shabby like himself, but also, like himself, made all the show it could)[64], he presented me to Mrs. Micawber, a thin and faded[65] lady, not at all young, who was sitting in the parlour (the first floor[66] was altogether unfurnished, and the blinds were kept down to delude the neighbours),[67] with a baby at her breast. This baby was one of twins; and I may remark here that I hardly ever, in all my experience of the family, saw both the twins detached from Mrs. Micawber at the same time. One of them was always taking refreshment.[68]

There were two other children; Master Micawber, aged about four, and Miss Micawbcr, aged about three. These, and a dark-complexioned young woman, with a habit of snorting,[69] who was servant to the family, and informed me, before half an hour had expired, that she was 'a Orfling,[70]' and came from St. Luke's workhouse,[71] in the neighbourhood, completed the establishment.[72] My room was at the top of the house, at the back: a close chamber;[73] stencilled all over with an ornament which my young imagination represented as a blue muffin;[74] and very scantily furnished.

'I never thought,' said Mrs. Micawber, when she came up, twin and all,[75] to show me the apartment, and sat down to take breath,'before I was married, when I lived with papa and mama,[76] that I should ever find it necessary to take a lodger. But Mr. Micawber being in difficulties, all considerations of private feeling[77] must give way.'

I said: 'Yes, ma'am.[78]'

'Mr. Micawber's difficulties are almost overwhelming just at present,' said Mrs. Micawber; 'and whether it is possible to bring him through them, I don't know. When I lived at home with papa and mama, I really should have hardly understood what the word[79] meant, in the sense in which I now employ it, but experientia does it[80] — as papa used to say.'

I cannot satisfy myself[81] whether she told me that Mr. Micawber had been an officer in the Marines,[82] or whether I have imagined it. I only know that I believe to this hour that he *was* in the Marines once upon a time, without knowing why. He was a sort of town traveller[83] for a number of miscellaneous houses,[84] now; but made little or nothing[85] of it, I am afraid.

'If Mr. Micawber's creditors *will not* give him time,' said Mrs. Micawber, 'they must take the consequences; and the sooner they bring it to an issue[86] the better. Blood cannot be obtained from a stone, neither can anything on account[87] be obtained at present (not to mention law expenses[88]) from Mr. Micawber.'

I never can quite understand whether my precocious self-dependence confused Mrs. Micawber in reference to my age,[89] or whether she was so full of the subject[90] that she would have talked about it to the very twins if there had been nobody else to communicate with, but this was the strain[91] in which she began, and she went on accordingly all the time I knew her.

Poor Mrs. Micawber! She said she had tried to exert herself; and so, I have no doubt, she had. The centre of the street door was perfectly covered with a great brass-plate, on which was engraved 'Mrs. Micawber's Boarding Establishment for Young Ladies'[92]: but I never found that any young lady had ever been to school there; or that the least preparation was ever made to receive any young lady. The only visitors I ever saw or heard of, were creditors. *They* used to come at all hours, and some of them were quite ferocious. One dirty-faced man, I think he was a boot-maker, used to edge himself into the passage[93] as early as seven o'clock in the morning, and call up the stairs to Mr. Micawber: 'Come! You ain't[94] out yet, you know. Pay us, will you? Don't hide, you know; that's mean. I wouldn't be mean if I was you. Pay us, will you? You just pay us, d'ye[95] hear? Come! ' Receiving no answer to these taunts, he would mount in his wrath to the words[96] 'swindlers' and 'robbers'; and these being ineffectual too, would sometimes go to the extremity of crossing the street, and roaring up at the windows of the second floor, where he knew Mr. Micawber was. At these times Mr. Micawber would be transported with grief and mortification,[97] even to the length (as I was once made aware by a scream from his wife) of making motions at himself with a razor; but within half an hour afterwards, he would polish up his shoes with extraordinary pains,[98] and go out, humming a tune with a greater air of gentility than ever. Mrs. Micawber was quite as elastic.[99] I have known her to be thrown into fainting fits by the king's taxes[100] at three o'clock, and to eat lamb chops breaded,[101] and drink warm ale (paid for with two teaspoons that had gone to the pawnbroker's) at four. On one occasion, when an execution had just been put in,[102] coming home through some chance as early as six o'clock, I saw her lying (of course with a twin) under the grate[103] in a swoon, with her hair all torn about her face; but I never knew her more cheerful than she was, that very same night, over a veal cutlet[104] before the kitchen fire, telling me stories about her papa and mama, and the company they used to keep.[105]

. . . .

Chapter XIII The Sequel of My Resolution

. . . .

Very stiff and sore of foot I was in the morning,[106] and quite dazed by the beating of drums and marching of troops, which seemed to hem me in on every side[107] when I went down towards the long narrow street. Feeling that I could go but a very little way that day, if I were to reserve any strength for getting to my journey's end, I resolved to make the sale of my jacket its principal business.[108] Accordingly, I took the jacket off, that I might learn to do without it;[109] and carrying it under my arm, began a tour of inspection of the various slop-shops.[110]

It was a likely place to sell a jacket in; for the dealers in second-hand clothes were numerous, and were, generally speaking, on the look-out for customers at their shop doors. But, as most of them had, hanging up among their stock, an officer's coat or two, epaulettes and all, I was rendered timid by the costly nature of their dealings,[111] and walked about for a long time without offering my merchandise[112] to any one.

This modesty of mine directed my attention to the marine-store shops,[113] and such shops as Mr. Dolloby's[114], in preference to the regular dealers. At last I found one that I thought looked promising[115] at the corner of a dirty lane, ending in an enclosure full of stingingnettles, against the palings of which some second-hand sailors' clothes, that seemed to have overflowed the shop,[116] were fluttering among some cots, and rusty guns, and oilskin hats, and certain trays full of so many old rusty keys of so many sizes that they seemed various enough to open all the doors in the world.

Into this shop, which was low and small, and which was darkened rather than lighted by a little window, overhung with clothes, and was descended into by some steps, I went with a palpitating heart; which was not relieved when an ugly old man, with the lower part of his face all covered with a stubbly grey beard, rushed out of a dirty den behind it, and seized me by the hair of my head. He was a dreadful old man to look at, in a filthy flannel waistcoat, and smelling terribly of rum. His bedstead, covered with a tumbled and ragged piece of patchwork, was in the den he had come from, where another little window showed a prospect of more stinging-nettles, and a lame donkey.

'Oh, what do you want?' grinned this old man, in a fierce, monotonous whine. 'Oh, my eyes and limbs,[117] what do you want? Oh, my lungs and liver, what do you want? Oh, goroo, goroo!'

I was so much dismayed by these words, and particularly by the repetition of the last unknown one,[118] which was a kind of rattle in his throat, that I could make no answer; hereupon the old man, still holding me by the hair, repeated:

'Oh, what do you want? Oh, my eyes and limbs, what do you want? Oh, my lungs and liver, what do you want? Oh, goroo!'—which he screwed out of himself, with an energy that made his eyes start in his head.[119]

'I wanted to know,' I said, trembling, 'if you would buy a jacket?'

'Oh, let's see the jacket!' cried the old man. 'Oh, my heart of fire, show the jacket to us! Oh, my eyes and limbs, bring the jacket out!'

With that he took his trembling hands, which were like the claws of a great bird, out of my hair; and put on a pair of spectacles, not at all ornamental,[120] to his inflamed eyes.

'Oh, how much for the jacket?' cried the old man, after examining it. 'Oh—goroo!—how much for the jacket?'

'Half a crown,'[121] I answered, recovering myself.

'Oh, my lungs and liver,' cried the old man, 'no! Oh, my eyes, no! Eighteenpence. Goroo!'

Every time he uttered this ejaculation, his eyes seemed to be in danger of starting out; and every sentence he spoke, he delivered in a sort of tune, always exactly the same, and more like a gust of wind, which begins low, mounts up high, and falls again, than any other comparison I can find for it.

'Well', said I, glad to have closed the bargain,[122] 'I'll take eighteenpence.'

'Oh, my liver!' cried the old man, throwing the jacket on a shelf. 'Get out of the shop! Oh, my lungs, get out of the shop! Oh, my eyes and limbs—goroo!—don't ask for money; make it an exchange.'[123]

I never was so frightened in my life, before or since; but I told him humbly that I wanted money, and that nothing else was of any use to me, but that I would wait for it, as he desired, outside, and had no wish to hurry him. So I went outside, and sat down in the shade in a corner. And I sat there so many hours, that the shade became sunlight, and the sunlight became shade again, and still I sat there waiting for the money.

There never was such another drunken madman in that line of business, I hope. That he was well known in the neighbourhood, and enjoyed the reputation of having sold himself to the devil,[124] I soon understood from the visits he received from the boys, who continually came skirmishing about the shop, shouting that legend,[125] and calling to him to bring out his gold. 'You ain't poor, you know, Charley, as you pretend. Bring out your gold. Bring out some of the gold you sold yourself to the devil for. Come! It's in the lining of the mattress, Charley. Rip it open and let's have some! ' This, and many offers to lend him a knife for the purpose,[126] exasperated him to such a degree, that the whole day was a succession of rushes on his part, and flights[127] on the part of the boys. Sometimes in his rage he would take me for one of them, and come at me, mouthing[128] as if he were going to tear me in pieces; then, remembering me, just in time, would dive into the shop, and lie upon his bed, as I thought from the sound of his voice, yelling in a frantic way, to his own windy tune, *The Death of Nelson,*[129] with an Oh! before every line, and innumerable Goroos interspersed.[130] As if this were not bad enough for me, the boys, connecting me with the establishment,[131] on account of the patience and perseverance with which I sat outside, half-dressed, pelted me, and used me very ill[132] all day.

He made many attempts to induce me to consent to an exchange; at one time coming out with a fishing-rod, at another with a fiddle, at another with a cocked hat,[133] at another with a flute. But I resisted all these overtures,[134] and sat there in desperation;[135] each time asking him, with tears in my eyes, for my money or my jacket. At last he began to pay me in half-pence at a time; and was full two hours at getting by easy stages to a shilling.[136]

'Oh, my eyes and limbs! ' he then cried, peeping hideously out of the shop, after a long pause, 'will you go for twopence more?'

'I can't,' I said, 'I shall be starved.'

'Oh, my lungs and liver, will you go for threepence?'

'I would go for nothing, if I could,'[137] I said, 'but I want the money badly.'

'Oh, go—roo! ' (it is really impossible to express how he twisted this ejaculation out of himself, as he peeped round the door-post at me, showing nothing but his crafty old head) 'will you go for fourpence?

I was so faint and weary that I closed with this offer;[138] and taking the money out of his claw, not without trembling, went away more hungry and thirsty than I had ever been, a little before sunset. But at an expense of threepence I soon refreshed myself completely;[139] and, being in better spirits then, limped seven miles upon my road.[140]

. . . .

Chapter LV Tempest

. . . .

'Don't you think that,' I asked the coachman, in the first stage out of London,[141] 'a very remarkable[142] sky? I don't remember to have seen one like it.'

'Nor I—not equal to it,' he replied. 'That's wind, sir. There'll be mischief done at sea, I expect, before long.'

It was a murky confusion—here and there blotted with a colour like the colour of the smoke from damp fuel—of flying clouds tossed up into most remarkable heaps, suggesting greater heights in the clouds than there were depths below them to the bottom of the deepest hollows in the earth,[143] through which the wild moon seemed to plunge headlong, as if, in a dread disturbance of the laws of nature,[144] she had lost her way and were frightened. There had been a wind all day; and it was rising then, with an extraordinary great sound. In another hour it had much increased, and the sky was more overcast, and blew hard.[145]

But as the night advanced, the clouds closing in and densely overspreading the whole sky, then very dark, it came on to blow, harder and harder. It still increased, until our horses could scarcely face the wind. Many times, in the dark part of the night (it was then late in September, when the nights were not short), the leaders[146] turned about, or came to a dead stop; and we were often in serious apprehension that the coach would be blown over. Sweeping gusts of rain came up before this storm like showers of steel; and, at those times, when there was any shelter of trees or lee walls[147] to be got, we were fain to stop,[148] in a sheer impossibility of continuing the struggle.

When the day broke, it blew harder and harder. I had been in Yarmouth when the seamen said it blew great guns,[149] but I had never known the like of this, or anything approaching to it. We came to Ipswich[150] — very late, having had to fight every inch of ground since we were ten miles out of London; and found a cluster of people in the marketplace, who had risen from their beds in the night, fearful of falling chimneys. Some of these, congregating about the inn-yard while we changed horses, told us of great sheets of lead having been ripped off a high church-tower, and flung into a by-street, which they then blocked up.[151] Others had to tell of country people,[152] coming in from neighbouring villages, who had seen great trees lying torn out of the earth, and whole ricks scattered about the roads and fields. Still there was no abatement in the storm, but it blew harder.

As we struggled on, nearer and nearer to the sea, from which this mighty wind was blowing dead on shore,[153] its force became more and more terrific. Long before we saw the sea, its spray was on our lips, and showered salt rain upon us. The water was out,[154] over miles and miles of the flat country[155] adjacent to Yarmouth; and every sheet and puddle[156] lashed its banks, and had its stress of little breakers setting heavily towards us.[157] When we came within sight of the sea, the waves on the horizon, caught at intervals above the rolling abyss,[158] were like glimpses of another shore with towers and buildings. When at last we got into the town, the people came out of their doors, all aslant,[159] and with streaming hair, making a wonder of the mail[160] that had come through such a night.

I put up[161] at the old inn, and went down to look at the sea; staggering along the street, which was strewn with sand and seaweed, and with flying blotches of sea-foam;[162] afraid of falling slates and tiles; and holding by people I met, at angry corners.[163] Coming near the beach, I saw, not only the boatmen, but half the people of the town, lurking behind buildings; some, now and then braving the fury of the storm to look away to sea, and blown sheer out of their course in trying to get zigzag back.[164]

Joining these groups, I found bewailing women whose husbands were away in herring or oyster boats,[165] which there was too much reason to think might have foundered before they could run in anywhere for safety. Grizzled old sailors were among the people, shaking their heads, as they looked from water to sky, and muttering to one another; ship-owners, excited and uneasy; children, huddling together, and peering into older faces; even stout mariners,[166] disturbed and anxious, levelling their glasses at the sea[167] from behind places of shelter, as if they were surveying an enemy.

The tremendous sea itself, when I could find sufficient pause to look at it,[168] in the agitation of the blinding wind, the flying stones and sand, and the awful noise, confounded me. As the high watery walls came rolling in, and, at their highest, tumbled into surf, they looked as if the least would engulf the town.[169] As the receding wave swept back with a hoarse roar, it seemed to scoop out deep caves in the beach, as if its purpose were to undermine the earth. When some white-headed billows thundered on, and dashed themselves to pieces before they reached the land, every fragment of the late whole seemed possessed by the full might of its wrath,[170] rushing to be gathered to the composition of another monster.[171] Undulating hills were changed to valleys, undulating valleys (with a solitary storm-bird sometimes skimming through them) were lifted up to hills; masses of water shivered and shook the beach with a booming sound; every shape triumphantly rolled on, as soon as made, to change its shape and place, and beat another shape and place away; the ideal shore on the horizon,[172] with its towers and buildings, rose and fell; the clouds flew fast and thick; I seemed to see a rending and upheaving of all nature.[173]

Not finding Ham among the people whom this memorable wind — for it is still remembered down there as the greatest ever known to blow upon that coast — had brought together, I made my way to his house. It was shut; and as no one answered to my knocking, I went, by back ways[174] and by-lanes, to the yard where he worked. I learned, there, that he had gone to Lowestoft,[175] to meet some sudden exigency of ship-repairing in which his skill was required; but that he would be back tomorrow morning, in good time.

I went back to the inn; and when I had washed and dressed, and tried to sleep, but in vain, it was five o'clock in the afternoon. I had not sat five minutes by the coffee-room fire, when the waiter coming to stir it,[176] as an excuse for talking, told me that two colliers[177] had gone down, with all hands, a few miles away; and that some other ships had been seen labouring hard in the Roads,[178] and trying, in great distress, to keep off shore. Mercy on them,[179] and on all poor sailors, said he, if we had another night like the last!

I was very much depressed in spirits; very solitary; and felt an uneasiness in Ham's not being there, disproportionate to the occasion.[180]

I was seriously affected, without knowing how much, by late events;[181] and my long exposure to the fierce wind had confused me. There was that jumble in my thoughts and recollections, that[182] I had lost the clear arrangement of time and distance. Thus,[183] if I had gone out into the town, I should not have been surprised, I think, to encounter someone who I knew must be then in London. So to speak, there was in these respects a curious inattention in my mind.[184] Yet it was busy, too, with all the remembrances the place naturally awakened; and they were particularly distinct and vivid.

In this state, the waiter's dismal intelligence[185] about the ships immediately connected itself, without any effort of my volition,[186] with my uneasiness about Ham. I was persuaded,[187] that I had an apprehension of his returning from Lowestoft by sea, and being lost.

This grew so strong with me,[188] that I resolved to go back to the yard,[189] before I took my dinner, and ask the boat-builder if he thought his attempting[190] to return by sea at all likely. If he gave me the least reason to think so, I would go over to Lowestoft and prevent it by bringing him with me.

I hastily ordered my dinner, and went back to the yard. I was none too soon[191]; for the boat-builder, with a lantern in his hand, was locking the yard-gate. He quite laughed when I asked him the question, and said there was no fear; no man in his senses, or out of them, would put off in such a gale of wind,[192] least of all Ham Peggotty,[193] who had been born to seafaring.

So sensible of this, beforehand, that[194] I had really felt ashamed of doing what I was nevertheless impelled to do, I went back to the inn. If such a wind could rise, I think it was rising. The howl and roar, the rattling of the doors and windows, the rumbling in the chimneys, the apparent rocking of the very house that sheltered me, and the prodigious tumult of the sea, were more fearful than in the morning. But there was now a great darkness besides; and that invested the storm with new terrors, real and fanciful.

I could not eat, I could not sit still, I could not continue steadfast to anything. Something within me, faintly answering to the storm without, tossed up the depths of my memory[195] and made a tumult in them. Yet, in all the hurry of my thoughts, wild running with the thundering sea—the storm and my uneasiness regarding Ham were always in the foreground.[196]

My dinner went away almost untasted, and I tried to refresh myself with a glass or two of wine. In vain. I fell into a dull slumber before the fire, without losing my consciousness, either of the uproar out of doors, or of the place in which I was. Both became overshadowed by a new and indefinable horror; and when I awoke — or rather when I shook off the lethargy that bound me in my chair — my whole frame thrilled with objectless and unintelligible fear.[197]

I walked to and fro, tried to read an old gazetteer, listened to the awful noises: looked at faces, scenes, and figures in the fire.[198] At length, the steady ticking of the undisturbed clock on the wall tormented me to that degree that I resolved to go to bed.

It was reassuring,[199] on such a night, to be told that some of the inn-servants had agreed together to sit up[200] until morning. I went to bed, exceedingly weary and heavy; but, on my lying down, all such sensations vanished, as if by magic, and I was broad awake, with every sense refined.[201]

For hours I lay there, listening to the wind and water; imagining, now, that I heard shrieks out at sea; now, that I distinctly heard the firing of signal guns; and now, the fall of houses in the town. I got up several times, and looked out; but could see nothing, except the reflection in the window-panes of the faint candle I had left burning, and of my own haggard face looking in at me from the black void.[202]

At length, my restlessness attained to such a pitch, that I hurried on my clothes, and went downstairs. In the large kitchen, where I dimly saw bacon and ropes of onions hanging from the beams, the watchers[203] were clustered together, in various attitudes,[204] about a table, purposely moved away from the great chimney, and brought near the door. A pretty girl, who had her ears stopped with her apron, and her eyes upon the door, screamed when I appeared, supposing me to be a spirit;[205] but the others had more presence of mind,[206] and were glad of an addition to their company. One man, referring to the topic they had been discussing, asked me whether I thought[207] the souls of the collier-crews who had gone down, were out in the storm.

I remained there, I dare say,[208] two hours. Once, I opened the yard-gate,[209] and looked into the empty street. The sand, the seaweed, and the flakes of foam, were driving by; and I was obliged to call for assistance before I could shut the gate again, and make it fast against the wind.[210]

There was a dark gloom in my solitary chamber, when I at length returned to it; but I was tired now, and, getting into bed again, fell—off a tower and down a precipice—into the depths of sleep.[211] I have an impression that for a long time, though I dreamed of being elsewhere and in a variety of scenes, it was always blowing in my dream. At length, I lost that feeble hold upon reality,[212] and was engaged with two dear friends,[213] but who they were I don't know, at the siege of some town in a roar of cannonading.

The thunder of the cannon was so loud and incessant, that I could not hear something I much desired to hear, until I made a great exertion and awoke. It was broad day—eight or nine o'clock; the storm raging, in lieu of the batteries,[214] and someone knocking and calling at my door.

'What is the matter?' I cried.

'A wreck![215] Close by!'

I sprung out of bed, and asked, what wreck?

'A schooner, from Spain or Portugal, laden with fruit and wine. Make haste, sir, if you want to see her! It's thought, down on the beach,[216] she'll go to pieces every moment.'

The excited voice went clamouring along the staircase; and I wrapped myself in my clothes as quickly as I could, and ran into the street.

Numbers of people were there before me, all running in one direction, to the beach. I ran the same way, outstripping a good many, and soon came facing the wild sea.

The wind might by this time have lulled a little, though not more sensibly than if the cannonading I had dreamed of had been diminished by the silencing of half a dozen guns out of hundreds.[217] But the sea, having upon it the additional agitation of the whole night,[218] was infinitely more terrific than when I had seen it last. Every appearance it had then presented, bore the expression of being *swelled*;[219] and the height to which the breakers rose, and, looking over one another, bore one another down, and rolled in, in interminable hosts,[220] was most appalling.

In the difficulty of hearing anything but wind and waves, and in the crowd, and the unspeakable confusion, and my first breathless efforts to stand against the weather, I was so confused that I looked out to sea for the wreck, and saw nothing but the foaming heads of the great waves. A half-dressed boatman, standing next me, pointed with his bare arn (a tattoo'd arrow on it,[221] pointing in the same direction) to the left. Then, O great Heaven, I saw it, close in upon us!

One mast was broken short off,[222] six or eight feet from the deck, and lay over the side, entangled in a maze of sail and rigging;[223] and all that ruin,[224] as the ship rolled and beat—which she did without a moment's pause, and with a violence quite inconceivable—beat the side as if it would stave it in.[225] Some efforts were even then being made, to cut this portion of the wreck away; for as the ship, which was broadside on,[226] turned towards us in her rolling, I plainly descried her people at work with axes, especially one active figure with long curling hair, conspicuous among the rest. But a great cry, which was audible even above the wind and water, rose from the shore at this moment; the sea, sweeping over the rolling wreck, made a clean breach[227], and carried men, spars, casks, planks, bulwarks,[228] heaps of such toys,[229] into the boiling surge.

The second mast was yet standing, with the rags of a rent[230] sail, and a wild confusion of broken cordage flapping to and fro. The ship had struck once,[231] the same boatman hoarsely said in my ear, and then lifted in[232] and struck again. I understood him to add that she was parting amidships,[233] and I could readily suppose so, for the rolling and beating were too tremendous for any human work[234] to suffer long. As he spoke, there was another great cry of pity from the beach; four men arose from the wreck out of the deep,[235] clinging to the rigging of the remaining mast; uppermost,[236] the active figure with the curling hair.

There was a bell on board; and as the ship rolled and dashed, like a desperate creature driven mad, now showing us the whole sweep of her deck,[237] as she turned on her beam-ends towards the shore,[238] now nothing but her keel,[239] as she sprung wildly over and turned towards the sea, the bell rang; and its sound, the knell of those unhappy men, was borne towards us on the wind. Again we lost her, and again she rose. Two men were gone. The agony on shore increased. Men groaned, and clasped their hands; women shrieked, and turned away their faces. Some ran wildly up and down along the beach, crying for help where no help could be. I found myself one of these, frantically imploring a knot of sailors whom I knew, not to let those two lost creatures[240] perish before our eyes.

They were making out to me, in an agitated way — I don't know how, for the little I could hear I was scarcely composed enough to understand — that[241] the lifeboat had been bravely manned an hour ago, and could do nothing; and that as no man would be so desperate as to attempt to wade off with a rope, and establish a communication wit the shore, there was nothing to try; when I noticed that some new sensation[242] moved the people on the beach, and saw them part, and Ham come breaking through them to the front.

I ran to him — as well as I know[243] — to repeat my appeal for help. But, distracted though I was by a sight so new to me and terrible,[244] the determination in his face, and his look out to sea — exactly the same look as I remembered in connection with the morning after Emily's flight[245] — awoke me to a knowledge of his danger.[246] I held him back with both arms; and implored the men with whom I had been speaking, not to listen to him, not to do murder, not to let him stir off that sand![247]

Another cry arose on shore; and looking to the wreck, we saw the cruel sail, with blow on blow, beat off the lower of the two men, and fly up iu triumph round the active figure left alone upon the mast.

Against such a sight, and against such determination as that of the calmly desperate man who was already accustomed to lead half the people present,[248] I might as hopefully have entreated the wind.[249] 'Mas'r Davy,'[250] he said, cheerily grasping me by both hands, 'if my time is come, 'tis come. If 'tan't, I'll bide it.[251] Lord above[252] bless you, and bless all! Mates, make me ready! I'm a-going[253] off! '

I was swept away, but not unkindly, to some distance, where the people around made me stay, urging,[254] as I confusedly perceived, that he was bent on going, with help or without, and that I should endanger the precautions for his safety by troubling those with whom they rested.[255] I don't know what I answered, or what they rejoined; but I saw hurry on the beach, and men running with ropes from a capstan that was there, and penetrating into a circle of figures that hid him from me. Then I saw him standing alone, in a seaman's frock and trousers: a rope in his hand, or slung to his wrist; another round his body; and several of the best men holding, at a little distance, to the latter,[256] which he laid out himself, slack upon the shore, at his feet.

The wreck, even to my unpractised eye,[257] was breaking up. I saw that she was parting in the middle, and that the life of the solitary man upon the mast hung by a thread. Still, he clung to it. He had a singular red cap on—not like a sailor's cap, but of a finer colour;[258] and as the few yielding planks between him and destruction rolled and bulged,[259] and his anticipative death-knell rung, he was seen by all of us to wave it.[260] I saw him do it now, and thought I was going distracted, when his action brought an old remembrance to my mind of a once dear friend.

Ham watched the sea, standing alone, with the silence of suspended breath behind him,[261] and the storm before,[262] until there was a great retiring wave, when, with a backward glance at those who held the rope which was made fast round his body, he dashed in after it, and in a moment was buffeting with the water: rising with thehills, falling with the valleys, lost beneath the foam; then drawn again to land. They hauled in hastily.

He was hurt. I saw blood on his face, from where I stood; but he took no thought of that. He seemed hurriedly to give them some directions for leaving him more free—or so I judged from the motion of his arm—and was gone as before.

And now he made for the wreck, rising with the hills, falling with the valleys, lost beneath the rugged foam, borne in towards the shore, borne on towards the ship, striving hard and valiantly. The distance was nothing,[263] but the power of the sea and wind made the strife deadly. At length he neared the wreck. He was so near, that with one more of his vigorous strokes he would be clinging to it — when, a high, green, vast hill-side of water, moving on shoreward, from beyond the ship, he seemd to leap up into it with a mighty bound, and the ship was gone!

Some eddying fragments[264] I saw in the sea, as if a mere cask had been broken, in running to the spot where they were hauling in. Consternation was in every face. They drew him to my very feet — insensible — dead. He was carried to the nearest house; and, no one preventing me now, I remained near him, busy, while every means of restoration were tried; but he had been beaten to death by the great wave, and his generous heart was stilled for ever.

As I sat beside the bed, when hope was abandoned and all was done,[265] a fisherman, who had known me when Emily and I were children, and ever since, whispered my name at the door.

'Sir,' said he, with tears starting to his weather-beaten[266] face, which, with his trembling lips, was ashy pale,[267] 'will you come over yonder?'[268]

The old remembrance that had been recalled to me,269 was in his look. I asked him, terror-stricken, leaning on the arm he held out to support me:

'Has a body come ashore?'

He said: 'Yes.'

'Do you know it?' I asked then.

He answered nothing.

But he led me to the shore. And on that part of it where she and I[270] had looked for shells, two children — on that part of it where some lighter fragments of the old boat,[271] blown down last night, had been scattered by the wind — among the ruins of the home he had wronged — I saw him lying[272] with his head upon his arm, as I had often seen him lie at school.

【作者简介】 Charles Dickens（查理·狄更斯，1812—1870），十九世纪英国伟大的小说家。幼年家贫，曾作徒工，成名后仍接近贫苦人民。一生创作辛勤，留下了二十几部小说，包括 *The Posthumous Papers of the Pickwick Club*（《匹克威克外传》，1836—1837 年），*Oliver Twist*（《奥立弗·推斯特》，1837—1838 年），*The Old Curiosity Shop*（《老古玩店》，1840—1841 年），*Dombey and Son*（《董贝父子》，1846—1848 年），*David Copperfield*（《大卫·科波菲尔》，1849—1850 年），*Hard Times*（《艰难时世》，1854 年），*A Tale of Two Cities*（《双城记》，1854 年），*Great Expectations*（《鸿运》，1860—1861 年）等。他的作品广泛地反映了英国中下阶层的生活，对劳苦人民的苦难和不幸寄予深切的同情，同时对英国资产阶级的贪婪、虚伪及其统治机构的腐败作了无情的揭露和鞭挞。但由于他从小资产阶级的人道主义的立场出发，不愿触动资本主义私有制，对社会问题多从善恶观念去解释，以至作品中经常出现发善心的有钱人并常以好人团圆、恶棍受惩的结局，减弱了作品的批判力量，狄更斯的小说情节曲折动人，人物形象鲜明生动，写景叙事真切而又富想象，有尖刻的讽刺，又有幽默的夸张，拥有广大读者，声誉至今不衰。

【题解与注释】

David Copperfield（《大卫·科波菲尔》）是狄更斯的一部重要作品，写于 1849—1850 年。作者在小说的序言里写道："我在自己的全部作品中最喜欢的是这一本（Of all my books, I like this the best）." 小说以孤儿 David Copperfield 的成长和遭遇为主要线索，与作者本人身世颇多吻合之处；又通过主人公的自叙，展开了丰富有趣的情节。狄更斯此书故事十分引人，笔调幽默而略带感伤，并且创造了一大群出色的人物形象。这里的四段分别选自该书第四、十一、十三、五十五章，现介绍如下。

第四、十一、十三章都是写 David Copperfield 的童年时代。David 是个遗腹子，在母亲和女仆 Peggotty 的爱抚下，度过了最初几个幸福的岁月。接着，年轻软弱的母亲改嫁，家中来了冷酷的继父——富商 Murdstone，和他的姊姊 Murdstone 小姐，从此母子俩受尽了 Murdstone 的虐待欺凌。第四章的选段就是描写 David 在 Murdstone 监视下读书时惊慌失措的情景。从这段家庭冲突的故事中可以看到狄更斯对被压迫者的同情，也可以看到他对儿童心理的了解和细腻描写。狄更斯在叙述 David 的回忆时用了动词的现在时态，使故事益加生动。

由于 Murdstone 的折磨，David 的母亲终于抑郁而死，年幼的 David 被送到伦敦去当徒工，寄居在穷跑街 Micawber 家中。Micawber 是狄更斯小说中典型的悲喜剧式的小人物，是他写得最成功的人物之一。心地善良的 Micawber 夫妇，一心想要发迹，但无情的资本主义社会逼得他们穷愁潦倒，债台高筑，然而他们又不甘向生活认输，总是巴望着有朝一日会碰到什么好运气。Micawber 先生穷得有时连饭也吃不上，却极力摆出绅士的架子，举止言词务求典雅。在第十一章里，狄更斯描述了 David 与这位可怜、可笑而又可爱的人物初次会面的情景以及 Micawber 一家的境遇。

David 不堪忍受徒工生活的劳累和屈辱，决定去离伦敦数十英里的 Dover 镇投奔他的有钱的祖姑母 Betsey Trotwood。刚一出门，不料遇上流氓，抢走了他仅有的衣物钱币，于是只得徒步而行。沿途风餐露宿，靠当卖身上的衣服买食物充饥，经过六昼夜的艰难历程，才找到那位老人。所选第十三章的片断是 David 变卖上衣遇欺的一场，其中收旧衣的店主是狄更斯爱写的怪人物之一。这个性情乖戾、面目可憎的老头和天真弱小的 David 形成了有趣的对照。

David 为祖姑母收留，在她供养下，读书成人，并且靠着自己努力，终于成了有名的作家，他娶了律师的女儿 Dora 为妻，两人性格虽然不同，但相爱至深。不幸，娇弱的爱妻竟一病不起，早早夭亡了。在此前后，David 一向崇拜的学友、贵族子弟 Steerforth，诱骗了女仆 Peggotty 家的养女 Emily，撕碎了她养父 Peggotty 先生（女仆的胞兄）和未婚夫 Ham 这两位善良渔民的心；Betsey Trotwood 的法律顾问 Wickfield 落入了奸诈的青年职员 Uriah Heep 的圈套，让他独揽了自己的全部事务，侵吞了 Betsey 的产业，还几乎把自己的爱女、David 的挚友 Agnes 许给了他。虽然 Emily 被 Steerforth 遗弃之后回到了她养父的身边，Uriah Heep 的阴谋也被揭穿，但这两场风波不能不使阅历尚浅的 David 大为震惊，加重了他丧妻的痛苦。生活对 David 的这些冲击，就构成了第五十五章大风暴的背景。David 为了摆脱精神上的痛苦与不安，也为了替即将随养父移居海外的 Emily 送信给 Ham，决定去 Yarmouth 海滨一行。车出伦敦不远，就遇上了风暴。这是英国文学中少有的大风暴，作者让自然界的狂风恶浪和主人公内心世界的翻腾激荡卷在一起了。

从小说的这四个片断中，我们可以看到狄更斯的艺术天才是多方面的。他善于描写儿童心理，用儿童的眼光去摄取周围世界的景象，他善于刻划形形色色的人物，总能替他们的容貌、举止、言语找到充分表露性格的特征，使他们的形象既夸张又逼真。他善于描述人物受苦受辱的情景，勾起读者的同情。他是创造气氛的能手，常以景物烘托感情，抓住读者的心。他既能具体而微地描写一家店铺、一间住房的陈设，又能勾画出惊心动魄的宏伟场面。他是幽默大师，总是用乐观的情绪来感染读者，却又用幽默来冲淡和回避现实社会的尖锐矛盾。不用说，他又最会讲故事。狄更斯这种多方面的才能和特点在 *David Copperfield* 这部代表作里得到了充分的表现。

CHAPTER IV

1. occasions: = chances, possibilities，可能性。

2. boarding-school: 寄宿学校。

3. my mother had of course agreed with them: David 的母亲性格软弱，在丈夫的淫威下只有百依百顺，因此作者用了 of course 一词。

4. found them: 指 those lessons。

5. that miscalled firmness: Murdstone 先生不许妻子流露自己的感情，不许她疼爱孩子，常以“坚定”（be firm）相诫，作者认为这根本不是什么“坚定”，因此称之为 miscalled（误称为的）firmness。

6. primer: 初级读本。

7. the puzzling novelty of their shapes: 字母的形状新奇（形容词 novel，名词 novelty）而令人不解（puzzling）；孩子初次认字，对各种形状的字母有一种新鲜而困惑之感。

8. the easy good-nature of O and Q and S: O, Q，S 等字母的圆形，给孩子以和善可亲的感觉。

9. recall: 引起…的回忆，使人忆起。

10. I seem to have walked along a path of flowers as far as the crocodile-book: David 在母亲改嫁前，常喜欢给女仆 Peggotty 读一本讲鳄鱼的故事书，那时候他的生活是幸福的，读书的心情是愉快的，所以说一直到读“鳄鱼书”的那段生活就象一条花径一般。

11. succeeded: 承继，接着。

12. not half so ready as Mr. Murdstone ..., or as Miss Murdstone: 远不如（Murdstone 先生或 Murdstone 小姐）那样一心等着我去上课；在敏感的 David 看来，Murdstone 姐弟专等着给 David 上课的机会，来训斥 Copperfield 母子。

13. stringing steel beads: 用线串钢珠子（Murdstone 小姐的首饰）。

14. (to be) at infinite pains to ...: 竭尽全力设法… pains = efforts.

15. By the bye: = by the way，顺便说一句。

16. take a last drowning look at the page: 对那页书贪婪地看了最后一眼；drowning 有“企图一眼把整页书都看进去”之意。

17. trip over a word: 背错了一个词；trip over 原义是“被…绊倒”，用在此处和上文 start off aloud at a racing pac（用赛跑般的速度开始大声背诵）相呼应，非常合适。

18. He knows his lesson, or he does not know it: 意即：他要末会背，要末不会背，没有什么商量余地。

19. awfully: 肃然可畏地，威严地；这里用的是此词的原义（词根 awe 是“敬畏”的意思），而在现代英语中通常仅作“非常”解，即等于 very, extremely。

20. the first clause of the injunction: 训令的第一条；这是故作庄重的幽默说法，injunction 即指上文母亲的最后一句话，the first clause 指“try once more”，the second 指“don't be stupid”。

21. the number of yards of net in Miss Murdstone's cap: Murdstone 小姐的帽子用了多少码的网线。

22. lays it by as an arrear: 把它放在一边，算是一项积欠。

23. abandon myself to my fate: 听天由命。

24. blunder on: 一个劲儿地错下去。

25. the greatest effect in these miserable lessons: 这些倒霉的功课中戏剧效

果最大的场面（反语）。

26. give me the cue: 给我提词。

27. lying in wait: 埋伏着守候；意即：偷偷地看着母亲专等她向我暗示这一着。

28. colours: = reddens.

29. the worst is yet to happen, in the shape of an appalling sum: 最糟糕的还在后头呢，那就是一道可怕的算术题；in the shape of 原义为“以…形式出现的”。

30. 'If I go into a cheesemonger's shop, …': “假如我上干酪铺去买五千块双格罗斯特干酪，而每块干酪的价格是四个半便士，那么总计该付多少钱？” Gloucester [ˈglɔstə] 是一种干酪的名称，产于英国 Gloucestershire [ˈglɔstoʃiə]，其中牛乳少的称为 single-Gloucester，牛乳多的称为 double-Gloucester。

31. pore over: 埋头钻研，苦苦思索。

32. made a Mulatto of myself: 把自己弄成个黑白混血儿似的；Mulatto [mjuˈlætəu]，白种人与黑种人结亲的后裔。

33. I have a slice of bread to help me out with the cheeses: 他们就给我一片面包，来帮忙处理这些干酪。to help me out with 有双关意义，即“好让我就着这些干酪吃下去”和“帮我解决关于干酪的这道算术题”；而这又是个反讥的说法，真正的意思是“我做不出这道关于干酪的算术题，因此晚饭就只给我吃一片面包，作为惩罚”。

34. am considered in disgrace for the rest of the evening: 那一晚就被当作坏孩子看待了。

CHAPTER XI

35. the counting-house clock: 帐房墙上的挂钟。David 在继父 Murdstone 的公司 Murdstone and Grinby 的一所仓库内当徒工，仓库里间是徒工们工作的地方，外间是帐房，中间有玻璃窗隔开。

36. Mr. Qniniun [ˈkwiniən]: 小说中 Murdstone and Grinby 公司经理酒业的经纪人。

37. surtout: 一种袖子肥大的外套。

38. tights: 紧身的裤子。

39. which he turned full upon me: 他把那张大脸转过来，正对着我。

40. had an imposing shirt-collar on: 戴了一条很显眼的衣领。欧洲男子的衬衣和衣领常常是分开的，衣着体面的人总要戴一条白硬领。

41. a jaunty sort of stick: 带着一根手杖，神态显得很轻快潇洒。

42. rusty tassels: 古色古香的流苏。

43. quizzing-glass: 单片眼镜。

44. with a certain condescending roll in his voice: 说话声音洪亮带着一种自感优越的腔调。

45. a certain indescribable air of doing something genteel: 有一种莫可名状的神气，好象在做什么高雅的事情。

46. Master Copperfield: Copperfield 少爷。姓氏之前加 master 是对男孩子的

称呼。

47. in short: 简而言之；Micawber 先生的口头禅。

48. in a burst of confidence: 忽然对我说了体己的话。

49. He takes orders for us on commission: 他替我们承揽定货，赚取佣金。

50. Windsor [ˈwinzə] **Terrace:** 一排楼房的名称；英国城市中成排的住宅常以 terrace 为名。

51. your peregrinations in this metropolis，你在这大都会的游历。

52. penetrating the arcana of the Modern Babylon: 穿过这现代巴比伦城的迷宫。arcana [ɑːˈkeinə]（arcanum 的复数），原义为"奥秘"；Babylon [ˈbæbilən]，幼发拉底河谷的古代名城，为古代巴比伦的首都。

53. install you in the knowledge of the nearest way: 使你获得关于最近的途径的知识；意即：带你走最近便的路。

54. I beg to wish you good day: 谨祝您日安；古雅的道别语。

55. was clear of: 走出了。

56. formally engaged me to be as useful as I could: 正式地雇佣了我，让我尽力而为。

57. from my uncertainty on this head: 从我对这一点（指究竟是六先令还是七先令）的不肯定来判断。

58. He paid me a week down: 他先付给我一周的工资；pay … down 意为"一次付清一笔款项"。

59. Mealy: 与 David 一起做工的另一徒工的外号。

60. a turn at a neighbouring pump: 在就近的酒店里喝上一杯；pump 此处指汲啤酒的唧筒，转指酒店，a turn 意为打开一次龙头，即要一杯啤酒。

61. to do the greater honour to his gentility: 为了更好地对他的高雅风度表示敬重。

62. the shapes of corner houses: 马路拐角处房屋的形状。

63. that: = so that.

64. made all the show it could: 尽量装点门面。

65. faded: 已现苍老的。

66. the first floor: 此处指一层，即 ground floor.

67. to delude the neighbours: 好瞒过四邻的眼睛。

68. taking refreshment: 原义为"吃点心"，此处幽默地指婴儿吃奶。

69. with a habit of snorting: 鼻子老爱打哼哼。

70. 'a Orfling': = an orphan. orphan 在未受过教育的人的口语里变了形，就成了 orfling。

71. St. Luke's workhouse: 圣路加贫民习艺所；workhouse 是英国资产阶级残酷剥削失去生活依靠的贫苦人民的场所，根据 1834 年的贫民法而设，英国劳动人民称之为"穷人的巴士底狱"（The Poor Man's Bastille），狄更斯对此始终给以最猛烈的抨击。

72. (These, and a dark-complexioned young woman ...) completed the establishment:（把这两个孩子连同一个皮肤黑黝黝的姑娘都算上）这一家子就齐了。

73. a close chamber: 房间又小又挤。

74. stencilled all over with an ornament which my young imagination represented as a blue muffin: 四周墙上用蓝漆印上了一种图案，在我童年的想象里，就象一个个蓝色的松饼一样。

75. twin and all: 抱着那个吃奶的双生子一块儿（上来）。

76. papa and mama: 老式或贵族人家子女对父母的称呼。

77. all considerations of private feeling: 一切个人情感（爱恶）的考虑。

78. ma'am [mɑːm]: = madam，对妇人的尊称。

79. the word: 指 difficulties。

80. but experientia does it: = but experience taught me to understand what the word means; Micawber 太太的父亲（不如说 Micawber 太太自己？）故意用 experientia 这样的拉丁字，以示典雅。

81. I cannot satisfy myself: = I cannot be certain

82. the Marines: 海军陆战队。

83. town traveller: 跑街，掮客。

84. houses: 公司，厂家。

85. made little or nothing of it: 几乎一无所得。

86. bring it to an issue: 把事情了结了。

87. anything on account: 帐目上的债款。

88. law expenses: 诉讼费用；债主和 Micawber 先生打官司花的钱，要打输了的 Micawber 负担。

89. Whether my precocious self-dependence confused Mrs. Micawber in reference to my age: 也许因为我过早自立，使 Micawber 太太弄错了我的年龄。

90. she was so full of the subject: 关于这件事她有一肚子话要说。

91. strain: 指 Micawber 太太把 David 当作大人那样跟他说话的语气。

92. Boarding Establishment for Young Ladies: 女子寄宿学校。

93. edge himself into the passage: 侧着身子挤到过道里来。

94. ain't: = are not；俗语。

95. d'ye: = do you；口语体的形式。

96. mount in his wrath to the words ...: 越说越生气，用起…的字眼来。

97. transported with grief and mortification: 伤心羞辱之至。

98. pains: = efforts, care.

99. elastic: 能屈能伸的，乐观的。

100. thrown into fainting fits by the king's taxes: 因为交不出捐税，急得晕厥过去。

101. lamb chops breaded: 大块羊肉，外面裹有面包屑。

102. when an execution lad just been put in:（因还不起债）刚刚被人没收去

了一批家产。资本主义社会中负债人到期还不起债，债主有权要求官方没收其产业并予拍卖，以为抵偿。

103. lying under the grate: 躺在火炉前；grate，炉挡。

104. veal cutlet: 小牛肉。

105. the company they used to keep: 过去与她家来往的亲友。

CHAPTER XIII

106. Very stiff and sore of foot I was in the morning: David 离开伦敦去 Dover 寻找祖姑母，在路上已过了两夜一天，这一天他一气走了二十三英里，然后在靠近海湾的 Chatham ['tʃætəm] 镇外的一座炮台上睡了一夜，第二天醒来，感到腰酸腿痛。

107. which seemed to hem me in on every side:（Chatham 驻有军队）营地上喧闹的鼓声和军队的操练声就象从四面八方向我围拢来似的。

108. its principal business: 那一天的主要任务；its = the day's.

109. that I might learn to do without it: = so that I might get used to doing without it，好习惯一下只穿衬衫不穿上衣；David 在出走的第一个晚上因为衣物钱币都给抢走了，只好卖了一件背心买食物充饥，现在卖背心得的钱已用完，又得卖上衣，这样身上就只剩一件衬衣了。

110. slop-shops: 旧衣店。

111. I was rendered timid by the costly nature of their dealings: 我以为他们做的都是大买卖，胆子就变小了。

112. my merchandise: 即指 David 的上衣。

113. marine-store shops: 买卖水手衣物的旧货店。

114. Mr. Dolloby's: David 前一天卖背心的那家旧货店。

115. promising: 有希望的。

116. that seemed to have overflowed the shop: 仿佛从铺子里泛滥出来似的。

117. my eyes and limbs: 惊叹语，是这老头的口头禅，下文 my lungs and liver, my heart on fire 等同此。

118. the last unknown one: 指老头打酒嗝的声音 goroo (one = word)；它当然算不上是什么“词”，只是 Dickens 幽默地如此称呼罢了。

119. which he screwed out of himself, with an energy that made his eyes start in his head: 这怪声就象从他的身体里费力地绞出来似的，以至连眼珠都快爆出来了。

120. not at all ornamental: 丝毫没有给他增添什么风采。

121. crown: 英国钱币名，相当于五先令（shillings）；现已不通用，但仍有 half-crown.

122. closed the bargain: 谈妥了价钱。

123. make it an exchange: 来个物物交换吧；it 指这次交易。

124. enjoyed the reputation of having sold himself to the devil: 四邻众口一

是地说他已经把自己出卖给了魔鬼。

125. that legend: 即指 having sold himself to the devil。

126. for the purpose: = for that purpose = for the purpose of ripping open the mattress.

127. flights: 逃跑。

128. mouthing: 咆哮。

129. yelling in a frantic way, to his own windy tune, *The Death of Nelson*: 发疯似地用他那风啸般的调子高唱着《纳尔逊之死》的小曲。

130. with an Oh! before every line, and innumerable Goroos interspersed: 每一句歌词前都要加一个 oh，中间还穿插了无数个 Goroo。

131. the establishment: 指老头的旧货店。

132. used me very ill: = treated me very badly；这种说法在现代英语中已不常见。

133. cocked hat: 旧时欧洲人戴的卷边三角帽。

134. overtures: = offers.

135. sat there in desperation: 顽固地坐着不走。

136. was full two hours at getting by easy stages to a shilling: 花了整整两小时，才一点一点地给足了一先令；to get to (a place) by easy stages 原义是分程搭车，从容不迫地到达一地。

137. I would go for nothing, if I could: 要是我真有办法的话，我情愿一个子儿也不要就走。

138. closed with this offer: 同意了他出的价钱。

139. refreshed myself completely: 饱饱地吃了一顿，精神完全恢复过来。

140. limped seven miles upon my road: 一颠一跛地一口气走了七英里路。

CHAPTER LV

141. in the first stage out of London: 车出伦敦不到一站路的工夫。火车发明以前，在英国长途旅行都要坐分程公共马车（stage-coach），马车分站换马，甲乙两站间的一程路便称为 a stage. 马车除载旅客外，还兼送邮件。David 答应 Peggotty 先生去 Yarmouth 替他的养女捎信给船工 Ham，就在那天傍晚搭公共马车前往。

142. remarkable: 不寻常的。

143. suggesting greater heights ... in the earth: 云层的高度看去比从云端到地下最深的洞底还要深远。suggest 此处意为"给人以…的印象"。

144. in a dread disturbance of the laws of nature: 受到自然界法则的可怕的惊扰。

145. In another hour ..., and blew bard: 此句结构较松，谓语动词 blew 的主语是 it; and the sky was more overcast 有插入语的性质。

146. the leaders: 领头的马。分程公共马车一般有四匹马拉，两前两后，前头的称为 leaders。

147. lee walls: 背风的墙。

148. we were fain to stop: 我们只有停下来；fain 是古词，现代英语中不用。

149. I had been in Yarmouth when the seamen said it blew great guns: 以前我在海员们说的刮大炮那样的风里也到过 Yarmouth. Yarmouth [ˈjɑːməθ]，英格兰东部海港，在伦敦东北。

150. Ipswich [ˈipswitʃ]**:** 伦敦东北一市镇，位于 Yarmouth 以南。

151. which they then blocked up: 这些铅皮（they）就把那条小巷（which）堵住了。

152. Others had to tell of country people: = others had country people to tell of，另外的人谈到有些乡下人…。

153. was blowing dead on shore: 正对着海岸刮来。

154. The water was out: 水都泛滥开了。

155. flat country: 平原。

156. every sheet and puddle: 每一片、每一洼的洪水。

157. had its stress of little breakers setting heavily towards us:（洪水）用它那有力的小浪猛烈地向我们冲来。

158. caught at intervals above the rolling abyss: 不时地可以在翻滚着的深渊上空瞥见。caught = caught by our eyes；近处波浪滔天，因此远处地平线上的浪涛只能在近处波浪的起伏间偶尔瞥见。

159. all aslant: 都侧着身子（不敢面对狂风）。

160. making a wonder of the mail: 对（David 乘坐的）这辆邮车惊讶不已。

161. put up: 借宿。

162. and (strewn) with flying blotches of sea-foam: 给暴风刮来的海浪打得东一滩西一滩的。

163. holding by people I met, at angry corners: 在暴风雨肆虐的拐角处抓住碰见的人。

164. blown sheer out of their course in trying to get zigzag back: 当他们踉跄着走回来时，简直给刮得东倒西歪。to be blown out of one's course 原义指船只被风刮得离开了原来的航向。

165. herring or oyster boats: 捕鲱鱼或牡蛎的船。

166. stout mariners: 勇敢的水手。

167. levelling their glasses at the sea: 拿望远镜对着海上。

168. when I could find sufficient pause to look at it: 在风势较弱，容许我仔细看一眼的时候。

169. as if the least would engulf the town: 仿佛这些大浪中最小的一部分就可以吞没整个市镇。

170. every fragment of the late whole seemed possessed by the full might of its wrath: 原先完整的浪头的每一碎片好象都饱含着它全部的愤怒力量。

171. rushing to be gathered to the composition of another monster: 又赶忙

聚集成另一个怪物。

172. the ideal shore on the horizon: 地平线上幻想的海岸，即前面提到的远处的波涛。

173. a rending and upheaving of all nature: 整个宇宙都在崩裂翻腾。

174. back ways: 小路。

175. Lowestoft [ˈləustɔft]: 海港名，离 Yarmouth 不远。

176. coming to stir it: 进来拨火，it 指 fire.

177. colliers: 运煤船。

with all hands: 全船人员（都沉没了）。

178. the Roads: = the road stead,（航海用语）港口外船舶抛锚的浅水区。

179. mercy on them: = May God have mercy on them，但愿上帝保佑他们。

180. felt an uneasiness ... disproportionate to the occasion: 因 Ham 不在而感到过分的不安。disproportionate to the occasion 原义是"与（引起不安的）原因不相称的"。

181. late events: 不久前发生的一系列事情，即指 David 爱妻 Dora 之死，旧友 Steerforth 先拐走后又遗弃 Emily，奸人 Uriah Heep 霸占律师 Wickfield 的业务，侵吞 David 祖姑母的产业，并几乎强娶 David 的挚友 Agnes.

182. that jumble ... that ...: = such a jumble ... that ....

183. Thus, etc.: 此句意为：（由于思绪万千，神情恍惚）我要是到镇上去一次，那末即使我碰上一个当时应当是在伦敦的人，也一定不会觉得奇怪。

184. a curious inattention in my mind: 我的心神有一种奇怪的恍忽之感。

185. dismal intelligence: 凄惨的消息。

186. without any effort of my volition: 不由自主地。

187. I was persuaded: 我委实觉得。

188. This grew so strong with me: 我这种担忧变得如此强烈。

189. yard: = ship-yard，造船厂。

190. if he thought his attempting ...: 这里 he 指 boat-builder, his 指 Ham。

191. I was none too soon: 我去得正是时候。

192. no man in his senses, or out of them, would put off in such a gale of wind: 任何一个神志清醒的人，甚至是发了疯的人，也不会在这样的大风里起航。

193. least of all Ham Peggotty: 更不用说 Ham Peggotty 了。

194. So sensible of this, beforehand, that ...: 因为我来以前就知道这些道理（this 指前句造船工劝慰 David 的话），所以…。

195. Something with in me, faintly answering to the storm without, tossed up the depths of my memory: 我内心里似乎有什么和外界的风暴隐约相当的东西卷起了我记忆深处的波浪。

196. were always in the foreground: 在我脑中总是最清楚的。foreground 原义为"画面的前景"。

197. my whole frame thrilled with objectless and unintelligible fear: 我

的整个躯体都感到一种不明由来的（objectless 原义是“没有对象的”）、不可理解的恐惧。

198. looked at faces, scenes, and figures in the fire: 看着火中的各种幻影：一张张的人脸，一件件的往事，一个个的身影。

199. reassuring: 令人安心的。

200. to sit up: 不睡觉，守夜。

201. with every sense refined: 每一个感官都变得分外警觉。

202. looking in at me from the black void: 从窗外的一片漆黑里向我看着。

203. the watchers: 指旅店内守夜的侍者。

204. in various attitudes: 各有各的姿态。

205. spirit: 鬼魂。

206. had more presence of mind: 头脑要比她冷静。

207. whether I thought ...: 依我看来，那些葬身海底的运煤船船员的鬼魂有没有在暴风雨里出来游荡。

208. I dare say: = I think.

209. the yard-gate: 此处指朝院子开的旅店大门。

210. make it fast against the wind: 把门紧紧关上，不让风吹开。fast = tight.

211. fell—off a tower and down a precipice—into the depths of sleep: 就象从一座高塔上跌下悬崖峭壁，堕入了沉睡的深渊。

212. I lost that feeble hold upon reality: 我失掉了对现实世界仅有的那点知觉。

213. engaged with two dear friends: 和两个好友一起在打仗。

214. the storm raging, in lieu of the batteries: 暴风雨在怒吼，而不是（梦中的）大炮轰击了。

215. A wreck!: 一条船出事了！

216. It's thought, down on the beach: 海滩上的人都说。

217. though not more sensibly than ... out of hundreds: 风力虽有减弱，却极有限，犹如我梦中所听的炮轰，即使少了五六尊炮，也不会使人感到有多少差别一样。

218. having upon it the additional agitation of the whole night: 加上了前一夜的激荡。

219. bore the expression of being *swelled*: 显出水势澎涨的样子。swell 指风暴过后海水的澎涨，因是海员渔民们的用语，故有 swelled 这个过去分词形式，而不是通常的 swollen。

220. in interminable hosts: 一群跟着一群，没有尽头。

221. a tattoo'd arrow on it: 在手臂（it）上用药水针刺出了一支箭的图形。

222. was broken short off: 给猛然截断了。

223. lay over the side, entangled in a maze of sail and rigging: 倒在船舷外面，裹在帆布绳索当中，乱成一团。

224. all that ruin: 即指断了的桅杆。

225. as if it would stave it in: 前一个 it 指 all that ruin，后一个 it 指 the side，

意即断了的桅杆猛烈地撞击着船舷，好象要把它砸烂一样。

226. which was broadside on:（航海用语）船舷朝着我们。

227. made a clean breach:（航海用语）冲走了甲板上几乎所有的东西。

228. bulwarks [ˈbulwəːks]：舷板。

229. heaps of such toys: 作者用 toys 一词来表示在凶猛的巨浪里船上的设备用具变得脆弱无用。

230. rent: 撕裂了的，为动词 rent 的过去分词。

231. The slip had struck once: 船已经触过一次礁了。

232. lifted in: 浮了起来。

233. I understood him to add that she was parting amidships: 我还听他说那条船正在拦腰裂开。作者用 I understood him to add 而不说 He added，意为风浪声音太大，David 无法听清那船工的话，只能约略知其大意。

234. any human work: 任何人造的东西。

235. the deep: = the sea，海洋的别称，通常见于诗中。

236. uppermost: 在桅杆上爬得最高的。

237. showing us the whole sweep of her deck: 让我们看到了甲板的全长。

238. she turned on her beam-ends towards the shore: = She turned her broadside on the shore，船舷横对着海岸。

239. now nothing but her keel: = now showing us nothing but her keel，有时候只看到船底的龙骨；意即船身几乎完全侧了过来。

240. those two lost creatures: 船上仅剩的两名遭难的船员。

241. They were making out to me ... that ...: 他们向我解释说。

242. some new sensation: 一阵新的激动。

243. as well as I know: = as far as I remember now，就我现在记起来的；David 已经记不清在这紧张的时刻自己的一言一行了。

244. a sight so new to me and terrible: 指货船遇险的惨景。

245. exactly the same look as I remembered in connection with the morning after Emily's flight: Ham 的未婚妻 Emily 出走后的第二天早晨，David 在海滩上见到他眼望着海，脸上有一副严峻坚定的表情，这里说的就是当时 Ham 的表情。狄更斯在前面就为 Ham 的结局下了伏笔。

246. awoke me to a knowledge of his danger: 使我突然意识到他处于危险的时刻。

247. stir off that sand: 离开沙滩一步。

248. who was already accustomed to lead half the people present:（由于他勇敢坚定）他已经惯于使至少象在场人数一半那样多的群众听他的话行动。

249. I might as hopefully have entreated the wind: 我这样求他不要下海，就如同去求狂风一样没有希望。

250. Mas'r Davy: = Master Davy; Ham 没有受过教育，说话又带乡音，作者通过拼法的变化，表现了这种语言。

251. If 'tan't, I'll bide it: = If it ain't, … = If it isn't (my time), I'll bide it (my time). 如果我的日子还没到头，那我就会活下去 . to bide one's time 意为“等待时机”。

252. Lord above: = God.

253. a-going: = gong，原为古体，现见于未受教育者的语言中。

254. urging: 劝说道。

255. with whom they rested: 那些安全准备就要靠他们来作。they 指 precautions.

256. the latter: 指 another round his body，即绕在他身上的那根绳。

257. even to my unpractised eye: 即使在我这个外行的眼里看来。

258. of a finer colour: 颜色要更加鲜艳一些。

259. the few yielding planks between him and destruction rolled and bulged: 使他暂免毁灭的那几条脆弱的木板滚动了，崩裂了。

260. to wave it: it 指 a red cap.

261. with the silence of suspended breath behind him: 他后面的人群屏住呼吸，一声不响地期待着。

262. and the storm before: = and with the storm before him.

263. The distance was nothing: 船离开海岸的距离是微不足道的。

264. eddying fragments: 打着漩涡的几块碎片。

265. all was done: = all was over，一切都完了。

266. weather-beaten: 饱经风霜的。

267. ashy pale: 死灰一般地苍白。

268. yonder: = over there，在现代英语中已不常见。

269. The old remembrance that had been recalled to me: 即指第 29 页第 19—20 行提到的：an old remembrance … of a once dear friend.

270. she and I: she 指 Emily, David 幼年时到 Peggotty 家作客，和 Emily 一起在海滩上游戏。

271. the old boat: Peggotty 先生在海滩上的住房，因为它是一只旧船改建的，人称为 the old boat.

272. among the ruins of the home he had wronged—I saw him lying …: 这里 he 和 him 都是指 Steerforth，也就是船上最后剩下的那个挥动红帽子的人。这里狄更斯又巧妙地用了前后呼应的笔法。第一次提到船上人挥动帽子的姿势时，就说这勾起了 David 对过去一位好友的回忆，接着，船毁了以后，当有人要他出去看一看时，他就预感到是那位旧友遭殃了，最后，预感成了现实。这里作者始终没提 Steerforth 的名字，愈益显示出 David 对他这位毁了别人也毁了自己的旧友的宽大和怀念之深。正是在这等地方，我们看出了 David 的幻想和狄更斯的弱点。

42 WILLIAM MAKEPEACE THACKERAY 1811–1863

VANITY FAIR

(selections)

刘承沛　选注

CHAPTER I CHISWICK MALL

While the present century was in its teens,[1] and on one sunshiny morning in June, there drove up to the great iron gate of Miss Pinkerton's academy for young ladies, on Chiswick Mall,[2] a large family coach, with two fat horses in blazing harness, driven by a fat coachman in a three-cornered hat and wig,[3] at the rate of four miles an hour. A black servant, who reposed on the box beside the fat coachman, uncurled his bandy legs as soon as the equipage[4] drew up opposite Miss Pinkerton's shining brass plate,[5] and as he pulled the bell at least a score of young heads were seen peering out of the narrow windows of the stately old brick house. Nay, the acute observer might have recognized the little red nose of good-natured Miss Jemima Pinkerton herself, rising over some geranium-pots[6] in the window of that lady's own drawing-room.

"It is Mrs. Sedley's coach, sister," said Miss Jemima. "Sambo, the black servant, has just rung the bell; and the coachman has a new red waistcoat."

"Have you completed all the necessary preparations incident to Miss Sedley's departure, Miss Jemima?"[7] asked Miss Pinkerton herself, that majestic lady; the Semiramis[8] of Hammersmith, the friend of Doctor Johnson,[9] the correspondent of Mrs. Chapone[10] herself.

"The girls were up at four this morning, packing her trunks, sister," replied Miss Jemima; "we have made her a bow-pot."

"Say a bouquet,[11] sister Jemima, 'tis more genteel."

"Well, a booky as big almost as a hay-stack; I have put up two bottles of gillyflower-water for Mrs. Sedley, and the receipt for making it, in Amelia's box."

"And I trust, Miss Jemima, you have made a copy of Miss Sedley's account.[12] This is it, is it? Very good — ninety-three pounds four shillings. Be kind enough to address it to John Sedley, Esquire,[13] and to seal this billet which I have written to his lady."

In Miss Jemima's eyes an autograph letter[14] of her sister, Miss Pinkerton, was an object of as deep veneration as would have been a letter from a sovereign.[15] Only when her pupils quitted the establishment,[16] or when they were about to be married, and once, when poor Miss Birch died of the scarlet fever, was Miss Pinkerton known to write personally to the parents of her pupils; and it was Jemima's opinion that if anything *could* console Mrs. Birch for her daughter's loss, it would be that pious and eloquent composition in which Miss Pinkerton announced the event.

In the present instance Miss Pinkerton's "billet" was to the following effect:

"THE MALL, CHISWICK, JUNE 15,18 — .

Madame: After her six years' residence at the Mall, I have the honor and happiness of presenting Miss Amelia Sedley to her parents, as a young lady not unworthy to occupy a fitting position in their polished and refined circle. Those virtues which characterize the young English gentlewoman, those accomplishments which become her birth and station,[17] will not be found wanting in the amiable Miss Sedley, whose *industry*[18] and *obedience* have endeared her to her instructors, and whose delightful sweetness of temper has charmed her *aged* and her *youthful* companions.

"In music, in dancing, in orthography, in every variety of embroidery and needlework, she will be found to have realized her friends' *fondest wishes*. In geography there is still much to be desired;[19] and a careful and undeviating use of the backboard,[20] for four hours daily during the next three years, is recommended as necessary to the acquirement of that dignified *deportment* and *carriage* so requisite for every young lady of *fashion*.

"In the principles of religion and morality, Miss Sedley will be found worthy of an establishment which has been honored by the presence of *The Great Lexicographer*,[21] and the patronage of the admirable Mrs. Chapone. In leaving the Mall, Miss Amelia carries with her the hearts of her companions, and the affectionate regards of her mistress, who has the honor to subscribe herself,

"Madame,

"Your most obliged humble servant,

"BARBARA PINKERTON.

"P. S.—Miss Sharp accompanies Miss Sedley. It is particularly requested that Miss Sharp's stay in Russell Square may not exceed ten days. The family of distinction with whom she is engaged desire to avail themselves of her services as soon as possible."

This letter completed, Miss Pinkerton proceeded to write her own name and Miss Sedley's in the fly-leaf of a Johnson's Dictionary—the interesting work which she invariably presented to her scholars, on their departure from the Mall On the cover was inserted a copy of "Lines addressed to a young lady on quitting Miss Pinkerton's school, at the Mall; by the late revered Doctor Samuel Johnson." In fact, the lexicographer's name was always on the lips of this majestic woman,[22] and a visit he had paid to her was the cause of her reputation and her fortune.

Being commanded by her elder sister to get "the Dictionary" from the cupboard, Miss Jemima had extracted two copies of the book from the receptacle in question.[23] When Miss Pinkerton had finished the inscription in the first, Jemima, with rather a dubious and timid air, handed her the second.

"For whom is this, Miss Jemima?" said Miss Pinkerton, with awful coldness.

"For Becky Sharp," answered Jemima, trembling very much, and blushing over her withered face and neck, as she turned her back on her sister. "For Becky Sharp; she's going, too."

"MISS JEMIMA!" exclaimed Miss Pinkerton, in the largest capitals. "Are you in your senses?[24] Replace the Dixonary[25] in the closet, and never venture to take such a liberty in future."

"Well, sister, it's only two-and-ninepence,[26] and poor Becky will be miserable if she don't get one."

"Send Miss Sedley instantly to me," said Miss Pinkerton. And so venturing rot to say another word, poor Jemima trotted off, exceedingly flurried and nervous.

Miss Sedley's papa was a merchant in London, and a man of some wealth; whereas Miss Sharp was an articled pupil,[27] for whom Miss Pinkerton had done, as she thought, quite enough, without conferring upon her at parting the high honor of the Dixonary.

Although schoolmistresses' letters are to be trusted no more nor less than churchyard epitaphs;[28] yet, as it sometimes happens that a person departs this life who is really deserving of all the praises the stone-cutter carves over his bones—who *is* a good Christian, a good parent, child, wife or husband; who actually *does* leave a disconsolate family to mourn his loss—so in academies of the male and female sex it occurs every now and then that the pupil is fully worthy of the praises bestowed by the disinterested[29] instructor. Now, Miss Amelia Sedley was a young lady of this singular species,[30] and deserved not only all that Miss Pinkerton said in her praise, but had many charming qualities which that pompous old Minerva[31] of a woman could not see, from the differences of rank and age between her pupil and herself.

For she could not only sing like a lark, or a Mrs. Billington,[32] and dance like Hillisberg[32] or Parisot,[32] and embroider beautifully, and spell as well as Dixonary itself, but she had such a kindly, smiling, tender, gentle, generous heart of her own as won the love of everybody who came near her, from Minerva herself down to the poor girl in the scullery and the one-eyed tart-woman's daughter, who was permitted to vend her wares once a week to the young ladies in the Mall. She had twelve intimate and bosom friends out of the twenty-four young ladies. Even envious Miss Briggs never spoke ill of her: high and mighty Miss Saltire (Lord Dexter's granddaughter) allowed[33] that her figure was genteel; and as for Miss Swartz, the rich woolly-haired mulatto from St. Kitt's, on the day Amelia went away, she was in such a passion of tears that they were obliged to send for Dr. Floss, and half tipsify her with sal volatile. Miss Pinkerton's attachment was, as may be supposed, from the high position and eminent virtues of that lady, calm and dignified; but Miss Jemina had already whimpered several times at the idea of Amelia's departure, and, but for[34] fear of her sister, would have gone off in downright hysterics, like the heiress (who paid double[35]) of St. Kitt's. Such luxury of grief,[36] however, is only allowed to parlor-boarders.[37] Honest Jemima had all the bills, and the washing, and the mending and the puddings, and the plate and crockery, and the servants to superintend. But why speak about her? It is probable that we shall not hear of her again from this moment to the end of time, and that when the great filigree iron gates are once closed on her, she and her awful sister will never issue therefrom into this little world of history.

But as we are to see a great deal of Amelia, there is no harm in saying, at the outset of our acquaintance, that she was a dear little creature; and a great mercy it is, both in life and in novels, which (and the latter especially) abound in villains of the most sombre sort, that we are to have for a constant companion so guileless and good-natured a person. As she is not a heroine, there is no need to describe her person; indeed I am afraid that her nose was rather short than otherwise, and her cheeks a great deal too round and red for a heroine; but her face blushed with rosy health, and her lips with the freshest of smiles, and she had a pair of eyes which sparkled with the brightest and honestest goodhumor, except, indeed, when they filled with tears, and that was a great deal too often; for the silly thing would cry over a dead canary-bird, or over a mouse that the cat haply had seized upon; or over the end of a novel, were it ever so stupid; and as for saying an unkind word to her, were any persons hardhearted enough to do so[38] — why, so much the worse for them.[39] Even Miss Pinkerton, that austere and god-like woman, ceased scolding her after the first time, and though she no more comprehended sensibility than she did algebra,[40] gave all masters and teachers particular orders to treat Miss Sodley with the utmost gentleness, as harsh treatment was injurious to her.

So that when the day of departure came, between her two customs of laughing and crying, Miss Sedley was greatly puzzled how to act. She was glad to go home, and yet most woefully sad at leaving school. For three days before, little Laura Martin, the orphan, followed her about, like a little dog. She had to make and receive at least fourteen presents — to make fourteen solemn promises of writing every week. "Send my letters under cover to my grandpapa, the Earl of Dexter," said Miss Saltire (who, by the way, was rather shabby); "Never mind the postage but write every day, you dear darling," said the impetuous and woolly-headed, but generous and affectionate, Miss Swartz; and the orphan, little Laura Martin (who was just in round-hand), took her friend's hand and said, looking up in her face wistfully, "Amelia, when I write to you I shall call you mamma." All which details, I have no doubt, JONES,[41] who reads this book at his club, will pronounce to be excessively foolish, trivial, twadding, and ultra-sentimental. Yes; I can see Jones at this minute (rather flushed with his joint of mutton and half pint of wine), taking out his pencil and scoring under the words "foolish, twaddling," etc., and adding to them his own remark of "quite true." Well, he is a lofty man of genius, and admires the great and heroic in life and novels; and so had better take warning and go elsewhere.[42]

Well, then. The flowers, and the presents, and the trunks, and bonnet-boxes of Miss Sedley having been arranged by Mr. Sambo in the carriage, together with a very small and weather-beaten old cow's skin trunk with Miss Sharp's card neatly nailed upon it, which was delivered by Sambo with a grin, and packed by the coachman with a corresponding sneer,[43] the hour for parting came; and the grief of that moment was considerably lessened by the admirable discourse which Miss Pinkerton addressed to her pupil. Not that the parting speech caused Amelia to philosophize,[44] or that it armed her in any way with a calmness, the result of argument; but it was intolerably dull, pompous, and tedious; and having the fear of her schoolmistress greatly before her eyes, Miss Sedley did not venture, in her presence, to give way to any ebullitions of private grief. A seed-cake and a bottle of wine were produced in the drawing-room, as on the solemn occasions of the visits of parents, and these refreshments being partaken of, Miss Sedley was at liberty to depart.

"You'll go in[45] and say good-by to Miss Pinkerton, Becky," said Miss Jemima to a young lady of whom nobody took any notice, and who was coming down-stairs with her own bandbox.

"I suppose I must," said Miss Sharp calmly, and much to the wonder of Miss Jemima; and the latter having knocked at the door, and received permission to come in, Miss Sharp advanced in a very unconcerned manner, and said in French, and with a perfect accent, "Ma demoiselle, je viens vous faire mes adieux."[46]

Miss Pinkerton did not understand French; she only directed those who did; but biting her lips and throwing up her venerable and Roman-nosed head (on the top of which figured a large and solemn turban), she said, "Miss Sharp, I wish you a good-morning." As the Hammersmith Semiramis spoke, she waved one hand, both by way of adieu and to give Miss Sharp an opportunity of shaking one of the fingers of the hand which was left out for that purpose.

Miss Sharp only folded her own hands with a very frigid smile and bow, and quite declined to accept the proffered honor; on which Semiramis tossed up her turban more indignantly than ever. In fact, it was a little battle between the young lady and the old one, and the latter was worsted.[47] "Heaven bless you, my child," said she, embracing Amelia, and scowling the while over the girl's shoulder at Miss Sharp. "Come away, Becky," said Miss Jemima, pulling the young woman away in great alarm, and the drawing-room door closed upon them forever.

Then came the struggle and parting below. Words refuse to tell it. All the servants were there in the hall — all the dear friends — all the young ladies — the dancing-master who had just arrived; and there was such a scuffing, and hugging, and kissing, and crying, with the hysterical *yoops*[48] of Miss Swartz, the parlor-boarder, from her room, as no pen can depict and the tender heart would fain pass over. The embracing was over; they parted — that is, Miss Sedley parted from her friends. Miss Sharp had demurely entered the carriage some minutes before. Nobody cried for leaving *her*.

Sambo of the bandy legs slammed the carriage-door on his young weeping mistress. He sprang up behind the carriage. "Stop!" cried Miss Jemima, rushing to the gate with a parcel.

"It's some sandwiches, my dear," said she to Amelia. "You may be hungry, you know; and Becky, Becky Sharp,[49] here's a book for you that my sister — that is, I — Johnson's Dixonary, you know; you mustn't leave us without that. Good-by. Drive on, coachman. God bless you!"

And the kind creature retreated into the garden, overcome with emotion.

But, lo! and just as the coach drove off, Miss Sharp put her pale face out of the window and actually flung the book back into the garden.

This almost caused Jemima to faint with terror. "Well, I never,[50]" said she. "What an audacious — " Emotion prevented her from completing either sentence. The carriage rolled away; the great gates were closed; the bell rang for the dancing lesson. The world is before two young ladies; and so, farewell to Chiswick Mall.

From CHAPTER XXXVI
HOW TO LIVE WELL ON NOTHING A YEAR

I suppose there is no man in this Vanity Fair of ours so little observant[51] as not to think sometimes about the worldly affairs of his acquaintances, or so extremely charitable[52] as not to wonder how his neighbor Jones, or his neighbor Smith, can make both ends meet[53] at the end of the year. With the utmost regard for the family,[54] for instance (for I dine with them twice or thrice in the season), I can not but own that the appearance of the Jenkinses[55] in the Park, in the large barouche, with the grenadier footmen,[56] will surprise and mystify me to my dying day; for though I know the equipage is only jobbed,[57] and all the Jenkins people are on board wages,[58] yet those three men and the carriage must represent an expense of six hundred a year at the very least — and then there are the splendid dinners, the two boys at Eton,[59] the prize governess and masters for the girls, the trip abroad, or to Eastbourne or Worthing,[60] in the autumn, the annual ball[61] with a supper from Gunter's[62] (who, by the way, supplies most of the *first-rate* dinners which J. gives, as I know very well, having been invited to one of them to fill a vacant place, when I saw at once that these repasts are very superior to the *common* run of entertainments for which the *humbler* sort of J. 's acquaintances get cards)[63] — who, I say, with the most good-natured feelings in the world, can help wondering how the Jenkinses make out matters? What *is* Jenkins? We all know — Commissioner of the Tape and Sealing Wax Office, with £1200 a year for a salary. Had his wife a private fortune? Pooh! — Miss Flint — one of eleven children of a small squire in Buckinghamshire. All she ever gets from her family is a turkey at Christmas, in exchange for which she has to board two or three of her sisters in the off season;[64] and lodge and feed her brothers when they come to town. How does Jenkins balance his income?

I say, as every friend of his must say, How is it that he has not been outlawed[65] long since; and that he ever came back (as he did, to the surprise of everybody) last year from Boulogne?[66]

"I" is here introduced to personify the world in general—the Mrs. Grundy[67] of each respected reader's private circle—every one of whom can point to some families of his acquaintance who live nobody knows how. Many a glass of wine have we all of us drank, I have very little doubt, hob-and-nobbing[68] with the hospitable giver, and wondering how the deuce he paid for it.[69]

Some three or four years after his stay in Paris, when Rawdon Crawley and his wife were established in a very small comfortable house in Curzon Street, May Fair, there were scarcely one of the numerous friends whom they entertained at dinner that did not ask the above question regarding them. The novelist, it has been said before, knows everything, and as I am in a situation to be able to tell the public how Crawley and his wife lived without any income, may I entreat the public newspapers which are in the habit of extracting portions of the various periodical works now published, *not* to reprint the following exact narrative and calculations—of which I ought, as the discoverer (and at some expense, too), to have the benefit? My son, I would say, were I blessed with a child[70]—you may by deep inquiry and constant intercourse with him, learn how a man lives comfortably on nothing a year. But it is best not to be intimate with gentlemen of this profession and to take the calculations at secondhand, as you do logarithms,[71] for to work them yourself, depend upon it, will cost you something considerable.

On nothing per annum,[72] then, and during a course of some two or three years, of which we can afford to give but a very brief history, Crawley and his wife lived very happily[72] and comfortably in Paris. It was in this period that he quitted the Guards,[73] and sold out of the army.[74] When we find him again, his mustachios and the title of colonel on his card[75] are the only relics of his military profession.

It has been mentioned that Rebecca, soon after her arrival in

Paris, took a very smart and leading position in the society of that capital, and was welcomed at some of the most distinguished houses of the restored French nobility.[76] The Englishmen of fashion in Paris courted her, too, to the disgust of the ladies their wives, who could not bear the parvenue. For some months the salons of the Faubourg St. Germain, in which her place was secured, and the splendors of the new court where she was received with much distinction, delighted and perhaps a little intoxicated Mrs. Crawley, who may have been disposed during this period of elation to slight the people[77]—honest young military men mostly—who formed her husband's chief society.

But the colonel yawned sadly among the duchesses and great ladies of the court. The old women who played *écarté*[78] made such a noise about a five-franc piece[79] that it was not worth Colonel Crawley's while to sit down at a card-table. The wit of their conversation he could not appreciate, being ignorant of their language. And what good could his wife get, he urged, by making courtesies every night to a whole circle of princesses? He left Rebecca presently to frequent these parties alone; resuming his own simple pursuits and amusements among the amiable friends of his own choice.[80]

The truth is, when we say of a gentleman that he lives elegantly on nothing a year, we use the word "nothing" to signify something unknown: meaning simply that we don't know how the gentleman in question defrays the expenses of his establishment.[81] Now, our friend the colonel had a great aptitude for all games of chance,[82] and exercising himself, as he continually did, with the card, the dicebox, or the cue,[83] it is natural to suppose that he attained a much greater skill in the use of these articles than men can possess who only occasionally handle them. To use a cue at billiards well is like using a pencil, or a German flute, or a small-sword—you can not master any one of these implements at first, and it is only by repeated study and perseverance, joined to a natural taste,[84] that a man can excel in the handling of either. Now Crawley, from being only a brilliant amateur, had grown to be a consummate master of billiards. Like a great general, his genius used to rise with the danger, and when the luck had been unfavorable to him for a whole game, and the bets were consequently against him, he would, with consummate skill and boldness, make some prodigious hits which would restore the battle,[85] and come in a victor at the end, to the astonishment of everybody—of everybody, that is, who was a stranger to his play.[86] Those who were accustomed to see it were cautious how they staked their money against a man of such sudden resources[87] and brilliant and overpowering skill.

At games of cards he was equally skilful; for though he would constantly lose money at the commencement of an evening, playing so carelessly and making such blunders, that newcomers were often inclined to think meanly of his talent, yet when roused to action, and awakened to caution by repeated small losses, it was remarked that Crawley's play became quite different, and that he was pretty sure of beating his enemy thoroughly before the night was over. Indeed, very few men could say that they ever had the better of him.[88]

His successes were so repeated that no wonder the envious and the vanquished[89] spoke sometimes with bitterness regarding them. And as the French say of the Duke of Wellington,[90] who never suffered a defeat, that only an astonishing series of lucky accidents enabled him to be an invariable winner; yet even they allow that he cheated at Waterloo,[91] and was enabled to win the last great trick—so it was hinted at head-quarters in England, that some foul play must have taken place in order to account for the continuous successes of Colonel Crawley.

Though Frascati's and the Salon[92] were open at that time in Paris, the mania for play was so widely spread that the public gamblingrooms did not suffice for the general ardor, and gambling went on in private houses as much as if there had been no public means for gratifying the passion.[93] At Crawley's charming little *réunions*[94] of an evening this fatal amusement commonly was practiced—much to good natured little Mrs. Crawley's annoyance. She spoke about her husband's passion for dice with the deepest grief, she bewailed it to everybody who came to her house. She besought the young fellows never, never to touch a box; and when young Green, of the Rifles,[95] lost a very considerable sum of money, Rebecca passed a whole night in tears, as the servant told the unfortunate young gentleman, and actually went on her knees to her husband to beseech him to remit the debt,[96] and burn the acknowledgment.[97] How could he? He had lost just as much himself to Blackstone of the Hussars,[98] and Count Punter of the Hanoverian Cavalry.[99] Green might have any decent time; but pay?—of course he must pay; to talk of burning I O U's[100] was child's play.

Other officers, chiefly young—for the young fellows gathered round Mrs. Crawley—came from her parties with long faces,[101] having dropped more or less money at her fatal cardtables. Her house began to have an unfortunate reputation. The old hands warned the less experienced of their danger. Colonel O'Dowd, of the—th regiment, one of those occupying in Paris, warned Lieutenant Spooney of that corps. A loud and violent fracas took place between the infantry colonel and his lady, who were dining at the Café de Paris, and Colonel and Mrs. Crawley who were also taking their meal there. The ladies engaged on both sides. Mrs. O'Dowd snapped her fingers in Mrs. Crawley's face,[102] and called her husband "no betther than a blackleg." Colonel Crawley challenged Colonel O'Dowd, C. B.[103] The commander-in-chief hearing of the dispute, sent for Colonel Crawley, who was getting ready the same pistols "which he shot Captain Marker," and had such a conversation with him that no duel took place. If Rebecca had not gone on her knees to General Tufto, Crawley would have been sent back to England; and he did not play, except with civilians, for some weeks after.

But in spite of Rawdon's undoubted skill and constant successes, it became evident to Rebecca, considering these things, that their position was but a precarious one, and that, even although they paid scarcely anybody, their little capital would end one day by dwindling into zero. "Gambling," she would say, "dear, is good to help your income, but not as an income itself. Some day people may be tired of play, and then where are we?" Rawdon acquiesced in the justice of her opinion,[104] and in truth he had remarked that after a few nights of his little suppers, etc., gentlemen *were* tired of play with him, and, in spite of Rebecca's charms, did not present themselves very eagerly.

....

At this juncture news arrived which spread among the many creditors of the colonel at Paris, and which caused them great satisfaction. Miss Crawley, the rich aunt from whom he expected his immense inheritance, was dying; the colonel must haste to her bedside. Mrs. Crawley and her child would remain behind until he came to reclaim them. He departed for Calais,[105] and having reached that place in safety, it might have been supposed that he went to Dover;[106] but instead he took the diligence to Dunkirk,[107] and thence travelled to Brussels,[108] for which place he had a former predilection. The fact is, he owed more money at London than at Paris; and he preferred the quiet little Belgian city to either of the more noisy capitals.

Her aunt was dead. Mrs. Crawley ordered the most intense mourning[109] for herself and little Rawdon. The colonel was busy arranging the affairs of the inheritance. They could take the premier[110] now, instead of the little entresol[111] of the hotel which they occupied. Mrs. Crawley and the landlord had a consultation about the new hangings,[112] an amicable wrangle about the carpets, and a final adjustment of everything except the bill.[113] She went off in one of his carriages, her French *bonne*[114] with her, the child by her side — the admirable landlord and landlady smiling farewell to her from the gate. General Tufto was furious when he heard she was gone, and Mrs. Brent furious with him for being furious; Lieutenant Spooney was cut to the heart; and the landlord got ready his best apartments previous to the return of the fascinating little woman and her husband. He *serréd*[115] the trunks which she left in his charge with the greatest care. They had been especially recommended to him by Madame Crawley. They were not, however, found to be particularly valuable when opened some time after.

....

And so, Colonel and Mrs. Crawley came to London; and it is at their house in Curzon Street, May Fair, that they really showed the skill which must be possessed by those who would live on the resources above named.

【作者简介】 萨克雷（William Makepeace Thackeray 1811—63），英国批判现实主义作家。父亲是英国东印度公司驻印度的税吏，在萨克雷四岁时死去，留下一笔可观的遗产，使他得以进公学，进剑桥大学，以至到德国游学。但是萨克雷对于当时的学校教育不感兴趣，在剑桥未得学位就离校。他学了法律，却又不愿当律师；学过绘画，但作品多为讽刺性的素描，不为当时社会所赏识。1833 年，他的存款因银行倒闭而丧失殆尽，他才立志以写作谋生，为报刊写文章，出过一些集子，颇得好评。1847 年，《名利场》开始分期发表，萨克雷才作为小说家而闻名。其后，又写了几部有名的小说：*The History of Pendennis, The History of Henry Esmond, The Newcomes, The Virginians.* 除了写小说，萨克雷还到各地讲学，*The Virginians* 就是到美国讲学以后写的。1860 年，萨克雷担任了 *Cornhill* 杂志的编辑，自己也为它写了不少文章。

萨克雷青少年时期生活优裕，他的社会经济地位使他有可能熟悉资产阶级的各个阶层，从中看到了资本主义社会环境对人的影响。因为他观察敏锐细致，所以刻划的人物有血有肉，叙述的情节逼真。他的文笔幽默，处处可感到他对资本主义社会中各种人物和现象的讽嘲。

【题解与注释】

《名利场》在英国小说史上有重要的地位。萨克雷最初想把书名定为《没有主角的小说》。也就是说，它不以一两个正面角色为中心，而是以某一特定时期的一个社会剖面为其描绘对象。其中人物，虽然各有其性格特点，但并不象当时一般小说中那样善恶分明。而且，在萨克雷笔下，几乎个个都是小人物，都有缺点。即以爱米丽亚而论，第一章里似乎是要把她写成一个善良的人物，到后来萨克雷却写她的自私、浅陋。利蓓加为人刻薄，工于心计，为了满足自己可以不择手段，然而她的聪敏、干练，她处于逆境中所表现的勇猛反抗，却也讨人喜欢和同情。

萨克雷在这本小说里所要写的，就是他所看到的社会。在他看来，在那个社会里，每个人都在追逐那不值得追逐的荣华富贵。因此，当他忽然在一个晚上想起约翰·班扬的《天路历程》(*The Pilgrim's Progress*)中的“名利场”时，他欣喜若狂，立刻用它作了书名，而把《没有主角的小说》作为副标题。

这里所选的第一章（全文）和第三十六章（节选），都有利蓓加出场。第一章描述她和爱米丽亚在女子学堂学习期满离校的情景。我们看到女校长的势利、不学无术，假道学；看到有钱人家的女儿爱米丽亚如何受到宠爱和逢迎；看到贫穷而出身低微的利蓓加如何受到冷落、歧视。然而最叫人吃惊的还是利蓓加的表现。她之所以能和高贵的小姐们一起上学，只是因为校长要利用她教别的女孩子们学法文，可以说是受了学校雇用的。临走那天，她利用道别的场合，明知校长不懂法文，却故意用法语向她说再见，而且还拒绝和校长握手。好心的吉米玛偷偷送她一本字典，她却把它扔了回去。利蓓加的亮相令人绝倒。

第三十六章叙述的是利蓓加和她丈夫罗登在巴黎靠招摇撞骗过日子，最后债主登门，实在混不下去了，忽然传来了消息，说罗登的姑母病危，罗登要回英国去继承一大笔遗产。这时，旅馆主人才又重新巴结他们。然而到头来罗登并没有从姑母的遗产中分得多少钱，亏得利蓓加聪明能干，把债主打发掉，他们才又在伦敦安顿下来。

1. in its teens: 此书写于 1847 年，in its teens 指十九世纪的第二个十年期间。

2. on Chiswick Mall: 在契息克林荫道上。Chiswick 读 ['tʃizik]。

3. three-cornered hat and wig: 马车夫戴这种帽子，而且还有假发，说明这家主人的排场。

4. equipage: 仍指那辆马车。

5. shining brass plate: 指平克顿女子学校门上的名牌。

6. little red nose ... rising over some geranium-pots: geranium 学名天竺葵，是一种开桔红色小花的草本。作者用这种对比方法来打趣 Jemima。萨克雷学过绘画，擅长漫画、速写。在这第一段里，他用了许多种颜色，给人以鲜明印象。

7. “Have you completed all the necessary preparations incident to Miss Sedley's departure, Miss Jemima?”: 平克顿小姐道貌岸然，根本不接过话题，反问她的妹妹有没有为赛德笠小姐离校做好一切准备。称自己的妹妹为 Miss Jemima 也是道貌岸然的表示。

8. Semiramis: 传说中巴比仑古国的王后，丈夫死后由她当政，与前面的 majestic 相呼应。Hammersmith 是伦敦西部的一个区，应是该女校所在地。

9. Doctor Johnson: 即 Samuel Johnson (1709–84)，以编纂了一本英文字典闻名。

10. Mrs. Chapone: 指 Hester Chapone (1727–1801)：女文人，但并非名家。作者把她搬出来，显然是因为她写过“Letters on the Improvement of the Mind”，符合平克顿小姐的口味。

11. “Say a bouquet, ...”: bouquet（法语）['bu:'kei] 花篮。下一行 Jemima 把它说成 booky，是作者嘲弄她不会说法语；她把花篮之大比作花堆，则是嘲弄她粗俗。事实上，平克顿小姐也不懂法语。

12. a copy of Miss Sedley's account: 赛德笠小姐的帐单。

13. John Sedley, Esquire: 爱米丽亚的父亲；Esquire 写在姓名之后，是旧时对绅士的一种尊称。

14. autograph letter: 亲笔信。

15. sovereign: 君王，国君。

16. the establishment: 指平克顿女子学校。

17. become her birth and station: 与她的门第相称。

18. industry: 勤劳。

19. In geography there is still much to be desired: 指 Amelia 对地理所知不多。

20. use of the backboard: 旧俗，妇女背部定时缠以平板，使腰背挺直。

21. The Great Lexicographer: 指 Dr. Johnson。

22. was always on the lips of this majestic woman: 平克顿小姐老是把约翰逊的名字挂在嘴上（以此炫耀自己）。

23. the receptacle in question: 即上文的 cupboard。

24. "Are you in your senses?": "你疯了吗？"

25. Dixonary: 作者用这个拼法，嘲弄平克顿小姐的读音。

26. two-and-nine pence: 两先令九便士。（先令已于 1971 年起废弃不用）

27. an articled pupil: 半工半读的学生（Becky Sharp 在该校兼教法语）。

28. churchyard epitaphs: 墓志铭。（萨克雷认为墓志铭对死者的赞扬往往言过其实，女校长们写的信也一样不可全信）

29. disinterested: impartial（指赞扬不是为了讨好孩子的父母）。

30. a young lady of this singular species: 难能可贵的小姐（指她无愧于人们的赞扬）。

31. Minerva: 罗马神话中的智慧女神，在这里用来嘲讽平克顿小姐。

32. Mrs. Billington, Hillisberg, Parisot: 都是当时的歌唱家、舞蹈家。

33. allowed: 承认。

34. but for: if it had not been for。

35. paid double: 付双倍费用。

36. luxury of grief: 指穷学生不许表示哀伤；哀伤对她们说是一种奢望。

37. parlour boarders: 待为上宾的寄宿学生。

38. were any persons hard-hearted to do so: = if any persons were hardhearted enough to do so.

39. so much the worse for them: 那就算她们更要倒楣了（指爱米丽亚会因此而哭得更不可开交）。

40. though she no more comprehended sensibility than she did algebra: 虽然她对于感情是什么并不理解，正如她对于代数一窍不通一样。

41. Jones: 琼斯（这是英国很普通的姓氏，作者用它来指任何一个在读这本书的读者，有些象中国某些旧章回小说中作者插话时提到的"看官"）。

42. had better take warning and go elsewhere: 最好还是听我的话听别的故事去吧（因为作者在书名里已声明这本书里没有什么伟大的英雄人物）。

43. with a grin; with a corresponding sneer:（作者借马车夫和仆人对利蓓加的旧衣箱的态度，表现了人的势利）。

44. to philosophize: 用豁达的态度对待事物（这里作者是说 Amelia 之所以不那么哭闹，不是因为平克顿小姐的话有什么哲理，而是她近在眼前使 Amelia 感到害怕）。

45. "You'll go in ...":（这是一种命令句，而不是指将来）。

46. "je viens vous faire mes adieux":（法语）我来向您辞行了。

47. worsted: = defeated 这里是说利蓓加拒绝握手，使平克顿小姐丢了脸。

48. yoops: 形声词，啜泣的声音。

49. Becky, Becky Sharp，: Jemima 好心肠，称利蓓加为 Becky 表示亲切，但又怕她的姐姐为此生气，才又改口，加上利蓓加的姓。

50. "Well, I never,": "真没见过！"

51. so little observant: 那么不善于观察事物。

52. charitable: 心地善良，与人为善。

53. make both ends meet: 不负债，收支两抵。

54. with the utmost regard for the family: 不是我不尊重这家人（这种短语往往引出与它相反的意思）。

55. the Jenkinses: 詹金斯一家人（这是虚构的任何一家人）。

56. grenadier footmen: 穿制服的听差。

57. jobbed: 租来的。

58. on board wages: 东家只管佣人的食宿，不给工钱。

59. Eton: 伊顿公学（英国有名的"贵族"学校，两个孩子在那里上学，费用是很大的）。

60. Eastbourne, Worthing: 英国的名胜地。

61. annual ball: 一年一度的舞会。

62. Gunter's: 饭馆名。

63. cards: = invitation cards 请帖。

64. the off season: 社交活动不忙的季节。

65. outlawed: 被宣布为罪犯，受法律制裁。

66. Boulogne: 法国北部地名。（这句话暗示去年詹金斯出国到布隆，肯定花销很大，欠了债，居然逃脱了债主回到英国）。

67. Mrs. Grundy: 格隆第太太（Thomas Morton 著 *Speed the Plough*（1798）书中的人物，是品行端正的象征，传统行为标准的维护者）。

68. hob-and-nobbing: = hobnobbing 欢笑着共饮。

69. how the deuce he paid for it: = how on earth he paid for it.

70. were I blessed with a child: = if I were blessed with a child，如果我真有福气生了个孩子的话。

71. as you do logarithms: 就象做（数学中的）对数题目一样。（指查对数表，而不是直接演算）。

72. Crawley and his wife lived happily on nothing per annum: 两夫妻全年毫无收入，快快活活地过日子。per annum = per year

73. the Guards: 近卫部队（罗登所属的部队）。

74. sold out of the army: 把军队里的官职卖给了别人。

75. card: 名片。

76. the restored French nobility: 由于拿破仑战败，早先的封建贵族又抬头了。the parvenue：新贵，暴发户（利蓓加的父亲只是个画家，母亲是唱歌剧的，本不属于贵族阶级，现在却走运了。）

77. disposed ... to slight the people:（因为得意，有点飘飘然）往往看不起别人。

78. écarté:（法语）一种牌戏。

79. made such a noise about a five-franc piece: 输赢五个法郎就闹得不可开交。

80. friends of his own choice: 他自己选择的朋友。

81. his establishment: 指罗登的一家大小。

82. a great aptitude for all games of chance: 擅长各种赌博。

83. the cue: 弹子赌博中用来打弹子的长棍，此处指打弹子这种赌博。

84. joined to a natural taste: 和天赋结合起来。

85. make some prodigious hits which would restore the battle: 打出几个精彩的球，转败为胜。

86. of every body, that is, who was a stranger to his play: 那是说，凡是不熟悉他的打法的人。

87. resourees: 随机应变。

88. had the better of him: 打败过他。

89. the envious and the vanquished: 嫉羡他的人和被他打败过的人。

90. Duke of Wellington: 威灵顿公爵，1815 年率英、德、荷、比联军击败拿破仑。

91. Waterloo: 在布鲁塞尔南郊，即法军被击败处。

92. Frascati's and the Salon: 两个赌场名。

93. the passion: 指嗜赌的急切情绪。

94. reunions（法语）**:** 聚会。

95. the Rifles:（英）步枪团队。

96. to remit the debt: 勾销债务。

97. burn the acknowledgment: 把债据销毁。

98. the Hussars: 指当时英军中一支骑兵，全名为 Black Hussars。

99. the Hanoverian Cavalry: 汉诺威骑兵。汉诺威在今西德境内，当时自成一邦，与英国为邦联关系，至维多利亚女王接位后始与英国分离。Green might have any decent time：可以适当放宽格林还债的期限。

100. I. O. U.:（I owe you 的缩写）：债据。

101. with long faces: 愁眉苦脸。

102. snapped her fingers in Mrs. Crawley's face: 这是轻蔑的表示。

103. C. B.: = Companion of the Bath：一种爵位封号。

104. Rawdon acquiesced in the justice of her opinion: 劳登承认她的意见有道理。

105. Calais: 加来（法国西北地名）。

106. Dover: 多佛尔（英国港口，与加来隔海相望）。

107. Dunkirk: 敦刻尔克（法国西北）。

108. Brussels: 布鲁塞尔（比利时首都）。

109. mourning: 丧服。

110. the premier: 正房（旅馆中比较高级的住室）。

111. entresol: 亭子间（楼房中两层之间楼道旁的房间）。

112. new hangings: 新的窗帘饰物。

113. a final adjustment of everything except the bill: 把一切都商量安排好了，只是没有付帐。

114. bonne:（法语）女佣。

115. serréd:（从法语 *serrer*: 锁）上锁。

43 LEWIS CARROLL
1832–1898

THROUGH THE LOOKING-GLASS

张谷若　选注

Chapter VI

HUMPTY DUMPTY[1]

However, the egg only got larger and larger, and more and more human: when she had come within a few yards of it, she saw that it had eyes and a nose and mouth; and when she had come close to it, she saw clearly that it was Humpty Dumpty himself. "It can't be anybody else!" she said to herself. "I'm as certain of it, as if his name were written all over his face!"

It might have been written a hundred times, easily, on that enormous face. Humpty Dumpty was sitting with his legs crossed, like a Turk,[2] on the top of a high wall — such a narrow one that Alice quite wondered how he could keep his balance[3] — and, as his eyes were steadily fixed in the opposite direction, and he didn't take the least notice of her, she thought he must be a stuffed figure.[4]

"And how exactly like an egg he is!" she said aloud, standing with her hands ready to catch him, for she was every moment expecting him to fall.

"It's very provoking,[5]" Humpty Dumpty said after a long silence, looking away from Alice as he spoke, "to be called an egg — very!"

"I said you looked like an egg, Sir," Alice gently explained. "And some eggs are very pretty,[6] you know," she added, hoping to turn her remark into a sort of compliment.

"Some people," said Humpty Dumpty, looking away from her as usual, "have no more sense than a baby!"

Alice didn't know what to say to this: it wasn't at all like conversation, she thought, as he never said anything to her; in fact, his last remark was evidently addressed to a tree — so she stood and softly repeated to herself:

"Humpty Dumpty sat on a wall:
Humpty Dumpty had a great fall.
All the King's horses and all the King's men
Couldn't put Humpty Dumpty in his place again."

"That last line is much too long for the poetry," she added, almost out loud, forgetting that Humpty Dumpty would hear her.

"Don't stand chattering to yourself like that," Humpty Dumpty said, looking at her for the first time, "but tell me your name and your business."

"My name is Alice, but — "

"It's a stupid name enough!" Humpty Dumpty interrupted impatiently. "What does it mean?"

"Must a name mean something?" Alice asked doubtfully.

"Of course it must," Humpty Dumpty said with a short laugh: "my name means the shape I am — and a good handsome shape it is, too. With a name like yours, you might be any shape, almost."

"Why do you sit out[7] here all alone?" said Alice, not wishing to begin an argument.

"Why, because there's nobody with me!"[8] cried Humpty Dumpty. "Did you think I didn't know the answer to that? Ask another."

"Don't you think you'd be safer down on the ground?" Alice went on, not with any idea of making another riddle, but simply in her good-natured anxiety for the queer creature. "That wall is so very narrow!"

"What tremendously easy riddles you ask!" Humpty Dumpty growled out. "Of course I don't think so! Why, if ever I did fall off —which there's no chance of[9]—but if I did—" Here he pursed up his lips,[10] and looked so solemn and grand that Alice could hardly help laughing. "If I did fall," he went on, "the King has promised me—ah, you may turn pale,[11] if you like! You didn't think I was going to say that, did you? The King has promised me—with his own mouth—to—to—"

"To send all his horses and all his men," Alice interrupted, rather unwisely.

"Now I declare[12] that's too bad!" Humpty Dumpty cried, breaking into a sudden passion.[13] "You've been listening at doors—and behind trees—and down chimneys—or you couldn't have known it!"

"I haven't, indeed!" Alice said very gently. "It's in a book."

"Ah, well! They may write such things in a book," Humpty Dumpty said in a calmer tone. "That's what you call a History of England, that is. Now, take a good look at me! I'm one that has spoken to a King, I am: mayhap[14] you'll never see such another: and to show you I'm not proud,[15] you may shake hands with me!" And he grinned almost from ear to ear,[16] as he leant forwards (and as nearly as possible fell off the wall in doing so) and offered Alice his hand. She watched him a little anxiously as she took it. "If he smiled much more, the ends of his mouth might meet behind," she thought: "and then I don't know what would happen to his head! I'm afraid it would come off!"

"Yes, all his horses and all his men," Humpty Dumpty went on. "They'd pick me up again in a minute, they would! However, this conversation is going on a little too fast: let's go back to the last remark but one."

"I'm afraid I can't quite remember it," Alice said very politely.

"In that case we may start fresh," said Humpty Dumpty, "and it's my turn to choose a subject—" ("He talks about it just as if it was a game!" thought Alice.) "So here's a question for you. How old did you say you were?"

Alice made a short calculation, and said, "Seven years and six months."

"Wrong!" Humpty Dumpty[17] exclaimed triumphantly. "You never said a word like it."

"I thought you meant, 'How old are you?'" Alice explained.

"If I'd meant that, I'd have said it," said Humpty Dumpty.

Alice didn't want to begin another argument, so she said nothing.

"Seven years and six months!" Humpty Dumpty repeated thoughtfully. "An uncomfortable sort of age. Now if you'd asked my advice, I'd have said, 'Leave off at seven'—but it's too late now."

"I never ask advice about growing," Alice said indignantly.

"Too proud?" the other inquired.

Alice felt even more indignant at this suggestion. "I mean,"she said, "that one can't help growing older."[18]

"One can't, perhaps," said Humpty Dumpty, "but two can. With proper assistance, you might have left off at seven."

"What a beautiful belt you've got on!" Alice suddenly remarked. (They had had quite enough of the subject of age, she thought: and if they were really to take turns in choosing subjects, it was her turn now.) "At least," she corrected herself on second thoughts, "a beautiful cravat, I should have said—no, a belt, I mean—oh, I beg your pardon!" she added in dismay, for Humpty Dumpty looked thoroughly offended, and she began to wish she hadn't chosen that subject. "If only I knew," she thought to herself, "which was neck and which was waist!"

Evidently Humpty Dumpty was very angry, though he said nothing for a minute or two. When he did speak again, it was in a deep growl.

"It is a-most-provoking-thing," he said at last, "when a person doesn't know a cravat from a belt!"

"I know it's very ignorant of me," Alice replied. in so humble a tone that Humpty Dumpty relented.

"It's a cravat, child, and a beautiful one, as you say. "It's a present from the White King and Queen.[19] There now!"

"Is it really?" said Alice, quite pleased to find she had chosen a good subject, after all.

"They gave it me," Humpty Dumpty continued thoughtfully, as he crossed one knee over the other and clasped his hands round it, "—for an un-birthday present."

"I beg your pardon?"[20] Alice said with a puzzled air.

"I'm not offended," said Humpty Dumpty.

"I mean, what is an un-birthday present?"

"A present given when it isn't your birthday, of course."

Alice considered a little. "I like birthday presents best," she said at last.

"You don't know what you're talking about!" cried Humpty Dumpty. "How many days are there in a year?"

"Three hundred and sixty-five," said Alice.

"And how many birthdays have you?"

"One."

"And if you take one from three hundred and sixty-five, what remains?"

"Three hundred and sixty-four, of course."

Humpty Dumpty looked doubtful. "I'd rather see that done on paper," he said.

Alice couldn't help smiling as she took out her memorandum-book, and worked the sum for him:

$$\begin{array}{r} 365 \\ \underline{\quad 1} \\ \underline{364} \end{array}$$

Humpty Dumpty took the book, and looked at it very carefully. "That seems to be done right—" he began.

"You're holding it upside down!" Alice interrupted.

"To be sure I was!" Humpty Dumpty said gaily, as she turned it round for him. "I thought it looked a little queer. As I was saying, that seems to be done right—though I haven't time to look it over thoroughly just now—and that shows that there are three hundred and sixty-four days when you might get un-birthday presents—"

"Certainly," said Alice.

"And only one for birthday presents, you know. There's glory for you![21]"

"I don't know what you mean by 'glory,'" Alice said.

Humpty Dumpty smiled contemptuously. "Of course you don't—till I tell you. I meant there's a nice knock-down argument for you!"

"But 'glory' doesn't mean 'a nice knock-down argument,'[22]" Alice objected.

"When I use aword," Humpty Dumpty said in rather a scornful tone, "it means just what I choose it to mean—neither more nor less."

"The question is," said Humpty Dumpty, "which is to be master—that's all."

Alice was too much puzzled to say anything, so after a minute Humpty Dumpty began again. "They've a temper, some of them—particularly verbs, they're the proudest-adjectives you can do anything with, but not verbs—however, I can manage the whole lot! Impenetrability! That's what I say!"

"Would you tell me, please," said Alice, "what that means?"

"Now you talk like a reasonable child," said Humpty Dumpty, looking very much pleased. "I meant by 'impenetrability' that we've had enough of that subject, and it would be just as well if you'd mention what you mean to do next, as I suppose you don't intend to stop here all the rest of your life."

"That's a great deal to make one word mean," Alice said in a thoughtful tone.

"When I make a word do a lot of work like that," said Humpty Dumpty, "I always pay it extra.[23]"

"Oh!" said Alice. She was too much puzzled to make any other remark.

"Ah, you should see'em[24] come round me of a Saturday night,[25]" Humpty Dumpty went on, wagging his head gravely from side to side: "for to get their wages,[26] you know."

(Alice didn't venture to ask what he paid them with; and so you see I can't tell you.)

"You seem very clever at explaining words, Sir," said Alice. "Would you kindly tell me the meaning of the poem 'Jabberwocky'[27]?"

"Let's hear it," said Humpty Dumpty. "I can explain all the poems that ever were invented — and a good many that haven't been invented just yet."

This sounded very hopeful, so Alice repeated the first verse:

" 'Twas brillig, and the slithy toves
    Did gyre and gimble in the wabe:
All mimsy were the borogoves,
    And the mome raths outgrabe."

"That's enough to begin with," Humpty Dumpty interrupted: "there are plenty of hard words there. 'Brillig' means four o'clock in the afternoon — the time when you begin broiling things for dinner."

"That'll do very well,"[28] said Alice: "and 'slithy'?"

"Well, 'slithy' means 'lithe and slimy.' 'Lithe' is the same as'active.' You see it's like a portmanteau[29] — there are two meanings packed up into one word."

"I see it now," Alice remarked thoughtfully: "and what are'toves'?"

"Well, 'toves' are something like badgers — they're something like lizards — and they're something like corkscrews."

"They must be very curious creatures."

"They are that," said Humpty Dumpty: "also they make their nests under sundials — also they live on cheese."

"And what's to 'gyre' and to 'gimble'?"

"To 'gyre' is to go round and round like a gyroscope. To'gimble' is to make holes like a gimlet."

"And 'the wabe' is the grass plot round a sundial, I suppose?"-said Alice, surprised at her own ingenuity.

"Of course it is. It's called 'wabe', you know, because it goes a long way before it, and a long way behind it — "

"And a long way beyond it on each side," Alice added.

"Exactly so. Well then, 'mimsy' is 'flimsy and miserable' (there's another portmanteau for you). And a 'borogove' is a thin shabby-looking bird with its feathers sticking out all round — something like a live mop."

"And then 'mome raths'?" said Alice. "If I'm not giving you too much trouble."

"Well, a 'rath' is a sort of green pig: but 'mome' I'm not certain about. I think it's short for 'from home' — meaning that they'd lost their way, you know."

"And what does 'outgrabe' mean?"

"Well, 'outgrabing' is something between bellowing and whistling, with a kind of sneeze in the middle: however, you'll hear it done, maybe — down in the wood yonder — and when you've once heard it you'll be quite content. Who's been repeating all that hard stuff to you?"

"I read it in a book," said Alice. "But I had some poetry repeated to me, much easier than that, by — Tweedledee,[30] I think."

"As to poetry, you know," said Humpty Dumpty, stretching out one of his great hands, "I can repeat poetry as well as other folk if it comes to that[31] — "

"Oh, it needn't come to that!" Alice hastily said, hoping to keep him from beginning.

"The piece I'm going to repeat," he went on without noticing her remark, "was written entirely for your amusement."

Alice felt that in that case she really ought to listen to it, so she sat down, and said "Thank you" rather sadly.

"In winter, when the fields are white,
I sing this song for your delight—
only I don't sing it," he explained.
"I see[32] you don't," said Alice.

"If you can see whether I'm singing or not, you've sharper eyes than most," Humpty Dumpty remarked severely. Alice was silent.

"In spring, when woods are getting green,
I'll try and tell you what I mean."
"Thank you very much," said Alice.
"In summer, when the days are long,
Perhaps you'll understand the song:
"In autumn, when the leaves are brown,
   Take pen and ink and write it down."
"I will, if I can remember it so long," said Alice.

"You needn't go on making remarks like that," Humpty Dumpty said: "they're not sensible, and they put me out.[33]"

"I sent a message to the fish:
I told them 'This is what I wish.'
"The little fishes of the sea,
They sent an answer back to me.
"The little fishes' answer was
'We cannot do it, Sir, because—'"

"I'm afraid I don't quite understand," said Alice.

"It gets easier further on," Humpty Dumpty replied.

"I sent to them again to say
'It will be better to obey.'
"The fishes answered with a grin,
'Why, what a temper you are in!'
"I told them once, I told them twice:
They would not listen to advice.
"I took a kettle large and new,
Fit for the deed I nad to do.

"My heart went hop, my heart went thump;
I filled the kettle at the pump.
"Then someone came to me and said
'The little fishes are in bed.'
"I said to him, I said it plain,
'Then you must wake them up again.'
"I said it very loud and clear;
I went and shouted in his ear."

Humpty Dumpty raised his voice almost to a scream as he repeated this verse, and Alice thought with a shudder, "I wouldn't have been the messenger for anything!"

"But he was very stiff and proud;
He said 'You needn't shout so loud!'
"And he was very proud and stiff;
He said 'I'd go and wake them, if —'
"I took a corkscrew from the shelf:
I went to wake them up myself.
"And when I found the door was locked,
I pulled and pushed and kicked and knocked.
"And when I found the door was shut,
I tried to turn the handle, but — "

There was a long pause.

"Is that all?" Alice timidly asked.

"That's all," said Humpty Dumpty. "Good-bye."

This was rather sudden, Alice thought: but, after such a very strong hint that she ought to be going, she felt it would hardly be civil to stay. So she held out her hand. "Good-bye, till we meet again!" she said as cheerfully as she could.

"I shouldn't know you again if we did meet," Humpty Dumpty replied in a discontented tone, giving her one of his fingers to shake[34]; "you're so exactly like other people."

"The face is what one goes by, generally," Alice remarked in a thoughtful tone.

"That's just what I complain of," said Humpty Dumpty. "Your face is the same as everybody has — the two eyes, so — " (marking their places in the air with his thumb) "nose in the middle, mouth under. It's always the same. Now if you had the two eyes on the same side of the nose, for instance — or the mouth at the top — that would be some help."

"It wouldn't look nice," Alice objected. But Humpty Dumpty only shut his eyes and said, "Wait till you've tried."

Alice waited a minute to see if be would speak again, but as he never opened his eyes or took any further notice of her, she said, "Good-bye!" once more, and, on getting no answer to this, she quietly walked away: but she couldn't help saying to herself as she went, "Of all the unsatisfactory — " (she repeated this aloud, as it was a great comfort to have such a long word to say) "of all the unsatisfactory people I ever met — " She never finished the sentence, fcr at this moment a heavy crash[35] shook the forest from end to end.

【作者简介】Lewis Carroll (1832–1898) 是本文作者的笔名，他的真名是 Charles Lutwidge Dodgson，本为英国牛津大学数学讲师，在数学方面，也有著作。但是他在那方面的著作，却早已为人所忘记，而他给儿童写的读物，却至今为人所传诵。在十九世纪的英国，他把儿童读物提到了一个高的水平。他的著作里，最有名的是《阿丽思漫游奇境记》(*Alice's Adventures in Wonderland*, 1865 年，简称 *Alice in Wonderland*) 和《镜中世界》(*Through the Looking-Glass*, 1871 年)。用儿童心理，作种种幻想，看来似乎荒谬，但亦时含深意，且间亦有讽刺之处。其总的背景，则为维多利亚时代的英国，其写作对象，则为英国当时中等阶级家庭的儿童，如书中说到儿童的礼貌，怎样说话不得罪人等，就反映了这样的意识形态。

【题解与注释】

《镜中世界》和《阿丽思漫游奇境记》一样，也是以阿丽思作主人公，说冬天下雪的时候，她坐在起坐间或客厅里，逗小猫玩儿，因刚刚玩过棋，棋子还在桌上。阿丽思教小猫学作红棋子中的王后。她后来渐渐入睡，在梦中迷离惝恍，遇到一些离奇的光景。先见棋子里的王和后，都成了活人。又到花园中，遇到会说话的花儿。又到了一铺子，有羊坐在铺子里打毛活儿，她在铺子里买了一个蛋，蛋后来渐变为 Humpty Dumpty.

阿丽思是一个七岁多的小女孩，中等家庭出身，由保姆教大，脑子里装满了儿歌，有初步的算术、地理等知识，家里有哥哥上学，念初步的拉丁文。她的迷离的梦境，都由这种种情况联想而来的，或以这种种情况作背景的。

Lewis Carroll 的故事内容，都是他的脑子里自然涌现出来的，他的语言也好象是他笔底下自然涌现出来的。其实他对于文字的修改润色，是不遗余力的，不过他的文字，虽然经过修改润色，却仍旧那样自然，那样流利，所以一点也看不出斧凿的痕迹来。他的书既然是为儿童写的（他的朋友的一个六岁的孩子就听了阿丽思漫游奇境记而拍手大叫），文字自然要浅显容易，但是他的浅显容易的文字，却又表达了含意深远（例如嘲笑 Humpty Dumpty 醜而却好自夸，喜人奉承，以及其它资产阶级社会的人情世故）的内容。这就是他的书同样为成年人所爱读的原故，也就是他的文字特色的所在。他的文字（除了极个别的例外）几乎没有一句不是日常用语，几乎没有一句不是习惯（idiomatic）英语，但是同时却又是文学语言。中国初学英语的人，每每想要找到文字又浅易又优美的作品，这样作品是不多的。而 Lewis Carroll 的两部名著是这样作品里比较出色的。他的风格（用字、造句等等）是中国人初学英语的好模范。

1. Humpty Dumpty: 本意为身短、腰粗、肩凸之男或女。英国有一个儿歌谜语（见第 2 页第 17—20 行），以他作主角，谜底是一个蛋。在儿歌书里，普通把他画成一个很大的圆脸，也就是在一个蛋的轮廓上，加耳目口鼻，再画上很小的身子和四肢，坐在墙头上。阿丽思这儿所见的 Humpty Dumpty，即由她脑子里所记的这种形象而来。

2. sitting with his legs crossed, like a Turk: sitting with his legs crossed 也可以说 sitting cross-legged. 这有两种意思:（1）盘膝坐着;（2）叠着腿坐着。如不加 like a Turk，则一般为第（2）意。加 like a Turk 则确定为第（1）意。第（1）意也可加 like tailors. 土耳其人或埃及人等，都（席地）盘膝而坐，英国旧式成衣匠亦然。crosslegged 或 with legs crossed，如形容人站着的时候，则为“扭着腿”。

3. keep his balance:“保持平衡”；此处为“坐得四平八稳地。”

4. stuffed figure: 草人；外作人形，饰以衣帽，中实以草（麦稭之类）。多用在纪念“火药暗杀案”（Gun-powder Plot）时，饰作恶人，供烧毁之用。本书一开始的时候，提到阿丽思看见有人收集烧柴，供第二天作 bonfire（纪念日烟火）之用。在烧 bonfire 的时候，往往也烧 stuffed figure. 阿丽思这儿想到 stuffed figure，或即由 bonfire 联想而来。

5. provoking: 惹人生气。

6. and some eggs are very pretty: 阿丽思在这儿所想的，可能是 Easter eggs，因那种 eggs，上面画有图形。

7. sit out: = sit in the open air.

8. Why, because there's nobody with me!: 因前面的儿歌是一个谜语，所以这

儿 Humpty Dumpty 认为阿丽思问他的话，都是谜语。阿丽思前面问的那句话，重点在 Why do you sit out. 但 Humpty Dumpty 却把 all alone 看作重点，故有此答。

9. Which there's no chance of: of which there is no chance (= possibility) 的口语形式。

10. pursed up his lips: 把嘴撮起来，表示庄严，和 pout（撅嘴）表示生气不同。

11. turn pale: 听到国王，吓得脸都白了。

12. I declare: 作惊叹词用。

13. breaking into a sudden passion: 一下发怒。

14. mayhap: perhaps（古字）。

15. to show you I'm not proud: 说不骄傲，正是骄傲。

16. grinned ... from ear to ear: "咧着嘴笑"的普通说法。因这样笑的时候，两个嘴角朝着两个耳朵咧去。

17. Humpty Dumpty: 问的那句话重点在 did you say. 阿丽思则认为重点在 How old you were.

18. 阿丽思那句话重点在 Can't help, Humpty Dumpty 则把重点放在 one 上，而且将 one 解作"一个人"，而阿丽思的原意则是"人们"。

19. the White King and Queen: 指白色棋子的"王"和"后"而言。

20. I beg your pardon: 普通有两种用法。（1）向人道歉；（2）请人重叙前言。阿丽思是第（2）种意思，Humpty Dumpty 认为是第（1）种意思。

21. There's glory for you: there = that，和 there's a dear 的用法同。glory 是反语，看下文自明。

22. a nice knock-down argument: knock down = irresistible 无可反驳的辩论。

23. extra: 这儿是 adverb。

24. 'em: = them.

25. of a Saturday night: 英国工资，一般一星期付一次。

26. for to get their wages: 现在或说 to get their wages，或说 for their wages. for to get 是老一些或土一点的说法。这儿这种说法，和前面的 'em，都表示土一些的说法。

27. "Jabberwocky": 见本书第一章，阿丽思在梦中所见到一本书里，有一首诗，叫作这个名字。Jabberwock 为 Carroll 所造的字，一般认为是一种怪物。"Jabberwocky"那一首诗，普通叫作 nonsense verse，为英国的一种文字游戏，在可解与不可解之间。Jabberwocky 就是这种文字游戏在英文里的代表作之一。

28. That'll do very well: that's quite satisfactory.

29. portmanteau words: 是英语文字的一种，因为这种字是把好几个意思'装'在一个字里，好象把几件东西装在一个手提皮箱里一样，故名。

30. Tweedledee: 为本书中人物之一，是 Tweedledum 的孪生兄弟，两人长得一样，见第四章。

31. if it comes to that: 如果要到那步田地的话，此处是，如果需要那样的话。

32. I see: 有两种意思：（1）我明白了；（2）我看见了。阿丽思说的是（1），Humpty Dumpty 认为的是（2）。

33. put me out: 打乱了我的话。

34. giving her one of his fingers to shake: 这是一种傲慢、侮辱的态度。

35. a heavy crash: 下一章一开始，说阿丽思看见国王的步队和马队从树林子里过，这个轰然震动整个树林子的声音，就指军队杂沓的声音而言。

44 WILLIAM MORRIS
1834–1896

NEWS FROM NOWHERE
(selections)

夏祖煃　选注

[HOW IT ALL BEGAN]

"On some comparatively trifling occasion a great meeting was summoned by the workmen leaders to meet in Trafalgar Square[1] (about the right to meet in which place there had for years and years been bickering)[2]. The civic[3] bourgeois guard (called the police) attacked the said meeting[4] with bludgeons,[5] according to their custom; many people were hurt in the *mêlée,*[6] of whom five in all died, either trampled to death on the spot, or from the effects of their cudgelling[7]; the meeting was scattered, and some hundred[8] of prisoners cast into gaol.[9] A similar meeting had been treated in the same way a few days before at a place called Manchester,[10] which has now disappeared. Thus the 'lesson' began.[11] The whole country was thrown into a ferment by this;[12] meetings were held which attempted some rough organization[13] for the holding of another meeting to retort on the authorities.[14] A huge crowd assembled in Trafalgar Square and the neighbourhood (then a place of crowded streets[15]), and was too big for the bludgeon-armed police to cope with;[16] there was a good deal of dry-blow fighting[17]; three or four of the people were killed and half a score of policemen were crushed to death in the throng,[18] and the rest got away as they could. This was a victory for the people as far as it went.[19] The next day all London (remember what it was in those days) was in a state of turmoil.[20] Many of the rich fled into the country; the executive[21] got together soldiery, but did not dare to use them; and the police could not be massed[22] in any one place, because riots or threats of riots[23] were everywhere. But in Manchester, where the people were not so courageous or not so desperate as in London, several of the popular[24] leaders were arrested. In London a convention[25] of leaders was got together from the Federation of Combined Workmen,[26] and sat under the old revolutionary name of the Committee of Public Safety;[27] but as they had no drilled and armed body of men[28] to direct, they attempted no aggressive measures,[29] but only placarded the walls[30] with somewhat vague appeals[31] to the workmen not to allow themselves to be trampled upon.[32] However, they called a meeting in Trafalgar Square for the day fortnight[33] of the last-mentioned skirmish.[34]

"Meantime[35] the town grew no quieter, and business came pretty much to an end.[36] The newspapers — then, as always hitherto,[37] almost entirely in the hands of the masters[38] — clamoured to the Government for[39] repressive measures[40]; the rich citizens were enrolled as an extra body of police,[41] and armed with bludgeons like them; many of these were strong, well-fed, full-blooded young men, and had plenty of stomach for fighting;[42] but the Government did not dare to use them, and contented itself with getting full powers voted to it by the Parliament for suppressing any revolt,[43] and bringing up[44] more and more soldiers to London. Thus passed the week after the great meeting; almost as large a one[45] was held on the Sunday, which went off peaceably on the whole, as no opposition to it was offered,[46] and again the people cried 'victory.' But on the Monday the people woke up to find that they were hungry.[47] During the last few days there had been groups of men parading the streets asking (or, if you please,[48] demanding) money to buy food; and what for goodwill, what for fear,[49] the richer people gave them a good deal. The authorities of the parishes[50] also (I haven't time to explain that phrase at present) gave willy-nilly[51] what provisions[52] they could to wandering people; and the Government, by means of its feeble national workshops,[53] also fed a good number of half-starved folk. But in addition to this, several bakers' shops and other provision stores[54] had been emptied without a great deal of disturbance. So fat, so good.[55] But on the Monday in question[56] the Committee of Public Safety, on the one hand afraid of general unorganised pillage,[57] and on the other emboldened by the wavering conduct of the authorities,[58] sent a deputation[59] provided with carts and all necessary gear[60] to clear out[61] two or three big provision stores in the centre of the town, leaving papers with the shop managers[62] promising to pay the price of them; and also in the part of the town where they were strongest they took possession of[63] several bakers' shops and set men at work in them for the benefit of the people;—all of which was done with little or no disturbance, the police assisting in keeping order at the sack[64] of the stores, as they would have done at a big fire.

"But at this last stroke[65] the reactionaries were so alarmed, that they were determined to force the executive into action. The newspapers next day all blazed into the fury of frightened people,[66] and threatened the people, the Government, and everybody they could think of, unless 'order were at once restored.'[67] A deputation of leading commercial people waited on[68] the Government and told them that if they did not at once arrest the Committee of Public Safety, they themselves would gather a body of men, arm them, and fall on[69] 'the incendiaries,'[70] as they called them.

"They, together with a number of the newspaper editors, had a long interview with the heads of the Government and two or three military men, the deftest in their art that the country could furnish.[71] The deputation came away from that interview, says a contemporary eye-witness,[72] smiling and satisfied,[73] and said no more about raising an anti-popular[74] army, but that afternoon left London with their families for their country seats[75] or elsewhere.

"The next morning the Government proclaimed a state of siege[76] in London, — a thing common enough amongst the absolutist governments on the Continent,[77] but unheard of in England in those days. They appointed the youngest and cleverest of their generals to command the proclaimed district; a man who had won a certain sort of reputation in the disgraceful wars in which the country had been long engaged from time to time. The newspapers were in ecstasies,[78] and all the most fervent of the reactionaries now came to the front;[79] men who in ordinary times were forced to keep their opinions to themselves or their immediate circle,[80] but who began to look forward to crushing once for all[81] the Socialist, and even democratic tendencies, which, said they, had been treated with such foolish indulgence for the last sixty years.

"But the clever general took no visible action;[82] and yet only a few of the minor newspapers[83] abused him; thoughtful men gathered from this that a plot was hatching.[84] As for the Committee of Public Safety, whatever they thought of their position, they had now gone too far to draw back;[85] and many of them, it seems, thought that the Government would not act. They went on quietly organising their food supply, which was a miserable driblet[86] when all is said;[87] and also as a retort to the state of siege, they armed as many men as they could in the quarter[88] where they were strongest, but did not attempt to drill or organise them, thinking, perhaps, that they could not at the best turn them into trained soldiers till they had some breathing space.[89] The clever general, his soldiers, and the police did not meddle with all this in the least in the word;[90] and things were quieter in London that week-end; though there were riots in many places of the provinces,[91] which were quelled by the authorities without much trouble. The most serious of these were at Glasgow[92] and Bristol.[93]

"Well, the Sunday of the meeting[94] came, and great crowds

came to Trafalgar Square in procession, the greater part of the Committee[95] amongst them, surrounded by their band of men armed somehow or other.[96] The streets were quite peaceful and quiet, though there were many spectators to see the procession pass. Trafalgar Square had no body of police[97] in it; the people took quiet possession of it, and the meeting began. The armed men stood round the principal platform, and there were a few others armed amidst the general crowd; but by far the greater part[98] were unarmed.

"Most people thought the meeting would go off peaceably; but the members of the Committee had heard from various quarters[99] that something would be attempted against them; but these rumours were vague, and they had no idea of[100] what threatened. They soon found out.

"For before the streets about the Square were filled, a body of soldiers poured into it from the north-west corner and took up their places by the houses that stood on the west side. The people growled at the sight of the red-coats;[101] the armed men of the Committee stood undecided, not knowing what to do; and indeed this new influx[102] so jammed the crowd together that, unorganised as they were, they had little chance of working through[103] it. They had scarcely grasped the fact of their enemies being there, when[104] another column of soldiers, pouring out of the streets which led into the great southern road going down to the Parliament House[105] (still existing, and called the Dung Market)[106], and also from the embankment[107] by the side of the Thames,[108] marched up, pushing the crowd into a denser and denser mass, and formed along the south side of the Square. Then any of those who could see what was going on, knew at once that they were in a trap, and could only wonder what would be done with them.

"The closely-packed crowd would not or could not budge,[109] except under the influence of the height of terror,.[110] which was soon to be supplied to them. A few of the armed men struggled to the front, or climbed up to the base of the monument which then stood there,[111] that they might face the wall of hidden fire[112] before them; and to most men (there were many women amongst them) it seemed as if the end of the world had come, and today seemed strangely different from yesterday. No sooner were the soldiers drawn up aforesaid[113] than,[114] says an eye-witness, 'a glittering officer on horseback came prancing out from the ranks on the south, and read something from a paper which he held in his hand; which something, very few heard;[115] but I was told afterwards that it was an order for us to disperse, and a warning that he had legal right to fire on the crowd else,[116] and that he would do so. The crowd took it as[117] a challenge of some sort,[117] and a hoarse threatening roar went up from them; and after that there was comparative silence for a little, till the officer had got back into the ranks. I was near the edge of the crowd towards the soldiers,' says this eye-witness, 'and I saw three little machines[118] being wheeled out in front of the ranks, which I knew for mechanical guns. I cried out, "Throw yourself down![119] they are going to fire!" But no one scarcely could throw himself down,[120] so tight as the crowd were packed. I heard a sharp order given,[121] and wondered where I should be the next minute; and then—It was as if the earth had opened, and hell had come up bodily[122] amidst us. It is no use trying to describe the scene that followed. Deep lanes were mowed amidst the thick crowd;[123] the dead and dying[124] covered the ground, and the shrieks and wails and cries of horror filled all the air, till it seemed as if there was nothing else in the world but murder and death. Those of our armed men[125] who were still unhurt cheered wildly'[126] and opened a scattering fire[127] on the soldiers. One or two soldiers fell; and I saw the officers going up and down the ranks urging the men to fire again; but they received the orders in sullen silence, and let the butts of their guns fall.[128] Only one sergeant ran to a machine-gun and began to set it going;[129] but a tall young man, an officer too,[130] ran out of the ranks and dragged him back by the collar; and the soldiers stood there motionless while the horror-stricken crowd, nearly wholly unarmed (for most of the armed men had fallen in that first discharge)[131], drifted out of the Square. I was told afterwards that the soldiers on the west side had fired also, and done their part of the slaughter. How I got out of the Square I scarcely know: I went, not feeling the ground under me,[132] what with rage and terror and despair."[133]

"So says our eye-witness. The number of the slain[134] on the side of the people in that shooting during a minute[135] was prodigious;[136] but it was not easy to come at the truth about it;[137] it was probably between one and two thousand. Of the soldiers, six were killed outright,[138] and a dozen wounded."

I listened, trembling with excitement.[139] The old man's eyes glittered and his face flushed as he spoke, and told the tale of what I had often thought might happen. Yet I wondered that he should have got so elated about a mere massacre, and I said:

"How fearful! And I suppose that this massacre put an end to[140] the whole revolution for that time?"

"No, no," cried Old Hammond; "it began it!"

He filled his glass and mine, and stood up and cried out, "Drink this glass to the memory[141] of those who died there, for indeed it would be a long tale to tell how much we owe them."

A LITTLE SHOPPING

As he spoke, we came suddenly out of the woodland into a short street of handsomely built houses, which my companion named to me at once as Piccadilly:[142] the lower part of these I should have called shops, if it had not been that, as far as I could see, the people were ignorant of the arts of buying and selling.[143] Wares were displayed in their finely designed fronts,[144] as if to tempt people in, and people stood and looked at them, or went in and came out with parcels under their arms, just like the real thing.[145] On each side of the street ran an elegant arcade[146] to protect foot-passengers, as in some of the old Italian cities. About half-way down, a huge building; of the kind I was now prepared to expect[147] told me that this also was a centre of some kind, and had its special public buildings.

Said Dick:[148] "Here, you see, is another market on a different plan from most others:[149] the upper stories of these houses are used for guest-houses;[150] for people from all about the country are apt to drift up hither[151] from time to time, as folk are very thick upon the ground,[152] which you will see evidence of presently, and there are people who are fond of crowds, though I can't say that I am."

I couldn't help smiling to see how long a tradition would last.[153] Here was the ghost of London.[154] still asserting itself as a centre,—an intellectual centre, for ought I knew.[155] However, I said nothing, except that I asked him to drive very slowly, as the things in the booths looked exceedingly pretty.

"Yes," said he, "this is a very good market for pretty things, and is mostly kept for the handsomer goods,[156] as the Houses-of-Parliament market,[157] where they set out[158] cabbages and turnips and such like things, along with beer and the rougher kind of wine, is so near."

Then he looked at me curiously, and said, "Perhaps you would like to do a little shopping, as 'tis called."[159]

I looked at what I could see of my rough blue duds,[160] which I had plenty of opportunity of contrasting with the gay attire of the citizens we had come across;[161] and I thought that if, as seemed likely,[162] I should presently be shown about as a curiosity[163] for the amusement of this most unbusinesslike[164] people, I should like to look a little less like a discharged ship's purser.[165] But in spite of all that had happened, my hand. went down into my pocket again,[166] where to my dismay it met nothing metallic except two rusty old keys, and I remembered that amidst our talk in the guest-hall at Hammersmith[167] I had taken the cash out of my pocket to show to the pretty Annie,[168] and had left it lying there. My face fell fifty per cent.,[169] and Dick, beholding[170] me, said rather sharply:

"Hilloa,[171] Guest! what's the matter now? Is it a wasp?"[172]

"No," said I, "but I've left it behind."[173]

"Well," said he, "whatever you have left behind, you can get in this market again, so don't trouble yourself about it."

I had come to my senses by this time,[174] and remembering the astounding customs of this country, had no mind for another lecture on social economy and the Edwardian coinage;[175] so I said only:

"My clothes — Couldn't I?[176] You see — What do you think could be done about them?"

He didn't seem in the least inclined to laugh, but said quite gravely:

"O don't get new clothes yet. You see, my greatgrandfather is an antiquarian,[177] and he will want to see you just as you are. And, you know, I mustn't preach to you, but surely it wouldn't be right for you to take away people's pleasure of studying your attire, by just going and making yourself like everybody else. You feel that, don't you?" said he, earnestly.

I did not feel it my duty to set myself up for a scarecrow[178] amidst this beauty-loving people, but I saw I had got across some ineradicable prejudice,[179] and that it wouldn't do to[180] quarrel with my new friend. So I merely said, "O certainly, certainly."

"Well," said he, pleasantly, "you may as well see what the inside of these booths is like:[181] think of something you want."

Said I: "Could I get some tobacco and a pipe?"[182]

"Of course," said he; "what was I thinking of, not asking you before?[183] Well, Bob[184] is always telling me that we non-smokers are a selfish lot,[185] and I'm afraid he is right. But come along; here is a place just handy."

Therewith[186] he drew rein[187] and jumped down, and I followed. A very handsome woman, splendidly clad in figured silk, was slowly passing by, looking into the windows as she went. To her quoth[188] Dick: "Maiden, would you kindly hold our horse while we go in for a little?" She nodded to us with a kind smile, and fell to patting the horse[189] with her pretty hand.

"What a beautiful creature!"[190] said I to Dick as we entered.

"What, old Greylocks?"[191] said he, with a sly grin.

"No, no," said I; "Goldylocks,[192]—the lady."

"Well, so she is," said he. "'Tis a good job there are so many of them that every Jack may have his Jill; else I fear that we should get fighting for them.[193] Indeed," said he, becoming very grave, "I don't say that it does not happen even now, sometimes. For you know love is not a very reasonable thing, and perversity and self-will are commoner than some of our moralists think." He added, in a still more sombre tone:[194] "Yes, only a month ago there was a mishap down by us,[195] that in the end cost the lives of two men and a woman, and, as it were, put out the sunlight for us for a while.[196] Don't ask me about it just now; I may tell you about it later on."

By this time we were within the shop or booth, which had a counter, and shelves on the walls, all very neat, though without any pretence of showiness, but otherwise not very different to what I had been used to.[197] Within were a couple of children—a brown-skinned boy of about twelve, who sat reading a book, and a pretty little girl of about a year older, who was sitting also reading behind the counter; they were obviously brother and sister.

"Good morning, little neighbours,"[198] said Dick. "My friend here wants tobacco and a pipe; can you help him?"

"O yes, certainly," said the girl with a sort of demure alertness[199] which was somewhat amusing. The boy looked up, and fell to staring at my outlandish attire,[200] but presently reddened and turned his head, as if he knew that he was not behaving prettily.

"Dear neighbour," said the girl, with the most solemn countenance of a child playing at keeping shop,[201] "what tobacco is it you would like?"

"Latakia,"[202] quoth I, feeling as if I were assisting at a child's game, and wondering whether I should get anything but make-believe.[203]

But the girl took a dainty little basket from a shelf beside her, went to a jar, and took out a lot of tobacco and put the filled basket down on the counter before me, where I could both smell and see that it was excellent Latakia.

"But you haven't weighed it," said I, "and — and how much am I to take?"

"Why," she said, "I advise you to cram[204] your bag, because you may be going where you can't get Latakia. Where is your bag?"

I fumbled about, and at last pulled out my piece of cotton print which does duty with me for a tobacco pouch.[205] But the girl looked at it with some disdain, and said:

"Dear neighbour, I can give you something much better than that cotton rag." And she tripped[206] up the shop and came back presently, and as she passed the boy whispered something in his ear, and he nodded and got up and went out. The girl held up in her finger and thumb a red morocco[207] bag, gaily embroidered, and said, "There, I have chosen one for you, and you are to have it: it is pretty, and will hold a lot."

Therewith she fell to cramming it with the tobacco, and laid it down by me and said, "Now for the pipe: that also you must let me choose for you; there are three pretty ones just come in,"[208]

She disappeared again, and came back with a bigbowled pipe in her hand, carved out of some hard wood very elaborately, and mounted in gold sprinkled with little gems.[209] It was, in short, as pretty and gay a toy as I had ever seen; something like the best kind of Japanese work, but better.

"Dear me!"[210] said I, when I set eyes on[211] it, "this is altogether too grand for me,[212] or for anybody but the Emperor of the World. Besides, I shall lose it: I always lost my pipes."

The child seemed rather dashed,[213] and said, "Don't you like it, neighbour?"

"O yes," I said, "of course I like it."

"Well, then, take it," said she, "and don't trouble about losing it. What will it matter if you do? Somebody is sure to find it, and he will use it, and you can get another."

I took it out of her hand to look at it, and while I did so, forgot my caution,[214] and said, "But however am I to pay for such a thing as this?"

Dick laid his hand on my shoulder as I spoke, and turning I met his eyes with a comical expression in them, which warned me against another exhibition of extinct commercial morality;[215] so I reddened and held my tongue,[216] while the girl simply looked at me with the deepest gravity, as if I were a foreigner blundering in my speech, for she clearly didn't understand me a bit.

"Thank you so very much," I said at last, effusively,[217] as I put the pipe in my pocket, not without a qualm of doubt as to whether I shouldn't find myself before a magistrate presently.[218]

"O, you are so very welcome," said the little lass, with an affectation of grown-up manners at their best which was very quaint. "It is such a pleasure to serve dear old gentlemen like you; specially when one can see at once that you have come from far over sea."

"Yes, my dear," quoth I, "I have been a great traveller."[219]

As I told this lie from pure politeness, in came the lad again, with a tray in his hands, on which I saw a long flask and two beautiful glasses. "Neighbours," said the girl (who did all the talking, her brother being very shy, clearly), "please to drink a glass to us before you go,[220] since we do not have guests like this every day."

Therewith the boy put the tray on the counter and solemnly poured out a straw-coloured wine into the long bowls. Nothing loth,[221] I drank, for I was thirsty with the hot day; and thinks I,[222] I am yet in the world, and the grapes of the Rhine[223] have not yet lost their flavour; for if ever I drank good Steinberg, I drank it that morning; and I made a mental note[224] to ask Dick how they managed to make fine wine when there were no longer labourers compelled to drink rot-gut[225] instead of the fine wine which they themselves made.

"Don't you drink a glass to us, dear little neighbours?" said I.

"I don't drink wine," said the lass; "I like lemonade[226] better: but I wish your health!"

"And I like ginger-beer[227] better," said the little lad.

Well, well, thought I, neither have children's tastes changed much.[228] And therewith we gave them good day[229] and went out of the booth.

....

[THE ROAD MENDERS]

We came just here on[230] a gang of men road-mending, which delayed us a little; but I was not sorry for it; for all I had seen hitherto[231] seemed a mere part of a summer holiday; and I wanted to see how this folk would set to[232] on a piece of real necessary work. They had been resting, and had only just begun work again as we came up; so that the rattle of the picks was what woke me from my musing. There were about a dozen of them, strong young men, looking much like a boating party at Oxford would have looked in the days I remembered, and not more troubled with their work;[233] their outer raiment[234] lay on the road-side in an orderly pile under the guardianship of a six-year-old boy, who had his arm thrown over the neck of a big mastiff, who was as happily lazy as if the summer day had been made for him alone. As I eyed the pile of clothes, I could see the gleam of gold and silk embroidery on it, and judged that some of these workmen had tastes akin to[235] those of the Golden Dustman of Hammersmith.[236] Beside them lay a good big basket that had hints about it of[237] cold pie and wine: a half-dozen of young women stood by watching the work or the workers, both of which were worth watching, for the latter smote[238] great strokes and were very deft in their labour, and as handsome clean-built fellows as you might find a dozen of in a summer day.[239] They were laughing and talking merrily with each other and the women, but presently their foreman looked up and saw our way stopped[240]. So he stayed his pick[241] and sang out, "Spell ho, mates![242] here are neighbours want to get past."[243] Whereon[244] the others stopped also, and drawing around us, helped the old horse by easing our wheels over the half undone road,[245] and then, like men with a pleasant task on hand, hurried back to their work, only stopping to give us a smiling good-day; so that the sound of the picks broke out again before Greylocks had taken to his jog-trot.[246] Dick looked back over his shoulder at them and said:

"They are in luck today: it's right down[247] good sport trying how much pick-work one can get into an hour;[248] and I can see those neighbours know their business well. It is not a mere matter of strength getting on quickly with such work;[249] is it, guest?"

"I should think not," said I, "but to tell you the truth, I have never tried my hand at it."

"Really?" said he gravely, "that seems a pity;[250] it is good work for hardening the muscles and I like it; though I admit it is pleasanter the second week than the first. Not that I am a good hand at it: the fellows used to chaff me at one job where I was working, I remember, and sing out to me, 'Well rowed, stroke![251] ' 'Put your back into it, bow! '[252]"

"Not much of a joke," quoth I.

"Well," said Dick, "everything seems like a joke when we have a pleasant spell of work on,[253] and good fellows merry about us;[254] we feel so happy, you know." Again I pondered[255] silently.

UP THE THAMES

The morning was now getting on, the morning of a jewel of a summer day;[256] one of those days which, if they were commoner in these islands, would make our climate the best of all climates, without dispute.[257] A light wind blew from the west;[258] the little clouds that had arisen at about our breakfast time had seemed to get higher and higher in the heavens; and in spite of the burning sun we no more longed for rain than we feared[259] it. Burning as the sun was, there was a fresh feeling in the air that almost set us alonging[260] for the rest of the hot afternoon, and the stretch of blossoming wheat seen from the shadow of the boughs.[261] No one unburdened with very heavy anxieties could have felt otherwise than happy that morning:[262] and it must be said that whatever anxieties might lie beneath the surface of things, we didn't seem to come across[263] any of them.

We passed by several fields where haymaking was going on, but Dick, and especially Clara,[264] were so jealous of our up-river festival[265] that they would not allow me to have much to say to them. I could only notice that the people in the fields looked strong and handsome, both men and women, and that so far from[266] there being any appearance of sordidness about their attire, they seemed to be dressed specially for the occasion[267]—lightly, of course, but gaily and with plenty of adornment.

Both on this day as well as yesterday we had, as you may think, met and passed and been passed by many craft[268] of one kind and another. The most part of these were being rowed like ourselves, or were sailing, in the sort of way that sailing is managed on the upper reaches of the river; but every now and then we came on barges, laden with hay or other country produce, or carrying bricks, lime, timber, and the like, and these were going on their way without any means of propulsion[269] visible to me—just a man at the tiller, with often a friend or two laughing and talking with him. Dick, seeing on one occasion this day that I was looking rather hard on one of these, said: "That is one of our force-barges;[270] it is quite as easy to work vehicles by force by water as by land."

I understood pretty well that these "force vehicles" had taken the place of our old steam-power carrying; but I took good care not to ask any questions about them, as I knew well enough both that I should never be able to understand how they were worked, and that in attempting to do so I should betray myself,[271] or get into some complication impossible to explain; so I merely said, "Yes, of course, I understand."

We went ashore at Bisham,[272] where the remains of the old Abbey and the Elizabethan house that had been added to them yet remained, none the worse for many years of careful and appreciative habitation.[273] The folk of the place, however, were mostly in the fields that day, both men and women; so we met only two old men there, and a younger one who had stayed at home to get on with some literary work, which I imagine we considerably interrupted. Yet I also think that the hard-working man who received us was not very sorry for the interruption. Anyhow, he kept on pressing us to stay over and over again, till at last we did not get away till the cool of the evening.

However, that mattered little to us; the nights were light, for the moon was shining in her third quarter,[274] and it was all one to Dick whether[275] he sculled or sat quiet in the boat: so we went away a great pace.[276] The evening sun shone bright on the remains of the old buildings at Medmenham; close beside which arose an irregular pile of building which Dick told us was a very pleasant house; and there were plenty of houses visible on the wide meadows opposite, under the hill; for, as it seems that the beauty of Hurley[277] had compelled people to build and live there a good deal. The sun very low down showed us Henley little altered in outward aspect from what I remembered it. Actual daylight failed us[278] as we passed through the lovely reaches of Margrave and Shiplake; but the moon rose behind us presently. I should like to have seen with my eyes what success the new order of things[279] had had in getting rid of the sprawling mess with which commercialism had littered the banks of the wide stream about Reading and Caversham: certainly everything smelt too deliciously in the early night for there to be any of the old careless sordidness of so-called manufacture; and in answer to my question as to what sort of a place Reading was, Dick answered:

"O, a nice town enough in its way; mostly rebuilt within the last hundred years; and there are a good many houses, as you can see by the lights just down under the hills yonder. In fact, it is one of the most populous places on the Thames round about here. Keep up your spirits, guest! we are close to our journey's end for the night. I ought to ask your pardon for not stopping at one of the houses here or higher up; but a friend, who is living in a very pleasant house in the Maple-Durham meads, particularly wanted me and Clara to come and see him on our way up the Thames; and I thought you wouldn't mind this bit of night travelling."

He need not have adjured me to keep up my spirits, which were as high as possible; though the strangeness and excitement of the happy and quiet life which I saw everywhere around me was, it is true, a little wearing off,[280] yet a deep content, as different as possible from languid acquiescence,[281] was taking its place, and I was, as it were, really new-born.

AN OLD HOUSE AMONGST NEW FOLK

As I stood there Ellen[282] detached herself from our happy friends who still stood on the little strand and came up to me. She took me by the hand, and said softly, "Take me on to the house at once; we need not wait for the others: I had rather not."[283]

I had a mind to say that I did not know the way thither,[284] and that the river-side dwellers should lead; but almost without my will my feet moved on along the road they knew.[285] The raised way led us into a little field bounded by a backwater[286] of the river on one side; on the right hand we could see a cluster of small houses and barns, new and old, and before us a grey stone barn and a wall partly overgrown with ivy, over which a few grey gables showed. The village road ended in the shallow of the aforesaid backwater. We crossed the road, and again almost without my will[287] my hand raised the latch of a door in the wall, and we stood presently on a stone path which led up to the old house to which fate in the shape of Dick had so strangely brought me in this new world of men.[288]

My companion gave a sigh of pleased surprise and enjoyment; nor did I wonder, for the garden between the wall and the house was redolent of the June flowers,[289] and the roses were rolling over one another with that delicious super-abundance of small well-tended gardens which at first sight takes away all thought from the beholder save that of beauty.[290] The blackbirds were singing their loudest, the doves were cooing on the roof-ridge, the rooks in the high elm-trees beyond were garrulous among the young leaves, and the swifts[291] wheeled whining about the gables. And the house itself was a fit guardian for all the beauty of this heat of summer.[292]

Onceagain Ellen echoed my thoughts[293] as she said: "Yes, friend, this is what I came out for to see;[294] this manygabled old house built by the simple country-folk of the long-past times, regardless of all the turmoil that was going on in cities and courts, is lovely still amidst all the beauty which these latter days[295] have created; and I do not wonder at our friends tending it carefully and making much of it.[296] It seems to me as if it had waited for these happy days, and held in it the gathered crumbs[297] of happiness of the confused and turbulent past."

She led me up close to the house, and laid her shapely sunbrowned hand and arm on the lichened wall as if to embrace it, and cried out, "O me![298] O me! How I love the earth, and the seasons, and weather, and all things that deal with it, and all that grows out of it,—as this has done!"

I could not answer her, or say a word. Her exultation[299] and pleasure were so keen and exquisite,[300] and her beauty, so delicate, yet so interfused[301] with energy, expressed it so fully, that any added word would have been commonplace[302] and futile. I dreaded lest the others should come in suddenly and break the spell she had cast about me;[303] but we stood there a while by the corner of the big gable of the house, and no one came. I heard the merry voices some way off presently, and knew that they were going along the river to the great meadow on the other side of the house and garden.

We drew back[304] a little, and looked up at the house: the door and the windows were open to the fragrant suncured air;[305] from the upper window-sills hung festoons of flowers in honour of the festival,[306] as if the others shared in the love for the old house.

"Come in," said Ellen. "I hope nothing will spoil it inside; but I don't think it will. Come! we must go back presently to the others. They have gone on to the tents; for surely they must have tents pitched for the haymakers — the house would not hold a tithe[307] of the folk, I am sure."

She led me on to the door, murmuring little above her breath[308] as she did so, "The earth and the growth of it and the life of it! If I could but say or show how I love it!"

We went in, and found no soul in any room as we wandered from room to room, — from the rose-covered porch to the strange and quaint garrets amongst the great timbers of the roof,[309] where of old time[310] the tillers and herdsmen of the manor slept, but which a-nights[311] seemed now, by the small size of the beds, and the litter of useless and disregarded matters — bunches of dying flowers, feathers of birds, shells of starlings' eggs, caddis worms[312] in mugs, and the like — seemed to be inhabited for the time[313] by children.

Everywhere there was but little furniture, and that only the most necessary, and of the simplest forms.[314] The extravagant love of ornament which I had noted in this people[315] elsewhere seemed here to have given place to the feeling that the house itself and its associations was the ornament of the country life amidst which it had been left stranded from old times,[316] and that to reornament it would but take away its use as a piece of natural beauty.

We sat down at last in a room over the wall which Ellen had caressed, and which was still hung with old tapestry,[317] originally of no artistic value, but now faded into pleasant grey tones[318] which harmonised[319] thoroughly well with the quiet of the place, and which would have been ill supplanted by brighter and more striking decoration.[320]

I asked a few random questions of Ellen as we sat there,[321] but scarcely listened to her answers, and presently became silent, and then scarce conscious of anything, but that I was there in that old room, the doves crooning from the roofs of the barn and dovecot beyond the window opposite to me.

My thought returned to me[322] after what I think was but a minute or two, but which, as in a vivid dream, seemed as if it had asted a long time, when I saw Ellen sitting, looking all the fuller of life and pleasure and desire from the contrast with the grey faded tapestry with its futile design,[323] which was now only bearable because it had grown so faint and feeble.

She looked at me kindly, but as if she read me through and through.[324] She said: "You have begun again your never-ending contrast between the past and this present. Is it not so?"

"True," said I. "I was thinking of what you, with your capacity and intelligence, joined to your love of pleasure, and your impatience of unreasonable restraint[325]—of what you would have been in that past. And even now, when all is won and has been for a long time,[326] my heart is sickened with thinking of all the waste of life that has gone on for so many years!"

"So many centuries," she said, "so many ages!"

"True," I said; "too true," and sat silent again.

She rose up and said; "Come, I must not let you go off into a dream again so soon. If we must lose you,[327] I want you to see all that you can see first before you go back again."

"Lose me?" I said—"go back again? Am I not to go up to the North with you? What do you mean?"

She smiled somewhat sadly, and said: "Not yet; we will not talk of that yet. Only, what were you thinking of just now?"

I said falteringly:[328] "I was saying to myself. The past, the present? Should she not have said the contrast of the present with the future: of blind despair with hope?"[329]

"I knew it," she said. Then she caught my hand and said excitedly, "Come, while there is yet time! Come!" And she led me out of the room; and as we were going downstairs and out of the house into the garden by a little side door which opened out of a curious lobby, she said in a calm voice, as if she wished me to forget her sudden nervousness:[330] "Come! we ought to join the others before they come here looking for us. And let me tell you, my friend, that I can see you are too apt to fall into mere dreamy musing; no doubt because you are not yet used to our life of repose amidst of energy; of work which is pleasure and pleasure which is work.[331]"

She paused a little, and as we came out into the lovely garden again, she said: "My friend, you were saying that you wondered what I should have been if I had lived in those past days of turmoil and oppression. Well, I think I have studied the history of them to know pretty well. I should have been one of the poor, for my father when he was working was a mere tiller of the soil.[332] Well, I could not have borne that;[333] therefore my beauty and cleverness and brightness" (she spoke with no blush or simper of false shame)[334] "would have been sold to rich men, and my life would have been wasted indeed; for I know enough of that to know that I should have had no choice, no power of will over my life; and that I should never have bought pleasure from the rich men, or even opportunity of action, whereby I might have won some true excitement. I should have been wrecked and wasted in one way or another, either by penury or by luxury.[335] Is it not so?"

"Indeed, it is," said I.

She was going to say something else, when a little gate in the fence, which led into a small elm-shaded field, was opened, and Dick came with hasty cheerfulness up the garden path, and was presently standing between us, a hand laid on the shoulder of each. He said: "Well, neighbours, I thought you two would like to see the old bouse quietly without a crowd in it. Isn't is a jewel of a house after its kind?[336] Well, come along, for it is getting towards dinner-time. Perhaps you, guest, would like a swim before we sit down to what I fancy will be[337] a pretty long feast?"

"Yes," I said, "I should like that."

"Well, good-bye for the present, neighbour Ellen," said Dick. "Here comes Clara to take care of you, as I fancy she is more at home[338] amongst our friends here."

Clara came out of the fields as he spoke; and with one look at Ellen I turned and went with Dick, doubting, if I must say the truth, whether I should see her again.[339]

【作者简介】 William Morris（威廉·莫理斯 1834—1896），是十九世纪后半叶英国著名的进步作家。他是个多才多艺、兴趣广泛的人。他既是小说家，政论家，诗人，又是建筑装饰与室内装饰设计家，木刻家，画家，印刷字型设计家与装帧艺术家。但在他丰富多采的一生中，最有意义的是他的进步的政治活动。

莫理斯出生于一个富裕的家庭，父亲是期票掮客。他象当时多数的资产阶级子弟一样，由贵族化的寄宿中学（Marlborough）升入牛津大学；在大学里他受到美学家罗斯金（John Ruskin）的影响，结交了许多爱好文学与艺术的学友，开始写诗，毕业后放弃了家庭期望他从事的牧师生涯，到一个专搞教堂重修工程的建筑师事务所里工作。这期间他受前拉菲尔画派（the Pre-Raphaelite School）的影响，与画家及诗人罗赛蒂（Dante Gabriel Rossetti）友善，对中世纪的哥德式（Gothic）宗教建筑产生了狂热的爱好，学习绘画，并从事建筑物的壁画装饰工作。1861 年他与友人们合组了莫理斯·马歇尔·福克纳公司，进行家具、金属用具的制造与绘画雕塑等工艺美术活动，设计了一些有名的糊墙花纸、壁毯、家具等。他反对室内装饰的蠢琢、浮华、庸俗的恶习，崇尚轻巧清新，实用朴雅，一时造成了社会上的新风气。他兼事书籍设计装帧、印刷铅字设计与织物印花染色，在繁忙的美术活动中创造出不少匠心独运的实用艺术品。与此同时，他从事文艺创作活动。起初他写以中世纪骑士美人生活为题材的故事诗（*The Defense of Guenevere and Other Poems, 1858; The Earthly Paradise,* 1868–1870）。接着他取材于冰岛和德国古代神话而创作史诗（*Sigurd the Volsung,* 1876; *The Fall of the Nibelungs,* 1876）。他的诗句逐渐由修饰纤细向纯真遒劲发展。此外他翻译了荷马的史诗《奥德赛》（*Odyssey*），维吉尔的史诗《伊尼特》（*Aeneid*），并把古英国史诗《贝奥乌夫》(*Beowulf*) 译为近代英语，也都能在原著上加上自己诗风的特色。当时英国资本主义制度的内在矛盾正在日益尖锐化，英国上层社会的腐蚀性也更加明显。他所精心设计的美术品只能供老爷太太们装饰豪华的客厅卧室。穷苦的人民连最起码的吃穿都顾不上，根本谈不到用他的花纸糊墙，或买他的花布做窗帘。而唯利是图的市侩们又大量仿制他的美术品，粗制滥造，骗取利润，糟践艺术家的才华。因此，象他自己所说的那样，他开始"从一个艺术家的眼光来看社会主义"；他认为艺术应该"表达人在劳动中所感到的愉快"，但是这样的"艺术不可能在市侩主义与追逐利润的现制度下取得真正的生命与成长"。痛心疾首的莫理斯在 1877 年就作了题为"装饰艺术"(*The Decorative Arts*) 的讲演，阐述美术家应当为美化人民的生活而服务的道理，并谴责资本主义剥削使艺术受到糟踏。经过了几年在自由主义的歧路上的徘徊之后，在英国工人斗争与马克思的著作的教育下，他终于走上了前进的道路。1883 年他加入了"民主协会"(Democratic Federation)；1884 年起他热切地阅读了马克思的著作，并于 1885 年脱离了受机会主义者摆布的"社会民主协会"(Social Democratic Federation)，参加并创建了"社会主义同盟"(Socialist League). 1886 年他写成了以巴黎公社革命运动为背景的长诗"希望的朝礼者"(*Pilgrims of Hope*)。从 1884 年起他进行了不计其数的街头宣传演讲与对贫民区工业区的访问座谈，并曾因此于 1885 年被捕。从 1885 到 1890 年他任"社会主义同盟"刊物《群福》(*The Commonweal*)的编者与主要撰稿人。1887 年他和工人群众一起走上街头，进行斗争，亲身经历了伦敦特拉法尔加广场工人集会遭受警察残酷镇压的惨案(即"血腥的星期日"事件)。这次资产阶级对工人运动的残酷镇压，成为他在 1890 年写的幻想小说《乌有乡消息》(*News from Nowhere*) 的重要情节。在此以前，他已写了幻想小说《约翰·鲍尔的梦》(*A Dream of John Ball*, 1888)，描绘英国十四世纪的农民武装起义。此外，他还写了一些富有战斗性的短诗，合称《社会主义者小唱》(*Chants for Socialists*)，表明他的诗才又有了新的发展。他在晚年脱离了"社会主义同盟"，另行组织了"汉麦斯密社会主义者协会"(Hammersmith Socialist Society)。1892 年英国政府欲以"桂冠诗人"的职位收买他，被他拒绝。1896 年他病死，享年六十三岁。

莫理斯虽然努力研读了马克思的著作与参加了工人运动，但受了他出身阶级与所受教育的限制，他并未能真正了解马克思主义。他过分着重美感，思想里还有怀恋中世纪的所谓纯朴生活的一面，空想的色彩较浓，对资产阶级的个人主义与自由主义也还未能分析批判。但他从一个前拉菲尔画派的唯美艺术家进而为英国工人运动的积极参与者，这一进步的发展在英国文学史上是少见的。晚年他在政治性小册子中强调工人阶级必须有自己的强大的先锋政党，反对“煤气与自来水式的社会主义”（即改良主义），反对梦想靠资产阶级国会来实现斗争目的，指出武装斗争的必要。这些看法说明他具有先进的思想。

【题解与注释】

“乌有乡消息”（*News from Nowhere*）是莫理斯在1890年先在“社会主义同盟”的机关刊物《群福》（*The Commonweal*）上连载，于1891年又以单行本行世的幻想小说。小说是以传统的记载梦境的形式，叙述作者设想的未来的“共产主义”英国的政治经济、风俗习尚、景物人情。书中的第一人称叙述者是十九世纪八十年代末伦敦的一个进步人士。一天晚上他在“社会主义同盟”与同志们讨论“革命后的明天会发生什么事情”，结局是各人看法不一，不欢而散。返寓后他思索久之，辗转入睡。第二天早上醒来却已身入了二十一世纪。英国的革命早已成功，英国人民已在理想的“共产主义”下生活了一百五十年左右了。在这个社会里机器、火车、大工厂都已不存在，城市乡村都安静清洁。大片的森林与草地又出现在泰晤士河两岸。人们已经不认得金钱是什么东西。青年男女都是美丽健康的，老人长寿而神智不衰。人们彬彬有礼，热爱生活，互以真诚相见，没有欺诈强夺，没有机心城府。人们都劳动，而且热爱劳动。人各有其专业，但又经常暂时互换专职，调剂身心。老少都爱美，个个都打扮得雅致大方。房屋家具、生活用具都是线条明朗，造型美观的。作者被乌有乡的青年们引导到“伦敦”去游逛，发现这万恶都市已面目全非，成为一个安详的小城市。在残留下来的“大英博物馆”里他遇见一个熟谙古今的老人，听他陈叙了革命的经过与新社会的各种制度风尚。原来英国是在“1952年”爆发了工人阶级的武装起义的。在起义前后，工人阶级由于幼稚和受改良主义思想影响，屡次受资产阶级的欺骗，遭受残酷的镇压与无耻的破坏，受了极大的损失，几乎功败垂成。（这一段叙述，表达了作者对于资产阶级的残暴狡诈的本性有一定的认识，并对改良主义对革命造成的危害有所体会。）在革命终于胜利后，也还经过了一段建立新的秩序与新的道德的时期，才形成作者所见的样子。

由于作者的复古主义思想，这个空想社会主义的乌托邦被描写成一种“小国寡民”不与外间往来的桃花源。被摒弃的不仅是资本主义制度，而也有科学与大机器生产。组成这个空想社会的基础的，只是手工工艺与简单体力劳动。至于在这样的生产基础上怎样能达到富足生活，作者则并无说明。在泰晤士河上虽有用“动力”驱策的无噪音无烟尘的船只，但农业却仍全然是手工化的。工厂被推到背景里去，火车是在哪里也看不到的，劳动者的自觉组织性纪律性也很少谈及。在作者的笔下，共产主义社会在人民武装斗争胜利之后就自然出现了，他不知道还必须经过一个无产阶级专政和继续深入进行阶级斗争的时期；而这个社会出现之后，又是毫无发展的，没有外部敌人，没有内部矛盾，没有生产斗争，没有前进的动力，人们满足于现状，社会陷于停顿。今日看来，共产主义的实际决非空想社会主义者所能梦见。

作者在梦乡的短暂盘桓，随着在泰晤士河上驾小舟溯流而上、渐渐达到了欢乐的高峰，最后在一所旧时代遗留下来的大宅子里，举行了欢庆丰收的晚宴，而也就在这里作者被突然从美好的梦境唤回到资本主义英国丑恶的现实。梦乡一切，宛然在目。他耳边响着梦中相识的友人 Ellen 的叮咛："回去吧，因为看见过我们而更愉快，因为给自己的斗争添加了一线希望而更高兴吧！好好生活下去，不管要受到什么样的痛苦，付出什么样的劳力，也要一点点地争取一个充满同志爱的，充满休息与幸福的新的一天的到来！"

作者的文笔清新而有力。他反对在十九世纪末年英国流行的油滑、浮夸的报纸文体，追求文学的拙朴之美，为此而多用较老的民间说法，复活了简单有力的中古词汇，文章自成一体。他叙述特拉法尔加广场大屠杀的一节，可作为对血腥镇压的控诉书来读。作者也有他的缺点——如同他的工艺美术作品一样，在某些地方，终不免令人感到刻意摹古，失于做作。人们甚至有以"假古董式的英文"（"Wardour Street English"）相讥者。但这一点在本书并不明显。

这里所选的是原书第十七章，第六章，第七章，第十四章中片段与第三十一章的全文。第十七章叙述革命的经过，在原书中是在作者见到博物馆中的老人时，由老人补述的；现为了阅读方便，转置篇首。每个片段的小标题或用原章名，或略加更动，或另起新名以与内容符合。

[HOW IT ALL BEGAN]

这是原书十七章 How the Change Came 中的一段，叙述作者在梦中来到二十一世纪的英国，在大英博物馆原址遇到了一个一百零五岁的老人 Hammond，和他畅谈往事。老人详细告诉他约一百五十年前革命是如何由非暴力走向暴力，终于推翻了统治阶级，在英国建立了"共产主义"社会的。这里选的一段集中描述了触发武装革命的 Trafalgar 广场大屠杀。作者虽把它安排在想像中的 1952 年，实际上是以作者亲身经历的 1887 年 11 月 13 日 Trafalgar 广场屠杀案（即历史上有名的"血腥的星期日"—Bloody Sunday）为蓝本的。

1. Trafalgar Square [trəˈfælgə ˈskwεə]**:** 伦敦的特拉法尔加广场，为纪念纳尔逊海军上将在 Trafalgar 战役中击败法国舰队而命名，广场上有高大的纪念石柱，柱顶立着纳尔逊的铜像。从十九世纪以来，Trafalgar Square 一直是伦敦劳动人民举行政治性游行示威并与反动军警搏斗的地方。

2. bickering: 争吵。

3. civic: 市政的，民政的。

4. the said meeting: 上述的集会。

5. bludgeons: 粗棒。

6. *mêlée* [ˈmelei]**:** 混战，交锋。

7. cudgelling [ˈkʌdʒliŋ]**:** 棒击。

8. some hundred: 约一百。

9. gaol: = jail，监狱。

10. Manchester ['mæntʃistə]**:** 曼彻斯特市，英国的重要工业城市。作者厌恶资本主义工业城市的喧嚣浊恶，故在小说中使大工业城市在革命后都被疏散改建，成为小城市。

11. Thus the 'lesson' began: 本书上文曾说资产阶级叫嚣要对要求"和平变革"的工人"给以教训"。("The people must be taught a lesson.")这两次对群众集会的镇压就是"教训"的开始。

12. the whole country was thrown into a ferment by this: 举国为此惶惶不可终日。*ferment* ['fə:ment]，骚动。

13. some rough organization: 某种粗略的组织工作。

14. to retort on the authorities: 向当局进行反击。

15. Then a place of crowded streets: 在作者笔下伦敦在革命后改建为小城市，狭窄拥塞的闹市廛街都一扫而空。

16. too big for the bludgeon-armed police to cope with: 群众人数太多，不是以短棒武装起来的警察所能应付得了的。

17. dry-blow fighting: 动拳斗殴。

18. crushed to death in the throng: 在人堆里被挤死。

19. as far as it went: 就其本身说来。

20. a state of turmoil ['tə:mɔil]**:** 骚乱状态。

21. the executive [ig'zekjutiv]**:** 执政当局。

22. mass :*v.* 集中。

23. threats of riots: 骚动的威胁，骚动的可能性。

24. popular: 人民的。

25. convention: 大会，集会。

26. the Federation of Combined Workmen: 各业工人联合会。

27. sat under the old revolutionary name of the Committee of Public Safety: 以"公安委员会"的古老的革命的名称开会。("公安委员会"是法国大革命时的革命权力机构。)

28. drilled and armed body of men: 经过操练，配有武装的队伍。

29. aggressive measures: 进攻性的措施。

30. placarded the walls: 在墙上贴大幅告示。

31. somewhat vague appeals: 措词略嫌含混的呼吁书。

32. to be trampled upon: 被践踏，被欺凌。

33. the day fortnight ['fɔ:tnait]**:** 两周后。

34. the last-mentioned skirmish: 上述的混战。

35. meantime: 与此同时。

36. business came pretty much to an end: 商业活动差不多终止了。

37. then, as always hitherto: 以前差不多一直如此，当时仍是如此。

38. the masters: 指资产阶级统治者。

39. clamoured for: 高声叫嚷，要求…

40. repressive measures: 镇压措施。

41. an extra body of police: 临时募集的警察队伍。

42. many of these were strong, well-fed, full-blooded young men, and had plenty of stomach for fighting: 其中许多人是身强力壮，营养充足的血气方刚的年青人，很想尝一下打仗的味道。

43. getting full powers voted to it by the Parliament for suppressing any revolt: 使国会投票通过授予政府全权镇压任何叛乱。

44. bringing up: 召集，调集。

45. almost as large a one: = almost as large a meeting，差不多同样盛大的一次集会。

46. which went off peaceably on the whole, as no opposition to it was offered: 由于没有人试图阻挠开会，总的说来集会是和平地过去了。

47. the people woke up to find that they were hungry: 本书上文里谈到1952年是经济危机的一年，工厂纷纷倒闭，大批工人失业，衣食不继。这里谈他们虽然开会成功，但并未能解决饥饿问题。

48. if you please: 换句话说；如果你愿意的话，也可以这样说。

49. what for goodwill, what for fear fear:（= what with … what with），半出于实好行善，半出于恐惧。

50. the authorities of the parishes: 教区当局。（英国地方行政，郡 county 下面分为教区 parish，约等于一个乡。教区当局除负责地方行政外，还掌管“救济”大权。）因为革命后这种统治机构与伪善的“救济”制度都已消灭，老人认为来访的客人必然不了解它是怎么一回事，但又没有时间详细解释，故接下去说“我现在没有时间解释这是什么”。

51. willy-nilly: 情愿也好，不情愿也好；不得不。

52. provisions: 食品，供应品。

53. its feeble national workshops:（政府设立的）薄弱的国家工厂。（上文说到在1952年以前英国资产阶级政府为了缓和阶级矛盾，欺骗人民，设立了一些“国家工厂”，妄图推行所谓“国家社会主义”。）

54. provision stores: 粮食仓库。

55. so far, so good: 至此为止，一切都还算不错。

56. the Monday in question: 我们谈到的这个星期一。

57. pillage: 掠夺，抢粮。

58. emboldened by the wavering conduct of the authorities，由于当局的犹豫不决而胆壮起来。

59. deputation: 代表队，执行任务的小组。

60. all necessary gear: 一切必要工具。

61. clear out: 出清货物。

62. leaving papers with the shop managers: 给店铺经理开了收据。

63. take possession of: 占领，征用。

64. sack: 洗劫。

65. at this last stroke: 指老人刚叙述过的征用了大商店的粮食分发给平民。*stroke* = 一击，一个行动。

66. blazed into the fury of frightened people ...: 反动派的报纸次日大肆恫吓，表现出由于畏惧而产生的暴怒。

67. unless 'order were at once restored': 引号以内系引反动报纸原来的话，云若不"马上恢复秩序，"则将如何如何。*were* 是虚拟语态。

68. wait on: 拜见。

69. fall on: 进攻，袭击。

70. 'the incendiaries': 纵火犯，放火的暴徒。引号说明这是上文 leading commercial people（商界领袖人士）口里所用的词，指群众的领袖们。

71. the deftest in their art that the country could furnish: 这两三个军人是英国所能找到的最谙习战争的艺术的军人。

72. says a contemporary eye-witness: 据当时目睹者的记述…。作者利用这一类插入语与引语，给他的假托出自乌有乡一老人之口的革命爆发情况的追述增加了生动诩实的感觉，刻划了革命与反革命的尖锐对立，也为故事抹上了沧桑话旧的情调。例如这里 contemporary（同代的，同时期的）一词，就使读者感到事情发生在很多年以前。这类插入语下文中很多，不再一一指出。

73. smiling and satisfied: 二形容词系紧跟上文动词 came away 的表语。意为"代表团会见当局后退出时，咸微笑满意"。

74. anti-popular: 反人民的。

75. left London ... for their country seats ...,: 离开伦敦前往自己在乡间的府邸。

76. proclaimed a state of siege: 宣布戒严。

77. the absolutist governments on the Continent: 大陆欧洲的君主专制国家政府。(指十九世纪的德奥等君主国。)

78. in ecstasies: 欣喜若狂，满纸呓语。

79. came to the front: 出头，挤到前列。

80. keep their opinions to themselves or their immediate circle: 把意见藏在自己心里或仅谈给最亲近的人听。

81. once for all: 一了百了，彻底、永远地。

82. took no visible action: 未采取任何明显行动。

83. minor newspapers: 较小的报纸，只有较小的报纸攻击这位将军，说明最大的反动报纸已知道他未采取任何明显的行动是有用意的，是在准备更阴险残酷的大镇压。

84. a plot was hatching: = a plot was being hatched. 正在搞着阴谋。动词 to hatch（孵育）常可用于主动与被动两种语态，如 the eggs hatched = the eggs were hatched.

85. had now gone too far to draw back: 已经把事情做得太过，无法回头。

86. a miserable driblet:（食物的来源）少得可怜。driblet，涓满。

87. when all is said:（语气短句），充其量。

88. quarter: 城市的一个区。

89. breathing space: 喘口气的工夫，转圜的时间。

90. did not meddle with all this in the least in the world: 一点也没有来干涉。

91. the provinces: 各省份，指英国首都以外的各郡市。

92. Glasgow [ˈglɑːsgəu]: 格拉斯哥市，苏格兰工业城市。

93. Bristol [ˈbristl]: 布列斯特尔，英格兰大工业城市。

94. the meeting: 即上文所述公安委员会决定在第一次特拉法尔加广场集会后二周召开的大会。

95. the greater part of the Committee: 公共安全委员会大多数的委员。

96. armed somehow or other: 杂拼乱凑地武装起来。

97. body of police: 大批警察。

98. by far the greater part: 绝大多数。

99. from various quarters: 从各方面。

100. had no idea of: 一点也不知道。

101. red-coats: 兵士，军队。到十九世纪为止英国军队制服还是红色的。作者虽虚构二十世纪的事，仍假定军队制服颜色未变。

102. influx: 涌入，蜂拥而至的人群。

103. working through: = working one's way through，推挤出一条路来穿行过去。

104. had scarcely ... when ...: 还未及…就已经…。

105. Parliament House：国会大楼，现通称 Parliament。

106. Dung Market: 粪便市场。

107. embankment: 堤岸。

108. the Thames [ðəˈtemz]: 泰晤士河。

109. would not or could not budge: 或则不肯退让一步，或则无法退让一步。

110. the height of terror: 最大的恐怖。

111. the monument which then stood there: 指纳尔逊的纪念柱与铜像。不言而喻，作者痛恨这个大英帝国的元勋的纪念柱，并预料人民革命成功后会把它毁掉。

112. hidden fire: 隐藏的火力。（指全副武装的军警。）

113. aforesaid：如上所述地。这个词通常当形容词用，这里当副词用，表示说话的人用的是通俗口语式的语言。

114. no sooner ... than ...: 一俟…马上…。

115. which something, very few heard: = very few heard the things that he read，他所宣读的东西很少有人听清是什么。作者在这段叙述中大量使用连绵不断的长句与非限制性定语从句。这种笔法给人一种娓娓不倦、历历如绘的感觉。

116. else: 假如不然的话。这种用法也是通俗而古拙的。

117. took it as ...: 把它当作…。**of some sort:** 某种的。

118. machines: 指杀伤力极大的机关枪。（即下文 mechanical guns，今通称 machine guns.）作者预见到这类武器必然会被反动统治阶级用来残杀人民。

119. Throw yourself down!: 扑倒！卧倒！

120. no one scarcely could throw himself down: 谁也没法卧倒。这里连用两个否定语气的词（no 与 scarcely）来表示否定，是不合正规语法的，但却十足是一个未受很多教育的人的口吻。

121. I heard a sharp order given: 我听见有人厉声发命令。

122. bodily: 有形体地，真实地。

123. deep lanes were mowed amidst the thick crowd:（机关枪）在密集的人群中扫射出了条条深长的血路。

124. the dead and dying: 已死者与将死者。这两个词是形容词实义化了当名词用。

125. our armed men: 我方的武装人员（指人民中的配有武装的人）。

126. cheered wildly: 狂呼。（此处 cheer 不作"欢呼"解，指为鼓舞自己士气而发的呼声。）

127. a scattering fire: 散乱的射击。

128. let the butts of their guns fall: 听任枪托降下（即不再做瞄准、准备放的姿态）。

129. set it going: 开动它（开始射击）。

130. an officer too: 还是个军官呢！

131. that first discharge: 第一次开枪。

132. not feeling the ground under me: 脚底下没觉得踩到地面。（形容大屠杀之后人们震惊失措，狂奔乱挤，把叙述人拥出了广场。）

133. what with rage and terror and despair: 既由于愤怒，又由于恐惧，又由于绝望。what with ... and ... 一则因为…一则因为…。

134. the slain: 被杀死的人。

135. that shooting during a minute: 那延续一分钟的枪击。

136. prodigious: 惊人的，巨大的。

137. it was not easy to come at the truth about it: 欲弄清事情真相不是容易的。

138. outright: 当时，马上。

139. I listened, trembling with excitement: 至此，引号部分完。

140. put an end to: 结束。

141. drink this glass to the memory of: 为纪念…而饮一杯酒。

A LITTLE SHOPPING

这是原书第六章（同名）的一部分，作者从十九世纪末叶的英国一梦而进入了革命胜利后的英国，与新相识的 Dick 驱车入市，观光新的伦敦的市容，初次进入"各取所需"的"商店"。

142. Piccadilly [ˌpikəˈdili]: = Piccadilly Circus. 辟卡迪里转盘道口，伦敦的著名繁华商场区域。作者在想象中已把革命后的伦敦加以改建，使房屋美雅，街道宽洁，与十九世纪末年伦敦的廛舍丑陋，街巷狭污成一对照。作者在建筑学上提倡实用自然之美，反对过事雕琢，繁琐缛丽的维多利亚时期的建筑趣味，他依照自己的趣味“改造”了伦敦。

143. the lower part of these I should have called shops, if it had not been that, as far as I could see, the people were ignorant of the arts of buying and selling: 倘若不是因为就我所见，人们根本不懂得买与卖的艺术的话，我本会把这些房屋的下半部称为商店的。（意谓看房屋陈列货物象是商店，但看人物行径，却又不像。此段描写可与《镜花缘》中“君子国”一段对照来看。）

144. fronts: 店面，门面。

145. just like the real thing: 人们虽不懂买卖生意，却也伫立店门观看货物，或入内取货外出，像煞是真在购物。

146. arcade: 柱廊，临街罩廊。

147. of the kind I was now prepared to expect: 其建筑风格，已为我现在所习以为常。（指作者所极力推崇的、只有在乌有之乡才能见到的实用、自然、不事雕琢的建筑风格。）

148. Dick: 为作者某一天一觉醒来，发现自己到了乌有乡之后，第一个认识的青年男友。

149. on a different plan from most others: 与大多数其它市场构筑不相同。

150. guest-houses: 宾馆，招待所。

151. to drift up hither: 游逛到这里（伦敦）来。

152.folk are very thick upon the ground: 人口很多。（这里用古老的英国本土词 folk 一词而不用从古法语来的 people，标帜了作者的散文风格。）

which you will see evidence of presently: 此事你不久就可看到明证。

153. how long a tradition would last: 一个传统会延续多么长久。

154. the ghost of London: 乌有之乡的伦敦已经变为玲珑美丽的小型城市，非复当年的庞大喧嚣的都会，故称它为旧伦敦的“幽灵”。

155. for ought I know: = for aught I know. 就我所知道的一点点来说。

156. handsomer goods: 较精巧细致的货物。

157. the Houses-of-Parliament market: 参阅前章 How It All Began 中 *Dung Market* 条。

158. set out: 摆摊，陈设。

159. Perhaps you would like to do a little shopping, as 'tis called: 也许你愿意去买点什么吧？ *as 'tis called* = as it is called，象人们习惯所说的那样。do a little shopping 在乌有之乡已是通用的说法，Dick 怕异乡来的客人不习惯于这个说法，故解释一下。在乌有乡没有钱，也不用 buy 这个词。

160. my rough blue duds: 我身上穿的粗蓝布衣裳。作者极力夸饰乌有之乡中人们生活富足，人人可以穿华丽大方工精料美的衣服，与当时英国劳动人民穿的衣服成一对比。

161. come across: 碰到，遇见。

162. as seemed likely: = which seemed likely，这事是很可能的。

163. be shown about as a curiosity: 被当作一件希罕的东西来到处展览。

164. unbusinesslike: 不会办事的，此处指非同凡俗的。

165. a discharged ship's purser: 被解雇的船舶出纳员。（指作者当时身上穿得很寒酸。）

166. But in spite of all that had happened, my hand went down into my pocket again: 尽管已经出过多少次笑话，我的手还是不由自主地伸到口袋里去（摸钱）。这是说他已有经验，知道在乌有乡是没有金钱也不使用金钱的，但商品社会的习惯，使他不由得先摸一下袋里有钱没有。

167. Hammersmith [ˈhæməsmiθ]: 伦敦的一个郊区。讲故事人在一天晚上在 Hammersmith 自己家中睡觉后清早醒来发现自己到了乌有之乡的一所宾馆里。地方仍在 Hammersmith，景象却已全非。

168. the pretty Annie: 他在宾馆中遇到的一个年轻女郎。

169. My face fell fifty per cent: 我的脸顿然拉长了一半。（表示沮丧。）

170. beholding: 看见。这是较古的文字中常用的词；William Morris 喜用这类词，使文章的风格古朴。

171. hilloa [hiˈləu]: = hullo，喂。

172. Is it a wasp? 是被黄蜂蜇了吗？

173. I've left it behind: 我把它（钱）留在家里了。说的人指钱，听的人不明白，因此说"不管你把什么东西留在家里了，你都可以在这市场上再得到，因此别发愁了"。

174. I had come to my senses by this time: 我到此时已经明白过来了。（想起了在乌有之乡是不使用钱的。）

175. had no mind for another lecture on social economy and the Edwardian coinage: 不想再听一次关于社会经济学与爱德华国王年代的钱币的讲课。（他上次把袋中的钱拿出来"付帐"时，曾被乌有乡的新朋友好好地教育了一顿。）

176. My clothes—Couldn't I?: = My clothes are rather shabby. Couldn't I get some new clothes? 这种行文中的简略，需通过对上下文的了解来推测领会。

177. antiquarian: 考古家，博古的人。（乌有乡是数百年以后的英国，讲故事的人一梦到了彼土，连身上的衣服都成了考古家研究的对象了。）

178. to set myself up for a scarecrow: 把我自己弄成个吓乌鸦用的假人，意为特别丑的人。

179. I had got across some ineradicable prejudice: 我碰上了一种无法消除的偏见。

180. it wouldn't do to ...: …是不行的。

181. you may as well see what the inside of these booths is like: 你既已来此，不如也看一下这些铺子内部是什么样子。

182. some tobacco and a pipe: 一些烟丝和一只烟斗。*tobacco* 这里指烟斗用的烟草。

183. what was I thinking of, not asking you before?: 我刚才想什么去了？都忘了问你是否需要烟丝。

184. Bob: Dick 的朋友。

185. we non-smokers are a selfish lot: 我们这种不吸烟的人是一群自私的人，意为不关心吸烟的人的痛痒。

186. Therewith: 这样说着，于是。这也是为 William Morris 所喜用的古字之一。

187. drew rein: 拉紧缰绳。（使马停下来。）

188. quoth（拟古）**:** = said.

189. fell to patting the horse: 开始用手抚拍马。

190. "What a beautiful creature!": "多美的生物呀！" creature 可指人与兽。故下文 Dick 故意误解。

191. old Greylocks: 老灰鬃（马名）。

192. Goldylocks: 金发的人（临时编的名字，与 Dick 的话针锋相对）。

193. 'Tis a good job there are so many of them that every Jack may have his Jill, else I fear that we should get fighting for them: 幸好女人很多，每个男孩子都可以得到自己的女孩子，不然我怕我们就会为她们打起架来了。（Jack 为常用的男人名，Jill 为常用女人名，现被用来指任何一个少年和姑娘。）下面一段说出作者对新社会的道德风格的想象是很受限制的。

194. in a still more sombre tone: 用更加阴郁的口气说。

195. only a month ago there was a mishap down by us: 就只一个月以前我们那边出了一件不幸的事。*down by us* 是较土气的说法。

196. that ... as it were, put out the sunlight for us for a while: 这件事，可以这样说，使我们有一段时间生活中失去了阳光（使我们感到不幸福）。

197. without any pretence of showiness, but otherwise not very different to what I had been used to: 没有任何故作排场气派的地方，但其它方面则与我所习见的店铺没有很大的不同。different to，现通用 different from.（作者痛恨维多利亚时期英国资产阶级崇尚雕琢浮夸的庸俗审美观念，主张建筑与装饰应在简单与实用的基础上略事淡雅的修饰，取得一种自然古朴的美。此处所谓其它方面与习见的店铺没有不同，正为下文"买东西不要钱"的根本不同打下伏笔。）

198. little neighbours: 乌有乡中没有地位尊卑之别，人们见面互以"邻居"或"朋友"相称。

199. demure alertness: 娴静庄重而应对敏捷。

200. fell to staring at my outlandish attire: 睁着大眼直盯着我的异乡人的装束看个不停。to fall to doing something，开始做某事。

201. playing at keeping shop: 玩"开铺子"。

202. Latakia [ˌlætəˈki(ː)ə]**:** 一种高级土耳其烟草，以叙利亚的 Latakia 港为集散地而得名。

203. wondering whether I should get anything but makebelieve: 心想可能只是装模作样地哄一下人，不会真买到烟草的。

204. cram: 装满，塞满。

205. my piece of cotton print which does duty with me for a tobacco pouch: 我那块权充烟荷包用的印花棉布。（作者极力刻划在乌有之乡人们生活一切都是美的，连最简单的生活用品都是如此，因而他从十九世纪英国带去的一切东西相形之下都是俗陋不堪，使他自惭形秽。）

206. tripped: 以轻巧的步子疾行。（作者喜欢多用一些"雅""美"的字来代替常用的简单字，这是他文体的一个特点，在当时也曾成为一种风尚，今日看来不能说不是一种文病。此处的 trip 与上文的 demure, prettily, dainty，下文中的 quaint，等均属此类。）

207. morocco: 摩洛哥皮，山羊皮。

208. just come in: 才来到；才进货。这里 come 是过去分词形容词。

209. mounted in gold sprinkled with little gems: 镶着金，嵌着小粒宝石。

210. Dear me!: 惊叹语。

211. set eyes on: 一眼看到，见到。

212. altogether too grand for me: 太好了，我不配用它。altogether（全然），在这里用来加强语气。

213. dashed: 气沮。

214. forgot my caution：一时疏忽，忘了应该警惕的事。（即在乌有乡不能提"钱"这样东西。）

215. another exhibition of extinct commercial morality：再一次流露出已绝迹的市侩道德观念。（即购物必须付钱。）

216. held my tongue：缄口不言。

217. effusively：滔滔地，谢不绝口地。

218. not without a qualm of doubt as to whether I shouldn't find myself before a magistrate presently：心中不免疑惧，是否不久会被捉去对簿公堂。qualm 恶心；良心不安。

219. I have been a great traveller：我走的路真是不算近了。（讲故事的人实际上足迹未出伦敦，但在时间上已经飞历了一个时代；他这里语义双关，感慨系之，听的人是个天真的小姑娘，只可能从字面来理解，故下文称之为"纯为礼貌之故而说的谎话"。）

220. please to drink a glass to us before you go：请在离开以前为我们（的健康）饮一杯酒。please to do something 在现代英语中通常说 please do something 而不用 to。

221. nothing loth：（拟古，loth 同 loath），很愿意地，求之不得地。

222. thinks I：这种动词与人称的组合在较古的文体与方言中是常见的，在现代规范英语中是不合语法的。此处显然是作者故意使用，以求古拙之趣。时态从过去改成现在，是为了叙述生动之故。

223. the grapes of the Rhine：莱茵河的葡萄。（莱茵河两岸多种葡萄，盛产葡萄酒。作者梦中一饮此酒，觉得香味酷似莱茵河德境威斯巴登附近所产有名的 Steinberger 白葡萄酒中的上品，故下文云云。）

224. made a mental note ...：暗自在心里记下…

225. rot-gut："烂肠酒"，劣质烈性酒。（犹如我国俗语"酒是穿肠毒药"。）

226. lemonade：柠檬水。

227. ginger-beer：（或 ginger-ale）姜汁汽水。

228. neither have children's tastes changed much：（事虽隔世，名酒的味道仍如一）而孩子们的口味也并没有变。

229. we gave them good day：道"日安"。（寒暄，告别。）

[THE ROAD MENDERS]

"修路的人"。这是原书第七章"Trafalgar Square"（"特拉法尔加广场"）的最后一段，叙述作者在"买"了烟草之后继续驱车游览伦敦"市"容，路上遇见一群健康愉快的修路者。作者抒情地讴歌了在他的空想社会中已经成为最大的愉快的简单体力劳动。这样的对新社会劳动者面貌的设想，显然是远远不足的。

230. came on: 碰到。

231. hitherto: 迄今为止。

232. set to: 动起手来，下力干活。

233. looking much like a boating party at Oxford would have looked in the days I remembered, and not more troubled with their work: 看来正象在我记得的旧时代里牛津大学的一批划船运动员，而且是同样兴高采烈，不感劳累。

234. outer raiment: 外衣。（raiment 也是作者故意使用的"雅字"。）

235. akin to: 类似于，接近于。

236. the Golden Dustman of Hammersmith: 汉迈斯密区的穿金绣衣服的倒垃圾人。（在本书前面第三章里，作者曾谈到在乌有乡的汉迈斯密区宾馆里有个倒垃圾人，名叫 Henry Johnson，全身衣服都用金线绣花。）

237. had hints about it of ...: 隐约能令人猜出里面装着…。

238. smote:（*smite* 的过去时态），打，击。（古词。）

239. and as handsome clean-built fellows as you might find a dozen of in a summer day: 象这样面貌清秀身材匀称的小伙子，敢说决不会比你在一个美好的夏日里找到的任何十二个小伙子要差。

240. saw our way stopped: 发现我们的路被挡住了。

241. stayed his pick: 停住了镐。*stay* 作"停住，阻止"解，在现代只用于文艺性语言中。

242. Spell ho, mates!: 伙计们，歇一下！

243. here are neighbours want to get past: 这儿有乡亲们要过去。（在 neighbours 后按规范语法应有关系代词 who. 这种省略出现在随意的语言及方言中。）

244. whereon: 此际，这时，这样一来。（古词，现代除文学及方言外很少使用。）

245. easing our wheels over the half undone road: 推挽车轮使能滚过已被半挖开的路面。

246. had taken to his jog-trot: 进入慢步小跑。*to take to*，开始。

247. right down:（强调语气词），真正，简直，地道。

248. it's right down good sport trying how much pick-work one can get into an hour: 试试看自己一小时里抡起铁镐能干多少活儿，真是快事。

249. it is not a mere matter of strength getting on quickly with such work: 要想干这种活儿干得快，不是光拼力气就可以的。*it* 代表真正主语 *getting on.*

250. that seems a pity: 这真可惜。（在乌有乡里虽有劳动的分工，但不同工种的人常交换工作，以免单调枯燥，影响身心的全面发展。Dick 因此认为异乡客人没有干过抡镐挖石头的力气活是很可惜的。他自己是个划船的人，故下文谈到某次在某工地干挖土的工作时姿式不对，别人打趣他说："划得很好！""把背部力气使上去！"等。）

251. stroke: 划船时靠舵手最近的一个桨手，责任最大。

252. bow: 离船首最近的桨手。

253. have ... on: 有…在进行着。

254. and good fellows merry about us:（ = and when we have good fellows merry about us），当我们周围有好小伙子们在开心地（干活）。

255. ponder: 沉思。（又一个"雅字"。）

UP THE THAMES

这是原书第二十四章的一段，述说作者与乌有乡的几个青年男女乘小舟溯泰晤士河而上，游览乡间景色。在文中作者幻想地描绘了被资本主义物质文明破坏了的英国乡野在革命之后恢复了天然的美丽，表达了他的"返朴归真"的幻想。

256. a jewel of a summer day: 象宝石一样明朗美好的夏日。英国气候阴湿寒冷，夏季为四季中较晴爽宜人的季节。下文 these islands 指英国"三岛"而言。

257. without dispute: 无庸置辩地。

258. a light wind blew from the west: 在西欧各国西风因墨西哥湾暖流的缘故带来温暖晴朗的天气。

259. we no more longed for rain than we feared it: 非但不渴求下雨，而且还怕下雨了。

260. a-longing: = longing.（作者喜用这种较古的构词方法。在动词现在分词前面任意加前缀 a-（= on），在今日只见于诗歌等文学作品与方言中。）

261. Burning ... the boughs: 此句意思是：尽管阳光灼人，但惠风清新，使人几乎渴望炎热的午后的到来，并想通过河畔树木枝叶空隙处看看正在吐穗扬花的大片麦地。

262. No one unburdened with very heavy anxieties could have felt otherwise than happy that morning: 在那天上午，任何一个人，如果没有焦虑的重担压在心上，他是只会感到快乐而不会感到别样的。

263. come across: 碰到。

264. Clara: Dick 的妻子。

265. jealous of our up-river festival: 主人已为客人安排好在河的上游举行宴游，故不愿他处处留连景色。jealous of 此处意为“顾惜”，“为…而担心”。

266. so far from: 远不是这样，不但不…。

267. dressed specially for the occasion: 专门为了进行割饲草的劳动而穿上特别的衣着。

268. craft: 船只（复数，集合名词）。

269. means of propulsion: 推动力，（车船的）动力设备。

270. force-barge: 能力驳船。（作者痛恨火车轮船的污浊与噪音，幻想在新社会中能返朴归真，取消这些东西而改用马车帆船之类简单的交通工具。但他也知道这样不能满足运输的需要，就想象用一种无声的洁净的能力装置来推动船只。）

271. betray myself: 暴露自己的无知。

272. Bisham: 地名，有著名的古教堂。作者对资本主义文明的另一深恶痛绝之点，是许多古老美丽的建筑园林被破坏、丑化或划为禁区而不能为人民大众所欣赏享用。他幻想在革命后的乐土中这些建筑园林都被加意保护，向人民公开。本书中屡次谈到这一点。

273. careful and appreciative habitation: 留意的爱护的居住，意为居住者爱好这些屋子，处处小心，不使受损。

274. third quarter: 相当于阴历每月十五到二十三左右。

275. it was all one to Dick whether ...: 究竟是…还是…对 Dick 都一样。

276. a great pace: = at a great pace，迅速地。

277. Hurley: 与第 4 行 Henley 均泰晤士河上游地名。下文中还有一些地名。

278. Actual daylight failed us ...: 白昼过去，夜晚降临。（在夏季这比日没时间要晚很多，故曰 actual daylight.）

279. the new order of things: 新秩序（指新的社会制度）。下面一句大意是：在作者“前世”时泰晤士河两岸的 Reading, Caversham 等地工厂商号仓库等建筑密集，破坏了自然的美景，现在他很想看一下新社会怎样恢复了河岸的原来面目，可惜天太黑了，看不清楚。但从空气清新，没有恶臭之气来判断，资本主义工业的污染已被消灭了。

280. wearing off: 磨掉，消失。

281. languid acquiescence: 消极被动的对事物的接受与赞同。

AN OLD HOUSE AMONGST NEW FOLK

这是原书第三十一章的全文，作者终于到达泰晤士河上游某地的一古老的宅舍。（实即作者 1871—1878 居住的 Kelmscott Manor.）好客的乌有乡人们为他安排了欢畅的宴游，但是他在梦乡游目骋怀的日子已尽，即将告别知己，回到污恶的维多利亚王朝的英国去了。“乐莫乐兮新相知，悲莫悲兮生别离”，怅惘迷离之情，溢于言表。在这一段文章里作者愤怒地抨击了资本主义社会使劳动者变成牛马，使美貌与青春成为满足富有者淫欲的商品。但是写得有点缠绵，作者笔下的新女性不够刚强。

282. Ellen：是乌有乡一个女郎；在泰晤士的旅程中作者与她相遇，她由于同情这异乡客，驾舟追来，与他结伴同游。

283. I had rather not: = I had rather not wait for them. 我宁愿不等候他们。

284. thither: 通向那里。（较古的词。）

285. the road they knew: = the road that they (my feet) knew. 作者在乌有乡来到了旅程终点的古老宅舍，因景象全非，不辨路途；但是由于这房子是他在"前生"所熟识与热爱的，故两只脚不知不觉地随着走熟了的小径走去。

286. backwater: 河水回滞处，港汊。

287. almost without my will: 差不多是不由自主地。*will*，意志力。

288. the old house to which fate in the shape of Dick had so strangely brought me in this new world of men: 在这人类的新世界里，命运之神假手 Dick 把我离奇地带到了这所古老的房舍。*in the shape of*...，以…的形式出现。

289. redolent of the June flowers: 由于开满了六月的鲜花而芬芳馥郁。

290. save that of beauty: = except the thought of beauty.

291. the swifts: 雨燕。

292. And the house itself was a fit guardian for all the beauty of this heat of summer: 意谓房子本身古老美丽，足以衬托百花齐放，众鸟飞鸣的盛夏美景，故曰不愧为此美景的守护者。

293. once again Ellen echoed my thoughts: 作者经过泰晤士河上几天的旅程，与 Ellen 朝夕相处，感情渐深。到此时已经心心相印；凡作者心有所动，Ellen 便相感应。尤其是对于即将到来的永别，Ellen 更似乎已有所知。下文中此种情况很多。

294. for to see: = (in order) to see.（方言用法，现代语法认为不规范。）

295. these latter days: 指革命后的日子。

296. making much of it: 重视它，把它很当一回事。

297. crumbs: 面包屑，碎片。**the gathered crumbs of happiness**，意谓旧时代中充满了苦难酸辛，人民生活中仅有一些破碎的欢乐，似乎都收聚在这所古老的房子中了。

298. O me!: 惊叹语。

299. exultation: 大喜，兴高采烈。

300. exquisite: 优雅，超绝。

301. interfused: 渗融。

302. commonplace: 庸俗，平淡无奇。

303. break the spell she had cast about me: 打破她在我周围造成的神奇境界。*spell*，魔力。

304. draw back: 退回，走回。

305. sun-cured air: 由于阳光蒸射而产生了香味的空气。*cure* 原意为用盐、香料腌渍或用烟熏等法处理食品以利保藏。

306. the festival: 是泰晤士河两岸人们为庆祝收获举行的盛大狂欢节日。在乌有乡每逢收获季节常有此种盛会。

307. tithe: 十分之一，一小部分（通常此词意为农民被迫向教会缴纳的什一税，作者此处又是拟古，不足为训）。

308. murmuring little above her breath: 轻声低语，仅仅可闻。

309. the great timbers of the roof: 房顶下粗大的梁檩。

310. of old time: 从前（革命前）。

311. a-nights: = of nights，在夜间。（拟古。）

312. caddis worms: 蛴螬，石蚕。

313. for the time: 暂时。

314. Everywhere there was but little furniture, and that only the most necessary, and of the simplest forms: William Morris 主张实用朴素的美，反对室内装修的雕琢铺张。不赞成在屋内放置过多的家具，并痛恨家具的笨重与过分富丽。

315. this people: 指乌有乡的人们。

316. left stranded from old times: 犹如在涨潮时被水困在一块较高的沙地上一样，成为新时代中硕果仅存的属于旧时代的东西。

317. tapestry: 织锦壁毯。（用丝绣织出各种人物图案。）

318. tones: 色调。

319. harmonised: 和谐，调和。

320. which would have been ill supplanted by brighter and more striking decoration: 如用更鲜明触目的装饰去代替它，会是很不合适的。

321. I asked a few random questions of Ellen as we sat there: 我们在那里坐着时，我漫不经心地问了 Ellen 几个问题。*random*，任意的，无心的。*to ask a question of somebody* = to ask somebody a question，注意这里介词用 of 而不用 to.

此段描写作者在刹那之间出神冥思，忘其所在。作者连用 but ... and presently ... and then ...，等省略主语的短句，很快地把读者带入忘我的意境，而不露雕琢的形迹。

322. My thought returned to me ...: ：我清醒了过来。

323. looking all the fuller of life and pleasure and desire from the contrast with the grey faded tapestry with its futile design ...: 因为有了那褪了色的灰暗的壁毯以及它的繁藻而无意义的花纹作衬托，Ellen 更显得充满了生命、欢乐与欲望。*all the fuller*（*better, etc.*）from ...，由于…而更加…

324. as if she read me through and through: 就好象她能极透彻地看穿我的心意。

325. your impatience of unreasonable restraint: 你对于不合理的限制的不能忍耐。

326. when all is won and has been for a long time: 现在一切均已被赢到手，而且已经赢到手很久了。（指革命胜利已很久。）*and has been* = and has been won.

327. If we must lose you: 假如我们非得放你走不可。（Ellen 明白作者在乌有

乡中逗留的期限将满。而作者自己尚蒙在鼓里以为还可以欢聚数日，故下文他惊问 What do you mean?）

328. falteringly: 欲说还休；不知怎样说是好。

329. The past the present? Should she not have said the contrast of the present with the future: of blind despair with hope?: 此段意谓：我刚才心中想的是：她（指 Ellen）为什么说“过去与现在的对比”呢？（指上文第 24 页第 25、26 行。）她难道不应该说“现在与将来，全盘的绝望与希望的对比吗？”（从 Ellen 的眼光来看，作者生活的黑暗时代已过去，现在是光明幸福的。而从作者的眼光看，他所生活在其中的维多利亚王朝的现实是恐怖绝望的，而 Ellen 的美好社会还在遥远的将来。故此 Ellen 说过去与现在的对比，而作者不自觉地认为应说成是现在与将来的对比。虚虚实实，扑朔迷离，说明故事的叙述者人在梦乡，而未能忘掉丑恶的现实。）

330. her sudden nervousness: 她的突然的紧张或害怕。（指 Ellen 突然抓着他的手说：“Come, while there is yet time! …”）

331. our life of repose amidst of energy; of work which is pleasure and pleasure which is work: 此数语道穿 William Morris 理想的新社会的神髓。*amidst of* = amidst.

332. my father when he was working was a mere tiller of the soil: 我父亲在年壮能劳动时只是个耕田的人。（在乌有乡劳动者年老就可以退休养老。）

333. I could not have borne that: 我将会是受不了贫苦的生活的（假如我生在旧社会的话）。

334. she spoke with no blush or simper of false shame: 她说话时并不因为虚假的羞耻感而脸红或痴笑。

下面这一段中，作者通过 Ellen 之口，简单有力地概括了在资本主义社会中妇女的美貌与聪明被财富与强权所污辱践踏的恶运。

335. either by penury or by luxury: 不论是由于贫困或者由于奢侈。注意 penury 与 luxury 押韵，是作者强调之一法。

336. Isn’t it a jewel of a house after its kind?: 这所房子难道不是象它这一类建筑中的一颗明珠吗？

337. what I fancy will be …: = what I imagine (or think) will be …

338. more at home: 更自在，更不拘束。

339. doubting … whether I should see her again: 作者的预感竟成事实。后文中说在最后的晚宴上，作者隔桌又望见了 Ellen 一面，但她正与邻座笑语，竟相见而不相识。而其后作者很快就离开了盛宴的厅堂，回到了恶浊的十九世纪资本主义英国。

45 OSCAR WILDE
1854–1900

THE IMPORTANCE OF BEING EARNEST
(selections)

章含之 选注

ACT I

……

LADY BRACKNELL. Mr. Worthing! Rise, sir, from this semi-recumbent posture.[1] It is most indecorous.[2]

GWENDOLEN. Mamma! [*He tries to rise; she restrains him.*] I must beg you to retire. This is no place for you. Besides, Mr. Worthing has not quite finished yet.

LADY BRACKNELL. Finished what, may I ask?

GWENDOLEN. I am engaged to Mr. Worthing,[3] mamma. [*They rise together.*]

LADY BRACKNELL. Pardon me, you are not engaged to anyone. When you do become engaged to someone, I, or your father, should his health permit him, will inform you of the fact. An engagement should come on a young girl as a surprise, pleasant or unpleasant, as the case may be.[4] It is hardly a matter that she could be allowed to arrange for herself …. And now I have a few questions to put to you, Mr. Worthing. While I am making these inquiries, you, Gwendolen, will wait for me below in the carriage.

GWENDOLEN. [*Reproachfully.*] Mamma!

LADY BRACKNELL. In the carriage, Gwendolen! [GWENDOLEN *goes to the door.* She and JACK *blow kisses to each other*[5] *behind* LADY BRACKNELL'S *back.* LADY BRACKNELL looks vaguely about as *if she could not understand what the noise was. Finally turns round.*] Gwendolen, the carriage!

GWENDOLEN. Yes, mamma. [*Goes out, looking back at* JACK.]

LADY BRACKNELL. [*Sitting down.*] You can take a seat, Mr. Worthing. [*Looks in her pocket for notebook and pencil.*]

JACK. Thank you, Lady Bracknell, I prefer standing.

LADY BRACKNELL. [*Pencil and notebook in hand.*] I feel bound to tell you[6] that you are not down on my list of eligible young men,[7] although I have the same list as the dear Duchess of Bolton has. We work together, in fact. However, I am quite ready to enter your name, should your answers be what a really affectionate mother requires. Do you smoke?

JACK. Well, yes, I must admit I smoke.

LADY BRACKNELL. I am glad to hear it. A man should always have an occupation[8] of some kind. There are far too many idle men in London as it is. How old are you?

JACK. Twenty-nine.

LADY BRACKNELL. A very good age to be married at. I have always been of opinion that a man who desires to get married should know either everything or nothing. Which do you know?

JACK. [*After some hesitation.*] I know nothing, Lady Bracknell.

LADY BRACKNELL. I am pleased to hear it. I do not approve of anything that tampers with[9] natural ignorance.[10] Ignorance is like a delicate exotic fruit; touch it and the bloom is gone. The whole theory of modern education is radically unsound.[11] Fortunately in England, at any rate, education produces no effect whatsoever. If it did, it would prove a serious danger to the upper classes, and probably lead to acts of violence in Grosvenor Square.[12] What is your income?

JACK. Between seven and eight thousand a year.

LADY BRACKNELL. [*Makes a note in her book.*] In land, or in investments?[13]

JACK. In investments, chiefly.

LADY BRACKNELL. That is satisfactory. What between[14] the duties expected of one during one's lifetime, and[15] the duties exacted from one after one's death,[16] land has ceased to be either a profit or a pleasure. It gives one position[17] and prevents one from keeping it up. That's all that can be said about land.

JACK. I have a country house with some land, of course, attached to it, about fifteen hundred acres, I believe; but I don't depend on that for my real income. In fact, as far as I can make out, the poachers[18] are the only people who make anything out of it.

LADY BRACKNELL. A country house! How many bedrooms?Well, that point can be cleared up afterwards. You have a town house, I hope? A girl with a simple, unspoiled nature,[19] like Gwendolen, could hardly be expected to reside in the country.

JACK. Well, I own a house in Belgrave Square,[20] but it is let by the year[21] to Lady Bloxham. Of course, I can get it back when ever I like, at six months' notice.[22]

LADY BRACKNELL. Lady Bloxham? I don't know her.

JACK. Oh, she goes about very little. She is a lady considerably advanced in years.[23]

LADY BRACKNELL. Ah, nowadays that is no guarantee of respectability of character.[24] What number in Belgrave Square?

JACK. 149.

LADY BRACKNELL. [*Shaking her head.*] The unfashionable side.[25] I thought there was something. However, that could easily be altered.

JACK. Do you mean the fashion, or the side?

LADY BRACKNELL. [*Sternly.*] Both, if necessary, I presume. What are your politics?

JACK. Well, I am afraid I really have none. I am a Liberal Unionist.[26]

LADY BRACKNELL. Oh, they count as Tories.[27] They dine with us. Or come in the evening, at any rate. Now to minor matters. Are your parents living?

JACK. I have lost both my parents.

LADY BRACKNELL. To lose one parent, Mr. Worthing, may be regarded as a misfortune; to lose both looks like carelessness. Who was your father? He was evidently a man of some wealth. Was he born in what the Radical papers[28] call the purple of commerce,[29] or did he rise from the ranks of aristocracy?

JACK. I am afraid I really don't know. The fact is, Lady Bracknell, I said I had lost my parents. It would be nearer the truth to say that my parents seem to have lost me .... I don't actually know who I am by birth. I was ... well, I was found.[30]

LADY BRACKNELL. Found!

JACK. The late Mr. Thomas Cardew,[31] an old gentleman of a very charitable and kindly disposition,[32] found me, and gave me the name of Worthing because he happened to have a first-class ticket for Worthing in his pocket at the time. Worthing is a place in Sussex.[33] It is a seaside resort.

LADY BRACKNELL. Where did the charitable gentleman who had a first-class ticket for this seaside resort find you?

JACK. [*Gravely.*] In a hand-bag.

LADY BRACKNELL. A hand-bag?

JACK. [*Very seriously.*] Yes, Lady Bracknell. I was in a hand-bag — a somewhat large, black leather hand-bag, with handles to ti — an ordinary hand-bag, in fact.

LADY BRACKNELL. In what locality did this Mr. James, or Thomas, Cardew come across this ordinary hand-bag?

JACK. In the cloak-room[34] at Victoria Station. It was given to him in mistake for his own.

LADY BRACKNELL. The cloak-room at Victoria Station?

JACK. Yes. The Brighton line.[35]

LADY BRACKNELL. The line is immaterial.[36] Mr. Worthing, I confess I feel somewhat bewildered by what you have just told me. To be born, or at any rate, bred in a hand-bag, whether it had handles or not, seems to me to display[37] a contempt for the ordinary decencies of family life that reminds one of the worst excesses[38] of the French Revolution.[39] And I presume you know what that unfortunate movement led to? As for the particular locality in which the hand-bag was found, a cloak-room at a railway station might serve to conceal a social indiscretion[40] — has probably, indeed, been used for that purpose before now — but it could hardly be regarded as an assured basis for a recognised position in good society.

JACK. May I ask you then what you would advise me to do?need hardly say I would do anything in the world to ensure Gwendolen's happiness.

LADY BRACKNELL. I would strongly advise you, Mr. Worthing, to try and acquire some relations as soon as possible, and to make a definite effort to produce at any rate one parent, of either sex, before the season[41] is quite over.

JACK. Well, I don't see how I could possibly manage to do that. I can produce the hand-bag at any moment. It is in my dressing room[42] at home. I really think that should satisfy you, Lady Bracknell.

LADY BRACKNELL. Me, sir! What has it to do with me? You can hardly imagine that I and Lord Bracknell would dream of allowing our only daughter — a girl brought up with the utmost care — to marry into[43] a cloak-room, and form an alliance[44] with a parcel? Good morning, Mr. Worthing!

[LADY BRACKNELL *sweeps out in reajestic indignation.*]

JACK. Good morning! [ALGERNON, *from the other room, strikes up the Wedding March.* JACK *looks perfectly furious, and goes to the door.*] For goodness' sake don't play that ghastly tune, Algy![45] How idiotic you are!

[*The music stops, and* ALGERNON *enters cheerily.*]

……

ACT II

……

MERRIMAN.[46] A Miss Fairfax[47] has just called to see Mr. Worthing. On very important business Miss Fairfax states.

CECILY. Isn't Mr. Worthing in his library?

MERRIMAN. Mr. Worthing went over in the direction of the Rectory[48] some time ago.

CECILY. Pray[49] ask the lady to come out here; Mr. Worthing is sure to be back soon. And you can bring tea.[50]

MERRIMAN. Yes, Miss. [*Goes out.*]

CECILY. Miss Fairfax! I suppose one of the many good elderly women who are associated with Uncle Jack in some of his philanthropic work in London. I don't quite like women who are interested in philanthropic work. I think it is so forward[51] of them.

[*Enter* MERRIMAN.]

MERRIMAN. Miss Fairfax.

[*Enter* GWENDOLEN.]

[*Exit* MERRIMAN.]

CECILY. [*Advancing to meet her.*] Pray let me introduce myself to you. My name is Cecily Cardew.

GWENDOLEN. Cecily Cardew? [*Moving to her and shaking hands.*] What a very sweet name! Something tells me[52] that we are going to be great friends. I like you already more than I can say. My first impressions of people are never wrong.

CECILY. How nice of you to like me so much after we have known each other such a comparatively short time. Pray sit down.

GWENDOLEN. [*Still standing up.*] I may call you Cecily, may I not?

CECILY. With pleasure!

GWENDOLEN. And you will always call me Gwendolen, won't you?

CECILY. If you wish.

GWENDOLEN. Then that is all quite settled, is it not?

CECILY. I hope so. [*A pause. They both sit down together.*]

GWENDOLEN. Perhaps this might be a favourable opportunity for my mentioning who I am.[53] My father is Lord Bracknell. You have never heard of papa, I suppose?

CECILY. I don't think so.

GWENDOLEN. Outside the family circle, papa, I am glad to say, is entirely unknown. I think that is quite as it should be. The home seems to me to be the proper sphere[54] for the man. And certainly once a man begins to neglect his domestic duties[55] he becomes painfully effeminate,[56] does he not? And I don't like that. It makes men so very attractive. Cecily, mamma, whose views on education are remarkably strict, has brought me up to be extremely short-sighted; it is part of her system; so do you mind my looking at you through my glasses?

CECILY. Oh! not at all, Gwendolen. I am very fond of being looked at.

GWENDOLEN. [*After examining CECILY carefully through a lorgnette.*[57]] You are here on a short visit, I suppose.

CECILY. Oh no! I live here.

GWENDOLEN. [*Severely.*] Really? Your mother, no doubt, or some female relative of advanced years, resides herealso?

CECILY. Oh no! I have no mother, nor, in fact, any relations.

GWENDOLEN. Indeed?

CECILY. My dear guardian,[58] with the assistance of Miss Prism,[59] has the arduous task of looking after me.

GWENDOLEN. Your guardian?

CECILY. Yes, I am Mr. Worthing's ward.

GWENDOLEN. Oh! It is strange he never mentioned to me that he had a ward. How secretive[60] of him! He grows more interesting hourly. I am not sure, however, that the news inspires me with feelings of unmixed delight. [*Rising and going to her.*] I am very fond of you, Cecily; I have liked you ever since I met you! But I am bound to state that now that I know that you are Mr. Worthing's ward, I cannot help expressing a wish you were—well just a little older than you seem to be—and not quite so very alluring in appearance.[61] In fact, if I may speak candidly—

CECILY. Pray do! I think that whenever one has anything unpleasant to say, one should always be quite candid.

GWENDOLEN. Well, to speak with perfect candour, Cecily, I wish that you were fully forty-two, and more than usually plain for your age.[62] Ernest has a strong upright nature. He is the very soul of truth and honour. Disloyalty would be as impossible to him as deception. But even men of the noblest possible moral character are extremely susceptible[63] to the influence of the physical charms[64] of others. Modern, no less than Ancient History,[65] supplies us with many most painful examples of what I refer to. If it were not so, indeed, History would be quite unreadable.

CECILY. I beg your pardon, Gwendolen, did you say Ernest?

GWENDOLEN. Yes.

CECILY. Oh, but it is not Mr. Ernest Worthing who is my guardian. It is his brother—his elder brother.

GWENDOLEN. [*Sitting down again.*] Ernest never mentioned to me that he had a brother.

CECILY. I am sorry to say they have not been on good terms for a long time.

GWENDOLEN. Ah! that accounts for it.[66] And now that I think of it I have never heard any man mention his brother. The subject seems distasteful to most men. Cecily, you have lifted a load from my mind. I was growing almost anxious. It would have been terrible if any cloud had come across a friendship like ours, would it not? Of course you are quite, quite sure that it is not Mr. Ernest Worthing who is your guardian?

CECILY. Quite sure. [*A pause.*] In fact, I am going to be his.

GWENDOLEN. [*Enquiringly.*] I beg your pardon?

CECILY. [*Rather shy and confidingly.*[67]] Dearest Gwendolen, there is no reason why I should make a secret of it to you. Our little county newspaper is sure to chronicle[68] the fact next week. Mr. Ernest Worthing and I are engaged to be married.

GWENDOLEN. [*Quite politely, rising.*] My darling Cecily, I think there must be some slight error. Mr. Ernest Worthing is engaged to me. The announcement will appear in the *Morning Post*[69] on Saturday at the latest.

CECILY. [*Very politely, rising.*] I am afraid you must be under some misconception. Ernest proposed to me exactly ten minutes ago. [*Shows diary.*]

GWENDOLEN. [*Examines diary through her lorgnette carefully.*] It is certainly very curious, for he asked me to be his wife yesterday afternoon at 5: 30. If you would care to verify the incident, pray do so. [*Produces diary of her own.*] I never travel without my diary. One should always have something sensational[70] to read in the train. I am so sorry, dear Cecily, if it is any disappointment to you, but I am afraid I have the prior claim.[71]

CECILY. It would distress me more than I can tell you, dear Gwendolen, if it caused you any mental or physical anguish, but I feel bound to point out that since Ernest proposed to you he clearly has changed his mind.

GWENDOLEN. [Me*ditatively.*] If the poor fellow has been entrapped into any foolish promise[72] I shall consider it my duty to rescue him at once, and with a firm hand.

CECILY. [*Thoughtfully and sadly.*] Whatever unfortunate entanglement[73] my dear boy may have got into, I will never reproach him with it after we are married.

GWENDOLEN. Do you allude to me, Miss Cardew, as an entanglement? You are presumptuous. On an occasion of this kind it becomes more than a moral duty to speak one's mind. It becomes a pleasure.

CECILY. Do you suggest, Miss Fairfax, that I entrapped Ernest into an engagement? How dare you? This is no time for wearing the shallow mask of manners. When I see a spade I call it a spade.[74]

GWENDOLEN. [*Satirically.*] I am glad to say that I have never seen a spade. It is obvious that our social spheres[75] have been widely different.

[*Enter* MERRIMAN, *followed by the footman. He carries a salver, table cloth, and plate stand.* CECILY *is about to retort. The presence of the servants exercises a restraining influence,*[76] *under which both girls chafe.*[77]]

MERRIMAN. Shall I lay tea here as usual, Miss?

CECILY. [*Sternly, in a calm voice.*] Yes, as usual. [MERRIMAN *begins to clear table and lay cloth. A long pause.* CECILY *and* GWENDOLEN *glare at each other.*]

GWENDOLEN. Are there many interesting walks in the vicinity, Miss Cardew?

CECILY. Oh! yes! a great many. From the top of one of the hills quite close one can see five counties.

GWENDOLEN. Five counties! I don't think I should like that. I hate crowds.

CECILY. [*Sweetly.*] I suppose that is why you live in town? [GWENDOLEN *bites her lip, and beats her foot nervously with her parasol.*]

GWENDOLEN. [*Looking round.*] Quite a well-kept garden this is, Miss Cardew.

CECILY. So glad you like it, Miss Fairfax.

GWENDOLEN. I had no idea there were any flowers in the country.

CECILY. Oh, flowers are as common here, Miss Fairfax, as people are in London.

GWENDOLEN. Personally I cannot understand how anybody manages to exist in the country, if anybody who is anybody does.[78] The country always bores me to death.

CECILY. Ah! That is what the newspapers call agricultural

depression,[79] is it not? I believe the aristocracy are suffering very much from it just at present. It is almost an epidemic amongst them, I have been told. May I offer you some tea, Miss Fairfax?

GWENDOLEN. [*With elaborate politeness.*] Thank you. [Aside.[80]] Detestable girl! But I require tea!

CECILY. [*Sweetly.*] Sugar?

GWENDOLEN. [*Superciliously.*] No, thank you. Sugar is not fashionable any more.

[CECILY *looks angrily at her, takes up the tongs and puts four lumps of sugar into the cup.*]

CECILY. [*Severely.*] Cake or bread and butter?

GWENDOLEN. [*In a bored manner.*] Bread and butter, please. Cake is rarely seen at the best houses[81] nowadays.

CECILY. [*Cuts a very large slice of cake, and puts it on the tray.*] Hand that to Miss Fairfax.

[MERRIMAN *does so, and goes out with footman.* GWENDOLEN *drinks the tea and makes a grimace. Puts down cup at once, reaches out her hand to the bread and butter, looks at it, and finds it is cake. Rises in indignation.*]

GWENDOLEN. You have filled my tea with lumps of sugar, and though I asked most distinctly for bread and butter, you have given me cake. I am known for the gentleness of my disposition, and the extraordinary sweetness of my nature, but I warn you, Miss Cardew, you may go too far.[82]

CECILY. [*Rising.*] To save my poor, innocent, trusting boy from the machinations of any other girl there are no lengths to which I would not go.[83]

GWENDOLEN. From the moment I saw you I distrusted you. I felt that you were false and deceitful. I am never deceived in such matters. My first impressions of people are invariably right.

CECILY. It seems to me, Miss Fairfax, that I am trespassing on your valuable time.[84] No doubt you have many other calls of a similar character to make in the neighbourhood.

[*Enter* JACK.]

GWENDOLEN. [*Catching sight of him.*] Ernest! My own Ernest!

JACK. Gwendolen! Darling! [*Offers to kiss her.*]

GWENDOLEN. [*Drawing back.*] A moment! May I ask if you are engaged to be married to this young lady? [*Points to* CECILY.]

JACK. [*Laughing.*] To dear little Cecily! Of course not! What could have put such an idea into your pretty little head?

GWENDOLEN. Thank you. You may! [*Offers her cheek.*]

CECILY. [*Very sweetly.*] I knew there must be some misunderstanding, Miss Fairfax. The gentleman whose arm is at present round your waist is my dear guardian, Mr. John Worthing.

GWENDOLEN. I beg your pardon?

CECILY. This is Uncle Jack.

GWENDOLEN. [*Receding.*] Jack! Oh!

[*Enter* ALGERNON.]

CECILY. Here is Ernest.

ALGERNON. [*Goes straight over to* CECILY *without noticing anyone else.*] My own love! [*Offers to kiss her.*]

CECILY [*Drawing back.*] A moment, Ernest! May I ask you—are you engaged to be married to this young lady?

ALGERNON. [*Looking round.*] To what young lady? Good heavens! Gwendolen?

CECILY. Yes! to good heavens, Gwendolen, I mean to Gwendolen.

ALGERNON. [*Laughing.*] Of course not! What could have put such an idea into your pretty little head?

CECILY. Thank you. [*Presenting her cheek to be kissed.*] You may. [ALGERNON *kisses her.*]

GWENDOLEN. I felt there was some slight error, Miss Cardew. The gentleman who is now embracing you is my cousin, Mr. Algernon Moncrieff.

CECILY. [*Breaking away from* ALGERNON.] Algernon Moncrieff! Oh! [T*he two girls move towards each other and put their arms* *round each other's waists as if for protection.*]

CECILY. Are you called Algernon?

ALGERNON. I cannot deny it.

CECILY. Oh!

GWENDOLEN. Is your name really John?

JACK. [*Standing rather proudly.*] I could deny it if I liked. I could deny anything if I liked. But my name certainly is John. It has been John for years.

CECILY. [*To* GWENDOLEN.] A gross deception has been practised on both of us.

GWENDOLEN. My poor wounded Cecily!

CECILY. My sweet wronged Gwendolen!

GWENDOLEN. [*Slowly and seriously.*] You will call me sister, will you not? [*They embrace.* JACK *and* ALGERNON *groan and walk up and down.*]

CECILY. [*Rather brightly.*] There is just one question I would like to be allowed to ask my guardian.

GWENDOLEN. An admirable idea! Mr. Worthing, there is just one question I would like to be permitted to put to you. Where is your brother Ernest? We are both engaged to be married to your brother Ernest, so it is a matter of some importance to us to know where your brother Ernest is at present.

JACK. [*Slowly and hesitatingly.*] Gwendolen-Cecily-it is very painful for me to be forced to speak the truth. It is the first time in my life that I have ever been reduced to such a painful position, and I am really quite inexperienced in doing anything of the kind. However I will tell you quite frankly that I have no brother Ernest. I have no brother at all. I never had a brother in my life, and I certainly have not the smallest intention of ever having one in the future.

CECILY. [*Surprised.*] No brother at all?

JACK. [*Cheerily.*] None!

GWENDOLEN. [*Severely.*] H ad you never a brother of any kind?

JACK. [*Pleasantly.*] Never. Not even of any kind.

GWENDOLEN. I am afraid it is quite clear, Cecily, that neither of us is engaged to be married to anyone.

CECILY. It is not a very pleasant position for a young girl suddenly to find herself in. Is it?

GWENDOLEN. Let us go into the house. They will hardly venture to come after us there.

CECILY. No, men are so cowardly, aren't they?

[*They retire into the house with scornful looks.*]

……

【作者简介】 Oscar Wilde（奥斯卡·王尔德，1854—1900）英国剧作家，小说家。著有喜剧 Lady *Windermere's Fan*（《少奶奶的扇子》，1892），*A Woman of No Importance*（《一个无足轻重的妇人》，1893），*An Ideal Husband*（《理想的丈夫》，1895），*The Importance of Being Earnest*（《认真的重要》，1895）等。所著小说有 *The Picture of Dorian Gray*（《格雷的画象》，1891）。王尔德并曾写过童话故事，如 *The Happy Prince and Other Tales*（《快乐的王子童话集》，1888），也曾写过诗歌，如晚年的 *The Ballad of Reading Gaol*（《累丁狱中歌》，1898）。他的作品有颓废气息，但也讽刺和揭发了当时伦敦上层社会的时髦人物，而文笔优美，词锋犀利，又素以风格著称。

【题解与注释】

The Importance of Being Earnest 是王尔德所写喜剧中最成功的一部。它出色地体现了作者所特有的机智和幽默，同时也相当真实地反映了十九世纪末伦敦上层社会的优闲寄生生活和英国绅士淑女们玩世不恭的态度。剧中人物谈话内容的浅薄可笑和他们说话的伶俐俏皮构成了贯穿全剧的巧妙对照。剧本故事的关键是主人公 John（即 Jack）Worthing 的真假教名 Ernest（与 earnest［英语的"认真"］适成双关）。他是年轻的富绅，为了经常能到伦敦寻乐而又不致败坏名誉，向外声称他在伦敦有个浪子弟弟 Ernest，常要他去接济；日子一久，连受他监护的美丽小姐 Cecily Cardew 也信以为真。他与一个伯爵的女儿 Gwendolen 相爱，但伯爵夫人却因他出身不明而不准他们成婚。他的朋友、伯爵夫人的外甥 Algernon Moncrieff 得知他是一位姑娘的监护人，遂下乡探视，佯称自己是他的弟弟 Ernest，求见 Cecily。两人一见锺情，订下婚约。Gwendolen 也来到了 John Worthing 的庄园，与 Cecily 相遇。言谈之间，两位少女发现

对方都与名叫Ernest的青年订婚，引起一场误会。直至John从城里赶回，Algernon再次出场，才解开了疑团。剧本的最后一幕，John终于弄清了自己的身世，发现自己的教名果然是Ernest，而且还是Algernon的亲兄弟。喜剧以有情人皆成眷属而告终。

这里所选的是第一幕中伯爵夫人Lady Bracknell发现John正向其女儿Gwendolen屈膝求婚后盘问John的一场和第二幕Gwendolen和Cecily相会的一场。在这两场中，读者可以看到王尔德如何用夸张的手法刻划出伯爵夫人母女这两个贵族女子的自负和势利，也可以欣赏作者运用语言的机智、诙谐与简练。

1. semi-recumbent posture: 半立半卧的姿态（指John向Gwendolen下跪求婚的姿势）。

2. indecorous: 不合礼节，不成体统。

3. engaged to Mr. Worthing: 与Worthing先生订了婚。

4. as the case may be: 视情况而定。

5. blow kisses to each other: 相互飞吻。

6. I feel bound to tell you: 我感到有必要告诉你。

7. eligible young men: 够格的、可入选的年轻人。

8. occupation: 有事做，不闲着（亦指“职业”）。

9. tampers with: 干扰。

10. natural ignorance: 天然的无知。

11. radically unsound: 根本站不住脚。

12. Grosvenor [ˈgrəuvnə] **Square:** 伦敦西区富人住宅区；一广场名。

13. in land, or in investments:（收入）来自地租还是企业投资。

14. what between ... and ...: 既有…又有…。

15. the duties expected of one during one's lifetime: 指地主一生所承担的种种义务。如维修庄园和本区的教堂等。

16. the duties exacted from one after one's death: 指有产者死后政府向其家属所征收的遗产税。

17. position: 社会地位。

18. poachers: 非法到别人庄地上去打猎的人。

19. a simple, unspoiled nature: 纯朴的，未经娇惯的天性。

20. Belgrave [ˈbelgreiv] **Square:** 伦敦西区广场名。

21. let by the year: 按年出租（次年续租须续订）。

22. at six months' notice: 发出通知后六个月（收回房屋）。

23. considerably advanced in years: 上了年纪的。

24. respectability of character: 人品端庄。

25. the unfashionable side: 不时髦的一边，按当时伦敦社会的习俗，人们都喜与世家名门共居广场一边，于是这一边就成了the fashionable side，而那被冷落的一边就自然是unfashionable了。

26. Liberal Unionist: 一党派成员名称。Liberal Unionists原为自由党的一个派系，1886年因与该党政见不一，遂与之脱离，并和保守党结成联盟。

27. Tories: 保守党员（members of the Conservative Party）。

28. Radical papers: 激进派的报纸，指当时左翼自由党人及其他改良主义派所出版的报纸。

29. purple of commerce: 意为商业贵族。按 purple（古意为"深红色"），原为国王王服的传统颜色。此处转指伦敦富商大贾。

30. found: 捡来的，即"弃儿"之意。

31. the late Mr. Thomas Cardew: 已去世的 Thomas Cardew 先生。

32. of a very charitable and kindly disposition: 乐善好施的。

33. Sussex [ˈsʌsiks]: 英国南部海岸一郡名。

34. cloak-room: 存物处。

Victoria [vikˈtɔːriə] **Station:** 伦敦主要火车站之一，通往南部及西部地区。

35. the Brighton line: 到 Brighton 去的铁路线。Brighton [ˈbraitən] 为当时上层社会的一个海滨休养地，位于英国南部海岸。

36. immaterial: 无关紧要。

37. the ordinary decencies of family life: 家庭生活的起码准则。

38. the worst excesses: 最可怕的过激行为。

39. the French Revolution: 指 1789 年法国资产阶级革命。

40. a social indiscretion: 原意指不检点的行为，此处特指遗弃私生子。

41. the season: 指伦敦的社交季节，一般从冬季开始延至翌年春末。

42. dressing room: 与卧室相连，供梳妆更衣用的房间。

43. to marry into: 原意为与某一阶级或阶层的成员结婚。如 to marry into a rich family 意为与有钱人家子弟结婚。此处 to marry into a cloak-room 既指嫁入存衣室内，又指与藏在存衣室内的私生子结婚。这个双关的含义产生特殊的幽默效果。

44. form an alliance with: 与…结亲。

45. Algy: Algernon 之昵称。

46. Merriman: 仆人名。

47. a Miss Fairfax: 有一位 Fairfax 小姐。

48. Rectory: 教区牧师寓所。

49. pray: 表示请求的语气词。现代英语中少用。

50. tea: 指下午的茶点，不仅指茶水。

51. forward: 举止过于随便 .

52. something tells me: 我有一种感觉。

53. who I am: 此处特指家庭出身和个人地位。

54. the proper sphere: 宜于活动之处。

55. domestic duties: 家庭职责，通常指主妇的各种家务。

56. Effeminate [iˈfeminit]:（男子）带有女气的。

57. lorgnette [lɔːˈnjet]: 一种带长柄的手持眼镜。

58. guardian: 保护人，受托负责监护未成年男女的人，被监护者则称为 ward.

59. Miss Prism: Cecily 的家庭女教师。

60. secretive: 过分保守秘密。

61. alluring in appearance: 容貌迷人。

62. more than usually plain for your age: 不但老，而且特别丑（以你的年龄来说是异乎寻常的丑陋）。

63. susceptible [sə'septibl]**:** 易动心的，易受…的诱惑。

64. physical charms: 外表的美。

65. Modern, no less than Ancient History, etc.: 意为古今历史上的英雄人物，每每为女色所惑。

66. that accounts for it: 原来如此。

67. confidingly: 信任地。

68. to chronicle: 记载，此词一般用于重大的历史事件。

69. Morning Post:《晨报》, 1872 年至 1937 年英国保守党的主要报纸。

70. sensational: 耸人听闻的。

71. the prior ['praiə] **claim:** 优先权。

72. entrapped into any foolish promise: 上了圈套，作出任何愚蠢的诺言。

73. entanglement: 纠葛。

74. when I see a spade I call it a spade: 来自成语 to call a spade a spade，直言不讳 .

75. social spheres: 社交的范围，即指社会地位。

76. exercises a restraining influence: 对（她们）起了节制作用。

77. chafe: 原意为骡马倔强不驯服时用身子磨擦韁绳或车把，此处转指两位小姐在仆人面前为了不失上等人的体面，勉强忍住怒气，暂时不吵下去。

78. if anybody who is anybody does: 如果真有任何有身份的人住在乡下的话；句中第二个 anybody 与作“有身份、有地位的人”解的 somebody 意义相当。

79. agricultural depression: 农业不景气（此处语意双关，一方面针对上文 Gwendolen 所言［“The country always bores me to death.”］，一方面指出靠地租收入过活的贵族现在生活大不如前）。

80. aside: 舞台上一演员装作不为他演员听到的旁白。

81. the best houses: 最体面的人家。

82. you may go too far: 你会做得太过分（而惹我生气）的。

83. there are no lengths to which I would not go: 我什么都做得出来。

84. trespassing on your valuable time: 占了您的宝贵时间。

46 THOMAS HARDY
1840–1928

1. *The Return of the Native* (selections)
2. *Poems*

张谷若　选注

1. *THE RETURN OF THE NATIVE*

(1) The Custom of the Country[1]

III

HAD a looker-on been posted in the immediate vicinity of the barrow,[2] he would have learned that these persons were boys and men of the neighbouring hamlets. Each, as he ascended the barrow, had been heavily laden with furze[3]-faggots, carried upon the shoulder by means of a long stake sharpened at each end for impaling them easily—two in front and two behind. They came from a part of the heath[4] a quarter of a mile to the rear, where furze almost exclusively prevailed as a product.

Every individual was so involved in furze by his method of carrying the faggots that he appeared like a bush on legs till he had thrown them down. The party had marched in trail, like a travelling flock of sheep; that is to say, the strongest first, the weak and young behind.

The loads were all laid together, and a pyramid of furze thirty feet in circumference now occupied the crown of the tumulus,[5] which was known as Rainbarrow for many miles round. Some made themselves busy with matches, and in selecting the driest tufts of furze, others in loosening the bramble bonds which held the faggots together. Others, gaain, while this was in progress, lifted their eyes and swept the vast expanse of country commanded by their position, now lying nearly obliterated by shade. In the valleys of the heath nothing save its own wild face was visible at any time of day; but this spot commanded a horizon enclosing a tract of far extent, and in many cases lying beyond the heath country. None of its features could be seen now, but the whole made itself felt as a vague stretch of remoteness.

While the men and lads were building the pile, a change took place in the mass of shade which denoted the distant landscape. Red suns and tufts of fire[6] one by one began to arise, flecking the whole country round. They were the bonfires of other parishes[7] and hamlets that were engaged in the same sort of commemoration. Some were distant,[8] and stood in a dense atmosphere, so that bundles of pale straw-like beams radiated around them in the shape of a fan.[9] Some were large and near,[10] glowing scarlet-red from the shade, like wounds in a black hide. Some were Maenades,[11] with winy faces and blown hair. These tinctured the silent bosom of the clouds[12] above them and lit up their ephemeral caves, which seemed thenceforth to become scalding caldrons.[13] Perhaps as many as thirty bonfires could be counted within the whole bounds of the district; and as the hour may be told on a clock-face when the figures themselves are invisible, so did the men recognize the locality of each fire by its angle and direction, though nothing of the scenery could be viewed.

The first tall flame[14] from Rainbarrow sprang into the sky, attracting all eyes that had been fixed on the distant conflagrations back to their own attempt in the same kind. The cheerful blaze streaked the inner surface of the human circle—now increased by other stragglers, male and female—with its own gold livery,[15] and even overlaid the dark turf around with a lively luminousness, which softened off into obscurity where the barrow rounded downwards out of sight. It showed the barrow to be the segment of a globe, as perfect as on the day when it was thrown up, even the little ditch remaining from which the earth was dug. Not a plough had ever disturbed a grain of that stubborn[16] soil. In the heath's barrenness[17] to the farmer lay its fertility to the historian. There had been no obliteration[18] because there had been no tending.[19]

It seemed as if the bonfire-makers were standing in some radiant upper storey of the world,[20] detached from and independent of the dark stretches below. The heath down there was now a vast abyss, and no longer a continuation of what they stood on; for their eyes, adapted to the blaze, could see nothing of the deeps[21] beyond its influence.[22] Occasionally, it is true, a more vigorous flare than usual from their faggots sent darting lights like aides-de-camp[23] down the incline[24] to some distant bush, pool, or patch of white sand, kindling these to replies[25] of the same colour, till all was lost in darkness again. Then the whole black phenomenon[26] beneath represented Limbo[27] as viewed from the brink by the sublime Florentine[28] in his vision, and the muttered articulations[29] of the wind in the hollows were as complaints and petitions from the 'souls of mighty worth' suspended therein.[30]

It was as if these men and boys had suddenly dived into past ages,[31] and fetched therefrom[32] an hour and deed which had before been familiar with this spot. The ashes[33] of the original British[34] pyre which blazed from that summit lay fresh and undisturbed in the barrow beneath their tread. The flames from funeral piles long ago kindled there had shone down upon the lowlands as these were shining now. Festival fires to Thor and Woden[35] had followed on the same ground and duly had their day.[36] Indeed, it is pretty well known that such blazes as this the heathmen[37] were now enjoying are rather the lineal descendants from jumbled Druidical[38] rites and Saxon[39] ceremonies than the invention of popular feeling about Gunpowder Plot.

Moreover to light a fire is the instinctive and resistant act of man when, at the winter ingress,[40] the curfew[41] is sounded throughout Nature. It indicates a spontaneous, Promethean[42] rebelliousness against the fiat[43] that this recurrent season shall bring foul times, cold darkness, misery and death. Black chaos[44] comes, and the fettered gods of the earth[45] say, Let there be light.[46]

The brilliant lights and sooty shades which struggled upon the skin and clothes of the persons standing round caused their lineaments and general contours to be drawn with Durereseque[47] vigour and dash. Yet the permanent moral expression[48] of each face it was impossible to discover, for as the nimble flames towered, nodded, and swooped through the surrounding air, the blots of shade and flakes of light upon the countenances of the group changed shape and position endlessly. All was unstable; quivering as leaves, evanescent as lightning. Shadowy eye-sockets, deep as those of a death's head,[49] suddenly turned into pits of lustre[50]: a lantern-jaw was cavernous, then it was shining; wrinkles were emphasized to ravines, or obliterated entirely by a changed ray. Nostrils were dark wells; sinews in old necks were gilt mouldings[51]; things with no particular polish on them were glazed; bright objects, such as the tip of a furze-hook one of the men carried, were as glass; eyeballs glowed like little lanterns. Those whom Nature had depicted as merely quaint became grotesque, the grotesque became preternatural; for all was in extremity.

(2) The figure against the sky

VI

WHEN the whole Egdon concourse[2] had left the site of the bonfire to its accustomed loneliness, a closely wrapped female figure approached the barrow from that quarter of the heath in which the little fire lay.[3] Had the reddleman[4] been watching[5] he might have recognized her as the woman who had first stood there so singularly, and vanished at the approach of strangers.

She ascended to her old position at the top, where the red coals of the perishing fire greeted her like living eyes in the corpse of day. There she stood still, around her stretching the vast night atmosphere, whose incomplete darkness[6] in comparison with the total darkness of the heath below it might have represented a venial beside a mortal sin.[7]

That she was tall and straight in build, that she was ladylike in her movements, was all that could be learnt of her just now, her form being wrapped in a shawl folded in the old cornerwise fashion, and her head in a large kerchief, a protection not superfluous at this hour and place.[8] Her back was towards the wind, which blew from the north-west; but whether she had avoided that aspect[9] because of the chilly gusts which played about her exceptional position, or because her interest lay in the southeast, did not at first appear.

Her reason for standing so dead still as the pivot of this circle of heath-country was just as obscure. Her extraordinary fixity, her conspicuous loneliness, her heedlessness of night, betokened among other things an utter absence of fear. A tract of country unaltered from that sinister condition which made Caesar[10] anxious every year to get clear of its glooms before the autumnal equinox, a kind of landscape and weather which leads travellers from the South to describe our island as Homer's Cimmerian land,[11] was not, on the face of it,[12] friendly to women.

It might reasonably have been supposed that she was listening to the wind, which rose somewhat as the night advanced, and laid hold of the attention. The wind, indeed, seemed made for the scene, as the scene seemed made for the hour. Part of its tone was quite special; what was heard there could be heard nowhere else. Gusts in innumerable series followed each other from the northwest, and when each one of them raced past the sound of its progress resolved into three. Treble,[13] tenor, and bass notes were to be found therein. The general ricochet of the whole over pits and prominences[14] had the gravest pitch of the chime.[15] Next there could be heard the baritone[16] buzz of a holly tree.[17] Below these in force, above them in pitch, a dwindled voice[18] strove hard at a husky tune,[19] which was the peculiar local sound alluded to. Thinner and less immediately traceable than the other two, it was far more impressive than either. In it lay what may be called the linguistic[20] peculiarity of the heath; and being audible nowhere on earth off a heath, it afforded a shadow of reason for the woman's tenseness, which continued as unbroken as ever.

Throughout the blowing of these plaintive November winds that note bore a great resemblance to the ruins of human song[21] which remain to the throat[22] of fourscore and ten.[23] It was a worn whisper,[24] dry and papery,[25] and it brushed so distinctly across the ear that, by the accustomed, the material minutiae[26] in which it originated could be realized as by touch. It was the united products of infinitesimal[27] vegetable causes, and these were neither stems, leaves, fruit, blades, prickles, lichen, nor moss.[28]

They were the mummied[29] heath-bells[30] of the past summer, originally tender and purple, now washed colourless by Michaelmas[31] rains, and dried to dead skins by October suns. So low was an individual sound from these that a combination of hundreds only just emerged from silence, and the myriads of the whole declivity[32] reached the woman's ear but as a shrivelled and intermittent recitative.[33] Yet scarcely a single accent among the many afloat to-night could have such power to impress a listener with thoughts of its origin. One inwardly saw the infinity of those combined multitudes; and perceived that each of the tiny trumpets was seized on, entered, scoured and emerged from by the wind as thoroughly as if it were as vast as a crater.

2. POEMS

(1) Hap

(2) Neutral Tones
(3) She At His Funeral
(4) The Darkling Thrush
(5) At Castle Boterel
(6) In Tenebris
(7) Shut Out That Moon
(8) Afterwards

(1) HAP[1]

If but[2] some[3] vengeful[4] god would call to me
From up the sky, and laugh: "Thou suffering thing,[5]
Know that thy sorrow is my ecstasy,[6]
That thy love's loss is my hate's profiting[7]!"

Then would I bear it,[8] clench myself,[9] and die,
Steeled[10] by the sense[11] of ire unmerited;[12]
Half-eased[13] in that[14] a Powerfuller than I[15]
Had willed[16] and meted me the tears I shed.

But not so. How arrives it[17] joy lies slain,
And why unblooms the best hope ever sown?
—Crass Casualty[18] obstructs[19] the sun and rain,
And dicing Time[20] for gladness casts[21] a moan[22]....
These purblined Doomsters[23] had as readily strown[24]
Blisses about my pilgrimage[25] as pain.[26]

(2) NEUTRAL[1] TONES

We stood by a pond that winter day,
And the sun was white, as though chidden of God,[2]
And a few leaves lay on the starving[3] sod;
　　—They hadfallen from an ash, and were gray.

Your eyes on me were as eyes that rove[4]

Over tedious riddles of years ago;[5]
And some words played between us to and fro[6]
On which lost the more by our love.[7]

The smile on your mouth was the deadest thing
Alive enough to have strength to die;[8]
And a grin of bitterness swept thereby
Like an ominous bird a-wing[9]....

Since then, keen lessons[10] that love deceives,[11]
And wrings with wrong[12], have shaped to me
Your face, and the God-curst sun, and a tree,
And a pond edged with grayish leaves.

(3) SHE AT HIS FUNERAL

They bear him to his resting-place[1]—
In slow procession sweeping[2] past:
I follow at a stranger's space[3];
His kindred they,[4] his sweet heart I.
Unchanged my gown of garish dye,[5]
Though sable-sad is their attire[6];
But they stand round with griefless eye,
While my regret[7] consumes like fire!

(4) THE DARKLING[1] THRUSH[2]

I leant upon a coppice[3] gate[4]
When Frost was spectre-gray,[5]
And winter's dregs[6] made desolate
The weakening eye of day.[7]
The tangled bine-stems[8] scored the sky[9]
Like strings of broken lyres,
And all mankind that haunted nigh[10]
Had sought their household fires.[11]

The land's sharp features[12] seemed to be
The Century's corpse[13] outleant,[14]
His crypt the cloudy canopy,[15]
The wind his death-lament.[16]
The ancient[17] pulse[18] of germ and birth
Was shrunken hard and dry,
And every spirit[19] upon earth,
Seemed fervourless as I.

AT once a voice arose among
The bleak twigs overhead
In a full-hearted[20] evensong[21]
Of joy illimited;
An aged thrush, frail, gaunt, and small,
In blast-beruffled plume,[22]
Had chosen thus to fling his soul,
Upon[23] the growing[24] gloom.

So little cause for carolings[25]
Of such ecstatic sound
Was written[26] on terrestrial[27] things
Afar or nigh[28] around,
That I could think there trembled through
His happy good-night air[29]
Some blessed[30] Hope, whereof he knew
And I was unaware.

(5) AT CASTLE BOTEREL[1]

As I drive to the junction of lane and highway,[2]
And the drizzle bedrenches[3] the waggonette,[4]
I look behind at the fading byway,[5]
And see on its slope,[6] now glistening[7] wet,
Distinctly yet

Myself and a girlish form benighted[8]
In dry March weather. We climb the road
Beside a chaise[9]. We had just alighted
To ease the sturdy pony's load
When he sighed[10] and slowed.

What we did as we climbed,[11] and what we talked of[12]
Matters not much, nor to what it led,[13]—
Something that life will not be balked of[14]
Without rude reason[15] till hope is dead,
And feeling fled.

It filled but a minute. But was there ever
A time of such quality,[16] since or before,
In that hill's story[17]? To one mind never,
Though it has been elimbed, foot-swift,[18] foot-sore,
By thousands more.

Primaeval rocks form the road's steep border,
And much have they faced[19] there, first and last,
Of the Transitory[20] in Earth's long order;[21]
But what they record in colour and cast[22]
Is — that we two passed.

And to me, though Time's unflinching rigour,[23]
In mindless rote,[24] has ruled[25] from sight
The substance[26] now, one phantom figure
Remains on the slope, as when that night
Saw us alight.

I look and see it there, shrinking, shrinking,
I look back at it amid the rain
For the very last time; for my sand is sinking,[27]

And I shall traverse old love's domain[28]
 Never again.

(6) IN TENEBRIS[1]

II

"Considerabam ad desteram, et videbam; et non erat qui cognosceret me .... Non est qui requirat animam meam." — Ps. cxLi.

When the clouds' swoln bosoms[2] echo back the shouts[3] of the many and strong
That things are all as they best may be, save a few to be right ere long,
And my eyes have not the vision in them to discern what to these is so clear,
The blot seems straightway in me alone; one better he were not here.[4]

The stout upstanders[5] say, All's well with us: ruers have nought to rue!
And what the potent[6] say so oft,[7] can it fail to be somewhat true?
Breezily go they, breezily[8] come; their dust smokes around their career,[9]
Till I think I am one born out of due time, who has no calling[10] here.

Their dawns[11] bring lusty[12] joys, it seems, their evenings all that is sweet;
Our times[13] are blessed times, they cry: Life shapes it[14] as is most meet,[15]
And nothing is much the matter; there are many smiles to a tear;

Then what is the matter is I, I say, Why should such an one[16]
be here?...

Let him[17] in whose ears the low-voiced[18] Best is killed by the
clash of the First,[19]
Who holds that if way to the Better there be, it exacts[20] a fall
look at the worst,
Who feels that delight is a delicate growth cramped by
crookedness, custom and fear,[21,22]
Get him[23] up and be gone as one shaped awry; he disturbs
the order here.

(7) SHUT OUT THAT MOON

Close up the casement, draw the blind,[1]
Shut out that stealing moon,[2]
She wears too much the guise[3] she wore
Before our lutes were strewn
With years-deep dust,[4] and names we read
On a white stone[5] were hewn.[6]

Step not forth[7] on the dew-dashed[8] lawn[9]
To view[10] the Lady's Chair,[11]
Immense Orion's[12] glittering form,
The Less and Greater Bear:[13]
Stay in; to such sights we were drawn
When faded ones were fair.

Brush not the bough[14] for midnight scents
That come forth lingeringly,
And wake the same sweet sentiments
They breathed to you and me,
When Living seemed a laugh, and love
All it was said to be.

Within the common lamp-lit[15] room
Prison[16] my eyes and thought;
Let dingy[17] details[18] crudely[19] loom,
Mechanic speech be wrought;[20]
Too fragrant was Life's early bloom,
Too tart[21] the fruit it brought!

(8) AFTERWARDS

When the present[1] has latched its postern[2] behind my tremulous stay,[3]
And the May month flaps its glad[4] green leaves like wings,
Delicate-filmed[5] as new-spun silk, will the neighbours say,
"He was a man who used to notice such things"?

If it be in the dusk when, like an eyelid's soundless blink,
The dewfall-hawk comes crossing the shades[6] to alight
Upon the wind-warped[7] upland thorn, a gazer may think,
"To him this must have been a familiar sight."

If I pass[8] during some nocturnal blackness,[9] mothy[10] and warm,
When the hedgehog travels furtively over the lawn[11],
One may say, "He strove that such innocent creatures should come to no harm,[12]
But he could do little for them; and now he is gone."
If, when hearing that I have been stilled[13] at last, they stand at the door,
Watching the full-starred heavens that winter sees,[14]
Will this thought rise on those who will meet my face no more,
"He was one who had an eye for such mysteries."

And will any say when my bell of quittance[15] is heard in the

gloom,
And a crossing[16] breeze cuts a pause in its autrollings,[17]
Till they rise again, as they were[18] a new bell's boom,
"He hears it not now, but used to notice such things"?

【作者简介】 托玛斯·哈代既是英国19世纪末期杰出的小说家，又是20世纪初期杰出的史诗家。而他的诗歌则贯串于他整个创作活动时期中。他生于英格兰西南部滨海农业区道塞特郡里的一个小村庄。他的小说大部分都是以这个地区作背景的。哈代的父亲是一个石匠，后来作了木厂老板。哈代在乡村和郡城上完了中小学之后，因家境关系，在郡城一名建筑师名下学习建筑，后又于1862年去伦敦，在另一名当时著名建筑师的公事房里工作了五年。先在学校时，他就熟悉了拉丁文学。在伦敦期间，文学兴趣更浓。1865年开始写诗（幼年之作不算），1867年开始写小说，但未发表。他第一部问世的作品是1871年发表的小说《铤而走险》（*Desperate Remedies*），但是到1872年发表了《绿树荫下》（*Under the Greenwood Tree*），1873年发表了《秋波湛蓝》（*A Pair of Blue Eyes*），才奠定了从事小说写作的基础。随后除了别的作品以外，发表了重要小说《远离尘嚣》（*Far From the Madding Crowd*）（1874），《还乡》（*The Return of the Native*）（1878），《凯特桥市长》（*The Mayor of Casterbridge*）（1886），《林地居民》（*The Woodlanders*）（1887）。最后发表的是《德伯家的苔丝》（*Tess of the D'Urbervilles*）（1891）和《无名的裘德》（*Jude the Obscure*）（1896）。这两部小说因触犯了当时习俗道德，受到卫道者的攻击，哈代愤而放弃小说的写作，而专从事诗歌。他把旧作新作，汇为一集，名为*Obscure Poems*，于1898发表，以后又继续发表诗歌七集，直至1928年。在1904与1907，哈代发表了他的史诗剧《列国》（*The Dynasts*），更较完整地表现了他的思想与艺术。

【题解与注释】

1. THE RETURN OF THE NATIVE

(1) The custom of the country

在哈代所写的十三四部长篇小说中，有人从艺术的角度看，认为《还乡》（The Return of the Native）是最优秀的作品，而《还乡》又有六七个‘镜头’，写得更阔大、深刻，精确，令人难忘。现从此种‘镜头’中，选出两个：一个以视为主，使人看到他所要人看到的景象；一个以听为主，使人听到他所要人听到的声音；都可以说是‘能作难写之状’。

1. The custom of the country: 这一个‘镜头’，是描写 bonfire。英国于 1604 年发生了一件阴谋案，叫作‘火药阴谋案’（Gunpowder Plot），原因是，英国天主教失势之后，受到压迫，阴图报复，想于十一月五日，埋火药于国会地窖中，乘国会开会之时，把国王、议员等人一齐炸死，谋泄未遂。英人每年于十一月五日夜间，聚薪而焚之，纪念其事，其事尤盛行于乡间，即此章标题所说的 the Custom of the Country。

2. barrow: 古冢。此处为英国新石器时代人的葬地，多踞山顶，为圆形。

3. furze: 为‘大荒原’上原始野生灌木之一种，当地人用作燃料。

4. heath: 英国道塞特郡东南部一片广大的沙质丘陵地带。上面不长庄稼。只长 furze, heather 等几种原始野生植物。

5. tumulus (pl. tumuli): = barrow. Rainbarrow 为 barrows 中之一。

6. red suns and tufts of fire etc.: 指远处和近处之 bonfires 总言之。'Red suns of fire，言 bonfire 有的象红日一团；tufts of fire 言有的象草丛四布。一片荒原，上有许多土阜山丘，每一个丘阜顶上都点起一个 bonfire，夜里看来，星星点点，远近不一。

7. parishes: 这儿等于 villages. 英国因管理宗教事宜，把全英格兰分为二 provinces，由大主教二人主之。Provinces 下分若干主教区，每个主教区有一所 Cathedral，每主教区下分若干 parishes. Parish 由一村或数小村组成，有一所 Church。

8. Some were distant etc.: 分写远近不同之 bonfires。

9. pale straw-like bearms ... fan: 远处的 bonfire，颜色淡黄如麦杆，形状辐射如扇子（也就是前面说的 tufts of fires）。

10. Some were large and near: 这是近一些的 bonfire. black hide，黑毛兽皮，这里喻夜色；wound 是伤口，血淋淋地赤红，喻 bonfire。

11. Some were Maenades: 希腊神话，酒神巴枯斯（Bacchus 或 Dionysus）之供奉女尼或妇女，谓之 Maenades，于酒神节日，狂饮纵舞，如痴如癫。Winy faces 指饮酒面红而言，此处以喻 bonfire 之火。Blown hair，头发随风飘扬，此处以喻 bonfire 之烟。这类 bonfire 离得最近，故连烟都可看见。那天夜里有风，故烟气斜向一面。Maenades 的图形，多作头发飘扬之状。

12. the bosom of the clouds: clouds，复数，是 masses of watery vapour floating in the air. Bosom 是总说，穹窿之下，浮云弥漫，其最深处有如‘胸’‘怀’。Caves 则为单举。浮云不匀或不平，有凹有凸，凹处如 caves. 此类 bonfire 上面，云近天低，故为 bonfire 映得彤红，且凹凸之形亦皆映出。Ephemeral 言云非固定不动，而是瞬息变化的。

13. caldron: 鼎镬。scalding，烧红而烫人。

14. The first tall flame: 以下写这些人自己点的 bonfire。

15. streaked ... with its own gold livery: livery 本为仆人之号衣，转为外表之

意，此处则指火之颜色而言。streak 是‘一条一条地射到…之上’。

16. stubborn: 在这儿是‘顽强而不受锄犁’之意。

17. barrenness: 硗瘠，对 fertility，（肥沃）而言。土地未经耕垦，才保持原始地形与生态，可供历史家研究古代之用。

18. obliteration: = blotting out，毁灭。这儿指耕垦。

19. tending: 经营，耕垦。

20. the world: 这儿指点 bonfire 的人们所据的丘阜。这个丘阜，好象分为两层，上层发光，下层昏黑。Dark stretch，一片昏黑的地方。

21. the deeps: deep 为名词，= pit, valley. 这儿等于 pits，也就是前面的 abyss.

22. influence: 火光所及者。

23. aide-de-camp: 一般译侍从参谋，但此处解作传令官，较恰。从前两军交战，主帅站在阵后高地观察，要传达命令，由身边的传令官跑下山坡，疾趋山下而行之。

24. incline: slope.

25. replies: reflections.

26. black phenomenon: 即前面的 dark abyss 和 the deeps。

27. Limbo: 但丁《神曲》里地狱的最外层，那儿收容的是耶稣降生前之贤人和未及受洗即夭亡之婴儿的灵魂。

28. the sublime Florentine: 指但丁而言。但丁为 Florence 人。

29. muttered articulations of the wind: = low, subdued sounds of the wind.

30. from the… suspended therein: 英人 H. F. Cary 译《神曲》，直名之为 “The Vision of Dante”.《神曲，地狱篇》第 4 章第 5 行以下说：

…… For certain, on the brink
I found me of the lamentable vale,
The dread abyss, that joins a thundrous sound
Of plaints innumerable. Dark and deep,
And thick with clouds o'erspread, mine eyes in vain
Explored its bottom, nor could aught discern.

又第 25 行以下：

Here, as mine ear could not, no plaint was heard
Except of sighs, that made the eternal air
Tremble, not caused by tortures, but from grief
Felt by those multitudes, many and vast,
Of men, women, and infants ……

又第 40 行以下：

…… for well I knew
Suspended in that Limbo many a soul
Of mighty worth ……（以上都是 Cary 的译文。）

31. dived into past ages: 时代古老，犹如水深。故回到古代，犹如扎入水中。

32. fetched therefrom: = brought back from past ages.

33. ashes: 古代人火葬，焚尸体于薪垛（pyre）之上，焚毕，以其余烬与骨灰同埋冢中。

34. British: 古代不列颠人的。哈代笼统用 Briton 一字称有史以前居住现英国地方的民族。

35. Thor and Woden: 均为英人祖先（即日耳曼人）所供奉之神。

36. had their day: = had their time of prosperity.

37. heathmen: = inhabitants on the heath.

38. Druidical: Druid 是古 Briton 人的祭司。Druidical rites 即前面所说的 British pyre。

39. Saxon: 449 年 Angles, Saxons, Jutes（原住现在的丹麦和德国之间）开始侵入不列颠。后来称现代英人之祖为 Angle，即 English，或称 Saxon，亦称 Anglosaxon. Saxon ceremonies 即前面的 festival fires。

40. the winter ingress: the coming of winter.

41. the curfew: 灭火熄灯（或蜡）之钟声。行于欧洲中古。现在晚上有的地方教堂鸣钟，即其遗风。这儿钟声指冬天的风声。冬天的寒风一来，天地晦暗，天寒地冱，有如 curfew 钟声一鸣，家家灭火熄烛，灭火则冷，熄烛则暗。

42. Prometheus: 希腊神话，Prometheus 为 Titans（巨神）之一，违反天帝宙斯之意，窃火与人，天神锁之于柱（或石、或山），但他终不屈。

43. fiat:（神或自然造化的）命令。

44. black chaos: 冬天风雪交加、天昏地暗，一片混沌，象天地开辟以前的景象。

45. fettered gods of the earth: 以神比人，见于莎士比亚、培根、和哥德（此处不具引）。这儿也以神比人，人即神，特别以 Prometheus 比人，人即 Prometheus，因皆反抗天帝或神，而皆为神所制，而皆不屈。fettered 即前注之锁。这种神（即人）与 Prometheus 所不同者为：一为天上之神，一为地上之神。

46. Let there be light:《创世纪》第 1 章，上帝创造光明之时所说的一句话。

47. Duresque: 象 Durer 的。A. Durer (1471–1528) 为德国大画家和雕印画家（engraver），其作品以线条刚劲、轮廓分明为其特点。

48. permanent moral expression: 一个人生来是什么性格，如有的忠厚老实，有的狡黠油滑，有的正派，有的奸诈等等，这种种性格，都表现在脸上，总谓之为 moral expression. 这种表现与生俱来，不易改变，故谓之为 permanent。

49. death's head: = skull，骷髅。

50. pits of lutre: holes or caverns（这儿指凹入的眼睛、鼻孔等而言）so full of bright light that they give out shining surfaces.

51. moulding: 镂模，俗称牙子（牙读 yá）。

(2) The figure against the sky

1. The figure against the sky: 人影一个，昂天而立。

Egdon 是哈代给《还乡》的主要背景荒原（heath）起的名字。它的底本实有其地，叫作大荒原（the Great Heath）。

2. Concourse: crowd, people gathered together.

3. that quarter of the heath in which the little fire lay: 前面说过，本书女主角在她自己门外也点了一个小 bonfire。

4. reddleman: 卖红土的。红土是一种红色含氧化铁的粘土，英国农民用它在羊身上作记号，以免和别人的羊混杂。

5. Had the reddleman been watching: 前面说过，有一个卖红土的，老远眺览这片光景。

6. incomplete darkness: 在山顶上的空中，自然不比山下那样黑暗。

7. a venial beside a mortal sin: 天主教教义，认为重罪（mortal sin）有七种，如骄傲、贪婪、淫行等，有这类罪恶的灵魂永不得救。可恕之罪恶为 venial sin. 黑暗是罪恶的象征，罪恶愈大，黑暗愈甚。

8. at this hour and place: 注意，时间为黑夜，地点为荒丘。

9. aspect: side, direction.

the pivot of this circle of heath-country：四围都是荒原，她站在荒原正中间的山丘上，象枢纽一样。

10. Caesar: Julius Caesar 于 55，54 B. C. 两次入侵不列颠，都在秋分（autumnal equinox）以前就撤兵退出，否则天气要变，见于他的《高卢之战》(De Bello Gallico) 第 5 卷第 23 章。这一句是说，现在英国的阴暗天气，仍和两千多年前 Caesar 入侵的时候一样。

11. travellers from the South ... Homer's Cimmerian land: Cimmerian land 见 Homer's Odyssey 第 11 卷 14 行以下：'There is the land and the city of the Cimmerians, Shrouded in mist and cloud, and never does the shiny sun look down on them with his rays ... deadly night is outspread over miserable mortals'（Butther and Lang's translation）. the South，对英国说，法、意等国，都是南方。这儿 Travellers 虽是多数，但应特指 H. A. Taine（法国文学艺术历史及批评家）而言。他曾数次旅英，且有一时期在英讲学，写有《旅英札记》。(*Notes sur L'Angleterre*，1872）. 在那本书的第一章里，他拿荷马的 Cimmerians 地方比英国。

12. On the face of it: to judge by appearance.

13. treble: = Soprano 女或童高音。

ricochet：本为枪子儿或石头子儿着地又跳起之意，这儿是说风扑到或掠过坑谷岗峦的情况。

14. pits and prominences: = 前面说的 mounds and hollows，高阜与低谷或堑。

15. gravest pitch of chime: 西洋教堂的钟多为一组，高下成调。其中最低沉的是 the gravest pitch. 这种声音，呈低沉的嗡嗡之声，和风声极相似。

16. baritone: 男中音，亦即前面的 tenor. 因风声并不能太准，不能一定合于某一种音调。

17. buzz of a holly tree: buzz 本意为嗡嗡之声，如蜜蜂、苍蝇之声。holly 是长

青植物，叶子冬天也不凋落，且较硬，风吹其上，亦发嗡嗡之声，但这个嗡嗡之声与前不同，这个嗡嗡比前面的高。

18. dwindled voice: dwindled 本是干瘪抽缩之意，嗓音变 dwindled，就是干而不润，细而不洪，尖而不沉。老人嗓音多如此。

19. husky tune: 粗哑的音调。老人或病人尖细虚弱的嗓子，而强要发粗哑的声音，结果如何，只有模仿才可得而闻。

20. linguistic: 这儿 = vocal.

21. ruins of human song: 歌声之残痕剩迹。老人唱歌，不能充分发出歌儿所应有的声音。

22. throat: = voice.

23. fourscore and ten: 九十岁的老人。

24. worn whisper: whisper 是低语，有气无声（即声带不动），所以说嘁嘁喳喳。用 worn 形容声音，应是声嘶力竭。本来就只是嘁嘁喳喳，再加上声嘶力竭，所以这种嘁嘁喳喳是更细小、更虚弱的。

25. papery: 象揉搓纸片。

26. minuteae: 琐碎细小的情况。

27. infinitesimal: very small.

28. stems, leaves, fruit, blades, prickles, lichen, moss: stems 和 leaves 可以发声，这是人人都可以听得见者。fruit 等也可以发声，这只有象 Hardy 这样观察精细的诗人才能听到。比较他在本书另一个地方所写：at dusk, when soft, strange ventriloquisms (= sounds) came from holes in the ground, hollow stalks, curled dead leaves, and other crannies wherein breezes, worms, and insects can work their will ….

29. mummied: dead, dry, shrivelled like a mummy（木乃伊）。

30. heath-bell: heath 与前作‘荒原’解者不同，是荒原上面长的矮灌木丛，也叫 heather，开一种铃形或钟形小花，紫色，丛生。

31. Michaelmas: feast of St. Michael, September 29.

32. declivity: slope.

33. recitative: 宜叙调，半唱半说，为 opera 四种组成部分之一。shrivelled：本意，干瘪抽绉。声音 shrivelled 之解释，已见前。

法国研究英国文学的学者 Louis Cazamian 在他和 Emile Legouis 合写的《英国文学史》里说，‘从来没有人象哈代那样抓到了，或者至少用文字表达了 -heather 干枯了的小小钟形花上面那种特别的飒飒风声。’

2. POEMS

哈代写诗先于其写小说。其所写之诗有年月可考者始于 1863 年，而少年之作（juvenilia）尚不在内。以后续有所作，而 1896 年后，因《德伯家的苔丝》和《无名的裘德》，受到“卫道者”的攻击，遂放弃小说之写作，注全力于诗歌，直至 1928 年他死以前。他一共写了 918 首诗，辑为八集（《列国》(The Dynasts）单行，不在此内）。现在从他早期的作品里把最能代表他的主导思想和风格的，选出数首，以作尝鼎一脔。遗珠之憾，诚属无可奈何。

哈代自己愿意别人称他为诗人，而不愿意别人称他为小说家。他所以写小说，只是出于不得已。他重视诗歌远远过于小说。他的《列国》写的是拿破仑战争，托尔斯泰的《战争与和平》，写的也是拿破仑战争，但一则采取诗歌形式（史诗剧），而一则采取小说形式，这也可以看出民族传统、个人偏好的不同。不但此也，哈代还认为，在诗歌里可以更自由地表达思想。他说，假使当年伽利略用诗歌表达他的主张，他也许就不至于受到宗教法庭的制裁和迫害了。既然在诗歌里可以自由表达思想，所以在这里对哈代的思想就不再作介绍，因为这种介绍，总不免有贴标签之嫌，笼统含糊，难以确切。不如让读者从所选的作品里自下判断。不然，把“悲观主义”、“宿命论”等字样抬出来，岂不省事！至于所选是否真正代表哈代的主导思想，当然可有不同见解。这也是不先作介绍、不先定调子的原因之一。所可注意者，哈代自己从没承认过他的思想成为体系。他只不过把他的意见和感想，用艺术的形式发表问世而已。

(1) HAP

1. hap: (archaic) (1) chance or fortune (good or bad) that falls to anyone; (2) absence of design or intent in relation to a particular event; chance or fortune considered as the cause or determiner of events. 这是 hap 普通的意思。这儿 hap 含有这两种意思，而且还含有更多的意思。它可以说等于诗里的 Crass Casualty，解见后。

2. but: only.

3. some: a certain.

4. vengeful: harbouring revenge; seeking vengeance; prone or inclined to avenge oneself，蓄意报仇；锐于报仇雪恨。按基督教的说法，上帝是仁爱慈悲的（merciful and benevolent），revengeful 是属于 malicious 的，与 benevolent 正相反。此处言，求仁爱慈悲之上帝，固不可得，即退一步想，求一 malicious 之上帝，亦不可得。

5. Thou suffering thing: Thou = you. thing 指人说，人而谓之 thing，现在只用以表示 contempt, reproach, pity, affection 等感情。此处当然表示 contempt. 此处之 thing 所表示之人，指人类全体而言。人皆为受苦者。耶稣基督之舍身，为全人类赎罪。释迦牟尼之弃王位，亦为全人类求解脱。Thou suffering thing，为呼其人而告之。

6. ecstacy: ecstacy 在此处为乐得忘其所以，乐得如痴似狂。

7. Thy love's loss is my hate's profiting: 与上句意同，不过是另一样的说法，或更进一步的表达。“Your loss in love is my gain in hate.”“汝之爱所受之失即我之恨所得之益。”

8. bear it: bear = endure. 比较 grin and bear it。

9. clench myself: close tightly my teeth or fists，为忍受之具体表现。

10. Steeled: hardened in feeling.

11. by the sense: because I know or understand.

12. ire unmerited: ire = anger, wrath, now chiefly poetical and rhetorical. Unmerited, undeserved, not well-earned，并非罪有应得，这儿这个 unmerited 可以说相当于“薄言往愬，逢彼之怒。”因为这儿所说的这个上帝，既专以报仇雪恨为事，所以不管对象是有功还是有过，是善还是恶，一概以愤怒对待。

13. half-eased: partly felt relieved from pain, not feeling so much pain.

14. in that: because I think that.

15. a Powerfuller than I: a Being more powerful than I.

16. willed: wished, desired (now obsolete or archaic) .

17. How arrives it: How does it happen.

why unblooms the hope ever sown: 'hope' is compared to the seed of plant. Unbloom, fail to bloom or to blossom, fail to come into flower. 'Hope' has been sown, but it fails to come into flower, why is that so?

18. Crass Casualty: 'Crass', gross, grossly dull or stupid, grossly insemitive. 'Casualty', a chance occurrence, an accident, 'Crass Casualty' 在这儿是哈代给上帝的名字。这个上帝的 blind, insensate, equally indifferent to the happiness or misery of mankind, and does his Work unconciously and automatically. He is called "the Imminent Will" in 'the Dynasts."

19. obstruct: block up, exclude. plants need sunshine and rain for their growth. Now sunshine and rain are excluded from them, they can get no sunshine, nor rain, so they cannot grow.

20. dicing Time: Time is personified as a god. Dicing, playing dice. Time as a god knows nothing but playing dice.

21. casts: throws.

22. for gladness casts a moan: = cast a moan for gladness. Time plays dice. But the dice are not real dice. Instead of dice, he uses moan, sorrow, misery, grief as dice. He casts these for his pleasure.

23. These purblined Doomsters: Doomsters 就是前面说的 Crass Casualty 和 Dicing Time，他们都是人类命运的主宰者，但都是半拉瞎子。其实他们都是有前面注释中所列举的那些性格的，purblind 只是举其一端，以溉其余。

24. strown: scattered. strow = strew (archaic).

25. pilgrimage: the way I travel from birth to death. 在这儿等于说 my life.

26. strown blisses about my pilgrimage as pain: scattered on the way, i. e. my life, what are blisses to them but pain to me.

总叙全诗之意如下：我在此世并不求公道、合理、仁爱、明智，那是根本不可能的。所以如果只有一个心怀恶意，专事仇恨的上帝，统治人世，以世人之苦为自己之乐，那我也甘心忍受，不事抵抗，宁愿死去，也不抱怨。因为我知道，我之所以烦恼痛苦，都是因为有一个比我强大得多的 Being 或神之所欲所为，我无法抗拒。我之所以惹得神对我发怒，只象“薄言往愬，逢彼之怒”一样，原无道理可讲。但是事实上，连这样的神都不可得。现在世上，播种而不开花，本应使人欢娱之事而却使人苦恼。希望已经下种，而却不能有所希望的结果，世事总是乖舛谬戾，龃龉参商；其所以如此者，只是因为宇宙之主宰，昏聩无知，有目无珠，视而不见，听而不闻，甚至不闻不见，只在无识无知中任其自然而行动；造化小儿且以人世之苦难为自己之快乐，视世人如骰子，随意一掷即定赢输，事事全出偶然。正是由于这种情况，现在的世界和人事才是现在这种样子。

哈代这种思想，当然非他个人所独有。相同或类似的思想，古代即已有之，如中国的老子所说，“天地不仁，以万物为刍狗”，希腊的 Plutarch 所说，‘儿童投石击青蛙是玩儿，但是青蛙因为石所击而死，却不是玩儿，而是性命交关。’莎士比亚所说，更和哈代近似。他说，“神们看待我们，就象顽童看待苍蝇。他们杀害我们，给自己开心。”

哈代同时代或稍前稍后的诗人，则有 Mathew Arnold，在他的诗 Resignation 末尾，发出为全体人类之命运呼吁的声音。连乐观主义诗人 Robert Browning，也在他最后一卷诗里，写出了 Reverie 这样的诗，认为世界之上，善恶混淆，“善”只能挣扎，而统治者终属于“恶”。至于悲观诗人 James Thomason (1834–82)，则在他的诗 The City of Dreadful Night 里，把近代都市，比作昏暗中的冥国，魔影憧憧，鬼声啾啾。至于 A. E. Housman, T. S. Eliot，更和哈代相似。但是象哈代在二十五六岁这样年轻的时候，就一下“看破红尘”，并且虽然不能说是 consistent，却得说是 persistent，用各样方式，从各种角度，在诗里表达了同一思想，并且在他晚年《列国》那样的鸿篇巨制里，用在他那个时候看来最多事之秋——拿破仑战争时期——的纷纭事实，杂沓人物，来阐明同一主题，这在哈代可以说是独一无二。一般批评家，都说他的主导思想，在诗里是 explicit 的，而在他的小说里只是 implicit 的。其实这种说法也不尽然。现在就从他的小说里抄出两段来，作为他这种思想在小说里也同样是 explicit 的例证，以结束这段已嫌冗长的简介。

在《还乡》第一卷第七章里，说到书中女主角 Eustacia 的性格，哈代写道：“假使能有一会儿的工夫，她把全世界和全人类，完全掌握在自己的手里，假使她把纺线锤、纺线杆和大剪刀（古希腊命运女神所执之物），一手自由管领，那时候，世界之上很少有人能看出来，天道易主，世事变局。那时候，世上之人仍旧要命不齐，仍旧要永远进退维谷，仍旧要或受眷宠、或受谴责，仍旧要先讲宽容，后论公道，仍旧要祸福无门，忧乐难测，和我们现在所遭际的完全一样。”在《德伯家的苔丝》第五章里，写到书中女主角苔丝偏偏和奸污她的那个花花公子碰见，哈代议论道，“因为世间万事，虽然计划得好，而实行得却糟，所以呼唤人的和被呼唤的，很少能互相应答；恋爱的人和恋爱的时机，也不容易凑巧相合。当着两个人见了面儿就能前途美满的时候，老天很难得对他那可怜的人说一声‘你瞧’！不等到那捉迷藏的把戏把人累得筋疲力尽的时候，他也很难得说一声‘这儿！’，指引那高呼‘哪儿？’的人。将来人类的文明进化到至高无上那一天，人类的直觉自然要比现在更锐敏的了，社会的机构自然要比掀腾颠簸我们的这一种更密切地互相关联的了；到了那时候，那种进化了的直觉和进化了的社会机构，是不是就能把这种事序颠倒的情况矫正化除了，我们也许很想知道。不过这样完美的文明，不能预言在先，甚至于也不能悬想为可能。我们只晓得，现在这件公案，也和几百万别的公案一样，并不是一个完全整体的两半，正当完全适宜的时候，两两相遇；而只是两半里的一半失去不见，却在蠢然无知的顽冥中独自到处游荡，希冀遇到知音，一直游荡到事过境非的时候。由于这种行动的拙笨迁延，就生出来了种种焦虑、失望、惊吓、灾祸、和非常离奇的命运。”

现在再把这首诗的体裁和风格稍稍一谈。这是一首十四行诗，按正常的规律写出，其中虽有的地方，似稍出常规，如 thou suffering thing 似多出一个音节来，blisses 又轻重音颠倒，但这不算毛病，在按规律而写的英诗中本来允许这种失律的情况出现，以减少太合规律的写作里那种单调。而且此处之 suffering 也可读作 suff'ring. 所以这首诗不合常规，倒不在格律方面，而在词法句法的结构方面。词法方面，如题目之 hap，为 archaic，现在自属少见，但仍可见。至 unbloom 则似为哈代所独造不见于字典（O. E. D. 未收此字），但其意很明显，且语首 un 一可活用，从古英语，经中古英语，直到现代，都可活用，（细情各时代当然不可能完全一样。）不过字样看起来使人觉得‘生’而已。至 my love's profitting, thy hate's loss, How arrives it, Why unblooms the best hope，确不合普通语法结构，但这也并非哈代自我作古，而他是受了 Robert Browning 的影响，或者是他有意模仿 Browning。Browning 的诗里有这样的句子：Irks care the crop-full birds? Frets doubt the … maw-crammed beast?（见其诗 Rabbi Ben Ezra，第四段），（= Does care irk the … bird? Does doubt fret the … beast? i. d., Birds and beasts are never troubled by such things as care and doubt），正同哈代这儿的 How arrives it … Why unblooms hope …. 至于 love's loss, hate's profiting 之结构，更属于 Browning 之特点。哈代在 Hap 这首诗里，有意识地采用了 Browning 那种 cacophony，以与诗的内容协调，如果诗句是 euphemistic 的，反倒与内容不协调了。这种风格也是哈代后来的诗所有的风格。所以 Hap 这首诗，虽然是他二十六岁的作品（可能后来经过润色），却一下就早已表现了他的主导思想和他的独特风格，不能认为是粗疏而不成熟的。

他为什么这样年轻而就有这样的思想呢？当然是由于他在伦敦（当时人事最纷纭、现象最复杂的世界上第一大都市）有所见闻，有所接触，有所亲受，再加以有所思考，有所探索，才形成的。而在这一切里，男女关系更为突出。

(2) NEUTRAL TONES

1. neutral: having no decided colour, of a bluish grayish appearance. Tone, a quality of colour, a tint, a shade. 'Neutral Tones' 这个题目，简截地说，只是‘灰色’，但其所示，远过于此。其时为冬季，自然天地灰黯，其月白，亦即灰，其树则直言其灰，gray，是一切景物皆为灰色。但更重要者，则为其人心情之暗淡、凄冷，亦是灰黯。所以这两个字，应兼 literally 及 metaphorically 或 symbolically 解之。

2. chidden of God: rebuked or scolded by God. 人受责时，则其首低俯，其颜惨淡。此以人受责时惨淡之颜，喻冬日惨淡之色。

3. starving: that is dying of hunger; here, 'starving sod' means that the earth was so barren that it was bare of vegetation.

4. rove over: 既非注视，也非瞥视，正刻画了对 tedious 之物的看法。

5. tedious riddles of years ago: riddles are something to be guessed at. Riddles unsolved for many years one must lose interest in. So they become wearisome or tedious. Here "riddles" refers to the man. 诗中女方永远认为男方是一个谜，一直加以揣度，不知道他是否真正爱她？他是否能在社会上爬到和她身分相等的地位？他究竟配得过配不过她？诸如此类的问题永远在她的脑子里盘旋，一直没得到答案。这也表明，女方一直在心里计算，永远也没 love the man for himself alone. 那也就是说，她从来没真正爱过他。

6. Some words played between us to and fro: Some words passed or said between us as if we were bantering.

7. on which lost the more by our love: about which one of us lost the more as a result of our love.

8. alive enough to have strength to die: 活的程度只有死去的劲儿那样大。这可以有两种解释，死不需要"劲儿"，所以活的程度只是临死前那样活法儿，几乎是不活。这是一种解释。另一种解释是：有的人临死的时候，要经过一番痛苦，所谓 the agony or agonies of death，或 death-agony 或 death-struggle. 在这种痛苦中要扎挣～番，扎挣当然需要'劲儿'。但后一种解释嫌 far-fetched。

9. an ominous bird a-wing: a bird bringing ill-luck flying past. Such birds as ravens are popularly regarded as birds of evil omen.

10. keen lessons: lessons go deep to one's heart, lessons which cut sharply or deeply.

11. love deceives: 这是这首诗的主题。

12. wrings with wrong: wrings the heart with the sense of being wronged.

此诗写男女情人最后诀别时会面的光景。于此次会面中，女面对男面表现极鄙夷之态度，证其以前之甜言蜜语尽属欺骗，给男方留下极痛心疾首的印象。诗中特以会面时之景物作衬托，如陆放翁之犹吊"遗踪"也。

此诗写于 1866 年，正是哈代在伦敦著名建筑师布露姆·菲勤得的公事房中工作的时候。

(3) SHE AT HIS FUNERAL

1. resting-place: final resting-place, grave.

2. sweeping: walking or moving in a stately manner, moving along majestically.

3. a stranger's space: The distance a stranger keeps.

4. His kindred they: they are his kinsrmen.

5. garish dye: bright colour.

6. sable-sad ... attire: black clothes which are symbolic of sadness, the conventional mourning worn by the relations of the dead as sign of sorrow.

7. regret: sorrow, grief.

(4) THE DARKLING THRUSH

1. Darkling: being in the dark.

2. thrush: 一般译为“画眉”，但 thrush 严格说来，并不同于中国的画眉。中国画眉以英语译之应为 mountain babbler. 真属于 thrush 者有一百余种。且此字用法复杂：有真属于 thrush 者，在英文中反不叫 thrush，亦有不属于 thrush 者，而反叫 thrush. 总之此处的 thrush 是英国的一种鸟儿，以善鸣著。

3. coppice: 也作 copse. 英国树林，有 forest, woods, plantation, grove, coppice 等，都有分别。coppice 则为 small wood of underwood and small tree, grown for periodical cutting.

4. gate: 栅栏门。英国田地、草场、林地，都有围篱或树篱围绕（enclosure），故须有 gate，才能出入。

5. spectre-grey: spectre = ghost. 英人观念，以 ghost 为白色，可能由于死者尸体都裹以 winding-sheet（白色）而起。spectre-grey: grey or white as a ghost. 这应为 hoar-frost。

6. winter's dregs: dregs（plured），本为酒渣之意。此处为 last remains, small remnant，残余。故 winter's dregs 为“残冬”。winter 的说法或算法不一，普通的说法为 December 至 February，或 November 至 January. 此处以后者为宜，因此诗作于 31st December。总之，December 为一年中最冷之月份。

7. The weakening eye of day: the eye of day = the sun. weakening becoming dimmer and dimmer.

8. bine-stems: twining stems of climbing plants.

9. scored the sky: marked the sky with lines.

10. haunted nigh: nigh = near (archaic or poetical). haunted nigh: frequented the neighbourhood.

11. fires: masses of burning material, e. g. on a hearth. Here it means the firesides, the hearths.

12. The land's sharp features: Here the contour and surface of the land are compared to the features of human face. “Sharp”, because the hills are high and valleys low, or there are “rounds and hollows” as Hardy himself has said elsewhere. It is associated with “thin”, or “lean”, or “gaunt”.

13. The Century's Corpse: “Time” is personified and given the name of “Century”. Time is old and dead; only his dead body remains reclining or lying supinely.

14. outleant: 由 out lean 变来，out lean 又由 lean out 变来。lean 为 reline 之意。此处 out leant 之用法，与 outspread (p. part.) 相同，亦可直以 outspread 解之，不过一为欹卧，一为平卧。

15. His crypt the cloudy canopy: The cloudy canopy was his crypt, canopy 本为覆于床、宝座、人等上面的帐幕（如华盖）一类之物，也以之喻为天（天覆于一切

之上)。现在的 cloudy canopy 更是天。Crypt 是(特别是教堂下面)拱形地下室,为贵人等坟墓。地下室当然也有屋顶(象居室之有 ceiling)。现在"Time"的尸体既欹(lean out)于大地之上,则他这个墓室的穹隆就是天空(天空也叫穹隆)。这种以天地为庐舍的想法,中国古代文人也有之,和贾谊之《鹏鸟赋》以及刘伶等人(此处不备引)。但状"Time"之苍老枯瘠,景物之萧瑟荒寒者(desolate),恐无过此者。(哈代以 Titan 等喻荒寒苍凉之大地者,亦逊此处之所写)。

16. The wind his death-lament: The wind was his death-lament. Deathlament = death-dirge, dirge.

17. ancient: aged, old, of great age (archaic).

18. pulse: throb of life.

19. spirit: breath of life.

20. full-hearted: full of feeling, indicative of strong emotion.

21. evensong: 本为 evening prayer 之意,此处则为 a song sung in the evening.

22. In blast-beruffled plume: beruffled 即 ruffled,如 bedrenched 之即为 drenched,同为 intensive. In blast-beruffled plume: with his feathers ruffled by the wind.

23. fling his soul upon: pour out or discharge vigorously all his emotional energy on.

24. growing: increasing, deepening.

25. caroling: singing joyously.

26. written: marked.

27. terrestrial: earthly.

28. afar or nigh: far or near.

29. good-night air: air: song-like music. melody. Good night is used attributively, as in "good-night kiss."

30. blessed: joyful, blissful, bringing or accompanied by blissing or happiness.

这首诗收在哈代的诗集 *Poems of the Past and the Present* 中,可能是受到 W. H. Hadson 的 *Nature in Downland* 里一段描写的启发而写的,但其表达音乐之美,则全为哈代自己所创造。另一位英国诗人 Alfred Noyes 对此诗之论断,可引作此诗之定评,他说,"Hardy's ... the Darkling Thrush is a lyric of rugged strength, that peculiar strength which comes from understatement and the sense of something in reserve; a lyric of such pathos and beauty as can be compared with the best that has ever been done in our great lyrical language; and that is to say one of the finest lyrics in the world. From the first line to the restrained and intense rapture of the close, the poem bears upon it the stamp of a truth and sincerity beyond praise." 前哈代散文选,选了两篇"状难写之景",这一首诗是有"有余不尽之味"。

(5) AT CASTLE BOTEREL

哈代和他头一位夫人,于 1870 年第一次相遇,于 1874 年结婚。在结婚前,他们常一同游过一些地方。他的夫人于1912病故。哈代为哀悼她，写了一些悼亡诗，总名为*Poems of 1912–13*，副题为*Veteris vestigia flammae*，拉丁文，意为vestiges of old flame. 这些诗里有一些是他到他们一同旧游之地凭吊遗踪之作。现在从这类诗里选出一首。

1. Castle Boterel: 是哈代给这个地方起的名字。它的真名为Boscastle，是一个小小渔港，有小涧入海，涧在小山间曲折而流，颇富画意。其地在英兰格最西南部之Cornwall郡东北角上。Cornwall郡几乎全部都为游览区，此为其中之一。哈代与其夫人婚前曾同游其地。其夫人故去后第二年，哈代重到其地，凭吊旧迹，追忆从前而作此诗。

2. lane and highway: lane两旁有树篱（hedges）夹路，较窄而曲。open highway则路旁无树篱。

3. bedrench: intensive of drench, = soak.

4. waggonette: 专供游览用的四轮单马或双马马车。

5. by-way: 即前面的lane。

6. its slope: Cornwall为一半岛，全部为山区，几乎无平地。

7. glistening: 地面为雨水所湿而发亮。

8. benighted: overtaken by the darkness of the night. 以下追忆从前光景。前面see on the slope ... distinctly ... myself and a girlish form，追忆前事，前事重现，如在目前，故look与climb都用现在式。

9. chaise: 与前面的waggonette几乎相同的一种马牛。

10. sighed: 表示weariness, dejection等感情。

11. what we did as we climed: possibly embracing and kissing.

12. what we talked of: possibly plighting lovers' vows.

13. to what it led: to marriage.

14. be balked of: be disappointed in. 此处of之用法，同于be deprived of, be robbed of中之of。

15. rude reason: rude有simple, roughly made, wanting accuracy诸意，故rude reason应为无理由之理由、不成理由之理由。Reason亦可与love相对而论。Pure love纯属感情，掺不得半点理智。故reason与love比较，则成rude，而love则subtle, gentle, refined，所谓"心有灵犀一点通"是也。

16. such guality: 这儿等于sterling quality, a quality pure as pure gold.

17. in that hill's story: in all which the hill has experienced.

18. foot-swift: swift of foot.

19. faced: confronted, seen.

20. the Transitory: what lasts only a short time; contrasted with "long order".

21. order: way things normally happen, regular course of events.

22. cast: form, mould.

23. unflinching rigour: unyielding harshness, strict enforcement.

24. in mindless rote: rote: mechanical performance or practice. Mindless: thoughtless, heedless, careless. 这儿也可作 unconscious 解。哈代在 *The Dynasts* 的序幕里有 by rapt rote，与此处之 in mindless rote 实同义。

25. ruled: shut out.

26. The substance: the corporeal body, form with sustance, contrasted with "phantom figure", form with out rubstance.

27. my sand is sinking: sand 这儿是 sand-glass 或 hour-glass 里的 sand. 这是以 sand-glass 喻生命。sand-glass 里的沙快漏尽，比喻生命快完结。

28. Traverse old love's domain: go through or pass the place which lovers visited in the past. 这里是具体与想象兼而言之。

Robert Browning 在他的 Cristina 一诗中，说到 "moments when the spirit's true endowment stands out plainly" 和 "in some such moment mine and her souls rushed together." 的话。在哈代这首诗里，重现了上叙的概念。这种概念，可以用"心有灵犀一点通"解之。但西人之"灵犀"更属于 soul 方面，更抽象、更缥缈、更空灵，超过中国之"灵犀"。这就牵涉到但丁之与 Beatrice, Shelley 的 Epipsychidion（只举二人为例）。同时也牵涉到中西对 love 的整个问题。这当然非此注所能详、所宜详。

(6) IN TENEBRIS

1. In Tenebris: 拉丁文。Tenebris 是 tenebrae 的 ablative case，属于名词 first dlecension. Tenebrae 有具体的 darkness，抽象的 darkness，以及 gloom 等义。这里为后者之意或偏重后者，即 in darkness 或 in gloom.

题下所引为拉丁文《圣经》《诗篇》（*Psalms*）第 141 篇第 3 节。英文圣经（Authorized Version）则为 142 篇第 4 节（拉丁文圣经与英文圣经，章节的分法有时不同）。其英译为：I looked on my right hand, and beheld, but there was no man that would know me: … no man cared my soul. 右手一般比左手强而有力，使用得更多。在圣经里，亦尚右，右边为上帝所在之处，为力量所在之处，为援助所在之处。故往右看以求力量，以求援助。

2. the clouds' swoln bosoms: clouds, visible masses of condensed watery vapour. When cloud is regarded as a substance, it is used in the singular. 哈代在 the Return of the Native 第 5 卷第 7 章里写道，"The scene without grew darker; mud-coloured clouds bellied downward from the sky like vast hammocks slung across it …" 正是这儿 The clouds' swoln (= swollen, swoln 为 arch.) bosoms 的注脚；不过那儿是暴风雨欲来之时，天空乌云弥漫并且下垂，所谓"天近云低"。是具体的景象。这儿有象征或比喻之意。

3. echo back the shouts: 汉语说"声闻于天"。《圣经》里说闻于上帝，莎士比亚则说"… against the welkin (= sky) volleys out his voice." 英语也说 rend the welkin，特别是 make the welkin ring. Ring 和 echo 在这儿同义。

4. one better he were not here: it would be better if such a one like him were not here.

5. upstanders: 'to stand up for somebody or something' is to support somebody or something, so upstanders are supporters.

6. the potent: the strong, the powerful (chicfly poetical or shetorical).

7. oft: often (archaic).

8. breezily: briskly.

9. their dust smokes around their career: they kick up or raise so much dust by their brisk coming and going that what they are doing is quite obscured.

10. calling: need, occasion, right.

11. dawns: mornings.

12. lusty: vigorous, lively.

13. times: (pl.) conditions of life, prevailing circumstances, of period.

14. Life shapes it: Life shapes itself.

15. meet: (archaic) suitable, fit, proper.

16. such an one: 旧式。现用 such a one.

17. Let him: 这儿 Let him 贯串后面三个 clauses. Let him in whose ears ..., let him who holds that ... let him who feels that ...

18. low-voiced: here "Cow-voiced" should be interpreted as "soft-spoken", "gentle-voiced". 比较 Shakespeare, *Antony and Cleapatra*, 111.3.14-15, "is she shrill-tongued or low?... she is low-voiced." 又 *King Lear*. V.3.273, "Her voice was ever soft, gentle, low, an excellent thing in woman."

19. the First: in music, The voice or instrument that takes the highest or chief part in its class; The upper part of a duet, trio, etc.

20. exacts: requires urgently, demands strongly.

21. growth cramped by crookedness, custom and fear: 比较 Tess, chaper XX, "Their position was perhaps the happiest of all positions in the social scale, being above the line at which neediness ends, and below the line at which the *convenances* begin to cramp natural feeling, and the stress of threadbare modishness makes too little of enough." Crookedness the quality or state of being dishonest or not straightforward; the state of deviating from rectitude or uprightness. 比较汉语"世道曲如弓。"

22. fear: the emotion of pain or uneasiness caused by the sense of impending danger, or by the prospect of some possible evil. "人生艰苦，使人惴惴不安"。

23. get him: get himself.

这个题目 *In Tenebris* 之下，本有诗三首。现所选为其中第二首。这一首的主旨为 If way to the Better there be, it exacts a full look at the worst. 但是英国维多利亚时期，一般人只看到表面，认为工商业繁荣，科学发达，就深自满，以为只此已足，而特寄人类幸福于科学，于是讳疾忌医。哈代此诗专对这种人而发。大有众人皆醉而我独醒之意。由其所引拉丁文《诗篇》更可见此意。

(7) SHUT OUT THAT MOON

这首诗作于 1904 年，在哈代的夫人死前八年。那时他们都已 60 岁上下，同时他们的感情据说已不太好。这首诗可能受这种情况的影响而写，抚今追昔，不胜感慨。其追昔，实甚温馨旖旎，其抚今，确系凄清萧索，为哈代极 lyrical 之作之一。

1. blind: curtain.

2. steading moon: moon which peeps into the room.

3. guise: attire, garb, (arch.).

4. strewn with years-deep dust: thickly covered with dust accumulated by long years.

5. stone: tomb-stone, grave-stone.

6. hewn: cut, carved.

7. step not forth: don't go out.

8. dew-dashed: drenched, bedabbled, or spangled with dew.

9. lawn: grass covered land.

10. view: survey with the eyes.

11. Lady's Chair: Cassiopeia，仙后座，有几颗亮星，列成椅状，故名，或以之为 M 状。

12. Orion: 猎户座，四颗最亮的星，列成长方形，如人之立。腰间有小星，列成腰带状，带上挂短剑。此所谓 immense form，即指此种形状而言。

13. Less and Greater Bear: 小熊座和大熊座。小熊座一般作 the Lesser Bear.

14. Brush not the bough ...: 此诗每段所写皆夜景，而此段更属 midnight. 盖夜深人悄，花树披离，抚树拈花，则芬芳馥郁，沾手染衣，此正温馨旖旎之时也。

15. lamp-lit: lighted or lit by a lamp.

16. prison: imprion, confine (poet).

17. dingy: dull coloured, because seen in the lamp light,

18. details: 本为 minor decorations in building, picture, etc.，此处或特指 furniture 的雕饰而言。哈代曾学过建筑，故对这类东西特注意。

19. crudely: 以其本色，不加雕琢，亦即虽本来有雕琢之饰，现在在暗淡的灯光下，亦不可见。

20. wrought: 为 work 的 past 及 past participle forms 之一，意为 made, constructed, manufactured，本不能与 speech 连用，但此处之 speech 既为 mechanic 的，则与工艺品同，故用 wrought 表之。

21. tart: acid, sharp-tasted. 汉语为“辛酸”与“辛辣”，此兼而有之。

(8) AFIERWARDS

此为哈代晚年的诗。等于是他给自己写的一首墓志铭，里面说，他死后人们要怎样评论他。

1. Present: personified.

2. latched its postern: fastened its door with latch, locked its door.

3. my tremulous stay: stay here means "stay on earth"，意为 sojourn in this world. 人生如寄寓，天地为万物之逆旅，"Present" 是逆旅的主人，我寄寓之后，店主东把门锁上，喻我死去。Tremulous = trembling，小心翼翼，战战兢兢。Life is full of danger. My earthly "pilgrimage" has been full of traps and pit-falls. I have made this pilgrimage timidly, tremblingly. Shelley 的 诗 *A Lament* 里 I "O world! O life! O time! On whose last steps I climb; Trembling at that where had stood before." 可能是哈代这里的 Tremulous 之所本。Keats 的 *Ode to a Nightingale* 里 "Where palsy shakes a few, sad, last grey hairs," 也可能有影响。Palsy = paralytic trembling.

4. glad: full of brightness or beauty, suggesting feelings of cheerfulness and delight.

5. delicate-filmed: having fine, slender films. Film = fine thread or filament. 这一句应特别注意。这是普通人所不注意或视而不见的。dewfall-hawk "dewfall" means "the time when dew begins to fall", i. e. to form or to deposit. Dewfall-hawk: hawk that begins its activities after dark. It must be the nighthawk, also called night-jar or goatsucker.

6. the shades: (pl.) darkness of night or evening。

7. wind-warped: bent, contorted or twisted out of shape by the wind.

8. pass: die.

9. nocturnal blackness: dark night. Black 比 dark 还黑。

10. mothy: when moths are active.

11. lawn: grass-covered land.

12. He strove ... harm: 哈代最爱护动物，为 The Royal Society for the Prevention of Cruelty to Animals 会员，写过一些反对残害动物的诗，为虐待动物的人被告而出庭作证，其写受害小动物最著者为其对 Waterloo 之战前夕受害小动物之描写（见 *The Dynasts*, Part III. Act VI, Scene VIII.）。

13. stilled: quieted, calmed. 这儿是"死了"的意思。

14. full-starred heavens that winter sees: heaven 一字，从 17 世纪起，一般单数用于诗，复数用于普通散文。在那时以前，单复数用法无别。这儿是旧用法。Fullstarred: full of stars. 天上星星最多的时候是冬夜。猎户座、大犬座、小犬座都在冬季出现。大熊座、小熊座更不用说。哈代关于星星的描写，可以说以 *Far from the Madding Crowd* 第二章所写为最出色。

15. quittance: quitting, leaving. Bell of quittance = knell.

16. crossing: moving across，在这儿可解作，由侧面而来。

17. outrollings: outroll = roll out or forth, unroll. 此处为 the spreading of the sound waves.

18. as they were: as if they were.

哈代另一首诗 *A Poet*，也写他自己，与此诗性质相类，但角度不同。可参看。

47 GEORGE BERNARD SHAW
1856–1950

PYGMALION[1]

王佐良　选注

from Act III

It is Mrs Higgins's at-home day.[2] *Nobody has yet arrived. Her drawing room, in a flat on Chelsea Embankment,*[3] *has three windows looking on the river; and the ceiling is not so lofty as it would be in an older house of the same pretension.*[4] *The windows are open, giving access to a balcony with flowers in pots. If you stand with your face to the windows, you have the fireplace on your left and the door in the right-hund wall dose to the corner nearest the windows.*

Mrs Higgins was brought up on Morris and Burne Jones;[5] *and her room, which is very unlike her son's room in Wimpole Street,*[6] *is not crowded with furniture and little tables and nicknacks.*[7] *In the middle of the room there is a big ottoman;*[8] *and this, with the carpet, the Morris wall-papers, and the Morris chintz window curtains and brocade covers of the ottoman and its cushions, supply all the ornament, and are much too handsome to be hidden by odds and ends*[9] *of useless things. A few good oil-paintings from the exhibitions in the Grosvenor Gallery thirty years ago (the Burne Jones, not the Whistler side of them)*[10] *are on the walls. The only landscape is a Cecil Lawson on the scale of a Rubens.*[11] *There is a portrait of Mrs Higgins as she was when she defied the fashion in her youth in one of the beautiful Rossettian costumes which, when caricatured by people who did not understand, led to the absurdities of popular estheticism in the eighteen-seventies.*[12]

In the corner diagonally opposite the door Mrs Higgins, now over sixty and long past taking the trouble to dress out of the fashion,[13] *sits writing at an elegantly simple writing-table with a bell button within reach of her hand. There is a Chippendale chair*[14] *further back in the room between her amd the window nearest her side. At the other side of the room, further forward, is an Elizabethan chair roughly carved in the taste of Inigo Jones.*[15] *On the same side a piano in a decorated case. The corner between the fireplace and the window is occupied by a divan cushioned in Morris chintz.*

It is between four and five in the afternoon.

The door is opened violently; and Higgins enters with his hat on.[16]

MRS HIGGINS. [*dismayed*] Henry! [*Scolding him*] What are you doing here today? It is my at-home day: you promised not to come. [*As he bends to kiss her, she takes his hat off, and presents it to him*].

HIGGINS. Oh bother![17] [*He throws the hat down on the table*].

MRS HIGGINS. Go home at once.

HIGGINS. [*kissing her*] I know, mother. I came on purpose.

MRS HIGGINS. But you mustnt.[18] I'm serious, Henry. You offend all my friends: they stop coming whenever they meet you.

HIGGINS. Nonsense! I know I have no small talk;[19] but people dont mind. [*He sits on the settee*].

MRS HIGGINS. Oh! dont they? Small talk indeed! What about your large talk? Really, dear, you mustnt stay.

HIGGINS. I must. Ive a job for you. A phonetic job.

MRS HIGGINS. No use, dear. I'm sorry; but I cant get round your vowels;[20] and though I like to get pretty postcards in your patent shorthand,[21] I always have to read the copies in ordinary writing[22] you so thoughtfully send me.

HIGGINS. Well, this isnt a phonetic job.

MRS HIGGINS. You said it was.

HIGGINS. Not your part of it. Ive picked up a girl.[23]

MRS HIGGINS. Does that mean that some girl has picked you up?

HIGGINS. Not at all. I dont mean a love affair.

MRS HIGGINS. What a pity!

HIGGINS. Why?

MRS HIGGINS. Well, you never fall in love with anyone under forty-five. When will you discover that there are some rather nice-looking young women about?[24]

HIGGINS. Oh, I cant be bothered with young women.[25] My idea of a lovable woman is somebody as like you as possible. I shall never get into the way of seriously liking young women:[26] some habits lie too deep to be changed. [*Rising abruptly and walking about, jingling his money and his keys in his trouser pockets*] Besides, theyre all idiots,

MRS HIGGINS. Do you know what you would do if you really loved me, Henry?

HIGGINS. Oh bother! What? Marry, I suppose.

MRS HIGGINS, No, Stop fidgeting and take your hands out of your pockets.[27] [*With a gesture of despair, he obeys and sits down again*]. Thats a good boy. Now tell me about the girl.

HIGGINS, She's coming to see you,

MRS HIGGINS. I dont remember asking her.[28]

HIGGINS. You didnt. I asked her, If youd known her you wouldnt have asked her,

MRS HIGGINS. Indeed! Why?

HIGGINS. Well, it's like this. She's a common flower girl. I picked her off the kerbstone.[29]

MRS HIGGINS, And invited her to my at-home!

HIGGINS. [*rising and coming to her to coax her*] Oh, thatll be all right. Ive taught her to speak properly; and she has strict orders as to her behavior. She's to keep to two subjects:[30] the weather and everybody's health—Fine day and How do you do,[31] you know—and not to let herself go on things in general.[32] That will be safe.

MRS HIGGINS. Safe! To talk about our health! about our insides![33] perhaps about our outsides![34] How could you be so silly, Henry?

HIGGINS. [*impatiently*] Well, she must talk about something. [*He controls himself and sits down again*]. Oh, she'll be all right: dont you fuss. Pickering is in it with me.[35] Ive a sort of bet on that I'll pass her off as a duchess[36] in six months. I started on her some months ago; and she's getting on like a house on fire.[37] I shall win my bet. She has a quick ear; and she's been easier to teach than my middle-class pupils because she's had to learn a complete new language. She talks English almost as you talk French.

MRS HIGGINS. Thats satisfactory, at all events.[38]

HIGGINS. Well, it is and it isnt.

MRS HIGGINS. What does that mean?

HIGGINS. You see, Ive got her pronunciation all right; but you have to consider not only how a girl pronounces, but what she pronounces; and that's where —

They are interrupted by the parlor-maid, announcing guests.

THE PARLOR-MAID. Mrs and Miss Eynsford Hill.[39] [*She withdraws*].

HIGGINS. Oh Lord! [*He rises; snatches his hat from the table; and makes for the door: but before he reaches it his mother introduces him*].

Mrs and Miss Eynsford Hill are the mother and daughter who sheltered from the rain in Covent Garden.[40] The mother is well bred, quiet, and has the habitual anxiety of straitened means.[41] The daughter has acquired a gay air of being very much at home in society: the bravado of genteel poverty.[42]

MRS EYNSFORD HILL. [*to Mrs Higgins*] How do you do? [*They, shake hands*].

MISS EYNSFORD HILL. How d'you do? [*She shakes*].

MRS HIGGINS. [*introducing*] My son Henry.

MRS EYNSFORD HILL. Your celebrated son! I have so longed to meet you, Professor Higgins.

HIGGINS. [*glumly, making no movement in her direction*] Delighted.[*He backs against the piamo and bows brusquely*].

MISS EYNSFORD HILL. [*going to him with confident famniliarity*][43] How do you do?

HIGGINS. [staring at her] Ive seen you before somewhere. I havnt the ghost of a notion where;[44] but Ive heard your voice. [*Drearily*] It doesnt matter. Youd better sit down

MRS HIGGINS. I'm sorry to say that my celebrated son has no manners.[45] You mustnt mind him.

MISS EYNSFORD HILL. [*gaily*] I dont. [*She sits in the Elizabethan chair*]

MRS EYNSFORD HILL. [*a little bewildered*] Not at all. [*She sits on the ottoman between her daughter and Mrs Higgms, who has turned her chair away from the writing-table*].

HIGGINS. Oh, have I been rude? I didnt mean to be.

He goes to the central window, through which, with his back to the company,[46] *he contemplates the river and the flowers in Battersea Park on the opposite bank as if they were a frozen desert.*[47]

The parlor-maid returns, ushering in Pickering.

THE PARLOR-MAID. Colonel Pickering. [*She withdraws.*]

PICKERING. How do you do, Mrs Higgins?

MRS HIGGINS. So glad youve come. Do you know Mrs Eynsford Hill-Miss Eynsford Hill? [*Exchange of bows.*[48] *The Colonel brings the Chippendale chair a little forward between Mrs Hill and Mrs Higgins, and sits down*].

PICKERING. Has Henry told you what weve come for?

HIGGINS. [*over his shoulder*[49]] We were interrupted: damn it![50]

MRS HIGGINS. Oh Henry, Henry, really![51]

MRS EYNSFORD HILL. [*half rising*] Are we in the way?[52]

MRS HIGGINS. [*rising and making her sit down again*] No, no. You couldnt have come more fortunately: we want you to meet a friend of ours.

HIGGINS. [*turning hopefully*] Yes, by George![53] We want two or three people. Youll do as well as anybody else.[54]

The parlor-maid returns, ushering Freddy.

THE PARLOR-MAID. Mr Eynsford Hill.

HIGGINS. [*almost audibly, past endurance*[55]] God of Heaven! another of them.[56]

FREDDY. [*shaking hands with Mrs Higgins*] Ahdedo?[57]

MRS HIGGINS. Very good of you to come. [*Introducing*] Colonel Pickering.

FREDDY. [*bowing*] Ahdedo?

MRS HIGGINS. I dont think you know my son, Professor Higgins.

FREDDY. [*going to Higgins*] Ahdedo?

HIGGINS. [*looking at him much as if he were a pickpocket*[58]] I'll take my oath Ive met you before somewhere. Where was it?

FREDDY. I dont think so.

HIGGINS. [*resignedly*] It dont matter,[59] anyhow. Sit down.

He shakes Freddy's hand, and almost slings him on to the ottoman with his face to the window; then comes round to the other side of it.

HIGGINS. Well, here we are, anyhow! [*He sits down on the ottoman next Mrs Eynsford Hill, on her left*]. And now, what the devil are we going to talk about[60] until Eliza comes?

MRS HIGGINS. Henry: you are the life and soul of the Royal Society's soirées;[61] but really youre rather trying[62] or more commonplace occasions.

HIGGINS. Am I? Very sorry. [*Beaming suddenly*] I suppose I

am, you know. [*Uproariously*] Ha, ha!

MISS EYNSFORD HILL. [*who considers Higgins quite eligible matrimonially*[63]] I sympathize. I havnt any small talk. If people would only be frank and say what they really think![64]

HIGGINS. [*relapsing into gloom*] Lord forbid![65]

MRS EYNSFORD HILL. [*taking up her daughter's cue*][66] But why?

HIGGINS. What they think they ought to think is bad enough, Lord knows; but what they really think would break up the whole show.[67] Do you suppose it would be really agreeable if I were to come out now with[68] what I really think?

MISS EYNSFORD HILL [*gaily*] Is it so very cynical?

HIGGINS. Cynical! Who the dickens[69] said it was cynical? I mean it wouldnt be decent.

MRS EYNSFORD HILL. [*seriously*] Oh! I'm sure you dont mean that, Mr Higgins.

HIGGINS. You see, we're all savages, more or less.[70] We're supposed to be civilized and cultured—to know all about poetry and philosophy and art and science, and so or; but how many of us know even the meanings of these names? [*To Miss Hill*] What do you know of poetry? [*To Mrs Hill*] What do you know of science? [*Indicating Freddy*] What does he know of art or science or anything else? What the devil do you imagine I know of philosophy?

MRS HIGGINS. [*warningly*] Or of manners,[71] Henry?

THE PARLOR-MAID. [*opening the door*] Miss Doolittle. [She withdraws].

HIGGINS. [*rising hastily and running to Mrs Higgins*] Here she is, mother. [*He stands on tiptoe and makes signs over his mother's head to Eliza to indicate to her which lady is her hostess*].

Eliza, who is exquisitely dressed, produces an impression of such remarkable distinction and beauty as she enters that they all rise, quite fluttered. Guided by Higgins's signals, she comes to Mrs Higgins with studied grace.[72]

LIZA. [*speaking with pedantic correctness of pronunciation*[73] *and great beauty of tone*] How do you do, Mrs Higgins? [*She gasps slightly in making sure of the H in Higgins,*[74] *but is quite successful*]. Mr Higgins told me I might come.

MRS HIGGINS. [*cordially*] Quite right: I'm very glad indeed to see you.

PICKERING. How do you do, Miss Doolittle?

LIZA. [*shaking hands with him*] Colonel Pickering, is it not?[75]

MRS EYNSFORD HILL. I feel sure we have met before, Miss Doolittle. I remember your eyes.

LIZA. How do you do? [*She sits down on the ottoman gracefully in the place just left vacant by Higgins*].

MRS EYNSFORD HILL. [*introducing*] My daughter Clara.

LIZA. How do you do?

CLARA. [*impulsively*] How do you do? [*She sits down on the ottoman beside Eliza, devouring her with her eyes*].[76]

FREDDY. [*coming to their side of the ottoman*] Ive certainly had the pleasure.[77]

MRS EYNSFORD HILL. [*introducing*] My son Freddy.

LIZA. How do you do?

Freddy bows and sits down in the Elizabethan chair, infatuated.

HIGGINS. [*suddenly*] By George, yes: it all comes back to me![78] [*They stare at him*]. Covent Garden! [*Lamentably*] What a damned thing![79]

MRS HIGGINS. Henry, please! [*He is about to sit on the edge of the table*]. Dont sit on my writing-table: youll break it.

HIGGINS. [*sulkily*] Sorry.

He goes to the divan, stumbling into the fender[80] *and over the fire-irons*[80] *on his way; extricating himself with muttered imprecations; and finishing his disastrous journey by throwing himself so impatiently on the divan that he almost breaks it. Mrs Higgins looks at him, but controls herself and says nothing.*

A long and painful pause ensues.

MRS HIGGINS. [*at last, conversationally*[81]] Will it rain, do you think?

LIZA. The shallow depression[82] in the west of these islands[83] is likely to move slowly in an easterly direction. There are no indications of any great change in the barometrical situation.[84]

FREDDY. Ha! ha! how awfully[85] funny!

LIZA. What is wrong with that, young man? I bet I got it right.[86]

FREDDY. Killing![87]

MRS EYNSFORD HILL. I'm sure I hope it wont turn cold. Theres so much influenza about. It runs right through our whole family regularly every spring.

LIZA. [*darkly*][88] My aunt died of influenza: so they said.

MRS EYNSFORD HILL. [*clicks her tongue sympathetically*] *!!!*

LIZA. [*in the same tragic tone*] But it's my belief they done the old woman in.[89]

MRS HIGGINS. [*puzzled*] Done her in?

LIZA. Y-e-e-e-es, Lord love you! Why should she die of influenza? She come through diphtheria right enough the year before.[90] I saw her with my own eyes. Fairly blue with it, she was.[91] They all thought she was dead; but my father he[92] kept ladling gin down her throat til she came to[93] So sudden that she bit the bowl off the spoon.

MRS EYNSFORD HILL. [*startled*] Dear me![94]

LIZA. [*piling up the indictment*][95] What call[96] would a woman with that strength in her have to die of influenza? What become or her new straw hat that should have come to me?[97] Somebody pinched it; and what I say is, them as pinched[98] it done her in.[99]

MRS EYNSFORD HILL. What does doing her in mean?

HIGGINS. [*hastily*] Oh, thats the new small talk. To do a person in means to kill them.[100]

MRS EYNSFORD HILL. [*to Eliza, horrified*][101] You surely dont believe that your aunt was killed?

LIZA. Do I not! Them she lived with[102] would have killed her for a hat-pin, let alone a hat.[103]

MRS EYNSFORD HILL. But it cant have been right for your father to pour spirits[104] down her throat like that. It might have killed her.

LIZA. Not her. Gin was mother's milk to her. Besides, he'd poured so much down his own throat that he knew the good of it.

MRS EYNSFORD HILL. Do you mean that he drank?

LIZA. Drank! My word![105] Something chronic.[106]

MRS EYNSFORD HILL. How dreadful for you!

LIZA. Not a bit.[107] It never did him no harm what I could see.[108] But then he did not keep it up regular.[109] [*Cheerfully*] On the burst,[110] as you might say, from time to time. And always more agreeable when he had a drop in.[111] When he was out of work, my mother used to give him fourpence and tell him to go out and not come back until he'd drunk himself cheerful and loving-like.[112] Theres lots of women has to make their husbands drunk to make them fit to live with.[113] [*Now quite at her ease*] You see, it's like this. If a man has a bit of a conscience, it always takes him when he's sober;[114] and then it makes him low-spirited. A drop of booze just takes that off[115] and makes him happy. [*To Freddy, who is in convulsions of suppressed laughter*] Here! what are you sniggering at?

FREDDY. The new small talk. You do it so awfully well.

LIZA. If I was doing it proper, what was you laughing at?[116] [*To Higgins*] Have I said anything I oughtnt?

MRS HIGGINS. [*interposing*] Not at all, Miss Doolittle.

LIZA. Well, thats a mercy,[117] anyhow. [*Expansively*][118] What I always say is —

HIGGINS. [*rising and looking at his watch*] Ahem!

LIZA. [*looking round at him; taking the hint; and rising*] Well: I must go. [*They all rise. Freddy goes to the door*]. So pleased to have met you.[119] Goodbye. [*She shakes hands with Mrs Higgins*].

MRS HIGGINS. Goodbye.

LIZA. Goodbye, Colonel Pickering.

PICKERING. Goodbye, Miss Doolittle. [*They shake hands*].

LIZA. [*nodding to the others*] Goodbye, all.

FREDDY. [*opening the door for her*] Are you walking across the Park, Miss Doolittle? If so —

LIZA. [*with perfectly elegant diction*[120]] Walk! Not bloody likely.[121] [*Sensation*]. I am going in a taxi. [*She goes out*].

Pickering gasps and sits down. Freddy goes out on the batcony to catch another glimpse of Eliza.

MRS EYNSFORD HILL. [*suffering from shock*] Well, I really cant get used to the new ways.

CLARA. [*throwing herself discontentedly into the Elizabethan chair*] Oh, it's all right, mamma, quite right. People will think we never go anywhere or see anybody if you are so old-fashioned.

MRS EYNSFORD HILL. I daresay I am very old-fashioned; but I do hope you wont begin using that expression, Clara. I have got accastomed to hear you talking about men as rotters,[122] and calling everything filthy and beastly; though I do think it horrible and unladylike. But this last is really too much.[123] Dont you think so, Colonel Pickering?

PICKERING. Dont ask me. Ive been away in India for several years; and manners have changed so much that I sometimes dont know whether I'm at a respectable dinner-table or in a ship's forecastle.[124]

CLARA. It's all a matter of habit. Theres no right or wrong in it. Nobody means anything by it. And it's so quaint, and gives such a smart emphasis to things that are not in themselves very witty. I find the new small talk delightful and quite innocent.

MRS EYNSFORD HILL. [*rising*] Well, after that, I think it's time for us to go.

Pickering and Higgins rise.

CLARA. [*rising*] Oh yes: we have three at-homes to go to still.[125]

Goodbye, Mrs Higgins. Goodbye, Colonel Pickering. Goodbye, Professor Higgins.

HIGGINS. [*coming grimly at her from the divan, and accompanying her to the door*] Goodbye. Be sure you try on that small talk at the three at-homes. Dont be nervous about it.[126] Pitch it in strong.[127]

CLARA. [*all smiles*] I will. Goodbye. Such nonsense, all this early Victorian prudery![128]

HIGGINS. [*tempting her*] Such damned nonsense!

CLARA. Such bloody nonsense!

MRS EYNSFORD HILL. [*convulsively*] Clara!

CLARA. Ha! ha! [*She goes out radiant, conscious of being thoroughly up to date, and is heard descending the stairs in a stream of silvery laughter*].

FREDDY. [*to the heavens at large*][129] Well, I ask you[130] — [*He gives it up, and comes to Mrs Higgins*]. Goodbye.

MRS HIGGINS. [*shaking hands*] Goodbye. Would you like to meet Miss Doolittle again?

FREDDY. [*eagerly*] Yes, I should, most awfully.[131]

MRS HIGGINS. Well, you know my days.[132]

FREDDY. Yes. Thanks awfully. Goodbye. [*He goes out*].

MRS EYNSFORD HILL. Goodbye, Mr Higgins.

HIGGINS. Goodbye. Goodbye.

MRS EYNSFORD HILL. [*to Pickering*] It's no use. I shall never be able to bring myself to use that word.

PICKERING. Dont. It's not compulsory, you know. Youll get on quite well without it.[133]

MRS EYNSFORD HILL. Only, Clara is so down on me[134] if I am not positively reeking with the latest slang.[135] Goodbye.

PICKERING. Goodbye [*They shake hands*].

MRS EYNSFORD HILL. [*to Mrs Higgins*] You mustnt mind Clara. [*Pickering, catching from her lowered tone*[136] *that this is not meant for him to hear, discreetly joins Higgins at the window*]. We're so poor! and she gets so few parties,[137] poor child! She doesnt quite know. [*Mrs Higgins, seeing that her eyes are moist, takes her hand sympathetically and goes with her to the door*]. But the boy is nice. Dont you think so?

MRS HIGGINS. Oh, quite nice. I shall always be delighted to see him.

MRS EYNSFORD HILL. Thank you, dear. Goodbye. [*She goes out*].

【作者简介】 George Bernard Shaw（萧伯纳，1856—1950），十九世纪末年、二十世纪前半期英国最重要的剧作家，写了大小剧本约五十个，其中著名的有 *Widowers' Houses*（《鳏夫的房产》，1892 年），*Mrs. Warren's Profession*（《华伦夫人的职业》，1893 年），*Arms and the Man*（《武器与人》，1894 年），*Caesar and Cleopatra*（《凯撒与克莉奥佩屈拉》，1898 年），*Man and Superman*（《人与超人》，1903 年），*John Bull's Other Island*（《英国佬的另一个岛》，1904 年），*Major Barbara*（《巴巴拉少校》，1905 年），*Pygmalion*（《劈克美梁》，1913 年），*Heartbreak House*（《伤心之屋》，1917 年），*Saint Joan*（《圣女贞德》，1923 年），*The Apple Cart*（《苹果车》，1929 年）等。萧出生在爱尔兰都柏林一个破落的资产阶级家庭，曾做地产公司小职员，二十岁迁居英国，卷入当时正在风起云涌的社会改革运动，对于资本主义社会的罪恶深有所感，因此写剧时也以揭发和谴责英国资产阶级为己任，在剧本里提出了一系列的社会问题，但由于他早受费边主义（Fabianism）即英国的资产阶级改良主义的深刻影响，他对于这些问题的剖析和解答都有严重的缺陷。他的卓越贡献是在戏剧艺术方面。由于他着重剧本主题的社会意义，在技巧上又另辟途径，不重悲欢离合的动人情节，而重问题的讨论与争辩，在戏剧语言的运用上又达到很高的成就，因此能一扫世纪末时装艳情戏的歪风，为英国戏剧打开了新的局面。

【题解与注释】

Pygmalion 自从 1913 年初次公演以来，一直受到观众欢迎，在舞台上获得巨大成功之外，又在三十年代拍成影片，也获好评；五十年代有人又据以编成喜歌剧 *My Fair Lady*，受到普遍欢迎。它在萧的剧本中自成一格。萧的剧本一般不重情节，在本剧则情节十分引人；从表面上看，剧本主题似与政治、经济无关，作者倒是将语音学

的奇妙处搬上了舞台，这在英国戏剧史上也是破天荒第一次。

剧本共分五幕。第一幕：语音学家 Henry Higgins 在歌剧院前初遇卖花女 Eliza Doolittle. 第二幕：Higgins 开始训练 Eliza 说上层社会的“文雅”英语，并与另一语音学家 Pickering 上校打赌，说是经过六个月训练，Eliza 定能冒充公爵夫人。第三幕：Eliza 出席 Higgins 的母亲的茶会，小试其“文雅”口音，再经训练后终于出席某大使的招待会，会众惊为天人，疑是某国公主光临。第四幕：招待会上极大成功后，Eliza 与 Higgins 争吵，负气出走。第五幕：Eliza 出现在 Higgins 的母亲家里，Higgins 追至，但 Eliza 已决心同一名 Freddy 的青年去结婚。我们这里选的是第三幕的前半，即 Eliza 在 Higgins 的母亲家初试口音的一景。

口音（accent）一节，看来似乎是小事，但在英国资产阶级社会则过去向来被看成一个人出身、家世、教育、交游、社会地位等等的标志之一。在某些势利鬼的耳朵里，只有一种流行在牛津、剑桥两大学府和伦敦西区贵妇客厅里的口音（即语言学家 Daniel Jones 称为 Received Pronunciation 的口音）才算文雅，其他口音——特别是大多数伦敦人所操的土话口音，即所谓 Cockney ——则一律斥为粗俗。今天情况不同了，但在有些地方 R. P. 仍是吃香的。萧伯纳抓住了口音，正是抓住了英国资产阶级人士所十分希罕的东西；接着他却通过这有点奇幻然而充分合理的剧情向他们指出：他们所希罕的东西毫不珍贵，毫不难得，任何人只消花点钱请个语音学教授来训练一下，就都能用“文雅”的口音说话。

在 Higgins 那样的语言学家的耳朵里，则口音无所谓高尚与粗鄙——对于他，伦敦土话里的响亮的母音（例如卖花女在第一幕里的一声大叫：ah-ah-ah-ow-ow-owoo!）可能就比英国上层人士的十分别扭的 [iə][ɛə] 等音要动听多了。在这一点上，他无疑是有道理的；可是将一切当作素材而等量齐观，追求纯粹客观而无视事物的社会属性，Higgins 身上又清楚地显示了资产阶级科学家的通病。他自视为天神，而将别人只看作科学实验的原料；实验一做完，就想将卖花女撇在一边了。不料这位生长在伦敦贫民窟的姑娘完全有她自己的主见，斗志也旺盛得很，倒使他感到无可奈何了。

这样的情节，这样的人物，应该能够引起学习英语的学生的兴趣——何况还有萧伯纳笔下的好英文。他的英文爽利，但又饶有余韵；速度快，但又最善强调；不事藻饰而自然优美；看起来似乎略有瘰瘠，实则词句带有智慧的闪光，还有那极为动听的节奏在不知不觉中滋润了它！萧伯纳的戏剧不是人人都喜欢的，他的议论也常有荒谬之处，但他的散文风格则连最苛刻的批评家也都佩服，在议论文中他是斯威夫特（Swift）之后第一人，在戏剧语言的运用上则萧是散文的大师，正同莎士比亚是韵文的大师一样。萧的语言长于争论，打击力强，树立了语言作为犀利武器的范例；它既是现代的口语，又不过分俚俗而具有较大的稳定性，当年既不特别时髦，今天也不陈腐。

在这里所选的片段里，还有特别值得语言学生研究的材料。首先，作者通过茶会的场合介绍了各种语气的说法：客气话，含蓄话，粗鲁话，发誓赌咒，为闲谈而闲谈，而初试锋芒的 Eliza 则提供了气象公报的官腔和会话手册的套语。其次，有几个层次（levels）的言语在此并存并形成对照。Eliza 一人就兼备两种言语，即原来的 Cockney 同新学的“文雅”英语，不仅口音不同，用词以及语法也有许多差异。关于

Cockney 的某些特点，我们在注里有所涉及，这里不再多说。在讲“文雅”英语的人物当中，也分几种情形。两位老太太讲的话大体上差不多，都是没有多少特色的一般上层人士的言语。Pickering 与 Freddy 也大体相似，说的都是所谓“贵族学校英语”（Public School English——这种 Public School 实际上都是收费昂贵的私立学校），他们由于要表示自己是爱好打猎等等的传统绅士（gentlemen），而不是所谓读书人或知识分子，用词趋于简易，故意不掉书袋，如多用 awfully, jolly, I say 之类，读音方面也有懒惰、含混的情况，如 Freddy 将 How do you do 说成 Ahdedo. Higgins 与 Clara 两人在社会身分上也属他们一伙，但都有明显个人特点。Higgins 不拘小节，动不动就要发誓，因此 damn it, what the devil, who the dickens 之类的 swear-words 特多。他用它们是为了强调，这也是英语过去与现在都有的表达方式之一，例如在今天英美人士之间，what the hell 与 hell, no! 之类的话还是经常听得见的。（当然另外又有“轻描淡写”法，即 understatement，而且常有以低调而求强调的情况）。不过 Higgins 用这些词，只是由于个人习惯，并非模仿别人；作为一个上层资产阶级知识分子，他是什么也看不起，任何人也不屑于模仿的，有时连语法也一脚踢开，可以说出“To do a person in means to kill *them*”之类的话。但是 Clara 却是狠狠打定主意要学时髦人士的。只因为听了那位由卖花女乔装的贵小姐的几句话，就也满口 bloody 起来，以为尽得最新的客厅谈吐（the new small talk）之妙了。其实这里萧的讽刺是双重的，既刺那些鹦鹉学舌的小资产阶级人士，也刺那些被模仿的上层人士本身：正因为他们的谈吐十分贫乏无聊，卖花女的里巷之言才显得那样生动活泼；而且，鹦鹉学舌的不止 Clara, Clara 学上层人士，而上层人士又常学下层人民——为了追求新奇或表示洒脱。自封为“文雅”的上层言语常常是空洞的，贫血的，充满了禁忌的，而被斥为粗鄙的下层谈吐则总是面对现实，言之有物，新鲜有力，充满了智慧，幽默和诗情的。然而二者又是相通的，言语虽然有别，但是作为基础的则是同一的全民语言；差异只在口音，少数词汇，几条语法，而基本上都是同一英语，在绝大多数情况下用的是同样语言材料，在少数不同的情况下也是互相听得懂，说得通的。萧在此剧里使我们知道在语言问题上采取势利态度之无聊，又让我们听见几种不同阶层的谈吐，而萧用来写本剧的百分之九十九部分的语言则是规范化的现代英语 .

1. Pygmalion: 古希腊神话中的塞浦路斯（Cyprus）国王，喜雕刻，曾雕一女像名 Galatea，极美，爱之不舍，终央爱神 Aphrodite 使雕像成为活人，娶以为妻。这个神话过去也有作家用过，如古罗马诗人奥维德（Ovid），十九世纪末英国诗人莫里斯（William Morris）等。萧在此剧中将语音学家 Henry Higgins 比作 Pygmalion，将卖花女 Eliza Doolittle 比作 Galatea，但是他们之间并未发生爱情，Higgins 仍然不娶，Eliza 终于另嫁。

2. Mrs Higgins's at-home day: Higgins 夫人（Henry Higgins 之母）接待客人的日子；at-home 在此有特殊意义，即在家招待客人的特定日子。

3. Her drawing room, in a flat on Chelsea Embankment: Higgins 夫人的客厅，设在伦敦 Chelsea 区靠泰晤士河岸的一套房间里；flat 指城市住家屋子里的一套房间。

4. the same pretension: 同样样式与气派（的房子）。

5. Mrs Higgins was brought up on Morris and Burne Jones: Higgins夫人

的审美观念是自幼在 Morris 与 Burne-Jones 两人的影响之下形成的。William Morris（1834—1896）与 Edward Burne-Jones (1833–1898) 都是十九世纪末的英国艺术家，都曾受先拉斐尔派（the Pre-Raphaelite Brotherhood）的影响，Morris 又是著名作家，后来转向社会主义，他由于不满当时质地低劣、样式庸俗的日用品，曾设计并制造耐用而美观的墙纸，地毯，织锦，家具，陶器，染料等等，对于英国室内装饰的改进起了重大作用。下文提到 the Morris wall-papers, the Morris chintz（有光印花棉布，作窗帘及沙发布用）即指 William Morris 所设计的一类或其仿制品而言。

6. very unlike her son's room in Wimpole Street: Higgins 与他母亲分居，他本人住在 Wimpole 街，住处充满各种语音学研究的用具（留声片等等），而他母亲的寓所则整洁雅致，处处表现出一种三十年前流行的先拉斐尔画派的艺术趣味。作者在下面对于房内陈设的一番描写便是要强调女主人的艺术趣味，以示与其子的科学家性格迥然不同。

7. nicknacks: 各种小陈设。

8. ottoman: 无靠背及扶手的软榻。

9. odds and ends: 零碎东西。

10. the Burne Jones, not the Whistler side of them: them 指上行的 the exhibitions in the Grosvenor [ˈgrəuvnə] Gallery, Burne-Jones 是在上面第 9 行注里提到过的画家，Whistler 指另一画家 James A. M. Whistler (1834–1903)，两人的作品都曾在十九世纪七十年代在伦敦 Grosvenor 画廊展出，但是属于两个对立的画派：Burne-Jones 追求细致逼真，多用绘画来表达文学意境；Whistler 原是美国人，受日本绘画影响，在绘画中追求音乐效果，在技巧上是后期印象主义的前驱。此处萧指出 Higgins 夫人所受的影响来自 Burne-Jones，而非 Whistler。

11. The only landscape is a Cecil Lawson on the scale of a Rubens: 墙上只挂了一张风景画，是 Cecil Lawson (1851–1882) 画的，大小约如十六、七世纪比利时北部大画家 Peter Paul Rubens (1577–1640) 的作品。注意这里用 a Cecil Lawson 与 a Rubens 来表示一张某某人的画。

12. when she defied the fashion in her youth in one of the beautiful Rossettian costumes which, when caricatured by people who did not understand, led to the absurdities of popular estheticism in the eighteen-seventies: 当时她的装束绝不随俗，画像时穿的是一件美丽的古式衣服，如先拉斐尔派领袖 Dante Gabriel Rossetti (1828–1882) 所作的画中人物。后来无知之徒纷纷效颦（caricature 原意是用模仿加以丑化，漫画化），也来穿此类古式服装，结果造成了十九世纪七十年代荒唐可笑的唯美主义风尚。

13. long past taking the trouble to dress out of the fashion: 早就过了竭力穿得与众不同（即故意不穿时兴式样的服装）的年龄了。

14. a Chippendale chair: 一把雕刻精美的十八世纪样式的椅子。Thomas Chippendale (c.1718–1779)，英国十八世纪著名木匠，其所设计与制作的精美木器至今有名。

15. an Elizabetban chair roughly carved in the taste of Inigo Jones: 一把

伊丽莎白朝（十六世纪）的椅子，椅上雕刻的线条豪放，风格如 Inigo Jones 的设计。Inigo Jones (1573–1652) 是十六、七世纪有名建筑师，但也从事舞台布景、服装、道具等的设计，对于建立装饰式样中的英国传统有开创之功。

16. The door is opened violently; and Higgins enters with his hat on: 这一行舞台说明表示 Higgins 是个不拘小节、不讲礼貌的任性的科学家，因此猛然开门，闯进他母亲请人茶会的客厅，而且进了门连帽子也不脱下。

17. Oh bother!: 呵，真要命！

萧常将 bother 当作 damn 来用，如在 *The Simpleton of the Unexpected Isles*（1936年）中有这样的一句：Oh, *bother* number four! They are all the same.

18. mustnt: mustn't, must not. 萧伯纳经常不用"'"号，因此他的作品中出现 dont (don't), havnt (haven't), Ive (I've), isnt (isn't), cant (can't)，thatll (that'll) 之类的形式；但是为了避免混淆，有些字里的"'"号仍然保留，例如 she'll, she's, it's, I'm 等仍如通常写法。

19. I have no small talk: 我不会同人聊天；small talk 指社交场合的闲谈，下文（第 10 行）large talk（谈正经大事）与此相对。

20. cant get round your vowels: 学不会你的那些元音；to get round 意为设法越过困难而达目的。

21. pretty postcards in your patent shorthand: 用你那独创（因而享有专利权）的速记符号写的漂亮的明信片。

22. the copies in ordinary writing: 用普通字母写的副本。Higgins 知道他母亲看不懂他的速记符号，因此同时又寄一个用通常英文写的副本。

thoughtfully，用心周到地。

23. Ive picked up a girl: 我找到了一个姑娘；pick up 有萍水相逢、随便结合之意。萧故意让 Higgins 作此惊人之语，来引起有趣的误解。

24. there are some rather nice-looking young women about: 这周围颇有几个好看的姑娘；about = around.

25. cant be bothered with young women: 才不肯为年轻女人麻烦哩。

26. I shall never get into the way of seriously liking young women: 我永远不会变得认真地喜欢年轻女人起来；get into the way, get into the habit.

27. Stop fidgeting and take your hands out of your pockets: 别那样坐立不安了，快把手从袋里拿出来。Higgins 仍被他母亲当作小孩子看待，因此下面紧接 **Thats a good boy**（这才是个好孩子）。

28. I dont remember asking her: 我可并没请她来呀！（比较含蓄的说法，意为"谁让你随便请她来着！"）

29. I picked her off the kerbstone: 我是从大街上把她捡来的；off the kerbstone，从人行道的边沿石上，意即从街上。

30. to keep to two subjects: 只谈两个题目；*to keep to*, to stick to.

31. How do you do: 您好（第一次被介绍给生人时说的套语）。

32. not to let herself go on things in general: 不要信口胡谈一般事情（因为

那样会露出马脚)；to let oneself go，随便地、放开地做事我说话。

33. insides: 身体内部器官种种。

34. outsides: 外表。

35. Pickering is init with me: 这事是 Pickering 同我合干的（指两人打赌之事，故下句有 bet 字样）。

36. pass her off as a duchess: 使她可以冒充一位公爵夫人。

37. she's getting on like a house on fire: 她学得快极了。

38. Thats satisfactory, at all events: 那倒也不错了（略带嘲讽）；at all events = in any case.

39. Mrs and Miss Eynsford Hill: Eynsford 读作 ['einsfəd]。

40. the mother and daughter who sheltered from the rain in Covent Garden: 指本剧第一幕情节：幕开时，大雨，Covent Garden 的歌剧院刚散场，观众都在找车或避雨，当时这对母女站在一家教堂门前等事，恰与 Higgins, Pickering, Eliza 等人碰上。

41. the habitual anxiety of straitened means: 由于经济困难而惯常流露的忧虑神情。

42. acquired a gay air of being very much at home in society: the bravado of genteel poverty：学得象是对于社交生活非常在行的洒脱神气，实则不过是穷酸人家硬撑门面而已：at home，自在，不感拘束；society，此处不泛指"社会"，而指有钱的时髦人物的圈子；bravado [brəˈvɑːdəu]，故作勇敢，豪放；genteel，本同 gentleman 中的 gentle 同一字，但意存挖苦。

43. with confident familiarity: 带着很有把握的亲热样子（表示她是交际场所的老手）。

44. I havnt the ghost of a notion where: = I haven't the slightest idea where; not the ghost of a notion，一点儿概念也没有，ghost 此处作影子解，是加重语气的词，例如 not the ghost of a chance = no chance at all.

45. has no manners: 没有礼貌：注意 manners 用复数。

You mustnt mind him，请你们不要见怪他。

46. with his back to the company: 背对客人；company，在场的客人。

47. he contemplates the river and the flowers in Battersea Park on the opposite bank as if they were a frozen desert: 他眼看着泰晤士河以及河对岸 Battersea 公园里的花而毫无所感，就象是在看一片荒凉的沙漠似的；contemplate = gaze upon.

48. Exchange of bows: 相对鞠躬。

49. over his shoulder: Higgins 仍是背对客人坐着，只是侧过头来对 Pickering 说了一句话。

50. We were interrupted: damn it!：我正同我母亲说着话，就给（这些人）打断了，真要命！

以上可见 Higgins 的言谈举止都极无礼（rude）. 注意他喜用 damn, by George,

what the devil, who the dickens 等不文雅的咒骂用语（swear words）。

51. really!: 劝阻词，意为“真是太不象话了！”

52. Are we in the way?: 我们在这里是不是碍你们的事？

53. by George!: = I swear by St. George. Saint George 是英国的“保护神”（patron saint）。

54. Youll do as well as anybody else: 你们或任何别人都成，意为阿猫阿狗都可充数 .

55. almost audibly, past endurance: 几乎说出声来，因为已经超过他能忍耐的限度。

56. another of them: 这一家人简直没完（又来了一个）！

57. Ahdedo: 即 How d'ye do = How do you do. 英国有一些阔人子弟说话喜欢音调含糊，用词也自成一格，如 awful, jolly, killing, beastly 之类，Freddy 虽然家道中落，然而上过阔人学校，交往也是阔人为多，因此染上这类习气。

58. much as if he were a pickpocket: 就象他是个小偷似的。

59. It dont matter: 用 don't 而不用 doesn't 似乎不合语法，实则英美本国人如此说者不少，唯不足为训耳。Higgins 本人亦不一致，上文（第 6 页第 16 行）作 It doesnt matter.

60. what the devil are we going to talk about: the devil 也是不文雅的咒骂用语，用来着重语气，同 what on earth 或 what the hell，实际中心意义都是 what。

61. the life and soul of the Royal Society's soirées: 皇家学会晚会上最活跃的人物。皇家学会是英国科学家的组织，类似别国的科学院，这句话透露 Higgins 有较高的学术地位；soirée，原是法文，读作 ['swɑ:rei]，社交性的晚会。

62. trying: 使人难于忍受。

63. quite eligible matrimonially：作为婚姻对象颇为合适。

64. If people would only be frank and say what they really think!: 如果人们都能坦白，说出他们真实的想法（那就好了）。这一类虚拟式的 if-clause 单独成句，下半句照例不说出。

65. Lord forbid!: = May God forbid! 天呀，那怎么成！

66. taking up her daughter's cue: 看出了她女儿的心意，因此接着她的话头说下去；cue，线索。

67. would break up the whole show: 就会使整台戏都唱不下去了，意为整个儿都糟了。

68. to come out with: 说出。

69. Who the dickens: = Who the devil，也是不文雅的强调说法。

70. more or less: in greater or less degree，程度不同地。

71. Or of manners: Or, what do I know of manners? 或者说，对于礼貌我又懂得什么呢？（老夫人挖苦儿子，警告他不得无礼。）

72. studied grace: 精心装扮出来的文雅样子。

73. pedantic correctness of pronunciation: 发音十分正确，过分拘泥细节则

如学究。

74. she gasps slightly in making sure of the H in Higgins: 她在发 Higgins 一字中的 h 音的时候，先停下喘一口气。伦敦土话中 h 经常不发音，Henry Higgins 读作 enry iggins; Eliza 怕读错，因此作了特别的努力来发 h 音。

75. Colonel Pickering, is it not?: 您该是 Pickering 上校吧？

76. devouring her with her eyes: 用眼睛贪婪地看她，恨不得一口吞下她去。

77. Ive certainly had the pleasure: I've certainly bad the pleasure of meeting you，我曾有幸见过您。

78. it all comes back to me!: 这一下我都记起来了！

79. What a damned thing!: 真倒霉！（意为又碰上这一家人，真没意思！）

80. fender: 壁炉的围栏；**fire-irons**，火钳。

81. conversationally: 为闲谈而闲谈地。

82. shallow depression: 低气压。

83. these islands: the British Isles.

84. the barometrical situation: 天气的情况，barometer，气压表，晴雨表。

注意 Eliza 这一段话措词完全象气象公报，原是她在 Higgins 严格训练下一个字一个字学会的，现在在茶会上突然来这样打官腔的一段，十分滑稽。

85. awfully: very.

86. I bet I got it right: 我敢打赌我说得一字不差。这时 Eliza 的话已经接近本来面目，不再文绉绉的了。

87. Killing: = extremely funny，好笑死了。

88. darkly: 神秘地。

89. they done the old woman in: Eliza 说的话露出了伦敦俚语的老底子，而且不合语法——done 应作 did. 关于这句话的意义，戏中自有解释。

90. She come through diphtheria right enough the year before: 前一年她得了白喉，没出事；come 按语法应作 came。

91. Fairly blue with it, she was: 她呀，已经是面无人色了。这种倒装结构的句法在伦敦土话里常见，例如 'E's naughty, is our 'Enry.

92. my father he: he 在此处重复 father，不合语法，但这种紧接名词的代名词的用法正是伦敦土话特点之一。

93. came to: = came to herself，醒了过来。

bowl，羹匙的圆形盛汤部分。

94. Dear me!: 惊叹语，表示惊奇。

95. piling up the indictment: 越说越气；pile up，堆积起来，即越来越多；indictment 意为“控诉”，读作 [in'daitmənt]。

96. What call: 有什么理由。

97. What become of her new straw hat that should have come to me: 她的那顶新帽子本来应该归我所有，可是后来的下落如何呢？此句中 become 按通常语法应作 became。

98. pinched: 偷走了。

99. them as pinched it done her in: they that pinched it did her in；这句中 them as 的用法不合语法，但这种用法又是伦敦土话的特点之一。

100. To do a person in means to kill them: 照通常语法 them 应作 him. Higgins 的说话亦不全合规范语法。

101. horrified: shocked，震惊（指说话人 Mrs Eynsford Hill，非指 Eliza）。

102. Them she lived with: = those whom she lived with，不合语法之又一例。

103. let alone a hat:（他们可以为了一根帽子上的别针就害死她，）更不必谈（为了）一顶帽子了。

104. spirits: 烈性酒，烧酒，下文 gin 即是这种烧酒。

105. My word!: = Upon my word. 此处意为：我可以赌咒，他确实喝酒喝得凶。

106. Something chronic: 伦敦土话成语，意为"糟透了"。

107. Not a bit: 这一大段话包含了伦敦土话的许多特点，我们将在下面择要注明。

108. It never did him no harm what I could see: = it never did him *any* harm *that* I could see. 这种双重反语（double negative）是伦敦土话的一个特点，其他英语地区的未受教育的人也常用它。

109. he did not keep it up regular: regular 应作 regularly。

110. On the burst: 痛饮一场；burst 通常作 bust。

111. when he had a drop in: 当他喝醉了的时候；a drop（一滴）是英国人说话喜欢"轻描淡写"（understatement）的一例。

112. loving-like: = somewhat loving，脾气和善一些。这一种放在形容词后的 like 用法，也是伦敦土话特点之一。

113. Theres lots of women has to make their husbands drunk to make them fit to live with: = there *are* lots of women *who have* to make their husbands drunk to make them fit to live with.

114. it always takes him when he's sober: 在他不醉的时候，他受不了自己良心的责备；it 指 conscience; takes him 意为 catches and worries him, won't leave him alone.

115. A drop of booze just takes that off: 喝一点酒恰好可以驱走忧虑；booze，酒（俚语）。

116. If I was doing it proper, what was you laughing at?: 这也是典型的伦敦土话；proper 应作 properly; was 应作 were。

117. thats a mercy: 那就谢天谢地了。

118. Expansively: 越说越高兴地。

119. So pleased to have met you: 至此 Eliza 又恢复了 Higgins 教她的文雅谈吐。

120. with perfectly elegant diction: 用完全文雅的字眼（萧的俏皮话，但也可能指 Eliza 用完全文雅的口音说下面的粗话）。

121. Not bloody likely: 意思即是 not likely, bloody 加重其意而已。但在长期讲究体面的英国资产阶级上层社会里，bloody 一字被认为是极其粗鄙，在萧写剧的当年

(1913年左右)，更是完全排斥在文雅谈吐之外的。因此当萧故意让Eliza在台上讲了此字，不仅戏中人愕然，看戏人也震惊，确是作家大胆的一笔。据说当时有女演员就因有此字而不愿演Eliza一角，而有些语言学家则认为萧将bloody一字搬上了舞台，实是创造了语言学上新页。在五十年后的今天，bloody一字已经不再骇世惊俗，不过作为一个强调词，它还是很有力量的，如bloody fool, bloody nuisance之类仍是常见的。在本剧里，因为有几种不同的用语并存，产生了一种对照效果，又因为此字出现在一段社交的套语(So pleased to have met you. Goodbye)之后，作为对一个青年的多情的问话(Freddy想陪她在公园走走，多亲近她一会儿)的回答，这个直率的字还是来得突然，有力，并不因为过了半世纪而减色多少。

122. rotters: 废物(指人)；filthy, beastly，都是"不好"，"坏"的意思，如说beastly weather, beastly wet之类。这几个字都是强调词。

123. this last is really too much: 这最后的那个字可真是太过分了；this last = this last expression，指bloody一字。这位老太太连此字的名也不愿提。

124. or in a ship's forecastle: 还是在船上的水手舱里；forecastle读作['fəuksl]，商船上水手住的部分。Pickering之流认为水手说话粗鲁。

125. we have three at-homes to go to still: 我们还要赴三个茶会。Clara说此话是表示她家交际广阔。

126. Dont be nervous about it: 不要害怕。

127. Pitch it in strong: 使劲多讲。

128. early Victorian prudery: 早期维多利亚女王时代的假道学。维多利亚时代，英国社会表面上讲道德，出现了一种假撇清的空气。

129. to the heavens at large: 仰首向天；heavens = the sky；at large意为(向)整个天空(呼吁)。

130. I ask you: 祈求词，you指上天。

131. most awfully: = very much indeed.

132. Well, you know my days: days指at-home days，即招待客人的日子。

133. Youll get on quite well without it: 不用这字，你也一样过得很好。

134. down on me: 对我凶极了；be down on = treat severely.

135. positively reeking with the latest slang: 满口最新的俚语，真是臭不可闻。

136. catching from her lowered tone: 从她突然放低的声音意识到。

137. she gets so few parties: 她没有多少机会出去做客。

48 WILLIAM BUTLER YEATS (1865–1939)

1. The Lake Isle of Innisfree
2. When You Are Old
3. The Wild Swans at Coole
4. An Irish Airman Foresees His Death
5. Easter, 1916
6. The Second Coming
7. Sailing to Byzantium

周珏良　选注

1. THE LAKE ISLE OF INNISFREE

I will arise and go now,[1] and go to Innisfree,
And a small cabin build there, of clay and wattles made:[2]
Nine bean-rows will I have there, a hive for the honey-bee,
And live alone in the bee-loud glade.[3]

And I shall have some peace there, for peace comes dropping slow,[4]
Dropping from the veils of the morning to where the cricket sings;[5]
There midnight's all a glimmer, and noon a purple glow,
And evening full of the linnet's[6] wings.

I will arise and go now, for always night and day[7]
I hear lake water, lapping with low sounds by the shore;
While I stand on the roadway, or on the pavements grey,

I hear it in the deep heart's core.

2. *WHEN YOU ARE OLD*

When you are old and grey and full of sleep,
And nodding by the fire,[1] take down this book,
And slowly read, and dream of the soft look
Your eyes had once, and of their shadows deep;[2]

How many loved your moments of glad grace,[3]
And loved your beauty with love false or true,
But one man loved the pilgrim soul in you,[4]
And loved the sorrows of your changing face;[5]

And bending down beside the glowing bars,[6]
Murmur, a little sadly, how love fled
And paced upon the mountains overhead
And hid his face amid a crowd of stars.

3. *THE WILD SWANS AT COOLE*

The trees are in their autumn beauty,
The woodland paths are dry,
Under the October twilight the water
Mirrors a still sky;[1]
Upon the brimming water among the stones
Are nine-and-fifty swans.

The nineteenth autumn has come upon me
Since I first made my count;[2]
I saw, before I had well finished,[3]
All suddenly mount
And scatter wheeling in great broken rings

Upon their clamorous wings.

I have looked upon those brilliant creatures,[4]
And now my heart is sore.
All's changed since I, hearing at twilight,
The first time on this shore,
The bell-beat of their wings[5] above my head,
Trod with a lighter tread.[6]

Unwearied still, lover by lover,[7]
They paddle in the cold
Companionable streams or climb the air;
Their hearts have not grown old;[8]
Passion or conquest, wander where they will,[9]
Attend upon them still.

But now they drift on the still water
Mysterious, beautiful;
Among what rushes will they build,[10]
By what lake's edge or pool
Delight men's eyes[11] when I awake some day
To find they have flown away?

4. AN IRISH AIRMAN FORESEES HIS DEATH

I know that I shall meet my fate[1]
Somewhere among the clouds above;
Those that I fight I do not hate,[2]
Those that I guard I do not love;
My country is Kiltartan Cross,[3]
My countrymen Kiltartan's poor,
No likely end could bring them loss[4]

Or leave them happier than before.
N or law, nor duty bade me fight,
Nor public men, nor cheering crowds,[5]
A lonely impulse of delight
Drove to this tumult in the clouds;[6]
I balanced all, brought all to mind,[7]
The years to come seemed waste of breath,
A waste of breath the years behind
In balance with this life, this death.

5. EASTER, 1916

I have met them[1] at close of day
Coming with vivid faces
From counter[2] or desk among grey
Eighteenth-century houses.[3]
I have passed with a nod of the head[4]
Or polite meaningless words,
Or have lingered awhile and said
Polite meaningless words,
And thought before I had done
Of a mocking tale or a gibe
To please a companion
Around the fire at the club,
Being certain that they and I
But lived where motley is worn:
All changed, changed utterly:[5]
A terrible beauty is born.[6]

That woman's days were spent[7]
In ignorant good-will,[8]
Her nights in argument
Until her voice grew shrill.[9]

What voice more sweet than hers[10]
When, young and beautiful,
She rode to harriers?
This man had kept a school[11]
And rode our wingèd horse;
This other[12] his helper and friend
Was coming into his force;
He might have won fame in the end,
So sensitive his nature seemed,
So daring and sweet his thought.
This other man I had dreamed
A drunken, vainglorious lout.[13]
He had done most bitter wrong
To some who are near my heart,[14]
Yet I number him in the song;
He, too has resigned his part
In the casual comedy;[15]
He, too, has been changed in his turn,[16]
Transformed utterly:
A terrible beauty is born

Hearts with one purpose alone[17]
Through summer and winter seem
Enchanted to a stone
To trouble the living stream.[18]
The horse that comes from the road[19]
The rider, the birds that range
From cloud to tumbling cloud,
Minute by minute they change;
A shadow of cloud on the stream
Changes minute by minute;
A horse-hoof slides on the brim,
And a horse plashes within it;

The long-legged moor-hens dive,
And hens to moor-cocks call;
Minute by minute they live:
The stone's in the midst of all.

Too long a sacrifice[20]
Can make a stone of the heart.
O when may it suffice?[21]
That is Heaven's part, our part[22]
To murmur name upon name,
As a mother names her child
When sleep at last has come
On limbs that had run wild.
What is it but nightfall?
No, no, not night but death;[23]
Was it needless death after all?
For England may keep faith
For all that is done and said.[24]
We know their dream; enough[25]
To know they dreamed and are dead;
And what if excess of love
Bewildered them till they died?
I write it out in a verse —
MacDonagh and MacBride
And Connolly[26] and Pearse
Now and in time to be,
Wherever green is worn,
Are changed, changed utterly:
A terrible beauty is born.

6. THE SECOND COMING

Turning and turning in the widening gyre[1]

The falcon cannot hear the falconer;[2]
Things fall apart; the centre cannot hold;[3]
Mere anarchy is loosed upon the world,[4]
The blood-dimmed tide is loosed, and everywhere
The ceremony of innocence is drowned;
The best lack all conviction, while the worst[5]
Are full of passionate intensity.

Surely some revelation is at hand;[6]
Surely the Second Coming is at hand.
The Second Coming! Hardly are those words out[7]
When a vast image out of *Spiritus Mundi*
Troubles my sight: somewhere in sands of the desert
A shape with lion body and the head of a man,
A gaze blank and pitiless as the sun,
Is moving its slow thighs, while all about it
Reel shadows of the indignant desert birds.
The darkness drops again; but now I know[8]
That twenty centuries of stony sleep
Were vexed to nightmare by a rocking cradle,
And what rough beast, its hour come round at last,
Slouches towards Bethlehem to be born?

7. SAILING TO BYZANTIUM

I

That is no country for old men. The young[1]
In one another's arms, birds in the trees,
—Those dying generations—at their song,
The salmon-falls, the mackerel-crowded seas,
Fish, flesh, or fowl, commend all summer long
Whatever is begotten, born, and dies.
Caught in that sensual music all neglect[2]

Monuments of unageing intellect.

II[3]

An aged man is but a paltry thing,
A tattered coat upon a stick, unless
Soul clap its hands and sing, and louder sing
For every tatter in its mortal dress,
Nor is there singing school but studying
Monuments of its own magnificence;
And therefore I have sailed the seas and come
To the holy city of Byzantium.

III[4]

O sages standing in God's holy fire
As in the gold mosaic of a wall,
Come from the holy fire, perne in a gyre,
And be the singing-masters of my soul.
Consume my heart away; sick with desire
And fastened to a dying animal
It knows not what it is; and gather me
Into the artifice of eternity.

IV

Once out of nature I shall never take[5]
My bodily form from any natural thing,
But such a form as Grecian goldsmiths make[6]
Of hammered gold and gold enamelling
To keep a drowsy Emperor awake;
O r set upon a golden bough to sing
To lords and ladies of Byzantium
Of what is past, or passing, or to come.

【作者简介】 威廉·帕特勒·叶芝(William Butler Yeats)生于1865年，卒于1939年。他是爱尔兰人，但用英语写作诗歌、戏剧、散文，是现代有很大影响的诗人。他曾于1923年获得诺贝尔文学奖金。

叶芝出身于新教家庭，父亲是肖像画家。他本人也曾在都柏林艺术学校学画。1885年他开始出版诗作。1887年他在伦敦认识了唯美主义者王尔德(Oscar Wilde)和摩利斯(William Morris)等，并着手编辑威廉·布莱克(William Blake)的诗集，很受到布莱克的影响。1894年他去巴黎，接触到当时的法国诗派。他的朋友英国诗人兼批评家亚瑟·赛门斯(Arthur Symons)帮助他了解象征派诗。唯美主义和象征主义对叶芝早年的诗很有影响。

他早年曾参加爱尔兰的独立运动，但后来脱离了政治运动，专心致志于文学工作，以为这是唤起爱尔兰民族意识，求得民族独立的途径。他于1896年认识爱尔兰戏剧家格雷格里夫人(Lady Augusta Gregory)，于1904年和她一起在都柏林创立了“亚培戏院”(The Abbey Theatre)，叶芝亲自管理，并创造了许多剧本。先此，在1889年他遇见茉德·贡(Maud Gonne)，并爱上了她。茉德是演员又是爱尔兰独立运动积极分子。虽然茉德多次拒绝他的求婚，叶芝对她却终身爱慕，至老不衰。他早期的剧本*Cathleen ni Houlihan*就是为茉德写的，由她任主角演出。以后的许多诗也是为她写的，下面选的*When You Are Old*就是较有名的一首。

1922—1928年叶芝曾任爱尔兰自由邦(The Irish Free State)的参议员。

叶芝早年起就对神秘主义有兴趣，曾参加并组织过这类结社。他一方面继承了当时仍存在于爱尔兰民间的相信魔法、幻求的传统，同时也受布莱克的影响。但不止此，叶芝还努力建立能贯串天人的自己的神秘主义和象征主义的体系，以求得宇宙观和艺术创作的统一。他的散文著作《幻象》(*The Vision*，1926，1937年出版)和后来写的《自传》(*Autobiographies*)都叙述了这个体系。但这个体系更多是满足叶芝艺术创作的需要，而不一定是哲学乃至神学的需要。下面所选的*The Second Coming*和*Sailing to Byzantium*两诗中对此都有反映。

【题解与注释】

1. THE LAKE ISLE OF INNISFREE

这是叶芝早年作的一首小诗。Innisfree是爱尔兰西部Sligo附近Lough Gill地方的一个小岛。Sligo是叶芝青年时代居住过的地方。在他的《自传》里叶芝对写作这首诗的情况有如下记载：

“我仍然有十几岁时在Sligo就有的想法，想仿效托罗，居住在Innisfree岛上。[Henry David Thoreau，1817—62，美国哲学家，散文家，曾在Concord地方瓦尔登池（Walden Pond）旁结茅为屋，居住两年多，以求接近自然，避去尘嚣，并把自己的感受写成散文集《瓦尔登》一书。]……一天我怀着浓厚的乡思走过舰队街（Fleet Street，伦敦街名，是新闻界集中的地方），忽然听见细细的滴水声，看见一家商店橱窗里装饰着一股小喷泉，喷出的水顶着一只小球，使它不断在空中旋转，不落下来。这使我想起了湖水。凭这一时的回想，我写出Innisfree这首诗，是我第一首具有自己的音调的抒情诗。我开始灵活运用音律以避免繁缛的修词和随之而来的人们惯发的感慨。但当时我还只是模糊地，而不是经常地意识到，为了达到这个目的，我应当只使用普通的句子结构。如果是晚几年的话，我就不会在第一行里使用‘Arise and go’这种陈旧的说法，也不会在最后一节里用上倒装句法了。”从叶芝以上的话里可以知道，诗人在这里抒发的感情和我国晋代诗人陶渊明诗中“羁鸟恋旧林，池鱼思故渊”等句所表现的感情很有相似之处。

1. I will arise and go now:《圣经》中《路加福音》(*Luke*）十五章十八节：“I will arise and go to my father”. 这一行和《圣经》的语言类似，所以叶芝说它是“陈旧的语言”。

2. of clay and wattles made: 指用树枝柳条敷上泥土造成的。

3. the bee-loud glade: glade是树林中的空旷地。bee-loud = loud with the buzzing of bees.

4. peace comes dropping slow: 闲适安静的境界（peace）是点滴聚成的（comes dropping slow），亦即慢慢形成的。

5. dropping from the veils of the morning to where the cricket sings: the veils of the morning，清晨的“面纱”应当是指清晨的薄薄烟雾。这是叶芝称之为“繁缛的修词”的一例。第五第六两行，原来叶芝是这样写的：

There from the dawn above me peace
　　will come down dropping slow,
Dropping from the veils of the morning
　　to where the house hold cricket sings;

所以这里的蟋蟀指的是生活在诗人的小屋中（cabin）的。从清晨的薄雾写到屋里的蟋蟀，显示出里外一片清静。用有声的蟋蟀来写静寂的境界，这是对比手法。我国古诗中不是有“蝉噪林愈静，鸟鸣山更幽”的名句么？当然，我们也未免想到英国浪漫诗人济慈（John Keats）的十四行诗 *On the Grasshopper and the Cricket*，在那诗里济慈也恰恰是把蟋蟀同静寂的境界加以对比的（见本选集济慈诗选），而正是这种联想使叶芝诗句的内容加深了一层。

6. linnet: 一种棕色的鸣禽。

7. 第9—12行： 这四行是说当诗人在城里时（roadway, pavements gray，都是城市的象征），总是从内心深处向往着（I hear it in the deep heart's core）Innisfree湖畔那湖水轻轻拍打（lapping）岸边的声音。

2. WHEN YOU ARE OLD

这首诗是叶芝为他的恋人 Maud Gonne 写的，借用了法国十六世纪诗人龙沙（Pierre Ronsard, 1524–1585）一首十四行诗的诗意（此诗无题，头一行是："Quand vouz sevez bien vielle, an soir à la chandelle"，"当你年老时，夜晚秉烛而坐，"）。

1. the fire: 指壁炉的炉火。

this book 指叶芝写信给 Maud Gonne 的诗。

2. and of their shadows deep: their 指眼睛。眼光深沉清澈，所以用 shadows deep 来描绘。

3. your moments of glad grace: 你欢乐（glad）时刻的魅力。这里讲的 glad grace 和下一行的 beauty 都指一般所爱慕的，表面上的，因而也是浅薄的东西，和下面叶芝说他所爱的 the pilgrim soul in you and sorrows of your changing face 成为对比。

4. But one man loved the pilgrim soul in you: 这行是诗人自指。pilgrim 是宗教的朝圣者。Maud Gonne 热心于爱尔兰独立运动，叶芝也曾参加，后来脱离了。pil grim soul 指 Mand Gonne 追求民族独立的精神，如同朝圣者之追求宗教真谛的虔诚。

5. the sorrows of your changing face: 一个美人如果只有外表的美而没有意态的美，只有静的、死的而没有活的、动的美，那不过是泥塑木雕。这里的 changing face 正是指常恋的意态。sorrows 对第六行的 beauty 而言。这里叶芝是说 Maud Gonne 的一般爱慕者只注重她的美貌，而自己爱的却是她的意态，她的 sorrows（泛指严肃深沉的感情）。

6. the glowing bars: 指被炉火照耀着的壁炉铁箅。

3. THE WILD SWANS AT COOLE

Coole Park 是叶芝的朋友格雷格里夫人（Lady Gregory）的住所，他从青年起就常去的地方。1897 年叶芝首次在 Coole 作客，这首诗作于 1917 年，距离十九年了。这首诗最初发表时，现在的最后一节原是第三节。

1. mirrors a slill sky: 反映着静谧的天空。

2. made my count: 数（天鹅）的数目。

3. 第 9 行： 以下四行写的是诗人十九年前看见的事。诗人在说：当时我正数着（before I had well finished），我看见（I saw）所有的天鹅一下子飞起来（all sudden mount），扑棱着翅膀（upon their clamorous wings），分散开，绕着不完整的大圈子飞翔（scatter wheeling in great broken wings）.

4. 第 13 行： 以下写的又是当前景色。brilliant creatures 指野天鹅。

5. the bell-beat of their wings: 同上面 12 行 upon their clamorous wings 指的是一件事。

6. trod with a lighter tread: 主语是 15 行的 I，这行是说我行走起来步子轻快得多（with a lighter tread），暗含的意思是说当时年青得多。

7. 第 19—21 行： 指天鹅并不厌倦（unwearied still），暗含说诗人自己可是厌倦了，成双作对（lover by lover，这是天鹅的习惯）或在宜人的淳流中（in the cold companionable streams）划行（paddle）或飞翔于空中（climb the air）。

8. their hearts have not grown old: 天鹅的心尚未老，反衬出人心已老。

9. 第 23—24 行： 不管它们漫游到何处（wander where they will），激情（passion）和追求（conquest）还可在它们的身上找到（attend upon them still）。

10. among what rushes will they build: 他们将在哪里的蒲苇中筑巢。

11. delight men's eyes: = [will] delight men's eyes.

4. AN IRISH AIRMAN FORESEES THEIR DEATH

叶芝的朋友格雷格里夫人的儿子罗伯特·格雷格里少校（Robert Gregory）于 1918 年 1 月 23 日在意大利前线阵亡。叶芝曾写过许多诗纪念他，这首是其中之一。诗中用一个在英国空军中的爱尔兰驾驶员口气描写他自己对参加这场战争的看法。他作为一个遭受英国人民族压迫的爱尔兰人，而去参加这场对老百姓毫无好处的战争，去保卫他并不爱的英国和打他并不恨的德国，这是无意义的。他之所以毕竟参加是为了找一点刺激（见 11—12 行）。这样就从一个侧面谴责了这场帝国主义战争，也反映了第一次大战时知识分子的彷徨空虚的心理。

1. meet my fate: 丧命。

2. 第 3—4 行： 见题解。

3. Kiltartan Cross: 离格雷格里夫人家不远的一个地方。

4. 第 7—8 行：［这个战争］可能有的任何结果（no likely end）都不会使 Kiltarlan 的穷人受到损失（could bring them loss）或者得到什么好处（leave them happier than before）。

5. nor public men, nor cheering crowds: = nor public men, nor cheering crowds [bade me fight]. public men 指政界或社会上知名之士，cheering crowds 指送人参军的欢呼人群。同上一行串起来讲就是说：我之所以参战既非有法律规定（law），也非由于责无旁贷（duty），既没有响应大人物的号召，也没有受到群众的欢送。

6. A lonely impulse of delight / Drove to this tumult in the clouds: 这两行诗连同上两行是一个倒装子句。上两行说明不是为什么，这两行说明为了什么诗中的爱尔兰人做出了参军的选择。促使（drove）他介入这场云层中的喧闹的（this tumult in the clouds，指空战）是一种"孤寂的"（lonely）"愉快的冲动"（impulse of delight）。这里 lonely 一字有几层意义。它可以指在空中作战总是一个人，虽然战争是"喧嚣的"，但也是孤寂的，也可以指上面两行所指的情况，没有集体的法律规定，或责任的必需，也没有别人的宣传鼓动或欢送动员，而只是他个人决定这样做。还可以连系到更上两行。他这样做也不是为了集体的利益，因为战争无论胜负对爱尔兰人并没有什么好处。

7. 第 13—16 行： 这几行成一完整的子句，说明他之所以做出上述选择是经过一番全面思考权衡之后（I balanced all, brought all to mind）觉得以现在这种虽生而随时可死的状况权衡一下（in balance with）将来（the years to come）不过是一句空话（waste of breath），过去（the years behind）也不过是一句空话。这里暗含的意思是，当前究竟还能享受一种“愉快的冲动”，所以比起过去和将来还是好一点的。这几行充分表现了一种徬徨空虚的心情。

5. EASTER, 1916

1916 年 4 月 24 日爱尔兰共和兄弟会（Irish Republican Brotherhood）在都柏林举行起义反对英格兰统治，宣布成立爱尔兰共和国。这次起义因时机不成熟，筹划不周，于四月廿九日被镇压下去，领导人被处决或判刑，其中多叶芝当年的友人。叶芝当时在法国，已脱离了爱尔兰独立运动多年。当他听到消息后，起初认为这一举动“使多年的工作毁于一旦”。但叶芝青年时代的恋人而又为他终生所爱慕的茉德·贡告诉他：“这一来悲剧性的尊严又回到了爱尔兰了。”叶芝很受感动。据叶芝死后，茉德·贡所写的回忆文章里记载，这首诗的创作过程和当时和她同在法国的叶芝的心情如下：“1911 年 9 月我们都站在诺曼底［Normandy，在法国西北部］海岸，他给我读了前一天晚上写出的一首诗，恳求我把崖石和它内在的火焰［按指本诗 57—58 行］忘掉，而去追求变幻的生活之美。但是他看到我心如木石，一心只想回爱尔兰。他还是那样友好和愿意帮忙。他帮助我克服了政治上和护照上的困难，并陪我一直到伦敦。我们在那里分手；我的生活道路和康丝坦丝·马凯维支（Constance de Markievicz），卡斯琳·克拉克（Cathleen Clarke）的一样，通向了监狱，而威利［指叶芝］的生活道路却是一条更加艰难的外表恬静而内心矛盾的道路，这在他晚年著作中是看得出来的”（见 Stephen Gwynn 编 *Scattering Branches*，1940，一书中 Maud Gonne: *Yeats and Ireland*, 31—32 页）。从这一段叙述和本诗中可以看出，叶芝受到这次起义的感动，但又对它很不了解。这首诗的准确写作日期是 1916 年 9 月 25 日。

本诗的第一节，第二节和第四节最后一行都是 A terrible beauty is born，这是叶芝对这次起义的总看法，总评价：这次起义是不幸的，甚至是错误的（terrible），但它又是悲壮的，因而是美的（beauty）.起义时正当复活节，是耶稣复活升天的日子，叶芝这里似乎有意把两者对比，所以用“降生”（born）这一个意象。

第一节 （1—16 行）诗人回忆过去和参加起义的这些人的关系。他和这些人是泛泛之交，见而不过打个招呼，或者寒暄两句（1—8 行），甚至还没有完，就转念头拿他们来寻开心，以博友人一笑（9—12 行），因为他知道，爱尔兰不过是一个人们互相取笑的地方（13—14 行）。但因为这次起义，一切都变了（18 行）。这次起义是不幸的，但又是美的（16 行）。

1. them: 指起义的领导人。

2. counter:（柜台）和 desk（办公桌）指明这些人的不同职业。

3. grey eighteenth-century houses: 当时都柏林的房子都是十八世纪英国式的灰砖建筑。

4. 第 5—14 行： 从 5 行到本诗节之末（16 行），这十二行是一个句子，但可分两层意思来讲。第 15—16 两行单独是一个意思，下面另讲。5—8 行描述了诗人通常和这些革命领导人见面时的情况，暗示关系一般，不过点个头（passed with a nod of the head），或说几句客套话（polite meaningless words），再进一步也就是停下来（lingered awhile），也无非说几句客套话。还不止此，他在背后还拿这些人开心，甚至在寒暄未了之际（before I had done）就想到下一次有机会在俱乐部的炉旁（一般是禁止外人入内的上层人物活动场所）如何拿这些人开玩笑（thought ... of a mocking tale or a gibe）以博听者一笑了（to please a companion）. 所以如此是因为诗人知道他和这些人［背后］都会开对方玩笑的。第13—14 行里说 they and I/But lived where motley is worn. Motley 是西方传统里，宫廷或贵族家中豢养，专以诙谐或嘲讽的言辞使主子高兴的丑角所穿的花衣服。这后一行说：他们和我都是住在爱尔兰这一穿丑角花衣服的处所，意指大家都在互寻开心。

5. 第 15 行：但起义一开始，一切完全变了（utterly changed）。

6. A terrible beauty is born: 见题解。

7. 第二节（17—40 行）：这一节具体讲到一女三男。一女是叶芝所敬慕的，三男之中有一个是叶芝所讨厌的（31—34 行）。人虽不同但都卷入了这场叶芝称之为偶然发生的闹剧（casual comedy）的起义之中，都发生了变化。这是不幸而又悲壮的。

8. 第 17—18 行：that woman 指叶芝从年青时就相识的康丝坦丝 · 马凯维支（Constance Markiewicz 1868–1927）。她是爱尔兰望族高尔 - 布斯（Gore-Booth）家的女儿，以美貌著称。她嫁了一位波兰公爵。叶芝认为她进行革命活动是出于好意，但十分天真无知（days were spent/In ignorant good-will）。

9. Her nights in argument/Until her voice grew shrill: 接上两行，等于 Her nights [were spent] in argument，意思是说，她夜晚参加讨论问题，吵起来嗓音刺耳。

10. 第 21—23 行：harrier 是一种猎兔犬。rode to harriers = 骑马携犬打猎。康丝坦丝是她家乡有名的女骑手。在这三行诗里诗人进行了对比，说她年青貌美，行围射猎时，声音的好听是没有人比得上的。这里有明显的惋惜之意。

11. 第 24—25 行：这里说的是帕屈里克 · 皮尔斯（Patrick Pearse 1878–1916）是一位学校校长、律师，起义后被选为共和国总统，数日后被英军擒住，遭杀害。他也用爱尔兰文和英文写诗，所以叶芝说 rode our wingèd horse. 这个 wingèd horse 是希腊神话里生翼的神马 Pegasus，代表诗的灵感，诗人也就常常被比喻为骑着这匹神驹。叶芝是诗人，皮尔斯也是诗人，所以说“我们的”（our）。

12. this other: 指汤姆斯 · 麦克都诺（Thomas MacDonagh 1878–1916）是都柏林大学学院的英文教授，诗人，戏剧家和文学批评家。第 28 行的 he 也指麦克都诺。

13. This other man I had dreamed/A drunken, vainglorious lout: 指茉德 · 贡的丈夫约翰 · 麦克勃莱德少校（Major John McBride）. vainglorious = 自命不凡。lout = 粗暴的家伙。所以用 dreamed 一字是因为叶芝因为他对茉德 · 贡不好而一向讨厌他，因之说一直“想象”他是这样一个人，但想不到他也彻底变了（见下 39 行）。

14. some who are near to my heart: 这里指茉德 · 贡。她与麦克勃莱德结婚后感情不合，后来分居。

15. the casual comedy: 指起义的事。因为是仓促上阵，所以说是 casual. 选择用这个字表现了叶芝对起义的矛盾心理，既说 A terrible beauty is born，但又认为有点欠考虑，所以称之为 comedy. 莫怪茉德 · 贡在回忆时说叶芝当时对此事感到“吃惊和迷惘”，她对叶芝的心情感到很难理解（见前引茉德 · 贡文 31 页）。

16. 第 38—39 行：这两行的口气是这样的：连他也变了，甚至彻底改变了。

17. 第三节（41—56 行）: 在这一段里，诗人以优美的形象表达了自己的感慨，叹息于执著一件事会使人僵如木石，而搅乱了生命中的一片天机。

18. 第 41—44 行: 这里说人心中若无冬立夏（through summer and winter）只有一件事（one purpose alone）就好象是着了魔，会僵如木石（seem enchanted to a stone）. 扰乱活跃的生命之流（to trouble the living stream）或者如上面所说的，搅乱了生命中的天机。

19. 第 45—56 行: 在这里诗人用了一系列来自自然界的优美意象作比喻以具体描绘上述的生命之流。在十行之中两次重复运动这一意象，一则曰：minute by minute they change，一则曰：change minute by minute 以强调有生命的东西都在不停运动。而到了 55 行就指明本意说：时刻变动的就是时刻在生活的（minute by minute they live），反过来说，僵化没有运动也就是没有生命了。于是在下一行（56）就说：僵如木石的心也就存在于这生命之流中，造成了鲜明对比。

20. 第四节（57—80 行）: 这一段描述了诗人对整个事件的迷惘心情。

21. O when may it suffice?: 上两行仍重复长期的革命牺牲使人心如木石这一主题，而这一句忽发一问：这到何时为了？

22. 第 60—65 行: 诗人对上述的一问试作回答，其实并没有回答，而只是作出了反应：这是老天爷的事（that's heaven's part）而我们只能念叨（our part [is] to murmur …）[死者的] 名字，如同母亲在孩子们玩闹够了（limbs that had run wild）而睡熟之后所做的那样（62—64 行）。这不也是夜晚来临，犹如梦寐吗？（What is it but night fall?）

23. 第 66—67 行: 但这可不是梦而是死亡（66 行），而归根结底，这是否是不需要的牺牲？（Was it needless death after all?）所以有此一问是因为当时有许多人认为起义是个错误。

24. 第 68—69 行: 这两行提出怀疑起义是否有需要的理由：尽管 1）英国因为大战延缓实行 1913 年已答应的爱尔兰自治（done 就是指这个）；并且 2）有谣言说要撤回国会已通过的爱尔兰自治法案（said 就指这个），英国仍有可能遵守信用的（England may keep faith）。

25. 第 70—73 行: 这四行成一句，里面有两重意义：1）我们知道他们梦想着什么，可是知道他们曾梦想过而现在死了，这也就够了。言外之意是说，我们还能做什么呢？（前两行）；2）如果过分的热情使他们迷惑，狂热（bewildered）- 直到死，我们又能如何呢？这四行表现了叶芝的迷惘心情，莫怪茉德·贡追忆当时情况说她觉得叶芝的心情是令人难以理解的了（见前引茉德·贡文）。

第 74—80 行　那么诗人怎么办呢？他只能以诗来纪念死者。他们无论现在或将来都是变了，彻底的变了，但起义也使爱尔兰具有了悲壮的美。

26. Connolly: 是 James Connolly（1870—1916），是爱尔兰的工人运动领袖，曾组织武装起义队伍，在战斗中受伤，后被杀害。

6. THE SECOND COMING

此诗作于1919年2月，反映了叶芝对英国派警备队去爱尔兰镇压共和党人的态度。题目是从《圣经》上借用的。在《马太福音》(*Mathew*)第廿四章中预言耶稣基督将重降人间(the Second Coming)带来太平圣世。在《约翰一书》(1 *John*)第二章十八节里预言一个行恶的"伪基督"(Antichrist)将在末日之前到来。叶芝把两者结合起来，以形象地表达当时存在于欧洲的危机感。一个新时代将要到来，但不是基督重来的太平盛世，而是伪基督降生的天下大乱。叶芝于1938年在一封信里曾引用这首诗来证明他对法西斯主义的兴起不是漠不关心或麻木不仁的。他说："在欧洲正发生的事使人毛骨悚然"("Every nerve trembles with horror at what is happening in Europe")，"无邪的礼法已遭淹没"("The ceremony of innocence is drowned.")这首诗形象地反映出这一点。

这首诗和下一首代表叶芝后期的诗风。

第一节(1—8行)：这一节只有一句，描述的是大变动到来之前的离心、混乱状况，和人心的浮动。

第1—2行：螺旋(gyre)是叶芝后期诗中常用的形象。他认为历史的发展是依照螺旋形的，从螺旋的顶点向外围发展。发展到圈子最大时也就是一个世代的终结，而新的世代又将从另一个螺旋形的顶点开始，又由小向大发展。耶稣降生后到公元两千年成为一个世代。写诗的时候(1919年)已接近这一世代的末期，是历史螺旋形扩展到近乎圈子最大的时期，一切处于失去中心，离心解体的状况。

1. 第1行：这里说的是上述螺旋式的扩大。

2. 第2行：这里用猎鹰的越飞圈子越大，再也听不见调鹰者(falconer)的呼声这一形象表明它已脱去了控制。

3. 第3行：这里说得更清楚：一切解体，再没有什么中心能控制一切。

4. 第4—6行：这三行里连用了两个loosed以表明一发不可复收。首先是无政府状态(anarchy)在全世界泛滥，然后是血汗的洪流不可控制(the blood-dimmed tide is loosed).这里叶芝具体地可能想到刚结束的世界大战，爱尔兰的动荡，甚至十月革命。第六行的ceremony一字是秩序和驯服的形象。

5. 第7—8行：这两行写人们的心理。最好的是失去了一切信念，而最坏的则狂热得不得了。

第二节(9—22行)这一节描述叶芝认为的"第二次降临"，或者说"伪耶稣"降临的情景。

6. 第9—10行：这两行强调"第二次降临"是不远了。

7. 第11—17行：这八行是一句。11行之前重复了"The Second Coming!"口气就象是说：不错，就要到了！然后就是那个"降临"下来的狮身人面，代表混乱、危机、灾难的"伪基督"的形象。*Spiritus Mundis*依叶芝说就是"一个为大家所公有而非属于哪个个人的意象储存库"("A general storehouse of images which have ceased to be the property of any personality or spirit")，叶芝的思想里有很多神秘主义。他相信魔法，说能看见常人见不到的东西。14—15行里的那个狮身人面怪，据叶芝的记载，是他在作魔法时看见的。后来他在《探索》(*Explorations* 1962)一书中又说他见过在他“身左，刚刚眼力不及的地方，有一个铜雕的带翅野兽，我把它和狞笑的破坏者联系起来”，并说在*The Second Coming*一诗中曾描绘过这个形象，想就是指第十四行以下所说的那个怪物。

8. 第18—22行：这几行共成一句，回顾耶稣纪元来近两千年的往事，并瞻望将来，充满疑虑。“twenty centuries of stony sleep”指耶稣降生以来的两千年。“were vexed to nightmare by a rocking cradle”摇篮象征耶稣的诞生。“were vexed to nightmare”被搅乱为一场恶梦。what rough beast，即上面的狮身人面的家伙。slouch = 缓慢笨拙地行进。Bethlehem [ˈbeθliəm] 是耶稣降生地，这里借用来指“伪耶稣”的降生地。

7. SAILING TO BYZANTIUM

此诗作于1926年，发表在叶芝1928年出版的诗集《塔》(*The Tower*)里。这时叶芝已是六十开外的老人。拜占庭(Byzantium)是现在的伊斯坦布尔(Istanbul)，也是过去东罗马帝国或叫拜占庭帝国(Byzantine Empire)首都和东正数(Orthodox Church)的中心。对叶芝来说拜占庭是一个内容丰富的象征物。它象征着永恒，是一个脱去了人间生死哀乐的乐园。青年人达不到这种境界，因为他们太沉湎于感官的享受(第一节)，仅仅是年老也达不到这种境界，因为老年人精神上肉体上都衰弱了(第二节)，而只有当灵魂脱去了肉体的牵扯而寄托于富有生命力的艺术品上时，才能达到这个境界，才能到达拜占庭(第四节)。这就是本诗的大意。

叶芝没有到伊斯坦布尔去过，但1924年他到过意大利西西里(Sicily)，看过拜占庭时代的嵌石画(mosaics)，在这以前还在意大利北部拉文那(Ravenna)看到过古建筑物墙上的圣徒(saints)和哲人(sages)的造像。第三节里所指的大约就是以此为根据的。

第一节(1—8行)在这首诗里，一位老年人叙述自己的心情和自己决心要到拜占庭去的理由。和戏剧或小说的情节类似，这位老人的认识的开始、发展、终结和起伏变化贯串了全诗。在这一节的开始他就说:“这不是老年人呆的地方(1行)。”这地方泛指所处的世界，为引出金诗的主题，即到拜占庭去，做张本。

1. 第1—6行：这六行是一句，讲这个世界是青年人的。句子的动词是commend，意为歌颂。主语是互相拥抱的青年情侣(the young in one another's arms)，在树荫里互相赓和的群鸟(birds in the trees ... at their song)，无论是鱼(fish)，兽(flesh，包括人在内)和鸟(fowl)都在歌颂孳生，繁殖，也就是在起着物质生命的基本作用。这里要注意的是“those dying generations”(3行)和“the salmon-falls, The mackerel-crowded seas”(4行)两处。前者指的是无论是青年或群鸟，虽然当前尽情享受感官的快乐，但都不是永恒的，都是在走向死亡的。后者说的是沙门鱼产子时要到河流的上游，鲭鱼产子时要到深海里去。这两个形象都是关于繁殖孳生的，因之也是和青年相连的。但头一个意象(dying generations)已暗示出青春不能长在。

2. 第7—8行：点明青年的缺点在沉湎(caught)于感官的享受(以sensual music作为代表)，他们都轻视不老的或不朽的(unageing)精神的伟大产品(monuments of intellect，指伟大的艺术品等)。

3. 第二节（9—16 行）：上节之末提到青年不足之处，那么是否老年就没有问题了呢？大是不然。老年可能更是一种可悲的境界，所以说他是无足轻重的（paltry thing），甚至是稻草人，是一件挂在竹竿上的破烂衣服（A tattered coat upon a stick）. 但是情况是可以不这样的。第二行 unless 一字之下讲的就是改变这种情况的条件：（1）11—12 行形象地说灵魂（soul）或说精神，必须为摆脱肉体的束缚而达到欢乐的境界（sing for every tatter in its mortal dress = 为它无常的外壳的剥落而歌唱）；但（2）灵魂必须先认识自己的美和力量，而这必须通过对灵魂的杰作冥思苦想地深入体会才能达到。所以 13 —14 行说 Nor is there singing school but studying/ Monuments of its own magnificence，意为哪能学会［欢乐］歌唱（singing school 是教唱的地方）而不是通过研究（but studying = but for studying）灵魂自己的杰作（Monuments of its own significance）呢？因此老人就要去追求青年人所不注意的东西，要去拜占庭，完全离开第一节中所说的青年人的世界（15—16 行）。

4. 第三节（17—24 行）：在这一段里老人面对拜占庭的艺术精品（亦即上面所说的灵魂的杰作），看到这些艺术品本身就是灵魂的寄托之所，不是死的而是活的。于是他祈求建筑物墙上嵌石画上的圣者（sages）来教导他的灵魂（be the singing-masters of my soul）。这里要解释一下 perne in a gyre 这一意象。螺旋（gyre）是叶芝常用的意象（参考 *Second Coming* 1—2 行注）。perne 一作 pern，是旋转的意思。这里老人祈求这些拜占庭艺术品中有灵魂的圣者造像，要他们从所处的无生死，无时间的螺旋的上端飘翔下来，到老人所处的有生死，有时间的世代来教导自己。老人具体祈求的事如下：（1）consume my heart away 心被认为是七情六欲的根源，因之他祈求在圣火中的圣者（standing in God's holy fire）来用圣火把这根源除去（consume）. 因为但凡束缚于肉体的残余（fastened to a dying animal 指老人已衰坏的身躯），受欲念的牵制（sick with desire），灵魂就不知自己身处在什么境界（It knows what it is）;（2）gather me into the artifice of eternity 祈求把他（指灵魂）带到艺术的永恒境界中去。

第四节（25—32 行）

5. 第 25—26 行：老人决心在他的灵魂摆脱躯壳的束缚（out of nature）之后，决不使他再寄托（take my bodily form）于任何人世的物体上（any natural thing）.

6. 第 27—32 行：But such a form as … = But [take] such a form as … 叶芝自注这首诗说：'我记得在什么地方读到过，在拜占庭的王宫里有一棵用金银铸成的树，树上有会唱歌的人工制成的鸟。' 诗里用这个意象表明老人的灵魂愿寄托于不朽的金银制成的拜占庭艺术品之上以获得永生。它将歌唱的去、来、今（what is past, or passing, or to come），三者加起来就是时间的永恒。这正好和第一节青年人和有生物如群鸟所歌唱的"what is begotten, born, and dies"所代表的生命的有限形成对比。老人终于达到了理想的境界。

49 LYTTON STRACHEY
1880–1933

1. Dr. Arnold
2. Gibbon

戴镏龄　选注

1. DR. ARNOLD (from *Eminent Victorians*)

The public schools of those days were still virgin forests, untouched by the hand of reform. Keate[1] was still reigning at Eton; and we possess, in the records of his pupils, a picture of the public school education of the early nineteenth century, in its most characteristic state. It was a system of anarchy tempered by despotism.[2] Hundreds of boys,[3] herded together in miscellaneous boardinghouses,[4] or in that grim "Long Chamber"[5] at whose name in after years aged statesmen and warriors would turn pale, livid, badgered[6] and over-awed by the furious incursions of an irascible little old man carrying a bundle of birch-twigs,[7] a life in which licensed barbarism[8] was mingled with the daily and hourly study of the niceties of Ovidian verse.[9] It was a life of freedom and terror, of prosody[10] and rebellion, of interminable floggings and appalling practical jokes. Keate ruled, unaided — for the under-masters[11] were few and of no account — by sheer force of character. But there were times when even that indomitable will was overwhelmed by the flood of lawlessness.[12] Every Sunday afternoon he attempted to read sermons to the whole school assembled;[13] and every Sunday afternoon the whole school assembled shouted him down. The scenes in Chapel[14] were far from edifying: while some antique Fellow[15] doddered in the pulpit, rats would be let loose to scurry among the legs of the exploding[16] boys.

From two sides, this system of education was beginning to be assailed by the awakening public opinion of the upper middle classes. On the one hand, there was a desire for a more liberal curriculum;[17] on the other, there was a desire for a higher moral tone. The growing utilitarianism[18] of the age viewed with impatience a course of instruction which excluded every branch of knowledge except classical philology;[20] while its growing respectability[19] was shocked by such a spectacle of disorder and brutality as was afforded by the Eton of Keate. "The Public Schools," said the Rev. Mr. Bowdler, "are the very seats and nurseries of vice."

Dr. Arnold agreed. He was convinced of the necessity for reform. But it was only natural that to one of his temperament and education it should have been the moral rather than the intellectual side of the question which impressed itself upon his mind. Doubtless it was important to teach boys something more than the bleak rigidities[21] of the ancient tongues; but how much more important to instil into them the elements of character and the principles of conduct! His great object, throughout his career at Rugby, was, as he repeatedly, said, to "make the school a place of really Christian education." To introduce "a religious principle into education," was his "most earnest wish," he wrote to a friend when he first became headmaster; "but to do this would be to succeed beyond all my hopes; it would be a happiness so great, that, I think, the world would yield me nothing comparable to it.[22]" And he was constantly impressing these sentiments upon his pupils. "What I have often said before," he told them, "I repeat now: what we must look for here is, first, religious and moral principle; secondly, gentlemanly conduct; thirdly, intellectual ability."

There can be no doubt that Dr. Arnold's point of view was shared by the great mass of English parents. They cared very little for classical scholarship; no doubt they would be pleased to find that their sons were being instructed in history or in French; but their real hopes, their real wishes, were of a very different kind. "Shall I tell him to mind his work, and say he's sent to school to make himself a good scholar?"[23] meditated old Squire Brown when he was sending off Tom for the first time to Rugby. "Well, but he isn't sent to school for that — at any rate, not for that mainly. I don't care a straw for Greek particles, or the digamma; no more does his mother. What is he sent to school for?... If he'll only turn out a brave, helpful, truth-telling Englishman, and a Christian, that's all I want."

That was all; and it was that that Dr. Arnold set himself to accomplish. But how was he to achieve his end? Was be to improve the character of his pupils by gradually spreading round them an atmosphere of cultivation and intelligence? By bringing them into close and friendly contact with civilised men, and even, perhaps, with civilised women? By introducing into the life of his school all that he could of the humane, enlightened, and progressive elements in the life of the community? On the whole, he thought not. Such considerations left him cold, and he preferred to be guided by the general laws of Providence. It only remained to discover what those general laws were. He consulted the Old Testament,[24] and could doubt no longer. He would apply to his scholars, as he himself explained to them in one of his sermons, "the principle which seemed to him to have been adopted in the training of the childhood of the human race itself" He would treat the boys at Rugby as Jehovah had treated the Chosen People: he would found a theocracy; and there should be Judges in Israel.[25]

For this purpose, the system, prevalent in most of the public schools of the day, by which the elder boys were deputed to keep order in the class-rooms, lay ready to Dr. Arnold's hand. He found the "Praepostor"[26] a mere disciplinary convenience, and he converted him into an organ of government. Every boy in the Sixth[27] Form became *ipso facto*[28] a Praepostor, with powers extending over every department of school life; and the Sixth Form as a body was erected into an authority responsible to the headmaster, and to the headmaster alone, for the internal management of the school.

This was the means by which Dr. Arnold hoped to turn Rugly into "a place of really Christian education." The boys were to work out their own salvation, like the human race. He himself, involved in awful grandeur,[29] ruled remotely, through his chosen instruments, from an inaccessible heaven. Remotely—and yet with an omnipresent force. As the Israelite of old knew that his almighty Lawgiver[30] might at any moment thunder[31] to him from the whirlwind[32], or appear before his very eyes, the visible embodiment of power or wrath, so the Rugby schoolboy walked in a holy dread of some sudden manifestation of the sweeping gown, the majestic tone, the piercing glance, of Dr. Arnold. Among the lower forms of the school his appearances were rare and transitory, and upon these young children "the chief impression," we are told, "was of extreme fear." The older boys saw more of him, but they did not see much. Outside the Sixth Form, no part of the school came into close intercourse with him; and it would often happen that a boy would leave Rugby without having had any personal communication with him at all. Yet the effect which he produced upon the great mass of his pupils was remarkable. The prestige of his presence and the elevation of his sentiments were things which it was impossible to forget. In class, every line of his countenance, every shade of his manner imprinted themselves indelibly on the minds of the boys who sat under him.

With the boys in the Sixth Form, and with them alone, the severe formality of his demeanour was to some degree relaxed. It was his wish, in his relations with the Praepostors, to allow the Master to be occasionally merged in[33] the Friend. From time to time, he chatted with them in a familiar manner; once a term he asked them to dinner; and during the summer holidays he invited them, in rotation, to stay with him in Westmoreland.[34]

It was obvious that the primitive methods of discipline which had reached their apogee under the dominion of Keate were altogether incompatible with Dr. Arnold's view of the functions of a headmaster and the proper governance of a public school. Clearly, it was not for such as he to[35] demean himself by bellowing and cuffing,[36] by losing his temper once an hour, and by wreaking his vengeance with indiscriminate flagellations. Order must be kept in other ways. The worst boys were publicly expelled; many were silently removed; and, when Dr. Arnold considered that a flogging was necessary, he administered it with gravity. For he had no theoretical objection to corporal punishment. On the contrary, he supported it, as was his wont, by an appeal to general principles. "There is," he said, "an essential inferiority in a boy as compared with a man"; and hence "where there is no equality, the exercise of superiority implied in personal chastisement" inevitably followed. He was particularly disgusted by the view that "personal correction,"[37] as he phrased it, was an insult or a degradtion to the boy upon whom it was inflicted; and to accustom young boys to think so appeared to him to be "positively mischievous." "At an age," he wrote, "when it is almost impossible to find a true, manly sense of the degradation of guilt or faults, where is the wisdom of encouraging a fantastic sense of the degradation of personal correction? What can be more false, or more adverse to the simplicity, sobriety, and humbleness of mind which are the best ornaments of youth, and offer the best promise of a noble manhood?" One had not to look far, he added, for "the fruits of such a system." In Paris, during the Revolution of 1830,[38] an officer observed a boy of twelve insulting the soldiers, and "though the action was then raging,[39] merely struck him with the fiat part of his sword, as the fit chastisement for boyish impertinence. But the boy had been taught to consider his person sacred, and that a blow was a deadly insult; he therefore followed the officer, and having watched his opportunity, took deliberate aim at him with a pistol and murdered him." Such were the alraming results of insufficient whipping.

Dr. Arnold did not apply this doctrine to the Praepostors; but the boys in the lower parts of the school felt its benefits with a double force. The Sixth Form was not only excused from chastisement; it was given the right to chasise. The younger children, scourged both by Dr. Arnold and by the elder children, were given every opportunity of acquiring the simplicity, sobriety, and humbleness of mind, which are the best ornaments of youth.

In the actual sphere of teaching, Dr. Arnold's reforms were tentative and few. He introduced modern history, modern languages, and mathematics into the school curriculum; but the results were not encouraging. He devoted to the teaching of history one hour a week; yet, though he took care to inculcate in these lessons a wholesome hatred of moral evil, and to point out from time to time the indications of the providential government of the world, his pupils never seemed to make much progress in the subject. Could it have been that the time allotted to it was insufficient? Dr. Arnold had some suspicions that this might be the case. With modern languages there was the same difficulty. Here his hopes were certainly not excessive. "I assume it," he wrote, "as the foundation of all my view of the case, that boys at a public school never will learn to speak or pronounce French well, under any circumstances." It would be enough if they could "learn it grammatically as a dead language." But even this they very seldom managed to do. "I know too well," he was obliged to confess, "that most of the boys would pass a very poor examination even in French grammar. But so it is with their mathematics; and so it will be with any branch of knowledge that is taught but seldom, and is felt to be quite subordinate to the boys' main study."

The boys' main study remained the dead languages of Greece and Rome. That the classics should form the basis of all teaching was an axiom with Dr. Arnold. "The study of language," he said, "seems to me as if it was given for the very purpose of forming the human mind in youth; and the Greek and Latin languages seem the very instruments by which this is to be effected." Certainly, there was something providential about it—from the point of view of the teacher as well as of the taught. If Greek and Latin had not been "given" in that convenient manner, Dr. Arnold, who had spent his life in acquiring those languages, might have discovered that he had acquired them in vain. As it was, he could set the noses of his pupils to the grindstone of syntax and prosody with a clear conscience.[40] Latin verses and Greek prepositions divided between them the labours of the week. As time went on, he became, he declared, "increasingly convinced that it is not knowledge, but the means of gaining knowledge which I have to teach." The reading of the school was devoted almost entirely to selected passages from the writers of antiquity. "Boys," he remarked, "do not like poetry." Perhaps his own poetical taste was a little dubious; at any rate, it is certain that he condidered the Greek Tragedians greatly overrated,[41] and that he ranked Propertius[42] as "an indifferent poet."As for Aristophanes,[43] owing to his strong moral disapprobation, he could not bring himself to read him until he was forty, when, it is true, he was much struck by the "Clouds." But Juvenal[44] the Doctor could never bring himself to read at all.

2. GIBBON (from *Portraits in Miniature)*

... Gibbon's style is probably the most exclusive[1] in literature. By its very nature it bars out a great multitude of human energies. It makes sympathy impossible,[2] it takes no cognisance of passion, it turns its back upon religion with a withering smile.[3] But that was just what was wanted. Classic beauty came instead. By the penetrating influence of style—automatically, inevitably—lucidity, balance and precision[4] were everywhere introduced; and the miracle of order was established over the chaos of a thousand years.

Of course, the Romantics raised a protest. 'Gibbon's style,' said Coleridge,[5] 'is detestable; but,' he added, 'it is not the worst thing about him.' Critics of the later nineteenth century were less consistent.[6] They admired Gibbon for everything except his style, imagining that his History would have been much improved if it had been written in some other way; they did not see that, if it had been written in any other way, it would have ceased to exist;[7] just as St. Paul's would cease to exist if it were rebuilt in Gothic.[8] Obsessed by the colour and movement of romantic prose, they were blind to the subtlety, the clarity, the continuous strength of Gibbon's writing. Gibbon could turn a bold phrase with the best of them — 'the fat[9] slumbers of the Church,' for instance — if he wanted to; but he very rarely wanted to; such effects would have disturbed the easy, closeknit, homogeneous surface of his work. His use of words is, in fact, extremely delicate. When, describing St. Simeon Stylites on his pillar,[10] he speaks of 'this last and lofty station,' he succeeds, with the least possible emphasis,[11] merely by the combination of those two alliterative[12] epithets with that particular substantive, in making the whole affair ridiculous. One can almost see his shoulders shrug. The nineteenth century found him pompous; they did not relish the irony beneath the pomp .... Gibbon's irony, no doubt, is the salt of his work; but, like all irony, it is the product of style. It was not for nothing that he read through every year the *Lettres Provinciales* of Pascal.[13] From this point of view it is interesting to compare him with Voltaire.[14] The irony of the great Frenchman was a flashing sword — extreme, virulent, deadly — a terrific instrument of propaganda. Gibbon uses the weapon with far more delicacy; he carves his enemy 'as a dish fit for the Gods';[15] his mocking is aloof, almost indifferent, and perhaps, in the long run, for that very reason, even more effective.

At every period of his life Gibbon is a pleasant thing to contemplate, but perhaps most pleasant of all in the closing weeks of it, during his last visit to England. He had hurried home from Lausanne[16] to join his friend Lord Sheffield,[17] whose wife had died suddenly, and who, he felt, was in need of his company. The journey was no small proof of his affectionate nature; old age was approaching; he was corpulent, gouty, and accustomed to every comfort; and the war of the French Revolution was raging in the districts through which he had to pass.[18] But he did not hesitate, and after skirting the belligerent armies in his chaise, arrived safely in England. After visiting

Lord Sheffield he proceeded to Bath, to stay with his stepmother. The amazing little figure, now almost spherical, bowled along the Bath Road in the highest state of exhilaration. 'I am always,' he told his friend, 'so much delighted and improved with this union of ease and motion, that, were not the expense enormous, I would travel every year some hundred miles, more especially in England,' Mrs. Gibbon,[19] a very old lady, but still full of vitality, worshipped her stepson, and the two spent ten days together, talking, almost always *tête-à-tête,* for ten hours a day. Then the historian went off to Althorpe,[20] where he spent a happy morning with Lord Spencer,[21] looking at early editions of Cicero.[22] And so back to London. In London a little trouble arose. A protuberance in the lower part of his person,[23] which, owing to years of characteristic *insouciance*, had grown to extraordinary proportions, required attention; an operation was necessary; but it went off well, and there seemed to be no danger. Once more Mr. Gibbon dined out. Once more he was seen, in his accustomed attitude, with advanced forefinger, addressing the company, and rapping his snuff box at the close of each particularly pointed phrase. But illness came on again — nothing very serious.[24] The great man lay in bed discussing how much longer he would live — he was fifty-six — ten years, twelve years, or perhaps twenty. He ate some chicken and drank three glasses of madeira. Life seemed almost as charming as usual. Next morning, getting out of bed for a necessary moment,[25] 'Je suis plus adroit,'[26] he said with his odd smile to his French valet. Back in bed again, he muttered something more, a little incoherently, lay back among the pillows, dozed, half-woke, dozed again, and became unconscious — for ever.[27]

【作者简介】 斯特拉契（Lytton Strachey）1880年生，出身于大官僚家庭，父亲是军人，替大英国统治印度有功，受到爵士的封号。他受的又是资产阶级教育，毕业于英国剑桥大学。

他一生主要以著述为业，直到1933年逝世以前，他的生活几乎完全在书斋、客厅和旅行中度过。主要文学作品有《法国文学里程碑》（*Landmarks in French Literature*, 1912);《维多利亚时代名人》(*Eminent Victorians*, 1918);《维多利亚女王》(*Queen Victoria*, 1921);《伊丽莎白女王及埃塞克斯》(*Elizabeth and Essex*, 1928);《人物小画像》(*Portraits in Miniature*, 1931),以及其它评论文字等。

斯特拉契主要是个传记家,但在文学评论方面,也有一定的地位。他的《法国文学里程碑》对法国古典文学作家评价很高,作为一本小册子,论述也算较详的,在若干方面颇能从一个英国读者的角度,就英法两国文学异同作出一些比较。这部书的缺点是偏重形式,花过多的篇幅去分析文字结构及修词技巧特色,对思想内容则谈得较少。

他的最著名的作品是《维多利亚时代名人》及《维多利亚女王》,这两本书都曾经享有广大的读者。尤其《维多利亚时代名人》,出版后轰动整个英国文艺界,被推为划时代的作品。他在这书里,把那些在千千万万人中长期受崇拜的英国十九世纪上层社会名流,从他们巍巍的宝座上拉下来,让读者耳目一新,认清楚这些名流的本来面貌,如大主教曼宁的世欲熏心,教育革新家亚诺德的颟顸顽固,护士慈善小姐娜婷该尔的乖戾任性,虔诚的基督教徒戈登将军的怪诞反常。斯特拉契打破传统的偏见,主张对人物作深刻的心理分析。因此他的作品,对于摧毁英国资产阶级社会的偶象,揭露那些绅士淑女特有的伪善,起了一定的作用。英国十九世纪传记界流行的阿谀主人翁的风气,可以说是斯特拉契纠正过来的。可是他对于维多利亚时代英国社会本质,阶级力量对比,什么是历史前进的动力等,一无所知。他把历史上发生的事件说成有时起于偶然,对一个人的贤愚得失往往用心理动机和性格习惯所形成的影响去评价,他认为历史不是科学,社会发展规律是不可知的。他把社会的光明,寄托在人的诚实的智力和健全的理性上,重复了过去思想家的这个唯心主义观点。在这方面,《维多利亚时代名人》和《维多利亚女王》都暴露了最大的弱点。

他的传记所以享有广大的读者,是部分和他的艺术造诣有密切联系的。他的文笔犀利简练,细腻含蓄!传记在他手里变成象小说一般富于兴味,传记文学又呈现了一种新的姿态。他的善于剪裁的经济表达手法,对于堆砌冗拓的过去英国传记,不失为一个很大的革新。不过他有时重视传奇式的情节,加以渲染,绘声绘色,甚至为了增加效果,不惜乞灵于主观想象,凭空臆造,这些都是不足为训的。

他的文章虽然一般是流畅自然的,但也偶尔露出矫揉造作的痕迹。大体说来,他是师承英国古典主义散文作家的,讲究用词精确,结构清楚,韵律和谐，也注意排偶、对称、比照等修词技巧。在现代英国作家中，他的散文颇能独标一格。对于根本不太重视文章组织形式、不习惯于词义细致辨别的读者，这样的散文能给以一定的帮助。

【题解与注释】

1. DR. ARNOLD

本文说的是一个英国公学校长怎样办学。公学（public school）是英国有六百年左右传统的教育机构，是指中等学校之一的统称。

所谓公学，既非直接由政府管理的公立学校，也不是无条件公之于众的、任何家庭的子女都可以随便进去学习的地方。名为公，它实是私立，是穷人子弟进不起的私立贵族学校，因为用费昂贵，且有排外倾向。公学的“公”可能指的这类学校有一个公共性质的由绅士财主拼凑起来的董事会对它进行领导和提供经费。它的学生，特别是过去，都来自豪富家庭。有几所历史悠久的著名公学，其毕业生基本上升入老牌英国大学，如牛津、剑桥。长期以来，英国上、下院及内阁成员大都出身牛津、剑桥，也就是说，出身于某些公学。这样，英国公学学生既和阀阅制度有不可分割的姻缘，毕业后又结成宗派，政治上朋比拉拢，用一付势利眼去看社会地位不如他们的人。

以上情况在十九世纪英国达到突出的程度。在英国处于资本主义极盛的一个时期，公学为它的统治阶级造就了许许多多得力的官员。公学几乎成为英帝国主义培养人才的一个重要基地。达也是英国公学得名的原因之一。

十九世纪英国有一个名人，他是亚诺德博士（Dr. Thomas Arnold）。此人所以得名，并非因为他是大诗人 Matthew Arnold 的父亲，也并非因为他担任过牛津大学的历史教授，而仅仅因为他曾是拉格比公学（Rugby School）校长。拉格比在过去是四大名公学之一，其它三个是伊顿（Eton），温切斯特（Winchester）及哈罗（Harrow）。自从一八二八年亚诺德担任校长后，拉格比的声名更加受到人们的注意。亚诺德通过整顿拉格比带动了其它公学，被认为对英国教育事业立下了功勋。

斯特拉契以写出《维多利亚时代名人》（*Eminent Victorians*）一书而名噪一时，成为英国近代文坛巨星，亚诺德博士便是书中描绘的名人之一。他很细腻地客观地描画出这个名人的颟顸顽固，所谓教育革新家的本来面目不过如此。

亚诺德是一个自命关心青年一代的道德生活和宗教信仰的人。在这个前提下，他还要他们将来配称得上是上流人，是绅士。至于学生的智力在他的心目中是排在末位的。总之，他的最根本的办学要求，是学生都成为象他那样的虔诚基督教徒。他重视古典语言学习，课程表上几无现代科目的地位。而古典语言学习，对于亚诺德，最主要的也还是为了提高学生的品德。他的一套管理学生的制度竟是来自他从《旧约》传说所受到的启发，其基础是他公认不讳的神权政治。过去许多英国政治家的偏见和无知，和亚诺德所大力推行这种公学教育有密切的联系。

这本传记是作为一本正式传记问世的，所以作者经常在文中引用主人翁自己或别人的话，去说明事实背景或分析心理状态，以示一切是有材料根据的，作者不曾参入己见。然而不管作者有意或无意，他对主人翁的弱点的揭露和讽刺，还是充分地呈现在纸上。作者艺术手法是相当高明的。

1. Keate: 即 John Keate (1773–1852)，在伊顿公学任职很久，1797—1809 助理校长，1809—1834 校长，对学生滥施体罚，曾一次鞭打学生至八十名之多。

2. a system of anarchy tempered by despotism: 无政府主义中杂有专制主义的一种制度。学生闹无政府主义，校长搞专制主义。

3. boys: 公学当时大都是为男生设的，入学年龄限于十三岁到十四岁，至十八岁或十九岁离校。

4. miscellaneous boarding-houses: 混杂的宿舍。学生不分年龄大小，都规定挤在宿舍中居住及自修。

5. "Long Chamber": "长寝室"。

6. turned ... badgered: 着恼，感到极不安。前面的 statesmen and warriors 是毕业多年的老校友。

7. the furious incursions of an irascible little old man carrying a bundle of birch-twigs: 一个暴躁矮小的老头子拿着一束桦条怒不可遏地闯进来。Keate 身材矮小。桦木条坚韧，故被用来作鞭挞工具。

8. licensed barbarism: 特许的野蛮行为（指校长有权滥施体罚）。

9. the niceties of Ovidian verse: 奥维德的诗行的精致之处。奥维德指 Ovid（公元前 43—公元后 17？），古代罗马的大诗人。Ovidian，奥维德的。

10. prosody: 诗律学。决定拉丁语诗歌格律的是诗行中各音节的长度。

11. under-masters: 指一般教师。

12. even that indomitable will was overwhelmed by the flood of lawlessness: 甚至那副不屈不挠的意志也淹没在无法无天的洪流中。这儿 flood 与 overwhelmed 在用词上有互相呼应的关系。校长尽管意志坚强，一人难以对付这种纪律荡然的局面。

13. the whole school assembled: 集会在一起的全校学生。这儿 assembled 是分词，修饰 school.

14. Chapel:（附属于这个公学的）教堂。

15. antique Fellow: 一个老古董般的教师。

16. exploding: 一下子哄起来的（因有人放出老鼠恶作剧）。

17. a more liberal curriculum: 较为开明的课程表（即不限于死钻古典语言）。

18. utilitarianism: 功利主义。这儿指讲求实用。当时英帝国主义在世界各地扩张势力，急需为其效劳的实用人才。

19. respectability: 体面（符合英国资产阶级社会上层人物的高雅身分等）。

20. classical philology: 古典语言学（指对希腊语、拉丁语的词源、语法、修辞等的研究）。

21. bleak rigidities: 枯燥无味的死板东西。

22. it: 指上文 happiness。

23. Shall I ...: 此处引文见 Thomas Hughes (1822–1896) 的 *Tom Brown's School-days*（《汤姆·勃朗的公学生活》）第四章。书中主人翁 Tom Brown（本文中 Squire Brown 的儿子）追述亚诺德任拉格比公学校长时他在该校学习情况。引文中 particles，指不变格的语助词；digamma，指古希腊语中原字母表上的第六个字母，后来废弃不用，只是在语言研究上可供考证同族各语言中相当音值的递变痕迹。

24. The Old Testament:《旧约》（基督教《圣经》的上部）。

25. He ... Israel: 据《旧约》中的传说，以色列（Israel）人部落的主神名耶和华（Jehovah）。所谓"选民"，乃指以色列人，即选出把自己奉献给耶和华的人。在以色列人部落当中，一度担任军政领袖的是士师（Judges），这样的士师，自称奉耶和华的意志办事，对百姓进行统治，这就形成一种神权政治（Theocracy）. 亚诺德竟然从《旧约》中这些记载，得到启发，想以耶和华自居，管理低班的高班生便是他的士师。参考下段。

26. Praepostor: = prepostor,（英国某些公学中）负责维持低班纪律的高班生。

27. the Sixth Form: 第六班，即最高班。

28. *ipso facto*:（拉丁语），根据这一事实，因此。

29. involved in awful grandeur: 笼罩在令人敬畏的庄严气氛中。

30. Lawgiver:（此处指）耶和华，上帝。

31. thunder:《旧约》中描述耶和华时，常用此词，旧译《圣经》中有时作"大发雷声"，兼有本义及借义，从打雷借比震怒，犹如汉语"发雷霆"。

32. whirlwind:《旧约》中描述耶和华时常用到的另一个词，一般译作"旋风"，形容耶和华在旋风中来去，威严飘渺，不可窥测。

33. be ... mergedin: 消失在……中。

34. Westmoreland: 过去英国的一个郡，今并入 Cumbria 郡，旅游胜地，部分为英国的著名湖区。今一般拼作 Westmorland.

35. it was not for such as he to ...: 象他这样的人不宜于……

36. bellowing and cuffing: 咆哮如雷，乱打巴掌。

37. "personal correction": 人身惩罚，体罚。（correction = punishment，可视为婉语。）

38. the Revolution of 1830: 指一八三〇年七月巴黎人民进行的革命，当时他们在街头筑起壁垒进行战斗，在三天内推翻了查利第十的专制统治，粉碎了他复辟旧制度的阴谋。

39. the action was then raging: 当时战斗行动激烈。

40. set ... conscience: 心安理得地要他的学生孜孜不息地苦攻句法和诗律。

41. he ... overrated: 接上文说明亚诺德的诗歌趣味不高。用诗行写作的希腊悲剧家在西方文学史上有极高的地位。

42. Propertius: 纪元前一世纪罗马诗人，他的作品风格卑靡，确如亚诺德所说，是一个极其普通的（indifferent）作家。

43. Aristophanes:（448？—380？公元前），古希腊的杰出喜剧家，他的《云》

(*The Clouds*) 有罗念生同志的汉译本 .

44. Juvenal (60? –140?): 古罗马的杰出的讽刺诗人。

2. GIBBON

本篇从他的《人物小画像》中名叫《吉本》的一篇文章摘出。* 原文是一种传记小品，篇幅不长，这儿摘的是末尾部分。

吉本（Edward Gibbon, 1737–1794）是十八世纪英国资产阶级杰出历史学家，代表作是《罗马帝国衰亡史》(*The Dedine and Fall of the Roman Empire*)。象当时的其他启蒙大师一样，他在书中嘲笑宗教，抨击愚昧，具有进步的意义，但是他对历史的解释是唯心主义的，表现了他的局限性。

斯特拉契在这篇文章里，简要地叙述了吉本的生平，较为详细地谈到《罗马帝国衰亡史》这本书，它的写作经过，并十分赞扬这部书在材料处理、讽刺手法、文章风格各方面取得的成就。这篇传记小品写得精炼明畅，一气呵成；夹叙带议，重点突出，文笔是相当出色的。

斯特拉契在文章里明白说出，历史是艺术而不是科学（按此段我们未选）。他把一部历史的文体看成极端重要，并且认为历史家可以凭主观意志对材料作任意的去取和随心所欲的安排，这就暴露了他的唯心主义观点。

当然，吉本《罗马帝国衰亡史》的文体是有名的，谈这部书时可以顺便提到它的文体，而斯特拉契本人作为一个文体家，不妨在这方面多发挥一下。但是没有必要把文体的作用过分夸大，这点我们在后面选文的注解里还要论及。这种文体的特点大致上是音律齐整，结构谨严，运思清彻精密，用语警策简洁，在英国古典主义散文中达到很高的境界。这种文体虽有时也有它本身铺张浮华的一面，但总地说来，和那种夸诞放浪文体的不守法度和摆脱纪律，恰巧形成一个对照。但是吉本文体不是一成不变的，他的有名的《自传》，信笔写来，平易自然，和他的历史，如出自两人之手，这也是我们所应当知道的。

斯特拉契的文体和吉本的历史文体相近，都属于英国古典散文的范畴，其特点已如上述。不善于学这种文体的人，往往变得矜持生硬，或是满纸浮腔滑调，夹杂着大量抽象拉丁化的多音节词，这是应该避免的。斯特拉契虽然比起吉本是文体更现代化了，但也缺少吉本那样的大气派。

1. The most exclusive: 最为专一而不阐入任何浮词的（题外枝节之谈一概删除）。

2. It makes sympathy impossible: 作者认为吉本的历史严格地限于事实叙述，不搀杂个人同情在内。

3. it turns its back upon religion with s withering smile: 吉本在他的历史中（尤其第十五章）揭露了关于基督教起源的迷信传说，加以嘲笑。那种嘲笑是摧毁性

---

* 本文最初于 1928 年发表于期刊 *The Nation and The Athenaeum* 上。

的，故说 a withering smile.

注意这儿全句包含三个子句：It makes sympathy impossible, it takes no cognisance of passion, it turns its back upon religion with a withering smile. 逐句深入，第三个子句拉得最长，语势也最强，整个的节奏是自然匀称的。另外的例如下面的句子：

(1) Once more Mr. Gibbon dined out.

Once more he was seen, in his accustomed attitude, with advanced forefinger, addressing the company, and rapping his snuff box at the close of each particularly pointed phrase.

(2) The great man lay in bed discussing how much longer he would live — he was fifty-six — ten years, twelve years, or perhaps twenty.

4. lucidity, balance and precision: 为了加强修词效果，三个名词叠在一起，也有时把形容词或加上分词这样安排的。这种手法在斯特拉契文章中常见。本文下面另有这样的例子：

(1) easy, close-knit, homogeneous.

(2) extreme, virulent, deadly.

(3) corpulent, gouty, and accustomed to every comfort.

5. Coleridge: 柯勒律治，即 Samuel Taylor Coleridge (1772–1834)，英国浪漫主义诗人及批评家。原语见他的《茶余酒后谈》(“Table Talk”) 中 1833 年 8 月 15 日谈话，是他逝世前一年的意见。

6. 总地说来，他们不满意吉本的文体，但并非一笔抹煞，举几个例子说明。

李顿（Edward Bulwer Lytton, 1803–1873）承认吉本文体过于庄严和讲究音调，但他觉得它写得清楚，决不晦涩；许多作家尽管用字通俗些，却不如吉本易读易懂。

萨克雷（W. M. Thackeray, 1811–1863）认为吉本的文章虽然做作，却曾获得一些读者的爱好，这是卡莱尔（Thomas Carlyle）的文章所不能比的。

巴哲特（Walter Bagehot, 1826–1877）看出吉本的文体铺张繁缛，不是一切场合可用；可是他肯定它的优点，即生动流畅，加强了叙述的连贯性。

7. 文章形式当然对内容有反作用，但内容毕竟优先于形式。斯特拉契把吉本文体对他的历史的影响看成是决定性的。

8. St. Paul's 全名为 St. Paul's Cathedral，伦敦圣保罗大教堂。这是伦敦的古老教堂之一，一六六六年几全毁于伦敦大火，它本是一座峨特式的（Gothic）建筑物。楞因（Christopher Wren）设计重建这个教堂，十七世纪后叶着手，十八世纪初完成，采取的古典建筑风格，加了一个新的大圆顶。峨特式和古典式建筑有截然不同的面貌，两者不能并存，因此斯特拉契这儿说的关于圣保罗教堂的话是对的。至于一部历史和它的文章风格的关系，以及一座教堂和它的建筑风格的关系，二者是难以相提并论的。作者这种比法，归根到底，乃是过分重视历史著述的形式。

9. fat: dull, indolent, inert.

10. St. Simeon Stylites: 中世纪某种苦行禁欲的基督教徒，居叙利亚沙漠的柱顶上，日夜祈祷，称 stylite，汉译作“柱上苦行者”，从希腊语 stylos（“柱”）转成。此处 Stylites 不是复数，乃是希腊语的原来形式，主要用于“Simeon Stylites”（柱上苦行者栖弥昂）一语中；在一般情形下，Stylites 可视为 stylite 的复数。这个柱上苦行者栖弥昂是五世纪人，相传在各种柱顶上修苦行数十年，每次移住更高的柱子，最后的一根柱有六七十英尺高，故此处原文引语用lofty；他移上柱子后，一直到死未下来，故用last一词，构成"this last and lofty station"一语，这是从吉本"罗马帝国衰亡史"第三十七章摘引的一个短语。St. Simeon中之St.可略去，吉本原文未用。

11. 注意文中带有夸大效果的副词或副词短语，除这儿with *the least possible* emphasis外，如：

(1) *probably the most exclusive* in literature.

(2) lucidity, balance and precision were *everywhere* introduced.

(3) *extremely* delicate.

(4) can *almost* see his shoulders shrug:

(5) now *almost* spherical.

(6) talking, *almost always tête-à-tête*.

(7) each *particularly* pointed phrase.

(8) *almost* as charming as usual.

12. alliterative: 头韵相同的，双声的，指前文"*l*ast and *l*ofly".

13. Pascal (1623–1662)**:** 法国古典主义散文家。*Lettres Provinciales* 一作 *Les provinciales*（《致外省某友人书》）共收书信十八通，于1656—1657年用匿名发表，攻击耶稣会派的褊狭及诡辩。吉本在《自传》里说过，他从这些书信里，学得了甚至对于神圣的宗教问题，也可以使用严肃而温和的讽刺武器。

14. Voltaire (1694–1778)**:** 法国著名启蒙主义思想家及文学家。吉本和他认识，并受到他的著述的影响。

15. 在莎士比亚《恺撒大将》第二幕第一景第一七三行，布鲁特和同谋者计议如何刺死恺撒时说，"Let's carve him as a dish fit for the gods."借喻把敌人精刳细剜，不必刀砍斧斫，这个手法适用于讽刺。

16. Lausanne: 在瑞士，以风景著称，吉本在这儿寄居很久，从事历史著述。

17. Lord Sheffield: 原名John Baker Holroyd, 1735–1821，吉本友人，编辑过吉本的著述。

18. 在法国资产阶级革命发生的年代里，吉本对这件震动世界的大事，似乎漠不关心。他是1793年从瑞士绕道革命火焰高烧的法国回到英国的，几个月后，次年年头就病死了。

19. Mrs. Gibbon: 吉本的孀居继母，未生子女，待吉本友善。

20. Althorpe: 英国地方，在英格兰中部偏东区域，位于Trent河上，富有阶级在此置田庄别墅。

21. Lord Spencer: 即George John Spencer (1758–1801)，英国十八世纪贵族兼藏书家。

22. Cicero（公元前106—43）**:** 古罗马作家。

23. the lower part of his person（婉语），指与性器官或与之相联的部分。

24. But illness came on again —nothing very serious. 一句中正反对比。斯特拉契文中这样的句法很多，如：

(1) Obsessed by the colour and movement of romantic prose, they were blind to the subtlety … of Gibbon's writing.

(2) Gibbon could turn a bold phrase … if he wanted to; but he very rarely wanted to …

(3) … his mocking is aloof, almost indifferent, and perhaps, in the long run, for that very reason, even more efiective.

(4) At every period of his life Gibbon is a pleasant thing to contemplate, but perhaps most pleasant of all in the closing weeks of it …

25. for a necessary moment:（婉语）上厕所。

26. "Je suis plus adroit':（法语）我手脚更灵便些了。

27. 斯特拉契每每刻画这样的小情节，绘声绘色，助长趣味。吉本从病到死这一段描写着墨不多，异常传神，异常具体。这种体裁宜于小品文字，用于正规传记，就不太妥当。

作为继承英国古典主义散文传统的作家，斯特拉契有时却避用拉丁语风和法国语风（Latinism and Gallicism），而代以许多浅易的撒克逊词和习语（Saxonism）。这是一种改进。如末段最后的几句话，以单音节词为主，是其明证。但有时他又用字过大，如 cognisance, belligerent, exhilaration 以及 protuberance 这些词散见于文中，可见上述语风尚多残余，从这些词所出现的场合，它们并非必用不可的，它们可以用更简易的词代替。作者不用 cognizance 这个较通行的拼法，而用 cognisance，古法语的影响是显然的（一般词典仅列 cognizance,《牛津英语词典》兼收 cognisance，却把它排在第二，以见其非主要通行的）。"Takes no cognisance of" 也不通俗，这儿的 cognisance 一般用 notice 或 heed 代替，to take no notice of 或 to take no heed of 都更自然现成。又文中 "insouciance" 一词，也受法语影响，其实改用 carelessness 这个常见词，既无损于文义，也不妨碍音调。

50 VIRGINIA WOOLF
1882–1941

1. Mrs. Dalloway (selections)

*2. Defoe (*from *The Common Reader)*

赵萝蕤　选注

1. MRS. DALLOWAY
(*from* Chapter I)

Mrs. Dalloway said she would buy the flowers herself.

For Lucy[1] had her work cut out for her.[2] The doors would be taken off their hinges[3]; Rumpelmayer's men[4] were coming. And then, thought Clarissa Dalloway, what a morning — fresh as if issued to children on a beach.

What a lark![5] What a plunge![6] For so it had always seemed to her, when, with a little squeak of the hinges, which she could hear now, she had burst open the French windows[7] and plunged at Bourton[8] into the open air. How fresh, how calm, stiller than this[9] of course, the air was in the early morning; like the flap of a wave; the kiss of a wave; chill and sharp and yet (for a girl of eighteen[10] as she then was) solemn, feeling as she did, standing there at the open window, that something awful was about to happen; looking at the flowers, at the trees with the smoke winding off them and the rooks rising, falling; standing and looking until Peter Walsh[11] said, "Musing among the vegetables?" — was that it?[12] — "I prefer men to cauliflowers" — was that it? He must have said it at breakfast one morning when she had gone out on to the terrace — Peter Walsh. He would be back from India one of these days, June or July, she forgot which, for his letters were awfully dull; it was his sayings one remembered; his eyes, his pocket-knife, [13] his smile, his grumpiness and, when millions of things had utterly vanished — how strange it was! — a few sayings like this[14] about cabbages.

She stiffened a little on the kerb, waiting for Durtnall's van[15] to pass. A charming woman, Scrope Purvis[16] thought her (knowing her as one does know people who live next door to one in Westminster[17]); a touch of the bird about her, of the jay, blue-green, light, vivacious, though she was over fifty, and grown very white since her illness. There she perched, never seeing him, waiting to cross, very upright.

For having lived in Westminster — how many years now? over twenty, — one feels even in the midst of the traffic, or waking at night, Clarissa was positive, a particular hush, or solemnity; an indescribable pause, a suspense (but that might be her heart, affected, they said, by influenza) before Big Ben[18] strikes. There! Out it boomed. First a warning, musical; then the hour, irrevocable.[19] The leaden circles[20] dissolved in the air. Such fools we are, she thought, crossing Victoria Street. For Heaven only knows why one loves it so, how one sees it so, making it up, building it round one, tumbling it, creating it every moment afresh; but the veriest frumps,[21] the most dejected of miseries sitting on doorsteps (drink their downfall) do the same; can't be dealt with, she felt positive, by Acts of Parliament for that very reason: they love life. In people's eyes, in the swing, tramp, and trudge;[22] in the bellow and the uproar; the carriages, motor cars, omnibuses, vans, sandwich men shuffling and swinging; brass bands; barrel organs; in the triumph and the jingle and the strange high singing of some aeroplane overhead was what she loved; life; London; this moment of June.

For it was the middle of June. The War[23] was over, except for some one like Mrs. Foxcroft at the Embassy last night eating her heart out[24] because that nice boy was killed and now the old Manor House must go to a cousin;[25] or Lady Bexborough who opened a bazaar, they said, with the telegram in her hand, John, her favourite, killed; but it was over; thank Heaven — over. It was June. The King and Queen were at the Palace. And everywhere, though it was still so early, there was a beating, a stirring of galloping ponies, tapping of cricket bats; Lords, Ascot, Ranelagh and all the rest of it; wrapped in the soft mesh of the grey-blue morning air, which, as the day wore on, would unwind them, and set down on their lawns and pitches the bouncing ponies, whose forefeet just struck the ground and up they sprung, the whirling young men, and laughing girls in their transparent muslins who, even now, after dancing all night, were taking their absurd woolly dogs for a run; and even now, at this hour, discreet old dowagers were shooting out in their motor cars on errands of mystery; and the shopkeepers were fidgeting in their windows with their paste and diamonds, their lovely old sea-green brooches in eighteenth-century settings to tempt Americans (but one must economise, not buy things rashly for Elizabeth)[26], and she, too, loving it as she did with an absurd and faithful passion, being part of it, since her people were courtiers once in the time of the Georges,[27] she, too, was going that very night to kindle and illuminate; to give her party. But how strange, on entering the Park,[28] the silence; the mist; the hum; the slow-swimming happy ducks; the pouched birds waddling; and who should be coming along with his back against the Government buildings, most appropriately, carrying a despatch box stamped with the Royal Arms,[29] who but Hugh Whitbread; her old friend Hugh — the admirable Hugh!

"Good-morning to you, Clarissa!" said Hugh, rather extravagantly, for they had known each other as children. "Where are you off to?"

"I love walking in London," said Mrs. Dalloway. "Really it's better than walking in the country."

They had just come up — unfortunately — to see doctors. Other people came to see pictures; go to the opera; take their daughters[30] out; the Whitbreads came "to see doctors." Times without number Clarissa had visited Evelyn Whitbread in a nursing home. Was Evelyn ill again? Evelyn was a good deal out of sorts, said Hugh, intimating by a kind of pout or swell of his very well-covered, manly, extremely handsome, perfectly upholstered body[31] (he was almost too well dressed always, but presumably had to be, with his little job at Court) that his wife had some internal ailment, nothing serious, which, as an old friend, Clarissa Dalloway would quite understand without requiring him to specify. Ah yes, she did of course; what a nuisance; and felt very sisterly and oddly conscious at the same time of her hat. Not the right hat for the early morning, was that it? For Hugh always made her feel, as he bustled on,[32] raising his hat rather extravagantly[33] and assuring her that she might be a girl of eighteen, and of course he was coming to her party to-night, Evelyn absolutely insisted, only a little late he might be after the party at the Palace to which he had to take one of Jim's boys,—she always felt a little skimpy[34] beside Hugh; schoolgirlish; but attached to him, partly from having known him always, but she did think him a good sort in his own way, though Richard[35] was nearly driven mad by him, and as for Peter Walsh, he had never to this day forgiven her for liking him.

She could remember scene after scene at Bourton—Peter furious; Hugh not, of course, his match in any way, but still not a positive imbecile as Peter made out; not a mere barber's block.[36] When his old mother wanted him to give up shooting or to take her to Bath[37] he did it, without a word; he was really unselfish, and as for saying, as Peter did, that he had no heart, no brain, nothing but the manners and breeding of an English gentleman, that was only her dear Peter at his worst; and he could be intolerable; he could be impossible; but adorable to walk with on a morning like this.

(June had drawn out every leaf on the trees. The mothers of Pimlico[38] gave suck to their young. Messages were passing from the

Fleet[39] to the Admiralty. Arlington Street and Piccadilly[40] seemed to chafe the very air in the Park and lift its leaves hotly, brilliantly, on waves of that divine vitality which Clarissa loved, To dance, to ride, she had adored all that.)

For they might be parted for hundreds of years, she and Peter; she never wrote a letter and his were dry sticks;[41] but suddenly it would come over her, If he were with me now what would he say?—some days, some sights bringing him back to her calmly, without the old bitterness; which perhaps was the reward of having cared for people; they came back in the middle of St. James's Park on a fine morning—indeed they did. But Peter—however beautiful the day might be, and the trees and the grass, and the little girl in pink—Peter never saw a thing of all that. He would put on his spectacles, if she told him to; he would look. It was the state of the world that interested him; Wagner,[42] Pope's[43] poetry, people's characters eternally, and the defects of her own soul. How he scolded her! How they argued! She would marry a Prime Minister and stand at the top of a staircase; the perfect hostess he called her (she had cried over it in her bedroom), she had the makings of the perfect hostess, he said.

So she would still find herself arguing in St. James's Park, still making out that she had been right—and she had too—not to marry him. For in marriage a little licence, a little independence there must be between people living together day in day out in the same house; which Richard gave her, and she him. (Where was he this morning for instance? Some committee, she never asked what.) But with Peter everything had to be shared; everything gone into. And it was intolerable, and when it came to that scene in the little garden by the fountain, she had to break with him or they would have been destroyed, both of them ruined, she was convinced; though she had borne about with her for years like an arrow sticking in her heart the grief, the anguish; and then the horror of the moment when some one told her at a concert that he had married a woman met on the boat going to India! Never should she forget all that! Cold, heartless, a prude, he called her. Never could she understand how he cared. But those Indian women did presumably — silly, pretty, flimsy nincompoops.[44] And she wasted her pity. For he was quite happy, he assured her — perfectly happy, though he had never done a thing that they talked of; his whole life had been a failure. It made her angry still.

She had reached the Park gates. She stood for a moment, looking at the omnibuses in Piccadilly.

She would not say of any one in the world now that they were this or were that. She felt very young; at the same time unspeakably aged. She sliced like a knife through everything;[45] at the same time was outside, looking on. She had a perpetual sense, as she watched the taxi cabs, of being out, out, far out to sea and alone; she always had the feeling that it was very, very dangerous to live even one day. Not that she thought herself clever, or much out of the ordinary. How she had got through life on the few twigs of knowledge Fraulein Daniels[46] gave them she could not think. She knew nothing; no language, no history; she scarcely read a book now, except memoirs in bed; and yet to her it was absolutely absorbing; all this; the cabs passing; and she would not say of Peter, she would not say of herself, I am this, I am that.

Her only gift was knowing people almost by instinct, she thought, walking on. If you put her in a room with some one, up went her back like a cat's; or she purred. Devonshire House, Bath House,[47] the house with the china cockatoo, she had seen them all lit up once; and remembered Sylvia, Fred, Sally Seton[48] — such hosts of people; and dancing all night; and the waggons plodding past to market; and driving home across the Park. She remembered once throwing a shilling into the Serpentine.[49] But every one remembered; what she loved was this, here, now, in front of her; the fat lady in the cab. Did it matter then, she asked herself, walking towards Bond Street,[50] did it matter that she must inevitably cease completely; all this must go on without her; did she resent it; or did it not become consoling to believe that death ended absolutely? but that somehow in the streets of London, on the ebb and flow of things, here, there, she survived, Peter survived, lived in each other, she being part, she was positive, of the trees at home; of the house there, ugly, rambling all to bits and pieces as it was; part of people she had never met; being laid out like a mist between the people she knew best, who lifted her on their branches as she had seen the trees lift the mist, but it spread ever so far, her life, herself. But what was she dreaming as she looked into Hatchards[51] shop window?What was she trying to recover? What image of white dawn in the country, as she read in the book spread open:

Fear no more the heat o' the sun[52]

Nor the furious winter's rages.

This late age of the world's experience had bred in them all, all men and women, a well of tears. Tears and sorrows; courage and endurance; a perfectly upright and stoical bearing. Think, for example, of the woman she admired most, Lady Bexborough, opening the bazaar.

There were Jorrocks' *Jaunts and Jollities;*[53] there were *Soapy Sponge* and Mrs. Asquith's *Memoirs*[54] and *Big Game Shooting in Nigeria,* all spread open. Ever so many books there were; but none that seemed exactly right to take to Evelyn Whitbread in her nursing home. Nothing that would serve to amuse her and make that indescribably dried-up little woman look, as Clarissa came in, just for a moment cordial; before they settled down for the usual interminable talk of women's ailments. How much she wanted it — that people should look pleased as she came in, Clarissa thought and turned and walked back towards Bond Street, annoyed, because it was silly to have other reasons for doing things. Much rather would she have been one of those people like Richard who did things for themselves, whereas, she thought, waiting to cross, half the time she did things not simply, not for themselves; but to make people thiuk this or that;

perfect idiocy she knew (and now the policeman held up his hand[55]) for no one was ever for a second taken in. Oh if she could have had her life over again! she thought, stepping on to the pavement, could have looked even differently!

She would have been, in the first place, dark like Lady Bexborough, with a skin of crumpled leather and beautiful eyes. She would have been, like Lady Bexborough, slow and stately; rather large; interested in politics like a man; with a country house; very dignified, very sincere. Instead of which she had a narrow pea-stick figure; a ridiculous little face, beaked like a bird's. That she held herself well was true; and had nice hands and feet; and dressed well, considering that she spent little. But often now this body she wore (she stopped to look at a Dutch picture), this body, with all its capacities, seemed nothing—nothing at all. (She had the oddest sense of being herself invisible; unseen; unknown; there being no more marrying, no more having of children now, but only this astonishing and rather solemn progress with the rest of them, up Bond Street, this being Mrs. Dalloway; not even Clarissa any more; this being Mrs. Richard Dalloway.)

Bond Street fascinated her; Bond Street early in the morning in the season; its flags flying; its shops; no splash; no glitter; one roll of tweed in the shop where her father had bought his suits for fifty years; a few pearls; salmon on an iceblock.

"That is all," she said, looking at the fishmonger's. "That is all," she repeated, pausing for a moment at the window of a glove shop where, before the War, you could buy almost perfect gloves. And her old Uncle William used to say a lady is known by her shoes and her gloves. He had turned on his bed one morning in the middle of the War. He had said, "I have had enough." Gloves and shoes; she had a passion for gloves; but her own daughter, her Elizabeth, cared not a straw for either of them.

Not a straw, she thought, going on up Bond Street to a shop where they kept flowers for her when she gave a party. Elizabeth really cared for her dog most of all. The whole house this morning smelt of tar. Still, better poor *Grizzle*[56] than Miss Kilman;[57] better distemper and tar and all the rest of it than sitting mewed in a stuffy bedroom with a prayer book! Better anything, she was inclin ed to say. But it might be only a phase, as Richard said, such as all girls go through. It might be falling in love. But why with Miss Kilman? who had been badly treated of course; one must make allowances for that, and Richard said she was very able, had a really historical mind. Anyhow they were inseparable, and Elizabeth, her own daughter, went to Communion;[58] and how she dressed, how she treated people who came to lunch she did not care a bit, it being her experience that the religious ecstasy made people callous (so did causes); dulled their feelings, for Miss Kilman would do anything for the Russians, starved herself for the Austrians,[59] but in private inflicted positive torture, so insensitive was she, dressed in a green mackintosh coat. Year in year out she wore that coat; she perspired; she was never in the room five minutes without making you feel her superiority, your inferiority; how poor she was; how rich you were; how she lived in a slum without a cushion or a bed or a rug or whatever it might be, all her soul rusted with that grievance sticking in it, her dismissal from school during the War — poor embittered unfortunate creature! For it was not her one hated but the idea of her, which undoubtedly had gathered in to itself a great deal that was not Miss Kilman; had become one of those spectres with which one battles in the night; one of those spectres who stand astride us and suck up half our life-blood, dominators and tyrants; for no doubt with another throw of the dice, had the black been uppermost and not the white, she would have loved Miss Kilman! But not in this world. No.

It rasped her, though, to have stirring about in her this brutal monster! to hear twigs cracking and feel hooves planted down in the depths of that leaf-encumbered forest, the soul; never to be content quite, or quite secure, for at any moment the brute would be stirring, this hatred, which, especially since her illness, had power to make her feel scraped, hurt in her spine; gave her physical pain, and made all pleasure in beauty, in friendship, in being well, in being loved and making her home delightful rock, quiver, and bend as if indeed there were a monster grubbing at the roots, as if the whole panoply of content were nothing but self love! this hatred!

Nonsense, nonsense! she cried to herself, pushing through the swing doors of Mulberry's the florists.

She advanced, light, tall, very upright, to be greeted at once by button-faced Miss Pym, whose hands were always bright red, as if they had been stood in cold water with the flowers.

There were flowers: delphiniums, sweet peas, bunches of lilac; and carnations, masses of carnations. There were roses; there were irises. Ah yes—so she breathed in the earthy garden sweet smell as she stood talking to Miss Pym who owed her help, and thought her kind, for kind she had been years ago; very kind, but she looked older, this year, turning her head from side to side among the irises and roses and nodding tufts of lilac with her eyes half closed, snuffing in, after the street uproar, the delicious scent, the exquisite coolness. And then, opening her eyes, how fresh like frilled linen clean from a laundry laid in wicker trays the roses looked; and dark and prim the red carnations, holding their heads up; and all the sweet peas spreading in their bowls, tinged violet, snow white, pale—as if it were the evening and girls in muslin frocks came out to pick sweet peas and roses after the superb summer's day, with its almost blue-black sky, its delphiniums, its carnations, its arum lilies was over; and it was the moment between six and seven when every flower—roses, carnations, irises, lilac—glows; white, violet, red, deep orange; every flower seems to burn by itself, softly, purely in the misty beds; and how she loved the grey-white moths spinning in and out, over the cherry pie, over the evening primroses!

And as she began to go with Miss Pym from jar to jar, choosing, nonsense, nonsense, she said to herself, more and more gently, as if this beauty, this scent, this colour, and Miss Pym liking her, trusting her, were a wave which she let flow over her and surmount that hatred, that monster, surmount it all; and it lifted her up and up when — oh! a pistol shot[60] in the street outside!

"Dear, those motor cars," said Miss Pym, going to the window to look, and coming back and smiling apologetically with her hands full of sweet peas, as if those motor cars, those tyres of motor cars, were all *her* fault.

2. DEFOE[*]

THE FEAR WHICH ATTACKS the recorder of centenaries[1] lest he should find himself measuring a diminishing spectre[2] and forced to foretell its approaching dissolution is not only absent in the case of *Robinson Crusoe* but the mere thought of it is ridiculous. It may be true that *Robinson Crusoe* is two hundred years of age upon the twenty-fifth of April 1919, but far from raising the familiar speculations as to whether people now read it and will continue to read it, the effect of the bi-centenary is to make us marvel that *Robinson Crusoe*, the perennial and immortal,[3] should have been in existence so short a time as that. The book resembles one of the anonymous productions of the race rather than the effort of a single mind; and as for celebrating its centenary we should as soon think of[4] celebrating the centenaries of Stonehenge[5] itself. Something of this we may attribute to the fact that we have all had *Robinson Crusoe* read aloud to us as children, and were thus much in the same state of mind towards Defoe and his story that the Greeks were in towards Homer. It never occurred to us that there was such a person as Defoe, and to have been told that *Robinson Crusoe* was the work of a man with a pen in his hand would either have disturbed us unpleasantly or meant nothing at all. The impressions of childhood are those that last longest and cut deepest. It still seems that the name of Daniel Defoe has no right to appear upon the title-page of *Robinson Cru soe*, and if we celebrate the bi-centenary of the book we are making a slightly unnecessary allusion to the fact that, like Stonehenge, it is still in existence.

The great fame of the book has done its author some injustice; for while it has given him a kind of anonymous glory[6] it has obscured the fact that he was a writer of other works which, it is safe to assert, were not read aloud to us as children. Thus when the Editor of the *Christian World* in the year 1870 appealed to "the boys and girls of England" to erect a monument upon the grave of Defoe, which a stroke of lightning had mutilated, the marble wasinscribed to the memory of the author of *Robinson Crusoe*. No mention was made of *Moll Flanders*.[7] Considering the topics which are dealt with in that book, and in *Roxana*,[8] *Captain Singleton*,[9] *Colonel Jack*[10] and the rest, we need not be surprised, though we may be indignant, at the omission. We may agree with Mr. Wright,[11] the biographer of Defoe, that these "are not works for the drawing-room table". But unless we consent to make that useful piece of furniture the final arbiter of taste,[12] we must deplore the fact that their superficial coarseness,[13] or the universal celebrity[14] of *Robinson* Crusoe, has led them to be far less widely famed than they deserve. On any monument worthy of the name of monument[15] the names of *Moll Flanders* and *Roxana*, at least, should be carved as deeply as the name of Defoe.[16] They stand among the few English novels which we can call indisputably great. The occasion of the bicentenary of their more famous companion may well lead us to consider in what their greatness, which has so much in common with his, may be found to consist.

Defoe was an elderly man when he turned novelist, many years the predecessor of Richardson[17] and Fielding,[18] and one of the first indeed to shape the novel and launch it on its way. But it is unnecessary to labour the fact[19] of his precedence, except that he came to his novel-writing with certain conceptions about the art which he derived partly from being himself one of the first to practise it. The novel had to justify its existence by telling a true story and preaching a sound moral."This supplying a story by invention is certainly a most scandalous crime", he wrote. "It is a sort of lying that makes a great hole in the heart, in which by degrees a habit of lying enters in."[20] Either in the preface[21] or in the text of each of his works, therefore, he takes pains to insist that he has not used his invention at all but has depended upon facts, and that his purpose has been the highly moral desire to convert the vicious or to warn the innocent. Happily these were principles that tallied very well with his natural disposition and endowments. Facts had been drilled into him by sixty years[22] of varying fortunes before he turned his experience to account in fiction. "I have some time ago summed up the Scenes of my life in this distich,[23]" he wrote:

No man has tasted differing fortunes more,
And thirteen times I have been rich and poor.

He had spent eighteen months in Newgate[24] and talked with thieves,[25] pirates, highwaymen, and coiners before he wrote the history of Moll Flanders. But to have facts thrust upon you by dint of living and accident is one thing; to swallow them voraciously and retain the imprint of them indelibly, is another.[26] It is not merely that Defoe knew the stress of poverty and had talked with the victims of it, but that the unsheltered life, exposed to circumstances and forced to shift for itself, appealed to him imaginatively as the right matter for his art. In the first pages of each of his great novels he reduces his hero or heroine to such a state of unfriended misery[27] that their existence must be a continued struggle, and their survival at all the result of luck and their own exertions. Moll Flanders was born in Newgate of a criminal mother; Captain Singleton was stolen as a child and sold to the gipsies; Colonel Jack, though "born a gentleman, was put 'prentice to a pickpocket"; Roxana starts under better auspices, but, having married at fifteen, she sees her husband go bankrupt and is left with five children in "a condition the most deplorable that words can express".

Thus each of these boys and girls has the world to begin and the battle to fight for himself. The situation thus created was entirely to Defoe's liking. From her very birth or with half a year's respite at most, Moll Flanders, the most notable of them, is goaded by "that worst of devils, poverty", forced to earn her living as soon as she can sew, driven from place to place, making no demands upon her creator for the subtle domestic atmosphere which he was unable to supply, but drawing upon him for all he knew of strange people and customs. From the outset the burden of proving her right to exist is laid upon her. She has to depend entirely upon her own wits and judgement, and to deal with each emergency as it arises by a rule-of-thumb morality[28] which she has forged in her own head. The briskness of the story is due partly to the fact that having transgressed the accepted laws at a very early age she has henceforth the freedom of the outcast.[29] The one impossible event is that she should settle down in comfort and security. But from the first the peculiar genius of the author asserts itself, and avoids the obvious danger of the novel of adventure. He makes us understand that Moll Flanders was a woman on her own account[30] and not only material for a succession of adventures. In proof of this she begins, as Roxana also begins, by falling passionately, if unfortunately, in love.[31] That she must rouse herself and marry some one else and look very closely to her settlements and prospects is no slight upon her passion, but to be laid to the charge of her birth; and, like all Defoe's women, she is a person of robust understanding. Since she makes no scruple of telling lies[32] when they serve her purpose, there is something undeniable about her truth when she speaks it. She has no time to waste upon the refinements of personal affection; one tear is dropped, one moment of despair allowed, and then "on with the story". She has a spirit that loves to breast the storm. She delights in the exercise of her own powers. When she discovers that the man she has married in Virginia is her own brother she is violently disgusted; she insists upon leaving him; but as soon as she sets foot in Bristol,[33] "I took the diversion of going to Bath, for as I was still far from being old so my humour, which was always gay, continued so to an extreme". Heartless she is not, nor can any one charge her with levity; but life delights her, and a heroine who lives has us all in tow.[34] Moreover, her ambition has that slight strain of imagination in it which puts it in the category of the noble passions. Shrewd and practical of necessity, she is yet haunted by a desire for romance and for the quality which to her perception makes a man a gentleman. "It was really a true gallant spirit he was of, and it was the more grievous to me. 'Tis something of relief even to be undone[35] by a man of honour rather than by a scoundrel", she writes when she had misled a highwayman as to the extent of her fortune.[36] It is in keeping with this temper that she should be proud of her final partner because he refuses to work when they reach the plantations[37] but prefers hunting, and that she should take pleasure in buying him wigs and silver-hilted swords "to make him appear, as he really was, a very fine gentleman". Her very love of hot weather is in keeping, and the passion with which she kissed the ground that her son[38] had trod on, and her noble tolerance of every kind of fault so long as it is not "complete baseness of spirit, imperious, cruel, and relentless when uppermost, abject and low-spirited when down". For the rest of the world she has nothing but goodwill.

Since the list of the qualities and graces of this seasoned old sinner is by no means exhausted we can well understand how it was that Borrow's[39] apple-woman on London Bridge called her"blessed Mary" and valued her book above all the apples on her stall; and that Borrow, taking the book deep into the booth, read till his eyes ached. But we dwell upon such signs of character only by way of proof that the creator of Moll Flanders was not, as he has been accused of being, a mere journalist and literal recorder of facts with no conception of the nature of psychology. It is true that his characters take shape and substance of their own accord, as if in despite of the author[40] and not altogether to his liking. He never lingers or stresses any point of subtlety or pathos, but presses on imperturbably as if they came there without his knowledge. A touch of imagination, such as that when the Prince sits by his son's cradle and Roxana observes how "he loved to look at it when it was asleep", seems to mean much more to us than to him. After the curiously modern dissertation upon the need of communicating matters of importance to a second person lest, like the thief in Newgate, we should talk of it in our sleep, he apologises for his digression. He seems to have taken his characters so deeply into his mind that he lived them without exactly knowing how; and, like all unconscious artists, he leaves more gold in his work than his own generation was able to bring to the surface.

The interpretation that we put on his characters might therefore well have puzzled him. We find for ourselves meanings which he was careful to disguise even from his own eye. Thus it comes about that we admire Moll Flanders far more than we blame her. Nor can we believe that Defoe had made up his mind as to the precise degree of her guilt, or was unaware that in considering the lives of the abandoned he raised many deep questions and hinted, if he did not state, answers quite at variance with his professions of belief.[41] From the evidence supplied by his essay upon the "Education of Women" we know that he had thought deeply and much in advance of his age upon the capacities of women, which he rated very high, and the injustice done to them, which he rated very harsh.

I have often thought of it as one of the most barbarous customs in the world, considering us as a civilised and a Christian country, that we deny the advantages of learning to women. We reproach the sex every day with folly and impertinence; which I am confident, had they the advantages of education equal to us, they would be guilty of less than ourselves.

The advocates of women's rights would hardly care, perhaps, to claim Moll Flanders and Roxana among their patron saints; and yet it is clear that Defoe not only intended them to speak some very modern doctrines upon the subject, but placed them in circum stances where their peculiar hardships are displayed in such a way as to elicit our sympathy. Courage, said Moll Flanders, was what women needed, and the power to "stand their ground"; and at once gave practical demonstration of the benefits that would result. Roxana, a lady of the same profession, argues more subtly against the slavery of marriage.[42] She "had started a new thing in the world"the merchant told her; "it was a way of arguing contrary to the general practise". But Defoe is the last writer to be guilty of bald preaching.[43] Roxana keeps our attention because she is blessedly unconscious that she is in any good sense an example to her sex and is thus at liberty to own that part of her argument is "of an elcvated strain which was really not in my thoughts at first, at all". The knowledge of her own frailties and the honest questioning of her own motives, which that knowledge begets, have the happy result of keeping her fresh and human when the martyrs and pioneers of so many problem novels have shrunken and shrivelled to the pegs and props of their respective creeds.[44]

But the claim of Defoe upon our admiration does not rest upon the fact that he can be shown to have anticipated some of the views of Meredith,[45] or to have written scenes which (the odd suggestion occurs) might have been turned into plays by Ibsen.[46] Whatever his ideas upon the position of women, they are an incidental result of his chief virtue, which is that he deals with the important and lasting side of things and not with the passing and trivial. He is often dull, He can imitate the matter-of-fact precision of a scientific traveller until we wonder that his pen could trace or his brain conceive what has not even the excuse of truth to soften its dryness.[47] He leaves out the whole of vegetable nature, and a large part of human nature. All this we may admit, though we have to admit defects as grave in many writers whom we call great. But that does not impair the peculiar merit of what remains. Having at the outset limited his scope and confined his ambitions he achieves a truth of insight which is far rarer and more enduring than the truth of fact which he professed to make his aim. Moll Flanders and her friends recommended themselves to him[48] not because they were, as we should say, "picturesque"; nor, as he affirmed, because they were examples of evil living by which the public might profit. It was their natural veracity, bred in them by a life of hardship, that excited his interest. For them there were no excuses; no kindly shelter obscured their motives. Poverty was their taskmaster.[49] Defoe did not pronounce more than a judgement of the lips upon their failings. But their courage and resource and tenacity delighted him. He found their society full of good talk, and pleasant stories, and faith in each other, and morality of a home-made kind.[50] Their fortunes had that infinite variety which he praised and relished and beheld with wonder in his own life. These men and women, above all, were free to talk openly of the passions and desires which have moved men and women since the beginning of time, and thus even now they keep their vitality undiminished. There is a dignity in everything that is looked at openly. Even the sordid subject of money, which plays so large a part in their histories, becomes not sordid but tragic when it stands not for ease and consequence but for honour, honesty, and life itself.[51] You may object that Defoe is humdrum, but never that he is engrossed with petty things.

He belongs, indeed, to the school of the great plain writers, whose work is founded upon a knowledge of what is most persistent, though not most seductive, in human nature. The view of London from Hungerford Bridge,[52] grey, serious, massive, and full of the subdued stir of traffic and business, prosaic if it were not for the masts of the ships and the towers and domes of the city, brings him to mind. The tattered girls with violets in their hands at the street corners, and the old weather-beaten women patiently displaying their matches and bootlaces beneath the shelter of arches, seem like characters from his books. He is of the school of Crabbe[53] and of Gissing,[54] and not merely a fellow-pupil in the same stern place of learning, but its founder and master.

【作者简介】 维吉尼亚·吴尔芙（VirginiaWoolf, 1882–1941）出生于文学世家，父亲莱士里·史蒂芬（Leslie Stephen, 1832–1904）是《国家名人传记》（*Dictionary of National Biography*）和《康希尔杂志》（*Cornhill Magazine*）的编者，写过许多评论、传记和哲学文章，交往都是文学界、学术界的名流。由于健康关系，维吉尼亚没有正式上过学，她父亲的极为丰富的藏书室是她上过的唯一大学。英国西南靠海的康沃尔郡和伦敦是她最熟悉的两地，见描写大海的著名小说《到灯塔去》（*To the Lighthouse*, 1927）和《海浪》（*The Waves*, 1931）和描写伦敦的《黛洛维夫人》（*Mrs. Dalloway*, 1925），散文《时常上街去走》（*Street Haunting*, 1930）等。父亲于1904年逝世后，她在伦敦的住地布鲁姆斯伯里（Bloomsbury）成为文学中心，座上客都是当时著名的作家、文人。那里的一个成员说，“布鲁姆斯伯里的这些人是由于才能的血缘关系结合在一起的。”1912年维吉尼亚和列诺德·吴尔芙（Leonard Woolf）结婚，1917年夫妻成立了著名的“何加斯出版社”。维吉尼亚于1941年三月投河自杀。

维吉尼亚·吴尔芙也是个出色的评论家，她的评论文章收集在《普通读者》（*The Common Reader*）两卷内。她的小说着重写人物的内心世界，常用“意识流”（stream of consciousness）手法。其他主要作品还有《远航》（*The Voyage Out*, 1920），《夜与日》（*Night and Day*, 1919），《奥兰多》（*Orlando*，1928），《年月》，（*The Years*，1937），《幕与幕之间》（*Between the Acts*, 1941）等。“意识流”的创作方法当时曾风靡一时，特别著名的作家是英国的詹姆斯·乔伊斯（James Joyce, 1882–1941）和法国的马赛尔·普鲁斯特（Marcel Proust, 1871 – 1922）。

【题解与注释】

1. MRS. DALLOWAY

《黛洛维夫人》是作者早期的佳作，写黛洛维夫人一天十二小时之内的生活，情节简单，但是作者描写了几个主要人物的活动，风格特点是抒情、深邃、细致的。黛洛维夫人的内心活动和行动是中心，另外描写得较多的两个主要人物是过去热爱过她、在印度长期工作过的彼得·瓦尔希（Peter Walsh），和曾经十分勇敢、立过战功、现在却患着严重精神病的退伍军士塞普铁木斯·华伦·斯密士（Septimus Warren Smith）。

黛洛维夫人始终没有和斯密士见面，但斯密士夫妇同一天也在伦敦街上经过并在公园里停留。伦敦街头的事情他们都同时经历了。后来斯密士跳楼自杀，这个不幸的消息也带到了夫人的晚会上，引起了她的严重不安。作者以不少篇幅描写了斯密士的心情。他在战争中受了严重的精神创伤，他最念念不忘的是他失去产生感情的能力，他已不复能感受：他不能感到他在爱着自己的妻子或悼念着他最亲热的、已经死去了的伙伴。他的妻子到处求医，但他病入膏肓，因为躲避医生的干扰而跳窗自杀，结束了他惘然的余生。

彼得·瓦尔希从印度回来的第二天就去看望黛洛维夫人，他也被邀请参加当天的晚会。他的思想活动大部分是回想当年在克莉莎（Clarissa，即后来的黛洛维夫人）父母家的情景。他和克莉莎曾经相爱，但是她终于嫁给了理查德·黛洛维。他在去印度途中和一个偶然相遇的女子结了婚；现在他回来准备为一个未来的妻子办离婚手续。他有才能，读书多，但他的一生是失败的一生。小说中的几个次要人物是斯密士的妻子莉齐亚，一个离开了故国随同丈夫来英国的寂寞的、意大利制帽女郎，她希望永不离开她的丈夫，希望他痊愈，希望有孩子。夫人的丈夫理查德·黛洛维是个保守的下议院议员。他在上流社会受到宠爱，但始终未能入阁。他是个拘谨的人，他想告诉他的妻子他爱她，但是没有说出口，只是给了她一束玫瑰花。黛洛维夫妇的女儿伊丽莎白有一个历史教师：她贫穷、丑陋、常穿着雨衣；她鄙视黛洛维夫人徒有社会地位、生活富裕，但却是空虚，不学无术。她向往苏联，热爱自己的出生地德国。伊丽莎白只十七岁，她热爱父亲，对父母所关心的事情不感兴趣，只喜欢她的狗，喜欢上街坐着公共汽车到处跑跑。莎莉·希登（Sally Seton）是夫人年轻时最好的朋友，性格豪放，后来嫁了一个工业资本家，生了五个儿子，已不复有当年的热情、美貌。小说最后以不少篇幅描写了晚会的情景。首相到了，还有许多上流社会的显贵人物，也有夫人不愿邀请的寒酸亲朋。作者对他们的描写微带讽刺。小说有主要人物和次要人物，但很难说有什么正面人物。作者注意到人物思想感情的敏捷、深邃，各有个性，每个人都有些缺点、弱点。她感兴趣的是人物的内心深处的活动，很自然，"意识流"就是最适宜的创作方法。她熟悉并描写了上流社会中人物和有一定文化教养者的思想感情，也描写了患精神病的退伍军人和他的妻子、女儿的历史教师、贫苦的旧相识艾莉·韩德森等的心情和思想意识。

这里的选段是小说的开始。大约是六月的某天早晨十点左右，黛洛维夫人为准备当天的晚会上街购买鲜花。作者细致地描写了一天时间的分配。全部活动大约十二小时。象吴尔芙夫人一样，黛洛维夫人喜欢在伦敦街上走，她在街上遇到熟人时说，"我喜欢在伦敦街上走"（107 行）。她对街上的每个角落，每个止步的地方，遇到的人物和情节都深感兴趣。她任凭自己的思想瞻前顾后，也停留在她所熟悉的某些人物身上。作者特别描写了她对人对事对地方的感情反应，文笔委婉，深具匠心。

早晨走出家门，想到需要把门卸下时，她回忆到自己十八岁在伦敦自己家里清早推门外出的情景。想到那一段生活也就使她联想到彼得·瓦尔希：他说过的话，他的神情，他的小动作，他不久会从印度回来。他曾经爱着她，要求和她结婚，但是她拒绝了。她一边想着，一边留意街上的一切：过路的车辆，报时的钟声，走在什么街上。她是热爱生活的：街上有马车，小汽车，公共汽车，铜管乐队，手摇风琴，头上飞过的飞机，六月中旬的气候。她想到刚刚结束的第一次世界大战，有些人失去了儿子和亲属。幸好战争已经结束，到处又是生气盎然：两旁的店铺陈列着各种商品，伙计们在走动，白金汉宫和贵族之家也有许多活动。她走进了圣詹姆斯公园，遇到了熟人，和他闲谈几句。因为是熟人，她又回想到自己少女时代的人物，他们的行为，见解，特别彼得的性格，爱好，他对她的评价，他的言论，他们之间的关系。她想到自己有限的文化教养，自己的优点、缺点。她想到其他的许多熟人。她来到了伦敦著名的商业区彭德大街，她想到死亡和莎士比亚的名句："不要再害怕夏日的盛暑和寒冬的严霜"。由此而联想到她经常读的书籍。此时她又折回到彭德大街。她想到她往往不是为事而作事，而是为了希望能得某人的某种反应。她希望能再从头活起，换一个样子做人！早晨的彭德街使她留恋，她有一些特别熟悉的店家。她想到女儿，丈夫，女儿的历史教师朵莉斯·坎尔门小姐，一个虔诚的教徒：她经常关起门来和女儿在一起祈祷，或带领她去领圣餐。她对此很不高兴。她想到了坎尔门小姐的许多特点，她的性格，她的好恶。她不喜欢这位对她抱着审查态度的历史教师。作者以比喻方法（亦即诗的方法）描写了她的这种厌恶心情："在她胸中蠕动的这个粗暴恶魔使她不安！听到枝条断折的声音，感到马蹄在那长满树叶的森林深处、亦即灵魂深处践踏，使她不安；她永远也不会很满足、很安心，因为那野兽随时都会蠕动；特别自从她有病以来，这种憎恶有力量使她感到被磨损，使她的脊骨感到疼痛；使她的身体感到疼痛，使一切有关美、友谊、为人所爱，使她的家象喜人的岩石一样等等概念，也受到动摇和歪曲，好象有个恶魔在根部刨掘，好象满足的全部戎装只是自我，这种憎恨就是这样！"

小说描写她走进了花店。她熟悉店主，和她的关系是好的。她看到闻到了许多鲜花。在这样的环境里她克服了憎恨这个恶魔。突然一声爆炸惊动了她和其他过路的行人。一个要人乘坐的汽车车胎爆炸了。小说从这里开始了有关塞普铁木斯·华伦·斯密士的情节和人物的内心活动。

1. **Lucy:** 黛洛维夫人家里的女仆。

2. **had her work cut out for her:** 已给她安排了工作。

3. **taken off their hinges:** 把门从铰链上卸下来。

4. **Rumpelmayer's men:** 前来卸门的工人。

5. **What a lark!:** 多畅快！

6. **What a plunge!:** 多好的一次投身（投身到新鲜空气中去）！

7. **French windows:** 落地长窗。

8. **Bourton:** 夫人少女时代。父母家的所在地。

9. **than this:** this 指伦敦街上。

10. **for a girl of eighteen:** 夫人回忆自己十八岁的时候。

11. **Peter Walsh:** 她青年时代的朋友，她曾经对他很有感情，但终久未和他结婚。

12. **was that it?:** 是这么说的吗？

13. **his pocket-knife:** 彼得心情紧张时，常取出小折刀修剪指甲。

14. **a few sayings like this:** 有些这类的话（却常常记得）。

15. **Durtnall's van:** 某商号的运货车。

16. **Scrope Purvis:** 大约是运货车的驾驶员或其他雇员。

17. **Westminstes:** 英国议院所在地。

18. **Big Ben:** 伦敦英国议院塔上的大钟。

19. **First a warning musical ...:** 这里描写的是听者的主观反应。第一响只是一种警告，一种好听的声音。然后是一声声报时的钟声，时间过去，使人有时不再来的感觉。

20. leaden circles: 沉闷的音浪。

21. frumps: 衣冠不整的人。

22. the swing, the tramp, and trudge: 大摇大摆，踏步走路、到处流浪，步履艰难的人。

23. the War: 第一次世界大战。

24. eating her heart out: 忧伤过度。

25. the old Manor House must go to a cousin: 地主庄园要落到一个表亲手里了。

26. Elizabeth: 夫人的女儿。

27. Georges: 英国有六个名乔治的国王（这里至多包括五个乔治）。

28. Park: 圣詹姆斯公园（St. James Park），参看 166，179—180 行。

29. Royal Arms: 皇家纹章。

30. take their daughters: 把女儿引进社交界。

31. perfectly upholstered body: 在这里 perfectly upholstered 和 perfectly well-dressed（118 行）是同义词：穿着得非常考究。

32. bustled on: 急匆匆地朝前走。

33. extravagantly: 过份地。

34. skimpy: 微感不足的。

35. Richard: Richard Dalloway，夫人的丈夫，保守的下议院议员。

36. a mere barbers block: 只是一个理发师的帽模，即‘愚蠢’的意思。

37. Bath: 英国一市镇，以温泉著名。

38. Pimlico: 伦敦西南一地区。

39. Flect: 舰队街，报馆集中地。Admiralty，英国海军部。

40. Piccadilly: 伦敦繁华区。

41. dry sticks: 枯燥无味的。参看 27 行，awfully dull，非常乏味。

42. Wagner: 德国音乐家，歌剧作者理查德·伐格纳（Richard Wagner, 1813–1883）。

43. Pope: 亚历山大·蒲伯（Alexander Pope, 1688–1744）英国诗人。

44. flimsy nincompoops: 轻薄的糊涂人。

45. sliced like a knife through everything:（她能够）象一把刀子似地切过一切事物（即深入内部）。

46. Fräulein Danicls: 旦尼尔斯小姐，夫人少年的德籍家庭女教师。

47. Devonshire House, Bath House: 伦敦著名古屋。

48. Sylva, Fred, Sally Seton: 夫人的亲友，小说特别描写了莎莉·希登。

49. the Serpentine: 海德公园附近一湖。

50. Bond Street: 伦敦繁华的商业大街。

51. Hatchard's: 店铺的名字。

52. Fear no more the heat o' the sun ...: 出自莎士比亚的晚期剧本《辛白林》（1609）两个弟兄之歌 .

53. *Jorrock's Jaunts and Jollities*:《乔劳克斯的短期游览和欢乐》（1838），是

瑟蒂斯（Robert Smith Surtees, 1805–1864）的诙谐小说。Soapy Sponge，或许也是他的小说《史本奇先生的游历》*Mr. Sponge's Sporting Tour*, 1853）。

54. Mrs. Asquith's Memoirs: 这里恐是指赫伯特·亨利·艾思奎斯（第一次世界大战前和大战中任英国首相）的夫人所著《自传》（1922）。

55. (and now the policeman held up his hand): 警察举手禁止行人通过。

56. poor Grizzle: 可怜的灰灰，伊利莎白的爱犬。

57. Miss Kilman: 坎尔门小姐，伊利莎白的历史教师。

58. Communion: 吃圣餐。

59. starved herself for the Austrians: 愿为奥地利人挨饿，因为她原为德国人，只有在德国时才过到了幸福生活。

60. a pistol shat: 手枪声，即汽车轮胎爆炸声。

最后一行 *her* fault，好象轮胎爆破是她的不是而表示歉意。这里写花店主人对夫人的过份礼貌。

2. *DEFOE*

吴尔芙夫人写过许多评论文章，1905 年就开始写书评，载各大文学报刊。她读书甚多，不限于文学，也涉猎历史方面的书籍。她的《普通读者》两集收集了她主要的评论文章。作为评论家她的特点不是分析评述，而是写她对作品的感受和印象。“普通读者”（The common reader）一词出自英国十八世纪著名作家和第一部英文辞典的编纂者约翰逊（见《格雷传》）。他认为“普通读者”最能公正评价作品，但吴尔芙夫人决非一个普通读者，她这样自称只是谦逊而已。她评论散文，小说，书信，诗歌，理论，俄国小说，涉猎广泛，作家包括伊丽莎白时代的剧作家，邓恩，笛福，柯勒律治，詹恩·奥斯丁，勃朗特姊妹，惠特曼，乔治。爱里奥特，哈代，亨利·詹姆斯，福斯特等。她十分敬佩俄国作家托尔斯泰，陀斯妥耶夫斯基，契诃夫，屠格涅夫。她贬低自然主义，推崇现实主义，重视深刻理解生活和性格。她前后撰写了大约三百多篇评论文章和散文，都首先刊载在当时著名的杂志报刊上。她的见解新颖，富有启发，文风委婉多姿，为评论家和读者所称道。

《笛福》（1919）一文是为了纪念《鲁滨逊飘流记》出版二百年整而写的。作者曾写过一篇专论这部小说的短文《鲁滨逊·克鲁索》，在这篇文章中她指出，“一个中产阶级出现了，他们能够读书而且急于想读的不只是王子和公主们的爱情故事，而是他们自己的经历和他们自己单调而平凡的生活细节。在一千枝笔上舒展着的是适应这种要求的散文，它使自己适应于表达生活的事实而不是在写诗。”这样的话按说不大可能出自吴尔芙夫人的手笔。因为她自己对生活的外部细节并不十分感兴趣而是着力写诗一般抒情的人物的内心活动和感情反应。但是她却完全服膺现实主义，在这里她对笛福的粗犷而生动的现实主义给予了应有的评价。然而 19 世纪 40 年代的权威评论家却说，“不幸，笛福的审美观念和处境使他大部分时间消耗在下层生活中，他笔下的人物是我们不能同情的。向他敞开大门的似乎是流氓诈骗和犯罪行为的全部奥秘…他原该更谨慎地选择他的题材，以免如此经常地步入到如此低下而令人生厌的罪恶的领地。但是他似乎完全缺乏道德和审美的鉴别力。”

在这篇文章里作者首先指出《鲁滨逊》和英国史前的石柱群一样是不可以百年计的，是永恒而不朽的杰作。英国读者对它的尊重犹如希腊人对待荷马史诗一样。值得注意的是作者匆匆说了这样几句后立即着重谈了笛福的其他小说，特别是《摩尔·弗兰德斯》（*Moll Flanders*, 1722）。她把《摩尔·弗兰德斯》和《罗莎娜》（*Roxana*, 1724）置于少数几部无可争辩的伟大英国小说的行列，还首先指出这是作者深入体验了生活以后选择的题材和内容：他深刻了解贫穷和在贫穷中挣扎着的人们并认为他们是他自己艺术的恰当内容。文章的作者以不少篇幅描写了摩尔·弗兰德斯的遭遇和她的所作所为：女主人公对生活和斗争的积极、乐观态度和她的聪明才干赢得了评论者的敬意。她说笛福象是亲自生活了他小说中人物的生活（205—206行）。

文章的作者特别提到笛福对妇女的态度，说他的观点比同时代人要先进许多：他高度评价妇女的才能，对待妇女的不公正态度使他强烈不满，并引用了笛福有关《妇女的教育问题》的文章。吴尔芙夫人自己就是个积极的女权运动者。她认为妇女必须有选举权，见《奥兰多》（*Orlando*, 1928），《自己的一间屋子》（*A Room of One's Own*, 1929），《三个畿尼》（*Three Guineas*, 1938）和许多书评、散文和日记中。在《自己的一间屋子》中她要求妇女应有均等机会，有一间自己的屋子，有和男子一样受教育的权利。她曾谈论过英国女工的生活状况，她经营的“何加斯出版社”出版了一册英国女工写的文章，吴尔芙夫人自己写了引言（Life as we have known it with an introduction by V. Woolf, published by the Hogarth Press, 1931）。她曾经参加过工人的集会，讨论缩短工作时间，增加工资，改进卫生条件和上学的机会等。1936年十二月她写了短文《为什么艺术追随着政治》（*Why Art Follows Politics*），登载在共产党的“工人日报”（*Daily Worker*）。她特别强烈要求妇女应有机会受教育，她心目中指的是有才能的妇女，因此有的批评家称她为“精神贵族”（an intellectual aristocrat）。她反对男人的世界和男子统治着的各种机构，她认为女子应该有机会参加各种职业。但是她指出笛福虽然意识到了妇女在社会中的地位，却绝对未曾赤裸裸地说教。她指出，写社会问题的小说都已随着它们的信条而消失，但是笛福作品中的人物却依然清新而生动活泼，因为他写的是重要而持久的事物，不是烦琐而暂短的东西。他笔下所写的人物都为穷困所迫，但是却在万难中表现出勇敢机智和百折不挠的精神。他们并非堕落而是具备朴素的道德品质和尊严。他笔下的一切显得单调而平凡，但决不猥琐。他属于那种伟大而平凡的一派，深刻懂得人类性格中最持久的品质。

最后，文章的作者忘不了她所热爱的伦敦景色。笛福的小说中的确也再现了伦敦常见的一些场景。吴尔芙注意的是从亨格福桥（Hungerford Bridge）眺望街景，看见的是港口，城中的塔楼拱顶，街角那些手中拿着紫罗兰的褴褛女孩，憔悴的老婆婆耐着性子展示着她们的商品：火柴和鞋带。

在这篇文章里读者看到了作者对笛福小说的崇高评价，也窥测到了作者自己所关心的问题和爱好。

* 题目　此文写于1919年。丹尼尔·笛福（Daniel Defoe, 1660?–1731），英国最早

的小说家。

1. centenaries: 百年或几百年的纪念日。

2. a diminishing spectre: 一个日益消亡的幽灵。

3. the perennial and immortal: 持久而不朽的。

4. we should as soon shink of: 我们就等于想要…

5. Stonchenge: 英国威尔特郡（Wiltshire）索尔兹伯里（Salisbury）平原的史前期巨大石柱群。

6. anonymous glory: 无名氏式的光荣。指作品的声誉超过了作者的声誉。

7. *Moll Flanders*:《摩尔·弗兰德斯》(1722）题目的全部是《著名的摩尔·弗兰德斯的幸与不幸遭遇》，题解是“她出生于纽盖特监狱，在六十年的一生中除幼年外十二年卖淫，结婚五次（一次嫁给了她自己的兄弟），十二年行窃，八年在维吉尼亚流放，最后致富，过着诚实的生活，死时悔过自新。根据她自己的备忘录写此…”

8. Roxana:《罗莎娜》(1724)，罗莎娜的父母是法国新教徒，在英国长大，为丈夫遗弃，带领着五个孩子，经历了各种遭遇，死时悔罪。

9. Captain Singleton:《辛格尔敦船长》(1720)，婴儿时被拐，在船上长大，参加了哗变，后来又成为海盗，最后成巨富。

10. Colonel Jack:《杰克上校》(1722)，自幼为父母遗弃成为小偷，后来参军潜逃，又被人拐骗到了维吉尼亚，最后赎身致富，痛悔前非。

11. Mr. Wright: 托马斯·赖特，写了《生平》(Life，1894，修订本，1931)。

12. final arbiter of taste: 最后的审美仲裁，亦即审美的最高裁判。

13. superficial coarseness: 表面的粗糙。

14. universal celebrity: 享有广泛的盛名。

15. On any monument worthy of the name of monument: 在任何名符其实的丰碑上。

16. should be carved as deeply as the name of Defoe: 应铭刻得象笛福的名字一样深。

17. Richardson: 撒缪尔·理查生（1689—1761），擅长带有感伤主义的书信体小说。

18. Fielding: 亨利·菲尔丁（1707—1754），十八世纪英国最杰出的现实主义小说家，著名小说有《大伟人江奈生·魏尔德传》(*Jonathan Wild the Great*, 1743)，《约瑟·安德鲁》(*Joseph Andrews*, 1742）和《汤姆·琼斯》(*Tom Jones*, 1749)。

19. labour the fact: 过份强调这个事实（过份在这一事实上花费精力）。

20. "It is a sort of lying that makes a great hole in the heart, in which by degrees a habit of lying enters in": 这种谎言会在心上剜出一个大洞，说谎的习惯就会逐渐渗入。

21. preface: 笛福的小说都有一篇前言。

22. sixty years: 笛福五十九岁时才出版了《鲁滨逊飘流记》。

23. distich: 自成单位的两行。

24. Newgate: 伦敦的著名监狱，1902 年废弃。

25. thieves: 摩尔是个成功的惯贼；pirates，辛格尔敦船长曾作过海盗；highway men，摩尔最后的一个丈夫是个拦路强盗；coiners，摩尔曾被些伪造钱币者包围，但她始终未参加。

26. But to have facts thrust upon you by dint of living and accident is one thing; to swallow them voraclously and retain the imprint of them indelibly, is another: 但是通过生活或偶然而把事实摆在你面前是一回事，狼吞虎咽把这些事实吞下了肚而且留下了不可磨灭的印象则又是一回事。

27. unfriended misery: 无倚无靠的苦难。

28. a rule-of-thumb morality: 凭借经验和实践证明可用的、粗糙的道德观。

29. the freedom of the outcast: 被排斥在社会以外的人的自由。

30. a woman on her own account: 一个倚靠自己生活的妇女。

31. by falling passionately, if unfortunately, in love: 摩尔·弗兰德斯第一次恋爱的对象是主人家的长子，但是后来被迫嫁给次子。

32. makes no scruple of telling lies: 没有怕说谎的顾虑。

33. Bristol: 布里斯托尔，英国西南一个靠海城市。

34. has us all in tow: 我们都是钦佩的。

35. to be undone: 被奸污，被糟踏。

36. misled a highway man as to the extent of her fortum: 这位路劫强盗最初娶了她是误以为她很有钱财。

37. when they reach the plantations: 他们夫妇俩都被放逐到美洲维吉尼亚的种植园去劳动。

38. her son: 她无意之间嫁给自己的兄弟时生下的儿子也在维吉尼亚，后来又重逢了。

39. Borrow: 乔治·伯乐（1803—81）写过一些骗子小说的英国十九世纪中叶作家，爱好笛福的小说。

40. as if in despite of the author: 好象作者是不得已的。

41. answers quite at variance with his professions of belief: 他的答复和他公开声明的信仰颇有出入。

42. the slavery of marriage: 结婚是受奴役。

43. bald preaching: 赤裸裸的说教。

44. shrunken and chrivelled to the pegs and props of their respective creeds: 已经和他们各自的信条的木栓和支柱一样瘦小而干瘪。

45. Meredith: 乔治·梅瑞狄斯（1828—1909），英国十九世纪末著名小说家，作品包括《理查·费弗洛尔的苦难》（1859），《利己主义者》（1879）等，对资产阶级有一定的揭露。

46. Ibsen: 亨利克·易卜生（Henrik Ibsen, 1828–1906），杰出的挪威戏剧家，写过许多著名的"社会问题剧"，如《社会栋梁》（1877），《玩偶之家》（1879），《群鬼》（1881），《人民公敌》（1882）等。

47. we wonder that his pen could trace or his brain conceive what has not

even the excuse of truth to soften its dryness: 我们奇怪他的笔竟能描出、他的头脑竟能想出甚至并非真实的东西来减少这种东西枯燥乏味。这里是说笛福的作品有时枯燥乏味（dull）。

48. recommended themselves to him: 使他乐意采纳。

49. poverty was their taskmaster: 贫穷在鞭策着他们。

50. morality of a home-made kind: 比较 125 行的 a rule-of-thumb morality，这两个短语是同义词；home-made 的含义是"按照自己的经验制造的。"

51. it stands not for ease and consequence but for honour, honesty and life itself: 金钱不只代表生活和社会地位，而是维持荣誉、诚实、甚至生命本身所必要的（意谓'没有金钱，连荣誉、诚实、生命都是不可能的'）。

52. Hungerford Bridge: 亨格福桥建于 1841—45，笛福时还不存在。

53. Crable: 乔治·克莱勃（1754—1832），擅长叙事诗，描写生活中的丑恶现实。

54. Gissing: 乔治·吉辛（1857—1903），英国小说家，写过《德谟斯——英国社会主义的故事》（*Demos*, 1886）等揭露资产阶级同情工人的小说。

51 JAMES JOYCE
1882–1941

1. *A Little Cloud* (from *Dubliners*)
2. *Ulysses*
   a. *[Ineluctable Modality]*
   b. *[Lestrygonians]*
   c. *[Penelope]*

王佐良　选注

1. *A LITTLE CLOUD*

EIGHT years before he had seen his friend off at the North Wall[1] and wished him godspeed. Gallaher had got on.[2] You could tell that at once by his travelled air,[3] his well-cut tweed suit and fearless accent[4] Few fellows had talents like his and fewer still could remain unspoiled by such success. Gallaher's heart was in the right place and he had deserved to win. It was something to have a friend like that.

Little Chandler's thoughts ever since lunch-time had been of his meeting with Gallaher, of Gallaher's invitation and of the great city London where Gallaher lived. He was called Little Chandler because, though he was but slightly under the average stature, he gave one the idea of being a little man. His hands were white and small, his frame was fragile, his voice was quiet and his manners were refined. He took the greatest care of his fair silken hair and moustache and used perfume discreetly on his handkerchief. The half-moons of his nails were perfect[5] and when he smiled you caught a glimpse of a row of childish white teeth.

As he sat at his desk in the King's Inns[6] he thought what changes those eight years had brought. The friend whom he had known under a shabby and necessitous guise[7] had become a brilliant figure on the London Press. He turned often from his tiresome writing to gaze out of the office window. The glow of a late autumn sunset covered the grass plots and walks. It cast a shower of kindly golden dust on the untidy nurses and decrepit old men who drowsed on the benches; it flicketed upon all the moving figures-on the children who ran screaming along the gravel paths and on everyone who passed through the gardens. He watched the scene and thought of life; and (as always happened when he thought of life) he became sad. A gentle melancholy took possession of him. He felt how useless it was to struggle against fortune, this being the burden of wisdom which the ages had bequeathed to him.[8]

He remembered the books of poetry upon his shelves at home. He had bought them in his bachelor days and many an evening, as he sat in the little room off the hall,[9] he had been tempted to take one down from the bookshelf and read out something to his wife. But shyness had always held him back; and so the books had remained on their shelves. At times he repeated lines to himself and this consoled him.

When his hour had struck he stood up and took leave of his desk and of his fellow-clerks punctiliously. He emerged from under the feudal arch[10] of the King's Inns, a neat modest figure, and walked swiftly down Henrietta Street. The golden sunset was waning and the air had grown sharp.[11] A horde of grimy children populated the street. They stood or ran in the roadway or crawled up the steps before the gaping doors or squatted like mice upon the thresholds. Little Chandler gave them no thought. He picked his way deftly through all that minute vermin-like life[12] and under the shadow of the gaunt spectral mansions[13] in which the old nobility of Dublin had roistered. No memory of the past touched him, for his mind was full of a present joy.[14]

He had never been in Corless's but he knew the value of the name. He knew that people went there after the theatre to eat oysters and drink liqueurs; and he had heard that the waiters there spoke French and German. Walking swiftly by at night he had seen cabs drawn up before the door and richly dressed ladies, escorted by cavaliers, alight and enter quickly.[15] They wore noisy dresses[16] and many wraps. Their faces were powdered and they caught up their dresses, when they touched earth, like alarmed Atalantas.[17] He had always passed without turning his head to look. It was his habit to walk swiftly in the street even by day and whenever be found himself in the city late at night he hurried on his way apprehensively and excitedly. Sometimes, however, be courted the causes of his fear.[18] He chose the darkest and narrowest streets and, as he walked boldly forward, the silence that was spread about his footsteps troubled him, the wandering silent figures troubled him; and at times a sound of low fugitive laughter made him tremble like a leaf.[19]

He turned to the right towards Capel Street. Ignatius Gallaher on the London Press![20] Who would have thought it possible eight years before? Still, now that he reviewed the past, Little Chandler could remember many signs of future greatness in his friend.[21] People used to say that Ignatius Gallaher was wild. Of course, he did mix with a rakish set of fellows[22] at that time, drank freely and borrowed money on all sides. In the end he had got mixed up in some shady affair,[23] some money transaction: at least, that was one version of his flight.[24] But nobody denied him talent.[25] There was always a certain ... something in Ignatius Gallaher that impressed you in spite of yourself. Even when he was out at elbows[26] and at his wits' end for money he kept up a bold face. Little Chandler remembered (and the remembrance brought a slight flush of pride to his cheek) one of Ignatius Gallaher's sayings when he was in a tight corner:

—Half time,[27] now, boys, he used to say light-heartedly. Where's my considering cap?[28]

That was Ignatius Gallaher all out;[29] and, damn it, you couldn't but admire him for it.

Little Chandler quickened his pace.[30] For the first time in his life he felt himself superior to the people he passed.[31]. For the first time his soul revolted against the dull inelegance of Capel Street.[32] There was no doubt about it: if you wanted to succeed you had to go away. You could do nothing in Dublin. As he crossed Grattan Bridge he looked down the river towards the lower quays and pitied the poor stunted houses.[33] They seemed to him a band of tramps, huddled together along the river-banks,[34] their old coats covered with dust and soot, stupefied by the panorama of sunset[35] and waiting for the first chill of night to bid them arise, shake themselves and begone. He wondered whether he could write a poem to express his idea. Perhaps Gallaher might be able to get it into some London paper for him.[36] Could he write something original? He was not sure what idea he wished to express but the thought that a poetic moment had touched him took life within him like an infant hope.[37] He stepped onward bravely.

Every step brought him nearer to London, farther from his own sober inartistic life. A light began to tremble on the horizon of his mind.[38] He was not so old-thirty-two. His temperament might be said to be just at the point of maturity.[39] There were so many different moods and impressions that he wished to express in verse. He felt them within him. He tried to weigh his soul to see if it was a poet's soul. Melancholy was the dominant note of his temperament, he thought, but it was a melancholy tempered by recurrences of faith and resignation and simple joy. If he could give expression to it in a book of poems perhaps men would listen. He would never be popular: he saw that. He could not sway the crowd[40] but he might appeal to a little circle of kindred minds.[41] The English critics, perhaps, would recognise him as one of the Celtic school[42] by reason of the melancholy tone of his poems; besides that, he would put in allusions.[43] He began to invent sentences and phrases from the notices which his book would get.[44] *Mr Chandler has the gift of easy and graceful verse. ... A wistful sadness pervades these poems. ... The Celtic note.* It was a pity his name was not more Irish-looking.[45] Perhaps it would be better to insert his mother's name before the surname: Thomas Malone Chandler, or better still: T. Malone Chandler. He would speak to Gallaher about it.

He pursued his revery so ardently[46] that he passed his street and had to turn back. As he came near Corless's[47] his former agitation began to overmaster him and he halted before the door in indecision.[48] Finally he opened the door and entered.

The light and noise of the bar held him at the doorway for a few moments. He looked about him, but his sight was confused by the shining of many red and green wine-glasses. The bar seemed to him to be full of people and he felt that the people were observing him curiously. He glanced quickly to right and left (frowning slightly to make his errand appear serious[49]), but when his sight cleared a little he saw that nobody had turned to look at him: and there, sure enough, was Ignatius Gallaher leaning with his back against the counter[50] and his feet planted far apart.[51]

—Hallo, Tommy,[52] old hero, here you are ! What is it to be?[53] What will you have? I'm taking whisky: better stuff than we get across the water.[54] Soda? Lithia?[55] No mineral?[56] I'm the same. Spoils the flavour.[57] ... Here, *garçon,*[58] bring us two halves of malt whisky,[59] like a good fellow.[60] ... Well, and how have you been pulling along since I saw you last? Dear God, how old we're getting! Do you see any signs of aging[61] in me-eh, what? A little grey and thin on the top[62]—what?

Ignatius Gallaher took off his hat and displayed a large closely cropped head.[63] His face was heavy, pale and cleanshaven.[64] His eyes, which were of bluish slate-colour,[65] relieved his unhealthy pallor[66] and shone out plainly above the vivid orange tie[67] he wore. Between these rival features the lips appeared very long and shapeless and colourless. He bent his head and felt with two sympathetic fingers the thin hair at the crown. Little Chandler shook his head as a denial.

Ignatius Gallaher put on his hat again.

—It pulls you down, he said, Press life.[68] Always hurry and scurry, looking for copy[69] and sometimes not finding it: and then, always to have something new in your stuff. Damn proofs and printers,[70] I say, for a few days. I'm deuced glad,[71] I can tell you, to get back to the old country. Does a fellow good, a bit of a holiday.[72] I feel a ton better[73] since I landed again in dear dirty Dublin. ... Here you are, Tommy. Water? Say when.[74]

Little Chandler allowed his whisky to be very much diluted.[75]

—You don't know what's good for you, my boy, said Ignatius Gallaher. I drink mine neat.[76]

—I drink very little as a rule, said Little Chandler modestly. An odd half-one or so[77] when I meet any of the old crowd: that's all.

—Ah, well, said Ignatius Gallaher, cheerfully, here's to us and to old times and old acquaintance.[78]

They clinked glasses and drank the toast.

—I met some of the old gang to-day, said Ignatius Gallaher. O'Hara seems to be in a bad way.[79] What's he doing?

—Nothing, said Little Chandler. He's gone to the dogs.[80]

—But Hogan has a good sit,[81] hasn't he?

—Yes; he's in the Land Commission.[82]

—I met him one night in London and he seemed to be very flush.[83] ... Poor O'Hara! Boose, I suppose?[84]

—Other things, too, said Little Chandler shortly.

Ignatius Gallaher laughed.

—Tommy, he said, I see you haven't changed an atom. You're the very same serious person that used to lecture me on Sunday mornings when I had a sore head and a fur on my tongue. You'd want to knock about a bit in the world. Have you never been anywhere, even for a trip?

—I've been to the Isle of Man,[85] said Little Chandler.

Ignatius Gallaher laughed.

—The Isle of Man! he said. Go to London or Paris: Paris, for choice. That'd do you good.

—Have you seen Paris?

—I should think I have! I've knocked about there a little.[86]

—And is it really so beautiful as they say? asked Little Chandler.

He sipped a little of his drink while Ignatius Gallaher finished his boldly.

—Beautiful? said Ignatius Gallaher, pausing on the word and on the flavour of his drink.[87] It's not so beautiful, you know. Of course, it is beautiful. ... But it's the life of Paris; that's the thing.[88] Ah, there's no city like Paris for gaiety, movement, excitement. ...

Little Chandler finished his whisky and, after some trouble, succeeded in catching the barman's eye. He ordered the same again.

—I've been to the Moulin Rouge,[89] Ignatius Gallaher continued when the barman had removed their glasses, and I've been to all the Bohemian cafés.[90] Hot stuff![91] Not for a pious chap like you,[92] Tommy.

Little Chandler said nothing until the barman returned with the two glasses: then he touched his friend's glass lightly and reciprocated the former toast. He was beginning to feel somewhat disillusioned. Gallaher's accent and way of expressing himself did not please him. There was something vulgar in his friend which he had not observed before. But perhaps it was only the result of living in London amid the bustle and competition of the Press.[93] The old personal charm[94] was still there under this new gaudy manner. And, after all, Gallaher had lived, he had seen the world. Little Chandler looked at his friend enviously.

—Everything in Paris is gay, said Ignatius Gallaher. They believe in enjoying life-and don't you think they're right? If you want to enjoy yourself properly you must go to Paris. And, mind you, they've a great feeling for the Irish there.[95] When they heard I was from Ireland they were ready to eat me,[96] man.

Little Chandler took four or five sips from his glass.

—Tell me, he said, is it true that Paris is so ... immoral as they say?

Ignatius Gallaher made a catholic gesture[97] with his right arm.

—Every place is immoral, he said. Of course you do find spicy bits in Paris.[98] Go to one of the students' balls,[99] for instance. That's lively, if you like, when the *cocottes*[100] begin to let themselves loose. You know what they are, I suppose?

—I've heard of them, said Little Chandler.

Ignatius Gallaher drank off his whisky and shook his head.

—Ah, he said, you may say what you like. There's no woman like the Parisienne-for style, for go.[101]

—Then it is an immoral city, said Little Chandler, with timid insistence-l mean, compared with London or Dublin?

—London! said Ignatius Gallaher. It's six of one and half-a-dozen of the other.[102] You ask Hogan, my boy. I showed him a bit about London when he was over there. He'd open your eye. … I say, Tommy, don't make punch of that whisky: liquor up.[103]

—No, really. …

—O, come on, another one won't do you any harm. What is it?The same again, I suppose?

—Well … all right.

—*François*, the same again.[104] … Will you smoke, Tommy? Ignatius Gallaher produced his cigar-case.[105] The two friends lit their cigars and puffed at them in silence until their drinks were served.

—I'll tell you my opinion, said Ignatius Gallaher, emerging after some time from the clouds of smoke in which he had taken refuge, it's a rum world.[106] Talk of immorality! I've heard of cases-what am I saying?—I've known them: cases of … immorality. …

Ignatius Gallaher puffed thoughtfully at his cigar[107] and then, in a calm historian's tone, he proceeded to sketch for his friend some pictures of the corruption which was rife abroad.[108] He summarised the vices of many capitals[109] and seemed inclined to award the palm to Berlin.[110] Some things he could not vouch for[111] (his friends had told him), but of others he had had personal experience. He spared neither rank nor caste.[112] He revealed many of the secrets of religious houses[113] on the Continent and described some of the practices which were fashionable in high society and ended by telling, with details, a story about an English duchess — a story which he knew to be true. Little Chandler was astonished.

— Ah, well, said Ignatius Gallaher, here we are m old jogalong Dublin[114] where nothing is known of such things.

— How dull you must find it, said Little Chandler, after all the other places you've seen!

— Well, said Ignatius Gallaher, it's a relaxation to come over here, you know. And, after all, it's the old country, as they say, isn't it? You can't help having a certain feeling for it. That's human nature. ... But tell me something about yourself. Hogan told me you had... tasted the joys of connubial bliss.[115] Two years ago, wasn't it?

Little Chandler blushed and smiled.

— Yes, he said. I was married last May twelve months.[116]

— I hope it's not too late in the day to offer my best wishes, said Ignatius Gallaher. I didn't know your address or I'd have done so at the time.[117]

He extended his hand, which Little Chandler took.

— Well, Tommy, he said, I wish you and yours every joy in life, old chap, and tons of money, and may you never die till I shoot you. And that's the wish of a sincere friend, an old friend. You know that?

— I know that, said Little Chandler.

— Any youngsters? said Ignatius Gallaher.

Little Chandler blushed again.

— We have one child, he said.

— Son or daughter?

— A little boy.

Ignatius Gallaher slapped his friend sonorously on the back.

— Bravo, he said, I wouldn't doubt you,[118] Tommy.

Little Chandler smiled, looked confusedly at his glass and bit his lower lip with three childishly white front teeth.

—I hope you'll spend an evening with us, he said, before you go back. My wife will be delighted to meet you. We can have a little music and—

—Thanks awfully, old chap, said Ignatius Gallaher, I'm sorry we didn't meet earlier. But I must leave to-morrow night.

—To-night, perhaps…?

—I'm awfully sorry, old man. You see I'm over here with another fellow, clever young chap he is too, and we arranged to go to a little card-party. Only for that …

—O, in that case. …

—But who knows? said Ignatius Gallaher considerately. Next year I may take a little skip over here[119] now that I've broken the ice. It's only a pleasure deferred.[120]

—Very well, said Little Chandler, the next time you come we must have an evening together. That's agreed now, isn't it?

—Yes, that's agreed, said Ignatius Gallaher. Next year if I come, *parole d'honneur*.[121]

—And to clinch the bargain,[122] said Little Chandler, we'll just have one more now.

Ignatius Gallaher took out a large gold watch and looked at it.

—Is it to be the last?[123] he said. Because you know, I have an a. p.[124]

—O, yes, positively, said Little Chandler.

—Very well, then, said Ignatius Gallaher, let us have another one as *a deoc an doruis*[125]—that's good vernacular for a small whisky,[126] I believe.

Little Chandler ordered the drinks. The blush which had risen to his face a few moments before was establishing itself. A trifle made him blush at any time:[127] and now he felt warm and excited. Three small whiskies had gone to his head[128] and Gallaher's strong cigar had confused his mind, for he was a delicate and abstinent person. The adventure of meeting Gallaher after eight years, of finding himself with Gallaher in Corless's surrounded by lights and noise, of listening to Gallaher's stories and of sharing for a brief space[129] Gallaher's vagrant and triumphant life, upset the equipoise of his sensitive nature.[130] He felt acutely the contrast between his own life and his friend's, and it seemed to him unjust. Gallaher was his inferior in birth and education. He was sure that he could do something better than his friend had ever done, or could ever do, something higher than mere tawdry journalism if he only got the chance. What was it that stood in his way?[131] His unfortunate timidity! He wished to vindicate himself in some way, to assert his manhood. He saw behind Gallaher's refusal of his invitation.[132] Gallaher was only patronising[133] him by his friendliness just as he was patronising Ireland by his visit.

The barman brought their drinks. Little Chandler pushed one glass towards his friend and took up the other boldly.

—Who knows? he said, as they lifted their glasses. When you come next year I may have the pleasure of wishing long life and happiness to Mr and Mrs Ignatius Gallaher.[134]

Ignatius Gallaher in the act of drinking closed one eye expressively over the rim of his glass. When he had drunk he smacked his lips decisively, set down his glass and said:

—No blooming fear of that,[135] my boy. I'm going to have my fling first[136] and see a bit of life and the world before I put my head in the sack—if I ever do.

—Some day you will, said Little Chandler calmly.

Ignatius Gallaher turned his orange tie and slate-blue eyes full upon his friend.

—You think so? he said.

—You'll put your head in the sack,[137] repeated Little Chandler stoutly, like everyone else if you can find the girl.

He had slightly emphasised his tone and he was aware that he had betrayed himself; but, though the colour had heightened in his cheek, he did not flinch from his friend's gaze. Ignatius Gallaher watched him for a few moments and then said:

—If ever it occurs, you may bet your bottom dollar there'll be no mooning and spooning about it.[138] I mean to marry money. She'll have a good fat account at the bank or she won't do for me.

Little Chandler shook his head.

—Why, man alive,[139] said Ignatius Gallaher, vehemently, do you know what it is? I've only to say the word and to-morrow I can have the woman and the cash. You don't believe it? Well, I know it. There are hundreds-what am I saying?—thousands of rich Germans and Jews, rotten with money, that'd only be too glad. ... You wait a while, my boy. See if I don't play my cards properly.[140] When I go about a thing I mean business, I tell you. You just wait.

He tossed his glass to his mouth, finished his drink and laughed loudly. Then he looked thoughtfully before him and said in a calmer tone:

—But I'm in no hurry. They can wait. I don't fancy tying myself up to one woman, you know.

He imitated with his mouth the act of tasting and made a wry face.

—Must get a bit stale,[141] I should think, he said.

. . . .

Little Chandler sat in the room off the hall, holding a child in his arms. To save money they kept no servant but Annie's young sister Monica[142] came for an hour or so in the morning and an hour or so in the evening to help. But Monica had gone home long ago. It was a quarter to nine. Little Chandler had come home late for tea and, moreover, he had forgotten to bring Annie home the parcel of coffee from Bewley's.[143] Of course she was in a bad humour[144] and gave him short answers.[145] She said she would do without any tea but when it came near the time at which the shop at the corner closed she decided to go out herself for a quarter of a pound of tea and two pounds of sugar. She put the sleeping child deftly in his arms and said:

—Here. Don't waken him.

A little lamp with a white china shade stood upon the table and its light fell over a photograph which was enclosed in a frame of crumpled horn. It was Annie's photograph. Little Chandler looked at it, pausing at the thin tight lips.[146] She wore the pale blue summer blouse which he had brought her home as a present one Saturday. It had cost him ten and elevenpence; but what an agony of nervousness it had cost him! How he had suffered that day, waiting at the shop door until the shop was empty, standing at the counter and trying to appear at his ease while the girl piled ladies' blouses before him, paying at the desk and forgetting to take up the odd penny of his change, being called back by the cashier, and, finally, striving to hide his blushes as he left the shop by examining the parcel to see if it was securely tied. When he brought the blouse home Annie kissed him and said it was very pretty and stylish; but when she heard the price she threw the blouse on the table and said it was a regular swindle to charge ten and elevenpence for that. At first she wanted to take it back but when she tried it on she was delighted with it, especially with the make of the sleeves, and kissed him and said he was very good to think of her.

Hm! …

He looked coldly into the eyes of the photograph and they answered coldly. Certainly they were pretty and the face itself was pretty. But he found something mean in it. Why was it so unconscious and lady-like? The composure of the eyes irritated him. They repelled him and defied him:[147] there was no passion in them, no rapture. He thought of what Gallaher had said about rich Jewesses. Those dark Oriental eyes, he thought, how full they are of passion, of voluptuous longing! … Why had he married the eyes in the photograpn?

He caught himself up at the question[148] and glanced nervously round the room. He found something mean in the pretty furniture which he had bought for his house on the hire system.[149] Annie had chosen it herself and it reminded him of her. It too was prim and pretty.[150] A dull resentment against his life awoke within him. Could he not escape from his little house? Was it too late for him to try to live bravely like Gallaher? Could he go to London? There was the furniture still to be paid for. If he could only write a book and get it published, that might open the way for him.

A volume of Byron's poems lay before him on the table. He opened it cautiously with his left hand lest he should waken the child and began to read the first poem in the book:

Hushed are the winds and still the evening gloom,[151]
Not e'en a Zephyr[152] *wanders through the grove,*
Whilst I return to view my Margaret's tomb
And scatter flowers on the dust[153] *I love.*

He paused. He felt the rhythm of the verse about him in the room. How melancholy it was! Could he, too, write like that, express the melancholy of his soul in verse? There were so many things he wanted to describe: his sensation of a few hours before on Grattan Bridge, for example. If he could get back again into that mood. …

The child awoke and began to cry. He turned from the page and tried to hush it: but it would not be husbed. He began to rock it to and fro in his arms but its wailing cry grew keener. He rocked it faster while his eyes began to read the second stanza:

Within this narrow cell redines her day,[154]
That day where once …

It was useless. He couldn't read. He couldn't do anything. The wailing of the child pierced the drum of his ear. It was useless, useless! He was a prisoner for life. His arms trembled with anger and suddenly bending to the child's face he shouted:

—Stop!

The child stopped for an instant, had a spasm of fright and began to scream. He jumped up from his chair and walked hastily up and down the room with the child in his arms. It began to sob piteously, losing its breath for four or five seconds,[155] and then bursting out anew.[156] The thin walls of the room echoed the sound. He tried to soothe it but it sobbed more convulsively. He looked at the contracted and quivering face of the child[157] and began to be alarmed. He counted seven sobs without a break between them and caught the child to his breast in fright. If it died! ...

The door was burst open and a young woman ran in, panting.

—What is it? What is it? she cried.

The child, hearing its mother's voice, broke out into a paroxysm of sobbing.[158]

—It's nothing, Annie ... it's nothing. ... He began to cry ...

She flung her parcels on the floor and snatched the child from him.

—What have you done to him? she cried, glaring into his face.

Little Chandler sustained for one moment the gaze of her eyes and his heart closed together as he met the hatred in them.[159] He began to stammer:

—It's nothing. ... He ... he began to cry. ... I couldn't ... I didn't do anything. ... What?

Giving no heed to him[160] she began to walk up and down the room, clasping the child tightly in her arms and murmuring:

—My little man! My little mannie![161] Was 'ou frightened,[162] love? ... There now, love! There now! ... Lambabaun![163] Mamma's little lamb of the world![164] ... There now!

Little Chandler felt his cheeks suffused with shame[165] and he stood back out of the lamplight. He listened while the paroxysm of the child's sobbing grew less and less; and tears of remorse started to his eyes.

2. ULYSSES

a. [Inel uctable Modality]

Ineluctable modality of the visible[1]: at least that if no more, thought through my eyes.[2] Signatures of all things[3] I am here to read,[4] seaspawn and seawrack,[5] the nearing tide,[6] that rusty boot.[7] Snotgreen, bluesilver, rust: coloured signs.[8] Limits of the diaphane.[9]

But he adds: in bodies.[10] Then he was aware of them bodies before of them coloured. How? By knocking his sconce against them,[11] sure. Go easy.[12] Bald he was and a millionaire,[13] *maestro di color che sanno.*[14] Limit of the diaphane[15] in. Why in? Diaphane, adiaphane. If you can put your five fingers through it, it is a gate, if not a door.[16] Shut your eyes and see.[17]

Stephen closed his eyes to hear[18] his boots crush crackling wrack and shells. You are walking through it howsomever.[19] I am, a stride at a time. A very short space of time through very short times of space. Five, six:[20] the *nacheinander,*[21] Exactly: and that is the ineluctable modality of the audible. Open your eyes. No. Jesus![22] If I fell over a cliff that beetles o'er his base,[23] fell through the *nebeneinander*[24] ineluctably. I am getting on nicely in the dark. My ash sword hangs at my side.[25] Tap with it: they do.[26] My two feet in his boots[27] are at the end of my legs, *nebeneinander*. Sounds solid: made by the mallet of *Los Demiurgos.*[28] Am I walking into eternity along Sandymount strand?[29] Crush, crack, crik, crick.[30] …

b. [Lestrygonians]

His heart astir he pushed in the door of the Burton restaurant. Stink gripped his trembling breath: pungent meatjuice, slop of greens.[1] See the animals feed.[2]

Men, men, men.[3]

Perched on high stools by the bar, hats shoved back, at the tables calling for more bread no charge,[4] swilling, wolfing gobfuls of sloppy food,[5] their eyes bulging, wiping wetted moustaches. A pallid suetfaced[6] young man polished his tumbler knife fork and spoon with his napkin.[7] New set of microbes.[8] A man with an infant's saucestained napkin tucked round him[9] shovelled gurgling soup down his gullet.[10] A man spitting back on his plate:[11] halfmasticated gristle:[12] no teeth to chewchewchew it.[13] Chump chop from the grill.[14] Bolting to get it over.[15] Sad booser's eyes. Bitten off more than he can chew.[16] Am I like that? See ourselves as others see us. Hungry man is an angry man. Working tooth and jaw.[17] Don't! O! A bone! That last pagan king of Ireland Cormac in the schoolpoem[18] choked himself at Sletty south ward of the Boyne.[19] Wonder what he was eating. Something galoptious.[20] Saint Patrick[21] converted him to Christianity. Couldn't swallow it all however.

—Roast beef and cabbage.[22]

—One stew.[22]

Smells of men. His gorge rose.[23] Spaton sawdust, sweetish warmish cigarette smoke, reek of plug, spilt beer, men's beery piss,[24] the stale of ferment.

Couldn't eat a morsel here. Fellow sharpening knife and fork, to eat all before him, old chap picking his tootles.[25] Slight spasm, full, chewing the cud.[26] Before and after. Grace after meals.[27] Look on this picture then on that. Scoffing up stewgravy with sopping sippets of bread.[28] Lick it off the plate, man![29] Get out of this.[30]

He gazed round the stooled and tabled eaters,[31] tightening the wings of his nose.

—Two stouts here.[32]

—One corned and cabbage.[32]

That fellow ramming a knifeful of cabbage down as if his life depended on it.[33] Good stroke.[34] Give me the fidgets to look.[35] Safer to eat from his three hands.[36] Tear it limb from limb.[37] Second nature to him.[38] Born with a silver knife in his mouth.[39] That's witty, I think.[40] Or no.[41] Silver means born rich. Born with a knife. But then the allusion is lost.[42]

An illgirt[43] server gathered sticky clattering plates. Rock, the bailiff, standing at the bar blew the foamy crown from his tankard.[44] Well up:[45] it splashed yellow near his boot. A diner, knife and fork upright, elbows on table, ready for a second helping stared towards the foodlift[46] across his stained square of newspaper. Other chap telling him something with his mouth full. Sympathetic listener. Table talk. I munched hum un thu Unchster Bunk un Munchday.[47] Ha? Did you, faith?[48]

Mr Bloom raised two fingers doubtfully to his lips. His eyes said,

—Not here. Don't see him.[49]

Out. I hate dirty eaters.

He backed towards the door. Get a light snack in Davy Byrne's.[50] Stopgap. Keep me going. Had a good breakfast.[51]

—Roast and mashed here.[52]

—Pint of stout.

Every fellow for his own, tooth and nail.[53] Gulp. Grub. Gulp. Gobstuff.[54]

He came out into clearer air and turned back towards Grafton street. Eat or be eaten. Kill! Kill![55]

c. [Penelope]

... let me see if I can doze off 1 2 3 4 5[1] what kind of flowers are those they invented like the stars the wall paper in Lombard street was much nicer the apron he gave me was like that something only I only wore it twice better lower this lamp and try again[2] so as I can get up early Ill go to Lambes[3] there beside Findlaters and get them to send us some flowers to put about the place in case he brings him home tomorrow[4] today I mean no no Fridays an unlucky day[5] first I want to do the place up someway[6] the dust grows in it I think while Im asleep then we can have music and cigarettes I can accompany him[7] first I must clean the keys of the piano with milk whatll I wear shall I wear a white rose or those fairy cakes in Liptons[8] I love the smell of a rich big shop at 7½d a 1b[9] or the other ones with the cherries in them and the pinky sugarlld a couple of 1bs[10] of course a nice plant for the middle of the table[11] Id get that cheaper in wait wheres this I saw them not long ago[12] I love flowers Id love to have the whole place swimming in roses God of heaven theres nothing like nature[13] the wild mountains then the sea and the waves rushing then the beautiful country with fields of oats and wheat and all kinds of things and all the fine cattle going about that would do your heart good to see rivers and 1akes and flowers all sorts of shapes and smells and colours springing up even out of the ditches primroses and violets nature it is as for them saying theres no God I wouldnt give a snap of my two fingers for all their learning why dont they go and create something[14] I often asked him atheists or whatever they call themselves go and wash the cobbles off themselves first[15] then they go howling for the priest and they dying[16] and why why because theyre afraid of hell on account of their bad conscience ah yes I know hem well who was the first person in the universe before there was anybody that made it all who ah that they dont know neither do I so there you are[17] they might as well try to stop the sun from rising tomorrow the sun shines for you he said[18] the day we were lying among the rhododendrons on Howth head in the grey tweed suit and his straw hat the day I got him to propose to me yes first I gave him the bit of seedcake out of my mouth and it was leapyear like now yes 16 years ago my God after that long kiss I nearly lost my breath yes he said I was a flower of the mountain yes so we are flowers all a womans body yes that was one true thing he said in his life and the sun shines for you today yes that was why I liked him because I saw he understood or felt what a woman is and I knew I could always get round him[19] and I gave him all the pleasure I could leading him on[20] till he asked me to say yes and I wouldnt answer first only looked out over the sea and the sky I was thinking of so many things he didnt know of Mulvey and Mr Stanhope and Hester and father and old captain Groves and the sailors[21] playing all birds fly and I say stoop and washing up dishes they called it on the pier and the sentry in front of the governors house with the thing round his white helmet poor devil half roasted[22] and the Spanish girls laughing in their shawls and their tall combs and the auctions in the morning the Greeks and the Jews and the Arabs[23] and the devil knows who else from all the ends of Europe and Duke street and the fowl market all clucking outside Larby Sharons[24] and the poor donkeys slipping half asleep and the vague fellows[25] in the cloaks asleep in the shade on the steps and the big wheels of the carts of the bulls and the old castle thousands of years old yes and those handsome Moors all in white and turbans like kings asking you to sit down in their little bit of a shop and Ronda with the old windows of the posadas[26] glancing eyes[27] a lattice hid for her lover to kiss the iron[28] and the wineshops half open at night and the castanets[29] and the night we missed the boat at Algeciras the watchman going about serene with his lamp and O that awful deepdown torrent O and the sea the sea crimson sometimes like fire and the glorious sunsets and the figtrees in the Alameda gardens[30] yes and all the queer little streets and pink and blue and yellow houses and the rosegardens and the jessamine and geraniums and cactuses and Gibraltar as a girl where I was a Flower of the mountain yes when I put the rose in my hair like the Andalusian girls used or shall I wear a red yes and how he kissed me under the Moorish wall[31] and I thought well as well him as another[32] and then I asked him with my eyes to ask again[33] yes and then he asked me would I yes to say yes my mountain flower and first I put my arms around him yes and drew him down to me so he could feel my breasts all perfume yes and his heart was going like mad and yes I said yes I will Yes.[34]

【作者简介】 詹姆斯·乔伊斯（1882—1941）生于爱尔兰都柏林，从小受天主教会的教育，等到上大学却改学拉丁系语言，毕业后决心献身文艺创作，由于觉得都柏林的风气太狭隘，于是从1904年后长期旅居瑞士和法国，除曾一度教授英语外，一生从事创作，1941年死于瑞士苏黎世。

他也曾写过诗和剧本，但主要作品全是小说，数量虽不大，却都是精心之作，而且每写一本都表现出他的小说艺术有了进一步的发展。第一部作品 *Dubliners*（《都柏林人》，1914）是短篇小说合集，作者用莫泊桑式和契诃夫式的现实主义手法写都柏林市民的生活，篇篇出色，其中 *The Dead*（《死者》）一篇更是公认为现代英语文学中的经典之作。第二部作品 *A Portrait of the Artist as a Young Man*（《青年艺术家的写照》，1916）是一个中篇，写艺术家必然会将自己放逐于社会之外，创作方法虽然主要仍是现实主义的，然而象征意味加强了。第三部作品 *Ulysses*（《优力息斯》，1922）是长篇小说，在题材和写法上都作了大胆的创新，特别是意识流（stream of consciousness）技巧的运用引起了很大的注意，但也因此而不易为一般读者看懂，同时书中有几处对于男女性关系的写实也遭受到社会上一些人的攻击，因而一直到1933年此书在英美都遭禁止。乔伊斯最后一部作品*Finnegans Wake*（《芬尼根的守灵夜》，1939）费时十四年，作者大量创造新词，并进而改革整部作品的结构，头即是尾，尾也是头，全书构成一个圆周式的整体。作者苦心经营，成品却比*Ulysses*更为难懂，经过一些研究者的阐释，人们才知其用意所在。

乔伊斯认为在现代西方的情况之下，一个真正的艺术家必然是一个社会的逐客，因此一生埋头创作，不问外事。其实他是一个有心人。虽然他在外国客居36年，所写则总是爱尔兰都柏林的人和事，可见并未忘怀祖国。他在技巧上是一个最为"现代化"的作家，然而他的杰作*Ulysses*却处处拿平凡的现代都市的小市民同古希腊的英雄人物相对照，整部小说实际上是对现代西方的精神生活的深刻评论。他的写作态度也是严肃的，所发掘的题材都是他认为有重大意义的，而且都来自他所熟悉的现实生活。他之所以要创造新词，革新小说结构，也是因为他认为文学语言的刷新能够促进人的感觉的敏锐，而敏感的增进又正是打破现代西方世界里精神生活之日趋平板、迟滞、一律化的途径。

乔伊斯已死去四十年，然而影响至今存在，公认为西方现代派小说艺术的大师。

【题解与注释】

1. A LITTLE CLOUD

这是收集在*Dubliners*内的短篇小说之一，描写Little Chandler同Ignatius Gallaher见面的情况。两人原是老朋友，Little Chandler受的教育比Gallaher高，但后来Gallaher离开爱尔兰去伦敦成为名记者，而Little Chandler却留在都柏林，做了一个小办事员。故事从Gallaher成名后回爱尔兰度假开始。作者着重写的是Gallaher自鸣得意的俗气，而且是把他当作一种久居外国的爱尔兰人的典型来写的。

这篇小说用的是现实主义的手法，从中可见Joyce最初是莫泊桑、契诃夫一类的短篇小说家。他安排情节的本领似莫泊桑，而善于模拟气氛又如契诃夫。就是到了后期，尽管他用了许多新的技巧，他的现实主义的"基本功"仍然是处处可见的。

作者本人是喜欢这篇小说的，曾写信给他的弟弟Stanislaus Joyce说："A page of *A Little Cloud* gives me more pleasure than all my verses"（*Letters of James Joyce*, vol. II, ed. Richard Ellmann, New York, 1966, p.182）.

标题A Little Cloud，来自《圣经》《列王记》第18章，44节："第七次仆人说：

我看见有一小片云从海里上来，不过如人手那样大。”当时撒玛利亚地方久旱，有大饥荒，但当居民重新信仰耶和华为上帝后，开始降雨。这里“一小片云”就是雨的前兆。

1. the North Wall: 都柏林市的码头，客轮从此开往各处。

2. Gallaher had got on: Gallaher had succeeded, Gallaher 混得不错。

3. his travelled air: 他那种见过世面的神气；travelled，去过许多大地方的。

4. fearless accent: 那种天不怕地不怕的口气。

5. the half-moons of his nails were perfect: 他把手指甲剪得很整齐，每一个都露出好看的半月形。

6. the King's Inns: 律师聚居之处，有如伦敦的 Inns of Court.

7. under a shabby and necessitous guise:（当时 Gallaher）衣服不整，一付穷相；under ... guise，在……外表下。

8. this being the burden of wisdom which the ages had bequeathed to him: 这就是过去世代传给他的智慧的要旨。

9. the little room off the hall: 门厅旁边的小房。

10. the feudal arch: 中古形式的拱门；feudal，封建时期的，即欧洲中古时期的。

11. the air had grown sharp: 空气中颇有寒意了。

12. all that minute vermin-like life: 所有那种琐碎的虫豸似的生活。在这一段里作者用了 a horde of grimy children, crawled up the steps, squatted like mice 等语来表示满街都是脏孩子，而 Little Chandler 平时是厌恶他们的（犹如他觉得整个都柏林的生活都平凡、枯燥一样），但今天他急于去见老朋友，也就无心计较。

13. under the shadow of the gaunt spectral mansions: 在高而尖的、鬼怪似的大楼的阴影下。

14. his mind was full of a present joy: 他心里充满了当前的欢乐。

15. escorted by cavaliers, alight and enter quickly: 由殷勤的绅士陪同，下来后很快就进去了。

16. wore noisy dresses: 穿着过分鲜艳的服装。

17. like alarmed Atlantas: Atlanta 是希腊神话里的美丽的女猎手，以优雅、灵活出名。

18. courted the causes of his fear: 故意去碰使他害怕的东西。

19. a sound of low fugitive laughter made him tremble like a leaf: 随便传来一声低笑就把他吓得直哆嗦。

20. London Press: 伦敦新闻界。

21. remember many signs of future greatness in his friend: 回忆起他朋友那时就有许多迹象，表明他将来会大有作为。

22. mix with a rakish set of fellows: 同一批放荡的人相混。

23. got mixed up in some shady affair: 卷入在一件不光采的事情里。

24. one version of his flight: 关于他匆匆离开的说法的一种。

25. denied him talent: 否认他的才能。

26. even when he was out at elbows: 即使在他很穷的时候。

27. Half time: 停一停，别急。

28. considering cap: 助思帽，意为：我会想出好办法来的。

29. That was Ignatius Gallaher all out: 完全是 Gallaher 的本色；all out = all over.

30. quickened his pace: 加快（他的）步伐。

31. superior to the people he passed: 比从他身边过去的人都优越。

32. his soul revolted against the dull inelegance of Capel Street: 他从内心深处对 Capel 大街上的单调无味的粗俗大起反感。

33. pitied the poor stunted houses: 对那些蹩脚的矮小的房屋觉得可怜。

34. a band of tramps, huddled together along the river-banks:（象是）一群流浪者，沿着河堤上挤作一团。

35. stupefied by the panorama of sunset: 被日落的全景骇得发呆，在美丽的夕照面前沉默无言。

36. to get it into some London paper for him: 把他的诗介绍到一家伦敦报纸上去发表。

37. took life within him like an infant hope: 象一个小小的希望那样在他的身上活跃起来了。

38. on the horizon of his mind: 在他的心的视野上，意为他看到了这样的远景。

39. at the point of maturity: 正在成熟。

40. sway the crowd: 影响群众。

41. might appeal to a little circle of kindred minds: 可能打动少数趣味相投的人。

42. the Celtic school: 凯尔特派，即爱尔兰派（的诗人），指 W. B. Yeats 与 AE 这些写爱尔兰题材的作家，他们写的诗在初期都带忧郁情调。

43. put in allusions: 放进一些（有关爱尔兰的）典故。

44. the notices which his book would get: 他的书将会得到的评论。

45. Irish-looking: 具有爱尔兰特色。

46. pursued his revery so ardently: 沉溺于强烈的幻想中，revery，亦作 reverie，幻想。

47. Corless's: 酒馆名。

48. halted before the door in indecision: 犹豫不定地在门前停了下来。

49. frowning slightly to make his errand appear serious: 微微皱眉，表示他是有正经事儿来的。

50. leaning with his back against the counter: 他的背靠着柜台。

51. his feet planted far apart: 他的两脚分得很开地站着。

52. Tommy: Chandler 的小名。

53. What is it to be?: 你喝什么酒？

54. better stuff than we get across the water: 这酒比我们在海那边喝的要好；water 指隔在爱尔兰与英格兰之间的爱尔兰海；across the water，指英格兰。

55. Lithia: 锂盐矿水，瓶装矿泉水。

56. No mineral?: 不加矿泉水吧？

57. I'm the same. Spoils the flavour ...: 我也一样不加矿泉水，它只会把酒味弄坏。

58. garcon: 法语，即英语的 waiter; Gallaher 用这词儿，表示他去过外面世界的高级酒馆，在那里顾客喜欢这样地叫服务的人。

59. two halves of malt whisky: 两客半杯威士忌酒。

60. like s good fellow:（这是有身分的顾客对服务的人说的话，类似）有劳了，费您神。

61. Signs of ageing: 变老的痕迹。

62. A little grey and thin on the top: 头发有点灰白了，头顶开始秃了。

What?——（并不是问“什么”，而是英国上层人士说的断句语），对不对？

63. a large closely cropped head: 满头剪得很短的头发。

64. clean-shaven: 胡须刮得很光。

65. bluish slate-colour: 兰灰色。

66. relieved his unhealthy pallor: 调剂一下他的不健康的苍白色的脸。

67. orange tie: 美国研究者有注云：'Orangemen (named after William of Orange) were the defenders of Anglo-Irish Protestantism. The colour implies that Gallaher owes his allegiance to England'.' (James Joyce, *Dubliners*, ed. by Robert Scholes and A. Walton Litz, Penguin Books, 1976, p.478). 意为他这橘红色领带表明他向英国效忠。

68. Press life: 记者生涯。

69. looking for copy: 老在找材料写文章；copy 指记者写的稿子。

70. proofs and printers: 校样和印刷厂的人。

71. I'm deuced glad: 我是非常高兴的。

72. a bit of a holiday: 是主语，前面 **does a fellow good** 则是谓语。

73. a ton better: 好多了。（用 ton 是为了强调）。

74. Say when:（替人往酒里加水时说的）够了就叫停。

75. allowed his whisky to be very much diluted: 让 Gallaher 把他的威士忌冲得很淡，即水加得过多。

76. I drink mine neat: 我喝纯威士忌，不加水。

77. An odd half-one or so: 偶然喝个半杯。

78. here's to us and to old times and old acquaintance: 让我们为我们自己、过去的交情和老相识而饮；here's to 是祝酒时的开始语，= here is a toast to ....

79. in a bad way: 境遇困难。

80. He's gone to the dogs: 他毁了。

81. —But Hogan has a good sit: Hogan 倒有一个好差使；a good sit = a good position or situation.

82. Land Commission: 土地委员会，主持将大地主的土地卖给佃户的机构，由于工作者经手大宗款项，被视为肥缺。

83. very flush: 很有钱。

84. Boose, I suppose: 我想 O'Hara 之穷是因为老喝酒之故。

85. Isle of Man: 岛名，在爱尔兰海中，离北爱尔兰不远。下句 Gallaher 听了大笑，认为去那种附近地方算不得旅行。

86. I've knocked about there a little: 我去那儿漫游过一些地方。

87. pausing on the word and on the flavour of his drink: 在这个字上停了一停，同时品尝着酒味。

88. that's the thing: 这才是真正重要的。

89. Moulin Rouge: 巴黎地区名，有许多戏院酒馆，是金迷纸醉的地方。

90. Bohemian cafés: 放荡的女人和艺术家之类常去的咖啡馆。

91. Hot stuff!: 了不得的玩意儿（指那些地方非常放荡）。

92. Not for a pious chap like you: 不是为象你这样虔诚的（讲道德的）人的。

93. amid the bustle and competition of the Press: 在新闻界的忙乱和竞争中。

94. The old personal charm: 过去的个人魅力。

95. they've a great feeling for the Irish there: 巴黎人很喜欢爱尔兰人。

96. they were ready to eat me: 他们简直要把我吞掉了，意为他在巴黎很吃得开。

97. made a catholic gesture: 做了一个什么也不在乎的手势；catholic 在此意为 broad-minded.

98. Of course you do find spicy bits in Paris: 你当然会在巴黎找到一些刺激；spicy，挑动情欲的。

99. the students' balls: 大学生跳舞会。

100. cocottes: 法语，妓女。

101. There's no woman like the Porisienne — for style, for go: 没有别地的女人能同巴黎女人比——不论是讲风度还是讲热劲。

102. It's six of one and half-a-dozen of the other: 半斤八两，相差不多。

103. don't make punch of that whisky: liquor up: 别老往威士忌酒倒水了，多喝点真酒吧。

104. François, the same again: 侍者，再来两杯同样的酒；François，法国人名，显然 Gallaher 熟悉这个酒馆里的侍者，所以叫得出他的名字来。

105. produced his cigar-case: 拿出他的雪茄烟盒。

106. it's a rum world: 这是个离奇的世界。

107. puffed thoughtfully at his cigar: 他沉思地一口一口抽着雪茄烟。

108. he proceeded to sketch for his friend some pictures of the corruption which was rife abroad: 他开始给他朋友概略地叙述在国外看到的堕落成风的情景。

109. the vices of many capitals: 许多首都的不道德行为。

110. seemed inclined to award the palm to Berlin: 似乎认为柏林最放荡；**award the palm to:** 把最高荣誉奖给，认为是第一。

111. Some things he could not vouch for: 有些事他不能担保，因为不是亲眼看见而是朋友告诉他的。

112. He spared neither rank nor caste: 他不照顾等级和社会地位，意为他谈这些不道德的事时牵涉到许多大人物。

113. religious houses: 宗教团体。

114. in old jog-along Dublin: 在缓慢平稳地过日子的老都柏林。

115. tasted the joys of connubial bliss: 尝到了婚姻幸福的乐趣。

116. last May twelve months: 一年前的五月份。

117. or I'd have done so at that time: 不然那时我就会来道贺的。

118. Bravo, I wouldn't doubt you: 好啊！我早知道你是行的。

119. may take a little skip over here: 可能再回来一趟。now that I've broken the ice，既然我今年已经开了头。

120. It's only a pleasure deferred: 这只是把好事推后罢了。

121. parole d'honneur: 法语，word of honour，庄严的保证，即明年如再来，一定上你家去。

122. And to clinch the bargain: 为了最后肯定这个交易，为了把这事说定。

123. Is it to be the last: 这是否最后一杯了？

124. an a. p.: an appointmnent，一个约会。

125. asa deoc an doruis: 作为离别前的一饮；*deoc an doruis* 是爱尔兰的 Gaelic 语，照字面可解为 to drink of the door，即再见之意。

126. that's good vernacular for a small whisky: 那是表示一小杯威士忌酒的好土话。

127. A trifle made him blush at any time: 平时一件小事就能使他红脸。

128. Three small whiskies had gone to his head: 三小杯威士忌已使他有点昏昏然了；go to sb.'s head，（酒）使人有醉意。

129. for a brief space: for a short time.

130. upset the equipoise of his sensitive nature: 他的敏感的性情被搅乱得失去了平衡。

131. What was it that stood in his way?：是什么东西使他不能前进的？什么阻碍了他，使他不能飞黄腾达？

132. He saw behind Gallaher's refusal of his invitation: 他看清了 Gallaher 不肯上他家去的真正原因。

133. patronising: 摆出屈尊俯就的样子。

134. have the pleasure of wishing long life and happiness to Mr and Mrs Ignatius Gallaher: 意为那时候你已结婚，我可以向你和新娘道喜了。

135. No blooming fear of that: 请别替我操心，即我不会结婚；blooming 是加重语气的话，= bloody.

136. to have my fling first: 先要开心一番，先要好好玩玩。

137. put my head in the sack: 把我的头放进口袋，意为受到婚姻的束缚。

138. you may bet your bottom dollar there'll be no mooning and spooning about it: 你可以用所有的钱同我打赌，如果我有一天结婚，我不会搞些可笑的谈情说

爱的。

139. man alive: 哎呀，我的天呀！

140. See if I don't play my cards properly: 你等着瞧吧，我是会有办法的。

141. Must get a bit stale:（如果让自己只同一个女人在一起），一定会感到乏味的。

142. Annle's young sister, Monica: Annie 是 Chandler 的妻子，她的妹妹 Monica 每天来两小时帮助家务。

143. Bewley's: 商店名。

144. in a bad humour: 情绪不好。

145. gave him short answers: 对他没说什么好听的话。

146. pausing at the thin tight lips: 他的眼睛停留在她那紧闭的薄薄的嘴唇上。

147. They repelled him and defied him: 这双眼睛拒绝了他，反抗了他。

148. He caught himself up at the question: 发现自己这样在问赶快停住。

149. on the hire system: 按照分期付款办法。

150. It too was prim and pretty: 家俱同 Annie 一样，一本正经，小有姿色。

151. Hushed are the winds ...: 诗行出自拜伦所作"On the Death of a Young Lady"（*Hours of Idleness*）.

152. Zephyr: 和风。

153. the dust: 遗骸。

154. Within this narrow cell reclines her clay: 她的身体躺在这狭窄的小屋（指坟墓）内。

155. losing its breath for four or five seconds: 孩子喘不过气来达四、五秒钟。

156. and then bursting out anew: 后来突然重新又大哭起来。

157. the contracted and quivering face of the child: 孩子抽搐抖动的脸。

158. broke out into a paroxysm of sobbing: 突然放声大哭。

159. his heart closed together as he met the hatred in them: 看见她眼睛里露出的对他的仇恨，他的心冷了。

160. Giving no heed to him: 根本不理他。

161. My little mannie: 我的小宝贝。

162. Was'ou frightened: 你吓着了。

163. Lambabaun: lamb-child，乖乖，宝贝儿。

164. Mamma's little lamb of the world: 妈妈的宝贝儿；在《圣经》及礼拜仪式用语中，耶稣常被称为 Lamb of God。

165. suffused with shame: 脸上一片羞愧的红色。

2. ULYSSES

在二十世纪现代派英文小说之中，最享盛名的恐怕得数 Joyce 的 *Ulysses*，最受人误解的可能也是它，人们说它象天书那样难懂，又有人把它看成专写男女性爱的淫书，因此它在 1922 年刚一出版就在英美都遭禁止，一直到 1933 年，它还是美国海关要查抄的对象。其实它写性爱之处不多，其用意也不在诲淫，而所谓难懂，主要也只是因为它运用了当时一般读者还不熟悉的新写法。

时至今日，此书所引起的争论已经大体消除，人们逐渐能够认真地、不带成见地阅读它了，而这样一读，也就发现它是现实主义同象征手法的卓越的结合。

它有坚实的现实主义作为基础。我们在前面已经说过，Joyce 原是法国式、俄国式现实主义的继承者。在 *Ulysses* 里面，现实主义仍然是主心骨。它的故事线索是明显的。它是 1904 年 6 月 16 日一天都柏林城里两个人的生活经历，一个是青年教师 Stephen Dedalus，另一个是广告经纪人 Leopold Bloom，前者代表同社会格格不入的艺术家，后者代表二十世纪西方都市的普通市民。两人各干各的，到晚上才碰上了，这时 Stephen 已喝醉了，Bloom 把他领到自己家里，请他吃了一顿晚饭。等到 Bloom 上床睡觉，已是清晨二时。他一直在怀疑他的妻子 Molly 同另一个男人有暧昧关系，全书就以 Molly 躺在床上自言自语的长篇独白作为结束。Joyce 通过他的人物（特别是 Bloom）的感官印象，写下了都柏林城的景色、建筑、街道、商店、市声，它的芸芸众生和它的几乎每一小时的变动，细节的描绘十分真实。

然而他更加着重写的却是人物的心理状态。他把他们对周围的人和物的反应、想法、感情、回忆都和盘托出，而且在语言上作了重大的创新：写 Stephen 的段落多用大字、抽象字、哲理字，表示他富于玄想，而所想又大都涉及精神领域；写 Bloom 则具体，平凡，牵涉到的是日常人生；写 Molly 则更多鲜艳的色彩，更多花草和其它生长的、蓬勃的东西，表示她代表繁殖力和丰满的生命。

用不同的风格、语言来写不同的人物性格本是古往今来许多作家都用的手法，Joyce 的不同在于他比谁都用得彻底，用得成功。除此之外，他还追求流动性，即叙述不是静止的，而是涌流向前的。为此他去掉一些普通小说中常见的联结和说明，不写“他想……，他感到……”之类的引语，而是直接把人物的思想写出来，从一个写法不经转接就跳到另一个，串连起来就形成了所谓“意识流”（stream of consciousness）Joyce 用这新颖的手法不是为了追求怪异的效果，而是为了使文学写作更敏锐，更真实。

那么，他的象征又在哪里？*Ulysses* 一书从头到尾都是象征，都是隐含的对比，作家拿现代市民 Bloom 同荷马史诗里的古代英雄 Ulysses 相比，拿青年艺术家 Stephen 同 Ulysses 的儿子 Telemachus 相比，拿男女关系上不严肃的 Molly 同始终忠于爱情理想的 Penelope 相比，每一章都是荷马史诗《奥德赛》中一个重要情节在二十世纪环境下的重演；他把书名定为 *Ulysses* 就是向读者交代了这一点。换言之，整部书是一个规模巨大、计划周详的现代史诗，只不过作者让我们看到：远古的英雄人物在二十世纪西方的条件下变成了或则琐碎、庸俗或则畸形发展的人物，光辉的英雄业绩也蜕化成了平凡、枯燥、肮脏的都市生活。这样，这部将近八百页的大书里不仅有传统的与现代的品质并存，而且作者将爱尔兰一个都市的情景同整个欧洲文化的中心问题——即它提供了怎样的生活和价值标准——连结了起来。这样的题材无疑是有头等重要的意义的，而作者又有卓越的艺术才能和想象力来深入地、生动地表现它，从而把小说写作推进到了一个新阶段，因此无论从哪一点说，*Ulysses* 都是一部杰作。

从任何书摘取片断都未必能表现它的真貌，而对于 *Ulysses* 来说，摘取更无异于支解；只有阅读全书才能真正体会它的丰富，深刻和流动性。然而从语言的角度出发，选读几段也许仍是有益的——总比只听别人的议论（而此书引起的议论也真不少）而完全不读原著要好。我们在此选了三段：

第一段写 Stephen 在海边走路时心中所思。用的难字、大字最多，牵涉到的背景知识也最深奥，而作家是有意如此的，因为只有这样才能比较真实地表现出 Stephen 是一个曾经读过神学、而现在却立意从事艺术创作的知识分子。

第二段写 Bloom 在一家饭馆里的见闻。同第一段的风格相反，这里的语言具体，来自实际人生，作者要表示这饭馆里一切粗俗、野蛮、可憎。

第三段摘自 Molly 的有名的独白，通过它读者可以多少看到一点 Joyce 是怎样运用“意识流”的技巧的。

书名 Ulysses，荷马史诗《奥德赛》的主人公俄底修斯的另一个名字。作者把 Leopold Bloom 看作一个现代的 Ulysses，把他的妻子 Molly 看作一个现代的 Penelope（通译珀涅罗珀）。这两对人物的性格不同——Bloom 没有 Ulysses 的英雄气概，Molly 不象 Penelope 那样忠于爱情理想——就象征了古今两个时代的精神生活的质的不同。

a. [Ineluctable Modality]

这两段选自描写 Stephen 独自在都柏林的海边走路的一章。他一边走路一边冥想事物形态的变化以及是否可以通过表相来认识实质。所选两段第一段涉及视觉，第二段涉及听觉，但主要是写 Stephen 心中的反应和联想。由于他曾经学过哲学、神学，所以有不少哲理名词和典故。标题是我们加的。

1. Ineluctable modality of the visible: 哲学名词，意为 the unavoidable way of knowing reality through the sense of sight，即无可避免的通过视觉来认识真实的途径；ineluctable，无法逃避的，不可避免的；modality, mode, way, avenue of sensation，感觉道（如视觉道）。

2. thought through my eyes: 通过视觉而思想。

3. Signatures of all things: 原是十六七世纪德国神秘主义者 Jakob Bohme (1575—1624) 的话，指上帝在所有的事物上都盖了他的标记。

4. I am here to read: read 在此意为理解，看懂。

5. seaspawn and seawrack: 作者所创复合词，前者指海中各种产物，后者指浮在海水上的各种毁坏物。

6. the nearing tide: 正在涌来的潮水。

7. that rusty boot: 那只浮在水上的旧皮鞋；rusty，赭色的，褪色的。

8. Snotgreen, bluesilver, rust: coloured signs: 指上述各物的颜色，而且大多是丑恶、使人不愉快的颜色，如 snotgreen 是指象鼻涕那样的绿色，此字也是 Joyce 自己复合的；coloured signs，有颜色的象征记号，与上文 signatures（上帝的标记）相应。

9. Limits of the diaphane: 透明性的极限；diaphane, transparency，透明性。这原是古希腊哲学家亚里士多德在其所作 *De Anima* 中提出的名词。

10. he adds: in bodies: he 指亚里士多德，他在提出“透明性的极限”时，曾补充说：“在身体之内的”。

11. By knocking his sconce against them: sconce，诙谐语，指头，脑袋。意为：亚里士多德是靠用头去碰别人的身体而了解到此点的。

12. Go easy: 此处意为：别信口开河了！

13. Bald he was and a millionaire: he 仍指亚里士多德，相传他秃头，有钱，承继了一大笔财产，后来他的学生亚历山大又送了他一笔钱，因此 Stephen 说他是百万富翁。

14. maestro di color che sanno: 意大利语，出自但丁《炼狱》，意为 the master of them that know，那些有知识的人的老师，仍指亚里士多德。

15. adiaphane: 意与 diaphane 正好相反，指不透明性。Stephen 性喜玄思，从一个词立刻想到其反义词。

16. If you can put your five fingers through it, it is a gate, if not a door: 此处仍是说凭感官接触来认识事物。

17. Shut your eyes and see: 此句中 see 并不指真用眼睛瞧，而指等待事情发展。

18. Stephen closed his eyes to hear: 从此起涉及听觉。

19. howsomever: 即 howsoever，无论如何，不管怎样。

20. Five, six: Stephen 在数他走的步数。

21. nacheinander: 德语，after one another, successively，一下又一下（指时间上的连续）。

22. Jesus: 天哪！

23. If I fell over a cliff that beetles o'er his base: 语出莎士比亚《哈姆雷特》第一幕第四场，全文为：

What if it tempt you toward the flood, my lord,
Or to the dreadful summit of the cliff
That beetles o'er his base into the sea
And there assume some other horrible form,
Which might deprive your sovereignty of reason
And draw you into madness?

—*Hamlet* I iv 69–74

（殿下，要是它把您诱到潮水里去，或者把您领到下临大海的峻峭的悬崖之巅，在那边它现出了狰狞的面貌，吓得您丧失理智，变成疯狂，那可怎么好呢？

——朱生豪译文）

beetles o'er his base: overhangs threateningly its base，可怕地高悬在山基之上。

24. nebeneinander: 德语，beside one another, side by side，一个靠一个（指空间上的并立），此处意为：如我从悬崖跌下去，必然要穿过紧靠悬崖的空间。

25. My ash sword hangs at my side: ash sword 指 walking stick of ash wood，梣木制成的手杖。

26. they do: they 指盲人，他们都用手杖点着路走。

27. in his boots: his 指与 Stephen 同住的医科学生 Buck Mulligan, Stephen 穷得连皮鞋也没有，所穿的一双是向 Mulligan 借的。

28. made by the mallet of *Los Demiurgos*: Los Demiurgos 即 the Demiurge，原意是“工匠”；按照柏拉图的哲学，世界万物都是一个神秘的工匠做的；mallet 指工匠制物时用的木槌。

29. Sandymount strand: 都柏林海边街名。

30. Crush, crack, crik, crick: 一系列的拟声词，形容在沙滩上走路时皮鞋踩在贝壳等物上的声音。

b. [Lestrygonians]

这是 Bloom 在中午步行都柏林街头所见的一个片断。他走进一家饭馆，想吃午饭，但一见那里顾客吃东西的各种可怕样子，感到恶心，赶紧走了出来。作者有意把这些顾客同《奥德赛》第十章里所写的吃人怪物 Lestrygonians 相比。在西欧现代文学作品中，把一个都市的饭馆的景象写得如此不堪的，似乎又只有 Joyce一人。这里用的手法是现实主义加意识流。标题非原有，是后人加的。

标题 Lestrygonians，又作 Lestrigons 或 Laestrygones，住在 Sicily 岛上的巨人，喜欢吃人。Ulysses 在其归家途中曾派两个水手和一个送信人去见他们的王，请求准许登陆，结果派去的一人为王所食。

1. slop of greens: greens 蔬菜，用 slop 一字表明是汤，而且是象厨房下脚那样的有臭味的汤。

2. See the animals feed: 瞧这些人吃饭多象野兽！（Bloom 心里这样想）。

3. Men, men, men: 可有二解：1. 到处都是人。2. 这就是人的真相！

4. calling for more bread no charge:（向服务员）要多给几片不另加钱的面包。

5. swilling, wolfing gobfuls of sloppy food: 这几字形容狼吞虎咽的样子和声音：swilling 大口吞饮；wolfing，狼吞虎咽地吃；gobfuls，大口大口的食物；sloppy food，带汤水的劣质食物。

6. suetfaced: 脸如板油的。

7. polished his tumbler knife fork and spoon with his napkin: 用餐巾擦拭他的酒杯，刀，叉和汤匙（注意 Joyce 故意不用逗号把 tumbler 以下几字隔开）——这是不雅的行为，一般有教养的人是不干的。

8. New set of microbes: 这是 Bloom 对上述一事的评论，不过藏在心里，并未说出，意思是：这样擦有什么用，无非留下新的细菌而已。

9. A man with an infant's saucestained napkin tucked round him: 成人而系着一块婴孩用的餐巾，巾上又尽是酱汁的痕迹，可见其人之庸俗与可笑。

10. shovelled gurgling soup down his gullet: 这又是形容吃相之不雅；shovelled，把食物大口大口塞进嘴巴；gurgling soup，发着响声的汤，形容喝汤时出声，而

这又是有教养的人要避免的；his gullet，他的食管。

11. A man spitting back on his plate: 有人把刚进口的食物吐回盘子上，这也是无教养的人干的。

12. halfmasticated gristle: 咀嚼得不够的软骨。

13. no teeth to chewchewchew it: 这里 chewchewchew 一词是 Joyce 特创的，意思就是 chew，不过加以强调，表示是细细地咀嚼。

14. chump chop from the grill: 现烤的一大块肉；chump chop，大块猪排或羊排；grill，烤架。

15. Bolting to get it over: 囫囵吞下，草草吃完。

16. Bitten off more than he can chew: 成语：贪多嚼不烂，此处实义与引伸意兼而有之。

17. Working tooth and jaw: 表示拼命地吃；这个短语可能是模仿成语 fighting tooth and nail 而成。参见下面第 53 注。

18. That last pagan king of Ireland Cormac in the schoolpoem: 小学教科书里一首诗中提到的爱尔兰国王 Cormac，他是爱尔兰最后一个异教徒国王。

19. at Sletty southward of the Boyne: 在 Boyne 河南边的 Sletty 地方。

20. Something galoptious: 这里 galoptious 是 Joyce 所创新词，可能是形容大块难吞的东西。

21. Saint Patrick: 相传 Saint Patrick（约 385—461）在五世纪时来爱尔兰传播基督教，从此他成为爱尔兰的守护神。

22. 第 19，20 行：这两行是顾客点菜的声音，**roast beef and cabbage:** 烤牛肉加洋白菜；**one stew:** 一盆炖肉。

23. His gorge rose: 他几乎要呕吐了。Spaton sawdust，在铺木屑的地板上吐痰；Joyce 故意联写 spat on 两字；一般下等饭馆地上铺木屑，以防顾客滑倒。

24. reek of plug, spilt beer, men's beery piss: 这里写各种臭味，plug 指抽水马桶的放水装置，spilt beer 指杯子里满出来的啤酒，men's beery piss 指男人的带啤酒味的尿。the stale of ferment，总结上面所说，都是发酵的陈腐气味。

25. old chap picking his tootles: 有一个老头儿在剔他的牙齿；tootles 是 Joyce 自创词，照上下文看指牙齿。

26. chewing the cud: 反刍（本指牛羊，此处移用于人）。

27. Grace after meals: 饭后的感恩祷告（基督徒在吃饭前后要祷告感谢上帝）。

28. Scoffing up stewgravy with sopping sippets of bread: 用湿透的小块面包擦着盘上余剩的肉汁贪婪地吃着。（注意此处 s 音的运用，擦盘子的声音清楚可闻。）

29. Lick it off the plate, man!（索性）用舌头把盘子舔干净好了，老兄！（这也是 Bloom 心里想说而未说的话）。

30. Get out of this: 这是 Bloom 对自己说的话：赶快离开这鬼地方！

31. the stooled and tabled eaters: 坐在凳子上和桌子旁的食客们。

32. 第 3，4 行：又是顾客点酒菜的声音：**two stouts**：两杯黑啤酒；**one corned and cabbage**：一盘咸牛肉加洋白菜。

33. That fellow ramming a knifeful of cabbage down as if his life depended on it: 那个人把一刀子的洋白菜猛塞进嘴巴，象是饿得靠这菜救命似的。

34. Good stroke: 通常意为：了不得的一招儿；但此处可能是指 a hearty appetite，旺盛的食欲（解见 *OED*, stroke, sb.1, 19；Swift 曾经如此用过）。

35. Give me the fidgets to look: 让我看了坐立不安。

36. his three hands: 意为那人既用双手，又用刀，所以等于用三只手吃东西。

37. Tear it limb from limb: tear it apart，（象野兽似的）撕着一块一块地（吃）。

38. Second nature to him: 对于那人这样的吃法已经是第二天性，习以为常了。

39. Born with a silver knife in his mouth: 有成语作 born with a silver spoon in his mouth（生而富贵），作者故意把 spoon 改成 knife，表示那个吃相可怕的人象是一生下来就在口上咬着一把刀似的。

40. That's witty, I think: 我看那样改一个字，倒也俏皮。（其实 Bloom 是一个平庸的市民，说不出什么俏皮话来。另外，请注意他同上一段里的 Stephen 不一样，脑里并无高雅或深奥的引语，所想到的只是一些普通的、近乎套话的成语。这是作者所用手法之一，以之写 Bloom 的性格、气质不同于艺术家 Stephen。）

41. Or no: 不行，那样改不行，因为原成语中有 silver 一词，表示有钱，而如去掉 silver，则改过的句子变成 born with a knife，那么离原成语的形式较远，又不象成语了。

42. But then the allusion is lost: 那样就看不出是引用成语了。

43. illgirt: 衣服不整的。

44. blew the foamy crown from his tankard: 把他那杯啤酒顶上的泡沫吹掉。

45. Well up: 吹得很高。

46. foodlift: 运送食物的吊车。

47. I munched hum un thu Unchster Bunk un Munchday: 这是模仿那个顾客由于满嘴塞满食物而说话不清所发出声音，意思大体可辨，可能是说：I met him in X Bank on Monday.

48. Did you, faith?: 此处 faith 是断句语，类似“真的么？”，= in faith, good faith，无特别意思；*OED* 曾引狄更斯一例云：‘I'd rather be in old John's chimney-corner, faith’.（Dickens, *Barnaby Rudge*）

49. Not here. Don't see him:（他用眼睛表示他是来找人的，而这个人）不在这里，看不见他。

50. Get a light snack in Davy Byrne's: 可以到 Davy Byrne's（小吃店名）去吃点小吃。

51. Stopgap. Keep me going. Had a good breakfast: 作为暂时对付，总可以维持下去，反正早饭吃得不少。

以上这些话都是 Bloom 对自己说的，是他的内心活动，也是一种“意识流”。

52. Roast and mashed here: 仍是顾客点菜的话：这儿要一客烤肉加土豆泥。下句是顾客要啤酒的话。

53. Every fellow for his own, tooth and nail: 这里又是借用成语而略改，使它具有新意；原意应是：人自为战，拼命以赴；现在的意思是：人各大吃，动牙也动手指；仍然表示人们的吃相不雅，无异野兽。

54. Gulp. Grub. Gulp. Gobstuff: 四字都与吃东西有关，作者把它们放在一起，声音也相似，以加强效果。Gulp，吞咽；**grub** = food, a feed; **gobful** = mouthful.

55. Fat or be eaten. Kill! Kill!: 仍是 Bloom 心中所想。

c. [Penelope]

这是本书最后一章 Molly 的长篇独白的最后一部分。作者在此用了“意识流”手法，写出 Molly 在深夜睡不着觉，头脑里有各种念头和回忆，从一事跳到另一事，又连想到许多其它的事，中间一点转接也没有，句子有时忽然中断，有时溶入另一句，因此整个长达 45 页的一章无一个标点，到全书之末才出现一个句号。

题名 Penelope 非作者原标，而是后人所加的，但也符合 Joyce 的本意，因为他确是在将现代的 Molly 同古希腊的 Penelope 对比，在写信给友人时曾这样点明。Penelope 在丈夫 Ulysses 外出的长远年月里，在家守着他，虽然不断有显赫人物要她改嫁，但她设计挫败了他们的阴谋，直到丈夫回家。在西方古典文学传统里，她是妇女贤慧的楷模。而 Molly 则显然不同。由于现代西方社会的生活环境和价值标准，她对于丈夫 Bloom 是不忠实的，为了自己能登台表演唱歌，不惜同音乐会的经理人 Blazes Boylan 勾搭。然而 Joyce 并不简单化，他笔下的 Molly 又是一个热爱生活的好心肠的妇女。

1. 1 2 3 4 5: 这是 Molly 为了能入睡在数数目。

2. lower this lamp and try again: 把灯放低，再想办法入睡。

3. Lambes: 卖花的商店名。

Findlaters，另一商店名。

4. in case he brings him home tomorrow: 万一明天 Bloom 把那人带回家来；第二个 him 指另一人，可能是 Stephen。

5. Fridays an unlucky day: Friday is ...：西俗：星期五由于是耶稣受难日，所以被人们认为是不吉利的一天。

6. to do the place up someway: 把房间收拾干净一点。

7. accompany him: 弹钢琴为他伴奏。

8. Liptons: 店名。

9. at 7½d a 1b:（即蛋糕的定价是）7 ½ 便士一磅。

10. 11d a couple of lbs: 11 便士两磅。

11. a nice plant for the middle of the table: 一株可以放在桌子中间的好看的花草。

12. get that cheaper in wait wheres this I saw them not long ago: in 后面缺一商店名，因为她记不起来了；**wait wheres this I saw them not long ago** 是插入语，如照普通写法加上标点，应作 get that cheaper in —wait, where's this [place] where I saw them not long ago?

13. theres nothing like nature: 没有什么能比大自然更好了；从此起她神往于野外的花草之类的自然景物。

14. as for them saying theres no God I wouldnt give a snap of my two fingers for all their learning why dont they go and create something: 至于那些说不

存在上帝的人，不管他们有多大学问，我都是看得一文不值，他们干吗不去创造出一点东西来呢？这里 Molly 是在驳斥无神论，她是信教的，认为世界万物皆上帝所造。

15. go and wash the cobbles off themselves first: 先把他们身上的脏东西洗干净吧；cobbles 指小煤块，此处可能指煤灰。

16. then they go howling for the priest and they dying: 而等到他们快死的时候却喊着要找神父（来替他们祷告）。

17. who ah that they dont know neither do I so there you are: 如打标点，此行应作：Who? Ah, that they don't know. Neither do I. So there you are.

18. the sun shines for you he said: 从此起 Molly 回想 Bloom 向她求婚那天的情景。

19. I knew I could always get round him: 我知道我什么时候都能有办法支配他的；get round，克服，智胜。

20. leading him on: 诱使他干下去。

21. so many things he didnt know of Mulvey and Mr Stanhope and Hester and old captain Groves and the sailors: 这里说的是 Molly 小时候在 Gibraltar（直布罗陀）所见的人和事。她记得清楚，脑子里充满了明丽的色彩。

22. poor devil half roasted: 可怜的家伙（指总督府的门卫），（老站在那里）几乎给太阳烤焦了。

23. the Spanish girls ... the Greeks and the Jews and the Arabs ...: 直布罗陀原属西班牙，后为英占，当地居民除西班牙人外，还有许多其它民族的人。

24. the fowl market all clucking outside Larby Sharons: 家禽市场设在 Larby Sharons（不详，可能是一家大商店名）外面，鸡鸭之类在咯咯地叫着。

25. the vague fellows: 那些情况不明（即有点神秘）的人。

26. posadas: 西班牙语，小客栈。

27. glancing eyes: 迅速掠过的亮眼。

28. a lattice hid for her lover to kiss the iron:（那双亮眼躲在）一个花格窗后面，让她的情人可以同铁格子亲吻。

29. the castanets: 伴奏的响板（指酒店里拿着响板作舞的舞女）。

30. the sea crimson sometimes like fire and the glorious sunsets and the figtrees in the Alameda gardens: 这些仍是 Molly 回忆在直布罗陀所见的自然景物，她很喜欢艳丽的色彩，也很有想象力。

31. and how he kissed me under the Moorish wall: 在那摩尔式（伊斯兰式）建筑的墙下面他是如何热切地吻我呵；从此起 Molly 的思绪又回到她诱使 Bloom 向她求婚的情景。

32. I thought well as well him as another: 我心想，好吧，就嫁他吧，他也不比别的人差；这句话表示 Molly 并不真的热爱 Bloom，带点游戏人间的味道。

33. then I asked him with my eyes to ask again: 我用眼神促使他再要求我答应他的要求。

34. and yes I said yes I will Yes: 于是我就说：好，好，我愿意；这是全书最后一语，全章到此才出现第一个标点。

52 D. H. LAWRENCE
(1885–1930)

SONS & LOVERS

王家湘　选注

from Chapter IV The Young Life of Paul

…………

All the children, but particularly Paul, were peculiarly *against* their father, along with their mother. Morel continued to bully and to drink. He had periods, months at a time, when he made the whole life of the family a misery. Paul never forgot coming home from the Band of Hope[1] one Monday evening and finding his mother with her eye swollen and discoloured,[2] his father standing on the hearthrug, feet astride, his head down, and William, just home from work, glaring at his father. There was a silence as the young children entered, but none of the elders[3] looked round.

William was white to the lips, and his fists were clenched. He waited until the children were silent, watching with children's rage and hate; then he said:

You coward, you daren't do it when I was in. '

But Morel's blood was up.[4] He swung round on his son. William was bigger, but Morel was hard-muscled, and mad with fury.

'Dossn't I?' he shouted. 'Dossn't I? Ha'e much more o' thy chelp, my young jockey, an' I'll rattle my fist about thee. Ay, an' I sholl that, dost see.'[5]

Morel crouched at the knees and showed his fist in an ugly, almost beast-like fashion. William was white with rage.

'Will yer?'[6] he said, quiet and intense. 'It 'ud be the last time, though.'

Morel danced a little nearer, crouching, drawing back his fist to strike. William put his fists ready. A light came into his blue eyes, almost like a laugh. He watched his father. Another word, and the men would have begun to fight. Paul hoped they would. The three children[7] sat pale on the sofa.

'Stop it, both of you,' cried Mrs Morel in a hard voice. 'We've had enough for *one* night. And *you,*' she said, turning on to her husband, 'look at your children!'

Morel glanced at the sofa.

'Look at the children, you nasty little bitch!' he sneered. 'Why, what have I done to the children, I should like to know? But they're like yourself; you've put 'em up to your own tricks and nasty ways[8]—you've learned 'em in it, you'ave.'

She refused to answer him. No one spoke. After a while he threw his boots under the table and went to bed.

'Why didn't you let me have a go at him[9]?' said William, when his father was upstairs. 'I could easily have beaten him.'

'A nice thing—your own father,' she replied.

' "*Father!*" ' repeated William. 'Call *him my* father!'

'Well, he is—and so—'

'But why don't you let me settle him?[10] I could do, easily.'

'The idea!' she cried. 'It hasn't come to that *yet.*'[11]

'No,' he said, 'it's come to worse. Look at yourself. *Why* didn't you let me give it him?'[12]

'Because I couldn't bear it, so never think of it,' she cried quickly.

And the children went to bed, miserably.

When William was growing up, the family moved from the Bottoms[18] to a house on the brow of the hill, commanding a view of the valley, which spread out like a convex cockle-shell, or a clampshell, before it. In front of the house was a huge old ash-tree. The west wind, sweeping from Derbyshire, caught the houses with full force,[14] and the tree shrieked again. Morel liked it.

'It's music,' he said. 'It sends me to sleep.'

But Paul and Arthur and Annie hated it. To Paul it became almost a demoniacal noise. The winter of their first year in the new house their father was very bad. The children played in the street, on the brim of the wide, dark valley, until eight o'clock. Then they went to bed. Their mother sat sewing below. Having such a great space in front of the house gave the children a feeling of night, of vastness, and of terror. This terror came in from the shrieking of the tree and the anguish of the home discord. Often Paul would wake up, after he had been asleep a long time, aware of thuds downstairs. Instantly he was wide awake. Then he heard the booming shouts of his mother, then the bang, bang of his father's fist on the table, and the nasty snarling shout as the man's voice got higher. And then the whole was drowned in a piercing medley of shrieks and cries from the great, windswept ash-tree. The children lay silent in suspense, waiting for a lull in the wind to hear what their father was doing. He might hit their mother again. There was a feeling of horror, a kind of bristling in the darkness, and a sense of blood.[15] They lay with their hearts in the grip of an intense anguish. The wind came through the tree fiercer and fiercer. All the cords of the great harp[16] hummed, whistled, and shrieked. And then came the horror of the sudden silence, silence everywhere, outside and downstairs. What was it? Was it a silence of blood?[17] What had he done?

The children lay and breathed the darkness. And then, at last, they heard their father throw down his boots and tramp upstairs in his stockinged feet. Still they listened. Then at last, if the wind allowed, they heard the water of the tap drumming into the kettle, which their mother was filling for morning, and they could go to sleep in peace.

So they were happy in the morning—happy, very happy playing, dancing at night round the lonely lamp-post in the midst of the darkness. But they had one tight place of anxiety in their hearts, one darkness in their eyes, which showed all their lives.[18]

Paul hated his father. As a boy he had a fervent private religion.

'Make him stop drinking,' he prayed every night. 'Lord let my father die,' he prayed very often. 'Let him not be killed at pit,' he prayed when, after tea, the father did not come home from work.[19]

That was another time when the family suffered intensely. The children came from school and had their teas. On the hob the big black saucepan was simmering, the stew-jack[20] was in the oven, ready for Morel's dinner. He was expected at five o'clock. But for months he would stop and drink every night on his way from work.

In the winter nights, when it was cold, and grew dark early, Mrs Morel would put a brass candlestick on the table, light a tallow candle to save the gas. The children finished their bread-and-butter, or dripping,[21] and were ready to go out to play. But if Morel had not come they faltered. The sense of his sitting in all his pit-dirt,[22] drinking, after a long day's work, not coming home and eating and washing, but sitting, getting drunk, on an empty stomach, made Mrs Morel unable to bear herself. From her the feeling was transmitted to the other children. She never suffered alone any more: the children suffered with her.

Paul went out to play with the rest. Down in the great trough of twilight,[23] tiny clusters of lights burned where the pits were. A few last colliers struggled up[24] the dim field-path. The lamplighter[25] came along. No more colliers came. Darkness shut down over the valley; work was gone. It was night.

Then Paul ran anxiously into the kitchen. The one candle still burned on the table, the big fire glowed red. Mrs Morel sat alone. On the hob the saucepan steamed; the dinner-plate lay waiting on the table. All the room was full of the sense of waiting, waiting for the man who was sitting in his pitdirt, dinnerless, some mile[26] away from home, across the darkness, drinking himself drunk. Paul stood in the doorway.

'Has my dad come?' he asked.

'You can see he hasn't,' said Mrs Morel, cross with the futility of the question.

Then the boy dawdled about near his mother. They shared the same anxiety. Presently Mrs Morel went out and strained the potatoes.[27]

'They're ruined and black,' she said; 'but what do I care? '

Not many words were spoken. Paul almost hated his mother for suffering because his father did not come home from work.

'What do you bother yourself for?' he said. 'If he wants to stop and get drunk, why don't you let him?'

'Let him! ' flashed Mrs Morel. 'You may well say "let him." '

She knew that the man who stops on the way home from work is on a quick way to ruining himself and his home. The children were yet young, and depended on the breadwinner. William gave her the sense of relief, providing her at last with someone to turn to if Morel failed. But the tense atmosphere of the room on these waiting evenings was the same.

The minutes ticked away. At six o'clock still the cloth lay on the table, still the dinner stood waiting, still the same sense of anxiety and expectation in the room. The boy could not stand it any longer. He could not go out and play. So he ran in to Mrs Inger, next door but one, for her to talk to him. She had no children. Her husband was good to her, but was in a shop, and came home late. So, when she saw the lad at the door, she called:

'Come in, Paul.'

The two sat talking for some time, when suddenly the boy rose saying:

'Well, I'll be going and seeing if my mother wants an errand doing.'

He pretended to be perfectly cheerful, and did not tell his friend what ailed him.[28] Then he ran indoors.

Morel at these times came in churlish and hateful.

'This is a nice time to come home,' said Mrs Morel.

'Wha's[29] it matter to yo'[30] what time I come whoam?'[31] he shouted.

And everybody in the house was still, because he was dangerous. He ate his food in the most brutal manner[32] possible and, when he had done, pushed all the pots in a heap away from him, to lay his arms on the table. Then he went to sleep.

Paul hated his father so. The collier's small, mean head, with its black hair slightly soiled with grey, lay on the bare arms, and the face, dirty and inflamed, with a fleshy nose and thin, paltry brows, was turned sideways, asleep with beer and weariness and nasty temper. If anyone entered suddenly, or a noise were made, the man looked up and shouted:

'I'll lay my fist about thy y'ead,[33] I'm tellin' thee, if tha[34] doesna[35] stop that clatter! Dost hear?'

And the two last words, shouted in a bullying fashion, usually at Annie, made the family writhe with hate of the man.

He was shut out from all family affairs. No one told him anything. The children, alone with their mother, told her all about the day's happenings, everything. Nothing had really taken place in them until it was told to their mother. But as soon as the father came in, everything stopped. He was like the scotch in the smooth, happy machinery of the home. And he was always aware of this fall of silence on his entry, the shutting off of life,[36] the unwelcome. But now it was gone too far to alter.

He would dearly have liked the children to talk to him, but they could not. Sometimes Mrs Morel would say:

'You ought to tell your father.'

Paul won a prize in a competition in a child's paper. Everybody was highly jubilant.

'Now you'd better tell your father when he comes in,' said Mrs Morel. 'You know how he carries on[37] and says he's never told anything.'

'All right,' said Paul. But he would almost rather have forfeited the prize than have to tell his father.

'I've won a prize in a competition, dad,' he said.

Morel turned round to him.

'Have you, my boy? What sort of a competition?'

'Oh, nothing—about famous women.'

'And how much is the prize, then, as you've got?'

'It's a book.'

'Oh, indeed!'

'About birds.'

'Hm—hm!'

And that was all. Conversation was impossible between the father and any other member of the family. He was an outsider. He had denied the God in him.[38]

The only times when he entered again into the life of his own people was when he worked, and was happy at work. Sometimes, in the evening, he cobbled the boots or mended the kettle or his pit-bottle.[39] Then he always wanted several attendants, and the children enjoyed it. They united with him in the work, in the actual doing of something, when he was his real self again.

He was a good workman, dexterous, and one who, when he was in a good humour, always sang. He had whole periods, months, almost years, of friction and nasty temper. Then sometimes he was jolly again. It was nice to see him run with a piece of redhot iron into the scullery, crying:

'Out of my road—out of my road!'

Then he hammered the soft, red-glowing stuff on his iron goose,[40] and made the shape he wanted. Or he sat absorbed for a moment, soldering. Then the children watched with joy as the metal sank suddenly molten, and was shoved about against the nose of the soldering-iron, while the room was full of a scent of burnt resin and hot tin, and Morel was silent and intent for a minute. He always sang when he mended boots because of the jolly sound of hammering.

And he was rather happy when he sat putting great patches on his moleskin pit trousers,[41] which he would often do, considering them too dirty, and the stuff too hard, for his wife to mend.

But the best time for the young children was when he made fuses. Morel fetched a sheaf of long sound wheat-straws from the attic. These he cleaned with his hand, till each one gleamed like a stalk of gold, after which he cut the straws into lengths of about six inches, leaving, if he could, a notch at the bottom of each piece. He always had a beautifully sharp knife that could cut a straw clean without hurting it.[42] Then he set in the middle of the table a heap of gunpowder, a little pile of black grains upon the white-scrubbed board.[43] He made and trimmed the straws while Paul and Annie filled and plugged them. Paul loved to see the black grains trickle down a crack in his palm into the mouth of the straw, peppering jollily down-wards till the straw was full. Then he bunged up the mouth with a bit of soap—which he got in his thumb-nail from a pat[44] in a saucer—and the straw was finished.

'Look, dad! ' he said.

'That's right, my beauty,' replied Morel, who was peculiarly lavish of endearments to his second son. Paul popped the fuse into the powder-tin, ready for the morning, when Morel would take it to the pit, and use it to fire a shot that would blast the coal down.

Meantime Arthur, still fond of his father,[45] would lean on the arm of Morel's chair, and say:

'Tell us about down pit, daddy.'

This Morel loved to do.

'Well, there's one little 'oss[46]—we call 'im[47] Taffy,' he would begin. 'An he's a fawce[48] un! '[49]

Morel had a warm way of telling a story. He made one feel Taffy's cunning.

'He's a brown un,'[50] he would answer, 'an' not very high. Well, he comes i ' th' stall wi' a rattle,[51] an' then yo' 'ear 'im sneeze.[52] " 'Ello,[53] Taff," you say, "what art sneezin' for? Bin ta'ein' some snuff'?"[54]

'An' 'e sneezes again. Then he slives[55] up an' shoves 'is 'ead on yer, that cadin.'[56]

'"What's want, Taff?" yo' say.'

'And what does he? ' Arthur always asked.

'He wants a bit o' bacca,[57] my duckey.'

This story of Taffy would go on interminably, and everybody loved it.

Or sometimes it was a new tale.

'An' what dost think, my darlin'? When I went to put my coat on at snap-time,[58] what should go runnin' up my arm but a mouse.

"Hey up, theer!"[59] I shouts.[60]

'An' I wor just in time ter get 'im by th' tail.'[61]

'And did you kill it?'

'I did, for they're a nuisance. The place is fair snied[62] wi' 'em.'

'An' what do they live on?'

'The corn as the 'osses drops—and they'll get in your pocket an'eat your snap, if you'll let 'em—no matter where yo' hing[63] your coat—the slivin', nibblin' little nuisances, for they are.'

These happy evenings could not take place unless Morel had some job to do. And then he always went to bed very early, often before the children. There was nothing remaining for him to stay up for, when he had finished tinkering, and had skimmed the headlines of the newspaper.

And the children felt secure when their father was in bed. They lay and talked softly awhile. Then they started as the lights went suddenly sprawling over the ceiling from the lamps that swung in the hands of the colliers tramping by outside, going to take the nine o'clock shift. They listened to the voices of the men, imagined them dipping down into the dark valley. Sometimes they went to the window and watched the three or four lamps growing tinier and tinier, swaying down the fields in the darkness. Then it was a joy to rush back to bed and cuddle closely in the warmth.

Paul was rather a delicate boy, subject to bronchitis.[64] The others were all quite strong; so this was another reason for his mother's difference in feeling for him. One day he came home at dinner-time feeling ill. But it was not a family to make any fuss.[65]

'What's the matter with *you*?' his mother asked sharply.

'Nothing,' he replied.

But he ate no dinner.

'If you eat no dinner, you're not going to school,' she said.

'Why?' he asked.

'That's why.'

So after dinner he lay down on the sofa, on the warm chintz cushions the children loved. Then he fell into a kind of doze. That afternoon Mrs Morel was ironing. She listened to the small, restless noise the boy made in his throat as she worked. Again rose in her heart the old, almost weary feeling towards him. She had never expected him to live. And yet he had a great vitality in his young body. Perhaps it would have been a little relief to her if he had died. She always felt a mixture of anguish in her love for him.[66]

He, in his semi-conscious sleep, was vaguely aware of the clatter of the iron on the iron-stand, of the faint thud, thud of the ironingboard. Once roused, he opened his eyes to see his mother standing on the hearthrug with the hot iron near her cheek, listening, as it were, to the heat. Her still face, with the mouth closed tight from suffering and disillusion and self-denial, and her nose, the smallest bit on one side, and her blue eyes so young, quick, and warm, made his heart contract with love.[67] When she was quiet, so, she looked brave and rich with life, but as if she had been done out of her rights. It hurt the boy keenly, this feeling about her that she had never had her life's fulfilment: and his own incapability to make up to her hurt him with a sense of impotence, yet made him patiently dogged inside. It was his childish aim.

She spat on the iron, and a little ball of spit bounded, raced off the dark, glossy surface. Then, kneeling, she rubbed the iron on the sack lining of the hearthrug vigorously. She was warm in the ruddy firelight. Paul loved the way she crouched and put her head on one side. Her movements were light and quick. It was always a pleasure to watch her. Nothing she ever did, no movement she ever made, could have been found fault with by her children. The room was warm and full of the scent of hot linen. Later on the clergyman came and talked softly with her.

Paul was laid up with an attack of bronchitis. He did not mind much. What happened happened, and it was no good kicking against the pricks.[68] He loved the evenings, after eight o'clock, when the light was put out, and he could watch the fire-flames spring over the darkness of the walls and ceiling; could watch huge shadows waving and tossing, till the room seemed full of men who battled silently.

On retiring to bed, the father would come into the sickroom. He was always very gentle if anyone were ill. But he disturbed the atmosphere for the boy.[69]

'Are ter asleep, my darlin'? ' Morel asked softly.

'No; is my mother comin'?'

'She's just finishin' foldin' the clothes. Do you want anything?'Morel rarely 'thee'd' his son.[70]

'I don't want nothing.[71] But how long will she be? '

'Not long, my duckie.'

The father waited undecidedly on the hearthrug for a moment or two. He felt his son did not want him. Then he went to the top of the stairs and said to his wife:

'This childt's axin' for thee;[72] how long art goin' to be?'

'Until I've finished, good gracious! Tell him to go to sleep.'

'She says you're to go to sleep,' the father repeated gently to Paul.

'Well, I want *her* to come,'insisted the boy.

'He says he can't go off[73] till you come,' Morel called downstairs.

'Eh, dear! I shan't be long. And do stop shouting downstairs. There's the other children—'

Then Morel came again, and crouched before the bedroom fire.

He loved a fire dearly.

'She says she won't be long,' he said.

He loitered about indefinitely. The boy began to get feverish with irritation. His father's presence seemed to aggravate all his sick impatience. At last Morel, after having stood looking at his son awhile, said softly:

'Good-night, my darling.'

'Good-night,' Paul replied, turning round in relief to be alone.

Paul loved to sleep with his mother. Sleep is still most perfect, in spite of hygienists,[74] when it is shared with a beloved. The warmth, the security and peace of soul, the utter comfort from the touch of the other, knits the sleep,[75] so that it takes the body and soul completely in its healing. Paul lay against her and slept, and got better; whilst she, always a bad sleeper, fell later on into a profound sleep that seemed to give her faith.

In convalescence he would sit up in bed, see the fluffy horses feeding at the troughs in the field, scattering their hay on the trodden yellow snow; watch the miners troop home — small, black figures trailing slowly in gangs across the white field. Then the night came up in dark blue vapour from the snow.[76]

In convalescence everything was wonderful. The snowflakes suddenly arriving on the window-pane, clung there a moment like swallows, then were gone, and a drop of water was crawling down the glass. The snowflakes whirled round the corner of the house, like pigeons dashing by. Away across the valley the little black train crawled doubtfully over the great whiteness.

While they were so poor, the children were delighted if they could do anything to help economically. Annie and Paul and Arthur went out early in the morning, in summer, looking for mushrooms, hunting through the wet grass, from which the larks were rising, for the white-skinned, wonderful naked bodies[77] crouched secretly in the green. And if they got half a pound they felt exceedingly happy: there was the joy of finding something, the joy of accepting something straight from the hand of Nature, and the joy of contributing to the family exchequer.

But the most important harvest, after gleaning for frumenty,[78] was the blackberries. Mrs Morel must buy fruit for puddings on the Saturdays; also she liked blackberries. So Paul and Arthur scoured the coppices and woods and old quarries, so long as a blackberry was to be found, every weekend going on their search. In that region of mining villages blackberries became a comparative rarity. But Paul hunted far and wide. He loved being out in the country, among the bushes. But he also could not bear to go home to his mother empty. That, he felt, would disappoint her, and he would have died rather.

'Good gracious! ' she would exclaim as the lads came in, late, and tired to death, and hungry, 'wherever have you been?'

'Well,' replied Paul, 'there wasn't any, so we went over Misk Hills. And look here, our mother! '

She peeped into the basket.

'Now, those are fine ones! ' she exclaimed.

'And there's over two pounds — isn't there over two pounds?'

She tried the basket.

'Yes,' she answered doubtfully.

Then Paul fished out a little spray. He always brought her one spray, the best he could find.

'Pretty! ' she said, in a curious tone, of a woman accepting a lovetoken.

The boy walked all day, went miles and miles, rather than own himself beaten and come home to her empty-handed. She never realized this, whilst he was young. She was a woman who waited for her children to grow up. And William occupied her chiefly.

【作者简介】 D. H. 劳伦斯（D. H. Lawrence, 1885–1930）是当代英国文学上一位大师，著名的现代派作家的代表之一。他在创作上摒弃了英国十九世纪传统的艺术表现形式，语言质朴，句子结构简单，短小精悍，大量使用淳朴的生活语言。在小说结构上不重情节的发展，不追求故事的离奇和戏剧性的高潮，而重在对人物的精神世界作细腻的刻画，探索人与人之间的关系，精于描绘几乎无法表达的各种情绪，写出人们感情上的冲突、矛盾和极为复杂的内心世界。

劳伦斯生活于资本主义高度发展的社会中，在他看来，这个时代最突出的特征就是人们灵魂的空虚。他蔑视礼教习俗，痛恨这社会的文明传统。他认为人生来是善良的，而是资本主义的物质文明和日益发展的“机械化”使人堕落了。他笔下的主要人物几乎没有一个是真正幸福的，因为他认为文明社会中的人是不幸的，其不幸源于工业化的发展，人被机器所操纵，使人性离开了它生根的自然界而造成了人性的畸形。他对工业化文明的不满和仇恨使他力图远离社会。他曾试图与三五知己建立乌托邦式的小社会未成；他远离英国去寻求资本主义前的社会形态，他去到澳大利亚、墨西哥、美国等地，广泛观察土著居民的生活。在澳大利亚之行后他写了《袋鼠》(*Kangaroo*, 1923)，墨西哥之行后写了《带羽巨蛇》(*The Plumed Serpent*, 1926)。然而他终究无法脱离社会而生存，于是他寻求在精神上脱离社会，遁入自我，把才智用于对人的精神世界的分析，研究人与人在精神世界中的关系。

劳伦斯作品中关于两性之情的描写比较多，这是因为他认为十九世纪的英国社会是一个对人类本性的各个方面都进行压抑的社会，其中包括性压抑，是与资本主义社会财产占有本性相关的社会压抑的一部分。对劳伦斯来说，肉体之情，正如精神之情一样，是人类天性的一部分，不能回避。

劳伦斯在诗歌创作上也极有成就。他抛弃了韵体诗，也不把诗分成节，而写不受格律约束的自由体诗。对于他，诗的潜在的情感结构比诗的外形结构更重要，灵感比机械的诗规更重要。

但是劳伦斯的作品并不都是同样出色的，他对性在人生活中的作用的强调也是我们所不能同意的。

劳伦斯出生于英国诺丁汉郡一个煤矿工人的家庭里，依靠奖学金读完大学。他从一九一一年写第一部小说到一九三〇年客死法国，二十年间写了大量的长、短篇小说、诗歌、评论等，称得上是个多产作家。他的第一部作品《白孔雀》(*The White Peacock*)发表于一九一一年，次年出版了《私闯者》(*The Trespasser*)，他的著名自传式小说《儿子们和情人们》(*Sons and Lovers*)写于一九一三年。此后陆续出版了《彩虹》(*The Rainbow*, 1915)，《迷失的少女》(*The Lost Girl*, 1920)《恋爱中的女人们》(*Women in Love*, 1921)，《阿伦之杖》(*Aaron's Rod*, 1922)等。他最后的一部长篇小说是《恰特利夫人的情夫》(*Lady Chatterley's Lover*)。

【题解与注释】

《儿子们和情人们》是D. H. 劳伦斯的名著之一，取材于作者童年及青少年时代的生活，是一部自传式的小说。一九一三年首次出版，流行极广，仅一九四八年收入“企鹅丛书”后，三十年间先后印行了三十一次。

小说展现了二十世纪初英国外省中下层社会的生活场景，背景主要是一个矿工村及其周围的乡村市镇。劳伦斯以其现实主义的笔触，使读者了解到书中人物的经济地位，感受到阶级社会对人物生活的巨大影响。小说以主人公保尔·莫雷尔(Paul Morel)的家庭本身以及家庭的情感生活为中心，没有什么惊人的情节，只是描述了保尔从出生到二十五岁时的生活，或者说小说以保尔的母亲和父亲结合开始，而以母亲的凄哀逝世告终。

保尔的父亲沃特·莫雷尔(Walter Morel)是个井下采煤工，而母亲娘家的社会地位则稍高。婚后“头三个月她极其幸福，半年内她非常幸福，”但当新婚的激情稍淡的时候，她发现自己的丈夫原来只是一个平平凡凡的矿工，贪杯、粗俗；她对他开始厌恶，以至仇恨，保尔甚至从母亲的乳汁里就吮吸了对父亲的憎恶。父亲被排除在欢乐的家庭生活之外，他唯一的作用便是挣钱养家。于是他只能从酒吧间里找安慰，经常酩酊而归，乱发脾气。而母亲，当她对丈夫完全绝望之后，便把自己的一切希望寄托在大儿子、保尔的哥哥威廉身上。她坚决不让他步父亲的后尘下矿挖煤，而给他谋到了一个小职员的位置。威廉为了不辜负母亲的愿望，勤奋工作，得到赏识，最后到了伦敦。但在英国这个等级森严的社会里，一个矿工的儿子混迹于中产阶级之间是很难完全适应而不遭白眼的。他生活得并不愉快，最后年轻轻地客死异乡。威廉死了以后，母亲便又把全部的爱、全部的希望寄托在保尔身上。保尔从童年时代起便对母亲有着奇特的依恋，他的孩童的心灵被对受到生活欺凌的母亲的爱和对横蛮的父亲的恨所占据。保尔在这样一种不正常的感情状态下成长起来，走向了生活，在一家假肢厂找到了工作。他爱上了一个娇羞美丽的农家姑娘密里安。他们在精神生活上有着共同的情趣。但是母亲不能忍受密里安在精神上对保尔的占有，三个人之间发生了冲突，母爱在保尔心中占了上风。他悲伤地承认，只要母亲活着，不可能有别的女人占有他的感情。另一方面，在假肢厂所在的市镇上保尔结识了一位具有相当风情的已婚妇女克拉拉。保尔意识到他们之间只有肉体上的吸引，这种关系只可能是短暂的，而母亲也并不反对他们，因为她知道她仍独占着保尔精神上的爱。保尔处于极度矛盾痛苦之中，他感到母亲的这种爱阻碍了他自己精神上、感情上的正常成长，然而又无法摆脱这种爱的束缚。最后母亲患了癌症，在极度痛苦中极其缓慢地死去。保尔和妹妹安妮目睹母亲所受的痛苦，感到精神上无法再忍受下去，在安妮默许下，保尔在牛奶中放入过量的吗啡给母亲喝下，以结束这双方都无法忍受的局面——死亡使母亲得到肉体上的解脱，使保尔得到精神上的解脱。但是二十五年感情上的支柱一旦倾倒，保尔变成了大海中的一叶弃舟，随波逐流，哀伤、无助，心中只有对死的怀念，活着只有一个记忆：那在孩提时代极为神圣而后却毁了他的母子之情。

在劳伦斯自己的生活中就有着与保尔相同的感情经历，他之所以写《儿子们和情人们》，用他一九一三年十月二十六日一封信中的话来说，就是“人在写书时摆脱自己的病态——把自己的情感复述再现，以便能够控制它们。”（One sheds one's sicknesses in books —repeats and presents again one's emotions, to be master of them.）劳伦斯在写这本小说的时候，受着母亲对父亲偏见的影响，在感情上是厌恶父亲的，但由于他成长在这个家庭里，熟悉矿工家庭生活中的一切，加上他敏锐的观察力，现实的、栩栩如生的细节描写，因此劳伦斯笔下的矿工沃特·莫雷尔实际上是一个热情的、充满活力的、热爱劳动的人，在我们节选的部分中可以清楚地看到这一点，因而他后来的酗酒、横蛮实际上是由当时矿工艰苦生活所造成的。他的妻子不实际地希望他成为一个在精神及物质生活上都超出一般矿工的人物，这在当时阶级和社会条件下是不可能的，因而造成了妻子梦想的破灭，把希望转寄在儿子身上，逐渐把莫雷尔从家庭生活中排除出去，造成了这种家庭悲剧。劳伦斯在后来的年月中也感到他在《儿子们与情人们》中对莫雷尔是不公平的，他感到母亲是错了，而在写书时却认为母亲一切都对。他说，“要是现在提笔，我会写出一部不同的《儿子们与情人们》”。

本文节选自《儿子们和情人们》第四章“少年保尔的生活”。这一部分出色地描写了一个父母不和的家庭的气氛。父母吵架时孩子们那种忐忑的心情；父亲不在家时那短暂的平静；父亲应归而未归时家里的焦急与等待；父亲回家后孩子们对他的恐惧与仇恨…。然而父亲终究是一个善良的矿工，劳伦斯在这里描写了父子们一起劳动、创造时的喜悦；父亲给孩子们讲故事时所表现的那劳动人民的乐观和幽默；保尔生病时父亲那关切、疼爱而又不知如何表示出来的尴尬场面；种种情景读后使人久久不能平静。我们无法不钦佩劳伦斯能把如此深沉的情感变成文字，而其文字又能如此深深地激动起读者的情感这一非凡的艺术才能。同时，这段选文也能帮助我们了解劳伦斯创作的一个特色，即小说没有结构严谨的情节，没有惊险入胜的故事，他写的只是许许多多的细节，但却文如行云流水，自然地随着人物的心情象电影镜头般化出化入而不留下任何剪辑的痕迹。作者文笔极为简炼，短短几笔便是一幅如生的画面，寥寥数语便刻画出人物极其复杂的心理。下面仅举二例：

> Annie and Paul and Arthur went out early in the morning, in summer, looking for mushrooms, hunting through the wet grass, from which the larks were rising, for the white-skinned, wonderful naked bodies crouched secretly in the green.

> In that region of mining villages blackberries became a comparative rarity. But Paul hunted far and wide. He loved being out in the country, among the bushes. But he also could not bear to go home to his mother empty. That, he felt, would disappoint her, and he would have died rather.

前一段是一幅多么美妙的夏日采蘑图，而后一段又多么生动地表现出一个孩子对母亲的爱。这种描写在书中俯拾皆是，这便是《儿子们与情人们》具有引人入胜的魅力之所在。

1. the Band of Hope: 儿童禁酒协会。儿童每周来此活动一次，唱赞美诗，听故事，旨在使他们永不沾酒。

2. discoloured: 红肿变色。

3. elders: 威廉是长子，比保尔大七岁多，已经挣钱了，所以也被看作是个大人。elders 用复数，把他包括在内。

4. blood was up: 发怒。

5. "Dossn't I? ... Ha'e much more o'thy chelp, my young jockey, an' I'll rattle my fist about thee. Ay, an'I sholl that, dost see.": 保尔父亲是个未受过多少教育的矿工，因此说话用方言，有口音，且常不合语法。

Dossn't I = Don't I　**Ha'e** = have　**o'** = of

an'I = and I　**sholl** = shall

dost = do you

chelp: insolence，无礼。

my young jockey: 小仔子。

6. Will yer?: 方言，Will you?

7. the three children: 指保尔，其姐安妮及弟亚瑟。

8. you've put'em up to your own tricks and nasty ways: 你怂恿他们按你的鬼花招恶劣行径办事。

9. have a go at him: 干他一下。

10. settle him: 教训教训他让他放老实点。

11. The idea! It hasn't come to *that* yet.: 什么念头！还没到那种程度呢。

12. give it him: 教训教训他；让他尝尝厉害。

13. the Bottoms: 矿工居住区，因建在小河谷中而得此名。

14. The west wind, sweeping from Derbyshire, caught the houses with full force: 从 Derbyshire 刮过来的西风迎头袭向这些住宅。

15. a sense of blood: 杀气；血腥味。

16. the great harp: 指屋前的老梣树，句中 all the cords 指老树的枝桠，作者把老树比作竖琴，枝桠比作琴弦。风抖动树枝如拨弄琴弦。

17. a silence of blood: 孩子们猜想是不是因为父亲把母亲打伤了因而一片死寂。

18. which showed all their lives: 在他们一生中都显露出来；影响了他们的一生。

19. 第 4—6 行： 注意这一小段中状语的运用。作者用 every night, very often 和 when ... 表达了小保尔的极为复杂的心情。作者在选词上极其讲究，能微妙地传达出人物的心情。如 1201 页 14 行 "Instantly he was wide awake" 中的 instantly 和 wide 二词。试想一个孩子熟睡中被什么声音吵醒时，往往是一翻身又睡着了，但小保尔却 instantly 变得 wide awake，这样，保尔紧张、担忧、对父母的不和极度敏感的心理状态就跃然纸上了。

20. stew-jack: 炖锅支架。

21. dripping: 猪油。当时英国贫穷人家吃不起黄油就吃猪油。

22. in all his pit-dirt: 浑身都是井下沾的煤污。

23. down in the great trough of twilight: 保尔家在山坡上，他往山谷下一看。是一片满盛着暮色的低地。

24. struggled up: 用 struggled up 极好地表现出劳累了一天的矿工拖着疲惫不堪的身子爬上小山坡回家时的情景。

25. lamplighter: 点灯人。当时这一带没有电灯，街灯都是煤气灯，每天傍晚有点灯人来把街灯点燃。

26. some mile: 此处 some 意为 about，即约一英里。

27. strained the potatoes: 把泡土豆的水倒掉。

28. what ailed him: 什么事使他烦恼。

29. wha's: = what does.

30. yo': = you.

31. whoam: = home.

32. brutal manner: 吃起东西来象个牲口（塞满一嘴食物，嚼、咽声音极响，等）；吃相极坏。这一句形容 Morel 的模样，用词完全反映了保尔对父亲的厌恶心理：*mean* head; *soiled* with grey; *paltry* brows.

33. y'ead: = head.

34. tha: = thou = you.

35. doesna: = doesnot.

36. the shutting on of life: 生活的突然中断。

37. carries on: 吵闹；絮絮叨叨地抱怨个不停。

38. He had denied the God in him: 他摒弃了他的良知。此处 God 指一个人身上美好的东西。

39. pit-bottle: 装上茶水带到井下去喝的水壶。

40. iron goose: 长柄铁熨斗。

41. moleskin pit trousers: 绒面厚斜纹布做的井下工作裤。

42. cut a straw clean without hurting it: 把麦管一下子齐齐地切割而不使撕裂。

43. the white-scrubbed board: 刷洗得发白的木板桌面。

44. a pat: 一小块肥皂。

45. still fond of his father: 注意此处 still 一词，用了这个词，读者立即领会到亚瑟由于年纪尚小，尚未完全被母亲对父亲的恶感所影响左右，因而"still"——仍然——fond of his father.

46. 'oss: = horse.

47. 'im: = him.

48. fawce: false，此处意为 cunning.

49. un: = one.

50. an': = and.

51. i' th' stall wi' a rattle: in the stall with a rattle.

52. an' then yo' 'ear 'im sneeze: and then you hear him sneeze.

53. 'Ello: = hello.

54. what art sneezin' for? Bin ta'ein' some snuff?: = What are you sneezing for? Been taking some snuff?

55. slives: sidles，鬼鬼祟祟地走上来。

56. cadin': cadging，乞讨。

57. bacca: = tobacco.

58. snap-time: 井下休息吃点心的时候。

59. theer: = there.

60. I shouts: Morel 说话时多有不合语法之处，选文中很多。

61. An' I wor just in time ter get 'im by th' tail: And I was just in time to get him by the tail.

62. snied: infested，大批出没。

63. hing: hang.

64. subject to bronchitis: 容易得气管炎。

65. But it was not a family to make any fuss: 但这不是一个一点事就大惊小怪的家庭。由于家庭经济的艰难，孩子们都不是娇生惯养的，作者用这一句话表现了母亲极为实际的一面。

66. 第 25—30 行：这一段描写母亲对保尔的复杂感情的缘由在本书前面提到过。保尔母亲怀着他的时候，和莫雷尔关系已很坏，她已经不爱自己的丈夫了，因此也不想要怀着的这个孩子。但当保尔出生以后，母亲对他产生了强烈的怜爱之情，她要以自己全部的心、全部的爱来爱他，以补偿她怀着他时的冷漠。她在看着婴儿时代保尔清澈如镜的眼睛时，总感到一阵痛苦和恐惧。她觉得孩子的眼中似乎有着对她的谴责，也许当他在她身体内、躺在她心脏下面的时候，听到了她的心声？

67. made his heart contract with love: 劳伦斯在《儿子们和情人们》一书中所描写的母子情和当时开始在英国流行的奥地利心理学家弗洛伊德（Sigmund Freud, 1856-1939）的精神分析学不期而同。其中一个方面就是所谓的 Oedipus complex—恋母情绪。根据弗洛伊德的理论，儿子对母亲有特殊的依恋而对父亲很仇恨；女儿对父亲有特殊的依恋而对母亲很仇恨；如果他（她）们在成年后仍有这种感情，就会形成心理上的不正常。在我们的选文中有不少地方描写保尔对母亲的感情酷似对情人的感情，这句便是一例。其它如本段的以下数行；1210 页第 8 行开始的一整段；以及第 1211 页 20—23 行，描写保尔采黑莓时总是采一枝带花的树枝，而母亲在接受时好象在接受 a love-token —爱情纪念品。

68. kicking against the pricks: 圣经成语之一，意为对不可避免的命运作无谓的反抗。

69. But he disturbed the atmosphere for the boy: 但对孩子来说，他把整个的气氛给破坏了。

70. Morel rarely "thee'd" his son: Morel 在对儿子讲话时很少用 thee, thou 这类客气的代词。

71. I don't want nothing: 双重否定，一般受教育不多的人用。

72. This childt's axin' for thee: This child is asking for you.

73. go off: 睡着。

74. in spite of hygienists: 尽管卫生学家有不同看法（认为不应两人睡在一起）。

75. knits the sleep: 使人睡得沉，而不是时睡时醒，睡不踏实。

76. Then the night came up in dark blue vapour from the snow: 暗蓝的夜幕从雪地升起。

77. the white-skinned, wonderful naked bodies: 指蘑菇。

78. frumenty: 牛奶麦粥。此处 glean for frumenty 指去收获后的田野中拾麦粒，拿回家好煮牛奶麦粥。

53 T. S. ELIOT
1888–1965

1. The Waste Land
I. The Burial of The Dead
II. A Game of Chess
2. The Metaphysical Poets

赵萝蕤　选注

1. THE WASTE LAND

I. The Burial of the Dead

April is the cruellest month, breeding
Lilacs out of the dead land, mixing
Memory and desire, stirring
Dull roots with spring rain.
Winter kept us warm, covering
Earth in forgetful snow,[1] feeding
A little life with dried tubers.
Summer[2] surprised us, coming over the Starnbergersee,[3]
With a shower of rain; we stopped in the colonnade,[4]
And went on in sunlight, into the Hofgarten,[5]
And drank coffee, and talked for an hour.
Bin gar keine Russin, stamm' aus Litauen, echt deutsch.[6]
And when we were children, staying at the archduke's,
My cousin's, he took me out on a sled,
And I was frightened. He said, Marie,
Marie, hold on tight. And down we went.

In the mountains, there you feel free.
I read, much of the night, and go south in the winter.

What are the roots that clutch, what branches grow[7]
Out of this stony rubbish? Son of man,[8]
You cannot say, or guess, for you know only
A heap of broken images,[9] where the sun beats,
And the dead tree gives no shelter, the cricket no relief,[10]
And the dry stone no sound of water. Only
There is shadow under this red rock,[11]
(Come in under the shadow of this red rock),
And I will show you something different from either
Your shadow at morning striding behind you
Or your shadow at evening rising to meet you;
I will show you fear in a handful of dust.
Frisch weht der Wind[12]
Der Heimat zu
Mein Irisch Kind,
Wo weilest du?
"'You gave me hyacinths[13] first a year ago;
"They called me the hyacinth girl."'
—Yet when we came back, late, from the hyacinth garden,
Your arms full, and your hair wet, I could not
Speak, and my eyes failed,[14] I was neitber
Living nor dead, and I knew nothing,
Looking into the heart of light, the silence.[15]
Oed' und leer das Meer.[16]

Madame Sosostris, famous clairvoyante,[17]
Had a bad cold, nevertheless
Is known to be the wisest woman in Europe,
With a wicked pack of cards.[18] Here, said she,
Is your card, the drowned Phceniciau Sailor,[19]

(Those are pearls that were his eyes. Look!)[20]
Here is Belladonna,[21] the Lady of the Rocks,
The lady of situations.[22]
Here is the man with three staves, and here the Wheel,[23]
And here is the one-eyed merchant.[24] and this card,
Which is blank,[25] is something he carries on his back,
Which I am forbidden to see. I do not find
The Hanged Man.[26] Fear death by water.
I see crowds of people,[27] walking round in a ring.[28]
Thank you. If you see dear Mrs. Equitone,[29]
Tell her I bring the horoscope myself:
One must be so careful these days.

Unreal City,[30]
Under the brown fog of a winter dawn,
A crowd flowed over London Bridge, so many,
I had not thought death had undone so many.[31]
Sighs, short and infrequent, were exhaled,[32]
And each man fixed his eyes before his feet.
Flowed up the hill and down King William Street,
To where Saint Mary Woolnoth[33] kept the hours[34]
With a dead sound on the final stroke of nine.[35]
There I saw one I knew, and stopped him, crying: "Stetson![36]
"You who were with me in the ships at Mylae![37]
"That corpse you planted last year in your garden,[38]
"Has it begun to sprout? Will it bloom this year?
"Or has the sudden frost disturbed its bed?
"O keep the Dog far hence, that's friend to men,[39]
"Or with his nails he'll dig it up again!
"You! hypocrite lecteur! — mon semblable, — mon frère!"[40]

II. A Game of Chess

The Chair she sat in, like a burnished throne,[41]

Glowed on the marble, where the glass
Held up by standards[42] wrought with fruited vines
From which a golden Cupidon[43] peeped out
(Another hid his eyes behind his wing)
Doubled the flames of sevenbranched candelabra
Reflecting light upon the table as
The glitter of her jewels rose to meet it,
From satin cases poured in rich profusion.
In vials of ivory and coloured glass
Unstoppered, lurked her strange synthetic perfumes,[44]
Unguent, powdered, or liquid[45]—troubled, confused
And drowned the sense in odours; stirred by the air
That freshened from the window,[46] these ascended
In fattening the prolonged candle-flames,[47]
Flung their smoke into the laquearia,[48]
Stirring the pattern on the coffered ceiling.
Huge sea-wood fed with copper[49]
Burned green and orange,[50] framed by the coloured stone,
In which sad light a carvèd dolphin swam.
Above the antique mantel was displayed
As though a window gave upon[51] the sylvan scene[52]
The change of Philomel,[53] by the barbarous king
So rudely forced;[54] yet there the nightingale
Filled all the desert with inviolable voice[55]
And still she cried, and still the world pursues,
"Jug Jug"[56] to dirty ears.
And other withered stumps of time[57]
Were told upon the walls; staring forms
Leaned out, leaning, hushing the room enclosed.[58]
Footsteps shuffled on the stair.
Under the firelight, under the brush, her hair
Spread out in fiery points
Glowed into words,[59] then would be savagely still.

"My nerves are bad to-night. Yes, bad. Stay with me.
"Speak to me, Why do you never speak. Speak.
"What are you thinking of? What thinking? What?
"I never know what you are thinking. Think."

I think we are in rats' alley
Where the dead men lost their bones.

"What is that noise?"
The wind under the door.[60]
"What is that noise now? What is the wind doing?"
Nothing again nothing.
"Do
You know nothing? Do you see nothing? Do you remember Nothing?"

I remember
Those are pearls that were his eyes.
"Are you alive, or not? Is there nothing in your head?"[61]
But
O O O O that Shakespeherian Rag— [62]
It's so elegant
So intelligent
"What shall I do now? What shall I do?"
"I shall rush out as I am, and walk the street
"With my hair down, so. What shall we do to-morrow?
"What shall we ever do?"
The hot water at ten.[63]
And if it rains, a closed car at four.
And we shall play a game of chess,[64]
Pressing lidless eyes[65] and waiting for a knock upon the door.

When Lil's husband got demobbed,[66] I said—

I didn't mince my words, I said to her myself,
HURRY UP PLEASE ITS TIME[67]
Now Albert's coming back, make yourself a bit smart.
He'll want to know what you done with that money he gave you
To get yourself some teeth. He did, I was there.
You have them all out, Lil, and get a nice set,
He said, I swear, I can't bear to look at you.
And no more can't I, I said, and think of poor Albert,
He's been in the army four years, he wants a good time,
And if you don't give it him, there's others will, I said.
Oh is there, she said. Something o' that, I said.
Then I'll know who to thank, she said, and give me a straight look.[68]
HURRY UP PLEASE ITS TIME
If you don't like it you can get on with it,[69] I said.
Others can pick and choose if you can't.
But if Albert makes off, it won't be for lack of telling.
You ought to be ashamed, I said, to look so antique.
(And her only thirty-one.)
I can't help it, she said, pulling a long face,
It's them pills I took, to bring it off,[70] she said.
(She's had five already, and nearly died of young George.)
The chemist[71] said it would be all right, but I've never been the same.
You *are* a proper fool, I said.
Well, if Albert won't leave you alone, there it is, I said,
What you get married for if you don't want children?
HURRY UP PLEASE ITS TIME
Well, that Sunday Albert was home, they had a hot gammon,[72]
And they asked me in to dinner, to get the beauty of it hot—
HURRY UP PLEASE ITS TIME
HURRY UP PLEASE ITS TIME

Goonight Bill. Goonight Lou. Goonight May. Goonight.
Ta ta. Goonight, Goonight.
Good night, ladies, good night, sweet ladies, good night, good
night.[73]

2. The Metaphysical Poets[1]

By collecting these poems[2] from the work of a generation more often named than read, and more often read than profitably studied[3], Professor Grierson[4] has rendered a service of some importance. Certainly the reader will meet with many poems already preserved in other anthologies, at the same time that he discovers poems such as those of Aurelian Townshend[5] or Lord Herbert of Cheroury[6] here included. But the function of such an anthology as this is neither that of Professor Saintsbury's admirable edition of Caroline poets[7] nor that of the *Oxford Book of English Verse.*[8] Mr. Grierson's book is in itself a piece of criticism and a provocation of criticism;[9] and we think that he was right in including so many poems of Donne,[10] elsewhere (though not in many editions) accessible, as documents[11] in the case of 'metaphysical poetry.' The phrase has long done duty[12] as a term of abuse[13] or as the label of a quaint and pleasant taste. The question is to what extent the so-called metaphysicals formed a school (in our own time we should say a'movement'), and how far this so-called school or movement is a digression from the main current.[14]

Not only is it extremely difficult to define metaphysical poetry, but difflcult to decide what poets practise it and in which of their verses. The poetry of Donne (to whom Marvell[15] and Bishop King[16] are sometimes nearer than any of the other authors) is late Elizabethan, its feeling often very close to that of Chapman.[17] The'courtly' poetry[18] is derivative from[19] Jonson,[20] who borrowed liberally from the Latin;[21] it expires in the next century with the sentiment and witticism of Prior.[22] There is finally the devotional verse[23] of Herbert,[24] Vaughan,[25] and Crashaw[26] (echoed long after by Christina Rossetti[27] and Francis Thompson[28]); Crashaw, sometimes more profound and less sectarian than the others, has a quality which returns through the Elizabethan period to the early Italians. It is difficult to find any precise use of metaphor, simile, or other conceit, which is common to all the poets and at the same time important enough as an element of style to isolate these poets as a group. Donne, and often Cowley,[29] employ a device, which is sometimes considered characteristically 'metaphysical'; the elaboration (contrasted with the condensation) of a figure of speech[30] to the farthest stage to which ingenuity can carry it.[31] Thus Cowley develops the commonplace comparison of the world to a chessboard through long stanzas[32] *(To Destiny)*, and Donne, with more grace, in *A Valediction,*[33] the comparison of two lovers to a pair of compasses. But elsewhere we find, instead of the mere explication of the content of a comparison, a development by rapid association of thought[34] which requires considerable agility[35] on the part of the reader.

On a round ball
A workman that hath copies by, can lay
An Europe, Afrique, and an Asia,
And quickly make that, which was nothing, all;[36]
So doth each tear,
Which thee doth wear,
A globe, yea, world, by that impression grow,[37]
Till thy tears mixed with mine do overflow
This world; by waters sent from thee, my heaven dissolvèd so[38]

Here we find at least two connections which are not implicit in the first figure, but are forced upon it by the poet: from the geographer's globe to the tear, and the tear to the deluge.

On the other hand, some of Donne's most successful and characteristic effects are secured by brief words and sudden contrasts:

A bracelet of bright hair about the bone,[39]

where the most powerful effect is produced by the sudden contrast of associations of 'bright hair' and of 'bone.' This telescoping of images[40] and multiplied associations is characteristic of the phrase of some of the dramatists of the period which Donne knew: not to mention Shakespeare, it is frequent in Middleton,[41] Webster,[42] and Tourneur,[43] and is one of the sources of the vitality of their language.[44]

Johnson,[45] who employed the term 'metaphisical poets,'apparently having Donne, Cleveland,[46] and Cowley chiefly in mind, remarks of them that 'the most heterogeneous ideas are yoked by violence together.'[47] The force of this impeachment lies in the failure of the conjunction, the fact that often the ideas are yoked but not united;[48] and if we are to judge of styles of poetry by their abuse, enough examples may be found in Cleveland to justify Johnson's condemnation. But a degree of heterogeneity of material compelled into unity[49] by the operation of the poet's mind is omnipresent in poetry. We need not select for illustration such a line as:

Notre âme est un trois-mâts cherchant son Icarie;[50]

we may find it in some of the best lines of Johnson himself *(The Vanity of Humam Wishes):*

His fate was destined to a barren strand,
A petty fortress, and a dubious hand;[51]
He left a name at which the world grew pale,
To point a moral, or adorn a tale.[52]

where the effect is due to a contrast of ideas, different in degree but the same in principle, as that which Johnson mildly reprehended. And in one of the finest poems of the age (a poem which could not have been written in any other age),the *Exequy*[53] of

Bishop King, the extended comparison is used with perfect success: the idea and the simile beeome one, in the passage in which the Bishop illustrates his impatience to see his dead wife, under the figure of a journey:

Stay for me there;[54] I will not fail
To meet thee in that hollow Vale.[55]
And think not much of my delay;[56]
I am already on the way,
And follow thee with all the speed
Desire can make, or sorrows breed.
Each minute is a short degree,[57]
And ev'ry hour a step towards thee.
At night when I betake to rest,[58]
Next morn I rise nearer my West[59]
Of life, almost by eight hours sail,
Then when sleep breathed his drowsy gale [60]
But hark! My pulse, like a soft drum
Beats my approach, tells Thee I come;
And slow howe'er my marches be,
I shall at last sit down by Thee.

(In the last few lines there is that effect of terror which is several times attained by one of Bishop King's admirers, Edgar Poe.[61]) Again, we may justly take these quatrains from Lord Herbert's Ode,[62] stanzas which would, we think, be immediately pronounced to be of the metaphysical school:

So when from hence we shall be gone,
    And be no more, nor you, nor I,
    As one another's mystery,
Each shall be both, yet both but one,[63]

This said, in her uplifted face,
    Her eyes, which did that beauty[64] crown,
    Were like two stars, that having faln down,

Look up again to find their place:

While such a moveless[65] silent peace
Did seize on their becalmèd sense,[66]
One would have thought some influence
Their ravished spirits did possess.[67]

There is nothing in these lines (with the possible exception of the stars, a simile not at once grasped, but lovely and justified) which fits Johnson's general observations on the metaphysical poets in his essay on Cowley. A good deal resides in the richness of association which is at the same time borrowed from and given to the word 'becalmed'; but the meaning is clear, the language simple and elegant. It is to be observed that the language of these poets is as a rule simple and pure; in the verse of George Herbert this simplicity is carried as far as it can go — a simplicity emulated without success by numerous modern poets. The *structure* of the sentences, on the other hand, is sometimes far from simple, but this is not a vice; it is a fidelity to thought and feeling.[68] The effect, at its best, is far less artificial than that of an ode by Gray.[69] And as this fidelity induces variety of thought and feeling, so it induces variety of music. We doubt whether, in the eighteenth century, could be found two poems in nominally the same metre, so dissimilar as Marvell's *Coy Mistress* and Crashaw's *Saint Teresa*;[70] the one producing an effect of great speed by the use of short syllables, and the other an ecclesiastical solemnity by the use of long ones:

Love, thou art absolute sole lord
Of life and death.

If so shrewd and sensitive (though so limited) a critic as Johnson failed to define metaphysical poetry by its faults, it is worth while to inquire whether we may not have more success by adopting the opposite method: by assuming that the poets of the seventeenth century (up to the Revolution[71]) were the direct and normal development of the precedent age; and, without prejudicing their case by the adjective 'metaphysical,' consider whether their virtue was not something permanently valuable, which subsequently disappeared, but ought not to have disappeared. Johnson has hit, perhaps by accident, on one of their peculiarities, when he observes that 'their attempts were always analytic'; he would not agree that, after the dissociation, they put the material together again in a new unity.

It is certain that the dramatic verse of the later Elizabethan and early Jacobean poets[72] expresses a degree of development of sensibility which is not found in any of the prose, good as it often is. If we except Marlowe,[73] a man of prodigious intelligence, these dramatists were directly or indirectly (it is at least a tenable theory[74]) affected by Montaigne.[75] Even if we except also Jonson and Chapman, these two were probably erudite, and were notably men who incorporated their erudition into their sensibility: their mode of feeling was directly and freshly altered by their reading and thought. In Chapman especially there is a direct sensuous apprehension of thought, or a recreation of thought[76] into feeling, which is exactly what we find in Donne:

in this one thing, all the discipline[77]
Of manners and of manhood is contained;
A man to join himself with th' Universe
In his main sway, and make in all things fit
One with that All,[78] and go on, round as it;
Not plucking from the whole his wretched part,
And into straits, or into nought revert,
Wishing the complete Universe might be
Subject to such a rag of it as he;
But to consider great Necessity.

We compare this with some modern passage:

No, when the fight begins within himself,[79]
A man's worth something. God stoops o'er his head,
Satan looks up between his feet — both tug —
He's left, himself, i' the middle; the soul wakes
And grows. Prolong that battle through his life!

It is perhaps somewhat less fair, though very tempting (as both poets are concerned with the perpetuation of love by offspring), to compare with the stanzas already quoted from Lord Herbert's Ode the following from Tennyson:[80]

One walked between his wife and child,
With measured footfall firm and mild,
And now and then he gravely smiled.
    The prudent partner of his blood
    Leaned on him, faithful, gentle, good,
    Wearing the rose of womanhood.
And in their double love secure,
The little maiden walked demure,
Pacing with downward eyelids pure.
    These three made unity so sweet,
    My frozen heart began to beat,
    Remembering its ancient heat.

The difference is not a simple difference of degree between poets. It is something which had happened to the mind of England between the time of Donne or Lord Herbert of Cherbury and the time of Tennyson and Browning; it is the difference between the intellectual poet and the reflective poet.[81] Tennyson and Browning are poets, and they think; but they do not feel their thought as immediately as the odor of a rose. A thought to Donne was an experience; it modified his sensibility. When a poet's mind is perfectly equipped for its work, it is constantly amalgamating disparate experience; the ordinary man's experience is chaotic, irregular, fragmentary. The latter falls in love, or reads Spinoza,[82] and these two experiences have nothing to do with each other, or with the noise of the typewriter or the smell of cooking; in the mind of the poet these experiences are always forming new wholes.

We may express the difference by the following theory: The poets of the seventeenth century, the successors of the dramatists of the sixteenth, possessed a mechanism of sensibility which could devour any kind of experience. They are simple, artificial, difficult, or fantastic, as their predecessors were; no less nor more than Dante,[83] Guido Cavalcanti,[84] Guinicelli,[85] or Cino.[86] In the seventeenth century a dissociation of sensibility set in, from which we have never recovered; and this dissociation, as is natural, was aggravated by the influence of the two most powerful poets of the century, Milton[87] and Dryden.[88] Each of these men performed certain poetic functions so magnificently well that the magnitude of the effect concealed the absence of others. The language went on and in some respects improved; the best verse of Collins,[89] Gray, Johnson, and even Goldsmith[90] satisfies some of our fastidious demands better than that of Donne or Marvell or King. But while the language became more refined, the feeling became more crude. The feeling, the sensibility, expressed in the *Country Churchyard* (to say nothing of Tennyson and Browning) is cruder than that in the *Coy Mistress*.

The second effect of the influence of Milton and Dryden followed from the first, and was therefore slow in manifestation. The sentimental age began early in the eighteenth century, and continued. The poets revolted against the ratiocinative,[91] the descriptive; they thought and felt by fits, unbalanced; they reflected. In one or two passages of Shelley's[92] *Triumph of Life*, in the second *Hyperion*,[93] there are traces of a struggle toward unification of sensibility. But Keats and Shelley died, and Tennyson and Browning ruminated.

After this brief exposition of a theory — too brief, perhaps, to carry conviction — we may ask, what would have been the fate of the 'metaphysical' had the current of poetry descended in a direct line from them, as it descended in a direct line to them? They would not, certainly, be classified as metaphysical. The possible interests of a poet are unlimited; the more intelligent he is the better; the more intelligent he is the more likely that he will have interests: our only condition is that he turn them into poetry, and not merely meditate on them poetically.[94] A philosophical theory which has entered into poetry is established, for its truth or falsity in one sense ceases to matter, and its truth in another sense is proved.[95] The poets in question have, like other poets, various faults. But they were, at best, engaged in the task of trying to find the verbal equivalent for states of mind and feeling. And this means both that they are more mature, and that they wear better, than later poets of certainly not less literary ability.

It is not a permanent necessity that poets should be interested in philosophy, or in any other subject. We can only say that it appears likely that poets in our civilization, as it exists at present, must be *difficult*. Our civilization comprehends great variety and complexity, and this variety and complexity, playing upon a refined sensibility,[96] must produce various and complex results. The poet must become more and more comprehensive, more allusive,[97] more indirect, in order to force, to dislocate if necessary, language into his meaning.[98] (A brilliant and extreme statement of this view, with which it is not requisite to associate oneself,[99] is that of M. Jean Epstein, *La Poésie d'aujourd'hui.*[100]) Hence we get something which looks very much like the conceit — we get, in fact, a method curiously similar to that of the 'metaphysical poets,' similar also in its use of obscure words and of simple phrasing.

> O géraniums diaphanes, guerroyeurs sortilèges,[101]
> Sacrilèges monomanes!
> Emballages, dévergondages, douches! O pressoirs

Des vendanges des grands soirs!
Layettes aux abois,
Thyrses au fond des bois!
Transfusions, représailles,
Relevailles, compresses et l'éternal potion,
Angélus! n'en pouvoir plus
De débâcles nuptiales! de débâcles nuptiales!

The same poet could write also simply;

Elle est bien loin, elle pleure,
Le grand vent se lamente aussi...[102]

Jules Laforgue, and Tristan Corbière[103] in many of his poems, are nearer to the 'school of Donne' than any modern English poet. But poets more classical than they have the same essential quality of transmuting ideas into sensations, of transforming an observation into a state of mind.[104]

Pour l'enfant, amoureux de cartes et d'estampes,
L'univers est égal à son vaste appétit.
Ah, que le monde est grand à la clarté des lampes!
Aux yeux du souvenir que le monde est petit![105]

In French literature the great master of the seventeenth century — Racine[106] — and the great master of the nineteenth — Baudelaire — are in some ways more like each other than they are like any one else. The greatest two masters of diction are also the greatest two psychologists, the most curious explorers of the soul. It is interesting to speculate whether it is not a misfortune that two of the greatest masters of diction in our language, Milton and Dryden, triumph with a dazzling disregard of the soul. If we continued to produce Miltons and Drydens it might not so much matter, but as things are it is a pity that English poetry has remained so incomplete. Those who object to the 'artificiality' of Milton or Dryden sometimes tell us to 'look into our hearts and write.' But that is not looking deep enough; Racine or Donne looked into a good deal more than the heart. One must look into the cerebral cortex, the nervous system, and the digestive tracts.

May we not conclude, then, that Donne, Crashaw, Vaughan, Herbert and Lord Herbert, Marvell, King, Cowley at his best, are in the direct current of English poetry,[107] and that their faults should be reprimanded by this standard rather than coddled by antiquarian affection?[108] They have been enough praised in terms which are implicit limitations[109] because they are 'metaphysical' or 'witty,' 'quaint' or 'obscure,' though at their best they have not these attributes[110] more than other serious poets. On the other hand, we must not reject the criticism of Johnson (a dangerous person to disagree with) without having mastered it, without having assimilated the Johnsonian canons of taste.[111] In reading the celebrated passage in his essay on Cowley we must remember that by wit he clearly means something more serious than we usually mean today; in his criticism of their versification[112] we must remember in what a narrow discipline he was trained, but also how well trained; we must remember that Johnson tortures[113] chiefly the chief offenders, Cowley and Cleveland. It would be a fruitful work, and one requiring a substantial[114] book, to break up the classification[115] of Johnson (for there has been none since) and exhibit these poets in all their difference of kind and of degree, from the massive music of Donne to the faint, pleasing tinkle of Aurelian Townshend — whose *Dialogue Between a Pilgrim and Time*[116] is one of the few regrettable omissions[117] from the excellent anthology of Professor Grierson.

【作者简介】 西方现代派文学大师艾略特（T. S. Eliot, 1888–1965）生于美国密苏里州圣路易，祖先是十七世纪中从英国移居美国的。他父亲虽是商人，但先人亲属中多著名学者和文人，在当时的美国就算是望族世家了。他在哈佛大学学哲学，1910 年在巴黎大学学文学哲学，又曾在德国和英国牛津就学。第一次世界大战期间他在英国。这时他已开始刊出诗歌，但是一直到 1922 年发表了《荒原》他才称雄英国诗坛。1927 年他入了英国籍，1948 年国王向他授勋，同年获得诺贝尔奖金。艾略特不仅是他那一代的、在西方几乎居于首位的诗人，也是个极有威望、多有创见的评论家和剧作家。他的主要文章有《传统和个人才能》(*Tradition and the Individual Talent*, 1917)，《批评的功能》(*The Function of Criticism*, 1923)，《玄学派诗人》(*The Metaphysical Poets*, 1921) 等；主要剧本有《大教堂内的凶杀案》(*Murder in the Cathedral*, 1935)，《合家重聚》(*The Family Reunion*, 1939)，《鸡尾酒会》(*The Cocktail Party*, 1950) 等，剧中有时有合唱队，基本用诗体。作为诗人，他早期名著有《J. 阿尔弗雷德·普鲁福劳克的情歌》(*The Love Song Of J. Alfred Prufrock*, 1917)，《一位夫人的写照》(*Portrait of a Lady*, 1917)，《老人》(*Gerontion*, 1920)，《空心人》(*The Hollow Men*, 1925)，《圣灰星期三》(*Ash Wednesday*, 1930) 和稍晚的《四个四重奏》(*Four Quartets*, 1943)。在 1926 年写的一篇文章中，艾略特声称他“在宗教上是英国国教式的天主教徒，在政治上是保皇派，在文学上是古典主义者，”说明他在思想上起码是保守的。

【题解与注释】

1. *THE WASTE LAND*

《荒原》(*The Waste Land*) 不论是内容或形式，都是一首划时代的极有影响的长诗，原长约一千行，经作者的好友美国诗人埃士勒·庞德 (Ezra Pound, 1885–1972) 删订，成为目前精炼的 433 行。作者将此诗献给了庞德，并称他为“最卓越的匠人”，着力称颂他写诗的功力和鉴别能力。这是一首不可能完全解释清楚、并非处处有明确含义的长诗。艾略特认为当代诗歌之晦涩难解是不可避免的，因为当今社会和个人生活十分复杂多变，不可捉摸。他还认为文学传统对诗人有极大影响；诗人的博学多才制约了他的创作方法；诗人的创作决非只是他个人的生活经历。在这首诗中，作者至少引用了三十五种不同作家的作品（特别是但丁）和流行歌曲，引入了六种外国语，包括梵文。但是他把这些看来毫不相干的引语和自己的创作锤炼成了一体，都为他的主题服务，而且大大丰富了主题。

《荒原》尖刻暴露、描写了第一次世界大战后西方社会生活的极度荒唐、贫乏、枯涩，没有希望。全诗共五节：死者葬仪，对弈，火诫，水里的死亡，雷霆的话；这里选用的是第一、二两节。在荒芜的欧洲，特别象伦敦这样的城市，没有春天，没有甘霖。四月本应是大地复苏，春天的开始，却被作者写成是最残忍的一个月，冬天反倒温暖。这是一个很突兀的开始，极写时代的绝望情绪：四月只是引起令人不快的回忆和欲望，冬天却使人们沉湎于遗忘。接着诗体突然转变，由缓慢变成快速。诗人用十多行口语化的诗句描写了中欧（慕尼黑）生活的一个短小片段（8—18 行），反映了轻浮、贫乏的上流社会生活。接着作者又改变了诗体（起势有点象抑扬格五音步无韵体），点出了诗的主题，“焦石间没有流水的声音”（24行）。为了使大地繁殖，需要水，但水也不是完全友善的，因为水里有死亡（55行）。诗中多次描写了两性关系，其基调是丑恶的，情欲的，是不利于大地回春的。可以设想，正常而美满的两性关系应该会给荒原带来生机和繁荣——但这是这首诗里所找不到的。马丹梭梭屈里士（Madame Sosostris）是个骗人的女相士，她手里拿着和圣杯传说有关的太洛纸牌（详细见注释）：如有持剑的英雄能找到圣杯就能使荒原恢复生命力，可惜这里没有英雄，只有死在水中的腓尼基水手和士麦拿商人；象征繁殖力的渔王，耶稣和带着三根杖的人（见46行注），也死的死了，病的病了，女相士手中欧洲大陆的命运是十分不堪的。第一节的结尾描写了当代伦敦。评论家指出艾略特的描写伦敦可以和法国诗人波得莱尔（Baudelaire）的描写巴黎比美，作者也确实想到了巴黎（见60行注）。不仅伦敦与巴黎，欧洲的许多曾有光荣传统的城市也正在崩溃（见第五节373—376行）：“倾塌着的城楼/耶路撒冷雅典亚历山大/维也纳伦敦/并无实体的”（Falling Towers/Jerusalem Athens Alexandria/Vienna London/Unreal）。

第二节“对弈”主要包括两个情节，写庸俗的、充满灾难的两性关系（上流社会和贫民中间的）。这一节一开始诗句壮丽，作者回顾了莎翁名剧中的埃及女王克莉奥佩特拉的仪态万方、雍容华贵，后来又暗示了象狄多那样的史诗中人物，但是“瓶里暗藏着她那些奇异的合成香料”（86行）这样的句子点出了这个女人只是当代一个上流社会、骄奢淫逸、精神颓唐的妇女。同一节诗里又有小酒馆里两个下层伦敦市民——丽儿和她的同伴的对话。作者在诗中引用的典故始终起着突出今昔异同和对比的作用。第三节火诫也用同样的手法描写泰晤士河畔的今昔，伦敦各种人物的猥琐生活。这节诗里用了火的形象。火是情欲之火，这是伦敦生活的主题，但火也能锻炼人，使复归纯真。第四节短短十行写水里的死亡——一个曾经是高大漂亮的腓尼基人，如今淹死在水里。第五节，也是最后一节写欧洲是一片荒原，没有水。作者还以否定的态度描写了东欧和俄罗斯的革命浪潮。最后雷霆的声音表达了吠陀经里的说教，规劝人要施舍，同情，克制，才能得到平安。

这里还应注意的是这首诗里诗体的多样和丰富多采。艾略特在这里极少用韵，多用口语形式，但又和自由体不同，在不规则中有规则，在没有固定节奏中有节奏，给人的印象不是舒展、粗犷、自由而是极其严谨、极其丰满、极有分寸。在《荒原》一诗中，诗体形式很多：有时间的徐疾，有诗句的长短，停顿的妥贴安排等。作者也利用了各种类型的辞藻，有土语，有十分口语化或比较抒情的片段，有讽刺的片段，等，都生动反映了不同性质的内容。

这首诗不仅题目，甚至它的规划和有时采用的象征手法也绝大部分受了魏士登女士（Miss Jessie L. Weston）有关圣杯传说（the Grail Legend）一书的启发：该书即《从祭仪到传奇》（From Ritual to Romance）（剑桥版）。确实，我从中得益甚深。它比我的注释更能解答这首诗中的难点。谁认为这首诗还值得一解的话，我就向他推荐这本书（何况它本身也是饶有兴趣的）。大体说来，我还得益于另一本人类学著作，这本书曾深刻影响了我们这一代人；我说的就是《金枝》（The Golden Bough）. 我特别利用了阿多尼士，阿帖士，欧西利士（Adonis, Attis, Osiris）这两卷。熟悉这些著作的人会立刻在这首诗里看出有些地方还涉及到有关繁殖的礼节。

I. The Burial of the Dead 死者葬仪

1. [**forgetful snow:** 助人遗忘的雪，和 3 行 memory and desire，回忆和欲望适成对比。] *

2. 第 8—18 行：[这段情节摘自 1913 年版玛丽·拉里希伯爵夫人（Countess Marie Larisch）的回忆录《我的过去》（*My Past*），反映了上流社会生活的空虚、无聊。]

3. [**Starnbergersee:** 斯丹卜基西是慕尼黑附近一湖，是一游乐之地，艾略特用它来代表欧洲中部的现代荒原。]

4. [**colonnade:** 柱廊。]

5. [**Hofgarten:** 按词义应为'御花园'，是慕尼黑的一个公园。]

6. 第 12 行：[这是伯爵夫人在慕尼黑遇到艾略特时说的话：I'm not Russian at all, I come from Lithuania, a pure German，我不是俄国人，我是从立陶宛来的，是个地道的德国人。]

7. 第 19—30 行：[这是荒原的景象。头两行的辞藻近似旧约约伯记第八章第十七节：他们的根盘绕石堆，扎入石地（His roots here wrapped about the heap, and seeth the place of stones.）。]

8. 第 20 行：参阅以西结书第二章第一节。[旧约圣经以西结书上说，"他对我说：'人子啊，你站起来，我要和你说话。'"（On he said unto me, Son of man, stand upon thy feet, and I will speak with thee.）在这里，上帝要以西结宣讲弥赛亚（救世主）的到来。]

9. [**a heap of broken images:** 一堆破碎的偶像，见以西结书六章六节："在你们一切的住处，城邑要变为荒场，丘坛必然凄凉，使你们的祭坛荒废，将你们的偶像打碎，你们的日像被砍倒，你们的工作被毁灭"（In all your dwelling places the cities shall be laid waste, and the high places shall be desolate; that your altars may be laid waste and made desolate, and your idols may be broken and cease and your images may be cut down, and your works may be abolished.）。]

10. 第 23 行：参阅传道书第十二章第五节。[旧约传道书上说："人怕高处，路上有惊慌，杏树开花，蚱蜢成为重担，人所愿的也都废掉，因为人归他永远的家，吊丧的在街上往来"（Also when they shall be afraid of that which is high, and fears shall be in the way, and the almond tree shall flourish, and the grass-hopper shall be a burden, and desire shall fail: because man goeth to his long home, and the mourners go about the streets:）。]

11. 第 25 行：[可参阅旧约以赛亚书第三十二章第二节："必有一人象避风所，和暴风雨的隐密处，又象河流在干旱之地，象大磐石的影子在疲乏之地"（And a man

---

* 原注：方括弧外的是作者原注，括弧以内的是选注者注。下同。

shall be as an hiding place from the wind, and a covert from the tempest; as rivers of water in a dry place, as the shadow of a great rock in a weary land.)。]

12. 第 31—34 行：见“特利斯坦和绮索尔德”（Tristan und Isolde）第一幕五至八行。[在伐格纳（Richard Wagner）这一歌剧中，第一幕第一景写特利斯坦和绮索尔德乘船离开爱尔兰到康沃尔去。这短短四行是一个水手唱的情歌，唱的是幸福和纯朴的爱情：]

Fresh blows the wind
To the Homeland,
My Irish child,
Where do you wait?
风吹着很轻快，
吹送我回家园，
爱尔兰的小孩，
你在哪里等待？

特利斯坦这时候已把绮索尔德的未婚夫杀害，自己也受了伤。绮索尔德正要复仇，见特利斯坦已受伤，便不忍下手。特利斯坦伤愈后，带着绮索尔德去康沃尔，打算把她献给马克王为后。此时他们还未尝到‘爱的迷魂药’，胸怀是清净的。

13. 第 35—38 行：[**hyacinth**：风信子。这里可参阅艾略特的一首法语诗《在饭馆内》（Dans le Restaurant, In the Restaurant）：

I'avais sept ans, elle était plus petite,
    Elle était toute mouilée, je lui ai donne des prsmevères,
I was seven years old, she was younger,
    She was all wet, I gave her cowlips.
我那时七岁，她比我还要小，
她全身都湿了，我给了她莲馨花。

风信子和莲馨花都象征爱情、复苏和春天。但是好景不长，饭馆的侍者终于成为一个失意的老人，和淹死在水里的腓尼基人联系在一起。]

14. [**my eyes failed:** 我的眼睛看不见。]

15. [**Looking into the heart of light, the silence:** 望着光亮的中心看时，是一片寂静。]

16. 第 42 行：见“特利斯坦和绮索尔德”第三幕，第二十四行。[后来特利斯坦和绮索尔德都尝了迷魂药，热烈地相爱。他们受到了严厉的惩罚，特利斯坦并受了重创，凄惶地回到老家去。他裹着伤等候绮索尔德的到来。地方上的牧羊人代他瞭望，但是他的回答是：“荒凉而空虚是那大海”（Od' und leer das Meer: Waste and empty the sea.）。]

17. 第 43 行：[女相士的名字出自赫胥黎（Aldous Huxley）的小说《铬黄》（*Chrome Yellow*, 1921）。clairvoyante 即女相士。]

18. 第 46 行：我并不熟悉太洛纸牌（Tarot pack of cards）的确切组成，只是用来适应我自己的方便。按照传统，这套纸牌中的成员之一是‘那被绞死的人’，他在两方面适应我的目的：在我思想中，他和福来泽［《金枝》的作者 James George Frazer］的‘被绞死的神’联系在一起，又和第五节中众使徒到埃摩司去的路上遇到的那个戴斗篷的人［即复活后的耶稣］联系在一起。腓尼基水手和商人出现较晚；“成群的人”和“水里的死亡”则见于第四节。“带着三根杖的人”（是太洛纸牌中的有确切根据的一员）我也相当武断地把他和渔王（Fisher King）本人联系起来。［这里有必要把《从祭仪到传奇》一书的有关部分概述如下：

（一）传说地方上的王，即渔王，患了病（或说他已年老，受了伤，等等）。由于他的患病与衰老，原为肥沃之地成了荒原。这时就需要一位少年英雄历尽艰险，携一把利剑寻找圣杯（the Holy Grail），以便医治渔王，使大地复苏。

（二）荒原在于没有温暖，没有太阳，最主要的是没有水。这种祭祀在纪元前三千多年的《吠陀经》（the Rig-Veda）里已经有所记载：就是求英居拉神（Indra）释放七条大水，使土地肥美。另一个印度故事说一个年轻的婆罗门隐居山林。邻国忽逢旱灾，缺乏粮食。国王在占卜之后得知只要年轻的婆罗门一天保持贞操，他的国土也就一天保持干旱。他派了一个美丽少女前去诱惑英雄，终于把他赚来，并把女儿赐他为妻。在结婚的那一天，他的国土又重获甘霖。

（三）圣杯代表女性，利剑代表男性，两者同时代表繁殖力。杯和剑都见于太洛纸牌。这是一套中世纪纸牌，共七十二张，四套：（a）杯——即红桃；（b）矛（棍或杖）——即方块；（c）剑——即黑桃；（d）碟——即梅花。

（四）在寻找圣杯时，要经过一座凶险的教堂（The Chapel Perilous），好比炼狱，经此而达到生命的顶峰。本诗的第五节 387—389 行出现了“一个空的教堂，仅仅是风的家。”但是这里没有持剑的英雄，也没有谁找到了圣杯。］

19. 第 47 行：［腓尼基水手见第四节。参阅 35—36 行注和 46 行作者原注。］

20. 第 48 行：［参阅莎士比亚《风暴》中的丧歌：

Full fathom five thy father lies;
　　Of his bones are coral made;
Those are pearls that were his eyes:
你的父亲睡得有五噚深；
他的尸骨已成了珊瑚；
这些珍珠是他的眼睛：］

21.［**Belladonna:** 即意大利文“美丽的女人”，也是一种含毒的花。岩石指荒原的岩石。］

22.［**The lady of situations:** 一个善于应变的女人。这里 l 为小写，不是称号，而是描写她是怎样的一个女人。］

23.［**the Wheel:** the Wheel of Fortune，命运的转轮，指人生变化无常；或指佛教的轮回。］

24.［**the one-eyed merchant:** 独眼商人，即 204—214 行的士麦拿商人，是卖小葡萄干、说粗俗的法语的那个商人。参考 46 行原注。］

25.［**this card / Which is blank**：太洛纸牌中没有空白的牌，此处不知何义。］

26.［**The Hanged Man:** 那被绞死的人，见 46 行原注。他和耶稣一样，如死后复活可以使土地肥沃。]

27. [**crowds of people:** 成群的人和 55 行 death by water，水里的死亡见 46 行原注。]

28. [**walking round in a ring:** 绕着圆圈走，‘圆圈’指迷宫或指佛教的轮回。]

29. [**Mrs. Equitone:** 爱奎东太太，女相士的主顾。]

30. 第 60 行： 参看波得莱尔的诗：

Fourmillante cité, cité pleine de rêves,
Ou le spectre en plein jour raccroche le passant.
[Swarming city, city full of dreams,
Where the ghost stops the passer-by in full daylight.
这拥挤的城，充满了迷梦的城，
鬼魂在大白天也抓过路的人。]

31. 第 63 行： 参阅《地狱》(*Inferno*) 第三节，五十五至五十七行：

si lunga tratta
di gente, ch'io non avrei mai creduto
che morte tanta n'avesse disfatta.

[so long a train
of people, that I should never have believed
death had undone so many.

这样长的
一队人，我没想到
死亡竟毁了这许多人。]

32. 第 64 行： 同上第四节二十五至二十七行：

Quivi, secondo che per ascoltare,
Non avea pianto, ma' che di sospiri,
che l'aura eterna facevan tremare.
[Here there was no plaint,
that could be heard, except of sighs
which caused the eternal air to tremble.
根据听到的声音判断，
这里没有其他痛苦的表现，只有叹息
使永恒的空气抖颤。

但丁此时是在未曾受过洗礼的婴儿所在地——地狱的边缘地带。]

33. [**Saint Mary Woolnoth:** 圣马利吴尔诺斯是伦敦威廉王大街的教堂。]

34. [**kept the hours:** 按钟点报时。]

35. 第 68 行： 这是我常注意到的一种现象。[九点是上班的时间。]

36. [**Stetson:** 斯代真是一种宽边呢帽的牌子．指一个戴这种帽子的人。]

37. [**Mylae:** 迈里战役是罗马人和迦太基人之间的一战（260 B. C.），目的是争夺地中海的商业霸权。迦太基人战败。]

38. 第 71—72 行：[已经埋葬了的记忆，不希望它再发芽。回忆是痛苦的事。又有一说是把神象埋葬入土，以祈来年丰收。耶稣和被绞死的神死后复苏都和繁殖力的解放有关。但是荒原中人都不信教，看见了耶稣也不认识。]

39. 第 74 行：见韦伯斯特（Webster）《白魔鬼》中的挽歌（The Dirge in *The White Devil.*）[韦伯斯特（1580？—1625？），英国剧作家，其诗曰；

Call for the robin red-breast and the wren,
Since o'er shady groves they hover.
And with leaves and flowers do cover
The friendless bodies of unburied men:
　　Call unto his funeral dole
　　The ant, the field-mouse, and the mole,
To rear him hillocks that shall keep him warm,
And, when tombs are robbed, sustain no harm;
But keep the wolf from thence, that's foe to man,
For with his nails he'll dig them up again.
叫上那些个鹪鹩和知更，
它们在葱郁的丛林里徘徊。
让那些叶和花一同遮盖
那些未曾下葬孤独的尸身。
　　把蚂蚁田鼠和鼹鼠
　　叫去参加他下葬时的哀呼，
给他造起几座小山，使他温暖，
在坟墓被盗窃时也不受灾难；
叫豺狼走远些，他是人类的仇敌，
不然它会用爪子又把他们掘起。

狗熊星或天狼星传说是使尼罗河两岸肥沃的星宿。关于韦伯斯特的挽歌，英国散文家兰姆（Lamb）曾说，"我从未见过比这个更好的丧歌，除非是《风暴》中福迪能王子在追忆淹死了的父亲时所唱的山歌。那是有关水的，充满了水，这是有关土地的，充满了土地的气息。"]

40. 第 76 行：见波得莱尔《恶之花》的序诗。[序名"致读者："——Hypocrite reader!——my likeness, my brother!——虚伪的读者——我的同类——我的兄弟！诗人认为读者和他一样，也是百无聊赖、无精打彩的。]

II. A Game of Chess 对弈[见 136 行注]

41. 第 77 行：见《安东尼与克莉奥佩特拉》、(*Antony and Cleopatra*) 第二幕第二景，第一百九十行。[这是莎士比亚的名剧，原句是：

The barge she sat in, like a burnished throne
Burned on the water.

她所坐的游艇，象发亮的宝座

在水上放光。

艾略特在诗中曾引用许多女人的名字，如岩石的女主人贝洛岛纳，莎士比亚剧中的克莉奥佩特拉，奥菲莉亚，《伊尼德》中的狄多，伊利莎白女王，翡绿眉拉和其他作品中的女性。艾略特在第218行注中曾说，“所有的女人只是一个女人，”但有时也着力暗示她们的不同行动与命运。]

42. [**standards:** 镜台。]

43. [**Cupidon:** 小爱神，爱神维纳斯所钟爱的美少年。]

44. [**synthetic perfumes:** 合成香料。]

45. [**Unguent, powdered, or liquid:** 膏状，粉状，或液体的。]

46. [**stirred by the air/That freshened from the window:** 受到/窗外新鲜空气的微微吹动。]

47. [**these ascended/In fattening the prolonged candle-fames:** 这些香气/在上升时，使点燃了很久的烛焰变得肥满。]

48. laquearia:（镶板的天花板）见《伊尼德》（*Aeneid*）第一卷，第七百二十六行：dependent lychni laquearibus aureis incensi, et noctem flammis funalia vincunt.[Flaming torches hang from the golden panelled ceiling and the torches conquer the night with flames，点亮的灯从镶板的金色房顶上挂下来，火把的烈焰征服了黑夜。

《伊尼德》是罗马诗人维吉尔（Virgil）创作的一首长十二卷的史诗，写特洛亚王子伊尼亚斯一度和迦太基女王狄多结婚，后来遗弃了她，致使狄多自杀。这句诗描写女王狄多盛宴招待伊尼亚斯。]

49. [**fed with copper:** 洒上铜粉。]

50. [**burned green and orange:** 亮着青绿和橙黄色的火焰。]

51. [**gave upon:** 面对，面临。]

52. sylvan scene:（田野景物），见弥尔敦《失乐园》（Paradise Lost）第四卷第一百四十行。

[and over head up grew
Insuperable highth of loftiest shade,
Cedar, and Pine, and Firr and branching Palm
A sylvan scene, and as the ranks ascend
Shade above shade, a woodie theatre
Of stateliest view.
上面长着
高不可攀的巨大树荫，
柏树、松树，杉木与棕树的枝干纵横
一幅田野景物，一层一层上升
一层一层的树荫，象林木构成的剧场
最庄严的景象。

53. 第99行： 见奥维德（Ovid）《变形记》（Metamorphosis）第六卷，翡绿眉拉

(Philomela).[国王铁卢欧斯(Tereus)秉性暴烈,在他娶潘迪恩(Pandion)的女儿泊劳克奈(Procne)时,出现了种种凶兆,生头生儿子依帖士(Itys)时也有不祥之兆。后来泊劳克奈想念妹妹翡绿眉拉,求丈夫接她来小住。铁卢欧斯看见翡绿眉拉美丽,就心怀不良。将到家时他把她诱入山洞,把她强奸了,并在她辱骂时割去了她的舌尖;把她禁闭在洞里。翡绿眉拉把自己的伤心故事织成锦绣托人送给姐姐。泊劳克奈在盛怒之下杀了儿子,煮熟了给丈夫吃。国王持刀杀死了姊妹俩,翡绿眉拉变为夜莺,姐姐变为燕子。]

54. [**rudely forced:** 遭受了强暴。]

55. 第 101—102 行:[注意动词时态:"filled,充塞"和"cried,叫唤"是过去时,"pursues,追逐"却是现在时,表示世界现在还在参预着国王的这一暴行。]

56. [**'Jug Jug':** 是夜莺的鸣声,也暗示性交,是唱给脏耳朵听的肮脏故事。]

57. [**other withered stumps of time:** 其他那些时间的枯树根,指墙上还留下了过去的其它类似的故事。]

58. [**hushing the room enclosed:** 使紧闭的房间一片静寂。]

59. [**Glowed into words:** 亮成话语:发出亮光,象在说话似的,一时打破了沉寂。]

60. 第 118 行: 见韦伯斯特:"风在门里吗?"[见韦氏的《魔鬼的公案》(*The Devil's Law Case*)。]

61. 第 126 行: 参看第一节三十七,四十八行。[参看第一节三十七行,不知何义;48 行是"水里的死亡"的一个主题,见《风暴》中仙童的歌。]

62. 第 128 行:[莎士比亚名字中加一'希'字是为了适应爵士乐的节奏。]

63. [**The hot water at ten:** 十点供开水。]

64. 第 136 行: 参阅弥德尔敦(Middleton)《女人谨防女人》(*Women Beware Women*)中的对弈。[弥德尔敦(1570?—1627),英国剧作家。剧中写佛罗棱斯公爵(Duke of Florence)爱上了女子卞安格(Bianca),请人设法和她相会;邻居栗维亚(Livia)设局把卞安格的婆婆叫来下棋,同时又偷偷引卞安格与公爵相会。在两人对弈时,卞安格为名利所诱,顺从了公爵。第二节题名'对弈',着力写两性关系。]

65. [**lidless eyes:** 老是守望着的、不知安息的眼睛。]

66. 第 138 行:[艾略特在这里竭力模仿下层社会的口语。demobbed:退伍。]

67. 第 140 行:[这是酒馆催客准备关门时的呼叫声。]

68. [**give me a straight look:** 瞪了我一眼。]

69. [**you can get on with it:** 你就听便吧。]

70. [**to bring it off:** 为打胎。]

71. [**The chemist:** 药店老板,药剂师。]

72. [**hot gammon:** 薰火腿。]

73. 第 170—171 行:[参阅《哈姆莱特》(*Hamlet*)第四幕第五景,奥菲利娅(Ophelia)发疯后、投水前的一段话(此时她的父亲已被杀死,兄弟还在远方):

I hope all will be well. We must be patient: but I cannot choose but weep, to think they should lay him in the cold ground. My brother shall know of it; and so I thank you for your good counsel—come, my coach!—Good-night, ladies; good-night, sweet ladies; good-night, good-night.

但愿一切都顺利。我们必须有耐心：但是我一想到他们竟把他埋进了寒冷的土里我就禁不住流泪。我要让我哥哥知道这件事；我谢谢你们的好意。——来啊，我的马车！——明天见，太太，明天见，好太太，明天见，明天见。

这是一段向生活告别的、很凄凉的话。]

2. THE METAPHYSICAL POETS

《玄学派诗人》(*The Metaphysical Poets*)是艾略特继《传统和个人才能》(1917)，和《批评的功能》(1923)之后的又一篇重要评论文章。文章的直接起因是1921年出版的赫伯特·格里厄森(Herbert J. C. Grierson)教授编集的《十七世纪玄学派诗歌》(*Metaphsical Lyrics and Poems of the Seventeenth Century: Donne to Butler*)一书。文章是有关这个诗集的一篇书评。但是更加重要的是它阐述了作者自己对英国诗歌的见解，反映了作者自己所深受影响的诗歌流派与作家。艾略特的不少论点是和格里厄森教授一致的，例如格里厄森在选集的长篇引论中谈到了玄学派诗人的博学多思，他们的思想常常带有强烈的感情并从属于感情(格里厄森用了passionate thinking热烈的思考这个词，艾略特的名句则是"立即感受到思想象闻到一朵玫瑰花的芬芳一样")，他们性格中的严肃的哲理倾向，深挚热烈的情操，生动、鲜明、真实的表达方法和高度创新而又强有力的、动人的、接近口语的语言风格。格里厄森也指出：和玄学派诗人，尤其是最杰出的诗人邓恩相比，弥尔顿的诗歌就显得不是那么自然、那么具有思想和感情的深度和广度。当然，艾略特又有许多发展。他更加明确地反对了十九世纪流行的浪漫主义诗歌(例如拜伦、雪莱、济慈)和后来的勃朗宁(Robert Browning)、丁尼生(Alfred Tennyson)的创作方法，认为从十七世纪中就开始了英国诗歌中的"感受力的涣散"(dissociation of sensibility，或译作感受力的游离)；他认为玄学派以后的作家背离了伊丽莎白晚期以来的诗歌传统；他们诚然也思考，但是却失去了对思想的强烈感受力和感情反应。艾略特认为"感受力的统一"(unification of sensibility，250—251行)就是"不断把根本不同的经验凝结成一体，"(见218—219行)，或把不同的经验"形成新的整体"(223—224行)，也就是"把概念变成感觉"，"把观感所及变成思想状态"(301—302行)，这他认为正是玄学派诗歌的特点。按照艾略特的说法，十八、十九世纪的英国诗歌背离了这个传统，却在法国诗人拉辛(古典主义时期，十七世纪)，波得莱尔(十九世纪中，象征派诗人)和较晚的象征派诗人于尔·拉福格和特里斯坦·高卑依(十九世纪后半)的作品中出现。如上所说，这里反映了艾略特的师承：他自己的诗歌创作深受伊丽莎白时代晚期的戏剧家和诗歌、玄学派诗歌(包括但丁)和法国象征派诗歌的影响。这种影响广泛见于他的诗歌创作，也见于《荒原》一诗。在这篇文章里也出现了作者的两个著名论断，即诗人的博学多才和整个文学传统对他的创作的影响力，和当代诗歌，由于复杂、多样的时代与社会的制约(273—276行)必然会变得艰涩的观点。

为了说明上述观点，艾略特进行了很多举例和分析。

英国玄学派诗歌在二十世纪初已逐渐为人们所注意，但格里厄森教授的选集和艾略特的推崇是很大的推动力，使这一派诗歌红极一时，尤其为文学研究者所必读。在此之前格里厄森已编了一部《邓恩诗集》共两卷（1912），第二卷附有详细的引论和评注。艾略特文章的主要内容之一是力图给玄学派诗歌下一个确切的定义，虽然他认为这是一件非常困难的事。他认为最杰出的代表邓恩是一位伊丽莎白时代晚期的作家，在精神上十分接近以翻译荷马史诗著名的乔治·查普门（1559？—1634），继承了伊丽莎白时代的优秀传统。属于这个流派的诗人不少，他特别提到了安德鲁·马佛尔，亨利·金，亚伯拉罕·卡乌里和神学诗人乔治·赫伯特，亨利·弗恩和理查德·克拉效。为了阐明玄学派诗歌的创作手法，艾略特举了许多例，作了许多分析。他列举了一些写作方法，如把比喻衍伸到相当的长度（如卡乌里把世界比作棋盘，邓恩把分离的情人比作圆规的两脚，39—43行），快速的一个接着一个的联想，（如邓恩从地球仪跃进到眼泪，又跃进到洪水，47—56行），言简意明的突兀对比（如邓恩描写白骨上象戴了镯子似地绕上一圈颜色鲜艳的头发，63行）等等。十八世纪的约翰逊博士认为这是“强把毫无共同点的概念栓缚在一起。”但是艾略特认为这恰恰是诗人们经常采用的方法，诗人们恰恰是这样完成了感受力的统一，并举了一节极为动人的诗为例，即亨利·金的《殡仪》。他把迫切想与已经死去的妻子重逢比作一次旅程。

艾略特指出玄学派诗歌的语言是简朴典雅的，但句子结构却不简单而是十分忠实地反映了思想感情，并且由于思想感情的多样化而具有多样化的音乐性。为了指出玄学派和他们的前人和同辈是一脉相承的，他说琼生和查普门也把他们的博学注入了他们的感受力，他们的感情由于他们的阅读与思考而经历了改造：思想升华为感情并成为感情。相反，在玄学派以后的诗歌中，这种特点就消失了，其实是不应该消失的（160—161行）。这种感受力的统一性在雪莱和济慈的诗歌中还残存着，而在勃朗宁和丁尼生的诗中则少见了。艾略特还在玄学派诗人和勃朗宁、丁尼生之间划了一条界线；称前者属于别具慧心的诗人（the intellectual poet），后者属沉思的诗人（the reflective poet）（211—214行）。他接着说，“丁尼生和勃朗宁是诗人，他们思考；但是他们没有立即感觉到他们的思想象闻到一朵玫瑰花的芬芳一样”（215—216行）。“对邓恩说来，一个思想是一种经验；它改变了他的感受力”（214—215行）。艾略特指出，这种“感觉力的涣散”（“感受力的游离”）已于十七世纪出现，并由于弥尔顿和德莱顿（Dryden）的巨大影响而加剧。十八世纪的诗人们对语言进行了加工，语言更加精炼了，但感情却显得格外粗糙。艾略特最后断言，象弥尔顿和德莱顿那样伟大的诗人之所以有欠缺，是因为他们没有窥测到灵魂深处。用他的话来说，“必须进入大脑皮层神经系统和消化通道”（321—322行），光是探测心脏还很不够；而拉辛，邓恩则是远远超出了心脏的范围。

如上所述，艾略特在这篇文章中主要探讨了玄学派的创作特点，提出了“感受力涣散”的论点，力图恢复玄学派诗歌在文学史中的崇高地位并说明它们的创作方法在现代仍有强大生命力。在这里，作者几乎没有触及诗歌内容的问题。格里厄森教授所编诗集的分类概括地说明了这些作品的主要题材：爱情诗，神学诗，杂诗（包括哀歌，书信体诗歌，讽刺诗等），其中以爱情诗的造诣最高。玄学派诗人在政治上大多是保皇派，宗教上大多是天主教徒。邓恩首先是个天主教徒，后来因生活的需要倾向于英国国教。

1. The Metaphysical Poets:《玄学派诗人》原是一篇书评，1921 年载于伦敦“泰晤士报文学增刊”。这篇文章提出了诗歌中“感受力的涣散”这个主要论点，影响到英史的写作。

2. these poems: 指赫伯特 J. C. 格里厄森的选集《十七世纪玄学派诗歌》（H. J. C. Grierson: Metaphysical Lyrics and Poems of the Seventeenth Century，1921），这个诗集附有四十五页的引论。

3. more often named than read. and more often read than profitably studied: 提我的人多，读的人少；读的人多，从研究（这些诗歌）中得益的人少。

4. Professor Grierson: 格里厄森教授（Herbert John Clifford, 1866—1960），苏格兰学者，曾在阿伯丁（1894）和爱丁堡（1915）任教授，于 1936 年受勋为爵士，有很多著述。

5. Aurelian Townshend: 奥里良·汤欣德（1583？—1651？），宫廷微臣，贫苦，以卖诗为生，从未出过诗集，直到 1912 年钱伯士（E. K. Chambers）编辑的《诗与假面具》（*Poems and Masks*）.

6. Lord Herbert of Cherbury: 丘伯里的赫伯特勋爵（1582—1648），宫臣，军人，外交家，历史学家，哲学家，玄学派诗人，神学诗人乔治·赫伯特的长兄。

7. Professor Saintsbury's admirable edition of Caroline poets: 这里指的是乔治 E. B. 辛兹伯里（George Edward Bateman Saintsbury, 1845—1933）编的《查理王朝的次要诗人》（*Minor Poets of the Caroline Period*），共三卷，1921 初版，1965 新版。这一诗集引导读者对十七世纪诗歌发生兴趣。

8. Oxford Book of English Verse: 指阿瑟·奎勒考契（Arthur Quiller-Couch, 1863–1944）编选的《牛津英国诗选 1250—1918》，1900 初版，1939 新版。这两本诗选包括了按各个时期选出的长期公认的代表作，不致引起争论。

9. in itself a piece of criticism and a provocation of criticism:（选集）本身就是一篇评论，而且会引起更多的评论。

10. Donne: 约翰·邓恩（1572—1631），玄学派诗人中最有成就的代表，留有许多爱情诗、神学诗和说教文。

11. documents: 文献。

12. has long done duty: 曾长期被当作。

13. a term of abuse: 贬词。

14. a digression from the main current: 一种背离主流的异端。

15. Marvell: 安德鲁·马佛尔（1621—1678）。他的一首著名的诗是《给他那若即若离的情人》（*To His Coy Mistress*），艾略特曾用于《荒原》。

16. Bishop King: 亨利·金（1592—1669）曾被封为主教，玄学派诗人。

17. Chapman: 乔治·查普门（1559？—1634），剧作家，诗人，荷马史诗的译者，重要的伊利莎白时期作家。

18. 'courtly' poetry: 宫廷诗歌，通称为骑士派诗歌。

19. derivative from: 出自。

20. Jonson: 本·琼生（Ben Jonson, 1572—1637），莎士比亚后的剧作家，以喜剧著称。

21. Latin: 罗马文学。

22. Prior: 马太·泊莱奥（1664—1721），诗人。

23. devotional verse: 神学诗或宗教诗。

24. Herbert: 乔治·赫伯特（1593—1633），以宗教诗著称。

25. Vaughan: 亨利·弗恩（1622—1695），以写宗教诗著称。

26. Crashaw: 理查·克拉效（1612？—1649），写了许多宗教诗，是一个热情的天主教徒。

27. Christina Rossetti: 克莉丝蒂娜·罗塞蒂（1830—1894），著名的唯美主义前拉斐尔派诗人但丁 G. 罗塞蒂的妹妹，以宗教诗著称。

28. Francis Thompson: 法兰西斯·汤姆森（1859—1907），他的宗教诗反映了克拉效的影响。

29. Cowley: 亚伯拉罕·卡乌里（1618—1667），玄学派诗人。

30. a figure of speech: 一种修辞手段，例如隐喻（metaphor）或显喻（simile）（见 33 行）。conceit 亦是一种修辞手段，有时作‘牵强的比喻’讲。an element of style，风格的一个成分，则是比‘一种修辞手段’更加概括的说法。

31. to the farthest stage to which ingenuity can carry it: 巧用心计地把比喻延伸到尽可能的长度。

32. long stanzas:《命运》一诗共四节，每节 15—17 行。

33. *A Valediction*:《告别：不许悼念》（*A Valediction: Forbidding Mourning*，）

34. rapid association of thought: 快速的联想。

35. considerable agility: 相当的敏捷。

36. make that, which was nothing, all: 使原来的一无所有变成有了一切。

37. So doth each tear .../A globe, yea, world, by that impression grow: 就是这样，每一滴泪按照这个模式而成长为一个地球，甚至可说是一个世界。

38. 第 47—56 行： 摘自邓恩的《告别：饮泣》10—18 行（A Valedirction: Of Weeping）.

39. 第 63 行： 摘自邓恩的《遗物》（*The Relic*）6 行。这里的‘骨’指死者的遗骨。

40. This telescoping of images: 这种形象与形象通过撞击而结连在一起。参看 69—70 行 the most heterogeneous ideas are yoked by violence together，完全不同的概念强制地栓缚在一起。

41. Middleton: 托马斯·弥德尔顿（1570？—1627），英国剧作家，著名剧本有《对弈》（A Game at Chess, 1624），《女人谨防女人》（*Women Beware Women*, 1657），等。

42. Webster: 约翰·韦伯斯特（1580？—1625？），英国剧作家，名剧有《白魔鬼》（*The White Devil*，1608），《马尔菲的公爵夫人》（*The Duchess of Malfi*, 1614），《魔鬼的公案》（*The Devil's Law Case*, 1623），等。

43. Tourneur: 塞瑞尔·图诺（Cyril Tourneur, 1575?–1626），在他名下的剧本

有二:《复仇者的悲剧》(*The Revenger's Tragedy*, 1607)和《无神论者的悲剧》(*The Atheist's Tragedy*, 1611).

44. 第 68—69 行: 艾略特深受这些剧作者的影响，在《荒原》中他引用了前二者。

45. Johnson: 撒缪尔·约翰逊(Samuel Johnson, 1709–1784)，著名作家，第一部英语辞典(1755)的编纂者，其他著作有《诗人传》(*Lives of the Poets*, 1781)，长诗《人类的愿望是徒劳的》(*The Vanity of Human Wishes*, 1749)等。参看本文78—79 行。

46. Cleveland: 约翰·克利夫兰(1613—1658)，保皇派诗人，曾创造一种政治讽刺诗，在当时很受欢迎。

47. 第 72—74 行: 见《诗人传》中的《卡乌里传》。

48. the ideas are yoked but not united: 概念只是栓缚在一起，没有结成一体。

49. compelled into unity: 硬结成一体。

50. Notre âme est un trois-mats cherchant son Icarie: Our soul is a threemaster seeking its Icarie，我们的灵魂是一条三根桅杆的航船正寻找它的理想国(见波得莱尔《航程》, *Le Voyage*).

51. a dubious hand: 听一只不可靠的手指挥。

52. To point a moral, or adorn a tale: 指出某种教益，或修饰一个故事。

53. "Exequy":《殡仪》。

54. Stay for me there: 在那里等着我。

55. hollow Vale: 幽谷是指死者所在的忧伤之地，即阴曹地府。

56. think not much of my delay: 不要因我的延误而过份担心。

57. a sbort degree: 很短的一步。

58. when I betake to rest: 在我休息的时候。

59. my West: 西方是太阳沉落的地方，也是征途的终点。

60. when sleep breathed his drowsy gale ...: 睡眠在吹动它的困人的微风时…，这里‘睡眠’人身化了。

61. Edgar Poe: 埃德加·艾伦·坡(Edgar Allan Poe, 1809–1849)美国小说家，诗人，评论家。他的短篇小说与诗歌常带神秘与恐怖气氛，他也是一个最早的侦探小说家。他在后来的法国象征派诗人中享有崇高地位。

62. Ode:《有人问爱情是否将永远继续下去的颂歌》(*Ode Upon a Question Moved, Whether Love Should Continue for Ever*).

63. Each shall be both, yet both but one: 一个人将抵两个人，而两人又其实是一个。

64. that beauty: 指脸部的美：眼睛是脸部最美的部分。

65. moveless: 静止的，毫无动作的。

66. becalmèd sense: 平静的感觉。平静是因为没有风的吹动而完全静止。

67. some influence/Their ravished spirits did possess: 它们(眼睛)的沉醉神情确实能施加影响。

68. fidelity to thought and feeling: 忠实于思想感情。在这里思想和感情是结合的，但后来思想和感情就分离了，即感受力的涣散或游离。

69. Gray: 托马斯·格雷（1716—1771），诗人，他的一首最著名的诗是《墓园哀歌》(*Elegy in a Country Churchyard*, 1750)。

70. *Saint Teresa*: 这是克拉效（Crashaw）最著名的诗，共181行，诗人在这首诗里表现了巨大的宗教热情。

71. the Revolution: 艾略特认为内战（1642—1646，1648—1651）给英国带来了思想上的巨大变化。人们通常把“革命”当作1688年的“光荣革命”。这一革命导致了君主立宪制；但是艾略特特别重视内战，称之为“伟大的叛乱”（见《安德鲁·马佛尔》(*Andrew Marvell*) 一文（1921)。

72. Jacobean poets: 英国詹姆士一世时期的诗人。伊利莎白一世时期为1533—1603。詹姆士一世时期为1603—1625。

73. Marlowe: 克里斯托弗·马娄（Christopher Marlowe, 1564–1593)。英国剧作家，写有著名剧本如《马尔他岛的犹太人》(*The Jew of Malta*, 1590）和《浮士德博士的悲剧》(*Tragedy of Dr. Faustus*, 1592–1593)。

74. a tenable theory: 站得住脚的理论。

75. Montaigne: 米舍勒·爱冈·德蒙田（Michel Eyquem de Montaigne, 1533–1592)，法国文艺复兴后期人文主义作家。

76. a direct sensuous apprehension of thought, or a recreation of thought into feeling: 从思想中直接产生出一种美的感觉，或把思想重造为感情。

77. 第178—187行： 见乔治·查普门的剧本《昂布瓦的布西的复仇》(*The Revenge of Bussy d'Ambois*，1607，四幕一景，133行)。

78. fit/One with that All: 以有限适应无限，或以局部从属于全部。

79. 第182—186行： 摘自罗伯特·勃朗宁（Robert Browning, 1812–1889）的长诗《勃鲁格兰姆主教的辩辞》(*Bishop Blougram's Apology*) 693—697行。

80. Tennyson: 艾尔弗雷德·丁尼生（Alfred Tennyson, 1809–1892）的《两个声音》(*Two Voices*) 412—423行。

81. 第213—214行： 这是艾略特理论的中心。他举的例子是否选得公正是个问题。这样处理英国诗歌的发展是否合适，后来的批评家曾提出疑问。

82. Spinoza: 斯宾诺莎（1632—1677），荷兰哲学家，泛神论者。

83. Dante: 但丁（1265—1321），意大利大诗人，《神曲》(*Divina Comedia, Divine Comedy*, 1307–1321）的作者，艾略特所十分推崇的诗人。

84. Guido Cavalcanti: 格维多·卡瓦尔康狄（c.1255—1300），但丁所谓的“甜蜜的新风格”一派（dolce stil nuovo, sweet new style）诗人中的重要成员。

85. Guido Guinicelli: 格维多·贵尼切里（1230/40—1276），也是“甜蜜的新风格”一派中的成员。

86. Cino: 辟斯多雅的契诺（Cino da Pistoia, c.1270–c.1336），和上述诗人同为一派。

87. Milton: 约翰·弥尔顿（1608—1674），杰出的英国诗人，《失乐园》(*Paradise Lost*, 1667)，《复乐园》(*Paradise Regained*, 1671）和《力士参孙》(Samson Agonistes,

1671）的作者。

88. Dryden: 约翰·德莱顿（1631—1700），复辟王朝的桂冠诗人，写过一些政治讽刺诗、宗教论争诗和剧本。

89. Coilins: 威廉·柯林斯（1721—1759），抒情诗人。

90. Goldsmith: 奥立佛·哥尔斯密（1730—1774），写了《威克菲牧师传》（*The Vicar or Wakefield*, 1768，小说），《委曲求全》（*She Stoops to Conquer*, 1773，剧本），《荒村》（*The Deserted Village*, 1770，诗）。

91. the ratiocinative: 推理的（东西）。

92. Shelley: 波西·比希·雪莱（Percy Bysshe Shelley, 1792–1822），浪漫主义诗人，写了许多优秀作品如《解放了的普罗米修斯》（*Prometheus Unbound*，1819），《西风颂》（*Ode to the West Wind*, 1819），和许多政治抒情诗。《生活的胜利》（*The Triumph of Life*）作于1822。

93. the second Hyperion:《海批里安》（1819）第二种本是约翰·济慈（John Keats, 1795–1821）的又一次尝试：《海批里安的受贬：一个梦》（*The Fall of Hyperion: a Dream*）。

94. not merely meditate on them poetically: 不只是思考着想把它们写成诗。这里的意思和把勃朗宁和丁尼生叫作思考的诗人（reflective poets，见214行）是一样的，说他们只是反复思考（见242行）而不能把思想转变成为感情。

95. 第261—264行： 这里是说一种哲学理论转化成诗后，它是否真理已不必深究，而且既已转化为诗，也就证明它是真理。

96. playing upon a refined sensibility: 在一个有精细感受力的人身上起作用时。

97. more comprehensive, more allusive: 更加包罗万象，更加要用隐晦的手法（如比喻和典故等）。

98. to force, to dislocate if necessary, language into his meaning: 强迫、并且在必要时打乱语言，使它变成自己脑中所想的东西。264—266行这句话的含义在当时起了很大影响。

99. not requisite to associate oneself: 没有必要把自己和这种说法联系在一起。

100. *La Poésie d'aujourd'hui*:（法文），《今日之诗歌》（*The Poetry of Today*）。

101. 第285—294行： 这几行诗摘自法国象征派诗人于尔·拉福格（Jules Laforgue, 1860–1887）的《最后诗集》（*Derniers Vers, Last Poems*, 1890）。这几行是诗人最杂乱、难解的诗句，姑译成英文、汉文如下：

O transparent geraniums, warriors, spells,
Monomaniac sacrileges!
Packing materials, shamelessness, showers! O wine presses!
Of the vintages of evening parties!
Baby-clothes under siege,
Thyrsus in the depths of the woods!
Transfusions, reprisals,
Churchings, compresses and the eternal potion,
Angelus! no more are possible
Nuptial disasters! Nuptial disasters!
啊，透明的石里红，武士的符咒，

偏执狂的渎圣行为！
包装材料，不知廉耻，淋浴！啊，榨汁机
为了提供晚会时的佳酿！
围困着的婴儿衣物，
瑟塞斯在树林深处！
渗透，报复行为，
产后的教堂礼拜，敷布和永恒的药剂，
召唤祈祷的钟声！已不再可能的
结婚的祸害！结婚的祸害！
（注：瑟塞斯是酒神手中之杖。）

102. Elle est bien .. se lamente aussi …:（法文）= She is far away, she weeps, / The great wind laments also …：她在远处，/ 她哭了，大风也一样哀伤…

103. Tristan Corbière: 特里斯坦·高卑依（1845—1875）法国象征派诗人。艾略特很推崇他和拉福格的诗歌创作，并曾受他们的很深影响。他认为他们很近似英国玄学派诗人和詹姆士一世时期的剧作家。

104. of transmuting ideas into sensations, of transforming an observation into a state of mind: 把概念变成感觉，把形成的看法转化成为一种思想状态。艾略特在这篇文章里曾反复阐述这一分析，如 174—176 行，从思想中直接产生出一种美的感觉，或把思想重造为感情；216—217 行，他们不能立即感受到他们的思想象一朵玫瑰花的芬芳一样；258—260 行，他愈是有头脑就愈有可能有多种兴趣：我们唯一的条件是请他把这些兴趣写成诗歌而不只是思考着想把它们写成诗，等等。

105. 第 303—306 行：这四句摘自波得莱尔（*Charles Baudelaire*, 1821–1867）的《航程》（*Le Voyage*）：For the child, in love with maps and prints, / The universe is equal to his vast appetite./Ah, how big the world is by lamplight! / And how small the world is to the eyes of memory! 对于爱好地图和图片的孩子来说，/ 宇宙和他的巨大胃口一样浩淼。/ 啊，灯光下的世界多么大！ / 记忆眼里的世界又是多么小！

106. Racine: 若望·拉辛（Jean Racine, 1639–1699），法国古典主义诗人，写过十一部悲剧一部喜剧。

107. in the direct current of English poetry: 是直接属于英国诗歌的源流的。

108. coddled by antiquarian affection: 因对古董有感情而受到宠爱。

109. implicit limitations: 固有的限度。

110. attributes: 特征。

111. canons of taste: 审美标准。

112. versification: 写诗方法。

113. tortures: 审议。

114. substantial: 篇幅较多，分量较重。

115. break up the classification: 打破这种分类法。

116. *Dialogue Between a Pilgrim and Time*:《朝圣者和时间之间的对话》。

117. regrettable omissions: 令人遗憾的遗漏。